IMPERIUM

ROBERT HARRIS

IMPERIUM

HUTCHINSON

LONDON

First published by Hutchinson in 2006

1 3 5 7 9 10 8 6 4 2

Copyright © Robert Harris 2006

Robert Harris has asserted his right under the Copyright, Designs
and Patents Act, 1988 to be identified as the author of this work

Map of Republican Rome by Reginald Piggott
Endpaper image: Close-up of one of the long sides of the Ara Pacis
Augustae, Rome. Courtesy of Fratelli Alinari/Alinari Archive, Florence

HUTCHINSON
The Random House Group Limited
20 Vauxhall Bridge Road, London SWIV 2SA

Random House Australia (Pty) Limited
20 Alfred Street, Milsons Point, Sydney
New South Wales 2061, Australia

Random House New Zealand Limited
18 Poland Road, Glenfield
Auckland 10, New Zealand

Random House (Pty) Limited
Isle of Houghton, Corner of Boundary Road & Carse O'Gowrie,
Houghton 2198, South Africa

Random House Publishers India Private Limited
301 World Trade Tower, Hotel Intercontinental Grand Complex,
Barakhamba Lane, New Delhi 110 001, India

The Random House Group Limited Reg. No. 954009
www.randomhouse.co.uk

A CIP catalogue record for this book is available from the British Library

Papers used by Random House are natural, recyclable products made from
wood grown in sustainable forests. The manufacturing processes conform to
the environmental regulations of the country of origin

Typeset in 12.5/16.5pt Dante MT by
Palimpsest Book Production Limited, Grangemouth, Stirlingshire
Printed and bound in Great Britain by Mackays of Chatham PLC

ISBN 9780091801250 (trade paperback – from Jan 2007)
ISBN 0091801257 (trade paperback)
ISBN 9780091800956 (hardback – from Jan 2007)
ISBN 0091800951 (hardback)
ISBN 0091795443 (Waterstone's edition)
ISBN 9780091795498 (leatherbound edition)

IN MEMORY OF
Audrey Harris
1920–2005
and for
Sam

TIRO, M. Tullius, the secretary of Cicero. He was not only the amanuensis of the orator, and his assistant in literary labour, but was himself an author of no mean reputation, and the inventor of the art of shorthand, which made it possible to take down fully and correctly the words of public speakers, however rapid their enunciation. After the death of Cicero, Tiro purchased a farm in the neighbourhood of Puteoli, to which he retired, and lived, according to Hieronymous, until he reached his hundredth year. Asconius Pedianus (in *Milon.* 38) refers to the fourth book of a life of Cicero by Tiro.

Dictionary of Greek and Roman Biography and Mythology, Vol. III, edited by William L. Smith, London, 1851

'*Innumerabilia tua sunt in me officia, domestica, forensia, urbana, provincialia, in re privata, in publica, in studiis, in litteris nostris . . .*'

'Your services to me are beyond count – in my home and out of it, in Rome and abroad, in private affairs and public, in my studies and literary work . . .'

Cicero, letter to Tiro, 7 November 50 BC

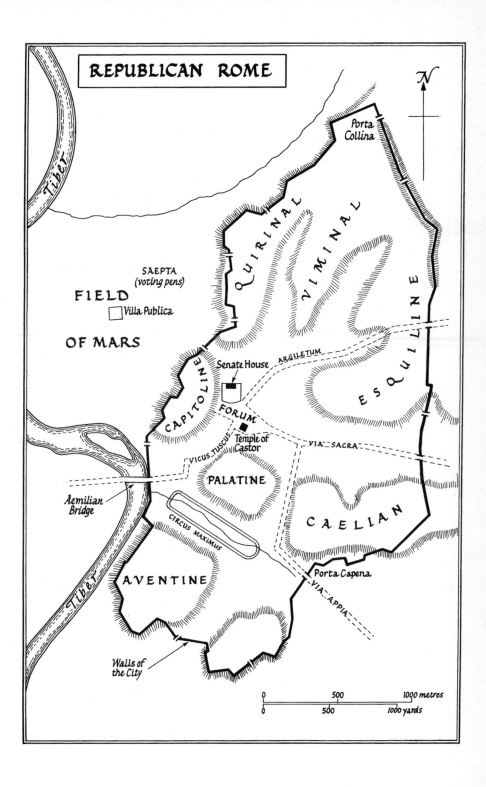

REPUBLICAN ROME

N

Tiber

Porta
Collina

SAEPTA
(voting pens)

FIELD

☐ Villa Publica

OF MARS

QUIRINAL

VIMINAL

ESQUILINE

CAPITOLINE

Senate House

ARGILETUM

FORUM

VICUS TUSCUS

Temple of
Castor

VIA SACRA

PALATINE

Aemilian
Bridge

CIRCUS MAXIMUS

CAELIAN

Porta Capena

Tiber

AVENTINE

VIA APPIA

Walls of
the City

0   500   1000 metres
0   500   1000 yards

PART ONE

SENATOR
79–70 BC

'Urbem, urbem, mi Rufe, cole et in ista luce viva!'

'Rome! Stick to Rome, my dear fellow, and live in the limelight!'

Cicero, letter to Caelius, 26 June 50 BC

I

My name is Tiro. For thirty-six years I was the confidential secretary of the Roman statesman Cicero. At first this was exciting, then astonishing, then arduous, and finally extremely dangerous. During those years I believe he spent more hours with me than with any other person, including his own family. I witnessed his private meetings and carried his secret messages. I took down his speeches, his letters and his literary works, even his poetry – such an outpouring of words that I had to invent what is commonly called shorthand to cope with the flow, a system still used to record the deliberations of the senate, and for which I was recently awarded a modest pension. This, along with a few legacies and the kindness of friends, is sufficient to keep me in my retirement. I do not require much. The elderly live on air, and I am very old – almost a hundred, or so they tell me.

In the decades after his death, I was often asked, usually in whispers, what Cicero was really like, but always I held my silence. How was I to know who was a government spy and who was not? At any moment I expected to be purged. But since my life is almost over, and since I have no fear of anything any more – not even torture, for I would not last an instant at the hands of the carnifex or his assistants – I have decided to offer this work as my answer. I shall base it on my memory, and on the documents

3

entrusted to my care. Because the time left to me inevitably must be short, I propose to write it quickly, using my shorthand system, on a few dozen small rolls of the finest paper – Hieratica, no less – which I have long hoarded for the purpose. I pray forgiveness in advance for all my errors and infelicities of style. I also pray to the gods that I may reach the end before my own end overtakes me. Cicero's final words to me were a request to tell the truth about him, and this I shall endeavour to do. If he does not always emerge as a paragon of virtue, well, so be it. Power brings a man many luxuries, but a clean pair of hands is seldom among them.

And it is of power and the man that I shall sing. By power I mean official, political power – what we know in Latin as *imperium* – the power of life and death, as vested by the state in an individual. Many hundreds of men have sought this power, but Cicero was unique in the history of the republic in that he pursued it with no resources to help him apart from his own talent. He was not, unlike Metellus or Hortensius, from one of the great aristocratic families, with generations of political favours to draw on at election time. He had no mighty army to back up his candidacy, as did Pompey or Caesar. He did not have Crassus's vast fortune to grease his path. All he had was his voice – and by sheer effort of will he turned it into the most famous voice in the world.

I was twenty-four years old when I entered his service. He was twenty-seven. I was a household slave, born on the family estate in the hills near Arpinum, who had never even seen Rome. He was a young advocate, suffering from nervous exhaustion, and struggling to overcome considerable natural disabilities. Few would have wagered much on either of our chances.

Cicero's voice at this time was not the fearsome instrument it later became, but harsh and occasionally prone to stutter. I believe the problem was that he had so many words teeming in his head that at moments of stress they jammed in his throat, as when a pair of sheep, pressed by the flock behind them, try at the same time to squeeze through a gate. In any case, these words were often too high-falutin for his audience to grasp. 'The Scholar', his restless listeners used to call him, or 'the Greek' – and the terms were not meant as compliments. Although no one doubted his talent for oratory, his frame was too weak to carry his ambition, and the strain on his vocal cords of several hours' advocacy, often in the open air and in all seasons, could leave him rasping and voiceless for days. Chronic insomnia and poor digestion added to his woes. To put it bluntly, if he was to rise in politics, as he desperately wished to do, he needed professional help. He therefore decided to spend some time away from Rome, travelling both to refresh his mind and to consult the leading teachers of rhetoric, most of whom lived in Greece and Asia Minor.

Because I was responsible for the upkeep of his father's small library, and possessed a decent knowledge of Greek, Cicero asked if he might borrow me, as one might remove a book on loan, and take me with him to the East. My job would be to supervise arrangements, hire transport, pay teachers and so forth, and after a year go back to my old master. In the end, like many a useful volume, I was never returned.

We met in the harbour of Brundisium on the day we were due to set sail. This was during the consulship of Servilius Vatia and Claudius Pulcher, the six hundred and seventy-fifth year after the foundation of Rome. Cicero then was nothing like the imposing figure he later became, whose features were so famous he could not walk down the quietest street unrecognised. (What has happened, I wonder, to all those thousands of busts and portraits, which once adorned so many private houses and public buildings? Can they really *all* have been smashed and burned?) The young man who stood on the quayside that spring morning was thin and round-shouldered, with an unnaturally long neck, in which a large Adam's apple, as big as a baby's fist, plunged up and down whenever he swallowed. His eyes were protuberant, his skin sallow, his cheeks sunken; in short, he was the picture of ill health. *Well, Tiro,* I remember thinking, *you had better make the most of this trip, because it is not going to last long.*

We went first to Athens, where Cicero had promised himself the treat of studying philosophy at the Academy. I carried his bag to the lecture hall and was in the act of turning away when he called me back and demanded to know where I was going.

'To sit in the shade with the other slaves,' I replied, 'unless there is some further service you require.'

'Most certainly there is,' he said. 'I wish you to perform a very strenuous labour. I want you to come in here with me and learn a little philosophy, in order that I may have someone to talk to on our long travels.'

So I followed him in, and was privileged to hear Antiochus of Ascalon himself assert the three basic principles of stoicism – that virtue is sufficient for happiness, that nothing except virtue is good, and that the emotions are not to be trusted – three simple rules which, if only men could follow them, would solve all the problems of the world. Thereafter, Cicero and I would often debate such questions, and in this realm of the intellect the difference in our stations was always forgotten. We stayed six months with Antiochus and then moved on to the real purpose of our journey.

The dominant school of rhetoric at that time was the so-called

Asiatic method. Elaborate and flowery, full of pompous phrases and tinkling rhythms, its delivery was accompanied by a lot of swaying about and striding up and down. In Rome its leading exponent was Quintus Hortensius Hortalus, universally considered the foremost orator of the day, whose fancy footwork had earned him the nickname of 'the Dancing Master'. Cicero, with an eye to discovering his tricks, made a point of seeking out all Hortensius's mentors: Menippus of Stratonicea, Dionysius of Magnesia, Aeschylus of Cnidus, Xenocles of Adramyttium – the names alone give a flavour of their style. Cicero spent weeks with each, patiently studying their methods, until at last he felt he had their measure.

'Tiro,' he said to me one evening, picking at his customary plate of boiled vegetables, 'I have had quite enough of these perfumed prancers. You will arrange a boat from Loryma to Rhodes. We shall try a different tack, and enrol in the school of Apollonius Molon.'

And so it came about that, one spring morning just after dawn, when the straits of the Carpathian Sea were as smooth and milky as a pearl (you must forgive these occasional flourishes: I have read too much Greek poetry to maintain an austere Latin style), we were rowed across from the mainland to that ancient, rugged island, where the stocky figure of Molon himself awaited us on the quayside.

This Molon was a lawyer, originally from Alabanda, who had pleaded in the Rome courts brilliantly, and had even been invited to address the senate in Greek – an unheard-of honour – after which he had retired to Rhodes and opened his rhetorical school. His theory of oratory, the exact opposite of the Asiatics', was simple: don't move about too much, hold your head straight, stick to the point, make 'em laugh, make 'em cry, and when you've won their sympathy, sit down quickly – 'For nothing,' said Molon, 'dries more quickly than a tear.' This was far more to Cicero's taste, and he placed himself in Molon's hands entirely.

Molon's first action was to feed him that evening a bowl of hard-boiled eggs with anchovy sauce, and, when Cicero had finished that – not without some complaining, I can tell you – to follow it with a lump of red meat, seared over charcoal, accompanied by a cup of goat's milk. 'You need bulk, young man,' he told him, patting his own barrel chest. 'No mighty note was ever sounded by a feeble reed.' Cicero glared at him, but dutifully chewed until his plate was empty, and that night, for the first time in months, slept soundly. (I know this because I used to sleep on the floor outside his door.)

At dawn, the physical exercises began. 'Speaking in the forum,' said Molon, 'is comparable to running in a race. It requires stamina and strength.' He threw a fake punch at Cicero, who let out a loud '*Oof!*' and staggered backwards, almost falling over. Molon had him stand with his legs apart, his knees rigid, then bend from the waist twenty times to touch the ground on either side of his feet. After that, he made him lie on his back with his hands clasped behind his head and repeatedly sit up without shifting his legs. He made him lie on his front and raise himself solely by the strength of his arms, again twenty times, again without bending his knees. That was the regime on the first day, and each day afterwards more exercises were added and their duration increased. Cicero again slept soundly, and now had no trouble eating, either.

For the actual declamatory training, Molon took his eager pupil out of the shaded courtyard and into the heat of midday, and had him recite his exercise pieces – usually a trial scene or a soliloquy from Menander – while walking up a steep hill without pausing. In this fashion, with the lizards scattering underfoot and only the scratching of the cicadas in the olive trees for an audience, Cicero strengthened his lungs and learned how to gain the maximum output of words from a single breath. 'Pitch your delivery in the middle range,' instructed Molon. 'That is where the power is. Nothing too high or low.' In the afternoons, for speech projection, Molon took him down to the shingle beach, paced out eighty yards (the maximum range of the human voice) and made him declaim against the boom and hiss of the sea – the nearest thing, he said, to the murmur of three thousand people in the open air, or the background mutter of several hundred men in conversation in the senate. These were distractions Cicero would have to get used to.

'But what about the content of what I say?' Cicero asked. 'Surely I will compel attention chiefly by the force of my arguments?'

Molon shrugged. 'Content does not concern me. Remember Demosthenes: "Only three things count in oratory. Delivery, delivery, and again: delivery."'

'And my stutter?'

'The st-st-stutter does not b-b-bother me either,' replied Molon with a grin and a wink. 'Seriously, it adds interest and a useful impression of honesty. Demosthenes himself had a slight lisp. The audience identifies with these flaws. It is only perfection which is dull. Now, move further down the beach and still try to make me hear.'

Thus was I privileged, from the very start, to see the tricks of oratory passed from one master to another. 'There should be no effeminate bending of the neck, no twiddling of the fingers. Do not move your shoulders. If you must use your fingers for a gesture, try bending the middle finger against the thumb and extending the other three – that is it, that is good. The eyes of course are *always* turned in the direction of the gesture, except when we have to reject: "O gods, avert such plague!" or "I do not think that I deserve such honour."'

Nothing was allowed to be written down, for no orator worthy of the name would dream of reading out a text or consulting a sheaf of notes. Molon favoured the standard method of memorising a speech: that of an imaginary journey around the speaker's house. 'Place the first point you want to make in the entrance hall, and picture it lying there, then the second in the atrium, and so on, walking round the house in the way you would naturally tour it, assigning a section of your speech not just to each room, but to every alcove and statue. Make sure each site is well lit, clearly defined, and distinctive. Otherwise you will go groping around like a drunk trying to find his bed after a party.'

Cicero was not the only pupil at Molon's academy that spring and summer. In time we were joined by Cicero's younger brother Quintus, and his cousin Lucius, and also by two friends of his: Servius, a fussy lawyer who wished to become a judge, and Atticus – the dapper, charming Atticus – who had no interest in oratory, for he lived in Athens, and certainly had no intention of making a career in politics, but who loved spending time with Cicero. All marvelled at the change which had been wrought in his health and appearance, and on their final evening together – for now it was autumn, and the time had come to return to Rome – they gathered to hear the effects which Molon had produced on his oratory.

I wish I could recall what it was that Cicero spoke about that night after dinner, but I fear I am the living proof of Demosthenes' cynical assertion that content counts for nothing beside delivery. I stood discreetly out of sight, among the shadows, and all I can picture now are the moths whirling like flakes of ash around the torches, the wash of stars above the courtyard, and the enraptured faces of the young men, flushed in the firelight, turned towards Cicero. But I do remember Molon's words afterwards, when his protégé, with a final bow of his head towards the imaginary jury, sat down. After a long silence he got to his feet and said, in a hoarse voice: 'Cicero, I congratulate you and I am amazed at you. It is Greece and her fate that I am sorry for. The only glory that was left to us was the supremecy of our eloquence, and now you have taken that as well. Go back,' he said, and gestured with those three outstretched fingers, across the lamplit terrace to the dark and distant sea, 'go back, my boy, *and conquer Rome.*'

Very well, then. Easy enough to say. But how do you do this? How do you 'conquer Rome' with no weapon other than your voice?

The first step is obvious: you must become a senator.

To gain entry to the senate at that time it was necessary to be at least thirty-one years old and a millionaire. To be exact, assets of one million sesterces had to be shown to the authorities simply to qualify to be a candidate at the annual elections in July, when twenty new senators were elected to replace those who had died in the previous year or had become too poor to keep their seats. But where was Cicero to get a million? His father certainly did not have that kind of money: the family estate was small and heavily mortgaged. He faced, therefore, the three traditional options. But making it would take too long, and stealing it would be too risky. Accordingly, soon after our return from Rhodes, he married it. Terentia was seventeen, boyishly flat-chested, with a head of short, tight black curls. Her half-sister was a vestal virgin, proof of her family's social status. More importantly, she was the owner of two slum apartment blocks in Rome, some woodland in the suburbs, and a farm; total value: one and a quarter million. (Ah, Terentia: plain, grand and rich – what a piece of work you were! I saw her only a few months ago, being carried on an open litter along the coastal road to Naples, screeching at her bearers to make better speed: white-haired and walnut-skinned but otherwise quite unchanged.)

So Cicero, in due course, became a senator – in fact, he topped the poll, being generally now regarded as the second-best advocate in Rome, after Hortensius – and then was sent off for the obligatory year of government service, in his case to the province of Sicily, before being allowed to take his seat. His official title was quaestor, the most junior of the magistracies. Wives were not permitted to accompany their husbands on these tours of duty, so Terentia – I am sure to his deep relief – stayed at home. But I went with him, for by this time I had become a kind of extension of himself, to be used unthinkingly, like an extra hand or foot. Part of the reason for my indispensability was that I had devised a method of taking down his words as fast as he could utter them. From small beginnings – I can modestly claim to be the man who invented the ampersand – my system eventually swelled to a handbook of some four thousand symbols. I found, for example, that Cicero was fond of repeating certain phrases, and these I learned to reduce to a line, or even a few dots – thus proving what most people already know, that politicians essentially say the same thing over and over again. He dictated to me from his bath and his couch, from inside swaying carriages and on country walks. He never ran short of words and I never ran short of symbols to catch and hold them for ever as they flew through the air. We were made for one another.

But to return to Sicily. Do not be alarmed: I shall not describe our work in any detail. Like so much of politics, it was dreary even while it was happening, without revisiting it sixty-odd years later. What was memorable, and significant, was the journey home. Cicero purposely delayed this by a month, from March to April, to ensure he passed through Puteoli during the senate recess, at exactly the moment when all the smart political set would be on the Bay of Naples, enjoying the mineral baths. I was ordered to hire the finest twelve-oared rowing boat I could find, so that he could enter the harbour in style, wearing for the first time the purple-edged toga of a senator of the Roman republic.

For Cicero had convinced himself that he had been such a great success in Sicily, he must be the centre of all attention back in Rome. In a hundred stifling market squares, in the shade of a thousand dusty, wasp-infested Sicilian plane trees, he had dispensed Rome's justice, impartially and with dignity. He had purchased a record amount of grain to feed the electors back in the capital, and had dispatched it at a record cheap price. His speeches at government ceremonies had been masterpieces of tact. He had even feigned interest in the conversation of the locals. He knew he had done well, and in a stream of official reports to the senate he boasted of his achievements. I must confess that occasionally I toned these down before I gave them to the official messenger, and tried to hint to him that perhaps Sicily was not entirely the centre of the world. He took no notice.

I can see him now, standing in the prow, straining his eyes at Puteoli's quayside, as we returned to Italy. What was he expecting? I wonder. A band to pipe him ashore? A consular deputation to present him with a laurel wreath? There was a crowd, all right, but it was not for him. Hortensius, who already had his eye on the consulship, was holding a banquet on several brightly coloured pleasure-craft moored nearby, and guests were waiting to be ferried out to the party. Cicero stepped ashore – ignored. He looked about him, puzzled, and at that moment a few of the revellers, noticing his freshly gleaming senatorial rig, came hurrying towards him. He squared his shoulders in pleasurable anticipation.

'Senator,' called one, 'what's the news from Rome?'

Cicero somehow managed to maintain his smile. 'I have not come from Rome, my good fellow. I am returning from my province.'

A red-haired man, no doubt already drunk, said, 'Ooooh! My *good fellow*! He's returning from his *province* . . .'

There was a snort of laughter, barely suppressed.

'What is so funny about that?' interrupted a third, eager to smooth things over. 'Don't you know? He has been in Africa.'

Cicero's smile was now heroic. 'Sicily, actually.'

There may have been more in this vein. I cannot remember. People began drifting away once they realised there was no city gossip to be had, and very soon Hortensius came along and ushered his remaining guests towards their boats. Cicero he nodded to, civilly enough, but pointedly did not invite to join him. We were left alone.

A trivial incident, you might think, and yet Cicero himself used to say that this was the instant at which his ambition hardened within him to rock. He had been humiliated – humiliated by his own vanity – and given brutal evidence of his smallness in the world. He stood there for a long time, watching Hortensius and his friends partying across the water, listening to the merry flutes, and when he turned away, he had changed. I do not exaggerate. I saw it in his eyes. *Very well*, his expression seemed to say, *you fools can frolic; I shall work.*

'This experience, gentlemen, I am inclined to think was more valuable to me than if I had been hailed with salvoes of applause. I ceased thenceforth from considering what the world was likely to hear about me: from that day I took care that I should be seen personally every day. I lived in the public eye. I frequented the forum. Neither my doorkeeper nor sleep prevented anyone from getting in to see me. Not even when I had nothing to do did I do nothing, and consequently absolute leisure was a thing I never knew.'

I came across that passage in one of his speeches not long ago and I can vouch for the truth of it. He walked away from the harbour like a man in a dream, up through Puteoli and out on to the main highway without once looking back. I struggled along behind him carrying as much luggage as I could manage. To begin with, his steps were slow and thoughtful, but gradually they picked up speed, until at last he was striding so rapidly in the direction of Rome I had difficulty keeping up.

And with this both ends my first roll of paper, and begins the real story of Marcus Tullius Cicero.

II

The day which was to prove the turning point began like any other, an hour before dawn, with Cicero, as always, the first in the household to rise. I lay for a little while in the darkness and listened to the thump of the floorboards above my head as he went through the exercises he had learned on Rhodes – a visit now six years in the past – then I rolled off my straw mattress and rinsed my face. It was the first day of November; cold.

Cicero had a modest two-storey dwelling on the ridge of the Esquiline Hill, hemmed in by a temple on one side and a block of flats on the other, although if you could be bothered to scramble up on to the roof you would be rewarded with a decent view across the smoky valley to the great temples on Capitol Hill about half a mile to the west. It was actually his father's place, but the old gentleman was in poor health nowadays and seldom left the country, so Cicero had it to himself, along with Terentia and their five-year-old daughter, Tullia, and a dozen slaves: me, the two secretaries working under me, Sositheus and Laurea, the steward, Eros, Terentia's business manager, Philotimus, two maids, a nurse, a cook, a valet and a doorkeeper. There was also an old blind philosopher somewhere, Diodotus the Stoic, who occasionally groped his way out of his room to join Cicero for dinner when his master needed an intellectual workout. So: fifteen of us in the household in all. Terentia complained endlessly about the cramped conditions, but Cicero would not move, for at this time he was still very much in his man-of-the-people phase, and the house sat well with the image.

The first thing I did that morning, as I did every morning, was to slip over my left wrist a loop of cord, to which was attached a small notebook of my own design. This consisted of not the usual one or two but four double-sided sheets of wax, each in a beechwood frame, very thin and so hinged that I could fold them all up and snap them shut. In this way I could take many more notes in a single session of dictation than the average secretary; but even so, such was Cicero's daily torrent of words, I always made sure to put spares in my pockets. Then I pulled back the curtain of my tiny room and walked across the courtyard into the tablinum, lighting the lamps and checking all was ready. The only piece of furniture was a sideboard, on which stood a bowl of chickpeas. (Cicero's name derived from *cicer*, meaning chickpea, and believing that an unusual name was an advantage in politics, he always took pains to draw attention to it.) Once I was satisfied, I passed through the atrium into the entrance hall, where the doorman was already waiting with his hand on the big metal lock. I checked the light through the narrow window, and when I judged it pale enough, gave a nod to the doorman, who slid back the bolts.

Outside in the chilly street, the usual crowd of the miserable and the desperate was already waiting, and I made a note of each man as he crossed the threshold. Most I recognised; those I did not, I asked for their names; the familiar no-hopers, I turned away. But the standing instruction was: 'If he has a vote, let him in', so the tablinum was soon well filled with anxious clients, each seeking a piece of the senator's time. I lingered by the entrance until I reckoned the queue had all filed in and was just stepping back when a figure with the dusty clothes, straggling hair and uncut beard of a man in mourning loomed in the doorway. He gave me a fright, I do not mind admitting.

'Tiro!' he said. 'Thank the gods!' And he sank against the door jamb, exhausted, peering out at me with pale, dead eyes. I guess he must have been about fifty. At first I could not place him, but it is one of the jobs of a political secretary to put names to faces, and gradually, despite his condition, a picture began to assemble in my mind: a large house overlooking the sea, an ornamental garden, a collection of bronze statues, a town somewhere in Sicily, in the north – Thermae, that was it.

'Sthenius of Thermae,' I said, and held out my hand. 'Welcome.'

It was not my place to comment on his appearance, nor to ask what he was doing hundreds of miles from home and in such obvious distress. I left him in the tablinum and went through to Cicero's study. The senator, who was due in court that morning to defend a youth charged with parricide, and who would also be expected to attend the afternoon session of the senate, was squeezing a small leather ball to strengthen his fingers, while being robed in his toga by his valet. He was listening to one letter being read out by young Sositheus, and at the same time dictating a message to Laurea, to whom I had taught the rudiments of my shorthand system. As I entered, he threw the ball at me – I caught it without thinking – and gestured for the list of callers. He read it greedily, as he always did. What had he caught overnight? Some prominent citizen from a useful tribe? A Sabatini, perhaps? A Pomptini? Or a businessman rich enough to vote among the first centuries in the consular elections? But today it was only the usual small fry and his face gradually fell until he reached the final name.

'Sthenius?' He interrupted his dictation. 'He's that Sicilian, is he not? The rich one with the bronzes? We had better find out what he wants.'

'Sicilians don't have a vote,' I pointed out.

'Pro bono,' he said, with a straight face. 'Besides, he does have bronzes. I shall see him first.'

So I fetched in Sthenius, who was given the usual treatment – the trademark smile, the manly double-grip handshake, the long and sincere stare into the eyes – then shown to a seat and asked what had brought him to Rome. I had started remembering more about Sthenius. We had stayed with him twice in Thermae, when Cicero heard cases in the town. Back then he had been one of the leading citizens of the province, but now all his vigour and confidence had gone. He needed help, he announced. He was facing ruin. His life was in terrible danger. He had been robbed.

'Really?' said Cicero. He was half glancing at a document on his desk, not paying too much attention, for a busy advocate hears many hard-luck stories. 'You have my sympathy. Robbed by whom?'

'By the governor of Sicily, Gaius Verres.'

The senator looked up sharply.

There was no stopping Sthenius after that. As his story poured out, Cicero caught my eye and performed a little mime of note-taking – he wanted a record of this – and when Sthenius eventually paused to draw breath, he gently interrupted and asked him to go back a little, to the day, almost three months earlier, when he had first received the letter from Verres. 'What was your reaction?'

'I worried a little. He already had a . . . *reputation*. People call him – his name meaning boar – people call him the Boar with Blood on his Snout. But I could hardly refuse.'

'You still have this letter?'

'Yes.'

'And in it did Verres specifically mention your art collection?'

'Oh yes. He said he had often heard about it and wanted to see it.'

'And how soon after that did he come to stay?'

'Very soon. A week at most.'

'Was he alone?'

'No, he had his lictors with him. I had to find room for them as well. Bodyguards are always rough types, but these were the worst set of thugs I ever saw. The chief of them, Sextius, is the official executioner for the whole of Sicily. He demands bribes from his victims by threatening to botch the job – you know, mangle them – if they do not pay up beforehand.' Sthenius swallowed and started breathing hard. We waited.

'Take your time,' said Cicero.

'I thought Verres might like to bathe after his journey, and then we could dine – but no, he said he wanted to see my collection straightaway.'

'You had some very fine pieces, I remember.'

'It was my life, Senator, I cannot put it plainer. Thirty years of travelling and haggling. Corinthian and Delian bronzes, pictures, silver – nothing I did not handle and choose myself. I had Myron's *The Discus Thrower* and *The Spear Bearer* by Polycleitus. Some silver cups by Mentor. Verres was complimentary. He said it deserved a wider audience. He said it was good enough for public display. I paid no attention till we were having dinner on the terrace and I heard a noise from the inner courtyard. My steward told me a wagon drawn by oxen had arrived and Verres's lictors were loading it with everything.'

Sthenius was silent again, and I could readily imagine the shame of it for such a proud man: his wife wailing, the household trauma-tised, the dusty outlines where the statues had once stood. The only sound in the study was the tap of my stylus on wax.

Cicero said: 'You did not complain?'

'Who to? The governor?' Sthenius laughed. 'No, Senator. I was alive, wasn't I? If he had just left it at that, I would have swal-lowed my losses, and you would never have heard a squeak from me. But collecting can be a sickness, and I tell you what: your Governor Verres has it badly. You remember those statues in the town square?'

'Indeed I do. Three very fine bronzes. But you are surely not telling me he stole those as well?'

'He tried. This was on his third day under my roof. He asked me whose they were. I told him they were the property of the town, and had been for centuries. You know they are four hundred years old? He said he would like permission to remove them to his residence in Syracuse, also as a loan, and asked me to approach the council. By then I knew what kind of a man he was, so I said I could not, in all honour, oblige him. He left that night. A few days after that, I received a summons for trial on the fifth day of October, on a charge of forgery.'

'Who brought the charge?'

'An enemy of mine named Agathinus. He is a client of Verres. My first thought was to face him down. I have nothing to fear as far as my honesty goes. I have never forged a document in my life. But then I heard the judge was to be Verres himself, and that he had already fixed on the punishment. I was to be whipped in front of the whole town for my insolence.'

'And so you fled?'

'That same night, I took a boat along the coast to Messana.'

Cicero rested his chin in his hand and contemplated Sthenius. I recognised that gesture. He was weighing the witness up. 'You say the hearing was on the fifth of last month. Have you heard what happened?'

'That is why I am here. I was convicted in my absence, sentenced to be flogged – and fined five thousand. But there is worse than that. At the hearing, Verres claimed fresh evidence had been produced against me, this time of spying for the rebels in Spain. There is to be a new trial in Syracuse on the first day of December.'

'But spying is a capital offence.'

'Senator – believe me – he plans to have me crucified. He boasts of it openly. I would not be the first, either. I need help. Please. Will you help me?'

I thought he might be about to sink to his knees and start kissing the senator's feet, and so, I suspect, did Cicero, for he quickly got up from his chair and started pacing about the room. 'It seems to me there are two aspects to this case, Sthenius. One, the theft of your property – and there, frankly, I cannot see what is to be done. Why do you think men such as Verres desire to be governors in the first place? Because they know they can take what they want, within reason. The second aspect, the manipulation of the legal process – that is more promising.

'I know several men with great legal expertise who live in Sicily – one, indeed, in Syracuse. I shall write to him today and urge him, as a particular favour to me, to accept your case. I shall even give him my opinion as to what he should do. He should apply to the court to have the forthcoming prosecution declared invalid, on the grounds that you are not present to answer. If that fails, and Verres goes ahead, your advocate should come to Rome and argue that the conviction is unsound.'

But the Sicilian was shaking his head. 'If it was just a lawyer in Syracuse I needed, Senator, I would not have come all the way to Rome.'

I could see Cicero did not like where this was leading. Such a case could tie up his practice for days, and Sicilians, as I had reminded him, did not have votes. Pro bono indeed!

'Listen,' he said reassuringly, 'your case is strong. Verres is obviously corrupt. He abuses hospitality. He steals. He brings false charges. He plots judicial murder. His position is indefensible. It can easily be handled by an advocate in Syracuse – really, I promise you. Now, if you will excuse me, I have many clients to see, and I am due in court in less than an hour.'

He nodded to me and I stepped forward, putting a hand on Sthenius's arm to guide him out. The Sicilian shook it off. 'But I need you,' he persisted.

'Why?'

'Because my only hope of justice lies here, not in Sicily, where Verres controls the courts. And everyone here tells me Marcus Cicero is the second-best lawyer in Rome.'

'Do they indeed?' Cicero's tone took on an edge of sarcasm: he hated that epithet. 'Well then, why settle for second best? Why not go straight to Hortensius?'

'I thought of that,' said his visitor artlessly, 'but he turned me down. He is representing Verres.'

I showed the Sicilian out and returned to find Cicero alone in his study, tilted back in his chair, staring at the wall, tossing the leather ball from one hand to the other. Legal textbooks cluttered his desk. *Precedents in Pleading* by Hostilius was one which he had open; Manilius's *Conditions of Sale* was another.

'Do you remember that red-haired drunk on the quayside at Puteoli, the day we came back from Sicily? "Ooooh! My *good fellow*! He's returning from his *province* . . ."'

I nodded.

'That was Verres.' The ball went back and forth, back and forth. 'The fellow gives corruption a bad name.'

'I am surprised at Hortensius for getting involved with him.'

'Are you? I'm not.' He stopped tossing the ball and contemplated it on his outstretched palm. 'The Dancing Master and the Boar . . .' He brooded for a while. 'A man in my position would have to be mad to tangle with Hortensius and Verres combined, and all for the sake of some Sicilian who is not even a Roman citizen.'

'True.'

'True,' he repeated, although there was an odd hesitancy in the way he said it which sometimes makes me wonder if he had not just then glimpsed the whole thing – the whole extraordinary set of possibilities and consequences, laid out like a mosaic in his mind. But if he had, I never knew, for at that moment his daughter Tullia ran in, still wearing her nightdress, with some childish drawing to show him, and suddenly his attention switched entirely on to her and he scooped her up and settled her on his knee. 'Did you do this? Did you *really* do this all by yourself . . . ?'

I left him to it and slipped away, back into the tablinum, to announce that we were running late and that the senator was about to leave for court. Sthenius was still moping around, and asked me when he could expect an answer, to which I could only reply that he would have to fall in with the rest. Soon after that

Cicero himself appeared, hand in hand with Tullia, nodding good morning to everyone, greeting each by name ('The first rule in politics, Tiro: never forget a face'). He was beautifully turned out, as always, his hair pomaded and slicked back, his skin scented, his toga freshly laundered; his red leather shoes spotless and shiny; his face bronzed by years of pleading in the open air; groomed, lean, fit: he *glowed*. They followed him into the vestibule, where he hoisted the beaming little girl into the air, showed her off to the assembled company, then turned her face to his and gave her a resounding kiss on the lips. There was a drawn-out 'Ahh!' and some isolated applause. It was not wholly put on for show – he would have done it even if no one had been present, for he loved his darling Tulliola more than he ever loved anyone in his entire life – but he knew the Roman elect-orate were a sentimental lot, and that if word of his paternal devotion got around, it would do him no harm.

And so we stepped out into the bright promise of that November morning, into the gathering noise of the city – Cicero striding ahead, with me beside him, notebook at the ready; Sositheus and Laurea tucked in behind, carrying the document cases with the evidence he needed for his appearance in court; and, on either side of us, trying to catch the senator's attention, yet proud merely to be in his aura, two dozen assorted peti-tioners and hangers-on, including Sthenius – down the hill from the leafy, respectable heights of the Esquiline and into the stink and smoke and racket of Subura. Here the height of the tene-ments shut out the sunlight and the packed crowds squeezed our phalanx of supporters into a broken thread that still somehow determinedly trailed along after us. Cicero was a well-known figure here, a hero to the shopkeepers and merchants whose inter-ests he had represented, and who had watched him walking past for years. Without once breaking his rapid step, his sharp blue eyes registered every bowed head, every wave of greeting, and it was rare for me to need to whisper a name in his ear, for he knew his voters far better than I.

I do not know how it is these days, but at that time there were six or seven law courts in almost permanent session, each set up in a different part of the forum, so that at the hour when they all opened one could barely move for advocates and legal officers hurrying about. To make it worse, the praetor of each court would always arrive from his house preceded by half a dozen lictors to clear his path, and as luck would have it, our little entourage debouched into the forum at exactly the moment that Hortensius – at this time a praetor himself – went parading by towards the senate house. We were all held back by his guards to let the great man pass, and to this day I do not think it was his intention to cut Cicero dead, for he was a man of refined, almost effeminate manners: he simply did not see him. But the consequence was that the so-called second-best advocate in Rome, his cordial greeting dead on his lips, was left staring at the retreating back of the so-called best with such an intensity of loathing I was surprised Hortensius did not start rubbing at the skin between his shoulder blades.

Our business that morning was in the central criminal court, convened outside the Basilica Aemilia, where the fifteen-year-old Caius Popillius Laenas was on trial accused of stabbing his father to death through the eye with a metal stylus. I could already see a big crowd waiting around the tribunal. Cicero was due to make the closing speech for the defence. That was attraction enough. But if he failed to convince the jury, Popillius, as a convicted parricide, would be stripped naked, flayed till he bled, then sewn up in a sack together with a dog, a cock and a viper and thrown into the River Tiber. There was a whiff of bloodlust in the air, and as the onlookers parted to let us through, I caught a glimpse of Popillius himself, a notoriously violent youth, whose eyebrows merged to form a continuous thick black line. He was seated next to his uncle on the bench reserved for the defence, scowling defiantly, spitting at anyone who came too close. 'We really must secure an acquittal,' observed Cicero, 'if only to spare the dog, the cock and the viper the ordeal of being sewn up in a sack with Popillius.' He always maintained that it was no business of the advocate to worry whether his client was guilty or not: that was for the court. He undertook only to do his best, and in return the Popillii Laeni, who could boast four consuls in their family tree, would be obliged to support him whenever he ran for office.

Sositheus and Laurea set down the boxes of evidence, and I was just bending to unfasten the nearest when Cicero told me to leave it. 'Save yourself the trouble,' he said, tapping the side of his head. 'I have the speech up here well enough.' He bowed politely to his client – 'Good day, Popillius: we shall soon have this settled, I trust' – then continued to me, in a quieter voice: 'I have a more important task for you. Give me your notebook. I want you to go to the senate house, find the chief clerk, and see if there is a chance of having this put on the order paper this afternoon.' He was writing rapidly. 'Say nothing to our Sicilian friend just yet. There is great danger. We must take this care-fully, one step at a time.'

It was not until I had left the tribunal and was halfway across the forum to the senate house that I risked taking a look at what he had written: *That in the opinion of this house the prosecution of persons in their absence on capital charges should be prohibited in the provinces.* I felt a tightening in my chest, for I saw at once what it meant. Cleverly, tentatively, obliquely, Cicero was preparing at last to challenge his great rival. I was carrying a declaration of war.

Gellius Publicola was the presiding consul for November. He was a blunt, delightfully stupid military commander of the old school. It was said, or at any rate it was said by Cicero, that when Gellius had passed through Athens with his army twenty years before, he had offered to mediate between the warring schools of philosophy: he would convene a conference at which they could thrash out the meaning of life once and for all, thus sparing themselves further pointless argument. I knew Gellius's secretary fairly well, and as the afternoon's agenda was unusually light, with nothing scheduled apart from a report on the military situation, he agreed to add Cicero's motion to the order paper. 'But you might warn your master,' he said, 'that the consul has heard his little joke about the philosophers, *and he does not much like it.*'

By the time I returned to the criminal court, Cicero was already well launched on his closing speech for the defence. It was not one of those which he afterwards chose to preserve, so unfortunately I do not have the text. All I can remember is that he won the case by the clever expedient of promising that young Popillius, if acquitted, would devote the rest of his life to military service – a pledge which took the prosecution, the jury, and indeed his client entirely by surprise. But it did the trick, and the moment the verdict was in, without pausing to waste another moment on the ghastly Popillius, or even to snatch a mouthful of food, he set off immediately westwards towards the senate house, still trailed by his original honour-guard of admirers, their number swelled by the spreading rumour that the great advocate had another speech planned.

Cicero used to say that it was not in the senate chamber that the real business of the republic was done, but outside, in the open-air lobby known as the senaculum, where the senators were obliged to wait until they constituted a quorum. This daily massing of white-robed figures, which might last for an hour or more, was one of the great sights of the city, and while Cicero plunged in among them, Sthenius and I joined the crowd of gawpers on the other side of the forum. (The Sicilian, poor fellow, still had no idea what was happening.)

It is in the nature of things that not all politicians can achieve greatness. Of the six hundred men who then constituted the senate, only eight could be elected praetor – to preside over the courts – in any one year, and only two of these could go on to achieve the supreme *imperium* of the consulship. In other words, more than half of those milling around the senaculum were doomed never to hold elected office at all. They were what the aristocrats sneeringly called the *pedarii*, the men who voted with their feet, shuffling dutifully to one side of the chamber or the other whenever a division was called. And yet, in their way, these citizens were the backbone of the republic: bankers, businessmen and landowners from all over Italy; wealthy, cautious and patriotic; suspicious of the arrogance and show of the aristocrats. Like Cicero, they were often 'new men', the first in their families to win election to the senate. These were his people, and observing him threading his way among them that afternoon was like watching a master-craftsman in his studio, a sculptor with his stone – here a hand resting lightly on an elbow, there a heavy arm clapped across a pair of meaty shoulders; with this man a coarse joke, with that a solemn word of condolence, his own hands crossed and pressed to his breast in sympathy; detained by a bore, he would seem to have all the hours of the day to listen to his dreary story, but then you would see his hand flicker out and catch some passer-by, and he would spin as gracefully as a dancer, with the tenderest backward glance of apology and regret, to work on someone else. Occasionally he would gesture in our direction, and a senator would stare at us, and perhaps shake his head in disbelief, or nod slowly to promise his support.

'What is he saying about me?' asked Sthenius. 'What is he going to do?'

I made no answer, for I did not know myself.

By now it was clear that Hortensius had realised something was going on, but was unsure exactly what. The order of business had been posted in its usual place beside the door of the senate house. I saw Hortensius stop to read it – *the prosecution of persons in their absence on capital charges should be prohibited in the provinces* – and turn away, mystified. Gellius Publicola was sitting in the doorway on his carved ivory chair, surrounded by his attendants, waiting until the entrails had been inspected and the auguries declared favourable before summoning the senators inside. Hortensius approached him, palms spread wide in enquiry. Gellius shrugged and pointed irritably at Cicero. Hortensius swung round to discover his ambitious rival surrounded by a conspiratorial circle of senators. He frowned, and went over to join his own aristocratic friends: the three Metellus brothers – Quintus, Lucius and Marcus – and the two elderly ex-consuls who really ran the empire, Quintus Catulus (whose sister was married to Hortensius), and the double-triumphator Publius Servilius Vatia Isauricus. Merely writing their names after all these years raises the hairs on my neck, for these were such men, stern and unyielding and steeped in the old republican values, as no longer exist. Hortensius must have told them about the motion, because slowly all five turned to look at Cicero.

Immediately thereafter a trumpet sounded to signal the start of the session and the senators began to file in.

The old senate house was a cool, gloomy, cavernous temple of government, split by a wide central aisle of black and white tile. Facing across it on either side were long rows of wooden benches, six deep, on which the senators sat, with a dais at the far end for the chairs of the consuls. The light on that November afternoon was pale and bluish, dropping in shafts from the unglazed windows just beneath the raftered roof. Pigeons cooed on the sills and flapped across the chamber, sending small feathers and even occasionally hot squirts of excrement down on to the senators below. Some held that it was lucky to be shat on while speaking, others that it was an ill omen, a few that it depended on the colour of the deposit. The superstitions were as numerous as their interpretations. Cicero took no notice of them, just as he took no notice of the arrangement of sheep's guts, or whether a peal of thunder was on the left or the right, or the particular flight-path of a flock of birds – idiocy all of it, as far as he was concerned, even though he later campaigned enthusiastically for election to the College of Augurs.

By ancient tradition, then still observed, the doors of the senate house remained open so that the people could hear the debates. The crowd, Sthenius and I among them, surged across the forum to the threshold of the chamber, where we were held back by a simple rope. Gellius was already speaking, relating the dispatches of the army commanders in the field. On all three fronts, the news was good. In southern Italy, the vastly rich Marcus Crassus – he who once boasted that no man could call himself wealthy until he could keep a legion of five thousand solely out of his income – was putting down Spartacus's slave revolt with great severity. In Spain, Pompey the Great, after six years' fighting, was mopping up the last of the rebel armies. In Asia Minor, Lucius Lucullus was enjoying a glorious run of victories over King Mithradates. Once their reports had been read, supporters of each man rose in turn to praise his patron's achievements and subtly denigrate those of his rivals. I knew the politics of this from Cicero and passed them on to Sthenius in a superior whisper: 'Crassus hates Pompey and is determined to defeat Spartacus before Pompey can return with his legions from Spain to take all the credit. Pompey hates Crassus and wants the glory of finishing off Spartacus so that he can rob him of a triumph. Crassus and Pompey both hate Lucullus because he has the most glamorous command.'

'And whom does Lucullus hate?'

'Pompey and Crassus, of course, for intriguing against him.'

I felt as pleased as a child who has just successfully recited his lesson, for it was all just a game then, and I had no idea that we would ever get drawn in. The debate came to a desultory halt, without the need for a vote, and the senators began talking among themselves. Gellius, who must have been well into his sixties, held the order paper up close to his face and squinted at it, then peered around the chamber, trying to locate Cicero, who, as a junior senator, was confined to a distant back bench near the door. Eventually Cicero stood to show himself, Gellius sat, the buzz of voices died away, and I picked up my stylus. There was a silence, which Cicero allowed to grow, an old trick to increase tension. And then, when he had waited so long it seemed that something must be wrong, he began to speak – very quietly and hesitantly at first, forcing his listeners to strain their ears, the rhythm of his words hooking them without their even knowing it.

'Honourable members, compared to the stirring accounts of

our men in arms to which we have lately listened, I fear what I say will sound small indeed.' And now his voice rose. 'But if the moment has come when this noble house no longer has ears for the pleas of an innocent man, then all those courageous deeds are worthless, and our soldiers bleed in vain.' There was a murmur of agreement from the benches beside him. 'This morning there came into my home just such an innocent man, whose treatment by one of our number has been so shameful, so monstrous and so cruel that the gods themselves must weep to hear of it. I refer to the honourable Sthenius of Thermae, recently resident in the miserable, misgoverned, misappropriated province of Sicily.'

At the word 'Sicily', Hortensius, who had been sprawling on the front bench nearest the consul, twitched slightly. Without taking his eyes from Cicero he turned and began whispering to Quintus, the eldest of the Metellus brothers, who promptly leaned behind him and beckoned to Marcus, the junior of the fraternal trio. Marcus squatted on his haunches to receive his instructions, then, after a brief bow to the presiding consul, came hurrying down the aisle towards me. For a moment I thought I was about to be struck – they were tough, swaggering fellows, those Metelli – but he did not even look at me. He lifted the rope, ducked under it, pushed through the crowd and disappeared.

Cicero, meanwhile, was hitting his stride. After our return from Molon, with the precept 'Delivery, delivery, delivery' carved into his mind, he had spent many hours at the theatre, studying the methods of the actors, and had developed a considerable talent for mime and mimicry. Using only the smallest touch of voice or gesture, he could, as it were, populate his speeches with the characters to whom he referred. He treated the senate that afternoon to a command performance: the swaggering arrogance of Verres was contrasted with the quiet dignity of Sthenius, the long-suffering Sicilians shrank before the vileness of the public executioner, Sextius. Sthenius himself could hardly believe what he was witnessing. He had been in the city but a day, and here he was, the subject of a debate in the Roman senate itself. Hortensius, meanwhile, kept glancing towards the door, and as Cicero began to work towards his peroration – 'Sthenius seeks our protection, not merely from a thief, but from the very man who is supposed to punish thieves!' – he finally sprang to his feet. Under the rules of the senate, a serving praetor always took precedence over a humble member of the *pedarii*, and Cicero had no choice but to give way.

'Senators,' boomed Hortensius, 'we have sat through this long enough! This is surely one of the most flagrant pieces of opportunism ever seen in this noble house! A vague motion is placed before us, which now turns out to relate to one man only. No notice is given to us about what is to be discussed. We have no means of verifying whether what we are hearing is true. Gaius Verres, a senior member of this order, is being defamed with no opportunity to defend himself. I move that this sitting be suspended immediately!'

Hortensius sat to a patter of applause from the aristocrats. Cicero stood. His face was perfectly straight.

'The senator seems not to have read the motion,' he said, in mock puzzlement. 'Where is there any mention here of Gaius Verres? Gentlemen, I am not asking this house to vote on Gaius Verres. It would not be fair to judge Gaius Verres in his absence. Gaius Verres is not here to defend himself. And now that we have established that principle, will Hortensius please extend it to my client, and agree that he should not be tried in his absence either? Or is there to be one law for the aristocrats and another for the rest of us?'

That raised the temperature well enough and set the *pedarii* around Cicero and the crowd at the door roaring with delight. I felt someone pushing roughly behind me and Marcus Metellus shouldered his way back into the chamber and walked quickly up the aisle towards Hortensius. Cicero watched his progress, at first with an expression of puzzlement, and then with one of realisation. He quickly held up his hand for silence. 'Very well. Since Hortensius objects to the vagueness of the original motion, let us reframe it so that there can be no doubt. I propose an amendment: *That whereas Sthenius has been prosecuted in his absence, it is agreed that no trial of him in his absence shall take place, and that if any such trial has already taken place, it shall be invalid.* And I say: let us vote on it now, and in the highest traditions of the Roman senate save an innocent man from the dreadful punishment of crucifixion!'

To mingled cheers and cat-calls, Cicero sat and Gellius rose. 'The motion has been put,' declared the consul. 'Does any other member wish to speak?'

Hortensius, the Metellus brothers and a few others of their party, such as Scribonius Curio, Sergius Catilina and Aemilius Alba, were in a huddle around the front bench, and it briefly seemed that the house would move straight to a division, which would have suited Cicero perfectly. But when the aristocrats finally settled back in their places, the bony figure of Catulus was revealed to be still on his feet. 'I believe I shall speak,' he said. 'Yes, I believe I shall have something to say.' Catulus was as hard and heartless as flint – the great-great-great-great-great-grandson (I believe that is the correct number of greats) of that Catulus who had triumphed over Hamilcar in the First Punic War – and a full two centuries of history were distilled into his vinegary old voice. 'I shall speak,' he repeated, 'and what I shall say first is that that young man' – pointing at Cicero – 'knows nothing whatsoever about "the highest traditions of the Roman senate", for if he did he would realise that no senator ever attacks another, except to his face. It shows a lack of breeding. I look at him there, all clever and eager in his place, and do you know what I think, gentlemen? I think of the wisdom of the old saying: "An ounce of heredity is worth a pound of merit"!'

Now it was the aristocrats who were rocking with laughter. Catilina, of whom I shall have much more to say later, pointed at Cicero, and then drew his finger across his throat. Cicero flushed pink but kept his self-control. He even managed a thin smile. Catulus turned with delight to the benches behind him, and I caught a glimpse of his grinning profile, sharp and beak-nosed, like a head on a coin. He swivelled back to face the chamber. 'When I first entered this house, in the consulship of Claudius Pulcher and Marcus Perperna . . .' His voice settled into a confident drone.

Cicero caught my eye. He mouthed something, glanced up at the windows, then gestured with his head towards the door. I understood at once what he meant, and as I pushed my way back through the spectators and into the forum, I realised that Marcus Metellus must have been dispatched on exactly the same errand. In those days, when time-keeping was cruder than it is now, the last hour of the day's business was deemed to begin when the sun dropped west of the Maenian Column. I guessed that must be about to happen, and sure enough, the clerk responsible for making the observation was already on his way to tell the consul. It was against the law for the senate to sit after sunset. Clearly, Hortensius and his friends were planning to talk out the remainder of the session, preventing Cicero's motion from being put to the vote. By the time I had quickly confirmed the sun's position for myself, run back across the forum and wriggled my way through the crowd to the threshold of the chamber, Gellius was making the announcement: 'The last hour!'

Cicero was instantly on his feet, wanting to make a point of order, but Gellius would not take it, and the floor was still with Catulus. On and on Catulus went, giving an interminable history of provincial government, virtually from the time since the she-wolf suckled Romulus. (Catulus's father, also a consul, had famously died by shutting himself up in a sealed room, kindling a charcoal fire, and suffocating himself with the fumes: Cicero used to say he must have done it to avoid listening to another speech by his son.) When he did eventually reach some sort of conclusion, he promptly yielded the floor to Quintus Metellus. Again Cicero rose, but again he was defeated by the seniority rule. Metellus had praetorian rank, and unless he chose to give way, which naturally he did not, Cicero had no right of speech. For a time Cicero stood his ground, against a swelling roar of protest, but the men on either side of him – one of whom was Servius, his lawyer friend, who had his interests at heart and could see he was in danger of making a fool of himself – pulled at his toga, and finally he surrendered and sat down.

It was forbidden to light a lamp or a brazier inside the chamber. As the gloom deepened, the cold sharpened and the white shapes of the senators, motionless in the November dusk, became like a parliament of ghosts. After Metellus had droned on for an eternity, and sat down in favour of Hortensius – a man who could talk on anything for hours – everyone knew the debate was over, and very soon afterwards Gellius dissolved the house. He limped down the aisle, an old man in search of his dinner, preceded by four lictors carrying his curule chair. Once he had passed through the doors, the senators streamed out after him and Sthenius and

37

I retreated a short distance into the forum to wait for Cicero. Gradually the crowd around us dwindled. The Sicilian kept asking me what was happening, but I felt it wiser to say nothing, and we stood in silence. I pictured Cicero sitting alone on the back benches, waiting for the chamber to empty so that he could leave without having to speak to anyone, for I feared he had badly lost face. But to my surprise he strolled out chatting with Hortensius and another, older senator, whom I did not recognise. They talked for a while on the steps of the senate house, shook hands and parted.

'Do you know who that was?' asked Cicero, coming over to us. Far from being cast down, he appeared highly amused. 'That was Verres's father. He has promised to write to his son, urging him to drop the prosecution, if we agree not to bring the matter back to the senate.'

Poor Sthenius was so relieved, I thought he might die from gratitude. He dropped to his knees and began kissing the senator's hands. Cicero made a sour face and gently raised him to his feet. 'Really, my dear Sthenius, save your thanks until I have actually achieved something. He has only promised to write, that is all. It is not a guarantee.'

Sthenius said, 'But you will accept the offer?'

Cicero shrugged. 'What choice do we have? Even if I re-table the motion, they will only talk it out again.'

I could not resist asking why, in that case, Hortensius was bothering to offer a deal at all.

Cicero nodded slowly. 'Now that is a good question.' There was a mist rising from the Tiber, and the lamps in the shops along the Argiletum shone yellow and gauzy. He sniffed the damp air. 'I suppose it can only be because he is embarrassed. Which in his case, of course, takes quite a lot. Yet it seems that even *he* would prefer not to be associated too publicly with such a flagrant criminal as Verres. So he is trying to settle the matter quietly. I wonder how much his retainer is from Verres: it must be an enormous sum.'

'Hortensius was not the only one who came to Verres's defence,' I reminded him.

'No.' Cicero glanced back at the senate house, and I could see that something had just occurred to him. 'They are all in it together, aren't they? The Metellus brothers are true aristocrats – they would never lift a finger to help anyone apart from themselves, unless it was for money. As for Catulus, the man is frantic for gold. He has undertaken so much building on the Capitol over the past ten years, it is almost more of a shrine to him than it is to Jupiter. I estimate we must have been looking at half a million in bribes this afternoon, Tiro. A few Delian bronzes – however fine, Sthenius, forgive me – would not be sufficient to buy that kind of protection. What *is* Verres up to down there in Sicily?' He suddenly began working his signet ring over his knuckle. 'Take this to the National Archive, Tiro, and show it to one of the clerks. Demand in my name to see all the official accounts submitted to the senate by Gaius Verres.'

My face must have registered my dismay. 'But the National Archive is run by Catulus's people. He is sure to hear word of what you are doing.'

'That cannot be helped.'

'But what am I looking for?'

'Anything interesting. You will know it when you see it. Go quickly, while there is still some light.' He put his arm round the shoulders of the Sicilian. 'As for you, Sthenius – you will come to dinner with me tonight, I hope? It is only family, but I am sure my wife will be delighted to meet you.'

I rather doubted that, but naturally it was not my place to say so.

The National Archive, which was then barely six years old, loomed over the forum even more massively than it does today, for back then it had less competition. I climbed that great flight of steps up to the first gallery, and by the time I found an attendant my heart was racing. I showed him the seal, and demanded, on behalf of Senator Cicero, to see Verres's accounts. At first he claimed never to have heard of Cicero, and besides, the building was closing. But then I pointed in the direction of the Carcer and told him firmly that if he did not desire to spend a month in chains in the state prison for impeding official business, he had better fetch those records now. (One lesson I had learned from Cicero was how to hide my nerves.) He scowled a bit and thought about it, then told me to follow him.

The Archive was Catulus's domain, a temple to him and his clan. Above the vaults was his inscription – *Q. Lutatius Catulus, son of Quintus, grandson of Quintus, consul, by a decree of the Senate, commissioned the erection of this National Archive, and approved it satisfactory* – and beside the entrance stood his life-size statue, looking somewhat more youthful and heroic than he had appeared in the senate that afternoon. Most of the attendants were either his slaves or his freedmen, and wore his emblem, a little dog, sewn on to their tunics. I shall tell you the kind of man Catulus was. He blamed the suicide of his father on the populist praetor Gratidianus – a distant relative of Cicero – and after the victory of the aristocrats in the civil war between Marius and Sulla he took the opportunity for revenge. His young protégé, Sergius Catilina, at his behest, seized Gratidianus, and whipped him through the streets to the Catulus family tomb. There, his arms and legs were broken, his ears and nose cut off, his tongue pulled out of his mouth and severed, and his eyes gouged out. In this ghastly condition his head was then lopped off, and Catilina bore it in triumph to Catulus, who was waiting in the forum. Do you wonder now why I was nervous as I waited for the vaults to be opened?

The senatorial records were kept in fireproof strongrooms, built to withstand a lightning strike, tunnelled into the rock of the Capitol, and when the slaves swung back the big bronze door I had a glimpse of thousands upon thousands of rolled papyri, receding into the shadows of the sacred hill. Five hundred years of history were encompassed in that one small space: half a millennium of magistracies and governorships, proconsular decrees and judicial rulings, from Lusitania to Macedonia, from Africa to Gaul, and most of them made in the names of the same few families: the Aemilii, the Claudii, the Cornelii, the Lutatii, the Metelli, the Servilii. This was what gave Catulus and his kind the confidence to look down upon such provincial equestrians as Cicero.

They kept me waiting in an antechamber while they searched for Verres's records, and eventually brought out to me a single document case containing perhaps a dozen rolls. From the labels on the ends I saw that these were all, with one exception, accounts from his time as urban praetor. The exception was a flimsy piece of papyrus, barely worth the trouble of unrolling, covering his work as a junior magistrate twelve years previously, at the time of the war between Sulla and Marius, and on which was written just three sentences: *I received 2,235,417 sesterces. I expended on wages, grain, payments to legates, the proquaestor, the praetorian cohort 1,635,417 sesterces. I left 600,000 at Ariminum.* Remembering the scores of rolls of meticulous accounts which Cicero's term as a junior magistrate on Sicily had generated, all of which I had written out for him, I could barely refrain from laughing.

'Is this all there is?'

The attendant assured me it was.

'But where are the accounts from his time in Sicily?',

'They have not yet been submitted to the treasury.'

'Not yet submitted? He has been governor for almost two years!'

The fellow looked at me blankly, and I could see that there was no point in wasting any more time with him. I copied out the three lines relating to Verres's junior magistracy and went out into the evening.

While I had been in the National Archive, darkness had fallen over Rome. In Cicero's house the family had already gone into dinner. But the master had left instructions with the steward, Eros, that I was to be shown straight into the dining room the moment I returned. I found Cicero lying on a couch beside Terentia. His brother, Quintus, was also there, with his wife, Pomponia. The third couch was occupied by Cicero's cousin Lucius and the hapless Sthenius, still clad in his dirty mourning clothes and squirming with unease. I could sense the strained atmosphere as soon as I entered, although Cicero was in good spirits. He always liked a dinner party. It was not the quality of the food and drink which mattered to him, but the company and the conversation. Quintus and Lucius, along with Atticus, were the three men he loved most.

'Well?' he said to me. I told him what had happened and showed him my copy of Verres's quaestorian accounts. He scanned it, grunted, and tossed the wax tablet across the table. 'Look at that, Quintus. The villain is too lazy even to lie adequately. Six hundred thousand – what a nice round sum, not a penny either side of it

– and where does he leave it? Why, in a town which is then conveniently occupied by the opposition's army, so the loss can be blamed on them! And no accounts submitted from Sicily for *two years*? I am obliged to you, Sthenius, for bringing this rogue to my attention.'

'Oh yes, *so* obliged,' said Terentia, with savage sweetness. '*So* obliged – for setting us at war with half the decent families in Rome. But presumably we can socialise with Sicilians from now on, so that will be all right. Where did you say you came from again?'

'Thermae, your ladyship.'

'Thermae. I have never heard of it, but I am sure it is delightful. You can make speeches to the town council, Cicero. Perhaps you will even get elected there, now that Rome is forever closed to you. You can be the consul of Thermae and I can be the first lady.'

'A role I am sure you will perform with your customary charm, my darling,' said Cicero, patting her arm.

They could needle away at one another like this for hours. Sometimes I believe they rather enjoyed it.

'I still fail to see what you can do about it,' said Quintus. He was fresh from military service: four years younger than his brother, and possessed of about half the brains. 'If you raise Verres's conduct in the senate, they will talk it out. If you try to take him to court, they will make sure he is acquitted. Just keep your nose out of it is my advice.'

'And what do you say, cousin?'

'I say no man of honour in the Roman senate can stand by and see this sort of corruption going on unchecked,' replied Lucius. 'Now that you know the facts, you have a duty to make them public.'

'Bravo!' said Terentia. 'Spoken like a true philosopher who has never stood for office in his life.'

Pomponia yawned noisily. 'Can we talk about something else? Politics is so dull.'

She was a tiresome woman whose only obvious attraction, apart from her prominent bust, was that she was Atticus's sister. I saw the eyes of the two Cicero brothers meet and my master give a barely perceptible shake of his head: ignore her, his expression said, it is not worth arguing over. 'All right,' he conceded, 'enough of politics. But I propose a toast.' He raised his cup and the others did the same. 'To our old friend Sthenius. If nothing else, may this day have seen the beginning of the restoration of his fortunes. Sthenius!'

The Sicilian's eyes were wet with tears of gratitude.

'Sthenius!'

'And Thermae, Cicero,' added Terentia, her small dark eyes, her shrew's eyes, bright with malice over the rim of her drink. 'Do not let us forget Thermae.'

I took my meal alone in the kitchen and went exhausted to bed with my lamp and a book of philosophy which I was too tired to read. (I was free to borrow whatever I liked from the household's small library.) Later, I heard the guests all leave and the bolts slam shut on the front door. I heard Cicero and Terentia mount the stairs in silence and go their separate ways, for she had long since taken to sleeping in another part of the house to avoid being woken by him before dawn. I heard Cicero's footsteps on the boards above my head, and then I blew out my lamp, and that was the last sound I heard as I surrendered myself to sleep – his footsteps pacing, up and down, up and down.

It was six weeks later that we heard the news from Sicily. Verres had ignored the entreaties of his father. On the first day of December, in Syracuse, exactly as he had threatened, he had judged Sthenius in his absence, found him guilty of espionage, sentenced him to be crucified, and dispatched his officials to Rome to arrest him and return him for execution.

III

The governor of Sicily's contemptuous defiance caught Cicero off his guard. He had been convinced he had struck a gentlemen's agreement which would safeguard his client's life. 'But then of course,' he complained bitterly, 'none of them is a gentleman.' He stormed around the house in an uncharacteristic rage. He had been tricked! They had played him for a fool! He would march down to the senate house right there and then and expose their villainous lies! I knew he would calm down before long, for he was only too aware that he lacked the rank simply to demand a hearing in the senate: he would risk humiliation.

But there was no escaping the fact that he was under a heavy obligation to protect his client, and on the morning after Sthenius had learned his fate, Cicero convened a meeting in his study to determine how best to respond. For the first time that I can remember, all his usual callers were turned away, and six of us crammed into that small space: Cicero, brother Quintus, cousin Lucius, Sthenius, myself (to take notes), and Servius Sulpicius, already widely regarded as the ablest jurist of his generation. Cicero began by inviting Servius to give his legal opinion.

'In theory,' said Servius, 'our friend has a right of appeal in

Syracuse, but only to the governor, that is to Verres himself; so that avenue is closed to us. To bring a prosecution against Verres is not an option: as a serving governor he has executive immunity; besides, Hortensius is the praetor of the extortion court until January; and besides both of these, the jury will be composed of senators who will never convict one of their own. You could table another motion in the senate, but you have already tried that, and presumably if you tried again you would merely meet with the same result. Continuing to live openly in Rome is not an option for Sthenius – anyone convicted of a capital crime is automatically subject to banishment from the city, so it is impossible for him to remain here. Indeed, Cicero, you are liable to prosecution yourself if you harbour him under your roof.'

'So what is your advice?'

'Suicide,' said Servius. Sthenius let out a terrible groan. 'No, really, I am afraid you should consider it. Before they catch hold of you. You do not want to suffer the scourge, the hot irons, or the torments of the cross.'

'Thank you, Servius,' said Cicero, cutting him off swiftly before he had an opportunity to describe those torments in further detail. 'Tiro, we need to find Sthenius a place where he can hide. He cannot stay here any longer. It is the first place they will look. As for the legal situation, Servius, your analysis strikes me as faultless. Verres is a brute, but a cunning brute, which is why he felt strong enough to press ahead with the conviction. In short, having thought about the matter overnight, it seems to me that there is only one slim possibility.'

'Which is?'

'To go to the tribunes.'

This suggestion produced an immediate stir of unease, for the tribunes were at that time an utterly discredited group.

Traditionally, they had checked and balanced the power of the senate by voicing the will of the common people. But ten years earlier, after Sulla had defeated the forces of Marius, the aristocrats had stripped them of their powers. They could no longer summon meetings of the people, or propose legislation, or impeach the likes of Verres for high crimes and misdemeanours. As a final humiliation, any senator who became a tribune was automatically disqualified from standing for senior office, that is the praetorship or the consulship. In other words, the tribuneship was designed to be a political dead end – a place to confine the ranting and the rancorous, the incompetent and the unpromotable: the effluent of the body politic. No senator of any nobility or ambition would go anywhere near it.

'I know your objections,' said Cicero, waving the room to be silent. 'But the tribunes still have one small power left to them, do they not, Servius?'

'That is true,' agreed Servius. 'They do have a residual *potestas auxilii ferendi*.' Our blank looks gave him obvious satisfaction. 'It means,' he explained with a smile, 'that they have the right to offer their protection to private persons against the unjust decisions of magistrates. But I must warn you, Cicero, that your friends, among whom I have long counted it an honour to number myself, will think much the less of you if you start dabbling in the politics of the mob. Suicide,' he repeated. 'Where is the objection? We are all mortal. For all of us it is only a matter of time. And this way you go with honour.'

'I agree with Servius about the danger we run if we approach the tribunes,' said Quintus. (It was usually 'we' when Quintus spoke about his elder brother.) 'Whether we like it or not, power in Rome nowadays lies with the senate and with the nobles. That's why our strategy has always been to build your reputation carefully, through your advocacy in the courts. We shall do ourselves irreparable damage with the men who really matter if the feeling gets around that you are merely another rabble-rouser. Also . . . I hesitate to raise this, Marcus, but have you considered Terentia's reaction if you were to follow this course?'

Servius guffawed at that. 'You will never conquer Rome, Cicero, if you cannot rule your wife.'

'Conquering Rome would be child's play, Servius, believe me, compared with ruling my wife.'

And so the debate went on. Lucius favoured an immediate approach to the tribunes, no matter what the consequences. Sthenius was too numb with misery and fear to have a coherent opinion on anything. At the very end, Cicero asked me what I thought. In other company this might have caused surprise, a slave's view not counting for much in most Romans' eyes, but these men were used to the way that Cicero sometimes turned to me for advice. I replied cautiously that it seemed to me that Hortensius would not be happy to learn of Verres's action, and that the prospect of the case becoming a public scandal might yet force him to put more pressure on his client to see sense: going to the tribunes was a risk, but on balance it was one worth taking. The answer pleased Cicero.

'Sometimes,' he said, summing up the discussion with an aphorism I have never forgotten, 'if you find yourself stuck in politics, the thing to do is start a fight – start a fight, even if you do not know how you are going to win it, because it is only when a fight is on, and everything is in motion, that you can hope to see your way through. Thank you, gentlemen.' And with that the meeting was adjourned.

★   ★   ★

There was no time to waste, for if the news from Syracuse had already reached Rome, it was a fair assumption that Verres's men were not far behind. Even while Cicero was talking, I had conceived an idea for a possible hiding place for Sthenius, and the moment the conference was over I went in search of Terentia's business manager, Philotimus. He was a plump and lascivious young man, generally to be found in the kitchen, pestering the maids to satisfy one or other, or preferably both, of his vices. I asked him if there was a spare apartment available in one of his mistress's tenement blocks, and when he replied that there was, I bullied him into giving me the key. I checked the street outside the house for suspicious loiterers, and when I was sure that it was safe I persuaded Sthenius to follow me.

He was in a state of complete dejection, his dreams of returning to his homeland dashed, in hourly terror of being arrested. And I fear that when he first saw the squalid building in Subura in which I said he would now have to live, he must have felt that even we had abandoned him. The stairs were rickety and gloomy. There was evidence of a recent fire on the walls. His room, on the fifth floor, was barely more than a cell, with a straw mattress in the corner and a tiny window which offered no view, except across the street to another, similar apartment, close enough for Sthenius to reach out and shake hands with his neighbour. For a latrine he had a bucket. But if it did not offer him comfort, it at least offered him security – dropped, unknown, into this warren of slums, it would be almost impossible for him to be found. He asked me, in a plaintive tone, to sit with him a while, but I had to get back and gather all the documents relating to his case, so that Cicero could present them to the tribunes. We were fighting time, I told him, and left at once.

The headquarters of the tribunes were next door to the senate house, in the old Basilica Porcia. Although the tribunate was only a shell, from which all the succulent flesh of power had been sucked, people still hung around its building. The angry, the dispossessed, the hungry, the militant – these were the denizens of the tribunes' basilica. As Cicero and I walked across the forum, we could see a sizeable crowd jostling on its steps to get a view of what was happening inside. I was carrying a document case, but still I cleared a way for the senator as best I could, receiving some kicks and curses for my pains, as these were not citizens with any great love for a purple-bordered toga.

There were ten tribunes, elected annually by the people, and they always sat on the same long wooden bench, beneath a mural depicting the defeat of the Carthaginians. It was not a large building, but packed, noisy and warm, despite the December cold outside. A young man, bizarrely barefoot, was haranguing the mob as we entered. He was an ugly, raw-faced youth with a brutal, grating voice. There were always plenty of cranks in the Basilica Porcia, and I took him at first to be just another, as his entire speech seemed to be devoted to arguing why one particular pillar should not, on any account, be demolished, or even moved one inch, to give the tribunes more room. And yet for some curious reason he compelled attention. Cicero began listening to him very carefully, and after a while he realised – from the constant references to 'my ancestor' – that this peculiar creature was none other than the great-grandson of the famous Marcus Porcius Cato who had originally built the basilica and given it his name.

I mention this here because young Cato – he was then twenty-three – was to become such an important figure, in both the life of Cicero and the death of the republic. Not that one would have guessed it at the time. He looked destined for nowhere more significant than the asylum. He finished his speech, and as he went by, wild-eyed and unseeing, he knocked into me. What remains in my mind is the animal stink of him, his hair matted with damp and the patches of sweat the size of dinner plates spreading under the armpits of his tunic. But he had won his point, and that pillar stayed absolutely in its place for as long as the building stood – which was not, alas, to be many years longer.

However, returning to my story, the tribunes were a poor lot on the whole, but there was one among them who stood out for his talent and his energy, and that was Lollius Palicanus. He was a proud man, but of low birth, from Picenum in the Italian north-east, the power base of Pompey the Great. It had been assumed that when Pompey returned from Spain he would use his influence to try to gain his fellow countryman a praetorship, and Cicero had been as surprised as everybody else earlier in the summer when Palicanus had suddenly announced his candidacy for the tribunate. But on this particular morning he looked happy enough with his lot. The fresh crop of tribunes always began their term of office on the tenth day of December, so he must have been very new in the job. 'Cicero!' he bellowed, the moment he saw us. 'I had been wondering when you would show up!'

He told us that he had already heard the news from Syracuse, and he wanted to talk about Verres. But he wanted to talk in private, for there was more at stake, he said mysteriously, than the fate of one man. He proposed meeting us at his house on the Aventine Hill in an hour, to which Cicero agreed, whereupon he immediately ordered one of his attendants to guide us, saying he would follow separately.

It turned out to be a rough and unpretentious place, in keeping with the man, close to the Lavernan Gate, just outside the city wall. The thing I remember most clearly is the larger-than-life-size bust of Pompey, posed in the headgear and armour of Alexander the Great, which dominated the atrium. 'Well,' said Cicero, after he had contemplated it for a while, 'I suppose it makes a change from the Three Graces.' This was exactly the sort of droll but inappropriate comment which used to get repeated around the town, and which invariably found its way back to its victim. Luckily, only I was present on this occasion, but I took the opportunity to pass on what the consul's clerk had said regarding his joke about Gellius mediating between the philosophers. Cicero pretended to be sheepish and promised to be more circumspect in future – he knew, he said, that people liked their statesmen to be dull – but naturally he soon forgot his resolution.

'That was a good speech you made the other week,' said Palicanus, the moment he arrived. 'You have the stuff in you, Cicero, you really have, if I may say so. But those blue-blooded bastards screwed you over, and now you are in the shit. So what exactly are you planning to do about it?' (This was more or less how he spoke – rough words in a rough accent – and the aristocrats used to have some sport with him over his elocution.)

I opened my case and handed the documents to Cicero, and he quickly laid out the situation regarding Sthenius. When he had finished he asked what chance there was of receiving any help from the tribunes.

'That depends,' said Palicanus, with a quick lick of his lips and a grin. 'Come and sit down and let us see what is to be done.'

He took us through into another room, small and completely overwhelmed by a huge wall painting of a laurelled Pompey, this time dressed as Jupiter, complete with lightning bolts shooting from his fingers.

'Do you like it?' asked Palicanus.

'It is remarkable,' said Cicero.

'Yes, it is,' he said, with some satisfaction. '*That* is art.'

I took a seat in the corner, beneath the Picenean deity, while Cicero, whose eye I dared not meet, settled himself at the opposite end of the couch to our host.

'What I am about to tell you, Cicero, is not to be repeated outside this house. Pompey the Great' – Palicanus nodded to the painting, in case we were in any doubt as to whom he meant – 'will soon be returning to Rome for the first time in six years. He will come with his army, so there can be no fancy double-dealing from our noble friends. He will seek the consulship. And he will get the consulship. And he will get it unopposed.'

He leaned forward eagerly, expecting shock or surprise, but Cicero received this sensational intelligence as coolly as if he were being told the weather.

'So in return for your helping me over Sthenius, I am to support you over Pompey?'

'You are a canny one, Cicero, you have the stuff in you. What do you think?'

Cicero rested his chin in his hand and gazed at Palicanus. 'Quintus Metellus will not be happy, for a start. You know the old poem – "In Rome Metelli are, 'tis fate, / Elected to the consulate." He has been scheduled since birth to have his turn next summer.'

'Has he indeed? Well he can kiss my backside. How many legions did Quintus Metellus have behind him, the last time you looked?'

'Crassus has legions,' Cicero pointed out. 'So has Lucullus.'

'Lucullus is too far away, and besides, he has his hands full. As for Crassus – well, it is true that Crassus hates Pompey's guts.

But the thing about Crassus is that he is not a proper soldier. He is a businessman, and that type always cuts a deal.'

'And then there is the little matter of its being completely unconstitutional. You have to be forty-two at the time of the consular election, and Pompey is how old?'

'Just thirty-four.'

'Indeed. Almost a year younger than me. And a consul is also required to have been elected to the senate and to have served as praetor, neither of which Pompey has achieved. He has never made a political speech in his life. To put the matter simply, Palicanus, seldom has a man been less qualified for the post.'

Palicanus made a dismissive gesture. 'All that may be true, but let us face facts – Pompey has run whole countries for years, and done it with proconsular authority to boot. He *is* a consul, in all but name. Be realistic, Cicero. You cannot expect a man such as Pompey to come back to Rome and start at the bottom, running for quaestor like some political hack. What would that do to his dignity?'

'I appreciate his feelings, but you asked my opinion, and I am giving it to you, and I tell you the aristocrats will not stand for it. All right, perhaps if he has ten thousand men outside the city they will have no choice but to let him become consul, but sooner or later his army will go home and then how will he— Ha!' Cicero suddenly threw back his head and started laughing. 'That is very clever.'

'You have seen it?' said Palicanus, with a grin.

'I have seen it.' Cicero nodded appreciatively. 'Very good.'

'Well, I am offering you the chance to be a part of it. And Pompey the Great does not forget his friends.'

At the time I had not the least idea of what they were talking about. Only when we were walking home afterwards did Cicero explain everything to me. Pompey was planning to seek the consulship on the platform of a full restoration of tribunician power. Hence Palicanus's surprising move in becoming a tribune. The strategy was not born of some altruistic desire on Pompey's part to give the Roman people greater liberty – although I suppose it is just possible he was occasionally pleased to lie in his bath in Spain and fancy himself a champion of citizens' rights – no: it was purely a matter of self-interest. Pompey, as a good general, saw that by advocating such a programme, he would trap the aristocrats in a pincer movement, between his soldiers encamped beyond the walls of Rome and the common people on the city's streets. Hortensius, Catulus, Metellus and the rest would have no choice but to concede both Pompey's consulship and the tribunes' restoration, or risk annihilation. And once they did, Pompey could send his army home, and if necessary rule by circumventing the senate and appealing directly to the people. He would be unassailable. It was, as Cicero described it to me, a brilliant stroke, and he had seen it in that flash of insight as he sat on Palicanus's couch.

'What exactly would be in it for me?' asked Cicero.

'A reprieve for your client.'

'And nothing else?'

'That would depend on how good you were. I cannot make specific promises. That will have to wait until Pompey himself gets back.'

'It is rather a weak offer, if I may say so, my dear Palicanus.'

'Well, you are in rather a weak position, if I may say so, my dear Cicero.'

Cicero stood. I could see he was put out. 'I can always walk away,' he said.

'And leave your client to die in agony on one of Verres's crosses?'

56

Palicanus also stood. 'I doubt it, Cicero. I doubt you are that hard.' He took us out then, past Pompey as Jupiter, past Pompey as Alexander. 'I shall see you and your client at the basilica tomorrow morning,' he said, shaking hands with Cicero on the doorstep. 'After that you will be in our debt, and we shall be watching.' The door closed with a confident slam.

Cicero turned on his heel and stepped into the street. 'If that is the kind of art he puts on public display,' he said, 'what do you suppose he keeps in the latrine? And do not warn me to guard my tongue, Tiro, because I do not care who hears it.'

He walked on ahead of me through the city gate, his hands clasped behind his back, his head hunched forward, brooding. Of course, Palicanus was right. Cicero had no choice. He could not abandon his client. But I am sure he must have been weighing the political risks of moving beyond a simple appeal to the tribunes to a full-blooded campaign for their restoration. It would cost him the support of the moderates, such as Servius.

'Well,' he said with a wry smile, when we reached his house, 'I wanted to get into a fight, and it seems I have succeeded.'

He asked Eros, the steward, where Terentia was, and looked relieved when he learned she was still in her room. At least that saved him from having to tell her the news for a few more hours. We went into his study, and he had just started dictating to me his speech to the tribunes – 'Gentlemen, it is an honour to stand before you for the first time' – when we heard shouts and a thump from the entrance. Cicero, who always liked to think on his feet and was prowling around, ran out to find out what was happening. I hurried after him. Six rough-looking fellows were crowded in the vestibule, all wielding sticks. Eros was rolling on the ground, clutching his stomach, with blood pouring from a split lip. Another stranger, armed not with a stick but with an official-looking document, stepped up to Cicero and announced that he had the authority to search the house.

'The authority of whom?' Cicero was calm – calmer than I would have been in his shoes.

'Gaius Verres, pro-praetor of Sicily, issued this warrant in Syracuse on the first day of December.' He held it up before Cicero's face for an insultingly short time. 'I am searching for the traitor Sthenius.'

'You will not find him here.'

'I shall be the judge of that.'

'And who are you?'

'Timarchides, freedman of Verres, and I shall not be kept talking while he escapes. You,' he said, turning to the nearest of his men, 'secure the front. You two take the back. The rest of you come with me. We shall start with your study, Senator, if you have no objection.'

Very soon the house was filled with the sounds of the search – boots on marble tile and wooden board, the screams of the female slaves, harsh male voices, the occasional crash as something was knocked and broken. Timarchides worked his way through the study upending document cases, watched by Cicero from the door.

'He is hardly likely to be in one of those,' said Cicero. 'He is not a dwarf.'

Finding nothing in the study, they moved on up the stairs to the senator's spartan bedroom and dressing room. 'Be assured, Timarchides,' said Cicero, still keeping his cool, but obviously with greater difficulty as he watched his bed being overturned, 'that you and your master will be repaid for this, one hundred-fold.'

'Your wife,' said Timarchides. 'Where does she sleep?'

'Ah,' said Cicero quietly. 'Now I really would not do that, if I were you.'

But Timarchides had his blood up. He had come a long way, was finding nothing, and Cicero's manner was chafing on his nerves. He ran along the passage, followed by three of his men, shouted, 'Sthenius! We know you're in there!' and threw open the door of Terentia's bedroom. The screech that followed and the sharp crack of her hand across the invader's face rang through the house. Then came such a volley of colourful abuse, delivered in such an imperious voice, and at such a volume, that Terentia's distant ancestor who had commanded the Roman line against Hannibal at Cannae a century and a half before must surely have sat bolt upright in his tomb. 'She fell on that wretched freedman,' Cicero used to say afterwards, 'like a tigress out of a tree. I almost felt sorry for the fellow.'

Timarchides must have realised his mission had failed and decided to cut his losses, for in short order he and his ruffians were retreating down the stairs, followed by Terentia, with little Tullia hiding behind her skirts and occasionally brandishing her tiny fists in imitation of her mother. We heard Timarchides calling to his men, heard a running of feet and the slam of the door, and after that the old house was silent except for the distant wailing of one of the maids.

'And this,' said Terentia, taking a deep breath and rounding on Cicero, her cheeks flushed, her narrow bosom rising and falling rapidly, '*this* is all because you spoke in the senate on behalf of that dreary Sicilian?'

'I am afraid it is, my darling,' he said sadly. 'They are determined to scare me off.'

'Well, you must not let them, Cicero.' She put her hands on either side of his head, gripped it tight – a gesture not at all of tenderness but of passion – and glared furiously into his eyes. 'You must *crush* them.'

The upshot was that the following morning, when we set out for the Basilica Porcia, Quintus was on one side of Cicero, Lucius was on the other, and behind him, magnificently turned out in the formal dress of a Roman matron and carried in a litter hired specially for the occasion, came Terentia. It was the first time she had ever troubled to see him speak, and I swear he was more nervous of appearing before her than he was of appearing before the tribunes. He had a big retinue of clients to back him up as he left the house, and we picked up more along the way, especially after we stopped off halfway down the Argiletum to retrieve Sthenius from his bolt-hole. A hundred or more of us must have surged across the forum and into the tribunes' hall. Timarchides followed at a distance with his gang, but there were far too many of us for him to risk an attack, and he knew that if he tried anything in the basilica itself he would be torn to bits.

The ten tribunes were on the bench. The hall was full. Palicanus rose and read the motion – *That in the opinion of this body the proclamation of banishment from Rome does not apply to Sthenius* – and Cicero stepped up to the tribunal, his face clenched white with nerves. Quite often he was sick before a major speech, as he had been on this occasion, pausing at the door to vomit into the gutter. The first part of his oration was more or less the same as the one he had given in the senate, except that now he could call his client to the front and gesture to him as need arose to stir the pity of the judges. And certainly a more perfect illustration of a dejected victim was never paraded before a Roman court than Sthenius on that day. But Cicero's peroration was entirely new, not at all like his normal forensic oratory, and marked a decisive shift in his political position. By the time he reached it, his nerves were gone and his delivery was on fire.

'There is an old saying, gentlemen, among the merchants in the Macellum, that a fish rots from the head down, and if there is something rotten in Rome today – and who can doubt that there is? – I tell you plainly that it has started in the head. It has started at the top. It has started in the senate.' Loud cheers and stamping of feet. 'And there is only one thing to do with a stinking, rotten fish-head, those merchants will tell you, and that is to cut it off – cut it off and throw it out!' Renewed cheers. 'But it will need quite a knife to sever this head, for it is an aristocratic head, and we all know what they are like!' Laughter. 'It is a head swollen with the poison of corruption and bloated with pride and arrogance. And it will need a strong hand to wield that knife, and it will need a steady nerve besides, because they have necks of brass, these aristocrats, I tell you: brass necks, all of them!' Laughter. 'But that man will come. He is not far away. Your powers will be restored, I promise you, however hard the struggle.' A few brighter sparks started shouting out Pompey's name. Cicero held up his hand, three fingers outstretched. 'To you now falls the great test of being worthy of this fight. Show courage, gentlemen. Make a start today. Strike a blow against tyranny. Free my client. And then free Rome!'

Later, Cicero was so embarrassed by the rabble-rousing nature of this speech that he asked me to destroy the only copy, so I must confess I am writing here from memory. But I recollect it very clearly – the force of his words, the passion of his delivery, the excitement of the crowd as he whipped them up, the wink he exchanged with Palicanus as he left the tribunal, and Terentia not moving a muscle, simply staring straight ahead as the common people around her erupted in applause. Timarchides, who had been standing at the back, slipped out before the ovation ended, no doubt to ride at full gallop to Sicily and report to his master what had happened – for the motion, I need hardly add, was passed by ten votes to nil, and Sthenius, as long as he stayed in Rome, was safe.

IV

Another of Cicero's maxims was that if you must do something unpopular, you might as well do it wholeheartedly, for in politics there is no credit to be won by timidity. Thus, although he had never previously expressed an opinion about Pompey or the tribunes, neither cause now had a more devoted adherent. And the Pompeians were naturally delighted to welcome such a brilliant recruit to their ranks.

That winter was long and cold in the city, and for no one, I suspect, more than Terentia. Her personal code of honour required her to support her husband against the enemies who had invaded her home. But having sat among the smelly poor, and listened to Cicero haranguing her own class, she now found her drawing room and dining room invaded at all hours by his new political cronies: men from the uncouth north who spoke with ugly accents and who liked to put their feet up on her furniture and plot late into the night. Palicanus was the chief of these, and on his second visit to the house in January he brought with him one of the new praetors, Lucius Afranius, a fellow senator from Pompey's homeland of Picenum. Cicero went out of his way to be charming, and in earlier years, Terentia, too, would have felt it an honour to have a praetor in her house. But Afranius had no decent family or breeding of any sort. He actually had the nerve to ask her if she liked dancing, and, when she drew back in horror, declared that personally he loved nothing more. He pulled up his toga, showed her his legs and demanded to know if she had ever seen a finer pair of calves.

These men were Pompey's representatives in Rome and they brought with them something of the whiff and manners of the army camp. They were blunt to the point of brutality; but then, perhaps, they had to be, given what they were planning. Palicanus's daughter, Lollia – a blowsy young piece, very much not to Terentia's taste – occasionally joined the menfolk, for she was married to Aulus Gabinius, another of Pompey's Picenean lieutenants, currently serving with the general in Spain. This Gabinius was a link with the legionary commanders, who in turn provided intelligence on the loyalty of the centuries – an important consideration, for, as Afranius put it, there was no point in bringing the army all the way to Rome to restore the powers of the tribunes, only to find that the legions would happily go over to the aristocrats if they were offered a big enough bribe.

At the end of January, Gabinius sent word that the final rebel strongholds of Uxama and Calagurris had been taken, and that Pompey was ready to march his legions home. Cicero had been active among the *pedarii* for weeks, drawing senators aside as they waited for debates, convincing them that the rebel slaves in the Italian north posed a gathering threat to their businesses and trade. He lobbied well. When the issue came up for discussion in the senate, despite the intense opposition of the aristocrats and the supporters of Crassus, the house voted narrowly to let Pompey keep his Spanish army intact and bring it back to the mother country to crush Spartacus's northern recruits. From that point on, the consulship was as good as his, and on the day the motion passed, Cicero came home smiling. True, he had been snubbed by the aristocrats, who now loathed him more than any other man in Rome, and the presiding consul, the super-snobbish Publius Cornelius Lentulus Sura, had even refused to recognise him when he tried to speak. But what did that matter? He was in the inner circle of Pompey the Great, and, as every fool knows, the quickest way to get ahead in politics is to get yourself close to the man at the top.

Throughout these busy months, I am ashamed to say, we neglected Sthenius of Thermae. He would often turn up in the mornings, and hang around the senator for the entire day in the hope of securing an interview. He was still living in Terentia's squalid tenement block. He had little money. He was unable to venture beyond the walls of the city, as his immunity ended at the boundaries of Rome. He had not shaved his beard nor cut his hair, nor, by the smell of him, changed his clothes since October. He reeked – not of madness exactly, but of obsession, forever producing small pieces of paper, which he would fumble and drop in the street.

Cicero kept making excuses not to see him. Doubtless he felt he had discharged his obligations already. But that was not the sole explanation. The truth is that politics is a country idiot, capable of concentrating only on one thing at a time, and poor Sthenius had become yesterday's topic. All anyone could talk about now was the coming confrontation between Crassus and Pompey; the plight of the Sicilian was a bore.

In the late spring, Crassus – having finally defeated the main force of Spartacus's rebels in the heel of Italy, killing Spartacus and taking six thousand prisoners – had started marching towards Rome. Very soon afterwards, Pompey crossed the Alps and wiped out the slave rebellion in the north. He sent a letter to the consuls which was read out in the senate, giving only the faintest credit to Crassus for his achievement and instead proclaiming that it was really he who had finished off the slave war 'utterly and entirely'. The signal to his supporters could not have been clearer: only one general would be triumphing that year, and it would not be Marcus Crassus. Finally, lest there be any remaining doubt, at the end of his dispatch Pompey announced that he too was moving on Rome. Little wonder that amid these stirring historical events, Sthenius was forgotten.

Sometime in May, it must have been, or possibly early June – I cannot find the exact date – a messenger arrived at Cicero's house bearing a letter. With some reluctance the man let me take it, but refused to leave the premises until he had received a reply: those, he said, were his orders. Although he was wearing civilian clothes, I could tell he was in the army. I carried the message into the study and watched Cicero's expression darken as he read it. He handed it to me, and when I saw the opening – *From Marcus Licinius Crassus, Imperator, to Marcus Tullius Cicero: Greetings* – I understood the reason for his frown. Not that there was anything threatening in the letter. It was simply an invitation to meet the victorious general the next morning on the road to Rome, close to the town of Lanuvium, at the eighteenth milestone.

'Can I refuse?' asked Cicero, but then he answered his own question. 'No, I can't. That would be interpreted as a mortal insult.'

'Presumably he is going to ask for your support.'

'Really?' said Cicero sarcastically. 'What makes you think that?'

'Could you not offer him some limited encouragement, as long as it does not clash with your undertakings to Pompey?'

'No. That is the trouble. Pompey has made that very clear. He expects absolute loyalty. So Crassus will pose the question: "Are

66

you for me or against me?" and then I shall face the politician's worst nightmare: the requirement to give a straight answer.' He sighed. 'But we shall have to go, of course.'

We left soon after dawn the following morning, in a two-wheeled open carriage, with Cicero's valet doubling up as coachman for the occasion. It was the most perfect time of day at the most perfect time of year, already hot enough for people to be bathing in the public pool beside the Capena Gate, but cool enough for the air to be refreshing. There was none of the usual dust thrown up from the road. The leaves of the olive trees were a glossy fresh green. Even the tombs that line the Appian Way so thickly along that particular stretch just beyond the wall gleamed bright and cheerful in the first hour of the sun. Normally, Cicero liked to draw my attention to some particular monument and give me a lecture on it – the statue of Scipio Africanus, perhaps, or the tomb of Horatia, murdered by her brother for displaying excessive grief at the death of her lover. But on this morning his usual good spirits had deserted him. He was too preoccupied with Crassus.

'Half of Rome belongs to him – these tombs as well, I should not wonder. You could house an entire family in one of these! Why not? Crassus would! Have you ever seen him in operation? Let us say he hears there is a fire raging and spreading through a particular neighbourhood: he sends a team of slaves round all the apartments, offering to buy out the owners for next to nothing. When the poor fellows have agreed, he sends another team equipped with water-carts to put the fires out! That is just one of his tricks. Do you know what Sicinnius calls him – always bearing in mind, by the way, that Sicinnius is afraid of no one? He calls Crassus "the most dangerous bull in the herd".'

His chin sank on to his chest and that was all he said until we had passed the eighth milestone and were deep into open country, not far from Bovillae. That was when he drew my attention to something odd: military pickets guarding what looked like small timber yards. We had already passed four or five, spaced out at regular half-mile intervals, and the further down the road we went, the greater the activity seemed – hammering, sawing, digging. It was Cicero who eventually supplied the answer. The legionaries were making crosses. Soon afterwards, we encountered a column of Crassus's infantry tramping towards us, heading for Rome, and we had to pull over to the far side of the road to let them pass. Behind the legionaries came a long, stumbling procession of prisoners, hundreds of them, vanquished rebel slaves, their arms pinioned behind their backs – a terrible, emaciated, grey army of ghosts, heading for a fate which we had seen being prepared for them, but of which they were presumably ignorant. Our driver muttered a spell to ward off evil, flicked his whip over the flanks of the horses and we jolted forwards. A mile or so later, the killing started, in little huddles off on either side of the road, where the prisoners were being nailed to the crosses. I try not to remember it, but it comes back to me occasionally in my dreams, especially, for some reason, the crosses with their impaled and shrieking victims being pulled upright by soldiers heaving on ropes, each wooden upright dropping with a thud into the deep hole that had been dug for it. That I remember, and also the moment when we passed over the crest of a hill and saw a long avenue of crosses running straight ahead for mile after mile, shimmering in the mid-morning heat, the air seeming to tremble with the moans of the dying, the buzz of the flies and the screams of the circling crows.

'So this is why he dragged me out of Rome,' muttered Cicero furiously, 'to intimidate me by showing me these poor wretches.'

He had gone very white, for he was squeamish about pain and death, even when inflicted on animals, and for that reason tried to avoid attending the games. I suppose this also explains his aversion to all matters military. He had done the bare minimum of army service in his youth, and was quite incapable of wielding a sword or hurling a javelin; throughout his career he had to put up with the taunt that he was a draft-dodger.

At the eighteenth milestone, surrounded by a ditch and ramparts, we found the bulk of Crassus's legions encamped beside the road, giving off that dusty smell of sweat and leather which always lingers over an army in the field. Standards fluttered over the gate, beside which Crassus's own son, Publius, then a brisk young junior officer, was waiting to conduct Cicero to the general's tent. A couple of other senators were being shown out as we arrived, and suddenly there was Crassus himself at the entrance, instantly recognisable – 'Old Baldhead', as his soldiers called him – wearing the scarlet cloak of a commander, despite the heat. He was all affability, waving goodbye to his previous visitors, wishing them a safe journey, and greeting us equally heartily – even me, whose hand he shook as warmly as if I were a senator myself, rather than a slave who might in other circumstances have been howling from one of his crosses. And looking back on it, and trying to fix precisely what it was about him which made him so disconcerting, I think it was this: his indiscriminate and detached friendliness, which you knew would never waver or diminish even if he had just decided to have you killed. Cicero had told me he was worth at least two hundred million, but Crassus talked as easily to any man as a farmer leaning on a gate, and his army tent – like his house in Rome – was modest and unadorned.

He led us inside – me as well: he insisted – apologising for the gruesome spectacle along the Appian Way, but he felt it was necessary. He seemed particularly proud of the logistics which had enabled him to crucify six thousand men along three hundred and fifty miles of road, from the victorious battlefield to the gates of Rome, without, as he put it, 'any scenes of violence'. That was seventeen crucifixions to the mile, which meant one hundred and seventeen paces between each cross – he had a wonderful head for figures – and the trick was not to cause a panic among the prisoners, or else one would have had another battle on one's hands. So, after every mile – or sometimes two or three, varying it to avoid arousing suspicion – the requisite number of recaptured slaves would be halted by the roadside as the rest of the column marched on, and not until their comrades were out of sight did the executions begin. In this way the job had been done with the minimum amount of disruption for the maximum deterrent effect – the Appian Way being the busiest road in Italy.

'I doubt whether many slaves, once they hear of this, will rise against Rome in the future,' smiled Crassus. 'Would you, for example?' he said to me, and when I replied very fervently that I most certainly would not, he pinched my cheek and ruffled my hair. The touch of his hand made my flesh shrivel. 'Is he for sale?' he asked Cicero. 'I like him. I'd give you a good price for him. Let us see . . .' He named an amount that was at least ten times what I was worth, and for a terrible moment I thought the offer might be accepted and I would lose my place in Cicero's life – a banishment I could not have borne.

'He is not for sale, at any price,' said Cicero. The journey had upset him; there was a hoarseness to his voice. 'And to avoid any misunderstanding, Imperator, I believe I should tell you right away that I have pledged my support to Pompey the Great.'

'Pompey the who?' mocked Crassus. 'Pompey the *Great*? As great as what?'

'I would rather not say,' replied Cicero. 'Comparisons can be odious.' At which remark even Crassus, for all his ironclad bonhomie, drew back his head a little.

There are certain politicians who cannot stand to be in the same room as one another, even if mutual self-interest dictates that they should try to get along, and it quickly became apparent to me that Cicero and Crassus were two such men. This is what the Stoics fail to grasp when they assert that reason rather than emotion should play the dominant part in human affairs. I am afraid the reverse is true, and always will be, even – perhaps especially – in the supposedly calculating world of politics. And if reason cannot rule in politics, what hope is there for it in any other sphere? Crassus had summoned Cicero in order to seek his friendship. Cicero had come determined to keep Crassus's goodwill. Yet neither man could quite conceal his distaste for the other, and the meeting was a disaster.

'Let us get to the point, shall we?' said Crassus, after he had invited Cicero to sit down. He took off his cloak and handed it to his son, then settled on the couch. 'There are two things I would like to ask of you, Cicero. One is your support for my candidacy for the consulship. I am forty-four, so I am more than old enough, and I believe this ought to be my year. The other is a triumph. For both I am willing to pay whatever is your current market rate. Normally, as you know, I insist on an exclusive contract, but, given your prior commitments, I suppose I shall have to settle for half of you. Half of Cicero,' he added with a slight bow of his head, 'being worth twice as much as the entirety of most men.'

'That is flattering, Imperator,' responded Cicero, bridling at the implication. 'Thank you. My slave cannot be bought, but I can, is that it? Perhaps you will allow me to think about it.'

'What is there to think about? Every citizen has two votes for the consulship. Give one to me and one to whomever else you please. Just make sure your friends all follow your example. Tell them Crassus never forgets those who oblige him. Or those who disoblige him, for that matter.'

'I would still have to think about it, I am afraid.'

Some shadow moved across Crassus's friendly face, like a pike in clear water. 'And my triumph?'

'Personally, I absolutely believe you have earned the honour. But, as you know, to qualify for a triumph it is necessary for the military action concerned to have extended the dominion of the state. The senate has consulted the precedents. Apparently, it is not enough merely to regain territory that has been lost previously. For example, when Fulvius won back Capua after its defection to Hannibal, he was not allowed a triumph.' Cicero explained all this with what seemed genuine regret.

'But this is a technicality, surely? If Pompey can be a consul without meeting any of the necessary requirements, why cannot I at least have a triumph? I know you are unfamiliar with the difficulties of military command, or even,' he added sinuously, 'with military service, but surely you would agree that I have met all the other requirements – killed five thousand in battle, fought under the auspices, been saluted imperator by the legions, brought peace to the province, withdrawn my troops? If someone of influence such as yourself were to put down a motion in the senate, he would find me very generous.'

There was a long pause, and I wondered how Cicero would escape from his dilemma.

'*There* is your triumph, Imperator!' he said suddenly, pointing in the direction of the Appian Way. '*That* is the monument to the kind of man you are! For as long as Romans have tongues to speak, they will remember the name of Crassus as the man who crucified six thousand slaves over three hundred and fifty miles, with one hundred and seventeen paces between the crosses. None of our other great generals would ever have done such a thing. Scipio Africanus, Pompey, Lucullus . . .' He flicked them away with contempt. 'None of them would even have *thought* of it.'

Cicero sat back and smiled at Crassus; Crassus smiled in return. Time went on. I felt myself begin to sweat. It became a contest to see whose smile would crack first. Eventually, Crassus stood and held out his hand to Cicero. 'Thank you so much for coming, my young friend,' he said.

When the senate met a few days later to determine honours, Cicero voted with the majority to deny Crassus a triumph. The vanquisher of Spartacus had to settle for an ovation, an altogether second-class award. Rather than entering the city riding on a chariot drawn by four horses, he would have to walk in; the customary fanfare of trumpets would be replaced by the trilling of flutes; and instead of the usual wreath of laurel he would only be permitted to wear myrtle. 'If the man has any sense of honour,' said Cicero, 'he will turn it down.' I need hardly add that Crassus quickly sent word of his acceptance.

Once the discussion moved on to honours for Pompey, Afranius pulled a clever trick. He used his praetorian rank to rise early in the debate and declare that Pompey would accept with humble gratitude whatever the house chose to grant him: he would be arriving outside the city with ten thousand men the following day, and hoped to thank as many of the senators in person as possible. *Ten thousand men?* After that, even the aristocrats were unwilling publicly to snub the conqueror of Spain, and the consuls were instructed by a unanimous vote to attend on Pompey at his earliest convenience and offer him a full triumph.

The next morning Cicero dressed with even more care than usual and consulted with Quintus and Lucius as to what line he should take in his discussions with Pompey. He decided on a bold approach. The following year he would be thirty-six, just eligible to stand for an aedileship of Rome, four of which were elected annually. The functions of the office – the maintenance of public buildings and public order, the celebration of various festivals, the issuing of trading licences, distribution of grain and so on – were a useful means of consolidating political support. That was what he would ask for, it was agreed: Pompey's backing for an aedileship. 'I believe I have earned it,' said Cicero.

After that was settled, we joined the throngs of citizens heading west towards the Field of Mars, where it was rumoured that Pompey intended to halt his legions. (It was, at least in those days, illegal to possess military *imperium* within the sacred boundaries of Rome; thus both Crassus and Pompey were obliged, if they wanted to keep command of their armies, to do their scheming from beyond the city's walls.) There was intense interest in seeing what the great man looked like, for the Roman Alexander, as Pompey's followers called him, had been away fighting for nearly seven years. Some wondered how much he might have changed; others – of whom I was one – had never set eyes on him at all. Cicero had already heard from Palicanus that Pompey intended to set up his headquarters in the Villa Publica, the government guest house next to the voting enclosures, and that was where we made for – Cicero, Quintus, Lucius and I.

The place was encircled with a double cordon of soldiers, and by the time we had fought our way through the crowds to the perimeter wall, no one was being allowed into the grounds unless they had authorisation. Cicero was most offended that none of the guards had even heard of him, and we were lucky that Palicanus was at that moment passing close to the gate: he was able to fetch his son-in-law, the legionary commander Gabinius, to vouch for us. Once we were inside we found that half of official Rome was already there, strolling around the shaded colonnades, humming with curiosity at being this close to power.

'Pompey the Great arrived in the middle of the night,' Palicanus informed us, adding grandly: 'The consuls are with him now.' He promised to return with more information as soon as he had any, then disappeared, self-importantly, between the sentries into the house.

Several hours passed, during which there was no further sign of Palicanus. Instead we noted the messengers rushing in and out, hungrily witnessed food being delivered, saw the consuls leave, and then watched Catulus and Isauricus, the elder statesmen, arrive. Waiting senators, knowing Cicero to be a fervent partisan of Pompey and believing him to be in his inner counsels, kept coming up to him and asking what was really happening. 'All in good time,' he would reply, 'all in good time.' Eventually I guess he must have found this formula embarrassing, for he sent me off to find him a stool, and when I returned, he set it against a pillar, leaned back and closed his eyes. Towards the middle of the afternoon, Hortensius arrived, squeezing his way through the curious onlookers held back by the soldiers, and was admitted immediately into the villa. When he was followed soon afterwards by the three Metellus brothers, it was impossible even for Cicero to pretend this was anything other than a humiliation. Brother Quintus was dispatched to see if he could pick up any gossip outside the senate house, while Cicero paced up and down the colonnades and ordered me for the twentieth time to try to find Palicanus or Afranius or Gabinius – anyone who could get him in to that meeting.

I hung around the crowded entrance, rising on tiptoe, trying to see over all the jostling heads. A messenger came out and briefly left the door half open, and for a moment I glimpsed white-robed figures, laughing and talking, standing around a heavy marble table with documents spread across it. But then I was distracted by a commotion from the street. With shouts of 'Hail Imperator!' and much cheering and yelling, the gate was swung open and, flanked by bodyguards, in stepped Crassus. He took off his plumed helmet and handed it to one of his lictors, wiped his forehead and looked around him. His gaze fell upon Cicero. He gave him a slight nod of the head accompanied by another of his plain man's smiles, and that was one of the few occasions, I should say, when Cicero was entirely lost for words. Then Crassus swept his scarlet cloak around him – rather magnificently, it must be admitted – and marched into the Villa Publica, while Cicero plonked down heavily on his stool.

I have frequently observed this curious of aspect of power: that it is often when one is physically closest to its source that one is least well informed as to what is actually going on. For example, I have seen senators obliged to step out of the senate chamber and dispatch their slaves to the vegetable market to find out what was happening in the city they were supposedly running. Or I have known of generals, surrounded by legates and ambassadors, who have been reduced to intercepting passing shepherds to discover the latest events on the battlefield. So it was that afternoon with Cicero, who sat within twenty feet of the room in which Rome was being carved up like a cooked chicken, but who had to hear the news of what had been decided from Quintus, who had picked it up from a magistrate in the forum, who had heard it from a senate clerk.

'It's bad,' said Quintus, although one could already tell that from his face. 'Pompey for consul and the rights of the tribunes restored, and with no opposition to be offered by the aristocrats. But in return – listen to this – *in return*, Hortensius and Quintus Metellus are to be consuls in the following year, with the full support of Pompey, while Lucius Metellus is to replace Verres as governor of Sicily. Finally, Crassus – *Crassus!* – is to rule with Pompey as joint consul, with both their armies to be dissolved on the day they take office.'

'But I should have been in there,' said Cicero, staring with dismay at the villa. '*I should have been in there!*'

'Marcus,' said his brother sadly, putting his hand on his shoulder, 'none of them would have you.'

Cicero looked stunned at the scale of this reversal – himself excluded, his enemies rewarded, Crassus elevated to the consulship – but then he shook his shoulder free and made angrily towards the doors. And perhaps his career might have been ended there by the sword of one of Pompey's sentries, for I believe, in his desperation, Cicero had resolved to force his way through to the negotiating table and demand his share. But it was too late. The big men, their deal struck, were already coming out, their aides scampering ahead of them, their guards stamping to attention as they passed. Crassus emerged first, and then, from the shadows, Pompey, his identity obvious at once not only from the aura of power around him – the way the proximate air seemed almost to crackle as he moved – but from the cast of his features. He had a broad face, wide cheekbones, and thick wavy hair that rose in a quiff, like the prow of a ship. It was a face full of weight and command, and he possessed the body to go with it, wide shoulders and a strong chest – the torso of a wrestler. I could see why, when he was younger, and famed for his ruthlessness, he had been called the Butcher Boy.

And so off they went, Baldhead and the Butcher Boy, noticeably neither talking nor even looking at one another, heading towards the gate, which swung open as they approached. A stampede of senators, seeing what was happening, set off in pursuit, and we were swept along in the rush, borne out of the Villa Publica and into what felt like a solid wall of noise and heat. Twenty thousand people must have gathered on the Field of Mars that afternoon, all bellowing their approval. A narrow avenue had been cleared by the soldiers, straining arms chain-linked at the elbows, feet scrabbling in the dust to hold back the crowd. It was just wide enough for Pompey and Crassus to walk abreast, although what their expressions were and whether they had started talking I could not see, as we were far back in the procession. They made slow progress towards the tribunal, where the officials traditionally stand at election time. Pompey heaved himself up first, to a renewed surge of applause, which he basked in for a while, turning his wide and beaming face this way and that, like a cat in sunshine. Then he reached down and hauled Crassus up after him. At this demonstration of unity between the two notorious rivals, the crowd let out another roar, and it came again and even louder when Pompey seized hold of Crassus's hand and raised it above his head.

'What a sickening spectacle,' said Cicero. He had to shout into my ear to make himself heard. 'The consulship demanded and conceded at the point of the sword. We are witnessing the beginning of the end of the republic, Tiro, remember my words!' I could not help reflecting, however, that if *he* had been in that conference, and had helped engineer this joint ticket, he would now be hailing it as a masterpiece of statecraft.

Pompey waved at the crowd for quiet, then began speaking in his parade-ground voice. 'People of Rome! The leaders of the senate have graciously conveyed to me the offer of a triumph, and I am pleased to accept it. They have also told me that I will be allowed to stand as a candidate for the consulship, and I am pleased to accept that as well. The only thing that pleases me more is that my old friend Marcus Licinius Crassus will be my colleague.' He concluded by promising that the following year he would hold a great festival of games, dedicated to Hercules, in honour of his victories in Spain.

Well, these were fine words, no doubt, but he spoke them all too quickly, forgetting to leave the necessary pause after every sentence, which meant that those few who had managed to hear what he said had no opportunity to repeat it to those behind who had not. I doubt if more than a few hundred out of that vast assembly knew what he was saying, but they cheered in any case, and they cheered even more when Crassus immediately, and cunningly, upstaged him.

'I hereby dedicate,' he said, in the booming voice of a trained orator, 'at the same time as Pompey's games – on the same day as Pompey's games – one tenth of my fortune – one tenth of my *entire* fortune – to providing free food to the people of Rome – free food for every one of you, for *three months* – and a great banquet in the streets – a banquet for every citizen – a banquet in honour of Hercules!'

The crowd went into fresh ecstasies. 'The villain,' said Cicero admiringly. 'A tenth of his fortune is a bribe of twenty million! But cheap at the price. See how he turns a weak position into a strong one? I bet you were not expecting *that*,' he called out to Palicanus, who was struggling towards us from the tribunal. 'He has made himself look Pompey's equal. You should never have allowed him a platform.'

'Come and meet the imperator,' urged Palicanus. 'He wants to thank you in person.' I could see Cicero was in two minds, but Palicanus was insistent, tugging at his sleeve, and I suppose he thought he ought to try to salvage something from the day.

'Is he going to make a speech?' shouted Cicero, as we followed Palicanus towards the tribunal.

'He doesn't really make speeches,' replied Palicanus over his shoulder. 'Not yet, anyway.'

'That is a mistake. They will expect him to say something.'

'Well, they will just have to be disappointed, won't they?'

'What a waste,' Cicero muttered to me in disgust. 'What I would not give to have an audience such as this! How often do you see so many voters in one place?'

But Pompey had little experience of public oratory, and besides, he was accustomed to commanding men, not pandering to them. With a final wave to the crowd, he clambered down from the platform. Crassus followed suit and the applause slowly died away. There was a palpable sense of anticlimax, as people stood around wondering what they should do next. 'What a waste,' repeated Cicero. '*I* would have given them a show.'

Behind the tribunal was a small enclosed area, where it was the custom for the magistrates to wait before going up to officiate on election-day. Palicanus conducted us into it, past the guards, and here, a moment or two later, Pompey himself appeared. A young black slave handed him a cloth and he began dabbing at his sweating face and wiping the back of his neck. A dozen senators waited to greet him and Palicanus thrust Cicero into the middle of the line, then drew back with Quintus, Lucius and myself to watch. Pompey was moving down the queue, shaking hands with each of the senators in turn, Afranius at his back to tell him who was who. 'Good to meet you,' said Pompey. 'Good to meet you. Good to meet you.' As he came closer I had a better opportunity to study him. He had a noble face, no question of it, but there was also a disagreeable vanity in those fleshy features, and his grand, distracted manner only emphasised his obvious boredom at meeting all these tedious civilians. He reached Cicero very quickly.

'This is Marcus Cicero, Imperator,' said Afranius.

'Good to meet you.'

He was about to move on, but Afranius took his elbow and whispered, 'Cicero is considered one of the city's foremost advocates, and was very useful to us in the senate.'

'Was he? Well, then – keep up the good work.'

'I shall,' said Cicero quickly, 'for I hope next year to be aedile.'

'Aedile?' Pompey scoffed at the very idea. 'No, no, I do not think so. I have other plans in that direction. But I'm sure we can always find a use for a clever lawyer.'

And with that he really did move on – 'Good to meet you . . . Good to meet you . . .' – leaving Cicero staring straight ahead and swallowing hard.

V

That night, for the first and last time in all my years in his service, Cicero drank too much. I could hear him arguing over dinner with Terentia – not one of their normal, witty, icily courteous disputes, but a row which echoed throughout the small house, as she berated him for his stupidity in ever trusting such an obviously dishonourable gang: Piceneans, all of them, not even proper Romans! 'But then of course, you are not a proper Roman either' – a dig at Cicero's lowly provincial origins which invariably got under his skin. Ominously, I did not hear what he said back to her – it was delivered in such a quiet, malevolent tone – but whatever it was, it must have been devastating, for Terentia, who was not a woman easily shaken, ran from the dining room in tears and disappeared upstairs.

I thought it best to leave him well alone. But an hour later I heard a crash, and when I went in Cicero was on his feet and swaying slightly, staring at a broken plate. The front of his tunic was stained with wine. 'I really do not feel well,' he said.

I got him up to his room by hooking his arm over my shoulder – not an easy procedure, as he was heavier than I – laid him on his bed, and unlaced his shoes. 'Divorce,' he muttered into his pillow, 'that is the answer, Tiro – divorce, and if I have to leave the senate because I can't afford it – well, so what? Nobody would miss me. Just another "new man" who came to nothing. Oh dear, Tiro!' I managed to get his chamber pot in front of him just before he was sick. Head down, he addressed his own vomit. 'We shall go to Athens, my dear fellow, and live with Atticus and study philosophy and no one here will miss us . . .' these last few words all running together into a long, self-pitying burble of slurred syllables and sibilant consonants which no shorthand symbol of mine could ever have reconstructed. I set the pot beside him, blew out the lamp and he was snoring even before I reached the door. I confess I went to bed that night with a troubled heart.

And yet, the next morning, I was woken at exactly the usual pre-dawn hour by the sound of him going through his exercises – a little more slowly than usual, perhaps, but then it was awfully early, for this was the height of summer, and he can hardly have had more than a few hours' sleep. Such was the nature of the man. Failure was the fuel of his ambition. Each time he suffered a humiliation – be it as an advocate in his early days when his constitution failed him, or on his return from Sicily, or now, with Pompey's offhand treatment – the fire in him was temporarily banked, but only that it might flare up again even more fiercely. 'It is perseverance,' he used to say, 'and not genius that takes a man to the top. Rome is full of unrecognised geniuses. Only perseverance enables you to move forward in the world.' And so I heard him preparing for another day of struggle in the Roman forum and felt the old, familiar rhythm of the house reassert itself.

I dressed. I lit the lamps. I told the porter to open the front door. I checked the callers. Then I went into Cicero's study and gave him his list of clients. No mention was ever made, either then or in the future, of what had happened the previous night, and I suspect this helped draw us even closer. To be sure, he looked a little green, and he had to screw up his eyes to focus on the names, but otherwise he was entirely normal. 'Sthenius!' he groaned, when he saw who was waiting, as usual, in the tablinum. 'May the gods have mercy upon us!'

'He is not alone,' I warned him. 'He has brought two more Sicilians with him.'

'You mean to say he is multiplying?' He coughed to clear his throat. 'Right. Let us have him in first and get rid of him once and for all.'

As in some curious recurring dream from which one cannot wake, I found myself yet again conducting Sthenius of Thermae into Cicero's presence. His companions he introduced as Heraclius of Syracuse and Epicrates of Bidis. Both were old men, dressed like him in the dark garb of mourning, with uncut hair and beards.

'Now listen, Sthenius,' said Cicero sternly, after he had shaken hands with the grim-looking trio, 'this has got to stop.'

But Sthenius was in that strange and remote private kingdom into which outside sounds seldom penetrate: the land of the obsessive litigant. 'I am most grateful to you, Senator. Firstly, now that I have obtained the court records from Syracuse,' he said, pulling a piece of paper from his leather bag and thrusting it into Cicero's hands, 'you can see what the monster has done. This is what was written before the verdict of the tribunes. And this,' he said, giving him another, 'is what was written afterwards.'

With a sigh, Cicero held the two documents side by side and squinted at them. 'So what is this? This is the official record of your trial for treason, in which I see it is written that you were present during the hearing. Well, we know that is nonsense. And here . . .' his words began to slow as he realised the implications, 'here it says that you were *not* present.' He looked up, his bleary eyes starting to clear. 'So Verres is falsifying the proceedings of his own court, and then he is falsifying his own falsification?'

'Exactly!' cried Sthenius. 'When he realised you had produced me before the tribunes, and that all of Rome knew I could hardly have been in Syracuse on the first day of December, he had to obliterate the record of his lie. But the first document was already on its way to me.'

'Well, well,' said Cicero, continuing to scrutinise the paper, 'perhaps he is more worried than we thought. And I see it also says here that you had a defence attorney representing you that day: "Gaius Claudius, son of Gaius Claudius, of the Palatine tribe." You are a fortunate man, to have your very own Roman lawyer. Who is he?'

'He is Verres's business manager.'

Cicero studied Sthenius for a moment or two. 'What else do you have in that bag of yours?' he said.

Out it all came then, tipped over the study floor on that hot summer's morning: letters, names, scraps of official records, scribbled notes of gossip and rumours – seven months' angry labour by three desperate men, for it transpired that Heraclius and Epicrates had also been swindled out of their estates by Verres, one worth sixty thousand, the other thirty. In both cases, Verres had abused his office to bring false accusations and secure illegal verdicts. Both had been robbed at around the same time as Sthenius. Both had been, until then, the leading men in their communities. Both had been obliged to flee the island penniless and seek refuge in Rome. Hearing of Sthenius's appearance before the tribunes, they had sought him out and proposed cooperation.

'As single victims, they were weak,' said Cicero, years later, reminiscing about the case, 'but when they joined in common cause, they found they had a network of contacts which spread across the entire island: Thermae in the north, Bidis in the south, Syracuse in the east. These were men sagacious by nature, shrewd by experience, accomplished by education, and their fellow countrymen had opened up the secrets of their suffering to them, as they would never have done to a Roman senator.'

Outwardly, Cicero still seemed the calm advocate. But as the sun grew stronger and I blew out the lamps, and as he picked up one document after another, I could sense his gathering excitement. Here was the sworn affidavit of Dio of Halaesa, from whom Verres had first demanded a bribe of ten thousand to bring in a not guilty verdict, and then stolen all his horses, tapestries and gold and silver plate. Here were the written testimonies of priests whose temples had been robbed – a bronze Apollo, signed in silver by the sculptor Myron, and presented by Scipio a century and a half earlier, stolen from the shrine of Aesculapius at Agrigentum; a statue of Ceres carried away from Catina, and of Victory from Henna; the sacking of the ancient shrine of Juno in Melita. Here was the evidence of farmers in Herbita and Agyrium, threatened with being flogged to death unless they paid protection money to Verres's agents. Here was the story of the wretched Sopater of Tyndaris, seized in midwinter by Verres's lictors and bound naked to an equestrian statue in full view of the entire community, until he and his fellow citizens agreed to hand over a valuable municipal bronze of Mercury that stood in the local gymnasium. 'It is not a province Verres is running down there,' murmured Cicero, in wonder, 'it is a fully fledged criminal state.' There were a dozen more of these grim stories.

With the agreement of the three Sicilians, I bundled the papers together and locked them in the senator's strongbox. 'It is vital, gentlemen, that not a word of this leaks out,' Cicero told them. 'By all means continue to collect statements and witnesses, but please do it discreetly. Verres has used violence and intimidation many times before, and you can be sure he will use them again to protect himself. We need to take the rascal unawares.'

'Does that mean,' asked Sthenius, hardly daring to hope, 'that you will help us?'

Cicero looked at him but did not answer.

Later that day, when he returned from the law courts, the senator made up his quarrel with his wife. He dispatched young Sositheus down to the old flower market in the Forum Boarium, in front of the Temple of Portunus, to buy a bouquet of fragrant summer blooms. These he then gave to little Tullia, telling her solemnly that he had a vital task for her. She was to take them in to her mother and announce they had come for her from a rough provincial admirer. ('Have you got that, Tulliola? A rough provincial admirer.') She disappeared very self-importantly into Terentia's chamber, and I guess they must have done the trick, for that evening, when – at Cicero's insistence – the couches were carried up to the roof and the family dined beneath the summer stars, the flowers had a place of honour at the centre of the table.

I know this because, as the meal was ending, I was unexpectedly sent for by Cicero. It was a still night, without a flicker of wind to disturb the candles, and the night-time sounds of Rome down in the valley mingled with the scent of the flowers in the warm June air – snatches of music, voices, the call of the watchmen along the Argiletum, the distant barking of the guard dogs set loose in the precincts of the Capitoline Triad. Lucius and Quintus were still laughing at some joke of Cicero's, and even Terentia could not quite hide her amusement as she flicked her napkin at her husband and scolded him that that was quite enough. (Pomponia, thankfully, was away visiting her brother in Athens.)

'Ah,' said Cicero, looking round, 'now here is Tiro, the master politician of us all, which means I can proceed to make my little declaration. I thought it appropriate that he should be present to hear this as well. I have decided to stand for election as aedile.'

'Oh, very good!' said Quintus, who thought it was all still part of Cicero's joke. Then he stopped laughing and said in a puzzled way, 'But that is not funny.'

'It will be if I win.'

'But you can't win. You heard what Pompey said. He doesn't want you to be a candidate.'

'It is not for Pompey to decide who is to be a candidate. We are free citizens, free to make our own choices. I choose to run for aedile.'

'There is no sense in running and losing, Marcus. That is the sort of pointlessly heroic gesture Lucius here believes in.'

'Let us drink to pointless heroism,' said Lucius, raising his glass.

'But we cannot win against Pompey's opposition,' persisted Quintus. 'And what is the point of incurring Pompey's enmity?'

To which Terentia retorted: 'After yesterday, one might better ask, "What is the point of incurring Pompey's friendship?"'

'Terentia is right,' said Cicero. 'Yesterday has taught me a lesson. Let us say I wait a year or two, hanging on Pompey's every word in the hope of favour, running errands for him. We have all seen men like that in the senate – growing older, waiting for half-promises to be fulfilled. They are hollowed out by it. And before they even know it, their moment has passed and they have nothing left with which to bargain. I would sooner clear out of politics right now than let that happen to me. If you want power, there is a time when you have to seize it. This is my time.'

'But how is this be accomplished?'

'By prosecuting Gaius Verres for extortion.'

So there it was. I had known he would do it since early morning, and so, I am sure, had he, but he had wanted to take his time about it – to try on the decision, as it were, and see how it fitted him. And it fitted him very well. I had never seen him more determined. He looked like a man who believed he had the force of history running through him. Nobody spoke.

'Come on!' he said with a smile. 'Why the long faces? I have not lost yet! And I do not believe I shall lose, either. I had a visit from the Sicilians this morning. They have gathered the most damning testimony against Verres, have they not, Tiro? We have it under lock and key downstairs. And when we do win – think of it! I defeat Hortensius in open court, and all this "second-best advocate" nonsense is finished for ever. I assume the rank of the man I convict, according to the traditional rights of the victorious prosecutor, which means I become a praetorian overnight – so no more jumping up and down on the back benches in the senate, hoping to be called. And I place myself so firmly before the gaze of the Roman people that my election as aedile is assured. But the best thing of all is that I do it – I, Cicero – and I do it without owing favours to anyone, least of all Pompey the Great.'

'But what if we lose?' said Quintus, finding his voice at last. 'We are defence attorneys. We never prosecute. You have said it yourself a hundred times: defenders win friends; prosecutors just make enemies. If you don't bring Verres down, there is a good chance he will eventually be elected consul. Then he will never rest until you are destroyed.'

'That is true,' conceded Cicero. 'If you are going to kill a dangerous animal, you had better make sure you do it with the first thrust. But then – don't you see? This way I can win everything. Rank, fame, office, dignity, authority, independence, a base of clients in Rome and Sicily. It opens my way clear through to becoming consul.'

This was the first time I had heard him mention his great ambition, and it was a measure of his renewed confidence that he felt able to utter the word at last. *Consul.* For every man in public life, this was the apotheosis. The very years themselves were distinguished from one another on all official documents and foundation stones by the names of the presiding consuls. It was the nearest thing below heaven to immortality. How many nights and days must he have thought of it, dreamed of it, nursed it, since his gawky adolescence? Sometimes it is foolish to articulate an ambition too early – exposing it prematurely to the laughter and scepticism of the world can destroy it before it is even properly born. But sometimes the opposite occurs, and the very act of mentioning a thing makes it suddenly seem possible, even plausible. That was how it was that night. When Cicero pronounced the word 'consul' he planted it in the ground like a standard for us all to admire. And for a moment we glimpsed the brilliant, starry future through his eyes, and saw that he was right: that if he took down Verres, he had a chance; that he might just – with luck – go all the way to the summit.

There was much to be done over the following months, and as usual a great deal of the work fell upon me. First, I drew up a large chart of the electorate for the aedileship. At that time, this consisted of the entire Roman citizenry, divided into their thirty-five tribes. Cicero himself belonged to the Cornelia, Servius to the Lemonia, Pompey to the Clustumina, Verres to the Romilia, and so forth. A citizen cast his ballot on the Field of Mars as a member of his tribe, and the results of each tribe's vote were then read out by the magistrates. The four candidates who secured the votes of the greatest number of tribes were duly declared the winners.

There were several advantages for Cicero in this particular electoral college. For one thing – unlike the system for choosing praetors and consuls – each man's vote, whatever his wealth, counted equally, and as Cicero's strongest support was among the men of business and the teeming poor, the aristocrats would find it harder to block him. For another, it was a relatively easy electorate to canvass. Each tribe had its own headquarters somewhere in Rome, a building large enough to lay on a show or a dinner. I went back through our files and compiled a list of every man Cicero had ever defended or helped over the past six years, arranged according to his tribe. These men were then contacted and asked to make sure that the senator was invited to speak at any forthcoming tribal event. It is surely amazing how many favours there are to be called in after six years of relentless advocacy and advice. Cicero's campaign schedule was soon filled with engagements, and his working day became even longer. After the courts or the senate had adjourned, he would hurry home, quickly bathe and change, and then rush out again to give one of his rousing addresses. His slogan was 'Justice and Reform'.

Quintus, as usual, acted as Cicero's campaign manager, while cousin Lucius was entrusted with organising the case against Verres. The governor was due to return from Sicily at the end of the year, whereupon – at the very instant he entered the city – he would lose his *imperium*, and with it his immunity from prosecution. Cicero was determined to strike at the first opportunity, and, if possible, give Verres no time to dispose of evidence or intimidate witnesses. For this reason, to avoid arousing suspicion, the Sicilians stopped coming to the house, and Lucius became the conduit between Cicero and his clients, meeting them in secret at various locations across the city. I thus came to know Lucius much better, and the more I saw of him the more I liked him. He was in many respects very similar to Cicero. He was almost the same age, clever and amusing, a gifted philosopher. The two had grown up together in Arpinum, been schooled together in Rome, and travelled together in the East. But there was one huge difference: Lucius entirely lacked worldly ambition. He lived alone, in a small house full of books, and did nothing all day except read and think – a most dangerous occupation for a man which in my experience leads invariably to dyspepsia and melancholy. But oddly enough, despite his solitary disposition, he soon came to relish leaving his study every day and was so enraged by Verres's wickedness that his zeal to bring him to justice eventually exceeded even Cicero's. 'We shall make a lawyer of you yet, cousin,' Cicero remarked admiringly, after Lucius had produced yet another set of damning affidavits.

Towards the end of December an incident occurred which finally brought together, and in dramatic fashion, all these separate strands of Cicero's life. I opened the door one dark morning to find, standing at the head of the usual queue, the man we had recently seen in the tribunes' basilica, acting as defence attorney for his great-grandfather's pillar – Marcus Porcius Cato. He was alone, without a slave to attend him, and looked as though he had slept out in the street all night. (I suppose he might have done, come to think of it, although Cato's appearance was usually dishevelled – like that of a holy man or mystic – so that it was hard to tell.) Naturally, Cicero was intrigued to discover why a man of such eminent birth should have turned up on his doorstep, for Cato, bizarre as he was, dwelt at the very heart of the old republican aristocracy, connected by blood and marriage to a webwork of Servilii, Lepidi and Aemilii. Indeed, such was Cicero's pleasure at having so high-born a visitor, he went out to the tablinum himself to welcome him, and conducted him into the study personally. This was the sort of client he had long dreamed of finding in his net one morning.

I settled myself in the corner to take notes, and young Cato, never a man for small talk, came straight to the point. He was in need of a good advocate, he said, and he had liked the way Cicero had handled himself before the tribunes, for it was a monstrous thing when any man such as Verres considered himself above the ancient laws. To put it briefly: he was engaged to be married to his cousin, Aemilia Lepida, a charming girl of eighteen, whose young life had already been blighted by tragedy. At the age of thirteen, she had been humiliatingly jilted by her fiancé, the haughty young aristocrat Scipio Nasica. At fourteen, her mother had died. At fifteen, her father had died. At sixteen, her brother had died, leaving her completely alone.

'The poor girl,' said Cicero. 'So I take it, if she is your cousin, that she must be the daughter of the consul of six years ago, Aemilius Lepidus Livianus? He was, I believe, the brother of your late mother, Livia?' (Like many supposed radicals, Cicero had a surprisingly thorough knowledge of the aristocracy.)

'That is correct.'

'Why, then, I congratulate you, Cato, on a most brilliant match. With the blood of those three families in her veins, and with her nearest relatives all dead, she must be the richest heiress in Rome.'

'She is,' said Cato bitterly. 'And that is the trouble. Scipio Nasica, her former suitor, who has just come back from Spain after fighting in the army of Pompey the so-called Great, has found out how rich she has become, now that her father and brother are gone, and he has reclaimed her as his own.'

'But surely it is for the young lady herself to decide?'

'She has,' said Cato. 'She has decided on him.'

'Ah,' replied Cicero, sitting back in his chair, 'in that case, you may be in some difficulties. Presumably, if she was orphaned at fifteen, she must have had a guardian appointed. You could always talk to him. He is probably in a position to forbid the marriage. Who is he?'

'That would be me.'

'You? You are the guardian of the woman you want to marry?'

'I am. I am her closest male relative.'

Cicero rested his chin in his hand and scrutinised his prospective new client – the ragged hair, the filthy bare feet, the tunic unchanged for weeks. 'So what do you wish me to do?'

'I want you to bring legal proceedings against Scipio, and against Lepida if necessary, and put a stop to this whole thing.'

'These proceedings – would they be brought by you in your role as rejected suitor, or as the girl's guardian?'

'Either.' Cato shrugged. 'Both.'

Cicero scratched his ear. 'My experience of young women,' he said carefully, 'is as limited as my faith in the rule of law is boundless. But even I, Cato, *even I* have to say that I doubt whether the best way to a girl's heart is through litigation.'

'A girl's heart?' repeated Cato. 'What has a girl's heart got to do with anything? This is a matter of principle.'

And money, one would have added, if he had been any other man. But Cato had that most luxurious prerogative of the very rich: little interest in money. He had inherited plenty, and gave it away without even noticing. No: it was principle that always motivated Cato – the relentless desire never to compromise on principle.

'We would have to go to the embezzlement court,' said Cicero, 'and lay charges of breach of promise. We would have to prove the existence of a prior contract between you and the Lady Lepida, and that she was therefore a cheat and a liar. We would have to prove that Scipio was a double-dealing, money-grubbing knave. I would have to put them both on the witness stand and tear them to pieces.'

'Do it,' said Cato, with a gleam in his eye.

'And at the end of all that, we would probably still lose, for juries love nothing more than star-crossed lovers, save perhaps for orphans – and she is both – and you would have been made the laughing-stock of Rome.'

'What do I care what people think of me?' said Cato scornfully.

'And even if we win – well, imagine it. You might end up having to drag Lepida kicking and screaming from the court through the streets of Rome, back to her new marital home. It would be the scandal of the year.'

'So this is what we have descended to, is it?' demanded Cato bitterly. 'The honest man is to step aside so that the rascal triumphs? And this is Roman justice?' He leapt to his feet. 'I need a lawyer with steel in his bones, and if I cannot find anyone to help me, then I swear I shall lay the prosecution myself.'

'Sit down, Cato,' said Cicero gently, and when Cato did not move, he repeated it: 'Sit, Cato, and I shall tell you something about the law.' Cato hesitated, frowned, and sat, but only on the edge of his chair, so that he could leap up again at the first hint that he should moderate his convictions. 'A word of advice, if I may, from a man ten years your senior. You must not take everything head-on. Very often the best and most important cases never even come to court. This looks to me like one of them. Let me see what I can do.'

'And if you fail?'

'Then you can proceed however you like.'

After he had gone, Cicero said to me: 'That young man seeks opportunities to test his principles as readily as a drunk picks fights in a bar.' Nevertheless, Cato had agreed to let Cicero approach Scipio on his behalf, and I could tell that Cicero relished the opportunity this would give him to scrutinise the aristocracy at first hand. There was literally no man in Rome with grander lineage than Quintus Caecilius Metellus Pius Cornelius Scipio Nasica – Nasica meaning 'pointed nose', which he carried very firmly in the air – for he was not only the natural son of a Scipio, but the adopted son of Metellus Pius, pontifex maximus and the titular head of the Metelli clan. Father and adopted son had only recently returned from Spain, and were presently on Pius's immense country estate at Tibur. They were expected to enter the city on the twenty-ninth day of December, riding behind Pompey in his triumph. Cicero decided to arrange a meeting for the thirtieth.

The twenty-ninth duly arrived, and what a day that was – Rome had not seen such a spectacle since the days of Sulla. As I waited by the Triumphal Gate it seemed that everyone in the city had turned out to line the route. First to pass through the gate from the Field of Mars was the entire body of the senate, including Cicero, on foot, led by the consuls and the other magistrates. Then the trumpeters, sounding the fanfares. Then the carriages and litters laden with the spoils of the Spanish war – gold and silver, coin and bullion, weapons, statues, pictures, vases, furniture, precious stones and tapestries – and wooden models of the cities Pompey had conquered and sacked, and placards with their names, and the names of all the famous men he had killed in battle. Then the massive, plodding white bulls, destined for sacrifice, with gilded horns hung with ribbons and floral garlands, driven by the slaughtering-priests. Then trudging elephants – the heraldic symbol of the Metellii – and lumbering ox-carts bearing cages containing the wild beasts of the Spanish mountains, roaring and tearing at their bars in rage. Then the arms and insignia of the beaten rebels, and then the prisoners themselves, the defeated followers of Sertorius and Perperna, shuffling in chains. Then the crowns and tributes of the allies, borne by the ambassadors of a score of nations. Then the twelve lictors of the imperator, their rods and axes wreathed in laurel. And now at last, to a tumult of applause from the vast crowd, the four white horses of the imperator's chariot came trotting through the gate, and there was Pompey himself, in the barrel-shaped, gem-encrusted chariot of the triumphator. He wore a gold-embroidered robe with a flowered tunic. In his right hand he held a laurel bough and in his left a sceptre. There was a wreath of Delphic laurel on his head, and his handsome face and muscled body had been painted with red lead, for on this day he truly was the embodiment of Jupiter. Standing beside him was his eight-year-old son, the golden-curled Gnaeus, and behind him a public slave to whisper in his ear that he was only human and all this would pass. Behind the chariot, riding on a black war-horse, came old Metellus Pius, his leg tightly bandaged, evidence of a wound incurred in battle. Next to him was Scipio, his adopted son – a handsome young fellow of twenty-four: no wonder, I thought, that Lepida preferred him to Cato – and then the legionary commanders, including Aulus Gabinius, followed by all the knights and cavalry, armour glinting in the pale December sun. And finally the legions of Pompey's infantry, in full marching order, thousand upon thousand of sunburnt veterans, the crash of their tramping boots seeming to shake the very earth, roaring at the top of their voices, *'Io Triumphe!'* and chanting hymns to the gods and singing filthy songs about their commander-in-chief, as they were traditionally permitted to do in this, the hour of his glory.

It took half the morning for them all to pass, the procession winding through the streets towards the forum, where, according to tradition, as Pompey ascended the steps of the Capitol to sacrifice before the Temple of the Jupiter, his most eminent prisoners were lowered into the depths of the Carcer and garrotted – for what could be more fitting than that the day which ended the military authority of the conqueror should also end the lives of the conquered? I could hear the distant cheering inside the city but spared myself that sight, and hung around the Triumphal Gate with the dwindling crowd to see the entry of Crassus for his ovation. He made the best of it, marching with his sons beside him, but despite the efforts of his agents to whip up some enthusiasm, it was a poor show after the magnificence of Pompey's dazzling pageant. I am sure he must have resented it mightily, picking his way between the horse shit and elephant dung left behind by his consular colleague. He did not even have many prisoners to parade, the poor fellow, having slaughtered almost all of them along the Appian Way.

The following day, Cicero set out for the house of Scipio, with myself in attendance, carrying a document case – a favourite trick of his to try to intimidate the opposition. We had no evidence; I had simply filled it with old receipts. Scipio's residence was on the Via Sacra, fronted by shops, although naturally these were not your average shops, but exclusive jewellers, who kept their wares behind metal grilles. Our arrival was expected, Cicero having sent notice of his intention to visit, and we were shown immediately by a liveried footman into Scipio's atrium. This has been described as 'one of the wonders of Rome', and indeed it was, even at that time. Scipio could trace his line back for at least eleven generations, nine of which had produced consuls. The walls around us were lined with the wax masks of the Scipiones, some of them centuries old, yellowed with smoke and grime (later, Scipio's adoption by Pius was to bring a further six consular masks crowding into the atrium), and they exuded that thin, dry compound of dust and incense which is to me the smell of antiquity. Cicero went round studying the labels. The oldest mask was three hundred and twenty-five years old. But naturally, it was that of Scipio Africanus, conqueror of Hannibal, which fascinated him the most, and he spent a long time bent down studying it. It was a noble, sensitive face – smooth, unlined, ethereal, more like the representation of a soul than of flesh and blood. 'Prosecuted, of course, by the great-grandfather of our present client,' sighed Cicero, as he straightened. 'Contrariness runs thick in the blood of the Catos.'

The footman returned and we followed him through into the tablinum. There, young Scipio lounged on a couch surrounded by a jumble of precious objects – statues, busts, antiques, rolls of carpet and the like. It looked like the burial chamber of some Eastern potentate. He did not stand when Cicero entered (an insult to a senator), nor did he invite him to sit, but merely asked him in a drawling voice to state his business. This Cicero proceeded to do, firmly but courteously, informing him that Cato's case was legally watertight, given that Cato was both formally betrothed to the young lady, and also her guardian. He gestured to the document case, which I held before me like a serving boy with a tray, and ran through the precedents, concluding by saying that Cato was resolved to bring an action in the embezzlement court, and would also seek a motion *obsignandi gratia*, preventing the young lady from having further contact with any person or persons material to the case. There was only one sure way of avoiding this humiliation, and that was for Scipio to give up his suit immediately.

'He really is a crackpot, isn't he?' said Scipio languidly, and lay back on his couch with his hands behind his head, smiling at the painted ceiling.

'Is that your only answer?' said Cicero.

'No,' said Scipio, 'this is my only answer. Lepida!' And at that, a demure young woman appeared from behind a screen, where she had obviously been listening, and moved gracefully across the floor to stand beside the couch. She slipped her hand into Scipio's. 'This is my wife. We were married yesterday evening. What you see around you are the wedding gifts of our friends. Pompey the Great came directly from sacrificing on the Capitol to be a witness.'

'Jupiter himself could have been a witness,' retorted Cicero, 'but that would not suffice to make the ceremony legal.' Still, I could see by the way his shoulders slumped slightly that the fight had gone out of him. Possession, as the jurists say, is nine tenths of the law, and Scipio had not merely the possession, but obviously the eager acquiescence, of his new bride. 'Well,' Cicero said, looking around at the wedding presents, 'on my behalf, I suppose, if not that of my client, I offer you both congratulations. Perhaps my wedding gift to you should be to persuade Cato to recognise reality.'

'That,' said Scipio, 'would be the rarest gift ever bestowed.'

'My cousin is a good man at heart,' said Lepida. 'Will you convey my best wishes, and my hopes that one day we shall be reconciled?'

'Of course,' said Cicero, with a gentlemanly bow, and he was just turning to go when he stopped abruptly. 'Now that is a pretty piece. That is a very pretty piece.'

It was a bronze statue of a naked Apollo, perhaps half the size of a man, playing on a lyre – a sublime depiction of graceful masculinity, arrested in mid-dance, with every hair of his head and string of his instrument perfectly delineated. Worked into his thigh in tiny silver letters was the name of the sculptor: Myron.

'Oh, that,' said Scipio, very offhand, 'that was apparently given to some temple by my illustrious ancestor, Scipio Africanus. Why? Do you know it?'

'If I am not mistaken, it is from the shrine of Aesculapius at Agrigentum.'

'That is the place,' said Scipio. 'In Sicily. Verres got it off the priests there and gave it to me last night.'

In this way Cicero learned that Gaius Verres had returned to Rome and was already spreading the tentacles of his corruption across the city. 'Villain!' exclaimed Cicero as he walked away down the hill. He clenched and unclenched his fists in impotent fury. 'Villain, villain, *villain!*' He had good cause to be alarmed, for it was fair to assume that if Verres had given a Myron to young Scipio, then Hortensius, the Metellus brothers and all his other prominent allies in the senate would have received even heftier bribes – and it was precisely from among such men that the jury at any future trial would be drawn. A secondary blow was the discovery that Pompey had been present at the same wedding feast as Verres and the leading aristocrats. Pompey had always had strong links with Sicily – as a young general he had restored order on the island, and had even stayed overnight in the house of Sthenius. Cicero had looked to him if not exactly for support – he had learned his lesson there – then at least for benign neutrality. The awful possibility now occurred to him that if he went ahead with the prosecution he might have every powerful faction in Rome united against him

But there was no time to ponder the implications of that now. Cato had insisted on hearing the results of Cicero's interview immediately, and was waiting for him at the house of his half-sister, Servilia, which was also on the Via Sacra, only a few doors down from Scipio's residence. As we entered, three young girls – none I would guess more than five years old – came running out into the atrium, followed by their mother. This was the first occasion, I believe, on which Cicero met Servilia, who was later to become the most formidable woman among the many formid-able women who lived in Rome. She was nearly thirty, hand-some but not at all pretty, about five years older than Cato. By her late first husband, Marcus Brutus, she had given birth to a son when she was still only fifteen; by her second, the feeble Junius Silanus, she had produced these three daughters in quick succession. Cicero greeted them as if he had not a care in the world, squatting on his haunches to talk to them while Servilia looked on. She insisted that they meet every caller, and so become familiar with adult ways, for they were her great hope for the future, and she wished them to be sophisticated.

Eventually a nurse came and took the girls away and Servilia

showed us through to the tablinum. Here, Cato was waiting with
Antipater the Tyrian, a Stoic philosopher who seldom left his
side. Cato took the news of Lepida's marriage quite as badly as
one would have predicted, striding around and swearing, which
reminds me of another of Cicero's witticisms – that Cato was
always the perfect Stoic, as long as nothing went wrong.

'Do calm yourself, Cato,' said Servilia after a while. 'It is
perfectly obvious the matter is finished, and you might as well
get used to it. You did not love her – you do not know what love
is. You do not even need her money – you have plenty of your
own. She is a drippy little thing. You can find a hundred better.'

'She asked me to bring you her best wishes,' said Cicero, which
provoked another outpouring of abuse from Cato.

'I shall not put up with it!' he shouted.

'Yes you will,' said Servilia. She pointed at Antipater, who
quailed. 'You tell him, philosopher. My brother thinks his fine
principles are all the product of his intellect, whereas they are
simply girlish emotions tricked out by false philosophers as manly
points of honour.' And then, to Cicero again: 'If he had had more
experience of the female sex, Senator, he would see how foolish
he is being. But you have never even lain with a woman, have
you, Cato?'

Cicero looked embarrassed, for he always had the equestrian
class's slight prudishness about sexual matters, and was unused
to the free ways of the aristocrats.

'I believe it weakens the male essence, and dulls the power of
thought,' said Cato sulkily, producing such a shriek of laughter
from his sister that his face turned as red as Pompey's had been
painted the previous day, and he stamped out of the room,
trailing his Stoic after him.

'I apologise,' said Servilia, turning to Cicero. 'Sometimes I almost think he is slow-witted. But then, when he does get hold of a thing, he will never let go of it, which is a quality of sorts, I suppose. He praised your speech to the tribunes about Verres. He made you sound a very dangerous fellow. I rather like dangerous fellows. We should meet again.' She held out her hand to bid Cicero goodbye. He took it, and it seemed to me that she held it rather longer than politeness dictated. 'Would you be willing to take advice from a woman?'

'From you,' said Cicero, eventually retrieving his hand, 'of course.'

'My other brother, Caepio – my full brother, that is – is betrothed to the daughter of Hortensius. He told me that Hortensius was speaking of you the other day – that he suspects you plan to prosecute Verres, and has some scheme in mind to frustrate you. I know no more than that.'

'And in the unlikely event that I was planning such a prosecution,' said Cicero, with a smile, 'what would be your advice?'

'That is simple,' replied Servilia, with the utmost seriousness. 'Drop it.'

VI

Far from deterring him, this conversation with Servilia and his visit to Scipio convinced Cicero that he would have to move even more quickly than he had planned. On the first day of January, in the six hundred and eighty-fourth year since the foundation of Rome, Pompey and Crassus took office as consuls. I escorted Cicero to the inaugural ceremonies on Capitol Hill, and then stood with the crowd at the back of the portico. The rebuilt Temple of Jupiter was at that time nearing completion under the guiding hand of Catulus, and the new marble pillars shipped from Mount Olympus and the roof of gilded bronze gleamed in the cold sunshine. According to tradition, saffron was burnt on the sacrificial fires, and those crackling yellow flames, the smell of spice, the shiny clarity of the winter air, the golden altars, the shuffling creamy bullocks awaiting sacrifice, the white and purple robes of the watching senators – all of it made an unforgettable impression on me. I did not recognise him, but Verres was also there, Cicero told me afterwards, standing with Hortensius: he was aware of the two of them looking at him, and laughing at some shared joke.

For several days thereafter nothing could be done. The senate met and heard a stumbling speech from Pompey, who had never before set foot in the chamber, and who was only able to follow what was happening by constant reference to a bluffer's guide to procedure which had been written out for him by the famous scholar Varro, who had served under him in Spain. Catulus, as usual, was given the first voice, and he made a notably states-manlike speech, conceding that, although he opposed it person-ally, the demand for the restoration of the tribunes' rights could not be resisted, and that the aristocrats had only themselves to blame for their unpopularity. ('You should have seen the looks on the faces of Hortensius and Verres when he said *that*,' Cicero told me later.) Afterwards, following the ancient custom, the new consuls went out to the Alban Mount to preside over the cele-brations of the Latin Festival, which lasted four days. These were followed by another two days of religious observance, during which the courts were closed. So it was not until the second week of the new year that Cicero was finally able to begin his assault.

On the morning that Cicero planned to make his announce-ment, the three Sicilians – Sthenius, Heraclius and Epicrates – came openly to the house for the first time in half a year, and together with Quintus and Lucius they escorted Cicero down the hill into the forum. He also had a few tribal officials in his train, mainly from the Cornelia and the Esquilina, where his support was particularly strong. Some onlookers called out to Cicero as he passed, asking where he was going with his three strange-looking friends, and Cicero responded cheerfully that they should come along and see – they would not be disappointed. He always liked a crowd, and in this way he ensured he had one as he approached the tribunal of the extortion court.

In those days, this court always met before the Temple of Castor and Pollux, at the very opposite end of the forum to the senate house. Its new praetor was Acilius Glabrio, of whom little was known, except that he was surprisingly close to Pompey. I say surprisingly because as a young man he had been required by the dictator Sulla to divorce his wife, even though she was then pregnant with his child, and yield her in marriage to Pompey. Subsequently, this unfortunate woman, whose name was Aemilia, died in childbirth in Pompey's house, whereupon Pompey returned the infant – a son – to his natural father; the boy was now twelve, and the joy of Glabrio's life. This bizarre episode was said to have made the two men not enemies but friends, and Cicero gave much thought as to whether this was likely to be helpful to his cause or not. In the end he could not decide.

Glabrio's chair had just been set up for him, the signal that the court was ready to open for business, and it must have been cold, for I have a very clear memory of Glabrio wearing mittens and sitting beside a charcoal brazier. He was stationed on that platform which runs along the front of the temple, halfway up the stairs. His lictors, their bundled rods slung over their shoulders, were standing in line, stamping their feet, on the steps beneath him. It was a busy spot, for as well as housing the extortion court, the temple was also the venue of the Bureau of Standards, where tradesmen went to check their weights and measures. Glabrio looked surprised to see Cicero with his train of supporters advancing towards him, and many other curious passers-by turned to watch. The praetor waved to his lictors to let the senator approach the bench. As I opened the document case and handed Cicero the *postulatus*, I saw anxiety in his eyes, but also relief that the waiting was finally over. He mounted the steps and turned to address the spectators.

'Citizens,' he said, 'today I come to offer my life in service to the Roman people. I wish to announce my intention to seek the office of aedile of Rome. I do this not out of any desire for personal glory, but because the state of our republic demands that honest men stand up for justice. You all know me. You know what I believe in. You know that I have long been keeping an eye on certain aristocratic gentlemen in the senate!' There was a murmur of approval. 'Well, I have in my hand an application to prosecute – a *postulatus*, as we lawyers call it. And I am here to serve notice of my intention to bring to justice Gaius Verres for the high crimes and misdemeanours committed during his term as governor of Sicily.' He waved it above his head, finally extracting a few muted cheers. 'If he is convicted he will not only have to pay back what he has stolen; he will lose all civil rights as a citizen. Exile or death will be his only choices. He will fight like a cornered animal. It will be a long, hard battle, make no mistake, and on its outcome I hereby wager everything – the office I seek, my hopes for the future, the reputation which I have risen early and toiled in the heat to gain – but I do so in the firm conviction that right will prevail!'

And with that he swung round and marched up the remaining few steps to Glabrio, who was looking mightily bemused, and gave him his application to prosecute. The praetor glanced at it quickly, then passed it to one of his clerks. He shook Cicero's hand – and that was it. The crowd began to disperse and there was nothing left to do except walk back up to the house. I am afraid the whole business had fallen embarrassingly flat, the trouble being that Rome was constantly witnessing individuals declaring their intention to run for some office or another – at least fifty were elected annually – and nobody saw Cicero's announcement in quite the same historic terms as he did. As for the prosecution, it was more than a year since he had stirred up the original excitement about Verres, and people, as he frequently remarked, have short memories; they had forgotten all about the wicked governor of Sicily. I could see that Cicero was suffering a dreadful sense of anticlimax, which even Lucius, who was usually good at making him laugh, could not shake him out of.

We reached the house, and Quintus and Lucius tried to amuse him by picturing the responses of Verres and Hortensius when they learned that a charge had been laid: the slave running back from the forum with the news, Verres turning white, a crisis meeting summoned. But Cicero would have none of it. I guessed he was thinking of the warning Servilia had given him, and the way Hortensius and Verres had laughed at him on inauguration day. 'They knew this was coming,' he said. 'They have a plan. The question is: what? Do they know our evidence is too weak? Is Glabrio in their pocket? What?'

The answer was in his hands before the morning was out. It came in the form of a writ from the extortion court, served upon him by one of Glabrio's lictors. He took it with a frown, broke open the seal, read it quickly, and then said a soft 'Ah . . .'

'What is it?' asked Lucius.

'The court has received a second application to prosecute Verres.'

'That is impossible,' said Quintus. 'Who else would want to do that?'

'A senator,' replied Cicero, studying the writ. 'Caecilius Niger.'

'I know him,' piped up Sthenius. 'He was Verres's quaestor, in the year before I had to flee the island. It was rumoured that he and the governor quarrelled over money.'

'Hortensius has informed the court that Verres has no objection to being prosecuted by Caecilius, on the grounds that he seeks "personal redress", whereas I, apparently, merely seek "public notoriety".'

We all looked at one another in dismay. Months of work seemed to be turning to dust.

'It is clever,' said Cicero ruefully. 'You have to say that for Hortensius. What a clever devil he is! I assumed he would try to have the whole case dismissed without a hearing. I never imagined that instead he would seek to control the prosecution as well as the defence.'

'But he cannot do that!' spluttered Quintus. 'Roman justice is the fairest system in the world!'

'My dear Quintus,' replied Cicero, with such patronising sarcasm it made me wince, 'where *do* you find these slogans? In nursery books? Do you suppose that Hortensius has dominated the Roman bar for the best part of twenty years by playing *fair*? This is a writ. I am summoned before the extortion court tomorrow morning to argue why I should be allowed to bring the prosecution rather than Caecilius. I have to plead my worth before Glabrio and a full jury. A jury, let me remind you, that will be composed of thirty-two senators, many of whom, you may be sure, will recently have received a new year's gift of bronze or marble.'

'But we Sicilians are the victims!' exclaimed Sthenius. 'Surely it must be for us to decide whom we wish to have as our advocate?'

'Not at all. The prosecutor is the official appointee of the court, and as such a representative of the Roman people. Your opinions are of interest, but they are not decisive.'

'So we are finished?' asked Quintus plaintively.

'No,' said Cicero, 'we are not finished,' and already I could see that some of the old fight was coming back into him, for nothing roused him to greater energy than the thought of being outwitted by Hortensius. 'And if we are finished, well then, at least let us go down with a fight. I shall start preparing my speech, and you, Quintus, will see if you can prepare me a crowd. Call in every favour. Why not give them your line about Roman justice being the fairest in the world, and see if you can persuade a couple of respectable senators to escort me to the forum? Some might even believe it. When I step up to that tribunal tomorrow, I want Glabrio to feel that the whole of Rome is watching him.'

No one can really claim to know politics properly until he has stayed up all night, writing a speech for delivery the following day. While the world sleeps, the orator paces around by lamplight, wondering what madness ever brought him to this occupation in the first place. Arguments are prepared and discarded. Versions of openings and middle sections and perorations lie in drifts across the floor. The exhausted mind ceases to have any coherent grip upon the purpose of the enterprise, so that often – usually an hour or two after midnight – there comes a point where failing to turn up, feigning illness and hiding at home seem the only realistic options. And then, somehow, under pressure of panic, just as humiliation beckons, the parts cohere, and there it is: a speech. A second-rate orator now retires gratefully to bed. A Cicero stays up and commits it to memory.

Taking only a little fruit and cheese and some diluted wine to sustain him, this was the process Cicero went through that evening. Once he had the sections in order, he released me to get some sleep, but I do not believe that he saw his own bed for even an hour. At dawn he washed in freezing-cold water to revive himself and dressed with care. When I went in to see him, just before we left for court, he was as restless as any prizefighter limbering up in the ring, flexing his shoulders and rocking from side to side on the balls of his feet.

Quintus had done his job well, and immediately the door was opened we were greeted by a noisy crowd of well-wishers, jammed right the way up the street. In addition to the ordinary people of Rome, three or four senators with a particular interest in Sicily had turned out to demonstrate their support. I remember the taciturn Gnaeus Marcellinus, the righteous Calpurnius Piso Frugi – who had been praetor in the same year as Verres, and despised him as a scoundrel – and at least one member of the Marcelli clan, the traditional patrons of the island. Cicero waved from the doorstep, hoisted up Tullia and gave her one of his resounding kisses, and showed her to his supporters. Then he returned her to her mother, with whom he exchanged a rare public embrace, before Quintus, Lucius and I cleared a passage for him and he thrust his way into the centre of the throng.

I tried to wish him luck, but by then, as so often before a big speech, he was unreachable. He looked at people but he did not see them. He was primed for action, playing out some inner drama, rehearsed since childhood, of the lone patriot, armed only with his voice, confronting everything that was corrupt and despicable in the state. As if sensing their part in this fantastic pageant the crowd gradually swelled in number, so that by the time we reached the Temple of Castor there must have been two or three hundred to clap him vigorously into court. Glabrio was already in his place between the great pillars of the temple, as were the panel of jurors, among whom sat the menacing spectre of Catulus himself. I could see Hortensius on the bench reserved for distinguished spectators, examining his beautifully manicured hands and looking as calm as a summer morning. Next to him, also very easy with himself, was a man in his mid-forties with reddish, bristling hair and a freckled face, whom I realised must be Gaius Verres. It was curious for me actually to set eyes on this monster, who had occupied our thoughts for so long, and to find him so ordinary-looking – more fox, in fact, than boar.

Two chairs had been put out for the contesting prosecutors. Caecilius was already seated, with a bundle of notes in his lap, and did not look up when Cicero arrived, but nervously pre-occupied himself with study. The court was called to order and Glabrio told Cicero that he, as the original applicant, must go first – a significant disadvantage. Cicero shrugged and rose, waited for absolute quiet, and started slowly as usual, saying that he assumed people might be surprised to see him in this role, as he had never before sought to enter any arena as a prosecutor. He had not wanted to do it now, he said. Indeed, privately he had urged the Sicilians to give the job to Caecilius. (I almost gasped at that.) But in truth, he said, he was not doing it simply for the Sicilians. 'What I am doing I do for the sake of my country.' And very deliberately he walked across the court to where Verres was sitting and slowly raised his arm to point at him. 'Here is a human monster of unparalleled greed, impudence and wickedness. If I bring this man to judgement, who can find fault with me for doing this? Tell me, in the name of all that is just and holy, what better service I can do my country at the present time!' Verres was not in the least put out, but grinned defiantly at Cicero, and shook his head. Cicero stared at him with contempt for a while longer, then turned to face the jury. 'The charge against Gaius Verres is that during a period of three years he has laid waste the province of Sicily – that he has plundered Sicilian communities, stripped bare Sicilian homes, and pillaged Sicilian temples. Could all Sicily speak with a single voice, this is what she would say: "All the gold, all the silver, all the beautiful things that once were in my cities, houses and temples: all these things you, Verres, have plundered and stolen from me; and on this account I sue you in accordance with the law for the sum of one million sesterces!" These are the words all Sicily would utter, if she could speak with a single voice, and as she cannot, she has chosen me to conduct her case for her. So what incredible impudence it is that *you*' – and now he finally turned to Caecilius – 'should dare to try to undertake their case when they have already said they will not have you!'

He strolled across to Caecilius, and stood behind him. He gave an exaggerated sigh of sadness. 'I am now going to speak to you as one friend to another,' he said, and patted Caecilius's shoulder, so that his rival had to twist round in his seat to see him – a fidgety movement which drew a good deal of laughter. 'I earnestly advise you to examine your own mind. Recollect yourself. Think of what you are, and what you are fit for. This prosecution is a very formidable and a very painful undertaking. Have you the powers of voice and memory? Have you the intelligence and the ability to sustain such a burden? Even if you had the advantage of great natural gifts, even if you had received a thorough educa-tion, could you hope to stand the strain? We shall find out this morning. If you can reply to what I am now saying, if you can use one single expression that is not contained in some book of extracts compiled from other people's speeches and given to you by your schoolteacher, then perhaps you will not be a failure at the actual trial.'

He moved towards the centre of the court, and now he addressed the crowd in the forum as well as the jury. '"Well," you may say, "what if that is so? Do *you* then possess all these qualities yourself?" Would that I did, indeed! Still, I have done my best, and worked hard from boyhood, in order to acquire them if I could. Everyone knows that my life has centred around the forum and the law courts; that few men, if any, of my age have defended more cases; that all the time I can spare from the business of my friends I spend in the study and hard work which this profession demands, to make myself fitter and readier for forensic practice. Yet even I, when I think of the great day when the accused man is summoned to appear and I have to make my speech, am not only anxious, but tremble physically from head to foot. *You*, Caecilius, have no such fears, no such thoughts, no such anxieties. You imagine that, if you can learn by heart a phrase or two out of some old speech, like "I beseech almighty and most merciful God" or "I could wish, gentlemen, had it only been possible", you will be excellently prepared for your entrance into court.

'Caecilius, you are nothing, and you count for nothing. Hortensius will *destroy* you! But he will never crush me with his cleverness. He will never lead me astray by any display of ingenuity. He will never employ his great powers to weaken and dislodge me from my position.' He looked towards Hortensius, and bowed to him in mock humility, to which Hortensius responded by standing and bowing back, eliciting more laughter. 'I am well acquainted with all this gentleman's methods of attack,' continued Cicero, 'and all his oratorical devices. However capable he may be, he will feel, when he comes to speak against me, that the trial is among other things a trial of his own capacities. And I give the gentleman fair warning well beforehand, that if you decide that I am to conduct this case, he will have to make a radical change in his methods of defence. If *I* conduct the case, he will have no reason to think that the court can be bribed without serious danger to a large number of people.'

The mention of bribery produced a brief uproar, and brought

the normally equable Hortensius to his feet, but Cicero waved him back into his place. On and on he went, his rhetoric hammering down upon his opponents like the ringing blows of a blacksmith in a forge. I shall not quote it all: the speech, which lasted at least an hour, is readily available for those who wish to read it. He smashed away at Verres for his corruption, and at Caecilius for his previous links with Verres, and at Hortensius for desiring a second-rate opponent. And he concluded by challenging the senators themselves, walking over to the jury and looking each of them in the eye. 'It rests with you, then, gentlemen, to choose the man whom you think best qualified by good faith, industry, sagacity and weight of character to maintain this great case before this great court. If you give Quintus Caecilius the preference over me, I shall not think I have been beaten by the better man. But Rome may think that an honourable, strict and energetic prosecutor like myself was not what you desired, and not what senators would ever desire.' He paused, his gaze coming to rest at last on Catulus, who stared straight back at him, and then he said very quietly: 'Gentlemen, see that this does not happen.'

There was loud applause, and now it was Caecilius's turn. He had risen from very humble origins, much more humble than Cicero's, and he was not entirely without merit. One could even say he had some prior claim to prosecute, especially when he began by pointing out that his father had been a freed Sicilian slave, that he had been born in the province, and that the island was the place he loved most in the world. But his speech was full of statistics about falling agricultural production and Verres's system of accounting. He sounded peevish rather than impassioned. Worse, he read it all out from notes, and in a monotone, so that when, after an hour, he approached his peroration,

Cicero slumped to one side and pretended to fall asleep. Caecilius, who was facing the jury and therefore could not see what everyone was laughing at, was seriously knocked off his stride. He struggled through to the end and then sat down, crimson with embarrassment and rage.

In terms of rhetoric, Cicero had scored a victory of annihilating proportions. But as the voting tablets were passed among the jury, and the clerk of the court stood ready with his urn to collect them, Cicero knew, he told me afterwards, that he had lost. Of the thirty-two senators, he recognised at least a dozen firm enemies, and only half as many friends. The decision, as usual, would rest with the floaters in the middle, and he could see that many of these were craning their necks for a signal from Catulus, intent on following his lead. Catulus marked his tablet, showed it to the men on either side of him, then dropped it in the urn. When everyone had voted, the clerk took the urn over to the bench, and in full view of the court tipped it out and began counting the tablets. Hortensius, abandoning his pretence of coolness, was on his feet, and so was Verres, trying to see how the tally was going. Cicero sat as still as a statue. Caecilius was hunched in his chair. All around me people who made a habit of attending the courts and knew the procedure as well as the judges were whispering that it was close, that they were re-counting. Eventually the clerk passed the tally up to Glabrio, who stood and called for silence. The voting, he said, was fourteen for Cicero – my heart stopped: he had lost! – thirteen for Caecilius, with five abstentions, and that Marcus Tullius Cicero was therefore appointed special prosecutor (*nominis delator*) in the case of Gaius Verres. As the spectators applauded and Hortensius and Verres sat down stunned, Glabrio told Cicero to stand and raise his right hand, and then had him swear the traditional oath to conduct the prosecution in good faith.

The moment that was finished, Cicero made an application for an adjournment. Hortensius swiftly rose to object: why was this necessary? Cicero said he wished to travel to Sicily to subpoena evidence and witnesses. Hortensius interrupted to say it was outrageous for Cicero to demand the right to prosecute, only to reveal in his next breath that he lacked an adequate case to bring to court! This was a valid point, and for the first time I realised how unconfident Cicero must be of the strength of his position. Glabrio seemed inclined to agree with Hortensius, but Cicero pleaded that it was only now, since Verres had left his province, that his victims felt it safe to speak out. Glabrio pondered the issue, checked the calendar, then announced, reluctantly, that the case would stand adjourned for one hundred and ten days. 'But be sure you are ready to open immediately after the spring recess,' he warned Cicero. And with that, the court was dismissed.

To his surprise, Cicero later discovered that he owed his victory to Catulus. This hard and snobbish old senator was, nevertheless, a patriot to his marrow, which was why his opinions commanded such respect. He took the view that the people had the right, under the ancient laws, to see Verres subjected to the most rigorous prosecution available, even though Verres was a friend of his. Family obligations to his brother-in-law, Hortensius, naturally prevented him from voting for Cicero outright, so instead he abstained, taking four waverers with him.

Grateful to be still in 'the Boar Hunt', as he called it, and delighted to have outwitted Hortensius, Cicero now flung himself into the business of preparing his expedition to Sicily. Verres's official papers were sealed by the court under an order *obsignandi gratia*. Cicero laid a motion before the senate demanding that the former governor submit his official accounts for the past three years (he never did). Letters were dispatched to every large town on the island, inviting them to submit evidence. I reviewed our files and extracted the names of all the leading citizens who had offered Cicero hospitality when he was a junior magistrate, for we would need accommodation throughout the province. Cicero also wrote a courtesy letter to the governor, Lucius Metellus, informing him of his visit and requesting official co-operation – not that he expected anything other than official harassment, but he reasoned it might be useful to have the notification in writing, to show that he had at least tried. He decided to take his cousin with him – Lucius having worked on the case for six months already – and to leave his brother behind to manage his election campaign. I was to go, too, along with both of my juniors, Sositheus and Laurea, for there would be much copying and note-taking. The former praetor, Calpurnius Piso Frugi, offered Cicero the services of his eighteen-year-old son, Gaius – a young man of great intelligence and charm, to whom everyone soon took a liking. At Quintus's insistence, we also acquired four strong and reliable slaves, ostensibly to act as porters and drivers, but also to serve as bodyguards. It was lawless country down in the south at that time – many of Spartacus's followers still survived in the hills; there were pirates; and no one could be sure what measures Verres might adopt.

All of this required money, and although Cicero's legal practice was now bringing in some income – not in the form of direct payments, of course, which were forbidden, but in gifts and lega-cies from grateful clients – he had nothing like the amount of ready cash necessary to mount a proper prosecution. Most ambitious young men in his position would have gone to see Crassus, who always gave loans to rising politicians on generous terms. But just as Crassus liked to show that he rewarded support, so he also took care to let people see how he punished opposition. Ever since Cicero had declined to join his camp, he had gone out of his way to demonstrate his enmity. He cut him dead in public. He poor-mouthed him behind his back. Perhaps if Cicero had grovelled sufficiently, he would have condescended to change his mind: his principles were infinitely malleable. But, as I have already said, the two men found it difficult even to stand within ten feet of one another.

So Cicero had no choice but to approach Terentia, and a painful scene ensued. I only became involved because Cicero, in a rather cowardly way, at first dispatched *me* to see her business manager, Philotimus, to enquire how difficult it would be to raise one hundred thousand from her estate. With characteristic malevolence, Philotimus immediately reported my approach to his mistress, who stormed down to find me in Cicero's study, and demanded to know how I dared poke my nose into her affairs. Cicero came in while this was happening and was consequently obliged to explain why he needed the money.

'And how is this sum to be repaid?' demanded Terentia.

'From the fine levied on Verres once he is found guilty,' replied her husband.

'And you are sure he *will* be found guilty?'

'Of course.'

'Why? What is your case? Let me hear it.' And with that she sat down in his chair and folded her arms. Cicero hesitated, but knowing his wife and seeing she was not to be shifted, told me to open the strongbox and fetch out the Sicilians' evidence. He took her through it, piece by piece, and at the end of it she regarded him with unfeigned dismay. 'But that is not enough, Cicero! You have wagered everything on *that*? Do you really think a jury of senators will convict one of their own because he has rescued some important statues from provincial obscurity and brought them back to Rome – where they properly belong?'

'You may be right, my dear,' conceded Cicero. 'That is why I need to go to Sicily.'

Terentia regarded her husband – arguably the greatest orator and the cleverest senator in Rome at that time – with the sort of look a matron might reserve for a child who has made a puddle on the drawing room floor. She would have said something, I am sure, but she noticed I was still there, and thought the better of it. Silently, she rose and left the study.

The following day, Philotimus sought me out and handed me a small money chest containing ten thousand in cash, with authorisation to draw a further forty thousand as necessary.

'Exactly half of what I asked for,' said Cicero, when I took it in to him. 'That is a shrewd businesswoman's assessment of my chances, Tiro – and who is to say she is wrong?'

VII

We left Rome on the Ides of January, on the last day of the
Festival of the Nymphs, with Cicero riding in a covered wagon
so that he could continue to work – although I found it a torment
even attempting to read, let alone write, in that rattling, creaking,
lurching *carruca*. It was a miserable journey, freezing cold, with
flurries of snow across the higher ground. By this time, most of
the crosses bearing the crucified rebel slaves had been removed
from the Appian Way. But some still stood as a warning, stark
against the whitened landscape, with a few rotted fragments of
bodies attached. Gazing at them, I felt as if Crassus's long arm
had reached out after me from Rome and was once again pinching
my cheek.

Because we had departed in such a hurry, it had proved impossible to arrange places to stay all along our route, and on three
or four nights when no inns were available we were reduced to
sleeping by the roadside. I lay with the other slaves, huddled
around the campfire, while Cicero, Lucius and young Frugi slept
in the wagon. In the mountains I would wake at dawn to find
my clothes starched with ice. When at last we reached the coast
at Velia, Cicero decided it would be quicker to board a ship and
hug the coast – this despite the risk of winter storms and pirates,
and his own marked aversion to travelling by boat, for he had

been warned by a sibyl that his death would somehow be connected with the sea.

Velia was a health resort, with a well-known temple to Apollo Oulius, then a fashionable god of healing. But it was all shuttered up and out of season, and as we made our way down to the harbour front, where the grey sea battered against the wharf, Cicero remarked that he had seldom seen a less enticing holiday spot. Aside from the usual collection of fishing boats, the port contained one huge vessel, a cargo ship the size of a trireme, and while we were negotiating our journey with the local sailors, Cicero happened to ask to whom it belonged. It was, we were told, a gift from the citizens of the Sicilian port of Messana to their former governor, Gaius Verres, and had been moored here for a month.

There was something infinitely sinister about that great ship, sitting low in the water, fully crewed and ready to move at a moment's warning. Our appearance in the deserted harbour had clearly already been registered and was causing something of a panic. Even as Cicero led us cautiously towards the vessel, we heard three short blasts sounded on a trumpet, and saw it sprout oars, like some immense water beetle, and edge away from the quayside. It moved a short distance out to sea, and dropped anchor. As the ship turned into the wind, the lanterns at its prow and stern danced bright yellow in the gloomy afternoon, and figures deployed along its heaving decks. Cicero debated with Lucius and young Frugi what to do. In theory, his warrant from the extortion court gave him authority to board and search any vessel he suspected of connection with the case. In truth, we lacked the resources, and by the time reinforcements could be summoned, the ship would be long gone. What it showed beyond doubt was that Verres's crimes were on a scale vastly bigger than anything even Cicero had imagined. He decided we should press on south at redoubled speed.

I guess it must be a hundred and twenty miles from Velia down to Vibo, running straight along the shin bone to the toe of Italy. But with a favourable wind and strong rowing we did it in just two days. We kept always within sight of the shore, and put in for one night to sleep on the sandy beach, where we cut down a thicket of myrtle to make a campfire and used our oars and sail for a tent. From Vibo we took the coast road to Regium, and here we chartered a second boat to sail across the narrow straits to Sicily. It was a misty early morning when we set off, with a saturating drizzle falling. The distant island appeared on the horizon as a dreary black hump. Unfortunately, there was only one place to make for, especially in midwinter, and that was Verres's stronghold of Messana. He had bought the loyalty of its inhabitants by exempting them from taxes throughout all his three years as governor, and alone of the towns on the island it had refused to offer Cicero any cooperation. We steered towards its lighthouse, and as we drew closer realised that what we had perceived as a large mast at the entrance to the harbour was not part of a ship at all, but a cross, facing directly across the straits to the mainland.

'That is new,' said Cicero, frowning as he wiped the rain from his eyes. 'This was never a place of execution in our day.'

We had no option but to sail straight past it, and the sight fell across our waterlogged spirits like a shadow.

Despite the general hostility of the people of Messana towards the special prosecutor, two citizens of the town – Basiliscus and Percennius – had bravely agreed to offer him hospitality, and were waiting on the quayside to greet us. The moment he stepped ashore, Cicero queried them about the cross, but they begged to be excused from answering until they had transported us away from the wharf. Only when we were in the compound of Basiliscus's house did they feel it safe to tell the story. Verres had spent his last days as governor living full-time in Messana, supervising the loading of his loot aboard the treasure ship which the grateful town had built for him. There had been a festival in his honour about a month ago, and almost it seemed as part of the entertainment, a Roman citizen had been dragged from the prison, stripped naked in the forum, publicly flogged, tortured, and finally crucified.

'A Roman citizen?' repeated Cicero incredulously. He gestured at me to begin making notes. 'But it is illegal to execute a Roman citizen without a full trial. Are you sure that is what he was?'

'He cried out that his name was Publius Gavius, that he was a merchant from Spain, and that he had done military service in the legions. Throughout his whipping he screamed, "I am a Roman citizen!" every time he received a blow.'

'"I am a Roman citizen",' repeated Cicero, savouring the phrase. '"I am a Roman citizen . . ." But what was alleged to be his crime?'

'Spying,' replied our host. 'He was on the point of boarding a ship for Italy. But he made the mistake of telling everyone he met that he had escaped from the Stone Quarries in Syracuse and was going straight to Rome to expose all Verres's crimes. The elders of Messana had him arrested and held until Verres arrived. Then Verres ordered him to be scourged, tortured with hot irons and executed on a cross looking out across the straits to Regium, so that he could see the mainland throughout his final agonies. Imagine that – being only five miles from safety! The cross has been left standing by the followers of Verres as a warning to anyone else who feels tempted to talk too freely.'

'There were witnesses to this crucifixion?'

'Of course. Hundreds.'

'Including Roman citizens?'

'Yes.'

'Could you identify any of them?'

He hesitated. 'Gaius Numitorius, a Roman knight from Puteoli. The Cottius brothers from Tauromenium. Lucceius – he is from Regium. There must have been others.'

I took down their names. Afterwards, while Cicero was having a bath, we gathered beside his tub to discuss this development. Lucius said, 'Perhaps this man Gavius really was a spy.'

'I would be more inclined to believe that,' replied Cicero, 'if Verres had not brought exactly the same charge against Sthenius, who is no more a spy than you or I. No, this is the monster's favoured method of operation: he arranges a trumped-up charge, then uses his position as supreme justice in the province to reach a verdict and pronounce sentence. The question is: why did he pick on Gavius?'

Nobody had an answer; nor did we have the spare time to linger in Messana and try to find one. Early the following morning we had to leave for our first official engagement, in the northern coastal town of Tyndaris. This visit set the pattern for a score which followed. The council came out to greet Cicero with full honours. He was conducted into the municipal square. He was shown the standard-issue statue of Verres, which the citizens had been obliged to pay for, and which they had now pulled down and smashed. Cicero made a short speech about Roman justice. His chair was set up. He listened to the complaints of the locals. He then selected those which were most eye-catching or most easily proved – in Tyndaris it was the story of Sopater, bound naked to a statue until the town yielded up its bronze of Mercury – and finally either I or one of my two assistants moved in to take statements, which would be witnessed and signed.

From Tyndaris we travelled on to Sthenius's home city of Thermae, where we saw his wife in his empty house, who sobbed as Cicero delivered letters from her exiled husband, and then ended the week in the fortress port of Lilybaeum, on the extreme western tip of the island. Cicero knew this place well, having been based here when he was a junior magistrate. We stayed, as so often in the past, at the home of his old friend Pamphilius. Over dinner on the first night, Cicero noticed that the usual decorations of the table – a beautiful jug and goblets, all family heirlooms – were missing, and when he asked what had become of them, was told that Verres had seized them. It quickly transpired that all the other guests in the dining room had similar tales to tell. Young Gaius Cacurius had been obliged to give up all his furniture, and Lutatius a citrus-wood table at which Cicero had regularly eaten. Lyso had been robbed of his precious statue of Apollo, and Diodorus of a set of chased silver cups by Mentor. The list was endless, and I should know, for I was the one summoned to compile it. After taking statements from each of them, and subsequently from all their friends, I began to think that Cicero had gone a little mad – did he plan to catalogue every stolen spoon and cream jug on the island? – but of course he was being cleverer than I, as events were to show.

We moved on a few days later, rattling down the unmade tracks from Lilybaeum to the temple city of Agrigentum, then up into the mountainous heart of the island. The winter was unusually harsh; the land and sky were iron. Cicero caught a bad cold and sat wrapped in his cloak in the back of our cart.

At Henna, a town built precipitously into the cliffs and surrounded by lakes and woods, the ululating priests all came out to greet us, wearing their elaborate robes and carrying their sacred boughs, and took us to the shrine of Ceres, from which Verres had removed the goddess's statue. And here for the first time our escort became involved in scuffles with the lictors of the new governor, Lucius Metellus. These brutes with their rods and axes stood to one side of the market square and shouted threats of dire penalties for any witness who dared to testify against Verres. Nevertheless, Cicero persuaded three prominent citizens of Henna – Theodorus, Numenius and Nicasio – to undertake to come to Rome and give their evidence.

Finally, we turned south-east towards the sea again, into the fertile plains below Mount Aetna. This was state-owned land, administered on behalf of the Roman treasury by a revenue-collection company, which in turn awarded leases to local farmers. When Cicero had first been on the island, the plains of Leontini had been the granary of Rome. But now we drove past deserted farmhouses and grey, untended fields, punctuated by drifting columns of brown smoke, where the homeless former tenants now lived in the open. Verres and his friends in the tax company had fanned out across the region like a ravaging army, commandeering crops and livestock for a fraction of their true value, and raising rents far beyond what most could pay. One farmer who had dared to complain, Nymphodorus of Centuripae, had been seized by Verres's tithe collector, Apronius, and hanged from an olive tree in the market place of Aetna. Such stories enraged Cicero, and drove him to fresh exertions. I still cherish the memory of this most urban of gentlemen, his toga hoisted around his knees, his fine red shoes in one hand, his warrant in the other, picking his way daintily across a muddy field in the pouring rain to take evidence from a farmer at his plough. By the time we came at last to Syracuse, after more than thirty days of arduous travels around the province, we had the statements of nearly two hundred witnesses.

Syracuse is by far the largest and fairest of Sicily's cities. It is four towns, really, which have merged into one. Three of these – Achradina, Tycha and Neapolis – have spread themselves around the harbour, and in the centre of this great natural bay sits the fourth settlement, known simply as the Island, the ancient royal seat, which is linked to the others by a bridge. This walled city-within-a-city, forbidden at night to Sicilians, is where the Roman governor has his palace, close by the great temples of Diana and Minerva. We had feared a hostile reception, given that Syracuse was said to be second only to Messana in its loyalty to Verres, and its senate had recently voted him a eulogy. In fact, the opposite was the case. News of Cicero's honesty and diligence had preceded him, and we were escorted through the Agrigentine gate by a crowd of cheering citizens. (One reason for Cicero's popularity was that, as a young magistrate, he had located in the overgrown municipal cemetery the one-hundred-and-thirty-year-old lost tomb of the mathematician Archimedes, the greatest man in the history of Syracuse. Typically, he had read somewhere that it was marked by a cylinder and a sphere, and once he had found the monument, he paid to have the weeds and brambles cleared away. He had then spent many hours beside it, pondering the transience of human glory. His generosity and respect had not been forgotten by the local population.)

But to resume. We were lodged in the home of a Roman

knight, Lucius Flavius, an old friend of Cicero's, who had plenty of stories of Verres's corruption and cruelty to add to our already bulging stock. There was the tale of the pirate captain, Heracleo, who had been able to sail right into Syracuse at the head of a squadron of four small galleys, pillage the warehouses, and leave without encountering any resistance. Captured some weeks later, further up the coast at Megara, neither he nor his men had been paraded as prisoners, and there were rumours that Verres had exchanged him for a large ransom. Then there was the horrible business of the Roman banker from Spain, Lucius Herennius, who had been dragged into the forum of Syracuse one morning, summarily denounced as a spy and, on Verres's orders, beheaded – this despite the pleadings of his friends and business associates, who had come running to the scene when they heard what was happening. The similarity of Herennius's case to that of Gavius in Messana was striking: both Romans, both from Spain, both involved in commerce, both accused of spying, and both executed without a hearing or a proper trial.

That night, after dinner, Cicero received a messenger from Rome. Immediately he had read the letter, he excused himself, and took Lucius, young Frugi and myself aside. The dispatch was from his brother Quintus, and it contained grave news. It seemed that Hortensius was up to his old tricks again. The extortion court had unexpectedly given permission for a prosecution to be brought against the former governor of Achaia. The prosecutor, Dasianus, a known associate of Verres, had undertaken to travel to Greece and back and present his evidence two days before the deadline set for Cicero's return from Sicily. Quintus urged his brother to return to Rome as quickly as possible to retrieve the situation.

'It's a trap,' declared Lucius immediately, 'to make you panic, and cut short your expedition here.'

'Probably so,' agreed Cicero. 'But I can't afford to take the risk. If this other prosecution slips into the court's schedule ahead of ours, and if Hortensius spins it out as he likes to do, our case could be pushed back until after the elections. By then Hortensius and Quintus Metellus will be consuls-elect. That youngest Metellus brother will no doubt be a praetor-elect, and this third will still be governor here. How will that be for having the odds stacked against us?'

'So what are we going to do?'

'We have wasted too much time pursuing the small fry in this investigation,' said Cicero. 'We need to take the war into the enemy's camp, and loosen some tongues among those who really know what has been going on – the Romans themselves.'

'I agree,' said Lucius. 'The question is: how?'

Cicero glanced around and lowered his voice before replying. 'We shall carry out a raid,' he announced. 'A raid on the offices of the revenue collectors.'

Even Lucius looked slightly green at that, for short of marching up to the governor's palace and attempting to arrest Metellus, this was about the most provocative gesture Cicero could make. The revenue collectors were a syndicate of well-connected men, of equestrian rank, operating under statutory protection, whose investors would certainly include some of the wealthiest senators in Rome. Cicero himself, as a specialist in commercial law, had built up a network of supporters among exactly this class of businessman. He knew it was a risky strategy, but he was not to be dissuaded, for it was here, he was sure, that the dark heart of Verres's murderous corruption was to be found. He sent the messenger back to Rome that same night with a letter for Quintus, announcing that he had only one more thing left to do, and that he would depart from the island within a few days.

Cicero now had to make his preparations with great speed and secrecy. He deliberately timed his raid to take place two days hence, at the least-expected hour – just before dawn on a major public holiday, Terminalia. The fact that this is the day sacred to Terminus, the ancient god of boundaries and good neighbours, only made it more symbolically attractive as far as he was concerned. Flavius, our host, agreed to come with us to point out the location of the offices. In the interim, I went down to the harbour in Syracuse and found the same trusty skipper I had used years before, when Cicero made his ill-judged return to Italy. From him I hired a ship and crew and told him to be ready to sail before the end of the week. The evidence we had already collected was packed in trunks and stowed aboard. The ship was placed under guard.

None of us got much sleep on the night of the raid. In the darkness before dawn we positioned our hired ox-carts at either end of the street to block it, and when Cicero gave the signal we all jumped out carrying our torches. The senator hammered on the door, stood aside without waiting for a reply, and a couple of our burliest attendants took their axes to it. The instant it yielded, we poured through into the passage, knocking aside the elderly nightwatchman, and secured the company's records. We quickly formed a human chain – Cicero, too – and passed the boxes of wax tablets and papyrus rolls from hand to hand, out into the street and on to the back of our carts.

I learned one valuable lesson that day, which is that if you seek popularity, there is no surer way of achieving it than raiding a syndicate of tax collectors. As the sun rose and news of our activity spread through the neighbourhood, an enthusiastic honour guard of Syracusans formed themselves around us, more than large enough to deter the director of the company, Carpinatius, when he arrived to reoccupy the building with a detachment of legionaries lent to him for the purpose by Lucius Metellus. He and Cicero fell into a furious argument in the middle of the road, Carpinatius insisting that provincial tax records were protected by law from seizure, Cicero retorting that his warrant from the extortion court overrode such technicalities. In fact, as Cicero conceded afterwards, Carpinatius was right. 'But,' he added, 'he who controls the street controls the law' – and on this occasion, at least, it was Cicero who controlled the street.

In all, we must have transported more than four cartloads of records back to the house of Flavius. We locked the gates, posted sentries, and then began the wearying business of sorting through them. Even now, remembering the size of the task that confronted us, I find myself starting to break into a sweat of apprehension. These records, which went back years, not only covered all the state land on Sicily, but itemised every farmer's number and quality of grazing animals, and every crop he had ever sown, its size and yield. Here were details of loans issued and taxes paid and correspondence entered into. And it quickly became clear that other hands had already been through this mass of material, and removed every trace of the name of Verres. A furious message arrived from the governor's palace, demanding that Cicero appear before Metellus when the courts reopened the following day, to answer a writ from Carpinatius that he return the documents. Meanwhile, yet another large crowd had started gathering outside and was chanting Cicero's name. I thought of Terentia's prediction, that her husband and she would be ostracised by Rome and end their days as consul and first lady of Thermae, and never did a prophecy seem more prescient than at that moment. Only Cicero retained his cool. He had represented enough shady revenue collectors in his time to know most of their tricks. Once it became apparent that the files specifically relating to Verres had been excised, he dug out an old list of all the company's managers, and hunted through it until he came to the name of the firm's financial director during the period of Verres's governorship.

'I'll tell you one thing, Tiro,' he said to me. 'I have never come across a financial director yet who didn't keep an extra set of records for himself when he handed over to his successor, just to be on the safe side.'

And with that we set off on our second raid of the morning.

Our quarry was a man named Vibius, who was at that moment celebrating Terminalia with his neighbours. They had set up an altar in the garden and there was some corn upon it, also some honeycombs and wine, and Vibius had just sacrificed a sucking pig. ('Always very pious, these crooked accountants,' observed Cicero.) When he saw the senator bearing down upon him, he looked a little like a sucking pig himself, but once he had read the warrant, which had Glabrio's praetorian seal attached to it, he reluctantly decided there was nothing he could do except cooperate. Excusing himself from his bemused guests, he led us inside to his tablinum and opened up his strongbox. Among the title deeds, account books and jewellery, there was a little packet of letters marked 'Verres', and as Cicero broke it open, Vibius's face bore an expression of utter terror. I guess he must have been told to destroy it, and had either forgotten or had thought to make some profit out of it.

At first sight, it was nothing much – merely some correspond-

ence from a tax inspector, Lucius Canuleius, who was responsible for collecting export duty on all goods passing through
Syracuse harbour. The letters concerned one particular shipment
of goods which had left Syracuse two years before, and upon
which Verres had failed to pay any tax. The details were attached:
four hundred casks of honey, fifty dining room couches, two
hundred chandeliers and ninety bales of Maltese cloth. Another
prosecutor might not have spotted the significance, but Cicero
saw it at once.

'Take a look at that,' he said, handing it to me. 'These are not
goods seized from a number of unfortunate individuals. *Four
hundred* casks of honey? *Ninety* bales of foreign cloth?' He turned
his furious gaze on the hapless Vibius. 'This is a *cargo*, isn't it?
Your Governor Verres must have stolen *a ship*.'

Poor Vibius never stood a chance. Glancing nervously over his
shoulder at his bewildered guests, who were staring open-
mouthed in our direction, he confirmed that this was indeed a
ship's cargo, and that Canuleius had been instructed never again
to attempt to levy tax on any of the governor's exports.

'How many more such shipments did Verres make?' demanded
Cicero.

'I am not sure.'

'Guess then.'

'Ten,' said Vibius fearfully. 'Perhaps twenty.'

'And no duty was ever paid? No records kept?'

'No.'

'And where did Verres acquire all these cargoes?' demanded
Cicero.

Vibius was almost swooning with terror. 'Senator, please . . .'

'I shall have you arrested,' said Cicero. 'I shall have you transported to Rome in chains. I shall break you on the witness stand

before a thousand spectators in the Forum Romanum and feed what's left of you to the dogs of the Capitoline Triad.'

'From ships, Senator,' said Vibius, in a little mouse voice. 'They came from ships.'

'What ships? Ships from where?'

'From everywhere, Senator. Asia. Syria. Tyre. Alexandria.'

'So what happened to these ships? Did Verres have them impounded?'

'Yes, Senator.'

'On what grounds?'

'Spying.'

'Ah, spying! Of course! Did ever a man,' said Cicero to me, 'root out so many spies as our vigilant Governor Verres? So tell us,' he said, turning back to Vibius, 'what became of the crews of these spy ships?'

'They were taken to the Stone Quarries, Senator.'

'And what happened to them then?'

He made no reply.

The Stone Quarries was the most fearsome prison in Sicily, probably the most fearsome in the world – at any rate, I never heard of a worse one. It was six hundred feet long and two hundred wide, gouged deep into the solid rock of that fortified plateau known as Epipolae, which overlooks Syracuse from the north. Here, in this hellish pit, from which no scream could carry, exposed without protection to the burning heat of summer and the cold downpours of winter, tormented by the cruelty of their guards and the debased appetites of their fellow prisoners alike, the victims of Verres suffered and died.

Cicero, with his notorious aversion to military life, was often charged with cowardice by his enemies, and certainly he was prone to nerves and squeamishness. But I can vouch that he was brave enough that day. He went back to our headquarters and collected Lucius, leaving young Frugi behind to continue his search of the tax records. Then, armed only with our walking sticks and the warrant issued by Glabrio, and followed by the now-usual crowd of Syracusans, we climbed the steep path to Epipolae. As always, the news of Cicero's approach and the nature of his mission had preceded him, and the captain of the guard, after receiving a withering harangue from the senator, threatening all manner of dire repercussions if his demands were not met, allowed us to pass through the perimeter wall and on to the plateau. Once inside, refusing to heed warnings that it was too dangerous, Cicero insisted on being allowed to inspect the Quarries himself.

This vast dungeon, the work of Dionysius the Tyrant, was already more than three centuries old. An ancient metal door was unlocked and we proceeded into the mouth of a tunnel, guided by prison guards who carried burning torches. The glistening walls, cankerous with lime and fungi, the scuttling of the rats in the shadows, the stench of death and waste, the cries and groans of the abandoned souls – truly this was a descent into Hades. Eventually we came to another massive door, and when this was unlocked and unbolted we stepped on to the floor of the prison. What a spectacle greeted our eyes! It was as if some giant had filled a sack with hundreds of manacled men and had then tipped them out into a hole. The light was weak, almost subaquatic, and everywhere, as far as one could see, there were prisoners. Some shuffled about, a few huddled in groups, but most lay apart from their fellows, mere yellowing sacks of bones. The day's corpses had not yet

been cleared, and it was hard to distinguish the living skeletons from the dead.

We picked our way among the bodies – those who had already
died, and those whose end had yet to come: there was no
discernible difference – and occasionally Cicero stopped and
asked a man his name, bending to catch the whispered reply.
We found no Romans, only Sicilians. 'Is any man here a Roman
citizen?' he demanded loudly. 'Have any of you been taken from
ships?' There was silence. He turned and called for the captain
of the watch and demanded to see the prison records. Like
Vibius, the wretch struggled between fear of Verres and fear of
the special prosecutor, but eventually he succumbed to Cicero's
pressure.

Built into the rock walls of the quarry were separate special
cells and galleries, where torture and execution were done, and
where the guards ate and slept. (The favoured method of execution, we discovered afterwards, was the garrotte.) Here, too,
was housed the administration of the prison, such as it was.
Boxes of damp and musty rolls were fetched out for us,
containing long lists of prisoners' names, with the dates of their
arrival and departure. Some men were recorded as having been
released, but against most was scratched the Sicilian word
edikaiothesan – meaning 'the death penalty was inflicted upon
them'.

'I want a copy of every entry for the three years when Verres
was governor,' Cicero said to me, 'and you,' he said to the prison
captain, 'when it is done, will sign a statement to say that we
have made a true likeness.'

While I and the other two secretaries set to work, Cicero and
Lucius searched through the records for Roman names.
Although the majority of those held in the Quarries during

Verres's time were obviously Sicilian, there was also a considerable proportion of races from all across the Mediterranean – Spaniards, Egyptians, Syrians, Cilicians, Cretans, Dalmatians. When Cicero asked why they had been imprisoned, he was told they were pirates – pirates and spies. All were recorded as having been put to death, among them the infamous pirate captain Heracleo. The Romans, on the other hand, were officially described as 'released' – including the two men from Spain, Publius Gavius and Lucius Herennius, whose executions had been described to us.

'These records are a nonsense,' said Cicero quietly to Lucius, 'the very opposite of the truth. No one saw Heracleo die, although the spectacle of a pirate on the cross invariably draws an enthusiastic crowd. But plenty saw the Romans executed. It looks to me as though Verres simply switched the two about – killed the innocent ships' crews and freed the pirates, no doubt on payment of a fat ransom. If Gavius and Herennius had discovered his treachery, that would explain why Verres had been so anxious to kill them quickly.'

I thought poor Lucius was going to be sick. He had surely come a long way from his philosophy books in sunlit Rome to find himself studying death lists by the guttering light of candles, eighty feet beneath the dripping earth. We finished as quickly as we could, and never have I been more glad to escape from anywhere than I was to climb the tunnel out of the Stone Quarries and rejoin humanity on the surface. A slight breeze had sprung up, blowing in across the sea, and I remember as if it were this afternoon rather than an afternoon more than half a century ago the way we all instinctively turned our faces to it and gratefully drank in the taste of that cold clear air.

'Promise me,' said Lucius after a while, 'that if ever you achieve this *imperium* you desire so much, you will never preside over cruelty and injustice such as this.'

'I swear it,' replied Cicero. 'And if ever, my dear Lucius, you should question why good men forsake philosophy to seek power in the real world, promise me in return that you will always remember what you witnessed in the Stone Quarries of Syracuse.'

By this time it was late afternoon, and Syracuse, thanks to Cicero's activities, was in a tumult. The crowd which had followed us up the steep slope to the prison was still waiting for us outside the walls of Epipolae. Indeed, it had grown larger, and had been joined by some of the most distinguished citizens of the city, among them the chief priest of Jupiter, all dressed up in his sacred robes. This pontificate, traditionally reserved for the highest-ranking Syracusan, was presently held by none other than Cicero's client, Heraclius, who had returned privately from Rome to help us – at considerable personal risk. He came with a request that Cicero should immediately accompany him to the city's senate chamber, where the elders were waiting to give him a formal civic welcome. Cicero was in two minds. He had much work to do, and not long left to do it, and it was undoubtedly a breach of protocol for a Roman senator to address a local assembly without the permission of the governor. However, it also promised to be a wonderful opportunity to further his enquiries. After a short hesitation, he agreed to go, and we duly set off on foot back down the hill with a huge escort of respectful Sicilians.

The senate chamber was packed. Beneath a gilded statue of Verres himself, the house's most senior senator, the venerable Diodorus, welcomed Cicero in Greek, and apologised for the fact that they had so far offered him no assistance: not until the events of today had they truly believed he was in earnest. Cicero, also speaking in Greek, and fired up by the scenes he had just witnessed, then proceeded to make a most brilliant off-the-cuff speech, in which he promised to dedicate his life to righting the injustices done to the people of Sicily. At the end of it, the Syracusan senators voted almost unanimously to rescind their eulogy to Verres (which they swore they had only agreed to after being pressured into it by Metellus). Amid loud cheers, several younger members threw ropes around the neck of Verres's statue and pulled it down, while others – more importantly – fetched out of the senate's own secret archives a wealth of new evidence which they had been collecting about Verres's crimes. These outrages included the theft of twenty-seven priceless portraits from the Temple of Minerva – even the highly decorated doors of the sanctuary had been carried away! – as well as details of all the bribes Verres had demanded to bring in 'not guilty' verdicts when he was a judge.

News of this assembly and the toppling of the statue had by now reached the governor's palace, and when we tried to leave the senate house we found the building ringed with Roman soldiers. The meeting was dissolved on Metellus's orders, Heraclius arrested, and Cicero ordered to report to the governor at once. There could easily have been a bloody riot, but Cicero leapt up on to the back of a cart and told the Sicilians to calm themselves, that Metellus would not dare to harm a Roman senator acting on the authority of a praetor's court – although he did add, and only half in jest, that if he had not emerged by nightfall, they might perhaps make enquiries as to his whereabouts. He then clambered down and we allowed ourselves to be conducted over the bridge and on to the Island.

The Metellus family were at this time approaching the zenith of their power. In particular, the branch of the clan that had produced the three brothers, Quintus, Lucius and Marcus – all then in their forties – looked set to dominate Rome for years to come. It was, as Cicero said, a three-headed monster, and this middle head – the second brother, Lucius – was in many ways the most formidable of all. He received us in the royal chamber of the governor's palace with the full panoply of his *imperium* – an imposing, handsome figure, seated in his curule chair beneath the unyielding marble gaze of a dozen of his predecessors, flanked by his lictors, with his junior magistrate and his clerks behind him, and an armed sentry on the door.

'It is a treasonable offence,' he began, without rising and without preliminaries, 'to foment rebellion in a Roman province.'

'It is also a treasonable offence,' retorted Cicero, 'to insult the people and senate of Rome by impeding their appointed representative in his duties.'

'Really? And what kind of Roman representative addresses a Greek senate in its native tongue? Everywhere you have gone in this province, you have stirred up trouble. I shall not have it! We have too small a garrison to keep order among so many natives. You are making this place ungovernable, with your damned agitation.'

'I assure you, Governor, the resentment is against Verres, not against Rome.'

'Verres!' Metellus banged the arm of his chair. 'Since when did you care about Verres? I shall tell you when. Since you saw a chance to use him as a way of advancing yourself, you shitty little seditious lawyer!'

'Take this down, Tiro,' Cicero said, without removing his steady gaze from Metellus. 'I want a verbatim record. Such intimidation is entirely admissible in court.'

But I was too frightened even to move, for there was a lot of shouting now from the other men in the room, and Metellus had jumped to his feet. 'I order you,' he said, 'to return the documents you stole this morning!'

'And I remind the governor,' replied Cicero calmly, 'with the greatest respect, that he is not on the parade ground, that he is addressing a free Roman citizen, and I shall discharge the duty I have been assigned!'

Metellus had his hands on his hips and was leaning forward, his broad chin thrust out. 'You will undertake to return those documents now, in private – or you will be ordered to return them tomorrow in court, before the whole of Syracuse!'

'I choose to take my chance in court, as always,' said Cicero, with a tiny inflection of his head. 'Especially knowing what an impartial and honourable judge I shall have in you, Lucius Metellus – the worthy heir of Verres!'

I know I have this conversation exactly right, because the moment we were outside the chamber – which was very soon after this last exchange – Cicero and I reconstructed it while it was still fresh in our memories, in case he did indeed have occasion to use it in court. (The fair copy remains to this day among his papers.)

'That went well,' he joked, but his hand and voice were trembling, for it was now plain that his whole mission, perhaps even his mortal safety, was in the gravest peril. 'But if you seek power,' he said, almost to himself, 'and if you are a new man, this is what you have to do. Nobody is ever going simply to hand it to you.'

We returned at once to the house of Flavius and worked all night, by the weak light of smoky Sicilian candles and stuttering oil lamps, to prepare for court the following morning. Frankly,

I did not see what Cicero could possibly hope to achieve, except humiliation. Metellus was never going to award judgement in his favour, and besides – as Cicero had privately conceded – the right of law lay with the tax company. But fortune, as the noble Terence has it, favours the brave, and she certainly favoured Cicero that night. It was young Frugi who made the breakthrough. I have not mentioned Frugi as often in this narrative as I should have done, chiefly because he had that kind of quiet decency which does not attract much comment, and which is only noticed when its possessor has gone. He had spent the day on the tax company records, and in the evening, despite having caught Cicero's cold, he refused to go to bed, and switched his attention instead to the evidence collected by the Syracusan senate. It must have been long after midnight when I suddenly heard him utter a cry, and then he beckoned us all over to the table. Laid out across it was a series of wax tablets, detailing the company's banking activities. Taken on their own, the lists of names, dates and sums loaned meant little. But once Frugi compared it with the list compiled by the Syracusans of those who had been forced to pay a bribe to Verres, we could see they tallied exactly: his victims had raised the funds they needed to buy him off by borrowing. Better still was the effect produced when he laid out a third set of accounts: the company's receipts. On the same dates exactly the same sums had been redeposited with the tax company by a character named 'Gaius Verrucius'. The depositor's identity was so crudely forged, we all burst out laughing, for obviously the name originally entered had been 'Verres', but in every case the last two letters had been scraped off and 'ucius' added as a replacement.

'So Verres demanded a bribe,' said Cicero, with growing

excitement, 'and insisted his victim borrow the necessary cash from Carpinatius – no doubt at an extortionate rate of interest. Then he reinvested the bribe with his friends in the tax company, so that he not only protected his capital but earned an extra share of the profits as well! Brilliant villain! Brilliant, greedy, stupid villain!' And after executing a brief dance of delight, he flung his arms around the embarrassed Frugi and kissed him warmly on both cheeks.

Of all Cicero's courtroom triumphs, I should say that the one he enjoyed the following day was among the sweetest – especially considering that technically it was not a victory at all but a defeat. He selected the evidence he needed to take back to Rome, and Lucius, Frugi, Sositheus, Laurea and I each carried a box of documents down to the Syracusan forum, where Metellus had set up his tribunal. An immense throng of local people had already gathered. Carpinatius was sitting waiting for us. He fancied himself as quite a lawyer, and presented his own case, quoting all the relevant statutes and precedents establishing that tax records could not be removed from a province, and generally giving the impression that he was merely the humble victim of an over-mighty senator. Cicero hung his head and put on such a mime of dejection I found it hard to keep a straight face. When at last he got to his feet he apologised for his actions, conceded he was wrong in law, begged forgiveness from the governor, promised gladly to return the documents to Carpinatius, but – he paused – *but* there was one small point he did not understand, which he would be very grateful to have cleared up first. He picked up one of the wax tablets and studied it in bafflement. 'Who exactly is Gaius Verrucius?'

Carpinatius, who had been smiling happily, looked like a man struck in the chest by an arrow fired from very short range, while

Cicero, in a puzzled manner, as if it were all a mystery far beyond his comprehension, pointed out the coincidence of names, dates and sums in the tax company's records and the claims of bribery compiled by the Syracusan senate.

'And there is another thing,' said Cicero pleasantly. 'This gentleman, who did so much business with you, does not appear in your accounts before his near-namesake, Gaius Verres, came to Sicily, and he has not done any business with you since Gaius Verres left. But in those three years when Verres was here, he was your biggest client.' He showed the accounts to the crowd. 'And it is unfortunate – do you see? – that whenever the slave who wrote up your records came to put down his name, he always made the same slip of his stylus. But there we are. I am sure there is nothing suspicious about it. So perhaps you could simply tell the court who this Verrucius is, and where he can be found.'

Carpinatius looked helplessly towards Metellus, as someone in the crowd shouted, 'He does not exist!' 'There never was anyone in Sicily called Verrucius!' yelled another. 'It is Verres!' And the crowd started chanting: 'It is Verres! It is Verres!'

Cicero held up his hand for silence. 'Carpinatius insists I cannot remove these records from the province, and I concede in law he is correct. But nowhere in law does it say I cannot make a copy, as long as it is fair, and properly witnessed. All I need is help. Who here will help me copy these records, so that I can take them back to Rome and bring this swine Verres to justice for his crimes against the people of Sicily?'

A plantation of hands sprang up. Metellus tried to call for silence, but his words were lost in the din of people shouting their support. Cicero, with Flavius to help him, picked out all the most eminent men in the city – Sicilian and Roman alike –

and invited them to come forward and take a share of the evidence, whereupon I handed each volunteer a tablet and stylus. I could see Carpinatius out of the corner of my eye frantically trying to struggle across to Metellus, and I could see Metellus with his arms folded scowling furiously down from his raised bench at the chaos of his court. Eventually, he simply turned on his heel and strode angrily up the steps and into the temple behind him.

Thus ended Cicero's visit to Sicily. Metellus, I am sure, would dearly have liked to have arrested him, or at least prevented him from removing evidence. But Cicero had won over too many adherents in both the Roman and the Sicilian communities. To have seized him would have caused an insurrection, and as Metellus had conceded, he did not have the troops to control the entire population. By the end of that afternoon, the copies of the tax company's records had been witnessed, sealed and transferred to our guarded ship in the harbour, where they joined the other trunks of evidence. Cicero himself remained only one more night on the Island, drawing up the list of witnesses he wished to bring to Rome. Lucius and Frugi agreed to remain behind in Syracuse to arrange their transportation.

The following morning they came down to the dock to see Cicero off. The harbour was packed with well-wishers, and he made a gracious speech of thanks. 'I know that I carry in this fragile vessel the hopes of this entire province. In so far as it lies within my power, I shall not let you down.' Then I helped him on to the deck, where he stood with fresh tears shining on his cheeks. Consummate actor that he was, I knew that he could summon any emotion at will, but I am sure that on that day his feelings were unfeigned. I wonder, indeed, looking back on it, if he somehow knew that he would never return to the island again. The oars dipped and stroked us out into the channel. The faces on the quayside blurred, the figures dwindled and disappeared, and slowly we headed out through the mouth of the harbour and into open water.

VIII

The journey back from Regium to Rome was easier than our progress south had been, for by now it was early spring, and the mainland was soft and welcoming. Not that we had much opportunity to admire the birds and flowers. Cicero worked every mile of the way, propped up, swaying and pitching in the back of his covered wagon, assembling the outline of his case against Verres. I would fetch documents from the baggage cart as he needed them, and trot along at the rear of his carriage taking down his dictation, which was no easy feat. His plan, as I understood it, was to separate the mass of evidence into four sets of charges – corruption as a judge, extortion in collecting taxes and official revenues, the plundering of private and municipal property, and, finally, illegal and tyrannical punishments. Witness statements and records were grouped accordingly, and even as he bounced along, he began drafting whole passages of his opening speech. (Just as he had trained his body to carry the weight of his ambition, so he had, by effort of will, cured himself of travel sickness, and over the years he was to do a vast amount of work while journeying up and down Italy.) In this manner, almost without his noticing where he was, we completed the trip in less than a fortnight and came at last to Rome on the Ides of March, exactly two months after we had left the city.

Hortensius, meanwhile, had not been idle, and an elaborate decoy prosecution was now underway. Of course, as Cicero had suspected, it had been designed partly as a trap to lure him into leaving Sicily early. Dasianus had not bothered to travel to Greece to collect any evidence. He had never even left Rome. But that had not stopped him from bringing charges against the former governor of Achaia in the extortion court, and the praetor, Glabrio, with nothing to do until Cicero returned, had found himself with little option but to let him proceed. And so there he was, day after day, this long-forgotten nonentity, droning away before a bored-looking jury of senators, with Hortensius at his side. And when Dasianus's loquacity flagged, the Dancing Master would rise in his graceful way, and pirouette about the court, making his own elaborate points.

Quintus, ever the well-trained staff officer, had prepared a daily campaign schedule while we had been away, and had set it up in Cicero's study. Cicero went to inspect it the moment he entered the house, and one glance revealed the shape of Hortensius's plan. Blobs of red dye marked the festivals when the court would not be sitting. Once those were removed, there were only twenty full working days until the senate went into recess. The recess itself lasted a further twenty days, and was followed immediately by the five-day Festival of Flora. Then there was the Day of Apollo, the Tarentine Games, the Festival of Mars, and so on. Roughly one day in four was a holiday. 'To put it simply,' said Quintus, 'judging by the way it is going, I think Hortensius will have no trouble occupying the court until almost the consular elections at the end of July. Then you yourself have to face the elections for aedile at the beginning of August. The earliest we are likely to be able to get into court, therefore, is the fifth. But then in the middle of August, Pompey's games begin – and they are scheduled to last for a full fifteen days. And then of course there are the Roman Games, and the Plebeian Games—'

'For pity's sake,' exclaimed Cicero, peering at the chart, 'does nobody in this wretched town do anything except watch men and animals kill one other?' His high spirits, which had sustained him all the way from Syracuse, seemed visibly to leak from him at that moment, like air from a bladder. He had come home ready for a fight, but Hortensius was far too shrewd to meet him head-on in open court. Blocking and attrition: these were to be his tactics, and they were nicely judged. Everyone knew that Cicero's resources were modest. The longer it took him to get his case to court, the more money it would cost him. Within a day or two, our first few witnesses would start arriving in Rome from Sicily. They would expect to have their travel and accommodation costs defrayed, and to be compensated for their loss of earnings. On top of this, Cicero was having to fund his election campaign for aedile. And assuming he won, he would then have to find the money to maintain himself in the office for a year, repairing public buildings and staging two more sets of official games. He could not afford to skimp these duties: the voters never forgave a cheapskate.

So there was nothing for it but to endure another painful session with Terentia. They dined alone together on the night of his return from Syracuse, and later I was summoned by Cicero and told to bring him the draft passages of his opening speech. Terentia was lying stiffly on her couch when I went in, stabbing irritably at her food; Cicero's plate, I noticed, was untouched. I was glad to hand him the document case and escape immediately. Already the speech was vast and would have taken at least two days to deliver. Later, I heard him pacing up and down, declaiming parts of it, and I realised she was making him rehearse his case, before deciding whether to advance him any more money. She must have liked what she heard, for the following morning Philotimus arranged for us to draw a line of credit for another fifty thousand. But it was humiliating for Cicero, and it is from around this time that I date his increasing preoccupation with money, a subject which had never previously interested him in the least.

I sense that I am dawdling in this narrative, having already reached my eighth roll of Hieratica, and need to speed it up a little, else either I shall die on the job, or you will be worn out reading. So let me dispense with the next four months very quickly. Cicero was obliged to work even harder than before. First of all in the mornings he had to deal with his clients (and of course there was a great backlog of casework to get through, which had built up while we were in Sicily). Then he had to appear in court or the senate, whichever was in session. He kept his head down in the latter, anxious in particular to avoid falling into conversation with Pompey the Great, fearful either that Pompey might ask him to drop his prosecution of Verres and give up his candidacy for aedile, or – worse – offer to help, which would leave him beholden to the mightiest man in Rome, an obligation he was determined to avoid. Only when the courts and senate adjourned for public holidays and recesses was he able to transfer all his energies to the Verres prosecution, sorting out and mastering the evidence, and coaching the witnesses. We were bringing around one hundred Sicilians to Rome, and as for virtually all of them it was their first visit, they needed to have their hands held, and this task fell to me. I became a kind of one-man tour agent, running around the city, trying to stop them falling prey to Verres's spies, or turning into drunks, or getting into fights – and a homesick Sicilian, let me tell you, is no easy charge. It was a relief when young Frugi returned from Syracuse to lend me a hand (cousin Lucius having remained in Sicily to keep the supply of witnesses and evidence flowing). Finally, in the early evenings, accompanied by Quintus, Cicero resumed his visits to the tribal headquarters to canvass for the aedileship.

Hortensius was also active. He kept the extortion court tied up with his tedious prosecution, using his mouthpiece Dasianus. Really, there was no end to his tricks. For example, he went out of his way to be friendly to Cicero, greeting him whenever they were standing around in the senaculum, waiting for a senate quorum, and ostentatiously steering him away for a private word about the general political situation. At first, Cicero was flattered, but then he discovered that Hortensius and his supporters were putting it about that he had agreed to take an enormous bribe deliberately to bungle the prosecution, hence the public embraces. Our witnesses, cooped up in their apartment blocks around the city, heard the rumours and started fluttering in panic, like chickens in a henhouse when a fox is about, and Cicero had to visit each in turn and reassure him. The next time Hortensius approached him with his hand outstretched, he showed him his back. Hortensius smiled, shrugged and turned away – what did he care? Everything was going his way.

I should perhaps say a little more about this remarkable man – 'the King of the Law Courts', as his claque of supporters called him – whose rivalry with Cicero lit up the Roman bar for a generation. The foundation of his success was his memory. In more than twenty years of advocacy, Hortensius had never been known to use a note. It was no trouble to him to memorise a four-hour speech, and deliver it perfectly, either in the senate or in the forum. And this phenomenal memory was not a dull thing, born of night-time study; it shone quick in the daylight. He had an alarming capacity to remember everything his opponents had said, whether in statement or cross-examination, and could hurl it back in their faces whenever he chose. He was like some doubly armoured gladiator in the arena of the law, lunging with sword and trident, protected by net and shield. He was forty-four years old that summer, and lived with his wife and teenaged son and daughter in an exquisitely decorated house on the Palatine Hill, next door to his brother-in-law, Catulus. *Exquisite* – that is the *mot juste* for Hortensius: exquisite in manners, exquisite in dress, in hairstyle, in scent, exquisite in his taste for all fine things. He never said a rude word to anyone. But his besetting sin was greed, which was already swelling to outrageous proportions – a palace on the Bay of Naples, a private zoo, a cellar containing ten thousand casks of the finest Chianti, a picture by Cydias bought for one hundred and fifty thousand, eels dressed in jewellery, trees watered with wine, the first man to serve peacock at dinner: the whole world knows the stories. It was this extravagance which had led him to form his alliance with Verres, who showered him with stolen gifts – the most notorious of which was a priceless sphinx, carved out of a single piece of ivory – and who paid for his campaign for the consulship.

Those consular elections were fixed to be held on the twenty-seventh day of July. On the twenty-third, the jury in the extortion court voted to acquit the former governor of Achaia of all the charges against him. Cicero, who had hurried down from working on his opening speech at home to await the result, listened impassively as Glabrio announced that he would begin hearing the case against Verres on the fifth day of August – 'when I trust your addresses to the court will be slightly shorter,' he said to Hortensius, who replied with a smirk. All that remained was to select a jury. This was accomplished the following day.

Thirty-two senators, drawn by lot, was the number laid down by the law. Each side was entitled to make six objections, but despite using up all his challenges, Cicero still faced a dauntingly hostile jury, including – yet again – Catulus and his protégé Catilina, as well as that other grand old man of the senate, Servilius Vatia Isauricus; even Marcus Metellus slipped on to the panel. Apart from these aristocratic hard-liners, we had also to write off cynics such as Aemilius Alba, Marcus Lucretius and Antonius Hybrida, for they would invariably sell themselves to the highest bidder, and Verres was lavish with his funds. I do not think I ever knew the true meaning of that old expression about someone looking like the cat that got the cream until I saw Hortensius's face on the day that jury was sworn in. He had it all. The consulship was in the bag, and with it, he was now confident, the acquittal of Verres.

The days which followed were the most nerve-racking Cicero had endured in public life. On the morning of the consular election he was so dispirited he could hardly bring himself to go out to the Field of Mars to vote, but of course he had to be seen to be an active citizen. The result was never in doubt, from the moment the trumpets sounded and the red flag was hoisted over the Janiculum Hill. Hortensius and Quintus Metellus were backed by Verres and his gold, by the aristocrats, and by the supporters of Pompey and Crassus. Nevertheless, there was always a race-day atmosphere on these occasions, with the candidates and their supporters streaming out of the city in the early-morning sunshine towards the voting pens, and the enterprising shopkeepers piling their stalls with wine and sausages, dice and parasols, and all else necessary to enjoy a good election. Pompey, as senior consul, in accordance with the ancient custom, was already standing at the entrance to the returning officer's tent, with an augur beside him. The moment all the candidates for consul and praetor, perhaps twenty senators, had lined up in their whitened togas, he mounted the platform and read out the traditional prayer. Soon afterwards the voting started and there was nothing for the thousands of electors to do except mill around and gossip until it was their turn to enter the enclosures.

This was the old republic in action, the men all voting in their allotted centuries, just as they had in ancient times, when as soldiers they elected their commander. Now that the ritual has become meaningless, it is hard to convey how moving a spectacle it was, even for a slave such as I, who did not have the franchise. It embodied something marvellous – some impulse of the human spirit that had sparked into life half a millennium before among that indomitable race who dwelled amid the hard rocks and soft marshland of the Seven Hills: some impulse towards the light of dignity and freedom, and away from the darkness of brute subservience. This is what we have lost. Not that it was a pure, Aristotelian democracy, by any means. Precedence among the centuries – of which there were one hundred and ninety-three – was determined by wealth, and the richest classes always voted earliest and declared first: a significant advantage. These centuries also benefited by having fewer members, whereas the centuries of the poor, like the slums of Subura, were vast and teeming; as a consequence, a rich man's vote counted for more. Still, it was freedom, as it had been practised for hundreds of years, and no man on the Field of Mars that day would have dreamed that he might live to see it taken away.

Cicero's century, one of the twelve consisting entirely of members of the equestrian order, was called around mid-morning, just as it was starting to get hot. He strolled with his fellows into the roped-off enclosure and proceeded to work the throng in his usual way – a word here, a touch of the elbow there. Then they formed themselves into a line and filed by the table at which sat the clerks, who checked their names and handed them their voting counters. If there was to be any intimidation, this was generally the place where it occurred, for the partisans of each candidate could get up close to the voters and whisper their threats or promises. But on this day all was quiet, and I watched Cicero step across the narrow wooden bridge and disappear behind the boards to cast his ballot. Emerging on the other side, he passed along the line of candidates and their friends, who were standing beneath an awning, paused briefly to talk to Palicanus – the roughly spoken former tribune was standing for a praetorship – and then exited without giving Hortensius or Metellus a second glance.

Like all those before it, Cicero's century backed the official slate – Hortensius and Quintus Metellus for consul; Marcus Metellus and Palicanus for praetor – and now it was merely a question of going on until an absolute majority was reached. The poorer men must have known they could not affect the outcome, but such was the dignity conveyed by the franchise, they stood all afternoon in the heat, awaiting their turn to collect their ballots and shuffle over the bridge. Cicero and I went up and down the lines as he canvassed support for the aedileship, and it was marvellous how many he knew personally – not just the voters' names, but their wives' names and the number of their children, and the nature of their employment: all done without any prompting from me. At the eleventh hour, when the sun was just starting to dip towards the Janiculum, a halt was called at last and Pompey proclaimed the winners. Hortensius had topped the poll for consul, with Quintus Metellus second; Marcus Metellus had won most votes for praetor. Their jubilant supporters crowded round them, and now for the first time we saw the red-headed figure of Gaius Verres slip into the front rank – 'The puppet-master comes to take his bow,' observed Cicero – and one would have thought that *he* had won the consulship by the way the aristocrats shook his hand and pounded him on the back. One of them, a former consul, Scribonius Curio, embraced Verres and said, loudly enough for all to hear, 'I hereby inform you that today's election means your acquittal!'

There are few forces in politics harder to resist than a feeling that something is inevitable, for humans move as a flock, and will always rush like sheep towards the safety of a winner. On every side now, one heard the same opinion: Cicero was done for, Cicero was finished, the aristocrats were back in charge, no jury would ever convict Gaius Verres. Aemilius Alba, who fancied himself a wit, told everyone he met that he was in despair: the bottom had dropped out of the market for Verres's jurors, and he could not sell himself for more than three thousand. Attention now switched to the forthcoming elections for aedile, and it was not long before Cicero detected Verres's hand at work behind the scenes here, as well. A professional election agent, Ranunculus, who was well disposed towards Cicero and was afterwards employed by him, came to warn the senator that Verres had called a night-time meeting at his own house of all the leading bribery merchants, and had offered five thousand to every man who could persuade his tribe not to vote for Cicero. I could see that both Cicero and his brother were worried. Worse was to follow. A few days later, on the eve of the actual election, the senate met with Crassus in the chair, to witness the praetors-elect draw lots to determine which courts they would preside over when they took office in January. I was not present, but

Cicero was in the chamber, and he returned home afterwards looking white and limp. The unbelievable had happened: Marcus Metellus, already a juror in the Verres case, had drawn the extortion court!

Even in his darkest imaginings, Cicero had never contemplated such an outcome. He was so shocked he had almost lost his voice. 'You should have heard the uproar in the house,' he whispered to Quintus. 'Crassus must have rigged the draw. Everyone believes he did it, but nobody knows *how* he did it. That man will not rest until I am broken, bankrupt and in exile.' He shuffled into his study and collapsed into his chair. It was a stiflingly hot day, the third of August, and there was hardly room to move among all the accumulated material from the Verres case: the piles of tax records and affidavits and witness statements, roasting and dusty in the heat. (And these were only a fraction of the total: most were locked in boxes in the cellar.) His draft speech – his immense opening speech, which kept on growing and growing, like some proliferating madness – was stacked in tottering piles across his desk. I had long since given up trying to keep track of it. Only he knew how it might come together. It was all in his head, the sides of which he now began massaging with the tips of his fingers. He asked in a croaking voice for a cup of water. I turned away to fetch it, heard a sigh and then a thump, and when I looked round he had slumped forwards, knocking his skull against the edge of his desk. Quintus and I rushed to either side of him and pulled him up. His cheeks were dead grey, with a livid streak of bright red blood trickling from his nose; his mouth hung slackly open.

Quintus was in a panic. 'Fetch Terentia!' he shouted at me. 'Quickly!'

I ran upstairs to her room and told her the master was ill. She came down at once and was magnificent in the way she took command. Cicero by now was feebly conscious, his head between his knees. She knelt beside him, called for water, pulled a fan from her sleeve, and starting waving it vigorously to cool his cheeks. Quintus in the mean time, still wringing his hands, had dispatched the two junior secretaries to fetch whatever doctors were in the neighbourhood, and each soon returned with a Greek medic in tow. The wretched quacks immediately began arguing between themselves about whether it was best to purge or bleed. Terentia sent both packing. She also refused to allow Cicero to be carried up to bed, warning Quintus that word of this would quickly get around, and the widespread belief that her husband was finished would then become an accomplished fact. She made him rise unsteadily to his feet and, holding his arm, took him out into the atrium, where the air was fresher. Quintus and I followed. 'You are not finished!' I could hear her saying sternly to him. 'You have your case – now make it!' Cicero mumbled something in reply.

Quintus burst out: 'That is all very well, Terentia, but you do not understand what has just happened.' And he told her about Metellus's appointment as the new president of the extortion court, and its implications. There was no chance of a guilty verdict being returned once *he* was in the judge's chair, which meant their only hope was to have the hearing concluded by December. But that was impossible, given Hortensius's ability to spin it out. There was simply too much evidence for the time available: only ten days in court before Pompey's games, and Cicero's opening statement alone would take up most of it. No sooner would he have finished outlining his case than the court would be in recess for the best part of a month, and by the time they came back the jury would have forgotten his brilliant points. 'Not that it matters,' Quintus concluded gloomily, 'as most of them are in the pay of Verres already.'

'It's true, Terentia,' said Cicero. He looked around him distractedly, as if he had only just woken up and realised where he was. 'I must pull out of the election for aedile,' he muttered. 'It would be humiliating enough to lose, but even more humiliating to win and not be able to discharge the duties of the office.'

'Pathetic,' replied Terentia, and she angrily pulled her arm free of his. 'You don't deserve to be elected, if this is how you surrender at the first setback, without putting up a fight!'

'My dear,' said Cicero beseechingly, pressing his hand to his forehead, 'if you will tell me how I am supposed to defeat time itself, then I will fight it bravely. But what am I to do if I only have ten days to set out my prosecution before the court goes into recess for weeks on end?'

Terentia leaned in close to him, so that her face was only inches from his. 'Make your speech shorter!' she hissed.

After his wife had retired to her corner of the house, Cicero, still not fully recovered from his fit of nerves, retreated to his study and sat there for a long time, staring at the wall. We left him alone. Sthenius came by just before sunset to report that Quintus Metellus had summoned all the Sicilian witnesses to his house, and that a few of the more timid souls had foolishly obeyed. From one of these, Sthenius had obtained a full report of how Metellus had tried to intimidate them into retracting their evidence. 'I am consul-elect,' he had thundered at them. 'One of my brothers is governing Sicily, the other is going to preside over the extortion court. Many steps have been taken to ensure that no harm can befall Verres. We shall not forget those who go against us.' I took down the exact quotation and tentatively went in to see Cicero. He had not moved in several hours. I read out Metellus's words, but he gave no sign of having heard.

By this stage I was becoming seriously concerned, and would have fetched his brother or wife again, if his mind had not suddenly re-emerged from wherever it had been wandering. Staring straight ahead, he said in a grim tone: 'Go and make an appointment for me to see Pompey this evening.' When I hesitated, wondering if this was another symptom of his malady, he glared at me. 'Go!'

It was only a short distance to Pompey's house, which was in the same district of the Esquiline Hill as Cicero's. The sun had just gone down but it was still light, and swelteringly hot, with a torpid breeze wafting gently from the east – the worst possible combination at the height of summer, because it carried into the neighbourhood the stench of the putrefying corpses in the great common graves beyond the city wall. I believe the problem is not so acute these days, but sixty years ago the Esquiline Gate was the place where everything dead and not worth a proper funeral was taken to be dumped – the bodies of dogs and cats, horses, donkeys, slaves, paupers and still-born babies, all mixed up and rotting together, along with the household refuse. The stink always drew great flocks of crying gulls, and I remember that on this particular evening it was especially acute: a rancid and pervasive smell, which one tasted on the tongue as much as one absorbed it through the nostrils.

Pompey's house was much grander than Cicero's, with a couple of lictors posted outside and a crowd of sightseers gathered opposite. There were also half a dozen canopied litters set down in the lee of the wall, their bearers squatting nearby playing bones – evidence that a big dinner party was in progress. I gave my message to the gatekeeper, who vanished inside, and returned a little later with the praetor-elect, Palicanus, who was dabbing at his greasy chin with a napkin. He recognised me, asked what it was all about, and I repeated my message. 'Right you are,' said Palicanus, in his blunt way. 'You can tell him from me that the consul will see him immediately.'

Cicero must have known Pompey would agree to meet, for when I returned he had already changed into a fresh set of clothes and was ready to go out. He was still very pale. He exchanged a last look with Quintus, and then we set off. There was no conversation between us as we walked, because Cicero, who hated any reminder of death, kept his sleeve pressed to his mouth and nose to ward off the smell from the Esquiline Field. 'Wait here,' he said, when we reached Pompey's house, and that was the last I saw of him for several hours. The daylight faded, the massy purple twilight ripened into darkness and the stars began to appear in clusters above the city. Occasionally, when the door was opened, the muffled sounds of voices and laughter reached the street, and I could smell meat and fish cooking, although on that foul night they all reeked of death to me, and I wondered how Cicero could possibly find the stomach for it, for by now it was clear that Pompey had asked him to join his dinner party.

I paced up and down, leaned against the wall, attempted to think up some new symbols for my great shorthand system, and generally tried to occupy myself as the night went on. Eventually, Pompey's guests started reeling out, half of them too drunk to stand properly, and it was the usual crew of Piceneans – Afranius, the former praetor and lover of the dance; Palicanus, of course; and Gabinius, Palicanus's son-in-law, who also had a reputation for loving women and song – a real old soldiers' reunion, it must have been, and I found it hard to imagine that Cicero could have enjoyed himself much. Only the austere and scholarly Varro – 'the man who showed Pompey where the senate house was', in Cicero's cutting phrase – would have been remotely congenial company, especially as he at least emerged sober. Cicero was the last to leave. He set off up the street and I hurried after him. There was a good yellow moon and I had no difficulty in making out his figure. He still kept his hand up to his nose, for neither the heat nor the smell had much diminished, and when he was a decent distance from Pompey's house, he leaned against the corner of an alley and was violently sick.

I came up behind him and asked him if he needed assistance, at which he shook his head and responded, 'It is done.' That was all he said to me, and all he said to Quintus, too, who was waiting up anxiously for him at the house when he got in: 'It is done.'

At dawn the following day we made the two-mile walk back to the Field of Mars for the second round of elections. Although these did not carry the same prestige as those for the consulship and the praetorship, they nevertheless had the advantage of always being much more exciting. Thirty-four men had to be elected (twenty senators, ten tribunes and four aediles), which meant there were simply too many candidates for the poll to be easily controlled: when an aristocrat's vote carried no more weight than a pauper's, anything could happen. Crassus, as junior consul, was the presiding officer at this supplementary election – 'But presumably even he,' said Cicero darkly, as he pulled on his red leather shoes, 'cannot rig this ballot.'

He had woken in an edgy, preoccupied mood. Whatever had been agreed with Pompey the previous night had obviously disturbed his rest, and he snapped irritably at his valet that his shoes were not as clean as they ought to be. He donned the same brilliant white toga he had worn on this day six years earlier, when he had first been elected to the senate, and braced himself before the front door was opened, as if he were about to shoulder a great weight. Once again, Quintus had done a fine job, and a marvellous crowd was waiting to escort him out to the voting pens. When we reached the Field of Mars, we found it was packed right down to the river's edge, for there was a census in progress, and tens of thousands had come to the city to register. You can imagine the noisy roar of it. There must have been a hundred candidates for those thirty-four offices, and all across the vast open field one could see these gleaming figures passing to and fro, accompanied by their friends and supporters, trying to gather every last vote before polling opened. Verres's red head was also conspicuous, darting all over the place, with his father beside him, and his son, and his freedman, Timarchides – the creature who had invaded our house – making extravagant promises to any who would vote against Cicero. The sight seemed to banish Cicero's ill humour instantly, and he plunged in to canvass. I thought on several occasions that our groups might collide, but the crowd was so huge it never happened.

When the augur pronounced himself satisfied, Crassus came out of the sacred tent and the candidates gathered at the base of his tribunal. Among them, I should record, making his first attempt to enter the senate, was Julius Caesar, who stood beside Cicero and engaged him in friendly conversation. They had known one another a long time, and indeed it was on Cicero's recommendation that the younger man had gone to Rhodes to study rhetoric under Apollonius Molon. Much hagiography now clusters around Caesar's early years, to the extent that you would think he had been marked out by his contemporaries as a genius ever since the cradle. Not so, and anyone who saw him in his whitened toga that morning, nervously fiddling with his thinning hair, would have been hard put to distinguish him from any of the other well-bred young candidates. There was one great difference, though: few can have been as poor. To stand for election, he must have borrowed heavily, for he lived in very modest accommodation in the Subura, in a house full of women – his mother, his wife, and his little daughter – and I picture him at this stage not as the gleaming hero waiting to conquer Rome, but as a thirty-year-old man lying sleepless at night, kept awake by the racket of his impoverished neighbourhood, brooding bitterly on the fact that he, a scion of the oldest family in Rome, had been reduced to such circumstances. His antipathy towards the aristocrats was consequently far more dangerous to them than Cicero's ever was. As a self-made man, Cicero merely resented and envied them. But Caesar, who believed he was a direct descendant of Venus, viewed them with contempt, as interlopers.

But now I am running ahead of myself, and committing the same sin as the hagiographers, by shining the distorting light of the future on to the shadows of the past. Let me simply record that these two outstanding men, with six years' difference in their ages but much in common in terms of brains and outlook, stood chatting amiably in the sun, as Crassus mounted the platform and read out the familiar prayer: 'May this matter end well and happily for me, for my best endeavours, for my office, and for the People of Rome!' And with that the voting started.

The first tribe into the pens, in accordance with tradition, were the Suburana. But despite all Cicero's efforts over the years, they did not vote for him. This must have been a blow, and certainly suggested Verres's bribery agents had earned their cash. Cicero,

however, merely shrugged: he knew that many influential men
who had yet to vote would be watching for his reaction, and it
was important to wear a mask of confidence. Then, one after
another, came the three other tribes of the city: the Esquilina,
the Collina and the Palatina. Cicero won the support of the first
two, but not the third, which was scarcely surprising, as it was
easily the most aristocratically inclined of Rome's neighbourhoods. So the score was two–two: a tenser start than he would
have liked. And now the thirty-one rustic tribes started lining up:
the Aemilia, Camilia, Fabia, Galeria . . . I knew all their names
from our office files, could tell you who were the key men in
each, who needed a favour and who owed one. Three of these
four went for Cicero. Quintus came up and whispered in his ear,
and for the first time he could perhaps afford to relax, as Verres's
money had obviously proved most tempting to those tribes
composed of a majority of city-dwellers. The Horatia, Lemonia,
Papiria, Menenia . . . On and on, through the heat and the dust,
Cicero sitting on a stool between counts but always rising whenever the voters passed in front of him after casting their ballots,
his memory working to retrieve their names, thanking them, and
passing on his respects to their families. The Sergia, Voltina,
Pupina, Romilia . . . Cicero failed in the last tribe, not surprisingly, as it was Verres's own, but by the middle of the afternoon
he had won the support of sixteen tribes and needed only two
more for victory. Yet still Verres had not given up, and could be
seen in huddled groups with his son and Timarchides. For a
terrible hour, the balance seemed to tilt his way. The Sabatini did
not go for Cicero, and nor did the Publilia. But then he just
scraped in with the Scaptia, and finally it was the Falerna from
northern Campania who put him over the top: eighteen tribes
out of the thirty which had so far voted, with five left to come

– but what did they matter? He was safely home, and at some point when I was not looking Verres quietly removed himself from the election field to calculate his losses. Caesar, whose own elevation to the senate had just been confirmed, was the first to turn and shake Cicero's hand. I could see Quintus triumphantly brandishing his fists in the air, Crassus staring angrily into the distance. There were cheers from the spectators who had been keeping their own tallies – those curious zealots who follow elections as fervently as other men do chariot racing – and who appreciated what had just happened. The victor himself looked stunned by his achievement, but no one could deny it, not even Crassus, who would shortly have to read it out, even though the words must have choked him. Against all odds, Marcus Cicero was an aedile of Rome.

A big crowd – they are always bigger after a victory – escorted Cicero from the Field of Mars all the way back to his house, where the domestic slaves were assembled to applaud him over the threshold. Even Diodotus the blind Stoic put in a rare appearance. All of us were proud to belong to such an eminent figure; his glory reflected on every member of his household; our worth and self-esteem increased with his. From the atrium, Tullia darted forward with a cry of 'Papa!' and wrapped her arms around his legs, and even Terentia stepped up and embraced him, smiling. I still hold that image of the three of them frozen in my mind – the triumphant young orator with his left hand on the head of his daughter and his right clasped about the shoulders of his happy wife. Nature bestows this gift, at least, on those who rarely smile: when they do, their faces are transformed, and I saw at that moment how Terentia, for all her

complaints about her husband, nonetheless relished his bril-
liance and success.

It was Cicero who reluctantly broke the embrace. 'I thank you
all,' he declared, looking around at his admiring audience. 'But
this is not the time for celebrations. That will only come when
Verres is defeated. Tomorrow, at long last, I shall open the prosecution in the forum, and let us pray to the gods that before too
many days have passed, fresh and far greater honour will descend
upon this household. So what are you waiting for?' He smiled
and clapped his hands. 'Back to work!'

Cicero retired with Quintus to his study, and beckoned to me
to follow. He threw himself into his chair with a gasp of relief
and kicked off his shoes. For the first time in more than a week
the tension in his face seemed to have eased. I assumed he would
now want to begin on the urgent task of pulling together his
speech, but apparently he had other plans for me. I was to go
back out into the city with Sositheus and Laurea, and between
us we were to visit all the Sicilian witnesses, give them the news
of his election, check that they were holding firm, and instruct
them all to present themselves in court the following morning.

'All?' I repeated in astonishment. 'All one hundred?'

'That is right,' he replied. The old decisiveness was back in his
voice. 'And tell Eros to hire a dozen porters – reliable men – to
carry every box of evidence down to court at the same time as
I go down tomorrow.'

'All the witnesses . . . A dozen porters . . . Every box of evidence
. . .' I was making a list of his orders. 'But this is going to take
me until midnight,' I said, unable to conceal my bewilderment.

'Poor Tiro. But do not worry – there will be time enough to
sleep when we are dead.'

'I am not worried about my sleep, Senator,' I said stiffly. 'I was wondering when I was going to have time to help you with your speech.'

'I shall not require your help,' he said with a slight smile, and raised a finger to his lips, to warn me that I must say nothing. But as I had no idea of the significance of his remark, there was hardly any danger of my revealing his plans, and not for the first time I left his presence in a state of some confusion.

IX

And so it came about that on the fifth day of August, in the consulship of Gnaeus Pompey Magnus and Marcus Licinius Crassus, one year and nine months after Sthenius had first come to see Cicero, the trial of Gaius Verres began.

Bear in mind the summer heat. Calculate the number of victims with an interest in seeing Verres brought to justice. Remember that Rome was, in any case, swarming with citizens in town for the census, the elections and the impending games of Pompey. Consider that the hearing pitched the two greatest orators of the day in head-to-head combat ('a duel of real magnitude', as Cicero later called it). Put all this together, and you may begin to guess something of the atmosphere in the extortion court that morning. Hundreds of spectators, determined to have a decent vantage point, had slept out in the forum overnight. By dawn, there was nowhere left to stand that offered any shade. By the second hour, there was nowhere left at all. In the porticoes and on the steps of the Temple of Castor, in the forum itself and in the colonnades surrounding it, on the rooftops and balconies of the houses, on the sides of the hills – anywhere that human beings could squeeze themselves into, or hang off, or perch on – there you would find the people of Rome.

Frugi and I scurried around like a pair of sheepdogs, herding our witnesses into court, and what an exotic and colourful assembly they made, in their sacred robes and native dress, victims from every stage of Verres's career, drawn by the promise of vengeance – priests of Juno and Ceres, the mystagogues of the Syracusan Minerva and the sacred virgins of Diana; Greek nobles whose descent was traced to Cecrops or Eurysthenes or to the great Ionian and Minyan houses, and Phoenicians whose ancestors had been priests of Tyrian Melcarth, or claimed kindred with the Zidonian Iah; eager crowds of impoverished heirs and their guardians, bankrupt farmers and corn merchants and ship owners, fathers bewailing their children carried off to slavery, children mourning for their parents dead in the governor's dungeons; deputations from the foot of Mount Taurus, from the shores of the Black Sea, from many cities of the Grecian mainland, from the islands of the Aegean and of course from every city and market town of Sicily.

I was so busy helping to ensure that all the witnesses were admitted, and that every box of evidence was in its place and securely guarded, that only gradually did I come to realise what a spectacle Cicero had stage-managed. Those evidence boxes, for example, now included public testimony collected by the elders of virtually every town in Sicily. It was only when the jurors started shouldering their way through the masses and taking their places on the benches that I realised – showman that he was – why Cicero had been so insistent on having *everything* in place at once. The impression on the court was overwhelming. Even the hard-faces, like old Catulus and Isauricus, registered astonishment. As for Glabrio, when he came out of the temple preceded by his lictors, he paused for a moment on the top step, and swayed half a pace backwards when confronted by that wall of faces.

Cicero, who had been standing apart until the last possible moment, squeezed through the crowd and climbed the steps to his place on the prosecutor's bench. There was a sudden quietness; a silent quiver of anticipation in the still air. Ignoring the shouts of encouragement from his supporters, he turned and shielded his eyes against the sun and scanned the vast audience, squinting to right and left, as I imagine a general might check the lie of the land and position of the clouds before a battle. Then he sat down, while I stationed myself at his back so that I could pass him any document he needed. The clerks of the court set up Glabrio's curule chair – the signal that the tribunal was in session – and everything was ready, save for the presence of Verres and Hortensius. Cicero, who was as cool as I had ever seen him, leaned back and whispered to me, 'After all that, perhaps he is not coming.' Needless to say, he *was* coming – Glabrio sent one of his lictors to fetch him – but Hortensius was giving us a foretaste of his tactics, which would be to waste as much time as possible. Eventually, perhaps an hour late, to ironic applause, the immaculate figure of the consul-elect eased through the press of spectators, followed by his junior counsel – none other than young Scipio Nasica, the love rival of Cato – then Quintus Metellus, and finally came Verres himself, looking redder than usual in the heat. For a man with any shred of conscience, it would surely have been a vision out of hell, to see those ranks of his victims and accusers, all ranged against him. But this monster merely bowed at them, as if he were delighted to greet old acquaintances.

Glabrio called the court to order, but before Cicero could rise to begin his speech, Hortensius jumped up to make a point of order: under the Cornelian Law, he declared, a prosecutor was entitled to call no more than forty-eight witnesses, but this prosecutor had brought to court at least double that number, purely for the purpose of intimidation! He then embarked on a long, learned and elegant speech about the origins of the extortion court, which lasted for what felt like another hour. At length, Glabrio cut him off, saying there was nothing in the law about restricting the number of witnesses present in court, only the number giving verbal evidence. Once again, he invited Cicero to open his case, and once again, Hortensius intervened with another point of order. The crowd began to jeer, but he pressed on, as he did repeatedly whenever Cicero rose to speak, and thus the first few hours of the day were lost in vexatious legal point-scoring.

It was not until the middle of the afternoon, when Cicero was wearily getting to his feet for the ninth or tenth time, that Hortensius at last remained seated. Cicero looked at him, waited, then slowly spread his arms wide in mock-amazement. A wave of laughter went round the forum. Hortensius responded by gesturing with a foppish twirl of his hand to the well of the court, as if to say, 'Be my guest.' Cicero bowed courteously and came forward. He cleared his throat.

There could scarcely have been a worse moment at which to begin such an immense undertaking. The heat was unbearable. The crowd was now bored and restless. Hortensius was smirking. There were only perhaps two hours left before the court adjourned for the evening. And yet this was to be one of the most decisive moments in the history of our Roman law – indeed, in the history of all law, everywhere, I should not wonder.

'Gentlemen of the court,' said Cicero, and I bent my head over my tablet and noted the words in shorthand. I waited for him to continue. For almost the first time before a major speech, I had no idea what he was going to say. I waited a little longer, my heart thumping, and then nervously glanced up to find him walking across the court away from me. I thought he was going to stop and confront Verres, but instead he walked straight past him and halted in front of the senators in the jury.

'Gentlemen of the court,' he repeated, addressing them directly, 'at this great political crisis, there has been offered to you, not through man's wisdom but almost as the direct gift of heaven, the very thing you most need – a thing that will help more than anything else to mitigate the unpopularity of your order and the suspicion surrounding these courts. A belief has become established – as harmful to the republic as it is to yourselves – that these courts, with you senators as the jury, will never convict any man, however guilty, if he has sufficient *money*.'

He put a wonderful, contemptuous stress on the last word. 'You are not wrong there!' shouted a voice in the crowd.

'But the character of the man I am prosecuting,' continued Cicero, 'is such that you may use him to restore your own good name. Gaius Verres has robbed the treasury and behaved like a pirate and a destroying pestilence in his province of Sicily. You have only to find this man guilty, and respect in you will be rightly restored. But if you do not – if his immense wealth is sufficient to shatter your honesty – well then, I shall achieve one thing at least. The nation will not believe Verres to be right and me wrong – but they will certainly know all they need to know about a jury of Roman senators!'

It was a nice stroke to start off with. There was a rustle of approval from the great crowd that was like a wind moving through a forest, and in some curious sense the focus of the trial seemed to shift all at once twenty paces to the left. It was as if the senators, sweating in the hot sun and squirming uncomfortably on their wooden benches, had become the accused, while the vast press of witnesses, drawn from every corner of the Mediterranean, was the jury. Cicero had never addressed such an immense throng before, but Molon's training on the seashore stood him in good stead, and when he turned to the forum his voice rang clear and true.

'Let me tell you of the impudent and insane plan that is now in Verres's mind. It is plain to him that I am approaching this case so well prepared that I shall be able to pin him down as a robber and a criminal, not merely in the hearing of this court but in the eyes of the whole world. But in spite of this, he holds so low an opinion of the aristocracy, he believes the senatorial courts to be so utterly abandoned and corrupt, that he goes about boasting openly that he has bought the safest date for his trial, he has bought the jury, and just to be on the safe side he has also bought the consular election for his two titled friends who have tried to intimidate my witnesses!'

This was what the crowd had come to hear. The rustle of approval became a roar. Metellus jumped up in anger, and so did Hortensius – yes, even Hortensius, who normally greeted any taunt in the arena with nothing more strenuous than a raised eyebrow. They began gesticulating angrily at Cicero.

'What?' he responded, turning on them. 'Did you count on my saying nothing of so serious a matter? On my caring for anything, except my duty and my honour, when the country and my own reputation are in such danger? Metellus, I am amazed at you. To attempt to intimidate witnesses, especially these timorous and calamity-stricken Sicilians, by appealing to their awe of you as consul-elect, and to the power of your two brothers – if this is not judicial corruption, I should be glad to know what is! What would you not do for an innocent kinsman if you abandon duty and honour for an utter rascal who is no kin of yours at all? Because I tell you this: Verres has been going round saying that you were only made consul because of his exertions, and that by January he will have the two consuls and the president of the court to suit him!'

I had to stop writing at this point, because the noise was too great for me to hear. Metellus and Hortensius both had their hands cupped to their mouths and were bellowing at Cicero. Verres was gesturing angrily at Glabrio to put a stop to this. The jury of senators sat immobile – most of them, I am sure, wishing they were anywhere but where they were – while individual spectators were having to be restrained by the lictors from storming the court. Eventually, Glabrio managed to restore order, and Cicero resumed, in a much calmer voice.

'So these are their tactics. Today the court did not start its business until the middle of the afternoon – they are already reckoning that today does not count at all. It is only ten days to the games of Pompey the Great. These will occupy fifteen days and will be followed immediately by the Roman Games. So it will not be until after an interval of nearly forty days that they expect to begin their reply. They count on being able then, with the help of long speeches and technical evasions, to prolong the trial until the Games of Victory begin. These games are followed without a break by the Plebeian Games, after which there will be very few days, or none at all, on which the court can sit. In this way they reckon that all the impetus of the prosecution will be spent and exhausted, and that the whole case will come up afresh before Marcus Metellus, who is sitting there on this jury.

'So what am I to do? If I spend upon my speech the full time allotted me by law, there is the gravest danger that the man I am prosecuting will slip through my fingers. "Make your speech shorter" is the obvious answer I was given a few days ago, and that is good advice. But, having thought the matter over, I shall go one better. Gentlemen, *I shall make no speech at all.*'

I glanced up in astonishment. Cicero was looking at Hortensius, and his rival was staring back at him with the most wonderful frozen expression on his face. He looked like a man who has been walking through a wood cheerfully enough, thinking himself safely alone, and has suddenly heard a twig snap behind him and has stopped dead in alarm.

'That is right, Hortensius,' said Cicero. 'I am not going to play your game and spend the next ten days in the usual long address. I am not going to let the case drag on till January, when you and Metellus as consuls can use your lictors to drag my witnesses before you and frighten them into silence. I am not going to allow you gentlemen of the jury the luxury of forty days to forget my charges, so that you can then lose yourselves and your consciences in the tangled thickets of Hortensius's rhetoric. I am not going to delay the settlement of this case until all these multitudes who have come to Rome for the census and the games have dispersed to their homes in Italy. I am going to call my witnesses at once, beginning now, and this will be my procedure: I shall read out the individual charge. I shall comment and elaborate upon it. I shall bring forth the witness who supports it, and question him, and then you, Hortensius, will have the same opportunity as me for comment and cross-examination. I shall do all this and I shall rest my case within the space of ten days.'

All my long life I have treasured – and for what little remains of it I shall continue to treasure – the reactions of Hortensius, Verres, Metellus and Scipio Nasica at that moment. Of course, Hortensius was on his feet as soon as he had recovered his breath and was denouncing this break with precedent as entirely illegal. But Glabrio was ready for him, and told him brusquely that it was up to Cicero to present his case in whatever manner he wished, and that he, for one, was sick of interminable speeches, as he had made clear in this very court before the consular elections. His remarks had obviously been prepared beforehand, and Hortensius rose again to accuse him of collusion with the prosecution. Glabrio, who was an irritable man at the best of times, told him bluntly he had better guard his tongue, or he would have his lictors remove him from the court – consul-elect or no. Hortensius sat down furiously, folded his arms and scowled at his feet, as Cicero concluded his opening address, once again by turning on the jury.

'Today the eyes of the world are upon us, waiting to see how far the conduct of each man among us will be marked by obedience to his conscience and observance of the law. Even as you will pass your verdict upon the prisoner, so the people of Rome will pass its verdict upon yourselves. The case of Verres will determine whether, in a court composed of senators, the condemnation of a very guilty and very rich man can possibly occur. Because all the world knows that Verres is distinguished by nothing except his monstrous offences and his immense wealth. Therefore if he is acquitted it will be impossible to imagine any explanation except the most shameful. So I advise you, gentlemen, for your own sakes, to see that this does not occur.' And with that he turned his back on them. 'I call my first witness – Sthenius of Thermae.'

I doubt very strongly whether any of the aristocrats on that jury – Catulus, Isauricus, Metellus, Catilina, Lucretius, Aemilius and the rest – had ever been addressed with such insolence before, especially by a new man without a single ancestral mask to show on his atrium wall. How they must have loathed being made to sit there and take it, especially given the deliriums of ecstasy with which Cicero was received by the vast crowd in the forum when he sat down. As for Hortensius, it was possible almost to feel sorry for him. His entire career had been founded on his ability to memorise immense orations and deliver them with the aplomb of an actor. Now he was effectively struck mute; worse, he was faced with the prospect of having to deliver four dozen mini-speeches in reply to each of Cicero's witnesses over the next ten days. He had not done sufficient research even remotely to attempt this, as became cruelly evident when Sthenius took the witness stand. Cicero had called him first as a mark of respect for the originator of this whole fantastic undertaking, and the Sicilian did not let him down. He had waited a long time for his day in court, and he made the most of it, giving a heart-wringing account of the way Verres had abused his hospitality, stolen his property, trumped up charges against him, fined him and tried to have him flogged, sentenced him to death in his absence and then forged the records of the Syracusan court – records which Cicero produced in evidence, and passed around the jury.

But when Glabrio called upon Hortensius to cross-examine the witness, the Dancing Master, not unnaturally, showed some reluctance to take the floor. The one golden rule of cross-examination is never, under any circumstances, to ask a question to which you do not know the answer, and Hortensius simply had no idea what Sthenius might say next. He shuffled a few documents, held a whispered consultation with Verres, then approached the witness stand. What could he do? After a few petulant questions, the implication of which was that the Sicilian was fundamentally hostile to Roman rule, he asked him why, of all the lawyers available, he had chosen to go straight to Cicero – a man known to be an agitator of the lower classes. Surely his whole motivation from the start was merely to stir up trouble?

'But I did not go straight to Cicero,' replied Sthenius in his ingenuous way. 'The first advocate I went to was you.'

Even some of the jury laughed at that.

Hortensius swallowed, and attempted to join in the merriment. 'Did you really? I can't say that I remember you.'

'Well you wouldn't, would you? You are a busy man. But I remember you, Senator. You said you were representing Verres. You said you didn't care how much of my property he had stolen – no court would ever believe the word of a Sicilian over a Roman.'

Hortensius had to wait for the storm of cat-calls to die down. 'I have no further questions for this witness,' he said in a grim voice, and with that the court was adjourned until the following day.

It had been my intention to describe in detail the trial of Gaius Verres, but now I come to set it down, I see there is no point. After Cicero's tactical masterstroke on that first day, Verres and his advocates resembled nothing so much as the victims of a siege: holed up in their little fortress, surrounded on every side by their enemies, battered day after day by a rain of missiles, and with tunnels undermining their crumbling walls. They had no means of fighting back. Their only hope was somehow to withstand the onslaught for the full nine days remaining, and then try to regroup during the lull enforced by Pompey's games. Cicero's objective was equally clear: to obliterate Verres's defences so completely that by the time he had finished laying out his case not even the most corrupt senatorial jury in Rome would dare to acquit him.

He set about this mission with his usual discipline. The prosecution team would gather before dawn. While Cicero performed his exercises, was shaved and dressed, I would read out the testimony of the witnesses he would be calling that day, and run through our schedule of evidence. He would then dictate to me the rough outline of what he intended to say. For an hour or two he would familiarise himself with the day's brief and thoroughly memorise his remarks, while Quintus, Frugi and I ensured that all his witnesses and evidence boxes were ready. We would then parade down the hill to the forum – and parades they were, for the general view around Rome was that Cicero's performance in the extortion court was the greatest show in town. The crowds were as large on the second and third days as they had been on the first, and the witnesses' performances were often heartbreaking, as they collapsed in tears recounting their ill treatment. I remember in particular Dio of Halaesa, swindled out of ten thousand sesterces, and two brothers from Agyrium forced to hand over their entire inheritance of four thousand. There would have been more, but Lucius Metellus had actually refused to let a dozen witnesses leave the island to testify, among them Heraclius of Syracuse, the chief priest of Jupiter – an outrage against justice which Cicero neatly turned to his advantage. 'Our allies' rights,' he boomed, 'do not even include permission to complain of their sufferings!' Throughout all this, Hortensius, amazing to relate, never said a word. Cicero would finish his examination of a witness, Glabrio would offer the King of the Law Courts his chance to cross-examine, and His Majesty would regally shake his head, or declare grandly, 'No questions for this witness.' On the fourth day, Verres pleaded illness and tried to be excused attendance, but Glabrio was having none of it, and told him he would be carried down to the forum on his bed if necessary.

It was on the following afternoon that Cicero's cousin Lucius at last returned to Rome, his mission in Sicily accomplished. Cicero was overjoyed to find him waiting at the house when we got back from court, and embraced him tearfully. Without Lucius's support in dispatching witnesses and boxes of evidence back to the mainland, Cicero's case would not have been half as strong. But the seven-month effort had clearly exhausted Lucius, who had not been a strong man to begin with. He was now alarmingly thin, and had developed a painful, racking cough. Even so, his commitment to bringing Verres to justice was unwavering – so much so that he had missed the opening of the trial in order to take a detour on his journey back to Rome. He had stayed in Puteoli and tracked down two more witnesses: the Roman knight Gaius Numitorius, who had witnessed the crucifixion of Gavius in Messana, and a friend of his, a merchant named Marcus Annius, who had been in Syracuse when the Roman banker Herennius had been judicially murdered.

'And where are these gentlemen?' asked Cicero eagerly.

'Here,' replied Lucius. 'In the tablinum. But I must warn you, they do not want to testify.'

Cicero hurried through to find two formidable men of middle age – 'The perfect witnesses from my point of view,' as he afterwards described them, 'prosperous, respectable, sober, and – above all – not Sicilian.' As Lucius had predicted, they were reluctant to get involved. They were businessmen, with no desire to make powerful enemies, and did not relish the prospect of taking starring roles in Cicero's great anti-aristocratic production in the Roman forum. But he wore them down, for they were not fools, either, and could see that in the ledger of profit and loss, they stood to gain most by aligning themselves with the side that was winning. 'Do you know what Pompey said to Sulla, when the old man tried to deny him a triumph on his twenty-sixth birthday?' asked Cicero.

'He told me over dinner the other night: "More people worship a rising than a setting sun."' This potent combination of name-dropping and appeals to patriotism and self-interest at last won them round, and by the time they went into dinner with Cicero and his family, they had pledged their support.

'I knew if I had them in your company for a few moments,' whispered Lucius, 'they would do whatever you wanted.'

I had expected Cicero to put them on the witness stand the very next day, but he was too smart for that. 'A show must always end with a climax,' he said. By now he was ratcheting up the level of outrage with each new piece of evidence, having moved on through judicial corruption, extortion and straight-forward robbery, to cruel and unusual punishment. On the eighth day of the trial, he dealt with the testimony of two Sicilian naval captains, Phalacrus of Centuripa and Onasus of Segesta, who described how they and their men had only escaped floggings and executions by bribing Verres's freedman, Timarchides (present in court, I am glad to say, to experience his humiliation personally). Worse: the families of those who had not been able to raise sufficient funds to secure the release of their relatives had been told they would still have to pay a bribe to the official executioner, Sextius, or he would deliber-ately make a mess of the beheadings. 'Think of that unbear-able burden of pain,' declaimed Cicero, 'of the anguish that racked those unhappy parents, thus compelled to purchase for their children by bribery not life but a speedy death!' I could see the senators on the jury shaking their heads at this, and muttering to one another, and each time Glabrio invited Hortensius to cross-examine the witnesses, and Hortensius simply responded yet again, 'No questions,' they groaned. Their position was becoming intolerable, and that night the first rumours reached us that Verres had already packed up the contents of his house and was preparing to flee into exile.

Such was the state of affairs on the ninth day, when we brought Annius and Numitorius into court. If anything, the crowd in the forum was bigger than ever, for there were now only two days left until Pompey's great games. Verres came late, and obviously drunk. He stumbled as he climbed the steps of the temple up to the tribunal, and Hortensius had to steady him as the crowd roared with laughter. As he passed Cicero's place, he flashed him a shattered, red-eyed look of fear and rage – the hunted, cornered look of an animal at bay. Cicero got straight down to business and called as his first witness Annius, who described how he had been inspecting a cargo down at the harbour in Syracuse one morning, when a friend had come running to tell him that their business associate, Herennius, was in chains in the forum and pleading for his life.

'So what did you do?'

'Naturally, I went at once.'

'And what was the scene?'

'There were perhaps a hundred people crying out that Herennius was a Roman citizen, and could not be executed without a proper trial.'

'How did you all know that Herennius was a Roman? Was he not a banker from Spain?'

'Many of us knew him personally. Although he had business in Spain, he had been born to a Roman family in Syracuse and had grown up in the city.'

'And what was Verres's response to your pleas?'

'He ordered Herennius to be beheaded immediately.'

There was a groan of horror around the court.

'And who dealt the fatal blow?'

'The public executioner, Sextius.'

'And did he make a clean job of it?'

'I am afraid he did not, no.'

'Clearly,' said Cicero, turning to the jury, 'Herennius had not paid Verres and his gang of thieves a large enough bribe.'

For most of the trial, Verres had sat slumped in his chair, but on this morning, fired by drink, he jumped up and began shouting that he had never taken any such bribe. Hortensius had to pull him down. Cicero ignored him and went on calmly questioning his witness.

'This is an extraordinary situation, is it not? A hundred of you vouch for the identity of this Roman citizen, yet Verres does not even wait an hour to establish the truth of who he is. How do you account for it?'

'I can account for it easily, Senator. Herennius was a passenger on a ship from Spain which was impounded with all its cargo by Verres's agents. He was sent to the Stone Quarries, along with everyone else on board, then dragged out to be publicly executed as a pirate. What Verres did not realise was that Herennius was not from Spain at all. He was known to the Roman community in Syracuse and would be recognised. But by the time Verres discovered his mistake, Herennius could not be allowed to go free, because he knew too much about what the governor was up to.'

'Forgive me, I do not understand,' said Cicero, playing the innocent. 'Why would Verres want to execute an innocent passenger on a cargo ship as a pirate?'

'He needed to show a sufficient number of executions.'

'Why?'

'Because he was being paid bribes to let the real pirates go free.'

Verres was up on his feet again shouting that it was a lie, and this time Cicero did not ignore him, but took a few paces towards him. 'A lie, you monster? A lie? Then why in your own prison records does it state that Herennius was released? And why do they further state that the notorious pirate captain, Heracleo, was executed, when no one on the island ever saw him die? I shall tell you why – because you, the Roman governor, responsible for the safety of the seas, were all the while taking bribes from the very pirates themselves!'

'Cicero, the great lawyer, who thinks himself so clever!' said Verres bitterly, his words slurred by drink. 'Who thinks he knows everything! Well, here is something you don't know. I have Heracleo in my private custody, here in my house in Rome, and he can tell you all himself that it's a lie!'

Amazing now, to reflect that a man could blurt out something so foolish, but the facts are there – they are in the record – and amid the pandemonium in court, Cicero could be heard demanding of Glabrio that the famous pirate be fetched from Verres's house by the lictors and placed in official custody, 'for the public safety'. Then, while that was being done, he called as his second witness of the day Gaius Numitorius. Privately, I thought that Cicero was rushing it too much: that he could have milked the admission about Heracleo for more. But the great advocate had sensed that the moment for the kill had arrived, and for months, ever since we had first landed in Sicily, he had known exactly the blade he wished to use. Numitorius swore an oath to tell the truth and took the stand, and Cicero quickly led him through his testimony to establish the essential facts about Publius Gavius: that he was a merchant travelling on a ship from Spain; that his ship had been impounded and the passengers all taken to the Stone Quarries, from which

Gavius had somehow managed to escape; that he had made his way to Messana to take a ship to the mainland, had been apprehended as he went aboard, and handed over to Verres when he visited the town. The silence of the listening multitudes was intense.

'Describe to the court what happened next.'

'Verres convened a tribunal in the forum of Messana,' said Numitorius, 'and then he had Gavius dragged before him. He announced to everyone that this man was a spy, for which there was only one just penalty. Then he ordered a cross set up overlooking the straits to Regium, so that the prisoner could gaze upon Italy as he died, and had Gavius stripped naked and publicly flogged before us all. Then he was tortured with hot irons. And then he was crucified.'

'Did Gavius speak at all?'

'Only at the beginning, to swear that the accusation was not true. He was not a foreign spy. He was a Roman citizen, a councillor from the town of Consa, and a former soldier in the Roman cavalry, under the command of Lucius Raecius.'

'What did Verres say to that.'

'He said that these were lies, and commanded that the execution begin.'

'Can you describe how Gavius met his dreadful death?'

'He met it very bravely, Senator.'

'Like a Roman?'

'Like a Roman.'

'Did he cry out at all?' (I knew what Cicero was after.)

'Only while he was being whipped, and he could see the irons being heated.'

'And what did he say?'

'Every time a blow landed, he said, "I am a Roman citizen."'

'Would you repeat what he said, more loudly please, so that all can hear.'

'He said, "I am a Roman citizen."'

'So just that?' said Cicero. 'Let me be sure I understand you. A blow lands' – he put his wrists together, raised them above his head and jerked forwards, as if his back had just been lashed – 'and he says, through gritted teeth, "I am a Roman citizen." A blow lands' – and again he jerked forwards – '"I am a Roman citizen." A blow lands. *"I am a Roman citizen –"*'

These flat words of mine cannot begin to convey the effect of Cicero's performance upon those who saw it. The hush around the court amplified his words. It was as if all of us now were witnesses to this monstrous miscarriage of justice. Some men and women – friends of Gavius, I believe – began to scream, and there was a growing swell of outrage from the masses in the forum. Yet again, Verres shook off Hortensius's restraining hand and stood up. 'He was a filthy spy!' he bellowed. 'A spy! He only said it to delay his proper punishment!'

'*But he said it!*' said Cicero, triumphantly, wheeling on him, his finger jabbing in outrage. 'You admit he said it! Out of your own mouth I accuse you – the man claimed to be a Roman citizen and you did nothing! This mention of his citizenship did not lead you to hesitate or delay, even for a little, the infliction of this cruel and disgusting death! If you, Verres, had been made a prisoner in Persia or the remotest part of India, and were being dragged off to execution, what cry would you be uttering, except that you were a Roman citizen? What then of this man whom you were hurrying to his death? Could not that statement, that claim of citizenship, have saved him for an hour, for a day, while its truth was checked? No, it could not – not with you in the judgement seat! And yet the poorest man, of humblest birth, in whatever savage land, has always until now had the confidence to know that the cry "I am a Roman citizen" is his final defence and sanctuary. It was not Gavius, not one obscure man, whom you nailed upon that cross of agony: it was the universal principle that Romans are free men!'

The roar which greeted the end of Cicero's tirade was terrifying. Rather than diminishing after a few moments, it gathered itself afresh and rose in volume and pitch, and I became aware, at the periphery of my vision, of a movement towards us. The awnings under which some of the spectators had been standing as protection against the sun began to collapse with a terrible tearing sound. A man dropped off a balcony on to the crowd beneath. There were screams. What was unmistakably a lynch mob began storming the steps to the platform. Hortensius and Verres stood up so quickly in their panic that they knocked over the bench behind them. Glabrio could be heard yelling that the court was adjourned, then he and his lictors hastened up the remaining steps towards the temple, with the accused and his eminent counsel in undignified pursuit. Some of the jury also fled into the sanctuary of the holy building (but not Catulus: I distinctly remember him standing like a sharp rock, staring unflinchingly ahead, as the current of bodies broke and swirled around him). The heavy bronze doors slammed shut. It was left to Cicero to try to restore order by climbing on to his own bench and gesturing for calm, but four or five men, rough-looking fellows, ran up and seized his legs and lifted him away. I was terrified, for both his safety and my own, but he stretched out his arms as if he was embracing the whole world. When they had settled him on their shoulders they spun him around to face the forum. The blast of applause was like the opening of a furnace door and the chant of 'Cic-er-o! Cic-er-o! Cic-er-o!' split the skies of Rome.

And that, at last, was the end of Gaius Verres. We never learned exactly what went on inside the temple after Glabrio suspended the sitting, but Cicero's belief was that Hortensius and Metellus made it clear to their client that further defence was useless. Their own dignity and authority were in tatters: they simply had to cut him adrift before any more harm was done to the reputation of the senate. It no longer mattered how lavishly he had bribed the jury – no member of it would dare to vote to acquit him after the scenes they had just witnessed. At any rate, Verres slipped out of the temple when the mob had dispersed, and fled the city at nightfall – disguised, some say, as a woman – riding full pelt for southern Gaul. His destination was the port of Massilia, where exiles could traditionally swap their hard-luck stories over grilled mullet and pretend they were on the Bay of Naples.

All that remained to do now was to fix the level of his fine, and when Cicero returned home he convened a meeting to discuss the appropriate figure. Nobody will ever know the full value of what Verres stole during his years in Sicily – I have heard an estimate of forty million – but Lucius, as usual, was eager for the most radical course: the seizure of every asset Verres possessed. Quintus thought ten million would be about right. Cicero was curiously silent for a man who had just recorded such a stupendous victory, and sat in his study moodily toying with a metal stylus. Early in the afternoon, we received a letter from Hortensius, relaying an offer from Verres to pay one million into court as compensation. Lucius was particularly appalled –

'an insult', he called it – and Cicero had no hesitation in sending the messenger away with a flea in his ear. An hour later he was back, with what Hortensius called his 'final figure': a settlement of one and a half million. This time, Cicero dictated a longer reply:

From: Marcus Tullius Cicero
To: Quintus Hortensius Hortalus
Greetings!
In view of the ludicrously low sum your client is proposing as compensation for his unparalleled wickedness, I intend asking Glabrio to allow me to continue the prosecution tomorrow, when I shall exercise my right to address the court on this and other matters.

'Let us see how much he and his aristocratic friends relish the prospect of having their noses rubbed further into their own filth,' he exclaimed to me. I finished sealing the letter, and when I returned from giving it to the messenger, Cicero set about dictating the speech he proposed to deliver the next day – a slashing attack on the aristocrats for prostituting their great names, and the names of their ancestors, in defence of such a scoundrel as Verres. Urged on by Lucius in particular, he poured out his loathing. 'We are aware with what jealousy, with what dislike, the merit and energy of "new men" are regarded by certain of the "nobles"; that we have only to shut our eyes for a moment to find ourselves caught in some trap; that if we leave them the smallest opening for any suspicion or charge of misconduct, we have to suffer for it at once; that we must never relax our vigilance, and never take a holiday. We have enemies – let us face them; tasks to perform – let us shoulder them; not forgetting that an open and declared enemy is less formidable than one who hides himself and says nothing!'

'There go another thousand votes,' muttered Quintus.

The afternoon wore on in this way, without any answer from Hortensius, until, at length, not long before dusk, there was a commotion from the street, and soon afterwards Eros came running into the study with the breathless news that Pompey the Great himself was in the vestibule. This was indeed an extraordinary turn-up, but Cicero and his brother had time to do no more than blink at one another before that familiar military voice could be heard barking, 'Where is he? Where is the greatest orator of the age?'

Cicero muttered an oath beneath his breath, and went out into the tablinum, followed by Quintus, then Lucius, and finally myself, just in time to see the senior consul come striding out of the atrium. The confines of that modest house made him bulk even larger than he did normally. 'And there he is!' he exclaimed. 'There is the man whom everyone comes to see!' He made straight for Cicero, threw his powerful arms around him, and embraced him in a bear hug. From where I was standing, just behind Cicero, I could see Pompey's crafty grey eyes taking in each of us in turn, and when he released his embarrassed host, he insisted on being introduced, even to me, so that I – a humble domestic slave from Arpinum – could now boast, at the age of thirty-four, that I had shaken hands with both the ruling consuls of Rome.

He had left his bodyguards out in the street and had come into the house entirely alone, a significant mark of trust and favour. Cicero, whose manners as always were impeccable, ordered Eros to tell Terentia that Pompey the Great was downstairs, and I was instructed to pour some wine.

'Only a little,' said Pompey, putting his large hand over the cup. 'We are on our way to dinner, and shall only stay a moment. But we could not pass our neighbour without calling in to pay our respects. We have been watching your progress, Cicero, over these past few days. We have been receiving reports from our friend Glabrio. Magnificent. We drink your health.' He raised his cup, but not a drop, I noticed, touched his lips. 'And now that this great enterprise is successfully behind you, we hope that we may see a little more of you, especially as I shall soon be merely a private citizen again.'

Cicero gave a slight bow. 'That would be my pleasure.'

'The day after tomorrow, for example – how are you placed?'

'That is the day of the opening of your games. Surely you will be occupied? Perhaps some other time . . .'

'Nonsense. Come and watch the opening from our box. It will do you no harm to be seen in our company. Let the world observe our friendship,' he added grandly. 'You enjoy the games, do you not?'

Cicero hesitated, and I could see his brain working through the consequences, of both refusal and acceptance. But really he had no choice. 'I adore the games,' he said. 'I can think of nothing I would rather do.'

'Excellent,' beamed Pompey. At that moment Eros returned, with a message that Terentia was lying down, unwell, and sent her apologies. 'That is a pity,' said Pompey, looking slightly put out. 'But let us hope there will be some future opportunity.' He handed me his untouched wine. 'We must be on our way. No doubt you have much to do. Incidentally,' he said, turning on the threshold of the atrium, 'have you settled on the level of the fine yet?'

'Not yet,' replied Cicero.

'What have they offered?'

'One and a half million.'

'Take it,' said Pompey. 'You have covered them in shit. No need to make them eat it, too. It would be embarrassing to me personally and injurious to the stability of the state to proceed with this case further. You understand me?' He nodded in a friendly way and walked out. We heard the front door open and the commander of his bodyguard call his men to attention. The door closed. For a little while, nobody spoke.

'What a ghastly man,' said Cicero. 'Bring me another drink.' As I fetched the jug, I saw Lucius frowning.

'What gives him the right to talk to you like that?' he asked. 'He said it was a social visit.'

'A social visit! Oh, Lucius!' Cicero laughed. 'That was a visit from the rent collector.'

'The rent collector? What rent do you owe him?' Lucius might have been a philosopher, but he was not a complete idiot, and he realised then what had happened. 'Oh, I understand!' A look of disgust came across his face, and he turned away.

'Spare me your superiority,' said Cicero, catching his arm. 'I had no choice. Marcus Metellus had just drawn the extortion court. The jury was bribed. The hearing was fixed to fail. I was this far' – Cicero measured an inch with his thumb and forefinger – 'from abandoning the whole prosecution. And then Terentia said to me, "Make your speech shorter," and I realised that was the answer – to produce every document and every witness, and do it all in ten days, and *shame* them – that was it, Lucius: you understand me? – *shame* them before the whole of Rome, so they had no alternative except to find him guilty.'

In such a way did he speak, working all his persuasive powers upon his cousin, as if Lucius were a one-man jury which he needed to convince – reading his face, trying to find within it clues to the right words and arguments which would unlock his support.

'But *Pompey*,' said Lucius, bitterly. 'After what he did to you before!'

'All I needed, Lucius, was one thing – one tiny, tiny favour – and that was the assurance that I could proceed as I wished, and call my witnesses straight away. No bribery was involved; no corruption. I just knew I had to be sure to secure Glabrio's consent beforehand. But I could hardly, as the prosecutor, approach the praetor of the court myself. So I racked my brains: who could?'

Quintus said, 'There was only one man in Rome, Lucius.'

'Exactly!' cried Cicero. 'Only one man to whom Glabrio was honour-bound to listen. The man who had given him his son back, when his divorced wife died – Pompey.'

'But it was not a tiny favour,' said Lucius. 'It was a massive interference. And now there is a massive price to be paid for it – and not by you, but by the people of Sicily.'

'The people of Sicily?' repeated Cicero, beginning to lose his temper. 'The people of Sicily have never had a truer friend than me. There would never have been a prosecution without me. There would never have been an offer of one and a half million without me. By heaven, Gaius Verres would have been *consul* in two years' time but for me! You cannot reproach me for abandoning the people of Sicily!'

'Then refuse to pay his rent,' said Lucius, seizing hold of his hand. 'Tomorrow, in court, press for the maximum damages, and to hell with Pompey. You have the whole of Rome on your side. That jury will not dare to go against you. Who cares about Pompey? In five months' time, as he says himself, he will not even be consul. Promise me.'

Cicero clasped Lucius's hand fervently in both of his and gazed deep into his eyes – the old double-grip sincere routine, which I had seen so often in this very room. 'I promise you,' he said. 'I promise you I shall think about it.'

Perhaps he did think about it. Who am I to judge? But I doubt it can have occupied his mind for more than an instant. Cicero was no revolutionary. He never desired to set himself at the head of a mob, tearing down the state: and that would have been his only hope of survival, if he had turned Pompey against him as well as the aristocracy. 'The trouble with Lucius,' he said putting his feet up on the desk after his cousin had gone, 'is that he thinks politics is a fight for justice. Politics is a profession.'

'Do you think Verres bribed Pompey to intervene, to lower the damages?' asked Quintus, voicing exactly the possibility which had occurred to me.

'It could be. More likely he simply wants to avoid being caught in the middle of a civil war between the people and the senate. Speaking for myself, I would be happy to seize everything Verres possesses, and leave the wretch to live on Gaulish grass. But that is not going to happen,' he sighed, 'so we had better see how far we can make this one and a half million stretch.'

The three of us spent the rest of the evening compiling a list of the most worthy claimants, and after Cicero had deducted his own costs, of close to one hundred thousand, we reckoned he could just about manage to fulfil his obligations, at least to the likes of Sthenius, and to those witnesses who had travelled all the way to Rome. But what could one say to the priests? How could one put a price on looted temple statues made of gems and precious metals, long since broken up and melted down by

Verres's goldsmiths? And what payment could ever recompense the families and friends of Gavius and Herennius and the other innocents he had murdered? The work gave Cicero his first real taste of what it is like to have power – which is usually, when it comes down to it, a matter of choosing between equally unpalatable options – and fairly bitter he found it.

We went into court in the usual manner the following morning, and there was the usual big crowd in their usual places – everything the same, in fact, except for the absence of Verres, and the presence of twenty or thirty men of the magistrates' patrol, stationed around the perimeter of the tribunal. Glabrio made a short speech, opening the session and warning that he would not tolerate any disturbances similar to those which had occurred the previous day. Then he called on Hortensius to make a statement.

'Due to ill health,' Hortensius began, and there was the most wonderful shout of laughter from all sides. It was some time before he was able to proceed. 'Due to ill health,' he repeated, 'brought on by the strain of these proceedings, and wishing to spare the state any further disruption, my client Gaius Verres no longer proposes to offer a defence to the charges brought by the special prosecutor.'

He sat down. There was applause from the Sicilians at this concession, but little response from the spectators. They were waiting to take their lead from Cicero. He stood, thanked Hortensius for his statement – 'somewhat shorter than the speeches he is in the habit of making in these surroundings' – and demanded the maximum penalty under the Cornelian Law: a full loss of civil rights, in perpetuity, 'so that never again can the shadow of Gaius Verres menace his victims or threaten the just administration of the Roman republic'. This elicited the first real cheer of the morning.

'I wish,' continued Cicero, 'that I could undo his crimes, and restore to both men and gods all that he has robbed from them. I wish I could give back to Juno the offerings and adornments of her shrines at Melita and Samos. I wish Minerva could see again the decorations of her temple at Syracuse. I wish Diana's statue could be restored to the town of Segesta, and Mercury's to the people of Tyndaris. I wish I could undo the double injury to Ceres, whose images were carried away from both Henna and Catina. But the villain has fled, leaving behind only the stripped walls and bare floors of his houses here in Rome and in the country. These are the only assets which can be seized and sold. His counsel assesses the value of these at one and a half million sesterces, and this is what I must ask for and accept as recompense for his crimes.'

There was a groan, and someone shouted, 'Not enough!'

'It is not enough. I agree. And perhaps some of those in this court, who defended Verres when his star was rising, and others who promised him their support if they found themselves among his jurors, might inspect their consciences – might inspect, indeed, the contents of their villas!'

This brought Hortensius to his feet to complain that the prosecutor was talking in riddles.

'Well,' responded Cicero in a flash, 'as Verres provided him with an ivory sphinx, the consul-elect should find no difficulty solving riddles.'

It cannot have been a premeditated joke, as Cicero had no idea what Hortensius was going to say. Or perhaps, on second thoughts, having written that, I am being naïve, and it was actually part of that store of spontaneous witticisms which Cicero regularly laid up by candlelight to use should the opportunity arise. Whatever the truth, it was proof of how important humour can be on a public occasion, for nobody now remembers a thing about that last day in court except Cicero's crack about the ivory sphinx. I am not even sure, in retrospect, that it is particularly funny. But it brought the house down, and transformed what could have been an embarrassing speech into yet another triumph. 'Sit down quickly' – that was always Molon's advice when things were going well, and Cicero took it. I handed him a towel and he mopped his face and dried his hands as the applause continued. And with that, his exertions in the prosecution of Gaius Verres were at an end.

That afternoon, the senate met for its final debate before it went into a fifteen-day recess for Pompey's games. By the time Cicero had finished smoothing matters over with the Sicilians, he was late for the start of the session, and we had to run together from the Temple of Castor, right across the forum to the senate house. Crassus, as the presiding consul for the month, had already called the house to order and was reading the latest dispatch from Lucullus on the progress of the campaign in the East. Rather than interrupt him by making a conspicuous entry, Cicero stood at the bar of the chamber, and we listened to Lucullus's report. The aristocratic general had, by his own account, scored a series of crushing victories, entering the kingdom of Tigranes, defeating the king himself in battle, slaughtering tens of thousands of the enemy, advancing deeper into hostile territory to capture the city of Nisibisis, and taking the king's brother as hostage.

'Crassus must feel like throwing up,' Cicero whispered to me gleefully. 'His only consolation will be to know that Pompey is even more furiously jealous.' And, indeed, Pompey, sitting beside Crassus, his arms folded, did look sunk in a gloomy reverie.

When Crassus had finished speaking, Cicero took advantage of the lull to enter the chamber. The day was hot and the shafts of light from the high windows lit jewelled swirls of midges. He walked purposefully, head erect, watched by everyone, down the central aisle, past his old place in obscurity by the door, towards the consular dais. The praetorian bench seemed full, but Cicero stood patiently beside it, waiting to claim his rightful place, for he knew – and the house knew – that the ancient reward for a successful prosecutor was the assumption of the defeated man's rank. I do not know how long the silence went on, but it seemed an awfully long time to me, during which the only sound came from the pigeons in the roof. It was Afranius who finally beckoned to him to sit beside him, and who cleared sufficient space by roughly shoving his neighbours along the wooden seat. Cicero picked his way across half a dozen pairs of outstretched legs and wedged himself defiantly into his place. He glanced around at his rivals, and met and held the gaze of each. No one challenged him. Eventually, someone rose to speak, and in a grudging voice congratulated Lucullus and his victorious legions – it might have been Pompey, now I come to think of it. Gradually the low drone of background conversation resumed.

I close my eyes and I see their faces still in the golden light of that late-summer afternoon – Cicero, Crassus, Pompey, Hortensius, Catulus, Catilina, the Metellus brothers – and it is hard for me to believe that they, and their ambitions, and even the very building they sat in, are now all so much dust.

PART TWO

PRAETORIAN

68–64 BC

'Nam eloquentiam quae admirationem non habet nullam iudico.'

'Eloquence which does not startle I don't consider eloquence.'

Cicero, letter to Brutus, 48 BC

X

I propose to resume my account at a point more than two years after the last roll ended – an elision which I fear says much about human nature, for if you were to ask me: 'Tiro, why do you choose to skip such a long period in Cicero's life?' I should be obliged to reply: 'Because, my friend, those were happy years, and few subjects make more tedious reading than happiness.'

The senator's aedileship turned out to be a great success. His chief responsibility was to keep the city supplied with cheap grain, and here his prosecution of Verres reaped him a great reward. To show their gratitude for his advocacy, the farmers and corn merchants of Sicily not only helped him by keeping their prices low: on one occasion they even gave him an entire shipment for nothing. Cicero was shrewd enough to ensure that others shared the credit. From the aediles' headquarters in the Temple of Ceres, he passed this bounty on for distribution to the hundred or so precinct bosses who really ran Rome, and many, out of gratitude, became his clients. With their help, over the following months, he built an electoral machine second to none (Quintus used to boast that he could have a crowd of two hundred on the streets within an hour whenever he chose), and henceforth little occurred in the city which the Ciceros did not know about. If some builders or a shopkeeper, for example, needed a particular licence, or wished to have their premises put on to the water supply, or were worried about the state of a local temple, sooner or later their problems were likely to come to the notice of the two brothers. It was this laborious attention to humdrum detail, as much as his soaring rhetoric, which made Cicero such a formidable politician. He even staged good games – or, rather, Quintus did, on his behalf – and at the climax of the Festival of Ceres, when, in accordance with tradition, foxes were released into the Circus Maximus with flaming torches tied to their backs, the entire crowd of two hundred thousand rose to acclaim him in the official box.

'That so many people can derive so much pleasure from such a revolting spectacle,' he said to me when he returned home that night, 'almost makes one doubt the very premise on which democracy is based.' But he was pleased nevertheless that the masses now thought of him as a good sport, as well as 'the Scholar' and 'the Greek'.

Matters went equally well with his legal practice. Hortensius, after a typically smooth and untroubled year as consul, spent increasingly lengthy periods on the Bay of Naples, communing with his bejewelled fish and wine-soaked trees, leaving Cicero in complete domination of the Roman bar. Gifts and legacies from grateful clients soon began flowing in such profusion that he was even able to advance his brother the million he needed to enter the senate – for Quintus had belatedly set his heart on a political career, even though he was a poor speaker and Cicero privately believed that soldiering was better suited to his temperament. But despite his increasing wealth and prestige, Cicero refused to move out of his father's house, fearing it would tarnish his image as the People's Champion to be seen swanking around on the Palatine Hill. Instead, without consulting Terentia, he borrowed heavily against his future earnings to buy a grand country villa, thirteen miles from the prying eyes of the city voters, in the Alban Hills near Tusculum. She pretended to be annoyed when he took her out to see it, and maintained that the elevated climate was bad for her rheumatics. But I could tell that she was secretly delighted to have such a fashionable retreat, only half a day's journey from Rome. Catulus owned the adjoining property, and Hortensius also had a house not far away, but such was the hostility between Cicero and the aristocrats that, despite the long summer days he spent reading and writing in his villa's cool and poplared glades, they never once invited him to dine. This did not disturb Cicero; rather, it amused him, for the house had once belonged to the nobles' greatest hero, Sulla, and he knew how much it must irritate them to see it in the hands of a new man from Arpinum. The villa had not been redecorated for more than a decade, and when he took possession an entire wall was devoted to a mural showing the dictator receiving a military decoration from his troops. Cicero made sure all his neighbours knew that his first act as owner was to have it whitewashed over.

Happy, then, was Cicero in the autumn of his thirty-ninth year: prosperous, popular, well rested after a summer in the country, and looking forward to the elections the following July, when he would be old enough to stand for a praetorship – the final stepping-stone before the glittering prize of the consulship itself.

And at this critical juncture in his fortunes, just as his luck was about to desert him and his life become interesting again, my narrative resumes.

At the end of September it was Pompey's birthday, and for the third year in succession Cicero received a summons to attend a dinner in his honour. He groaned when he opened the message, for he had discovered that there are few blessings in life more onerous than the friendship of a great man. At first, he had found it flattering to be invited into Pompey's inner circle. But after a while he grew weary of listening to the same old military anecdotes – usually illustrated by the manoeuvring of plates and decanters around the dinner table – of how the young general had outwitted three Marian armies at Auximum, or killed seventeen thousand Numidians in a single afternoon at the age of twenty-four, or finally defeated the Spanish rebels near Valencia. Pompey had been giving orders since he was seventeen and perhaps for this reason had developed none of Cicero's subtlety of intellect. Conversation as the senator enjoyed it – spontaneous wit, shared gossip, sharp observations which might be spun off mutually into some profound or fantastic dissertation on the nature of human affairs – all this was alien to Pompey. The general liked to hold forth against a background of respectful silence, assert some platitude, and then sit back and bask in the flattery of his guests. Cicero used to say he would sooner have all his teeth drawn by a drunken barber in the Forum Boarium than listen to another of these mealtime monologues.

The root of the problem was that Pompey was bored. At the end of his consulship, as promised, he had retired into private life with his wife, young son and baby daughter. But then what? Lacking any talent for oratory, there was nothing to occupy him in the law courts. Literary composition held no interest for him. He could only watch in a stew of jealousy as Lucullus continued his conquest of Mithradates. Not yet forty, his future, as the saying went, seemed all behind him. He would make occasional forays down from his mansion and into the senate, not to speak but to listen to the debates – processions for which he insisted on an immense escort of friends and clients. Cicero, who felt obliged to walk at least part of the way with him, observed that it was like watching an elephant trying to make itself at home in an anthill.

But still, he was the greatest man in the world, with a huge following among the voters, and not to be crossed, especially with an election less than a year away. Only that summer he had secured a tribuneship for his crony Gabinius: he still kept a hand in politics. So on the thirtieth day of September, Cicero went off as usual to the birthday party, returning later in the evening to regale Quintus, Lucius and myself with an account of events. Like a child, Pompey delighted in receiving presents, and Cicero had taken him a manuscript letter in the hand of Zeno, the founder of stoicism, two centuries old and extremely valuable, which had been acquired for him in Athens by Atticus. He would dearly have loved to have kept it for his own library in Tusculum, but he hoped that by giving it to Pompey he could begin to tempt the general into an interest in philosophy. Instead, Pompey had barely glanced at it before setting it aside in favour of a gift from Gabinius, of a silver rhino horn containing some Egyptian aphrodisiac made of baboon excrement. 'How I wish I could have retrieved that letter!' groaned Cicero, flopping down on to a couch, the back of his hand resting on his forehead. 'Even now it's probably being used by some kitchen maid to light the fire.'

'Who else was there?' asked Quintus eagerly. He had only been back in Rome for a few days, following his term as quaestor in Umbria, and was avid for the latest news.

'Oh, the usual cohort. Our fine new tribune-elect Gabinius, obviously, and his father-in-law, the art connoisseur Palicanus; Rome's greatest dancer, Afranius; that Spanish creature of

Pompey's, Balbus; Varro, the household polymath. Oh, and Marcus Fonteius,' he added lightly, but not so lightly that Lucius did not immediately detect the significance.

'And what did you talk about with Fonteius?' enquired Lucius, in the same clumsy attempt at an offhand manner.

'This and that.'

'His prosecution?'

'Naturally.'

'And who is defending the rascal?'

Cicero paused, and then said quietly, 'I am.'

I should explain, for those not familiar with the case, that this Fonteius had been governor of Further Gaul about five years earlier, and that one winter, when Pompey was particularly hard pressed fighting the rebels in Spain, he had sent the beleaguered general sufficient supplies and fresh recruits to enable him to survive until the spring. That had been the start of their friendship. Fonteius had gone on to make himself extremely rich, in the Verres manner, by extorting various illegal taxes out of the native population. The Gauls had at first put up with it, telling themselves that robbery and exploitation have ever been the handmaids of civilisation. But after Cicero's triumphant prosecution of the governor of Sicily, the chief of the Gauls, Induciomarus, had come to Rome to ask the senator to represent them in the extortion court. Lucius had been all for it; in fact it was he who had brought Induciomarus to the house: a wild-looking creature, dressed in his barbarian outfit of jacket and trousers – he gave me quite a shock when I opened the door to him one morning. Cicero, however, had politely declined. A year had passed, but now the Gauls had finally found a credible legal team in Plaetorius, who was a praetor-elect, and Marcus Fabius as his junior. The case would soon be in court.

'That is outrageous,' said Lucius, hotly. 'You cannot defend him. He is as guilty as Verres was.'

'Nonsense. He has neither killed anyone nor falsely imprisoned anyone either. The worse that can be said is that he once imposed excessive duties on the wine traders of Narbonne, and made some locals pay more than others to repair the roads. Besides,' added Cicero quickly, before Lucius could challenge this somewhat generous interpretation of Fonteius's activities, 'who are you or I to determine his guilt? It is a matter for the court to decide, not us. Or would you be a tyrant and deny him an advocate?'

'I would deny him *your* advocacy,' Lucius responded. 'You have heard from Induciomarus's own lips the evidence against him. Is all that to be cancelled out, simply because Fonteius is a friend of Pompey?'

'It has nothing to do with Pompey.'

'Then why do it?'

'Politics,' said Cicero, suddenly sitting up and swinging himself round so that his feet were planted on the floor. He fixed his gaze on Lucius and said very seriously: 'The most fatal error for any statesman is to allow his fellow countrymen, even for an instant, to suspect that he puts the interests of foreigners above those of his own people. That is the lie which my enemies spread about me after I represented the Sicilians in the Verres case, and that is the calumny which I can lay to rest if I defend Fonteius now.'

'And the Gauls?'

'The Gauls will be represented perfectly adequately by Plaetorius.'

'Not as well as they would be by you.'

'But you say yourself that Fonteius has a weak case. Let the weakest case be defended by the strongest advocate. What could be fairer than that?'

Cicero flashed him his most charming smile, but for once Lucius refused to be parted from his anger. Knowing, I suspect, that the only sure way to defeat Cicero in argument was to with-draw from the conversation altogether, he stood and limped across to the atrium. I had not realised until that moment how ill he looked, how thin and stooped; he had never really recovered from the strain of his efforts in Sicily. 'Words, words, words,' he said bitterly. 'Is there no end to the tricks you can make them perform? But, as with all men, your great strength is also your weakness, Marcus, and I am sorry for you, absolutely I am, because soon you will not be able to tell your tricks from the truth. And then you will be lost.'

'The truth,' laughed Cicero. 'Now there is a loose term for a philosopher to use!' But he was addressing his witticism to the air, for Lucius had gone.

'He will be back,' said Quintus.

But he did not come back, and over the following days Cicero went about his preparations for the trial with the determined expression of a man who has resigned himself to some distasteful but necessary surgical procedure. As for his client: Fonteius had been anticipating his prosecution for three years, and had used the time well, to acquire a mass of evidence to support his defence. He had witnesses from Spain and Gaul, including officers from Pompey's camp, and various sly and greedy tax farmers and merchants – members of the Roman community in Gaul, who would have sworn that night was day and land sea if it would have turned them a reasonable profit. The only trouble, as Cicero realised once he had mastered his brief, was that Fonteius was plainly guilty. He sat for a long time staring at the wall in his study, while I tiptoed around him, and it is important that I convey what he was doing, for it is necessary in order to understand his character. He was not merely trying, as a cyncial and second-rate advocate might have done, to devise some clever tactic in order to outwit the prosecution. *He was trying to find something to believe in.* That was the core of his genius, both as an advocate and as a statesman. 'What convinces is conviction,' he used to say. 'You simply must believe the argument you are advancing, otherwise you are lost. No chain of reasoning, no matter how logical or elegant or brilliant, will win the case, if your audience senses that belief is missing.' Just one thing to believe in, that was all he needed, and then he could latch on to it, build out from it, embellish it, and transform it just for the space of an hour or two into the most important issue in the world, and deliver it with a passion that would obliterate the flimsy rationality of his opponents. Afterwards he would usually forget it entirely. And what did he believe in when it came to Marcus Fonteius? He gazed at the wall for many hours and concluded only this: that his client was a Roman, being assailed within his own city by Rome's traditional enemy, the Gauls, and that whatever the rights and wrongs of the case, that was a kind of treachery.

Such was the line which Cicero took when he found himself once again in the familiar surroundings of the extortion court before the Temple of Castor. The trial lasted from the end of October until the middle of November, and was most keenly fought, witness by witness, right up until the final day, when Cicero delivered the closing speech for the defence. From my place behind the senator, I had, from the opening day, kept an eye out for Lucius among the crowd of spectators, but it was only on that last morning that I fancied I saw him, a pale shadow, propped against a pillar at the very back of the audience. And if it was him – and I do not know it was – I have often wondered what he thought of his cousin's oratory, as he tore into the evidence of the Gauls, jabbing his finger at Induciomarus – 'Does he actually know what is meant by giving evidence? Is the greatest chief of the Gauls worthy to be set on the same level as even the meanest citizen of Rome?' – and demanding to know how a Roman jury could possibly believe the word of a man whose gods demanded human victims: 'For who does not know that to this very day they retain the monstrous and barbarous custom of sacrificing men?' What would he have said to Cicero's description of the Gaulish witnesses, 'swaggering from end to end of the forum, with proud and unflinching expressions on their faces and barbarian menaces upon their lips'? And what would he have made of Cicero's brilliant *coup de théâtre* at the very end, of producing in court, in the closing moments of his speech, Fonteius's sister, a vestal virgin, clad from head to toe in her official garb of a flowing white gown, with a white linen shawl around her narrow shoulders, and who raised her white veil to show the jury her tears – a sight which made her brother also break down weeping? Cicero laid his hand gently on his client's shoulder.

'From this peril, gentlemen, defend a gallant and blameless citizen. Let the world see that you place more confidence in the evidence of our fellow countrymen than in that of foreigners, that you have greater regard for the welfare of our citizens than for the caprice of our foes, that you set more store by the entreaties of she who presides over your sacrifices than by the effrontery of those who have waged war against the sacrifices and shrines of all the world. Finally, gentlemen, see to it – and here the dignity of the Roman people is most vitally engaged –

see to it that you show that the prayers of a vestal maid have more weight with you than the threats of Gauls.'

Well, that speech certainly did the trick, both for Fonteius, who was acquitted, and for Cicero, who was never again regarded as anything less than the most fervent patriot in Rome. I looked up after I had finished making my shorthand record, but it was impossible to discern individuals in the crowd any more – it had become a single, seething creature, aroused by Cicero's technique to a chanting ecstasy of national self-glorification. Anyway, I sincerely hope that Lucius was not present, and there must surely be a chance that he was not, for it was only a few hours later that he was discovered at his home quite dead.

Cicero was dining privately with Terentia when the message came. The bearer was one of Lucius's slaves. Scarcely more than a boy, he was weeping uncontrollably, so it fell to me to take the news in to the senator. He looked up blankly from his meal when I told him, and stared straight at me, and said irritably, 'No,' as if I had offered him the wrong set of documents in court. And for a long time that was all he said: 'No, no.' He did not move; he did not even blink. The working of his brain seemed locked. It was Terentia who eventually spoke, and suggested gently that he should go and find out what had happened, whereupon he started searching dumbly for his shoes. 'Keep an eye on him, Tiro,' she said quietly to me.

Grief kills time. All that I retain of that night, and of the days which followed, are fragments of scenes, like some luridly brilliant hallucinations left behind after a fever. I recall how thin and wasted Lucius's body was when we found it, lying on its right side in his cot, the knees drawn up, the left hand laid flat across his eyes, and how Cicero, in the traditional manner, bent over him with a candle, to call him back to life. 'What was he seeing?' – that was what he kept asking: 'What was he seeing?' Cicero was not, as I have indicated, a superstitious man, but he could not rid himself of the conviction that Lucius had been presented with a vision of unparalleled horror at the end, and that this had somehow frightened him to death. As to how he died – well here I must confess to carrying a secret all these years, of which I shall be glad now to unburden myself. There was a pestle and mortar in the corner of that little room, with what Cicero – and I, too, at first – took to be a bunch of fennel lying beside it. It was a reasonable supposition, for among Lucius's many chronic ailments was poor digestion, which he attempted to relieve by a solution of fennel oil. Only later, when I was clearing the room, did I rub those lacy leaves with my thumb, and detect the frightful, musty, dead-mouse odour of hemlock. I knew then that Lucius had tired of this life, and for whatever reason – despair at its injustices, weariness with his ailments – had chosen to die like his hero, Socrates. This information I always meant to share with Cicero and Quintus. But for some reason, in the sadness of those days, I kept it to myself, and then the proper time for disclosure had passed, and it seemed better to let them continue to believe he had died involuntarily.

I also recall how Cicero spent such a great sum on flowers and incense that, after Lucius had been cleaned and anointed and laid on his funeral couch in his finest toga, his skinny feet pointing towards the door, he seemed, even in that drab November, to be in an Elysian grove of petals and fragrant scent. I remember the surprising number, for such a solitary man, of friends and neighbours who came to pay their respects, and the funeral procession at dusk out to the Esquiline Field, with young Frugi weeping so hard he could not catch his breath. I recall the dirges and the music, and the respectful glances of the citizens along the route – for this was a Cicero they were bearing to meet his ancestors, and the name now counted for something in Rome. Out on the frozen field, the body lay on its pyre under the stars, and the great orator struggled to deliver a brief eulogy. But his words would not perform their tricks for him on that occasion, and he had to give up. He could not even collect himself sufficiently to apply the torch to ignite the wood, and passed the task instead to Quintus. As the flames shot high the mourners threw their gifts of scent and spices on to the bonfire, and the perfumed smoke, flecked with orange sparks, curled up to the Milky Way. That night I sat with the senator in his study as he dictated a letter to Atticus, and it is surely a tribute to the affection which Lucius also inspired in that noble heart that this was the first of Cicero's hundreds of letters which Atticus chose to preserve:

'Knowing me as well as you do, you can appreciate better than most how deeply my cousin Lucius's death has grieved me, and what a loss it means to me both in public and in private life. All the pleasure that one human being's kindness and charm can give another I had from him.'

Despite having lived in Rome for many years, Lucius had always said that he wished to have his ashes interred in the family vault in Arpinum. Accordingly, on the morning after the cremation, the Cicero brothers set off with his remains on the three-day journey east, accompanied by their wives, having sent word ahead to their father of what had happened. Naturally, I went too, for although Cicero was in the mourning period, his legal and political correspondence could not be neglected.

Nevertheless, for the first – and, I think, the only – time in all our years together, he transacted no official business on the road, but simply sat with his chin in his hand, staring at the passing countryside. He and Terentia were in one carriage, Quintus and Pomponia in another, endlessly bickering – so much so that I saw Cicero draw his brother aside and plead with him, for the sake of Atticus, if for no one else, to make the marriage work. 'Well,' retorted Quintus, with some justice, 'if the good opinion of Atticus is that important to you, why do *you* not marry her?' We stayed the first night at the villa in Tusculum, and had reached as far as Ferentium on the Via Latina when a message reached the brothers from Arpinum that their father had collapsed and died the previous day.

Given that he was in his sixties and had been ailing for many years, this was obviously less of a shock than the death of Lucius (the news of which had apparently proved the final blow to the old man's fragile health). But to leave one house festooned with the pine and cypress boughs of mourning and to arrive at another similarly adorned was the height of melancholy, made worse by the mischance that we reached Arpinum on the twenty-fifth day of November, that date kept sacred to Proserpina, Queen of Hades, who carries into effect the curses of men upon the souls of the dead. The Ciceros' villa lay three miles out of the town, down a winding stony road, in a valley ringed by high mountains. It was cold at this altitude, the peaks already draped with the vestal veils of snow which they would wear till May. I had not been back for ten years, and to see it all as I remembered aroused strange feelings in me. Unlike Cicero, I had always preferred the country to the town. I had been born here; my mother and father had both lived and died here; for the first quarter-century of my life, these springy meadows and crystal streams, with their tall poplars and verdant banks, had been the limit of my world. Seeing how much I was affected, and knowing how devoted I had been to the old master, Cicero invited me to accompany him and Quintus to the funeral couch, to say goodbye. In a way, I owed their father almost as much as they did, for he had taken a shine to me when I was a lad, and educated me so that I could help with his books, and then had given me the chance to travel with his son. As I bent to kiss his cold hand, I had a strong sense of returning home, and then the idea came to me that perhaps I could remain here, and act as steward, marry some girl of equal station, and have a child of my own. My parents, despite their status as domestic slaves rather than farm labourers, had both died in their early forties; I had to reckon on having, at best, only ten years left myself. (Little do we know how the fates will play us!) I ached to imagine that I might depart the earth without issue and I resolved to raise the matter with Cicero at the earliest opportunity.

Thus it was that I came to have rather a profound conversation with him. On the day after our arrival, the old master was buried in the family vault, then Lucius's ashes in their alabaster vase were interred beside him, and finally a pig was sacrificed to keep the spot holy. The next morning Cicero took a tour around his newly inherited estate, and I went with him in case he needed to dictate any notes, for the place (which was so heavily mortgaged as to be virtually worthless) was in a dilapidated state, and much work needed to be done. Cicero observed that it was originally his mother who had managed the property; his father had always been too much of a dreamer to cope with land agents and agricultural suppliers; after her death, he had slowly let it all go to ruin. This was, I think, the first time in more than a decade in his service that I had heard Cicero mention his mother. Helvia was her name. She had died twenty years earlier, when he was in his teens, by which time he had left for Rome to be educated. I could barely remember anything of her myself, except that she had a reputation for terrible strictness and meanness – the sort of mistress who marked the jars to check if the slaves had stolen anything, and took great pleasure in whipping them if she suspected that they had.

'Never a word of praise from her, Tiro,' he said, 'either for myself or my brother. Yet I tried so hard to please her.' He stopped and stared across the fields to the fast-moving, ice-cold river – the Fibrenus it was called – in the centre of which was a little island, with a wooded grove and a small pavilion, half tumbled down. 'That was where I used to go and sit as a boy,' he said wistfully. 'The hours I spent there! In my mind I was going to be another Achilles, albeit of the law courts rather than the battlefield. You know your Homer: "Far to excel, out-topping all the rest!"'

He was silent for a while, and I recognised this as my opportunity. And so I put my plan to him – I gabbled it out, fairly ineptly I suppose: that I might remain here and bring the farm back up to scratch for him – and all the while he kept looking at that childhood island of his. 'I know exactly what you mean,' he said with a sigh when I had finished. 'I feel it, too. This is the true fatherland of myself and my brother, for we are descended from a very ancient family of this place. Here are our ancestral cults, here is our race, here are many memorials of our forefathers. What more need I say?' He turned to look at me, and I noticed how very clear and blue his eyes were, despite all his recent weeping. 'But consider what we have seen this week – the empty, senseless shells of those we loved – and think what a terrible audit Death lays upon a man. Ah!' He shook his head vigorously, as if emptying it of a bad dream, then returned his attention to the landscape. After a while he said, in a very different voice: 'Well, I tell you, for my part, I do not propose to die leaving one ounce of talent unspent, or one mile of energy left in my legs. And it is your destiny, my dear fellow, to walk the road me.' We were standing side by side; he prodded me gently in the ribs with his elbow. 'Come on, Tiro! A secretary who can take down my words almost as quickly as I can utter them? Such a marvel cannot be spared to count sheep in Arpinum! So let us have no more talk of such foolishness.'

And that was the end of my pastoral idyll. We walked back up to the house, and later that afternoon – or perhaps it was the following day: the memory plays such tricks – we heard the sound of a horse galloping very fast along the road from the town. It had started to rain, that much I do remember, and everyone was cooped up irritably indoors. Cicero was reading, Terentia sewing, Quintus practising drawing his sword, Pomponia lying down with a headache. (She still maintained that politics was 'boring', which drove Cicero into a quiet frenzy. 'Such a stupid thing to say!' he once complained to me. 'Politics? Boring? Politics is history on the wing! What other sphere of human activity calls forth all that is most noble in men's souls, and all that is most base? Or has such excitement? Or more vividly exposes our strengths and weaknesses? Boring? You might as well say that life itself is boring!') Anyway, at the noise of hooves clattering to a halt, I went out to greet the rider, and took from him a letter bearing the seal of Pompey the Great. Cicero opened it himself and let out a shout of surprise. 'Rome has been attacked!' he announced, causing even Pomponia to rouse herself briefly from her couch. He read on rapidly. The consular war fleet had been set on fire in its winter anchorage at Ostia.

Two praetors, Sextilius and Bellinus, together with their lictors and staff, had been kidnapped. It was all the work of pirates and designed to spread terror, pure and simple. There was panic in the capital. The people were demanding action. 'Pompey wants me with him straightaway,' said Cicero. 'He is calling a council of war at his country estate the day after tomorrow.'

XI

Leaving the others behind and travelling hard in a two-wheeled carriage (Cicero never went on horseback if he could avoid it), we retraced our route, reaching the villa at Tusculum by nightfall the following day. Pompey's estate lay on the other side of the Alban Hills, only five miles to the south. The lazy household slaves were stunned to find their master back so quickly and had to scramble to put the place in order. Cicero bathed and went directly to bed, although I do not believe he slept well, for I fancied I heard him in the middle of the night, moving around his library, and in the morning I found a copy of Aristotle's *Nicomachean Ethics* half unrolled on his desk. But politicians are resilient creatures. When I went into his chamber he was already dressed and keen to discover what Pompey had in mind. As soon as it was light we set off. Our road took us around the great expanse of the Alban Lake, and when the sun broke pink over the snowy mountain ridge we could see the silhouettes of the fishermen pulling in their nets from the glittering waters. 'Is there any country in the world more beautiful than Italy?' Cicero murmured, inhaling deeply, and although he did not express it, I knew what he was thinking, because I was thinking it too: that it was a relief to have escaped the enfolding gloom of Arpinum, and that there is nothing quite like death to make one feel alive.

At length we turned off the road and passed through a pair of imposing gates on to a long driveway of white gravel lined with cypresses. The formal gardens to either side were filled with marble statues, no doubt acquired by the general during his various campaigns. Gardeners were raking the winter leaves and trimming the box hedges. The impression was one of vast, quiet, confident wealth. As Cicero strode through the entrance into the great house he whispered to me to stay close by, and I slipped in unobtrusively behind him, carrying a document case. (My advice to anyone, incidentally, who wishes to be inconspicuous, is always to carry documents: they cast a cloak of invisibility around their bearer that is the equal of anything in the Greek legends.) Pompey was greeting his guests in the atrium, playing the grand country seigneur, with his third wife, Mucia, beside him, and his son, Gnaeus – who must have been eleven by this time – and his infant daughter, Pompeia, who had just learned to walk. Mucia was an attractive, statuesque matron of the Metellus clan, in her late twenties and obviously pregnant again. One of Pompey's peculiarities, I later discovered, was that he always tended to love his wife, whoever she happened to be at the time. She was laughing at some remark which had just been made to her, and when the originator of this witticism turned I saw that it was Julius Caesar. This surprised me, and certainly startled Cicero, because up to this point we had seen only the familiar trio of Piceneans: Palicanus, Afranius and Gabinius. Besides, Caesar had been in Spain for more than a year, serving as quaestor. But here he was, lithe and well built, with his lean, intelligent face, his amused brown eyes, and those thin strands of dark hair which he combed so carefully across his sunburnt pate. (But why am I bothering to describe him? The whole world knows what he looked like!)

In all, eight senators gathered that morning: Pompey, Cicero and Caesar; the three Piceneans mentioned above; Varro, Pompey's house intellectual, then aged fifty; and Caius Cornelius, who had served under Pompey as his quaestor in Spain, and who was now, along with Gabinius, a tribune-elect. I was not as conspicuous as I had feared, as many of the principals had also brought along a secretary or bag-carrier of some sort; we all stood respectfully to one side. After refreshments had been served, and the children had been taken away by their nurses, and the Lady Mucia had graciously said goodbye to each of her husband's guests in turn – lingering somewhat over Caesar, I noticed – slaves fetched in chairs so that everyone could sit. I was on the point of leaving with the other attendants when Cicero suggested to Pompey that, as I was famous throughout Rome as the inventor of a marvellous new shorthand system – these were his words – I might stay and keep a minute of what was said. I blushed with embarrassment. Pompey looked at me suspiciously, and I thought he was going to forbid it, but then he shrugged and said, 'Very well. That might be useful. But there will only be one copy made, and I shall keep it. Is that acceptable to everyone?' There was a noise of assent, whereupon a stool was fetched for me and I found myself sitting in the corner with my notebook open and my stylus gripped in a sweaty hand.

The chairs were arranged in a semicircle, and when all his guests were seated, Pompey stood. He was, as I have said, no orator on a public platform. But on his own ground, among those whom he thought of as his lieutenants, he radiated power and authority. Although my verbatim transcript was taken from me, I can still remember much of what he said, because I had to write it up from my notes, and that always causes a thing to stick in my mind. He began by giving the latest details of the pirate attack on Ostia: nineteen consular war triremes destroyed, a couple of hundred men killed, grain warehouses torched, two praetors – one of whom had been inspecting the granaries and the other the fleet – seized in their official robes, along with their retinues and their symbolic rods and axes. A ransom demand for their release had arrived in Rome yesterday. 'But for my part,' said Pompey, 'I do not believe we should negotiate with such people, as it will only encourage them in their criminal acts.' (Everyone nodded in agreement.) The raid on Ostia, he continued, was a turning point in the history of Rome. This was not an isolated incident, but merely the most daring in a long line of such outrages, which included the kidnapping of the noble Lady Antonia from her villa in Misenum (she whose own father had led an expedition against the pirates!), the robbery of temple treasures from Croton, and the surprise attacks on Brundisium and Caieta. Where would be struck next? What Rome was facing was a threat very different from that posed by a conventional enemy. These pirates were a new type of ruthless foe, with no government to represent them and no treaties to bind them. Their bases were not confined to a single state. They had no unified system of command. They were a worldwide pestilence, a parasite which needed to be stamped out, otherwise Rome – despite her overwhelming military superiority – would never again know security or peace. The existing national security system, of giving men of consular rank a single command of limited duration in an individual theatre, was clearly inadequate to the challenge.

'Long before Ostia, I had been devoting much careful study to this problem,' declared Pompey, 'and I believe this unique enemy demands a unique response. Now is our opportunity.' He clapped his hands and a pair of slaves carried in a large map of the Mediterranean, which they set up on a stand beside him. His audience leaned forwards to get a better look, for they could see mysterious lines had been drawn vertically across both sea and land. 'The basis of our strategy from now on must be to combine the military and the political spheres,' said Pompey. 'We hit them with everything.' He took up a pointer and rapped it on the painted board. 'I propose we divide the Mediterranean into fifteen zones, from the Pillars of Hercules here in the west to the waters of Egypt and Syria here in the east, each zone to have its own legate, whose task will be to scour his area clean of pirates and then to make treaties with the local rulers to ensure the brigands' vessels never return to their waters. All captured pirates are to be handed over to Roman jurisdiction. Any ruler who refuses to cooperate will be regarded as Rome's enemy. Those who are not with us are against us. These fifteen legates will all report to one supreme commander, who will have absolute authority over all the mainland for a distance of fifty miles from the sea. I shall be that commander.'

There was a long silence. It was Cicero who spoke first. 'Your plan is certainly a bold one, Pompey, although some might consider it a disproportionate response to the loss of nineteen triremes. You do realise that such a concentration of power in a single pair of hands has never been proposed in the entire history of the republic?'

'As a matter of fact, I *do* realise that,' replied Pompey. He tried to keep a straight face, but in the end he could not stop it breaking into a broad grin, and quickly everyone was laughing, apart from Cicero, who looked as if his world had just fallen apart – which in a sense it had, because this was, as he put it afterwards, a plan for the domination of the world by one man, nothing less, and he had few doubts where it would lead. 'Perhaps I should have walked out there and then,' he mused to me later on the journey home. 'That is what poor, honest Lucius would have urged me to do. Yet Pompey would still have gone ahead, either with me or without me, and all I would have done is earned his enmity, and that would have put paid to my chances of a praetorship. Everything I do now must be viewed through the prism of that election.'

And so, of course, he stayed, as the discussion meandered on over the next few hours, from grand military strategy to grubby political tactics. The plan was for Gabinius to place a bill before the Roman people soon after he took office, which would be in about a week, setting up the special command and ordering it be given to Pompey; then he and Cornelius would dare any of the other tribunes to veto it. (One must remember that in the days of the republic only an assembly of the people had the power to make laws; the senate's voice was influential, but not decisive; their task was to implement the people's will.)

'What do you say, Cicero?' asked Pompey. 'You have been very quiet.'

'I say that Rome is indeed fortunate,' replied Cicero carefully, 'to have a man with such experience and global vision as yourself to call on in her hour of peril. But we must be realistic. There will be huge resistance to this proposal in the senate. The aristocrats, in particular, will say that it is nothing more than a naked grab for power dressed up as patriotic necessity.'

'I resent that,' said Pompey.

'Well, you may resent it all you like, but you will still need to demonstrate that it is not the case,' retorted Cicero, who knew that the surest way to a great man's confidence, curiously enough, is often to speak harshly back to him, thus conveying an appearance of disinterested candour. 'They will also say that this commission to deal with the pirates is simply a stepping-stone to your true objective, which is to replace Lucullus as commander of the Eastern legions.' To that, the great man made no response other than a grunt – he could not, because that really was his true objective. 'And finally, they will set about finding a tribune or two of their own, to veto Gabinius's bill.'

'It sounds to me as though you should not be here, Cicero,' sneered Gabinius. He was something of a dandy, with thick and wavy hair slicked back in a quiff, in imitation of his chief. 'To achieve our objective will require bold hearts, and possibly stout fists, not the quibbles of clever lawyers.'

'You will need hearts and fists *and* lawyers before you are done, Gabinius, believe me,' responded Cicero. 'The moment you lose the legal immunity conferred by your tribuneship, the aristocrats will have you in court and fighting for your life. You will need a clever lawyer, well enough, and so will you, Cornelius.'

'Let us move on,' said Pompey. 'Those are the problems. Do you have any solutions to offer?'

'Well,' replied Cicero, 'for a start, I strongly urge that your name should not appear anywhere in the bill setting up the supreme command.'

'But it was my idea!' protested Pompey, sounding exactly like a child whose game was being taken over by his playmates.

'True, but I still say it would be prudent not to specify the actual name of the commander at the very outset. You will be the focus of the most terrible envy and rage in the senate. Even the sensible men, whose support we can normally rely on, will baulk at this. You must make the central issue the defeat of the pirates, not the future of Pompey the Great. Everyone will know the post is designed for you; there is no need to spell it out.'

'But what am I to say when I lay the bill before the people?' asked Gabinius. 'That any fool off the street can hold the office?'

'Obviously not,' said Cicero, with a great effort at patience. 'I would strike out the name "Pompey" and insert the phrase "senator of consular rank". That limits it to the fifteen or twenty living ex-consuls.'

'So who might be the rival candidates?' asked Afranius.

'Crassus,' said Pompey at once: his old enemy was never far from his thoughts. 'Perhaps Catulus. Then there is Metellus Pius – doddery, but still a force. Hortensius has a following. Isauricus. Gellius. Cotta. Curio. Even the Lucullus brothers.'

'Well, I suppose if you are really worried,' said Cicero, 'we could always specify that the supreme commander should be any ex-consul whose name begins with a P.' For a moment, no one reacted, and I was certain he had gone too far. But then Caesar threw back his head and laughed, and the rest – seeing that Pompey was smiling weakly – joined in. 'Believe me, Pompey,' continued Cicero in a reassuring tone, 'most of these are far too old and idle to be a threat. Crassus will be your most dangerous rival, simply because he is so rich and jealous of you. But if it comes to a vote you will defeat him overwhelmingly, I promise you.'

'I agree with Cicero,' said Caesar. 'Let us clear our hurdles one at a time. First, the principle of the supreme command; then, the name of the commander.' I was struck by the authority with which he spoke, despite being the most junior man present.

'Very well,' said Pompey, nodding judiciously. 'It is settled. The central issue must be the defeat of the pirates, not the future of Pompey the Great.' And on that note, the conference adjourned for lunch.

There now followed a squalid incident which it embarrasses me to recall, but which I feel I must, in the interests of history, set down. For several hours, while the senators lunched, and afterwards strolled in the garden, I worked as rapidly as I could to translate my shorthand notes into a fair manuscript record of proceedings, which I could then present to Pompey. When I had finished, it occurred to me that perhaps I should check what I had written with Cicero, in case there might be something in it to which he objected. The chamber where the conference had been held was empty, and so was the atrium, but I could hear the senator's distinctive voice, and set off, clutching my roll of paper, in the direction from which I judged it was coming. I crossed a colonnaded courtyard, where a fountain played, then followed the portico round to another, inner garden. But now his voice had faded altogether. I stopped to listen. There was only birdsong, and the trickling of water. Then, suddenly, from somewhere very close, and loud enough to make me jump, I heard a woman groan, as if in agony. Like a fool, I turned, and took a few more steps, and through an open door was confronted by the sight of Caesar with Pompey's wife. The Lady Mucia did not see me. She had her head down between her forearms, her dress was bunched up around her waist, and she was bent over a table, gripping the edge so tightly her knuckles were white. But Caesar saw me well enough, for he was facing the door, thrusting into her from behind, his right hand cupped around her swollen belly, his left resting casually on his hip, like a dandy standing on a street corner. For exactly how long our eyes met I cannot say, but he stares back at me even now – those fathomless dark eyes of his gazing through the smoke and chaos of all the years that were to follow – amused, unabashed, challenging. I fled.

By this time, most of the senators had wandered back into the conference chamber. Cicero was discussing philosophy with Varro, the most distinguished scholar in Rome, of whose works on philology and antiquities I was deeply in awe. On any other occasion I would have been honoured to be introduced, but my head was still reeling from the scene I had just witnessed and I cannot remember a thing of what he said. I handed the minutes to Cicero, who skimmed them quickly, took my pen from me, and made a small amendment, all the while still talking to Varro. Pompey must have noticed what he was doing, for he came across with a big smile on his wide face, and pretended to be angry, taking the minutes away from Cicero and accusing him of inserting promises he had never made – 'though I think you can count on my vote for the praetorship,' he said, and slapped him on the back. Until a short while earlier, I had considered Pompey a kind of god among men – a booming, confident war hero – but now, knowing what I did, I thought him also sad. 'This is quite remarkable,' he said to me, as he ran his huge thumb down the columns of words. 'You have captured my voice exactly. How much do you want for him, Cicero?'

'I have already turned down an enormous sum from Crassus,' replied Cicero.

'Well, if ever there is a bidding war, be sure that I am included,' said Caesar, in his rasping voice, coming up behind us. 'I would dearly love to get my hands on Tiro.' But he said it in such a friendly way, accompanying it with a wink, that none of the others heard the menace in his words, while I felt almost faint with terror.

'The day that I am parted from Tiro,' said Cicero, prophetically as it turned out, 'is the day that I quit public life.'

'Now I am doubly determined to buy him,' said Caesar, and Cicero joined in the general laughter.

After agreeing to keep secret everything that had been discussed, and to meet in Rome in a few days' time, the group broke up. The moment we turned out of the gates and on to the road to Tusculum, Cicero let out a long-pent-up cry of frustration and struck the side of the carriage with the palm of his hand. 'A criminal conspiracy!' he said, shaking his head in despair. 'Worse – a *stupid* criminal conspiracy. This is the trouble, Tiro, when soldiers decide to play at politics. They imagine that all they need to do is issue an order, and everyone will obey. They never see that the very thing which makes them attractive in the first place – that they are supposedly these great patriots, above the squalor of politics – must ultimately defeat them, because either they *do* stay above politics, in which case they go nowhere, or they get down in the muck along with the rest of us, and show themselves to be just as venal as everyone else.' He stared out at the lake, darkening now in the winter light. 'What do you make of Caesar?' he said suddenly, to which I returned a noncommittal answer about his seeming very ambitious. 'He certainly is that. So much so, there were times today when it occurred to me that this whole fantastic scheme is actually not Pompey's at all, but Caesar's. That, at least, would explain his presence.'

I pointed out that Pompey had described it as his own idea.

'And no doubt Pompey thinks it is. But that is the nature of the man. You make a remark to him, and then you find it being repeated back to you, as if it were his own. "The central issue must be the defeat of the pirates, not the future of Pompey the Great." That is a typical example. Sometimes, just to amuse myself, I have argued against my own original assertion, and waited to see how long it was before I heard my rebuttal coming back at me too.' He frowned and nodded. 'I am sure I am right. Caesar is quite clever enough to have planted the seed and left it to flower on its own. I wonder how much time he has spent with Pompey. He seems very well bedded in.'

It was on the tip of my tongue then to tell him what I had witnessed, but a combination of fear of Caesar, my own shyness, and a feeling that Cicero would not think the better of me for spying – that I would in some sense be contaminated myself by describing the whole sordid business – caused me to swallow my words. It was not until many years later – after Caesar's death, in fact, when he could no longer harm me and I was altogether more confident – that I revealed my story. Cicero, then an old man, was silent for a long time. 'I understand your discretion,' he said at last, 'and in many ways I applaud it. But I have to say, my dear friend, that I wish you *had* informed me. Perhaps then things might have turned out differently. At least I would have realised earlier the kind of breathtakingly reckless man we were dealing with. But by the time I did understand, it was too late.'

The Rome to which we returned a few days later was jittery and full of rumours. The burning of Ostia had been clearly visible to the whole city as a red glow in the western night sky. Such an attack on the capital was unprecedented, and when Gabinius and Cornelius took office as tribunes on the tenth day of December, they moved quickly to fan the sparks of public anxiety into the flames of panic. They caused extra sentries to be posted at the city's gates. Wagons and pedestrians entering Rome were stopped and searched at random for weapons. The wharves and warehouses along the river were patrolled both day and night, and severe penalties were promulgated for citizens convicted of hoarding grain, with the inevitable result that the three great food markets of Rome in those days – the Emporium, the Macellum, and the Forum Boarium – immediately ran out of supplies. The vigorous new tribunes also dragged the outgoing consul, the hapless Marcius Rex, before a meeting of the people, and subjected him to a merciless cross-examination about the security lapses which had led to the fiasco at Ostia. Other witnesses were found to testify about the menace of the pirates, and that menace grew with every retelling. They had a thousand ships! They were not lone raiders at all, but an organised conspiracy! They had squadrons and admirals and fearsome weapons of poison-tipped arrows and Greek fire! Nobody in the senate dared object to any of this, for fear of seeming complacent – not even when a chain of beacons was built all along the road to the sea, to be lit if pirate vessels were seen heading for the mouth of the Tiber. 'This is absurd,' Cicero said to me, on the morning we went out to inspect these most visible symbols of the national peril. 'As if any sane pirate would dream of sailing twenty miles up an open river to attack a defended city!' He shook his head in dismay at the ease with which a timorous population can be moulded by unscrupulous politicians. But what could he do? His closeness to Pompey had trapped him into silence.

On the seventeenth day of December, the Festival of Saturn began and lasted for a week. It was not the most enjoyable of holidays, for obvious reasons, and although the Cicero family went through the normal rituals of exchanging gifts, even allowing us slaves to have the day off and sharing a meal with us, nobody's heart was in it. Lucius used to be the life and soul of these events, and he was gone. Terentia, I believe, had hoped she was pregnant, but had discovered she was not, and was becoming seriously worried that she would never bear a son. Pomponia nagged away at Quintus about his inadequacies as a husband. Even little Tullia could not cheer the mood.

As for Cicero, he spent much of Saturnalia in his study, brooding on Pompey's insatiable ambition, and the implications it had for the country and for his own political prospects. The elections for the praetorship were barely eight months away, and he and Quintus had already compiled a list of likely candidates. From whichever of these men was eventually elected, he could probably expect to find his rivals for the consulship. The two brothers spent many hours discussing the permutations, and it seemed to me, although I kept it to myself, that they missed the wisdom of their cousin. For although Cicero used to joke that if he wanted to know what was politically shrewd, he would ask Lucius his opinion and then do precisely the opposite, nevertheless he had offered a fixed star to steer by. Without him, the Ciceros had only one another, and despite their mutual devotion, it was not always the wisest of relationships.

It was in this atmosphere, around the eighth or ninth day of January, when the Latin Festival was over and serious politics resumed, that Gabinius finally mounted the rostra to demand a new supreme commander. I am talking here, I should explain, about the old republican rostra, which was very different to the wretched ornamental footstool we have today. This ancient structure, now destroyed, was the heart of Rome's democracy: a long, curved platform, twelve feet high, covered with the statues of the heroes of antiquity, from which the tribunes and the consuls addressed the people. Its back was to the senate house, and it faced out boldly across the widest expanse of the forum, with six ships' battering rams, or 'beaks' – those *rostra* which gave the platform its name – thrusting from its heavy masonry (the beaks had been captured from the Carthaginians in a sea battle nearly three centuries earlier). The whole of its rear was a flight of steps, if you can imagine what I am saying, so that a magistrate might leave the senate house or the tribunes' headquarters, walk fifty paces, ascend the steps, and find himself on top of the rostra, facing a crowd of thousands, with the tiered façades of the two great basilicas on either side of him and the Temple of Castor straight ahead. This was where Gabinius stood on that January morning and declared, in his smooth and confident way, that what Rome needed was a strong man to take control of the war against the pirates.

Cicero, despite his misgivings, had done his best, with the help of Quintus, to turn out a good-sized crowd, and the Piceneans could always be relied upon to drum up a couple of hundred veterans. Add to these the regulars who hung about the Basilica Porcia, and those citizens going about their normal business in the forum, and I should say that close on a thousand were present to hear Gabinius spell out what was needed if the pirates were to be beaten – a supreme commander of consular rank with *imperium* lasting for three years over all territory up to fifty miles from the sea, fifteen legates of praetorian rank to assist him, free access to the treasury of Rome, five hundred warships and the right to levy up to one hundred and twenty thousand infantry and five thousand cavalry. These were staggering numbers and the demand caused a sensation. By the time Gabinius had finished the first reading of his bill, and had handed it to a clerk to be pinned up outside the tribunes' basilica, both Catulus and Hortensius had come hurrying into the forum to find out what was going on. Pompey, needless to say, was nowhere to be seen, and the other members of the group of seven (as the senators around Pompey had taken to calling themselves) took care to stand apart from one another, to avoid any suggestion of collusion. But the aristocrats were not fooled. 'If this is your doing,' Catulus snarled at Cicero, 'you can tell your master he will have a fight on his hands.'

The violence of their reaction was to prove even worse than Cicero had predicted. Once a bill had been given its first reading, three weekly market days had to pass before it could be voted on by the people (this was to enable country-dwellers to come into the city and study what was proposed). So the aristocrats had until the begining of February to organise against it, and they did not waste a moment. Two days later, the senate was summoned to debate the *lex Gabinia*, as it would be called, and despite Cicero's advice that he should stay away, Pompey felt that he was honour-bound to attend, and stake his claim to the job. He wanted a good-sized escort down to the senate house, and because there no longer seemed much point in secrecy, the seven senators formed an honour-guard around him. Quintus also joined them, in his brand-new senatorial toga: this was only his third or fourth visit to the chamber. As usual, I stayed close to Cicero. 'We should have known we were in trouble,' he lamented afterwards, 'when no other senator turned up.'

The walk down the Esquiline Hill and into the forum went well enough. The precinct bosses had played their part, delivering plenty of enthusiasm on the streets, with people calling out to Pompey to save them from the menace of the pirates. He waved to them like a landlord to his tenants. But the moment the group entered the senate house they were met by jeers from all sides, and a piece of rotten fruit flew across the chamber and splattered on to Pompey's shoulder, leaving a rich brown stain. Such a thing had never happened to the great general before, and he halted and looked around him in stupefaction. Afranius, Palicanus and Gabinius quickly closed ranks to protect him, just as if they were back on the battlefield, and I saw Cicero stretch out his arms to hustle all four to their places, no doubt reasoning that the sooner they sat down, the sooner the demonstration would be over. I was standing at the entrance to the chamber, held back with the other spectators by the familiar cordon of rope slung between the two doorposts. Of course, we were all supporters of Pompey, so the more the senators inside jeered him, the more we outside roared our approval, and it was a while before the presiding consul could bring the house to order.

The new consuls in that year were Pompey's old friend Glabrio, and the aristocratic Calpurnius Piso (not to be confused with the other senator of that name, who will feature later in this story, if the gods give me the strength to finish it). A sign of how desperate the situation was for Pompey in the senate was that Glabrio had chosen to absent himself, rather than be seen in open disagreement with the man who had given him back his son. That left Piso in the chair. I could see Hortensius, Catulus, Isauricus, Marcus Lucullus – the brother of the commander of the Eastern legions – and all the rest of the patrician faction

poised to attack. The only ones no longer present to offer opposition were the three Metellus brothers: Quintus was abroad,
serving as the governor of Crete, while the younger two, as if
to prove the indifference of fate to the petty ambitions of men,
had both died of the fever not long after the Verres trial. But
what was most disturbing was that the *pedarii* – the unassuming,
patient, plodding mass of the senate, whom Cicero had taken so
much trouble to cultivate – even they were hostile, or at best
sullenly unresponsive to Pompey's megalomania. As for Crassus,
he was sprawled on the consular front bench opposite, with his
arms folded and his legs casually outstretched, regarding Pompey
with an expression of ominous calm. The reason for his sangfroid
was obvious. Sitting directly behind him, placed there like a pair
of prize animals just bought at auction, were two of that year's
tribunes, Roscius and Trebellius. This was Crassus's way of telling
the world that he had used his wealth to purchase not just one,
but two vetoes, and that the *lex Gabinia*, whatever Pompey and
Cicero chose to do, would never be allowed to pass.

Piso exercised his privilege of speaking first. 'An orator of the
stationary or quiet type' was how Cicero condescendingly
described him many years later, but there was nothing stationary
or quiet about him that day. 'We know what you are doing!' he
shouted at Pompey, as he came to the end of his harangue. 'You
are defying your colleagues in the senate and setting yourself up
as a second Romulus – slaying your brother so that you may rule
alone! But you would do well to remember the fate of Romulus,
who was murdered in his turn by his own senators, who cut up
his body and carried the mangled pieces back to their homes!'
That brought the aristocrats to their feet, and I could just make
out Pompey's massive profile, stock still and staring straight ahead,
obviously unable to believe what was happening.

Catulus spoke next, and then Isauricus. The worst, though, was Hortensius. For almost a year, since the end of his consulship, he had hardly been seen in the forum. His son-in-law, Caepio, the beloved elder brother of Cato, had recently died on army service in the East, leaving Hortensius's daughter a widow, and the word was that the Dancing Master no longer had the strength in his legs for the struggle. But now it seemed that Pompey's over-reaching ambition had brought him back into the arena revitalised, and listening to him reminded one of just how formidable he could be on a big set-piece occasion such as this. He never ranted or stooped to vulgarity, but eloquently restated the old republican case: that power must always be divided, hedged around with limitations, and renewed by annual votes, and that while he had nothing personally against Pompey – indeed, felt that Pompey was more worthy of supreme command than any other man in the state – it was a dangerous, un-Roman precedent that would be set by the *lex Gabinia*, and that ancient liberties were not to be flung aside merely because of some passing scare about pirates. Cicero was shifting in his place and I could not help but reflect that this was exactly the speech which he would have made if he had been free to speak his mind.

Hortensius had just about reached his peroration when the figure of Caesar rose from that obscure region at the back of the chamber, close to the door, which had once been occupied by Cicero, and asked Hortensius to give way. The respectful silence in which the great advocate had been heard fractured immediately, and one has to admit that it was brave of Caesar to take him on in such an atmosphere. Caesar stood his ground until at last he could be heard, and then he started to speak, in his clear, compelling, remorseless way. There was nothing un-Roman, he said, about seeking to defeat pirates, who were the scum of the sea; what was un-Roman was to will the end of a thing but not the means. If the republic functioned as perfectly as Hortensius said it did, why had this menace been allowed to grow? And now that it was grown monstrous, how was it to be defeated? He had himself been captured by pirates a few years back when he was on his way to Rhodes, and held to ransom, and when at last he had been released, he had gone back and hunted down every last man of his kidnappers, and carried out the promise he had made to them when he was their prisoner – had seen to it that the scoundrels were crucified! 'That, Hortensius, is the Roman way to deal with piracy – and that is what the *lex Gabinia* will enable us to do!'

He finished to a round of boos and cat-calls, and as he resumed his seat, with the most magnificent display of disdain, some kind of fight broke out at the other end of the chamber. I believe a senator threw a punch at Gabinius, who turned round and punched him back, and very quickly he was in difficulties, with bodies piling in on top of him. There was a scream and a crash as one of the benches toppled over. I lost sight of Cicero. A voice in the crowd behind me cried that Gabinius was being murdered and there was such a surge of pressure forwards that the rope was pulled from its fixings and we tumbled into the chamber. I was lucky to scramble to one side as several hundred of Pompey's plebeian supporters (who were a rough-looking lot, I must admit) poured down the aisle towards the consular dais and dragged Piso from his curule chair. One brute had him by the neck, and for a few moments it looked as though murder would be done. But then Gabinius managed to struggle free and pull himself up on to a bench to show that, although he had been somewhat knocked about, he was still alive. He appealed to the demonstrators to let go of Piso, and after a short argument the consul was reluctantly released. Rubbing his throat, Piso declared hoarsely that the session was adjourned without a vote – and so, by the very narrowest of margins, for the moment at least, the commonwealth was saved from anarchy.

Such violent scenes had not been witnessed in the heart of Rome's governing district for more than fourteen years, and they had a profound effect on Cicero, even though he had managed to escape the mêlée with barely a ruffle in his immaculate dress. Gabinius was streaming blood from his nose and lip and Cicero had to help him from the chamber. They came out some distance after Pompey, who walked on, looking neither right nor left, with the measured tread of a man at a funeral. What I remember most is the silence as the mingled crowd of senators and plebeians parted to let him through. It was as if both sides, at the very last moment, had realised that they were fighting on a cliff-edge, had come to their senses and drawn back. We went out into the forum, with Pompey still not saying anything, and when he turned into the Argiletum, in the direction of his house, his supporters all followed him, partly for want of anything else to do. Afranius, who was next to Pompey, passed the word back that the general wanted a meeting. I asked Cicero if there was anything he required and he replied, with a bitter smile, 'Yes, that quiet life in Arpinum!'

Quintus came up and said urgently, 'Pompey must withdraw, or be humiliated!'

'He already has been humiliated,' retorted Cicero, 'and we with him. Soldiers!' he said to me in disgust. 'What did I tell you? I would not dream of giving them orders on the battle-field. Why should they believe they know better than I about politics?'

We climbed the hill to Pompey's house and filed inside, leaving the muted crowd in the street. Ever since that first conference I had been accepted as the minute-taker for the group, and when I settled into my usual place in the corner, no one gave me a second glance. The senators arranged them-selves around a big table, Pompey at the head. The pride had entirely gone out of his massive frame. Slumped in his throne-like chair he reminded me of some great beast that had been captured, shackled, baffled and taunted in the arena by crea-tures littler than himself. He was utterly defeatist and kept repeating that it was all over – the senate would clearly never stand for his appointment, he had only the support of the dregs on the streets, Crassus's tame tribunes would veto the bill in any case: there was nothing left for it but death or exile. Caesar took the opposite view – Pompey was still the most popular man in the republic, he should go out into Italy and begin recruiting the legions he needed, his old veterans would provide the backbone of his new army, the senate would capitulate once he had sufficient force. 'There is only one thing to do if you lose a throw of the dice: double your stake and throw again. Ignore the aristocrats, and if necessary rule through the people and the army.'

I could see that Cicero was preparing himself to speak, and was sure he did not favour either of these extremes. But there is as much skill in knowing how to handle a meeting of ten as there is in manipulating a gathering of hundreds. He waited until everyone had had their say, and the discussion was exhausted, before coming fresh to the fray. 'As you know,

Pompey,' he began, 'I have had some misgvings about this under-taking from the outset. But after witnessing today's débâcle in the senate, I have to tell you, they have vanished entirely. Now we simply have to win this fight – for your sake, for Rome's, and for the dignity and authority of all those of us who have supported you. There can be no question of surrender. You are famously a lion on the battlefield; you cannot become a mouse in Rome.'

'You watch your language, lawyer,' said Afranius, wagging his finger at him, but Cicero took no notice.

'Can you conceive of what will happen if you give up now? The bill has been published. The people are clamouring for action against the pirates. If you do not assume the post, someone else will, and I can tell you who it will be: Crassus. You say yourself he has two tame tribunes. He will make sure this law goes through, only with his name written into it instead of yours. And how will you, Gabinius, be able to stop him? By vetoing your own legislation? Impossible! Do you see? We cannot abandon the battle now!'

This was an inspired argument, for if there was one thing guaranteed to rouse Pompey to a fight, it was the prospect of Crassus stealing his glory. He drew himself up, thrust out his jaw and glared around the table. I noticed both Afranius and Palicanus give him slight nods of encouragement. 'We have scouts in the legions, Cicero,' said Pompey, 'marvellous fellows who can find a way through the most difficult terrain – marshes, mountain ranges, forests which no man has penetrated since time began. But politics beats any obstacle I have ever faced. If you can show me a route out of this mess, you will have no truer friend than I.'

'Will you place yourself in my hands entirely?'

'You are the scout.'

'Very well,' said Cicero. 'Gabinius, tomorrow you must summon Pompey to the rostra, to ask him to serve as supreme commander.'

'Good,' said Pompey belligerently, clenching his massive fist. 'And I shall accept.'

'No, no,' said Cicero, 'you will refuse absolutely. You will say you have done enough for Rome, that you have no ambitions left in public life, and are retiring to your estate in the country.' Pompey's mouth fell open. 'Don't worry. I shall write the speech for you. You will leave the city tomorrow afternoon, and you will not come back. The more reluctant you seem, the more frantic the people will be for your recall. You will be our Cincinnatus, fetched from his plough to save the country from disaster. It is one of the most potent myths in politics, believe me.'

Some of those present were opposed to such a dramatic tactic, considering it too risky. But the idea of appearing modest appealed to Pompey's vanity. For is this not the dream of every proud and ambitious man? That rather than having to get down in the dust and fight for power, the people should come crawling to him, begging him to accept it as a gift? The more Pompey thought about it, the more he liked it. His dignity and authority would remain intact, he would have a comfortable few weeks, and if it all went wrong, it would be someone else's fault.

'This sounds very clever,' said Gabinius, who was dabbing at his split lip. 'But you seem to forget that it is not the people who are the problem; it is the senate.'

'The senate will come round once they wake up to the implications of Pompey's retirement. They will be faced with a choice of either doing nothing about the pirates, or awarding the supreme command to Crassus. To the great majority, neither will be acceptable. Apply a little grease and they will slide our way.'

'That is clever,' said Pompey admiringly. 'Is he not clever, gentlemen? Did I not tell you he was clever?'

'These fifteen legateships,' said Cicero. 'I propose you should use at least half of them to win over support inside the senate.' Palicanus and Afranius, seeing their lucrative commissions in jeopardy, immediately objected loudly, but Pompey waved them to be quiet. 'You are a national hero,' continued Cicero, 'a patriot above petty political squabbles and intrigue. Rather than using your patronage to reward your friends, you should use it to divide your enemies. Nothing will split the aristocratic faction more disastrously than if some can be persuaded to serve under you. They will tear each other's eyes out.'

'I agree,' said Caesar, with a decisive nod. 'Cicero's plan is better than mine. Be patient, Afranius. This is only the first stage. We can wait for our rewards.'

'Besides,' said Pompey sanctimoniously, 'the defeat of Rome's enemies should be reward enough for all of us.' I could see that in his mind's eye, he was already at his plough.

Afterwards, as we were walking home, Quintus said, 'I hope you know what you are doing.'

'I hope I know what I am doing,' replied Cicero.

'The nub of the problem, surely, is Crassus and those two tribunes of his, and his ability to veto the bill. How are you going to get round that?'

'I have no idea. Let us hope that a solution presents itself. One usually does.'

I realised then just how much Cicero was relying on his old dictum that sometimes you have to start a fight to discover how to win it. He said good night to Quintus and walked on, head down in thought. From being a reluctant participant in Pompey's grand ambition, he had now emerged as its chief organiser, and he knew that this would put him in a hard place, not least with his own wife. In my experience, women are far less willing than men to forget past slights and it was inexplicable to Terentia that her husband should still be dancing attendance on the 'Prince of Picenum', as she derisively called Pompey, especially after that day's scenes in the senate, about which the whole city was talking. She was waiting for Cicero in the tablinum when we arrived home, all drawn up in full battle order and ready to attack. She flew at him immediately. 'I cannot believe things have reached such a pass! There is the senate on one side and the rabble on the other – and where is my husband to be found? As usual, with the rabble! Surely even you will sever your connection with him now?'

'He is announcing his retirement tomorrow,' Cicero soothed her.

'What?'

'It is true. I am going to write his statement myself this evening. Which means I shall have to dine at my desk, I am afraid, if you will excuse me.' He eased past her, and once we were in his study he said, 'Do you think she believed me?'

'No,' I replied.

'Nor do I,' he said, with a chuckle. 'She has lived with me too long!'

He was rich enough by now to have divorced her if he wanted, and he could have made himself a better match, certainly a more beautiful one. He was disappointed she had not been able to give him a son. And yet, despite their endless arguments, he stayed with her. Love was not the word for it – not in the sense that the poets use it. Some stranger, stronger compound bound them.

She kept him sharp, that was part of it: the whetstone to his blade. At any rate, she did not bother us for the rest of that night, as Cicero dictated the words he thought that Pompey should say. He had never written a speech for anyone else before, and it was a peculiar experience. Nowadays, of course, most senators employ a slave or two to turn out their speeches; I have even heard of some who have no idea of what they are going to say until the text is placed in front of them: how these fellows can call themselves statesmen defeats me. But Cicero found that he rather enjoyed composing parts for others. It amused him to think of lines that great men ought to utter, if only they had the brains, and later he would use the technique to considerable effect in his books. He even thought of a phrase for Gabinius to deliver, which afterwards became quite famous: 'Pompey the Great was not born for himself alone, but for Rome!'

The statement was deliberately kept short and we finished it long before midnight, and early the following morning, after Cicero had performed his exercises and greeted only his most important callers, we went across to Pompey's house and gave him the speech. Overnight, Pompey had contracted a bad dose of cold feet, and now he fretted aloud whether retirement was such a good idea after all. But Cicero saw that it was nervousness about going up on to the rostra as much as anything else, and once Pompey had his prepared text in his hands, he began to calm down. Cicero then gave some notes to Gabinius, who was also present, but the tribune resented being handed his lines like an actor, and questioned whether he should really say that Pompey was 'born for Rome'. 'Why?' teased Cicero. 'Do you not believe it?' Whereupon Pompey gruffly ordered Gabinius to stop complaining and say the words as written. Gabinius fell silent, but he glowered at Cicero and from that moment I believe became

his secret enemy – a perfect example of the senator's recklessness in causing offence by his repartee.

An enormous throng of spectators had gathered in the forum,
eager to see the sequel to the previous day's performance. We
could hear the noise as we came down the hill from Pompey's
house – that awesome, oblivious swelling sound of a great excited
multitude, which always reminds me of a huge sea rolling against
a distant shore. I felt my blood begin to pulse faster in anticipation. Most of the senate was there, and the aristocrats had brought
along several hundred supporters of their own, partly for their
protection, and also to howl down Pompey when, as they
expected, he declared his desire for the supreme command. The
great man briefly entered the forum escorted, as before, by Cicero
and his senatorial allies, but kept to the edge of it, and immediately went to the back of the rostra, where he paced around,
yawned, blew on his freezing hands, and generally gave every
indication of nerves, as the roar of the crowd increased in volume.
Cicero wished him luck, then went round to the front of the
rostra to stand with the rest of the senate, for he was keen to
observe their reactions. The ten tribunes filed up on to the platform and sat on their bench, then Gabinius stepped forward and
shouted dramatically, 'I summon before the people Pompey the
Great!'

How important appearance is in politics, and how superbly
Pompey was fashioned by nature to carry the look of greatness!
As that broad and familiar figure came plodding up the steps and
into view, his followers gave him the most tremendous ovation.
He stood there as solid as a full-grown bull, his massive head
tilted back slightly on his muscular shoulders, looking down on
the upturned faces, his nostrils flared as if inhaling the applause.
Normally, the people resented having speeches read to them

rather than delivered with apparent spontaneity, but on this occasion there was something in the way that Pompey unrolled his short text and held it up that reinforced the sense that these were words as weighty as the man delivering them – a man above the smooth oratorical tricks of the law and politics.

'People of Rome,' he bellowed into the silence, 'when I was seventeen I fought in the army of my father, Gnaeus Pompeius Strabo, to bring unity to the state. When I was twenty-three I raised a force of fifteen thousand, defeated the combined rebel armies of Brutus, Caelius and Carrinas, and was saluted imperator in the field. When I was twenty-four I conquered Sicily. When I was twenty-five I conquered Africa. On my twenty-sixth birthday, I triumphed. When I was thirty, and not even a senator, I took command of our forces in Spain with proconsular authority, fought the rebels for six years, and conquered. When I was thirty-six I returned to Italy, hunted down the last remaining army of the fugitive slave Spartacus, and conquered. When I was thirty-seven I was voted consul and triumphed for a second time. As consul, I restored to you the ancient rights of your tribunes, and staged games. Whenever danger has threatened this commonwealth, I have served it. My entire life has been nothing but one long special command. Now a new and unprecedented menace has arisen to threaten the republic. And to meet that danger, an office with new and unprecedented authority is rightly proposed. Whoever you choose to shoulder this burden must have the support of all ranks and all classes, for a great trust is involved in bestowing so much power on a single man. It is clear to me, after the meeting of the senate yesterday, that I do not have their trust, and therefore I want to tell you that however much I am petitioned, I shall not consent to be nominated; and if nominated, I shall not serve. Pompey the Great has had his fill of special commands. On this day I renounce all ambition for public office and retire from the city to till the soil like my forefathers before me.'

After a moment of shock, a terrible groan of disappointment broke from the crowd, and Gabinius darted to the front of the rostra, where Pompey was standing impassively.

'This cannot be permitted! Pompey the Great was not born for himself alone, but for Rome!'

Of course, the line provoked the most tremendous demonstration of approval, and the chant of 'Pompey! Pompey! Rome! Rome!' bounced off the walls of the basilicas and temples until one's ears ached with the noise. It was some time before Pompey could make himself heard.

'Your kindness touches me, my fellow citizens, but my continued presence in the city can only impede your deliberations. Choose wisely, O people of Rome, from the many able former consuls in the senate! And remember that although I now quit Rome altogether, my heart will remain among your hearths and temples for ever. Farewell!'

He raised his roll of papyrus as if it were a marshal's baton, saluted the wailing crowd, turned, and trudged implacably towards the back of the platform, ignoring all entreaties to remain. Down the steps he went, watched by the astonished tribunes, first the legs sinking from view, and then the torso, and finally the noble head with its crowning quiff. Some people standing close to me began weeping and tearing at their hair and clothes, and even though I knew the whole thing was a ruse, it was all I could do not to break into sobs myself. The assembled senators looked as if some weighty missile had dropped among them – a few were defiant, many were shaken, the majority simply blank with wonder. For almost as long as anyone could remember,

Pompey had been the foremost man in the state, and now he had – gone! Crassus's face in particular was a picture of conflicting emotions, which no artist ever born could have hoped to capture. Part of him knew that he must now, at last, after a lifetime in Pompey's shadow, be the favourite to seize the special command; the shrewder part knew that this had to be a trick, and that his whole position was threatened by some unforeseen jeopardy.

Cicero stayed just long enough to gauge the reactions to his handiwork, then hurried round to the back of the rostra to report. The Piceneans were there, and the usual crush of hangers-on. Pompey's attendants had brought a closed litter of blue and gold brocade to ferry him to the Capena Gate, and the general was preparing to clamber into it. He was like many men I have seen immediately after they have delivered a big speech, in the same breath both arrogant with exhilaration and anxious for re-assurance. 'That went extremely well,' he said. 'Did you think it was all right?'

'Superb,' said Cicero. 'Crassus's expression is beyond descrip-tion.'

'Did you like the line about my heart remaining among the hearths and temples of Rome for ever?'

'It was the consummate touch.'

Pompey grunted, highly pleased, and settled himself among the cushions of his litter. He let the curtain drop, then quickly pulled it aside again. 'You are sure this is going to work?'

'Our opponents are in disarray. That is a start.'

The curtain fell, then parted once more.

'How long before the bill is voted on?'

'Fifteen days.'

'Keep me informed. Daily at the least.'

Cicero stepped aside as the canopied chair was hoisted on to the shoulders of its bearers. They must have been strong young fellows, for Pompey was a great weight, yet they set off at the double, past the senate house and out of the forum – the heavenly body of Pompey the Great trailing his comet's tail of clients and admirers. 'Did I like the line about hearths and temples?' repeated Cicero under his breath as he watched him go. 'Well, naturally I did, you great booby – I wrote it!' I guess it must have been hard for him to devote so much energy to a chief he did not admire and a cause he believed to be fundamentally specious. But the journey to the top in politics often confines a man with some uncongenial fellow passengers and shows him strange scenery, and he knew there was no turning back now.

XII

For the next two weeks there was only one topic in Rome, and that was the pirates. Gabinius and Cornelius, in the phrase of the time, 'lived on the rostra' – that is, every day they kept the issue of the pirate menace before the people by issuing fresh proclamations and summoning more witnesses. Horror stories were their speciality. For example, it was put about that if one of the pirates' prisoners announced that he was a Roman citizen, his captors would pretend to be frightened, and beg forgiveness. They would even fetch a toga for him to wear, and shoes for his feet, and bow whenever he passed, and this game would go on for a long time, until at last, when they were far out at sea, they would let down a ladder and tell him he was free to go. If their victim refused to walk, he would be flung overboard. Such tales enraged the audience in the forum, who were accustomed to the magical incantation 'I am a Roman citizen' guaranteeing deference throughout the world.

Cicero himself did not speak from the rostra. Oddly enough, he had never yet done so, having decided early on to hold back until a moment in his career when he could make the maximum impact. He was naturally tempted to make this the issue on which he broke his silence, for it was a popular stick with which to beat the aristocrats. But in the end he decided against it, reasoning that the measure already had such overwhelming backing in the streets, he would be better employed behind the scenes, plotting strategy and trying to tempt over waverers in the senate. For this reason, his crucial importance has been frequently neglected. Instead of the fiery public orator he played the moderate for a change, working his way up and down the senaculum, listening to the complaints of the *pedarii*, promising to relay messages of commiseration and entreaty to Pompey, and dangling – very occasionally – half-offers of preferment to men of influence. Each day a messenger came to the house from Pompey's estate in the Alban Hills bearing a dispatch containing some fresh moan or enquiry or instruction ('Our new Cincinnatus does not seem to be spending much time ploughing,' observed Cicero with a wry smile), and each day the senator would dictate to me a soothing reply, often giving the names of men it might be useful for Pompey to summon out for interview. This was a delicate task, since it was important to maintain the pretence that Pompey was taking no further part in politics. But a combination of greed, flattery, ambition, realisation that some kind of special command was inevitable, and fear that it might go to Crassus eventually brought half a dozen key senators into Pompey's camp, the most significant of whom was Lucius Manlius Torquatus, who had only just finished serving as praetor and was certain to run for the consulship the following year.

Crassus remained, as always, the greatest threat to Cicero's schemes, and naturally he was not idle during this time either. He, too, went around making promises of lucrative commissions, and winning over adherents. For connoisseurs of politics it was fascinating to observe the perennial rivals, Crassus and Pompey, so evenly poised. Each had two tame tribunes; each could therefore veto the bill; and each had a list of secret supporters in the senate. Crassus's advantage over Pompey was the support of most of the aristocrats, who feared Pompey more than any other man in the republic; Pompey's advantage over Crassus was the popularity he enjoyed among the masses on the streets. 'They are like two scorpions, circling each other,' said Cicero, leaning back in his chair one morning, after he had dictated his latest dispatch to Pompey. 'Neither can win outright, yet each can kill the other.'

'Then how will victory ever be achieved?'

He looked at me, then suddenly lunged forward and slammed his plam down on his desk with a speed that made me jump. 'By the one which strikes the other by surprise.'

At the time he made that remark, there were only four days left before the *lex Gabinia* was due to be voted on by the people. He still had not thought of a means of circumventing Crassus's veto. He was wearied and discouraged, and once again began to talk of our retiring to Athens and studying philosophy. That day passed, and the next, and the next, and still no solution presented itself. On the final day before the vote, I rose as usual at dawn and opened the door to Cicero's clients. Now that he was known to be so close to Pompey, these morning levees had doubled in size compared to the old days, and the house was crowded with petitioners and well-wishers at all hours, much to Terentia's annoyance. Some of them had famous names: for example, on this particular morning, Antonius Hybrida, who was the second son of the great orator and consul Marcus Antonius, and who had just finished a term as tribune; he was a fool and a drunk, but protocol dictated he would have to be seen first. Outside it was grey and raining and the callers had brought in with them a wet-dog smell of moist stale clothes and damp hair. The black and white mosaic floor was streaked with tracks of mud and I was just contemplating summoning one of the household slaves to mop up when the door opened again and who should step in but Marcus Licinius Crassus himself. I was so startled, I briefly forgot to be alarmed, and gave him as natural a greeting as if he had been a nobody, come to request a letter of introduction.

'And a very good morning to you, Tiro,' he returned. He had only met me once, yet he still remembered my name, which frightened me. 'Might it be possible to have a word with your master?' Crassus was not alone but had brought with him Quintus Arrius, a senator who followed him around like a shadow, and whose ridiculously affected speech – always adding an aspirate to a vowel: 'Harrius' was how he pronounced his name – was to be so memorably parodied by that cruellest of poets, Catullus. I hurried through into Cicero's study, where he was doing his usual trick of dictating a letter to Sositheus while signing documents as quickly as Laurea could produce them.

'You will never guess who is here!' I cried.

'Crassus,' he replied, without looking up.

I was immediately deflated. 'You are not surprised?'

'No,' said Cicero, signing another letter. 'He has come to make a magnanimous offer, which is not really magnanimous at all, but which will show him in a better light when our refusal to agree to it becomes public. He has every reason to compromise, while we have none. Still, you had better show him in before he bribes all my clients away from me. And stay in the room and take a note, in case he tries to put words into my mouth.'

So I went out to fetch Crassus – who was indeed glad-handing his way around Cicero's tablinum, to the awed amazement of all concerned – and showed him into the study. The junior secretaries left, and there were just the four of us – Crassus, Arrius and Cicero all seated, and myself standing in the corner and taking notes.

'You have a very nice house,' said Crassus, in his friendly way. 'Small but charming. You must tell me if you think of selling.'

'If it ever catches fire,' responded Cicero, 'you will be the first to know.'

'Very droll,' said Crassus, clapping his hands and laughing with great good humour. 'But I am perfectly serious. An important man such as yourself should have a larger property, in a better neighbourhood. The Palatine, of course. I can arrange it. No, please,' he added, as Cicero shook his head, 'do not dismiss my offer. We have had our differences, and I should like to make a gesture of reconciliation.'

'Well, that is handsome of you,' said Cicero, 'but alas, I fear the interests of a certain gentleman still stand between us.'

'They need not. I have watched your career with admiration, Cicero. You deserve the place you have won in Rome. It is my view that you should achieve the praetorship in the summer, and the consulship itself two years after that. There – I have said it. You may have my support. Now what do you say in reply?'

This was indeed a stunning offer, and at that moment I grasped an important point about clever men of business – that it is not consistent meanness which makes them rich (as many vulgarly assume), but rather the capacity, when necessary, to be unexpectedly, even extravagantly generous. Cicero was entirely caught off balance. He was effectively being offered the consulship, his life's dream, on a platter – an ambition he had never even dared voice in the presence of Pompey, for fear of arousing the great man's jealousy.

'You overwhelm me, Crassus,' he said, and his voice was so

thick with emotion he had to cough to clear it before he could continue. 'But fate has once again cast us on different sides.'

'Not necessarily. On the day before the people vote, surely the time has arrived for a compromise? I accept that this supreme command is Pompey's conception. Let us share it.'

'A shared supreme command is an oxymoron.'

'We shared the consulship.'

'Yes, but the consulship is a joint office, based on the principle that political power should always be shared. Running a war is entirely different, as you know far better than I. In warfare, any hint of division at the top is fatal.'

'This command is so huge, there is easily room enough for two,' said Crassus airily. 'Let Pompey take the east, and I the west. Or Pompey the sea and I the land. Or vice versa. I do not mind. The point is that between us we can rule the world, with you as the bridge that links us.'

I am sure that Cicero had expected Crassus to come in threatening and aggressive, tactics which a career in the law courts had long since taught him how to handle. But this unexpectedly generous approach had him reeling, not least because what Crassus was suggesting was both sensible and patriotic. It would also be the ideal solution for Cicero, enabling him to win the friendship of all sides. 'I shall certainly put your offer to him,' promised Cicero. 'He shall have it in his hands before the day is out.'

'That is no use to me!' scoffed Crassus. 'If it were a matter of merely putting a proposal, I could have sent Arrius here out to the Alban Hills with a letter, could I not, Arrius?'

'Hindeed you could.'

'No, Cicero, I need you actually to bring this about.' He leaned in close and moistened his lips; there was something almost lecherous about the way Crassus talked of power. 'I shall be frank with you. I have set my heart upon resuming a military career. I have all the wealth a man could want, but that can only be a means and not an end in itself. Can you tell me what nation ever erected a statue to a man because he was rich? Which of the earth's many peoples mingles the name of some long-dead millionaire in its prayers because of the number of houses he once possessed? The only lasting glory is on the page – and I am no poet! – or on the battlefield. So you see, you really must deliver the agreement of Pompey for our bargain to stick.'

'He is not a mule to be driven to market,' objected Cicero, whom I could see was starting to recoil again from the crudeness of his old enemy. 'You know what he is like.'

'I do. Too well! But you are the most persuasive man in the world. You got him to leave Rome – do not deny it! Now surely you can convince him to come back?'

'His position is that he will come back as the sole supreme commander, or he will not come back at all.'

'Then Rome will never see him again,' snapped Crassus, whose friendliness was beginning to peel away like a thin layer of cheap paint on one of his less salubrious properties. 'You know perfectly well what is going to happen tomorrow. It will unfold as predictably as a farce at the theatre. Gabinius will propose your law and Trebellius, on my behalf, will veto it. Then Roscius, also on my instructions, will propose an amendment, setting up a joint command, and dare any tribune to veto *that*. If Pompey refuses to serve, he will look like a greedy child, willing to spoil the cake rather than share it.'

'I disagree. The people love him.'

'The people loved Tiberius Gracchus, but it did him no good in the end. That was a horrible fate for a patriotic Roman, which you might do well to remember.' Crassus stood. 'Look to your own interests, Cicero. Surely you can see that Pompey is leading you to political oblivion? No man ever became consul with the aristocracy united against him.' Cicero also rose and warily took Crassus's proferred hand. The older man grasped it hard and pulled him close. 'On two occasions,' he said in a very soft voice, 'I have offered the hand of friendship to you, Marcus Tullius Cicero. There will not be a third.'

With that, he strode out of the house, and at such a pace I could not get in front of him to show him out, or even open the door. I returned to the study to find Cicero standing exactly where I had left him, frowning at his hand. 'It is like touching the skin of a snake,' he said. 'Tell me – did I mishear him, or is he suggesting that Pompey and I might suffer the same fate as Tiberius Gracchus?'

'Yes: "a horrible fate for a patriotic Roman",' I read from my notes. 'What was the fate of Tiberius Gracchus?'

'Cornered like a rat in a temple and murdered by the nobles, while he was still tribune, and therefore supposedly inviolable. That must have been sixty years ago, at least. Tiberius Gracchus!' He clenched his hand into a fist. 'You know, for a moment, Tiro, he almost had me believing him. But I swear to you, I would sooner never be consul than feel that I had only achieved it because of Crassus.'

'I believe you, Senator. Pompey is worth ten of him.'

'A hundred, more like – for all his absurdities.'

I busied myself with a few things, straightening the desk and collecting the morning's list of callers from the tablinum, while Cicero remained motionless in the study. When I returned again, a curious expression had come over his face. I gave him the list and reminded him that he still had a houseful of clients to receive, including a senator. Absent-mindedly he selected a couple of names, among them Hybrida's, but then he suddenly said, 'Leave things here to Sositheus. I have a different task for you to perform. Go to the National Archive and consult the Annals for the consular year of Mucius Scaevola and Calpurnius Piso Frugi. Copy down everything relating to the tribuneship of Tiberius Gracchus and his agrarian bill. Tell nobody what you are doing. If anyone asks you, make something up. Well?' He smiled for the first time in a week and made a shooing gesture, flicking his fingers at me. 'Go on, man. Go!'

After so many years in his service I had become used to these bewildering and peremptory commands, and once I had wrapped myself up against the cold and wet I set off down the hill. Never had I known the city so grim and hard pressed – in the depths of winter, under a dark sky, freezing, short of food, with beggars on every corner, and even the occasional corpse in the gutter of some poor wretch who had died in the night. I moved quickly through the dreary streets, across the forum and up the steps to the Archive. This was the same building in which I had discovered the meagre official records of Gaius Verres and I had been back on many errands since, especially when Cicero was aedile, so my face was familiar to the clerks. They gave me the volume I needed without asking any questions. I took it over to a reading desk beside the window and unrolled it with my mittened fingers. The morning light was weak, it was very draughty, and I was not at all sure what I was looking for. The Annals, at least in those days before Caesar got his hands on them, gave a very straight and full account of what had happened in each year: the names of the magistrates, the laws passed, the wars fought, the famines endured, the eclipses and other natural phenomena observed. They were drawn from the official register that was written up each year by the pontifex maximus, and posted on the white board outside the headquarters of the college of priests.

History has always fascinated me. As Cicero himself once wrote: 'To be ignorant of what occurred before you were born is to remain always a child. For what is the worth of human life, unless it is woven into the life of our ancestors by the records of history?' I quickly forgot the cold and could have spent all day happily unwinding that roll, poring over the events of more than sixty years before. I discovered that in this particular year, Rome's six hundred and twenty-first, King Attalus III of Pergamon had died, bequeathing his country to Rome; that Scipio Africanus Minor had destroyed the Spanish city of Numantia, slaughtering all of its five thousand inhabitants, apart from fifty whom he saved to walk in chains in his triumph; and that Tiberius Gracchus, the famous radical tribune, had introduced a law to share out the public land among the common people, who were then, as always, suffering great hardship. Nothing changes, I thought. Gracchus's bill had infuriated the aristocrats in the senate, who saw it as threatening their estates, and they had persuaded or suborned a tribune named Marcus Octavius to veto the law. But because the people were unanimous in their support for the bill, Gracchus had argued from the rostra that Octavius was failing in his sacred duty to uphold their interests. He had therefore called upon the people to begin voting Octavius out of office, tribe by tribe, which they at once proceeded to do. When the first seventeen of the thirty-five tribes had voted overwhelmingly for Octavius's removal, Gracchus had suspended the polling and appealed to him to withdraw his veto. Octavius had refused, whereupon Gracchus had 'called upon the gods to witness that he did not willingly wish to remove his colleague', had balloted the eighteenth tribe, achieved a majority, and Octavius had been stripped of his tribuneship ('reduced to the rank of a private citizen he departed unobserved'). The agrarian law had then been passed. But the nobles, as Crassus had reminded Cicero, had exacted their revenge a few months later, when Gracchus had been surrounded in the Temple of Fides, beaten to death with sticks and clubs, and his body flung in the Tiber.

I unfastened the hinged notebook from my wrist and took out my stylus. I remember how I glanced around to make sure I was alone before I opened it and started copying the relevant passages from the Annals, for now I understood why Cicero had been so emphatic about the need for secrecy. My fingers were freezing and the wax was hard; the script I produced was atrocious. At one point, when Catulus himself, the patron of the Archive, appeared in the doorway and stared straight at me, I felt as if my heart would shatter the bones of my breast. But the old man was short-sighted, and I doubt he would have known who I was in any case; he was not that sort of politician. After talking for a while with one of his freedmen, he left. I finished my transcription and almost ran out of that place, down the icy steps and back across the forum towards Cicero's house, carrying my wax tablet pressed close to me, sensing I had never done a more significant morning's work in my life.

When I reached the house, Cicero was still ensconced with Antonius Hybrida, although as soon as he saw me waiting near the door, he drew their conversation to a close. Hybrida was one of those well-bred, fine-boned types, who had ruined himself and his looks with wine. I could smell his breath even from where I stood: it was like fruit rotting in a gutter. He had been thrown out of the senate a few years previously for bankruptcy and loose morals – specifically, corruption, drunkenness, and buying a beautiful young slave girl at an auction and living openly with her as his mistress. But the people, in that peculiar way of theirs, rather loved him for his rakish ways, and now that he had served a year as their tribune, he had worked his way back into the senate. I waited until he had gone before I gave Cicero my notes. 'What did he want?' I asked.

'My support in the elections for praetor.'

'He has a nerve!'

'I suppose he has. I promised to back him, though,' said Cicero carelessly, and seeing my surprise he explained: 'At least with him as praetor I shall have one fewer rival for the consulship.'

He laid my notebook on his desk and read it carefully. Then he put his elbows on either side of it, rested his chin in the palms of his hands, hunched forward and read it again. I pictured his quick thoughts running ahead in the way that water runs along the cracks in a tiled floor – first onwards, and then spreading to either side, blocked in one spot, advancing in another, widening and branching out, all the little possibilities and implications and likelihoods in shimmering fluid motion. Eventually, he said, half to himself and half to me, 'Such a tactic had never been tried before Gracchus used it, and has never been attempted since. One can see why. What a weapon to put into any man's hands! Win or lose, we should have to live with the consequences for years.' He looked up at me. 'I am not sure, Tiro. Perhaps it would be better if you erased it.' But when I made a move towards the desk, he said quickly, 'And then again perhaps not.' Instead, he told me to fetch Laurea and a couple of the other slaves and have them run around to all the senators in Pompey's inner group, asking them to assemble after the close of official business that afternoon. 'Not here,' he added quickly, 'but in Pompey's house.' Thereupon he sat down and began writing out, in his own hand, a dispatch to the general, which was sent off with a rider who had orders to wait and return with a reply. 'If Crassus wants to summon up the ghost of Gracchus,' he said grimly, when the letter had gone, 'he shall have him!'

Needless to say, the others were agog to hear why Cicero had summoned them, and once the courts and offices were shut for the day, everyone turned up at Pompey's mansion, filling all the seats around the table, except for the absent owner's great throne, which was left empty as a mark of respect. It may seem strange that such clever and learned men as Caesar and Varro were ignorant of the precise tactics which Gracchus had used as tribune, but remember that he had been dead by then for sixty-three years, that huge events had intervened, and that there was not yet the mania for contemporary history which was to develop over the coming decades. Even Cicero had forgotten it until Crassus's threat dislodged some distant memory from the time when he was studying for the bar. There was a profound hush as he read out the extract from the Annals, and when he had finished, an excited hubbub. Only the white-haired Varro, who was the oldest present, and who remembered hearing from his father about the chaos of the Gracchus tribunate, expressed reservations. 'You would create a precedent,' he said, 'by which any demagogue could summon the people, and threaten to dispose of any of his colleagues whenever he felt he had a majority among the tribes. Indeed, why stop at a tribune? Why not remove a praetor, or a consul?'

'We would not create the precedent,' Caesar pointed out impatiently. 'Gracchus created it for us.'

'Exactly,' said Cicero. 'Although the nobles may have murdered him, they did not declare his legislation illegal. I know what Varro means, and to a degree I share his unease. But we are in a desperate struggle, and obliged to take some risks.'

There was a murmur of assent, but in the end the most decisive voices in favour were those of Gabinius and Cornelius, the men who would actually have to stand before the people and push the legislation through, and who would, as a consequence, be chiefly liable to the nobles' retaliation, both physical and legal.

'The people overwhelmingly want this supreme command, and they want Pompey to be given it,' declared Gabinius. 'The fact that Crassus's purse is deep enough to buy two tribunes should not be allowed to frustrate their will.'

Afranius wanted to know if Pompey had expressed an opinion.

'This is the dispatch I sent to him this morning,' said Cicero, holding it up, 'and here on the bottom is the reply he sent back instantly, and which reached me here at the same time as you all did.' Everyone could see what Pompey had scrawled, in his large, bold script: the single word, *Agreed*. That settled the matter. Afterwards, Cicero instructed me to burn the letter.

The morning of the assembly was bitterly cold, with an icy wind whipping around the colonnades and temples of the forum. But the chill did not deter a vast assembly from turning out. On major voting days, the tribunes transferred themselves from the rostra to the Temple of Castor, where there was more space to conduct the ballot, and workmen had been busy overnight, erecting the wooden gangways up which the citizens would file to cast their votes. Cicero arrived early and discreetly, with only myself and Quintus in attendance, for as he said as he walked down the hill, he was only the stage manager of this production and not one of its leading performers. He spent a little while conferring with a group of tribal officers, then retreated with me to the portico of the Basilica Aemilia, from where he would have a good view of proceedings and could issue instructions as necessary.

It was a dramatic sight, and I guess I must be one of the very few left alive who witnessed it – the ten tribunes lined up on their bench, among them, like hired gladiators, the two matched pairs of Gabinius and Cornelius (for Pompey), versus Trebellius and Roscius (for Crassus); the priests and the augurs all standing at the top of the steps to the temple; the orange fire on the altar providing a flickering point of colour in the greyness; and spread out across the forum the great crowd of voters, red-faced in the cold, milling around the ten-foot-high standard of their particular tribe. Each standard carried its name proudly in large letters – *AEMILIA, CAMILIA, FABIA*, and so on – so that its members, if they wandered off, could see where they were supposed to be. There was much joking and horse-trading between the groups, until the trumpet of the herald called them to order. Then the official crier gave the legislation its second reading in a penetrating voice, after which Gabinius stepped forward and made a short speech. He had joyful news, he said: the news that the people of Rome had been praying for. Pompey the Great, deeply moved by the sufferings of the nation, was willing to reconsider his position, and serve as supreme commander – but only if it was the unanimous desire of them all. 'And is it your desire?' demanded Gabinius, to which there was a huge demonstration of enthusiasm. This went on for some time, thanks to the tribal officers. In fact, whenever it seemed the volume might be waning, Cicero would give a discreet signal to a couple of these officers, who would relay it across the forum, and the tribal standards would start waving again, rekindling the applause. Eventually Gabinius motioned them to be quiet. 'Then let us put it to the vote!'

Slowly – and one had to admire his courage in standing up at all, in the face of so many thousands – Trebellius rose from his place on the tribunes' bench and came forward, his hand raised to signal his desire to intervene. Gabinius regarded him with contempt, and then roared to the crowd, 'Well, citizens, should we let him speak?'

'No!' they screamed in response.

To which Trebellius, in a voice made shrill by nerves, shouted: 'Then I veto the bill!'

At any other time in the past four centuries, excepting the year when Tiberius Gracchus was tribune, this would have been the end of the legislation. But on that fateful morning, Gabinius motioned the jeering crowd to be silent. 'Does Trebellius speak for you all?'

'No!' they chanted back. 'No! No!'

'Does he speak for anyone here?' The only sound was the wind: even the senators who supported Trebellius dared not raise their voices, for they were standing unprotected among their tribes, and would have been set upon by the mob. 'Then, in accordance with the precedent set by Tiberius Gracchus, I propose that Trebellius, having failed to observe the oath of his office and represent the people, be removed as tribune, and that this be voted on immediately!'

Cicero turned to me. 'And now the play begins,' he said.

For a moment, the citizenry simply looked at one another. Then they started nodding, and a sound grew out of the crowd of realisation – that is how I think of it now, at any rate, as I sit in my little study with my eyes closed and try to remember it all – a realisation that they could do this, and that the grandees in the senate were powerless to stop them. Catulus, Hortensius and Crassus, in great alarm, started pushing their way towards the front of the assembly, demanding a hearing, but Gabinius had stationed a few of Pompey's veterans along the bottom steps and they were not allowed to pass. Crassus, in particular, had lost all his usual restraint. His face was red and contorted with rage as he tried to storm the tribunal, but he was pushed back. He noticed Cicero watching and pointed at him, and shouted something, but he was too far away and there was too much noise for us to hear. Cicero smiled at him benignly. The crier read out Gabinius's motion – 'That the people no longer desire Trebellius to be their tribune' – and the electoral clerks dispersed to their stations. As usual, the Suburana were the first to vote, filing up the gangplank two abreast to cast their ballots, then down the stone steps at the side of the temple and back into the forum. The city tribes followed one after the other, and every one of them voted for Trebellius to be stripped of his office. Then the rural tribes started balloting. This all took several hours, and throughout it Trebellius looked grey with anxiety, and frequently conferred with his companion, Roscius. At one point he disappeared from the tribunal. I did not see where he went, but I guess it must have been to plead with Crassus to release him from his obligation. All across the forum, small huddles of senators gathered as their tribes finished voting, and I noticed Catulus and Hortensius going, grim-faced, from group to group. Cicero also did the rounds, leaving me behind as he circulated among the senators, talking to some of those, such as Torquatus and his old ally Marcellinus, whom he had secretly persuaded to switch to Pompey's camp.

At length, after seventeen tribes had voted to oust Trebellius, Gabinius ordered a pause in the balloting. He summoned Trebellius to the front of the tribunal and asked him whether he was prepared now to bow to the will of the people, and by so doing keep his tribunate, or whether it would be necessary to hold an eighteenth ballot and cast him out of office. This was Trebellius's chance to enter history as the hero of his cause, and I have often wondered whether, in his old age, he looked back on his decision with regret. But I suppose he still had hopes of a political career. After a short hesitation, he signalled his assent and his veto was withdrawn. I need hardly add that he was subsequently despised by both sides and never heard of again.

All eyes now turned to Roscius, Crassus's second tribune, and it was at this point, some time in the early afternoon, that Catulus appeared again at the foot of the temple steps, cupped his hands to his mouth, and shouted up to Gabinius, demanding a hearing. As I have mentioned before, Catulus commanded great respect among the people for his patriotism. It was therefore hard for Gabinius to refuse him, not least because he was regarded as the senior ex-consul in the senate. He gestured to the veterans to let him pass, and Catulus, despite his age, shot up the steps like a lizard. 'This is a mistake,' Cicero muttered to me.

Gabinius told Cicero afterwards that he thought the aristocrats, seeing that they had lost, might now be willing to concede in the interests of national unity. But not at all. Catulus railed against the *lex Gabinia* and the illegal tactics being used to drive it through. It was madness, he declared, for the republic to entrust its security to one man. Warfare was a hazardous business, especially at sea: what would happen to this special command if Pompey was killed? Who would be his replacement? A cry went up of 'You!' which, however flattering, was not at all the response that Catulus wanted. He knew he was far too old to go off soldiering. What he really wanted was a dual command – Crassus and Pompey – because even though he detested Crassus personally, he reckoned that the richest man in Rome would at least provide a counterweight to Pompey's power. But by now Gabinius had begun to realise his error in letting Catulus speak. The winter days were short. He needed to finish the voting by sunset. He roughly interrupted the former consul and told him he had had his say: it was time to put the matter to the ballot. Roscius thereupon sprang forward and tried to make a formal proposal splitting the supreme command in two, but the people were becoming exasperated, and refused to give him a hearing. In fact they set up such a defeaning clamour it was said that the noise killed a raven flying overhead and sent it plummeting to the earth. All Roscius could do against the uproar was raise two fingers to veto the legislation and signify his belief that there should be two commanders. Gabinius knew that if he had to call yet another ballot to remove a tribune, he would lose the light, and with it the chance of establishing the supreme command that day – and who could tell what lengths the aristocrats might go to if they had a chance to regroup overnight? So he responded by turning his back on Roscius and ordering the bill to be put regardless.

'That's it,' said Cicero to me, as the voting clerks sprang to their stations. 'It's done. Run up to Pompey's house, and tell them to send a message to the general immediately. Write this down: "The bill is passed. The command is yours. You must set out for Rome at once. Be sure to arrive tonight. Your presence is required to secure the situation. Signed, Cicero."' I checked I had his words correctly, then hurried off on my errand, while Cicero plunged back into the crowded forum to practise his art – cajoling, flattering, sympathising, even occasionally threatening – for there was nothing, according to his philosophy, that could not be made or undone or repaired by words.

★ ★ ★

Thus was passed, by a unanimous vote of all the tribes, the *lex Gabinia*, a measure which was to have immense consequences – for all those personally concerned, for Rome, and for the world.

As night fell, the forum emptied and the combatants retired to their respective headquarters – the aristocratic diehards to the home of Catulus, on the brow of the Palatine; the adherents of Crassus to his own, more modest dwelling, lower down the same hill; and the victorious Pompeians to the mansion of their chief, on the Esquiline. Success had worked its usual fecund magic, and I should think that at least twenty senators crammed themselves into Pompey's tablinum to drink his wine and await his victorious return. The room was brilliantly illuminated by candelabra, and there was that thick atmosphere of drink and sweat and the noisy racket of masculine conversation which often follows the release of tension. Caesar, Afranius, Palicanus, Varro, Gabinius and Cornelius were all present, but the newcomers outnumbered them. I cannot remember all their names. Lucius Torquatus and his cousin, Aulus, were certainly present, along with another notable young pair of bluebloods, Metellus Nepos and Lentulus Marcellinus. Cornelius Sisenna (who had been one of Verres's most enthusiastic supporters) made himself thoroughly at home, putting his feet up on the furniture, as did the two ex-consuls, Lentulus Clodianus and Gellius Publicola (the same Gellius who was still smarting from Cicero's joke about the philosophy conference). As for Cicero, he sat apart in an adjoining chamber, composing an acceptance speech for Pompey to deliver the next day. At the time, I could not understand his curious quietness, but with hindsight I believe he may have had an intuition that something had just cracked in the commonwealth which it would be hard even for his words to repair. From time to time he sent me out to the vestibule to check on Pompey's whereabouts.

Shortly before midnight, a messenger arrived to say that Pompey was approaching the city along the Via Latina. A score of his veterans had been stationed at the Capena Gate to escort him home by torchlight, in case his enemies resorted to desperate tactics, but Quintus – who had spent much of the night touring the city with the precinct bosses – reported to his brother that the streets were quiet. Eventually, cheering outside announced the great man's arrival, and suddenly there he was among us, bigger than ever, grinning, shaking hands, clapping backs; even I received a friendly punch on the shoulder. The senators clamoured for Pompey to make a speech, at which Cicero remarked, a touch too loudly, 'He cannot speak yet: I have not written what he should say.' Just for a moment I saw a shadow flash across Pompey's face, but yet again Caesar came to Cicero's rescue, howling with laughter, and when Pompey suddenly grinned and wagged his finger in mock-reproach, the atmosphere relaxed into the joshing humour of an officers' mess, where the triumphant commander expects to be ribbed.

Whenever I picture the word *imperium* it is always Pompey who comes into my mind – Pompey that night, hovering over his map of the Mediterranean, distributing dominion over land and sea as casually as he dispensed his wine ('Marcellinus, you can have the Libyan sea, while you, Torquatus, shall have eastern Spain . . .'), and Pompey the following morning, when he went down into the forum to claim his prize. The annalists later reckoned that twenty thousand crammed into the centre of Rome to see him anointed world commander. It was such a throng that even Catulus and Hortensius dared not commit some last act of resistance, although I am sure they would have liked to, but were instead obliged to stand with the other senators, putting the best face on it they could; Crassus, typically, could not even manage that, and stayed away altogether. Pompey did not say much, mostly a few protestations of humble gratitude, crafted by Cicero, and an appeal for national unity. But then he did not have to say anything: his presence alone had caused the price of grain in the markets to halve, such was the confidence he inspired. And he finished with the most wonderful theatrical flourish, which can only have come from Cicero: 'I shall now put on again that uniform once so dear and so familiar to me, the sacred red cloak of a Roman commander in the field, and I shall not take it off again until victory in this war is won – or I shall not survive the outcome!' He raised his hand in salute and left the platform – was wafted from the platform would be a better way of putting it, on a wind of acclamation. The applause was still going on when suddenly, beyond the rostra, he came into view again – steadily climbing the steps of the Capitol, now wearing the *paludamentum*, that bright scarlet cloak which is the mark of every Roman proconsul on active service. As the people went wild with enthusiasm, I glanced across to where Cicero was standing next to Caesar. Cicero's expression was one of amused distaste, but Caesar's was enraptured, as if he were already glimpsing his own future. Pompey carried on into the precincts of the Capitoline Triad, where he sacrificed a bull to Jupiter, and left the city immediately afterwards, without saying goodbye to Cicero or to anyone else. It was to be six years before he returned.

XIII

In the annual elections for praetor that summer, Cicero topped the poll. It was an ugly, scrappy campaign, fought in the aftermath of the struggle over the *lex Gabinia*, when trust between the political factions had broken down. I have before me the letter which Cicero wrote to Atticus that summer, expressing his disgust at all things in public life: 'It is unbelievable in how short a time how much worse you will find them than when you left.' Twice the balloting had to be abandoned halfway through when fighting broke out on the Field of Mars. Cicero suspected Crassus of hiring thugs to disrupt the voting, but could not prove it. Whatever the truth, it was not until September that the eight praetors-elect were finally able to assemble in the senate house to determine which court each would preside over in the coming year. The selection, as usual, was to be settled by drawing lots.

The most coveted office was that of urban praetor, who in those days ran the justice system and was ranked third in the state, behind the two consuls; he also had responsibility for staging the Games of Apollo. If that was the plum, then the post to be avoided at all costs was the embezzlement court, a job of stunning tedium. 'Of course, I should like the urban praetorship,' Cicero confided to me as we walked down to the senate that morning. 'And frankly, I should rather hang myself than sort out embezzlement for a year. But I shall willingly settle for anything in between.' He was in a buoyant mood. The elections were concluded at last and he had won the most votes. Pompey was gone not only from Rome but from Italy, so he had no great man looming over him. And he was getting very close to the consulship now – so close he could almost feel that ivory chair beneath him.

There was always a full chamber for these lot-drawing ceremonies, combining as they did high politics with a game of chance, and by the time we arrived the majority of the senators had already gone in. Cicero entered to a noisy reception, with cheers from his old supporters among the *pedarii* and abusive shouts from the aristocrats. Crassus, stretched out in his usual position on the consular front bench, regarded him through half-closed eyes, like a big cat pretending to be asleep while a little bird hops by. The election had turned out much as Cicero had expected, and if I give you here the names of the other praetors-elect, I believe you will have a good sense of how politics stood at that time. Apart from Cicero, there were only two other men of obvious ability waiting calmly to draw their lots. By far the most talented was Aquilius Gallus, who some say was a better lawyer even than Cicero, and who was already a respected judge; in fact, he was something of a paragon – brilliant, modest, just, kindly, a man of supreme taste, with a magnificent mansion on the Viminal Hill; Cicero had it in mind to approach the older man to be his running-mate for consul. Next to Gallus, at least in gravitas, was Sulpicius Galba, of a distinguished aristocratic family, who had so many consular masks in his atrium, it was inconceivable he would not be one of Cicero's rivals for the consulship; but although he was honest and able, he was also harsh and arrogant – that would count against him in a tight election. Fourth in talent, I suppose, although Cicero sometimes burst out laughing at his absurdities, was Quintus Cornificius, a rich religious fundamentalist, who talked endlessly about the need to revive Rome's declining morals – 'the candidate of the gods', Cicero called him. After that, I am afraid, there was a great shelving-away in ability: remarkably, all the other four praetors-elect were men who had previously been expelled from the senate, for deficiencies in either funds or morals. The oldest of these was Varinius Glaber, one of those clever, bitter men who expect to succeed in life and cannot believe it when they realise they have failed – already a praetor seven years earlier, he had been given an army by the senate to put down the revolt of Spartacus; but his legions were weak and he had been beaten repeatedly by the rebel slaves, eventually retiring from public life in humili-ation. Then there was Caius Orchivius – 'all push and no talent', as Cicero characterised him – who had the support of a big voting syndicate. In seventh place when it came to brains Cicero placed Cassius Longinus – 'that barrel of lard' – who was some-times called the fattest man in Rome. Which left, in eighth, none other than Antonius Hybrida, the drinker who kept a slave girl for a wife, whom Cicero had agreed to help in the elections on the grounds that here, at least, would be one praetor whose ambitions he would not have to worry about. 'Do you know why they call him "Hybrida"?' Cicero asked me one day. 'Because he's half man, half imbecile. I wouldn't award him the half, person-ally.'

But those gods to whom Cornificius was so devoted have a way of punishing such hubris, and they duly punished Cicero that day. The lots were placed in an ancient urn which had been used for this purpose for centuries, and the presiding consul, Glabrio, called up the candidates in alphabetical order, which meant that Antonius Hybrida went first. He dipped his trembling hand into the urn for a token and gave it to Glabrio, who raised an eyebrow and then read out: 'Urban praetor.' There was a moment of silence, and then the chamber rang with such a shout of laughter that the pigeons roosting in the roof all took off in a great burst of shit and feathers. Hortensius and some of the other aristocrats, knowing that Cicero had helped Hybrida, pointed towards the orator and clapped their sides in mockery. Crassus almost fell off his bench with delight, while Hybrida himself – soon to be the third man in the state – stood beaming all around him, no doubt misinterpreting the derision as pleasure at his good fortune.

I could not see Cicero's face, but I could guess what he was thinking: that his bad luck would surely now be completed by drawing embezzlement. Gallus went next and won the court which administered electoral law; Longinus the fat man received treason; and when candidate-of-the-gods Cornificius was awarded the criminal court, the odds were starting to look decidedly grim – so much so that I was sure the worst was about to happen. But thankfully it was the next man up, Orchivius, who drew embezzlement. When Galba was given responsibility for hearing cases of violence against the state, that meant there were only two possibilities left for Cicero – either his familiar stamping-ground of the extortion court, or the position of foreign praetor, which would have left him effectively the deputy of Hybrida: a grim fate for the cleverest man in the city. As he stepped up to the dais to draw his lot, he gave a rueful shake of his head – you can scheme all you like in politics, the gesture seemed to say, but in the end it all comes down to luck. He thrust his hand into the urn and drew out – extortion. There was a certain pleasing symmetry in that it was Glabrio, the former president of this very court in which Cicero had made his name, who read out the announcement. So that left the foreign praetorship to Varinius, the victim of Spartacus. Thus the courts were settled for the following year, and the preliminary field lined up for the consulship.

Amid all this rush of political events, I have neglected to mention that Pomponia had become pregnant in the spring – proof, as Cicero wrote triumphantly to Atticus when he passed on the news, that the marriage with Quintus must be working after all. Not long after the praetorian elections, the child was born, a healthy boy. It was a matter of great pride to me, and a mark of my growing standing within the family, that I was invited to attend the lustrical, on the ninth day following the birth. The ceremony was held at the Temple of Tellus, next to the family house, and I doubt whether any nephew could have had a more doting uncle than Cicero, who insisted on commissioning a splendid amulet from a silversmith as a naming-present. It was only after baby Quintus had been blessed by the priest with holy water, and Cicero took him in his arms, that I realised how much he missed having a boy of his own. A large part of any man's motivation in pursuing the consulship must surely have been that his son, and grandson, and sons of his sons to infinity, could exercise the right of *ius imaginum*, and display his likeness after death in the family atrium. What was the point in founding a glorious family name if the line was extinct before it even started? And glancing across the temple to Terentia, carefully studying her husband as he stroked the baby's cheek with the back of his little finger, I could see that the same thought was in her mind.

The arrival of a child often prompts a keen reappraisal of the future, and I am sure this was what led Cicero, shortly after the birth of his nephew, to arrange for Tullia to become betrothed. She was now ten years old, his cynosure as ever, and rare was the day, despite his legal and political work, when he did not clear a little space to read to her or play some game. And it was typical of his mingling of tenderness and cunning that he first raised his plan with her, rather than with Terentia. 'How would you like,' he said to her one morning, when the three of us were in his study, 'to get married one day?' When she replied that she would like that very much, he asked her whom in all the world she would most like to have as a husband.

'Tiro!' she cried, flinging her arms around my waist.

'I am afraid he is much too busy helping me to have time to take a wife,' he replied solemnly. 'Who else?'

Her circle of grown-up male acquaintances was limited, so it was not long before she raised the name of Frugi, who had spent so much time with Cicero since the Verres case, he was almost a part of the family.

'Frugi!' exclaimed Cicero, as if the idea had never before occurred to him. 'What a wonderful thought! And you are sure this is what you want? You are? Then let us go and tell your mama immediately.'

In this way Terentia found herself outmanoeuvred by her husband on her own territory as skilfully as if she had been some cretinous aristocrat in the senate. Not that she could have found much to object to in Frugi, who was a good enough match even for her – a gentle, diligent young man, now aged twenty-one, from an extremely distinguished family. But she was far too shrewd not to see that Cicero, by creating a substitute whom he could train and bring on to a public career, was doing the next best thing to having a son of his own. This realisation no doubt made her feel threatened, and Terentia always reacted violently to threats. The betrothal ceremony in November went smoothly enough, with Frugi – who was very fond of his fiancée, by the way – shyly placing a ring on her finger, under the approving gaze of both families and their households, with the wedding fixed for five years hence, when Tullia would be pubescent. But that night Cicero and Terentia had one of their most ferocious fights. It blew up in the tablinum before I had time to get out of the way. Cicero had made some innocuous remark about the Frugis being very welcoming to Tullia, to which Terentia, who had been ominously quiet for some time, responded that it was indeed very good of them, *considering*.

'Considering what?' asked Cicero wearily. He had obviously decided that arguing with her that night was as inevitable as vomiting after a bad oyster, and that he might as well get it out of the way at once.

'Considering the connection they are making,' she responded, and very quickly she was launched on her favourite line of attack – the shamefulness of Cicero's lackeying towards Pompey and his coterie of provincials, the way that this had set the family in opposition to all who were most honourable in the state, and the rise of mob rule which had been made possible by the illegal passage of the *lex Gabinia*. I cannot remember all of it, and in any case what does it matter? Like most arguments between husband and wife it was not about the thing itself, but a different matter entirely – that is, her failure to produce a son, and Cicero's consequent semi-paternal attachment to Frugi. Nevertheless, I do remember Cicero snapping back that, whatever Pompey's faults, no one disputed that he was a brilliant soldier, and that once he had been awarded his special command and had raised his troops and put to sea, he had wiped out the pirate threat in only forty-nine days. And I also recall her crushing retort, that if the pirates really had been swept from the sea in seven weeks, perhaps they had not been quite the menace that Cicero and his friends had made them out to be in the first place! At that point, I managed to slip out of the room and retreat to my little cubicle, so the rest was lost to me. But the mood in the house during the following days was as fragile as Neapolitan glass.

'You see how hard pressed I am?' Cicero complained to me the next morning, rubbing his forehead with his knuckles. 'There is no respite for me anywhere, either in my business or my leisure.'

As for Terentia, she became increasingly preoccupied with her supposed barrenness, and took to praying daily at the Temple of the Good Goddess on the Aventine Hill, where harmless snakes roamed freely in the precincts to encourage fertility and no man was allowed to set eyes upon the inner sanctum. I also heard from her maid that she had set up a small shrine to Juno in her bedroom.

Secretly, I believe Cicero shared Terentia's opinion of Pompey. There was something suspicious as well as glorious about the speed of his victory ('Organised at the end of winter,' as Cicero put it, 'started at the beginning of spring, and finished by the middle of the summer'), which made one wonder whether the whole enterprise could not have been handled perfectly well by a commander appointed in the normal way. Still, there was no denying his success. The pirates had been rolled up like a carpet, driven from the waters of Sicily and Africa eastwards, through the Illyrian Sea to Achaia, and then purged from the whole of Greece. Finally, they had been trapped by Pompey himself in their last great stronghold, Coracesium, in Cilicia, and in a huge battle on sea and land, ten thousand had been killed and four hundred vessels destroyed. Another twenty thousand had been captured. But rather than have them crucified, as no doubt Crassus would have done, Pompey had ordered the pirates to be resettled inland with their wives and families, in the depopulated towns of Greece and Asia Minor – one of which he renamed, with characteristic modesty, Pompeiopolis. All this he did without reference to the senate.

Cicero followed his patron's fantastic progress with mixed feelings ('Pompeiopolis! Dear gods, the *vulgarity* of it!'), not least because he knew that the more swollen with success Pompey became, the longer the shadow he would cast over his own career. Meticulous planning and overwhelming numerical superiority: these were Pompey's favourite tactics, both on the battlefield and in Rome, and as soon as phase one of his campaign – the destruction of the pirates – was completed, phase two began in the forum, when Gabinius started agitating to have the command of the Eastern legions stripped from Lucullus and awarded to Pompey. He used the same trick as before, employing his powers as tribune to summon witnesses to the rostra, who gave the people a sorry picture of the war against Mithradates. Some of the legions, unpaid for years, had simply refused to leave their winter camp. The poverty of these ordinary fighting men Gabinius contrasted with the immense wealth of their aristocratic commander, who had shipped back so much booty from the campaign that he had bought an entire hill just outside the gates of Rome and was building a great palace there, with all the state rooms named after the gods. Gabinius subpoenaed Lucullus's architects and had them brought to the rostra, where he forced them to show to the people all their plans and models. Lucullus's name from that time on became a synonym for outrageous luxury, and the angry citizens burned his effigy in the forum.

In December, Gabinius and Cornelius stood down as tribunes, and a new creature of Pompey's, the tribune-elect, Caius Manilius, took over the safeguarding of his interests in the popular assemblies. He immediately proposed a law granting command of the war against Mithradates to Pompey, along with the government of the provinces of Asia, Cilicia and Bithynia – the latter two held by Lucullus. Any thin hopes that Cicero might have entertained of lying low on the issue were destroyed when Gabinius came to see him bearing a message from Pompey. This briskly conveyed the general's good wishes, along with his hopes that Cicero would support the *lex Manilia* 'in all its provisions', not only behind the scenes but also in public, from the rostra.

'"In all its provisions",' repeated Gabinius, with a smirk. 'You know what that means.'

'I presume it means the clause which appoints you to the command of the legions on the Euphrates, thus giving you legal immunity from prosecution now that your term as tribune has expired.'

'You have it.' Gabinius grinned and did a passable impersonation of Pompey, drawing himself up and puffing out his cheeks: '"Is he not clever, gentlemen? Did I not tell you he was clever?"'

'Calm youself, Gabinius,' said Cicero wearily. 'I assure you there is no one I would rather see heading off to the Euphrates than you.'

It is dangerous in politics to find oneself a great man's whipping boy. Yet this was the role in which Cicero was now becoming trapped. Men who would never have dared directly to insult or criticise Pompey could instead land blows on his lawyer-surrogate with impunity, knowing that everyone would guess their real target. But there was no escaping a direct order from the commander-in-chief, and so this became the occasion of Cicero's first speech from the rostra. He took immense trouble over it, dictating it to me several days beforehand, and then showing it to Quintus and Frugi for their comments. From Terentia he prudently withheld it, for he knew he would have to send a copy to Pompey and it was therefore necessary for him to ladle on the flattery. (I see from the manuscript, for example, that Pompey's 'superhuman genius as a commander' was amended at Quintus's suggestion to 'Pompey's superhuman *and unbelievable* genius as a commander'.) He hit upon a brilliant slogan to sum up Pompey's success – 'one law, one man, one year' – and fretted over the rest of the speech for hours, conscious that if he failed on the rostra, his career would be set back and his enemies would say he did not have the common touch to move the plebs of Rome. When the morning came to deliver it, he was physically sick with nerves, retching again and again into the latrine while I stood next to him with a towel. He was so white and drawn that I actually wondered if he would have the legs to get all the way down to the forum. But it was his belief that a great performer, however experienced, must always be frightened before going on stage – 'the nerves should be as taut as bowstrings if the arrows are to fly' – and by the time we reached the back of the rostra he was ready. Needless to say, he was carrying no notes. We heard Manilius announce his name and the applause begin. It was a beautiful morning, clear and bright; the crowd was huge. He adjusted his sleeves, drew himself erect, and slowly ascended into the noise and light.

Catulus and Hortensius once again were the leaders of the opposition to Pompey, but they had devised no new arguments since the *lex Gabinia*, and Cicero had some sport with them. 'What is Hortensius saying?' he teased. 'That if one man is to be put in supreme command, the right man is Pompey, but that supreme

command ought not to be given to one man? That line of
reasoning is now out of date, refuted not so much by words as
by events. For it was you, Hortensius, who denounced that courageous man Gabinius for introducing a law to appoint a single
commander against the pirates. Now I ask you in Heaven's name
– if on that occasion the Roman people had thought more of
your opinion than of their own welfare and their true interests,
should we today be in possession of our present glory and our
worldwide empire?' By the same token, if Pompey wanted
Gabinius as one of his legionary commanders, he should have
him, for no man had done more, apart from Pompey, to defeat
the pirates. 'Speaking for myself,' he concluded, 'whatever devotion, wisdom, energy or talent I possess, whatever I can achieve
by virtue of the praetorship which you have conferred upon me,
I dedicate to the support of this law. And I call on all the gods
to witness – most especially the guardians of this hallowed spot
who see clearly into the hearts of all who enter upon public life
– that I am acting not as a favour to Pompey, nor in the hope of
gaining favour from him, but solely in the cause of my country.'
He left the rostra to respectful applause. The law was passed,
Lucullus was stripped of his command and Gabinius was given
his legateship. As for Cicero, he had surmounted another obstacle
in his progress to the consulship, but was more hated than ever
by the aristocrats.

Later, he had a letter from Varro, describing Pompey's reaction
at the moment when he received the news that he now had
complete control of Rome's forces in the East. As his officers
crowded round him at his headquarters in Ephesus to congratulate him, he frowned, struck himself on the thigh, and said ('in
a weary voice', according to Varro): 'How sad it makes me, this
constant succession of labours! Really I would rather be one of

those people whom no one has heard about, if I am never to have any relief from military service, and never to be able to escape from being envied so that I can live quietly in the country with my wife.' Such play-acting was hard to stomach, especially when the whole world knew how much he had desired the command.

The praetorship brought an elevation in Cicero's station. Now he had six lictors to guard him whenever he left the house. He did not care for them at all. They were rough fellows, hired for their strength and easy cruelty: if a Roman citizen was sentenced to be punished, they were the ones who carried it out, and they were adept at floggings and beheadings. Because their posts were permanent, some had been used to power for years, and they rather looked down on the magistrates they guarded as mere transitory politicians, here today and gone tomorrow. Cicero hated it when they cleared the crowds out of his way too roughly, or ordered passers-by to remove their headgear or dismount in the presence of a praetor, for the people being so humiliated were his voters. He instructed the lictors to show more politeness, and for a time they would, but they soon snapped back into their old ways. The chief of them, the *proximus lictor*, who was supposed to stand at Cicero's side at all times, was particularly obnoxious. I forget his name now, but he was always bringing Cicero tittle-tattle of what the other praetors were up to, gleaned from his fellow lictors, not realising that this made him deeply suspect in the eyes of Cicero, who was well aware that gossip is a trade, and that reports of his own actions would be being offered as currency in return. 'These people,' Cicero complained to me one morning, 'are a warning of what happens to any state which has a permanent staff of officials. They begin as our servants and end up imagining themselves our masters!'

My own status rose with his. I discovered that to be known as the confidential secretary of a praetor, even if one was a slave, was to enjoy an unaccustomed civility from those one met. Cicero told me beforehand that I could expect to be offered money to use my influence on behalf of petitioners, and when I insisted hotly that I would never accept a bribe, he cut me off. 'No, Tiro, you should have some money of your own. Why not? I ask only that you tell me who has paid you, and that you make it clear to whoever approaches you that my judgements are not to be bought, and that I will decide things on their merits. Aside from that, I trust you to use your own discretion.' This conversation meant a great deal to me. I had always hoped that eventually Cicero would grant me my freedom; permitting me to have some savings of my own I saw as a preparation for that day. The amounts which came in were small – fifty or a hundred here and there – and in return I might be required to bring a document to the praetor's attention, or draft a letter of introduction for him to sign. The money I kept in a small purse, hidden behind a loose brick in the wall of my cubicle.

As praetor, Cicero was expected to take in promising pupils from good families to study law with him, and in May, after the senate recess, a new young intern of sixteen joined his chambers. This was Marcus Caelius Rufus from Interamnia, the son of a wealthy banker and prominent election official of the Velina tribe. Cicero agreed, largely as a political favour, to supervise the boy's training for two years, at the end of which it was fixed that he would move on to complete his apprenticeship in another household – that of Crassus, as it happened, for Crassus was a business associate of Caelius's father, and the banker was anxious that his heir should learn how to manage a fortune. The father was a ghastly money-lending type, short and furtive, who seemed to regard his son as an investment which was failing to show an adequate yield. 'He needs to be beaten regularly,' he announced, just before he brought him in to meet Cicero. 'He is clever enough, but wayward and dissolute. You have my permission to whip him as much as you like.' Cicero looked askance at this, having never whipped anyone in his life, but fortunately as it turned out he got on very well with young Caelius, who was as dissimilar to his father as it was possible to imagine. He was tall and handsome and quick-witted, with an indifference towards money and business which Cicero found amusing; I less so, for it generally fell to me to do all the humdrum tasks which were Caelius's responsibility, and which he shirked. But still, I must concede, looking back, that he had charm.

I shall not dwell on the details of Cicero's praetorship. This is not a textbook about the law, and I can sense your eagerness for me to get on to the climax of my story – the election for the consulship itself. Suffice it to say that Cicero was considered a fair and honest judge, and that the work was easily within his competence. If he encountered a particularly awkward point of jurisprudence, and needed a second opinion, he would either consult his old friend and fellow pupil of Molon, Servius Sulpicius, or go over to see the distinguished praetor of the election court, Aquilius Gallus, in his mansion on the Viminal Hill. The biggest case over which he had to preside was that of Caius Licinius Macer, a kinsman and supporter of Crassus, who was impeached for his actions as governor of Macedonia. The hearing dragged on for weeks, and at the end of it Cicero summed up very fairly, except that he could not resist one joke. The nub of the prosecution case was that Macer had taken half a million in illegal payments. Macer at first denied it. The prosecution then produced proof that the exact same sum had been paid into a money-lending company which he controlled. Macer abruptly changed his story and claimed that, yes, he remembered the payments, but thought that they were legal. 'Now, it may be,' said Cicero to the jury, as he was directing them on points of evidence, 'that the defendant believed this.' He left a pause just long enough for some of them to start laughing, whereupon he put on a mock-stern face. 'No, no, he may have believed it. In which case' – another pause – 'you may reasonably conclude perhaps that he was too *stupid* to be a Roman governor.' I had sat in sufficient courts by then to know from the gale of laughter that Cicero had just convicted the man as surely as if he had been the prosecuting counsel. But Macer – who was not stupid at all, but on the contrary, very clever: so clever that he thought everyone else a fool – did not see the danger, and actually left the tribunal while the jury was balloting in order to go home and change and have a haircut, in anticipation of his victory celebration that night. While he was absent, the jury convicted him, and he was just leaving his house to return to the court when Crassus intercepted him on his doorstep and told him what had happened. Some say he dropped dead on the spot from shock, others that he went straight back indoors and killed himself to spare his son the humiliation of his exile. Either way, he died, and Crassus – as if he needed one – had a whole new reason for hating Cicero.

The Games of Apollo on the sixth day of July traditionally marked the start of the election season, although in truth it always seemed to be election season in those days. No sooner had one campaign come to an end than the candidates began anticipating the start of the next. Cicero joked that the business of governing the state was merely something to occupy the time between polling days. And perhaps this is one of the things that killed the republic: it gorged itself to death on votes. At any rate, the responsibility for honouring Apollo with a programme of public entertainment always fell to the urban praetor, which in this particular year was Antonius Hybrida.

Nobody had been expecting much, or indeed anything at all, for Hybrida was known to have drunk and gambled away all his money. So it was a vast surprise when he staged not only a series of wonderful theatrical productions, but also lavish spectacles in the Circus Maximus, with a full programme of twelve chariot races, athletic competitions and a wild-beast hunt involving panthers and all manner of exotic animals. I did not attend, but Cicero gave me a full account when he came home that evening. Indeed, he could talk of nothing else. He flung himself down on one of the couches in the empty dining room – Terentia was in the country with Tullia – and described the parade into the Circus: the charioteers and the near-naked athletes (the boxers, the wrestlers, the runners, the javelin throwers and the discus men), the flute players and the lyre players, the dancers dressed as Bacchanalians and satyrs, the incense burners, the bulls and the goats and the heifers with their gilded horns plodding to sacrifice, the cages of wild beasts and the gladiators . . . He seemed dizzy with it. 'How much must it have all cost? That is what I kept asking myself. Hybrida must be banking on making it all back when he goes out to his province. You should have heard the cheers they gave to him when he entered and when he left! Well, I see nothing for it, Tiro. Unbelievable as it seems, we shall have to amend the list. Come.'

We went together into the study and I opened the strongbox

and pulled out all the papers relating to Cicero's consular campaign. There were many secret lists in there – lists of backers, of donors, of supporters he had yet to win over, of towns and regions where he was strong and where he was weak. The key list, however, was of the men he had identified as possible rivals, together with a summary of all the information known about them, pro and anti. Galba was at the top of it, with Gallus next to him, and then Cornificius, and finally Palicanus. Now Cicero took my pen and carefully, in his neat and tiny writing, added a fifth, whose name he had never expected to see there: Antonius Hybrida.

And then, a few days later, something happened which was to change Cicero's fortunes and the future of the state entirely, although he did not realise it at the time. I am reminded of one of those harmless-looking specks which one occasionally hears about, that a man discovers on his skin one morning, and thinks little of, only to see it gradually swell over the following months into an enormous tumour. The speck in this instance was a message, received out of the blue, summoning Cicero to see the pontifex maximus, Metellus Pius. Cicero was mightily intrigued by this, since Pius, who was very old (sixty-four, at least) and grand, had never previously deigned even to speak to him, let alone demand his company. Accordingly, we set off at once, with the lictors clearing our way.

In those days, the official residence of the head of the state religion was on the Via Sacra, next to the House of the Vestal Virgins, and I remember that Cicero was pleased to be seen entering the premises, for this really was the sacred heart of Rome, and not many men ever got the chance to cross the threshold.

We were shown to a staircase and conducted along a gallery which looked down into the garden of the vestals' residence. I secretly hoped to catch a glimpse of one of those six mysterious white-clad maidens, but the garden was deserted, and it was not possible to linger as the bow-legged figure of Pius was already waiting for us impatiently at the end of the gallery, tapping his foot, with a couple of priests on either side of him. He had been a soldier all his life and had the cracked and roughened look of something made of leather which has been left outside for years and only lately brought indoors. There was no handshake for Cicero, no invitation to be seated, no preliminaries of any sort. Pius merely said immediately, in his hoarse voice, 'Praetor, I need to talk to you about Sergius Catilina.'

At the mere mention of the name, Cicero stiffened, for Catilina was the man who had tortured to death his distant cousin, the populist politician Gratidianus, by breaking his limbs and gouging out his eyes and tongue. A jagged streak of violent madness ran through Catilina, like lightning across his brain. At one moment he could be charming, cultured, friendly; then a man would make some seemingly innocuous remark, or he would catch another looking at him in a way he thought dis-respectful, and he would lose all self-restraint. During the proscriptions of Sulla, when death lists were posted in the forum, Catilina had been one of the most proficient killers with the hammer and knife – *percussores*, as they were known – and had made a lot of money out of the estates of those he executed. His own brother-in-law was among the men he had murdered. Yet he had an undeniable charisma, and for each person he repulsed by his savagery, he attracted two or three more by his equally reckless displays of generosity. He was also sexually licentious. Seven years previously, he had been

prosecuted for having sexual relations with a vestal virgin –
none other, in fact, than Terentia's half-sister, Fabia. This was
a capital offence, not only for him but for her, and if he had
been found guilty she would have suffered the traditional
punishment for a vestal virgin who broke her sacred vows of
chastity – burial alive in the tiny chamber reserved for the
purpose beside the Colline Gate. But the aristocrats, led by
Catulus, had rallied around Catilina and secured his acquittal,
and his political career had continued uninterrupted. He had
been praetor the year before last, and had then gone out to
govern Africa, thus missing the turmoil surrounding the *lex
Gabinia*. He had only just returned.

'My family,' continued Pius, 'have been the chief patrons of
Africa since my father governed the province half a century ago.
The people there look to me for protection, and I have to tell
you, Praetor, I have never seen them more incensed by any man
than they have been by Sergius Catilina. He has plundered that
province from end to end – taxed them and murdered them,
stolen their temple treasures and raped their wives and daughters. The Sergii!' he exclaimed in disgust, retching up a great gob
of yellow phlegm into his mouth and spitting it on to the floor.
'Descended from the Trojans, or so they boast, and not a decent
one among them for two hundred years! And now they tell me
you are the praetor responsible for bringing his type to book.'
He looked Cicero up and down. 'Amazing! I cannot say that I
know who the hell you are, but there it is. So what are you going
to do about it?'

Cicero was always cool when someone tried to insult him. He
merely said, 'Do the Africans have a case prepared?'

'They do. They already have a delegation in Rome seeking a
suitable prosecutor. Who should they go to?'

'That is hardly a matter for me. I must remain the impartial president of the court.'

'Blah blah. Spare me the lawyer's talk. Privately. Man-to-man.' Pius beckoned Cicero to come closer. He had left most of his teeth behind on various battlefields and his breath whistled when he tried to whisper. 'You know the courts these days better than I. Who could do it?'

'Frankly, it will not be easy,' said Cicero. 'Catilina's reputation for violence precedes him. It will take a brave man to lay a charge against such a brazen killer. And presumably he will be standing for the consulship next year. There is a powerful enemy in the making.'

'Consul?' Pius suddenly struck himself very hard on the chest. The thump made his priestly attendants jump. 'Sergius Catilina will not be consul – not next year or any year – not as long as this old body has any life left in it! There must be someone in this city who is man enough to bring him to justice. And if not – well, I am not quite such a senile fool that I have forgotten how to fight in Rome. You just make sure, Praetor,' he concluded, 'that you leave enough time in your calendar to hear the case,' and he shuffled off down the corridor, grumbling to himself, pursued by his holy assistants.

As he watched him go, Cicero frowned and shook his head. Not comprehending politics nearly as well as I should have done, even after thirteen years in his service, I was at a loss to understand why he should have found this conversation so troubling. But he certainly was shaken, and as soon as we were back on the Via Sacra, he drew me out of the keen hearing of the *proximus lictor* and said, 'This is a serious development, Tiro. I should have seen this coming.' When I asked why it mattered to him whether Catilina was prosecuted or not, he replied, in a withering tone,

'Because, *bird-brain*, it is illegal to stand for election if you have charges pending against you. Which means that if the Africans do find a champion, and if a charge is laid against Catilina, and if it drags on into next summer, he will be barred from standing for the consulship until the case is resolved. Which means that if by any chance he is acquitted, *I* shall have to fight him in *my* year.'

I doubt whether there was another senator in Rome who would have tried to peer so far into the future – who would have piled up so many *ifs* and discerned a reason for alarm. Certainly, when he explained his anxiety to Quintus, his brother dismissed it with a laugh: 'And *if* you were struck by lightning, Marcus, and *if* Metellus Pius were able to remember what day of the week it was . . .' But Cicero continued to fret, and he made discreet enquiries about the progress of the African delegation as they searched for a credible advocate. However, as he suspected, they were finding it hard going, despite the immense amount of evidence they had collected of Catilina's wrongdoing, and the fact that Pius had carried a resolution in the senate censuring the former governor. No one was anxious to take on such a dangerous opponent, and risk being discovered floating face-down in the Tiber late one night. So, for the time being at least, the prosecution languished, and Cicero put the matter to the back of his mind. Unfortunately, it was not to remain there for long.

XIV

At the end of his term as praetor, Cicero was entitled to go abroad and govern a province for a year. This was the normal practice in the republic. It gave a man the opportunity to gain administrative experience, and also to replenish his coffers after the expense of running for office. Then he would come home, assess the political mood, and if all seemed promising, stand for the consulship that summer: Antonius Hybrida, for example, who had obviously incurred tremendous liabilities by the cost of his Games of Apollo, went off to Cappadocia to see what he could steal. But Cicero did not take this course, and waived his right to a province. For one thing, he did not want to put himself in a position where a trumped-up charge might be laid against him and he would find himself with a special prosecutor dogging his footsteps for months. For another, he was still haunted by that year he had spent as a magistrate in Sicily, and ever afterwards he had hated to be away from Rome for longer than a week or two. There can seldom have been a more urban creature than Cicero. It was from the bustle of the streets and the courts, the senate and the forum that he drew his energy, and the prospect of a year of dreary provincial company, however lucrative, in Cilicia or Macedonia, was anathema to him.

Besides, he had committed himself to an immense amount of advocacy, starting with the defence of Caius Cornelius, Pompey's former tribune, who had been charged with treason by the aristocrats. No fewer than five of the great patrician senators – Hortensius, Catulus, Lepidus, Marcus Lucullus and even old Metellus Pius – lined up to prosecute Cornelius for his part in advancing Pompey's legislation, charging him with illegally ignoring the veto of a fellow tribune. Faced with such an onslaught, I was sure that he was bound to be sent into exile. Cornelius thought so too, and had actually packed up his house and was ready to leave. But Cicero was always inspired by the sight of Hortensius and Catulus on the other side, and he rose to the occasion, making a most effective closing speech for the defence. 'Are we really to be lectured,' he demanded, 'on the traditional rights of the tribunes by five gentlemen, all of whom supported the legislation of Sulla abolishing exactly those rights? Did any of these illustrious figures step forward to support the gallant Gnaeus Pompey when, as the first act of his consulship, he restored the tribunes' power of veto? Ask yourself, finally, this: is it really a new-found concern for the traditions of the tribunes which drags them from their fish-ponds and private porticoes into court? Or is it, rather, the product of certain other "traditions" much dearer to their hearts – their tradition of self-interest and their traditional desire for revenge?'

There was more in a similar vein, and by the time he had finished, the five distinguished litigants (who had made the mistake of all sitting in a row) were looking half their previous size, especially Pius, who obviously found it hard to keep up, and who had his hand cupped to his ear and kept twisting in his seat as his tormentor prowled around the court. This was to be one of the old soldier's last appearances in public before the long twilight of his illness descended upon him. After the jury had voted to acquit Cornelius of all the charges, Pius left the court to jeers and mocking laughter, wearing an expression of elderly bafflement which I fear nowadays I recognise all too well as the natural set of my own features. 'Well,' said Cicero, with a certain satisfaction, as we prepared to walk home, 'at any rate, I believe that now he knows who I am.'

I shall not mention every case which Cicero took on at this time because there were dozens, all part of his strategy to place as many influential men as possible under an obligation to support him at the consular election, and to keep his name constantly in the voters' minds. He certainly chose his clients carefully, and four of them at least were senators: Fundanius, who controlled a big voting syndicate; Orchivius, who had been one of his colleagues as praetor; Gallius, who was planning to run for a praetorship; and Mucius Orestinus, charged with robbery, who was hoping to become tribune, and whose case tied up the practice for many days.

I believe that never before had any candidate approached the business of politics as exactly that – a business – and every week a meeting was convened in Cicero's study to review the campaign's progress. Participants came and went, but the inner core consisted of five: Cicero himself, Quintus, Frugi, myself, and Cicero's legal apprentice, Caelius, who, although still very young (or perhaps because of it), was adept at picking up gossip around the city. Quintus was once again the campaign manager, and insisted on presiding. He liked to suggest, by the occasional indulgent smile or raised eyebrow, that Cicero, genius though he was, could be something of an airy-fairy intellectual, and needed the blunt common sense of his brother to keep his feet on the earth; and Cicero, with a reasonably good grace, played along.

It would make an interesting study, if only I had the life left in me to write it: the story of brothers in politics. There were the Gracchi, of course, Tiberius and Caius, who devoted themselves to distributing wealth from the rich to the poor, and who both perished violently as a result. And then in my own time there were Marcus and Lucius Lucullus, patrician consuls in successive years, as well as any number of siblings from the Metellus and Marcellus clans. In a sphere of human activity in which friendships are transitory and alliances made to be broken, the knowledge that another man's name is forever linked to yours, however the fates may play, must be a powerful source of strength. The relationship between the Ciceros, like that between most brothers, I expect, was a complicated mixture of fondness and resentment, jealousy and loyalty. Without Cicero, Quintus would have been a dull and competent officer in the army, and then a dull and competent farmer in Arpinum, whereas Cicero without Quintus would still have been Cicero. Knowing this, and knowing that his brother knew it too, Cicero went out of his way to conciliate him, generously wrapping him in the glittering mantle of his fame.

Quintus spent a long time that winter compiling an election handbook, a distillation of his fraternal advice to Cicero, which he liked to quote from whenever possible, as if it were Plato's *Republic. Consider what city this is,* it began, *what it is you seek, and who you are. Every day, when you go down to the forum, repeat to yourself: 'I am a new man. I seek the consulship. This is Rome.'* I can still recall some of the other little homilies it preached. *All things are full of deceit, snares and treachery. Hold fast to the saying of Epicharmus, that the bone and sinew of wisdom is 'Never trust rashly'*

. . . See to it that you show off both the variety and number of your friends . . . I am very anxious that you should always have a crowd about you . . . If someone asks you to do something, do not decline, even if you cannot do it . . . Lastly, see that your canvass is a fine show, brilliant, resplendent and popular; and also, if it can be managed, that there should be scandalous talk about the crimes, lusts and briberies of your competitors.

Quintus was very proud of his handbook, and many years later he actually had it published, much to the horror of Cicero, who believed that political mastery, like great art, depends for its effects on the concealment of all the cunning which lies behind it.

In the spring Terentia celebrated her thirtieth birthday and Cicero arranged a small dinner party in her honour. Quintus and Pomponia came, and Frugi and his parents, and fussy Servius Sulpicius and his unexpectedly pretty wife, Postumia; there must have been others, but the flow of time has washed them from my memory. The household was assembled briefly by Eros the steward to convey our good wishes, and I remember thinking, when Terentia appeared, that I had never seen her looking quite so fine, or in a more cheerful mood. Her short dark curly hair was lustrous, her eyes bright, and her normally bony frame seemed fuller and softer. I said as much to her maid after the master and mistress had led their guests in to dinner, at which she glanced around to check that no one was observing us, linked her hands and made a circular gesture outwards over her stomach. At first I did not understand, which gave her a fit of the giggles, and it was only after she had run back upstairs, still laughing, that I realised what a fool I had been; and not just me, of course.

A normal husband would surely have noticed the symptoms sooner, but Cicero was invariably up at dawn and back at dusk, and even then there was always a speech to write or a letter to be sent – the miracle was that he should have found time to perform his conjugal duties at all. Anyway, midway through the dinner, a loud shout of excitement, followed by applause, confirmed that Terentia had taken the opportunity of the celebration to announce her pregnancy.

Later that evening, Cicero came into the study with a wide smile. He acknowledged my congratulations with a bow. 'She is certain it is a boy. Apparently, the Good Goddess has informed her of the fact, by means of certain supernatural signs understood only by women.' He rubbed his hands vigorously in anticipation; he really could not stop smiling. 'Always a wonderful addition at election time, Tiro, a baby – suggestive of a virile candidate, and a respectable family man. Talk to Quintus about scheduling the infant's campaign appearances.' He pointed to my notebook. 'I am joking, you idiot!' he said, seeing my dumb-struck expression, and pretended to cuff my ear. But I am un-decided who it says most about, him or me, that I am still not entirely convinced he *was* joking.

From this time on, Terentia became much stricter in her observance of religious rituals, and on the day following her birthday she made Cicero accompany her to the Temple of Juno on Capitol Hill, where she bought a small lamb for the priest to sacrifice, in gratitude for her pregnancy and marriage. Cicero was delighted to oblige her, for he was genuinely overjoyed at the prospect of another child, and besides, he knew how much the voters lapped up these public displays of piety.

★   ★   ★

And now I fear I must return to the growing tumour that was Sergius Catilina.

A few weeks after Cicero's summons to see Metellus Pius, that year's consular elections were held. But such was the flagrant use of bribery by the winning ticket, the result was swiftly annulled and in October the poll was held again. On this occasion Catilina submitted his name as a candidate. Pius swiftly put a stop to his chances – I suppose it must have been the last successful battle the old warrior fought – and the senate ruled that only those whose names were on the original ballot would be permitted to stand. This drove Catilina into one of his furies, and he began hanging around the forum with his violent friends, making all kinds of threats, which were taken sufficiently seriously by the senate that they voted an armed bodyguard to the consuls. Not surprisingly, no one had been brave enough to come forward and take up the Africans' case in the extortion court. I actually suggested it to Cicero one day, wondering if it might be a popular cause for him to espouse – after all, he had brought down Verres, and that had made him the most famous advocate in the world. But Cicero shook his head. 'Compared to Catilina, Verres was a kitten. Besides, Verres was not a man anyone much liked, whereas Catilina undeniably has a following.'

'Why is he so popular?' I asked.

'Dangerous men always attract a following, although that is not what concerns me. If it were simply a question of the mob in the street, he would be less of a threat. It is the fact that he has widespread aristocratic support – Catulus certainly, which probably also means Hortensius.'

'I should have thought him much too uncouth for Hortensius.'

'Oh, Hortensius knows how to make use of a street fighter

when the occasion demands it. Many a cultured house is protected by a savage dog. And Catilina is also a Sergius, do not forget, so they approve of him on snobbish grounds. The masses and the aristocracy: that is a potent combination in politics. Let us hope he can be stopped in the consular elections this summer. I am only grateful that the task does not look like falling to me.'

I thought at the time that this was the sort of remark which proves there are gods, because whenever, in their celestial orbits, they hear such complacency, it amuses them to show their power. Sure enough, it was not long afterwards that Caelius Rufus brought Cicero some disturbing news. Caelius by this time was seventeen, and, as his father had stated, quite ungovernable. He was tall and well built and could easily have passed for a man in his early twenties, with his deep voice and the small goatee beard which he and his fashionable friends liked to sport. He would slip out of the house when it was dark and Cicero was preoccupied with his work and everyone else was asleep; often he would not return until just before dawn. He knew that I had a little money put by, and was always pestering me to advance him small loans; one evening, after I had refused yet again, I retired to my cubicle to discover that he had found my hiding place and taken everything I possessed. I spent a miserable, sleepless night, but when I confronted him the next morning and threatened to report him to Cicero, tears came into his eyes and he promised to pay me back. And, in fairness to him, he did, and with generous interest; so I changed my hiding place and never said a word about it.

He drank and whored around the city at night with a group of very disreputable young noblemen. One of them was Gaius Curio, a twenty-year-old whose father had been consul and a great supporter of Verres. Another was Mark Antony, the nephew of Hybrida, who I reckon must then have been eighteen. But the real leader of the gang, chiefly because he was the eldest and richest and could show the others ways of getting into mischief they had never even dreamed of, was Clodius Pulcher. He was in his middle twenties and had been away for eight years on military service in the East, getting into all sorts of scrapes, including leading a mutiny against Lucullus – who also happened to be his brother-in-law – and then being captured by the very pirates he was supposed to be fighting. But now he was back in Rome, and looking to make a name for himself, and one night he announced that he knew exactly how he was going to do it – it would be a lark, a dare, risky and amusing (these were his actual words, according to Caelius) – *he would prosecute Catilina.*

When Caelius rushed in to tell Cicero the following morning, the senator at first refused to believe him. All he knew of Clodius were the scandalous rumours, widely circulating, that he had slept with his own sister – indeed these rumours had lately taken on a more substantial form, and had been cited by Lucullus himself as one of the grounds on which he had divorced his wife. 'What would such a creature be doing in the law courts,' scoffed Cicero, 'except as a defendant?' But Caelius, in his cheeky way, retorted that if Cicero wanted proof of what he was saying, he need only pay a visit to the extortion court in the next hour or two, when Clodius was planning to submit his application to prosecute. Needless to say, this was a spectacle Cicero could not resist, and once he had seen his more important clients, he went down to his old haunt at the Temple of Castor, taking me and Caelius with him.

Already, in that mysterious way it does, news that something dramatic was about to happen had spread, and there was a crowd of a hundred or more hanging around the foot of the steps. The current praetor, a man named Orbius, afterwards governor of Asia, had just sat down in his curule chair and was looking around him, no doubt wondering what was up, when a group of six or seven smirking youths appeared, strolling from the direction of the Palatine, apparently without a care between them. They clearly fancied themselves the height of fashion, and I suppose they were, with their long hair and their little beards, and their thick, embroidered belts worn loosely around their waists. 'By heavens, what a spectacle!' muttered Cicero, as they pushed past us, trailing a fragrant wake of crocus oil and saffron unguents. 'They look more like women than men!' One of their number detached himself from the rest and climbed the steps to the praetor. Midway up, he paused, and turned to the crowd. He was, if I may express it vulgarly, 'a pretty boy', with long blond curls, thick, wet red lips and a bronzed skin – a kind of young Apollo. But his voice when he spoke was surprisingly firm and masculine, marred only by his slangy, mock-plebeian accent, which rendered his family name as 'Clodius' instead of 'Claudius': another of his fashionable affectations.

'I am Publius Clodius Pulcher, son of Appius Claudius Pulcher, consul, grandson of consuls in the direct line for the past eight generations, and I come this morning to lay charges in this court against Sergius Catilina for the crimes he lately committed in Africa.'

At the mention of Catilina's name there was some muttering and whistling, and a big brute standing close to us shouted, 'You want to watch your backside, girlie!'

But Clodius did not seem in the least concerned. 'May my

ancestors and the gods bless this undertaking, and bring it to a fruitful conclusion.' He trotted briskly up to Orbius and gave him the *postulatus*, all neatly bound up in a cylinder, with a seal and a red ribbon, while his supporters applauded noisily, Caelius among them, until Cicero silenced him with a look. 'Run and find my brother,' he said to him. 'Inform him of what has happened, and tell him we need to meet at once.'

'That is a job for a slave,' objected Caelius, with a pout, no doubt worried about losing face in front of his friends. 'Surely Tiro here could go and fetch him?'

'Do as you are ordered,' snapped Cicero, 'and while you are at it, find Frugi as well. And be grateful I have not yet told your father of the disreputable company you are keeping.' That made Caelius shift himself, and he disappeared out of the forum towards the Temple of Ceres, where the plebeian aediles were normally to be found at that hour of the morning. 'I have spoiled him,' Cicero said wearily, as we climbed the hill back to the house, 'and do you know why? It is because he has charm, that most cursed of all the gifts, and I never can stop myself indulging someone with charm.'

As punishment, and also because he no longer fully trusted him, Cicero refused to let Caelius attend the day's campaign meeting, but sent him off instead to write up a brief. He waited until he was out of the way before describing the morning's events to Quintus and Frugi. Quintus was inclined to take a sanguine view, but Cicero was absolutely convinced that he would now have to fight Catilina for the consulship. 'I have checked the calendar of the extortion court – you remember what that is like – and the truth is there is simply no chance of Catilina's case being heard until July, which makes it impossible for him to be a consular candidate in this year. Therefore he comes inevitably

into mine.' He suddenly pounded his fist on the desk and swore
– a thing he rarely did. 'I predicted exactly this outcome a year
ago – Tiro is my witness.'

Quintus said, 'Perhaps Catilina will be found guilty and sent
into exile?'

'With that perfumed creature as his prosecutor? A man whom
every slave in Rome knows to have been the lover of his own
sister? No, no – you were right, Tiro. I should have taken down
Catilina myself, when I had the chance. He would have been
easier to beat in court than he will be in the ballot.'

'Perhaps it is not too late,' I suggested. 'Perhaps Clodius could
be persuaded to yield the prosecution to you.'

'No, he will never do that,' said Cicero. 'You had only to look
at him – the arrogance of the fellow – a typical Claudian. This
is his chance for glory, and he will not let it slip. You had better
bring out our list of potential candidates, Tiro. We need to find
ourselves a credible running-mate – and quickly.'

In those days consular candidates usually submitted themselves to the electorate in pairs, for each citizen cast two votes
for consul and it was obviously good tactics to form an alliance
with a man who would complement one's own strengths during
the canvass. What Cicero needed to balance his ticket was
someone with a distinguished name who had wide appeal among
the aristocracy. In return, he could offer them his own popularity
among the *pedarii* and the lower classes, and the support of the
electoral machine which he had built up in Rome. He had always
thought that this would be easy enough to arrange when the
time came. But now, as we reviewed the names on the list, I saw
why he was becoming so anxious. Palicanus would bring nothing
to the ticket. Cornificius was an electoral no-hoper. Hybrida had
only half a brain. That left Galba and Gallus. But Galba was so

aristocratic, he would have nothing to do with Cicero, and Gallus – despite all Cicero's pleadings – had said firmly that he had no interest in becoming consul.

'Can you believe it?' complained Cicero, as we huddled around his desk, studying the list of likely runners. 'I offer the man the greatest job in the world, and he has to give me nothing in return except to stand at my side for a day or two. Yet he still says he would prefer to concentrate on jurisprudence!' He took up his pen and crossed out Gallus's name, then added Catilina's to the bottom of the list. He tapped his pen beside it idly, underlined it, circled it, then glanced at each of us. 'Of course, there is one other potential partner we have not mentioned.'

'And who is that?' asked Quintus.

'Catilina.'

'*Marcus!*'

'I am perfectly serious,' said Cicero. 'Let's think it through. Suppose, instead of attempting to prosecute him, I offer to defend him. If I secure his acquittal, he will be under an obligation to support me for consul. On the other hand, if he is found guilty, and goes into exile – then that is the end of him. Either outcome is acceptable as far as I am concerned.'

'You would defend *Catilina*?' Quintus was well used to his brother, and it took a great deal to shock him, but on that day he was almost speechless.

'I would defend the blackest devil in hell if he was in need of an advocate. That is our system of law.' Cicero frowned and shook his head irritably. 'But we went over all this with poor Lucius just before he died. Come on, brother – spare me the reproachful face! You wrote the book: "I am a new man. I seek the consulship. This is Rome." Those three things – they say it all. I am a new man, therefore there is no one to help me but myself, and you few friends. I seek the consulship, which is immortality – a prize worth fighting for, yes? And this is Rome – *Rome* – not some abstract place in a work of philosophy, but a city of glory built on a river of filth. So yes, I will defend Catilina, if that is what is necessary, and then I will break with him as soon as I can. And he would do the same to me. That is the world we live in.' Cicero sat back in his chair and raised his hands. 'Rome.'

Cicero did not make a move immediately, preferring to wait and see whether the prosecution of Catilina would definitely go ahead. There was a widespread view that Clodius was simply showing off, or perhaps trying to distract attention from the shame of his sister's divorce. But in the lumbering way of the law, as the summer came on, the process passed through all its various stages – the *postulatio*, *divinatio*, and *nominis delatio* – a jury was selected and a date was fixed for the start of the trial in the last week of July. There was no chance now that Catilina would be free of litigation in time for the consular elections; nominations had already closed.

At this point, Cicero decided to let Catilina know that he might be interested in acting as his advocate. He gave much thought as to how to convey the offer, for he did not wish to lose face by being rebuffed, and he also wanted to be able to deny ever making an approach in case he was challenged in the senate. In the end he hit upon a characteristically subtle scheme. He called Caelius to his study, swore him to secrecy, and announced that he had it in mind to defend Catilina: what did he think? ('But not a word to anyone, mind!') This was exactly the sort of gossip which Caelius most delighted in, and naturally he could not resist sharing the confidence with his friends, among them Mark Antony

– who, as well as being the nephew of Hybrida, was also the adopted son of Catilina's close friend, Lentulus Sura.

I guess it must have taken all of a day and a half for a messenger to turn up on Cicero's doorstep, bearing a letter from Catilina asking him if he would care to visit, and proposing – in the interests of confidentiality – that the rendezvous be conducted after dusk. 'And so the fish bites,' said Cicero, showing me the letter, and he sent back with the slave a verbal reply that he would attend on Catilina in his house that same night.

Terentia was now very close to parturition, and was finding the heat of Rome in July insufferable. She lay, restless and groaning, on a couch in the stifling dining room, Tullia on one side reading to her in a piping voice, a maid with a fan on the other. Her temper, warm in the best of circumstances, was in these days permanently inflamed. As darkness fell and the candelabra were lit, she saw that Cicero was preparing to leave, and immediately demanded to know where he was going. When he gave a vague reply, she tearfully insisted that he must have taken a concubine and was visiting her, for why else would a respectable man go out of doors at this hour? And so, reluctantly, he told her the truth, that he was calling on Catilina. Of course this did not mollify her in the slightest, but only enraged her further. She demanded to know how he could bear to spend a moment in the company of the monster who had debauched her own sister, a vestal virgin, to which Cicero responded with some quip about Fabia having always been 'more vestal than virgin'. Terentia struggled to rise but failed and her furious invective pursued us all the way out of the house, much to Cicero's amusement.

It was a night very like the one on the eve of the elections for aedile, when he had gone to see Pompey. There was the same oppressive heat and feverish moonlight; the same slight breeze stirred the smell of putrefaction from the burial fields beyond the Esquiline Gate and spread it over the city like an invisible moist dust. We went down into the forum, where the slaves were lighting the street lamps, past the silent, darkened temples, and up on to the Palatine, where Catilina had his house. I was carrying a document case, as usual, and Cicero had his hands clasped behind his back and was walking with his head bowed in thought. Back then the Palatine was less built up than it is today, and the buildings were spaced further apart. I could hear the sound of a stream nearby and there was a scent of honeysuckle and dog rose. 'This is the place to live, Tiro,' said Cicero, halting on the steps. 'This is where we shall come when there are no more elections to be fought, and I need take less account of what the people think. A place with a garden to read in – imagine that – and where the children can play.' He glanced back in the direction of the Esquiline. 'It will be a relief to all concerned when this baby arrives. It is like waiting for a storm to break.'

Catilina's house was easy to find, for it was close by the Temple of Luna, which was painted white and lit up at night by torches, in honour of the moon goddess. A slave was waiting in the street to guide us, and he took us straight into the vestibule of the mansion of the Sergii, where a most beautiful woman greeted Cicero. This was Aurelia Orestilla, the wife of Catilina, whose daughter he was supposed to have seduced initially, before moving on to the mother, and for whose sake, it was rumoured, he had murdered his own son by his first marriage (the lad having threatened to kill Aurelia rather than accept such a notorious courtesan into the family). Cicero knew all about her, and cut off her effusive greeting with a curt nod. 'Madame,' he said, 'it is your husband I have come to see, not you,' at which she bit her lip and fell silent. It was one of the most ancient houses in Rome, and its timbers creaked as we followed the slave into the interior, which smelled of dusty old drapes and incense. One curious feature I remember was that it had been stripped almost bare, and obviously recently, for one could see the blurred rectangular outlines of where pictures had once hung, and circles of dust on the floor marked the absence of statues. All that remained in the atrium were the dingy wax effigies of Catilina's ancestors, jaundiced by generations of smoke. This was where Catilina himself was standing. The first surprise was how tall he was when one got close up – at least a head higher than Cicero – and the second was the presence behind him of Clodius. This must have been a terrific shock to Cicero, but he was far too cool a lawyer to show it. He shook hands quickly with Catilina, and then with Clodius, politely refused an offer of wine, and the three men turned straight to business.

Looking back, I am struck by how alike Catilina and Clodius were. This was the only time I ever saw them in a room together, and they might have been father and son, with their drawling voices, and the way they stood together so languidly, as if the world was theirs to own. I suppose this is what is called 'breeding'. It had taken four hundred years of intermarriage between the finest families in Rome to produce those two villains – as thoroughbred as Arab bloodstock, and just as quick and headstrong and dangerous.

'This is the deal as we see it,' said Catilina. 'Young Clodius here will make a brilliant speech for the prosecution and everyone will say he is the new Cicero and I am bound to be convicted. But then you, Cicero, will make an even more brilliant argument for the defence in reply, and therefore no one will be surprised when I am acquitted. At the end of it, we shall have put on a good show and we shall all emerge with our positions enhanced.

I am declared innocent before the people of Rome. Clodius is acknowledged as the brave and coming man. And you will have won yet another splendid triumph in the courts, defending someone a cut above your usual run of clients.'

'And what if the jury decides differently?'

'You need not be concerned about them.' Catilina patted his pocket. 'I have taken care of the jury.'

'The law is *so* expensive,' said Clodius with a smile. 'Poor Catilina has had to sell his heirlooms to be sure of justice. It really is a scandal. How *do* people manage?'

'I shall need to see the trial documents,' said Cicero. 'How soon before the hearing opens?'

'Three days,' said Catilina, and he gestured to a slave who was standing at the door. 'Does that give you long enough to prepare?'

'If the jury has already been convinced, I can make the speech in six words: "Here is Catilina. Let him go."'

'Oh, but I want the full Ciceronian production!' protested Catilina. 'I want: "This n-n-noble m-m-man . . . the b-b-blood of centuries . . . behold the tears of his w-w-wife and f-f-friends . . ."' He had his hand in the air and was twirling it expressively, crudely imitating Cicero's almost imperceptible stutter. Clodius was laughing; they were both slightly drunk. 'I want "African s-s-savages s-s-sullying this ancient c-c-court . . ." I want Carthage and Troy to be conjured before us, and Dido and Aeneas—'

'You will get,' said Cicero, coldly cutting him off, 'a professional job.' The slave had returned with the papers for the trial and I began rapidly piling them into my document case, for I could sense the atmosphere beginning to worsen as the drink took hold and I was anxious to get Cicero out of there. 'We shall need to meet to discuss your evidence,' he continued, in the same chilly tone. 'Tomorrow it had better be, if that is convenient to you.'

'By all means. I have nothing better to do. I had been expecting to stand for the consulship this summer, as you well know, until this young mischief-maker put a stop to it.'

It was the agility that was so shocking in a man of such height. He suddenly lunged forward and wrapped his powerful right arm around Clodius's neck and dragged the younger man's head down, so that Clodius was bent double. Poor Clodius – who was no weakling, incidentally – let out a muffled cry, and his fingers clawed feebly at Catilina's arm. But the strength of Catilina was appalling, and I wonder if he might not have broken his visitor's neck with a quick upward flick of his forearm, if Cicero had not said calmly, 'I must advise you, Catilina, as your defence attorney, that it would be a grievous mistake to murder your prosecutor.'

On hearing that, Catilina swung round and frowned at him, as if he had momentarily forgotten who Cicero was. Then he started laughing. He ruffled Clodius's blond curls and let him go. Clodius staggered backwards, coughing and massaging the side of his head and throat, and for an instant he gave Catilina a look of pure murder, but then he too started laughing, and straightened up. They embraced, Catilina called for some more wine, and we left them to it. 'What a pair,' exclaimed Cicero, as we passed by the Temple of Luna on our way back home. 'With any luck they will have killed one another by morning.'

By the time we had returned to Cicero's house, Terentia was in labour. There was no mistaking it. We could hear the screams from the street. Cicero stood in the atrium, white with shock and alarm, for he had been away when Tullia was born, and nothing in his philosophy books had prepared him for what was happening. 'Dear heavens, it sounds as though she is being tortured. Terentia!' He started towards the staircase which led to her room, but one of the midwives intercepted him.

We passed a long vigil in the dining room. He asked me to stay with him, but was at first too anxious to do any work. Sometimes he lay stretched out on the same couch Terentia had been occupying when we left, and then, when he heard another scream, he would jump up and pace around. The air was hot and heavy, the candle flames motionless, their black threads of smoke as rigid as plumb-lines suspended from the ceiling. I busied myself by emptying my case of the court papers I had carried back from Catilina's house and sorting them into categories – charges, depositions, summaries of documentary evidence. Eventually, to distract himself, Cicero, still prone on the couch, stretched out a hand and started reading, picking up one roll after another and holding it to the lamp which I placed beside him. He kept flinching and wincing, but I could not tell whether it was the continuing howls from upstairs or the horrific allegations against Catilina, for these were indeed the most appalling accounts of violence and rape, dispatched by almost every town in Africa, from Utica to Thaenae, and from Thapsus to Thelepte. After an hour or two, he tossed them aside in disgust and asked me to fetch some paper so that he could dictate a few letters, beginning with one to Atticus. He lay back and closed his eyes in an effort to concentrate. I have the very document before me now.

It is a long time since I had a line from you. I have already written to you in detail about my election campaign. At the moment I am proposing to defend my fellow candidate Catilina.

We have the jury we want, with full cooperation from the prosecution. If he is acquitted I hope he will be more inclined to work with me in the campaign. But should it go otherwise, I shall bear it philosophically.

'Ha! That is certainly true enough.' He closed his eyes again.

I need you home pretty soon. There is a decidedly strong belief going around that your noble friends are going to oppose my election.

And at that point my writing stops, because instead of a scream we heard a different sound from above us – the gurgling cry of a baby. Cicero sprang from the couch and ran upstairs to Terentia's room. It was some time before he reappeared, and when he did he silently took the letter from me and wrote across the top in his own hand:

I have the honour to inform you that I have become the father of a little son. Terentia is well.

How transformed a house is by the presence of a healthy newborn baby! I believe, although it is seldom acknowledged, that this must be because it is a double blessing. The unspoken dreads which attend all births – of agony, death and deformity – are banished, and in their place comes this miracle of a fresh life. Relief and joy are intertwined.

Naturally, I was not permitted upstairs to see Terentia, but a few hours later Cicero brought his son down and proudly showed him off to the household and his clients. To be frank, there was not much that was visible, apart from an angry little red face and a lick of fine dark hair. He was wrapped up tight in the woollen swaddling clothes which had performed the same service for Cicero more than forty years earlier. The senator also had a silver rattle preserved from his infancy which he tinkled above the tiny face. He carried him tenderly into the atrium and pointed to the spot where he dreamed that one day his consular image would hang. 'And then,' he whispered, 'you will be Marcus Tullius Cicero, son of Marcus Tullius Cicero the *consul* – how does that sound? Not bad, eh? There will be no taunts of "new man" for you! Here you are, Tiro – make the acquaintance of a whole new political dynasty.' He offered the bundle to me, and I held it nervously, in that way the childless do when handed a baby, and was relieved when the nurse took him from me.

Cicero meanwhile was once again contemplating the blank spot on his atrium wall, and had fallen into one of his reveries. I wonder what it was he was seeing there: his death mask, perhaps, staring back at him, like a face in the mirror? I enquired after the health of Terentia, and he said, distractedly, 'Oh, she is very well. Very strong. You know what she is like. Strong enough, at least, to resume belabouring me for making an alliance with Catilina.' He dragged his gaze away from the empty wall. 'And now,' he sighed, 'I suppose we had better keep our appointment with the villain.'

When we reached the house of Catilina, we found the former governor of Africa in a charming humour. Cicero later made a list of his 'paradoxical qualities' and I give it here, for it was nicely put: 'To attach many by friendship, and to retain them by devotion; to share what he possessed with all, and to be at the service of all his friends in time of need, with money, influence, effort, and – if necessary – with reckless crime; to control his natural temper as occasion required, and to bend and turn it this way and that; to be serious with the strict, easy with the liberal, grave with the old, amiable with the young, daring with criminals, dissolute with the depraved . . .' This was the Catilina who was waiting for us that day. He had already heard about the birth of Cicero's son, and pumped his advocate's hand in warm congratulation, and then produced a beautiful calfskin box, which he insisted Cicero open. Inside was a baby's silver amulet which Catilina had acquired in Utica. 'It is merely a local trinket to ward off ill health and evil spirits,' he explained. 'Please give it to your lad with my blessing.'

'Well,' replied Cicero, 'this is handsome of you, Catilina.' And it was indeed quite exquisitely engraved, certainly no mere trinket: when Cicero held it to the light I saw all manner of exotic wild animals chasing each another, linked by a motif of curling serpents. For one last moment he toyed with it, and weighed it in his palm, but then he replaced it in its box and handed it back to Catilina. 'I am afraid I cannot accept it.'

'Why?' asked Catilina, with a puzzled smile. 'Because you are my advocate, and advocates cannot be paid? Such integrity! But this is only a trifle for a baby!'

'Actually,' said Cicero, drawing in his breath, 'I have come to tell you I am not going to be your advocate.'

I was in the act of unpacking all the legal documents on to a small table which stood between the two men. I had been watching them in a sideways fashion but now I put my head down and carried on. After what seemed to me a long silence, I heard Catilina say, in a quiet voice, 'And why is that?'

'To speak frankly: because you are so obviously guilty.'

Another silence, and then Catilina's voice, when it came, was once again very calm. 'But Fonteius was guilty of extortion against the Gauls, and you represented him.'

'Yes. But there are degrees of guilt. Fonteius was corrupt but harmless. You are corrupt and something else entirely.'

'That is for the court to decide.'

'Normally I would agree. But you have purchased the verdict in advance, and that is not a charade I wish to be a part of. You have made it impossible for me to convince myself that I am acting honourably. And if I cannot convince myself, then I cannot convince anyone else – my wife, my brother; and now, perhaps more importantly, my son, when he is old enough to under-stand.'

At this point I risked a look at Catilina. He was standing completely motionless, his arms hanging loosely by his sides, and I was reminded of an animal that has suddenly come across a rival – it was a type of predatory stillness: watchful and ready to fight. He said lightly, but it seemed to me the lightness was now more strained: 'You realise this is of no consquence to me, but only to yourself? It does not matter who is my advocate; nothing changes for me. I shall be acquitted. But for you now – instead of my friendship, you will have my enmity.'

Cicero shrugged. 'I prefer not to have the enmity of any man, but when it is unavoidable, I shall endure it.'

'You will never have endured an enmity such as mine, I promise you that. Ask the Africans.' He grinned. 'Ask Gratidianus.'

'You removed his tongue, Catilina. Conversation would be diffi-cult.'

Catilina swayed forward slightly, and I thought he might do to Cicero what he had only half done to Clodius the previous evening, but that would have been an act of madness, and Catilina was never wholly mad: things would have been far easier if he had been. Instead he checked himself and said, 'Well then, I suppose I must let you go.'

Cicero nodded. 'You must. Leave the papers, Tiro. We have no need of them now.'

I cannot remember if there was any further conversation; I do not believe there was. Catilina and Cicero simply turned their backs on one another, which was the traditional means of signalling enmity, and so we left that ancient, empty, creaking mansion, and went out into the heat of the Roman summer.

XV

Now began a most difficult and anxious period in Cicero's life, during which I am sure he often regretted that he had made such an enemy of Catilina, and had not simply found some excuse to wriggle out of his commitment to defend him. For there were, as he often observed, only three possible outcomes to the coming election, and none was pleasant. Either he would be consul and Catilina would not – in which case who could tell what lengths his resentful and defeated rival might be willing to go to? Or Catilina would be consul and he would not, and all the resources of the office would be turned against him. Or – and this, I think, alarmed him most of all – he and Catilina might be consuls together, in which case his dream of supreme *imperium* would degenerate into a year-long running battle, and the business of the republic would be paralysed by their acrimony.

The first shock came when the trial of Catilina opened a couple of days later, because who should step forward to act as chief defence advocate but the senior consul himself, Lucius Manlius Torquatus, head of one of the oldest and most respected patrician families in Rome. Catilina was escorted into court by all the traditional old guard of the aristocracy – Catulus, of course, but also Hortensius, Lepidus and the elder Curio. The only consolation for Cicero was that Catilina's guilt was utterly manifest, and Clodius, who had his own reputation to consider, actually made quite a decent job of drawing out the evidence. Although Torquatus was an urbane and precise attorney, he could only (to use the crude phrase of the time) apply so much perfume to this particular turd. The jury had been bribed, but the record of Catilina's behaviour in Africa was sufficiently shocking that they very nearly found him guilty, and he was only acquitted *per infamiam* – that is, he was dishonourably discharged from the court. Clodius, fearful of retaliation from Catilina and his supporters, departed the city soon afterwards, to serve on the staff of Lucius Murena, the new governor of Further Gaul. 'If only I had prosecuted Catilina myself!' groaned Cicero. 'He would be with Verres in Massilia by now, watching the waves coming in!' But at least he had avoided the dishonour of serving as Catilina's defender – for which, incidentally, he gave much credit to Terentia, and thereafter he was always more willing to listen to her advice.

Cicero's campaign strategy now called for him to leave Rome for four months, and travel north to canvass, all the way up to the borders of Italy in Nearer Gaul. No consular candidate, as far as I am aware, had ever done such a thing before, but Cicero, even though he loathed to leave the city for so long, was convinced it was worth it. When he stood for aedile, the number of registered electors was some four hundred thousand; but now those rolls had been revised by the censors, and with the extension of the franchise as far north as the River Po, the electorate had increased to almost one million. Very few of these citizens would ever bother to travel all the way to Rome to cast their votes in person. But Cicero reckoned that if he could only persuade just one in ten of those he met to make the effort, it could give him a decisive edge on the Field of Mars.

He fixed his departure for after the Roman Games, which began that year as usual on the fifth day of September. And now came Cicero's second – I will not call it a shock exactly, but it was certainly more troubling than a mere surprise. The Roman Games were always given by the curule aediles, one of whom was Caesar. As with Antonius Hybrida, nothing much was expected of him, for he was known to be hard up. But Caesar took the whole production over, and in his lordly way declared that the games were in honour not only of Jupiter, but of his dead father. For days beforehand he had workmen in the forum building colonnades, so that people could stroll around and see the wild beasts he had imported, and the gladiators he had bought – no fewer than three hundred and twenty pairs, clad in silver armour: the greatest number ever produced for a public spectacle. He laid on banquets, held processions, staged plays, and on the morning of the games themselves the citizens of Rome woke to discover that he had, overnight, erected a statue of the populist hero, Marius – the aristocrats' great hate-figure – within the precincts of the Capitol.

Catulus immediately insisted that a session of the senate be called, and tabled a motion demanding that the statue be removed at once. But Caesar replied to him with contempt, and such was his popularity in Rome, the senate did not dare to press the matter further. Everyone knew that the only man who could possibly have lent Caesar the money for such an extravaganza was Crassus, and I remember how Cicero returned from the Roman Games in the same dejected manner that he had come back from Hybrida's Games of Apollo. It was not that Caesar, six years his junior, was ever likely to run against him personally in an election, but rather that Crassus was clearly up to something, and he could not work out what. Cicero described to me that night a part of the entertainment. 'Some poor wretch, a criminal, was led out naked into the centre of the Circus, armed with a wooden sword, and then they released a panther and a lion to attack him, which no doubt they had starved for weeks. And actually he put on a reasonable show, using the only advantage he had – his brains – dashing this way and that, and for a while it looked as though he might succeed in making the beasts attack one another instead of him. The crowd were cheering him on. But then he tripped and the creatures tore him to pieces. And I looked to one side of me at Hortensius and the aristocrats, all laughing and applauding, and at Crassus and Caesar side by side on the other, and I thought to myself, Cicero: that man is you.'

His personal relations with Caesar were always cordial, not least because Caesar enjoyed his jokes, but he had never trusted him, and now that he suspected he was in alliance with Crassus, he began to keep a greater distance. There is another story I should tell about Caesar. Around this time Palicanus came to call, seeking Cicero's support for his own bid for the consulship. Oh dear – poor Palicanus! He was a cautionary lesson in what can happen in politics if one becomes too dependent on the favour of a great man. He had been Pompey's loyal tribune, and then his loyal praetor, but he had never been given his share of the spoils once Pompey had achieved his special commands, for the simple reason there was nothing left he could offer in return; he had been bled dry. I picture him, day after day sitting in his house, staring at his gigantic bust of Pompey, or dining alone beneath that mural of Pompey as Jupiter – truthfully, he had about as much chance of becoming consul as I did. But Cicero tried to let him down kindly, and said that although he could not form an electoral alliance with him, he would at least try to do something for him in the future (of course, he never did). At the end of the interview, just as Palicanus was rising, Cicero, keen to end on a friendly note, asked to be remembered to his daughter, the blowsy Lollia, who was married to Gabinius.

'Oh, do not talk to me about that whore!' responded Palicanus. 'You must have heard? The whole city is talking about it! She is being screwed every day by Caesar!'

Cicero assured him he had not heard.

'Caesar,' said Palicanus bitterly. 'Now there is a duplicitous bastard! I ask you: is that any time to bed a comrade's wife – when he is a thousand miles away, fighting for his country?'

'Disgraceful,' agreed Cicero. 'Mind you,' he observed to me after Palicanus had gone, 'if you are going to do such a thing, I should have thought that was the ideal time. Not that I am an expert on such matters.' He shook his head. 'Really, though, one has to wonder about Caesar. If a man would steal your wife, what else wouldn't he take from you?'

Yet again I almost told him what I had witnessed in Pompey's house; and yet again I thought the better of it.

It was on a clear autumn morning that Cicero bade a tearful goodbye to Terentia, Tullia and little Marcus, and we left the city to begin his great campaign tour of the north. Quintus, as usual, remained behind to nurse his brother's political interests, while Frugi was entrusted with the legal casework. As for young Caelius, this became the occasion of his finally leaving Cicero and going to the household of Crassus to complete his internship.

We travelled in a convoy of three four-wheeled carriages, pulled by teams of mules – one carriage for Cicero to sleep in, another specially fitted out as an office, and a third full of luggage and documents; other, smaller vehicles trailed behind for the use of the senator's retinue of secretaries, valets, muleteers, cooks, and heaven knows who else, including several thick-set men who acted as bodyguards. We left by the Fontinalian Gate, with no one to see us off. In those days, the hills to the north of Rome were still pine-clad, apart from the one on which Lucullus was just completing his notorious palace. The patrician general had now come back from the East, but was unable to enter the city proper without forfeiting his military *imperium* and with it his right to a triumph. So he was lingering out here amid his spoils of war, waiting for his aristocratic cronies to assemble a majority in the senate to vote him *triumphator*, but the supporters of Pompey, among them Cicero, kept blocking it. Mind you, even Cicero glanced up from his letters long enough to take a look at this colossal structure, the roof of which was just visible over the treetops, and I secretly hoped that we might catch a glimpse of the great man himself, but of course he was nowhere to be seen. (Incidentally, Quintus Metellus, the sole survivor of the three Metelli brothers, had also recently returned from Crete, and was also holed up outside the city in anticipation of a triumph which, again, the ever-jealous Pompey would not allow. The plight of Lucullus and Metellus was a source of endless amusement to Cicero: 'A traffic jam of generals,' he called them, 'all trying to get into Rome through the Triumphal Gate!') At the Mulvian Bridge we paused while Cicero dashed off a final note of farewell to Terentia. Then we crossed the swollen waters of the Tiber and turned north on to the Flaminian Way.

We made extremely good time on that first day, and shortly before nightfall we reached Ocriculum, about thirty miles north of the city. Here we were met by a prominent local citizen who had agreed to give Cicero hospitality, and the following morning the senator went into the forum to begin his canvass. The secret of effective electioneering lies in the quality of the staff work done in advance, and here Cicero was very fortunate to have attached to his campaign two professional agents, Ranunculus and Filum, who travelled ahead of the candidate to ensure that a decent crowd of supporters would always be waiting in each town when we arrived. There was nothing about the electoral map of Italy which these two rascals did not know: who among the local knights would be offended if Cicero did not stop to pay his respects, and who should be avoided; which were the most important tribes and centuries in each particular district, and which were most likely to come his way; what were the issues which most concerned the citizens, and what were the promises they expected in return for their votes. They had no other topic of conversation except politics, yet Cicero could sit with them late into the night swapping facts and stories, as happily as he could converse with a philosopher or a wit.

I would not weary you with all the details of the campaign, even if I could remember them. Dear gods! What a heap of ash most political careers amount to, when one really stops to consider them! I used to be able to name every consul for the past one hundred years, and most praetors for the past forty. Now, they have almost entirely faded out of my memory, quenched like lights at midnight around the Bay of Naples. Little wonder that the towns and crowds of Cicero's consular campaign have all merged into one generalised impression of hands shaken, stories listened to, bores endured, petitions received, jokes told, undertakings given, and local worthies smoothed and flattered. The name of Cicero was famous by this time, even outside Rome, and people turned out to see him en masse, especially in the larger towns where law was practised, for the speeches he had prepared for the prosecution of Verres – even those he had not delivered – had been extensively copied and circulated. He was a hero to both the lower classes and the respectable knights, who saw him as a champion against the rapacity and snobbery of the aristocracy. For this reason, there were not many grand houses which opened their doors to him, and we had to endure taunts and even occasionally missiles whenever we passed close to the estates of one or other of the great patricians.

We pressed on up the Flaminian Way, devoting a day to each of the decent-sized towns – Narnia, Carsulae, Mevania, Fulginiae, Nuceria, Tadinae and Cales – before finally reaching the Adriatic coast about two weeks after leaving Rome. It was some years since I had gazed upon the sea, and when that line of glittering blue appeared above the dust and scrub I felt as thrilled as a child. The afternoon was cloudless and balmy, a straggler left behind by a distant summer which had long since retreated. On impulse, Cicero ordered that the wagons be halted so that we could all walk on the beach. How odd the things which *do* lodge in one's mind, for although I cannot now recall much of the serious politics, I can still remember every detail of that hour-long interlude – the smell of the seaweed and the taste of salt spray on my lips, the warmth of the sun on my cheeks, the rattle of the shingle as the waves broke and the hiss as they receded, and Cicero laughing as he tried to demonstrate how Demosthenes was supposed to have improved his elocution by rehearsing his speeches with a mouth full of pebbles.

A few days later, at Ariminum, we picked up the Aemilian Way and swung west, away from the sea, and into the province of Nearer Gaul. Here we could feel the nip of winter coming on. The black and purple mountains of the Apenninus rose sheer to our left, while to our right, the Po delta stretched grey and flat to the horizon. I had a curious sensation that we were mere insects, creeping along the foot of a wall at the edge of some great room. The passionate political issue in Nearer Gaul at that time was the franchise. Those who lived to the south of the River Po had been given the vote; those who lived to the north had not. The populists, led by Pompey and Caesar, favoured extending citizenship across the river, all the way to the Alps; the aristocrats, whose spokesman was Catulus, suspected a plot further to dilute their power, and opposed it. Cicero, naturally, was in favour of widening the franchise to the greatest extent possible, and this was the issue he campaigned on.

They had never seen a consular candidate up here before, and in every little town crowds of several hundred would turn out to listen to him. Cicero usually spoke from the back of one of the wagons, and gave the same speech at every stop, so that after a while I could move my lips in synchronicity with his. He denounced as nonsense the logic which said that a man who lived on one side of a stretch of water was a Roman and that his cousin on the other was a barbarian, even though they both spoke Latin. 'Rome is not merely a matter of geography,' he would proclaim. 'Rome is not defined by rivers, or mountains, or even seas; Rome is not a question of blood, or race, or religion; Rome is an ideal. Rome is the highest embodiment of liberty and law that mankind has yet achieved in the ten thousand years since our ancestors came down from those mountains and learned how to live as communities under the rule of law.' So if his listeners had the vote, he would conclude, they must be sure to use it on behalf of those who had not, for that was their fragment of civilisation, their special gift, as precious as the secret of fire. Every man should see Rome once before he died. They should go next summer, when the travelling was easy, and cast their ballots on the Field of Mars, and if anyone asked them why they had come so far, 'You can tell them Marcus Cicero sent you!' Then he would jump down, and pass among the crowd while they were still applauding, doling out handfuls of chickpeas from a sack carried by one of his attendants, and I would make sure I was just behind him, to catch his instructions and write down names.

I learned much about Cicero while he was out campaigning. Indeed, I would say that despite all the years we had spent together I never really knew him until I saw him in one of those small towns south of the Po – Faventia, say, or Claterna – with the late autumn light just starting to fade, and a cold wind blowing off the mountains, and the lamps being lit in the little shops along the main street, and the upturned faces of the local farmers gazing in awe at this famous senator on the back of his wagon, with his three fingers outstretched, pointing towards the glory of Rome. I realised then that, for all his sophistication, he was really still one of them – a man from a small provincial town with an idealised dream of the republic and what it meant to be a citizen, which burned all the fiercer within him because he, too, was an outsider.

For the next two months Cicero devoted himself entirely to the electors of Nearer Gaul, especially those around the provincial capital of Placentia, which actually lies on the banks of the Po and where whole families were divided by the vexed question of citizenship. He was given great assistance in his campaigning by the governor, Piso – that same Piso, curiously enough, who had threatened Pompey with the fate of Romulus if he pressed ahead with his desire for the special command. But Piso was a pragmatist, and besides, his family had commercial interests beyond the Po. He was thus in favour of extending the vote; he even gave Cicero a special commission on his staff, to enable him to travel more freely. We spent the festival of Saturnalia at Piso's headquarters, imprisoned by snow, and I could see the governor becoming more and more charmed by Cicero's manners and wit, to the extent that one evening, after plenty of wine, he clapped him on the shoulder and declared, 'Cicero, you are a good fellow after all. A better fellow and a better patriot than I realised. Speaking for myself, I would be willing to see you as consul. It is only a pity it will never happen.'

Cicero looked taken aback. 'And why are you so sure of that?'

'Because the aristocrats will never stand for it, and they control too many votes.'

'It is true they have great influence,' conceded Cicero. 'But I have the support of Pompey.'

Piso roared with laughter. 'And much good may it do you! He is lording it around at the other end of the world, and besides – haven't you noticed? – he never stirs for anyone except himself. Do you know who I would watch out for if I were you?'

'Catilina?'

'Yes, him too. But the one who should really worry you is Antonius Hybrida.'

'But the man is a halfwit!'

'Cicero, you disappoint me. Since when has idiocy been a bar to advancement in politics? You take it from me – Hybrida is the man the aristocrats will rally around, and then you and Catilina will be left to fight it out for second place, and do not look to Pompey for help.'

Cicero smiled and affected unconcern, but Piso's remarks had obviously struck home, and as soon as the snowfall melted we set off back to Rome at maximum speed.

★   ★   ★

We reached the city in the middle of January, and to begin with all seemed well. Cicero resumed his hectic round of advocacy in the courts, and his campaign team once again met weekly under the supervision of Quintus, who assured him his support was holding firm. We were minus young Caelius, but his absence was more than made up for by the addition of Cicero's oldest and closest friend, Atticus, who had returned to live in Rome after an absence in Greece of some twenty years.

I must tell you a little about Atticus, whose importance in Cicero's life I have so far only hinted at, and who was about to become extremely significant indeed. Already rich, he had recently inherited a fine house on the Quirinal Hill together with twenty million in cash from his uncle, Quintus Caecilius, one of the most loathed and misanthropic money-lenders in Rome, and it says much about Atticus that he alone remained on reasonable terms with this repulsive old man right up to his death. Some might have suspected opportunism, but the truth was that Atticus, because of his philosophy, had made it a principle never to fall out with anyone. He was a devoted follower of the teachings of Epicurus – 'that pleasure is the beginning and end of living happily' – although I hasten to add that he was an Epicurean not in the commonly misunderstood sense, as a seeker after luxury, but in the true meaning, as a pursuer of what the Greeks call *ataraxia*, or freedom from disturbance. He consequently avoided arguments and unpleasantness of any kind (needless to say, he was unmarried) and desired only to contemplate philosophy by day and dine by night with his cultured friends. He believed that all mankind should have similar aims, and was baffled that they did not: he tended to forget, as Cicero occasionally reminded him, that not everyone had inherited a fortune. He never for an instant contemplated undertaking anything as upsetting or dangerous as a political career, yet at the same time, as an insurance against future mishap, he had taken pains to cultivate every aristocrat who passed through Athens – which, over two decades, was a lot – by drawing up their family trees, and presenting them as gifts, beautifully illustrated by his slaves. He was also extremely shrewd with money. In short, there can never have been anyone quite so worldly in their pursuit of unworldliness as Titus Pomponius Atticus.

He was three years older than Cicero, who stood somewhat in awe of him, not only because of his wealth but also because of his social connections, for if there is one man guaranteed to enjoy an automatic entrée into smart society it is a rich and witty bachelor in his middle forties with an unfeigned interest in the genealogy of his host and hostess. This made him invaluable as a source of political intelligence, and it was from Atticus that Cicero now began to realise how formidable was the opposition to his candidacy. First, Atticus heard over dinner from his great friend Servilia – the half-sister of Cato – that Antonius Hybrida was definitely running for the consulship. A few weeks after that, Atticus reported a comment of Hortensius (another of his acquaintances) to the effect that Hybrida and Catilina were planning to run on a joint ticket. This was a serious blow, and although Cicero tried to make light of it – 'Oh well, a target that is double the size is twice as easy to hit' – nevertheless I could see that he was shaken, for he had no running-mate of his own, and no serious prospect at this stage of finding one.

But the really bad news came just after the senatorial recess in the late spring. Atticus sent a message that he needed to see the Cicero brothers urgently, so when the courts had closed for the day all three of us made our way up to his house. This was a perfect bachelor set-up, built on a promontory next to the

Temple of Salus – not large, but with the most wonderful views across the city, especially from the library, which Atticus had made the centrepiece of the house. There were busts of the great philosophers around the walls, and many little cushioned benches to sit on, for Atticus's rule was that while he would never lend a book, any of his friends were free whenever they liked to come up and read or even make their own copies. And it was here, beneath a head of Aristotle, that we found Atticus reclining that afternoon, dressed in the loose white tunic of a Greek, and reading, if I remember rightly, a volume of *Kyriai doxai*, the principal doctrines of Epicurus.

He came straight to the point. 'I was at dinner last night on the Palatine, at the home of Metellus Celer and the Lady Clodia, and among the other guests was our former consul, no less an aristocrat than' – he blew on an imaginary trumpet – 'Publius Cornelius Lentulus Sura.'

'By heavens,' said Cicero with a smile, 'the company you keep!'

'Did you know that Lentulus is trying to make a comeback, by standing for a praetorship this summer?'

'Is he really?' Cicero frowned and rubbed his forehead. 'He is of course a great friend of Catilina. I suppose they must be in alliance. See how the gang of rascals grows?'

'Oh yes, it is quite a political movement – him, and Catilina and Hybrida, and I got the impression there were others, but he would not give me their names. At one point, he produced a piece of paper with the prediction of some oracle written upon it, that he would be the third of the Cornelii to rule as dictator in Rome.'

'Old Sleepy-Head? Dictator? I trust you laughed in his face.'

'No I did not,' replied Atticus. 'I took him very seriously. You ought to try it some time, Cicero, instead of just delivering one of your crushing witticisms which simply shuts everybody up. No, I encouraged him to ramble on, and he drank more of Celer's excellent wine, and I listened more, and he drank more, and eventually he swore me to secrecy and he told me his great secret.'

'Which is?' said Cicero, leaning forward in his seat, for he knew that Atticus would not have summoned us for nothing.

'They are being backed by Crassus.'

There was a silence.

'Crassus is voting for them?' asked Cicero, which I think was the first time I had ever heard him say something seriously stupid: I ascribe it to the shock.

'No,' said Atticus irritably. 'He is backing them. You know what I mean. Financing them. Buying them the whole election, according to Lentulus.'

Cicero seemed temporarily deprived of the power of speech. After another long pause it was Quintus who spoke up. 'I do not believe it. Lentulus must have been well in his cups to make such a ridiculous boast. What possible reason would Crassus have for wanting to see such men in power?'

'To spite me,' said Cicero, recovering his voice.

'Nonsense!' exclaimed Quintus angrily. (Why was he so angry? I suppose because he was frightened that the story was true, in which case he would look a fool, especially in the light of all the assurances he had given his brother that the campaign was in the bag.) 'Absolute nonsense!' he repeated, although with slightly less certainty. 'We already know that Crassus is investing heavily in Caesar's future. How much would it cost him in addition to buy two consulships and a praetorship? You are talking not just about a million, but four million, five million. He hates you, Marcus, everyone knows it. But does he hate you so much more than he loves his money? I doubt it.'

'No,' said Cicero firmly, 'I am afraid you are wrong, Quintus. This story has the ring of truth, and I blame myself for not recognising the danger earlier.' He was on his feet now, and pacing around, as he always did when he was thinking hard. 'It started with those Games of Apollo given by Hybrida – Crassus must have paid for those. The games were what brought Hybrida back from the political dead. And could Catilina really have raised the funds to bribe his jury simply by selling a few statues and pictures? Of course not. And even if he did, who is paying his campaign expenses now? Because I have been inside his house and I can tell you: that man is bankrupt.' He wheeled around, his gaze darting to right and left, bright and unseeing, his eyes working as rapidly as his thoughts. 'I have always known in my bones that there was something wrong about this election. I have sensed some invisible force against me from the very outset. Hybrida and Catilina! These creatures should never even have been *candidates* in any normal canvass, let alone the front-runners. They are merely the tools of someone else.'

'So we are fighting Crassus?' said Quintus, sounding resigned to it at last.

'Crassus, yes. Or is it really Caesar, using Crassus's money? Every time I look around, I seem to see a flash of Caesar's cloak, just disappearing out of view. He thinks he is cleverer than anyone, and perhaps he is. But not on this occasion. Atticus –' Cicero stopped in front of him, and took his hands in both of his '– my old friend. I cannot thank you enough.'

'For what? I merely listened to a bore, and then plied him with a little drink. It was hardly anything.'

'On the contrary, the ability to listen to bores requires stamina, and such stamina is the essence of politics. It is from the bores that you really find things out.' Cicero squeezed his hands warmly, then swung around to his brother. 'We need to find some evidence, Quintus. Ranunculus and Filum are the men who can sniff it out – not much moves at election time in this city that those two are not aware of.'

Quintus agreed, and in this way the shadow-boxing of the consular election finally ended, and the real fight began.

XVI

To discover what was going on, Cicero devised a trap. Rather than simply asking around about what Crassus was up to – which would have got him nowhere, and would also have alerted his enemies that he was suspicious – he called Ranunculus and Filum to him, and told them to go out into the city and let it be known that they were representing a certain anonymous senator who was worried about his prospects in the forthcoming consular ballot, and was willing to pay fifty sesterces per vote to the right electoral syndicate.

Ranunculus was a runtish, almost half-formed creature, with a flat, round face at the end of a feeble body, who well deserved his nickname of 'Tadpole'. Filum was a giant spindle, an animated candlestick. Their fathers and grandfathers had been bribery agents before them. They knew the score. They disappeared into the back streets and bars, and a week or so later reported back to Cicero that something very strange was going on. All the usual bribery agents were refusing to cooperate. 'Which means,' as Ranunculus put it, in his squeaky voice, 'either that Rome is full of honest men for the first time in three hundred years, or that every vote that was up for sale has already been bought.'

'There must be someone who will crack for a higher price,'

insisted Cicero. 'You had better do the rounds again, and this time offer a hundred.'

So back they went, and back they returned after another week with the same story. Such was the huge amount that the bribery agents were already being paid, and such was their nervousness about antagonising their mysterious client, that there was not a single vote to be had, and not a breath of rumour as to who that client might be. Now you might well wonder, given the thousands of votes involved, how such an immense operation could remain so tight a secret. The answer is that it was very cleverly organised, with perhaps only a dozen agents, or *interpretes* as they were called, knowing the identity of the buyer (I regret to say that both Ranunculus and Filum had acted as *interpretes* in the past). These men would contact the officials of the voting syndicates and strike the initial bargain – such-and-such a price for fifty votes, say, or five hundred, depending on the size of the syndicate. Because naturally no one trusted anyone else in this game, the money would then be deposited with a second category of agent, known as the *sequestres*, who would hold the cash available for inspection. And finally, when the election was over and it was time to settle up, a third species of criminal, the so-called *divisores*, would distribute it. This made it extremely difficult to bring a successful prosecution, for even if a man was arrested in the very act of handing over a bribe, he might genuinely have no idea of who had commissioned the corruption in the first place. But still Cicero refused to accept that someone would not talk. 'We are dealing with bribery agents,' he shouted, in a rare show of anger, 'not an ancient order of Roman knights! Somewhere you will find a man who will betray even as dangerous a paymaster as Crassus, if the money is good enough. Go and track him down and find his price – or must I do everything myself?'

By this time – I suppose it must have been well into June, about a month before the election – everyone knew that something strange was going on. It was turning into one of the most memorable and closely fought campaigns in living memory, with a field of no fewer than seven for the consulship, a reflection of the fact that many men fancied their chances that year. The three front-runners were reckoned to be Catilina, Hybrida and Cicero. Then came the snobbish and acerbic Galba, and the deeply religious Cornificius. The two no-hopers were the corpulent ex-praetor Cassius Longinus, and Gaius Licinius Sacerdos, who had been governor of Sicily even before Verres, and who was at least a decade older than his rivals. (Sacerdos was one of those irritating candidates who enter elections 'not out of any personal ambition', as they like to say, but solely with the intention of 'raising issues' – 'Always beware of the man who says he is not seeking office for himself,' said Cicero, 'for he is the vainest of the lot.') Realising that the bribery agents were unusually active, the senior consul, Marcius Figulus, was prevailed upon by several of these candidates to bring before the senate a severe new law against electoral malpractice: what he hoped would become the *lex Figula*. It was already illegal for a candidate to offer a bribe; the new bill also made it a criminal offence for a voter to accept one.

When the time came for the measure to be debated in the senate, the consul first went round each of the candidates in turn to ask for his opinion. Sacerdos, as the senior man, spoke first, and made a pious speech in favour; I could see Cicero squirming with irritation at his platitudes. Hybrida naturally spoke against, but in his usual bumbling and unmemorable way – no one would ever have believed his father had once been the most eagerly sought advocate in Rome. Galba, who was going to lose badly in any case, took this opportunity to withdraw from the election, loftily announcing that there was no glory in participating in such a squalid contest, which disgraced the memory of his ancestors. Catilina, for obvious reasons, also spoke against the *lex Figula*, and I must concede that he was impressive. Utterly without nerves, he towered over the benches around him, and when he came to the end of his remarks he pointed at Cicero and roared that the only men who would benefit from yet another new piece of legislation were the lawyers, which drew the usual cheers from the aristocrats. Cicero was in a delicate position, and as he rose I wondered what he would say, because obviously he did not wish to see the legislation fail, but nor, on the eve of the most important election of his life, did he want to alienate the voting syndicates, who naturally regarded the bill as an attack on their honour. His response was adroit.

'In general I welcome this bill,' he said, 'which can only be a terror to those who are guilty. The honest citizen has nothing to fear from a law against bribery, and the dishonest should be reminded that a vote is a sacred trust, not a voucher to be cashed in once a year. But there is one thing wrong with it: an imbalance which needs to be redressed. Are we really saying that the poor man who succumbs to temptation is more to be condemned than the rich man who deliberately places temptation in his way? I say the opposite: that if we are to legislate against the one, we must strengthen the sanctions against the other. With your permission, therefore, Figulus, I wish to propose an amendment to your bill: *That any person who solicits, or seeks to solicit, or causes to be solicited, the votes of any citizen in return for money should be liable to a penalty of ten years' exile.*' That produced an excited and long-drawn-out 'Oohh!' from all around the chamber.

I could not see Crassus's face from where I was standing, but

Cicero delightedly assured me afterwards that it turned bright red, for that phrase, *or causes to be solicited*, was aimed directly at him, and everyone knew it. The consul placidly accepted the amendment, and asked if any member wished to speak against it. But the majority of the house were too surprised to react, and those such as Crassus who stood to lose most dared not expose themselves in public by openly opposing it. Accordingly, the amendment was carried without opposition, and when the house divided on the main bill, it was passed by a large margin. Figulus, preceded by his lictors, left the chamber, and all the senators filed out into the sunshine to watch him mount the rostra and give the bill to the herald for an immediate first reading. I saw Hybrida make a move towards Crassus, but Catilina caught his arm, and Crassus walked rapidly away from the forum, to avoid being seen with his nominees. The usual three weekly market days would now have to elapse before the bill could be voted upon, which meant that the people would have their say almost on the eve of the consular election.

Cicero was pleased with his day's work, for the possibility now opened up that if the *lex Figula* passed, and if he lost the election because of bribery, he might be in a position to launch a prosecution not only against Catilina and Hybrida, but also against his arch-enemy Crassus himself. It was only two years, after all, since a previous pair of consuls-elect had been stripped of their offices for electoral malpractice. But to succeed in such an action he would require evidence, and the pressure to find it became even more intense. Every waking hour he now spent canvassing, going about with a great crowd of supporters, but never with a *nomenclator* at his elbow to whisper the names of the voters: unlike his opponents Cicero took great pride in being able to remember thousands of names, and on the rare occasion when he met someone whose identity he had forgotten, he could always bluff his way through.

I admired him greatly at this time, for he must have known that the odds were heavily against him and the chances were that he was going to lose. Piso's prediction about Pompey had proved amply correct, and the great man had not lifted a finger to assist Cicero during the campaign. He had established himself at Amisus, on the eastern edge of the Black Sea – which is about as far away from Rome as it is possible to get – and there, like some great Eastern potentate, he was receiving homage from no fewer than twelve native kings. Syria had been annexed. Mithradates was in headlong retreat. Pompey's house on the Esquiline had been decorated with the captured beaks of fifty pirate triremes and was nowadays known as the *domus rostra* – a shrine to his admirers all across Italy. What did Pompey care any more about the pygmy struggles of mere civilians? Cicero's letters to him went unanswered. Quintus railed against his ingratitude, but Cicero was fatalistic: 'If it is gratitude you want, get a dog.'

Three days before the consular election, and on the eve of the vote on the bribery law, there was at last a breakthrough. Ranunculus came rushing in to see Cicero with the news that he had found a bribery agent named Gaius Salinator, who claimed to be in a position to sell three hundred votes for five hundred sesterces apiece. He owned a bar in the Subura called the Bacchante, and it had been agreed that Ranunculus would go to see him that very night, give him the name of the candidate for whom the bribed electors were to vote, and at the same time hand over the money to one of the *sequestres*, who was trusted by them both. When Cicero heard about this he became very excited, and insisted that he would accompany Ranunculus to the meeting, with a hood pulled down to conceal his well-known face. Quintus was against the plan, considering it too dangerous, but Cicero was insistent that he needed to gather evidence at first hand. 'I shall have Ranunculus and Tiro with me for protection,' he said (I assume this was one of his jokes), 'but perhaps you could arrange for a few loyal supporters to be drinking in the neighbourhood, just in case we need more assistance.'

I was by this time almost forty, and after a life devoted exclusively to clerical duties my hands were as soft as a maiden's. In the event of trouble it would be Cicero, whose daily exercises had given him an imposing physique, who would be called upon to protect *me*. Nevertheless, I opened up the safe in his study and began counting out the cash we needed in silver coin. (He had a well-stocked campaign fund, made up of gifts from his admirers, which he drew on to pay for such expenses as his tour of Nearer Gaul: this money was not bribes, as such, although obviously it was comforting for the donors to know that Cicero was a man who famously never forgot a name.) Anyway, this silver was fitted into a money belt which I had to strap around my waist, and with a heavy tread, in both senses of the phrase, I descended with Cicero at dusk into the Subura. He cut a curious figure wearing a hooded tunic borrowed from one of his slaves, for the night was very warm. But in the crowded slums of the poor, the bizarrely dressed are an everyday sight, and when people saw a man with a hood pulled down low over his face they gave him a wide berth, perhaps fearing that he had leprosy or some disfiguring complaint which they might catch. We followed Ranunculus, who darted, appropriately tadpole-like, through the labyrinth of narrow, squalid alleys which were his natural habitat, until at last we came to a corner where men were sitting leaning against the wall, passing back and forth a jar of wine. Above their heads, beside the door, was a painting of Bacchus with his groin thrust out, relieving himself, and the spot had the smell to match the sign. Ranunculus stepped inside and led us behind the counter and up some narrow wooden stairs to a raftered room, where Salinator was waiting, along with another man, the *sequester*, whose name I never learned.

They were so anxious to see the money, they paid little attention to the hooded figure behind me. I had to take off my belt and show them a handful of coins, whereupon the *sequester* produced a small pair of scales and began weighing the silver. Salinator, who was a flabby, lank-haired, pot-bellied creature, watched this for a while, then said to Ranunculus, 'That seems well enough. Now you had better give me the name of your client.'

'I am his client,' said Cicero, throwing back his hood. Needless to say, Salinator recognised him at once, and stepped back in alarm, crashing into the *sequester* and his scales. The bribery agent struggled to recover, hopelessly trying to turn his stumble into a sequence of bows, and began some improvised speech about what an honour it was and so forth to help the senator in his campaign, but Cicero shut him up quickly. 'I do not require any help from the likes of you, wretch! All I require is information.'

Salinator had just begun to whine that he knew nothing when suddenly the *sequester* dropped his scales and made a dive for the staircase. He must have got about halfway down before he ran into the solid figure of Quintus, who spun him around, hauled him up by his collar and the seat of his tunic and threw him back into the room. I was relieved to see, coming up the stairs behind Quintus, a couple of stout young lads who often served as Cicero's attendants. At the sight of so many, and confronted by the most famous advocate in Rome, Salinator's resistance began to weaken. What finished it altogether was when Cicero threatened to hand him over to Crassus for trying to sell the same votes twice. He was more scared of retribution at Crassus's hands than of anything, and I was reminded of that phrase about Old Baldhead which Cicero had repeated years before: 'the most dangerous bull in the herd'.

'Your client is Crassus, then?' asked Cicero. 'Think carefully before you deny it.'

Salinator's chin twitched slightly: the nearest he dared come to a nod.

'And you were to deliver three hundred votes to Hybrida and Catilina for the consulship?'

Again he gave the ghost of a nod. 'For them,' he said, 'and the others.'

'Others? You mean Lentulus Sura for praetor?'

'Yes. Him. And the others.'

'You keep saying "the others",' said Cicero, frowning. 'Who are these "others"?'

'Keep your mouth shut!' shouted the *sequester*, but Quintus kicked him in the stomach and he groaned and rolled over.

'Ignore him,' said Cicero affably. 'He is a bad influence. I know the type. You can tell me.' He put an encouraging hand on the bribery agent's arm. 'The others?'

'Cosconius,' said Salinator, casting a nervous glance at the figure writhing on the floor. Then he took a breath and said rapidly, in a quiet voice: 'Pomptinus. Balbus. Caecilius. Labienus. Faberius. Gutta. Bulbus. Calidius. Tudicius. Valgius. And Rullus.'

As each new name was mentioned, Cicero looked more and more astonished. 'Is that it?' he said, when Salinator had finished.

'You are sure there is no one left in the senate you have forgotten?' He glanced across at Quintus, who was looking equally amazed.

'That is not just two candidates for consul,' said Quintus. 'That is three candidates for praetor and *ten* for tribune. Crassus is trying to buy the entire government!'

Cicero was not a man who liked to show surprise, but even he could not disguise it that night. 'This is completely absurd,' he protested. 'How much is each of these votes costing?'

'Five hundred for consul,' replied Salinator, as if he were selling pigs at market. 'Two hundred for praetor. One hundred for tribune.'

'So you are telling me,' said Cicero, frowning as he performed the calculation, 'that Crassus is willing to pay three quarters of a million merely for the three hundred votes in your syndicate?'

Salinator nodded, this time more vigorously, even happily, and with a certain professional pride. 'It has been the most magnificent canvass anyone can remember.'

Cicero turned to Ranunculus, who had been keeping watch at the window in case of any trouble in the street. 'How many votes do you think Crassus will have bought altogether at this sort of price?'

'To feel confident of victory?' replied Ranunculus. He pondered the matter judiciously. 'It must be seven or eight thousand.'

'*Eight thousand?*' repeated Cicero. 'Eight thousand would cost him *twenty million.* Have you ever heard the like? And at the end of it, he is not even in office himself, but has filled the magistracies with ninnies like Hybrida and Lentulus Sura.' He turned back to Salinator. 'Did he give you any reason for such an immense exercise?'

'No, Senator. Crassus is not a man much given to answering questions.'

Quintus swore. 'Well, he will answer some fucking questions now,' he said, and to relieve his frustration he aimed another kick at the belly of the *sequester*, who had just started to rise, and sent the fellow groaning and crashing back to the floor.

Quintus was all for beating the last scrap of information out of the two hapless agents, and then either marching them round to the house of Crassus and demanding that he put a stop to his schemes, or dragging them before the senate, reading out their confessions, and calling for the elections to be postponed. But Cicero kept a cooler head. With a straight face he thanked Salinator for his honesty, told Quintus to have a cup of wine and calm down, and me to gather up our silver. Later, when we had returned home, he sat in his study and tossed that little leather exercise ball of his from one hand to the other, while Quintus raged that he had been a fool to let the two bribery agents go, that they would surely now alert Crassus or flee the city.

'They will not do either,' replied Cicero. 'To go to Crassus and tell him what has happened would be to sign their own death warrants. Crassus would never leave such incriminating witnesses alive, and they know it. And flight would merely bring about the same result, except that it would take him longer to track them down.' Back and forth, back and forth went the ball. 'Besides, no crime has been committed. Bribery is hard enough to prove at the best of times – impossible to establish when not a vote has been cast. Crassus and the senate would merely laugh at us. No, the best thing is to leave them at liberty, where at least we know where to find them again, and be ready to subpoena them if we lose the election.' He threw the ball higher and caught it with a swiping motion. 'You were right about one thing, though, Quintus.'

'Was I really?' said Quintus bitterly. 'How kind of you to say so.'

'Crassus's action has nothing to do with his enmity for me. He would not spend twenty million simply to frustrate *my* hopes. He would only invest twenty million if the likely return were *huge*. What can it be? On that issue I must confess myself baffled.' He stared at the wall for a while. 'Tiro, you always got on well with young Caelius Rufus, didn't you?'

I remembered the shirked tasks which I had been obliged to complete for him, the lies I had told to keep him out of trouble, the day he stole my savings and persuaded me not to report his thieving to Cicero. 'Reasonably well, Senator,' I replied cautiously.

'Go and talk to him tomorrrow morning. Be subtle about it. See if you can extract any clues from him about what Crassus is up to. He lives under the same roof, after all. He must know something.'

I lay awake long into the night, pondering all of this, and feeling increasingly anxious for the future. Cicero did not sleep much either. I could hear him pacing around upstairs. The force of his concentration seemed almost to penetrate the floorboards, and when sleep did at last come to me, it was restless and full of portents.

The following morning I left Laurea to deal with Cicero's press of visitors and set off to walk the mile or so to the house of Crassus. Even today, when the sky is cloudless and the mid-July heat feels oppressive even before the sun is up, I whisper to myself, 'Election weather!' and feel again that familiar clench of excitement in my stomach. The sound of hammering and sawing rose from the forum, where the workmen were finishing the erection of the ramps and fences around the Temple of Castor, for this was the day on which the bribery bill was to be put to the vote of the people. I cut through behind the temple and paused to take a drink from the tepid waters of the fountain of Juturna. I had no idea what I was going to say to Caelius. I am a most inexpert liar – I always have been – and I realised I should have asked Cicero to advise me on some line to take, but it was too late now. I climbed the path to the Palatine, and when I reached the house of Crassus I told the porter that I had an urgent message for Caelius Rufus. He offered to let me wait inside but I declined. Instead, while he went off to fetch the young man, I crossed the street and tried to make myself as inconspicuous as possible.

Crassus's house, like the man himself, presented a very modest façade to the world, although I had been told that this was deceptive, and that once you got inside it went back a long way. The door was dark, low and narrow, but stout, flanked by two small, barred windows. Ivy climbed across peeling walls of light ochre. The terracotta roof was also ancient, and the edges of the tiles where they overhung the pavement were cracked and black, like a row of broken teeth. It might have been the home of an unwise banker, or some hard-up country landowner who had allowed his town house to fall into disrepair. I suppose this was Crassus's way of showing that he was so fabulously rich, he had no need to keep up a smart appearance, but of course in that street of millionaires it only drew attention to his wealth, and there was something almost vulgar in this studied lack of vulgarity. The dark little door was constantly opening and shutting as visitors scurried in and out, revealing the extent of the activity within: it put me in mind of a buzzing wasps' nest, which shows itself only as a tiny hole in the masonry. None of these men was recognisable to me until Julius Caesar stepped out. He did not see me, but walked straight off down the street in the direction of the forum, trailed by a secretary carrying a document case. Shortly afterwards, the door opened again and Caelius appeared. He paused on the threshold, cupped his hand above his eyes to shield them from the sun and squinted across the street towards me. I could see at once that he had been out all night as usual, and was not in a good humour at being woken. Thick stubble covered his handsome chin, and he kept sticking out his tongue, swallowing and wincing, as if the taste of it was too horrible to hold it in his mouth. He walked carefully towards me, and when he asked me what in the name of the gods I wanted, I blurted out that I needed to borrow some money.

He squinted at me in disbelief. 'What for?'

'There is a girl,' I replied helplessly, simply because it was the sort of thing he used to say to me when he wanted money and I had not the wit to come up with anything else. I tried to steer him along the street a little way, anxious that Crassus might come out and see us together. But he shook me off and stood swaying in the gutter.

'A girl?' he repeated incredulously. 'You?' And then he began to laugh, but that obviously hurt his head, so he stopped and put his fingers gently to his temple. 'If I had any money, Tiro, I should give it to you willingly – it would be a gift, bestowed simply for the pleasure of seeing you with any living person other than Cicero. But that could never happen. You are not the type for girls. Poor Tiro – you are not any kind of type, that I can see.' He peered at me closely. 'What do you really need it for?' I could smell the stale wine hot on his breath, and could not prevent myself flinching, which he mistook for an admission of guilt. 'You are lying,' he said, and then a grin spread slowly across his stubbled face. 'Cicero sent you to find out something.'

I pleaded with him to move away from the house, and this time he did. But the motion of walking evidently did not agree with him. He halted again, turned very white and held up a warning finger. Then his eyes and throat bulged, he gave an alarming groan, and out came such a heavy gush of vomit it reminded me of a chambermaid emptying a bucket out of an upstairs window into the street. (Forgive these details, but the scene just came entirely back into my mind after an absence of sixty years, and I could not help but laugh at the memory.) Anyway, this seemed to act as a purge; his colour returned and he became much brighter. He asked me what it was that Cicero wanted to know.

'What do you think?' I replied, a little impatiently.

'I wish I could help you, Tiro,' he said, wiping his mouth with the back of his hand. 'You know I would if I could. It is not nearly as pleasant living with Crassus as it was with Cicero. Old Baldhead is the most awful shit – worse even than my father. He has me learning accountancy all day, and a duller business was never invented, except for commercial law, which was last month's torture. As for politics, which does amuse me, he is careful to keep me away from all that side of things.'

I tried asking him a few more questions, for instance about Caesar's visit that morning, but it quickly became clear that he was genuinely ignorant of Crassus's plans. (I suppose he might have been lying, but given his habitual garrulity, I doubted it.) When I thanked him anyway and turned to leave, he grabbed my elbow. 'Cicero must be really desperate,' he said, with an expression of unaccustomed seriousness, 'to ask for help from me. Tell him I am sorry to hear it. He is worth a dozen of Crassus and my father put together.'

I did not expect to be seeing Caelius again for a while, and banished him from my mind for the remainder of the day, which was entirely given over to the vote on the bribery bill. Cicero was very active among the tribes in the forum, going from one to another with his entourage, and urging the merits of Figula's proposal. He was especially pleased to find, under the standard marked *VETURIA*, several hundred citizens from Nearer Gaul, who had responded to his campaign and turned out to vote for the first time. He talked to them for a long while about the importance of stamping out bribery, and as he turned away he had the glint of tears in his eyes. 'Poor people,' he muttered, 'to have come so far, only to be mocked by Crassus's money. But if we can get this bill through, I may yet have a weapon to bring the villain down.'

My impression was that his canvassing was proving effective, and that when it came to a vote the *lex Figula* would pass, for the majority were not corrupt. But simply because a measure is honest and sensible does not guarantee that it will be adopted; rather the opposite, in my experience. Early in the afternoon, the populist tribune Mucius Orestinus – he, you may remember, who had formerly been a client of Cicero's on a charge of robbery – came to the front of the rostra and denounced the measure as an attack by the aristocrats on the integrity of the plebs. He actually singled out Cicero by name as a man 'unfit to be consul' – those were his precise words – who posed as a friend of the people, but never did anything for them unless it furthered his own selfish interests. That set half the crowd booing and jeering and the other half – presumably those who were accustomed to selling their votes, and wished to continue doing so – yelling their approval.

This was too much for Cicero. He had, after all, only the year before, secured Mucius's acquittal, and if such a glossy rat as this was leaving his sinking ship, it really must be halfway to the sea bed already. He shouldered his way to the steps of the temple, his face red with the heat and with anger, and demanded to be allowed to answer. 'Who is paying for *your* vote, Mucius?' he shouted, but Mucius pretended not to hear. The crowd around us were now pointing to Cicero, pushing him forward and calling on the tribune to let him speak, but obviously that was the last thing Mucius wanted. Nor did he want a vote on the bill which he might lose. Raising his arm, he solemnly announced that he was vetoing the legislation, and amid scenes of pandemonium, with scuffles between the rival factions, the *lex Figula* was lost. Figulus immediately announced that he would summon a meeting of the senate the following day to debate what should be done.

It was a bitter moment for Cicero, and when at last we reached his house and he was able to close the door on the crowd of his supporters in the street, I thought he might collapse again, as on the eve of the elections for aedile. For once he was too tired to play with Tullia. And even when Terentia came down with little Marcus, and showed him how the infant had learned to take a wobbly step or two unaided, he did not hoist him up and toss him into the air, which was his usual greeting, but simply patted his cheek and squeezed his ear in an absent-minded way, and then passed on towards his study – only to stop dead in surprise on the threshold, for who should be sitting at his desk but Caelius Rufus.

Laurea, who was waiting just inside the door, apologised to Cicero and explained that he would have told Caelius to wait in the tablinum, like every other visitor, but he had been insistent that his business was so confidential he could not be seen in the public rooms.

'That is all right, Laurea. I am always pleased to see young Caelius. Although I fear,' he added, shaking Caelius's hand, 'that you will find me dull company at the end of a long and dispiriting day.'

'Well then,' said Caelius with a grin, 'perhaps I might have just the news to cheer you up.'

'Crassus is dead?'

'On the contrary,' laughed Caelius, 'very much alive, and planning a great conference tonight in anticipation of his triumph at the polls.'

'Is he indeed?' said Cicero, and immediately, at this touch of gossip, I saw him start to revive a little, like some wilted flower after a sprinkle of rain. 'And who will be at this conference?'

'Catilina. Hybrida. Caesar. I am not sure who else. But the chairs were being set out as I left. I have all this from one of Crassus's secretaries, who went around the city with the invitations while the popular assembly was in progress.'

'Well, well,' murmured Cicero. 'What I would not give to have an ear at that keyhole!'

'But you could have,' responded Caelius. 'This meeting is in the chamber where Crassus transacts all his business affairs. Often – but not tonight, I am told by my informant – he likes to keep a secretary close at hand, to make a note of what is said, but without the other person being aware of it. For that purpose he has had a small listening post constructed. It is just a simple cubicle, hidden behind a tapestry. He showed it to me when he was giving me lessons in how to be a man of business.'

'You mean to tell me that Crassus eavesdrops on *himself*?' asked Cicero in wonder. 'What sort of statesman would do that?'

'"There is many a rash promise made by a man who thinks there are no witnesses" – that was what he said.'

'So you think that you could hide yourself in there, and make an account of what is said?'

'Not me,' scoffed Caelius. 'I am no secretary. I was thinking of Tiro here,' he said, clapping me on the shoulder, 'with his miraculous shorthand.'

I would like to be able to boast that I volunteered readily for this suicidal assignment. But it would not be true. On the contrary, I threw up all manner of practical objections to Caelius's scheme. How would I enter Crassus's house undetected? How would I leave it? How would I determine which speaker was which from the babble of voices if I was concealed behind a screen? But to all my questions Caelius had answers. The essential fact was that I was terrified. 'What if I am caught,' I protested to Cicero, finally coming to the crux of what really bothered me, 'and tortured? I cannot claim to be so courageous that I would not betray you.'

'Cicero can simply deny any knowledge of what you were doing,' said Caelius – unhelpfully, I thought, from my point of view. 'Besides, everyone knows that evidence obtained under torture is unreliable.'

'I am beginning to feel faint,' I joked feebly.

'Compose yourself, Tiro,' said Cicero, who had become increasingly excited the more he heard. 'There would be no torture and no trial. I would make sure of that. If you were detected, I would negotiate your release, and I would pay any price to see that you were unharmed.' He took both my hands in that sincere double grip of his, and looked deep into my eyes. 'You are more my second brother than my slave, Tiro, and have been ever since we sat and learned philosophy together in Athens all those years ago – do you remember? I should have discussed your freedom with you before now, but somehow there has always seemed to be some fresh crisis to distract me. So let me tell you now, with Caelius here as my witness, that it is my intention to give you your liberty – yes, and that simple life in the country you have long desired so much. And I see a day when I shall ride over from my place to your little farm, and sit in your garden, and as we watch the sun go down over some distant, dusty olive grove or vineyard, we shall discuss the great adventures we have had together.' He let go of my hands, and this rustic vision trembled on the warm dusky air an instant longer, then faded. 'Now,' he said briskly, 'this offer of mine is not conditional in any way on your undertaking this mission – let me make that clear: you have earned it many times over already. I would never order you to put yourself in danger. You know how badly my cause stands tonight. You must do whatever you think best.'

Those were very nearly his exact words: how could I forget them?

XVII

The conference was set for nightfall, which meant there was no time to be lost. As the sun vanished behind the brow of the Esquiline, and as I climbed the slope of the Palatine Hill for the second time that day, I had a disturbing premonition that I was walking into a trap. For how could I, or Cicero for that matter, be certain that Caelius had not transferred his loyalty to Crassus? Indeed, was 'loyalty' not an absurd word to apply to whatever shifting, temporary focus of amusement seized the fancy of my young companion? But there was nothing to be done about it now. Caelius was already leading me down a small alley towards the back of Crassus's house. Pulling aside a thick curtain of trailing ivy, he uncovered a tiny, iron-studded door, which looked to have long since rusted shut. But a sharp jab from his shoulder caused it to swing silently open and we jumped down into an empty storeroom.

Like Catilina's, the house was very old, and had been added to over the centuries, so that I quickly lost track of our route as we followed the winding passages. Crassus was famous for the number of highly skilled slaves he owned – he hired them out, as a kind of employment agent – and with so many swarming around on duty it seemed impossible that we could reach our destination undetected. But if Caelius had developed any skill during his years of legal study in Rome, it was for illicit entry and exit. We cut across an inner courtyard, hid in an antechamber while a maid went by, then stepped into a big, deserted room, hung with fine tapestries from Babylon and Corinth. Perhaps twenty gilt chairs had been arranged in the centre in a semicircle, and numerous lamps and candelabra were lit around the perimeter. Caelius quickly seized one of the lamps, crossed the floor and lifted the edge of a heavy woollen tapestry depicting Diana bringing down a stag with a spear. Behind it was an alcove, of the sort in which a statue might stand, just high enough and deep enough to take a man, with a little ledge near the top for a lamp. I stepped inside smartly, for I could hear loud male voices coming closer. Caelius put a finger to his lips, winked at me, and carefully replaced the tapestry. His rapid footsteps faded and I was alone.

To begin with I was blind, but gradually I became used to the weak glow of the oil lamp just behind my shoulder. When I put my eye to the tapestry I found that there were tiny spyholes, bored through the thick material in such a way as to give me a complete view of the room. I heard more footsteps, and then abruptly my vision was obscured by the back of a wrinkled bald pink head, and Crassus's voice rang very loud in my ears – so loud I almost stumbled forward in shock – calling genially to his visitors to follow him. He moved away, and the shapes of other men passed by on their way to take their places: the loose-limbed Catilina; Hybrida, with his drinker's face; Caesar, looking sleek and dandified; the impeccable Lentulus Sura; Mucius, the hero of the afternoon; and a couple of notorious bribery agents – these I recognised, together with various other senators who were seeking the tribuneship. They all seemed in an excellent mood, joking with one another, and Crassus had to clap his hands to get their attention.

'Gentlemen,' he said, standing before them with his back to me, 'thank you for attending. We have much to discuss and not long in which to do it. The first item on the agenda is Egypt. Caesar?'

Crassus sat, and Caesar stood. He stroked back a stray sparse hair and tucked it behind his ear with his index finger. Very carefully, so as not to make a sound, I opened my notebook, withdrew my stylus, and, as Caesar started to speak in that unmistakable harsh voice of his, started to write.

It is, if you will forgive a little immodesty at this juncture, the most wonderful invention, my shorthand system. Although I concede that Xenophon had some primitive version nearly four centuries before me, that was more of a private aid to composition than proper stenography, and besides, it was only suitable for Greek, whereas mine compresses the whole of Latin, with its large vocabularly and complex grammar, into four thousand symbols. And it does so, moreover, in such a way that the system can be taught to any willing pupil; in theory even a woman could become a stenographer.

As those who have the skill will know, few things wreak greater havoc with shorthand than trembling fingers. Anxiety renders the digits as dextrous as Lucanian sausages, and I had feared my nervousness that night would be an impediment to a fast script. But once I was underway I found the process oddly soothing. I did not have time to stop and consider what I was writing. I heard the words – Egypt, colonists, public land, commissioners – without remotely comprehending their meaning; my ambition was merely to keep pace with their delivery. In fact, the greatest practical difficulty I had was the heat: it was like a furnace in that confined place; the sweat ran in stinging rivulets into my eyes and the perspiration from my palms made my stylus slippery to grip. Only occasionally, when I had to lean forward and press my eye to the fabric to check the identity of the speaker, did I realise the enormity of the risk I was taking. Then I experienced a sensation of terrifying vulnerability, made worse by the fact that the audience often seemed to be staring directly at me. Catilina in particular appeared fascinated by the scene on the tapestry which concealed me, and my worst moment of the night by far came right at the end, when Crassus declared the conference over. 'And when we meet again,' he said, 'the destiny of all of us, and of Rome, will have been changed for ever.' The moment the applause was finished, Catilina rose from his seat and walked directly towards me, and as I shrank back against the wall, he ran his palm down the tapestry, barely a hand's breadth from my sweating face. The way that bulge travelled before my gaze still has the power to wake me in the night with a shout. But all he wished to do was compliment Crassus on the workmanship, and after a brief discussion about where it had been purchased, and – inevitably with Crassus – how much it had cost, the two men moved away.

I waited a long time, and when at last I dared to look out through my spyhole, I saw that the room was empty. Only the disarrangement of the chairs proved that there had been a meeting at all. It took an effort to restrain myself from wrenching aside the tapestry and making a run for the door. But the agreement was that I would wait for Caelius, so I forced myself to sit hunched in that narrow space, my back to the wall, my knees drawn up and my arms clasped around them. I have no idea how long the conference had lasted, except that it was long enough to fill the four notebooks I had brought with me, nor how long I sat there.

It is even possible I fell asleep, because when Caelius returned, the lamps and candles, including my own, had all burned away to darkness. I jumped when he pulled back the tapestry. Without speaking, he put out his hand to help me, and together we crept back through the sleeping house to the storeroom. After I had scrambled up stiffly into the alley, I turned to whisper my thanks.

'No need,' he whispered in return. I could just make out the excited gleam of his eyes in the moonlight – eyes so wide and bright that when he added, 'I enjoyed it,' I knew that it was not mere bravado, but that the young fool was telling the truth.

It was well after midnight when I finally returned home. Everyone else was asleep, but Cicero was waiting up for me in the dining room. I could tell he had been there for hours by the scattering of books around the couch. He sprang up the moment I appeared. 'Well?' he said, and when I nodded to signify my mission had succeeded, he pinched my cheek and declared me the bravest and cleverest secretary any statesman ever had. I pulled the notebooks from my pocket to show him. He flipped one open and held it to the light. 'Ah, of course, they are all your damned hieroglyphics,' he said with a wink. 'Come and sit down and I shall fetch you some wine, and you can tell me everything. Would you like something to eat?' He looked around vaguely; the role of waiter was not one which came naturally to him. Soon I was sitting opposite him with an untouched cup of wine and an apple, my notebooks spread before me, like a schoolboy called to recite his lesson.

I no longer possess those wax tablets, but Cicero kept my subsequent transcription among his most secret papers, and looking at it now I am not surprised that I could not follow the original discussion. The conspirators had obviously met many times before, and their deliberations that night presupposed a good deal of knowledge. There was much talk of legislative timetables, and amendments to drafts of bills, and divisions of responsibilities. So you must not imagine that I simply read out what I had written and all was clear. It took the two of us many hours of puzzling over various cryptic remarks, and fitting this to that, until at last we had the whole thing plainly in sight. Every so often Cicero would exclaim something like 'Clever devils! They are such clever devils!' and get up and prowl around, then return to work some more. And to cut it short, and give you the gist, it turned out that the plot which Caesar and Crassus must have been hatching over many months fell into four parts. First, they aimed to seize control of the state by sweeping the board in the general elections, securing not only both consulships, but also all ten tribunates, and a couple of praetorships besides: the bribery agents reported that the thing was more or less a fait accompli, with Cicero's support slipping daily. The second stage called for the introduction by the tribunes of a great land reform bill in December, which would demand the breaking up of the big publicly owned estates, in particular the fertile plains of Campania, and their immediate redistribution as farms to five thousand of the urban plebs. The third step involved the election in March of ten commissioners, headed by Crassus and Caesar, who would be given immense powers to sell off conquered land abroad, and to use the funds thereby released to compulsorily purchase further vast estates in Italy, for an even greater programme of resettlement. The final stage demanded nothing less than the annexation of Egypt the following summer, using as a pretext the disputed will of one of its dead rulers, King Ptolemy the something-or-other, drawn up some seventeen years earlier, by which he had supposedly bequeathed his entire country to the Roman people; again, the revenue from this was to be given to the commissioners, for further acquisition of land in Italy.

'Dear gods: it is a *coup d'état* disguised as an agrarian reform bill!' cried Cicero, when we finally reached the end of my record. 'This commission of ten, led by Crassus and Caesar, will be the real masters of the country; the consuls and the other magistrates will be mere ciphers. And their domination at home will be maintained in perpetuity by the proceeds of extortion abroad.' He sat back and was silent for a long while, his arms folded, his chin on his chest.

I was drained by what I had endured and longed only for sleep. Yet the early summer light now beginning to seep into the room showed we had worked right through the night and it was already election eve. I was aware of the dawn chorus starting up outside, and soon after that heard the tread of someone coming down the stairs. It was Terentia in her nightdress, her hair awry, her unmade-up face soft with sleep, a shawl drawn around her narrow shoulders. I stood respectfully and looked away in embarrassment. 'Cicero!' she exclaimed, taking no notice of me. 'What on earth are you doing down here at this hour?'

He looked up at her and wearily explained what had happened. She had a very quick mind for anything political or financial – had she not been born a woman, and given her spirit, there is no telling what she might have done – and naturally, the moment she grasped it, she was horrified, for Terentia was an aristocrat to her core, and the notion of privatising state land and giving it to the plebs was, to her, a step on the road to the destruction of Rome.

'You must lead the fight against it,' she urged Cicero. 'This could win you the election. All the decent men will rally to you.'

'Ah, but will they?' Cicero picked up one of my notebooks. 'Outright opposition to this could rebound on me badly. A large faction in the senate, half of them patriotic and the other half just plain greedy, has always favoured seizing Egypt. And out on the streets, the cry of "Free farms for all!" is far more likely to gain Catilina and Hybrida votes than cost them. No, I am trapped.' He stared at the transcript of the conference and shook his head slowly, like an artist ruefully contemplating the work of some talented rival. 'It really is an extraordinary scheme – a stroke of true political genius. Only Caesar could have dreamed it up. And as for Crassus – for a down-payment of just twenty million, he can expect to gain control of most of Italy and the whole of Egypt. Even you would concede that that is a good return on your investment.'

'But you have to do *something*,' persisted Terentia. 'You cannot simply allow it to happen.'

'And what exactly would you have me do?'

'And you are supposed to be the cleverest man in Rome?' she asked in exasperation. 'Is it not obvious? Go to the senate this morning and expose what they are plotting. Denounce them!'

'A brilliant tactic, Terentia,' responded Cicero sarcastically. (I was beginning to find my position between them increasingly uncomfortable.) 'I both reveal the existence of a popular measure and denounce it at the same time. You are not listening to me: the people who stand to benefit the most from this are *my* supporters.'

'Well then, you have only yourself to blame for depending on such a rabble in the first place! This is the problem with your demagoguery, Cicero – you may think you can control the mob, but the mob will always end up devouring you. Did you seriously believe you could beat men like Crassus and Catilina when it came to a public auction of principles?' Cicero grunted irritably; however, I noticed he did not argue with her. 'But tell me,' she continued, needling away at him, 'if this "extraordinary scheme", as you call it – or "criminal enterprise", as I should prefer it – really is as popular as you say, why all this skulking around at night? Why do they not come out with it openly?'

'Because, my dear Terentia, the aristocrats think like you. They would never stand for it. First it will be the great public estates that are broken up and redistributed, next it will be their private domains. Every time Caesar and Crassus give a man a farm, they will create another client for themselves. And once the patricians start to lose control of the land, they are finished. Besides, how do you think Catulus or Hortensius would react to being ordered around by a ten-man commission elected by the people? The people! To them it would seem like a revolution – Tiberius Gracchus all over again.' Cicero threw the notebook back on to the dining table. 'No, they would scheme and bribe and kill to preserve the status quo, just as they always have done.'

'And they would be right!' Terentia glowered down at him. Her fists were clenched; I almost expected her to hit him. 'They were right to take away the powers of the tribunes, just as they were right to try to stop that provincial parvenu Pompey. And if you had any sense, you would go to them now with this, and you would say to them, "Gentlemen, this is what Crassus and Caesar are proposing to do – support me and I shall try to put a stop to it!"'

Cicero sighed in exasparation and slumped back on to the couch. For a while he was silent. But then he suddenly glanced up at her. 'By heavens, Terentia,' he said quietly, 'what a clever shrew you are.' He jumped up and kissed her on the cheek. 'My brilliant, clever shrew – you are quite correct. Or rather, half correct, for there is actually no need for *me* to do anything with it at all. I should simply pass it to Hortensius. Tiro, how long would it take you to make a fair copy of this transcript – not of all of it necessarily, just enough to whet Hortensius's appetite?'

'A few hours,' I said, bewildered by his dramatic change of mood.

'Quick!' he said, more alive with excitement than I can ever remember seeing him. 'Fetch me a pen and paper!'

I did as I was ordered. He dipped the nib in the inkpot, thought about it for a moment, and then wrote the following, as Terentia and I watched over his shoulder:

From: Marcus Tullius Cicero
To: Quintus Hortensius Hortalus
Greetings!
I feel it is my patriotic duty to share with you in confidence this
record of a meeting held last night at the home of M. Crassus,
involving G. Caesar, L. Catilina, G. Hybrida, P. Sura, and
various candidates for the tribuneship whose names will be
familiar to you. I intend to tackle certain of these gentlemen in
a speech to the senate today, and if you would care to discuss
the matter further, I shall be afterwards at the home of our
esteemed mutual friend T. Atticus.

'That should do the trick,' he said, blowing on the ink to dry it. 'Now, Tiro, make as full a copy of your notes as you can, being sure to include all the passages which will make their blue blood run cold, and deliver it, together with my letter, personally into the hands of Hortensius – personally, mark you: not to any aide – at least an hour before the senate meets. Also, send one of the lads with a message to Atticus, asking him to call on me before I leave.' He gave me the letter and hurried out of the door.

'Do you want me to ask Sositheus or Laurea to bring in your clients?' I called after him, for by now I could hear them queuing outside in the street. 'When do you want the doors opened?'

'No clients in the house this morning!' he shouted in reply, already halfway up the stairs. 'They can accompany me to the senate if they wish. You have work to do and I have a speech to compose.'

His footsteps thumped along the boards above our heads to his room and I found myself alone with Terentia. She touched her hand to her cheek where her husband had kissed her and looked at me in puzzlement. 'Speech?' she said. 'What speech is he talking about?'

But I had to confess that I had no idea, and thus can claim no hand in, or even prior knowledge of, that extraordinary piece of invective which all the world knows by the name of *In toga candida*.

I wrote as quickly and as neatly as my tiredness would allow, setting out my document like the script of a play, with the name of the speaker first, and then his remarks. I excised a great deal of what I considered irrelevant material, but then at the end I wondered if I was really competent enough to judge. Therefore I decided to keep my notebooks with me, in case I might need to refer to them during the day. Once it was done, I sealed it and placed it in a cylinder, and set off. I had to push my way through the throng of clients and well-wishers blocking the street, who clutched at my tunic and demanded to know when the senator would appear.

Hortensius's house on the Palatine was subsequently bought,

many years later, by our dear and beloved emperor, so that gives you an idea of how fine it was. I had never been to it before and I had to stop several times and ask for directions. It was right at the top of the hill, on the south-western side overlooking the Tiber, and one might have been in the country rather than the city, with its view over the dark green trees to the gentle silver curve of the river and the fields beyond. His brother-in-law Catulus, as I think I have mentioned, owned the house next door, and the whole spot – fragrant with the scent of honeysuckle and myrtle, and silent save for the twittering of the birds – was redolent of good taste and old money. Even the steward looked like an aristocrat, and when I said I had a personal message for his master from Senator Cicero, you might have thought I had farted, such an exquisite expression of distaste spread across his bony face at the mention of the name. He wanted to take the cylinder from me, but I refused, so he bade me wait in the atrium, where the masks of all Hortensius's consular ancestors stared down at me with their blank, dead eyes. Displayed on a three-legged table in the corner was a sphinx, wonderfully carved from a single huge piece of ivory, and I realised that this must be the very sphinx which Verres had given to his advocate all those years ago, and which Cicero had made his joke about. I was just stooping to examine it when Hortensius came into the room behind me.

'Well,' he said, as I stood up, feeling guilty, 'I never thought to see a representative of Marcus Cicero under the roof of my ancestors. What is all this about?'

He was wearing his full senatorial rig, but with slippers on his feet instead of shoes, and was obviously still getting ready to depart for the morning's debate. It seemed strange to me, too, to see the old enemy unarmoured, as it were, outside the arena.

I gave him Cicero's letter, which he broke open and read in front of me. Immediately he saw the names it mentioned he gave me a sharp glance, and I could tell that he was hooked, although he was too well bred to show it.

'Tell him I shall inspect it at my leisure,' he said, taking the document from me, and strolled back the way he had come, as if nothing less interesting had ever been placed in his manicured hands – although I am sure that the moment he was out of sight he must have run to his library and broken open the seal. For myself, I went back out into the fresh air and descended to the city by the Caci Steps, partly because I had time to kill before the senate convened and could afford to take a long way round, and partly because the other route took me nearer to the house of Crassus than I cared to go. I came out into that district on the Etruscan road where all the perfume and incense shops are located, and the scented air and the weight of my tiredness combined to make me feel almost drugged. My mood was oddly separated from the real world and its concerns. By this time tomorrow, I remember thinking, the voting on the Field of Mars would be well underway, and we would probably know whether Cicero was to be consul or not, and in either event the sun would shine and in the autumn it would rain. I lingered in the Forum Boarium and watched the people buying their flowers and their fruit and all the rest of it, and wondered what it would be like not to have any interest in politics, but simply to live, as the poet has it, *vita umbratilis*, 'a life in the shade'. That was what I planned to do when Cicero gave me my freedom and my farm. I would eat the fruit I grew and drink the milk of the goats I reared; I would shut my gate at night and never give a fig for another election. It was the closest to wisdom I have ever come.

By the time I eventually reached the forum, two hundred or

more senators had assembled in the senaculum and were being watched by a crowd of curious gawpers – out-of-towners to judge by their rustic dress, who had come to Rome for the elections. Figulus was sitting on his consular chair in the doorway of the senate house, the augurs beside him, waiting for a quorum, and every so often there was a minor commotion as a candidate erupted into the forum with his corona of supporters. I saw Catilina arrive, with his curious mixture of young aristocrats and the dregs of the streets, and then Hybrida, whose rackety assemblage of debtors and gamblers, such as Sabidius and Panthera, seemed quite respectable by comparison. The senators began to file into the chamber, and I was just beginning to wonder if some mishap had befallen Cicero when, from the direction of the Argiletum, came the noise of drums and flutes and then two columns of young men rounded the corner into the forum, carrying freshly cut boughs above their heads, with children scampering excitedly all around them. These were followed by a mass of respectable Roman knights led by Atticus, and then came Quintus with a dozen or so backbench senators. Some maids were scattering rose petals. It was a vastly better show than any of its rivals had managed, and the crowd around me greeted it with applause. At the centre of all this whirling activity, as in the eye of a tornado, walked the candidate himself, clad in the gleaming *toga candida* which had already seen him through three victorious election campaigns. It was rare that I was able to watch him from a distance – usually I was tucked in behind him – and for the first time I appreciated what a natural actor he was, in that when he donned his costume he found his character. All those qualities which the traditional whiteness was supposed to symbolise – clarity, honesty, purity – seemed to be personified in his solid frame and steady gaze as he walked, unseeing, past me. I could tell by the way he moved, and his air of detachment, that he was heavy with a speech. I fell in at the back of the procession and heard the cheers from his supporters as he entered the chamber, and the answering cat-calls of his opponents.

We were kept back until the last of the senators had gone in, and then permitted to run to the bar of the house. I secured myself my usual decent vantage point beside the door jamb and was immediately aware of someone squeezing in beside me. It was Atticus, looking white with nerves. 'How does he find it within himself to do this?' he asked, but before I could say anything, Figulus got up to report on the failure of his bill at the popular assembly. He droned on for a while, and then called on Mucius to explain his conduct in vetoing a measure which had been adopted by the house. There was an oppressive, restless air in the chamber. I could see Catilina and Hybrida among the aristocrats, with Catulus seated just in front of them on the consular bench, and Crassus a few places along from him. Caesar was on the same side of the chamber, on the bench reserved for ex-aediles. Mucius got up and in a dignified way explained that his sacred office called on him to act in the interests of the people, and that the lex Figula, far from protecting those interests, was a threat to their safety and an insult to their honour.

'Nonsense!' shouted a voice from the opposite side of the aisle, which I recognised at once as Cicero's. 'You were bought!'

Atticus gripped my arm. 'Here he goes!' he whispered.

'My conscience—' continued Mucius.

'Your conscience had nothing to do with it, you liar! You sold yourself like a whore!'

There came that low grumble of noise which is caused by several hundred men all muttering to one another at once, and

375

suddenly Cicero was on his feet, his arm outstretched, demanding the floor. At that same moment I heard a voice behind me calling to be let through, and we shuffled out of the way to allow a late-arriving senator, who proved to be Hortensius, access to the chamber. He hurried down the aisle, bowed to the consul, and took his place next to Catulus, with whom he quickly struck up a whispered conversation. By this time Cicero's supporters among the *pedarii* were bellowing that he should be allowed to speak, which, given that he was a praetorian, and outranked Mucius, he was undeniably entitled to do. Very reluctantly, Mucius allowed himself to be pulled down by the senators seated around him, whereupon Cicero pointed at him – his white-draped arm held out straight and rigid, like some statue of avenging Justice – and declared: 'A whore you are, Mucius – yes, and a treacherous one at that, for only yesterday you declared to the popular assembly that I was not fit to be consul – I, the first man to whom you turned when you were prosecuted for robbery! Good enough to defend you, Mucius, but not good enough to defend the Roman people, is that it? But why should I care what you say about me, when the whole world knows you were paid to slander me?'

Mucius turned scarlet. He shook his fist and started shouting insults in return, but I could not make them out over the general tumult. Cicero regarded him with contempt, then held up his hand for silence. 'But who is Mucius in any case?' he said, spitting out the name and dismissing it with a flick of his fingers. 'Mucius is just one solitary whore in a whole hired troupe of common prostitutes. Their master is a man of noble birth, bribery his chosen instrument – and believe me, gentlemen, he plays it like a flute! He is a briber of juries, a briber of voters and a briber of tribunes. Little wonder he loathed our bill against bribery, and that the method he used to stop it should have been – bribery!'

He paused and lowered his voice. 'I should like to share some information with the house.' The senate now went very quiet. 'Last night, Antonius Hybrida and Sergius Catilina met, together with others, at the house of this man of noble birth—'

'Name him!' shouted someone, and for a moment I thought that Cicero might actually do so. He stared across the aisle at Crassus with such calculated intensity that he might as well have gone over and touched him on the shoulder, so clear was it whom he had in mind. Crassus sat up slightly in his seat and slowly leaned forward, never taking his eyes from Cicero: he must have wondered what was coming. One could feel the entire chamber holding its breath. But Cicero had different quarry to chase, and with an almost palpable effort of will, he dragged his gaze away from Crassus.

'This man, as I say, of noble birth, having bribed away the bribery bill, has a new scheme in mind. He intends now to bribe his way to the consulship, not for himself but for his two creatures, Hybrida and Catilina.'

Naturally, both men instantly jumped up to protest, as Cicero must have calculated they would. But as their rank was no higher than his, he was entitled to leave them standing. 'Well, there they are,' he said, turning to the benches behind him, 'the best that money can buy!' He let the laughter build and chose the perfect moment to add: 'As we lawyers say – *caveat emptor*!'

Nothing is more injurious to a politician's dignity and authority than to be mocked, and if it happens it is vitally important to appear entirely unconcerned. But Hybrida and Catilina, buffeted by gusts of merriment from every side, could not decide whether to remain defiantly standing or to sit and feign indifference. They ended up trying to do both, bobbing up and down like a pair of workmen at either end of a pump-handle, which only increased the general hilarity. Catilina in particular was obviously losing his temper, for like many arrogant men the one thing he could not abide was to be teased. Caesar tried to come to their rescue, rising to demand what point Cicero was trying to make, but Cicero refused to acknowledge his intervention and the consul, enjoying himself like everyone else, declined to call Cicero to order.

'Let us take the lesser first,' continued Cicero, after both his targets had finally sunk back in to their seats. 'You, Hybrida, should never even have been elected praetor, and would not have been had I not taken pity on you, and recommended you to the centuries. You live openly with a courtesan, you cannot speak in public, you can barely remember your own name without the assistance of a *nomenclator*. You were a thief under Sulla, and a drunkard thereafter. You are, in short, a joke; but a joke of the worst sort – a joke that has gone on too long.'

The chamber was much quieter now, for these were insults which would oblige a man to be your enemy for life, and as Cicero turned towards Catilina, Atticus's anxious grip on my arm tightened. 'As for you, Catilina, is it not a prodigy and a portent of evil times that you should hope for, or even think of, the consulship? For from whom do you ask it? From the chiefs of the state, who, two years ago, refused even to allow you to stand for it? Do you ask it from the order of knights which you have slaughtered? Or from the people, who still remember the monstrous cruelty with which you butchered their leader – my kinsman – Gratidianus, and carried his still-breathing head through the streets to the Temple of Apollo? Do you ask it from the senators, who by their own authority had almost stripped you of all your honours, and surrendered you in chains to the Africans?'

'I was acquitted!' roared Catilina, leaping back to his feet.

'Acquitted!' mocked Cicero. 'You? Acquitted? You – who disgraced yourself by every sort of sexual perversion and profligacy; who dyed your hands in the wickedest murder, who plundered the allies, who violated the laws and the courts of justice? You, who married in adultery the mother of the daughter you first debauched? Acquitted? Then I can only imagine that Roman knights must have been liars; that the documentary evidence of a most honourable city was false; that Quintus Metellus Pius told lies; that Africa told lies. Acquitted! O wretched man, not to see that you were not acquitted by that decision, but only reserved for some more severe tribunal, and some more fearful punishment!'

This would have been too much even for an equable man to sit through, but in Catilina it induced nothing short of murderous insanity. He gave an animal's bellow of primitive rage and launched himself over the bench in front of him, crashing between Hortensius and Catulus, and diving across the aisle in an effort to reach his tormentor. But of course this was precisely the reaction Cicero had been trying to goad him into. He flinched but stood his ground as Quintus and a few other ex-soldiers scrambled to form a cordon around him – not that there was any need, for Catilina, big though he was, had been seized at once by the consul's lictors. His friends, among them Crassus and Caesar, quickly had him by the arms and started dragging him back to his seat as he writhed and roared and kicked in fury. The whole of the senate was on its feet, trying to see what was happening, and Figulus had to suspend the session until order was restored.

When the sitting resumed, Hybrida and Catilina, as custom dictated, were given the opportunity to respond, and each man, quivering with outrage, tipped a bucketful of the usual insults over Cicero's head – ambitious, untrustworthy, scheming, 'new man', foreigner, evader of military service, coward – while their supporters cheered them dutifully. But neither had Cicero's flair for invective, and even their most dedicated partisans must have been dismayed by their failure to answer his central charge: that their candidacies were based on bribery by a mysterious third party. It was noticeable that Hortensius and even Catulus offered them only the most half-hearted applause. As for Cicero, he put on a professional mask and sat smiling and unconcerned throughout their shrill tirades, seemingly no more concerned than a duck in a rainstorm. Only afterwards – after Quintus and his military friends had escorted him rapidly out of the chamber to prevent a further assault by Catilina, and only after we had reached the safety of Atticus's house on the Quirinal and the door had been locked and barred – only then did he appear to realise the enormity of what he had done.

XVIII

There was nothing left for Cicero now except to wait for the reaction of Hortensius. We passed the hours in the dry stillness of Atticus's library, surrounded by all that ancient wisdom, under the gaze of the great philosophers, while beyond the terrace the day ripened and faded and the view over the city became yellower and dustier in the heat of the July afternoon. I should like to record that we took down the occasional volume and spent the time swapping the thoughts of Epicurus or Zeno or Aristotle, or that Cicero said something profound about democracy. But in truth no one was much in the mood for political theory, least of all Quintus, who had scheduled a campaign appearance in the busy Porticus Aemilia and fretted that his brother was losing valuable canvassing time. We relived the drama of Cicero's speech – 'You should have seen Crassus's face when he thought I was about to name him!' – and pondered the likely response of the aristocrats. If they did not take the bait, Cicero had placed himself in a highly dangerous position. Every so often, he would ask me if I was absolutely certain that Hortensius had read his letter, and yet again I would reply that I had no doubt, for he had done so right in front of me. 'Then we shall give him another hour,' Cicero would say, and resume his restless pacing, occasionally stopping to make some cutting remark to Atticus: 'Are they always this punctual, these smart friends of yours?' or 'Tell me, is it considered a crime against good breeding to consult a clock?'

It was the tenth hour by Atticus's exquisite sundial when at last one of his slaves came into the library to announce that Hortensius's steward had arrived.

'So now we are supposed to negotiate with his servants?' muttered Cicero. But he was so anxious for news that he hurried out into the atrium himself, and we all went with him. Waiting there was the same bony, supercilious fellow whom I had encountered at Hortensius's house that morning; he was not much more polite now. His message was that he had come in Hortensius's two-seater carriage to collect Cicero and convey him to a meeting with his master.

'But I must accompany him,' protested Quintus.

'My orders are simply to bring Senator Cicero,' responded the steward. 'The meeting is highly sensitive and confidential. Only one other person is required – that secretary of his, who has the quick way with words.'

I was not at all happy about this, and nor was Quintus – I out of a cowardly desire to avoid being cross-examined by Hortensius, he because it was a snub, and also perhaps (to be more charitable) because he was worried for his brother's safety. 'What if it is a trap?' he asked. 'What if Catilina is there, or intercepts you on your journey?'

'You will be under the protection of Senator Hortensius,' said the steward stiffly. 'I give you his word of honour in the presence of all these witnesses.'

'It will be all right, Quintus,' said Cicero, laying a reassuring hand on his brother's arm. 'It is not in Hortensius's interests for any injury to befall me. Besides,' he smiled, 'I am a friend of Atticus here, and what better guarantee of safe passage is there than that? Come along, Tiro. Let us find out what he has to say.'

We left the relative safety of the library and went down into the street, where a smart *carpentum* was waiting, with Hortensius's livery painted on its side. The steward sat up at the front next to the driver, while I sat in the back with Cicero and we lurched off down the hill. But instead of turning south towards the Palatine, as we had expected, we headed north, towards the Fontinalian Gate, joining the stream of traffic leaving the city at the end of the day. Cicero had pulled the folds of his white toga up over his head, ostensibly to shield himself from the clouds of dust thrown up by the wheels, but actually to avoid any of his voters seeing him travelling in a vehicle belonging to Hortensius. Once we were out of the city, however, he pulled his hood down. He was clearly not at all happy to be leaving the precincts of Rome, for despite his brave words he knew that a fatal accident out here would be very easy to arrange. The sun was big and low, just beginning to set behind those massive family tombs which line the road. The poplars threw elongated shadows which fell jet black across our path, like crevasses. For a while we were stuck behind a plodding bullock cart. But then the coachman cracked his whip and we raced forward, just narrowly managing to overtake it before a chariot rattled past us, heading towards the city. I guess we both must have realised by then where we were going, and Cicero pulled his hood up again and folded his arms, his head down. What thoughts must have been spinning through his mind! We turned off the road and began climbing a steep hillside, following a driveway freshly laid with gravel. It took us on a winding journey over gushing brooks and through gloomy, scented pine groves where pigeons called to one another in the dusk, until eventually we came to a huge pair of open gates, and beyond them an immense villa set in its own park, which I recognised from the model Gabinius had displayed to the jealous mob in the forum as the palace of Lucullus.

For years thereafter, whenever I smelt fresh cement and wet paint, I would think of Lucullus and that echoing mausoleum he had built for himself beyond the walls of Rome. What a brilliant, melancholy figure he was – perhaps the greatest general the aristocrats had produced for fifty years, yet robbed of ultimate victory in the East by the arrival of Pompey, and doomed by the political intrigues of his enemies, among them Cicero, to linger outside Rome for years, unhonoured and unable even to attend the senate, for by crossing the city's boundaries he would forfeit his right to a triumph. Because he still retained military *imperium*, there were sentries in the grounds, and lictors with their bundles of rods and axes waited sullenly in the hall – so many lictors, in fact, that Cicero calculated that a second general on active service must be on the premises. 'Do you think it's possible that Quintus Metellus is here as well?' he whispered, as we followed the steward into the cavernous interior. 'Dear gods, I think he must be!'

We passed through various rooms stuffed with loot from the war until at last we reached the great chamber known as the Room of Apollo, where a group of six were talking beneath a mural of the deity shooting a fiery arrow from his golden bow. At the sound of our footsteps on the marble floor, the conversation ceased and there was a loud silence. Quintus Metellus was indeed among them – stouter, greyer and more weather-beaten following his years of command in Crete, but still very much the same man who had attempted to intimidate the Sicilians into dropping their case against Verres. On one side of Metellus was his old courtroom ally Hortensius, whose bland and handsome face was expressionless, and on the other, Catulus, as thin and sharp as a blade. Isauricus, the grand old man of the senate, was also present – seventy years old he must have been on that July evening, but he did not look it (he was one of those types who never look it: he was to live to be ninety, and attend the funerals of almost everyone else in the room); I noticed he was holding the transcript I had delivered to Hortensius. The two Lucullus brothers completed the sextet. Marcus, the younger, I knew as a familiar figure from the senate front bench. Lucius, the famous general, paradoxically I did not recognise at all, for he had been away fighting for eighteen out of the past twenty-three years. He was in his middle fifties, and I quickly saw why Pompey was so passionately jealous of him – why they had literally come to blows when they met in Galatia to effect the handover in the Eastern command – for Lucullus had a chilly grandeur which made even Catulus seem slightly common.

It was Hortensius who ended the embarrassment, and who stepped forward to introduce Cicero to Lucullus. Cicero extended his hand, and for a moment I thought Lucullus might refuse to shake it, for he would only have known Cicero as a partisan of Pompey, and as one of those populist politicians who had helped engineer his dismissal. But finally he took it, very gingerly, as one might pick up a soiled sponge in a latrine. 'Imperator,' said Cicero, bowing politely. He nodded to Metellus as well: 'Imperator.'

'And who is that?' demanded Isauricus, pointing at me.

'That is my secretary, Tiro,' said Cicero, 'who recorded the meeting at the house of Crassus.'

'Well, I for one do not believe a word of it,' replied Isauricus, brandishing the transcript at me. 'No one could have written down all of this as it was uttered. It is beyond human capacity.'

'Tiro has developed his own system of stenography,' explained Cicero. 'Let him show you the actual records he made last night.'

I pulled out the notebooks from my pocket and handed them around.

'Remarkable,' said Hortensius, examining my script intently. 'So these symbols substitute for sounds, do they? Or for entire words?'

'Words mostly,' I replied, 'and common phrases.'

'Prove it,' said Catulus belligerently. 'Take down what I say.' And giving me barely a moment to open a fresh notebook and take up my stylus, he went on rapidly: 'If what I have read here is true, the state is threatened with civil war as a result of a criminal conspiracy. If what I have read is false, it is the wickedest forgery in our history. For my own part, I do not believe it is true, because I do not believe such a record could have been produced by a living hand. That Catilina is a hothead, we all know well enough, but he is a true and noble Roman, not a devious and ambitious outsider, and I will take his word over that of a new man – always! What is it you want from us, Cicero? You cannot seriously believe, after all that has happened between us, that I could possibly support you for the consulship? So what is it?'

'Nothing,' replied Cicero pleasantly. 'I came across some information which I thought might be of interest to you. I passed it along to Hortensius, that is all. You brought me out here, remember? I did not ask to come. I might more appropriately

PRAETORIAN

ask: What do *you* gentlemen want? Do you want to be trapped between Pompey and his armies in the East, and Crassus and Caesar and the urban mob in Italy, and gradually have the life squeezed out of you? Do you want to rely for your protection on the two men you are backing for consul – the one stupid, the other insane – who cannot even manage their own households, let alone the affairs of the nation? Is that what you want? Well, good then. I at least have an easy conscience. I have done my patriotic duty by alerting you to what is happening, even though you have never been any friends of mine. I also believe I have demonstrated by my courage in the senate today my willingness to stand up to these criminals. No other candidate for consul has done it, or will in the future. I have made them my enemies and shown you what they are like. But from you, Catulus, and from all of you, *I* want *nothing,* and if all you wish to do is insult me, I bid you a good evening.'

He spun around and began walking towards the door, with me in tow, and I guess that must have felt to him like the longest walk he ever took, because we had almost reached the shadowy antechamber – and with it, surely, the black void of political oblivion – when a voice (it was that of Lucullus himself) shouted out: 'Read it back!' Cicero halted, and we both turned around. 'Read it back,' repeated Lucullus. 'What Catulus said just now.'

Cicero nodded at me, and I fumbled for my notebook. '"If what I have read here is true",' I began, reciting in that flat, strange way of stenography being read back, '"the state is threatened with civil war as a result of a criminal conspiracy if what I have read is false it is the wickedest forgery in our history for my own part I do not believe it is true because I do not believe such a record could have been produced by a living hand—"'

387

'He could have memorised that,' objected Catulus. 'It is all just a cheap trick, of the sort you might see done by a conjuror in the forum.'

'And the latter part,' persisted Lucullus. 'Read out the last thing your master said.'

I ran my finger down my notation. '". . . never been any friends of mine I also believe I have demonstrated by my courage in the senate today my willingess to stand up to these criminals no other candidate for consul has done it or will in the future I have made them my enemies and shown you what they are like but from you Catulus and from all of you I want nothing and if all you wish to do is insult me I bid you a good evening."'

Isauricus whistled. Hortensius nodded, and said something like 'I told you' or 'I warned you' – I cannot remember exactly – to which Metellus responded, 'Yes, well, I have to say, that is proof enough for me.' Catulus merely glared at me.

'Come back, Cicero,' said Lucullus, beckoning to him. 'I am satisfied. The record is genuine. Let us put aside for the time being the question of who needs whom the most, and start from the premise that each of us needs the other.'

'I am still not convinced,' grumbled Catulus.

'Then let me convince you with a single word,' said Hortensius impatiently. 'Caesar. Caesar – with Crassus's gold, two consuls and ten tribunes behind him!'

'So, really, we must talk with such people?' Catulus sighed. 'Well, Cicero perhaps,' he conceded. 'But we certainly do not need you,' he snapped, pointing at me, just as I was moving, as always, to follow my master. 'I do not want that creature and his tricks within a mile of me, listening to what we say, and writing everything down in his damned untrustworthy way. If anything is to pass between us, it must never be divulged.'

Cicero hesitated. 'All right,' he said reluctantly, and he gave me an apologetic look. 'Wait outside, Tiro.'

I had no business to feel aggrieved. I was merely a slave, after all: an extra hand, a tool – a 'creature', as Catulus put it. But nevertheless I felt my humiliation keenly. I folded up my notebook and walked into the antechamber, and then kept on walking, through all those echoing, freshly stuccoed state rooms – Venus, Mercury, Mars, Jupiter – as the slaves in their cushioned slippers moved silently with their glowing tapers among the gods, lighting the lamps and candelabra. I went out into the soft warm dusk of the park, where the cicadas were singing, and for reasons which I cannot even now articulate I found that I was weeping, but I suppose I must have been very tired.

It was almost dawn when I awoke, stiff in my limbs and damp with cold from the dew. For a moment I had no idea where I was or how I had got there, but then I realised I was on a stone bench close to the front of the house, and that it was Cicero who had woken me. His face looming over me was grim. 'We have finished here,' he said. 'We must get back to the city quickly.' He glanced across to where the carriage was waiting, and put his finger to his lips to warn me not to say anything in front of Hortensius's steward. So it was in silence that we clambered into the *carpentum*, and as we left the park I remember turning for a final look at the great villa, the torches still burning along its terraces, but losing their sharpness now as the pale morning light came up; of the other aristocrats there was no sign.

Cicero, conscious that in little more than two hours he would have to leave his house to go down to the Field of Mars for

the election, kept urging the driver to make better speed, and
those poor horses must have been whipped until their hides
were raw. But we were lucky that the roads were empty, save
for a few very early voters walking into town for the election,
and we hurtled along at a great speed, reaching the Fontinalian
Gate just as it was opening, and then rattled up the paved
slopes of the Esquiline Hill faster than a man could sprint. Just
before the Temple of Tellus, Cicero told the driver to stop and
let us out, so that we could walk the last part of the way – an
order which puzzled me, until I realised that he wanted to
avoid being seen by the crowd of his supporters which was
already beginning to assemble in the street outside his front
door. He strode on ahead of me in that way of his, with his
hands clasped behind his back, still keeping his thoughts to
himself, and I noticed that his once-brilliant white toga was
stained with dirt. We went down the side of the house and
through the little door at the back which the servants used,
and there we bumped into Terentia's business manager, the
odious Philotimus, who was obviously on his way back from
some nocturnal assignation with one of the slave girls. Cicero
did not even see him, so preoccupied was he with what had
happened and what was to come. His eyes were red with tiredness, his face and hair brown with dust from the journey. He
told me to go and open up the door and let the people in.
Then he went upstairs.

Among the first across the threshold was Quintus, who naturally demanded to know what was happening. He and the others
had waited for our return in Atticus's library until nearly
midnight, and he was furious and anxious in equal measure.
This put me in an awkward spot, and I could only stammer
that I would prefer it if he addressed his questions directly to

his brother. To be honest, seeing Cicero and his bitterest enemies all together in such a setting now seemed so unreal to me, I could almost have believed I had dreamed it. Quintus was not satisfied, but fortunately I was saved further embarrassment by the sheer number of visitors pouring through the door. I escaped by pretending I had to check everything was ready in the tablinum, and from there I slipped into my little cubicle and rinsed my neck and face with tepid water from my basin.

When I next saw Cicero, an hour later, he once again demonstrated those remarkable powers of recuperation which I have observed to be the distinguishing mark of all successful politicians. Watching him come down the stairs in a freshly laundered white toga, his face washed and shaved and his hair combed and scented, no one could have guessed that he had not slept for the past two nights. The cramped house by this time was packed with his supporters. Cicero had the infant Marcus, whose first birthday it was, carefully balanced on his shoulders, and such a cheer went up when the two of them appeared, it must have shaken off several roof tiles: no wonder the poor child started crying. Cicero quickly lifted him down, lest this be seen as a bad omen for the day, and handed him to Terentia, who was standing behind him on the stairs. He smiled at her, and said something, and at that moment I realised for the first time just how close they had become over the years: that what had started as a marriage of convenience was now a most formidable partnership. I could not hear what passed between them, and then he came down into the crowd.

So many people had turned out it was hard for him to struggle through the tablinum to the atrium, where Quintus, Frugi and Atticus were surrounded by a very decent showing of senators.

Among those present to demonstrate their support were Cicero's old friend Servius Sulpicius; Gallus, the renowned scholar of judisprudence, who had refused to run himself; the elder Frugi, with whom Cicero was forming a family connection; Marcellinus, who had supported him ever since the Verres trial; and all those senators he had represented in the courts, such as Cornelius, Fundanius, Orchivius, and also Fonteius, the corrupt ex-governor of Gaul. Indeed, as I struggled through the rooms after Cicero, it was as if the past ten years had all sprung back to life, so many half-forgotten courtroom struggles were represented there; even Popillius Laenas, whose nephew Cicero had rescued from a charge of parricide on the day Sthenius came to see us. The atmosphere was more akin to a family festival than an election day, and Cicero as ever was in his element on these occasions: I doubt if there was one supporter whose hand he did not shake, and with whom he did not establish one brief moment of rapport, sufficient to leave the other man feeling he had been specially singled out.

Just before we left, Quintus pulled him to one side to ask, quite angrily as I recall it, where on earth he had been all night – he had almost sent men out looking for him – to which Cicero, conscious of the people all around him, replied quietly that he would tell him later. But that only made Quintus more aggrieved. 'Who do you think I am?' he demanded. 'Your maid? Tell me now!' And so Cicero told him then very rapidly about the journey out to the palace of Lucullus and the presence there of Metellus and Catulus, as well as Hortensius and Isauricus.

'The whole patrician gang!' whispered Quintus excitedly, his irritation entirely forgotten. 'My gods, whoever would have thought it? And are they going to support us?'

'We talked for hour after hour, but in the end they would

not commit themselves until they had spoken to the other great families,' replied Cicero, glancing nervously around in case anyone was listening, but the din was too great for him to be overheard. 'Hortensius, I think, would have agreed on the spot. Catulus remains instinctively opposed. The others will do what self-interest dictates. We shall just have to wait and see.'

Atticus, who had heard all this, said, 'But they believed in the truth of the evidence you showed them?'

'I think so, yes. Thanks to Tiro. But we can discuss all this later. Put on your bravest faces, gentlemen,' he said, gripping the hands of each of us in turn, 'we have an election to win!'

Seldom can a candidate have staged a more splendid show than Cicero did during his walk down to the Field of Mars, and for that much credit must go to Quintus. We made up a parade of three or four hundred, with musicians, young men carrying green boughs wound with ribbons, girls with rose petals, actor friends of Cicero's from the theatre, senators, knights, merchants, stall-holders, regular spectators from the law courts, guild officers, legal clerks, representatives from the Roman communities in Sicily and Nearer Gaul. We set up a terrific noise of cheering and whistling as we came on to the campus and there was a great surge of voters towards us. It is always said of elections, in my experience, that whichever one is in progress at the time is the most significant there has ever been, and on that day, at least, it was arguably true, with the added excitement that no one knew how it would turn out, given the activity among the bribery agents, the sheer number of candidates and the enmity between them following Cicero's attack on Catilina and Hybrida in the senate.

We had anticipated trouble, and Quintus had taken the

precaution of stationing some of our heftier supporters immediately behind and in front of his brother. As we approached the
voting pens I felt increasingly worried, for I could seen Catilina
and his followers up ahead, waiting beside the returning officer's
tent. Some of these ruffians jeered us as we arrived at the enclosure, but Catilina himself, after a brief and contemptuous glance
in Cicero's direction, resumed talking to Hybrida. I muttered to
young Frugi that I was surprised he did not at least put on a
show of intimidation – that, after all, was his usual tactic – to
which Frugi, who was no fool, responded: 'He does not feel he
needs to – he is so confident of victory.' His words filled me with
unease.

But then a very remarkable thing happened. Cicero and all
the other senators seeking either the consulship or the praetorship – perhaps two dozen men – were standing in the small
area reserved for the candidates, surrounded by a low sheep
fence to separate them from their supporters. The presiding
consul, Marcius Figulus, was talking to the augur, checking
that all was propitious for the ballot to begin, when just at that
moment Hortensius appeared, followed by a retinue of about
twenty men. The crowd parted to let him through. He
approached the fence and called to Cicero, who interrupted
his conversation with one of the other candidates – Cornificius,
I think it was – and went over to him. This in itself surprised
people, for it was known that there was little love lost between
the two old rivals, and there was a stir among the onlookers;
Catilina and Hybrida certainly both turned to stare. For a
moment or two, Cicero and Hortensius regarded one another,
then simultaneously they nodded, and each reached out and
slowly shook the hand of the other. No word was uttered, and
with the handclasp still in place, Hortensius half turned to the

men behind him and raised Cicero's arm above his head. A great shout of applause, mingled with some boos and groans, broke out from the watching crowd, for there was no doubt what the gesture meant: I certainly never expected to see anything like it. *The aristocrats were supporting Cicero!* Immediately, Hortensius's attendants turned and disappeared into the throng, presumably to spread the word among the nobles' agents in the centuries that they were to switch their support. I risked a look at Catilina and saw on his face an expression of puzzlement rather than anything else, for the incident, though obviously significant – people were still buzzing about it – was so fleeting that Hortensius was already walking away. An instant later, Figulus called to the candidates to follow him to the platform so that the voting could begin.

You can always spot a fool, for he is the man who will tell you he knows who is going to win an election. But an election is a living thing – you might almost say, the most vigorously alive thing there is – with thousands upon thousands of brains and limbs and eyes and thoughts and desires, and it will wriggle and turn and run off in directions no one ever predicted, some-times just for the joy of proving the wiseacres wrong. This much I learnt on the Field of Mars that day, when the entrails were inspected, the skies were checked for suspicious flights of birds, the blessings of the gods were invoked, all epileptics were asked to leave the field (for in those days an attack of epilepsy, or *morbus comitialis*, automatically rendered proceed-ings void), a legion was deployed on the approaches to Rome to prevent a surprise attack, the list of candidates was read, the trumpets were sounded, the red flag was hoisted over the

Janiculum Hill, and the Roman people began to cast their ballots.

The honour of being the first of the one hundred and ninety-three centuries to vote was decided by lot, and to be a member of this *centuria praerogativa*, as it was known, was considered a rare blessing, for its decision often set the pattern for what followed. Only the richest centuries were eligible for the draw, and I remember how I stood and watched as that year's winners, a stalwart collection of merchants and bankers, filed self-importantly over the wooden bridge and disappeared behind the screens. Their ballots were quickly counted, Figulus came to the front of his tribunal and announced that they had put Cicero in first place and Catilina second. At once a gasp went up, for all those fools I was speaking of had predicted it would be Catilina first and Hybrida second, and then the gasp quickly turned into cheers as Cicero's supporters, realising what had happened, began a noisy demonstration which spread across the Field of Mars. Cicero was standing under the awning beneath the consul's platform. He permitted himself only the most fleeting of smiles, and then, such was the actor in the man, he composed his features into an expression of dignity and authority appropriate to a Roman consul. Catilina – who was as far away from Cicero as it was possible to get, with all the other candidates lined up between them – looked as if he had been struck in the face. Only Hybrida's expression was blank – whether because he was drunk as usual or too stupid to realise what was happening I cannot say. As for Crassus and Caesar, they had been loitering and chatting together near to the place where the voters emerged after casting their ballots, and I could have laughed aloud as they looked at one another in disbelief. They held a hurried consultation and then darted off in different directions, no doubt to demand how the expenditure of twenty million sesterces had failed to secure the *centuria praerogativa*.

If Crassus really had purchased the eight thousand votes which Ranunculus had estimated, that would normally have been enough to swing the election. But this ballot was unusually heavy, thanks to the interest aroused all across Italy, and as the voting went on throughout the morning it became apparent that the briber-in-chief had fallen just short of his target. Cicero had always had the equestrian order firmly behind him, plus the Pompeians and the lower orders. Now that Hortensius, Catulus, Metellus, Isauricus and the Lucullus brothers were delivering the blocs of voters controlled by the aristocrats, he was winning a vote from every century, either as their first or second preference, and soon the only question was who would be his consular colleague. Throughout the morning, it looked as if it would be Catilina, with my notes (which I found the other day) showing that at noon the voting was:

Cicero	81 centuries
Catilina	34 centuries
Hybrida	29 centuries
Sacerdos	9 centuries
Longinus	5 centuries
Cornificius	2 centuries

But then came the voting of the six centuries composed exclusively of the aristocrats, the *sex suffragia*, and they really put the knife into Catilina, so that if I retain one image above all from that memorable day it is of the patricians, having cast their ballots, filing past the candidates. Because the Field of

Mars lies outside the city limits, there was nothing to stop Lucius Lucullus, and Quintus Metellus with him, both in their scarlet cloaks and military uniforms, turning out to vote, and their appearance caused a sensation – but nothing like as great an uproar as greeted the announcement that their century had voted Cicero first and then Hybrida. After them came Isauricus, the elder Curio, Aemilius Alba, Claudius Pulcher, Junius Servilius – the husband of Cato's sister, Servilia – old Metellus Pius, the pontifex maximus, too sick to walk but carried in a litter, followed by his adopted son, Scipio Nasica . . . And again and again the announcement was the same: Cicero first, and next Hybrida; Cicero first, and next Hybrida; Cicero first . . . When, finally, Hortensius and Catulus passed by, it was noticeable that neither man could bring himself to look Catilina in the eye, and once it was declared that their century, too, had voted for Cicero and Hybrida, Catilina must have realised his chances were finished. At that point Cicero had eighty-seven centuries to Hybrida's thirty-five and Catilina's thirty-four – for the first time in the day, Hybrida had eased in front of his running-mate, but more importantly, the aristocrats had publicly turned on one of their own, and in the most brutal manner. After that, Catilina's candidacy was effectively dead, although one had to give him high marks for his conduct. I had anticipated that he would storm off in a rage, or lunge at Cicero and try to murder him with his bare hands. But instead he stood throughout that long, hot day, as the citizens went past him and his hopes of the consulship sank with the sun, and he maintained a look of imperturbable calm, even when Figulus came forward for the final time to read the result of the election:

Cicero	193 centuries
Hybrida	102 centuries
Catilina	65 centuries
Sacerdos	12 centuries
Longinus	9 centuries
Cornificius	5 centuries

We cheered until our throats ached, although Cicero himself seemed very preoccupied for a man who had just achieved his life's ambition, and I felt oddly uneasy. He was now permanently wearing what I later came to recognise as his 'consular look': his chin held ever-so-slightly high, his mouth set in a determined line, and his eyes seemingly directed towards some glorious point in the distance. Hybrida held out his hand to Catilina, but Catilina ignored it, and stepped down from the podium like a man in a trance. He was ruined, bankrupt – surely it would be only a year or two before he was thrown out of the senate altogether. I searched around for Crassus and Caesar, but they had quit the field hours earlier, once Cicero had passed the number of centuries needed for victory. So, too, had the aristocrats. They had gone home for the day the instant Catilina had been safely disposed of, like men who had been required to perform some distasteful duty – put down a favourite hunting-dog, say, which had become rabid – and who now wanted nothing more than the quiet comfort of their own hearths.

Thus did Marcus Tullius Cicero, at forty-two, the youngest age allowable, achieve the supreme *imperium* of the Roman consulship – and achieve it, amazingly, by a unanimous vote of the centuries, and as a 'new man', without family, fortune or force

of arms to assist him: a feat never accomplished before or afterwards. We returned that evening from the Field of Mars to his
modest home, and once he had thanked his supporters and sent
them away, and received the congratulations of his slaves, he
ordered that the couches from the dining room be carried up on
to the roof, so that he could dine beneath the open sky, as he
had done on that night – so long ago it seemed – when he had
first disclosed his ambition to become consul. I was honoured
to be invited to join the family group, for Cicero was insistent
that he would never have achieved his goal without me. For a
delirious moment I thought he might be about to award me my
freedom and give me that farm right there and then, but he said
nothing about it, and it did not seem the appropriate time or
setting to bring it up. He was on one couch with Terentia, Quintus
was with Pomponia, Tullia was with her fiancé, Frugi, and I
reclined with Atticus. I can recall little at my great age of what
we ate or drank, or any of that, but I do remember that we each
went over our particular memories of the day, and especially of
that extraordinary spectacle of the aristocracy voting en masse
for Cicero.

'Tell me, Marcus,' said Atticus, in his worldly way, once plenty
of good wine had been consumed, 'how did you manage to
persuade them? Because, although I know you are a genius with
words, these men despised you – absolutely loathed everything
you said and stood for. What did you offer them, besides stopping Catilina?'

'Obviously,' replied Cicero, 'I had to promise that I will lead
the opposition to Crassus and Caesar and the tribunes when they
publish this land reform bill of theirs.'

'That will be quite a task,' said Quintus.

'And that is all?' persisted Atticus. (It is my belief, looking back, that he was behaving like a good cross-examiner, and that he knew the answer to the question before he asked it, probably from his friend Hortensius.) 'You really agreed to nothing else? Because you were in there for many hours.'

Cicero winced. 'Well, I did have to undertake,' he said reluctantly, 'to propose in the senate, as consul, that Lucullus should be awarded a triumph, and also Quintus Metellus.'

Now at last I understood why Cicero had seemed so grim and preoccupied when he left his conference with the aristocrats. Quintus put down his plate and regarded him with undisguised horror. 'So first they want you to turn the people against you by blocking land reform, and then they demand that you should make an enemy out of Pompey by awarding triumphs to his greatest rivals?'

'I am afraid, brother,' said Cicero wearily, 'that the aristocracy did not acquire their wealth without knowing how to drive a hard bargain. I held out as long as I could.'

'But why did you agree?'

'Because I needed to win.'

'But to win what, exactly?'

Cicero was silent.

'Good,' said Terentia, patting her husband's knee. 'I think all those policies are good.'

'Well, you would!' protested Quintus. 'But within weeks of taking office, Marcus will have no supporters left. The people will accuse him of betrayal. The Pompeians will do the same. And the aristocrats will drop him just as soon as he has served his purpose. Who will be left to defend him?'

'I shall defend you,' said Tullia, but for once no one laughed at her precocious loyalty, and even Cicero could only manage a faint smile. But then he rallied.

'Really, Quintus,' he said, 'you are spoiling the whole evening. Between two extremes there is always a third way. Crassus and Caesar have to be stopped: I can make that case. And when it comes to Lucullus, everyone accepts that he deserves a triumph a hundred times over for what he achieved in the war against Mithradates.'

'And Metellus?' cut in Quintus.

'I am sure I shall be able to find something to praise even in Metellus, if you give me sufficient time.'

'And Pompey?'

'Pompey, as we all know, is simply a humble servant of the republic,' replied Cicero, with an airy wave of his hand. 'More importantly,' he added, deadpan, 'he is not here.'

There was a pause, and then, reluctantly, Quintus started to laugh. 'He is not here,' he repeated. 'Well, that is true.' After a while, we all laughed; one had to laugh, really.

'That is better!' Cicero smiled at us. 'The art of life is to deal with problems as they arise, rather than destroy one's spirit by worrying about them too far in advance. Especially tonight.' And then a tear came into his eye. 'Do you know who we should drink to? I believe we should raise a toast to the memory of our dear cousin, Lucius, who was here on this roof when we first talked of the consulship, and who would so much have wanted to see this day.' He raised his cup, and we all raised ours with him, although I could not help remembering the last remark Lucius ever made to him: *Words, words, words. Is there no end to the tricks you can make them perform?*

Later, after everyone had gone, either to their home or to their bed, Cicero lay on his back on one of the couches, with his hands clasped behind his head, staring up at the stars. I sat quietly on the opposite couch with my notebook ready in case he needed anything. I tried to stay alert. But the night was warm and I was swooning with tiredness, and when my head nodded forward for the fourth or fifth time, he looked across at me and told me to go and get some rest: 'You are the private secretary of a consul-elect now. You will need to keep your wits as sharp as your pen.' As I stood to take my leave, he settled back into his contemplation of the heavens. 'How will posterity judge us, eh, Tiro?' he said. 'That is the only question for a statesman. But before it can judge us, it must first remember who we are.' I waited for a while in case he wanted to add something else, but he seemed to have forgotten my existence, so I went away and left him to it.

AUTHOR'S NOTE

Although *Imperium* is a novel, the majority of the events it describes did actually happen; the remainder at least *could* have happened; and nothing, I hope (a hostage to fortune, this), demonstrably *did not* happen. That Tiro wrote a life of Cicero is attested both by Plutarch and Asconius; it vanished in the general collapse of the Roman Empire.

My principal debt is to the twenty-nine volumes of Cicero's speeches and letters collected in the Loeb Classical Library and published by Harvard University Press. Another invaluable aid has been *The Magistrates of the Roman Republic, Volume II, 99 B.C.–31 B.C.* by T. Robert S. Broughton, published by the American Philological Association. I should also like to salute Sir William Smith (1813–93), who edited the *Dictionary of Greek and Roman Biography and Mythology*, the *Dictionary of Greek and Roman Antiquities* and the *Dictionary of Greek and Roman Geography* – three immense and unsurpassed monuments to Victorian classical scholarship. There are, of course, many other works of more recent authorship which I hope to acknowledge in due course.

R.H.
16 May 2006

L
re
L.
v.
P

Waiting in the Wings

Waiting in the Wings

DONNA HAY

ORION

Copyright © 2000 Donna Hay

The right of Donna Hay to be identified as
the author of this work has been asserted by her in
accordance with the Copyright, Designs and Patents Act 1988

This edition first published in Great Britain in 2000 by
Orion
An imprint of Orion Books Ltd
Orion House, 5 Upper St Martin's Lane, London WC2H 9EA

A CIP catalogue record for this book is
available from the British Library

Typeset by Deltatype Ltd, Birkenhead, Merseyside
Printed and bound in Great Britain
by Clays Ltd, St Ives plc

For Ken and Harriet

Acknowledgements

First of all, to Marina Oliver and everyone at the RNA for their help, advice and encouragement. Also to my pals on the New Writers' Scheme, especially Val McManus, Pauline Case and Heather Jan Brunt. Even if all this had never happened, it would have been worth it just to get to know them.

To my agent Sarah Molloy, and to Jane Wood and Selina Walker at Orion, for taking me on, for never being too busy to answer stupid questions and for knowing a lot more than I do.

To the many actors and actresses who have graciously offered me insights into everything from auditions to first-night nerves.

To my best friend June Smith Sheppard, because I promised if I ever wrote a book I'd mention her (although I absolutely refuse to put 'the wind beneath my wings', as she insisted I should).

Last but by no means least, to my husband Ken and daughter Harriet, the unsung heroes who lived through every agonising page of this book, and without whose endless support and sacrifice it would never have been written.

London

Chapter 1

According to *Every Woman's Self Help Guide to Relation-ships*, there were four stages to the classic break-up: Denial, Self-Recrimination, Anger and Resolution.

Strange they didn't mention Compulsive Eating, Annie reflected, delving into the box of Coco Pops she clutched to her bosom like a much-loved teddy bear. Max had only been gone three weeks and she'd already worn quite a furrow in the stretch of carpet from the sofa to the fridge. At this rate, by the time she got to the Resolution bit she'd look like she'd swallowed a duvet.

If she ever got there. At the moment she was still hanging on by what was left of her finger-nails to Denial, before she made the long, dismal freefall into Self-Recrimination.

Julia had been typically blunt. 'You're letting yourself go,' she'd bawled down the telephone earlier. 'I bet you're wearing that sad old cardigan, aren't you? And when was the last time you washed your hair?'

Annie ran a hand through her tangled curls. 'Mind your own business. You're my agent, not my mother.'

'I'm just protecting my investment. Carry on like this

and I'll be lucky to get you a guest appearance as a dosser on *Casualty*.'

'Look, I just want to be left alone, okay? I'm depressed.'

'And don't we know it.' Julia sighed.

'I think I've got a right to be slightly cheesed off. My husband walked out on me three weeks ago.'

'Exactly,' Julia snapped. 'Three weeks ago. So don't you think it's time you pulled yourself together?'

Annie picked at a chocolate stain on her shapeless grey cardie. How could she expect Julia to understand? When it came to the men in her life, she had the boredom threshold of a black widow spider. Her idea of commitment was to give a man her phone number. And half the time it wasn't her real one.

Whereas Annie was more like a swan, mating for life. Or so she'd thought, until Max swam off in search of a new, more attractive pond.

'I know what you need,' Julia said.

Annie groaned. Julia Gold had a serious interferiority complex. She could just imagine her sitting at her desk overlooking Soho Square, lighting up her twentieth Silk Cut of the morning, strong black Java blend coursing through her veins. 'I'm not interested in your cast-off men, if that's what you mean.'

'And I dare say they wouldn't be interested in you, either. Let's face it, you're hardly Claudia Schiffer at the moment, are you?'

Julia could be very cruel sometimes. She was a frighteningly elegant forty-something, with a Nicky Clarke blonde bob and a designer wardrobe to die for. She also had two divorces behind her and a contacts book that read like a *Who's Who* of British theatre. It had been fear at first sight when Annie met her straight from drama

4

school. After seven years together Julia still refused to treat her like a grown-up.

'No,' she went on briskly, 'what you need is a job. And I've got just the one for you.'

Annie shovelled down another handful of Coco Pops as Julia described the 'fantastic new opportunity' she'd lined up for her. Some downbeat repertory theatre in an unheard-of part of Yorkshire was reopening after many years and the new artistic director was casting for its opening production.

And for some reason Julia seemed to think it was just what she needed.

'I know it's not exactly the RSC, darling, but it's six weeks' work,' she'd purred down the phone.

Annie straightened her shoulders. Her husband might have run off with her best friend, leaving her with a mortgage to pay, a terrifyingly huge Barclaycard bill and the self-esteem of the last sandwich in a railway buffet, but professionally speaking she still had her pride. 'I couldn't possibly do it,' she said, with as much hauteur as she could muster through a mouthful of breakfast cereal.

'Don't be silly, darling, I'm sure it won't be that difficult.' Annie listened as Julia drew long and hard on her ciggie. 'Besides, even if you do make a complete arse of yourself, no one will see it, will they? I mean, who'd be desperate enough to go all that way?'

'How reassuring.'

'Seriously, this guy's an absolute genius, so they say.' Julia had obviously realised she wasn't doing too good a sales job. 'He's got some fantastic ideas for the first season. They're opening with *Much Ado*. You know you've always wanted to play Beatrice.'

'I don't think I could any more.' Once she might have

taken Beatrice's sparky, feisty character in her stride. These days, it was all she could do to fetch in the milk from the front step.

'Nonsense, you could do it with your eyes closed,' Julia insisted. 'And you've got too much talent to waste it sitting around stuffing your face and waiting for that bastard to come home.'

'What makes you think I'm doing that?' Annie shoved a half-empty Quality Street box under the sofa with her foot.

'Because I know you. You won't get him back by eating yourself into blimpdom, you know.'

Too late for that, Annie thought, plucking at the baggy knees of her leggings, which were well into their fourth day of wear and looking the worse for it. 'Who says I want him back?'

'You mean if he came through that door now you wouldn't welcome him back with open arms?'

'Not necessarily.' Annie crossed her fingers.

'And you don't jump on the phone every time it rings?'

'Oh, please!' No need to tell her she took it to bed every night, along with an old flannel shirt that still held lingering traces of his CKBe.

'So you're not just existing from day to day, hanging on to the hope that he'll come back?'

'I do have my own life to live, you know.' Annie abandoned the Coco Pops and foraged under the sofa for the Quality Street box. So what if she chose to spend it huddled up on the sofa with the curtains closed, eating chocolate and watching Richard and Judy phone-ins.

'I'm glad to hear it. So there's nothing to stop you taking this job then, is there?'

There was a penetrating silence. Julia was extremely good at them.

Annie wasn't. 'I'm grieving,' she mumbled.

'What on earth for?'

'My marriage.' She felt tears rising again and sniffed them back.

'Oh, for God's sake!' Julia snapped. 'Anyone can see you're better off without that egotistical little shit. If I were you I'd be changing the locks and hanging out the bloody flags.'

As Julia launched into her well-rehearsed speech on Why Max Kennedy Wasn't Worth Spitting On, Annie tuned out, her gaze drifting around her strangely sparse living-room. Max had already removed most traces of himself – his books, his CDs and his collection of priceless Broadway sound-tracks. But he'd left behind a freakish piece of modern art, a twisted mass of knotted perspex and metal that occupied far too large a space in one corner of the room. Annie loathed it, but he'd always been extremely fond of the piece – called, inexplicably, *Freedom*. Now she latched on to it as a vital sign that one day he would come home.

Since Max had gone she'd become obsessed with signs and portents. She devoured her horoscope every day, searching for clues that he might return. She even made bets with herself. If she could get through *Coronation Street* without a ciggie he'd come back. If Trevor McDonald scratched his ear during the news he wouldn't. Sometimes she wondered if her grief had unhinged her.

And here was another sign. A narrow shaft of July sunlight had managed to edge its way through the closed curtains, illuminating their wedding photo, propped up on the half-empty bookshelves. Max had also left that behind,

7

although he had taken the framed photo of him meeting Lord Attenborough – or Dickie, as he called him – that had once stood beside it.

Annie smiled at the photo. Max grinned back at her from outside Chelsea Register Office, that slow, sexy smile that still made her stomach curl. He was reaching up to push his flopping blond hair out of those denim-blue eyes. She was clinging to his arm and looking slightly startled, as if she couldn't believe her luck in landing such a beautiful man.

She felt the hot sting of tears behind her eyes again. She knew Julia was right: he was a shit and she was better off without him. But even with all her drama school training she still couldn't summon up the appropriate emotions.

'God knows what possessed you to marry him in the first place,' Julia droned on. 'He held you back from the moment you met. You could have taken that RSC contract and become a huge star if he hadn't stood in your way.'

'He didn't stand in my way.' Annie wedged the phone between her chin and shoulder as she unwrapped a Strawberry Creme. 'It was my decision not to take that job.'

'Only because he said he wouldn't marry you if you did!'

'He didn't want us to start our married life apart –'

'Bollocks! He just didn't want you to outshine him. Not that it's too difficult,' Julia added waspishly. 'A twenty-watt bulb could outshine that talentless—'

'Is that all you wanted?' Annie cut her off.

There was another long silence. This time Annie bit her lip to stop herself breaking it.

'What you need is a complete change.' Having failed

8

with bullying, Julia decided to try conciliation. 'That's what's so wonderful about this job. You can go away for six weeks, put your career back on track, get your personal life sorted out. And you know what they say: success is the best revenge.'

'Is it?' Annie said bleakly. Up until now she'd been getting a kind of grim satisfaction from pouring Max's aftershave down the plughole and fantasizing about sending his Ralph Lauren suits to the local Oxfam shop.

'Anyway, I think you should meet this guy,' Julia went on. 'And I happen to know he'll be at Alex Wingate's party tonight. I haven't told him about you yet. I thought if you could just casually turn up and bump into him –'

But Annie wasn't listening. 'A party? Tonight?' She accidentally inhaled the Strawberry Creme. 'But I can't!'

'Of course you can.' Julia laughed. 'For heaven's sake, it's only a party.'

Only a party. She couldn't have been more terrified if Julia had invited her to take part in a Satanic bonding ritual. At least then she wouldn't have been faced with the awful, insurmountable task of making herself look decent. 'I can't do it,' she whispered, shrinking back into the sofa cushions. 'It's too soon. I – I'm not ready for it.'

'For God's sake, Annie, stop acting like a grief-stricken widow! Max has walked out, he hasn't died.'

More's the pity, Annie thought, gripping the phone. It might have been easier if he had died. At least then she wouldn't have to face the thought of him being happy with someone else. 'But what if everyone knows?' she wailed. 'I couldn't stand it if they were all looking at me, talking about me –'

'You should be so lucky! Besides, that didn't seem to

worry you at the Lloyd Webber party, when you stood on that table and —'

'That was different. I was drunk.'

'Well, for God's sake don't get drunk tonight,' Julia warned. 'I want this guy to know what a highly talented and consummate professional you are. That's not going to happen if you start doing one of your party pieces.'

'No chance of that,' Annie said firmly. 'I'm not going.'

'But you must. You don't know how hard I've worked to pin him down —'

'Well, you can call and unpin him, can't you?'

'Actually, I can't,' Julia said. 'He's in meetings all day and his mobile is switched off.'

'Liar.'

'And even if I could I'm not going to.' Julia ignored her. 'Because frankly you owe it to yourself and to me to stop being such a complete pain in the backside and get your life together. I know no one else would say this to you, but the fact is you've become extremely boring since this break-up business. And let's face it, the chances of Max coming back are about the same as me playing prop forward for Wigan Athletic, so it's about time you got used to it.' She paused. 'I'm only telling you as a friend.'

'Thanks a lot,' Annie said bitterly. Why did people think that gave them the right to deliver such devastating insults? As far as she was concerned, 'I'm only telling you as a friend' rated as almost the worst seven words in the English language. Just ahead of 'Don't worry it will soon grow back' and, shortly behind, 'I just thought you ought to know . . .'

That was what Suzy Carrington had said just before she broke the news that she had stolen her husband. Annie could still picture her standing in the kitchen, holding the cup of coffee that she had just made for her, her blue eyes wide and earnest in her porcelain-pretty face. She'd made it sound as if she was doing Annie a favour, telling her. What she didn't say was that the whole story would be appearing in Nigel Dempster the following morning, alongside a photo of Max and Suzy hand in hand slipping out of Joe Allen's together, and a hideously unflattering one of Annie when she played Lady Macbeth, plastered in heavy white make-up and looking about a hundred and fifty.

Later that day Max had slunk home, packed a bag and moved out of the house, leaving a huge gap in their wardrobe and an even bigger one in her heart. Annie cringed to think how she'd begged and pleaded with him not to go, how she'd clung to him, tearfully promising to change, to do anything he wanted, as long as he didn't leave her. All the while Max had gone on emptying his cupboards, stony-faced, not even looking at her.

That night he and Suzy had escaped to her father's house in Provence, leaving Annie to cope alone with the hordes of press men camping in her tiny front garden, trampling her herbaceous border and poking their zoom lenses through the letter-box.

For a full forty-eight hours she had crouched on the bed, whimpering with terror as she listened to the hammering on the door, hugging her knees under her chin, afraid to move because it hurt so much.

It was two days before she could summon the strength to venture downstairs, by which time a fresh scandal had broken and the paparazzi had scooted off to stake out an MP who'd been having an affair with a teenage call-girl in Hackney.

Gradually, moving slowly and painfully, she'd started to

get on with her daily life. She'd put the phone back on the hook. She'd done her best to reassure her anxious parents down in Sussex that she wasn't about to kill herself and that there was no need for them to catch the next train to London. The last thing she needed was to spend a week putting on a brave face when she was dying inside.

It had taken her two weeks to pluck up the nerve to go to the supermarket. Asking her to go to a party was like inviting an agoraphobic to a beach barbecue.

'Annie? Are you still there?' Julia's voice rang out on the other end of the phone. 'I'll expect you at nine, shall I?'

'Do what you like, I'm not coming,' Annie said sulkily.

'You won't forget, will you? The Mortimer Gallery at nine. I'll bike your invitation round to you.'

'I told you, I'm not coming.'

Julia sighed. 'If you don't, you can find yourself another bloody agent.'

'Suits me.'

There was a long pause. 'Actually, I think I might bring along one of my cast-off men after all,' Julia said. 'A decent, uncomplicated one-night stand with a real man might be just what you need. Maybe then you'll realise what you've been missing, married to that self-centred bastard all these years.'

'Julia –'

'I'll see you at nine.' She laughed and rang off.

Chapter 2

Alex Wingate's parties were legendary, at least to the readers of *Hello!* magazine and anyone who cared whether they were invited to them. Wingate Management was one of the biggest theatrical agencies in the country. Every summer Alex threw what he called with ironic modesty a 'little office bash' for his clients. But this was no run-of-the-mill office party: the guest list included directors, producers, Hollywood megastars who happened to be in town, plus anyone Alex wanted to poach from other agencies. This was where influential people met, talked and did their deals. Stratospheric careers had been launched over the champagne and canapés. It was a standing joke in the business that Wingate's party could start phones ringing all over the West End by the next morning.

No wonder invitations were difficult to come by. But Julia, of course, had managed to pull a few strings and wangle a couple.

Annie wished she hadn't bothered as, under the watchful eye of the cloakroom attendant, she reapplied her lipstick for the third time. She'd been hiding out in the

Ladies for so long she'd almost become rooted to the polished marble tiles.

The party was exactly the nightmare she'd feared it would be. It was being held in a fashionable Mayfair art gallery, very minimalist and monochrome on a Japanese theme. Oriental waiters, dressed in black, moved through the room with the swift, silent intent of Ninja assassins armed with trays of sushi.

Because she was so terrified of walking into a crowded room, Annie had deliberately got there early. But as soon as she arrived she'd realised the tactical error she'd made. At least in a crowd she could pass unnoticed. As she walked into that vast, echoing white space, her Doc Martens squeaking on the polished maple floor, all eyes turned to follow her. They went on following her as she grabbed a drink from a passing tray and fled to the loo.

And there she stayed. Her pounding heart had slowed down, but her sense of foreboding was still there.

Why had she ever agreed to come? At the time it seemed less exhausting than a full-scale argument with Julia. Now she was beginning to wish she'd stuck to her guns and stayed at home. She didn't want the bloody job anyway. How could she ever hope to win Max back when she was two hundred miles up the A1? And that's what she wanted to do, although she would never admit it to Julia. Julia would just tell her he wasn't worth it, or that she was wasting her time. All of which she already knew, but it didn't stop her clinging to that last shred of hope, like a *Titanic* survivor holding on to a lump of wreckage in a freezing ocean.

Julia kept talking about her rebuilding her life, but as far as she was concerned, she didn't want a life without Max.

Annie jumped as the door opened and a thin Sloaney

14

type came in. From beyond, the sound of laughter grated across her exposed nerves. She probably wouldn't get the job anyway. This director would take one look at her and decide she was too tall, or too gawky, or just too suicidal-looking for a merry romantic comedy. And he'd be right. She stared gloomily at her reflection. And she was dressed all wrong. Why hadn't Julia warned her everyone else would be sporting the understated designer look? Not that it would have made much difference, since she didn't own anything designer or understated. But in her dark-green velvet hippy-chic dress and jangling ethnic jewellery she stood out among the Amanda Wakeleys like a morris dancer at a funeral.

She offered the cloakroom attendant an ingratiating smile. The woman glared back, her meaty arms folded across her chest, as if she suspected Annie might at any moment try to make off with the paper towels, or attempt a smash-and-grab raid on the condom machine.

Behind her the toilet flushed and the Sloane emerged. Suddenly the cloakroom attendant underwent a dramatic transformation, smiling and fawning. 'Perfume, madam?' she asked. 'We have quite a selection.' Elbowing Annie aside, she threw open the door of the cupboard and drew out a tray full of goodies that looked like a small-scale version of Harrods' perfumery department.

'No, thanks.' The woman sent them all a dismissive look, dropped a pound coin in the saucer and headed off back to the party. Annie smiled again at the cloakroom attendant. Again, she glared back.

Annie's shoulders slumped. God, what chance did she have of networking when she couldn't even get the loo attendant to like her?

She jammed the top back on her lipstick and dropped it

into her bag. She didn't have to do this. She could just walk out and go home. In half an hour she could be watching *Inspector Morse* and eating cold rice pudding out of the tin.

'Bugger it,' she said out loud. Alarmed, the attendant took a step backwards. Annie seized her opportunity, lunged at the perfume display and gave herself a generous spritz of Escape.

Very appropriate under the circumstances, she thought, making for the door.

The room had filled up while she'd been lurking in the Ladies. She got halfway across the room and stopped dead. There was Julia, standing by the entrance, looking sharply elegant in a cream Jasper Conran trouser-suit, her shiny blonde bob swinging as she chatted to a man.

The dreaded director, no doubt. Annie studied the back of his head. Bulbous, balding and hunched inside a rather nasty houndstooth-check jacket. Her heart plummeted to her DMs. She didn't need to go any closer to know that he would have damp, sweating palms and eyes that would spend the whole evening searching out her cleavage like a heat-seeking missile.

Not that it mattered. He could have had the body of a love god and she still wouldn't be able to face him.

Annie swiped another glass from a passing Ninja waiter and tried to work out her next move. She'd never get past Julia's eagle eye. In fact, she'd probably situated herself by the door for that very reason. She searched the room for another route. Should she sidle around the room until she got on Julia's blind side, then make a dash for the door? Too risky. Should she create a diversion? She shuddered. Just what she wanted to avoid.

Or should she just approach Julia and say, straight out,

'Sorry, I've changed my mind'? That would be the sensible, grown-up thing to do. She dismissed it instantly.

Then she saw that a pair of fire-exit doors, discreetly masked by a Japanese paper screen, had been left half open to let in the warm summer air. With another quick glance around the room to make sure no one was watching, Annie edged towards them and slipped behind the screen.

She found herself amid the overflowing dustbins in a narrow back alley. She leaned against the wall, the balmy evening breeze cooling her face. The sound of crashing plates and pots came from the open back door of the Italian restaurant opposite, mingling with the impatient noise of the busy West End traffic streaming past the end of the alleyway.

Annie sighed with pleasure and relief. Alone at last.

She searched in her bag for a cigarette to calm her nerves. She found the packet, then delved again for her lighter. It wasn't there. She trawled through the mire of old bus tickets, Tampax, festering sweeties and other assorted gunge at the bottom of her bag, muttering under her breath.

'Allow me.' There was a soft click and a tiny flame flickered towards her.

Annie hesitated for a moment. A mugger? Not in a designer suit, surely. 'Um . . . thanks.' She leaned towards the lighter.

'Annie? Annie Mitchell?' His voice was deep, husky and strangely familiar.

Annie jerked back so quickly she nearly singed her eyebrow on the stranger's lighter. 'Who –'

'Don't tell me you don't remember me?'

Of course she remembered. The voice might have eluded her, but those eyes didn't. They were as dark as

17

sloes, warm, kind and, at that moment, on the verge of laughter. She could already see the faint crinkles forming at the corners the way they always used to.

'Hello, Annie,' said Nick Ryan, the man she'd jilted six years previously.

Chapter 3

Talk about out of the frying pan! Annie looked at him in horror. Performing a naked one-woman conga through the party crowd couldn't be as embarrassing as this.

Her brain groped for some appropriate greeting. But what could you say to the man you'd abandoned to run off with someone else? 'Long time no see' was a bit flippant under the circumstances.

He put her out of her misery. 'Small world.'

Annie squinted up at his white teeth, glinting in the fading light. Was he smiling, or just baring them? She gulped. 'Isn't it?'

'So are you with Wingate Management, then?'

'You must be joking! My agent would kill me if I ever left her.' Actually, Julia would probably kill her anyway, after tonight. 'Er — how about you?'

Nick shook his head. 'I'm just here to rub shoulders with the rich and famous, like everyone else.'

'Ah. Right.' The embarrassed silence between them lengthened. God, this was painful.

'Do you still want that light?'

She looked up, startled. 'Sorry?'

'For your cigarette.' She followed his gaze to the ciggie

she'd been nervously pleating between her fingers. Shit. And it was her last one.

As if he'd read her thoughts, Nick drew out a packet of Marlboros from his pocket. 'Here. Have one of mine,' he offered.

'Thanks.' As he leaned forward to light it for her, Annie couldn't resist giving him a quick once-over. He didn't look like the Nick she'd once known. The Scruffy Out of Work Actor Look had given way to the Man Who Can Afford Casual but Probably Expensive Italian Linen Suits Look. Even his tousled dark hair had been tamed with an expert trim. But as he glanced up and met her gaze she caught a glimpse of the old Nick. Those dark eyes, that strong-featured face, the shadowing of stubble around his jawline, that faint, irresistible citrus smell of his aftershave . . .

The last time she'd seen him he'd just splurged his life savings on a couple of one-way tickets to New York. But on the day they were supposed to be flying out to start their new life she'd married someone else.

She looked away guiltily and took a quick, nervous puff on her cigarette. 'I'm trying to give them up,' she gabbled. 'I've started limiting them to after meals.'

'And does it work?'

'Oh, yes. Except I'm on twenty meals a day now.' Oh, God, why did she always make stupid jokes when she was nervous?

Nick's dark eyes crinkled. 'Same old Annie,' he said softly. 'So what are you doing with yourself these days?'

'Oh, you know. This and that.'

'Still acting?'

'When I can get the work. That's why I'm here,

actually.' She could feel herself gabbling again. 'My agent is trying to fix me up with some rep company.'

'You don't sound too keen?'

'Hardly!' She curled her lip. 'I'm only here to keep her happy.'

She glanced up at him from under her lashes. It was quite disturbing, meeting up with him again after all these years. She could feel the burden of what she'd done to him like a great weight on her shoulders, making it difficult for her to look him in the eye.

Yet once they'd been really close. So close that there was even a time when Annie thought they might have become more than friends. Maybe they would have, if Max hadn't come along.

They had met seven years ago when Annie, fresh out of drama school, had joined Nick's community theatre company. Although 'company' was perhaps too strong a word for half a dozen actors who bummed around the country in a beaten-up old van, performing Shakespeare workshops in schools.

They all knew they were never going to get rich or famous doing it. They were supposed to split the profits, but after they'd paid for petrol there was usually hardly any left. Often they were so broke they had to sleep in the back of the van, curling up among the diesel-scented tarpaulins and scenery flats. But they'd laughed a lot and it was good experience. Annie had only joined to get her Equity card. But she ended up staying for nearly a year. Mainly because of Nick.

He was four years older than her and good-looking in a casual sort of way. But they were never lovers. It was difficult to become intimate with someone when you were sharing the back of a battered old Bedford van with four other people every night. The others used to tease them about their closeness and Annie knew one or two of the girls were jealous. But she never thought of Nick like that. To her, he was more like a best friend. She could talk to him about anything and know he'd understand. They'd lie awake on warm summer nights, talking, laughing, sharing their dreams while the others snored in the back of the van.

It was hearing Sinatra singing 'New York, New York' late one night on the van's crackly radio on the way down the M6 that gave them the idea to seek their fortunes in the States. Somehow Broadway seemed more glamorous than the West End.

They planned it all. They would head for New York, find a cheap apartment and get stop-gap jobs to support themselves until they found acting work.

And then along came the *Pericles* tour. Annie hadn't wanted to take the job, but her new agent had cajoled her into it. 'It's about time you did some proper acting,' Julia had said scathingly. 'Doing Ophelia to a bunch of sixth formers isn't going to get your name in lights.'

Ironically it was Nick who finally persuaded her to do it. As he pointed out, in three months she would have saved enough to tide them over for their first few weeks in the States. So they made a deal. She would take the job, go on tour and save her money. Meanwhile Nick would use his savings to buy the plane tickets. As soon as she came home they would be off.

Except she never came home. She met Max, fell in love and married him instead.

Cowardly to the end, she couldn't face Nick with the truth. Instead she'd sent him an invitation to the wedding.

He'd sent it back with a barbed refusal and their paths hadn't crossed since. Until tonight.

'So – er – are you still acting?' she asked.

Nick shook his head. 'I gave up that idea years ago. I'm more on the technical side now.' He smiled wryly. 'Let's face it, I was never going to make it as an actor.'

'But you were really good.'

'No, I wasn't. Six months out of work in New York soon cured me of any illusions I might have had.' He glanced at her. 'You were the one with all the talent, as I recall.'

Annie felt herself blushing. 'So are you still living in the States?'

'I was, until last week. I've got a new job over here.' He looked her up and down. 'You're looking great, by the way. How's married life?'

She opened her mouth, then closed it again. Of course, Nick wouldn't know about her break-up. So all encompassing was her pain that she somehow imagined it must show on her face. 'Fine,' she lied. 'Absolutely fine.'

They stood in awkward silence. Annie contemplated the glowing tip of her cigarette, willing it to burn faster. 'I like your suit,' she said at last.

'Thanks. My wife bought it for me. She said she'd rather I looked fashionably crumpled than just plain scruffy.'

But Annie wasn't listening. 'Your wife? You got married?'

'Don't look so surprised.' Nick grinned ruefully. 'I'm not that bad, am I?'

'No! Not at all. It's just – I can't imagine you with a wife.'

'Actually, I'm divorced. Nearly two years ago now.'

'Oh, I'm sorry.'

Nick shrugged. 'It was fairly amicable. Elizabeth's married to a doctor in Connecticut now. She seemed very happy last time I saw her.'

Annie's jaw dropped. 'You still see her?'

'Occasionally,' Nick said. 'Most of the time we phone, or write. She and Gil are hoping to come over, once I'm settled in my new place.'

Annie searched for signs of hidden anguish, some tell-tale glint in his eye that told her he would really like to drop-kick this Gil character's head off his shoulders. She couldn't see any.

Was there really such a thing as an amicable separation, she wondered? Would she ever reach the point where she could mention Max's and Suzy's names in the same breath without wanting to burst into tears? She could certainly never see herself exchanging Christmas cards or, heaven forbid, going round for a cosy dinner at their Chelsea love nest.

'Actually, Max and I –' She stopped. She couldn't tell him. Not now. Five minutes ago she'd been boasting everything was rosy. 'Actually, Max and I are very happy,' she finished, realising how awful and smug it sounded, especially after Nick had just been talking about his divorce. 'Very, very happy,' she added, unable to stop herself.

'Good for you.' Nick looked at her strangely.

Another silence. 'So you're not interested in this rep job, then?' he said finally. 'I thought you enjoyed working in the theatre.'

'That depends.' She stuck out her chin. 'If it were the West End I might consider it.'

'And there speaks a girl who once played Juliet in a

rugby club beer tent!' He grinned. 'Do you know, I can never watch the balcony scene without thinking of you dodging those empty lager cans.'

She smiled reluctantly. 'Why do you think I don't want to go back to it?'

Just then the back door of the Italian restaurant was flung open by one of the cooks, filling the warm evening air with the scent of garlic and flooding the gloomy alleyway with light. It was like the moment at the school dance when all the lights went on and you were confronted with the acne-ridden specimen you'd been canoodling with all evening. Annie stole a quick glance at Nick's rugged profile. If this had been a school dance, she thought, she wouldn't have been too disappointed.

The cook emptied a bowlful of vegetable peelings into the dustbin and retreated back inside, plunging them into darkness once more.

'Well,' Nick said briskly, 'I suppose I'd better be making a move.'

'You're not going back to the party?'

'I don't think there's much point in hanging around. Besides, I've got an early start in the morning.' He glanced at his watch, then at her. 'How about you? Shouldn't you go in and tell your agent you've changed your mind about that job?'

'No, thanks.' Annie shuddered. 'If Julia's going to tell me off, I'd rather be on the other end of a telephone.'

'In that case, can I offer you a lift home?'

She hesitated. 'I wouldn't want to put you to any trouble. I can easily catch the tube —'

'It's no trouble. My car's just around the corner.'

Why did I think this was a good idea, Annie wondered, as

the gleaming BMW made its way across Vauxhall Bridge. She sat rigidly upright, her hands knotted in her lap. She stared at the moonlight on the Thames and trawled her brain for something useful to say. Something that wouldn't touch on the last six years and all that had gone before. 'Nice car,' she said finally.

'Isn't it? It's only hired, unfortunately. But I could certainly get used to it.'

'It's got a lot of – er – buttons and things.'

'God knows what half of them do. But I did find this one.' Nick flicked a switch on the impressive-looking console and the sexy, smoky sound of Aretha Franklin drifted out. 'What do you think?' he asked.

She thought she'd like to close her eyes, sink into the soft leather seat and let the sheer luxury of it all wash over her. But she didn't. 'Very nice. It's certainly a lot better than that old heap you used to drive –' She closed her eyes. Oh, God, why did she say that?

Nick smiled. 'Your taste wasn't much better, I seem to remember. What about that ghastly old VW you had? It was forever conking out on you.'

It still is, Annie said silently, thinking of Beryl the Beetle which was at that moment rusting away quietly outside her house.

She cleared her throat. 'So – er – where are you living now you're back in England?'

'I'm kind of between addresses at the moment. I'm staying with a friend until I move into my new place. Do you remember Rob Masters?'

Of course I remember him, she was about to exclaim. Then her mouth closed like a trap. 'Can't say I do,' she mumbled.

'You must know Rob. We started up the theatre

company together. Tall, skinny guy? A bit hippyish. It was his old van we —'

'Doesn't ring any bells.' Annie cut him off abruptly. Just to press home the point, she leaned across and turned Aretha's volume up.

Nick's jaw was clenched, although whether this was from annoyance or because he was negotiating the Wandsworth one-way system she couldn't be sure.

Annie had her key in her hand by the time they pulled up outside the terraced cottage. Without thinking, she glanced up at the windows, looking as she always did for the light that would tell her Max was home. The little house slumbered in darkness under its shaggy ramparts of clematis.

She stifled a sigh. 'Well, thanks for the lift. I'd invite you in for coffee —' But I can't wait to get away from you, she added silently.

'No problem. It's getting late.' He peered out of the windscreen. 'Nice place,' he remarked. 'It must be great at this time of year, being so close to the river.'

'We like it.' She groped around in the darkness for the door handle.

'I see you've still got that car.'

'Yes, well, it's more out of pity these days. I can't sell her and I can't bring myself to send her to the scrapyard. She's like an ageing relative I've been saddled with.' At last! She found the door handle and yanked at it. Nothing happened.

'Here, let me.' Nick leaned across and lifted the lock. Annie shrank away as his arm brushed hers. He turned his face towards her, until she could feel his warm breath fanning her cheek. He's going to kiss me, she thought in panic.

The next moment the door was open, Nick was back in his seat and Annie was wondering if she'd imagined the whole thing.

'Well, it was nice seeing you again,' he said calmly.

'And you.' She got out of the car and looked up at the little house, with its dark windows. Suddenly she had a horrible vision of herself, huddled in her dressing-gown, watching *Newsnight* all alone. Just her and Jeremy Paxman.

'Nick!' He was pulling away from the kerb. She flung herself at the car and wrenched the door open. He slammed on the brake so hard she would have been catapulted on to the bonnet if she hadn't been clinging to the handle.

He leaned across, his face pale in the lamplight. 'Christ, Annie, you certainly know how to get someone's attention. What is it?'

'I was just wondering —' She did her best to sound casual. 'Maybe you'd like coffee after all?'

Chapter 4

'Won't Max mind?' Nick asked.

'Max doesn't care what I do.' That was the truth, at any rate. 'The sitting-room's through here.'

As Annie flicked on the lamp she remembered the mess she'd left behind. She saw the room through Nick's eyes, littered with coffee cups and discarded chocolate wrappers. On the coffee table an unfinished bowl of cereal provided an attractive centrepiece.

'Sorry about the mess.' She rescued a banana skin from behind the cushion just as Nick sat down. 'Max is away at the moment, so I've let the housework slide. Well, not so much a slide as an avalanche, really.' She smiled apologetically.

'It looks very – lived in.' Nick's gaze roamed around the room, then stopped abruptly when it reached the corner. 'My God, what's that?' he said, staring at *Freedom*. It was looking particularly gruesome, the lamplight striking off its many sharp angles.

Annie stuck out her chin defensively. 'It belongs to Max. It's Art.'

'It looks like a road accident.'

'It's a very significant new work.' Annie parroted Max's own words. 'It's a shocking metaphor of –'

'It's shocking, all right.' Nick frowned at her. 'Don't tell you me you actually like it?'

'Of course.' Since it was Max's she was prepared to defend it as if it were her first-born.

'Then you two must really be made for each other.'

'We are. We're happy. Very, very happy,' she said firmly.

'So you keep telling me.'

She caught the sardonic glint in his eyes, and felt herself blushing. 'I'll make that coffee,' she mumbled and fled.

In the kitchen she put the kettle on and stood for a while to collect herself. What was she doing? She didn't want Nick here. She didn't want anyone. She liked being alone. She didn't have to smile, or pretend to function. She could slob around on the sofa, eating junk food and wallowing in her own self-pity.

And even if she did want company there were plenty of friends she could call on. She certainly didn't need Nick Ryan. She couldn't look at him without feeling swamped with guilt. More than that, he reminded her of how incredibly, over the moon in love she and Max had once been.

Like every other female in the *Pericles* company, Annie had developed a huge crush on Max Kennedy. But she never dreamed he'd look at her twice. He was everything she wasn't – outspoken, self-assured, extremely ambitious. He had a gorgeous body, irresistible faded-blue eyes, a devastatingly sexy smile and the kind of aristocratic cheek-bones most women would go under the knife for. He also had an entourage of beautiful women whom he treated with casual neglect. He was always taking calls from some frustrated, abandoned girlfriend on his mobile. Occasionally one would turn up tearfully at the stage door to confront him. Depending on his mood, Max would either whisk them off to bed or instruct the stage doorkeeper to turn them away.

'Scenes are so boring,' he'd drawl in that world-weary way of his. Annie would be torn between pity for them and quiet satisfaction that there was one less rival to worry about.

She was determined not to make a fool of herself. Worried that her every move and glance might give her away, she steered clear of him. After each performance she would scurry back to her digs, avoiding the clique that drifted down to the pub for last orders. Little did she realise that her unwitting indifference was just the kind of behaviour guaranteed to pique Max's interest. He wasn't used to women turning their backs on him. He was intrigued.

Annie never imagined anything would happen between them. She was playing Marina to his Lysimachus but, despite refusing to surrender her virginity to him on-stage every night, she was stunned and delighted when it happened for real in a grotty seafront hotel in Brighton.

From that moment she was lost. She had never been so hopelessly and passionately in love before. It almost hurt. She couldn't eat, she couldn't sleep. Sometimes, when Max was on the phone to one of his female friends, or flirting with one of the other women in the cast, she could hardly breathe. One minute her emotions were soaring and she felt light-headed with happiness that he wanted her, the next she was writhing in a pit of black despair, terrified of losing him. For the first time in her life she found herself feeling jealous of every woman who crossed his path.

Max did little to ease her agony. He could see what she was going through, but he carried on flirting and teasing regardless. Sometimes she wondered if he got some kind of perverse satisfaction from seeing her suffer. She longed for him to give up his other women, but she didn't have the courage to ask him. She knew how Max hated possessiveness and the last thing she wanted was to be seen as clingy.

And then, one night in Bath, Nick turned up. The curtain had just come down and Annie was in her dressing-room taking off her make-up when the stage doorkeeper called.

She felt the cold grip of panic in her chest. Oh, God. This was it. The moment she'd been dreading. She'd been feeling vaguely guilty about Nick ever since she and Max got together. She had kept meaning to write to him, but it was easier not to get round to it. Now he was here and there was no putting it off any longer.

In a panic, she rushed to Max's dressing-room. She wanted advice, moral support. Most of all, she wanted him to offer to do her dirty work for her.

But he didn't. 'Just don't see him,' he said flatly.

'But I've got to,' Annie reasoned. 'I promised I'd go to America with him. He's bought the tickets. I owe him an explanation, at least.'

'You don't owe him anything. You and I are together now. That's all there is to it.'

He turned away and she stared in frustration at the back of his head. It might be that simple for Max, who discarded girlfriends like other people threw away paper hankies. But she'd never been in this situation before. Nick was her friend and she didn't want to hurt him.

'Couldn't you come with me?' she pleaded.

'God, no! I'm not going anywhere near him. And I don't think you should either.' He reached for his cigarettes and lit one up. 'You know what will happen, darling. He'll make you feel guilty and the next thing you know you'll be right back where he wants you, in that grubby little theatre group.'

'That won't happen,' Annie said, but Max wasn't listening.

'You're too good for him,' he drawled. 'Anyone can see he's going nowhere. He even has to put on his own tinpot little shows because no one will employ him.'

His laughter grated. She might not love Nick the way she loved Max, but he deserved her loyalty. 'It's not like that. He runs that theatre group because he believes in it. He likes to have artistic control.'

'Well, he's certainly got control of you, hasn't he?' Max's eyes narrowed. 'The way you're talking, anyone would think you had the hots for him.'

'I don't!' Annie protested. 'I just want to be fair –'

'What about being fair to me?' His voice rose. 'You say you love me, but the minute this guy turns up you're falling over yourself to see him.'

'That's not true.'

'Prove it.' He snatched up his mobile and thrust it into her face. 'Send him away.'

'I can't –'

'You mean you won't.' He sent the phone skittering across his dressing-table. 'So bloody well go to him, if that's what you want.'

He gazed moodily at his reflection in the mirror.

Annie stared at him, shocked. Then it dawned on her. 'You're jealous,' she whispered.

'So what if I am?' He jabbed his cigarette out on the dressing-table, not caring that he missed the ashtray. 'Look, this isn't bloody easy for me. You know I hate possessiveness. I just never thought I'd feel like this myself.' He glared at her. 'I love you. I'm scared of losing you. And I know that's what will happen if you see him again. Okay?'

It was the first time he'd ever shown how he really felt and it was as if a great bubble had suddenly exploded in her chest, filling her with so much warmth and happiness she could hardly breathe. 'It won't happen,' she said gently, reaching for his hand. Max's fingers closed around hers. 'But I've got to talk to him,' she pleaded. 'He's come all this way —'

The hand was quickly withdrawn. Annie suddenly felt cold, as if he'd taken his love away too.

'Go, then,' he snapped. 'Bugger off to America with him.'

'Max —' She stood for a moment, staring at his stubbornly turned back. Then, with a defeated sigh, she turned away.

She was almost at the door when Max said, 'Marry me.'

He whispered it so quietly she stopped dead, wondering if she'd really heard him. Slowly she turned to face him.

'Marry me,' he repeated. His blue eyes searched hers. 'Please?'

Somehow, after that, Nick just didn't seem important any more.

She was just spooning out the coffee when the phone

34

rang, followed a moment later by her own cheery voice inviting the caller to leave a message.

It was bound to be Julia, calling to give her an earful for not turning up. That particular conversation could wait until morning.

Then she heard Max's familiar drawl on the machine and a surge of panic ran through her. Dropping the spoon, she ran into the living-room. But it was too late. Before she could reach the answer-machine, Max was already announcing loud and clear that he would be round to pick up the rest of his stuff the following day.

'I think it's best if you're not around when I get there,' he concluded. 'We don't want another scene like last time, do we?'

She couldn't bring herself to look at Nick. Instead she kept her gaze fixed on the answer-machine long after the message had clicked off, staring hard at the tiny flashing red light.

'Why didn't you tell me?' Nick broke the silence.

'There's nothing to tell.' She forced a shrug. 'It's — it's just a temporary separation. No big deal.'

'When did he leave?'

'A couple of weeks ago. I can't remember.' Annie shook her hair back impatiently. 'Like I said, it's no big deal.' She turned away and fled back to the kitchen.

Chapter 5

There was a bottle of brandy somewhere, long buried at the back of a kitchen cupboard. Annie clawed her way among the bottled fruits and jars of pasta sauce and dug it out. Sod the coffee. She needed something stronger. She dusted off the bottle, sloshed some brandy into a glass and downed it in one.

'Oh, my God!' She clutched her throat as the first fiery mouthful seared its way down her windpipe, making her gasp for breath. She stopped spluttering, wiped her streaming eyes on her sleeve and topped up her glass defiantly.

She slumped against the cupboard door. So now it was official. Her life couldn't get any worse. Not only did Nick know that Max had abandoned her, he also thought she was a compulsive liar and mentally unhinged into the bargain.

Screwing her eyes shut, Annie took another gulp of the brandy. Actually, it wasn't so bad once she got used to it. The first lot must have burned away her throat lining, so this went down quite easily, spreading a pleasant warmth through her limbs and bringing barely a tear to her eye.

She peered into the depths of her glass, distracted for a

moment from the terrible mess that was her life. She couldn't face Nick. If she stayed here long enough, perhaps he'd take the hint and go away.

No such luck.

'Annie?'

She sensed him standing there in the doorway behind her. 'Go away.'

'Does this mean I don't get my coffee?'

'There's an all-night café on the corner if you're that desperate.' She didn't move. Neither did Nick. 'Look, I just want to be alone, okay?'

'So you can drink yourself into a stupor? I don't think that's going to help.'

'Well, I do.' She poured another brandy, threw back her head defiantly and gulped the lot. It went down with barely a shudder this time. She was getting good at this.

She could feel Nick watching her with disapproval. 'So I take it this isn't just a temporary separation?' he said at last.

'No, it isn't. He's gone. For good. With my best friend, if you must know.' She fired out every word like bullets from a gun.

That shocked him. 'Jesus,' he whispered. 'I'm sorry. Why didn't you tell me?'

She stared down at his well-polished brogues. 'I don't know,' she admitted. 'Maybe I just wanted to go on pretending for a little while longer. Or perhaps I was afraid you'd laugh.'

'Why should I do that?'

'Because I deserve it.' She forced herself to look at him. 'I did the same to you, didn't I? I let you down when I went off with Max. What goes around comes around and all that.'

Nick ran his hand through his dark hair, so it stood up in cropped spikes. 'Let me get this straight,' he said slowly. 'You reckon I could get some kind of satisfaction out of seeing you suffer, just because you dumped me?'

Annie looked into her glass. 'Why not? I couldn't blame you, after what I did.'

'But that was years ago. I'd have to lead a pretty sad and empty life to harbour a grudge against you for all this time.'

Annie scuffed her boots on the polished wood floor. Put like that it did seem slightly foolish. 'But we were going to America,' she said. 'You'd bought the tickets and everything –'

'Yes and I was pretty pissed off when you didn't turn up. But do you really think I'd spend six years brooding over it?' He shook his head. 'Life goes on, Annie.'

She pushed her hair uncertainly out of her eyes. 'So everyone keeps telling me.'

Annie settled back into the squashy comfort of her sofa and topped up her glass again, marvelling at how steady her hand seemed, considering the paralysis creeping up her arm. The hellish fire of the brandy had faded quickly into an agreeable warmth, which spread through her limbs, giving her an inner glow.

It was nice to have someone to talk to, she reflected, beaming at Nick across the room. Someone who actually wanted to listen. Most of her friends had got so bored with her pouring out her troubles that now they either changed the subject or just left the room whenever Max's name was mentioned.

Not that she really needed anyone around when she wanted to talk. She could unburden herself emotionally to a plant stand if she was desperate enough. When it came to her marriage break-up, Annie knew she could bore for England.

But Nick was really interested. At least he *seemed* interested. Although after all that brandy it was difficult to see whether his eyes had glazed over or not. Annie squinted at him. It was hard to make out if he even had eyes any more.

She'd already given him the full, unexpurgated story of how Max and Suzy had gone on that *Separate Tables* tour. How she'd fretted about him being away, how she'd even begged Suzy to keep an eye on him for her.

'I might have known,' she muttered. 'It was like asking a wolf to watch over a flock of sheep.' And Max was like a lamb to the slaughter.

Everyone knew, it seemed, except her. Max had come home every weekend with a bag full of dirty socks and underwear, and she'd never suspected a thing. Until the tour ended.

Annie had spent all day planning a special romantic evening to welcome him home. She had Marks & Spencer beef *medallions* in the oven, Krug in the fridge and a sensational La Perla bustier under her dress when Suzy turned up. Alone.

Even then she'd been stupidly blind. She'd made Suzy a cup of coffee and settled down for a gossip, never imagining that the juicy titbit her friend had to tell her was about her own husband.

Nick listened to the whole sorry story. Although he might have been nodding off, she couldn't really be sure.

'It's my fault. I shouldn't have let him go.'

'You weren't to know,' Nick said.

'That's just it,' Annie insisted. 'I did know.' In her heart

39

of hearts she had always known. Just as she'd always known it was only sheer fluke that had won her Max in the first place. And she also knew it was only a matter of time before someone more worthy claimed him.

She just never imagined it would be her best friend.

Strange, really, when she'd been so watchful of other women throughout their marriage, that she should ignore the danger on her own doorstep. She remembered Suzy's pole-axed expression when she met Max for the first time. Up until then, Suzy had always been the one with the fabulous boyfriends. At drama school she was known as the Gorgeous Blonde. Annie was Her Friend. Tall, gawky and tawny-haired, Annie had felt she was destined for a lifetime of blind dates with the friends of whichever Adonis happened to be after Suzy at the time.

But then along came Max and suddenly it was as if, in the Great Game Show of Love, Annie had swanned off with the holiday in St Lucia, while Suzy had been left with the Crackerjack pencil.

She took a steadying gulp of her drink. She could feel herself sliding dangerously towards self-pity. 'I've always known I'd lose him in the end. He was so sexy and gorgeous –'

'Really? He sounds a bit of a bastard to me.'

Annie's head jerked back. 'How can you say that? You don't even know him.'

'I know any man who can sleep with his wife's best friend is hardly going to be an all-round nice guy.'

'It was her fault. She lured him into it.'

'I don't suppose he took much luring. Seems like he was about as hard to get as a flu bug.'

Annie ignored him. 'You don't know what she's like,' she protested. 'Max didn't stand a chance.'

40

She took another swig of her drink. When it came to men, her career or anything else, 'No' wasn't a word in Suzy's limited vocabulary. That fluffy blonde exterior hid a steely inner core. She was like a lump of granite wrapped in candyfloss.

'She's beautiful. And successful. How can I compete with that?'

'You could be successful too, if you wanted to be.' Annie noticed with a touch of annoyance that he didn't mention the beautiful bit. 'You've got tons of talent.'

'I'd rather be gorgeous,' she muttered into her glass.

'You are.'

'Oh, please!'

'I mean it. Any man would fancy you.'

She squinted at him across the room, just to make sure he wasn't making fun of her. His gaze was as direct and honest as she'd always remembered. She could feel herself blushing. 'Thanks,' she whispered. But as she lifted her drink, her hand was shaking so much the glass rattled against her teeth. 'You too. Not that men would fancy you, of course,' she added hastily. 'I mean they might, but I'm not saying you're gay or anything. Not that there's anything wrong with being gay, but –'

'I know what you mean.' Nick grinned as she floundered helplessly.

I'm bloody glad someone does, Annie thought, crashing the bottle against her glass as she refilled it. It was true what they said about brandy being good in a crisis. Very calming and relaxing. In fact, she was so relaxed she was in danger of sliding off the sofa and straight into a coma under the coffee table.

She stared across at Nick, trying to focus on him. He

seemed to have sprouted three wavering heads. And none of them was drinking. 'Drink up,' she encouraged.

'I'm driving.'

'Oh. Oh well, that means more for me.'

'Don't you think you've had enough?'

'God no. There's still tons left.' She held up the bottle and squinted into it.

'That doesn't mean you have to drink it all.'

'I'm drowning my sorrows,' she told him huffily.

'I reckon they're well and truly drowned by now, don't you?'

'Actually, no,' she said. 'They're just coming up for air again. My sorrows are very strong swimmers, if you must know. Every time I think I've drowned the little buggers they surface again.'

'I see.' Nick smiled once more. He had a wonderful, warm smile, she reflected squiffily. And gorgeous eyes, very dark and soulful. She racked her brains, trying to remember if they were brown or very dark grey. In her current state she couldn't even remember what colour her own eyes were.

And Nick listened. He'd always been a good listener. Not like Max, who would rather have undergone colonic irrigation than discuss matters of the heart. In fact, all their most meaningful conversations had been conducted with him safely hidden behind a copy of *The Stage*.

'How did someone like you ever end up getting divorced?' She looked round, wondering who'd had the cheek to ask such a question. And why were they shouting?

'It's a long story.'

'You can tell me if you like,' Annie offered. 'I mean,

I've been boring you all evening. Now it's your turn.' Her eyes widened. Had she really just said that?

'Some other time, maybe. Anyway, it's all ancient history now. Elizabeth and I have come out of it good friends and that's all that matters.'

'I can't imagine ever being good friends with Max.' Annie shuddered.

'I know. The emotions are too raw at the moment. But you'll get over it, I promise.'

'That's what people keep telling me. But I don't want to get over it. I just want Max!'

'Even after everything he's done?'

'I told you, it wasn't his fault.'

Nick looked as if he was about to say something, then thought better of it.

Annie finished her drink. The pleasant warm feeling was starting to give way to an alarming numbness. She could feel the paralysis spreading up through her feet. What would happen when it reached her brain?

She looked at Nick lopsidedly. He was definitely attractive, in a dark, rugged kind of way. Not like Max, of course, who was as flawlessly beautiful as a Greek god. She frowned. Was she always going to measure every man she met against him? 'I suppose you must have masses of girl-friends?' she asked.

'A few. No one serious.'

'I should never have dumped you like that.'

'Oh, I don't know. As Dear John letters go, a wedding invitation was pretty original.'

'I mean, maybe we should have stayed together. After all, we've both made a mess of our other relationships, haven't we?' Her mouth seemed to have declared UDI from her brain. It couldn't be trusted. 'Do you ever wonder what would have happened if I'd come with you to America?'

'It's not something that keeps me awake at nights.' She noticed he wasn't smiling any more, but that didn't stop her.

'Do you think we would have stayed together? It might have been fun —'

'We'll never know, will we?' Nick cut her off abruptly.

He put down his glass and stood up. Annie looked at him in panic. 'You're not going?'

'I've got to go. Like I said, I've got an early start in the morning.'

A flash of perception pierced the alcoholic fog in her brain. 'I've upset you, haven't I?' she said. 'Talking about us . . .'

'It's not a good idea to rake up the past, Annie.' So much for him still carrying a torch for her after all these years. Their brief friendship was obviously so meaningless he could hardly bring himself to think about it. She fought the urge to offer him another drink, or coffee, or anything at all to make him stay. She might be paralytic, but even she could recognise a brush-off when she saw it.

Well, if he was going she could at least be dignified about it. But as Annie hauled herself off the sofa she felt a huge rush of blood to her head and a simultaneous rush of alcohol to her legs. She turned, took a step forward, tripped over the coffee table and fell headlong towards the door. There was a painful crash, and she found herself lying dazed and confused amid a tangle of metal.

'Are you okay?' Nick's face swam into focus above her.

'I've flattened *Freedom*,' she wailed, disentangling herself with difficulty from the clawing metal arms. Max's pride and joy. He would never forgive her.

44

'It's about time someone did.' Nick held out his hand.

'But you don't understand.' She allowed him to haul her to her feet. 'It was Art. It was conceptual —' It also cost more than the average family saloon.

They both stood there for a moment, staring in solemn silence at the squashed jumble of metal.

'Actually, I think you've improved it,' Nick remarked at last.

Annie glanced at his twitching smile, then suddenly the absurdity of it all hit her and she started laughing too. At the same moment her legs inexplicably turned to elastic, pitching her forward into Nick's arms. They closed around her, crushing her to him. At nearly five feet nine, it took quite a man to make her feel small and fragile, but somehow he managed it.

She looked up into his face. His eyes were charcoal grey, almost black, she remembered. 'Nick?' she whispered.

He frowned down at her. 'What?'

She closed her eyes. 'Kiss me,' she said. And passed out.

Chapter 6

She woke up several hours later, sprawled across the bed, sweating and shivering in the chilly grey light of dawn, and realised she was dead.

She couldn't feel like this and still be living. Her body had been crushed by a Chieftain tank. A whole regiment of them, in fact. The regiment in question was still in her head now, doing drill practice. And, oh God, they'd been cleaning their filthy boots on her tongue.

Annie opened her eyes and wished she hadn't, as her eyeballs ricocheted around in their sockets. For a minute or two she lay, clutching her head. She would never, ever drink brandy again. In fact, she would never drink anything again. The way she felt, she would probably never move again. This was God's punishment to her for – she frowned. For what, exactly?

Slowly, painfully, she tried to piece together what had happened the night before. She remembered being stupendously drunk, of course. She remembered falling over, and Nick picking her up, and then –

Annie caught sight of her bra dangling from the bedpost and groaned. It was all coming back to her now. That kiss. She couldn't remember the actual details, but it must have been quite something because she'd passed out. She remembered coming round just as Nick was putting her – well, all right, dumping her – on the bed. She'd reached up for him, pulled him down on top of her, and they'd both collapsed in a frenzy of pent-up passion . . . Or had they?

She sat up quickly – a bad mistake, as her stomach shot to her throat like a high-speed lift – and looked around. All that remained of the previous night were her own clothes, scattered with wild abandon around the room. There was no sign of Nick.

He'd done a runner. Annie didn't blame him. She would have fled too, if some complete and utter berk had launched a drunken pass at her.

Then she spotted the note on the bedside table. It was propped up against a glass of water, beside a packet of Nurofen. Annie groped for it, her hand shaking.

'Dear Annie,' it said, 'thought you might need these. Nick.'

She didn't know whether to feel relieved or just mortified. Surely the only thing worse than waking up after a one-night stand was waking up and realising you'd been turned down.

She rolled over, clutching her head and groaning with pain and misery. Not only had she failed dismally at marriage, she couldn't even manage a night of casual sex.

Julia would have been ashamed of her.

Julia, as it turned out, was more furious than ashamed. 'You blew it,' she yelled, when Annie finally summoned up the strength to answer the phone later that morning. 'For God's sake, what happened to you last night?'

'I – I couldn't make it.'

'You mean, you bottled out!'

Annie clutched her head against the verbal onslaught, too sick to fight back. A handful of Nurofen, a piece of dry toast and several cups of strong black coffee had failed to stem her relentless hangover. A feeble 'sorry' was all she could manage in her defence.

'You will be,' Julia threatened. 'And why are you mumbling? You sound like Marlon Brando.'

'I don't feel very well.'

'Well, you'd better make a quick recovery. Your audition's at eleven.'

'What audition?'

'The one I've just fixed you up with. For the rep company. You wouldn't believe the trouble I've had to go to. He practically refused to see you, after last night.'

'But I can't,' Annie croaked. 'I'm dying.'

'Nonsense. Have a stiff drink and you'll be fine.'

Annie's stomach lurched protestingly. She took a deep breath and braced herself. 'Look, Julia, I've been thinking about this and I really don't want the job –'

'I know you don't, but you need it,' Julia said. 'Besides, you owe me. I had to do a lot of heavy-duty grovelling for this. The least you can do is turn up and meet the man.'

'I suppose so.' So much for being assertive.

'At least you're thinking clearly.'

I don't know about that, Annie thought as she scribbled down the details Julia gave her.

'So what did happen to you last night?' Julia asked suddenly.

'You wouldn't believe me if I told you.'

'Let me guess. You chickened out and rushed home to your lonely marital bed with just a photo of darling Max for company.'

'Actually, I picked up a gorgeous man and brought him home.'

There was a shocked silence, then an insulting laugh rang out from the other end of the phone.

I told you you wouldn't believe me, Annie thought, putting down the receiver.

Chapter 7

It was a warm July morning outside, but the draughty church hall had all the welcoming cheer of a morgue. With its peeling paintwork and musty smell of old hymn books, it was like every other rehearsal room Annie had ever been in.

Around the room people were talking about work: discussing who was and who wasn't, comparing notes on recent auditions, gossiping about other people and furtively scribbling down potential leads in their address books. Annie, meanwhile, sat shivering on her hard plastic chair, sheltering behind her Ray-Bans and wondering if anyone would notice if she was sick into her rucksack.

In spite of endless pain-killers washed down with coffee, her monster hangover still hadn't abated. Neither had her burning sense of shame.

She couldn't help replaying last night's horrific scene over and over in her head. And every time her brain hit the rewind button, some fresh and humiliating detail appeared.

Like the way she'd toyed with the curling hair at the nape of Nick's neck as he hauled her up the stairs. And how she'd dragged him down on top of her as she lay on the bed. And the moment when he'd averted his face as she tried to kiss him.

She shifted in her seat and closed her eyes with a shudder. Her only consolation was that she would never, ever have to see him again.

'Well, of course I could go into mainstream West End if I wanted to, but I actually prefer experimental theatre.' A woman's voice sliced into her troubled thoughts. 'It's much more broadening, don't you think?'

There was a general murmur of agreement. Annie smiled to herself. She knew that, like everyone else, the woman would gladly have given up wearing bin bags and smearing herself with axle grease in the name of art for a sniff at the new Tom Stoppard.

Like most other auditions, the room was pretty evenly divided into the Haves and the Have Nots. The Haves, who already had a job or at least a couple of hopeful call-backs, exuded an air of blasé confidence, as they gossiped to each other about work. The Have Nots, whose phones had remained stubbornly silent for too long, gave off a nervous, sweating despair. Annie gazed sympathetically at the lanky young man opposite her. From his bobbing Adam's apple and the bony, white-knuckled hands clutching his CV, it was clear the only role he'd played recently was Man in Dole Queue.

Not that she looked much better. Her face had the greyish pallor of unbaked dough, in stark contrast to the huge black circles under her eyes. Her hair, which she couldn't bring herself to wash, was scraped back in a rubber band. If they'd been auditioning for one of the witches in *Macbeth* she would have walked it.

The door to the audition room opened and a woman with cropped two-tone hair and a black *Les Miserables*

T-shirt stuck her head out and announced they were running forty-five minutes late. Everyone groaned. Annie closed her eyes against the throbbing pain in her head and wondered if she had alcohol poisoning. Perhaps she would die. If so, she hoped it would be soon.

She began to day-dream that Max found out she was dead and was filled with remorse. Would alcohol poisoning be romantic enough, she wondered? Perhaps it should be something else. A lingering but rather beautiful illness, like Greta Garbo in *Camille*. Then Max could sob at her bedside while she made a touching farewell speech, bestowing love and forgiveness, while at the same time making sure he was too grief-stricken and guilty ever to go near Suzy Carrington again.

Annie frowned. What was it Garbo had in that film? Consumption, maybe? Although didn't that involve coughing up blood? She winced. Hardly romantic. She could just imagine what Max's reaction to that might be.

She moved on to her funeral. Small and dignified, yet big enough for Max to see how much she was adored, by everyone else if not by him. There would be touching eulogies from her friends. Then someone, probably Julia, would say they should be celebrating her life, not mourning her death. She'd tell some suitable anecdotes, revealing Annie's sensitive, caring side as well as her sense of humour (she would have to check these in advance, just to make sure none started with 'I remember when Annie was so pissed . . .'). Then someone else would whip out a guitar and play some heart-breaking music, everyone would sob and Suzy Carrington would become a social leper from that day on.

'Tip? I'll give you a tip, mate. Don't come via the bloody North Circular next time.' Everyone exchanged glances as heavy footsteps thudded up the stairs. Moments later the doors burst open and a diminutive figure fell through them, staggering under the weight of several Pied A Terre carriers.

'Shit,' she muttered, as the doors swung closed on her, trapping her bags. 'Shit, shit, shit!' She wrenched them impatiently, ripping the handles.

Annie blinked in recognition at the flushed angry urchin face framed by cropped black hair. It couldn't be, could it?

Who else but Caroline Wilde could make an entrance like that? Chaos was her middle name. The last year at drama school when they'd shared a flat it had been like living in a soap opera, with its relationship dramas, financial crises and general angst, not to mention a supporting cast of bastard boyfriends and eccentric relatives. The quiet life it wasn't, but it had certainly been fun.

Needless to say, Caz was one of the many aspects of her former life of which Max didn't approve. And the feeling was obviously mutual. Annie had done her best to make them like each other, but after one too many tense dinner parties even she had to admit defeat. Gradually their girls' nights out had dwindled to exchanging Christmas cards.

She'd often thought of picking up the phone and making contact again, especially since Max had walked out. But she was too afraid of what Caz's response would be.

She snatched up her magazine and ducked her head behind it, just as Caz flopped into the chair beside her. Great, just great. Now she'd have to spend the next hour hunched motionless behind *Hello!*.

'I don't know why you're bothering to hide. With that

hair and those legs you're about as inconspicuous as a nun on a hen night,' Caz said after about ten minutes.

'Hmm?' Annie squeaked.

'Oh, for God's sake!' Caz snatched the magazine out of her hands. 'I don't know about you, but I'm dying for a ciggie.'

'Me too.' They grinned at each other and suddenly it was as if the years separating them hadn't happened. They were final-year students again, nipping out of the mime and mask workshop for a sly smoke.

Caz propped her feet up on the seat opposite and lit up a Marlboro Light, casually ignoring the No Smoking signs. She was as small and slender as a dancer, but there was nothing fragile about her tight black Levis and leather biker's jacket. 'I hear you've given that bastard the push,' she said bluntly. 'About bloody time too.'

Annie glanced around the room. Suddenly everyone seemed to be looking at her. 'It was more the other way round,' she admitted sheepishly.

'I know.' Caz blew a perfect smoke ring into the air. 'I bet that's the first time Suzy Carrington's ever done anyone a favour. If you ask me, those two deserve each other.'

Annie fiddled with the zip on her rucksack, wishing Caz would shut up. If she'd wanted her private life dissected in public, she could have gone on the *Vanessa* show. But at least she wasn't avoiding her, like most people. Annie had known old friends cross the street when they saw her coming. Overnight she'd become a social embarrassment.

'Anyway, he'll regret it,' Caroline went on. 'Once he finds out what a bitch she really is.'

'Do you think so?' Annie ventured.

''Course.' Caz shrugged. 'And she's a crap actress. Everyone knows she only gets work because of her family.'

That was true. Suzy came from an acting dynasty that made the Redgraves look positively *arriviste*. Her grandparents were veterans of the British theatre, her uncle a film director, her father a famous TV detective. The Carringtons practically had their own section in *Spotlight*.

Suzy had cornered the market playing demure young heroines in lavish costume dramas. No Dickens or Hardy adaptation was complete without her, blonde tendrils framing her innocent face, her bosom spilling out of sprigged muslin. It was kind of ironic, Annie thought, that her husband had run off with a professional virgin.

'I mean, did you see her in that Jane Austen?' Caz went on, warming to her subject. 'She was so bloody wooden the director had to keep moving her around in case someone mistook her for a chest of drawers.'

Annie grinned. She hadn't had a decent bitching session in ages. Nor had she realised how much she'd missed her old friend.

'Been working?' Caz changed the subject.

'Oh, you know. This and that. How about you?'

'Don't ask.' She aimed another moody smoke ring at the ceiling. 'I've been working as a children's entertainer. You know, kids' parties and stuff?'

'That must be − er − nice.'

'No, it bloody well isn't.' Caz looked indignant. 'Have you ever been shut in with a bunch of hyperactive six-year-olds with only a comedy wig and a box of magic tricks for protection?'

'Can't say I have.'

'Well, it's no joke, I can tell you. Do you know, I once

spent two hours locked in an airing cupboard while the little buggers ran riot?'

Annie was horrified. 'They locked you in?'

'Did they, hell! I locked myself in.'

'Still, it must pay well?' Annie eyed the carrier bags around Caz's feet.

'This is retail therapy. I need it to survive.' Caz shifted her shoulders with a creak of ancient leather. 'The more depressed I'm feeling, the more I get this urge to go out and buy shoes. I reckon a quick splurge in Pied A Terre is better than a couple of Prozac any day.' She stubbed out her cigarette. 'Although I must say, my bank balance is beginning to suffer. That's why I need this job. It sounds really interesting, don't you think?'

Annie did her best to look interested.

'I haven't done any Shakespeare for ages. And my agent reckons there's a good chance he'll be looking for people for the rest of the season. Just think – no more kids' parties.'

Annie listened with a growing sense of guilt as she nattered on about the theatre's forthcoming season. Poor Caz was desperate for this job. Unlike her, who'd only turned up because her agent had threatened her with a fatwah if she didn't.

Although, listening to Caroline, it did sound interesting. She hadn't done any theatre for a long time. And she'd always enjoyed Shakespeare. Perhaps Julia was right. Maybe this job might be just what she needed. It wouldn't be for ever. And it might even do Max some good to see her getting on with her life. Sitting at home moping was all very well, but there was nothing sexy about a doormat.

She was running through her audition piece in her head when the door opened and the woman with two-tone hair stuck out her head and yelled, 'Annie Mitchell, please.'

Annie's stomach lurched. Suddenly she was desperate for the loo. 'I'm going to be sick,' she muttered through clenched teeth.

'You haven't got time,' Caroline hissed back, giving her a shove.

The woman introduced herself as Mel Bushell, the Assistant Director. Annie remembered to wipe her clammy palms down her jeans before shaking hands.

'Don't be nervous,' Mel reassured her. 'We've heard great things about you.'

Annie smiled back. Holding on to the contents of her stomach grimly, she followed Mel into the audition room. The squeak of her boots on the polished floorboards echoed up into the cavernous ceiling.

'Take a seat, would you?' Mel pointed to chair in front of a long trestle table, but Annie didn't move.

Her eyes were fixed on the line of faces seated on the other side of the table. There was an efficient-looking girl with mousy hair held in place by a black velvet Alice band. Her clipboard was poised. At the other end of the table another girl with blonde hair in drastic need of a roots job doodled with great concentration on hers.

And between them, his scuffed Timberland boots up on the table, was Nick Ryan.

Chapter 8

He'd swopped his designer suit for faded Levis and an ancient grey sweat-shirt, but she'd know those dark eyes and that sardonic grin anywhere.

Annie hardly listened as Mel introduced the girl in the Alice band as Fliss, the Deputy Stage Manager, and the messy blonde as Debbie, the Casting Assistant. She tried to concentrate, but horrifying images of herself, half dressed and completely plastered, trying to lasso Nick with her bra, kept rising up to haunt her.

'And this is Nick Ryan, our Artistic Director.' Mel smiled. 'But of course, you two know each other already, don't you?'

'What?' Annie stared at him in panic.

Nick's eyes twinkled. 'I told Mel we once worked together.'

'Oh. Yes. Worked together. Of course.' Annie's tongue clung to the roof of her mouth in terror.

'Nick tells us you're quite something,' Mel said.

Annie glanced at Nick. He was studying his notes, but she could see his lips twitching as his dark head bent over his clipboard.

He was enjoying this, the bastard! She closed her eyes. It

could only happen to her. Other women had one-night stands that disappeared with the dawn. Hers came back to haunt her.

'Annie?' Mel sounded concerned. 'Are you okay?' she asked. 'You look a bit pale.'

'I'm fine,' Annie lied. 'Only a bit of a headache, that's all.'

'Probably just audition nerves,' Mel said. 'I used to suffer terribly.'

Annie felt a stab of fury. This was all Nick's fault. Why hadn't he told her who he was last night? He could have saved her from all this embarrassment, instead of letting her make a complete fool of herself. She cringed. Well, even if she did want this job, she'd more than talked herself out of it.

Mel began to ask her about her background and experience. As Annie mumbled her replies, she kept catching the glances Fliss was giving her. God knows what she must have thought of her, slumped zombie-like in the chair, reeking of stale booze and ciggies. If only she'd done something with her hair. Or put on some make-up. Or never been born.

Once the interview was over, it was time for her audition piece. Annie rose to her feet, sweat prickling on her upper lip as she tried to stop the room spinning. Nick wasn't even looking at her, as he flicked through his notes. Annie felt another surge of rage that cleared her head. How dare he ignore her! She knew there was no way he was going to give her a job, but she could still make him sit up and take notice.

She'd chosen a speech from *A Midsummer Night's Dream*, where the spurned Helena confronts her love rival Hermia. It wasn't until she began to speak that she realised how appallingly appropriate it was. There was Helena, full of jealousy that the man she adored was in love with another woman. Every word she uttered could have come straight from Annie's own wounded heart.

"'O teach me how you look, and with what art you sway the motion of Demetrius' heart.'" She'd never made this speech with so much real feeling. If she could be more like Suzy, maybe she could sway Max's heart too.

The room was still for a moment after she'd finished. Annie knew she'd impressed them. Even Nick was looking at her with respect. 'Thank you,' he said softly.

There was a quick, huddled conference. Annie tried to compose herself and push all thoughts of Max aside. It was like trying to stop herself breathing.

Then Nick looked up. 'Would you mind sight-reading something for us?' he asked.

'Of course.' Why was he doing this to her? They both knew he had no intention of hiring her.

The piece was from *Much Ado*, taken from the opening scene. 'I'll read Benedick,' Nick said, coming from behind the table to stand in front of her.

'Great.' Annie took the text from him, her hands shaking.

Nick peered into her face. 'Are you okay?'

'Fine. Let's get on with it, shall we?'

She might have known he wouldn't. Nick was a perfectionist. Every couple of lines he stopped her, pointing out some new expression he wanted her to try. 'Let's have a bit more bantering,' he suggested. 'This is meant to be a battle of wits, remember?'

Annie nodded. She had never felt less witty and bantering in her life. Now she'd started thinking about Max again, she couldn't seem to stop.

'"Then is Courtesy a turn-coat. But it is certain I am loved of all ladies, only you excepted."' Nick was looking at her. '"And I would I could find it in my heart that I had not a hard heart, for truly I love none."'

'"I thank God and my cold blood I am of your humour for that."' Annie bent her head over her script. '"I had rather hear my dog bark at a crow than a man swear he loves me."' Her voice caught on the words. She would never hear Max swearing he loved her again.

'"God keep your ladyship still—"' Nick broke off. As she looked up at him, a tear escaped and rolled down her cheek. 'Annie?' he whispered. He reached out to brush it off, but she flinched away from him.

'I'm sorry,' she blurted out. 'I – I can't do this.' She looked at the bemused faces of Mel, Debbie and Fliss. 'I'm really, really—' But her last words were choked on a sob as she fled from the room.

'Perhaps it wasn't as bad as you thought?' Caz said encouragingly, as they perched on high stools in the Costa Coffee at Waterloo station an hour later.

Annie shook her head. 'Believe me, it was.'

'You wait, these things are never the way they seem –'

'Caz, I cried my eyes out! How much worse can it get?' She buried her face in her hands, trying to shut out the awful picture. The last twelve hours had been the most mortifying of her life and it was only lunch-time. 'God knows what he must think of me.'

'Perhaps he'll see the funny side,' Caz suggested.

Annie pushed a handful of curls out of her eyes. 'There wasn't one,' she said gloomily.

'But it could happen to anyone.'

'Has it ever happened to you?'

'Well, no, but –'

'There you are then.' Her hands trembled as she wrapped them around her black coffee. 'He probably thinks I'm having some kind of nervous breakdown. What with that, and –' She slammed her mouth shut.

It was too much to hope Caz wouldn't notice. 'Is there something you're not telling me?' she asked, eyes narrowed.

Reluctantly, Annie admitted the whole story. How she'd once dumped Nick and how disastrously their paths had crossed again the night before. By the time she'd finished, Caz was wiping away the tears.

'It's not funny,' Annie grumbled, toying with a sugar lump.

'Are you kidding? It's the funniest thing I've heard all year.' Caz shook her head. 'And you're actually telling me you ditched him for Max?'

Annie's chin rose defensively. 'What's that supposed to mean?'

'Nothing.' But she could see the incredulous look on Caz's face. She knew not everyone liked Max. He could be quite outspoken at times, but it was hardly his fault if people mistook it for arrogance. And Caz wasn't the only one of her friends who'd been edged out of their social life. Annie could still remember a couple of excruciating nights out when Max had watched her friends' antics in haughty silence. But his honesty was something she had always appreciated.

And it wasn't as if he was antisocial. God no, he had a huge circle of friends. He was forever talking about the mates he'd met at first night parties – Ken and Helena, Ralphie Fiennes, Judi and Mike. He used to show off the phone numbers he'd collected. So what if some people found him a bit pompous? Annie thought he was adorable.

She still did. She took a huge gulp of scalding coffee, which did nothing to ease the lump of misery in her throat.

'He's gorgeous though, isn't he?' Caz skimmed the froth off her cappuccino. 'Very sexy in a world-weary kind of way, don't you think?'

'Who?'

'Nick Ryan, of course. I'm not surprised you tried to get him into bed last night.'

'I didn't!'

'Oh, right. So dragging him up the stairs was you playing hard to get, was it?' Caz sent her a sly look. 'I don't think you've got anything to worry about, anyway. Nick's bound to give you a job. Even if it is out of pity.'

'Somehow I don't think so.' It was a good thing she hadn't set her heart on it.

'I know what you need,' Caz said later as they were leaving the café.

'What?' A nose job? A personality transplant? Annie was prepared to try anything.

'Some retail therapy.' Caz grinned. 'How about going on a mad splurge in South Molton Street?'

Annie shook her head. 'No, thanks. I've got next month's mortgage to think about.' That was something else pecking away at her troubled mind. Max had always handled the finances. How was she going to cope with paying the bills, especially if she didn't have a job?

'Suit yourself.' Caz planted a kiss on her cheek. 'Take care of yourself, won't you? And don't forget to let me know if you hear from the lovely Nick.'

'I will.' Although she was already expecting the 'thanks

but no thanks' message to be waiting on her answering-machine when she got home.

'Anyway, cheer up!' Caz called over her shoulder as she headed towards the Northern Line. 'Things could be worse.'

Annie thought about it as she made her way home. She had been dumped by her husband and betrayed by her best friend. She was out of work, out of luck and out of cash. Short of being struck down by some rare virus that caused her to gain three stone and lose all her hair, could her life really get any worse?

Then she let herself into the house, saw Max standing there, and realised it probably could.

Chapter 9

It wasn't meant to be like this. When she met Max again in her day-dreams she was always cool, poised and desirable. She was not hungover and wearing a *Rocky Horror Show* T-shirt that could have doubled as a dishrag.

He was standing at the hall table, flicking through his post. Annie took one look at him in his white polo shirt and faded Levis, streaky blond and gorgeous, and felt her stomach contract with lust.

He glanced up at her. 'Did you know this Barclaycard bill was due last Friday?' His voice was clipped with irritation. 'Why didn't you send it on to me?'

'I had other things on my mind.' She walked past him quickly, hoping he wouldn't detect the whiff of stale ciggies. 'What are you doing here, anyway?'

'Collecting the rest of my things. I called last night, remember?'

Did she ever! 'You should have waited until I got back. You can't just walk in here whenever you feel like it, you know.'

'What's the problem?' His lip curled. 'You haven't got a man here, have you?'

'I might have.'

'Yeah, right.' He grinned. 'That's why you're all dressed up.' He looked her up and down insultingly.

'Oh, fuck off!' She was too tired to fight him. After dreaming for three weeks of this moment, suddenly all she wanted him to do was to go away. 'I'd still rather you waited until I was here.'

'Why? So you can make another scene?'

'What scene? I don't make scenes.'

'You're making one now.'

She opened her mouth, then closed it again.

'Anyway, my name's still on the mortgage,' Max went on. 'So this place is still technically half mine, remember?'

'In that case, you still technically owe me half the phone bill.'

He smiled that maddeningly handsome smile of his and pushed the blond hair out of his eyes. 'I'll write you a cheque, shall I? Only I'll have to send it on. I'm changing bank accounts at the moment. Which reminds me, there are some papers you've got to sign. About closing our joint account.'

Annie felt her lip trembling. 'The joint account?'

'Well, it makes sense, doesn't it?' Max said briskly. 'We don't need it now we're separated.'

Annie wasn't listening. The joint bank account was one of the last shreds of hope she was clinging on to. Like his Ralph Lauren boxer shorts in the chest of drawers, it was a sign that one day Max might, just might, come back to her.

'I hope you're going to be sensible about this?' he warned. 'My God, it's only a bank account.'

She stared at his back as he turned away to flick through his post. Only a bank account. Like their marriage certificate was only a piece of paper.

'So what happened to *Freedom*?' he asked. Annie felt confused. Was he after some kind of philosophical discussion? '*Freedom*,' he repeated slowly, as if talking to a backward child. 'The Art. It's wrecked.'

How can you tell, she wanted to ask. 'It was an accident.'

'Of course it was.' He smiled knowingly.

'I didn't do it on purpose, if that's what you're thinking. If you must know, I got pissed and fell on it.' She saw his face fall and added weakly, 'I'll pay for it, of course. I know how much you loved it —'

'Forget it.' Max aimed a *Reader's Digest* Prize Draw letter at the waste-paper bin. 'Suzy wouldn't have it in the house anyway. She reckons all that post-Modernist stuff's crap.'

Annie breathed in sharply. She'd always thought it was crap too, but that hadn't stopped Max insisting it take up half the sitting-room.

She went into the kitchen. Max followed her. Too late, she remembered the unwashed dishes festering in a sinkful of cold, greasy water.

'I see the place has gone to pot since I left.' Max leaned against the doorway, his mocking eyes taking in the scene.

'And Suzy's utterly perfect, I suppose.' Annie snatched up the kettle with unnecessary force. 'Don't tell me, she gets up at dawn to serve you breakfast with a rose between her teeth?'

Max grinned. 'Actually, it's me who usually gets up first. Suzy's hopeless until she's had her first cup of Earl Grey.'

Annie crashed cups around. How dare he swan in and start discussing his domestic arrangements with her. Did he honestly think she wanted to hear what he and Suzy got up to in the bedroom, or anywhere else for that matter?

And when was the last time he'd brought her tea in bed? Not once, in six years of marriage. She could have been struck down with the bubonic plague and he wouldn't have offered her so much as a Lemsip. And yet Suzy got the star treatment every day.

She caught sight of herself in the mirror over the sink and flinched. Bloody Suzy, she thought. And bloody Max, too. Why did he have to turn up now, when she was looking like something other people scraped off their boots?

'So have you finished packing the rest of your things?'

'Not yet.' He folded his arms. 'What's the rush? Anyone would think you wanted to get rid of me.'

'Well spotted.' She banged the kettle down on the work top and fumbled for the switch. 'If you must know, I want to go to bed. I didn't sleep too well last night.'

'Not because of me, I hope?'

'Don't flatter yourself! I happen to have a hellish hangover.'

'Oh, I get it.' He grinned knowingly. 'I suppose you've had the coven round for a few girly bitching sessions? I thought my ears were burning.'

'Actually there were only two of us,' she said haughtily. 'And we had better things to talk about.'

'I see.' His gaze fell on the two glasses sitting side by side on the draining board, waiting to be washed. 'So this friend of yours,' he said casually. 'Anyone I know?'

'No.'

'Male or female?'

'What's that got to do with you?'

'I just wondered, that's all.'

She glared at him. 'It was a man. Is that a problem?'

68

'No,' he said quickly. 'No, not at all.' But he looked shaken, she noticed.

'Good,' she said. 'I mean, it would be a bit rich under the circumstances, wouldn't it?' She raised her chin. 'I am a free woman. What's sauce for the goose and all that.'

They stood in silence for a moment, both watching the kettle as it failed to boil. Finally Annie sighed. 'I don't think I'll bother with the coffee after all. I'm going for a bath instead.' She eyed him coldly. 'Don't forget to lock the door on your way out, will you?'

It was amazing what a generous slosh of Body Shop Aromatherapy Bath Oil could do, she reflected some time later, as she sank beneath the hot, steaming water. Already she could feel her headache easing and the life slowly ebbing back into her aching limbs. Any minute now she might start to feel almost human again.

She could hear Max moving around downstairs. She was beginning to regret being so offhand with him. Not that he didn't deserve it, but she wondered if she hadn't gone too far. Being cool was one thing, but she didn't want to put him off completely.

She grabbed a towel off the rail. She would catch him before he left, try to make amends. God knows when she'd get another chance.

She was out of the bath when she heard footsteps on the stairs. She barely had time to wrap the towel around herself before the door opened and Max appeared, mug in hand.

'You could have knocked.' She pushed her damp hair out of her eyes.

'Why? It's not as if I haven't seen you naked before.' He ran his eyes slowly and disturbingly down her body.

She distracted herself quickly. 'I see you've made yourself at home. Who said you could use my coffee?'

'Actually, it's for you. I thought it might help the hangover.'

She inhaled sharply in disbelief. Max making coffee? She wasn't sure he even knew how. 'Thanks,' she muttered, fumbling with the towel. Should she pull it down so it decently covered her thighs and risk leaving too much bosom exposed, or should she tweak it up so it covered her boobs but barely skimmed her bottom? And did it really matter when every inch of her was blushing furiously?

'Just take the bloody thing off.' Max was watching her with amusement. Annie trembled. If only he weren't so gorgeous it might be a lot easier to hate him.

He took a step closer. She could feel the heat of his body. 'Where do you want it?' he whispered.

'What?'

'Your coffee.' His smile was sexy and knowing. 'Shall I leave it here, or would you rather have it in the bedroom?'

'I'll take it,' Annie said shakily. Clutching her towel with one hand, she made a hasty grab for the mug.

'You look like a mermaid, with your hair like that.' Max reached out to touch a damp curl. 'It's beautiful, like the colour of sherry. The finest Oloroso –'

His touch was electric. Annie flinched away, splashing hot coffee over her hand. 'I thought you preferred blondes these days,' she snapped.

Max smiled. '*Touché.*'

Annie suddenly felt as self-conscious as a teenager. 'I'll go and get dressed,' she muttered, moving to push past him.

Max stood in her way. 'Do you have to? I prefer you the way you are. All kind of sexy and rumpled.'

She felt her knees buckling and her carefully built-up defences melting like wax. In spite of her pain and anger, he could still do it to her.

'Annie –' Next moment his hands were cupping her face, drawing her towards him.

'What about Suzy?' she whispered. Max's face was so close to hers she could see the dark-blue flecks in his eyes.

'What about her?'

What indeed, Annie thought, as he began to trace a tingling line of kisses along her collarbone. Had Suzy spared a thought for her while she and Max were cavorting in her dressing-room after the curtain came down?

Next moment the towel was at her feet and she was in Max's arms, kissing him hungrily, ripping at the buttons on his shirt, desperate to touch him, to feel the warmth of his skin under her fingers.

'What about your boyfriend?' he asked suddenly.

'Hmm?' She went on fumbling at his shirt buttons.

'The guy from last night?' Max caught her wrists, pulling her away from him.

She felt cold and shivery. All she could think about was getting back into his arms. 'What boyfriend?' she mumbled.

It seemed like the right answer. Max smiled an odd little smile, almost triumphant, before his mouth claimed hers again.

They'd made it all the way to the bedroom and collapsed on to the bed when the phone rang, shattering the mood. At first Annie ignored it.

It was Max who pulled away. 'Aren't you going to answer it?' he asked.

'No.' Annie dragged his mouth back to hers. She couldn't have stopped even if she'd wanted to. Her whole body was molten with lust.

Max jerked away, lifting himself up on to his elbow. He could never ignore a ringing phone. 'But it might be important,' he insisted.

Annie stretched out for the receiver, picked it up, then slammed it down again. The sudden silence was deafening.

'They hung up.' She grinned mischievously, reaching for him. Almost immediately it rang again.

'Look, you'd better answer it.' Max picked up his shirt.

Annie began to panic. 'You're not going?' She raised her voice above the insistent ringing.

'I've got to.'

She touched his skin, feeling its warmth under her hand. 'Stay,' she pleaded.

'I can't.'

Annie watched him button up his shirt. 'You're going back to her,' she said in a small, flat voice.

And still the phone kept ringing. 'Can't you answer that bloody thing?' he shouted.

She picked it up and slammed it down again, her eyes never leaving his face. 'How can you go back to her, after – after what we've just done?'

Max sighed. 'I don't want to, but – it's complicated.'

'What do you mean?'

'I mean it's just – complicated, that's all.' He cupped her chin in his hand. 'Look, I don't know how I feel at the moment. Everything's totally confused.'

You're confused? Annie pulled the duvet around her.

He wasn't the one being abandoned one minute and seduced the next.

Her throat felt tight. 'So are you coming back?' she whispered. She hated herself for sounding so pathetic, but she had to know.

'I —' The wretched phone started ringing again. Max glanced at it, then at her. He bent down, dropped a quick kiss on the top of her head, then ruffled her hair affectionately. 'I'll call you,' he promised.

'Max —' But she was already talking to his retreating back as it disappeared through the door.

'We'll talk later,' he yelled. 'Now answer that bloody thing!'

As his footsteps echoed down the stairs, Annie reached across and snatched up the phone. 'Yes?' she hissed. If it was a double-glazing salesman, he was in serious trouble.

But it wasn't.

Chapter 10

'Have I called at a bad time?' Nick asked.

Downstairs the front door banged shut. Max was gone. Annie swung round and directed all her frustration down the phone. 'What do you want?'

'How are you feeling?'

Annie gritted her teeth. 'Fine.'

Gathering the duvet round her she went over to the window and looked into the narrow, tree-lined street, trying to catch a glimpse of Max. But he'd already gone.

If only the wretched phone hadn't rung, she might have held on to him long enough to make him change his mind. This was all Nick's fault. And if Max never came back, if he stayed with Suzy bloody Carrington, that would be all his fault too.

'Are you sure? It's just the way you left –'

'I told you, I'm fine.' Max wouldn't really stay with Suzy, would he? Not after what had happened.

'I was surprised to see you at the audition today,' Nick was saying.

'I could say the same thing!' Annie dragged her thoughts away from Max. 'You could have told me who you were last night. It might have saved us both a lot of embarrass-ment.'

'How was I to know you were the one I was supposed to be meeting? All I knew was that when Julia Gold phoned, begging me to meet her client, she made it sound like you were the greatest thing since Kate Winslet. I never imagined it would be you.'

'Thanks a lot,' Annie muttered.

'That's not what I meant, and you know it. Anyway, by the time I realised it was you, you'd made it so clear you didn't want the job I decided it was best not to mention it. I was trying not to embarrass you,' he said pointedly. 'I didn't know your agent would be on the phone the next morning, begging me to give you an audition.'

Annie rolled over on the bed and caught a glimpse of herself in the wardrobe mirror. Her cheek-bones were stained with hectic colour, her eyes as brilliant as topaz. It was an after-sex face. Almost.

Now that the post-Max euphoria was beginning to fade she felt cold and uncertain. She'd nearly let him make love to her and now he was gone. What did that tell her?

'So why did you do it?' Nick asked.

Annie stared at the phone, startled. 'What?'

'The audition. What made you change your mind?'

'Julia.' She bit her lip. Where had she gone wrong? Had she made it too easy for Max? She had a vague idea that falling into bed with him wasn't the shrewdest move she'd ever made. But he only had to touch her and she melted. God, why was she such a wimp?

'Ah, yes, I can understand that. Very – er – forceful, isn't she?'

'She could bully for Britain.' But maybe she'd got it wrong? Maybe Max really did want to come home?

75

Perhaps living with Suzy had made him realise how much he'd missed her. Quite how that could have happened she didn't know, but didn't Max say he was confused? A small bubble of hope rose within her.

'Annie? Are you still there?'

She realised that she hadn't heard a word Nick had said for the last two minutes. 'Sorry, what was that?'

'It doesn't matter. Look, are you sure I haven't called at a bad time? I can ring back if it isn't convenient.'

'No, no. Now is fine.' She didn't want to risk tying up the phone lines if Max was trying to get through later on.

Besides, she felt she owed him some kind of apology. A pretty big one, in fact.

'I'm sorry about last night.' She blurted out the words, gripping the phone cord tighter.

'Oh, that.' She could hear the smile in his voice again.

'I don't know what made me do it.'

'A gallon of brandy might have helped.'

Annie pressed her lips together in annoyance. 'Anyway, I'm sorry it happened.'

'Forget it,' Nick said. 'I hope you understand that it was nothing personal – me turning you down like that?'

'No.' She could feel the blush creeping up from her ankles.

'It's just when I go to bed with a woman I prefer her to remember it in the morning.'

Oh, I remember it all right, Annie thought. Was she ever going to be able to forget it?

She reached across for her dressing-gown and glanced at the bedside clock. Three thirty-seven. Maybe Max was already trying to get through?

'Well,' she said briskly, 'if that's all you wanted, I'm pretty busy –'

'Wait,' said Nick. 'There was something else.'

She stifled a sigh. 'What?'

'How would you like to play Beatrice?'

Annie froze, the phone wedged against her shoulder, one arm in her dressing-gown. 'You're not serious? But my audition —'

'— was one of the best I've seen in a very long time,' Nick finished for her. 'Although to be honest, I would have offered you the job anyway.'

'Because you feel sorry for me?'

'Because you're good. I've seen you work. I know what you can do.'

He began to outline his offer. The Phoenix Theatre, Middlethorpe, was due to reopen in early September. Rehearsals for *Much Ado* would begin in a fortnight, with four weeks' rehearsal before they opened. As Caz had predicted, Nick was also casting for the rest of the season and there was a good chance that she would be offered more work if things turned out well.

The whole time he was talking, Annie's mind was racing. A few hours ago she might have been tempted. But Max's unexpected reappearance had thrown everything into chaos.

'Well?' Nick's voice broke into her thoughts. 'What do you say?'

Annie twisted the phone cord in her hands. 'Look, it's very sweet of you to offer,' she said, biting her lip. 'But I can't do it.'

There was a long silence. 'You're turning it down?'

'Yes.'

'I see.' His voice could have frozen the phone line. 'So why did you bother turning up for the audition if you think this job's so far beneath you?'

'It's not that —' Annie took a deep breath. She would have to tell him, she decided. After the way she'd poured her heart out to him he'd want to know. 'It's Max,' she said.

'What about him?'

'I think —' oh, God, please don't let her be wrong '— I think he's decided to come home.'

There. She'd said it. For a minute she thought Nick had hung up.

'What makes you think that?' he said at last.

'He was here. Just now. When you rang. And he's changed. I really think he knows he's made a mistake —'

'Did he tell you that?' Nick cut her off abruptly.

'What?'

'Did he tell you he'd made a terrible mistake? Did he beg you to take him back?'

'Not exactly —'

'So where is he now?'

'I — I don't know,' she faltered. 'He had to leave.'

'I see.'

'At least I know he still cares,' Annie protested. The chill of the wooden floor was beginning to seep through her bare feet. 'I thought you'd be happy for me.'

Nick sighed wearily. 'I am,' he said. 'If that's what you really want.'

'It is.'

There was a heavy silence. 'Then I wish you luck,' Nick said, and put down the phone.

Annie held on to the dead line, her happiness evaporating like mist. How dare Nick go and spoil it all? He was only put out because she'd turned down his stupid job offer.

She put down the receiver and sat for a moment, half

expecting Max to ring back straight away. But he didn't. Annie spent the rest of the day and evening in a state of agitation, full of restless energy, waiting for him to call. She sorted through her knicker drawer, cleaned the kitchen floor and even found herself washing the windows so she could keep an eye on the road. She would have weeded the window boxes too, but she was worried about getting soil under what was left of her nails.

And all the time she prowled around the phone, waiting for it to ring.

Her nerves were in tatters by the time it did ring, just after nine. She was flopped in front of the *Nine O'Clock News*, watching Michael Buerk with the sound turned down.

She pounced on the receiver. 'Thank God!' she cried. 'I've been waiting hours. Max, what's going on?'

'I was rather hoping you could tell me that.' Suzy's voice was cool on the other end of the line. 'I think it's time we met, don't you?'

Chapter 11

They arranged to have lunch in the Garden restaurant the next day. They'd often met there in the past, but this time Annie doubted if girly gossip would be on the menu.

She sat at the corner table, staring out over the sunny Covent Garden piazza and wondering what Max had told Suzy. She'd tried to call him, but his mobile had been switched off all morning.

Whatever he'd said, Suzy had been tight-lipped on the phone. Had he told her he was leaving? Annie tried to quell the unworthy surge of spiteful triumph at the thought of Suzy pacing tearfully around her Chelsea love nest, shredding soggy tissues and chewing her manicured nails.

She mustn't gloat, she told herself firmly, as she tried to catch a passing waiter's eye. She would have Max back and that was all that mattered. Although maybe Dempster should be told, just to set the record straight.

She'd arrived at the restaurant a fashionable fifteen minutes late, only to find Suzy still wasn't there. Maybe she wasn't coming? Perhaps she was still at home, desperately trying to repair her tear-ravaged face?

Annie took out her mirror and cautiously examined her

own appearance. She'd taken hours to get ready and for once she was satisfied with herself. Her war-paint was just right, the blend of gold shadows bringing out the tigerish amber in her eyes, which was reflected in her tobacco-coloured silk shirt. Her hair had been moussed, serumed and pinned into submission. She snapped her mirror shut, feeling confident. Then the waiter arrived.

Annie could tell that, like most of the staff, he was an out-of-work actor. As he appeared at her table his restless gaze was skimming the crowd, searching for the famous face who might offer him his big break. He'd already given Annie her place in his sucking-up order. And by the impatient way he was tapping his pen against his order book it wasn't near the top.

She dithered over the drinks menu. Should she have a glass of wine to steady her nerves? Or should she keep a clear head and order mineral water?

In the end she opted for the water. 'Yeah, go mad, why don't you?' the waiter said in a bored voice, scribbling on his pad before drifting off to the bar.

Five minutes later he was still leaning there, deep in conversation with two other waitresses, while Annie waited for her drink. She'd just lit a cigarette in desperation when Suzy turned up.

She looked blonde, glowing and not the least bit heart-broken. She was wearing a brief white lacy top and skin-tight pink pedal pushers which should have looked idiotic on anyone over seven years old, but on her looked irritatingly cute and sex kittenish.

Annie was so shocked to see her she took a wrongly judged puff and swallowed a lungful of smoke.

'Oh, my God, are you all right?' Suzy banged her on the back, taking the rest of her breath away.

'I'm fine.' Annie shook her off. So much for being cool, she thought, mopping her streaming eyes with her sleeve.

'Are you sure? Let me get you a glass of water.'

You'll be lucky, Annie was about to gasp. But Suzy had barely raised her finger the merest fraction of an inch before the waiter came scampering over, his notebook poised. Annie felt sick, and not because she'd just swallowed half her cigarette.

Suzy ordered the water, then turned back to Annie. 'Haven't I told you smoking's bad for you?' She smiled. It wasn't the smile of someone who had just been dumped by her lover. It was more the supremely confident, hundred-kilowatt, teeth-dazzling smile of someone who knew she had the upper hand.

Annie fumbled in her bag for a tissue. Typically, all she could find was a tattered, disconcertingly crispy scrap she'd once used to wipe the mud off her boots. She was just wondering if she could get away with using an old bus ticket when Suzy handed over a pristine hankie.

'Here, have one of mine,' she offered. 'Don't worry, I haven't got any germs.'

I bet you haven't, Annie thought, dabbing her eyes. Everything about Suzy was as squeaky clean and fresh as an advert for bathroom cleaner. Except her conscience.

The waiter came scuttling back with the water. He stood over Suzy as she dithered prettily over the menu. Any minute now he'd be on his back, begging her to tickle his tummy, Annie thought bitchily.

Normally at such a lunch Annie would have demolished the day's special and still found room for the chocolate fudge brownie with extra whipped cream. But today her stomach was knotted with tension. Gloomily she closed her menu and ordered a salad.

'Do you want fries with that?' the waiter asked, eyeing her thighs unkindly. Annie glared at him.

'How about some wine?' Suzy suggested.

'Why not?' Annie sipped her water grimly. Forget abstinence. It would take more than a bottle of Perrier to get her through this ordeal.

Suzy ordered house white and a fresh orange juice for herself. 'I'm not drinking at the moment,' she said smugly. 'But I'm sure you won't have any trouble finishing the bottle.'

Annie stared at Suzy's nauseatingly perfect face and wondered how she had ever considered her a friend. Not only was she a cheating, man-stealing cow, but she was also without a shred of human failing. She was the only person Annie knew who not only belonged to a gym, but actually went there regularly. She'd never demolished a family-sized bar of Whole Nut in one sitting. In fact, she was unnaturally perfect. How could she have ever felt close to a woman for whom cellulite was something that only happened to other people?

'So.' Suzy leaned forward with the hushed, concerned tone normally reserved for visiting patients in secure establishments. 'How are you?'

'Fine. Never better.' Annie tossed her curls defiantly.

'That's good.' Suzy leaned even further. 'You know, I've really missed you,' she confided. 'It's been awful, not being able to call you for a gossip like I used to.'

Was she for real? 'Well, yes, it did make things a teeny bit awkward,' Annie said. 'You running off with my husband like that.'

Suzy nodded earnestly. She wouldn't have recognised sarcasm if it turned round and bit her on her sickeningly pert backside. She sat across the table, her smooth skin the colour of orange-blossom honey, her rosebud mouth a little circle of concern. 'That's why I'm here,' she said. 'To get things sorted out between us. I hope when this is over we can still be friends.'

Annie was saved from answering by the waiter speeding over with their drinks. As he poured Annie's wine he turned to Suzy and said bashfully, 'I hope you don't mind me asking, Miss Carrington, but can I have your autograph?'

'Of course.' Suzy reached flirtatiously into his apron pocket, took out his notepad and scribbled something on it. Annie watched as she added a few extravagant kisses and handed it back, reducing the waiter to a mass of quivering hormones.

'I'm trying to break into acting myself,' he babbled, turning his back on Annie. 'I just wondered if you had any advice –'

'Yes. Don't give up the day job.' Annie snatched her glass away as he filled it to the brim. He shot her a mean look, then flounced off towards the kitchen.

Suzy sighed. 'Don't you get tired of that happening?'

'Constantly,' Annie said. The last time she'd signed her autograph was on a Save the Whale petition.

Suzy sipped primly at her orange juice. Finally Annie could stand it no longer. 'So why did you want to meet?'

'I thought it was time we cleared the air.' Suzy toyed with her napkin. 'Max told me – about yesterday.'

Annie nearly took a bite out of her wineglass. 'Oh, yes?'

'Yes.' Suzy's thickly lashed eyes came up to meet hers. 'And I must say I'm very disappointed.'

Disappointed? Annie stared at her. *Disappointed*? Blind fury she could understand. Devastated – well, she'd been there too. But disappointed? That was what you felt when

84

your lottery numbers didn't come up, not when your boy-friend unexpectedly snogged his estranged wife.

But then Suzy had all the depth of a car-park puddle. You only had to watch her act to see that.

'It's not going to work, you know,' she went on. 'Max isn't going to fall for it.'

'What are you talking about?'

'You know.' Suzy sent her an accusing look. 'Actually, I feel rather sorry for you, stooping to that kind of emotional blackmail. I thought you had more self-respect than that –'

'Now hang on a minute!' Annie banged down her glass. 'What exactly has Max been telling you?'

'The truth.' There was a hint of cold steel in her blue eyes. 'That he came round to collect his things and that you got very emotional, as usual.'

'Anything else?'

Suzy's lips tightened. 'He told me you threw yourself at him. He didn't want to say anything at first but I knew something had happened.' She lifted her chin. 'I found your hair on his shirt collar.'

'And did he also tell you he tried to get me into bed?' An unnerving hush fell over the entire restaurant. Even the waiters stopped gossiping and looked round.

Suzy's face lost a little of its doll-like pinkness, but she regained her composure quickly. 'Oh, Annie.' She sighed. 'When are you going to give up?'

'But it's true.'

'You mean you'd like it to be.' Suzy gave her a sorrowful look that wouldn't have shamed a daytime TV agony auntie. 'Max is right. You really won't accept it, will you? Perhaps you should get some help –'

The waiter sidled up with their food. He paused just

long enough to give Suzy a winning smile and Annie a look that said he hoped she'd choke on her radicchio before racing off, elbows out against the other waiters, to schmooze Trevor Nunn on the other side of the room.

Annie poked listlessly about in her salad. Maybe she did need help. She must be mad, letting Max hurt her like that again. She knew she hadn't imagined the way he'd looked at her, the way he'd touched her. She'd been so sure he wanted her back. But now, in the cold light of day, she was beginning to see how things really were. This wasn't about Max wanting her again. This was Max wanting to prove no one else could have her.

Looking back on it, she could see how his attitude had changed when he found out about Nick. Had he tried to seduce her just to prove he still could? That even though there was another man in her life, he was still the one she really wanted?

Annie let her fork fall, her stomach burning with anger. She felt used and humiliated. And yet, deep down, she knew she would do it all again, just for the chance to be in Max's arms, even for a second.

'Look, I'm sorry.' Suzy was back to her relentless pitying mode. 'I didn't mean to upset you. That's not what I came here for at all.'

'Then why did you come?'

'To try and build some bridges. And to let you know we're here for you, Max and I.'

She put out a hand. Annie picked up her fork again hurriedly. Suzy had been watching too much *Oprah*, she decided. Any minute now she'd be suggesting they all got together for a group hug.

'I know it's not what you wanted to hear,' Suzy droned on, 'but your marriage is over. It's left you emotionally shattered, I can understand that. But you've got to face up to reality. You and Max just aren't right for each other. You never were. You've got to move on, rebuild your life –'

Annie jabbed at her salad with tightly controlled agitation. If they hadn't been in a crowded restaurant she would have pinned Suzy to the floor with a fork at her throat by now. 'We were fine until you came along,' she muttered.

'But you weren't, were you?' Suzy speared a cherry tomato. 'You were having problems long before that. Anyone could see you two weren't really happy.' She leaned forward. 'You were stifling him, Annie.'

Annie winced. 'I loved him.'

'Yes, but that wasn't the kind of love he needed, was it?' Suzy leaned over again. Any further and she'd be face down in her salad. 'You never gave him any space –'

Look what happened when I did, Annie thought furiously. 'Spare me the psychology. You wanted him, and that's all there was to it.'

'I fell in love with him.' Suzy looked hurt. 'I couldn't help it. You've got to realise how painful this has been for me.'

'For you?' Annie took a swig of her wine. 'You're not the one who got dumped, remember? You're not the one whose so-called best friend ran off with her husband.'

'Before you blame me, perhaps you should ask yourself why he left.'

Annie's blood froze in her veins. 'What's that supposed to mean?'

'If Max had been happy with you, why did he want me?' There was steely determination in that porcelain-pretty face.

87

Annie regarded the acres of smooth, honey-skinned bosom rising out of her off-the-shoulder top, her baby-blonde hair piled on top of her head, tendrils falling around her provocatively innocent face. There was absolutely no answer to that, she decided.

'Anyway, I haven't come here to spread doom and gloom.' Suzy went back to her salad, as if she had been chatting about the weather instead of tearing the last six years of Annie's life apart.

Annie stared into the murky green depths of her bowl. After a few minutes she heard a word that made her look up. 'Film? What film?'

'Oh, didn't Max tell you? Uncle Victor's making a film of *The Tenant of Wildfell Hall*. He wants Max and me to star in it.' Suzy smiled. 'I suppose he thought it would be interesting, given our real-life relationship –'

Good old Uncle Victor, Annie thought bitterly. She wondered how much Suzy had had to beg him to give Max a part. Well, that was it. She'd never get him back now. If it was a choice between her and a starring role in a Victor Carrington film, she might as well sign those divorce papers right now. 'Very clever,' she said.

Suzy blinked. 'I don't know what you mean.'

'Oh, come on! You know Max has always wanted to be in films. He won't leave you while you're dangling that little prize in front of him.'

'He won't leave me anyway.' Suzy twirled a piece of lollo rosso around her fork with great concentration.

'Really? And what makes you so sure?'

There was a spark of defiance in Suzy's blue eyes. 'I'm pregnant,' she said.

Chapter 12

'Max wanted to tell you himself.' Suzy broke the stunned silence. 'That's partly why he came round yesterday. But you were so emotional he never got the chance.'

Annie was so numb with shock she let this pass without comment. 'When?' she heard herself whisper. 'How long —'

'Five weeks. The baby's due next March.' Suzy smoothed her flat stomach with her hand. 'It happened on tour. If it's a boy we're going to call him Terence, after Terence Rattigan. You know, *Separate Tables*? Or do you think that's a bit kitsch?'

Annie gripped the table-cloth, her fingers white against the red-checked fabric, fighting the terrible urge to tip up the table and scream with rage. Was Suzy deliberately being cruel, or was she just too stupid to realise what she was saying?

'Max is thrilled, of course,' Suzy went on. 'He's completely ecstatic. You should see him, he's treating me like I'm a piece of priceless Dresden. He won't let me lift a finger. Anyone would think I was the first woman in the world to conceive.' She popped another cherry tomato in her mouth. 'It is a bit awkward, though, what with the film and everything. But we should have finished in a couple of months. And Uncle Victor says if I get too huge he'll just shoot my head.'

Someone bloody well should, Annie thought, focusing on Suzy's pink glossy mouth. If she had a gun she'd do it herself.

'Of course, we'll have to find somewhere else to live,' Suzy was saying. 'We'll probably keep the Cheyne Walk flat on because it's so convenient, but London's hardly the place to bring up a child, is it? And I've seen a fabulous place in *Country Life*. A barn conversion in Hampshire. Way out of our price range, of course, but Daddy says he'll chip in and help us.' She giggled. 'It's got masses of land. Can you imagine, me keeping chickens and gorgeous little lambs and things?'

Annie watched her, sick with jealousy. She'll be asking if I want to be a godmother next, she thought.

Suzy appeared to notice her stunned look. 'I'm sorry if this has all been a shock. I didn't mean it to come out this way. But you never know, perhaps this baby will bring us all closer together.' Her blue eyes gleamed. 'How would you like to be a godmother?'

Annie's unequivocal reply was silenced by the trill of Suzy's mobile phone.

'Hello? Oh, hello, darling.' Annie knew straight away it was Max calling. 'Yes, I'm fine. Yes, yes, I'm sure. Oh, you are so sweet —'

It only took a few seconds of Annie glaring for even Suzy to realise that this wasn't the most tactful thing she could do. Excusing herself, she slid from her seat and headed over to the door to continue her conversation.

Alone at last, Annie finally gave in to her feelings. The

hurt was physical, a terrible crushing pain in her chest. She could hardly breathe.

She couldn't remember a time when she hadn't longed for a baby. Max's baby. They'd only been married a few weeks when she first brought up the subject. Max had just talked her out of signing a contract with the RSC, saying it was no way to start their married life, with her a hundred miles away up the M1. Annie assumed it was because, like her, he wanted to start a family immediately.

But he'd insisted it was too soon. 'Of course I want kids, darling,' he had reassured her. 'But for God's sake, the ink's hardly dry on the marriage certificate. Can't we wait a while?'

So she'd waited. Two years on they'd bought a house, Max had got a bit part in *EastEnders* and she was working in the theatre. It seemed like the perfect time to her. But not to Max.

'Give it time,' he'd said again. 'We're only just getting ourselves established. Do you really want to ditch your career to change nappies and wipe snotty noses all day?'

Actually, she did. And besides, she was only working in Theatre in Education, performing Shakespeare workshops to uninterested sixth formers. Taking a break was hardly going to do her career any serious harm. 'We could work round it,' she suggested. 'Maybe we could get a nanny –'

'No way!' Max was adamant. 'No kid of mine is being brought up by strangers.'

And so it went on. Either they were working and didn't have the time to devote to bringing up a child, or they were out of work and didn't have the money.

'We'll know when it's right,' Max kept saying. But somehow it never was.

In the end Annie had stopped mentioning it, knowing

how much it annoyed him. But that didn't take away the wanting, the physical ache that made her look yearningly at pregnant women in the street.

And now he was 'thrilled' and 'ecstatic' because Suzy was having his baby. This betrayal cut more deeply than their affair ever could.

Suzy hadn't just stolen her husband, she'd stolen her dream. That should have been *her* barn conversion in Hampshire. Those should have been *her* chickens and sheep. Most of all, those should have been *her* children, hers and Max's, romping around in their OshKosh dungarees, shrieking after the chickens and soaking each other with the garden hose while she looked on lovingly.

'The bloody bitch has pinched my life,' she hissed. The couple at the next table shot her a wary glance and edged away their chairs.

Suzy came back as she was refilling her wineglass. 'Everything all right?' she asked brightly.

'Fine,' Annie replied through gritted teeth.

'By the way, no one else knows about the baby, so I'd be grateful if you could keep it to yourself for now,' Suzy said. 'We don't want any fuss for a while. At least not until we've finished filming.'

Annie could already see the soft-focus spread in *Hello!* 'I'm hardly likely to tell the world, am I?'

'And we're going to be away on location most of the time, so you won't have to worry about running into us all over the place.' Suzy reached over and gave her hand a reassuring pat.

Annie snatched it away. How dare she pity me, she thought furiously. 'Actually, I'm going to be out of town myself.'

'Really?' Suzy smiled. 'Taking a little holiday, are you? Good idea.'

'As a matter of fact, I've got a job.' The words seemed to come out of nowhere.

The blue gaze sharpened. 'What kind of job?'

'I'm going back to the theatre.'

'Really? Where?'

Annie racked her brains. What was that name? 'The – er – Phoenix, Middlethorpe.'

'Rep? You're going into rep?' Suzy gave a tight little smile of malice. No wonder, Annie thought. To someone as well-connected as her it was the acting equivalent of joining the Foreign Legion.

'I know, but I just couldn't resist it,' Annie lied airily. 'It was such a tempting offer. And the new Artistic Director is a genius, so I've heard. He's just finished directing Shakespeare in Central Park. The RSC has been after him for months.'

It was an outrageous lie, but at least it brought a gleam of envy to Suzy's eyes. She might have made it on TV playing bosomy heroines, but she still liked to consider herself a serious actress and she'd always wanted to play the real classics.

'What's his name?' she asked. 'Maybe Uncle Victor knows him?' But Annie had decided the time had come for a swift exit.

'Is that the time? I really must go.' She stood up as the waiter swanned past the table.

'Leaving already?' he said, looking at her untouched bowl. 'What do you want me to do with your salad?'

'Let her have it,' Annie glanced at Suzy. 'She seems to enjoy my leftovers.'

Her moment of self-righteous triumph carried her

through the restaurant and out into the street. She was halfway down the Strand before her fragile emotions finally gave way. It was like an anaesthetic wearing off, leaving her with a raw, agonising wound. She stood, sobbing, in front of the baby accessories display in Boots window.

It might have brought her a brief moment of satisfaction, lying to Suzy about the job, but it was going to look pretty hollow in a few weeks when she was still jobless and stuck at home.

Oh, God, she thought. What have I done?

Middlethorpe

Chapter 13

Oh, God, what have I done, Annie thought again two weeks later as she sat at the window, watching rivulets of rain trickle down the glass.

It couldn't even rain properly in this town. There was no drenching downpour, no dramatic storm lighting up the roof-tops. Just the same depressing, half-hearted drizzle that had been falling ever since she had first arrived.

The window overlooked the town square, a grim quandrangle bordered by discount shops offering cut-price toiletries and plastic kitchenware. In the middle of it all stood a statue of a dour-looking Victorian gentleman, his bewhiskered chin held high despite the fact he was ankle deep in discarded Coke cans and old Burger King wrappers. This, she had been told, was Josiah Blanchard, founder of the once prosperous mill town of Middlethorpe.

He wouldn't have recognised the place now, Annie thought. The Victorian architecture had been swept aside to make way for a soulless landscape of concrete, enlivened here and there by flyposters and graffiti. Litter blew down the pedestrian precinct.

Depressed, she shifted her gaze away from the window and back to the gathering. It was the first time the newly formed Phoenix Theatre Company had met and Nick had organised a get-together in the upstairs room of the local pub, the Millowners' Arms. People filled the room, talking, hugging, laughing.

And probably thinking how much older they all looked since the last time they'd worked together, Annie thought cynically.

Then she caught Nick's eye. He was on the other side of the room talking to Adam Gregory, the actor playing Claudio, but she could feel him watching her. They'd hardly spoken since that humiliating phone call she'd made, begging him for a job. To his credit, he had never asked why, or even said 'I told you so'. He didn't have to. It hung unspoken in the air between them like a great black cloud.

'Everything all right?' Caz appeared, looking chirpy. At least she was enjoying herself. Nick had offered her the part of Margaret, the saucy lady-in-waiting.

'Fine.'

'They seem like a great crowd, don't they?'

Annie glanced around the room. There was Clive Seymour, with his lugubrious, bloodhound face, perfect for the comical Dogberry. And there, helping himself to a sly snifter of whisky from his hip-flask, was Henry Adams, who was to play Beatrice's uncle, Leonato. He came from the old school, before TV taught young actors to mumble their lines. The huge voice that rumbled from his grizzled beard could warn shipping.

'They're okay. I hate all this bonding stuff, though.'

'Come on, it could be a lot worse. At least it's not one of those terrible touchy-feely sessions.' Caz giggled. 'I remember one job where we had to spend three days rolling around on the floor giving each other back rubs. And that was only for a dog food commercial. Mind you –' her gaze strayed across to the far side of the room '– I wouldn't mind rubbing *his* back – or anything else, come to think of it.'

Annie craned her neck. The only person she could see was the lanky Irishman playing Don John. 'Not Brendan O'Brien?'

'No, you idiot. That guy talking to him. The tall blond one.' Caz narrowed her eyes speculatively. 'Who is he, I wonder?'

'No idea. I imagine he's playing Benedick.'

'You mean you get to snog him every night? You lucky thing!'

'I suppose so,' Annie agreed listlessly.

'You could show a bit more interest.' Caz shook her head. 'God, he's wasted on you. The state you're in, you could be kissing Robin Cook every night and not even notice.'

She had a point. Ever since Annie had found out about Suzy's baby it felt as if all her feelings had shut down. Nothing seemed to touch her any more. But there was no point trying to explain that to Caz, whose emotions were like a white-knuckle ride, hurtling from high to low in a matter of seconds.

Just as she was wondering whether she could plead a headache and go home, something happened.

'Oh, God!' Annie stared at the door. 'It can't be.'

Caz swung round. 'Oh shit! No one told me she was going to be here.'

They both watched, transfixed with horror, as Georgia Graham made her noisy entrance. She made sure all eyes were on her before she shrugged off her coat, revealing a figure-hugging black linen shift dress.

Annie's heart plummeted. Georgia was a notoriously difficult actress to work with. In a business where success depended on actors working together, she was famous for upstaging and stealing scenes. And as if that wasn't a good enough reason to hate her, she was also a friend of Suzy Carrington.

'I bet you anything she's playing Hero,' Caz said.

'Just what I need.' Annie groaned. It was like finding herself strapped to the school bully in the three-legged race on sports day.

They watched her sashay across the room to where Nick was standing. Flicking her long, glossy black hair off her face, she moved in for a full-on kiss.

'Nothing like going straight to the top, is there?' Caz remarked. 'I wonder if she's slept with him yet?'

'No!'

'Why not? She's famous for it. How do you think she gets most of her work?' Her lip curled. 'Just look at them. He's hardly fighting her off, is he?'

'I thought he had more taste.'

'He's a man, isn't he? And besides –' Caz suddenly clutched at her arm. 'Oh, God, she's seen us. Quick, look busy!'

But it was too late. Georgia was already homing in on them. 'My God, you two!' Annie nearly choked on a cloud of Arpège as she swept them both into her arms. 'Imagine you being here. I had no idea.'

'Me neither.' If she'd had the faintest hint, she would never have got on that train.

'Well, of course, I don't usually do theatre.' Georgia's deep, breathy voice sounded like it had just crawled out of

100

bed after a heavy night. 'But when Nick asked me to come up here as a favour to him, I simply couldn't refuse. He's such a dear, *close* friend.' Annie felt Caz's 'I told you so' look burning into the side of her head. 'Anyway, it looks as if the poor darling needs all the help he can get. I mean, this lot are hardly the cream of the acting world, are they? Present company excepted, of course,' she added insincerely.

Annie bristled. 'What do you mean?'

'Darling, just look around you.' Georgia's slanted green eyes were full of contempt. 'Poor Henry's hardly ever off the booze these days. And old Edwin's just working his ticket until they find him a place in the Old Actors' Home. And as for Brendan O'Brien –' she leaned forward confidingly '– the rumour is he had to get out of London sharpish. Owed a lot of money to the wrong kind of people, if you know what I mean.'

Annie frowned. No doubt she'd be dishing the dirt to Suzy about her later on.

'What about the blond guy?' Caz did her best to sound casual.

'Him? Oh, that's Dan. Daniel Oliver. He's playing Benedick. You must know him, darling. He's being tipped as the next Ralph Fiennes. Or at least he was, until –'

'Until what? What?'

'Poor Dan.' Georgia sighed. 'He turned down an offer from Hollywood because his wife didn't want to go. But he'd no sooner torn up his contract than she ran off with someone else. A car mechanic from Bushey Heath, can you believe it?'

'God, how awful,' Annie murmured.

'Well, quite. I mean, she could have been sipping martinis in the Beverly Hills Hotel by now, if she'd played her cards right.' Georgia missed the point entirely. 'Dan's devastated, as you can imagine. But I think he's more upset at losing his kids than the Hollywood deal.'

Annie gazed across the room, feeling instant sympathy for him. He was smiling as he chatted to Brendan, but she could see in his eyes the shell-shocked look of a fellow survivor.

Caz gulped back the rest of her wine. 'I'll just get another drink,' she said.

'I'll come with –' Annie started to say, but Caz interrupted her.

'No, I'll get them. You stay and talk to Georgia.'

They watched her drift across the room towards Daniel. 'She'll be lucky,' Georgia commented. 'The poor darling's still hopelessly smitten with his wife.' She turned to Annie. 'Perhaps you should talk to him? I mean, you'll know what he's going through, won't you?' She tilted her head. 'How are you coping, by the way?'

'Fine.'

'So brave of you to try and rebuild your life like this,' Georgia went on. 'It can't be easy for you. Especially with Max and Suzy practically on your doorstep –'

Annie's gaze sharpened. 'What are you talking about?'

'Didn't you know, darling? This film they're making. Apparently they're on location somewhere around here. Well, I suppose they'd have to, it being a Brontë classic. They couldn't very well film it in Torquay, could they?'

But Annie wasn't listening. 'Where?' she demanded.

'Sorry, darling?'

'Where are they filming it?'

Georgia shrugged. 'God knows. Suzy did tell me. Out on some ghastly moors, I think. Why? Are you thinking of paying them a visit?'

At that moment Nick arrived. Annie's head was still reeling so much she barely noticed how Georgia snuggled up to him. Across the room, Caz had accidentally on purpose spilt her drink over Daniel and was helping him wipe down his jeans with rather more enthusiasm than was decent. The whole world seemed to be paired off, except her.

'Excuse me,' she mumbled.

Out in the square, the rain seeped through her sweater as she huddled at the huge stone feet of old Josiah.

Max was here and she didn't know whether to be appalled or excited at the prospect. Part of her didn't want him near her. Why couldn't he be safely in London, far out of temptation's reach? She'd done what everyone wanted her to do, she'd sent herself into exile, made a stab at rebuilding her life. It wasn't fair of him to end up here, where she could bump into him at any time.

But part of her felt it must be A Sign. She'd done her best to get away from him, yet Fate had thrown him in her path again. There must be a reason why it had happened.

Rain dripped off her nose as she looked across the square. It was early evening, the discount shops were putting up their shutters and people were emerging from their offices to begin the weary trek home. As they struggled with their umbrellas and bags, none of them bothered to glance at the other side of the square, to the building that stood empty and forlorn, its face shrouded in a veil of scaffolding and tarpaulin.

This was the Phoenix: the theatre that was to be her home for the next six weeks.

'Not much to look at, is it?' She'd been so deep in thought she hadn't heard Nick approaching.

'I'm sure it'll be very nice when it's finished,' she said.

'I don't know about that. I doubt if it'll ever win any prizes for architectural beauty. But as they say, it's what's inside that counts.' He handed her an umbrella. 'I thought you might need this.'

She smiled up at him, wet curls sticking to her neck and dripping down her face. 'It's a bit late now, but thanks anyway.'

Nick nodded back at the theatre. 'Of course, you're not really seeing it at its best. You should see it when the sun's shining. It looks so —' He searched for the word.

'Radiant?' Annie suggested.

'Dull.'

She laughed. Then Nick said, 'What was Georgia saying to you?'

'Sorry?'

'I know she must have said something for you to rush out like that. What was it?'

'It doesn't matter.'

Nick frowned. 'You mustn't take any notice of her. You know what she's like.'

Annie hoped he might go back inside and leave her alone, but he didn't. He sat down next to her. For a long time they sat in silence, staring at the theatre. 'So what changed your mind?' he asked suddenly.

'What do you mean?'

'This job. You never told me why you decided to come.' He glanced at her. 'I take it the reconciliation with Max didn't work out?'

'You could say that.' She thought of telling him about the baby, but the words wouldn't come.

'But now you're not so sure you did the right thing, running away?'

She blinked at him. 'What makes you say that?'

'It's been written all over your face ever since you got here. You look like you've just been handed a life sentence.'

Annie twisted the umbrella in her hands. 'I'm sorry. I didn't mean to seem ungrateful. You were good enough to give me the job –'

'I didn't do it out of the kindness of my heart. I did it because we need you. I need you.' His eyes met hers, honest and direct. 'But I'll understand if you want to go back to London. It won't do either of us any good if your heart's not in this.'

Annie looked up at the theatre. The tattered tarpaulin flapped in the breeze like the sails of a battle-scarred galleon. 'I don't want to leave,' she said.

'Really? But I thought –'

'I've changed my mind. I want to stay.'

'I see. Can I ask why?'

'I just feel it's something I need to do.' No need to tell him about Max being here. She doubted if he'd understand.

He looked at her for a long time. 'Well, I can't promise you won't regret it,' he said finally. 'It'll be hard work. And even then there's no guarantee we'll sell a single ticket –'

'Keep talking and I might change my mind!' she joked.

Nick wiped the rain off his face. 'Tell you what, why don't we go out for a drink tonight?'

'I've already told you I'm staying. You don't have to bribe me with alcohol.'

'Call it a celebration. I'll meet you in the pub at eight, shall I?'

'If you like.'

They watched the throng of early-evening commuters

dispersing across the square. 'I'm glad you're here,' Nick said.

Annie thought about Max, somewhere out on those wind-swept Yorkshire moors. 'So am I,' she said.

Chapter 14

Annie sprinted through the rain to where her ancient Beetle was parked on its own behind the shops, surrounded by a gaggle of adolescents in ski hats and shiny track suits. They eyed her as she flung herself at the door. Then one of them muttered something and they all started laughing.

She edged her way in behind the wheel, stung by their unspoken criticism. She knew what they were thinking. There was no point in stealing the tyres when they were balder than Duncan Goodhew. And anything they could do to the rusting paintwork could only be an improvement.

She turned the key in the ignition, aware that the gang was watching her with interest. 'Please start,' she whispered. 'Please, please start!' Beryl the Beetle cleared her throat, spluttered a little, then died. Gritting her teeth, Annie tried again. This time the car gave an irritable whine. Gingerly she began to lift her foot off the clutch. Everything died.

The youths were sniggering now. Annie wound down the window. 'Haven't you got any phone boxes to smash up?' she yelled. But this convulsed them even more.

'Oh, bog off!' She wiped her face with her sleeve.

'I hope you're not talking to me?' Caz stared through the gap in the window, her dark hair plastered to her face. 'You could have waited,' she accused.

'Sorry.' Annie reached over and yanked at the stubborn lock on the passenger side.

Caz dived in. 'You left a bit sharpish. Why didn't you wait for me?'

'I didn't know if you'd be coming. You and Daniel seemed to be getting on so well –'

'No such luck,' Caz grumbled. 'And why have you got that window open? It's freezing in here.'

Annie wound up the window laboriously. 'The car won't start.'

'What a pile of junk!' Caz snorted. 'When are you going to sell it for scrap and get yourself a nice new one?'

Annie took a deep breath and turned the key in the ignition. This time it coughed into life.

Caz settled back into her seat with a satisfied smile. 'See?' she said. 'You've just got to show it who's boss.'

'I think it already knows.' Annie noticed the youths hanging around on the corner and veered deliberately through a puddle towards them, sending an arc of muddy spray over their white trainers.

'So why were you in such a hurry tonight?' Caz gave her a sly look.

'Sorry?'

'Don't worry, I won't let on.' Caz pulled off her boot and examined the soaked purple suede. 'I just happened to hear him telling Georgia, that's all.'

'What are you talking about?' Annie crunched the gears.

'Come on, don't go all coy. You're seeing Nick tonight, aren't you?'

'Oh, that.'

'You're a quick worker. You've only been here five minutes and you're already dating the boss. Georgia was furious.'

'It's not like that.' Annie peered through the blurred windscreen. The rain was more than a match for her creaking wipers.

'Of course not.' Caz looked knowing. 'Still,' she sighed, 'at least you've got a date tonight. I was that far from getting Daniel to ask me out, until that old drunk Henry Adams butted his big red nose in. Half an hour of flirting and where's it got me? Nowhere!'

'Give him time,' Annie said. 'His wife's just left him, remember?'

'But that was months ago,' Caz protested. 'Anyway, how can he still be pining for her, after the way she's treated him?'

'How indeed?' Annie sighed. No one could have treated her worse than Max, yet she still pined for him. 'He's probably still in shock. I know how he feels.'

'But it hasn't taken you very long to find someone else, has it?'

'I told you, Nick and I are just friends, that's all.' She glimpsed a flash of movement through the streaming windscreen and jammed on the brakes just as a juggernaut rumbled out in front of her.

'If you say so.' There was a pause. 'You don't think he's gay, do you?'

'Who? Nick?'

'No! That man's testosterone on legs.' Caz shook her head. 'I mean Daniel.'

'Caz, he's got two kids.'

'That doesn't mean anything these days. And there's got to be a reason why his wife left him.'

'Maybe she just fell out of love.'

'That's what he says,' Caz muttered darkly. 'But is he telling the truth? I mean, he's hardly likely to admit she walked out because she caught him in bed with a minicab driver called Frank, is he?'

Annie laughed. 'And this is all because he didn't ask you out?'

'Well, can you think of another reason?'

'Maybe you're just not his type?'

Caz swung round, shocked. 'Don't be ridiculous!'

It must be wonderful to have such unshakeable self-esteem, Annie decided.

'So where's he taking you?' Caz asked.

'Who?'

'Nick. Romantic dinner *à deux*, is it?'

'I told you, we're just –'

'Friends. Yes, I know.' Caz raised her eyes heavenwards. 'I reckon he fancies you.'

'He doesn't,' Annie said firmly. 'And even if he did, I don't fancy him. Okay?'

Caz shot her a shrewd look, but said no more.

Number 19 Bermuda Gardens stood out from all the other neat little post-war semis in the street. It might have been the rose-coloured stone cladding, the Elizabethan lattice windows or the row of mock crenellations along the roof edge, but whatever it was, it sat among its sober neighbours like a drag queen at a WI meeting.

Annie turned into the drive, carefully negotiating her way through the minefield of Grecian urns, stone cherubs and ornamental wheelbarrows overflowing with petunias. A regiment of gnomes glared up at her from their sentry duty around the miniature wishing well. Apparently it played 'Three Coins in the Fountain' when you dropped money into it, so Caz had informed her gleefully.

It was like no theatrical digs Annie had ever known. But then, Jeannie Acaster was like no other landlady she'd ever known, either.

There were no house rules. In fact, Mrs Acaster positively encouraged lewd behaviour after lights out. She seemed disappointed that they'd been there for two days and neither had yet brought home a single decent-looking young actor.

She didn't seem to mind when they used the kitchen, mainly because she seldom ventured in there herself, except to get some ice for her gin and tonic. 'I don't cook and I don't clean up after people,' she told them bluntly. 'I had enough of that when my miserable old sod of a husband was alive.'

In fact, living chez Acaster might have been perfect, except for one thing.

Trixie.

As they got out of the car Caz eyed the front door nervously. 'Do we have to go in?'

'It'll be fine,' Annie reassured her. 'As long as we stick together and remember not to slam the –'

But it was too late. Caz let the car door go with a resounding bang. The next moment there was a volley of frantic yapping and the thud of something flinging itself repeatedly against the other side of the door inside the house.

They hesitated on the step. 'You go first,' Annie pleaded.

'And let that thing rip my new trousers to shreds? No thanks.'

'Then there's only one thing for it.' They looked at each other then, as one, they both made a dash for the back door.

They almost made it. As they got into the kitchen there was a low-flying blur of blonde fluff and pink ribbon, and Trixie launched herself at their ankles.

As a dog, she was a pathetic specimen. Shave off her great bouffant of peroxide fur – which Annie had been sorely tempted to do – and she would be the size of a malnourished hamster. But whether it was her size or the ludicrous ribbon she was forced to wear, something had given Trixie the need to prove to the world she was more than just a powder-puff on legs. Like a canine kamikaze, she would take on anything that moved. Which at that moment was Annie's boot.

'That dog's got a serious attitude problem,' Caz said.

'She'll have a serious dental problem if she even thinks of biting me.'

'Is that you, girls?' Jeannie Acaster called from up the hall.

They went into the living-room, Trixie still snarling around Annie's ankles. The room was decorated in Soho massage parlour chic, with lurid pink satin, scarlet velvet and gold tassles everywhere. In the middle of it all, reclining on her chaise longue watching the Home Shopping Channel, was Jeannie Acaster.

'What do you think of that pendant?' She nodded towards the screen.

'Very nice.'

'Do you think so? Not too flashy?'

Annie glanced at Jeannie's well-upholstered, pink-satin-clad body. Despite it being only six o'clock she was already in full glamour make-up, her bleached hair piled up on top of her head. Her ear-rings could have picked up Sky Sport. 'I think you could carry it off,' she said tactfully.

Jeannie looked pleased. 'Did you remember my fags, by the way?'

'I've got them here.' Caz handed them over.

'Good lass. But I hope you didn't get them from the corner shop. I said I'd never go in there since that tight old bastard stopped my tick.' She beamed at Annie. 'Playing with my little Trixie, are you? That's nice. She's got a real soft spot for you, I can tell.'

I've got one for her, too, Annie thought grimly. Out in the back garden, under the ornamental pond.

'So, did you have a nice time, girls?' Jeannie fluttered her false eyelashes at them. 'Meet any nice men?'

'It's funny you should say that –' Caz plonked herself down on the chaise and launched into a blow-by-blow account of Daniel. Annie managed to escape from Trixie and left them gossiping while she went up to run herself a bath.

Like the rest of the house, their bedroom was a psychedelic nightmare. Animal prints on the walls vied with black satin on the beds. Tarzan meets Lily Savage, Caz called it. It appealed to her sense of retro kitsch. But after two days of living there, Annie had begun to crave Laura Ashley.

While she waited for her bath to run, she pulled her case out from under the bed to finish unpacking. Most of it was already done, but there were still a few bits and pieces to sort out.

Like her self-help books. Annie took out a handful and

glanced through the titles. *Loving a Difficult Man. Women Who Love Too Much. Women Who Need Too Much.*

How about *Women Who Read Too Much*, she thought, tossing them on to the bed. They hadn't done her much good so far.

Perhaps she was going about it all the wrong way? Maybe Caz had the right idea. If one relationship breaks down, just move on to the next. No regrets, no looking back. It seemed to work for her. But then Caz changed her men as often as she changed her shampoo brand. It was easier saying goodbye to someone after six weeks than six years.

As if to prove it, there was their wedding photo, staring up at her from the bottom of the suitcase. Annie picked it up and hid it in her bedside drawer, trying not to meet Max's eye. So much for not looking back. There were some things she could never leave behind, no matter what.

She closed the drawer, then changed her mind and opened it again. A photo wasn't enough. Knowing he was so near, she couldn't resist the chance to see him just one more time.

It only took a couple of phone calls on her mobile to find the information she needed. She pressed the off button, feeling pleased with herself.

'What do you think you're playing at?'

She swung round in alarm. 'Do you have to sneak up on people? You nearly gave me a heart attack.'

'You're the one being sneaky.' Caz stood in the doorway. 'Who were you whispering to on the phone?'

'I wasn't.'

'You were calling Carrington Productions, weren't you? And don't bother to lie, I heard everything.'

'I don't know what you're talking about.' Annie stalked past her into the bathroom. Caz followed.

'Georgia told me about Max being up here.' She folded her arms across her chest. 'Why, Annie? Why do you want to track him down, after everything he's done to you? For God's sake, haven't you got any pride?'

'You wouldn't understand.'

'You're right, I don't. Bloody hell, he couldn't make it any more obvious that he doesn't care. Why don't you just take the hint?'

'I have. I just – I can't explain it. I just have to see him again, okay?' She tested the bathwater with her hand and turned off the taps.

'You realise this is how stalkers start?' Caz persisted. 'Next thing you know you'll have a restraining order slapped on you.'

'Caz –'

'Can't you see how pathetic you're being? Catch me making a fool of myself over some man.'

'That's rich! You were practically cleaning Daniel's boots with your tongue this afternoon.'

'At least he's available,' Caz pointed out coldly. 'Anyway, what about Nick? You were supposed to be meeting him tonight, or had you forgotten?'

She had forgotten. But she wasn't about to admit that when Caz was in such a disapproving mood. 'I'm not seeing him until later. Anyway, he'll understand.'

'So you're determined to go ahead and make a complete prat of yourself?'

'Caz –'

'Fine. I'll expect the call from the police station in a couple of hours, shall I?' Caz turned on her heel and walked out of the room.

Chapter 15

Caz was right, Annie reflected some time later, as she sat shivering behind the steering wheel looking at the Roebuck Hotel. She was crazy. Why else would she be out here, in the middle of nowhere, trying to catch a glimpse of her husband and his new girlfriend?

It had taken her a while to find the place. Several times she had to pull off the narrow country lane to consult the directions the woman at Carrington Productions had given her. And the further she strayed from Middlethorpe, the more her doubts grew. It would be dark in an hour or so, and the rain was coming down more heavily. Beryl the Beetle's lights had never been her most reliable feature. Suppose she ended up stranded out here in the middle of the moors? It all looked pretty bleak.

Then, just when she was beginning to wonder if she should give up and turn back, she found it. An old country inn, nestling in the valley.

Annie pulled her car off the road behind some trees where she could get a good view of the pub and waited. The Roebuck looked warm and welcoming, its lights twinkling invitingly. She crouched behind the wheel, the sound of the rain drumming on the roof, punctuated by the half-hearted squeak of the windscreen wipers.

Now what, she wondered as she sat there, her fingers cramped from gripping the steering wheel. The compulsion that had brought her all the way out here seemed to be ebbing away, leaving her feeling cold and rather foolish.

She was just about to start the engine when the location bus rumbled into the car-park. Annie sank down behind the wheel, pulling up the collar of her jacket. She watched the crew tumbling off the bus, squinting through the rain-blurred windscreen to make out the shapes. And then she saw him.

She knew straight away it was Max. Annie pressed her face closer to the window, straining to catch another glimpse of him. As she did, he turned around suddenly.

She dived down in her seat again, bashing her head against the steering wheel. But she was trembling so much from the adrenalin pumping round her body that she hardly noticed.

What if he saw the car? What if he suddenly appeared at the window and demanded to know what she was doing? What if –

Slowly she edged her way back up to risk another peek. He was still standing there. Then she realised with a shock that he hadn't recognised her. He was too busy looking at Suzy.

Annie watched as he put out a hand to help her off the bus. The rain was soaking him, but he didn't seem to care as he slipped off his jacket and draped it protectively round her shoulders.

How did Suzy describe it? Like a piece of priceless Dresden? Annie hadn't really believed it until now. It was so different from the Max she'd known. This was not a man who would knowingly take all the hot water or make her sleep on the edge of the bed.

He bent his head and whispered something to her. Suzy laughed and lifted her face to his. There they were, the two of them, looking so – in love.

Annie couldn't bear to watch any more. Her hand shaking, she turned the ignition key. The engine whined, then stalled.

Oh, God, not now. Please not now, she prayed, turning the key again. Silence. She turned it again and again, more frantically each time.

'Need any help?' A man was coming towards her across the car-park. Annie spotted the green Carrington Productions logo on his bomber jacket.

'Start, damn you!' Panic-stricken, she wrenched the key in the ignition. Beryl the Beetle coughed, spluttered and sprang to life.

'Thank God.' Annie lifted her foot off the clutch. Beryl strained forward, but didn't move. She listened to the ominous whizzing sound.

'Looks like your back wheel's stuck,' the man yelled. 'Hang on a sec. I'll get some of the lads to give you a push.'

'No!' But he was already ambling back across the car-park.

Annie leaped from the car. The freezing mud sucked at her boots as she scrambled round to the back. She had to shift Beryl before he came back with the others. He might bring Max! Not that she could imagine him turning out on a rainy night to rescue a damsel in distress, but she couldn't take any chances.

She leaned her full weight against Beryl and heaved

hard. Her feet slipped and skidded in the mud, but she kept on pushing.

She'd heard stories of people who developed super-human strength in times of crisis, but she'd never believed it was possible until, incredibly, Beryl began to inch forward.

The men were coming out of the pub. Annie flung open Beryl's door and dived behind the wheel. Crunching the gears in her panic to get away, she'd reached the lane before they got halfway across the car-park.

Luckily there were no other cars on the road that night as she drove, her foot slammed on the accelerator, taking corners recklessly. She didn't even try to read her map and it was only by sheer fluke that she ended up on the road back to Middlethorpe.

She found herself in the town centre, the rain-washed streets empty and desolate, even though it was still only just after nine o'clock. Annie slumped in her seat, feeling wrung-out. Her clothes and shoes were splattered in mud, and cold had seeped right through to her bones. She would just nip into the pub, buy some ciggies and head for home.

Then it dawned on her. The pub. Nick. Oh hell.

Chapter 16

It was Talent Nite in the Millowners' Arms. A middle-aged man with thatched hair and a spangly waistcoat was sweating his way through 'Copacabana' as Annie peered through the dense, smoky haze, looking for Nick.

Of course he wasn't there. How could she expect him to wait over an hour for her? Especially on Talent Nite. It was more than flesh and blood could stand.

Annie came out of the pub into the wet night, feeling guilty. Poor Nick. She'd completely forgotten about him in her desperation to see Max. Now that craving had subsided she felt deeply ashamed of herself.

She was heading back across the square when she spotted the light in one of the upper windows of the theatre. Someone was moving about up there, a dark shape outlined in the light.

It must be Nick. He had become tired of waiting for her and gone back to the theatre to catch up with some work instead. Annie walked towards the building.

The stage door was open. The street lamps outside cast a dim, eerie light down the narrow corridor, which smelled strongly of wet paint and sawdust. Annie's breath made coils in the air as she picked her way towards the door at the end.

After a lot of tripping and cursing in the dark she found herself on the stage, looking out into the empty auditorium. In front of her the rows of seats, swathed in dust-sheets, made eerie shapes in the gloom. A sense of foreboding crept through her veins.

'Nick?' Her voice sounded like a gunshot in the dense silence. The only other sound was her heart, thudding somewhere below her tonsils.

She groped her way to the front of the stage, her hands moving over crumbling patches of ornate plasterwork. Something brushed past her in the darkness, briefly touching her face.

Annie's shriek of terror echoed around the building. She wasn't easily spooked, but this was just too creepy. And there was a strange smell, too, mingling with the wet paint: dark, aromatic and smoky. Annie lifted her chin, sniffing the icy air. It smelled just like –

'Turkish cigarettes. They were her favourites.'

The voice croaked out of the darkness behind her. Annie swung round and found herself trapped in a beam of torchlight as the stooped figure shuffled out of the shadows. He was the oldest man she'd ever seen, so crooked with age his nose was pointing at the bare boards of the stage.

' 'Course, she'd smoke 'owt if she had to, even my Capstans. But them Sobrani things was always her favourite.' He cocked his head to fix her with rheumy, yellowed eyes. His skin hung in wrinkled folds off his bones. 'I suppose you'll be one of them new lot?'

'I'm Annie Mitchell.' She flinched as he aimed the torchbeam straight into her face. She wondered where

Nick had dug him up. 'Dug up' being the operative phrase.

'Aye, she told me you'd be coming.' He nodded approvingly. 'She likes you. Not everyone can sense her, y'know. Only them she trusts.'

'Really?' Annie took a step backwards. 'That's – er – nice.'

He tweaked at his old cardigan with a shaking hand. 'You'll do well here, you will. You'll come to no harm. Jessie Barron takes care of them she likes. Not like some.'

'Oh – good.' He was obviously rambling. Oh well, better humour him. 'So you look after this place, do you? You and your – er – friend Jessie?'

A cackle wheezed up from his thin chest. 'That's right.' He chuckled. 'Me and Jessie look after things now. Been here all my life, I have. Right from a lad. I was here when the place closed down, thirty years back.'

'Really?' Judging from his musty smell, Annie wondered if he'd been stored away in an old props basket somewhere backstage.

' 'Course, there's some as said the place should never be opened up again. Not after all that's happened.' He fixed her with a beady look. 'Told you about the curse, have they?'

'What curse?'

'Didn't think they would. Wouldn't want you running away, would they?'

'All right, Stan. I'm sure Annie doesn't want to hear any of your fairy stories.' Annie nearly collapsed with relief as the house lights went on and Nick emerged from the wings.

'They ain't fairy stories!' Stan looked indignant. 'It's the truth!'

'Whatever you say.'

'And I'll tell you summat else true an' all. It weren't her that started that fire.' He looked them up and down defiantly.

'So you keep telling me, Stan.' Nick put his hand on the old man's shoulder. Next to him, Stan's frail, stooped body was like a child's. 'Now, I think it's time we locked up for the night, don't you?'

Stan touched his cap. 'Right you are, Mr Ryan, sir.'

As he shuffled off, jangling his keys, Annie turned to Nick. 'Thank God you turned up. He was giving me the creeps.'

Nick smiled at her. 'Take no notice of old Stan. He's barking mad, but harmless.'

'Where did you get him from? A youth opportunities scheme?'

'He found me. He heard word the theatre was reopening and came to see me about a week ago. Apparently he's worked here on the stage door all his life. So I took him on as a caretaker.'

'He doesn't look as if he can take care of himself, let alone this place,' Annie said doubtfully.

'I know, but I couldn't just send him away. And it's got to be better than mouldering in a day centre, staring at the walls and waiting to die.'

'What about his wife? Is she as decrepit as he is?'

'I've no idea. I didn't even know he had any family.'

'So who's this Jessie character he's been going on about?'

'Ah, you mean Jessie Barron.' Nick's brows lifted.

'That's right. I hope she's not going to leap out of the woodwork as well?'

'I very much doubt it. She's been dead for nearly sixty years.'

'What? But he said —'

'Stan likes to live in the past. Besides, you wouldn't be bothered by a ghost, would you? Most theatres have them.'

'Yes, I know.' Annie shivered. 'But I never imagined I'd be sharing a dressing-room with one.'

'Don't worry, you won't have to. I've been here nearly two weeks and I haven't seen a thing.'

Annie thought of the strange, cloying smell and the thing that had brushed her face in the dark, but said nothing. 'And what about this curse?' she asked. 'Is that a figment of Stan's imagination too?'

Nick's smile disappeared. 'There is no curse,' he said flatly.

For some reason Annie didn't feel reassured. 'But Stan said —'

'Stan's wrong,' Nick cut her off. 'If there's any ill will towards this place, it's from the living, not the dead.' He noticed her dismayed expression. 'Sorry.' He sighed. 'I didn't mean to snap. I've just had a lot on my mind tonight.'

'Problems?'

'Nothing a couple of thousand extra pounds wouldn't sort out.' Nick rubbed his eyes. 'I've just spent the last hour on the phone to the builders. They reckon they've found some new kind of rot under the stage. Apparently the whole thing's got to be ripped out and replaced.'

'Sounds expensive.'

'It will be. I shouldn't think the trustees will be too happy about it when they find out.'

'The trustees?'

'The people who own the lease on this building.' He explained how a group of local business men and women had got together to buy it. 'The council wanted to redevelop it. If the trustees hadn't stepped in when they did, this place might have been a department store by now.' His face was grim. 'I think they're beginning to wonder if they did the right thing.'

Annie noticed the lines of fatigue etched in his face and felt guilty. Poor Nick. He looked as if he could have done with some cheering up tonight.

'I didn't think you were coming.' He seemed to read her thoughts.

'I know – I'm sorry. I – er – got delayed.'

'Nothing serious, I hope?'

'No.' Her brain raced. 'It was Caz's fault. She – er – wanted me to help her.'

'I see.'

'She's going out, you see, and she needed me to help her find something to wear.'

'For an hour? She must have quite an extensive wardrobe.'

'Well, not for a whole hour, obviously.' She could feel herself squirming. 'She wanted me to do her hair too. And her make-up. She was in a terrible state, poor thing.'

'Funny,' Nick said. 'She sounded quite calm when I phoned earlier.' His eyes raked her. 'It's all right, Annie. You can stop lying. I know you've been to see Max.'

Chapter 17

One look at his face and she knew there was no point in denying it. 'Caz told you?'

He nodded. 'I called your house when you didn't turn up. I was worried about you.'

He was worried about her. And all the time she'd been hanging around on the moors, trying to catch a glimpse of a man who didn't give a damn.

Annie looked at his hurt face and felt even more guilty. She'd behaved appallingly. Nick deserved much better than this. 'I'm really sorry,' she said. 'You must be furious.'

'Only with myself.' His voice was bitter. 'I thought you'd come up here because you wanted this job. I might have known he'd be the reason behind it.'

'But I didn't know Max was going to be here.'

'Don't tell me it's just a coincidence? Come on, I'm not that stupid. Why else would you have taken it? You said yourself, it's hardly a great career move.'

'I had no idea Max was here until Georgia told me. I came because I wanted to get away from him.'

'Which is why you took off across the moors looking for him the minute you found out?'

He had a point, she realised. Why should he believe her? Why should he ever trust her again after the way she'd behaved? 'You're right,' she admitted. 'It was completely stupid. I just wanted to see him again.'

'And did you?'

'Oh, yes. I saw him all right. And her.' Tears stung her eyes. 'They looked so – perfect. Like they were meant to be together.'

'Maybe they are.'

'Maybe.' She took a deep, steadying breath. 'But it's not easy to accept, is it? That the person you love most in all the world wants someone else?'

'No,' Nick said softly. 'No, it's not easy at all.' There was a silence. 'So what are you going to do now?' he asked.

'What else can I do? Start doing what everyone's been telling me and get over him, I suppose.'

'Do you think you can?'

'I don't know.' She swallowed the lump in her throat. 'But I don't think I've got much choice, have I?' She looked at him again. Perhaps he really did care about her, she thought. In spite of everything. She made up her mind that if he gave her another chance, she wasn't going to blow it. She was going to buckle down, work hard and show Nick the best Beatrice he'd ever seen. And maybe, in the process, she would forget about her aching heart.

'I am sorry,' she said again.

'I don't like being lied to.'

'It won't happen again, I promise.' She glanced up at him and crossed her fingers surreptitiously. 'I'll understand, though – if you don't want me around.' She bit her lip, waiting.

At last he spoke. 'I don't know about you, but I need that drink,' he said.

Talent Nite was just reaching its riotous conclusion. They stood outside the Millowners' Arms for a moment, listening to the sounds of crashing furniture and smashing glass.

'Let's go back to my place,' Nick suggested. 'You can leave your car here. I'll drive you back to collect it later.'

He lived just outside town, at the end of a long row of old millworkers' cottages clinging to the hillside overlooking Middlethorpe.

'Sorry about the state of the place,' he said, turning the key in the lock. 'I wasn't expecting any visitors.'

Inside, the house was warm and cosy. Lamps cast soft pools of light over the kelim rugs and bookshelves. The living-room was dominated by two huge squashy sofas, strewn with sections of the *Sunday Times*. It was endearingly untidy, welcoming and the kind of place Annie could have stayed in for ever.

She sighed enviously as she took off her muddy boots on the doormat. 'This is certainly better than our digs.'

'Why? What's your place like?'

'The knocking shop from hell!' She grimaced. 'The landlady's okay, but the place looks like Lily Savage has been let loose on it.'

Nick laughed. 'Sounds delightful. Now, shall I open some wine? Or would you prefer a brandy? I've just got the one bottle. Do you think that will be enough?' He dodged the cushion that Annie hurled at him. 'I'll take that as a no, shall I?'

'Just coffee, thank you,' Annie said primly.

While he was clattering about in the kitchen, she took a look around the room. Like her, Nick appeared to be a compulsive collector of clutter. Books, photos, old news-papers – he didn't seem to throw anything away.

'You know, you can tell a lot about a person from his bookshelves,' she commented, browsing through the titles on the spines.

'So what do mine say?'

Annie frowned at the overloaded shelves, buckling under the weight of Pinter and Shaw, with elderly copies of *Beano* and *Private Eye* piled haphazardly on top for good measure. 'Same as mine. Disorganised and on the point of collapse.'

'Sounds about right.'

She moved across to the photos on the dresser, each with a handful of bills and old letters stuffed behind them. Nick's filing system seemed remarkably like hers too. Then one of the photos caught her eye. It was Georgia, draped over a chair, wearing black stockings, a bowler hat and a come-hither smile. 'To darling Nick. Thanks for everything,' was scrawled across her bosom.

And what exactly was *everything*, Annie wondered. 'So how long have you known Georgia?'

'A couple of years. I directed her in *Cabaret*.'

'That must have been interesting.'

'I know she can be a bit difficult at times, but she's pretty talented,' Nick said. 'She just needs careful hand-ling.'

Annie was about to ask how much handling had gone on when she noticed her reflection in the mirror. 'Oh, my God!' she shrieked. 'Why didn't you tell me?'

'About what?' Nick stuck his head round the door. 'Oh, that. You don't look bad.'

'Not bad?' Annie stared at her dirt-streaked face and

wild hair. She looked as if she'd been mud-wrestling – and the mud had won.

'Your clothes are worse,' Nick pointed out mildly.

'Thanks a lot. May I use your bathroom?'

'Upstairs, first on the left. There are some clean clothes in the wardrobe if you want to change.'

After their bathroom at home, which looked liked stock-taking day at the Boots No. 7 counter, Nick's seemed positively minimal. Annie quickly dragged a brush through her curls and washed her face. The towels smelled of Nick – clean, fresh and lemony.

Then she wandered next door to his bedroom to find something to wear. It felt strange to be there, among his clothes, his books, his most personal things, as if she was somehow intruding on his private space. But at the same time she couldn't resist looking around and taking in the details: the simple, iron-framed bed with its navy quilt; the script, covered in scribbled notes, left carelessly on the pillow ready for tomorrow's rehearsal; the old pine chest of drawers, crowded with yet more photos. Annie crept across the room to look. Nick's parents, his brothers – she'd never met them but she couldn't miss the resemblance. A laughing blonde stretched out on a sun lounger. His sister? Couldn't be. His wife? Annie peered closer, curious to see the woman Nick had fallen in love with.

Then she noticed another photo, of her and the rest of the gang, taken the last time they were on the road. Annie grimaced. God, she was so young! And her hair – it certainly wasn't her most flattering angle. There were Rob and Ian and Claire. And there was Nick, standing beside her, his arm round her shoulders, easily the most handsome of them all.

She heard Nick calling from downstairs and dropped

the photo guiltily. It fell with a clatter, skittering all the others.

'Annie? Are you okay up there?'

'I'm fine.' She set them straight hurriedly, worried Nick would appear and find her snooping. 'I – er – won't be a minute.'

When she came downstairs he was pouring the coffee. 'That's an improvement,' he remarked.

'Thanks.' Annie cinched in the thick leather belt that held up his faded Levis. She'd grabbed the first shirt and jeans she could find. It seemed all wrong to be up there, poking around in his wardrobe. 'I'll let you have them back as soon as I've washed them.'

'Whenever.' He pushed a mug towards her. 'White, no sugar. That's how you like it, isn't it?'

'You still remember after all these years? I'm impressed.' She curled up on the sofa and tucked her bare feet under her.

'So how exactly did you end up covered in mud?' Nick asked.

'My car got stuck so I had to push it.' She explained about the minibus and the man, and how desperate she'd been to get away. 'I don't know how I managed to get it out of the mud, but I knew –' She broke off, seeing Nick's face. 'Are you laughing?'

'No.'

'Yes, you are. It wasn't funny. You should try being face down in mud some time and see how you like it.'

'I did once. Don't you remember, that night Rob managed to put the van into a ditch?'

'And you came up with the brilliant idea of levering it out?' Annie started to laugh. 'Serves you right for being such a know-all. I told you we should have called the AA.'

'Yes, you did. And as I recall, you were still telling me when I was pulling myself out of the mud.'

'Not just mud. There were cows in that field, re-member?'

Nick grimaced. 'Don't remind me. I can't think why we decided to leave it all behind and head for the bright lights of Broadway, can you?'

There was an awkward silence. Annie thought about the photo upstairs, of her grinning lopsidedly into the camera, Nick's arm casually round her shoulders. It all seemed such a long time ago. 'So what was it like in America?' she asked.

'Pretty tough, at first. I think I must have gone to every audition in town when I first arrived there.' Nick poured himself more coffee. 'I nearly caught the next plane back to England. But I promised I'd give myself a year to make it, so I decided to stick it out.'

'What happened then?'

'I was so desperate for cash I signed up to teach some acting classes. That's where I met this other guy, Mark Ellis. He was in the same boat as me, so we decided to get together and put on *A Streetcar Named Desire* off-Broad-way.' He sipped his coffee. 'Neither of us really expected much to come of it. We just did it to make the rent, really. But we struck lucky. Someone from the *New York Times* happened to see the show, wrote an incredible review and by the following week we were suddenly the hottest ticket in town.' He stretched out on the rug. 'Funny how things work out, isn't it? It could all have been so different.'

Indeed it could. Annie's hands tightened around her mug. 'So is that where you met your wife? In the theatre?'

'Kind of. She came along to the opening when we transferred to Broadway.'

'So she's not an actress?'

'Elizabeth? God, no.' He laughed. 'Her father would have had a fit. He was furious enough about her marrying me. I think he was hoping for a doctor or a lawyer as a son-in-law, not an impoverished theatrical. Lizzie came from an old Boston family, you see. Her father made it sound as if I was practically marrying into royalty.'

Annie thought of the smiling blonde in the photo. 'Is that what split you up?'

Nick shook his head. 'Things just fizzled out. There were no big bust-ups, or anything like that. We simply agreed to go our separate ways. Elizabeth packed her stuff, moved back in with her parents and a year later married a heart surgeon from Connecticut. Daddy whole-heartedly approves, so I'm told.' His mouth twisted wryly.

'And it doesn't hurt you to see her with someone else?'

'Not really. I think Lizzie only married me to annoy her folks and I was – well, let's just say my heart wasn't in it.' He put down his mug. 'I'm truly glad we both realised our mistake before it was too late. It would have been more difficult if there'd been kids involved.'

Annie felt a shaft of pain. Was that why Max had never wanted a baby? Because he knew he would leave her one day? 'I wonder if things would have been different if we'd had children?' she mused.

'I doubt it. Marriages break up even when there are kids involved. Look at Daniel Oliver. It's just more compli- cated and painful when they do.'

'You're probably right.' She'd never know now, anyway.

'What about you?' Nick asked. 'What made you fall for Max?'

Annie smiled mistily. 'He swept me off my feet.'

'Love at first sight, you mean?'

'Something like that.' Except in her case it had been stomach-melting lust at first sight. And in Max's – well, she didn't know how long it had taken him to notice her.

Nick yawned and stretched out his legs. 'I don't know if I've ever believed in all that stuff.'

'You mean you've never seen someone and realised they were the one?'

'I wish I had. By the time I'm aware of it, they've usually gone off with someone else.' His eyes met hers fleetingly over the rim of his mug.

Annie looked away. 'I just wish I could get over him as quickly as I fell for him.'

'You will,' Nick promised. 'Wait and see. In a few months' time you'll be able to listen to all your CDs without bursting into tears. And in a year or so you'll probably be able to look at your old photos and feel only mildly suicidal.'

'Now there's something to look forward to.' Annie sighed. 'Is that how long it took you to get over your wife?'

His eyes held hers. 'No,' he said. 'That's how long it took me to get over you.'

At first she thought he was joking, then realised with a shock that he wasn't. She knew some kind of response was called for, but what the hell did he expect her to say?

'Don't look so shocked.' Nick grinned. 'Surely you must have known how I felt about you?'

'I – I knew we were friends, but –' Yes, of course she knew. In her heart of hearts she'd always known. Why else would she have felt so terrible about dumping him?

'It's all ancient history now, of course.' Nick seemed to read her thoughts. 'A lot's happened since then. We've

134

both grown up. And it's never a good idea to try and turn back the clock, is it?'

'No.'

'Maybe I shouldn't have said anything.' He watched her carefully. 'I'd hate you to feel awkward about it.'

It was a bit late for that now. Annie experimented with a carefree laugh. It didn't work. 'Me? Awkward? Don't be silly.'

'That's okay, then. More coffee?' Nick picked up the pot. 'I can make some fresh, if you like?'

'God, is that the time?' Annie looked at her watch. 'I really should be going.' She headed over to the door where she'd left her boots.

'But it's only eleven.'

'I know, but we start rehearsals tomorrow, don't forget.' She knew she was gibbering as she found her boots and pulled them on. 'We don't want to be late on the first day.'

'I can't be late. I'm the director.' She could feel Nick watching her with amusement. 'Hang on, I'll fetch my car keys.'

'There's no need –'

'Your car's still in town, remember?' He smiled, his eyes crinkling. 'You can't walk all the way back to Middle-thorpe on your own.'

Oh, I don't know, Annie thought as she followed him reluctantly to the car. After what she'd heard tonight, some fresh air might be just what she needed.

Chapter 18

'I told you he fancied you!'

Caz sat on the end of the bed in her bra and knickers, drying her hair. Even with her head upside down, Annie could see her triumphant expression.

'I don't know what you're grinning about,' she grumbled.

'Oh, come on.' Caz switched off the hairdryer and fluffed up her spiky crop. 'It's not every day some gorgeous man tells you he's in love with you. Admit it, you must feel just a teeny bit flattered?'

'Not really,' Annie lied. 'And anyway, he doesn't feel that way about me any more. He said so.'

'So what are you panicking about?' Caz picked her way across to the wardrobe, threw it open and began hurling things out. 'He doesn't fancy you, you don't fancy him. What's the problem?'

'Don't you see? This makes things very awkward.' Annie dodged sideways to avoid a pair of low-flying pedal pushers. 'How can I face him after this? It's embarrassing.' She hadn't been able to sleep all night thinking about it.

'I know what's wrong with you.' Caz pulled out a flimsy scrap of black fabric and began to shake out the creases. 'You do like him. And you're terrified you might do something about it.'

'Don't talk rubbish,' Annie snapped. 'I'm not ready for a relationship. I'm still coming to terms with being alone –'

'Oh, yes? And which self-help book did you get that out of? *Learning To Love Celibacy*, or *How To Be a Boring Old Fart for the Rest of Your Life?*'

'You're not taking this seriously.'

'You're right, I'm not. Look, all I can see is you're single, he's single, you obviously like each other –'

'As friends,' Annie put in quickly.

'So why don't you forget about your horrible ex-husband and just get on with it?' Caz held up the shirt. 'Bugger, it's still all creased. I'll have to find something else.'

'You're making a lot of effort just for a read-through.' Annie remarked. 'This wouldn't have anything to do with Daniel, would it?'

'Ten out of ten.' Caz retrieved a skimpy-looking T-shirt from one of the assorted piles around the room. 'And you'd better get a move on too. Have you seen the time?'

'I don't know if I can face it. My throat feels a bit sore –'

'Liar. Come on, we'll be late.'

She was right. By the time Caz had finished slapping on her make-up and Beryl had creaked to life, it was already ten o'clock. It was nearly half past when they hurtled into the church hall they'd borrowed as a rehearsal room. Everyone else was already there, sitting in a circle. There was a noisy scraping of chairs as people turned round to look at them. Georgia consulted her watch ostentatiously.

Of course there were only two chairs left. And, of

course, one of them was right next to Nick. There was a moment of comic shuffling as Annie and Caz raced each other to the only other available seat. Caz got there first. Shooting her a mutinous look, Annie retreated to sit between Nick and Fliss, the Deputy Stage Manager she'd met at that fateful audition.

'Nick's been showing us the set,' Fliss explained.

Annie looked at the model box, the miniature mock-up of the stage with its tiny cardboard pillars and plinths. This was the working model that the designer produced for the director's approval, before work started on the real thing.

'The way I see it, there's really two love stories,' Nick was explaining. 'First there's Hero and Claudio. The golden couple. They've fallen in love for the first time and everything's incredibly idealistic and romantic.'

Just like Max and Suzy. Annie remembered the way they'd been together, bathed in the glow of love: a perfect pair.

'And then at the other end of the scale there's Beatrice and Benedick,' Nick went on. 'She's been through it all before, she's been hurt and now she's wary of getting involved again.' Annie looked up sharply. He could have been talking about her. 'Benedick's in the same boat. He's seen his friends lose their heads over women and he's not going to let it happen to him. Yet in spite of it all, there's an attraction between them they can't hide away from.' Their eyes met. 'No matter how much they try to fight it, in the end they know what's going to happen.'

Annie felt her mouth go dry. Then Georgia piped up, breaking the tension. 'I see your point, Nick darling, but I always think of their story as being subordinate to that of Hero and Claudio. I don't feel we should fall into the trap of making too much of it.'

'Not if it keeps you off the stage, anyway.' Adam Gregory, who played Claudio, raised his eyebrows at Annie.

'I agree. Which is why I plan to highlight the differences.' Nick reached down beside his chair and pulled out a portfolio of sketches. 'I got these costume ideas from the designer yesterday. As you can see, I want to emphasise the fact that Hero is young, fresh and idealistic, and Beatrice is –'

'A raddled old hag, by the sound of it.' Annie frowned.

'Representing the darker, more cynical side of love.' Nick grinned at her. Annie felt her stomach do a back flip. 'Do you think you can do that?' he asked.

'After the month I've had? On my head, I should imagine,' she replied.

They began the morning's work with a read-through. As everyone opened their texts, there was an immediate gasp of protest from Georgia. 'But shouldn't we spend some time on our characters first?' she asked. Like Caz, she'd dressed up for the occasion in a scarlet top and skin-tight black capri pants. Her glossy black hair was pinned on top of her head, showing off her bone structure. 'When I did *Cymbeline* at the National we spent a week exploring our inner depths –'

'Or inner shallows, in your case,' Henry Adams snorted through his beard. His eyes were suspiciously bloodshot this morning, Annie noticed.

'I'm sure it would be useful, but we don't have time,' Nick said tactfully. 'We open in less than four weeks.'

'Yes, but –'

'And I've never thought there was much to be gained by talking. Surely you can find out more by doing something than by sitting around discussing it?'

'Hear, hear,' muttered Cecily Taylor, the elderly actress playing Ursula. She had put down her text and was busy knitting.

'You're the director.' Georgia stuck out her lip.

'Thank you.'

'But don't expect me to give of my best. I don't work well under this kind of pressure.'

'I'll bear that in mind,' Nick said levelly. 'Now, if we could just get on with the read-through?'

They all picked up their texts again. Georgia gave a stifled moan. She continued to whimper through Act One, Scene One, between Annie, Henry – who played Beatrice's uncle Leonato – and a messenger, played by Clive Seymour.

Georgia had one line: 'My cousin means Signor Benedick of Padua.' She delivered it, then burst into noisy tears. 'It's no good, I can't do it.' She sobbed. 'I know nothing about my character.'

'Perhaps you should have read the play?' Adam pointed out kindly.

In the end, much to everyone else's disgust, Nick gave in. 'Okay,' he said. 'We'll do some character exercises. Get into pairs, everyone.'

There was another unseemly dash across the room, as Caz and Georgia raced each other to Daniel. Georgia won by a neck and a well-aimed elbow.

Caz retreated sulkily back to the empty seat beside Annie. 'Look at her.' She shot Georgia an evil look. 'If she sits any closer she'll be kissing him!'

'Let's just get on with it, shall we?' Annie had done this exercise a million times. Actors got into pairs and took it in turn to ask questions, which the other had to answer in character. 'What do you want to ask me?'

'I bet I know what she's asking *him*. Bloody harpy!'

Nobody except Georgia seemed to be taking it seriously. As they swopped partners around the room, Annie discussed Adam's pregnant wife's heartburn, the best bet for the two forty-five at Haydock with Brendan O'Brien and cooed over photos of Cecily's new grandchild. And all the time she could feel Nick watching her.

'Right, is everyone happy now?' he asked half an hour later. 'If we could just get on with the read-through?'

They did. They might have been sitting in a circle reading from their scripts, but it didn't take Annie long to forget her troubles and get caught up in the story that was unfolding. She began to feel herself taking on the character of feisty Beatrice. She understood her dilemmas. She had been let down in love and was reluctant to offer her wounded heart again. And there was Benedick – a friend, a soul mate, but a lover?

She glanced across at Nick. His head was bent over his script, following each line. The trouble was, he was extremely fanciable in a dark, rugged kind of way. Caz was right, she could easily go for him. But it was too soon. She should still be mourning her marriage, not looking around for someone new. Beatrice might be falling in love, but she couldn't. In her current state she needed a new man like she needed wider hips.

She was suddenly aware that all eyes were turned in her direction. 'Oh, God, sorry. Is it my line?' Blushing, she thumbed through her script.

'"Is Claudio thine enemy?"' Daniel came to her rescue. 'Line two ninety.'

'Thanks.' Annie didn't dare look up as she scrabbled for her place. What a great start. Her most important scene and she'd day-dreamed her way through it.

'I'm really sorry,' she said to Daniel as they broke for lunch later. 'I hope I didn't put you off too much, missing my cue like that?'

'Don't worry.' Daniel grinned. He had wicked green eyes, Annie noticed. No wonder Caz fancied him. 'We're all going down to the Millowners' for lunch. Are you coming?'

'We'd love to, wouldn't we?' Right on cue, Caz appeared.

'You go on. I'll join you later,' Annie looked across at Nick, who was deep in conversation with Fliss. She knew she should talk to him, maybe apologise for making such a hasty exit last night. After all, it was quite an ego boost to be told that someone had once secretly fancied you. Maybe she should ask him out to lunch? Just as friends, of course . . .

He looked up and smiled as she approached.

She wetted her lips nervously. 'I was just wondering if you'd like to –'

'Ready, Nick darling?' Georgia appeared and threaded her arm possessively through his. 'I thought we'd try that Italian in the High Street? It looks pretty dire but at least there's a chance the food will be edible.'

'Coming.' Nick looked back at Annie. 'Sorry. What was it you wanted?'

'It can wait.' So much for her fears about him fancying her, she thought. Like the man said, it was ancient history now.

Chapter 19

After lunch they began the blocking rehearsal. Fliss had marked out an area with tape to represent the stage, with different coloured markings to show any pillars, steps or props that would appear on the final set. She was sitting next to Nick, making technical notes in The Book.

This was the period in which the actors began to move around, trying to put movement to their speech. For Annie, it was the most exciting time as she looked for outward ways of expressing her character's inner feelings. She felt a familiar tingle, something she hadn't felt in a very long time. She was back where she belonged, doing something she loved. And she was enjoying herself.

But this didn't stop Georgia breaking everyone's concentration and offering unhelpful advice.

'Do you really think Beatrice would be that flirtatious?' she queried, as they stood on the sidelines, watching a scene between Benedick and Claudio. 'I mean, she's a bit of a social embarrassment, isn't she? Over the hill and still not married off.'

'How come you're not playing her, if you know so much about it?' Caz muttered.

'Too young, darling,' Georgia flashed back.

Annie skimmed her lines and tried to ignore their bickering. Then suddenly everything stopped.

'Wow!' Georgia whispered. 'Who's that?'

'No idea. But he's bloody gorgeous, whoever he is.'

Annie looked up and her heart shot like a high-speed lift into her throat. He was just like Max. Tall, fair-haired, in an immaculately tailored grey suit that obviously didn't come from Middlethorpe High Street. His cool gaze searched the room until it found Nick.

'My guess is he's one of the trustees.' Georgia ran the tip of her tongue over her lips. 'Maybe I should go over and introduce myself.'

But Nick beat her to it. Annie watched him talking to the stranger. From the agitated way his hand went through his dark hair she could tell they weren't exchanging pleasantries.

Finally he came over. 'I'm afraid we're going to have to end rehearsals for the day. Something's come up at the theatre.'

'Nothing serious, I hope?' Adam asked.

Annie noticed Nick's shoulders slump. 'So do I.'

There was an end-of-term feeling among the actors at the unexpected holiday.

As usual, on the drive home Caz could only talk about Daniel. 'I feel so sorry for him,' she said. 'Do you know, his wife wouldn't even let him take the kids for a holiday?'

'Maybe she doesn't want them upset.'

'Or maybe she's just being vindictive. She knows how much he adores those girls. She's just doing it to hurt him.' Caz put her feet up on the dashboard. 'And yet he still talks about her as if she's some kind of saint. He really

144

needs to find someone new. A person who'll really appreciate him.'

'Someone like you, you mean?'

'Why not? I'd be perfect for him.' Caz's chin lifted. 'The trouble is, how do I get him to realise it?'

'Perhaps it's just not meant to be.'

'Oh, spare me! I haven't let a man slip through my fingers since Matthew Hargreaves in my fourth year at school. And that was only because his family moved to Australia before I'd had a chance to snog him.' Her eyes flashed with the light of battle. 'No, I'm going to get Daniel if it's the last thing I do.'

'Why don't you just get him drunk and seduce him?' Annie had meant it as a joke, but she should have known better with Caz.

'That's it! That's the answer! Annie, you're a bloody genius.'

'Am I?' Annie looked blank. 'What did I say?'

'We'll have a dinner party.'

I don't remember saying that, she thought.

But Caz was already lost in her own fantasies. 'It's a brilliant idea. We can have soft lights, music, delicious food . . . He won't be able to keep his hands off me!'

'Aren't you forgetting something?'

'What? You mean the drink? Don't worry, we'll have loads.'

'You'll need it,' Annie said grimly. 'You can't cook, remember?'

'Of course I can.' Caz looked scornful. 'I cook all the time. I cooked the other night. My speciality.'

'Caz, this is a proper, grown-up dinner party we're talking about. Somehow I don't think a boil-in-the-bag curry is going to impress anyone.'

Caz looked crestfallen for about three seconds. 'You're right,' she said. 'I don't know how to cook. But you do.'

'Me? Oh, no, count me out.'

'Come on, Annie. What about all those posh dinners you used to cook for Max?'

'That was different. Dinner parties take planning, preparation –'

'You've got a couple of days, haven't you? Blimey, you're only planning a meal, not the D-Day landings.' She settled back in her seat. 'I suppose we'll have to invite quite a few people, just so it doesn't look like a set-up. We've got to be subtle about this.'

Annie glanced at Caz's glittery green nails and flimsy frock, and wondered if she understood the meaning of the word. She gritted her teeth. 'So how many were you thinking of inviting?'

'Oh, I don't know. Maybe eight or nine.'

'What?' Annie jammed on the brakes just in time to avoid skidding into a Volvo's rear end. 'And where were you thinking of holding this – this extravanganza? Will you be hiring a marquee?'

'At home, of course. I'm sure Jeannie will be cool about it.'

As predicted, Jeannie Acaster was extremely cool about it. Especially after Caz had primed her with a packet of Benson and Hedges.

'So you see?' Caz said brightly. 'There's really no problem, is there?'

None at all, Annie thought. Except that she had been saddled with cooking for a dinner party she didn't even want.

But there was worse to come. She was enjoying a

leisurely soak in the bath half an hour later when Caz came in and plonked herself on the furry leopardskin-covered toilet seat. 'I've been thinking,' she said, 'about this dinner party. Maybe entertaining eight people would be a bit ambitious.'

'Hurray.' Annie adjusted the gold dolphin taps with her toe. She'd been having a waking nightmare in which she had been trying to stretch a Lean Cuisine eight ways.

'I think we should stick to a nice round six, don't you? I've made a list.' Caz produced a scrap of paper and a pencil stub.

'Why bother?' Annie sank beneath the bubbles. 'Why not invite the whole bloody company and have done with it? Or ask Jeannie Acaster if she wants to bring a few friends home from Bingo –'

'Do you want to hear this list or not?' Without waiting for an answer, Caz went on, 'I thought we'd invite Daniel, of course, and Adam and his wife –'

'What about Georgia?'

'And watch her trying to get off with Daniel all night? No, thanks.' Caz chewed her pencil end. 'But we do need a spare man, so I thought we'd ask Nick.'

Chapter 20

Thankfully, Nick didn't turn up to rehearsal the following morning so Caz had no time to put her plan into action.

They were greeted by Mel, the Assistant Director. 'Nick's busy so I'll be looking after things for today,' she told them.

'A director too busy to direct his own play? Whatever next?' Henry Adams remarked, not looking up from his text.

'There's no problem, is there?' Adam Gregory asked.

'Nothing serious. Just bit a bit of a crisis at the theatre, that's all.'

'Crisis? What kind of crisis?'

Mel shrugged. 'A burst pipe or something. Nick just needs to be there to sort it out. Now, shall we get started?'

But Annie knew it would take something more drastic than a burst pipe to keep Nick away from rehearsal. So after they finished for the day she made her way to the theatre to see for herself.

And she was right. As soon as she walked in through the stage door she stepped up to her ankles in cold, greasy water. The smell of damp filled the air. This was a small flood the way the Black Death was a nasty bug.

From the other end of the corridor came the sound of blaring pop music. She took off her boots, rolled up the legs of her jeans and followed the noise. There she found a couple of builders propped against the wall, smoking.

'Have you seen Nick?' she shouted over the din.

They looked up, dull-eyed.

'Eh?'

'Nick Ryan? The director?'

'Who?'

'Oh, forget it. I'll look for him myself.'

'I'd put your armbands on first, love.' As she walked away she heard them sniggering like schoolboys.

Someone had laid a makeshift path of boards over the puddles. Annie picked her way cautiously through it, her boots in her hand. The smell of damp and decay filled the air. Water dripped eerily from the ceiling. Every so often an icy drop would catch her and run down the back of her neck.

Then she heard it. Faint but unmistakable, the sound of music coming from upstairs. Scratchy, like an old gramophone. She strained her ears, trying to pick out the tune.

Annie followed the sound. Stumbling in the gloom, she made her way up the narrow staircase.

There it was again. More clearly this time. Annie stopped to listen. She remembered the tune now. From an old film, or was it a musical? *I'll see you again, whenever spring breaks through again.*

As she reached the upstairs landing, the music grew louder. It was coming from behind one of those doors. Annie made her way towards it. 'Nick?' she whispered. But when she opened the door, the music died away.

She fumbled for the light switch. Nothing.

'There's water in the electrics.'

Annie screamed and swung round. Even in the half-light she couldn't mistake the stooped figure in the doorway. 'My God, Stan, do you always creep up on people?' She put a hand to her thudding chest.

'Sorry, Miss. Thought you were intruders snooping around.' She noticed he was armed with a heavy-duty staple gun.

'And what were you going to do? Staple me to the wall until the police arrived?'

He grinned, displaying a sparse array of yellow stumpy teeth. 'Can't be too careful. Been all kinds of goings-on around here lately.'

'Maybe it's Jessie up to her old tricks?'

Stan stiffened defensively. 'Don't try to pin the blame on Jessie. She wouldn't do nowt to hurt this place, no matter what anyone says.' His beady eyes gleamed. 'No, Miss, it ain't the ghosts that bear this place any malice and that's a fact.'

Annie remembered what Nick had said about ill will coming from the living, not the dead. 'What do you mean?'

'It ain't really my place to say, Miss. But I'll tell you this.' He wagged a crooked finger. 'There were a lot of people in Middlethorpe didn't want this theatre to reopen. And there's a lot stands to gain if it doesn't.'

'What kind of people?'

Stan looked around him, then he leaned forward confidingly. 'Ever heard of Bob Stone, Miss?'

'No.'

'Well, I dare say he knows you. Ain't nothing goes on in this place that Bob Stone don't know about.' His eyes darted around. 'He's got eyes and ears everywhere, has Bob.'

Annie backed away from his graveyard breath.

'He was the one wanted to put a stop to this place. He's on the council, see.'

Frankly, she didn't. 'But why would he want to do that? Surely the council would be pleased to see the theatre reopen?'

'Not Bob.' Stan shook his head. 'His old friend Blanchard was after the land. He wanted to tear the old building down and put up some big shop thing here instead.'

'Blanchard? As in that bloke out in the square? The one with the pigeons on his head?' Oh, dear. Looked like old Stan had got stuck in his parallel reality again.

'No, not him. He's been dead donkey's years.' Stan sent her a withering look. 'His great-great-grandson or summat. He wanted hold of this land, and Bob Stone as good as promised it him. Until the trustees snatched it out from under his nose. Bob weren't pleased about it, I can tell you. He tried all ways to put a stop to it.' He clutched at her sleeve, pulling her closer. Annie held her breath and tried not to gag. 'Might still be trying, for all we know.'

'You think Bob Stone might be behind all this?' Annie touched the damp plasterwork.

'I don't think nothing, Miss. It ain't my business to think.' Stan's face was closed. 'All I know is there's a few people round here I wouldn't trust further than I could throw 'em!' He broke into a toothless smile. 'Still, Mr Ryan will sort it all out. I reckon he's got his head screwed on right.'

'Where is Nick? Have you seen him?'

'He was here earlier, Miss. With that Mr Brookfield.'

Annie couldn't help noticing his distaste when he said the name. 'Mr Brookfield?'

'One of them trustees. You must have seen him? Tall, fair-haired fella, very full of himself? Always hanging around here he is, making a bloody nuisance of himself, poking and prying into things that don't concern him.'

'Sounds as if you don't like him.'

'I don't! And he don't like me, neither. He tried to get rid of me, but Mr Ryan wouldn't hear of it. I'll give him old and useless.' He shook with fury. 'Jessie don't like him, either. She told me.'

Here we go again, Annie thought. She began to edge away. 'Will you be all right here on your own, Stan?'

'I'm not on my own, am I?'

Annie smiled nervously. 'I suppose Jessie's with you?'

'No, Miss. But the builders are.'

I suppose I asked for that one, she thought. 'By the way, how did you get your music to work without the electricity?'

'Music, Miss? I ain't been playing no music. But if you mean that racket downstairs –'

'No, this was more old-fashioned. Sort of like a –'

'A gramophone? Playing "I'll See You Again", I suppose?'

'That's right.' A cold trickle ran down her spine. 'Oh, God, don't tell me.'

'It were Jessie's favourite, Miss. She were always playing it in her dressing-room.' He cackled. 'I told you she liked you.'

Annie made her way back downstairs. As she reached the corridor the two builders were still leaning against the wall, still smoking.

She stopped. 'Shouldn't you be doing something?'

'We are. We're having a fag.' The bigger of the two spoke up. 'We're on our break.'

'But you were on your break half an hour ago.'

'That were a different break.' His mate chortled at this startling piece of wit. 'Besides, we can't do nowt till t'blow heaters arrive.'

'You could make a start clearing up this mess.'

'Oh, no, we couldn't do that. That's ancillary work, that is.'

'So?'

'So we're skilled labour. Ancillary work ain't in our contract.'

It was like arguing with a brick wall with learning difficulties. 'Couldn't you do it anyway?' she pleaded. 'Just to help out?'

They looked at each other, deeply affronted. 'Are you asking us to break the terms of our labour agreement? That's harassment, that is. We could down tools over that.'

'You'd have to pick them up first.' Annie was exasperated. No wonder Nick looked so exhausted all the time. Dealing with prima donnas like Georgia must seem like a breeze after tiptoeing round these sensitive egos.

'Besides,' he went on, 'we're on –'

'Your break. Yes, I know.' She gritted her teeth. 'You call this a break? I've known shorter retirements.'

'She's right.' Annie swung round. The man who'd interrupted yesterday's rehearsal was standing behind her. His fair hair glinted in the half-light, his immaculate suit out of place amid the chaos.

The workmen straightened their shoulders, instantly humble. 'But we were told –'

'Never mind what you were told.' He cut through their protests with impressive authority. 'I want this mess cleared up before you go home, or you won't have a job in the morning.'

Grumbling, the men threw their cigarette stubs into the nearest puddle with a sizzle.

Annie smiled at him. 'How did you do that?'

'Years of practice.' The man held out his hand. 'I'm James Brookfield.'

'Annie Mitchell.'

'Ah, yes. Our Beatrice.' Was it her imagination, or did he hold her hand a fraction longer than necessary? 'So what brings you here?'

'I was just curious. And I was looking for Nick.'

'I'm afraid you've missed him. He went home half an hour ago. Won't I do?'

She shook her head. 'I need to see Nick.'

'Lucky Nick.' This time she knew she hadn't imagined the gleam in his blue eyes.

Annie went home, but she was restless and worried. The flood was worse than she'd imagined and she wondered how Nick was taking the set-back. She longed to see him, but she didn't feel she could just turn up on his doorstep.

Then inspiration struck. The clothes she'd borrowed. Surely he wouldn't think it was strange if she returned them?

It took a moment for him to answer the door. He looked slightly flustered to see her. 'Annie! What are you doing here?'

'I brought these back.' She thrust the shirt and jeans through the narrow gap in the door.

'Oh, right. Thanks.'

'I would have left them until tomorrow but if Caz gets hold of them there's no knowing if you'd ever see them again.' She waited to be invited in. 'I've – er – been to see the flood.'

He grimaced. 'Not good, is it?'

'Put it this way, the builders were constructing an ark.'

'At least they were constructing something. All I've seen them do is smoke cigarettes and read the paper.' There was an awkward pause. 'Look, I'd invite you in, but –'

'Red or white, Nick?' Annie's mouth fell open as Georgia appeared behind him, bearing a bottle in each hand.

'Georgia's here.'

'So I see.' And very cosy she looked, too, her hair loose around her catlike face.

Georgia sidled up to the doorway. 'Nick's very kindly helping me with my character,' she said.

'I'm sure he is. Well, I won't keep you. I expect you two have a lot to get on with.'

As she turned to go, Nick called her back. 'Actually, I've been meaning to ask you. Caz phoned and invited me to dinner on Saturday.'

'Oh yes?'

'I forgot to ask her at the time, but is it okay with you if I bring someone?'

You can bring the whole of the Dagenham Girl Pipers if you want, she thought silently. 'Why not? The more the merrier.' Her face muscles ached.

'What's this about a dinner party?' Georgia interrupted. 'Sounds like fun. When is it?'

'Saturday night.' If she'd had any kind of backbone at all, she told herself later, she would have left it at that. But Georgia fixed her expectantly with those cool green eyes and, as usual, she felt herself crumble. 'You're – er – welcome to come, of course.'

'Really? Who else is going to be there?'

Annie felt herself redden as she reeled off the guest list. Why did Georgia always make her feel like a schoolgirl?

'Is that all?' Georgia looked disappointed. 'I'll have to check my diary and get back to you. Okay if I tell you tomorrow?'

Annie nodded, wondering how Georgia had managed to turn it round so she sounded as if she was doing them a favour.

She scurried back to her car, burning with curiosity. Whoever Nick was planning to bring, it certainly wasn't Georgia. So who the hell was it?

Chapter 21

Annie stood at the sink with a potato peeler in her hand and murder in her heart. So much for Caz's dinner party. For the past two hours she had chopped onions, julienned carrots – and most of her finger-nails – and ribboned courgettes. All Caz had done was languish in the bath humming Spice Girls songs.

She listened in a fury to the sounds of splashing coming from upstairs. The guests would be arriving in half an hour. She was red-faced and sweating, her hair had frizzled in the steamy heat of the kitchen and she had potato dirt ingrained in her cuticles. She hadn't prepared the starters. And she was still smarting from the conversation they'd had earlier that afternoon.

'What difference does it make who Nick brings?' Caz had asked as she watched her chopping the onions. 'Unless you're jealous?'

'Don't be stupid!' Annie cursed in frustration as the knife slipped. 'I told you, I'm not interested in Nick. I love Max.'

'Really? Then how come you haven't mentioned his name for days?'

'What do you mean?'

'When we first got here, all you ever talked about was Max. Now it's Nick. What does that mean, do you suppose?'

Annie opened her mouth to protest, then closed it again. 'I'm not even going to have this conversation.'

'Suit yourself. Anyway who cares who Nick brings, as long as it's not Georgia bloody Graham. I don't think I could stand seeing her across the dinner table all night.' She shuddered.

Annie looked anxious. 'Actually, I've been meaning to talk to you about that . . .' She began to explain what had happened.

Caz listened in unnerving silence. 'Oh, God, you didn't!' she whispered. 'Please tell me you didn't invite her.'

'I had no choice —'

'You could have said no! I bloody well would have.' Caz paced the kitchen furiously. 'She'll be all over Daniel. I won't stand a chance. And now that Nick's bringing someone, it means we're two spare men down. I'm going to have to do some phoning around.'

'But you're meant to be helping me.'

'I can't now, can I?' Caz shot her an accusing look. 'You do realise this dinner party's going to be a disaster, thanks to you?' She'd grabbed her address book, disappeared upstairs and hadn't been seen since.

Annie plunged her hands into the sinkful of muddy water, searching around for more potatoes. They were supposed to be grated and shaped into rosti, but she was buggered if she was going to do it. Life was too short and so was her temper.

She dried her hands, lit a ciggie and puffed mutinously.

She had a good mind to go down to the pub and leave Caz to stuff her own mushrooms.

And as for all that nonsense about Max – how could Caz even think she was getting over him? Okay, so she hadn't mentioned him for a while, but that didn't mean he wasn't on her mind constantly. Or at least when she wasn't rehearsing, or learning her lines. Or thinking about Nick . . .

She inhaled deeply. She was just curious about him, that was all. All right, if truth be told, she did fancy him a bit. But not enough to do anything about it. And besides, whatever Nick had once felt for her, it was obviously over and forgotten now. He seemed to have women swarming round him like flies these days. And he wasn't exactly fighting them off, either.

Jeannie came down in a cloud of cerise chiffon as Annie was making a start on the garlic-stuffed mushrooms. 'Right lovie, I'm off to Bingo,' she announced, looking suspiciously overdressed for a night out at the local Mecca. 'I've locked Trixie in the bedroom so she won't make a nuisance of herself.' She watched Annie struggling with the gooey breadcrumbs. 'What's that you're doing?'

'I'm stuffing these mushrooms.'

'And what's the point of that, then?'

What indeed, Annie thought, blowing a damp curl out of her eyes.

'Smells nice, anyway.' Jeannie sniffed appreciatively. 'What is it you're having?'

'Roast lamb with a rosemary and sun-dried-tomato stuffing.' She hadn't dared open the oven to check it yet, but the herby aroma filling the kitchen seemed hopeful.

Jeannie's nose wrinkled. 'I don't hold with all this fancy foreign stuff myself. They do say the way to a man's heart is through his stomach, but personally I've always found the other way's a lot more fun.' She roared with laughter. 'Take a tip from me, love. Put on a nice low-cut top and he won't even notice what he's eating.'

Jeannie left and Annie lit up another cigarette to calm her temper. It was Saturday night and she should have been curled up in front of the TV watching *Blind Date*, not feeding the five thousand.

Caz swanned into the room just as she was finishing the last mushroom. 'How do I look?' she asked, doing a quick twirl.

'Wonderful.' Annie didn't look up.

'You don't think it's a bit too much?'

Annie glanced up. 'Bloody hell!' she breathed.

Even by Caz's eccentric standards it was over the top. The black lycra catsuit clung like a second skin, finished off by vampish thigh-length boots with lethal spiked heels. All she needed was a whip and a studded dog collar, and she could have had her own exposé in the *News of the World*.

'I don't know how I'm going to wee in it, but who cares?' Caz shrugged. 'By the way, shouldn't you be getting ready? They'll be here in ten minutes.'

'Ten minutes!' Annie dropped the mushroom. 'Oh, my God, I've barely got enough time for a bath –'

'You've barely got enough water, either.' Caz looked sheepish. 'I used it all. Sorry.'

'Thanks a lot.' Annie's grip tightened on the palette knife. She thought about beating Caz around the head with it, but that would only waste more time.

Shouting instructions about taking the carrots off the heat, she rushed upstairs to get ready. She had a lightning bath and washed her hair in four inches of tepid water, rinsing it under the cold tap.

She was still in her tatty dressing-gown drying her hair when she heard the tinny sound of 'Que Sera Sera' on the doorbell, closely followed by Trixie's frenzied yapping as she hurled herself at Jeannie's bedroom door.

'Don't worry, I'll get it.' Caz's heels clattered up the hall, followed moments later by the sound of voices. Annie strained to listen. There were Adam and his wife Becky, Brendan O'Brien – was he really Caz's idea of a spare man? – and Daniel.

She could hear everyone in the sitting-room, getting stuck into the wine. The soulful voice of Lauryn Hill drifted up the stairs, mingling with the sound of laughter and the strangely acrid smell of –

'The carrots!'

Still in her dressing-gown, Annie flung herself downstairs. But she was too late. The carrots had not only boiled dry, they'd welded themselves to the blackened bottom of the pan. Cursing Caz, she thrust it under the cold tap, where it sent up a huge hiss and a cloud of evil-smelling steam.

Just then the doorbell rang. 'Door!' she yelled, but everyone ignored her. 'Can someone get the door?' The sound of laughter in the sitting-room grew louder.

'Bloody hell, do I have to do everything around here?' Still clutching the pan, Annie stomped to open it.

'God, I hope that's not our dinner?' Georgia's arched brows rose in mild disgust. She swept into the hall and threw off her white cashmere pashmina to reveal a strappy cream dress that showed off acres of tan. She looked Annie up and down. 'I didn't know it was a come as you are, darling.'

But Annie barely noticed her cutting comment. She was too busy watching Nick and his mystery guest getting out of their car. It couldn't be. Surely not . . .

'I know. Amazing, isn't it?' Georgia followed her gaze. 'Close your mouth, sweetie. You'll catch flies.'

But Annie's jaw seemed glued to the doorstep as she watched Nick and his companion coming up the path.

Chapter 22

'Thanks ever so much for inviting me.' Fliss's grey eyes shone behind her owlish specs.

'Any time.' Annie's mind raced. Nick and *Fliss*? It didn't make sense. She was much too young for him for a start. What on earth did he see in her?

'I hope we're not too early?' Nick said.

'No, it's fine. We're just –' She looked down in horror at her tatty towelling dressing-gown and realised what he meant. 'Oh, hell! Excuse me.' She dashed upstairs, blitzed her wardrobe and finally decided on a flowing black skirt and white lace top. She slapped on some make-up and raced back to join the party.

They were all in the living-room, getting stuck into the wine. Adam and Becky, who was heavily pregnant, were squashed together on the chaise longue. Daniel was in the armchair, with Caz draped over the arm. So much for subtlety, Annie thought. Brendan and Georgia were having hysterics over the musical mini bar in the corner. Brendan kept topping up his whisky just to hear it play 'Begin the Beguine'.

And there, on the red velvet sofa, were Nick and Fliss. She was fiddling with her mousy hair, her drab beige sweater and trousers a bizarre contrast to Caz's outrageous bondage queen outfit. Annie couldn't take her eyes off them. It was too unbelievable to be true.

'More drink, anyone?' she asked and everyone started talking at once.

'Could I have a mineral water?' Becky patted her bump. 'Sorry to be boring. I'll pretend it's a gin and tonic.'

'Could I have a mineral water as well?' Fliss asked.

'Don't tell me you're pregnant too?' Georgia smiled slyly. 'Or are you just boring?'

Annie noticed Fliss's embarrassed flush and felt a twinge of pity for her. Then she saw Nick's arm go round her shoulders and her sympathy vanished.

'Fliss is driving me home,' he explained.

Annie was uncorking the wine when Caz came into the kitchen. 'So, what do you think about Nick's mystery girl-friend? I would never have believed it, would you?'

'Why not?' Annie's voice was tight. 'Fliss is a nice girl –'

'I know, but she's hardly his type, is she?' Caz giggled. 'I feel a bit sorry for her, actually. Georgia's taking the piss out of her endlessly, but she's either too nice or too dim to realise it.'

'And what about Nick?' Annie couldn't stop herself asking.

'He's spitting, but he daren't show it because he doesn't want to embarrass Fliss.' Caz helped herself to a handful of peanuts. 'You should go in and have a look. It's hilarious.'

'No, thanks. I hate blood sports.' Annie glugged some wine into her glass and downed it so quickly it made her head spin.

'Careful with that! You'll be plastered before we start eating.'

'Good.' She refilled her glass defiantly. 'Anyway, what

are you watching me for? Shouldn't you be keeping your eye on Dan? Georgia could have him pinned to the sofa by now.'

'Oh, God, you're right!' Caz grabbed a handful of drinks and dashed off.

Annie found the oven gloves and took the leg of lamb out of the oven. At least something was going right. Now all she had to do was put the mushrooms under the grill, finish off the vegetables and she could enjoy the rest of the evening.

Who was she kidding? When it came to enjoyment, this dinner party was right up there with having a wisdom tooth out.

As she refilled her glass, she sensed someone come into the kitchen behind her. 'Yes, I am having another drink,' she said loudly, thinking it was Caz. 'And no, I don't care if I am under the table by the time the starters arrive.'

'Sounds like fun.'

Annie swung round. Standing in the doorway, holding a bottle of Pinot Noir, was James Brookfield. 'I rang the bell, but no one answered.' He handed her the bottle. 'Seems as if I've got a bit of catching up to do.'

They stood there, appraising each other. He reminded her of Max, with his flopping blond hair and lazy, sexy smile that lit up his deep-blue eyes. It was a smile that made her want to rush upstairs and check her make-up.

'Sorry about the greeting,' she said. 'Things are getting a bit frazzled, as you can see.'

'Really? You look perfectly in control to me.'

'Yeah, right.'

'You do. Serene, in fact.'

'The others are in the sitting-room if you want to join them.' Her mouth was dry suddenly.

'Couldn't I just stay here with you?' Annie realised with a shock that he really was flirting with her this time.

Caz appeared in the doorway. 'When are we going to eat? Brendan's already half cut, and –' She caught sight of James. 'Oh, hi. I'm Caz Wilde. We spoke on the phone.'

'Of course.'

'Sorry the invite was at such short notice. I hope you didn't mind me ringing you out of the blue?'

'Not at all. I'm delighted you asked me.' James gave Annie a look that made her toes curl.

'Just go through and introduce yourself. I'll be with you in a minute.' As he disappeared off into the hall, Caz turned to Annie. 'What do you think?' she said gleefully. 'Did I come up trumps with a spare man or what?'

'He seems – very nice.'

'Nice? He's gorgeous. And he's rich, too. He's a lawyer. They earn pots of money, don't they?' She grinned. 'I tell you, Georgia owes me one for this.'

'Sorry?'

'For fixing her up with James. He's just her type, isn't he? And it'll help keep her sticky paws off Dan.' She stuffed a handful of peanuts into her mouth. 'Now tell me I'm a genius.'

Annie sighed. 'You're a genius,' she agreed wearily.

To her embarrassment, Annie found herself seated next to James, with Georgia on his other side. She picked at her stuffed mushrooms. Why did everyone always seem to be paired off but her, she wondered, not for the first time. Caz had attached herself to Dan. Adam and Becky were feeding each other. And there, across the table, were Nick and Fliss. He was whispering something to her, making her laugh. She was staring up at him with those doe eyes, hanging on to his every word.

'Look at them. Love's young dream,' Brendan whispered beside her.

'Hardly.' Annie took a vicious stab at a mushroom.

'I suppose that just leaves you and me.' He sighed. 'I don't suppose you fancy a quick snog, do you?'

'Brendan!'

'Well, it sometimes works.' He looked injured.

She tried not to laugh. 'You amaze me.'

'Mind you, it helps that they're usually half cut when I ask them.' He reached for the bottle and topped up her glass. 'So there's not much point in me wasting my second chat-up line on you, then?'

'Ask me again when this bottle's empty.' She took a sip of her wine. Brendan cracked a few jokes and for the first time that evening she began to feel more cheerful. So what if Nick and Fliss were a couple? So what if the dinner party had about as much atmosphere as the surface of Mars? She could still have a laugh, even if it was only at Georgia's heavy-handed flirting with James.

'I'm just slipping upstairs to freshen up.' Georgia glided out of her seat, making sure James got a good look down her cleavage as she did so. 'See you in a moment.' With a final meaningful flash of her green eyes she was gone.

Annie watched her leave. 'I think you're meant to follow her,' she pointed out.

'Why? I don't want to freshen up. Besides, I'd rather stay here with you. I've been longing to talk to you all evening.'

Of course, Annie thought. That's why you've been staring at Georgia's cleavage. She wondered how she could have fancied him, however fleetingly. The guy's charm could cause a North Sea oil slick.

'So what do you think of our little theatre?' he asked.

'I'm looking forward to working there.'

'And you're not worried about the curse? I thought you actors were meant to be such a superstitious bunch.'

His comment was like an electric cattle prod, startling the others to attention.

'Curse? What curse?' Caz looked panic-stricken.

'Oh, fock, I knew it,' Brendan groaned. 'No wonder the bloody nags have been letting me down.'

Annie looked round at their shocked faces. James was right. Actors were notoriously superstitious. She knew some who would refuse to go on if they heard whistling backstage.

'Of course, it's probably nonsense,' James went on. 'But the locals reckon the place is built on the same spot they used to burn witches back in the seventeenth century. They believe the site's been cursed ever since.'

A heavy silence followed his words.

'Rubbish,' Nick said flatly.

'A lot of people believe it.'

'A lot of people believe they've been abducted by aliens, but that doesn't make it true.'

Annie looked from one to the other. There was no love lost between them, that was for sure.

'So how do you explain the strange things that have been going on lately?' James asked. 'That flood, the rot under the stage, the problems with the builders – it's got to be more than a coincidence, hasn't it?'

'I agree. But you know as well I do it's got nothing to do with the supernatural.'

James broke the tense silence. 'More wine anyone?' He picked up the bottle and everyone started talking again.

'I don't think your boss likes me,' he whispered to Annie.

'What did he mean, "you know as well as I do"?'

'No idea. Maybe he thinks there's someone out to get us.'

'You mean like Councillor Bob Stone?'

James's smile dropped. 'What do you know about him?'

Not as much as you, obviously, she thought, noticing how pale he'd gone. 'Just something I'd heard,' she said. 'Do you think he's got anything to do with all the things that have been going wrong at the theatre?'

'If I did, I wouldn't go around telling other people. Not if I wanted to keep my kneecaps.'

Annie laughed. 'Come on, he can't be that bad.'

'No?' James looked troubled. 'Let's just say I've had a few dealings with Councillor Stone in the past. I know what he's capable of.'

Annie was about to ask more. But before she could say anything, Georgia came back. 'I don't know if this is important,' she said, 'but there's some kind of rodenty thing eating your joint.'

'What?' Annie shot out of her chair, sending it clattering backwards.

'I was on my way back from the bathroom when I heard this yapping, so I just opened the door and this horrid little thing shot past me.' Georgia looked at the faces around the table. 'Don't look at me like that. It's not my fault. Anyway, I've probably saved you from a social faux-pas. No one eats red meat these days.'

'Oh, my God! Trixie!' Annie ran into the kitchen, but

it was too late. Trixie was gone and so was most of the lamb. All that remained was a mangled bone.

'I'm going to kill you.' Fired up with fury, she grabbed a skewer off the draining board. 'Come out, you little —'

'What are you planning to do with that?' Nick stood in the doorway, his arms folded.

'Kebab that bloody dog, when I find it.'

Nick touched her shoulder. 'Have a drink,' he advised. 'You'll see things differently.'

She didn't. Half a glass of Cabernet Sauvignon later, she could still see a thoroughly chewed leg of lamb on a plate in front of her. If anything, it looked even worse.

She bit her lip. 'I wonder if I could disguise it with some kind of sauce —'

'Annie, a witness protection scheme couldn't disguise that.'

Tears spilled down her cheeks. She rubbed them away with her fists. 'What am I going to do?' she wailed.

'Can I help?' Fliss's earnest face appeared around the door. Then she saw the lamb remains. 'Oops!'

Annie glared. 'If that's all you can say —'

'Thanks, Fliss, but I think the situation's beyond help.' Nick cut her off.

Fliss inspected the joint. 'Couldn't you cook something else?'

'Of course. Why didn't I think of that? I'll just whip up a quick Beef Wellington, shall I?'

'I think that might take a bit too long.' The dart of sarcasm seemed to go over Fliss's head. 'Why don't we see what else we've got?' Annie watched as she delved in the fridge. 'There are a couple of big bags of prawns, and some — oh, well, that's it really.' Her face brightened. 'Prawns it will have to be, then.'

'Terrific.' Annie felt even more gloomy. 'So it's prawn sandwiches all round?'

'I think we can do better than that.' Fliss rolled up her sleeves. 'Now, I'm going to need a few extra things. I don't suppose there's a late-night grocer anywhere?'

'Only Patel's, on the corner.'

'That'll do. Nick, if I give you a list, can you go down there and fetch a couple of bits and pieces? Just some extra vegetables and some spices and things. They shouldn't be too hard to find.'

'No problem,' Nick said.

'Tell you what.' Annie refilled her glass. 'Why don't you pick up a couple of loaves and fishes while you're down there? Because I reckon we're going to need a bloody miracle.'

It was like watching an alchemist turning lead into gold. Fliss moved around the kitchen, grinding pepper here, adding a touch of spice there and filling the air with delicious aromas. Within what seemed like minutes she had produced a dish of fragrant stir-fried prawns, served with rice and spiced vegetables.

'I hope it's okay,' she said modestly. 'By the way, I don't know if you've noticed but your dog has just thrown up behind the dresser.'

By the time dinner was served, everyone had heard the sorry tale. Fliss almost received a standing ovation when she brought her culinary masterpiece to the table.

Annie sat among the rapturous congratulations, feeling depressed. She knew she should be grateful to her for saving the day and she was, but she couldn't help feeling a little resentful. Why was it everything she did seemed to go so terribly wrong?

'I'm sure your meal would have been wonderful,' James whispered.

'I doubt it. Even the wretched dog couldn't keep it down.'

'Maybe your talents lie elsewhere?'

She flinched as his hand came to rest on her knee. Carefully she shifted her leg away. 'So how did you become a trustee?' she asked. 'Are you interested in the theatre?'

'To be honest, I don't know my Aristophanes from my elbow.' James grinned. 'I only took on the job because my firm handled the lease transfer.'

'And is that how you met Bob Stone?'

'You're very interested in him, aren't you?' His smile didn't quite reach his eyes. 'If you must know, Councillor Stone and I had some disagreements over the terms of the lease.'

'You mean he didn't want us to have it?'

'Let's just say he didn't make it easy.' He moved closer. 'Look, do we have to talk about the theatre? I'd much rather talk about you.'

Annie felt the warm, firm pressure of his hand on her leg again. She started to move away, then thought better of it. James obviously knew more about the notorious Mr Stone than he was letting on. And if flirting with him was the only way to find out, it was worth a try.

Trouble was, after all these years she'd forgotten how.

'So, are you married?' James asked.

Annie felt herself sobering up at the question. 'Not so you'd notice.'

'Annie's husband ran off with her best friend,' Georgia chimed in. 'She's broken-hearted, aren't you, darling?'

'Really? I'll have to do something about that.' James

picked a prawn off his plate and offered it to her. 'Broken hearts are my speciality.'

Mending them or causing them, Annie wondered.

'So what exactly does a trustee do?' Georgia fluttered her eyelashes. 'Do you have a lot of power? I've never been able to resist a powerful man.'

As Annie reached for the bottle, she caught Nick staring at her across the table, his eyes like flint. Why was he in such a bad mood, she wondered. He wasn't presiding over the worst dinner party since the Last Supper.

'I suppose you could call it power, in a way. The ten of us jointly own the lease on the building. It's our job to make sure the theatre opens on schedule and within budget. Neither of which looks likely at the moment, I have to say.' He glanced at Nick.

'It'll be fine,' Caz said. 'Everything always looks like chaos until we get to the first night.'

'*If* we get there.' James's words hung in the air for a moment, then everyone started talking at once.

'Are you saying there's a chance we won't?' Brendan asked.

'I certainly hope we will. But to be honest, things are beginning to look doubtful.' James shrugged apologetically. 'We're way behind schedule and the building costs are rocketing. There comes a point where you start to wonder if you might be better off cutting your losses –'

'Can we talk about this later?' A muscle moved in Nick's jaw.

'But they can't pull the plug.' Adam looked worried. 'I turned down a sitcom to come up here.'

'The Phoenix will open.' Nick looked around the table, his steady gaze taking them all in one by one. 'Your jobs are safe. You can count on it.'

'I don't know if you can make those kind of promises,' James said. 'I've been looking at the figures. The trustees –'

'I'll talk to them.'

'Look, I know you think you're invincible, but even you can't magic money out of thin air.'

'I said I'll talk to them.' Nick's eyes were dark and forbidding.

Annie stood up quickly, rattling plates to distract him. 'Let's have pudding, shall we?'

Alone in the kitchen, she dumped the plates in the sink, forgetting to scrape them clean first. She ran the taps full blast, watching as a few remaining prawns bobbed one by one to the surface.

Wearily, she took the chocolate roulade out of the fridge and was searching around in the drawer for a suitable cutting implement when she felt a pair of hands cupping her bottom.

'That looks good.' James's breath was warm against her ear.

'Thanks.' She felt the hardness of his hips grinding into her back. 'I – er – take it you haven't come to help with the washing up?'

'Hardly!' James's arms twined around her, pulling her into him. 'You don't know how much I've wanted to touch you all night.'

'Look, James –' She turned around to disentangle herself and, instead, found herself locked in his arms, her back pressing against the work top. She felt her hips sink into something unpleasantly squidgy. 'Oh, no – the roulade!'

'Fuck the roulade,' James groaned. A second later, his mouth was on hers.

As Annie finally struggled up for air, she realised Nick was standing in the doorway watching them.

Chapter 23

'Am I interrupting something?' he asked coldly.

Annie pushed James away and smoothed down her skirt guiltily.

James, meanwhile, seemed unruffled. 'Yes, as a matter of fact.' He straightened his tie.

Nick looked as if he wanted to punch him. 'I need to talk to Annie.'

'Can't it wait?'

'No.'

James gave in with a shrug. 'Fine, I'll leave you to it, then.' Annie winced as he planted a kiss on the top of her head. 'See you later, sweetheart,' he said and sauntered off.

As the door closed, Annie let out a sigh of relief. 'Thank God you came in.' She picked up a cloth and started dabbing cream off her skirt. 'It was like wrestling with an octopus.'

'What did you expect?'

She stopped dabbing and looked up. 'What's that supposed to mean?'

'Oh, come on! You've been flirting with the guy all night. You didn't think he was going to end the evening with a handshake, did you?'

'I wasn't flirting with him.' Annie's face grew hot with indignation. 'If you must know, we were talking about the theatre –'

'How intellectual. Was that before or after he put his hand on your leg?' Nick's mouth curled. 'What are you playing at, Annie? One minute you're moaning you'll never love anyone again, the next you've got your tongue down someone's throat.'

'I was fighting him off!'

'Not too hard, I noticed. Didn't take you long to get over Max, did it?'

That hurt. Any ideas she'd had of telling him what she'd discovered about Bob Stone and the theatre disappeared instantly in a rush of white-hot anger. 'Don't you get all self-righteous with me! I'm not the one with the bloody harem.'

Nick's eyes narrowed. 'What?'

'You and all your women. First I come round and there's Georgia looking very cosy at your place. The next minute you're turning up here with Fliss Burrows.'

'You don't know what you're talking about.'

'Oh, so it's okay for you to lecture me about my love life, but yours is out of bounds, is that it?'

'If you must know, I invited Fliss because it was her birthday and she had no one to spend it with. And as for Georgia,' he went on, as Annie opened her mouth to interrupt, 'I told you she came round to work and that's all it was. Work.'

She ignored the flutter of relief in the pit of her stomach. 'I couldn't care less what you get up to in your private life.' She turned away and stared at the squashed remains of the roulade. 'Just stay out of my life and I'll stay out of yours, okay?'

'My pleasure,' Nick growled. He stalked out, slamming the door after him.

Annie continued to stare at the roulade, too rigid with fury to move. How dare he condemn her, especially when she was only trying to help. Did he really think she'd seriously be interested in someone like James Brookfield? And he hadn't even had the good grace to listen to what she had to say. She picked up a ladle and slammed it on the work top. Well, sod him! In future he could sort out his own problems.

She was still seething when she got back to the dining-room. She banged what was left of the roulade down on the table, making the cutlery tremble.

'Don't ask!' She shot a furious look around the table. 'I sat in it, okay?' No one said a word. Even Georgia could only manage a faint smirk.

'Not hungry?' James whispered, as she pushed her pudding around her plate ten minutes later.

'I've lost my appetite.'

'Been giving you a hard time, has he? Take no notice of him.' Annie felt his hand on her knee and jerked her leg away. She didn't feel like playing that game any more.

'Oops, it must have been serious.' James grinned. 'Don't tell me, he told you I was a big bad wolf and you were to keep away from me?'

'Something like that.'

'He's probably right.' James sent her a challenging look. 'Still, it's a pity. I was going to ask you to come out to dinner with me.'

Annie glanced at Nick from under her lashes. He was still watching them, his mouth a narrow line of disapproval. How dare he try to dictate what she did with her life?

She lifted her chin and met his gaze with defiance. 'I'd love to,' she said.

Two hours later, Annie was already regretting it.

'I don't know what you're moaning about.' Caz sat at the dressing-table, creaming off her make-up before bed. 'He's gorgeous. And he's loaded. I never thought he'd be interested in you.'

'Thanks a lot.'

'You know what I mean.' Caz was in a good mood because Dan had finally asked her out.

'But I haven't been on a date since Duran Duran were in the charts,' Annie wailed. 'How will I know what to do?'

'Just do what you used to do, I suppose.'

'I used to go to the Odeon and pretend to be old enough to get into an X film.' Somehow she couldn't imagine James being too impressed by that idea.

She didn't even want to go out with him. Now her defiance had worn off, she could see what a mistake she'd made.

'You'll be fine,' Caz reassured her. 'Just make sure you've sussed out the four Ss, that's all.'

'The what?'

'The four Ss. Don't tell me you haven't heard of them? Single, Straight, Solvent and Sexually Compatible?'

Annie stared at her. 'You mean he might not be?'

'You can't be too careful,' Caz said wisely. 'I mean, he could have a girlfriend locked away somewhere – or even a boyfriend. And you don't want to end up in the bedroom and find out he's got some kind of weird fetish.'

'We won't get that far.'

'You never know.' Caz waggled her brows. 'Still, at least you can be sure he's solvent.'

'As if that matters.'

'There speaks someone who's never been on a date to the local Burger King.' Caz smiled pityingly. 'I can see you've got a lot to learn.'

But I don't want to learn, Annie thought. I don't want to be single and out there picking my way through the dating minefield. I want to be happily attached and never have to worry about whether men are married or commitment phobic or fetishistically addicted to vinyl handbags. 'I want to be married,' she wailed.

'Don't we all?' Caz sighed. 'But let's see if you can get through the first date, shall we?'

But before that she had to get through Monday's blocking rehearsal. And it wasn't going to be easy. Nick was in a foul mood. He sat at one end of the hall, his script bunched in his fist, watching them from under lowered brows.

The atmosphere was leaden. Aware of his black mood, the actors tiptoed around, giving each other wary looks and following Nick's suggestions, which were beginning to sound more like orders.

The mutterings began when he finally called a lunch break. 'About bloody time,' Brendan moaned. 'I've already missed the one thirty at Sedgefield.'

'Why don't you complain to the boss?' Adam suggested.

'And get my ear chewed off? No focking thanks!'

'I can't understand what's got into him. He's always been so courteous and professional,' Henry grumbled.

Annie was just glad to escape. Perhaps it was paranoia, but Nick seemed to be picking on her more than anyone else. She couldn't say a line without him pouncing on this inflection or that, making her repeat the scene over and over again, changing his mind until she neither knew nor cared which was the right way. Then he'd snapped at her for not knowing her lines, even though everyone knew actors seldom let go of their scripts until much later in rehearsal.

Henry was right. Nick was usually so calm and in control. He listened to everyone's ideas and made them feel as if they were really contributing something. But not today. Even Fliss looked near to tears as he shouted at her yet again.

'Bugger this,' Caz whispered. 'Let's go shopping.'

'Do you think we should?' Annie had planned to spend her lunch break going over her lines, determined Nick shouldn't find fault with her again.

'Look, we're not called again until three. And I'm not going to sit around here waiting for him to start bellowing at me again.'

'You're right.' Annie agreed. She had the feeling she could have been word perfect and Nick would still have picked on her.

Middlethorpe wasn't exactly the fashion capital of the north. There were precisely two clothes shop in the whole town, if you included the one that sold nothing but crimplene trouser-suits for the fuller figure. But it still took Caz ages to make up her mind what to buy. They crossed the precinct again and again while she dithered between the red leather miniskirt or the leopardskin sling-backs.

'Just buy them both!' Annie glanced at her watch. 'Come on, it's ten to three. We don't want to be late back, do we?'

Everyone looked up as they stumbled through the door twelve minutes later. The only one smiling was Georgia.

In the middle of them all sat Nick, his fingers steepled together in front of his face. His expression was blank. He seemed to be gathering all his strength to speak. 'Where the fuck have you been?' His voice was filled with icy menace.

'We're only two minutes late.' Caz protested.

'Not you – her.' He pointed at Annie. 'You were called at two thirty.'

'No, I wasn't. It was three o'clock.'

'Two thirty. It's there on your call sheet, if you'd cared to look.'

'But –' Annie was about to get out her call sheet and show him, then she saw Fliss's stricken face and it all became clear. The poor girl had given her the wrong time. Now she was trembling, waiting for her terrible mistake to be exposed. 'You're right,' Annie said. 'I should have checked. I'm sorry.'

'Sorry!' Nick's jaw tightened. 'That's all you can say, is it? So it's okay to keep the rest of us waiting here for half an hour, just because you can't be bothered to read your bloody call sheet properly.'

Annie looked at Fliss again. Her eyes were swimming with tears.

'But I suppose the normal rules of courtesy don't apply to you, do they?' Nick stood up and walked towards her, measuring out the distance between them with his long strides. 'Perhaps it doesn't matter to you that the rest of us have been standing around like idiots for the past half-hour, waiting for you to grace us with your presence?'

His words bit deep. She was transported back to the third form, being carpeted by a sadistic form mistress over her lost maths homework. She felt a dull flush of embarrassment creep up her face, aware of everyone's pity.

Fliss stepped forward. 'Nick —'

He didn't even flicker. 'Well?' he snapped.

'I said I'm sorry.' Annie stared at a crack in the floorboards.

'Look, it's no big deal.' Adam tried to lighten the atmosphere. 'Everyone's late once in a while —' Nick swung round, making him flinch. He was a big man, but even he cowered under the director's steely gaze.

'I'll decide if it's a big deal. And this isn't just about being late. It's about attitude.' He turned back to Annie. 'I think yours leaves a lot to be desired. I realise you think it's all a bit beneath you, but the rest of us are working bloody hard to make a success of this place. And I'd appreciate it if you showed a little more commitment.'

As he turned away, Annie found herself retaliating. 'I'm working just as hard as everyone else.'

'Are you? It seems to me if you spent as much time worrying about your work as you do about your love life, we might start to see some results.'

Annie gasped. 'That's not fair.'

'No, you're right. It isn't. It isn't fair on me and it isn't fair on anyone else. I think we've all made more than enough allowances for your fragile emotional state. From now on, I want one hundred per cent commitment. If you're not prepared to give me that then you might as well leave now.'

A shocked silence followed his words. Even Georgia stood rigid.

Annie took a deep breath to stop herself trembling. 'Fine,' she said. 'I will.' With the weight of everyone's gaze on her she picked up her bag and walked out.

Chapter 24

Annie yelped as she jabbed the mascara wand in her eye for the third time. She rubbed at the black streaks on her cheek, then gave up and tossed the brush down in frustration. It was no good. After the day she'd had, her brain just wasn't up to putting on make-up.

How could he have fired her! Never mind that she'd chosen to walk out. He hadn't given her much choice. And he certainly hadn't tried to talk her out of it. She'd spent most of the afternoon seething by the phone, willing him to ring so she could tell him exactly what she thought of him. But he hadn't.

Instead, she'd had to wait for Caz to come home. 'What a bastard!' she'd declared, throwing off her leather jacket. 'He had no right to talk to you like that. You did the right thing, walking out.'

'What happened after I left?'

'Well, Nick couldn't believe it. He went a bit quiet and stared at the door like this.' Caz made a face like a dazed haddock. 'Serves him right, the high-handed sod.' She looked around. 'Where's Jeannie?'

'Having a bath. She's got a big date tonight, apparently.'

'She's not the only one. I hope she doesn't take all the hot water.'

Annie ignored her. 'So what happened then?'

'What? Oh, you mean Nick? Well, he sort of sat there with his head in his hands for a while. Then he started bitching about your lack of professionalism. He said it was a good thing you'd gone and if the rest of us had a problem with the way he'd treated you we were welcome to go too. Of course, no one did.'

'Thanks.'

'Not that we're not all totally behind you, of course. But we need the work.' Caz shrugged apologetically.

'He'll be sorry,' Annie fumed. 'How's he going to cope with no Beatrice?'

Caz blushed. It was a rare sight. 'He's – um – asked Georgia if she'll read it.'

'What?'

'You said yourself, he's got to find someone to do it. And since you're not coming back –'

Who said I'm not coming back, Annie was about to say. Up until now, she'd thought of her walk-out as a kind of token protest, to show Nick she wouldn't be pushed around. Suddenly it occurred to her he might not actually want her back.

'Maybe James could help get your job back?' Caz suggested. 'He's one of the trustees, isn't he? Perhaps he could put in a good word with Nick?'

Yes, and she could imagine what that would do. Nick hated James even more than he hated her. Which was really saying something at the moment.

'I'm not sure I want the stupid job anyway.' She sniffed.

Caz shook her head. 'You and Nick Ryan are as

stubborn as each other. You know, I'm sure he'd love to have you back, if only you'd –'

'Go crawling to him? Forget it. I'm not that desperate.'

'Suit yourself.' Caz stood in front of her wardrobe, tossing clothes on to the floor as she rejected them. 'This needs a wash, this is too boring, he's seen me in this –' She turned away in disgust. 'What are you wearing tonight?'

'You're looking at it.'

'That?' Caz wrinkled her nose.

'What's wrong with it?' Annie glanced down at her ankle-skimming black skirt and little grey twinset.

'Nothing – if you're a librarian. Why don't you dress up a bit?'

'This *is* dressed up.'

Caz plunged her hand into her wardrobe and dragged out a sliver of dark-red satin that looked like a hankie on a coat hanger. 'No, *this* is dressed up.' She pulled it off the hanger and tossed it at Annie. 'Try it on. You'll look sensational.'

'Sensational is right. I'd get arrested wearing this.' It would have looked indecent on a Barbie.

'Go on. Just see what it looks like.'

Ten minutes later Annie stood gawping at her reflection in the full-length mirror. Caz stood beside her, surveying her creation proudly. 'Well? What do you think?'

'It's a bit short, isn't it?' Annie yanked at the hem. The satin fabric slithered through her fingers.

'It's supposed to be. Besides, you've got amazing legs. You should show them off, instead of hiding them under those frumpy skirts.'

'I like to be comfortable.' She took a step closer to the mirror and nearly fell off the spiked heels Caz had bullied her into wearing. 'Can I take these things off now, before I break my neck?'

'No. They go with the dress. Besides, your Doc Martens will look stupid with sheer black tights.' Caz tweaked at a stray curl. 'Perfect.' She sighed. 'You should wear your hair loose more often. You look like a Pre-Raphaelite painting.'

'I feel like a hooker on her night off.' But she had to admit Caz had done wonders with her hair. Set free from its restraining pony-tail, it flowed like a copper river over her bare shoulders. 'Can I put my clothes back on now?' she begged.

'No. You're going out like that and that's final.' Caz grinned. 'James won't be able to keep his hands off you.'

That's what I'm worried about. Annie's amber eyes stared back at her from the mirror. She'd agreed to have dinner with him out of a mixture of spite and curiosity. He obviously knew more about the sinister happenings at the theatre than he was letting on. She had hoped to charm him into telling her more about Bob Stone. But now that the Phoenix was nothing to do with her any more it seemed pointless going on with the charade. Why should she help Nick, when he so obviously didn't give a damn about her?

She'd tried to call James to tell him dinner was off, but he was out of the office all day and no one could get a message to him. Annie sighed. It was too much to hope he'd stand her up.

On the dot of eight, James's sleek silver Mercedes convertible turned the corner into Bermuda Gardens.

'Right on time,' Caz said gleefully, peering through the net curtains. 'He must be keen. Where's he taking you?'

187

'I'm not sure. Some Italian place, I think.'

Caz sighed. 'God, I envy you. We're going to the Millowners' Arms. I might get a packet of cheese and onion crisps if I'm lucky.'

James leaned back in the driver's seat, the slight breeze ruffling his fair hair. He looked like something out of a glossy car ad, in his immaculately pressed chinos and white Versace shirt that showed off his tan.

'My God, you look gorgeous.' His eyes devoured her as she got into car. 'What do you say we skip dinner and I'll eat you instead?'

Annie smiled feebly and pulled at her hem. Why had she ever let Caz talk her into wearing this obscene dress? Now she was going to have to spend the whole evening fighting him off.

But perhaps she shouldn't? After all, she was virtually a single woman and he was an attractive man, if a bit too slick and charming for her liking. Perhaps she should just do what everyone had been telling her to do – get on with her life and enjoy herself. But as he leaned across to kiss her, she couldn't help averting her face so he only caught the corner of her mouth.

Luckily he didn't seem to notice, as he started up the engine with a macho burst of revs. 'So how are things at the Phoenix?' he shouted over the roar.

Annie swung round to face him. 'Why? What have you heard?'

'Nothing.' He sent her a sideways look. 'Don't tell me there are more problems?'

'Just a few – artistic differences, that's all.' She certainly wasn't going to ruin her appetite talking about Nick. 'I'm not Mr Ryan's favourite person at the moment.'

'Join the club.' James laughed. 'I'm afraid I'm permanently in his bad books. Especially now.' He glanced at her.

'Why?'

'He's pissed off I'm going out with you.' His mouth twisted. 'Come on, you must know he's got the hots for you?'

'No.'

'It's true. You saw the steam coming out of his ears when he caught us together the other night. He's jealous because I got to you first.' Annie squirmed uncomfortably as his gaze travelled the exposed length of her thighs.

'I gathered you two weren't the best of friends.' She changed the subject quickly.

'You could say that. Nick doesn't understand about money. He doesn't like it that I have to keep hold of the purse strings. He can't seem to realise we aren't a bottomless pit for his artistic whims.' He pulled up at the traffic lights and drummed impatiently on the steering wheel. 'The only reason he hasn't been hauled over the coals before now is that half the trustees are too senile to take in how much money he's spending. And he's got the head of them on his side. Lady Carlton won't hear a word said against him. I reckon the old trout fancies him.' The lights changed and he roared off, casually cutting in front of an elderly couple in a Metro. 'Bloody idiots! Shouldn't be allowed on the road.' He grinned at her frozen expression. 'Why are we talking about Nick, anyway? I want to forget about him tonight.'

'Me too,' Annie replied with feeling.

But after a moment or two she realised they didn't actually have anything else to talk about. 'It's – um – a very nice car,' she commented at last.

James beamed with pride. 'Mercedes CLK coupé. There's a three-year waiting list for these at the Stuttgart factory. But I pulled a few strings and got mine in two months.'

Annie tried to look impressed as he went into great detail about his car-getting coup. It all sounded terribly complicated. She was about to ask why he didn't just go to a dealer and buy a car like everyone else, but something told her that wasn't the point.

Thankfully, they had arrived at the smart Italian restaurant on the outskirts of town. Annie expected the usual trattoria décor, but there wasn't a chianti bottle or a faded poster of Firenze in sight. It was all very white and minimalist with splashy modern art on the walls and black marble tables. From the way the maître d' fluttered up to James, he was obviously a valued customer.

'Very exclusive, this place,' he whispered as they were shown to their table. 'People kill to get a table here. Luckily I've got a few contacts –'

'It looks wonderful,' Annie said quickly before he got started on another story of how many strings he'd pulled.

She glanced around, conscious of the knowing smiles the waiters were giving her. 'Why do they keep staring at me?'

'Because you're the most beautiful woman in the room.' James reached across to stroke her bare arm. 'And they're crazy with jealousy because you're coming home with me.' Annie tried not to flinch as his fingers brushed her breast. God, how embarrassing, she thought. Not to mention presumptuous.

The same thought crossed her mind a few minutes later when the waiter arrived to take their order. Annie was still making up her mind between the lemon sole and the chicken cacciatore, but James insisted on ordering for her.

'They do a marvellous pasta arrabiata here,' he said. 'Take it from me, it's the best thing on the menu.'

Annie controlled her irritation. You're supposed to be enjoying this, she reminded herself firmly. She couldn't help feeling that she would have enjoyed herself far more in the Millowners' Arms with Caz and the others.

But she was there to winkle out information and that was what she was going to do. 'So,' she said, when they'd finished ordering. 'You were going to tell me all about Bob Stone.'

'Was I? I don't remember that.'

'How well do you know him?' she persisted.

'Everyone knows Bob Stone. He's one of our most eminent local councillors, he runs several businesses in the area, his wife's a stalwart of the WI. He's a real pillar of the community.'

'Then why is everyone so afraid of him?'

'Shall we order some wine?' James picked up the wine list. 'Which do you prefer, red or white?'

'Everyone I speak to clams up whenever his name's mentioned. What is he – some kind of gangster?'

'Red's probably best. They do a very good Pinot Noir here –'

'I've also heard he wanted to sell the Phoenix site to his friends the Blanchards for their department store.'

That worked. James's eyes flicked to hers. 'Who told you that?'

'It's true, then? That's why Bob Stone wants the theatre to fail.'

'They're your words, not mine.'

'But you said yourself, all those things going wrong at the theatre aren't an accident.'

James went back to the wine list. Annie looked at him in exasperation. 'You promised you'd tell me.'

'I didn't promise you anything.' James slammed the menu shut, startling her. 'Look, you don't know what you're getting into. The Blanchards have owned most of this town for years. Their reputation is whiter than white. And they like to make sure it stays that way.' His mouth tightened.

'And what about Bob Stone?'

'Bob Stone is a dangerous enemy to have. I should know.'

'Why? What's he ever done to you?'

'So it's a bottle of the Pinot Noir, then.' James lifted his finger to summon the waiter.

Annie waited impatiently until he'd finished ordering. All kinds of thoughts were going through her mind. 'What did he do, James?' she asked. 'Why are you so afraid of him?'

James stared at her, his blue gaze steady. 'If you must know, he threatened to ruin me.'

The waiter arrived, bearing their wine with a Latin flourish. Ignored by both of them, he filled their glasses and retreated.

'Are you saying he tried to blackmail you?' Annie whispered.

'Not at first. When we met initially he couldn't have been more charming. He even offered me money to mess up some paperwork over the lease. It was only when I said no that he turned nasty.'

'So what did he do?'

James leaned across the table and took her hands in his. 'Can you keep a secret?'

'Of course.'

'Promise to tell no one? Not even Nick?' Annie nodded. James took a deep breath. 'He threatened to tell everyone I was – illegitimate.'

For a moment she sat in stunned silence, wondering if she'd heard him properly. 'But that's nothing to be ashamed of, surely?' she said. Where she came from, it was positively trendy.

James looked affronted. 'It may not seem like a lot to you, but in a little place like Middlethorpe it could be enough to finish me,' he said. 'This place is a social time warp. I've spent years building up my reputation, trying to forget who I am and where I came from. This could ruin my professional reputation.'

But everyone knows all lawyers are bastards. Annie bit back the joke. 'Why didn't you go to the police?'

'And tell them everything? What good would it do? Bob Stone's brother-in-law just happens to be the Chief Constable.' He shook his head. 'As it turned out, Stone never went through with his threat.'

'He changed his mind?'

'Or had it changed for him. You see, exposing me would have meant exposing my father too.' James's eyes met hers. 'And my father is Philip Blanchard.'

Chapter 25

He smiled cynically at her stunned expression. 'I know, I had very much the same reaction when I found out.'

'But wha—? How?'

'My mother worked for them when she was a teenager. I suppose she must have caught the boss's eye. When she found out she was pregnant the family closed ranks and tried to force her into an abortion. The Blanchards didn't want a hint of scandal attached to their great name.' He looked bitter. 'She refused, so they offered her a pay-off. A huge sum of money to sign a contract saying she would never make a claim against the Blanchard name, or tell anyone the identity of her baby's father. Not even me.'

'So how did you find out?'

'Well, she told me in the end. She felt she had to. Besides, I was entitled to know.' There was a touch of defiance in his hard blue eyes. 'Everyone has a right to be acknowledged by their own father.'

'And were you?'

'No.' He sipped his wine broodingly. 'Once I'd qualified as a lawyer the first thing I did was to check over that contract my mother had signed. It was watertight. There was no way either of us could make any claim on them. Those bastards robbed me of my birthright.' He caught her looking at him in dismay and his face relaxed. 'So, now you know why I got involved with the Phoenix,' he said. 'As soon as I found out the trustees were trying to stop the Blanchards getting hold of the site I was determined to help them. That's why I got myself voted on to the board. I may not have your friend Nick's artistic vision, but I've got a damn good reason for wanting to see the theatre succeed.'

No one could argue with that, Annie thought. She felt an unexpected surge of pity for him. Under that slick exterior lurked a sad, scared man.

Their food arrived and she stared in horror at her plate. Oh, God. Who in their right mind ordered spaghetti on a first date? Spaghetti was for that stage in your relationship when you'd given up wearing make-up for bed. It was impossible to eat impressively. Either you shovelled it in and risked disgusting your new partner, or you twirled it decorously around your fork all night and slowly starved to death.

Annie opted for twirling. James, she noticed, ploughed through it like a JCB. 'What I don't understand', she said, 'is what Bob Stone has to gain by trying to stop the theatre opening? I mean, the lease is ours now, isn't it? There's nothing anyone can do.'

'Don't you believe it.' James slurped a few stray pasta strands noisily. 'It's not as simple as that. Our friend Mr Stone still has one more trump card up his sleeve. He made sure our lease was conditional. We have to prove the project is viable within a certain time. If we fail, the council has the right to close us down and renegotiate the lease.'

'Sell it to Blanchards, in other words.' She fought the

urge to dab sauce off his chin. 'So how long have they given us?'

'Until this time next year.'

Annie dropped her fork with a clatter. 'A year? But that's ridiculous!' No wonder Nick was so stressed. Annie knew even a potentially successful theatre needed a couple of seasons to settle down before it started making money. Bob Stone had set them an impossible task.

'So you see what he's doing? The more delays and problems we have, the less time we'll have to make a profit. You've got to hand it to him, he's a clever swine.'

'And Nick knows about all this?'

'Of course he does. But he won't let us tell anyone, especially you lot. He keeps saying it's his problem and he'll deal with it. Talk about sticking your head in the sand.' He nodded towards her untouched plate. 'Aren't you going to eat that?'

'I'm not hungry.' Annie pushed it away. Poor Nick. No wonder he was under so much pressure. And now she'd just added to his problems by walking out.

The rest of the meal seemed to drag by. She did her best to keep the conversation going, but her heart wasn't in it. She couldn't stop thinking about Nick and his doomed task at the theatre.

Not that James seemed to notice. He was quite happy to talk about himself, needing only the minimum of nods and vague smiles from her to keep going. It was a relief when the evening ended and they left the restaurant for the warm air outside.

'So,' James said, as they walked back towards his car, 'are you coming back to my place?'

'I'd rather go home, if you don't mind.' She was about

to launch into a complicated litany of excuses, but James cut her off.

'Fine.' He shrugged. 'Your place it is, then.'

He'd taken her refusal well, Annie thought as she sat beside him in the car, the soothing sounds of the Lighthouse Family washing over her. Too well, in fact. She was beginning to wonder whether he'd got the message. She looked at him sideways. She could hardly ask, could she?

'Are you okay?'

She jumped at the question. 'Of course. Any reason why I shouldn't be?'

'No. You've just gone very quiet, that's all.' He reached over and stroked her thigh. Annie edged out of his reach until she was right up against the door.

As they drove through the town square, Annie found herself gazing longingly at the Millowners' Arms. It was a lively night, as usual. Three men were brawling around the fountain, egged on by a couple of women waving handbags.

James sighed. 'And Nick thinks these people need cultural entertainment.'

Annie smiled back. But deep down she was thinking what fun it would be to drop in for last orders.

'I see the Ghost of Theatre Past is still hanging around.' James nodded towards the stage door, where the slight, stooped figure of Stan the Stage Door Man was fumbling shakily with his keys. 'Look at him. How can Nick call him a caretaker?'

'He's harmless.'

'Exactly. We need someone with a bit more muscle. Especially with Bob Stone's heavies hanging around. But as usual Mr Ryan knows best. I told him, you can give the old sod a job, but there's no way we're paying him.'

'You mean Stan works for nothing?'

'He would if I had my way.' James frowned. 'No. Nick pays him directly out of his own wages. Talk about a soft touch!'

Annie felt a twinge. 'What does Stan say about it?'

'He doesn't know. That's what's so pathetic about the whole thing.' 'Nick insists we have to go through this great sham of sending him a payslip like everyone else. He reckons it's something to do with his pride. As if an old crock like that had any.'

'I suppose he'd be better off watching game shows all day at the local OAP centre,' she suggested, remembering what Nick had said to her.

'Absolutely.' James didn't notice the ironic tone in her voice. 'There are enough people on the payroll as it is.'

'There'll be one less after today.' Annie sighed deeply. 'I suppose I'd better tell you, as you'll probably find out anyway. I've resigned.'

James nearly swerved off the road. 'You're joking! Christ, when did that happen?'

'This afternoon.' She explained about their bust-up. 'It was partly my fault. I had no idea Nick was under so much pressure –'

'That's no excuse to take it out on you. Bloody hell, I bet he's panicking now.'

'I feel terrible. The last thing I wanted to do was add to his problems.' Annie knotted her fingers in her lap. 'I suppose I'd better apologise, try to get things straightened out –'

'No way! After the way he's treated you? If anyone apologises, it should be him.'

'Yes, but —'

'I mean it, Annie. Don't you dare go crawling to him. If I were you I'd pack my bags and go straight back to London. You were always too good for this place anyway.'

Annie frowned. James might have the best interests of the theatre at heart, but he couldn't resist having a jibe at Nick.

When they got back to Bermuda Gardens, Annie thanked him quickly and got out of the car. But by the time she reached the front gate he was there ahead of her, opening it for her. 'Don't I even get a coffee?'

'Well, I —' Annie hesitated. 'I suppose so.'

The house was in darkness. Annie cursed silently. She was hoping Caz or Jeannie would be at home. But it seemed that even Trixie wasn't there to protect her. As she slid her key into the lock all she could hear were frustrated yaps coming from upstairs.

'So — coffee, then?'

'I'd rather have you.'

He had pinned her against the wall before she had time to put away her key. Annie disentangled herself firmly. 'I'll put the kettle on,' she said, heading for the kitchen.

By the time she came back with the tray, James was sprawled out on the chaise longue. He'd helped himself to whisky, Annie noticed.

'Be careful, you're driving,' she warned.

'I could always stay the night.'

She forced a smile. 'What about Caz?'

'I don't fancy Caz.'

'We share a bedroom.' She put down the tray and picked up his cup.

'Really? Sounds very cosy.' He caught her wrist as she

put down his coffee, pulling her gently towards him. 'She's not into threesomes, is she?'

Whether it was deliberate or not she wasn't sure, but as their mouths were about to collide, her hand holding the cup jerked downwards, splashing hot coffee everywhere. There was a howl of agony as James danced round the room, clutching his groin.

'Oh, God, I'm sorry!' Annie put her hands to her mouth. 'Here, let me help you −'

'Get off me,' James managed to gasp. 'You've already done enough damage.'

'There's a cloth in the kitchen −'

'I don't need a cloth. I need bloody surgery.' He was doubled up with pain. 'Where's your bathroom?'

'Upstairs on the left.'

Annie listened to him hobbling up the stairs, then quickly reached for the phone.

It took her several minutes to get through to Caz at the Millowners' Arms. Annie crouched behind the sofa, listening to the background of noisy drunkenness at the other end and praying James wouldn't come downstairs.

'Hello?' Caz shouted at last.

Relief flooded through her. Caz would know what to do. 'You've got to help me!'

'Who is this?' Her voice was slurred.

'It's Annie.'

'Annie? Where the bloody hell are you? Listen. I'm having the most pig awful time. You'll never guess −'

'Never mind that. James is here and he wants to sleep with me.'

'But why are you calling me? Sounds as if you're doing all right on your own.' Caz cackled down the phone.

'That's just it, I'm not.' Annie glanced nervously

towards the door. 'He seems to think I want to sleep with him, but I don't. And now I can't—' She broke off, aware that Caz was no longer listening to her. 'Caz? Are you still there?'

'Speak up! It's a bad line.'

'I can't, he might hear me.'

Speaking as slowly as her thudding heart would allow, Annie told her the whole story.

'You're kidding! You mean he's in the bathroom nursing third-degree burns and you're hiding behind the sofa phoning me?' Caz spluttered.

'It's not funny!'

'So what do you expect me to do about it?'

'I don't know.' She chewed her thumbnail. 'Couldn't you come home early and save me?'

'Forget it,' Caz said. 'Georgia's circling Daniel like a shark. I daren't leave them alone. Which reminds me —'

There was silence at the other end of the phone. Annie listened to a few agonising minutes of static before Caroline's voice came crackling down the line again. 'Sorry about that.' She chuckled. 'Brendan's just been telling me the most hilarious joke. There was this Irishman in a bacon factory —'

'Caz!'

'Oh, God. Sorry, I forgot. Now, what did you want to ask me again?'

'What am I going to do about James?' Annie pleaded.

'I don't know.' A burst of music exploded on the other end of the phone. 'Why don't you just sleep with him?'

Annie lowered her voice. 'Look, I don't fancy him. I don't even like him that much. How do I tell him I don't want to sleep with him?'

'How about to his face?' She looked up sharply. There, leaning in the doorway, was James.

Chapter 26

He would have made an amusing picture in shirt-tails and damp underpants, if he hadn't been so furious. 'I've had some disastrous dates in my time, but no one's ever actually rung the Samaritans before.'

Annie slammed down the phone. 'Look, I can explain –' she started to say, but James held up his hand.

'I can work it out for myself, thanks.' He winced painfully. 'I think it's best if I go home, don't you?'

'Are you all right?' She knew instantly it was the wrong thing to say.

'I may need a skin graft, but apart from that –' He moved gingerly towards the door. 'I'll put my trousers on again.'

He was still limping when she saw him to the door. 'I'm sorry,' she apologised for the fiftieth time.

He didn't smile. 'A word of advice. If you want a man to get the message there are easier ways than scalding off his private parts.'

Annie bit her lip. 'One day you'll look back on this and laugh.'

'I doubt it.' James sent her an icy look. 'As a matter of fact I've a good mind to sue you for loss of amenity.'

She went back into the living-room and sank wearily on to the chaise longue. It had been a hell of a day, even by her chaotic standards. And it had started to rain again. Annie closed her eyes and listened to it pattering against the glass. Didn't it ever stop? At least she wouldn't miss the dismal weather when she went back to London.

Back to London. She shuddered at the thought of packing all her things and returning to her empty house. Not to mention telling Julia what had happened. Annie could already imagine what her reaction would be.

Unbelievable as it seemed, she would miss Middle-thorpe. She was just beginning to realise how much the place meant to her. She'd miss Caz and Adam and Daniel, and even Brendan. She'd miss Jeannie and the Millowners' Arms. She'd even miss Trixie trying to take chunks out of her ankle every time she set foot inside the front door.

And she'd miss Nick. Talking to James tonight had made her see him in an entirely new light. She'd never understood how much pressure he was under, with the future of the theatre and everyone who worked there riding on his shoulders. Yet in spite of it, until today he'd always been good to her. He took time to listen to her. He'd shown superhuman patience even when she was droning on about her marriage break-up. He was kind, warm, funny . . .

And now she'd blown it. Annie swallowed hard. The thought of not being there with the others on opening night filled her with misery.

She was just summoning up the energy to go to bed when there was a knock on the door. She looked at the clock. It was nearly eleven. No doubt Caz had stumbled home too drunk to find her key.

But it wasn't Caz.

'Where is he?' Nick stood on the doorstep, rain flattening his dark hair and dripping down his face. He was breathing hard as if he'd been running.

'Who?'

'That sod Brookfield.' He shouldered past her into the hall.

'Halfway home, I should think. Why?'

Nick swung round, his eyes narrowed to black slits. 'Did he touch you?'

'Sorry?'

'Did he force himself on you?' His mouth tightened with suppressed rage. 'If he laid a finger on you I swear I'll kill the bastard.'

Annie stared at him for a moment. Then slowly it dawned on her. 'You were in the pub. When I phoned Caz –'

'She made it sound like you were being date raped, or something.'

Annie sighed. Trust Caz. She could just imagine her broadcasting it to the whole pub. It was a wonder the landlord of the Millowners' Arms hadn't sent a lynch mob over. Thank heavens James had gone, she thought, looking at Nick's angry face. 'It was nothing, really.'

'Are you sure?'

She nodded. 'Just a misunderstanding, that's all.'

They stood in the hall, like strangers caught in the same bus queue.

'Well, I'll be off then.'

'Thanks for coming over.'

He was halfway out of the door when suddenly he turned back, his eyes blazing. 'Look, I can't stand this! I've got to know. Are you going back to London or not?'

She was taken aback. 'Is that – what you want me to do?'

'Of course it bloody well isn't.' He raked his hand through his wet hair. 'Do you think I'd have come all the way over here if it were? Do you really think I'd care?' His shoulders slumped. 'Look, Fliss told me it was her fault you were late today. I know I've said some unforgivable things to you and I'm sorry. I wouldn't blame you if you did decide to go.' His eyes met hers. 'But I want you to stay. I need you here.'

She could hardly breathe for the lump in her throat. 'Do you?' she whispered.

'I don't think I can do this without you.' For a moment they looked at each other. Then he dragged his gaze away, breaking the spell. 'We open in three weeks,' he said gruffly. 'The last thing I need right now is to have to find a new leading lady.'

'Yes, I can see that.' Annie wondered at the plummeting feeling in the pit of her stomach.

'Do you think we could discuss this inside?' Nick turned up his collar against the drenching downpour.

'Oh, God, yes – I'm sorry.' She stood back to let him in. He shrugged off his dripping coat. His wet hair was plastered to his head. 'Come into the kitchen and get warmed up.'

She fetched a towel so that he could dry his hair, then put on the kettle. As she concentrated on spooning coffee into the mugs she tried hard not to notice how the damp fabric of his shirt clung to his broad shoulders and the flat, tapering planes of his stomach.

He idled in the doorway. She could feel him watching her.

'That dress you're wearing –'

'It's Caz's.' She yanked self-consciously at the hem. 'I know. Awful, isn't it? I don't know how she talked me into putting it on.'

'I was going to say it looks great.'

'Thanks.' She could feel herself blushing like a school-girl. 'I – I think it's me that owes you the apology actually,' she stammered. 'You're right, I have been a bit selfish lately. I didn't think of the pressure you might be under.' She glanced over her shoulder at him. 'I know about Bob Stone and the lease.'

Nick's face hardened. 'I suppose James has been whining to you? I told him not to say anything.'

'Why didn't you tell us what was happening?'

'And worry you all even more? You know how much everyone's invested in this place. They're anxious enough as it is, without me making it worse. This is my problem and I'll deal with it. That's what I'm being paid for, after all.'

Annie felt a twinge of sympathy. How could she not have noticed those shadows etched under his eyes, or the grim lines of tension around his mouth?

She knotted her hands in her lap, resisting the sudden, urge to reach out and massage those rigid shoulders. 'So do you think we'll be able to pull it off?'

'I don't know. But I'm damned if I'm going to give up without a fight.'

As they talked about the theatre, the atmosphere between them seemed to thaw.

'Caz told me you'd asked Georgia to read my part.' Annie said.

'Only to shut her up,' Nick groaned. 'I'd already spent two hours listening to her telling me why she should do it.'

'So – um – how was she?'

'Okay, I suppose. But nothing like you. The whole time she was reading I just kept imagining you standing there.'

Annie looked into his crinkly, laughing eyes. Suddenly her mouth went dry and she felt a jolt in the pit of her stomach.

Whatever had just happened to her seemed to hit him at the same moment. His eyes moved from hers to linger on her mouth and back again.

She knew what was going to happen and it filled her with panic. She turned away and focused on the kitchen clock instead. She could feel Nick's stare still fixed on her.

'Annie?' Slowly she turned to face him. They were so close she only had to breathe to touch him –

'Cooee! Anyone home?'

The crashing of the front door was like a bucket of icy water. They sprang apart as the kitchen door flew open. There was Jeannie, her cerise lips smudged and her blonde beehive slightly askew.

'You go on up, Bobby love, I'll be there in a minute,' she called up the stairs. 'Don't start without me, will you?' She gave a shriek of laughter, which nearly toppled her as she collapsed into the room.

'Oops, sorry love, I didn't know you had company.' Jeannie's appraising gaze fell on Nick. 'This is James, is it?'

'Actually, it's Nick.' Annie felt herself going red.

'Two in one night?' Jeannie grinned, oblivious to the sexual tension that crackled around the room. 'Bloody hell, lass, and I thought I was a fast worker.' She peered flirtatiously at Nick from under her false lashes. 'I was just about to have a little drinkie,' she slurred. 'Can I get you something? Gin? Whisky? You look like a Jack Daniels man to me.'

'I'm just leaving.'

'Surely not? Don't go on my account, love. I'll just get those drinks.'

'Sorry about that.' Annie grimaced, as Jeannie tottered off towards the sitting-room.

'She's scary.'

'I think she quite likes you.'

'That's what frightens me.'

'Do you have to go?'

His eyes met hers. 'I think I should.'

Annie followed him into the hall. Suddenly they were back to being polite strangers again.

'So I'll see you tomorrow? At rehearsal?'

'Fine.' She stared at the carpet.

There was a long pause. She could feel his eyes on her. 'Annie?' he said softly.

'Yes?'

He's going to kiss me, she thought. Her heart did a lambada in her chest – and nearly stopped when he planted a light peck on top of her head. 'I'll see you tomorrow.'

And then he was gone. Fighting off an unexpected feeling of frustration and disappointment, Annie watched him striding down the path.

Jeannie was reclining on the chaise longue, one sling-back dangling seductively, when Annie came in alone. Her heavily made-up face fell. 'Oh,' she said. 'Your friend Dick gone, has he?'

'Nick. Yes, he's gone.'

'Pity.' Jeannie sighed. 'He's gorgeous, isn't he? Married?'

'No.'

'Good.' A thought struck her. 'He doesn't – you know, travel on the other bus?'

Annie smiled in spite of herself. 'No.'

'I thought not. I can usually tell.' Jeannie smiled back. 'You want to snap him up, love, before someone else beats you to it.'

I think I'm already too late, Annie thought. Six years too late. 'I'm going to bed.'

'Goodnight, love. Oh, and watch yourself up there, won't you? I've brought a friend home.' Jeannie looked coy.

At least someone's got her love life sorted out, Annie thought, trailing up the stairs.

As she reached the landing the bathroom door suddenly flew open and a stranger appeared. He was short, stocky and wearing nothing but a plastic shower cap jauntily over his private parts. 'Come on, my little Yorkshire pudding! Naughty Bobby's ready for his bed bath.' He lunged at Annie, then stopped and peered at her. 'You're not Jeannie,' he accused.

'No.' Thank God, Annie thought, averting her eyes. This was the second near-naked man she'd seen in as many hours. Poor Caz, and she had to go out for her entertainment.

'Oh, bloody hell! Sorry lass, I can't see a thing without my glasses.'

She watched him hurry into Jeannie's bedroom and slam the door. A second later it opened again and a small, yapping scrap of fur flew out. 'Bugger off, Trixie,' he grunted, as the door closed again.

Annie smiled ruefully. 'Well, Trixie old pal, it looks like we're both alone tonight.'

Chapter 27

A week later the renovations were nearly finished and rehearsals moved to the theatre.

Even on a sunny morning, the building echoing with gossip and laughter, a chill crept through Annie's veins as she stood on the bare stage, looking out over the empty auditorium. The smell of sawdust and paint still hung in the air.

'God, this place gives me the creeps.' Georgia sat on an upturned box at the side of the stage, huddled under several layers of sweaters. 'Is anyone else freezing? I hope there's central heating in the dressing-rooms.'

'I hate to break this to you, but at the moment there aren't even any dressing-rooms.' Caz didn't look up from *The Stage*.

'You're kidding? What are they expecting us to do, then? Get changed in a phone box like Superman or something?'

'Nick says it'll all be sorted out by opening night,' Cecily Taylor said soothingly over the frantic click of her knitting needles.

'Nick? Where the bloody hell is he while all this is

going on?' Georgia grumbled. 'He should have been here half an hour ago.'

'Fliss says he's stuck in a meeting with the set builders.'

Georgia tutted. 'It was never like this at the National.'

Why don't you go back there, then, Annie thought. Everyone was very tense. There were just over two weeks to go until the show opened and Nick was looking more exhausted every day. He spent all his time running from rehearsals to meetings and overseeing the last of the building work. They hadn't been alone together since that night at her place. Annie was beginning to wonder if he was avoiding her.

Someone who wasn't avoiding her, unfortunately, was James Brookfield. He'd taken to appearing at rehearsals, watching over them.

He was hanging around them now as they sat in a circle, warming their hands on their lighted cigarettes. He still moved very cautiously, Annie couldn't help noticing.

'Of course, you know this place is haunted?' he said casually.

'I knew it,' Georgia said. 'My aura's been disturbed all morning.'

'All theatres are haunted.' Cecily didn't look up from her knitting. 'It's a tradition.'

'Ah, but not all of them have a ghost like Jessica Barron.'

'What's so special about Jessica Barron, whoever she is?' Caz asked.

'She hates this theatre and everyone in it.'

'Oh, great. You mean she sits in the audience and heckles?' Brendan said.

'Worse than that.' James's face was sombre. 'If I were

you I'd be very worried. Jessica's been known to do some rather sinister things.'

'So who is she?' Georgia asked. They were waiting for him to tell his story. Only Annie tried to ignore him as she carried on skimming her lines.

'She and her husband Leonard starred in the original Phoenix repertory company, nearly seventy years ago. But Leonard had an eye for the ladies. He had an affair with one of the chorus girls – Sara something, I think her name was. Anyway, she wanted Leonard to leave Jessica and marry her, but he wouldn't. He was worried about what the scandal might do to his career.'

'Typical,' Caz muttered.

'So they decided to kill Jessica,' James went on. 'They reckoned once Leonard was a grieving widower there'd be nothing to stop them marrying. The plan was that Sara would start a fire in Jessie's dressing-room just before the curtain came down. Jessie ended up getting trapped.'

'And that's how she died?'

James shook his head. 'The plan went wrong. The fire swept out of control through the building and several other people were killed. Sara managed to escape and so did Leonard. But instead of saving himself, he had a fit of remorse and went back for Jessica. He died saving her.' James looked round at the circle of rapt faces. 'Jessica lived although, as it turned out, it might have been kinder if she had perished. The fire left her badly disfigured.'

'So what happened then?'

'She became a recluse. After she finally died, they found all the mirrors in her house smashed to pieces. But not only that, for years everyone blamed her for starting the fire. The rumour was she'd left a cigarette burning in her dressing-room. She went to her grave a broken woman, shunned by the theatrical world she had once loved.'

'So when did they find out the truth?' Caz asked.

'Not until Sara died many years later. She left a note attached to her will confessing everything. But of course by then it was too late for Jessica.' He paused, letting the full effect of his words sink in. 'They rebuilt the place, but they reckon she still walks the dressing-rooms and corridors, wreaking havoc on the theatre that turned its back on her. Some people say if you listen you can hear her gramophone playing and smell her cigarettes to this day –'

'Not to mention the unmistakable whiff of bullshit.' They all turned round. Nick was watching them with lazy amusement. 'What is this? Stories round the camp fire?'

'I was just filling them in with a bit of local history.' James looked defensive.

'Filling them with crap, you mean.' Nick smiled, but his eyes were cold. 'Thanks for the entertainment,' he said. 'But if you don't mind we've got work to do.'

James shot him a look of barely veiled dislike. Relations between them were even worse than usual, it seemed.

'Nobody told me I'd be working in a bloody psychic minefield,' Georgia grumbled, as they settled down to rehearsal.

'Oh, come on, you don't really believe that stuff, do you?' Caz teased.

'Why not? I told you my aura had been disturbed. And what about that curse? And all the things that have been going wrong with this place? You've got to admit it's weird.' She turned to Annie. 'What do you think?'

Annie thought about Stan and the cigarettes, and the distant scratchy sound of the gramophone. *I'll see you again, whenever spring breaks through again* . . . 'I think we've got better things to worry about than a ghost,' she said.

'Well, I don't.' Georgia shuddered. 'In fact, I'm thinking of phoning my agent.'

'Me too,' Brendan agreed. 'I've always had a bad feeling about this place.'

Annie glanced around. They were all shuffling their feet and looking awkward. James had obviously got to them. She thought of telling them about Bob Stone, but that would only make them more paranoid. And she'd promised Nick she wouldn't breathe a word.

'But if we give up now, what have we got left?' She turned to Brendan. 'Do you really want to go back to London still owing money to all those people? And you –' She swung round to face Caz. 'You do realise if this falls through you'll be doing those kids' parties again?'

'Oh God, anything but that.' Caz recoiled.

There was a general mumbling of discontent. Then, to her relief, they picked up their scripts and went back to work.

'Thanks.' Annie jumped as Nick whispered in her ear. 'I think you've averted a mutiny.'

Were the four layers of jumpers and thermals finally doing the trick, or was it being so close to him that made her feel so much warmer?

'James seems to get a kick out of causing trouble.' His mouth thinned.

'Everyone's a bit jumpy, that's all. They'll calm down.'

'I know. Look, I'm sorry I haven't been here much.'

'You've been busy.' She looked around. 'This place is great, by the way.'

'It's taking shape at last. Who knows, if we carry on like this we might even end up with a theatre on opening night.' They both laughed. This is crazy, Annie thought. Why did she suddenly find it so hard to meet his eye?

'I was thinking,' Nick said. 'Why don't we go out one night? We deserve a break, after all our hard work.'

'That sounds like a good idea,' Annie agreed. 'I'm sure the others will appreciate it.'

'I wasn't thinking of the others. I was thinking about us.'

'You and me?' Annie looked blank. 'You mean, like a date?'

'You make us sound like a couple of sixteen-year-olds.' Nick grinned. 'Don't look so terrified. I was only asking you out to dinner.'

'That would be very nice,' Annie said stiffly.

'Great.'

She stood there, her tongue glued to the roof of her mouth, wondering what to say next.

In the end, Nick saved her the trouble. 'I suppose we'd better get back to this rehearsal, shall we?'

As the morning went on, she found it increasingly difficult to take her eyes off him. She watched the way his dark eyes crinkled when he smiled; how he raked his hand through his hair whenever he was thinking. To her dismay, she even found herself remembering what his body was like under his faded denim shirt.

He glanced round suddenly and caught her. He winked. Annie blushed and buried her face in her script, forcing herself to concentrate on her scene with Daniel. It was near the end of the play and Beatrice and Benedick were still indulging in their favourite sparring.

'I can't seem to get this right,' Daniel's brows knitted in frustration. 'I mean, what's Benedick actually saying here?

If they're so crazy about each other, why don't they just come out and admit it?'

'Because they're scared.' Nick came over and took the script from him. 'You're right, they've both realised how much they love each other, but they're hiding behind their usual war of words.' He turned to Annie. 'Benedick's feelings have overtaken him, whether he likes it or not. Or maybe he knows falling for someone like Beatrice isn't going to be easy. Look, he says here – "I do suffer love indeed for I do love thee against my will."'

His eyes met hers, honest and direct. '"Thou and I are too wise to woo peaceably,"' he said softly. Annie held her breath.

'And what about Beatrice?' Daniel asked.

'Beatrice is too scared to let her guard down and make herself vulnerable.' With a last quick look at Annie he handed the script back to Daniel.

'What's going on between you two?' Caz whispered, as they sat in the wings sharing a bag of wine gums half an hour later. On-stage, the villains Don John and Borachio were plotting how to discredit the virtuous Hero in the eyes of her husband-to-be.

'What do you mean?'

'Oh, come on! My God, you two can hardly keep your eyes off each other.'

'That's not true.'

'Oh, well, if you don't want to tell me what's going on –' Caz delved into the bag.

'There's nothing going on.'

'But you'd like there to be, is that it?'

Annie was saved from answering as Caz jumped up, sending the wine gums flying. 'What the hell –'

'Look out!' Adam suddenly leaped at Brendan with a flying tackle that sent them both skidding across the stage, just as one of the lights fell from the overhead gantry and landed with a splintering crash.

For a moment no one moved. Then everyone started talking at once.

'Jesus, how did that happen?'

'I thought the bloody roof was coming in for a minute.'

'Someone could have been killed.'

Slowly, still dazed, Brendan sat up and began to pick off the shards of glass. His long, pale face was even whiter than usual as he stared up at the gantry, then at the smashed remains of light where he'd been standing moments earlier. 'Focking hell,' was all he could say.

'Brendan, are you okay?' Nick ran over to him.

'I – I think so.' Brendan rubbed his eyes with a shaking hand. 'Focking hell.'

As everyone gathered around him, James looked on cynically. 'What did I tell you?' he murmured. 'Jessica Barron strikes again.'

'Shut the fuck up!' Nick swung round, grabbed him savagely by the collar and shook him like a rat. 'This is no time for your stupid bloody jokes. If you haven't got anything constructive to say, why don't you just bugger off and shuffle some papers, or whatever it is you do.' He released him, sending him staggering backwards.

They held their breath, waiting for a fight.

James straightened his tie with as much dignity as he could muster. 'I'll be in the office if anyone wants me.' He stalked off, scattering people in his path. But he left a lot of discontent behind him. Everyone ignored Fliss as she tried to marshal them all back to rehearsal.

'That's it, I'm definitely going to call my agent.'

Georgia shuddered. 'There's no way I'm going to work here.'

'Why don't you just shut up?' Annie glanced at Nick. He didn't seem to be aware of what was going on. He stared at the shattered light in his hand, like a man in a trance. 'It was an accident, that's all.'

'Some bloody accident,' Georgia hissed. 'I could have been killed.'

'We should be so lucky.' Caz raised her eyes heavenwards.

'Look, why don't we all try to calm down?' Adam said reasonably. 'We've all had a shock, but luckily no one was hurt –'

'Until the next time.' Georgia snorted.

Suddenly there was a lot of shouting. Georgia and Caz were sniping at each other; Brendan was still shaking; Adam was trying to calm everyone down and Henry was taking a sly swig from his hip-flask.

In the middle of it all, Fliss was desperately trying to make herself heard. 'If we could all just get back to work?' she pleaded.

'I am definitely not staying here.' Georgia tossed her dark hair petulantly. 'I'm not setting foot inside this building again until there's been a proper health and safety inspection.'

'But –'

'Georgia's right.' They all turned as Nick spoke quietly. 'It's going to take a while to clear this lot up. There's no point trying to carry on. Everyone take the rest of the day off.'

No one needed telling twice. As they hurried off to get their bags, Annie turned to Nick. He was sitting on an upturned box, looking utterly defeated.

'Is there anything I can do?' she asked.

He looked up at her, his face etched with lines of fatigue. 'Take me away from all this.'

Chapter 28

They ended up in York, partly because it was a beautiful and ancient city, which Annie had always wanted to visit, and partly because it was the furthest Beryl could go without needing a spell in intensive care.

But as they explored the narrow streets and trawled the museums and shops, Annie could have been there alone for all Nick noticed of his surroundings. He might have been by her side, but she could tell his thoughts were back in Middlethorpe.

Finally they visited the Minster. Inside, it was dark, cool and full of shadows, an oasis of peace after the bright, busy streets. Annie went on ahead, quoting from the guidebook. She halted in front of the famous rose window.

'Shall we go up the tower? There's meant to be a brilliant view.'

'If you like.'

'And then I thought we could take off all our clothes and throw ourselves off the parapet?'

'Whatever.'

Annie sighed. 'Or we could just go home, if you'd prefer?'

'Is it that obvious?' Nick smiled ruefully. 'Sorry I'm not very good company. I've got a lot on my mind.'

'I know. But try not to dwell on it. At least no one was hurt.'

'It's not just that.' The shadows cast harsh dark planes across his worried face.

'You're not telling me you've started to believe all that stuff about Jessie Barron, have you?'

'I wish I did. But ghosts don't cut through cables, do they? That light coming down was no accident. Someone deliberately tampered with it.'

Annie gasped. 'How do you know that?'

'I checked the cable. Besides, I was there when they were putting up the lighting. There was no way that fitting was loose when it went up.'

Fear crackled down Annie's spine. 'But who could have done it?'

'Someone who doesn't want the theatre to open, I suppose.'

'Bob Stone.' She frowned. 'I still can't believe anyone would go that far. I mean, what does he stand to gain?'

'Quite a lot, from what I've been told.' Nick looked weary. 'Apparently Blanchards promised him a sizeable backhander if the deal went through. It looks like he's got his way, doesn't it? Even if we do make it to opening night, we may not have a cast.'

'Don't take any notice of Georgia. She's always having a tantrum about something. She'll calm down eventually.'

'And what about the others? You saw their faces. They're terrified of what's going to happen next. And frankly, I don't blame them.' His hand rasped over the stubble on his chin. 'How can I put them through this when there's so much danger around? Someone could be seriously hurt next time.'

'Yes, and I could go up that tower and fall off,' Annie said. 'Look, none of us knows what's around the corner. Look at me. If you'd told me a month ago I'd be here, I'd have said you needed certifying. And now –'

'Now you're wondering if you're the one who should be certified.' Nick smiled. 'Thanks for the pep talk, but I think you're too late. Everyone's given up on the Phoenix.'

'No, they haven't. But they might if they think you have.' Annie grabbed his hand impulsively. 'Don't give up, Nick. Not when we're so close.'

She felt his long fingers tightening around hers. He lifted her hand to his lips, his eyes lingering on her face. 'What would I do without you?' he whispered.

Annie pulled her hand away, worried that he might notice how clammy her palm was. 'Come on,' she said. 'I'll race you to the top of the tower.'

From then on they talked and laughed, and he was more like the Nick she knew. But she could still see the tell-tale shadows in his eyes. He was trying to keep it from her, but she knew he was troubled.

They stopped for dinner in a country hotel on the way home. It was a former monastery – an old, ivy-clad building set amid acres of rambling grounds.

'It says they've got four-poster beds.' Annie flipped idly through the brochure as they waited for their table. 'I've always wanted to try one.'

Nick's eyes glinted. 'Is that an invitation?'

'Absolutely not!' Annie stuffed the brochure back into the rack, blushing furiously.

They ate on a moonlit terrace overlooking the lake. The scent of honeysuckle and roses hung in the warm, still air. It was a perfect evening. Or it would have been, if the waitress hadn't taken such an obvious shine to Nick. Much to Annie's irritation, she flirted with him shamelessly.

When she'd flashed her cleavage at him again over the coffee, Annie finally snapped. 'Where's the manager? I'm going to complain.'

'Why? I don't mind.' Nick gave the waitress a devastating smile, which sent her cannoning haphazardly into the wall with the dessert trolley. 'She's quite pretty, actually.'

'That's not the point. You're supposed to be with me.'

His eyes glinted mockingly. 'Don't tell me you're jealous?'

'No.'

'Just like you weren't jealous when I brought Fliss to your dinner party?'

'Certainly not!'

'Or when you found Georgia at my place that night?'

'Georgia Graham makes a point of sleeping with all her directors.' Annie's chin lifted. 'It was only a matter of time before she made a play for you.'

'And it doesn't bother you?'

'Why should it?' she lied. Then she ruined it all by adding, 'So – did Georgia get what she wanted?'

'Oh, yes.' He grinned at her outraged expression. 'She told me she wanted to work on her scenes and that's exactly what we did.'

'Especially her love scenes, I'll bet.' Her voice had a bitter edge.

'You *are* jealous.' Nick looked triumphant. 'Look, if

you're asking did I go to bed with her the answer is no. You're right, she did try a few approaches, but I made it clear I wasn't interested.'

'Why not? She's a very attractive woman.'

'I know. But the only woman I want to take to bed is you.'

There was a silence. Annie picked up an after-dinner mint and started unwrapping it.

'Not that I haven't made it pretty obvious already,' Nick went on ruefully. 'You must have noticed how mad I get when another man goes near you. Christ, I even find myself watching Daniel like a hawk during rehearsals in case he goes too far.

'And as for James Brookfield –' His face was brooding. 'I know I shouldn't have lost my temper with you the way I did. But I couldn't stand watching him flirt with you. And then when you agreed to go out with him –'

'I only did that to find out more about Bob Stone. I thought I could help.'

'I wish you'd told me. It might have stopped me behaving like a jealous maniac.' He smiled. 'Although, on second thoughts, I'd probably still have wanted to kill him.'

There was a silence. Annie abandoned the mint and started unwrapping another.

'It's okay. You can relax.' Nick looked rueful. 'I'm not going to try to seduce you, if that's what you're worried about. I know I'd be wasting my time.'

'Oh?'

'I realise you're still getting over Max. The last thing you need is me coming on to you. But I thought I should tell you how I feel. Just in case it ever entered your head to take a chance.' He reached for her hand. 'I've probably got this all wrong, but that night round at your place, after James left. There was a moment when I thought you might – you know, feel the same?'

She did know and that was what frightened her. It wasn't just that she fancied Nick. If she wasn't careful she could even imagine herself falling in love with him. But she was still in love with Max. At least that's what she kept telling herself, although as the days went by she was finding it harder and harder to believe it. Instead of being a solid, constant presence, Max now floated through her thoughts like an insubstantial wraith. If she got involved with Nick she might forget him completely. And the idea of letting go frightened her.

Just in case it occurred to you to take a chance, Nick had said. But she didn't think her heart could withstand another bruising.

They drove home in silence. Annie tried hard to quell the ridiculous feelings of disappointment that swamped her. If she'd done the right thing, why did it feel so wrong? Why couldn't she stop thinking about her and Nick together?

'I hate to tell you this, but I think you've got a puncture.'

'Sorry?' She glanced across at him, shaken out of her troubled thoughts.

'A flat tyre. Don't tell me you haven't noticed?' Nick frowned. 'Pull over. I'll take a look at it.'

Annie drew in to the verge and he got out. A moment later he stuck his head through the window. 'Flat as a pancake,' he declared. 'I'm going to have to change the wheel.'

'What, now?'

'It would seem to be a sensible idea. Unless you think

we should sit here and wait for the wheel fairy to come along and replace it for us?' His brows lifted.

'Do you – er – want me to help?' Annie inspected what was left of her nails.

'Have you ever changed a wheel before?'

'Well no, but –'

'Then I suggest you don't.'

Annie snuggled down in her seat as Nick got to work. It was so nice, she thought, having a practical man around. Max would have thrown a tantrum and called for the AA. They would have been shivering on the verge for hours.

She checked herself for such disloyal thoughts. Not everyone could be practically minded. Max more than made up for it in other ways, she was certain.

It was just that she couldn't think of any, at that precise moment.

Then she thought of something else. Her eyes flicked open and she jerked upright in her seat just as Nick flung open the door and said, 'You don't appear to have a spare wheel.'

'Um – no.'

Nick sighed. 'Don't you think you should have mentioned it earlier?'

'Sorry.'

'So what do you suggest we do?'

She picked his mobile off the passenger seat. 'Do you know the wheel fairy's number?'

He smiled reluctantly. 'We might be better off phoning the local garage and getting a tow.'

'Do you know where it is, or what it's called, let alone the phone number? No, I've got an even better idea.' She wetted her lips nervously. It was now or never. 'The name and number of that hotel are on the bill. Why don't we ring and get them to have us towed back there?'

'Are you sure about this?' Nick asked for the tenth time. Annie nodded, but when they finally reached the reception desk her legs were trembling so much she wasn't sure how long they would hold her up.

She let Nick do all the talking. But she couldn't help seeing the receptionist's disapproving gaze when she noticed they had no luggage.

'Did you see that look she gave me?' Annie hissed as they made their way up to their room. 'I feel really guilty.'

'Why? You haven't done anything – yet.' Nick's eyes glinted wickedly.

By the time they were in their room she was so excited she nearly forgot to breathe. It was heavenly, very olde worlde, with stone walls and narrow lattice windows looking out over the grounds. But it was a long way from the monastic cell it had once been, dominated as it was by a huge canopied bed.

'A four-poster!'

'You did say you wanted to try one.'

Annie smiled up at him. 'You are aware we don't have a toothbrush between us?'

'Who's got time to brush their teeth?' Nick kicked the door closed and pulled her to him.

Annie was shocked to realise how often she'd fantasised about the moment he would kiss her. She gave herself up to the dizzying sensation as his tongue plundered her mouth, gentle, persuasive and lethally expert.

But as they approached the bed she was seized with panic. She'd never been to bed with anyone who wasn't

Max. What if she did it all wrong? What if she took off all her clothes and Nick suddenly didn't fancy her any more?

'Are you sure you're okay?' He read the apprehension in her eyes. 'We don't have to do this, you know – not if you don't want to.'

'I do. I do.' Shakily she began to unbutton her shirt, her fingers fumbling.

'Let me.' Nick gently took over. Annie closed her eyes, praying she was wearing a decent bra.

But he didn't seem to care about the state of her underwear, and neither did she as he unfastened her jeans and traced a flickering line with his tongue over her breasts and down the flat plane of her stomach. Annie groaned, her body arched convulsively, feeling the urgent, pulsing beat of desire. She tore at his clothes, her shyness forgotten, pulling at the buttons of his shirt, desperate to touch him. His skin felt warm, his muscles hard under her fingers.

They fell on the bed, their clothes discarded, exploring each other with hands, tongues, eyes and fingertips, discovering each other for the first time, their desire spiralling until they couldn't stand it any more and their bodies cried out for the inevitable release.

She'd always thought sex with Max was wonderful, but never in her wildest dreams had she ever imagined it could be like this. Max made love like he was giving a virtuoso performance, with her the appreciative audience. There was none of the raw, explosive pleasure she felt now, as she and Nick clung together, their sated bodies drenched in sweat.

Afterwards she lay on the warm, creased sheets, happiness enveloping her like a tight hug.

'Well?' Nick whispered. 'Was the four-poster all you'd hoped it would be?'

'Better.' She curled up against him, her hot skin sticking to his, feeling the rough hair of his chest under her fingers. 'Much, much better.'

She gazed up at the canopy of apricot chintz, trying to imprint every detail in her memory. Outside, the birds were beginning to herald the first chilly light of dawn. She was afraid Nick would say they had to leave. She wanted to hold on to every precious moment for as long as she could.

She listened to the rise and fall of his breathing. 'What are you thinking?' he asked at last.

A chill ran over her skin as the cold wind of reality blew in.

He turned his head to look at her. 'Well?' he whispered.

How could she answer him? How could she tell him she was falling in love with him, but was terrified of the way she felt? She'd given herself body and soul to Max and he'd nearly destroyed her. Her heart told her Nick would never hurt her like that, but her head told her it was better not to take the chance.

' "I do suffer love indeed, for I love thee against my will," ' Annie quoted under her breath. Now she knew how Benedick felt.

'I'm scared about the future,' she whispered. 'About how things will change.'

For a moment he was silent. 'So don't think about it,' he said softly. 'Let's enjoy what we've got now.'

Then his arms went round her, and suddenly the here and now was all she could think about.

They said goodbye outside Nick's cottage. It was after

eight, and the sun was already shining over the town below. Thanks to the hotel organising a mechanic to come and change the wheel, Beryl was now on the road again.

'Are you sure you won't come in?' he said, as they came up for air after another long, lingering kiss. 'There aren't any rehearsals today. We could go back to bed.'

'Don't!' The idea was all too tempting. 'I haven't got used to being a scarlet woman yet.'

'Maybe you need more practice?' Nick kissed her again.

She still had a grin plastered on her face as she drove back to Bermuda Gardens. She was so happy she could barely summon up more than an irritated sigh as Trixie flung herself at her ankles the moment she opened the door.

She tiptoed up the stairs, her shoes in her hand, and nearly fainted with shock when Caz appeared on the landing in her dressing-gown.

'There you are.' Her cropped hair stuck up in spikes around her accusing face. 'Where the hell have you been? I've been ringing round everywhere looking for you.'

Annie thought about telling her, then decided it could wait. 'Why? What's happened?' She was expecting the latest tragic instalment of Caz's love life.

'Prepare yourself for a shock.' Caz took a deep breath. 'Max is here.'

Chapter 29

'He arrived last night,' Caz said. 'I told him you weren't here, but he insisted on waiting for you.'

Annie looked down at the sleeping figure, bundled under a quilt on the chaise longue. 'What does he want?'

'You'd better ask him that.' Caz yawned. 'I'm going to make some coffee.'

Annie couldn't take her eyes off Max. She used to love to watch him sleeping. Sometimes she'd lie awake, just gazing at his beautiful face, the perfect curve of his mouth, the way his long lashes brushed his cheek-bones.

His eyes flicked open and Annie found herself pinned by that oh-so-familiar blue gaze. 'Annie?' He looked around him, disorientated. 'What time is it?'

'Half past eight.'

He struggled to sit up, wincing as he stretched his limbs. 'God, I ache all over. I feel like I've spent the night on the hard shoulder of the M1.' He gave her his most disarming smile. 'I don't suppose you could be an angel and make me some coffee?'

Damn right I couldn't. 'Caz is doing it.' She looked away from his bare chest.

'Caz!' Max groaned. 'She wasn't too pleased to see me

last night. I'd have got a warmer welcome at an Eskimo convention.'

Annie didn't return his smile. 'What are you doing here, Max?'

'Ah, well, that's a long story.' He flung the quilt aside and stood up. He was wearing nothing but a snugly fitting pair of Calvin Kleins.

'Perhaps you'd better start telling it, then.'

He opened his mouth to speak, but shut it again as Caz came in with two steaming mugs. She gave one to Annie, then curled up in the armchair with the other one.

'Nothing for me?' Max made a mock-sorrowful face.

'I didn't think you'd be staying long enough to drink it.'

'You'd probably try to poison me, anyway.'

'Poison you? You'll be lucky.' Caz glared at him. 'Nothing so painless for you, you conniving bastard!'

Annie left them sniping at each other and trudged off to the kitchen to find another mug. Obviously she wasn't going to hear what Max had to say until she did.

She stood at the sink, staring out over the garden, and waited for her emotions to kick in. Where was the excitement, the panic? Where was the sexual meltdown that happened whenever she was in the same room as him? All she felt was numb. Perhaps she was too tired, she told herself, as she poured water into the mug.

Back in the sitting-room, Max and Caz had retreated into glaring silence. Annie sensed Caz's accusing eyes on her back as she handed him his coffee.

'Thanks, angel.' He gave her a smile that once would have sent her pulse into orbit. To her surprise, she felt nothing more than a flicker.

'So.' She seated herself well out of his flirting range. 'Are you going to tell me why you're here?'

'Can you call off your pet Rottweiler first? She's making me nervous.'

They both looked at Caz, who slammed down her mug. 'I'm going to have a shower,' she grumbled. 'I'll be upstairs if you need me.'

'Don't worry, I'm not going to ravish her while your back's turned,' Max drawled.

Caz shot him a look of dislike. 'Just don't take any crap from him, okay?' she warned, before stomping off upstairs.

'I don't think your little friend likes me.' Max stretched out on the sofa. 'Don't tell me she's a lesbian who thinks all men should be castrated?'

'Only you.' Annie eyed him bleakly. Max ignored her pointed remark.

'What are you doing here, Annie? This place is a dump.' He looked around him. 'And as for those oddballs you live with, Christ, I know you've been a bit down on your luck lately, but shacking up with Lily Savage and the Man Hater from Hell —'

'What do you want, Max?' She felt edgy and impatient. 'I'm sure you haven't come all this way because you were worried about my domestic arrangements.'

'You're right, I haven't.' She detected a trace of unease in those faded-denim eyes. 'It's about me and Suzy.'

'Now what? You're getting married? Expecting trip-lets?' Nothing could shock her any more.

'We've split up.'

Except that. 'When?' she heard herself ask.

'Two days ago.'

'You mean she threw you out?'

'No, I left. I walked out on the film. I've given up everything.' His eyes met hers in direct challenge. 'Call her yourself and ask her if you don't believe me.'

Annie groped in her bag for her cigarettes, playing for time. 'What brought this on?'

'It's been building up for a while. We had a big row on set a couple of days ago and I left. I wanted to tell you myself, before the press got hold of the story.'

Strange that he hadn't shown that much concern when he and Suzy ran off together. 'So what are you going to do now?' she asked, flicking at her lighter. For some reason her hand wouldn't stay steady enough to make the damn thing catch.

'Well, that depends on you, doesn't it?' Smiling, he took the lighter and lit her cigarette for her. His eyes met hers. 'I want you back.'

Upstairs she could hear the rushing water of the shower. Everything was so normal and yet she seemed to be trapped in a bubble of unreality. She felt as if all the breath had been kicked out of her.

'Well, say something.'

'What do you want me to say?'

'Welcome home would be nice.' He laughed. 'I thought you'd be delighted. I mean, it's what you wanted, isn't it?'

Annie took a deep drag on her cigarette and considered it. Once she would have been organising a street party to celebrate. But now – she felt nothing. Maybe it still hadn't sunk in?

Meanwhile, Max was still talking: 'I knew as soon as Suzy and I came up here I'd made a terrible mistake. She's nothing like you. She's self-centred, egotistical –'

'What about the baby?' Annie interrupted him.

'Sorry?'

'Your child. The one Suzy's carrying. Are you walking out on that too?'

He looked genuinely surprised. 'Why should you care?'

Even she didn't know the answer to that one, but she did. Whatever Max and Suzy had done, the baby was an innocent victim.

'Actually, Suzy and I have discussed it,' Max admitted. 'We're going to share the upbringing. Suzy will have custody, of course, but we'll do our share – you know, at weekends and so on.'

'We?'

'Of course. You don't think I'd leave you out, do you, angel?' Max smiled compassionately at her. 'I've learned my lesson. From now on we do everything together.'

'Including taking responsibility for your love child?'

Max looked perplexed. 'I thought you'd be pleased. You were always on about having kids.'

'Yes, but not someone else's.'

'We can have one of our own too. A whole bloody house full, if it'll make you happy.' He put down his mug and leaned forward. 'All I want is for us to be together. That's what you want too, isn't it?'

Annie was silent. Three weeks ago she would have said yes without hesitation. She would have taken Suzy's baby into her home and loved it like her own, if it meant not losing Max. But a lot had happened since then. 'It's not that simple,' she said.

'Why not? Don't tell me you've found someone else?'

Annie thought of Nick. 'Maybe.'

'Yeah, right. Another one of your make-believe lovers, I suppose?'

She felt the terrible urge to wipe the smirk off his face. 'Where do you think I was last night?'

That shook him. His smile wavered slightly. 'I don't believe you.'

'I can show you the hotel bill, if you like?'

Max stood up and paced over to the window. 'So who is it?'

'I'm not telling you.'

'Is it someone from the theatre?' She kept her lips pressed together but her rising blush gave her away. 'I knew it. It is, isn't it?' He shook his head. 'My God, I would never have believed it. You – having a one-night stand!'

She glanced at him. He looked more intrigued than angry.

'I can hardly blame you, can I?' He shrugged. 'After everything I've done –'

'It wasn't a one-night stand.'

He frowned. 'What?'

'It wasn't a one-night stand.' Her chin lifted. 'I love him. And I want to spend the rest of my life with him.'

The words shocked her as much as they did Max. But in a flash she realised they were true. All this time she had been holding on to a dream, trying to compare Nick with a man who didn't exist except in her imagination. Max didn't love her. It wasn't his fault, or hers. He was too vain, shallow and self-centred to love anyone.

And she'd never loved him, either. She had idolised him, like a teenager with a crush on a pop star, grateful for any crumbs of attention he'd thrown her way. But Nick was real. He could make her laugh, make her cry, make her feel cherished one minute and infuriated the next. She could talk to him about anything and know he'd listen. She could argue with him and know he wouldn't leave her. With Nick she could finally be herself.

'You're lying,' Max said flatly. 'You're only saying it because you're angry with me. You want to hurt me –'

'No, I don't. I don't care enough to want to hurt you, not any more.' She shook her head wearily. 'Max, this isn't about you. It's about me. I don't want you any more. I'm in love with someone else.'

He looked uncertain for a moment. Then he shook his head. 'Not you,' he said. 'You know you love me. I'm not saying I've done anything to deserve it, but that's just the way you are.'

He smiled indulgently. 'You'll see. You'll take me back. You always have and you always will.'

Chapter 30

'Lift up your arm for me, would you, darling?' Silence. 'Sweetie?' Vince tutted through a mouthful of pins. 'Look, do you want to go on stage looking like Quasimodo, or what?'

'Hmm?' Annie looked up vaguely.

'Lift. Your. Arm.' He jerked her into position. 'Thank you.' He sighed. 'God, you're in another world, aren't you?'

No, but I wish I were, Annie thought. She wasn't looking forward to this morning's rehearsal.

Maybe she should have phoned Nick last night. Or better still, gone round to his place. A busy rehearsal room was hardly the place to tell someone she loved him. Or to break the news that her ex-husband was back on the scene. She didn't know which she was dreading most.

She reached for her cigarettes. Vince slapped her hand. 'Not until I've finished pinning. You knows those things bring on my chest.'

She put them back.

'You are in a state, aren't you? Don't tell me – man trouble?'

'How did you guess?'

240

'Just call me Mystic Meg, love.' It certainly suited him better than Vince. 'If I had a fiver for every lovesick lady I've had in here I wouldn't be pinning frocks for a living, I can tell you. So what is it this time? Boyfriend dumped you?'

I wish, Annie thought. A day had passed since Max had arrived and, despite her efforts to get him to go back to London, he had insisted on checking into a local hotel outside Middlethorpe. She had a nasty feeling he wasn't going to give up on her that easily. With Max hanging around, she knew it was only a matter of time before he and Nick came face to face. Which was why it was so important that she told him how she felt first.

On stage, Georgia was pacing around, miming a scene, her rehearsal skirt swishing over the bare boards. Dan and Adam were lying on the ground doing their voice warm-up exercises. Nick and Fliss were at the side of the stage, going over the notes for the day's rehearsal. As Annie approached them, he looked up and smiled.

'Can I talk to you?' she whispered.

'Of course.' Nick gave a final instruction to Fliss, took Annie's arm and guided her towards the darkness of the wings.

'It's about –'

'Shh. Hang on a sec.' Pulling the curtain around them, he bent over and gave her a long, lingering kiss. 'Sorry about that.' He grinned, pulling away. 'I just wanted to make sure I wasn't dreaming yesterday.' He reached out and pushed a stray curl off her face. 'I haven't stopped thinking about you.'

'Me neither.'

'I nearly drove over to see you last night.'

'I wish you had.' She stared at the buttons on his shirt. 'Look, Nick, there's something I've got to tell you –'

'Nick, the musicians have arrived. They want to know what you want for the wedding – oops!' Fliss flung back the curtain and turned red.

'Tell them I'll be right there.' Nick turned back to Annie. 'You were saying?'

'It can wait.' She couldn't just gabble it out in two minutes flat.

He planted a quick kiss on the top of her head. 'We'll talk later,' he promised. And then he was gone.

There wasn't much chance to talk for the rest of the day. Every time she managed to get close to Nick, someone was always there before her, demanding his attention. Then, when they broke for lunch, he was side-tracked by a meeting with the lighting men.

Just as they were wrapping up for the evening Stan appeared in a state of high agitation. 'I tried to stop him, Mr Ryan. I told him he couldn't come in, but he wouldn't listen.' His palsied limbs shook so much he seemed in a state of perpetual motion.

'Told who, Stan?' But before Nick could get an answer, a man appeared from the wings, wearing a shiny suit and an affable expression.

'Sorry to trouble you all like this. I was looking for Annie Mitchell?'

'I'm Annie.' She regarded him warily. She knew that smile. She'd seen dozens like it through her windows on the day Max left.

'Annie. Wonderful to meet you.' He stretched out his hand. 'Dennis Webster, *Goss* magazine. I'm here about the interview.'

'What interview?'

'The exclusive you promised us. About your reconciliation?' His smile dropped. 'Oh, dear, hasn't your husband spoken to you? He said it would be okay when we talked on the phone earlier.'

Annie glanced at Nick. His face was taut, his eyes watchful. 'I – I don't know what you're talking about,' she stammered.

'Don't you? Oh, well, not to worry.' Dennis rallied quickly. 'We've already got Max's side of the story. Now we just need some quotes from you – you know, how delighted you are to be back together, looking forward to the future, etc. Our readers love a happy ending.' He took out his notebook. 'Then later, we'll get some nice romantic shots of the two of you together.'

Annie could feel her face growing hot as everyone stared at her. 'I've got nothing to say to you.'

'But your husband said –'

'You heard her. She's got nothing to say.' Nick stepped between them. 'Now, if you don't mind, we're trying to work.'

'But there must be some mistake. We've already drawn up the contract –' His voice faded as Nick propelled him forcibly back into the wings. 'I'll have to speak to the editor about this,' Annie heard him shout as the stage door slammed.

'Well, well.' Georgia's brows rose. 'This is a surprise. Suzy called last night and told me she'd kicked Max out. I didn't realise he'd come crawling back to you.'

An uneasy silence fell as Nick returned. Annie tried to catch his eye but he didn't glance in her direction as he grabbed his script from Fliss. She could tell from the rigid lines of his body that he was angry. And she knew it wouldn't be long before she felt the full force of it.

She was right.

As everyone drifted off he took her arm and held her back. 'So when were you going to tell me?' he asked. 'Or were you just going to send me a wedding invitation like last time?'

'I – I tried.' She flinched at the harshness in his voice. 'I've been trying to talk to you all day.'

'Shame you didn't try harder, isn't it?' He released her abruptly and turned his back on her. 'So when did all this happen?'

'Yesterday morning.'

'Yesterday?' He swung round. 'And it didn't occur to you to pick up the phone and tell me? I suppose you were too busy enjoying your romantic reconciliation.' His mouth twisted. 'So what did he do? Turn up with a big bunch of flowers? Promise to be a good boy? I don't suppose I even entered your head, did I?'

Annie looked at him sharply. How could he even think that? Did he really believe she could forget about him or their night together that easily? But the warm, gentle man who'd made love to her seemed a million miles away from the harsh, accusing figure who faced her now. He was the one who'd forgotten, not her. 'It wasn't like that,' she said. 'There is no romantic reconciliation. Max and I are not together.'

He frowned. 'That's not what that journalist said.'

'Well, he didn't get the story from me.' Tears of frustration pricked her eyes. 'I told you, Max and I aren't back together. How do you think I could go back to him after what happened between us?'

He looked at her for a moment. 'Because it's what you

want,' he said finally. 'It's what you've always wanted. My God, you've told me so yourself often enough, remember?'

'That's not true.'

'Of course it's true.' Nick's eyes blazed. 'Christ, don't you think I've had long enough to get used to the idea? It's always been him. No matter what I said, no matter what we did, he's always been there.'

'He wasn't there in the hotel,' Annie said quietly.

'That night in the hotel was a mistake.'

His words hit her like a blow. 'You can't mean that.' She reached for him, but he jerked away.

'Can't I? We both got carried away, that's all. I was depressed about the theatre, and you were feeling low over Max. I told you we should enjoy what we had and that's what we did. But now it's over.'

She stared at his cold implacable face in disbelief. This wasn't how it was meant to be. She wanted to tell him how she felt, how things had changed. And he was implying that they hadn't changed at all.

'So what are you saying?' she asked. He didn't answer. 'Nick?'

He couldn't even bring himself to look at her. 'I'm saying,' he said, 'that it might have been better for both of us if that night had never happened.'

Chapter 31

Max came out to greet Annie as she screeched into the hotel car-park amid a hail of skittering gravel and an ominous smell of scorched brake linings.

'Bloody hell, you're in a bit of a hurry,' he observed. 'Couldn't wait to see me, is that it?'

'You bastard!' She slammed the door so hard that Beryl's wing mirror fell off. 'What's this about an interview?'

'Oh, that.' Max smirked. 'I was going to ring you. It was quite a brainwave, wasn't it? A nice pre-emptive strike before the Carrington PR machine grinds into action. I'd like to see them put a positive spin on that one.'

'But it's not true,' Annie shouted. 'We're not together!'

'But that's only a matter of time, isn't it?' He went to put his arm round her, but she shrugged him off.

'I want you to tell them not to print it.'

'I can't do that. How do you think it would make me look?'

'I don't care. You should have consulted me first.'

'I didn't think you'd mind.'

'Mind? *Mind*? Have you any idea how much trouble you've caused me?'

'You're really angry, aren't you?' Amazingly, he clicked. 'Come and have a drink and we'll talk about it.'

As it turned out, Max did most of the talking. Annie sat in the hotel bar, nursing a glass of dry white wine and listening to his litany of complaints, mostly about Suzy and the miserable time he'd had with her.

'Do you know, she wouldn't even introduce me to her family?' he grumbled. 'Apparently her darling daddy didn't like the idea of his daughter getting involved with a married man. As if that randy old sod doesn't have a few skeletons in his closet. Just because he's got a good press agent –'

Annie crunched on a lemon pip and thought about Nick. If only that wretched reporter hadn't turned up. If only he'd let her explain how she felt . . .

'And then there's the film,' Max droned on. 'Of course, I knew it was going to be a fiasco right from the start. We were supposed to have equal billing, but you wouldn't have believed it from the way I was treated. Do you know, I even had to share a trailer with one of the supporting cast?'

Although she was probably wasting her time, she reflected. After what Nick had said about wishing they had never made love, it was pretty obvious he didn't feel the same way.

'Meanwhile, of course, she got treated like a bloody megastar.' Max's mouth tightened. 'I'm telling you, it was sickening the way everyone flocked around her.'

How could Nick say those things, she wondered. Their night together had turned her life around and she had been sure that it had changed things for Nick too. But now he seemed to think it was all pretty unimportant.

'But then, what can you expect when her uncle's the

director? Not that he's any good, of course. That man couldn't direct traffic.'

Annie watched Max's mouth moving. Well, it had been important for her. And with Max's help, she had managed to ruin everything.

She banged down her glass. 'Max, I want you to call that reporter and tell him the truth.'

'I told you, angel, I can't.' He shrugged helplessly. 'Besides, it *is* the truth. I love you. Why else would I be hanging around this dump? My God, they can't even chill a bottle of Chardonnay properly.' He picked up the bottle and peered critically at the label.

'But I don't love you.'

'Of course you do.' He smiled indulgently. 'You're just not admitting it because you want to punish me.'

Annie stared at him, open-mouthed. Why had she never noticed what a self-centred berk he was before?

'You'll see,' Max went on. 'Once we get back to London —'

'London? I'm not going back to London.'

'You've got to go back some time, darling. You can't stay in this hell-hole for the rest of your life.'

'I'm staying for the next four weeks. I've got a job here.'

'So you keep saying.' He patted her hand. 'But don't worry, I expect Julia can work some magic and get you out of the contract. After all, it's her fault for sending you here in the first place.'

'But I don't want to get out of it.' Annie's voice rose stubbornly. 'I like it here.'

Max looked blank. 'Don't you want us to be together? I don't think we should be apart, you know. It's very bad for a marriage.'

Her hands clenched in frustration. Hadn't he listened to a word she'd said? 'I told you, we don't have a marriage,' she said. 'I'm in love with someone else.' Even if he doesn't feel the same, she added silently.

Their eyes clashed. 'Then I suppose I'll have to stay around until you change your mind,' Max said.

Her temples were beginning to throb. 'Do what you like,' she said wearily.

'Well, I can hardly go back to London on my own, can I? I can just imagine what Suzy and her press gang will make of that.' He gave a martyred sigh. 'I don't suppose you'd consider moving in here with me?'

'No.'

'Then how about dinner tonight?'

'I'm running through my lines with Caz.'

'Lunch tomorrow, then? Surely that won't hurt?'

He looked so injured she had to relent. Max the vulnerable little boy was always more deadly than Max the predator, she remembered. 'I suppose not.'

'I'll pick you up at twelve.' He insisted on walking her out to her car. When she opened the door he tried to kiss her, but she averted her face so he just caught the side of her cheek. 'I love you.'

As she drove away, Annie glanced in her rear-view mirror. He was still there, standing forlornly in the car-park, watching her go. Amazing, she thought. All these years while she'd tried to please him she'd never realised how much a bit of indifference could do for a relationship.

Perhaps I should try it on Nick, she thought, then knew she couldn't. Whatever else she felt about him, the one thing she could never be was indifferent.

As it turned out, Caz had invited Daniel over to help with

her lines, leaving Annie to play gooseberry. She sat huddled in the armchair, watching them curled up on the sofa together.

What was Nick doing now, she wondered. It was all she could do to force herself not to phone him, just to hear his voice. She could feel herself turning into a lovesick teenager.

She'd imagined everything would be so different now. But here she was, still alone, still without the man she loved — it just happened to be a different man.

'Why don't you go out?' Caz eyed her meaningfully. 'I'm sure the others are at the Millowners', if you want to join them?'

'No, thanks.' Any minute now she'll be offering me a fiver and sending me off to the pictures, Annie thought sourly.

In the end she settled for a bath and an early night with the latest Maeve Binchy. Downstairs, she could hear Caz and Daniel whispering and giggling together. They'd abandoned their lines and switched on the telly. She'd never felt so lonely in her life.

Not only that, she was forced to listen to Caz bragging when she finally came upstairs.

'He kissed me.' She bounded on to Annie's bed. 'He actually kissed me! Do you think I could be getting somewhere?'

You mean apart from on my nerves? Annie yanked up the bedclothes. She knew it wasn't Caz's fault that she was so miserable, but her happiness grated.

'I hope you've sent that bastard packing?' Caz changed the subject as she began to undress. 'God, he's got a nerve, trying to wheedle his way in here.'

Annie pulled the duvet over her head and pretended to be asleep. The last thing she needed was another lecture.

She tossed and turned for what seemed like hours. Then, just as she'd fallen into a fitful doze, she was woken up by the harsh sound of the phone ringing. A moment later Trixie joined in the chorus with her frenzied yapping.

'Christ, who's that?' Caz's cropped head appeared from under her duvet. 'What time is it?'

'Ten past five.'

'Bloody hell!' She disappeared again, muttering under her breath.

'I'll get it.' Annie tumbled out from under the quilt, her bare feet sinking into the shag pile.

She stumbled past Jeannie's bedroom door, which was shut firmly. She'd probably taken one of her sleeping pills. With a Temazepam inside her, you could strap Jeannie to the front of the Gatwick Express and she still wouldn't wake up.

She grabbed the phone, turning her back on Trixie's hysterics from beyond the kitchen door. 'Hello?'

'Annie? It's Dan.'

'Dan? *Dan*? Do you know what time it is?'

'Yes – sorry. But I had to ring.' Something in his urgent tone snapped her into wakefulness. 'It's about the theatre –'

Chapter 32

They could smell the smoke before they turned the corner. News had spread and a gaggle of people stood looking up at the building. Some were even taking photos.

'Look at them. Bloody vultures!' Caz started to cry.

Annie put her arms around her. 'Come on,' she coaxed. 'It doesn't look too bad from outside.' She grimaced at the blackened holes where the upper windows used to be.

James was waiting for them by the cordoned-off doorway. 'It happened in the early hours.' His face was grim. His usually immaculate clothes looked as if they'd been slept in. 'They reckon it started in one of the dressing-rooms. Probably an electrical fault of some kind. Luckily some passers-by saw the smoke before it brought the place down completely.'

'How bad is the damage?' Caz sniffed.

'Come and take a look.' James cast them a sidelong glance. 'You'd better prepare yourselves for a shock.'

But nothing could have prepared them for what they saw as they picked their way past the firemen's cordon and into the charred, blackened building. The acrid smell of smoke filled their mouths, choking them. The fire had devoured the foyer, leaving black streaks where its tongue had licked the walls. Its teethmarks were in the charred shreds that hung from the ceiling. It had savaged the staircase, reducing it to ugly, blackened stumps.

The sodden carpet squished under their feet as they walked around, looking at everything. A lump rose in Annie's throat. It had always been a bleak, unlovely building, but it had never really had a chance. Seeing it like this she felt as if her heart had been torn out.

Adam and Daniel were already there, picking their way around the mess. Their expressions said it all. Caz let out a sob and flew into Daniel's arms. Adam hugged Annie. No one spoke.

James led them through the dripping, blackened remains towards the door marked Stalls.

Annie stopped. 'I can't go in there,' she whispered. 'I don't want to see it. Not if it's like this.'

'Come on, pet. It's not too bad.' Adam squeezed her shoulders. 'There's a bit of water damage, but luckily the fire didn't spread that far.'

He was right. It was gloomy, icy cold and the bitter tang of smoke still filled her nose and mouth, but mercifully it was unharmed.

'Does Nick –' No sooner had she started to speak than she saw him. He was on the far side of the auditorium, sitting on the edge of the stage.

'Nick!' Annie immediately moved towards him, but Adam held her back.

'Best leave him,' he said gruffly. 'He's taken it very badly.'

Annie stood still, watching him, tears brimming. He didn't look up. He had never felt so out of her reach.

'It's a bloody mess, isn't it?' Daniel said grimly. 'That old bloke was lucky to get out alive, I reckon.'

Annie's head snapped back. 'What old bloke?'

'That old caretaker guy who's been hanging around here. What's his name —'

'Not Stan?' Annie whispered.

'That's it. Apparently he was in here last night, locking up.'

'Oh, God!' Adam steadied her as her legs threatened to give way. 'Is he — is he going to be all right?'

'No one knows. He's on the critical list, so I've heard. Another few minutes and he would have been a goner.'

Annie felt sick. This couldn't be happening. It was like some terrible nightmare.

They stood silently, looking around, all lost in their own thoughts.

'How long will it take to rebuild it, do you reckon?' Daniel asked the question that was on everyone's minds.

Adam shrugged. 'No idea. At least the damage in here isn't too bad, so we could still open —'

'I doubt it.' James's voice was calm. 'You haven't seen upstairs. It's completely gutted.'

'So you think they'll put off the first night?'

'I shouldn't think there'll be a first night. Or any other night, come to that.'

They turned round. Nick was standing behind them. It shocked her to see how much older he'd become. His face was gaunt and tired, etched with deep lines. She ached to reach out and take him in her arms but he hardly seemed to notice she was there.

'What do you mean?' Caz asked.

'I mean we can't afford to rebuild this place.'

There was an uneasy silence. Then James laughed

nervously. 'Aren't you being a bit pessimistic? Once we get the insurance sorted out –'

'There isn't any insurance,' Nick said curtly. 'I've been talking to the chief fire officer. He reckons the fire was started deliberately. Which means the insurance people won't pay out.'

His words sank into the silence. Then everyone started talking at once.

'Deliberate?'

'But who'd do a thing like that?'

'Your guess is as good as mine.' Nick glanced at Annie. She could see the pain in his dark, hollowed eyes.

'So we're out of a job.' Adam groaned. 'Oh, Christ!'

'But surely if we explained it wasn't our fault –' Caz faltered. James looked at her pityingly.

'Do you really think they'd believe us? This place is in dire financial trouble. Then out of the blue someone starts a fire and burns it down. It's got to look suspicious, hasn't it?' He looked around. 'Mind you, I've got a good idea who did start it.'

'Who?'

'That old fool Stan Widderburn. He could have dropped a cigarette, or spilt something accidentally. He's so old and senile he probably wouldn't even know what he'd done.'

Annie looked at Nick but for once he didn't rise to the bait. He just stood there, his shoulders hunched in weary resignation, letting it all fall around him. They might have lost their jobs, but he'd lost much more. The Phoenix was his dream. And now it had been taken away from him.

She clenched her fists at her sides to stop herself reaching out to him.

'Strange, isn't it?' Caz said as the four of them left the

theatre. James had stayed behind to talk to Nick. 'They say the fire started upstairs, in the dressing-rooms.'

'So?'

'So that's where it started the night Jessica Barron's husband was killed, wasn't it? And that was deliberate too.'

'Oh, for God's sake!' Adam looked impatient. 'You don't think this bloody mess was caused by a ghost, do you?'

'I'm just saying it's strange, that's all. Don't you think so?'

'No,' said Adam. 'I think it's bloody tragic.' He sighed. 'Oh well, I suppose I'd better go and break the news to Becky. I just hope this doesn't send her into early labour.' He plodded off across the square, ignoring the reporters who had gathered around the building.

The three of them stood forlornly on the pavement. 'I suppose it's too early for a drink?' Daniel said hopefully, looking across at the locked doors of the Millowners' Arms. 'I don't feel like being alone at the moment.'

'We could get some breakfast somewhere.' Despite her heart-break, Caz was never one to pass up a dating opportunity. 'There's a café open around the corner, I think.' She turned to Annie. 'Are you coming?'

She shook her head. 'I think I'll wait for Nick.'

She lingered outside the building for nearly half an hour, but he didn't appear. She thought about going back inside to look for him, then decided against it. He probably wanted to be alone.

It was a dull grey morning. As she trudged across the square past old Josiah's statue, Annie was lost in her thoughts.

Surely no one could have started that fire deliberately?

Who could have hated them so much they'd put an old man's life in danger?

She drove home, changed, then headed to the hospital to visit Stan.

Chapter 33

'Are you a relative?' The ward sister eyed Annie with suspicion. 'Mr Widderburn's very poorly. It's close family only.'

No, I'm a phantom hospital visitor, preying on unsuspecting pensioners. 'I'm his granddaughter.' Annie smiled sweetly through an armful of foliage.

The nurse looked doubtful. 'No more than five minutes,' she warned. 'And don't excite him.'

Annie resisted the urge to point out it took her a lot longer than five minutes to excite a man these days, even with a box of Milk Tray and an extravagant bunch of chrysanthemums. Meekly she followed the ward sister down the corridor, trying not to breathe in the horrible boiled cabbage and antiseptic smell.

She ushered her into a side ward. 'Remember, no more than five minutes.'

Annie stopped short. Nick was already at the old man's bedside. They looked at each other for a moment, both at a loss.

'I – I didn't know you'd be here,' she managed to say.

'I thought someone should be with him – in case he woke up.'

'Me too.'

He got to his feet. 'I'd better go.'

'Please don't!' She felt herself blushing. 'Stan would – er – want you here.' Nick hesitated, then sank back into his seat. They both looked towards the bed. Stan lay propped up against a bank of pillows, his face covered by an oxygen mask, his frail body lost under a mass of wires and tubes. A bleeping machine punctuated the silence. Annie's heart contracted with pity. Poor Stan. He looked so thin and old and vulnerable, his bones sticking out from under his wrinkled white skin.

She put down her flowers and pulled the covers up around him. He deserved his dignity.

'How did you get past the nurse?' she asked.

'I told them he was my grandfather.'

'Me too. I suppose that makes us brother and sister?' They smiled warily at each other. Annie looked back at Stan. 'I don't suppose he's got much family.'

'He never talks about them.'

Her throat ached from trying not to cry. 'Have they – said how he is?'

'Not really. You know what they're like. But from what I can gather he's not suffered any serious burns. The main problem is smoke inhalation.' His voice was gruff with emotion. 'The trouble is, he's so old and frail they think he might have suffered permanent lung damage.'

Suddenly the tears she'd been fighting off all day overwhelmed her. She put her face in her hands and wept.

'Shh. It's okay.' She felt Nick close and for a moment she thought he might take her in his arms. Then a crumpled tissue was pushed into her hands.

'I just wish there was something I could do –'

'How do you think I feel? It's my fault all this has happened.'

Annie looked up, mopping her eyes. 'You? Why?'

'I should never have given him the job. I knew he was getting on and couldn't manage it. I only did it to make him happy. And now this –' His face was bleak. 'James is right. He would have been better off in an OAP home.'

'You know that's not true.' Annie dabbed at her nose. 'He would have died a lonely old man. You gave him something to live for, a reason to get up in the morning –'

'And look what happened.' Nick's hands balled into fists. 'My God, if only I could get my hands on the bastard who did this.'

They were silent, both lost in their own thoughts.

'What's happening about the theatre?' Annie said at last.

Nick shrugged. 'God knows. They're holding an emergency trustees' meeting in the morning. I suppose they'll be voting on whether to go ahead with the project.'

He didn't have to say any more. They both knew what that meant. Annie longed to touch him, but she could feel him shutting her out.

'I'm sorry,' she whispered. 'About Max, I mean. I didn't want you to find out like that.'

'I had to some time.'

She twisted her fingers and wondered what to say next. 'Look, I know this isn't easy, but we've got to go on working together,' she ventured. 'It would help if we could stay friends.'

At last he turned his head to look at her. 'That's what you want, is it?'

Of course it's not what I want, she longed to shout. But she couldn't bear being enemies, either. 'I think it would be best.'

Annie read the inscription, her anger welling. 'Well, Mr Stone,' she said aloud. 'I think it's about time we met.'

Chapter 34

As Annie headed across the hospital car-park she was astonished to see Max coming towards her. 'What are you doing here?'

'Your landlady told me where to find you. We had a lunch date, remember? An hour ago.'

Annie felt dazed. 'Sorry.'

'Why are you here, anyway?' He frowned. 'Are you ill or something?'

'I had to see someone.'

'You could have called me.'

'I forgot.'

Max looked disbelieving. 'I know what you're up to. You're doing this to punish me, aren't you? I can't say I don't deserve it, but frankly this playing hard to get thing is beginning to get on my –'

'Why does it always have to be about you? Just leave me alone, will you?'

She walked towards her car, Max following. 'Where are you going? What about our lunch date?'

'Some other time.' He would never believe the world didn't revolve around him and she didn't have time to argue.

She got into the car and turned the ignition key. Beryl coughed, then died. Bugger! She tried again. This time the car couldn't even raise a cough. Annie slumped back in her seat. Beryl's timing was impeccable, as usual. Now what was she going to do?

Meanwhile, Max was still whining. 'What about me?' he was saying. 'How am I supposed to entertain myself in this dump?'

Frustrated and angry, Annie stuck her head out of the window to tell him exactly what he could do – and spotted his shiny Mazda parked not far away. Grabbing her bag off the passenger seat, she got out of the car and headed for it.

'I knew it!' Max grinned triumphantly. 'I knew you were just fooling around.' He opened the door for her. 'So where shall we go? I spotted a nice country place not far from –'

'Middlethorpe Golf Club.'

'What?'

'I'll explain on the way.' Annie clicked her seat-belt. 'Just drive, will you?'

'So how do you know this Bob Stone guy will be there?' Max asked, when she'd told him about the fire.

'I called his office on my mobile from the hospital. They told me he always plays golf on Thursdays.'

'Did they know who you were?'

Annie shook her head. 'I said I was from a charity and we wanted him to be guest of honour at our celebrity ball. Apparently Mr Stone likes doing things for charity.'

Max looked at her with admiration. 'Very resourceful,' he remarked. 'You've certainly changed in the last few weeks.'

'I know.'

'I'm getting used to the new you. Actually, it's quite a turn-on —'

'Right at the next set of lights.' Annie diverted him swiftly.

'But you're not planning to tackle this guy? You've got no evidence. You can't just go around accusing people.'

'I've got to do something.'

Max sent her a sidelong glance. 'This place really means a lot to you, doesn't it?'

When they arrived at the golf club, Annie was grateful that Beryl hadn't started. Here in the car-park, amid the Jaguars and the BMWs, she would have stuck out like a vegetarian at a hog roast.

'Are you sure about this?' Max asked again. 'What if he turns nasty?'

'On a golf-course? What's he going to do, clobber me with a number five iron and bury me in a bunker?' Annie looked scathing. 'If you're that worried, you can always come with me.'

'No, thanks.' Max switched off the engine. 'You can make a fool of yourself without any help from me.'

Despite all her bravado, Annie's heart was sinking as she approached the clubhouse. Max was right, she had no proof Bob Stone was involved. What if he did threaten her? She'd already seen the evidence of how ruthless he could be.

The clubhouse was full of middle-aged men dressed in pastel Pringle sweaters. She stood in the doorway, feeling underdressed in her ripped jeans and T-shirt.

'What are you doing here? This is members only.' One of the men, holding a gin and tonic, bore down on her.

'I'm looking for Mr Stone,' Annie said sweetly. 'Could you tell me where I might find him?'

'What do you want Bobby Stone for? He's far too old for you. Wouldn't I do instead?' The man leered, showing off large yellow teeth. 'Why don't you stay and have a little drinkie? I'm sure I could keep you entertained.' The alcohol fumes from his breath nearly knocked her sideways.

Annie lowered her eyes to conceal her anger. 'Some other time, maybe.' Like when hell freezes over, she added silently. 'I really need to find Mr Stone.'

The man sighed. 'He'll probably be on the eighteenth hole by now. I'll show you which way to go.'

Annie fought the urge to turn round and slap his face as he guided her outside, his hand hovering on her bottom. 'Thanks,' she interrupted his long-winded directions. 'I think I'll be able to find it.'

'Sure you wouldn't like me to run you up there?'

Annie shuddered. 'No, thanks.' She surveyed the rolling green, dotted here and there with pastel-coloured golfers. 'Er, how will I know which one is Bob Stone?'

'You can't miss him. He'll be the one with the entourage. Old Bob never goes anywhere without his heavies.'

Annie pictured him, surrounded by a wall of huge black-suited men, like a scene from *Reservoir Dogs*. How reassuring, she thought.

Nearly half an hour later she was beginning to wonder if a lift with Tombstone Teeth wouldn't have been a small price to pay. At least she wouldn't still be walking round in circles. She sat down on a grassy mound to ease her aching feet. Surely a golf-course shouldn't be this big? Had she passed that clump of trees before? Or that big sand-filled thingy? She had visions of wandering for years, her skeleton being finally unearthed from the sixteenth hole some time in the twenty-second century.

Worse still, exhaustion had dissipated her anger. She had a feeling that once she met Bob Stone she would be so relieved to see another face that she'd fall at his feet with gratitude and beg him to take her home.

Then she did see him. As she puffed her way up to the crest of a slope he was suddenly below her, surrounded, as Tombstone Teeth had predicted, by ten other pastel-clad men.

She remembered Stan lying in that hospital bed and Nick, his face drawn with fatigue and strain, and all the anger she thought had gone came surging back in an adrenalin rush that sent her storming, red-faced and breathless, down the hill.

They turned to look at her. All except Bob Stone, who didn't seem to notice her as he lined up his next putt, waggling his stocky hips into position.

As she advanced towards them, a tall, thin man with sparse hair blocked her way. 'Can I help you, young lady?'

'Not you. Him!' Annie jabbed a finger towards Bob Stone. 'I hope you're bloody well satisfied,' she shouted.

Bob Stone calmly watched the ball roll into the hole with a muted clunk. Finally, he turned to face her. 'Not really. I'm three up on my handicap.' The pale sun glinted off his glasses. 'Do I know you?'

'I suppose you know the Phoenix has burned down?'

The hint of a smile crossed his face. 'Oh, aye. I did hear summat about that.' He shook his head. 'Bad business.'

'Don't give me that! You got what you wanted, didn't you?'

His eyes narrowed. 'Are you from the press?'

'No, I'm one of the people you've just put out of work. All so you can hand the site over to your friends the Blanchards and collect your backhander. I don't know how you can sleep at night.'

He was bending down to collect his ball from the hole. Slowly, he straightened up. 'I hope you're not suggesting I had anything to do with that fire?'

They stared at each other. Annie could see why people were afraid of him. That square, blunt face was menacing. Yet there was something familiar about him and his gruff voice. It hovered out of reach at the back of her memory.

She took a deep breath. 'I'm not suggesting anything. I know you did it.'

There was a collective gasp. 'Shall I get security, Bob?' one of the men asked.

Bob Stone shook his head. 'It's all right, Tony. I think I can handle this.' He looked her up and down. 'Look, lass, I can see you're upset. But that theatre's an old building. It wasn't safe. It could have burned down at any time –'

'The fire was started deliberately,' Annie said. 'And you did it.'

'And someone saw me, did they? Someone actually saw me coming out of there with a petrol can in my hand?'

'No,' Annie faltered, 'but –'

'I've got a couple of hundred witnesses who saw me at a civic function last night.' Bob thrust his face close to hers. 'So where's your proof?'

He had the upper hand and he knew it. One of the men muttered something about women with over-active im-aginations. 'Over-active hormones, more like,' someone else sneered and they laughed.

Annie clenched her fists in impotent rage. 'So much for

Bob Stone, the caring councillor,' she hissed. 'I wonder if the voters would find it so funny if they knew what you were up to.'

Something inside him seemed to snap. Letting his golf-bag drop, he grabbed her, his fingers biting into her flesh. 'Those are very serious allegations you're making, young lady.' His face was mottled with fury. 'And in front of witnesses too. Now bugger off before I have you for defamation.'

As he released her and turned to walk away, it suddenly dawned on her where she'd seen him before. That short, stocky figure, that brush of greying curls: it all came back to her. Except of course he hadn't been wearing Rupert Bear golfing trousers then . . .

'Thank you, Jeannie Acaster,' she murmured.

The effect was electric. Bob Stone froze, his expression rigid with shock. The others were too far away to hear. He grabbed her arm again. 'What did you say?' he hissed.

Annie smiled. 'Ready for your bed bath, Mr Stone – or should I say Bobby?' She looked him up and down. 'I didn't recognise you with your clothes on.'

His jowly face quivered. 'I don't know why you came here, but if you're expecting me to wring my hands and say I'm sorry the theatre's gone, then I'm not.' Beneath the bluster she could tell he was rattled. 'I made no secret of the fact that I considered it a waste of civic money. And I don't care that it won't go ahead.' He turned away from her and snatched up his golf-bag.

'And don't you care that an old man was nearly killed? You do realise that if old Stan dies you'll be up on a manslaughter charge?'

He stopped. 'Old Stan Widderburn was in that fire?'

'Whoever started it left him trapped in there to die. Don't tell me you didn't know.'

Bob Stone went very pale. 'I had no idea —'

'Your friends the Blanchards must have made it really worth your while for you to stoop to murder.'

One of his cronies stepped between them. 'That's enough! You've had your say and Mr Stone's been very patient with you. Now get lost before I call security and have you thrown off.'

Annie watched them walking away. From the look Bob Stone gave her over his shoulder she had a terrible feeling she might have made a big mistake.

'You must be mad!' Caz looked appalled. 'You actually went to see this guy?'

'I know.' Now some of her white-hot anger had worn off, she felt incredibly foolish. 'I think I might have made things worse.'

'I should say. I wouldn't be surprised if you ended up at the bottom of Middlethorpe reservoir with your DMs full of concrete.'

'Thanks. That thought had occurred to me too.' Along with various other grisly deaths. She'd obviously watched too many Bob Hoskins films.

'And you say this Bob Stone and Jeannie are – you know?' Caz giggled.

Annie nodded. 'Doctors and nurses.'

'Bloody hell! And at their age, too.' She considered for a moment. 'We could always try blackmailing him.'

'I've thought of that, but what good would it do?' It wouldn't bring the Phoenix back. And it certainly wouldn't help poor Stan.

She watched Caz apply her lipstick. She was in tearing

spirits now she and Daniel were finally going out on a proper date.

'I think this might be the night,' Caz had confided.

'I don't know how you can leave me,' Annie grumbled. 'What if he sends round one of his heavies?'

'Then you've only got yourself to blame.' Caz dropped her lipstick back into her bag. 'Now, can I borrow your wonderbra?'

Left alone in the house, Annie tried to comfort herself with a giant bag of Maltesers and an episode of *Casualty* she'd taped from the weekend before. She usually enjoyed spotting her actor friends in the waiting room of Holby City, dripping blood and having seizures. But tonight she couldn't concentrate. Especially when the victim of a gangland shooting was wheeled in.

Would Bob Stone be that unsubtle, she wondered. Or would she just find Beryl's brakes had been tampered with one night?

The phone rang, making her scream. Trixie sprang off the chaise longue and lunged at it, attacking it into submission. It took a while to wrench it from her jaws, by which time it was dripping with doggy drool.

Annie grimaced and held it away from her ear. 'Hello?'

'Are you alone?'

She'd heard the expression about blood running cold, but she'd never believed it was possible until she heard Bob Stone's gruff voice on the other end of the line. 'No.'

'Liar.' He laughed harshly. 'I know Jeannie's out and I've just seen your mate leave with her boyfriend.'

Annie felt light-headed with fear. 'What do you want?'

'I think we should talk, don't you?' There was a heavy silence. 'I didn't like what you were implying this afternoon. You could do me a lot of damage with rumours like that.'

His voice seemed to fill the room. Annie wondered if anyone had remembered to lock the back door. 'So?' she squeaked. 'What are you going to do about it?'

'I think it's time we set the record straight. I've kept quiet about this for long enough. But if old Stan Widderburn dies, I don't see why I should take the blame.' There was a long silence. 'I didn't set fire to your theatre, lass. But I know who did.'

Chapter 35

Annie was already ten minutes late by the time she found James's office, a sleek glass building in the middle of town. Despite her haste, she had time to be impressed. How like James, she thought, as she entered the vast reception area, her footsteps muted by the expanse of tasteful grey carpet.

She wasn't sure if she was doing the right thing, turning up to this meeting. She'd spent most of the night fretting about it. But by the morning she knew she had to go. Someone should be there to tell them the truth.

Her first instinct was to talk to Nick. But there was no answer from his cottage and he wasn't at the theatre. Annie was beginning to feel desperate. She just prayed he would be at the meeting. She didn't think she could do this by herself.

A chic blonde sat behind a sweeping curve of pale wood that looked more like a spaceship console than a reception desk. She looked down her narrow nose as Annie rushed up breathlessly. 'Can I help you?'

'Has the trustees meeting started yet?'

'Are they expecting you?'

'Does it matter?' Annie felt her facial muscles going into spasm. 'I need to be there. I've got something important to tell them.' The blonde eyed her dubiously. 'Look, can you just tell James I'm here?'

'You mean Mr Brookfield?'

Annie could feel a vein in her head about to pop. It was like talking to a Speak Your Weight machine. 'That's right. James Brookfield. Can I speak to him?'

'I'm afraid that won't be possible. He's in a meeting at the moment.'

Annie contemplated grabbing her designer lapels and shaking her. Then she heard James's voice coming from beyond the door to her right. She hitched her bag on to her shoulder and headed for it.

'Wait a minute, you can't go in there!'

Annie ploughed past the secretary's waving arms, pushed open the door and went inside.

The room fell silent as she entered. They were sitting around a long glass table. Annie looked at the strangers' faces and her nerve began to fail her.

James rose from his seat at the other end. 'Annie. What on earth are you doing here?'

'Where's Nick?'

'He hasn't turned up. Couldn't face it, I suppose.' James came towards her. 'I'm afraid you can't stay. This meeting's for trustees only.' He was already shepherding her back towards the door.

'But I've got to be here.' Annie stared at the trustees. Most of them seemed very ordinary. It could have been a meeting of the local parish council. One or two of them appeared quite friendly, although the old dear at the other end of the table seemed a bit Lady Bracknell, with her blue rinse and frosty expression.

'Who is this person, Mr Brookfield?' She peered over her spectacles at Annie.

275

'She's an actress, Lady Carlton. From the repertory company.' James turned back to Annie. 'I can see you're upset. Why don't you go and have some coffee in reception? We can talk when all this is over.'

'I'm not going anywhere.' She shook him off. 'Not until I've said what I came to say.' She glanced around the room again. 'You need to know the truth, before you do something you'll regret.'

'Annie, you're making a fool of yourself,' James hissed. 'I really think you should go now, before —'

'Oh, shut up, James!' Annie focused on the friendliest face, a bearded man in a hand-knitted pullover. 'I know you're here to vote on the future of the Phoenix,' she said. 'But before you do, I think you should know who started that fire.'

There was a moment's shocked silence. James gripped her wrist. 'For God's sake, you're hysterical —'

'Let her speak.' It worked. The man in the pullover was smiling encouragingly at her. 'If the lass has something to say, I reckon we should hear it.'

'But she has no authority —' James began to protest.

Lady Carlton interrupted. 'I'll decide who has authority to address this meeting.' She turned to Annie. 'So who started the fire, Miss — er —'

'Mitchell. Annie Mitchell.' She took a deep breath. Everyone was looking at her expectantly. She felt as if she was on top of a roller coaster, poised on the edge on a deep plunge, and there was nothing she could do but hang on and hope for the best.

She turned to James, who was still hanging on to her wrist. 'He did.'

There was a long silence, then James began to laugh. 'I

told you she was hysterical. Now perhaps you'll let me throw her out?'

'Just a moment, Mr Brookfield.' Lady Carlton turned to Annie. Her watery blue eyes were full of intelligence. 'I want to know how Miss Mitchell has come up with such an extraordinary idea.'

Annie's chin lifted. 'Bob Stone told me.'

'Bob Stone?' James laughed again. 'My God, this just gets better and better.'

'It's true.' Annie felt her temper flare. 'I confronted him about the fire and he told me what happened.'

'And what did you expect him to do? Get down on his knees and confess?' James retreated behind the table. 'Bob Stone's the biggest crook this side of the A1. He wouldn't know the truth if he fell over it.'

There was a low rumble of laughter around the table.

Annie felt her confidence sinking. He was making a fool of her. 'Maybe not,' she agreed slowly. 'But he's not too pleased at taking the blame for something he didn't do. In fact,' she added, 'he's very, very angry. Did you know Stan was an old friend of his father's?' James paled, she noticed.

'But why would he say Mr Brookfield was responsible? I don't understand.' Lady Carlton frowned.

'Neither do I.' James glared at Annie. 'Look, this is turning into a farce,' he complained. 'I know we're all upset. None of us wants to see the Phoenix fail –'

'Except you,' Annie put in bitterly.

'This is Nick Ryan's fault.' James sent her a withering look. 'Somehow he's made everyone believe I'm the bad guy. Just because I've had to make a few hard financial decisions. The fact that they've been endorsed by the rest of the board –'

'Bob Stone told me you'd been bribing his men to hold up the building work,' Annie cut in.

James's eyes bulged. 'That's ridiculous!' He slammed his fists down on the table. 'What could I possibly have to gain from closing the theatre down? I'm one of the trustees, for God's sake.'

Annie met his gaze unflinchingly. 'You're also Philip Blanchard's son.'

Everyone started talking at once. James, she noticed, had gone very still.

Lady Carlton turned to him. 'Is this true?'

His mouth was a thin line. 'Yes, it's true. But it isn't something I choose to talk about.' He looked at Annie. Suddenly she was glad the table separated them.

'Surely we should have been informed?' Lady Carlton spoke for all of them. 'This is a clear conflict of interests.'

'I don't see why,' James said coldly.

'Your father is head of the company that wants to buy the Phoenix land.'

'That's true. And I agree, it would have been a conflict of interests if I'd had anything to gain from the deal. But I don't. Entirely the opposite, in fact.' Annie sensed the anger beneath his icy calm. 'As I told Miss Mitchell, my mother signed a contract when I was ten years old, relinquishing all rights and claims on the Blanchard family. In return for a certain sum of money she agreed never to reveal my father's identity.' His chin lifted. 'So you see, if I'd declared anything to you, I would have been breaking the terms of the agreement. I'm only telling you all this now under extreme duress.' He stared at Annie with loathing. 'Not only do I have nothing to gain from the Blanchard deal, I also have good reason to resent them for the shabby way they've treated my mother and myself over the years.'

Everyone looked at each other. Then Lady Carlton spoke. 'I see.' She took a deep breath. 'I'm sorry you had to go through all that, Mr Brookfield. I appreciate how painful it must have been for you.' There was a misty look in her eyes.

She's crying, Annie thought. He's played her like a Stradivarius. She caught the glint in his eye. And he knew it too, the bastard. 'If you feel so sorry for your mother, why haven't you spoken to her for the last ten years?' she asked.

James blanched. 'I really don't see what that has to do with you —'

'It's because you're angry, isn't it? You're angry at her for selling your birthright. It's thanks to her and that stupid contract you'll never be able to take your rightful place as a Blanchard heir. No wonder you've never forgiven her.'

'That's not true!' A muscle flickered in his jaw. 'I detest that family and all they stand for.'

'Then why did you offer them the Phoenix site?' There was a collective gasp from around the table. 'That's why you got involved with this place, isn't it? You didn't want to save it from being redeveloped, or to stop Blanchards getting their hands on it. You wanted to run it into the ground so the trustees would have no choice but to hand the lease back to the council.' She took a deep breath. 'You couldn't break that contract, so you decided to wheedle your way back into the family by offering them what they wanted most. The Phoenix.'

James looked as if he was going to explode. 'That's the most ludicrous idea I've ever heard!'

'Really? Philip Blanchard told Bob Stone all about it. He's even kept the letters you sent him.'

Suddenly, James had the look of a cornered animal – a cornered, very dangerous animal. 'I suggest we end this meeting here, since the whole thing had turned into a charade.' He appeared to be fighting for control. 'And as for you.' He turned to Annie. 'I'll see you in court for defamation.'

'And I'll see you there for attempted murder.' They swung round. Nick stood in the doorway. Annie hardly recognised him, he looked so angry. 'Stan Widderburn, the man you left to die in that fire? He's ready to identify you.'

Chapter 36

'You know what the really ironic thing is? Blanchards don't even want the site now.'

They were in the theatre, just the two of them. The acrid smell of smoke still hung in the air.

'You're kidding? Why not?'

'They've invested heavily in a new flagship store in Leeds. They're not interested in Middlethorpe any more.' Nick lit a cigarette. 'I'd like to see James's face when he finds out.'

'I don't care if I never see his face again.' Annie shuddered. A weekend had gone by since the meeting but it still unsettled her. She dreaded to think what would have happened if Nick hadn't been there.

Amazingly, James had somehow managed to keep his cool. He'd gone on protesting his innocence in the face of all the evidence. He'd even accused Nick of organising a personal vendetta against him. Then he'd packed up his papers and stalked out, declaring that no one had any real proof against him and he'd sue them all if they breathed a word of their outrageous lies.

'I should have known it was him,' Nick said. 'The way he was always hanging around here, pretending to be everyone's friend, and all the time he was just stirring up trouble.'

'And letting other people take the blame.' Annie felt sick, thinking how he'd even tried to blame poor old Stan. That was one thing she couldn't forgive him for: not only had he started the fire, but he had left a man to die.

And he might have got away with it, if Bob Stone hadn't decided enough was enough.

'At least he's safe behind bars now,' she said.

'For the time being,' Nick pointed out. 'I wonder if he'll get any of his wealthy friends to stand bail for him?'

'Perhaps he should ask the Blanchards?'

They were both silent.

Annie watched the smoke drifting up from her cigarette. The coldness between her and Nick had thawed slightly since the confrontation in James's office, but nevertheless she could feel an invisible barrier there. Among other things the unspoken subject of Max still loomed between them. 'At least the trustees have agreed not to pull the plug on this place,' she said.

'So what?' Nick's face was bleak. 'How are we going to open in this state? And you heard what they said at that meeting. There's no more money for repairs.'

Annie stubbed out her cigarette. 'But there must be something we can do. Couldn't we raise the funds ourselves?'

'What do you suggest? A whist drive at the local church hall?'

'At least I'm trying to think of something,' Annie retorted. 'I'm not ready to give up yet.'

'Do you think I want to?' Nick's dark eyes blazed. 'Don't you think I've had all the same crazy ideas as you?'

He shook his head. 'I'm just being realistic, Annie. It's not going to happen.'

'Well, I'm not giving up.'

'Why do you care so much?'

She looked up and their eyes met. For a moment she thought she saw her own yearning mirrored in his dark gaze.

Because you do, she wanted to say. And because this theatre is the only thing stopping us from drifting apart. Her mouth went dry. 'Nick –'

'Hello, hello. Hope I'm not interrupting anything?'

They both swung round as Bob Stone stepped out of the shadows, flanked by two grim-looking men. He looked like Mr Toad, with his tweed suit and smug expression.

Nick was immediately hostile. 'What do you want?'

'I've come to look at the damage.'

'Come to gloat, you mean.' Annie pushed her hair out of her eyes.

He ignored her, his spectacles glinting in the gloom as he looked around. 'What a bloody mess. That James Brookfield never could do anything right. I'll tell you summat, if I'd wanted this place burned down it would have been nowt but a pile of ash by now.'

'Disappointed?' Annie asked.

Bob tutted. 'Now then, lass. What have I told you about jumping to conclusions.'

'Oh, come on. You might not have started the fire but you don't care what happens to this place. You want it to fail.'

'Then how come I'm here to help?'

'It's a bit late for that, isn't it?' Nick snapped.

Bob shook his head. 'I'll grant you, there's a fair bit to

put right, but nowt that can't be done by a couple of skilled craftsmen like my lads here.' Annie turned to the shaven-headed men with him. They looked as if they'd be more skilled with crowbars.

'I don't believe this.' Nick shook his head as if to clear it. 'You do your damnedest to put us out of business and now you have the nerve to come round here offering to quote us for repairs?'

'You won't get a better job done anywhere in Yorkshire, I'll tell you that.'

'You're wasting your time. We haven't got a penny.'

'Who says it'll cost owt?' Bob Stone polished his glasses on his waistcoat. 'Look, I know I was against this place reopening. I still am, if truth be told. And I won't deny I've stood in your way more than once. But whatever folks might say about me, I don't hold with doing things the way the likes of James Brookfield do them. Especially when he drags my good name into it.' He looked around, sizing up the damage. 'I still don't think you can make a go of it. But I reckon you deserve a fair chance to try.'

'And you'll do the repairs for nothing?' Annie looked disbelieving.

'Now then, I said I'd help, I didn't say I was Father bloody Christmas, did I?' His eyes twinkled behind his glasses. 'I'm a Yorkshireman, lass. We don't do owt for nowt, you should know that. But I'm prepared to offer you some easy terms. Maybe we could work out a deal so you pay me out of your profits. If there are any,' he added grimly. 'As far as I'm concerned, you've got about as much chance of filling this place as Middlethorpe has of hosting the next Olympics.'

Annie's gloom was beginning to lift, but Nick brought her back down to earth with a bump. 'It's very kind of you,' he said wearily. 'But even if you did do the work for nothing we still wouldn't have it finished in time for opening night.'

'Now that's where you're wrong. We're used to tight schedules. I told you, we're skilled craftsmen.'

'You could be bloody fairies and you still wouldn't get the job done.'

'Who are you calling a bloody fairy?' One of the men took a step towards Nick. Bob Stone held him back.

'We will get it done. We'll work round the clock if needs be.' He stuck out his hand. 'You'll get your theatre for opening night, Mr Ryan. You have my word on it.'

Nick shook his hand. He looked dazed. 'What can I say, except – thank you.'

'Don't thank me, lad. It's this lass of yours you ought to be grateful to. You've got yourself a good 'un there. Even if she is a bit mouthy at times.' He winked at Annie.

'I know,' Nick said quietly.

'Besides,' Bob Stone went on, 'you've made a right bloody nuisance of yourselves around here. People have started to notice this place and they've decided they want to keep it. So I don't suppose it'll do me any harm to be seen doing my bit for the community.'

As Nick discussed repairs with the two men, Bob took Annie aside. 'I hope this means you won't be showing up at the golf club again.' he said. 'I didn't appreciate being made a fool of, I can tell you.'

'Sorry,' Annie said meekly.

'And I hope it's the last we hear of that other little – er – business.' He eyed her meaningfully. 'Jeannie Acaster is an old family friend. That night you saw me – we were just catching up on old times, that's all.'

'Of course.' Annie fought to keep a straight face. 'Don't worry, I won't be going to the press.'

'It's not the press I'm worried about,' Bob said gruffly. 'Bloody hell, I own the local paper anyway. But if you breathe a word of this to my wife –'

'I won't.' Impulsively she threw her arms round his neck. 'Mr Stone, you're an angel.'

'Now then, lass, it's Councillor Stone to you.' He turned slightly pink. 'We don't want your boyfriend getting the wrong idea, do we?'

They spent the next half-hour discussing repairs to the theatre. As he left, Bob turned back and said, 'By the way, in case you were wondering, your pal Brookfield is up before the magistrates this morning. I've got the feeling he'll be in for a nice long stretch.'

'Unless he gets bail,' Annie said grimly.

'Oh, I shouldn't think that's very likely, lass. You see, a good friend of mine just happens to be sitting on the bench today.' With a wink he was gone.

'I can't credit it!' Nick laughed. 'You realise this means we might just make opening night after all?'

'I know. Who'd have believed Bob Stone would turn out to be our knight in shining armour?'

She looked at Nick and realised he wasn't laughing any more. 'Thanks,' he said quietly.

'What for?'

'Bob Stone was right. None of this would have happened if it hadn't been for you. I'm very grateful.'

Grateful! Was that the best he could do? 'You heard what he said. We make a great team.'

Then, suddenly, they were in each other's arms, hugging. Annie clung to him, breathing him in, feeling his reassuring warmth. For a moment it seemed as if Nick

286

might be feeling the same powerful rush of emotions. His arms tightened round her. Then, abruptly, he let her go.

'I'd better go and let the others know the good news.' He turned and walked away.

Annie watched him go, a lump rising in her throat. So that was that. She'd proved how much she loved him and it still wasn't enough. What more could she do?

Chapter 37

'Did you see that? She's limping now. Fucking *limping*, for Christ's sake!'

It was the last rehearsal before opening night and tensions were running high. The rehearsal was supposed to be for the benefit of the stage crew, but as usual Georgia couldn't resist stirring things up.

'I just thought it might bring some reality into the scene.' She appealed to Nick, who sat staring up at the ceiling. 'I mean, it doesn't say in the text that Hero didn't have a limp, does it?'

'It doesn't say Leonato didn't have three heads and walk like a fucking fairy, but you don't see me doing that, do you?' muttered Henry.

'There's no need to be offensive.' Georgia sniffed. 'Tell him, Nick.'

'Lose the limp, Georgia.' Nick sighed.

'I don't see why –'

'Because I say so.' Nick levelled his gaze at her. 'Because we open in two days. This is a lighting rehearsal and it's too late to start making changes.'

Georgia stared at him. After all his soothing and cajoling

of past weeks, it was as if her pet lap-dog had leaped up and gone for the jugular.

'Look, I appreciate your need to interpret the role,' he went on, as her lip trembled on the verge of yet another tantrum. 'But not everyone has your – instincts. They need to predict what's going to happen next.'

'If you say so.' Georgia looked huffy.

'And that includes not suddenly making up your own lines because you can't be bothered to learn your bloody script,' Brendan added in an undertone.

Georgia shot him a pained look as she stalked off back to her spot, her long skirts swishing.

'I'll be glad when she's dead,' Caz muttered to Annie, who was busy adjusting her corset.

'Except she'll probably take half an hour to do it.' They might as well not be on stage when Georgia was there. Even when she wasn't in the scene she was usually ad libbing noisily in the background.

She caught Nick's wry smile and her stomach did its usual backflip. He looked so damned sexy, his black jeans and sweater emphasising his lean body. She found it hard to breathe, even without her rib-crushing corset.

Poor Nick. He was dealing with everything with his usual weary patience, although Annie noticed he was on his fourth Marlboro and was shredding the packet. He looked as if he hadn't slept for a week.

Not that they needed to worry. Bob Stone had been as good as his word. Having decided to embrace the Phoenix, he had put his best men on the job and made sure the renovations were better than any of them could have hoped. He'd also got himself voted on to the board of trustees and insisted on giving the local press a guided tour around the theatre. From the way he talked about 'our' plans, anyone would have thought the whole idea had been his from the start.

But at least it had brought some good publicity. THE PHOENIX RISES FROM THE ASHES, the local newspaper headlines had said. The box-office was doing good business and the theatre had started to attract more than casual glances. For the first time, people dared to believe it might work.

Annie should have been elated, but she couldn't shake off a lingering feeling of depression. She and Nick were still avoiding each other. Meanwhile, Max was refusing to take the hint and go home.

While Dogberry and the Sexton were playing their scene, she and Caz sneaked off to the green-room for a smoke.

Caz was in a foul mood. 'Daniel's wife's coming to the first night. Apparently she thinks they should make a go of it for the kids' sake.' She was an incongruous sight, her cropped hair covered with a lace cap, long skirts tucked up around her, puffing angrily on a ciggie.

'Oh, no!'

'I know why she's really doing it. It's because she's found out about me. She wants to prove she can take Dan back whenever she feels like it.'

'Surely he won't fall for that?'

'Don't you believe it. She's got the kids, remember? Dan dotes on them. As soon as he heard the news he was off to Toys R Us to buy the place.' Her lip trembled. 'How do I compete?'

'You can't,' Annie agreed. 'But would you really want to, if it meant keeping him away from them?'

'I suppose not.' Caz brushed ash off the front of her

crinoline. 'God, why can't I just fall in love with someone who loves me back?'

I know what you mean, Annie thought. She looked up at the monitor, which showed what was happening on stage. Dogberry was in the middle of his comical scene, but the only one she noticed was Nick. He had his long legs tucked under him, watching the actors with a fixed concentration that made her heart lurch.

'You still really like him, don't you?' Caz's voice broke into her thoughts.

'Yes.' She'd given up denying it a long time ago, even to herself.

'So what's stopping you? Why don't you just tell him how you feel?'

'Because I know it's not what he wants to hear.'

'But everyone can see he's crazy about you.'

Well, he's got a funny way of showing it, Annie thought. Sometimes she caught an unguarded look or smile that made her think he might still care about her. But then the shutters would come down and she'd realise they were as far apart as they'd ever been.

'Maybe he's just pissed off because Max is still around,' Caz suggested.

'Don't you think I know that?' Annie's gaze drifted away from the screen. 'I've tried to explain how I feel about Max, but Nick doesn't want to know. I suppose I'll just have to face it. He's not interested enough to care.'

'You're sure you're not letting Max hang around because you're thinking of going back to him?' Caz looked worried.

'Are you serious?' Max was like a Spandau Ballet poster she'd once drooled over but now wondered what she'd ever seen in it. 'It would be a lot easier if I could hate him. But to tell the truth I just feel sorry for him.'

'Sorry? For that selfish bastard? I wouldn't waste my time.'

'I know, but I can't help it. I just wish he'd take the hint and leave.' Unfortunately, her efforts to make him go only seemed to make him more attentive. He sent her flowers and phoned her several times a day. Once or twice, much to her embarrassment, he'd even turned up at the stage door to take her home. Fortunately she'd managed to put him off that one.

'So what are you going to do?' Caz asked.

'I don't know. But I can't stay here.' The idea of leaving was tearing her apart, but seeing Nick every day and knowing they were growing further apart was much worse. 'You know, I don't think I can stand much more of this. If I have to go on acting cool and professional any longer, I think I'll scream –'

She realised Caz was making frantic eye-rolling gestures, turned and saw Georgia, Adam and Nick in the doorway. One look at his rigid expression told her he'd heard every word of her last remark.

'Can you see my nipples?' Annie adjusted her corset and turned to face Caz on the other side of the dressing-room.

It was the first night and the place was in chaos. The surfaces were littered with flowers, mostly from Georgia's admirers. Annie's mirror was lined with cards, including a huge pink satin heart from Jeannie and Trixie, and a more discreet one from Julia, wishing her well and threatening never to speak to her again if she messed this up. The scent of roses and freesias mingled in the air with the nervous sweat of pre-show panic.

'Hard to miss them, in that frock.' Caz didn't look up from her *Marie Claire*.

'That's what I was afraid of.' Annie yanked at the plunging neckline of her gold-embroidered bodice. The dress was beautiful, deep-green velvet that set off her tumbling curls. But either her boobs had grown or Vince had messed up on the measurements, because it was positively indecent.

'At least you can breathe in yours.' Georgia leaned into the mirror, applying a layer of false eyelashes. She looked as beautiful as ever, her dark colouring emphasised by the virginal white of her gown. Never was a costume more inappropriate, Annie thought.

'If you want to breathe you'll have to wait until the interval.' Greta the dresser bustled in with an armful of roses. She looked as if she was wrestling a small shrub.

Georgia looked up expectantly. 'For me? How sweet.'

'Not this time.' Greta smirked as she dumped them on Annie's dressing-table. Georgia had had her running around all afternoon, fetching and carrying her ioniser, her cigarettes and her throat pastilles.

'Ooh, I wonder who they're from?'

'As if we didn't know.' Georgia's mouth twisted. 'He's certainly trying, isn't he?'

Annie threw the card into the bin without emotion. Once upon a time Max sending her flowers would have made her heart race. Now, with a house full of expensive blooms, all she felt was a deep weariness.

It was less than ten minutes to curtain up and from down the corridor came the rich baritone of Henry Adams doing his voice warm-up exercises. Over the tannoy they could hear rustling and murmuring as the audience shuffled into the seats. The show was a sell-out.

And from somewhere, much further away, came another sound.

'Can anyone hear that?' Annie tilted her head, listening.

'Hear what?'

'That music. Sort of scratchy, like a –' She stopped. Like an old-fashioned gramophone. 'It's nothing.' She touched her curls. 'Just my imagination, that's all.'

She could still hear the music, faint but unmistakable. *I'll see you again, whenever spring breaks through again . . .* Strangely, she didn't find it scary any more.

'Is everyone okay?'

She didn't turn round. She didn't need to look at him. It was as if all her senses sprang to attention at once.

'Nick, darling!' Georgia got up and kissed him. 'You look gorgeous.'

Annie risked a glance in the mirror and her heart stopped. He was attractive enough in his rumpled old clothes, but dressed up in an immaculately tailored suit he knocked her sideways.

'I thought I'd make the effort.' He caught her eye in the mirror. 'What do you think?'

What she thought was that she wanted to rip off his jacket, mess up his dark hair and make love to him on the spot, but she managed to control herself. 'Very smart,' she said.

'You look great, too.' For a moment it appeared as if the same thought had been going through his mind. 'I just came to wish you all the best.'

'What do you think of Annie's flowers?' Georgia broke in. 'Max sent them. Isn't he a darling?'

'Very.' Suddenly the softness was gone from his gaze.

'It must be love, don't you think?' Annie willed her to shut up.

Luckily, before she could say any more, Fliss's voice came over the tannoy.

'This is your Act One beginners' call, please. LX and sound operators stand by. Stage staff stand by on OP and Prompt Side doors. This is your Act One beginners.'

Annie rose shakily. 'Well, this is it.'

Nick nodded. 'It looks like it.'

Waiting in the wings, her heart crashing against her ribs, she fought the urge to peer out at the audience, knowing that if she did she would be lost. As the house lights dimmed the heat seemed to drain from her veins.

'Here we go, sweetie.' Henry squeezed her hand. Giving herself a mental shove, like a parachutist about to dive from a plane, Annie closed her eyes and forced her feet forward and on to the stage.

Chapter 38

The moment the curtain went up all her nerves vanished. It was the magic of the theatre, the heady combination of playing to a real audience and the adrenalin that pumped through her veins like a class A drug, lifting her high. Scenes that she'd dreaded in rehearsal suddenly seemed to flow. Even Georgia's atrocious attempts at scene stealing hardly seemed to bother her any more. As feisty Beatrice, she teased her staid Uncle Leonato and tormented her old friend Benedick, giving just the merest hint of her real feelings for him. They circled each other like sword fighters, parrying with words, pretending indifference when deep down they felt anything but.

Just like Nick and me. The thought struck as she and Daniel were in the middle of the emotional scene where Benedick and Beatrice finally break down and admit their true feelings for each other.

"'I do love nothing in the world so well as you, is that not strange?'" Daniel dropped to his knees where she sat, his hand clutching hers.

Stiffly, she withdrew it. "'As strange as the thing I know not: it were as possible for me to say I loved nothing so well as you —'" Without thinking, her gaze lifted, seeking

Nick out in the wings. He was there, as always, watching her intently.

She felt a hard squeeze on her hand and looked round. Daniel was still kneeling in front of her. Beads of perspiration had broken out on his lip. "'But believe me not, and yet I lie not.'" She saw the relief in his eyes as she supplied his cue. "'I confess nothing, nor I deny nothing.'"

Gratefully, he plunged into his next line. Annie glanced up again. Nick had gone.

And then it was all over. Annie stood on the edge of the stage, hand in hand with Daniel, Adam and the others, listening to the thunderous applause echoing through the building as they took their final bow. The lights felt hot on her face. Rivulets of sweat trickled down between her jacked-up breasts. Then Daniel grabbed her hand and dragged her downstage to take her final bow.

As she did, she allowed herself to seek out the faces in the front rows for the first time. There was Jeannie Acaster, a vibrant splash of cerise and orange in the front row, Trixie clutched to her bosom, wearing a matching bow and looking suitably embarrassed. Beside them, in the best seat in the house just as she'd promised, sat Stan, dabbing his eyes. There was Julia, beaming proudly. Further along the row, beside Lady Carlton, was Bob Stone. Annie smiled down at them, tears of happiness mingling with the perspiration on her face. She'd forgotten how good this felt.

She left the stage with the others, the applause still ringing in her ears, and almost cannoned straight into Nick.

'Well done, everyone. Great show.' His eyes swept over them all and then he was gone again.

'Charming,' Caz grumbled. 'My God, two weeks ago we didn't even have a theatre. You'd think he'd be a bit more enthusiastic.'

'He was.' Adam watched him disappear down the corridor. 'Couldn't you see the poor guy was choked?'

'I don't know what he means about a great show.' Daniel glanced back at Georgia as she lingered on stage, extracting the last of the applause from an exhausted audience. 'Did you see how long she took to collapse at the end of the wedding scene?'

'I was too distracted by the speech impediment to notice,' Brendan said gloomily. 'Can someone explain why she developed a lisp in the second act?'

Annie left them chattering and went back to her dressing-room. Her heart sank as she saw Max was lounging in her chair, his feet up on the dressing-table.

'Hi, angel,' he drawled. 'I see you got the flowers.'

'Yes. Thanks.' She shooed him off her chair and sat down.

Max leaned against the wall, watching her. 'I thought I'd get roses. I know they're your favourites.'

'I'm surprised you remembered.'

'How could I forget? You carried them on our wedding day.'

She looked at him sharply. Of course she remembered. Their scent never failed to bring back that chilly grey morning outside Chelsea Register Office. But for all Max seemed aware, she could have been carrying a bouquet of stinging nettles.

He guessed her thoughts. 'I know you think I'm an unfeeling bastard, but there are some things I don't forget.

Like how beautiful you looked that day. And how much I loved you.'

Annie dragged her gaze away, picked up the nearest jar and began applying the contents. Too late, she realised she was smearing her face with hand cream.

'Still, all that's going to change,' he said. 'I realise now how much I need you. I'm a different person.'

So am I. Annie tissued off the cream with a shaking hand. That's the trouble.

'You'll see, once we get back to London −'

'I told you, I'm not going back to London yet.'

Consternation flickered in his blue eyes. 'But you said −'

'No, *you* said. You just assumed I'd go along with your plans.'

'But I don't understand. What's keeping you here?'

What indeed, Annie thought, scrunching up her tissue and aiming it at the bin. It missed.

'Anyway, we don't have to discuss it now,' Max went on. 'I've booked a quiet supper back at the hotel, just the two of us. We can talk about it then.'

'But what about the party?'

'You mean that bun-fight at the local?' He looked scornful. 'You don't want to go there.'

'I do.' Their eyes clashed. Max made a big show of giving in.

'Okay, okay, if that's what you want. We'll go to the party. Just don't expect me to enjoy it, that's all. Making small talk with a bunch of inbreds isn't my idea of a good time.'

'You don't have to come,' Annie pointed out.

'Of course I do. You're my wife.' He came up behind her and squeezed her shoulders. 'You look incredibly sexy in that dress, by the way.' 'I spent the whole first act fantasising about unlacing that corset with my teeth.'

Annie wriggled away from him and got up. 'Do you mind?' she asked. 'I want to get changed and have a shower.'

'I don't mind at all.' Max sat in her vacated chair, his hands clasped behind his head. 'You go ahead.'

'Max!' Annie shot him a look.

'Spoilsport!' He got up grudgingly. 'At least let me help you out of that dress?'

'I can manage, thank you.'

There was a knock on the door. Max strode over and flung it open.

Nick stood outside. 'Annie, I –' His expression froze. 'Sorry, I didn't realise you were busy.'

'Er – Nick, this is Max. My – um –'

'Husband.' Max greeted him in a friendly manner. 'You must be the director. I was just telling Annie how much I enjoyed *Much Ado*.'

'Thanks.' Nick's face, by contrast, had all the warmth of a Siberian winter.

'Did you – er – want me for something?' Annie broke the tense silence.

'I'd like to see you in my office. When you've got a moment.' Shooting Max a final look of dislike he left, slamming the door behind him so hard that all the jars rattled on the counter tops.

'Nice to meet you too!' Max called after him. 'What a fun guy,' he drawled.

Annie didn't reply. She stared at the door, full of sadness.

'Oh, I get it.' A slow smile spread across Max's face. 'You and he are – involved, is that it?' Annie said nothing.

'My God, you really were serious when you said there was someone else. And I thought you were just trying to make me jealous.'

'I've got to see him.' She couldn't leave it like this. Not any more.

Annie stood outside Nick's office for a moment, gathering her thoughts. But as she entered the tiny room and saw him standing behind the desk, his expression was so forbidding that her brain went blank.

'I wanted to give you this.' He picked up a piece of paper off the desk.

'What is it?'

'Your contract.' As she watched, horrified, he tore it slowly down the middle. 'As of now, you no longer work for the Phoenix company.'

'You – you're sacking me?'

'I'm releasing you. Now you can leave.' He watched her closely.

So he *had* heard what she said to Caz. 'But what about the show?' she stammered. 'How will you cope?'

'I'll think of something.' He rasped his hand over his chin. 'That's my problem, not yours.'

'You want me to go?'

'I don't want you if your heart's not in it.' He lifted weary eyes to meet hers. 'Let's face it, you've never really belonged here, have you?'

So this was it. He couldn't have made his feelings clearer if he'd gone round to Jeannie's and packed her bags for her himself.

'I'll make up your pay until the end of the week, if that's okay?' Suddenly he was brisk, discussing the practical details. Annie watched his mouth move but barely heard the words. Was this really the same man who had taken her in his arms in that hotel four-poster and told her he loved her? That he'd always loved her? She fought the overwhelming urge to rush to him, to beg him not to send her away. But it was no use. She had done that once to Max and it had got her nowhere. At least this time she'd escaped with a shred of pride. Although what use that was going to be to her during the long, lonely days and nights to come she had no idea.

She bit her lip, determined to be brave. 'Can I at least have a hug? Just for old times' sake?'

He hesitated for a moment. Then slowly, reluctantly, he lifted his arms to her. Annie rushed into them and for a moment they clung to each other, both knowing it was for the last time.

Max was waiting for her in the corridor outside. 'Well? What happened? Have you two kissed and made up, or what?'

Annie dashed away a tear with the back of her hand, hoping he wouldn't notice.

But Max was too quick for her. 'Christ, Annie, what is it?' Then he saw the fragments of paper in her hand. 'What's that?'

She held it out to him.

As he scanned the words, a slow smile spread across his face. 'Oops,' he said. 'Looks like the end of a beautiful friendship, doesn't it? Cheer up, angel. Now there's nothing to stop you coming back to London, is there?' He put his arm round her shoulders. This time she didn't bother to fight him off.

Chapter 39

The landlord of the Millowners' Arms had never thrown a first night party before, but luckily he was resourceful. Glittery streamers and bunches of balloons bearing the words 'Happy 21st' decked the ceilings. Coloured disco lights flashed, Abba blared from the speakers and, with the champagne flowing, no one seemed to notice that the paper table-cloths all had Christmas trees on them.

'Christ, it's like the school disco from hell.' Max whispered as they walked in. He gripped her hand possessively. It was a novelty after all the parties where he'd dumped her at the door like an old coat while he disappeared in search of booze and some juicy gossip. 'You look stunning,' he whispered. 'You always did look amazing in gold.'

Annie forced a smile. The silk sheath dress had cost a fortune, but it was worth it. It slithered over her body, its rich tobacco colour bringing out the amber of her eyes and the glowing highlights in her hair. But she painfully aware that she had bought it with another man in mind.

'Don't look now, but the paparazzi are waiting.' Max nodded towards the girl reporter and photographer who huddled together under a brolly outside the pub. 'I suppose it's not often this dump hosts a glittering celebrity event.'

'Who's this, Annie?' The girl called out as they passed.

'I'm her husband.' Annie cringed as he squeezed her hand. 'Max Kennedy.' He peered over her shoulder, making sure she spelled his name right.

'Fancy not knowing who I was.' He tutted as they walked away. 'Don't they have TV up here, or something?'

Just then Bob Stone appeared, surrounded as usual by his entourage, all self-consciously togged up in bow ties and looking like a night-club bouncers' convention.

'Well done, lass!' He gathered her into his arms for a hug as a flashbulb exploded in their faces. 'That was a great show you put on. Absolutely cracking.'

'You really liked it?' She blinked at him.

'Well, to tell you the truth I fell asleep, but the wife enjoyed it. It's an asset to Middlethorpe,' he added loudly, for the benefit of the reporter, who was standing nearby. 'And to think that if I hadn't stepped in at the last minute to rescue the place it might have been lost to the community.' He winked at Annie, then turned away to answer more questions from the eager reporter.

'Alone at last,' Max whispered.

'There's Caz.' Annie distracted him, waving across the room.

He groaned. Caz was sending him the kind of look she normally reserved for something unpleasant stuck to the bottom of her Kurt Geiger sling-backs. 'It looks like she wants to speak to you.' He nodded to where Caz was doing a little war-dance of excitement. 'You go and see what she wants. I'll try and find something decent to drink.'

As he disappeared into the crowd, Caz was already bearing down on her. 'Guess what? Dan's finally split up from his wife.'

'You're kidding? But I thought it was all on again?'

'It was. Until this morning.' Caz jiggled up and down, spilling most of her champagne. 'You know she was supposed to be coming up here for the first night? Well, she rang to say she'd changed her mind. Apparently the car mechanic's come up with a better offer. He's taking them all to Disneyland Paris for the weekend. Poor Dan was furious. I think it finally dawned on him what kind of woman she really is.' She grinned. 'Just think, I might end up being a wicked stepmother.'

'Hang on! He's just got rid of one wife. He might not want another.'

'Just you wait.' Caroline's dark eyes gleamed with a sense of purpose. 'I'll have him up that aisle faster than you can say big white wedding with all the trimmings.'

Only two days ago she was ready to give up on him, Annie thought. When it came to her love life, Caz was as resilient as a bungee rope.

She gazed across at Max. Yet how could she talk? Who could have guessed a few months ago that her feelings for Max would change so completely?

'Is he still here?' Caz followed her gaze across the room. 'You'd better get rid of him before Nick arrives. He'll be furious.'

'I don't think he'll care.' Annie's voice was emotionless. 'He's already told me to go back to him.'

'Nick told you that? I don't believe it! You two were made for each other.'

'He obviously doesn't think so.'

'What about you? Don't you love him?'

'I don't think that really matters –'

'Of course it matters! Do you love him?'

Annie looked at the floor. 'Yes.'

'Then fight for him. Go and tell him how you feel.'

'And what good would that do? I'd only end up humiliated.'

'So you'd rather lose him, is that it?' Caz grabbed her arm. 'Talk to him, Annie. Before you both do something you'll regret.'

She walked off, leaving Annie staring at the sandwiches. The noise of the party drifted around her. Gary Glitter was exhorting everyone to come on, come on. Bob Stone was punching the air drunkenly. Everyone was having a marvellous time, except her.

She grabbed a plastic cup of champagne from the bar and took a swig. It was warm and slightly flat, but it was enough to numb her senses.

Then, from across the room, she heard Georgia's voice.

'So he asked me if I'd consider taking the part on, and of course I said yes,' she was telling Adam and Henry, and anyone else within a two-mile radius. 'I've always felt Beatrice and Benedick were central to the play's theme. I mean, it's their story more than anyone else's, isn't it?' Annie felt a vein throbbing dangerously in her temple. 'And of course I felt I could bring a more sensitive interpretation to the role. I'm not saying Annie isn't a competent actress, but –'

She turned away, crunching the plastic cup in her fist, and walked straight into Julia.

'So this is where you're hiding.' Julia looked distinctly

out of place in a tasteful black Ben de Lisi. 'Why aren't you soaking up all the adulation with the others?'

'I don't feel like it.'

'But you deserve it. You've put this place on the theatrical map. And now what you require is some serious work. I've got a couple of roles in mind that will be perfect for you.'

'Two months ago you told me this was just what I needed!'

'Yes, and I was right, wasn't I?' Julia smiled. 'But now it's time for something more broadening.'

'And what if I don't want anything more broadening?'

'Sorry?'

'I just wish people would stop trying to run my life for me.'

Julia looked blank. 'But I'm your agent. That's my job.' She ploughed on without waiting for an answer. 'Now, I've been talking to an old contact of mine and he reckons they'll be casting for the new Sir Walter Scott adaptation soon. There could well be a part in it for you. I don't suppose you can milk a goat, by any chance?'

'I'm not going to Scotland.'

'Of course you are, darling.'

'No, she's not.' Max sidled up to join them, a cup in each hand. 'She's coming back to London with me, aren't you, angel? We're going to rebuild our marriage.'

'At the expense of her career, I suppose?'

'Some things are more important than work, Julia. Although I don't expect someone like you to understand that.'

'At least I've got her best interests at heart. Let's face it, you only want her back because –'

Annie tuned out as the argument raged around her.

Why did they all think they knew best? Julia, Max, Caz — even Nick. In all this mess, no one had bothered to ask what *she* really wanted.

Well, it was about time she told someone, before the rest of her life was mapped out for her.

She left them arguing and went outside. Across the square, a dim light glowed in one of the upper windows of the theatre. Annie headed for it purposefully.

Chapter 40

Annie's heart was beating a salsa rhythm against her ribs as she pushed open the stage door and went inside.

'Hello?' Her whisper sounded like a gunshot in the dense silence.

Then she heard it. Drifting down the stairs, the unmistakable sound of an old gramophone.

'Nick?' she croaked. There was no answer. But from somewhere above her she heard the noise of a woman's laughter.

She froze. Then, slowly, she urged her feet forward down the narrow corridor into the darkness, her hands tracing the cold walls. As she went, she could feel the hairs stirring on the back of her neck, as if someone was behind her.

She walked on stage. It felt strange to look out over the empty auditorium, where only a couple of hours before row upon row of faces had looked up at her. She stood for a moment, lost in thought, remembering the applause ringing in her ears.

'It was quite a night, wasn't it?' She swung round, as Nick emerged from the shadows.

'I'll never forget it,' she said.

'Neither will I.' They stood in silence for a moment, both staring out over the empty theatre. Finally, he spoke. 'What are you doing here?'

'I came to talk to you.'

He rubbed the back of his neck wearily. 'I think we've said all there is to say, don't you?'

He started to turn away from her but Annie grabbed his arm, dragging him back. 'No,' she said. 'So far everyone else has done the talking. Now it's my turn.'

His face darkened. 'What –'

'Don't!' Her voice echoed around the empty theatre. 'Don't you dare say a word until I've finished.'

He sighed and sat down in a carved chair at the side of the stage, his legs stretched out in front of him. 'Okay, then. Let's hear it.'

She took a deep breath and stared out at the rows of empty seats, unable to look at him. 'I just wanted to know what I've done wrong,' she said. 'Why do you hate me so much?' Nick opened his mouth to speak, but Annie silenced him. 'Okay, so I made a mistake and fell in love with you. It's not such a great crime, is it? You didn't have to fire me.'

'What did you say?'

She ignored the interruption. 'I mean, now you've made it clear you don't feel the same, I can respect that. I think I'm grown-up enough to move on. And I hope I'm professional enough to –'

'Annie!' She turned round and he was there, standing right behind her, close enough to touch. Close enough to kiss. 'Why the hell didn't you tell me all this before?'

'I tried, remember? When Max came back. But you wouldn't listen.'

'I thought you were just trying to let me down gently. I

was so upset and furious that I wasn't in the mood to listen to anything.' He looked her straight in the eyes. 'You really mean it?'

She never thought she'd see that look on his face again. But at the same time she couldn't resist teasing him. 'I think I should,' she said. 'If only to stop you giving my part to Georgia and making the biggest mistake of your life.'

'I've already done that,' he admitted. 'The biggest mistake of my life was letting you walk out of here.'

'Then why did you?'

'Because I thought I knew how you felt about Max. When he turned up, I assumed you'd jump at the chance to go back to him.'

'So you pretended you didn't care?'

'I did it before, when you married Max. I thought I could do it again.' He paused. 'I was scared to tell you how I felt, if you must know, in case you didn't feel the same.'

'I can understand that.' Hadn't she been through the same agonies herself?

'Only this time it wasn't so easy. I nearly cracked tonight after the show. That's why I came to see you in your dressing-room. I was going to tell you how I felt, lay my cards on the table. And then I saw him with you and I knew I couldn't do it.'

'I wish you had.'

'So do I,' he admitted. 'That's why I stayed away from the party. I knew if I saw you together, again I'd end up punching him, or making an even bigger fool of myself. I let you go once and I ended up regretting it. I don't think I could go through losing you again.'

He took her in his arms and kissed her for a long time.

This time there was no thought of letting each other go. This was where she belonged.

'What about my contract?' she asked, when she finally came up for air.

'I've been thinking about that.' Nick grinned his old familiar lopsided grin that made her heart lurch. 'As a matter of fact, I wondered if you'd consider taking on a new one. Something different. I thought we could go down to the register office and get one drawn up?'

She controlled her shiver of excitement. 'I don't know,' she said. 'I'll have to get Julia to check it over. Will it involve a performance every evening?'

'Almost certainly.' His smile was devastatingly sexy. 'And probably a few matinées too. And absolutely no chance of an understudy.'

'Sounds perfect.' She grabbed his collar and pulled him towards her for another kiss.

As they stood in each other's arms, a spotlight suddenly picked them out in the middle of the stage. And from somewhere up in the gods came the distant sound of applause.

CORSAIR

CORSAIR

CLIVE CUSSLER
with JACK DU BRUL

A NOVEL FROM
THE *OREGON*® FILES

MICHAEL JOSEPH
an imprint of
PENGUIN BOOKS

MICHAEL JOSEPH

Penguin (...4, USA
Penguin Group (...anada M4P 2Y3

Penguin Irela... ...Books Ltd)
Penguin Gr... ..., Australia

Penguin Books In... – 110 017, India
Penguin ... ...ealand

Penguin Books (Sou... 2196, South Africa

Pengui... ...gland

www.penguin.com

First published in the United States of America by G. P. Putnam's Sons,
part of the Penguin Group (USA) Inc. in 2009
First published in Great Britain in 2009

1

Printed in Great Britain by Clays Ltd, St Ives plc

A CIP catalogue record for this book is available from the British Library

Hardback ISBN: 978-0-718-15444-8
OM paperback ISBN: 978-0-718-15445-5

www.greenpenguin.co.uk

Mixed Sources
Product group from well-managed
forests and other controlled sources
www.fsc.org Cert no. SA-COC-1592
© 1996 Forest Stewardship Council

Penguin Books is committed to a sustainable future
for our business, our readers and our planet.
The book in your hands is made from paper
certified by the Forest Stewardship Council.

". . . that it is founded on the Laws of their Prophet, that it is written in their Koran, that all nations who should not have acknowledged their authority were sinners, that it is their right and duty to make war upon them wherever they could be found, and to make slaves of all they could take as Prisoners, and that every Musselman who should be slain in Battle are sure to go to Paradise."

—Thomas Jefferson's testimony to the Continental Congress explaining the justification given to him by the Barbary ambassador to England, Sidi Haji Abdul Rahman Adja, concerning their preying on Christian ships, 1786

"We ought not to fight them at all unless we determine to fight them forever."

—John Adams on the Barbary pirates, 1787

THE BAY OF TRIPOLI
FEBRUARY 1803

N O SOONER HAD THE SQUADRON SIGHTED THE FORTIFIED
walls of the Barbary capital than a storm struck suddenly,
forcing the ketch *Intrepid* and the larger brig *Siren* back out into the
Mediterranean. Through his spyglass, Lieutenant Henry Lafayette,
the *Siren*'s First Officer, had just by chance spotted the towering
masts of the USS *Philadelphia*, the reason the two American warships had ventured so close to the pirates' lair.

Six months earlier, the forty-four-gun *Philadelphia* had chased a
Barbary corsair too close to Tripoli's notoriously treacherous harbor and grounded in the shallow shoals. At the time, the frigate's
captain, William Baimbridge, had done all he could to save his
ship, including heaving her cannons over the side, but she was hard
aground, and high tide was hours away. Under threat of a dozen
enemy gunboats, Baimbridge had no choice but to strike the colors
and surrender the massive warship to the Bashaw of Tripoli. Letters
from the Dutch Consul residing in the city reported that Baimbridge
and his senior officers were being treated well, but the fate of the
Philadelphia's crew, like that of most others who fell to the Barbary
pirates, was slavery.

It was decided among the American commanders of the Mediterranean fleet that there was no hope of recapturing the *Philadelphia* and sailing her out of the harbor, so they determined she would burn instead. As to the fate of her crew, through intermediaries it was learned that Tripoli's head of state was amenable to releasing them for a cash settlement, totaling some half a million dollars.

For centuries, the pirates of the Barbary Coast had raided all along Europe's coastline, rampaging as far north as Ireland and Iceland. They had pillaged entire towns and carried captives back to North Africa, where the innocents languished as galley slaves, laborers, and, in the case of the more attractive women, as concubines in the various rulers' harems. The wealthiest captives were given the chance to be ransomed by their friends and family, but the poor faced a lifetime of drudgery and anguish.

In order to protect their merchant fleets, the great naval powers of England, Spain, France, and Holland paid exorbitant tributes to the three principal cities of the Barbary Coast—Tangiers, Tunis, and Tripoli—so the raiders would not attack their vessels. The fledgling United States, having been under the protection of the Union Jack until independence, also paid a tribute of nearly one-tenth her tax revenue to the potentates. That all changed when Thomas Jefferson took office as the third President, and he vowed that the practice would cease immediately.

The Barbary States, sensing a bluff by the young democracy, declared war.

Jefferson replied by dispatching an armada of American ships.

The very sight of the frigate *Constitution* convinced the Emperor of Tangiers to release all American sailors in his custody and renounce his demand for tribute. In return, Commodore Edward Preble returned to him the two Barbary merchant ships he'd already captured.

The Bashaw of Tripoli wasn't so impressed, especially when

his sailors captured the USS *Philadelphia* and renamed her *Gift of Allah*. Having taken one of America's capital ships, the Bashaw felt emboldened by his success and rebuffed any attempt at negotiation, save the immediate payment of his tribute. There was little concern on the Americans' part that the Barbary pirates would be able to sail the square-rigged ship and use her as a corsair, but the thought of a foreign flag hanging from her jack staff was enough to gall even the most novice seaman.

For five days after the Americans espied the *Philadelphia*, protected by the one hundred and fifty guns of Tripoli's inner harbor, the skies and seas raged in a battle as fierce as any aboard the two warships had seen. Despite the best efforts of their captains, the squadron became separated and drifted far to the east.

As bad as it was aboard the *Siren*, First Officer Lafayette couldn't imagine what the crew of the *Intrepid* faced during the tempest. Not only was the ketch much smaller than his ship, coming in at a mere sixty-four tons, but until the previous Christmas the *Intrepid* had been a slave ship called *Mastico*. She'd been captured by the *Constitution*, and when her holds were inspected the Americans discovered forty-two black Africans chained below. They were to be a gift of tribute to the Sultan in Istanbul from Tripoli's Bashaw.

No amount of lye could mask the stench of the human misery.

The storm finally abated on February twelfth, but it wasn't until the fifteenth that the two ships rendezvoused at sea and made their way back to Tripoli. That night, Captain Stephen Decatur, the squadron commander, convened a war council aboard the plucky little *Intrepid*. Henry Lafayette, along with eight heavily armed seamen, rowed over to join him.

"So you get to wait out the storm in comfort and now come aboard looking for glory, eh?" Decatur teased, reaching out to give Lafayette a hand over the low gunwale. He was a handsome, broad-shouldered man, with thick dark hair and captivating brown eyes, who wore the mantle of command easily.

"Wouldn't miss it for the world, sir," Lafayette replied. Though the two men shared the same rank, were the same age, and had been friends since their midshipmen days, Lafayette deferred to Decatur as the squadron commander and captain of the *Intrepid*.

Henry was as tall as Decatur but had the slender build of a master fencer. His eyes were so dark they appeared black, and in the native garb he had donned as a disguise he cut as dashing a figure as the legendary pirate they hoped to one day face, Suleiman Al-Jama. Born in Quebec, Lafayette had crossed into Vermont as soon as he turned sixteen. He wanted to be part of America's experiment in democracy. He already spoke passable English, so he anglicized his first name from Henri and became an American citizen. He joined the Navy after a decade working the timber schooners of Lake Champlain.

There were eighty men crammed onto the sixty-foot ketch, though only a few wore disguises. The rest were to hide behind her gunwale or wait in the hold when the *Intrepid* sailed past the stone breakwater and into Tripoli's principal anchorage.

"Henry, I'd like you to meet Salvador Catalano. He's going to be our pilot once we near the harbor."

Catalano was thickset and swarthy, with a massive bush of a beard that spread across his chest. His head was covered with a filthy linen turban, and in his belt was stuck a wickedly curved knife with a red semiprecious stone set into its pommel.

"I assume he didn't volunteer," Lafayette whispered to Decatur as he moved to shake the pilot's hand.

"Cost us a king's ransom, he did," Decatur retorted.

"Pleased to meet you, Mr. Catalano," Henry said, grasping the Maltese's greasy palm. "And on behalf of the crew of the USS *Siren*, I want to thank you for your brave service."

Catalano threw a wide, gap-toothed grin. "The Bashaw's corsairs have raided my ships enough times that I thought this is fitting revenge."

"Good to have you with us," Lafayette replied absently. His attention was already on his new, temporary home.

The *Intrepid*'s two masts stood tall, but several of her stays sagged, and the sails she presented to the wind were salt-crusted and oft-patched. Though her deck had been scrubbed with both lye and stones, a fetid miasma rose from the oak timbers. Henry's eyes swam with the stench.

She was armed with only four small carronades, a type of naval cannon that slid on tracks mounted to the deck rather than rolling backward on wheels when fired. The men of the raiding party lay sprawled where they could find space on the deck, each with a musket and sword within easy reach. Most still looked like they were suffering the aftereffects of the five-day storm.

Henry grinned at Decatur. "Hell of a command you have here, sir."

"Aye, but she's mine. To the best of my knowledge, Mr. Lafayette, no one has yet called you captain in all your years of service."

"True enough"—Lafayette threw a smart salute—"Captain."

Another night would pass before the winds picked up enough for the *Intrepid* to make her approach on Tripoli. Through a brass telescope, Decatur and Lafayette watched the walled city slowly emerge from the vast, trackless desert. Spread along the high defensive wall and sprouting from the ramparts of the Bashaw's castle were more than a hundred and fifty guns. Because of the seawall, called the mole, which stretched across the anchorage, they could see only the tops of the *Philadelphia*'s three masts.

"What do you think?" Decatur asked Henry, whom he had appointed his First Officer for the attack. They stood shoulder to shoulder behind the Maltese pilot.

Henry looked up at the *Intrepid*'s spread of canvas and at the wake trailing behind the little ketch. He judged their speed to be four knots. "I think if we don't slow down we are going to enter the harbor long before sunset."

"Should I order the topsail and jib reefed, Captain?" asked Salvador Catalano.

"It's best we do. The moon's going to be bright enough later on."

Shadows lengthened until they began to merge, and the last of the sun's rays set over the western horizon. The ketch entered Tripoli Bay and began closing in on the imposing walls of the Barbary city. The rising crescent moon made the stones of the mole, fortress, and the Bashaw's castle gleam eerily, while the black gun emplacements dotting the fortifications exuded an air of menace. Peeking over the wall was the thin silhouette of a minaret, from which the men on the *Intrepid* had just heard the call to prayer moments before sundown.

And at anchor directly below the castle lay the USS *Philadelphia*. She appeared in good shape, and the Americans could see that her once-discarded cannons had been salvaged and refitted in her gunports.

The sight of her sent conflicting emotions through Henry Lafayette. He was stirred by her beautiful lines and sheer size, while his anger boiled at the thought of the Tripolian flag hanging over her stern and the knowledge that her three-hundred-and-seven-man crew were hostages in the Bashaw's prison. He would like nothing more than for Decatur to order his men to swarm the castle and free the prisoners, but he knew that command would never come to pass. Commodore Preble, the commander of the entire Mediterranean squadron, had made it clear that he wouldn't risk the Barbary pirates getting more American prisoners than they already had.

Clustered around the harbor and tied along the breakwater were dozens of other ships, lateen-rigged merchantmen and rakish pirate craft bristling with cannons. Lafayette stopped counting after twenty.

A new emotion tightened his chest. Fear.

If things didn't go as planned, the *Intrepid* would never make it back out of the harbor, and every man aboard her would be dead— or, worse, a prisoner destined for slavery.

Henry's mouth was suddenly dry, and the countless hours he'd trained with his cutlass seemed not nearly enough. The pair of mismatched .58 caliber flintlock pistols tucked into the sash he'd wound around his waist felt puny. Then he glanced down at the sailors hiding behind the *Intrepid*'s gunwales. Armed with axes, pikes, swords, and daggers, they looked to be as bloodthirsty as any Arab pirate. They were the finest men in the world, volunteers all, and he knew they would carry the day. A midshipman was moving among them, making certain the squad leaders had their lamps lit and their lengths of whale-oil fuse ready.

He again looked to the *Philadelphia*. They were close enough now to see a trio of guards standing at her rail, their curved scimitars plainly visible. But with the wind so light, it took a further two hours before they were in comfortable hailing distance.

Catalano called out in Arabic, "Ahoy, there."

"What do you want?" one shouted back.

"I am Salvador Catalano," the Maltese pilot said, keeping to the script Decatur and Lafayette had worked out. "This is the ship *Mastico*. We are here to buy livestock for the British base on Malta but were caught in a storm. Our anchor was torn off so we cannot moor. I would like to tie up to your magnificent ship for the night. In the morning, we will dock properly and effect repairs."

"This is it," Decatur whispered to Henry. "If they don't go for it, we're going to be in trouble."

"They will. Look at us from their perspective. Would you be concerned about this little ketch?"

"No. Probably not."

The guard captain scratched his beard, eyeing the *Intrepid* warily, before finally shouting back, "You may tie up, but you must leave at dawn."

"Thank you. Allah has a special place in His heart for you," Catalano called out, then switched to English and whispered to the two officers. "They have agreed."

Lafayette stood at Decatur's shoulder as the light breeze slowly pushed the *Intrepid* closer and closer to the side of the *Philadelphia*. The big frigate's cannons were run out and the protective tampions removed from the barrels. The nearer they drew, the more the muzzles seemed to grow in size. If the pirates became suspicious, a broadside at this range would turn the ketch into kindling and rip the eighty men aboard to shreds.

Drawing nearer still, the pirates lining the rail were a good fifteen feet above the *Intrepid*'s deck. They began muttering among themselves and pointing as they made out the shapes of men cowering behind the ketch's gunwales.

Ten feet still separated the ships when one pirate shouted. *"Americanos!"*

"Tell your men to attack," Catalano wailed.

"No order to be obeyed but that of the commanding officer," Decatur said evenly.

Above them, the Barbary pirates were drawing their swords, and one fumbled with the blunderbuss strapped across his back. A cry went up just as the oak hulls came together, and Decatur shouted, "Board her!"

Henry Lafayette touched the Bible he kept on him at all times and leapt for an open gunport, hooking one hand around the wooden edge and clasping the warm bronze cannon with the other. He kicked his legs through the gap between the gun and the side of the ship and came up on his feet, his blade keening as he drew it from its scabbard. By the light of a single lamp hanging from the low ceiling, he saw two pirates wheeling back from another gun-port as more men scrambled aboard. One of the pirates turned and saw him. The pirate's broad scimitar was suddenly in his hand as his bare feet pounded the decking. He shrieked as he charged, a technique most appropriate when confronting unarmed and untrained merchant sailors.

Henry wasn't fazed. The fear he had been sure would paralyze him had turned to cold rage.

He let the man come, and as the pirate began a hip-high cutting stroke that would have sliced Henry in half Henry stepped forward lightly and sank his blade into the other man's chest. The force of the pirate's charge ran the steel through his ribs and out his back. The heavy scimitar clattered to the deck as the corsair slumped against Lafayette. He had to use his knee as leverage to pull his blade from the pirate's chest. Henry whirled at a moving shadow and ducked under the swinging arc of an ax aimed at his shoulder. He counter-cut back with his sword, the edge slicing through cloth, skin, and muscle. He hadn't had the angle to eviscerate his foe, but the amount of blood that gushed from the wound told him the pirate was out of the fight.

The gun deck was a scene out of hell. Dark figures hacked and slashed at one another with abandon. The crash of steel on steel was punctuated by screams of pain when blade met skin. The air was charged with the smell of gunpowder, but above it Henry could detect the coppery scent of blood.

He waded into the fray. With its low ceilings, the gun deck wasn't an ideal field to battle with a sword or pike, but the Americans fought doggedly. One of them went down when he was struck from behind. Henry saw that the corsair who had hit him towered over everyone else. His turban almost brushed the support beams. He swung his scimitar at Henry, and, when Henry parried, the power of the blow made his entire arm go numb. The Arab swung again, and it took every once of strength for Lafayette to raise his blade enough to deflect the flashing sword.

He staggered back, and the pirate pressed his advantage, swinging wildly, keeping Henry on his back foot and always on the defensive. Decatur had been adamant during their planning that the raid was to be as silent as possible because of the massive pirate armada lying at anchor in the harbor. With his strength quickly waning, Lafayette had no choice but to yank his pistol from the sash around his waist. He pulled the trigger even before he had acquired his target. The small measure of powder in the pan flashed, and as the gun came up the main charge blew with a sharp report. The .58 caliber ball smashed into the pirate's chest.

The shot would have dropped a normal man to the deck before he had time to blink, but the giant kept coming. Henry had just an instant to raise his sword as the scimitar swiped at him again. His blade saved him from having his arm cut off, but the stunning momentum tossed him bodily across the gun deck. He fell against one of the *Philadelphia*'s eighteen-pounders. With Decatur's orders about silence still ringing in his ears, Lafayette fumbled for the lit oil lamp slung in a pouch around his waist and held the flame to the bronze cannon's touchhole. He could smell the powder charge burning, although the sizzle barely registered above the sounds of the fight still raging across the ship. He kept his body between the great gun and his attacker, trusting that with his years of experience manning naval cannons his timing would be perfect.

The pirate must have sensed his opponent was spent by the way Lafayette just stood there, as if accepting the inevitable. The pirate raised his Saracen sword and started to swing, his body anticipating the resistance of the blade cutting through flesh and bone. Then the American leapt aside. The Arab was too committed to check his swing or to notice the smoke coiling from the back of the cannon. It roared an instant later in a gush of sulfurous smoke.

There were thick hemp lines designed to retard the force of the recoil and keep the gun from careening across the deck, but they still let the cannon rocket back several feet. The butt of the gun hit the pirate square in the groin, shattering his pelvis, crushing his hip joints, and splintering both thighbones. His limp body was flung against a beam, and he collapsed to the deck, folded in half—backward.

Henry took a second to peer out the gunport. The eighteen-pound cannonball had smashed into the fortress across the harbor, and an avalanche of rubble tumbled from the gaping hole.

"Two with one shot. Not bad, *mon ami* Henri, not bad at all." It was John Jackson, the big bosun.

"If Captain Decatur asks, it was one of these rotters who fired the gun, eh?"

"That's what I saw, Mr. Lafayette."

The cannon going off had acted like a starter's pistol at the beginning of a race. The Arab pirates abandoned their defense and began rushing for the gunports, leaping and falling into the calm waters of the harbor. Those scrambling up the ladders for the main deck would doubtless run into Decatur and his men.

"Let's get to work."

The men returned to the starboard side of the ship where crewmates aboard the *Intrepid* were standing by, ready to start passing combustibles up to the raiding party. Followed by Jackson and six others burdened with kegs of black powder, Henry Lafayette descended a ladder, passing crews' quarters where hammocks still hung from the rafters but all other gear had been scavenged. They dropped lower still, to the orlop deck, the lowest on the frigate, and entered one of the ship's holds. Most of the naval stores had been taken, but enough remained for the men to start burning the frigate.

They worked quickly. Henry decided where they would lay their fuses, and when they were set he lit them with his oil lamp. The flames grew quickly, much quicker than any of them had anticipated. In an instant, the hold filled with reeking smoke. They started back up, holding their sleeves over their mouths so they could breathe. The ceiling above them suddenly burst into flames with a roar like a cannon blast. John Jackson was knocked off his feet and would have been crushed by a burning timber if Henry hadn't grabbed one of his legs and dragged him across the rough planking. He helped the bosun up, and they started running, their team at their heels. They had to leap and duck as chunks of flaming wood continued to crash down from above.

They reached a ladder, and Henry turned, urging his men upward. "Go, go, go, damn you, or we're going to die down here."

He followed Jackson's ponderous rump as a jet of fire raced down the corridor. Henry rammed his shoulder into Jackson's backside and heaved with everything he had. The two emerged from the hatch, rolling to the side, as a volcanic eruption of flame bellowed up from the hold, hit the ceiling, and spread like an unholy canopy.

They were in a sea of fire. The walls, deck, and ceiling were sheathed in flames, while the smoke was so thick that tears streamed from Henry's eyes. Running blindly, he and Jackson found the next ladder and emerged on the gun deck. Smoke streamed out the ports, but enough fresh air reached them that for the first time in five minutes they could fill their lungs without coughing.

A small explosion shook the *Philadelphia*, knocking Henry into John Jackson.

"Let's go, lad."

They clambered out one of the ports. Men on the *Intrepid* were there to help them settle in on the small ketch. Crewmen slapped Henry's back several times. He thought they were congratulating him on a job well done, but in fact they were putting out the smoldering cloth of his native shirt.

Above them on the rail, Stephen Decatur stood with one boot up on the bulwark.

"Captain," Lafayette shouted, "lower decks are clear."

"Very good, Lieutenant." He waited for a couple of his men to climb down ropes and then descended to his ship.

The *Philadelphia* was engulfed in fire. Flames shot from her gunports and were starting to climb her rigging. Soon, the heat would be intense enough to cook off the powder charges in her cannons, eight of which were aimed directly at the *Intrepid*.

The forward line holding the ketch to the frigate was cast off easily enough, but the stern line jammed. Henry pushed men aside and drew his sword. The rope was nearly an inch thick, and his blade, dulled by combat, still sliced it clean with one blow.

With the fire consuming so much air, the ketch couldn't fill her sails, and the jib was dangerously close to tangling with the *Philadelphia*'s burning rigging. The men used oars to try to force their vessel away from the floating pyre, but as soon as they pushed free the conflagration drew them back in again.

Bits of burning sail from the frigate's mainmast fell like confetti. One sailor's hair caught fire.

"Henry," Decatur bellowed, "unship the boat and tow us free."

"Aye, aye."

Henry, Jackson, and four others lowered the dinghy. With a line secured to the *Intrepid*'s bow, they pulled away from the ketch. When the rope came taut, they heaved against the oars, straining to gain inches. When they pulled the paddles from the water for another stroke, half the distance they had gained was lost to the fire-born wind.

"Pull, you sons of dogs," Henry shouted. "Pull!"

And they did. Heaving against the sixty-four deadweight tons of their ship and the powerful suction of the fire, they fought stubbornly. The men hauled on the oars until the vertebrae crackled in their backs and veins bulged from their necks. They pulled their ship and crew away from the *Philadelphia* until Decatur could get sails up her mainmast and fill them with the slight breeze now blowing in from the desert.

There was a sudden bloom of light high up on the castle wall. A moment later came the concussive roar of a cannon. The shot landed well beyond the ketch and rowboat, but it was followed by a dozen more. The water came alive with tiny dimples—small-arms fire from lookouts and guards running along the breakwater.

Aboard the *Intrepid*, men manned the oars, rowing for everything they were worth, while behind them the *Philadelphia* suddenly flared as the remainder of her canvas caught fire.

For twenty tense minutes, the men pulled while, around them, shot after shot hit the water. One ball passed through the *Intrepid*'s topgallant sail, but other than that the ship wasn't struck. The small-arms fire died away first, and then they were beyond the reach of the Bashaw's cannons. The exhausted men collapsed into each other, laughing and singing. In their wake, the walls of the fortress were lit with the wavering glow of the burning ship.

Henry brought the dinghy about and slipped it under the davits.

"Well done, my friend." Decatur was smiling, his face reflecting the ethereal glimmer behind them.

Too exhausted to do anything but pant, Henry threw Decatur a weak salute.

All eyes suddenly turned toward the harbor as the raging towers that were the *Philadelphia*'s masts slowly collapsed across her port side in an explosion of sparks. And then, as a final salute, her guns cooked off, an echoing cannonade that sent some balls across the water and others into the castle walls.

The men roared at her act of defiance against the Barbary pirates.

"What now, Captain?" Lafayette asked,

Decatur stared across the sea, not looking at Henry when he spoke. "This won't end tonight. I recognized one of the corsairs in the harbor. It was Suleiman Al-Jama's. She's called the *Saqr*. It means falcon. You can bet your last penny that he's making ready to sail against us this very moment. The Bashaw won't take vengeance on our captured sailors for what we did tonight—they are too valuable to him—but Al-Jama will want revenge."

"He was once a holy man, right?"

"Up until a few years ago," Decatur agreed. "He was what the Muslims called an Imam. Kind of like a priest. Such was his hate for Christendom that he decided preaching wasn't enough, and he took up arms against any and all ships not flying a Muslim flag."

"I heard tell that he takes no prisoners."

"I've heard the same. The Bashaw can't be too happy about that since prisoners can be ransomed, but he holds little sway over Al-Jama. The Bashaw made a deal with the devil when he let Al-Jama occasionally stage out of Tripoli. I've also heard he has no end of volunteers to join him when he goes raiding. His men are suicidal in their devotion to him.

"Your rank-and-file Barbary pirate sees what he is doing as a profession, a way to make a living. It is something they've been doing for generations. You saw tonight how most of them fled the *Philadelphia* as soon as we boarded. They weren't going to get themselves killed in a fight they couldn't win.

"But Al-Jama's followers are a different breed altogether. This is a holy calling for them. They even have a word for it: jihad. They will fight to the death if it means they can take one more infidel with them."

Henry thought about the big pirate who had come at him relentlessly, battling on even after he'd been shot. He wondered if he was one of Al-Jama's followers. He hadn't gotten a look at the man's eyes, but he'd sensed a berserker insanity to the pirate, that somehow killing an American was more important to him than preventing the *Philadelphia* from being burned.

"Why do you think they hate us?" he asked.

Decatur looked at him sharply. "Lieutenant Lafayette, I have never heard a more irrelevant question in my life." He took a breath. "But I'll tell you what I think. They hate us because we exist. They hate us because we are different from them. But, most important, they hate us because they think they have the right to hate us."

Henry remained silent for a minute, trying to digest Decatur's answer, but such a belief system was so far beyond him he couldn't get his mind around it. He had killed a man tonight and yet he hadn't hated him. He was just doing what he'd been ordered to do. Period. It hadn't been personal and he couldn't fathom how anyone could make it so.

"What are your orders, Captain?" he finally asked.

"The *Intrepid*'s no match for the *Saqr*, especially as overcrowded as we are. We'll link up with the *Siren* as we planned, but rather than return to Malta in convoy I want you and the *Siren* to stay out here and teach Suleiman Al-Jama that the American Navy isn't afraid of him or his ilk. Tell Captain Stewart that he is not to fail."

Henry couldn't keep the smile off his face. For two years, they had seen little action, with the exception of capturing the *Intrepid* and now burning the *Philadelphia*. He was excited to take the fight to the corsairs directly.

"If we can capture or kill him," he said, "it will do wonders for our morale."

"And severely weaken theirs."

• • •

AN HOUR AFTER DAWN, the lookout high atop the *Siren*'s mainmast called down, "Sail! Sail ho! Five points off the starboard beam."

Henry Lafayette and Lieutenant Charles Stewart, the ship's captain, had been waiting for this since sunup.

"About damned time," Stewart said.

At just twenty-five years of age, Stewart had received his commission a month before the Navy was officially established by Congress. He had grown up with Stephen Decatur, and, like him, Stewart was a rising star in the Navy. Shipboard scuttlebutt had it that he would receive a promotion to captain before the fleet returned to the United States. He had a slender build, and a long face with wide-apart, deep-set eyes. He was a firm but fair disciplinarian, and whatever ship he served on was consistently considered lucky by its crew.

Sand in the hourglass drizzled down for ten minutes before the lookout shouted again. "She's running parallel to the coast."

Stewart grunted. "Bugger must suspect we're out here, number one. He's trying to end around us and then tack after the *Intrepid*." He then addressed Bosun Jackson, who was the ship's sailing master. "Let go all sails."

Jackson bellowed the order up to the men hanging in the rigging, and in a perfectly choreographed flurry of activity a dozen sails unfurled off the yards and blossomed with the freshening breeze. The foremast and mainmast creaked with the strain as the two-hundred-and-forty-ton ship started carving through the Mediterranean.

Stewart glanced over the side at the white water streaming along the ship's oak hull. He estimated their speed at ten knots, and knew they would do another five in this weather.

"She's spotted us," the lookout shouted. "She's piling on more sail."

"There isn't a lateen-rigged ship in these waters that's faster than us," Henry said.

"Aye, but he draws half the water we do. If he wants, he can stay in close to shore and beyond the range of our guns."

"When I spoke with Captain Decatur, I had the impression this Suleiman Al-Jama isn't afraid of a fight."

"You think he'll come out to meet us?"

"Decatur thinks so."

"Good."

For the next fourteen hours, the *Siren* doggedly pursued the *Saqr*. With a greater spread of canvas, the American brig was several knots faster than Al-Jama's raider, but the Arab captain knew these waters better than anyone. Time and again he would lure the *Siren* danger-ously close to shoals and force her to tack off the chase in search of deeper water. The *Saqr* also managed to find stronger winds close to the shore, winds driven off the searing desert beyond the cliffs that towered over the coastline in unending ramparts.

The gap between the ships noticeably shrank when the sun started to set and the inshore breeze slowed.

"We'll have him within the hour," Stewart said, accepting a glass of tepid water from his cabin steward.

He surveyed the open gun deck. Crews were standing by their cannons, the keen edge of expectation in their eyes. Shot and pow-der charges were laid in and at the ready, though not too much in case a gun took a direct hit. Powder monkeys—boys as young as ten—were ready to scamper back and forth to the magazine to keep the weapons fed. Men were aloft in the rigging, ready to alter sail as the battle dictated. And pairs of Marine marksmen were making their way to the fighting tops on the foremast and mainmast. Two were brothers from Appalachia, and while no one on the crew could understand them when they spoke they both could load and shoot four times a minute and score bull's-eyes with all four shots.

Two white plumes suddenly obscured the *Saqr*'s fantail, and a moment later came the boom of the shots. One ball landed fifty yards off the *Intrepid*'s port bow while the other landed well astern.

Stewart and Lafayette looked at each other. Henry gave voice to their mutual concern. "Her stern chasers are long guns. Double our range at the very least."

"Mr. Jackson, come about to port ten degrees," Stewart ordered, to throw off the *Saqr*'s gunners. "Standing order for a similar maneuver with every shot fired. Turn toward where the closest ball falls."

"And your orders if we're hit?" the big bosun asked before he could stop himself.

Stewart could have had Jackson lashed for such an insolent comment; instead, he said, "Dock yourself a day's pay, and hope we have more ship than you have salary."

The wind close to shore suddenly died. The *Saqr*'s large triangular sails lost tension and flapped uselessly while those aboard the *Intrepid* remained taut. They came in astern of the pirate ship at a slight angle, so as to avoid her aft guns. At a hundred and fifty yards, three of the *Saqr*'s cannons fired, blowing a wall of smoke over the corsair's flank that completely hid her from view. Two rounds went high, while the third struck the *Siren*'s hull but didn't penetrate.

Stewart remained silent, closing the distance, increasing his chances of a hit with each foot gained. He saw they weren't yet targeted by any of the other guns, so he waited until the Arab crew was running out the weapons they had just cleaned and reloaded.

"Fire as you bear!"

Four carronades went off with one throaty roar that beat in on Henry's chest as if he'd been kicked. The bow was enveloped in smoke that whipped along the length of the *Intrepid*'s hull as she charged the *Saqr*. On the fighting tops, the Marines were busy with their muskets, picking off pirates on the *Saqr*'s deck who thought they were invisible behind the ship's railings.

Two more cannons roared before anyone could see if their first salvo scored. The *Saqr* responded with a raking broadside that had been perfectly aimed. One ball smashed a carronade with a lit fuse, knocking the weapon on its side as it fired. That ball hit the adjacent gun crew, killing two men and maiming another. Bags of powder burned like incandescent flares. Another of the *Saqr*'s shots smashed the *Intrepid*'s mainmast, though not enough to topple it, while others ripped needle-sharp splinters from the bulwarks with enough velocity to run a man through.

"Mr. Jackson," Stewart shouted over the sounds of battle, "take some sail off the mainmast before we lose it entirely. Mr. Lafayette, take charge up on the bow. Get those fires out and the carronades sorted."

"Aye, aye, sir." Henry threw a quick salute and raced for the bow as musket fire from the *Saqr* raked the decks.

He looked over to see a fire raging on the Barbary ship. The *Intrepid* was giving as good as she got. He could see one figure shouting orders, not in a panicked way but with a calm that belied the situation. He wore clean white robes and had a contrasting dark beard shot through with two lines of white whiskers falling from the corners of his mouth. His nose was large and so heavily hooked it could almost touch his upper lip.

Suleiman Al-Jama must have felt the scrutiny, because he chose that moment to look across at the American ship. At a hundred yards, Henry could feel the hatred radiating off the man. A fresh blast from the guns obscured the pirate captain for a moment, and Henry had to duck as the railing behind him burst apart. When he looked again, Al-Jama was still staring.

Henry looked away.

He reached the bow and quickly organized a bucket brigade to douse the flames. The one carronade that had been hit was destroyed, but the gun next to it was in good order. Henry took command of it himself. The teenage midshipman who had been in charge of this section of guns was burned beyond recognition.

He aimed the loaded gun and touched the fuse with a length of smoldering slow match. The gun bellowed, sliding back on its guide rails in the blink of an eye. Lafayette had men swabbing the barrel before he checked the *Saqr* for damage. Their ball had hit next to one of the gunports, and through the hole it had blown into the wood he could see that men were down, writhing in agony.

"Reload!"

At nearly point-blank range the two ships pounded on each other like prizefighters who don't know when to quit. It was getting darker now, but they were so close that the crews could aim using the glow of the fires that flashed and ebbed.

The weight of shot from the *Saqr* began to die down. The Americans were destroying her cannons one by one. And when no return fire came from the Tripolian vessel for nearly a minute, Stewart ordered the *Siren* in tighter.

"Boarding parties at the ready."

Sailors took up grappling hooks to bind the two ships fast, while others passed out pikes, axes, and swords. Henry checked the priming pans of the two pistols tucked into his belt and drew his cutlass.

Pushing a swell of white water off her bow, the *Siren* charged the *Saqr* like a bull, and when the ships were a dozen feet apart the hooks were thrown. The instant the hulls smashed into each other, Henry leapt across to the other ship.

No sooner had his feet touched the deck than a series of blistering explosions raced along the length of the pirate vessel. Her cannons hadn't been silenced at all. They had pretended to be unarmed to lure the *Siren* in close. Twelve guns poured their shot into the American brig, raking the line of men at her rail. Stewart had to veer off sharply. Sailors hacked at the grappling ropes in a desperate bid to get free.

Seeing his shipmates cut down like that pained Henry as if it were his own flesh torn apart. But he didn't have time to jump back aboard before his ship had put twenty feet between herself and the pirate vessel. He was trapped on the *Saqr*. Musket balls from the Marines whined over his head.

The Arabs manning the *Saqr*'s guns hadn't noticed him leap. The only course open to Henry was to jump into the sea and pray he was a strong enough swimmer to reach the distant shore. He started creeping for the far rail and had almost made it when a figure suddenly loomed above him.

He instinctively went on the charge before the man could fully comprehend what he was seeing. Henry pulled one of his pistols with his left hand and fired an instant before his shoulder collided with the man's chest.

As they tumbled over the railing, he recognized the distinctive white streaks in the other man's beard: Suleiman Al-Jama.

They hit the bath-warm water tangled together. Henry broke the surface to find Al-Jama next to him, gasping to fill his lungs. He was thrashing wildly, but oddly, too. It was then that Henry noticed the dark stain on the otherwise white robe. The ball from his pistol had hit the captain at the shoulder joint, and he couldn't lift that arm.

Looking quickly, he saw the *Saqr* was already fifty feet away and was again trading broadsides with the *Siren*. There was no way anyone on either ship could hear Henry shouting, so he didn't bother.

Al-Jama's efforts to keep his head above water were growing weaker. He still couldn't get his lungs to reinflate, and his heavy robes were dragging him under. Henry had been a strong swimmer his entire life, but it was clear the Arab was not. His head vanished below the surface for a moment, and he came up sputtering. But not once did he cry out for help.

He went under again, longer this time, and when he returned to the surface he could barely keep his lips out of the water. Henry kicked off his heavy boots and used his dirk to slice open Al-Jama's robe. The clothing floated free, but Al-Jama wouldn't last another minute.

The coastline was at least three miles distant, and Henry Lafayette wasn't sure if he could make it at all let alone while towing the pirate, but Suleiman Al-Jama's life was in his hands now and he had the responsibility to do everything in his power to save him.

He reached around Al-Jama's bare chest. The captain thrashed to push him off.

Henry said, "The moment we fell off the ship, you stopped being my enemy, but I swear to God that if you fight me I'll let you drown."

"I would rather," Suleiman replied in heavily accented English.

"Have it your way, then." With that, Henry pulled his second pistol and smashed it into Al-Jama's temple. Grabbing the unconscious man under one arm, he started paddling for shore.

ONE

WASHINGTON, D.C.

S<small>T. JULIAN PERLMUTTER SHIFTED HIS CONSIDERABLE BULK</small> in the backseat of his 1955 Rolls-Royce Silver Dawn. He plucked a tulip flute of vintage champagne off the fold-down table in front of him, took a delicate sip, and continued reading. Stacked next to the champagne and a plate of canapés were photocopies of letters sent to Admiral Charles Stewart over the length of his incredible career. Stewart had served every President from John Adams to Abraham Lincoln, and had been awarded more commands than any officer in American history. The original letters were safely tucked away in the Rolls's trunk.

As perhaps the leading naval historian in the world, Perlmutter deplored the fact that some philistine had subjected the letters to the ravages of a photocopier—light damages paper and fades ink—but he wasn't above taking advantage of the gaffe, and he started reading the copies as soon as he had settled in for the drive back from Cherry Hill, New Jersey.

He'd been after this collection for years, and it had taken his considerable charm, and a rather large check, to see that it wasn't given to the government and archived in some out-of-the-way location.

If the letters turned out to be uninteresting, he planned to keep the copies for reference and donate the originals for the tax benefit.

He glanced out the window. The traffic into the nation's capital was murder, as usual, but Hugo Mulholland, his longtime chauffeur and assistant, seemed to be handling it well. The Rolls glided down I-95 as if it were the only car on the road.

The collection had passed through numerous generations of the Stewart family, but the branch that held them now was dying out. The only child of Mary Stewart Kilpatrick, whose row house Perlmutter had just left, had no interest in it, and her only grandchild was severely autistic. St. Julian really didn't begrudge the price he'd paid, knowing the money would help support the boy.

The letter he was reading was to the Secretary of War, Joel Roberts Poinsett, and had been written during Stewart's first command of the Philadelphia Navy Yard between 1838 and 1841. The letter's contents were rather dry: lists of supplies needed, progress on the repairs of a frigate, remarks about the quality of sails they had received. Though competent at his job, it was clear in the writing that Stewart would much rather captain a ship again than oversee the facility.

Perlmutter set it aside, popped a canapé in his mouth, and washed it down with another sip of champagne. He leafed through a couple more letters, settling on one written to Stewart by a bosun who had served under his command during the Barbary Wars. The writing was barely legible, and the author, one John Jackson, appeared to have had limited schooling. He reminisced about being a part of the raid to burn the USS *Philadelphia* and the subsequent gun battle with a pirate ship called the *Saqr*.

St. Julian was well aware of these exploits. He'd read Captain Decatur's firsthand account of the burning of the American frigate, although there wasn't much material on the fight with the *Saqr* other than Stewart's own report to the War Department.

Reading the letter, St. Julian could almost smell the gun smoke and hear the screams as the *Saqr* lured the *Siren* in close then let loose with a surprise broadside.

In the letter, Jackson asked the admiral about the fate of the brig's second-in-command, Henry Lafayette. Perlmutter recalled that the young lieutenant had leapt aboard the Tripolian ship a moment before her cannons fired, and he presumably had been killed since no ransom had ever been asked for his return.

He read on, piqued as he realized he had it wrong. Jackson had seen Lafayette fighting the *Saqr*'s captain, and both had gone over the port rail together. "The lad fell into the sea with that fiend (spelled *feinde*) Suleiman Al-Jama."

The name jolted Perlmutter. It wasn't the historical context that surprised him—he dimly recalled the *Saqr*'s captain's name. Rather, it was the present-day incarnation of the name that tripped him up: Suleiman Al-Jama was the nom de guerre of a terrorist only slightly less wanted than Osama bin Laden.

The *modern* Al-Jama had starred in several beheading videos and was the spiritual inspiration for countless suicide bombers throughout the Middle East, Pakistan, and Afghanistan. His crowning achievement had been leading an assault on a remote Pakistani Army outpost that left more than a hundred soldiers dead.

St. Julian searched though the letters to see if Stewart had responded and kept a copy, as had been his practice. Sure enough, the next letter in the stack was addressed to John Jackson. He read it once, rushing through it in astonishment, then read it again more slowly. He sat back so the leather seat creaked under his weight. He wondered if there were any contemporary implications to what he had just read and decided there probably weren't.

He was about to start perusing another letter when he reconsidered. What if the government could use this information? What would it gain them? Most likely nothing, but he didn't think it was his call to make.

Normally, when he came across something interesting in his research, he would pass it along to his good friend Dirk Pitt, the Director of the National Underwater and Marine Agency, but he wasn't sure if this fell under NUMA's sphere of influence quite yet. Perlmutter was an old Washington hand and had contacts throughout the city. He knew just who to call.

The car's telephone had a Bakelite handset and rotary dial. Perlmutter detested cell phones and never carried one. His thick finger barely fit in the telephone dial's little holes, but he managed.

"Hello," a woman answered.

St. Julian had called her direct line, thus avoiding an army of assistants.

"Hi, Christie, it's St. Julian Perlmutter."

"St. Julian!" Christie Valero cried. "It's been ages. How have you been?"

Perlmutter rubbed his bulging stomach. "You know me. I'm wasting away to nothing."

"I sure that's the case." She laughed. "Have you made my mother's Coquilles St.-Jacques since you cajoled her secret recipe out of me?"

Apart from his vast knowledge of ships and shipping, Perlmutter was a legendary gourmand and bon vivant.

"It's now part of my regular repertoire," he assured her. "Whenever you'd like, give me a call and I'll make it for you."

"I'll take you up on that. You know I can't follow cooking instructions more sophisticated than 'Pierce outer wrapper to vent and place on microwave-safe dish.' So is this a social call or is there something on your mind? I'm a little swamped here. The conference is still months away, but the dragon lady is running us ragged."

"That is no way to refer to her," he admonished mildly.

"Are you kidding? Fiona loves it."

"I'll take your word for it."

"So what's up?"

"I've just now come across something rather interesting and I thought you might like first crack at it." He relayed what he'd read in Charles Stewart's letter to his former shipmate.

When he finished, Christie Valero had just one question. "How soon can you be in my office?"

"Hugo," St. Julian said when he replaced the telephone on its cradle, "change of plans. We're going to Foggy Bottom. Our Undersecretary of State for Mideast Affairs would like to have a chat."

TWO

THE INDIAN OCEAN WAS A SHIMMERING JEWEL, PERFECTLY clear and blue. But on its surface was a flaw in the shape of a five-hundred-and-sixty-foot freighter. The ship was barely making headway, though her single stack belched copious amounts of noxious black smoke. It was clear the vessel was plying the sea-lanes far beyond her intended life span.

She was so low in the water that she had been forced on a circuitous route from Mumbai to avoid any storms because seas much above four feet would wash across her deck. Her port side would ship water in smaller swells because she had a slight list to that side. The hull was painted a scabrous green, with patches of other colors where the crew had run out of the primary shade. Tongues of scaly rust ran from her scuppers, and large metal plates had been welded to her sides to shore up structural deficiencies.

The tramp freighter's superstructure was just aft of amidships, giving her three cargo holds on her foredeck and two aft. The three cranes towering over the decks were heavily rusted and their cables frayed. The decks themselves were littered with leaky barrels, broken machinery, and clutter. Where pieces of her railing had rusted away, the crew had hung lengths of chain.

To the men studying her from a nearby fishing boat, the freighter didn't appear promising, but they were in no position to ignore the opportunity she presented.

The Somali captain was a wiry, hatchet-faced man missing a tooth in the center of his mouth. The other teeth around the gap were badly rotted, and his gums were black with decay. He conferred with the three other men on the crowded bridge before plucking a hand mic from the two-way transceiver and thumbing the button. "Ahoy, nearby freighter." His English was heavily accented but passable.

A moment later a voice burst over the tinny speaker. "Is this the fishing boat off my port beam?"

"Yes. We are in need of doctor," the captain said. "Four of my men are very sick. Do you have?"

"One of our crew was a Navy medic. What are their symptoms?"

"I do not know this word *sim-toms*."

"How are they sick?" the radio operator on the freighter asked.

"They throw up bad for days. Bad food, I think."

"Okay. I think we can handle that. Come abeam of us just ahead of the superstructure. We will slow as much as we can, but we won't be able to stop completely. Do you understand?"

"Yes, yes. I understand. You no stop. Is okay." He shot a wolfish grin at his comrades, saying in his native tongue, "They believe me. They're not going to stop, probably because the engines wouldn't refire, but that isn't a problem. Abdi, take the helm. Put us alongside near the superstructure and match their speed."

"Yes, Hakeem."

"Let's get on deck," the captain said to the other two.

They met up with four men who had been in the cabin below the wheelhouse. These men had ragged blankets draped over their thin shoulders and moved as if crippled with cramps.

The freighter dwarfed the sixty-foot fishing boat, though with her so low in the water the ship's rail wasn't that far above their own. Crewmen had hung truck tires for fenders and retracted a section of railing near the superstructure to make it easier to transfer the stricken men aboard. Hakeem counted four of them. One, a short Asian man, wore a uniform shirt with black epaulettes. Another was a large African or Caribbean islander, and the other two he wasn't sure.

"Are you the captain?" Hakeem called to the officer.

"Yes. Captain Kwan."

"Thank you for doing this. My men are very sick, but we must stay at sea to catch fish."

"It is my duty," Kwan said rather haughtily. "Your boat will have to stay close by while we treat your men. We're headed to the Suez Canal and can't detour to take them ashore."

"That is not a problem," Hakeem said with an oily smile as he handed up a line. The African crewman secured it to a rail stanchion.

"Okay, let's have them," Kwan said.

Hakeem helped one of his men step onto their boat's railing. The gap between the two vessels was less than a foot, and in these calm seas there was little chance of his slipping. The two of them stepped up and across to the freighter's deck and moved aside for two more at their heels.

It was when the fourth jumped nimbly onto his ship that Captain Kwan became wary.

As he opened his mouth to question the seriousness of their condition, the four men with the blankets let them drop away. Concealed underneath were AK-47s with the wooden butts crudely cut off. Aziz and Malik, the two other crewmen from the fishing boat, grabbed matching weapons from a wooden chest and rushed aboard.

"Pirates!" Kwan yelled, and had the muzzle of one weapon rammed into his stomach.

He dropped to his knees, clutching his abdomen. Hakeem pulled an automatic pistol from behind his back while the other armed men hustled the freighter's crew away from the rail and out of sight of anyone who may have been on the bridge wing high overhead.

The Somali leader dragged the captain to his feet, pressing the barrel of his pistol into Kwan's neck. "Do as you are told and no one will be hurt."

There was a momentary spark of defiance behind Kwan's eyes, something he couldn't suppress, but it was fleeting, and the pirate hadn't noticed. He nodded awkwardly.

"You will take us to the radio room," Hakeem continued. "You will make an announcement to your crew that they are to go to the mess hall. Everyone must be there. If we find anyone walking around the ship, he will be killed."

While he was talking, his men were cuffing the stunned crew with plastic zip ties. They used three on the muscle-bound black man, just in case.

While Aziz and Malik took charge of the other crewmen, Kwan led Hakeem and the four "sick" pirates into the superstructure, a pistol pressed to his spine. The interior of the ship was only a few degrees cooler than outside, thanks to a barely functioning air-conditioning system. The halls and passageways looked as if they hadn't been cleaned since the freighter had slipped down the ways. The linoleum flooring was cracked and peeling, and dust bunnies the size of jackrabbits lurked in every corner.

It took less than a minute to climb up to the bridge, where a helmsman stood behind the large wooden wheel and another officer was hunched over a chart table littered with plates of congealing food and a chart so old and faded it could have depicted the coastline of Pangaea. The windows were nearly opaque with rimed salt.

"How'd it go with the fishermen?" the officer asked without looking up. His voice had an odd British inflection that wasn't quite right. He lifted his head and blanched. His big, innocent eyes went wide. The four pirates had the entire room covered with their assault rifles, and the captain's head was bent sideways with the pressure of the pistol jammed into his neck.

"No heroics," Kwan said. "They promised not to harm anyone if we just follow their orders. Open a shipwide channel please, Mr. Maryweather."

"Aye, Captain." Moving deliberately, the young officer, Duane Maryweather, reached for the intercom button located next to the ship's radio. He handed the microphone to his captain.

Hakeem screwed the pistol deeper into Kwan's neck. "If you give any warning, I will kill you now, and my men will slaughter your crew."

"You have my word," Kwan said tightly. He keyed the mic, and his voice echoed from loudspeakers placed all over the vessel. "This is the captain speaking. There is a mandatory meeting in the mess hall for all crew members immediately. On-duty engineering staff are not exempt."

"That is enough," Hakeem snapped, and took away the microphone. "Abdul, take the wheel." He waved his pistol at Maryweather and the helmsman. "You two, over next to the captain."

"You can't leave just one man at the helm," Kwan protested.

"This is not the first ship we have taken."

"No. I suppose it isn't."

With no discernible government, Somalia was ruled by rival warlords, some of whom had turned to piracy to fund their armies. The waters of this Horn of Africa country were some of the most dangerous in the world. Ships were attacked on an almost daily basis, and while the United States and other nations maintained a naval presence in the region the seas were simply too vast to protect every ship that steamed along the coast. Pirates usually used fast speedboats and mostly robbed the ships of any cash or valuables, but what started out as simple larceny had expanded. Now entire ships were being hijacked, their cargoes sold on the black market and their crews either abandoned in lifeboats, held for ransom to the vessel's owners, or killed outright.

So, too, had the sizes of the targeted ships increased along with the savagery of the attacks. Where once only small coastal freighters were the primary targets, the pirates now preyed on tankers and containerships, and had once raked a cruise liner with automatic fire for fifteen minutes. Recently, a new warlord had started putting a stranglehold on other pirates along the north coast, consolidating his power base until every pirate in the region was loyal to him alone.

His name was Mohammad Didi, and he'd been a fighter in the capital, Mogadishu, during the chaotic days of the mid-1990s, when the United Nations was trying to stave off epidemic starvation in the drought-ridden country. He had secured a name for himself plundering trucks loaded with emergency food and supplies, but it was during the Black Hawk Down incident that he cemented his reputation. He had led the charge against an American position and destroyed a Humvee with an RPG. He had then dragged the bodies from the burning wreckage and hacked them to pieces with a machete.

After the inglorious withdrawal of the U.S. Marine Corps, Didi continued to build his power base until he was one of only a handful of warlords controlling the country. Then, in 1998, he had been linked to the Al-Qaeda bombings of the American embassies in

Kenya and Tanzania. He had given the bombers safe haven for the weeks leading up to the attack, as well as several men to act as look-outs. With an indictment at the World Court in The Hague and a half-million-dollar price on his head, Didi knew it was only a matter of time before one of his rivals would try to collect on the bounty. He moved his operation out of Mogadishu and into an area of coastal swamps three hundred miles to the north.

Before his arrival, most victims of piracy were set free immediately. It was Didi who had initiated the ransom demands. And if they were not met, or the negotiations seemed to be faltering, he unceremoniously had the crews killed. It was rumored that he wore a necklace of teeth with gold fillings extracted from the men he had personally murdered. It was to Didi that the pirates taking control of the old freighter had pledged their oath.

Hakeem and one of his men forced Captain Kwan to take them to his office, while the other pirates escorted the bridge staff to the mess hall. Kwan's office was attached to his cabin one deck below the pilothouse. The rooms were spartan but clean, with just a couple of tacky velvet clown paintings on the otherwise bare metal walls. There was a framed photograph of Kwan and a woman, most likely his wife, on the empty desk.

Brassy light blazed through the single porthole.

"Show me crew manifest," Hakeem demanded.

There was a small safe bolted to the deck in the corner of the office behind Kwan's desk. The captain stooped over it and began to work the combination.

"You will step back when you open the door," the pirate ordered.

Kwan glanced over his shoulder. "I assure you we have no weapons." But he did as he was told. He swung open the door and took a step back from the safe.

With his assistant covering Kwan with his AK, Hakeem bent

over the safe, pulling out files and folders and dumping everything on the captain's desk. He made a sound when he opened one particularly thick envelope and discovered bundles of cash in several currencies. He fanned a wad of hundred-dollar bills under his beaky nose, inhaling as if testing a fine wine.

"How much you have?"

"Twelve thousand dollars, maybe a bit less."

Hakeem stuffed the envelope into his shirt. He rifled through the papers until he found the crew's manifest. He couldn't read his native Somali, let alone English, but he recognized the various passports. There were twenty-two in all. He checked them, pulling out Kwan's, Duane Maryweather's, and that of the helmsman. He also found the passports belonging to the three men who had been on deck when they had boarded the ship. He was pleased. They had already accounted for a quarter of the crew.

"Now, take us to the mess hall."

When they arrived, the brightly lit room was packed with men. A few smoked cigarettes, so the air was as thick as smog, but it masked the stench of nervous sweat. They were a mix of races, and even without the weapons pointing at them they were a dour lot. These were down-on-their-luck men who could find no better employment than aboard a broken-down old tramp freighter. They had maintained her well beyond her years for the simple reason that they would never find another after she was gone.

One of Kwan's people held a bloody rag to the back of his head. He had obviously said or done something to set off one of the hijackers.

"What's going on, Captain?" asked the chief engineer. His jumpsuit was streaked with grease.

"What does it look like? We've been boarded by pirates."

"Silence," Hakeem roared.

He went through the stacks of passports he'd brought from Kwan's office, comparing the photographs to the men seated around the mess until he was certain every member of the crew was accounted for. He had once made the mistake of trusting a captain about his ship's complement, only to find that there had been two others who had beaten one of Hakeem's men to death and almost managed to radio a Mayday before they were discovered.

"Very good. No one is playing hero." He set aside the passports and looked around the room. He was an excellent judge of fear and liked what he saw. He sent one of his men out to the deck to cast off their fishing boat with orders for Abdi to make for their base as quickly as he could with the news they had captured the freighter. "My name is Hakeem, and this ship is now mine. If you follow my orders, you will not be killed. Any attempt to escape and you will be shot and your body fed to the sharks. Those are the two things you must remember at all times."

"My men will follow orders," Kwan said resignedly. "We'll do whatever you say. We all want to see our families again."

"That is very wise, Captain. With your help, I will contact the ship's owners to negotiate your release."

"Bastards won't spring for a gallon of paint," the engineer muttered to a table companion. "Fat luck they'll pay to save our hides."

Two of the gunmen had been in the kitchen gathering up anything that could be used as a weapon. They emerged dragging a linen bag full of forks, steak knives, kitchen knives, and cleavers. One gunman remained in the mess while the other continued to haul the bag out into the hallway, where it would most likely be thrown over the side.

"These guys know what they're doing," Duane whispered to the ship's radio operator. "I would have gone for a knife as soon as their guard was down."

Maryweather hadn't realized one of the pirates was directly

behind him. The Kalashnikov crashed down on the back of his neck hard enough to drive his face into the Formica-topped table. When he straightened, blood dripped from a nostril.

"Talk again and you will die," Hakeem said, and from the tone of his voice it was clearly the last warning. "I see there is a bathroom attached to the mess hall, so you will all remain here. There is only one way in or out of this room, and it will be barred from the outside and guarded at all times." He switched to Somali and said to his men, "Let's go see what they are carrying for cargo."

They filed out of the mess and secured the door with heavy-duty wire wrapped around the handle and tied to a handrail on the opposite wall of the passageway. Hakeem ordered one of his men to stay outside the door while he and the others systematically searched the vessel.

Given the ship's large external dimensions, the interior spaces were remarkably cramped, and the holds smaller than expected. The aft holds were blocked by rows of shipping containers so tightly packed that not even the skinniest pirate could squeeze by. They would have to wait until they reached harbor and the containers were unloaded before they would know what was inside them. What they discovered in the forward three holds made whatever was in the containers superfluous. Amid the crates of machine parts, Indian-made car engines, and table-sized slabs of steel plate, they found six pickup trucks. When mounted with machine guns, the vehicles were known as technicals and were a favored weapons platform across Africa. There was another, larger truck, but it looked so dilapidated it probably didn't run. The ship was also carrying pallets of wheat in bags stenciled with the name of a world charity, but the greatest prize were hundreds of drums of ammonium nitrate. Used primarily as a potent fertilizer, the nitrate compound, when mixed with diesel fuel, became a powerful explosive. There was enough in the hold to level half of Mogadishu, if that's what Mohammad Didi wanted to do with it.

Hakeem knew that Didi's exile into the swamps wasn't permanent. He always talked about returning to the capital and taking on the other warlords in a final confrontation. This massive amount of explosives would surely give him the edge over the others. In a month or less, Hakeem was sure Didi would be the ruler of all of Somalia, and he was just as sure that his reward for taking the freighter would be greater than anything he could imagine.

He now wished he hadn't sent Abdi ahead so quickly, but there was nothing he could do about it. Their little radio couldn't pick up anything beyond a couple of miles, and the fishing boat was already out of range.

He returned to the bridge to enjoy the Cuban cigar he had pilfered from the captain's cabin. The sun was sinking fast over the horizon, turning the great ocean into a sheet of burnished bronze. Dusk's beauty was lost on men like Hakeem and his band of pirates. They existed on an ugly, cruel level where everything was judged based on what it could do for them. Some would argue that they were the product of their war-ravished country, that they never stood a chance against the brutality of their upbringing. The truth was that the vast majority of Somalia's population had never fired a gun in their lives, and the men who aligned themselves with a warlord like Didi did it because they enjoyed the power it gave them over others, like the crew of this ship.

He liked seeing the captain's head bowed in defeat. He liked the fear he saw in the sailors' eyes. He had found a picture of the captain and a woman in the office, the captain's wife he assumed. Hakeem had the power to make that woman a widow. For him, there was no greater rush in the world.

Aziz and Malik entered the bridge. They had helped themselves to some new clothes from the officers' quarters. Aziz, only twenty-five but a veteran of a dozen hijackings, was so slender that he'd had to cut extra holes in the belt to keep his new jeans up around his waist. Malik was in his forties, and had fought at Mohammad Didi's side against the United Nations and the Americans. Shrapnel from a street fight with a rival gang had left the right side of his face in ruin, and the blow had affected his mind. He rarely spoke, and, when he did, little of what he said made sense. But he followed orders to the letter, which was all Hakeem demanded of him.

"Go get the captain. I want to talk to him about the company that owns this ship. I want to know how much he thinks they will be willing to pay." He studied Aziz's eyes. "And lay off the bang." He used the African nickname for marijuana.

The two pirates descended the stairs to the main deck. With the sun setting, the interior of the ship was gloomy. There were only a few functioning lamps, so shadows clung to the ceilings and walls like moss. Aziz nodded to the guard to untie the wire. He and Malik had their weapons at the ready when the door creaked inward. All three men gaped.

The mess hall was empty.

THREE

MALIK AND AZIZ HAD JUST STEPPED INTO THE EMPTY MESS hall when the guard felt a presence down the hall. He peered into the gloom, raising his rifle. Had he not been so spooked by the crew vanishing, he would have calmly explored the passageway. But every nerve in his body tingled with electricity as if a mild current had been applied to his skin. His finger curled around the trigger, and he unleashed a wild, ten-round burst. The juddering flame from the barrel of his AK-47 revealed the hall was deserted, while the bullets did nothing more than scrape more paint off the dingy walls.

"What is it?" Aziz demanded.

"I thought I saw someone," the guard stammered.

Aziz made his decision quickly. "Malik, go with him and search this deck. I will tell Hakeem what has happened."

The pirate leader had heard the gunfire and met up with Aziz halfway down from the bridge. He was holding his pistol like he had seen in music videos, arched at arm's length and turned flat on its side, and his eyes were bright with anger.

"Who was shooting, and why?" He didn't slow his pace when they met, forcing Aziz to double back quickly.

"The mess hall is empty, and Ahmed thought he saw someone. He and Malik are searching now."

Hakeem wasn't sure what he was hearing. "What do you mean the mess hall is empty?"

"The crew is all gone. The wire was still on the door and Ahmed was awake, but somehow they are gone."

The mess door was barely ajar when they arrived, so Hakeem kicked it open with all his strength. It crashed against the doorstop with a booming echo. Just as they had left the crew hours earlier, all twenty-two members were still seated around the tables. They all had tense, anxious expressions.

"What was that gunfire?" Captain Kwan asked.

Hakeem gave Aziz a murderous look. "A rat."

He grabbed the younger man by the arm and pushed him from the room. As soon as the door was closed behind Hakeem, he slapped Aziz across the face and backhanded him in a perfect follow-through. "You fool. You're so stoned right now, you don't know which is your dung hand."

"No, Hakeem. I swear it. We all saw—"

"Enough! I catch you smoking bang during one of my operations again, I will shoot you where you stand. Got it?" Aziz's eyes were cast down, and he said nothing. Hakeem grabbed Aziz's jaw so their eyes met. "Got it?" he repeated.

"Yes, Hakeem."

"Retie this door, and find Malik and Ahmed before they shoot up more of the ship."

Aziz did as he was ordered while Hakeem lingered. Hakeem pressed his ear to the door but couldn't hear anything through the thick metal. He glanced around the empty corridor. There was nothing out of the ordinary, but he had the sudden sense that some- one was watching him. The sensation tingled at the base of his skull and raced down his back so that he visibly quivered. *Damn fools will have me chasing shadows next.*

●　　●　　●

TWO DECKS BELOW THE MESS, in a section of the ship the pirates couldn't dream existed, Juan Rodriguez Cabrillo watched the Somali shiver. A slight smile played at the corners of his mouth.

"Boo," he said at the image on the large, flat-panel display that dominated the front of the room known as the Operations Center.

The op center was the high-tech brains of the vessel, a low-ceilinged space that glowed faintly blue from the countless computer screens. The floors were covered in antiskid, antistatic rubber, and the consoles were done in smoky grays and black. The effect, as was the intention, was a darker version of the bridge of television's star-ship *Enterprise*. The two seats directly in front of the main display panel were the ship's helm and weapons-control station. Ringing the room were workstations for radio, radar, sonar, engineering, and damage control.

In the middle sat what was known as the Kirk Chair. From it, Cabrillo had an unobstructed view of everything taking place around him, and from the computer built into the arm of the well-padded seat he could take control of any function aboard his ship.

"You shouldn't have let them do that," admonished Max Hanley, the president of the Corporation. Cabrillo held the title of chairman. "What if Mohammad Didi's boys came back when the secret door was open?"

"Max, you worry like my grandmother. We would have retaken the *Oregon* from them and gone to plan B."

"Which is?"

"I'd tell you as soon as I came up with it." Juan stood and stretched his arms over his head.

He was solidly built, topping out near six feet, with a strong, weathered face and startlingly blue eyes. He kept his hair in a long crew cut. An upbringing on the beaches of southern California and a lifetime of swimming had bleached it white blond. Though he was on the other side of forty, it was still thick and stiff.

There was a compelling aura about Cabrillo that people picked up almost immediately but could never really put their fingers on. He didn't have the polish of a corporate heavy hitter or the rigidity of a career soldier. It was more a sense that he knew what he wanted out of life and made certain he got it every day. That, and he possessed a wellspring of confidence that knew no bottom—a confidence earned over a lifetime of achievement.

Max Hanley, on the other hand, was in his early sixties and a veteran of two tours in Vietnam. He was shorter than Cabrillo, with a bright, florid face and a halo of ginger curls in the shape of a horseshoe around his balding head. He could stand to lose a few pounds, something Juan delighted in teasing him about, but Max was rock solid in every sense of the word.

The Corporation had been Cabrillo's brainchild, but it was Max's steady hand that made it such a success. He managed the day-to-day affairs of the multimillion-dollar company and also acted as the *Oregon*'s chief engineer. If any man loved the ship more than Juan, it was Max Hanley.

Despite the seven heavily armed pirates roaming the vessel and the twenty-two crew members held "captive" in the mess hall, there was no concern in the op center, especially on Cabrillo's part.

This operation had been planned with meticulous attention to detail. When the pirates had first come aboard—arguably, the most critical moment, because no one knew how they were going to treat the crew—snipers positioned in the bows had held all seven Somalis in their sights. Also, the deck crew wore micro-thin body armor, which was still under development in Germany for NATO.

There were pinhole cameras and listening devices secreted in every hallway and room in the "public" parts of the ship, so the gunmen were observed at all times. Wherever they went, at least two members of the Corporation shadowed them from inside the *Oregon*'s hidden compartments, ready to react to any situation.

The old freighter was really two ships in one. On the outside, she was little more than a derelict trying to stay one step ahead of the breaker's yard. However, that was all a façade to deflect her true nature from customs inspectors, harbor pilots, and anyone else who happened to find themselves aboard her. Her state of dilapidation was meant to make anyone seeing the *Oregon* immediately forget her.

The rust streaks were painted on, the debris cluttering her deck was placed there intentionally. The wheelhouse and cabins in the superstructure were nothing more than stage sets. The pirate currently manning the helm had zero control over the ship. The helmsman in the Operations Center was fed data from the wheel through the computer system, and he made the appropriate course corrections.

All this was a shell over perhaps the most sophisticated intelligence-gathering ship in the world. She bristled with hidden weapons, and had an electronics suite to rival any Aegis-class destroyer. Her hull was armored enough to repel most low-tech weapons used by terrorists, such as rocket-propelled grenades. She carried two minisubs that could be deployed through special doors along her keel, and a McDonnell Douglas MD-520N helicopter in her rear hold, hidden by a wall made to look like stacked containers.

As for the crew's accommodations, they rivaled the grandest

rooms on a luxury cruise ship. The men and women of the Corporation risked their lives every day, so Juan wanted to ensure they were
as comfortable as possible.

"Where's our guest?" Max asked.

"Chatting up Julia again."

"Think it's the fact she's a doctor or a looker?"

"Colonel Giuseppe Farina, as his name implies, is Italian. And
I happen to know he considers himself the best, so he is after her
because she is female. Linda Ross and all the other women have
blown him off enough since he first came aboard. Our good Dr.
Huxley is the last one left, and since she can't leave medical in case
there's an emergency Colonel Farina has a captive audience."

"Damned waste to have an observer with us in the first place,"
Max said.

"You go with the deal you've got, not the one you want," Juan pontificated. "The powers that be don't want anything to go wrong during the trial once they get their hands on Didi. Farina's here to make
sure we follow by the engagement parameters they set out for us."

A sour look crossed Max's pug face. "Fighting terrorists using the
Marquis of Queensbury rules? Ridiculous."

"It isn't so bad. I've known 'Seppe for fifteen years. He's all right.
With no way to extradite Didi through legal channels, because
Somalia doesn't have a functioning court system—"

"Or anything else."

Juan ignored the interruption. "We offered an alternative. The
price we pay is 'Seppe's presence until we get Didi into international
waters and the U.S. Navy takes him off our hands. All Didi has to
do is set foot on this ship and we've got this in the bag."

Max nodded reluctantly. "And we've loaded what looks like
enough explosives aboard so he'll want to see it for himself."

"Exactly. The right bait for the right vermin."

The Corporation had taken on what was an unusual job for them. They typically worked for the government, tackling operations deemed too risky for American soldiers or members of the intelligence community, on a strictly cash-only basis. This time they were working through the CIA to help the World Court bring Mohammad Didi to justice. U.S. authorities wanted Didi sent straight to Guantánamo, but a deal was hashed out with America's allies that he be tried in Europe, provided he could be captured in a manner that didn't include rendition.

Langston Overholt, the Corporation's primary contact in the CIA, had approached his protégé, Juan Cabrillo, with the difficult task of grabbing Didi in such a way that it couldn't be construed as kidnapping. True to form, Cabrillo and his people had come up with their plan within twenty-four hours while everyone else involved had been scratching their heads for months.

Juan glanced at the chronometer set in one corner of the main view screen. He checked the ship's speed and heading and calculated they wouldn't reach the coast until dawn. "Care to join me for dinner? Lobster Thermidor, I think."

Max patted his belly. "Hux has me scheduled on the StairMaster for thirty minutes."

"Battle of the Bulge redux," Juan quipped.

"I want to see *your* waistline in twenty years, my friend."

•   •   •

THE SHIP REACHED the coastline a little after dawn. Here, mangrove swamps stretched the entire width of the horizon. Hakeem took the wheel himself because he was most familiar with the secret deepwater channels that would allow them access to their hidden base. While this was the largest vessel they had ever taken, he was confident he could reach their encampment without grounding, or at least get close enough so they wouldn't have much trouble unloading their cargo.

The air was hazy and heavy with humidity, and the moment the sun peeked over the horizon the temperature seemed to spike.

As the big freighter eased deeper into the swamp, her wake turned muddy brown from the silt her engines churned up. Hakeem had no idea how to read the fathometer mounted on a bulkhead at the helm, but only eight feet of water separated the ship's bottom from the muck. The trees grew denser still, hemming in the ship, until their branches almost met overhead.

The channel was barely wide enough for him to maneuver. He didn't remember it being so small, but then again he had never seen it from the wheelhouse of such a large vessel. The bow plowed into a submerged log that would have holed his fishing boat, but to the freighter it was a mere annoyance scraping along the hull. There was one more turn before they reached their base, but it was the tightest one yet. The opposite bank looked closer than the length of the ship.

"Do you think you can do it?" Aziz asked.

Hakeem didn't look at him. He was still angry about the incident the night before. "We're less than a kilometer from camp. Even if I don't, we can unload the ship and ferry everything back."

He tightened his grip on the wheel, bracing his feet a little farther apart. The prow eased into the corner, and he waited until the last second to start cranking the wheel. The ship didn't respond as quickly as he had hoped and continued to drive toward the far bank.

Then, ever so slowly, the bows started to come about, but it was a little too late. They were going to hit. Hakeem slammed the engine telegraph to full reverse in hopes of lessening the impact.

Several decks below, Cabrillo sat in his customary seat in the op center. Eric Stone was by far the *Oregon*'s best ship handler; however, he was currently locked in the mess hall pretending to be Duane Maryweather. In this instance, Cabrillo wouldn't have had him at the conn anyway. For waters this tight, Juan trusted no one but himself in control of his ship.

Though Hakeem had called for full reverse, Cabrillo ignored his command and hit the bow thruster instead. He also turned the nozzles of the directional pump jets that powered the ship as far as they would go.

Back on the bridge, it had to have seemed that a miracle wind had come up suddenly, although none of the trees moved. The bow swung sharply around as if pushed by an invisible hand. Hakeem and Aziz exchanged a startled look. They couldn't believe the freighter could turn so quickly, and neither realized the vessel had also righted itself in the channel after coming out of the turn. Hakeem uselessly turned the wheel anyway, still believing he had control.

"Allah has surely blessed this mission from the start," Aziz said, although neither man was particularly religious.

"Or maybe I know what I am doing," Hakeem said sharply.

The pirate camp lay on the right-hand bank, where it rose until it was almost level with the freighter's deck. The high ground protected the area from tides and spring flooding. There was a hundred-foot-long wooden dock built along the shore, accessible from the bank by several flights of steel stairs dug into the hard soil. The stairs had been taken from one of the first ships they had hijacked. Hakeem's boat was tied to the jetty along with two other small fishing vessels.

Beyond the bank lay the camp, a sprawl of haphazardly placed buildings made of whatever could be salvaged. There were tents once meant for refugees and traditional mud huts, plus structures built of native timber and sheathed in corrugated metal. It was home to more than eight hundred people, three hundred of them children. The perimeter was defined by four watchtowers made of lengths of pipe and weatherworn planks. The grounds were littered with trash and human waste. Half-feral dogs roamed in lean, mangy packs.

Throngs of cheering people lined the riverbank and crowded the dock to the point there was a real danger of its collapsing. There were half-naked kids, women in dusty dresses with infants strapped to their backs, and hundreds of men carrying their assault rifles. Many were firing into the air, the concussive noise so common here that the babies slept right through it. Standing in the center of the dock, and surrounded by his most trusted aides, was Mohammad Didi.

Despite his fearsome reputation, Didi wasn't a physically imposing man. He stood barely five foot six, and his self-styled uniform hung off his thin body like a scarecrow's rags. The lower half of his face was covered in a patchy beard that was shot through with whorls of gray. His eyes were rheumy and ringed in pink, while the whites were heavily veined with red lines. Didi was so slender that the big pistol hanging from his waist made his hips cock as if he suffered from scoliosis.

There was no trace of a smile, or any other expression, on his face. That was another of his trademarks. He never showed emotion—not when killing a man, not when holding one of his countless children for the first time—never.

Around his throat was a necklace made of irregular white beads that on closer inspection revealed themselves to be human teeth fitted with gold fillings.

It took Hakeem fifteen frustrating minutes to maneuver the big freighter to the dock, once approaching so fast that the people standing on it fled back to the riverbank. It would have taken longer, but Cabrillo finally had enough of the Somali's pathetic attempts and docked the ship himself. Pirates on the rail threw ropes down to the crowd below, and the ship was made fast against the pier.

The thick smoke that had poured from the funnel trickled off to a wisp. Hakeem gave a blast on the horn, and the crowd redoubled their cheers. He sent Aziz to find help lowering the boarding stairs so Mohammad Didi could see for himself what they had captured.

● ● ●

IN THE OP CENTER, Giuseppe Farina pointed at the monitor. "There's our man right in the center."

"The one with the chicken feathers growing off his face?" Max Hanley asked.

"*Si*. He is not much to look at, but he is a hardened killer." Farina wore Italian Army fatigues, and black boots so shiny they looked like patent leather. He was handsome, with dark eyes and hair, olive skin, and a sculpted face. The laugh lines at the corners of his mouth and across his forehead were earned from having a well-developed sense of fun and mischief. When Juan had been in the CIA working a Russian contact in Rome, he and 'Seppe had torn up the town on more than one occasion.

"Just so our orders are clear, we have to wait until Didi boards the *Oregon*, right?" Juan asked. Farina nodded, so he added, "Then what?"

"Then you capture him any way you want. This is a flagged vessel, and therefore the sovereign property of . . . Where is this ship registered?"

"Iran."

"You joke."

"Nope," Juan said with a lazy smile. "Can you think of a better country to deflect suspicion of us being an American-backed espionage ship?"

"No," Giuseppe conceded with a nervous frown, "but that might raise eyebrows in The Hague."

"Relax, 'Seppe. We also carry papers listing the *Oregon* as the *Grandam Phoenix*, registered in Panama."

"Odd name."

"It was a ship in a book I read years go. Kinda liked it. There won't be any problems once you get Didi to the World Court."

"*Sí*. As soon as he steps foot on your ship, he is no longer in Somalia. So he is, ah, fair game."

"How are you guys going to explain in court that an Italian colonel happened to be on a freighter hijacked by a guy who's got a half-million-dollar bounty on his head and a standing indictment?"

"We don't," Farina said. "Your involvement will never be known. I have brought a drug with me that will wipe out his memories of the past twenty-four hours. He will awake with the worst hangover in history, but there is no permanent harm. We have a captured fishing boat standing by beyond Somalia's twelve-mile territorial limit. You transfer Didi to it in international waters, and then the American cruiser, performing interdiction duties, boards her and finds the prize. Slick and simple, and no rendition."

"Madness," Max grumbled.

"Chairman," Mark Murphy said to get Juan's attention. Murph was the ship's defenses operator. From his workstation next to the helm, he could unleash the awesome array of weapons built into the former lumber carrier. He could launch torpedoes, surface-to-surface and surface-to-air missiles, fire any number of .30 caliber machine guns hidden aboard as well as the radar-guided 20mm Vulcan cannons, the 40mm Orlikon, and the big 120mm gun in its bow redoubt.

Cabrillo looked past Murphy and saw on the screen that the boarding stairs were down and Mohammad Didi was moving toward them.

"'Come into my web,' said the spider to the fly."

FOUR

BAHIRET EL BIBANE,
TUNISIA

ALANA DIDN'T MIND THE SAND OR THE TREMENDOUS HEAT that blasted out of the desert in unending waves. What got to her were the flies. No matter how much cream she slathered onto her skin or how often she checked her tent's mosquito netting at night, there seemed to be no relief from the winged devils. After nearly two months on the dig, she couldn't tell where one welt ended and its neighbor began. To her dismay, the local workers didn't seem to even notice the biting insects. To make herself feel a little better, she'd tried to think up some discomfort in her native Arizona that these people couldn't handle but couldn't come up with anything worse than traffic congestion.

There were eleven Americans and nearly fifty hired laborers on the archaeological dig, all under the leadership of Professor William Galt. Six of the eleven were postdocs like Alana Shepard. The other five were still in grad school at the University of Arizona. Men outnumbered women eight to three, but so far that hadn't become an issue.

Ostensibly, they were here digging at a Roman site a half mile inland from the Mediterranean. Long believed to be a summer retreat

for Claudius Sabinus, the regional governor, the complex of crumbling buildings was turning out to be far more interesting. There
appeared to be a large temple of some kind completely unknown
before. The buzz around the camp among the archaeologists is that
Sabinus was the head of a sect, and, given the time he ruled the area,
there was speculation he might have become a Christian.

Professor Bill, as Galt liked to be called, frowned on conjecture,
but he couldn't stop his people from discussing it around meals.

But that was just for cover. Alana and her small team of three
were here for something quite different. And while it had an archaeological component, their mission wasn't about discovering the past
but rather saving the future.

So far, things were not going well. Seven weeks of searching had
turned up nothing, and she and the others were beginning to think
they had been sent on a fool's errand.

She recalled being excited about the project when she'd first been
approached by Christie Valero from the State Department, but the
desert had burned away any remaining enthusiasm long ago.

Standing just five foot four, Alana Shepard was often confused for
one of her students though she was a year shy of her fortieth birthday. Twice divorced—the first was a big mistake she made when she
was eighteen, the second an even bigger mistake she made in her late
twenties—she had one son, Josh, who stayed with her mother when
Alana was in the field.

Because it was easier to maintain short hair in the desert, her dark
bangs were cut across her forehead, and the hair at the back of her
head barely covered the nape of her neck. She wasn't particularly
beautiful, but Alana was so petite that she was universally considered cute—a term she professed to hate but secretly loved. She had
a double doctorate from the University of Arizona in geology and
archaeology, which made her particularly suited to the job, but no

number of sheepskins hanging on her office wall in Phoenix would help her find something that wasn't even there.

She and her team had combed the dried-up riverbed for miles inland without seeing any sort of anomaly. The sandstone canyon carved by the river millions of years ago was as featureless as a utility corridor until it reached what once had been a waterfall.

There had been no need to search farther upstream than that. When the river was flowing two hundred years ago, the falls would have been an insurmountable obstacle.

The sound of a rock drill broke Alana from her reverie. The machine was mounted on the back of a truck and positioned horizontally so it could bore into the cliff face. The diamond-tipped bit chewed through the friable sandstone with ease. Mike Duncan, a geologist from Texas with oil-field experience, manned the controls at the rear corner of the rig. They used the cutter head to probe old landslides to see if they hid any sort of cavern or cave. After more than a hundred such holes, they had nothing to show but a half dozen worn-out bits.

She watched for several minutes, pausing to wipe perspiration from her throat. When forty feet of the drill had been rammed into the ground, Mike killed the diesel engine. Its roar faded until Alana could hear the wind again.

"Nothing," he spat.

"I still say we should have shot a few more holes in that rock slide about a mile downstream." This from Greg Chaffee. He was their government minder. Alana suspected CIA but didn't want to know if she was right. Chaffee had no academic or professional qualifications to be with them, so his opinion was generally ignored. At least he did his share of whatever job she set out for him, and he spoke Arabic like a native.

Emile Bumford was the fourth member of the little group. Bumford was an expert on the Ottoman Empire, with a particular focus on the Barbary States. He was a prissy lout, in Alana's estimation. He refused to leave the camp set up near the Roman ruins, saying that his expertise wasn't needed until they actually found something.

This was true, but back in Washington, D.C., when they had met Undersecretary Valero, he had boasted of vast field experience, saying he "loved the feel of dirt under his fingernails." So far, he hadn't lifted one of those manicured nails to do anything other than constantly straighten the safari jacket he wore as an affectation.

"Another one of your feelings?" Mike asked Chaffee. They shared a common interest in horse racing and trusted their guts with the ponies as much as the information they read in the racing forms.

"Can't hurt." Chaffee shrugged.

"Won't help either," Alana said a little harsher than she intended. She lowered herself to the ground in the truck's shadow. "Sorry, that sounded worse than I wanted it to. But the cliffs are too tall and steep there. It wouldn't have been possible to lead camels down to unload a ship."

"Are we sure this is even the right old riverbed?" Mike asked. "You don't find too many large caverns in sandstone. It's too soft. The roof would collapse before erosion could make it large enough to hide a boat."

Alana had thought the same thing. They should be looking for limestone, which is perfect for caverns because it was soft enough to erode but tough enough to withstand the aeons. The problem was they hadn't found anything other than the sandstone and a few basalt outcroppings.

"The Charles Stewart letter was pretty clear as to the location of Al-Jama's secret base," she said. "Remember, Henry Lafayette stayed

there for two years before the old pirate's death. Satellite imagery shows this to be the only possible riverbed within a hundred miles of where Lafayette said they lived."

"Hey, at least it's on this side of the Libyan border," Greg added. His blond hair and fair skin made him especially susceptible to the sun, so he wore long sleeves and a big straw hat. His shirts were always stained at the collar and under the arms and had to be washed out every night. "Despite the upcoming summit in Tripoli, I don't think old Muammar Qaddafi would like us digging around in his backyard."

Mike said, "My father worked the Libyan oil fields before Qaddafi nationalized them." He was taller and leaner than Greg, hardened by a lifetime of working outdoors so the wrinkles around his blue eyes never vanished. His hands were callused like the bark of an oak tree, and the corner of his mouth bulged with a wad of tobacco the size of a golf ball. "He told me the Libyan people are about the nicest in the world."

"People, yes. Government, not so much." Alana took a swig from her canteen. It was as warm as bathwater. "Even with them hosting the peace thing, I don't see them really changing their tune." She looked at Greg Chaffee, asking pointedly, "Doesn't the CIA believe they once sheltered Suleiman Al-Jama, the terrorist who took his name from the pirate we're looking for?"

He didn't rise to the bait. "What I read in the papers is that Al-Jama tried to enter the country but wasn't allowed in."

"We've been up and down this wash for weeks. There's nothing here," Mike said disgustedly. "This mission is a complete waste of time."

"The nabobs in the know don't seem to think so," Alana answered, but with reservations.

She thought back to her meeting in Washington with Christie Valero. In the Foggy Bottom office with Undersecretary Valero had been one of the largest men Alana had ever seen. He had the unforgettable name of St. Julian Perlmutter, and he reminded her of Sydney Greenstreet, except while the old actor had always seemed sinister Perlmutter was the quintessential jovial fat man. His eyes were as bright blue as Alana's were green. Valero was a trim, pretty blonde a few years older than Alana. The walls of her office were decorated with photographs of the places she'd been stationed in her twenty-year career, all in the Middle East.

She had risen from her desk when Alana had been shown into the room, but Perlmutter remained on the sofa and shook her hand sitting down.

"Thank you for agreeing to meet with us," Christie said.

"It's not every day I get an offer to meet with an Undersecretary."

"They're a dime a dozen in this town." Perlmutter chuckled. "Turn on a light at a party and they scurry like cockroaches."

"Another crack like that," Christie said, "and I'll have you black-listed from all the embassy dinners."

"That's hitting below the belt," St. Julian said quickly, then laughed. "Actually, that's hitting the belt line precisely."

"Dr. Shepard—"

"Alana. Please."

"Alana, we have a particularly interesting challenge that's suited to your talents. A few weeks ago, St. Julian came across a letter written by an admiral named Charles Stewart in the 1820s. In it, he describes a rather incredible tale of survival by a sailor lost during the Barbary Coast War of 1803. His name was Henry Lafayette."

Christie Valero outlined Lafayette's role in the burning of the *Philadelphia* and how he was presumably lost at sea following the attack on the *Saqr*. St. Julian picked it up from there.

"Lafayette and Suleiman Al-Jama made it to shore, and Henry removed the pistol ball with his bare fingers and packed the wound with salt he scraped from rocks. The pirate captain was delirious for three days, but then his fever broke and he made a full recovery. Fortunately for them, Henry managed to gather rainwater to drink, and he was skilled at foraging for food along the shore.

"Now, you must understand that Al-Jama was a pirate not because of the financial reward. He did it because of his hate for the infidel. The man was the Osama bin Laden of his day."

"Is this where Suleiman Al-Jama gets his name?" Alana asked, referencing the modern-day terrorist.

"Yes, it is."

"I had no idea his name had a historical context."

"He chose it very carefully. To many in the radicalized side of Islam, the original Al-Jama is a hero and a spiritual guide. Before turning to piracy he was an Imam. Most of his writings survive to this day, and are closely studied because they give so many justifications for attacking nonbelievers."

"There was a painting done of him before his first sea voyage," Undersecretary Valero said. "We often find pictures of it in places of honor whenever there's a raid on a terrorist stronghold. He is an inspiration to terrorists throughout the Muslim world. To them, he's the original jihadist, the first to take the fight to the West."

Alana was confused, and said, "I'm sorry, but what does any of this have to do with me? I'm an archaeologist."

"I'm getting to that," St. Julian replied. His stomach grumbled, so he gave it an affectionate rub. "And I'll make it brief.

"Now, Lafayette and Al-Jama couldn't have been more different if one of them had been from Mars. But they shared a rather strange bond. You see, Henry had saved Suleiman's life not once but twice. First by towing him to shore, then by nursing him back from the bullet wound. It was a debt the Muslim simply couldn't ignore. Also,

Henry, who was French Canadian, looked exactly like Al-Jama's long-dead son.

"They were stranded in the desert at least a hundred miles from Tripoli. Suleiman knew that if he returned Henry there, the Bashaw would imprison him with the crew from the *Philadelphia*, or, worse, try him for burning the ship and execute him.

"However, there was an alternative. You see, apart from using the city, Al-Jama also had a secret base in the desert far to the west. It was from there he staged many of his raids, allowing him to avoid any naval blockade. He assumed that his ship would defeat the *Siren* and that his men would meet him at their *lair*."

A natural storyteller, Perlmutter put extra emphasis on the last word to bolster the drama.

"So they headed west, walking along the shore whenever they could, but they were oftentimes forced to trek inland. Henry didn't know how many days it took them. Four weeks, was a rough estimate, and it must have been utter hell. Water was always scarce, and on more than one occasion both thought they were going to die from thirst. 'Water, water, every where, / Nor any drop to drink.' Coleridge had it right. They were saved by the occasional rain squall and the juice of clams they found.

"A funny thing happened, too. The two men began to become friends. Al-Jama spoke some English, and because Henry was already bilingual he was able to pick up Arabic very quickly. I can't imagine what they discussed, but talk they did. By the time they reached the hideout, Al-Jama wasn't keeping Henry alive because of an obligation. He did it because he genuinely liked the young man. Later, he would call Henry 'son,' and Henry referred to him as 'father.'

"At the secret base, they discovered the *Saqr*, but the men, who had thought their captain dead, had returned to their homes along the Barbary Coast. In his report to the Navy Department, Charles Stewart stated the *Saqr* was burning heavily and sinking after they broke off the engagement, but obviously it survived.

"By Henry's account, the hideout was well provisioned, and there was an elderly servant to attend to their needs. Every few months, a camel caravan would come by to barter for food in exchange for some of the plunder Al-Jama had hoarded, though he made them promise not to tell his men he was alive."

"Plunder?" Alana asked.

"Henry's exact words were 'a mountain of gold,'" Perlmutter replied. "Then there's the belief that Al-Jama was in possession of the Jewel of Jerusalem."

Alana looked to Undersecretary Valero. "Do you want to send me on some sort of treasure hunt?"

Christie nodded. "In a manner of speaking, but we're not interested in gold or some mythical gemstone. What do you know about fatwas?"

"Isn't that some kind of proclamation for Muslims? There was one issued to kill Salman Rushdie for writing *The Satanic Verses*."

"Exactly. Depending on who issues them, they carry tremendous influence in the Muslim world. Ayatollah Khomeini issued one during Iran's war with Iraq, giving permission for soldiers to blow themselves up in suicide attacks. You must be aware that suicide is expressly forbidden in the Koran, but Khomeini's forces were being routed by Saddam's, and he was desperate. So he said it was okay to blow yourself up if you're taking your enemies with you. His strategy worked—maybe too well, from our perspective. The Iranians pushed back Iraq's Army and eventually came to a cease-fire, but his fatwa remained in place, and is still used as the justification for suicide bombers from Indonesia to Israel. If it could somehow be countered by an equally respected cleric, then we might see a drop in suicide bombings all over the world."

Alana was beginning to understand. "Suleiman Al-Jama?"

St. Julian leaned forward, the couch's leather creaking. "According to what Henry told Charles Stewart after his return to the United States, Al-Jama did a complete reversal of his earlier position concerning Christians. He had never even spoken to one until Henry rescued him. Henry read to him from the Bible he carried, and Al-Jama began to focus on the similarities between faiths rather than the differences. In the two years before he died in the hideout, he studied the Koran like never before, and wrote extensively on how Christianity and Islam should coexist in peace. That is why I believe he didn't want his sailors to know he had survived the attack, because they would want to go raiding again and he did not."

Christie Valero interrupted. "If those documents exist, they could be a powerful tool in the war on terrorism because it would cut the underpinnings of many of the most fanatical terrorists. The killers who so blindly follow Al-Jama's early edicts on murdering Christians would be honor-bound to at least consider what the old pirate had written later in his life.

"I don't know if you are aware," she continued, "that there is a peace conference in Tripoli, Libya, in a couple of months. This is going to be the largest gathering of its kind in history, and perhaps our greatest shot at ending the fighting once and for all. All sides are talking serious concessions, and the oil states are willing to pledge billions in economic aid. I would love for the Secretary of State to have the opportunity to read something Al-Jama wrote about reconciliation. I think it would tip the scales in favor of peace."

Alana made a face. "Wouldn't that be, I don't know, largely symbolic?"

"Yes, it would," St. Julian answered. "But so much of diplomacy is symbolism. The parties want reconciliation. Hearing about it from a revered Imam, a powerful inspiration for violence who changed his mind, would be a diplomatic coup, and the very thing these talks need to be a success."

Alana recalled feeling excited about helping to bring stability to the Middle East following her meeting with Valero and Perlmutter, but now, after weeks searching vainly for Al-Jama's secret base, she felt nothing but tired, hot, and dirty. She pushed herself to her feet. Their break was over.

"Come on, guys. We have another hour or so before we have to head back to the Roman ruins and check in with the dig supervisor." As part of their deal for tagging along with that other expedition, Alana and her team had to return to camp every night. It was an onerous burden, but the Tunisian authorities insisted that no one spend a night alone in the desert. "Might as well check where Greg's gut is telling him our discovery awaits, 'cause the geology isn't telling me squat."

FIVE

ABRILLO'S PLAN TO CAPTURE MOHAMMAD DIDI WAS SIMPLE. As soon as he and his entourage entered the superstructure, armed teams would surround them with overwhelming force. The surprise alone should ensure the capture went down smooth and easy. Once they had him, they would back away from the pier and make their way out into the open ocean. None of the fishing boats had a chance at catching the disguised freighter, and Juan hadn't seen any signs the rebels had a helicopter.

He was so confident that he wasn't bothering to participate. Eddie Seng, who had pretended to be Captain Kwan, would lead the team. Eddie was another CIA veteran, like Cabrillo, and was one of the most proficient fighters on the *Oregon*. Backing him, as always, would be Franklin Lincoln. The big former SEAL had been on deck when the pirates came aboard, and they had wrongly assumed he was African. Linc was a Detroit native and about the most unflappable man Cabrillo knew.

But as Cabrillo watched the view screen, he saw his plans fly out the window.

The camera was mounted high atop one of the ship's gantry

cranes and had an unobstructed view of the dock. Moments before Didi was to step onto the boarding stairs, he paused, spoke a few words to his followers, and moved aside. Dozens of Somalis raced up the gangplank, shouting and whooping like banshees.

"Chairman!" Mark Murphy cried as the multitude swarmed the ship.

"I see it."

"What are you going to do?" Giuseppe Farina asked.

"Give me a second." Juan couldn't tear his eyes away from the screen. He keyed a mic button built into his chair. "Eddie, you copying this?"

"I'm watching it on a monitor down here. Looks like plan A is out. What do you suggest?"

"Stay in the staging area and out of sight until I think of something."

Mohammad Didi finally started to climb the gangway, but already there were at least a hundred natives aboard the old ship and more were trickling up behind their leader.

Juan thought through and discarded his options. The *Oregon* and her crew carried enough firepower to kill every last Somali, but that was one option he didn't even consider. The Corporation was a mercenary outfit, a for-profit security and surveillance company, but there were lines they would never cross. Indiscriminately targeting civilians was something he would never condone. Taking out the guys brandishing AKs wouldn't weigh on Juan's conscience too much, but there were women and children mixed with the crowd.

Eric Stone raced into the Operations Center from an entrance at its rear. He was still dressed as Duane Maryweather. "Sorry I'm late. Looks like the party's bigger than we intended."

He took his seat at the navigation station, tapping knuckles with Murph. The two were best friends. Stone had never gotten over being a shy, studious high school geek, despite his four years at Annapolis and six in the Navy. He dressed mostly in chinos and button-down shirts, and wore glasses rather than bother with contact lenses.

Murph, on the other hand, cultivated a surfer-punk persona that he couldn't quite pull off. A certified genius, he had been a weapons designer for the military, which was where he'd met Eric. Both were in their late twenties. Mark usually wore black, and kept his hair a dark shaggy mess. He was in his second month of trying to grow a goatee, and it wasn't going well.

Polar opposites in so many ways, they still managed to work as one of the best teams on the ship, and they could anticipate Cabrillo as if able to read his mind.

"Depress the—" Cabrillo started.

"—water-suppression cannons," Murph finished. "Already on it."

"Don't fire until I give the order."

"Righto."

Juan looked over to Linda Ross. She was the Corporation's vice president of operations. Another Navy squab, Linda had done stints on an Aegis cruiser and had worked as an assistant to the Joint Chiefs, making her equally skilled at naval combat and staff duties. She had an elfin face, with bright almond eyes and a dash of freckles across her cheeks and nose. Her hair, which changed routinely, was currently strawberry blond and cut in what she called the "Posh." She also had a high, almost girlish voice that was incongruous with belting out combat orders. But she was as fine an officer as any of her male shipmates.

"Linda," Cabrillo said, "I want you to monitor Didi. Don't lose him on the internal cameras, and tell me the minute he enters the hold."

"You got it."

"'Seppe, are you satisfied that Didi came onto this ship of his own free will?"

"He's all yours."

Juan keyed the microphone again. "Eddie, Linc, meet me down in the Magic Shop, double time."

Juan slipped a portable radio into a pocket and fitted headphones over his ears so he could stay on the communications grid. As he ran from the room, he asked over his shoulder for Hali Kasim to patch him in to Kevin Nixon, the head magician of the Magic Shop. Launching himself down teak-paneled stairwells rather than wait for one of the elevators, Cabrillo told the former Hollywood makeup artist what he had in mind. After that, he got in touch with Max Hanley and gave him his orders. Max grumbled about what Juan wanted to do, knowing it would make for a maintenance headache for his engineers later on, but he admitted it was a good idea.

Cabrillo reached the Magic Shop on Eddie and Linc's heels. The room looked like a cross between a salon and a storage shed. There was a makeup counter and mirror along one wall, while the rest of the space was given over to racks of clothing, special effects gear, and all manner of props.

The two gundogs, as Max called them, wore black combat uniforms festooned with pouches for extra ammunition, combat knives, and other gear. They also carried Barrett REC7 assault rifles, a possible successor to the M16 family of weapons.

"Lose the hardware," Cabrillo said brusquely.

Kevin bustled into the Magic Shop from one of the large storerooms where he kept disguises. In his arms were garments called *dishdashas*, the long nightshirt-type clothes commonly worn in this part of the world. The cotton had once been white but had been artfully stained to appear old and worn out. He gave one to each man, and they shrugged them over their clothes. Linc looked like he was stuffed into a sausage casing, but the shirt covered everything but his combat boots.

Nixon also gave them headscarves, and as they started winding them around their skulls he applied makeup to darken Eddie's and Juan's skin. A perfectionist, Kevin detested doing anything slipshod, but Cabrillo's impatience radiated off of him in waves.

"It doesn't have to be perfect," Juan said. "People see what they expect to see. That's the number one rule in disguise."

Linda's voice came over Juan's microphone. "Didi is about two minutes from the main hold."

"Too soon. We're not ready. Is there anyone on the bridge?"

"A couple of kids are playing with the ship's wheel."

"Hit the foghorn and pipe it down to the hold through the speakers."

"Why?"

"Trust me," was all Juan said.

The horn bellowed across the mangrove swamp, startling birds to flight and sending the mongrel camp dogs cowering with their tails tucked between their legs. Inside the corridor where Mohammad Didi and his retainers were walking toward their prize, the sound was a physical assault on the senses. Clamping their hands to their heads did little to mitigate the effect.

"Good call," Linda told the Chairman. "Didi has stopped to send one of his men back to the wheelhouse. Those kids are in for it when he gets there."

"What's going on everywhere else?"

"The horn hasn't stopped people from looting. I see two women carrying the mattresses out of the captain's cabin. Another pair are taking those hideous clown pictures. And don't ask me why he's bothering, but a guy is working on pulling up the toilet."

"A throne by any other name," Juan quipped.

Kevin had finished with their makeup by the time Didi's lieutenant arrived on the bridge and cuffed the two boys behind the ears.

Linda disengaged the horn when the pirate reached for the controls, though he looked at the panel oddly because he hadn't actually hit any button. He shrugged and hurried back to be with the warlord.

An armorer had arrived in the Magic Shop and handed over three Kalashnikov AK-47s. The weapons looked as battle worn as the ones the pirates carried, but like every facet of the *Oregon* this was a ruse. These rifles were in perfect working order. He also gave them filter masks that they tucked into the pockets of their dishdashas.

"You got us down here," Linc said, "and got you boys looking like a couple of imitation homeys, but I don't know the plan."

"We couldn't waltz up to Didi dressed like a bunch of ninjas with so many armed rebels roaming the ship. We need to get close to him without raising an alarm."

"Hence the mufti," Eddie surmised.

"In all the excitement," Juan explained, "we'll blend in and wait for our moment."

"If Didi decides to open the drums of ammonium nitrate and discovers they're filled with seawater, he's going to sense a trap and hightail it off the *Oregon*."

"Why do you think I'm rushing, big man? Kevin?"

Nixon stepped back and looked at his handiwork. He rummaged in a desk drawer and handed Juan and Eddie aviator-style sunglasses. Their skin tone was right, but without latex appliances there wasn't much he could do about their features. Given enough time, he could make either of them a twin of Didi, but the addition of the shades made him satisfied. He gave a nod, and was going to pronounce his work complete, but Juan was already leading the others out of the room.

"Linda, where is Didi now?" Cabrillo asked over the radio.

"They're just outside the hold. There are probably twelve men with him. All of them are armed to the teeth. Speaking of which, our pirate leader, Hakeem, is grinning ear to ear."

"I bet he is," Juan replied. "But not for long."

He led Linc and Eddie to an unmarked door on one of the *Oregon*'s elegant corridors. He opened a peephole on a two-way mirror, and when he saw the room beyond was dark he swung open the door and the three men stepped through. A pull on an overhead fixture revealed they were in a utility closet, with a mop sink, buckets, and shelves loaded with cleaning supplies. This was one of the many secret passages between the *Oregon*'s two sections.

It was only when Juan put his hand on the knob to open the door to the public part of the ship that he thought about the fact he was potentially entering a combat situation. A jolt of adrenaline hit him like a narcotic. The old feelings were there—fear, anxiety, and a dose of excitement, too—but the more times he faced danger, the longer it took to quell those feelings and empty his mind of distraction.

This was the moment none of the Corporation operators ever discussed or acknowledged in any way. He could imagine Linc's and Eddie's horror if he turned to them and asked if they were as scared as he was. This was the essence of any good soldier, the ability to admit he is afraid while having the discipline to channel it into something useful in combat.

Juan didn't pause. He pushed open the door and stepped into the public part of the ship. Two Somali women hustled by carrying rolled-up carpet they must have pulled from one of the cabins. They didn't give Cabrillo's party a second glance.

The three men rushed aft until they found a stairwell leading them deeper into the freighter. There was an armed guard stationed at the foot of the stairs, and when Juan tried to pass he grabbed for his arm, saying something in Somali that Cabrillo didn't understand.

"I need to speak with Lord Didi," Juan said in Arabic, hoping the man knew the language.

"No. He is not to be disturbed," the guard replied haltingly.

"Have it your way," Juan muttered in English, and coldcocked the man with a haymaker that lifted the slightly built Somali off his feet.

Cabrillo shook out his wrist while Linc and Eddie dragged the guard under the metal scissor stairs.

"Make sure we don't forget that guy when this is over," Juan said, and started off toward the hold. According to Linda Ross, Moham-mad Didi had been in there for three minutes so far and was still inspecting the trucks.

"What's his mood?"

"Like a kid in a candy store."

"Okay, I think it's time. Tell Max to start pumping out the smoke and to get ready on those water cannons. Remember, I want people getting off, not rushing aboard to grab anything else."

"Roger."

Perhaps the *Oregon*'s single greatest hidden feature was the fact she wasn't powered by traditional marine diesels. Instead, she employed something called magnetohydrodynamics. Magnets cooled by liquid helium stripped free electrons out of the seawater and gave the ship a near-limitless supply of electricity. This was used to power four jet pumps that shot water through a pair of directional drive tubes deep in the hull. The revolutionary propulsion system could move her eleven thousand tons through the waves at unimaginable speeds. But to maintain the illusion that she was a derelict vessel, she had smudge generators that could belch smoke from her stack to simulate poorly maintained engines.

It was this smoke that Max was redirecting into the ventila-tion system in the parts of the ship the Somali pirates thought they controlled.

Approaching the open door to the number three cargo hold, Juan noted soot boiling out of the ventilation grilles set into the low ceiling.

It would take no more than fifteen minutes to fill the ship with the noxious gas. They could hear voices echoing from inside the hold.

"Ready?" Juan asked. Linc and Eddie nodded.

They rushed into the hold, Juan screaming, "Fire! Fire!"

Didi and his dozen-strong entourage looked over from where they were examining one of the heavy-duty pickups. "What's all this?"

"There is a fire. Smoke," Juan said, knowing he spoke Arabic with a Saudi accent that must sound strange to the Somali. "It is coming from everywhere."

Didi glanced at the drums of ammonium nitrate. Juan wasn't sure if he was thinking about taking them before flames engulfed the ship or if he was concerned they could detonate. They could smell the smoke now in the unventilated hold. A pall of it hung near the entry door. Juan looked over at Hakeem. The pirate sensed he was being studied and looked back. He had no idea what was going on behind the sunglasses Cabrillo wore, and would have drawn his pistol and fired if he knew the depths of hatred Juan had for pirates.

Linda's voice came over the headset hidden under his turban. "Just so you know the women and young children are making for the gangplank, but not many of the soldiers seemed concerned."

"Have you seen the flames yourself?" asked Mohammad Didi.

"Er, no, sir."

A wary look flashed behind the strongman's eyes. "I do not know you. What is your name?"

"Farouq, sir."

"Where are you from?"

Juan couldn't believe it. There was a potential fire raging on the ship, Didi had seen the smoke, and he wanted a life history.

"Sir, there isn't time."

"Oh, all right. Let's see what has you so spooked. Someone probably just burned food in the galley."

Juan motioned for Eddie to lead them back down the corridor to the stairwell. Didi walked slowly and stayed in the middle of his group, despite Juan's urging him to rush. Eddie looked back just before stepping over the coaming of a watertight door. Cabrillo nodded.

The instant Mohammad Didi, preceded by Juan and Linc, stepped over the threshold, a steel panel concealed in the ceiling came down under hydraulic force. It happened so fast that the men trapped on the other side didn't have time to react. One second the path was open and the next a metal barrier barred them from leaving the corridor.

The trapdoor had cut the number of guards in half, but it was still too many to take on in such close quarters.

"What's going on?" Didi asked no one in particular.

Hakeem remembered Malik's and Aziz's wild story about the mess hall being empty. He looked around with superstitious dread. There was something not right with this ship, and his heightened desire to get off had nothing to do with the possibility of a fire.

Two pirates tried unsuccessfully to lift the slab of steel, while their comrades pounded on the metal from the other side. The smoke was growing thicker.

"Leave them," Didi shouted, also feeling that things were not what they seemed.

He led the charge up the stairs, not noticing that the guard he had posted earlier wasn't there. What started as a fast walk turned into a jog and then an outright sprint.

This guy has the instincts of a rat, Juan thought. He slowed his pace so he could talk to the op center without attracting attention. "Linda, are you tracking us?"

"I've got you."

"I can't grab Didi with all these guards. When we break out onto the deck I want you to hit us. Got it?"

"Got it."

They climbed up past the corridor with the nearest secret entrance and emerged on the main deck by the gangplank. The moment they set foot outside the superstructure and into the burning sun, a lance of water from a fire-suppression cannon hit Didi square in the chest. The blast sent him back into his men, dropping three of them. Linc wrapped his big arms around two who had managed to stay on their feet and crashed their heads together with a dull knock. Had he wanted to, he could have cracked their skulls, but he was satisfied when they dropped to the deck.

Hakeem ignored the torrent sloshing across his feet and stared at Juan in disbelief. The gush of seawater had scoured the makeup from his face and torn away the sunglasses to reveal his piercing blue eyes. His shout of alarm rose above the wail of women doused by the blast. He was swinging his AK to his hip when Juan slammed into him with his shoulder, driving the pirate into the ship's rail. The impact was enough to curl the pirate's finger around the trigger.

A juddering blast of autofire ripped from the gun. Fortunately, it passed harmlessly over the heads of the milling women and children, but it turned what had been an orderly exodus into a stampede and caught the attention of other armed men.

Juan vented his rage into the Somali by ramming an elbow into his stomach. Hakeem's Kalashnikov clattered to the deck. As the pirate's eyes goggled and his mouth worked to suck air into his deflated lungs, Cabrillo hit him again on the point of the jaw hard enough to fling him over the rail. Juan glanced over to see Hakeem had the bad luck of landing not in the narrow band of water separating the ship from the dock but on the transom of the fishing boat he'd first used in his attack on the *Oregon*. By the way Hakeem's neck was twisted, Juan knew it was broken and the pirate was dead.

He couldn't be more pleased.

He pushed through the panicked throng of Somalis. Water continued to fountain from the fire cannon, splattering against the ship, so it was like running through a cyclone. No one seemed to notice his white skin until a boy of maybe six carrying a stack of sheets and towels saw him and opened his mouth to shout a warning. Juan pinched his arm in the hopes of making the kid start crying, a sound coming from dozens of wailing children trying to get off the ship with their mothers. Instead, the boy dropped to the deck and wrapped his arms around Juan's leg. Cabrillo tried to pull away, but the boy hung on with the tenacity of a moray eel. Then he made the mistake of trying to bite Cabrillo's calf. Having never seen or even heard of a dentist, the boy clamped down as hard as he could and managed to snap off four of his baby teeth. He started to bawl as blood dripped from his blubbering lips.

Cabrillo shook the kid loose and reached his teammates. "Come on, guys."

Mohammad Didi was almost on his feet. The water had torn away his shirt, revealing a chest riddled with shrapnel scars, while water dripped from his beard. Looking like a drowned rat, he was more determined than ever to get off the *Oregon*. He lunged forward and ran into the proverbial immovable object.

Franklin Lincoln towered over the Somali warlord.

"Not so fast, my friend," the big man said, and grabbed Didi around the upper arm while at the same time pulling the pirate's pistol from its holster.

"Help me!" Didi shouted to his men.

The powerful jet of water and the spatter it kicked up when it hit the deck made it impossible to see what was happening just ten feet away, but the yell galvanized Didi's men. They started forward, shielding their eyes from the spray, their rifles held one-handed. Fingers were an ounce of pressure away from loosening a barrage.

"Let's go!" Juan helped drag Didi deeper into the superstructure, with Eddie covering their rear.

The pirates broke through the waterfall-like cascade, and as soon as their eyes adjusted to the dim interior they realized that their leader was in trouble. One of them triggered off a half dozen rounds, ignoring the danger to Didi.

Juan felt the heat of the bullets singe his neck before they hit the ceiling and ricocheted down the passageway.

Running backward, Eddie put the gunman down with a double tap from his AK, then thumbed the selector to automatic and fired a wild volley of his own. The three remaining pirates dove flat, giving the team time to round a corner.

Juan took point position, listening to Linda in his ear for warnings about other pirates still on board. He paused at a corner when she told him there was an armed Somali a few feet from him. He peeked around the junction, saw the man's back was to him, and gave him a rap on the back of the head with the AK's butt.

Either he had miscalculated or the pirate had the hardest skull in the world, because the man turned on Juan and rammed his gun into Juan's stomach, shoving him far away enough so he could take a shot.

Juan kicked out with his left foot as the gun swung toward him, pinning the barrel against the wall. The gunman tried to yank it free but couldn't. Cabrillo swung his AK like a baseball bat and hit the pirate in the head a second time. The blow opened a gash on his cheek and sent him sprawling.

Linda's next warning came the instant Juan looked farther up the corridor. Two more pirates emerged from the mess hall, their guns blazing. Juan took a bullet just above his right ankle, the impact making him stagger. He lost his balance and was falling when Eddie grabbed his arm and yanked him back around the corner.

"You okay?" Seng asked.

Juan flexed his knee. "Peg leg seems all right." Below the knee, Juan Cabrillo had a prosthetic leg thanks to a hit from an artillery shell from a Chinese destroyer during a mission for the National Underwater and Marine Agency. It is what the boy on deck broke his teeth on.

Cabrillo adjusted his headset, which had come loose. "Talk to me, Linda."

"The two who just fired are taking cover positions at the mess hall door and you've got a half dozen more coming up from behind."

"Eddie, watch our back."

Juan ran across the hall to one of the cabins. The door was locked, and there hadn't been enough time for the Somalis to force it open and strip the cabin bare. Juan rammed a master key into the handle and threw the door open. The cabin was supposed to be for the ship's chief engineer, so it was smaller than the captain's cabin Eddie had used earlier. The furniture was still cheap to maintain the ruse that the *Oregon* was little more than a scow, and the décor consisted of Spanish bullfighting posters and models of sailing ships in bottles. He strode through the cabin and into the small head. Above the porcelain sink was a mirror affixed to the bulkhead with glue. He jabbed the barrel of his AK into the glass and smashed it to fragments. He plucked one the size of a playing card off the linoleum floor and raced out of the room.

He edged up to the corner again and eased the fragment of mirror out into the hallway so he could see the two gunmen. They were crouched at the mess door as Linda had said, one hunched down and the other standing over him. Both had their weapons trained on the corner, but in the uneven light couldn't see the mirror.

As slowly as a cobra lulling its prey, Cabrillo inched the barrel of his assault rifle around the corner, so only a tiny bit was showing.

Some call it the sixth sense—the body's ability to know its position relative to its surroundings, its orientation in space. Cabrillo's sixth sense was so honed that even looking at a mirror reflection, crouched on the floor, and with six terrorists gunning for them, he could feel the precise angle he had to raise the Kalashnikov's barrel. He brought it up a fraction of an inch and fired.

The stream of bullets smashed into the wall next to the mess hall door and ricocheted off with enough force to impact the door and slam it into the protruding barrels of the pirates' guns. Cabrillo was moving even as the door was swinging closed, using his fusillade as cover fire. The pirates made no attempt to withdraw their weapons or open the door with rounds pounding it from the outside, which allowed Juan enough time to reach it without being seen. He jammed the barrel of his gun into the crack between the door and frame and fired off another burst at point-blank range. Blood sizzled on the hot barrel when he pulled his weapon clear. He looked through the opening and saw both gunmen were down, their bodies riddled with bullet holes.

He waved to his men, and they charged after him, Linc nearly lifting the Somali warlord off his feet to keep him moving.

"They're coming," Linda warned.

Juan knew she meant the six tangos she'd mentioned earlier. He dropped the magazine from the AK's receiver and slapped home a fresh one. There was a round still in the chamber—no matter how hot things got in combat, Cabrillo knew to never let his gun empty completely—so he didn't need to cock it. As soon as he saw the flicker of shadow moving around the corner they had just used for cover, he opened up, firing past his men in a desperate bid to buy them the time they needed to reach cover.

The sound was deafening in the enclosed space, and the combination of smoke pumping through the ventilators and the pall left from so much gunfire made it impossible to breathe or see that well.

A blast of light from the end of the hall was a burst of return fire. Eddie Seng went sprawling, as if suddenly shoved from behind. Unable to stop his fall with his hands, he crashed to the deck and slid into the Chairman. One-handed, Juan grabbed him by the collar and dragged him into the mess, all the while firing with his left.

Didi continued to struggle in Linc's powerful grip as he was man-handled into the mess hall. All the furniture was gone, and, unbelievably, a pair of men was wrestling the stove out the kitchen door despite the gun battle raging just outside. When the pair realized the men who had rushed into the room weren't their friends, they dropped their burden and reached for the weapons they'd left lying across the burners.

Juan fired fast and from the hip but still managed amazing accuracy. Both men's chests erupted in a gush of blood and torn meat.

A secret door seamlessly built into a bulkhead clicked open. Linda had been watching them with the hidden camera and had men standing by to help. A pair of operatives rushed into the room, and ten seconds later Mohammad Didi had FlexiCuffs around his wrists. They hustled him back through the door and closed it behind them. Eddie was groaning and trying to get to his feet. Juan gently lifted him up and helped him through the door. Once through, Juan fell back on the wall with his hands on his knees, dripping water onto the plush carpet. It took him a moment to catch his breath.

"That could have gone better," he panted.

"You can say that again," Eddie agreed.

"You okay?"

"The bullet grazed a plate in my flak jacket. Hurts like hell, but I'm good to go. Just give me a minute."

Giuseppe Farina approached with Dr. Huxley. Hux wore her de rigueur white lab coat over a pair of surgical scrubs and had a leather medical bag gripped in her right hand. She was in her early forties, with dark hair pulled back in a ponytail, and a no-nonsense look in her eyes.

"Not being too cowboy for you, are we?" Juan grinned at the Italian observer.

Farina cast a murderous look at Didi, and said, "I had hoped, maybe, for a little more."

"Who are you people?" Didi demanded in accented English. "You cannot take me. I am a Somali citizen. I have rights."

"Not once you set foot on this ship before it had cleared customs," Juan informed him. "You're on my territory now." It took all his willpower not to rip the grisly necklace from around Didi's neck and cram it down his throat.

Julia set her bag on the deck, rummaged through it, and stood holding a syringe and a pair of surgical scissors. With Didi firmly in Linc's grip, she cut away part of his sleeve and swabbed his skin with alcohol.

"What are you doing?" Didi's eyes had gone wide. He tried to wiggle free, but Linc's arms were like iron bands around his body. "This is torture."

Juan was in front of the warlord before anyone knew he was moving. He pulled Didi from Linc's grip. With one hand around Didi's throat, Juan used the leverage of the corridor wall to lift the Somali off his feet so they were eye to eye. Didi began to gag, but no one made a move to help him. Even their European observer was spellbound by the utter rage that puffed up the Chairman's face and turned his skin red.

"You want to see torture? I will show you torture, you murderous piece of filth." He used the thumb and index finger of his other hand and pinched a nerve bundle in Didi's shoulder. Didi must have felt as if he'd been seared with a hot poker, because he let out a wail that echoed down the corridor. Juan dug in deeper, changing the pitch of the pirate's scream as if he were playing a musical instrument.

"That's enough, Juan," Dr. Huxley said.

Cabrillo released his grip and let Didi, who clutched at his throat and shoulder, fall to the floor. He was weeping, and a silver string of saliva oozed out of the corner of his mouth.

"Like I figured," Juan said as if the outburst had not occurred, "in the heart of every bully lies a coward. I wish your men could see you now."

Hux bent over the prostrate killer and slid the needle home. A moment later, Didi's eyes fluttered and rolled back into his skull so only the whites showed. Hux bent over him a second time and thumbed down the lids.

"Congratulations, Juan." 'Seppe extended his hand. "Mission accomplished."

"Not until we're clear of Somali waters and that scumbag is off my boat." He tapped his radio. "Linda, tell Max to cut the smoke and give me a sit rep."

"The pirates who were chasing you are milling around the mess hall. One is checking on the guys you took down, but those boys aren't in any condition to tell them much. On deck, the water cannons are having the desired effect. People are scrambling off the ship as fast as they can."

"How many do you estimate are still aboard?"

"Forty-three precisely. And that includes the rebels you trapped down near the hold. The guard you left unconscious under the stairs has already been taken care of. He came awake the moment he was tossed into the water."

"Tell Eric to make ready to pull away from the dock."

"What do we do with the pirates still roaming around the super-structure?" Linda asked.

"Lock it down, and get the armorer up here with tranq guns and NVGs."

In the op center, Linda relayed Juan's orders. On the big monitor she watched as a group of kids was trying to dodge the powerful spray from one of the water cannons, turning it into a game of dare. From her seat in the middle of the room, she hit a toggle to take command of that particular cannon and cut the flow of water. The kids stopped dashing around, looking like their favorite toy had been taken away. Linda adjusted the aim and electronically opened the valve again. The blast caught the boys at the knees, knocking all six flat and tumbling them like flotsam toward the boarding stairs. They didn't stop rolling until they landed on the dock in a sodden tangle of limbs. The boys quickly got to their feet and fled into the village.

"Locking down now," Mark Murphy said after typing at his workstation for a moment. He made the last keystroke, and all over the ship hidden steel shutters slammed closed over every door, hatch, and window, effectively sealing the entire superstructure.

A cat might have been able to maneuver in such darkness, but a man without night vision goggles was as good as blind.

Linda switched the internal cameras to thermal imaging and scanned the feeds until she had checked every compartment and hallway. There were still thirteen people locked inside the ship. When she switched the cameras to low-light mode, she made out that they were all armed men. Over the speakers, she could hear them calling out to one another, but no one dared move from where he stood.

Just as Linda finished her sweep, Juan came over the radio. "How do we look?"

"We've got thirteen. The pirates who were in the mess are out in the hallway now with the others you tangled with, so I'd say you're clear."

"Good enough for me."

"Happy hunting."

Two decks above, Juan doused the lights in the hallway and slid a pair of third-generation night vision goggles over his eyes. In his hand he carried a sleek-looking pistol with walnut grips and an especially long barrel. Powered by compressed gas, the tranquilizer gun could fire ten needles laced with a sedative so potent it would drop an average-sized man in ten seconds. While that may sound like a short amount of time, it could give a gunman ample opportunity to loosen an entire magazine from an automatic weapon—hence the darkness.

Eddie and Linc were similarly armed.

Cabrillo opened the secret door again. Through the goggles, the world had gone an eerie shade of green. Reflective surfaces shone a bright white that could be distracting had Juan and his people not been so used to NVGs. When the hatch closed behind them, they padded forward until they were pressed to the mess hall door. The air still smelled sharply of smoke.

"There are three of them to your right," Linda said over the tactical net. "Ten feet down the corridor and moving away from you."

Using hand signals, Juan relayed the information to his men and like wraiths out of a nightmare they slid out the mess and took aim simultaneously. The tranquilizer guns gave a soft whisper, and even before the darts found their marks Cabrillo and the others were back in the mess.

The barbs hit the men in their shoulders, the ultrafine needles having no trouble piercing clothing and lodging in flesh. The sharp sting made all three whirl around, and one opened fire in panic. The muzzle flash revealed an empty corridor, and for the second time in twelve hours Malik and Aziz were chasing ghosts.

"This ship is crewed by evil djinns," Aziz managed to wail before he was overtaken by the drug. Malik, who was a larger man, swayed for a moment before he, too, tumbled flat, landing on the unconscious third rebel.

"Ten to go," Linda said. "But we've got another problem."

"Talk to me," Juan said tersely.

"The pirates on shore are getting organized. There's some guy rallying them to reboard the *Oregon*. He has maybe twenty-five or thirty looking like they're going to try it."

"Am I on the speakers?"

"Affirmative."

"Mark, pop open one of the deck .30s and scatter that crowd. Eric, pull us away."

Eric Stone and Mark Murphy shot each other a grin and made to carry out Cabrillo's order. Murphy keyed in the command to one of the .30 caliber machine guns hidden in an oil barrel on deck.

The barrel's lid hinged open and the weapon emerged in a vertical position before its gimbal it until the barrel was pointed at the earthen embankment behind the dock. On Murphy's computer, a camera slaved to the M60 gave him a sight picture, including an aiming reticle.

He loosened a volley over the heads of the crowd, the gun barking and a string of empty shell casings falling to the deck in a metal rain. The armed pirates either dropped flat or vanished over the embankment. A few lying prone returned fire, raking the area where the remotely operated gun still smoked. Their 7.62mm rounds were as effective as hitting a rhino with a spitball.

Next to Murphy, Eric Stone dialed up the power from the magnetohydrodynamic engines. The water this deep into the swamp was brackish from having mixed with fresh, but it maintained enough salinity for him to ramp the ship up to eighty percent capacity. He engaged reverse thrust. The power of the massive hydro pumps boiled the water at the *Oregon*'s bow, and the great ship began to back away from the wooden dock.

The ropes the pirates had used to secure the vessel lost their slack, then went as taut as bowstrings before the old hemp broke. Eric eased the ship back from the dock a good fifty feet and then engaged the dynamic positioning system to keep the *Oregon* at those exact GPS coordinates.

There was no way he would attempt to maneuver the ship out of the swamp without the Chairman on deck to lend a hand if he got into trouble.

But then his mind was changed for him.

Like a barrage from a group of archers, a flurry of rocket-propelled grenades came sizzling over the embankment. The smoke they trailed seemed to fill the sky from horizon to horizon.

SIX

ERIC SLAMMED HIS FIST ON THE COLLISION ALARM BUTTON. The electronic cry would carry to every deck and compartment on the ship. It was a sound the crew knew well.

At this close range there wasn't enough time to deploy the 20mm Gatling close-in defense system; however, Mark Murphy was getting it ready for the second salvo he was sure to follow.

A few of the rockets went radically off course, corkscrewing into the water or into the mangroves to detonate harmlessly. Even with the bow facing the attack, the *Oregon* was still a large enough target to make it difficult to miss. RPGs slammed into her prow, blowing off her fore railing and tearing a fluke off one of her anchors. Others skimmed over the bow and exploded against the superstructure below the closed-off bridge windows.

Had this been any other ship, the onslaught would have turned the vessel into scrap. But the *Oregon*'s armor held. A few craters had been cored into the steel, and paint had been burned off all over the superstructure, but none of the rocket grenades had penetrated. There remained vulnerable areas, however. The ship wasn't entirely impervious to a rocket attack. The smokestack shielded the ship's sophisticated radar dish, and a lucky shot could easily destroy it.

"Incoming," Juan heard over the radio earbud an instant before the first RPG homed in on his ship.

The blasts at the bow gave him and his team enough warning to clamp their hands over their ears and leave their mouths open to prevent unequal pressure in their sinuses that would blow out their eardrums.

The superstructure rang as though it were a giant bell. Each explosion sent the men reeling back, though they were nowhere near the sections getting pummeled. In those compartments, the staggering concussions were lethal. One pirate, who had been leaning against a wall that took one of the rocket strikes, had his insides jellied by the blast, while the two men with him permanently lost their hearing.

"Tell Eric to get us the hell out of here," Juan shouted into his microphone. He could barely hear his own voice, while Linda's was an unintelligible squeal.

As soon as Eric had mashed the collision alarm, he disengaged the GPS and reconfigured the view on the main screen so half of it showed a camera shot over the *Oregon*'s fantail while the other monitored the pirate lair. There was neither time nor room to turn the five-hundred-foot ship.

He moved the throttles once again into reverse.

The channel looked so narrow he felt like he was going to thread a needle while wearing oven mitts. At least the first mile was straight, so he added more power, backing the big freighter as carefully as he possibly could. It didn't help that a breeze had picked up, and the hull and superstructure were acting like a sail.

A pair of RPGs was launched from the dock. This time, Mark

had the redoubt opened for the six-barreled Gatling gun, and it spooled up to nearly a thousand rpms.

The Vulcan shrieked and the Russian-made rocket-propelled grenades ran into the solid curtain of the 20mm rounds it had spewed. Both warheads detonated over the water, while the embankment beyond was chewed apart by the slugs that overshot. Mark saw that pirates were getting ready to follow the *Oregon* in their fishing boats. They wouldn't be an issue once they reached the sea, but until Eric maneuvered them through the mangroves the fishing boats had the edge.

Mark aimed low along the hull of the first boat and unleashed a one-second burst. The shells ripped open the water immediately adjacent to the boat, dousing the rebels and, more important, warning them. They dove off the boat and were halfway down the dock when Murph unleashed the autocannon again.

The small trawler disintegrated in a mushrooming cloud of shredded wood, splintered glass, and torn metal. When the gas tank erupted, the blast knocked the pirates flat, as greasy smoke rose into the air.

The men on the second boat had pulled away from the dock before they realized they were next. Mark almost chuckled at how comically they leapt from the doomed boat, giving little thought to their comrades. When it was clear of men, he fired. The pilothouse was blown away like a garden shed caught in a tornado. So much of the bow was destroyed that, with the throttles open, water poured into the hull until the boat vanished entirely. It reminded him of a submarine sinking beneath the waves, only this craft was never surfacing again.

Up in the superstructure, Juan and his two teammates took up the chase again. Still unable to hear Linda because his ears continued to ring, Cabrillo relied on his hunter's instincts. They moved slowly and methodically, checking and clearing the area room by room. When they discovered the grisly chamber where one of the rockets had hit, they darted the two deafened pirates. The third man looked like a rag doll with half its stuffing removed.

The explosions, and the fact that they could feel the ship under way, sent the rebels into near panic. They screamed for one another in the blackness, and the ones who found a sealed door clawed at the metal with their bare hands. They had no idea they were being stalked until a dart shot out of nowhere.

Had these men not preyed on unsuspecting ships off the coast, Juan could almost dredge up some pity for them. But he had a mariner's special loathing for pirates and piracy, so he felt nothing when he fired the final time and sent the last of them into dreamland.

"Okay, Linda, that's it," Juan reported. "Unseal the superstructure and get some support in here. Tell Hux to treat the wounded as best she can, but I want this scum off the ship in thirty minutes."

Cabrillo stripped off the cumbersome night vision goggles when the plates over the exterior doors and ports lifted and the fluorescent lights flickered to life. His wiped the sweat from his forehead with his sleeve. It came away soaked, and he knew that the temperature was only partially responsible for the perspiration. His limbs trembled with the aftereffects of the adrenaline high.

A few moments later, the superstructure was crawling with personnel to deal with the unconscious gunmen. Giuseppe appeared at Juan's side and handed him a water bottle glistening with dew. He walked with Juan as the Chairman headed for the op center. The Italian had to lengthen his stride to keep pace.

"I was thinking, *amico*, it might be wise to take a few of these men with us when we put Didi on the fishing boat we have."

Cabrillo drank deeply, then said, "Better cover story than Didi out on his own sunset cruise?"

"*Sí.*"

"Did you have enough of that amnesia drug?"

"I have enough for two more, I should think."

"Fine by me," Juan said casually as they entered the ship's nerve center.

With one sweep of his eyes, Cabrillo took in the operational situation. They were far enough from the rebel compound that they were no longer under threat of attack from the RPGs, and since he didn't see any boats in pursuit he assumed Murph had taken care of them. Eric had backed up the *Oregon* until she was almost in the tight turn.

"How are you doing, Mr. Stone?" he asked.

"It's like pushing string, sir. Between the incoming tide, rising wind, and shoaling bottom, I don't see how you got us into this jam in the first place."

"Want me to take over?"

"I'd like to give it a try myself first."

"Incoming!" Murph suddenly shouted.

Unknown to the crew, there was a causeway running alongside the channel that the rebels had cleared to make a road. While the ship was slowly backing out of the swamp, armed rebels had boarded several trucks and raced after the lumbering freighter. When it paused in the tight confines of the turn, they opened fire with more RPGs.

Murph still had the Gatling port opened, but he had let the gun barrels stop rotating. He spun it up with the press of a button and opened fire. He was too slow for the first two rockets, which hit the hull and detonated harmlessly, but he managed to swat two more out of the air.

"I have the conn," Cabrillo said.

"Roger," Eric replied instantly.

Where Eric was approaching the tricky turn slowly and methodically, Juan ramped up the engines and engaged the bow thruster, remembering that they were in reverse so he had to call on the opposite side.

The Vulcan sounded like an industrial saw when it screamed again. On the causeway, one of the technicals had its front axle torn off. The vehicle catapulted over its truncated front end, scattering men, weapons, and a cascade of broken glass. It landed on its roof and dug a deep furrow into the rocky soil, its rear wheels spinning.

A second pickup was hit broadside. The kinetic energy of the tungsten shells flipped the two-ton truck onto its side and the gas tank exploded. It erupted in a blooming rose of flame and smoke. Mark had a bead on the third when it vanished behind a thick tangle of vegetation. He waited for it to reemerge on the other side of the copse of trees, but seconds trickled by with no firm sighting.

Watching the undergrowth through the zoom camera lens, he thought he saw movement yet still held his fire. With the ship accelerating down the channel, the angle continued to shift. In a moment, he would have to switch from the Vulcan mounted along the *Oregon*'s flank near the bow to the second gun located at the stern. Mark activated the hydraulics that would open the fantail doors. The plates slid aside to reveal the multibarrel weapon, but it would take a moment for it to be run out and the camera switched on his monitor. The jungle he'd been watching erupted in blinding flashes that came in a continuous blur. A second later, 20mm rounds from a truck-mounted antiaircraft cannon raked the *Oregon*. Unlike the RPGs, the cannon's hardened rounds tore into the ship's armor, gouging divots into the steel, and when two hit the same spot they bored through and began to wreak havoc on the interior spaces.

The only saving grace was that the ship's ballast tanks were full to make her look heavily laden, so only one of her secret decks was exposed. One round penetrated the executive boardroom and blew through a pair of leather-backed chairs before embedding itself in the far wall. Another entered the pantry and tore apart a pallet of flour so the air became a solid-white curtain of dust. A third exploded into the cabin of an off-duty engineer. He'd been sitting at his desk, watching the battle on the ship's closed-circuit television system, which saved his legs from the blast of shrapnel, but his back and neck were shredded as though he'd been mauled.

This all happened in the blink of an eye. Mark watched helplessly. He was impotent until the computer told him the second gun was ready.

"Wepps, what the hell?" Juan growled without taking his attention off the delicate maneuver of turning the big ship.

"One more sec . . ."

Murphy's board turned green, and he unleashed the weapon. The jungle where the technical lay hidden was swept away by the onslaught. Trees up to a foot thick were mowed down like wheat before a combine. One trunk plummeted to the earth, a halo of wood chips choking the area. It smashed into the technical's bed, silencing its twin cannons, but Mark kept up the remorseless torrent of rounds until the trees were gone and all that remained of the truck and crew was a smoldering ruin of torn metal and rended flesh.

The *Oregon* was halfway through the turn. Cabrillo had judged it precisely. He backed his ship with the expertise of a truck driver parallel-parking a big rig. The stern came mere inches from the muddy bank. They were so close that someone standing near the jack staff could have plucked leaves from the trees. Then she swung around, almost pivoting on a dime, so her fantail was pointed eastward toward the open ocean.

Eric gave Cabrillo a look of respect bordering on hero worship. He never would have dared maneuver the ship so fast through such a tight channel.

"Think you can take it from here?" the Chairman asked his helmsman.

"I got her, boss man." The ship automatically recorded its position using the constellation of GPS satellites. All Stone had to do now that the trickiest corner had been negotiated was run a reverse course through the nava-computer and the ship would steer herself around the tricky swamps and shifting shoals. He already had the coordinates where the derelict fishing boat awaiting Mohammad Didi had been pre-positioned.

Juan got up from his command chair and turned to Giuseppe Farina. "Let's figure out who you want to keep and who's going over the side. I want the pirates off the ship before we clear the mangroves."

He led the Italian observer down several decks to the *Oregon's* boat garage. Here, near the waterline, was a large door that could be opened to the sea. There was a ramp built into the ship, covered in Teflon to make it slick. From it, the crew could launch Zodiacs, Jet Skis, or her RHIB—rigid-hull inflatable boat. That particular craft was built for the Navy SEALs, with a bladder of air around its hull to give it buoyancy in any conditions and a pair of powerful outboards that could shoot it across the waves at better than fifty knots. The lighting was white fluorescents, but red battle lamps could be lit for night operations.

The crew had already inflated a large black raft, and the unconscious forms of the pirates had been loosely bound to it. Once they awoke, they would be able to free one another and paddle the raft back to shore. Hux still had the wounded in the medical bay, while the dead would be given burials at sea.

"We'll take this one and this one and that guy on the far side," Farina said, pointing to Malik and Aziz. "When they took the ship, they appeared to have some leadership role. Who knows, they might prove to be an intelligence asset."

"The younger one probably isn't worth it. Guy smokes more dope than a hippie at a Grateful Dead concert."

"They no longer tour, you know," 'Seppe teased.

"You know what I mean."

"We'll use him anyway. A little forced detoxification might do him some good."

Thirty minutes later, Hux arrived in the boat garage with a couple of crewmen acting as orderlies. They wheeled down several gurneys for the injured pirates.

"How are they?" Juan asked.

"We have a casualty," Hux told him.

"What? Why wasn't I told?"

"No sense informing you until I had him stable."

"Who is it? What happened?"

"One of those triple-A rounds penetrated Sam Pryor's cabin. He took some shrapnel to his back. I pulled out about twenty small fragments. He lost a good amount of blood, and there's some torn muscle, but he's going to be fine."

"Thank God," Juan breathed, thinking about the reprimand Mark Murphy had coming. He should have had the stern Gatling online much sooner. "So what about these guys?"

"Two have hearing loss," Dr. Huxley replied in a no-nonsense tone. "I don't know if it's permanent, and there isn't much I could do either way. Couple more have superficial wounds. I dug out the shrapnel, cleaned and dressed them, and pumped them with as much antibiotic as I dared. If they get infected, they're in for a rough time of it, considering the conditions they live in."

The two Somalis who'd been shot had been given a nylon satchel. Cabrillo guessed they contained additional medication and written instructions on how to use it. He also guessed the men wouldn't take the drugs and they would end up on Somalia's booming black market.

The wounded were set on the raft and the outer door was cranked open. Juan called up to the op center for Eric to bring the ship to a stop. At the leisurely speed they were doing, it took only a few minutes for the pump jets to slow the ship until she was wallowing in the gentle waves like an old sow. Water lapped just below the bottom edge of the ramp. Beyond, Cabrillo could see they were just about to break out of the mangroves. With the tide coming in, the raft would drift westward until it became entangled in the swamp. The men would wake in about an hour, so other than mild dehydration they would be fine.

He helped push the raft until it was sliding down the ramp. It hit the water without a splash, and its momentum carried it a few yards from the ship.

Juan tapped the intercom button again. "Okay, Eric, take us away nice and easy, and when they're a quarter mile astern open her up and get us to the fishing boat."

"Roger that."

A half hour later, Juan and 'Seppe Farina were outside, standing on the wing bridge. Crewmen were at work repairing the cosmetic damage caused by the RPG attacks. Railings were being replaced and scorch marks covered in thick marine paint. Men were slung over the side on bosun's chairs welding patches to the hull where the antiaircraft rounds had pierced the armor. Other men were inside, restoring the cabins with mattresses and furniture from the ship's stores. Max Hanley was compiling a list of everything they would need to buy in order to put the old freighter back to her former "glory."

The *Oregon* plowed through the calm waves at better than thirty knots, far from her maximum speed, when Linda Ross's already high-pitched voice squeaked from the tinny speaker. "Chairman, we have a radar contact four miles dead ahead."

Juan swung a pair of binoculars to his eyes and a moment later saw a speck on the otherwise deserted ocean. It took a few more minutes for it to resolve itself into a fishing boat much like the one that had initially attacked.

"When is the American destroyer going to be in this area?" Juan asked his friend.

"Dawn tomorrow. More than enough time for us to steal off into the night. Didi and the others probably won't be awake yet, and, if they are, they will be so nauseated by the drug they'll be as docile as lambs. And do not worry, the boat has no radio or fuel, and the chance someone will happen across it before your Navy is absolutely zero."

Eric brought the *Oregon* alongside the old fishing vessel so that men in the boat garage could simply leap aboard her with lines to secure it to the freighter. Cabrillo and Farina personally carried Mohammad Didi onto the stinking boat. They lugged him into the cabin below the pilothouse, and when they tossed him on an unmade bunk they might accidentally have thrown him too hard. His head hit the frame with a satisfying clunk.

Cabrillo looked down on the warlord with utter contempt. "We should've had your ass Gitmo'd for all the suffering you've caused, but that wasn't my call. The worst cell in the worst jail in the world is too good for you. Imprisonment in Europe will probably feel like a vacation after living like you have, so all that I can hope is that when they hand down that life sentence you have the decency to die on the spot."

Back on deck he couldn't help but chuckle. Linc and Eddie had tied Aziz to a chair with a fishing rod in one hand and a bottle of beer taped in the other.

No sooner had the ropes been cast away than Hali Kasim, the *Oregon*'s communications specialist, came over the intercom. "Chairman, you have an urgent call from Langston Overholt."

"Pipe it down here." Juan waited a beat, and said, "Lang, it's Juan. Just so you know, you're on speakerphone. With me is our Italian liaison."

"I'll cut the pleasantries for now," Overholt said from his Langley office. "How soon can you be in Tripoli?"

"Depending on traffic through the Suez Canal, maybe four days. Why?"

"The Secretary of State was on her way there for some preliminary talks. We just lost communication with her plane. We fear it crashed."

"We'll be there in three."

SEVEN

WHEN HER FINGER SLIPPED OFF THE STRING, FIONA CURSED. She looked up quickly to make sure no one heard, even though she was alone in the private bedchamber in the rear of the aircraft. Her mother had been a strong believer in using soap in the mouth to discourage profanity, so her reaction was automatic even forty years later.

The violin was her refuge from the world. With bow in hand she could empty her mind of all distractions and concentrate solely on the music. There was no other activity or hobby that could quiet her thoughts so thoroughly. She often credited it with keeping her sane, especially since accepting the appointment to head the State Department.

Fiona Katamora was one of those rare creatures who come along once in a generation. By her sixth birthday, she was giving violin concerts as a soloist. Her parents, who had been interned during World War II because both had been born in Japan, had taught her Japanese while she taught herself Arabic, Mandarin, and Russian. She entered Harvard when she was fifteen and law school when she was eighteen. Before taking the bar exam, she took time off to sharpen her fencing skills, and would have gone on to the Olympics had she not torn a ligament in her knee a week before the opening ceremony.

She did all this and much more and made it look effortless. Fiona Katamora possessed a near-photographic memory, and required only four hours of sleep a night. Apart from her athletic, academic, and musical talents, she was charming, gracious, and possessed an infectious smile that could brighten any room.

Fiona had over a hundred job offers to consider when she passed the bar, including a teaching position at her alma mater, but she wanted to dedicate herself to serving the public trust. She joined a Washington think tank specializing in energy matters, and quickly made a name for herself with her ability to see causalities others simply couldn't. After five years, one of her papers was submitted as a doctoral thesis, and she was awarded a Ph.D.

Her reputation within the Beltway grew to the point that she was a regular consultant at the White House for Presidents of both parties. It was only a matter of time before she was tapped for a cabinet post.

Still unmarried at forty-six, Fiona Katamora remained a stunning beauty, with raven hair as glossy as obsidian and a smooth, unlined face. She was trim and, at five foot six, tall for her ancestry. In interviews, she said she was simply too busy for a family of her own, and while gossip magazines had tried to link her to various men of wealth and power she almost never dated.

In her two years as Secretary of State, she had worked wonders around the globe, restoring America's reputation as peacemaker and impartial arbiter. She had helped broker the longest cease-fire to date between the government of Sri Lanka and Tamil Tiger separatists, and had used her skills to settle a disputed election in Serbia that had threatened to become violent.

Fiona had shaken things up within the corridors of the State Department as well. She had garnered the nickname "dragon lady" because she had swept house at Foggy Bottom, cutting out layer upon layer of redundant staff, until State was the model of efficiency for the rest of the government.

And now she was headed for what could be the crowning moment of a remarkable career. The preliminary talks were meant to establish the framework for what was to be called the Tripoli Accords. If anyone could bring peace to the Middle East after ten presidential administrations failed, it would be Fiona Katamora.

She finished playing the Brahms piece she'd been practicing and set the violin and bow aside. She wiped her fingers on a monogrammed handkerchief and did some exercises to work out the mild cramping. She feared that arthritis was starting to make inroads.

There was a knock on the cabin door.

"Come in," she said.

Her personal assistant, Grace Walsh, popped her head around the jamb. Grace had been with Fiona for more than a decade, following her boss from plum job to plum job.

"You wanted me to tell you when it was four."

"Thanks, Gracie. What's our ETA?"

"Knew you'd ask, so I spoke with the pilot. We're about forty-five minutes out. We'll be over Libyan territory shortly. Can I get you anything?"

"A bottle of water would be great. Thanks."

Fiona buried herself in the stack of papers spread out on the bed. They were dossiers on all the major players expected at the upcoming summit, including brief biographies and photographs. She'd gone over them all before, committing most to memory, but she wanted to make sure she had everything just right. She quizzed herself on which ministers were related to their country's rulers, names of wives and children, educational backgrounds, anything to make this as personal as possible.

She was most intrigued by Libya's dynamic new Foreign Minister, Ali Ghami. His was by far the smallest dossier. Reportedly, Ghami had been a low-level civil servant until he'd come to the attention of Libya's President Muammar Qaddafi. Within days of a meeting between the two men, Ghami had been elevated to Foreign Minister. In the six months since, he had been on a whirlwind tour throughout the region, drumming up support for the peace conference. His reception in various Middle Eastern capitals had been cool at first, but his dynamic personality and utter charm had slowly started to change minds. In many ways, he was like Fiona, and maybe that's why she couldn't get her mind around what bothered her about him.

Grace knocked again and stepped into the bedroom. She set a bottle of Dasani on the nightstand and turned to go.

"Hold on a sec," Fiona said, and showed her the photograph of Ghami. "What does your woman's intuition tell you about him?"

Grace took the picture and held it close to one of the Boeing 737's windows. In the official photograph, Ghami wore a Western-style suit cut perfectly for his physique. He had thick salt-and-pepper hair and a matching mustache.

Gracie gave her the picture back. "I'm the wrong person to ask. I fell in love with Omar Sharif when I saw *Doctor Zhivago* as a teenager, and this guy has that same vibe."

"Handsome, yes, but look at his eyes."

"What about them?" Gracie asked.

"I can't put my finger on it. There's something there, or something missing. I don't know."

"Could just be a bad picture."

"Maybe it's that I just don't like going into this knowing virtually nothing about our host."

"You can't have crib notes on everybody," Grace teased gently. "Remember when you did a background check on that cute lawyer you wanted to—"

A loud, jarring crash cut Grace off in midsentence. The two women looked at each other, eyes wide. Both had spent countless hours in the air over the years and knew whatever that sound was, it wasn't good.

They waited a beat to see if anything else was happening. After a few seconds, they simultaneously released a held breath and shared a nervous chuckle.

Fiona got to her feet to ask the pilot if anything was wrong. She was halfway to the door when the aircraft shuddered violently and started to fall from the sky. Grace screamed when the wild descent pressed her up against the ceiling. Fiona managed to keep on her feet by pushing her hands against the molded plastic overhead.

In the forward section of the executive jet, she could hear other staffers screaming as they fought the effects of temporary weightlessness.

"I don't know what happened," the pilot, an Air Force colonel, said over the intercom, "but everyone get yourselves strapped in as quickly as you can." He left the intercom on while he and his copilot tried to regain control of the hurtling aircraft, so Fiona and the others could hear the tension in his voice. "What do you mean you can't reach anyone? We were talking with Tripoli two minutes ago."

"I can't explain it," the copilot replied. "The radio's just dead."

"Don't worry about it now, help me—damn, the port engine just kicked out. Try to restart it." The intercom suddenly clicked off.

"Are we going to crash?" Grace asked. She had regained her feet, and she and Fiona clutched each other like little girls in a haunted house.

"I don't know," Fiona said more calmly than she felt. Her insides fluttered, and her palms had gone greasy.

"What happened?"

"I don't know. Something mechanical, I guess." That answer didn't satisfy her at all. There was no reason the plane should have plummeted like that with both engines functioning. It could even fly on one engine. Something else had to have caused their sudden drop. And what was that loud bang? Her first and only thought was that they had been hit by a missile, one meant to cripple the plane, not destroy it.

The gut-wrenching descent slowly started to even out. The pilots had managed to regain enough control so they were no longer in free fall, but they were still plunging toward earth at breakneck speed.

Fiona and Grace groped their way into the main cabin and strapped themselves into the big leather chairs. Secretary Katamora said a few reassuring words to her people, wishing she could do more to alleviate the fear she saw etched on their faces. The truth was that she was barely in control of her own emotions. She feared that if she spoke more her terror would rise to the surface and bubble over, like lava erupting from a volcano.

"Ladies and gentlemen"—it was the copilot—"we don't know what just happened. One of our engines is down and the other is barely producing thrust. We're going to have to land in the desert. I don't want anyone to worry. Colonel Markham has actually done this before in an F-16 during the first Gulf War. When I give the signal, I want everyone to assume the crash positions. Tuck your head between your knees and wrap your arms around them. As soon as the plane comes to a stop, I want the steward to open the cabin door as quickly as possible. Secretary Katamora's Secret Service detail is to get her off the plane first."

There was only one agent on board. The rest of Fiona's detail, plus a number of her staff, had been in Libya for nearly a week preparing for her arrival.

The agent, Frank Maguire, unbuckled his seat belt, paused until the aircraft stopped buffeting for a second, and switched seats so he was between Fiona and the door. He quickly strapped himself in as the Boeing lurched violently. When the time came, he could grab her and have her out of the door in seconds.

Holding Grace's hand, Fiona started to do something she hadn't in years: pray. But it wasn't for their lives. She prayed that if the worst did happen and they died in the crash, the momentous opportunity of the summit wouldn't be lost forever. Unselfish to the end, Fiona Katamora cared more about the cause of peace than her own life.

She chanced looking out the window. The terrain not far below the aircraft was rough desert punctuated by jagged hills. Not a pilot herself, she still knew the odds were long despite the crew's assurance.

"Okay, folks," the copilot announced, "this is it. Please assume the crash positions and hang on tight."

The passengers heard the pilot ask "Do you see th—" before the intercom went silent again. They had no idea what he had seen, and would be better off not knowing anyway.

EIGHT

ALANA SAT IN THE DRILL TRUCK'S PASSENGER'S SEAT WHILE Mike Duncan drove. The old riverbed was littered with rounded boulders. Some could be steered around, others they had to muscle over. Her backside was a sea of bruises after so many weeks traversing the same terrain.

At camp the night before, they had pleaded their case to the Tunisian representative, who believed they were searching for a Roman mill and waterwheel, that returning to the old ruins every night was an unnecessary precaution. They begged to be allowed to stay out for a few days, pointing out that Greg Chaffee had a satellite phone, so they would never really be out of contact with the main archaeological team.

While the legitimate members of the archaeological dig were making tremendous strides in excavating the Roman ruins, Alana's team still had nothing to show for their weeks of effort. It was hoped that if they could remain out in the desert longer, and thus roam wider, they might pick up the trail of the old Barbary corsair, Suleiman Al-Jama.

The only thing keeping her going now was her nightly e-mail

chat with her son back in Phoenix. She marveled at the advance in technology. Her first dig as an undergrad, at a site in the Arizona desert less than two hundred miles from school, had been more isolated than this godforsaken dust bowl, thanks to modern satellite communications.

The Tunisian government minder continued to refuse their request until Greg took him aside for about two minutes. When they had returned to the dining tent, the official beamed at Alana and granted them permission, provided they checked in every day and returned within seventy-two hours.

"Baksheesh," Greg had replied to her inquiring look.

Alana had paled. "What if he refused the money and reported you?"

"This is the Middle East. We would have been in trouble if he hadn't."

"But . . ." Alana didn't know what to say.

She had always lived her life by one simple dictum: Obey the rules. She had never cheated on a test, reported every penny on her tax return, and set her car's cruise control at the posted speed limit. For her, the world was very black-and-white, and this made things simple in one sense and incredibly difficult in another. She could always feel comfortable with the moral choices she made, but she was forced to live in a society that spent most of its time searching for the gray areas so it could avoid responsibility.

It wasn't that she was naïve to the way the world worked, she just couldn't allow its petty corruptions into her life. It never would have occurred to her to bribe the representative from Tunisia's archaeological ministry because it was wrong.

On the other hand, she certainly wouldn't turn down the opportunity Greg's actions presented. So they were driving again, with the intention of finding a way past the waterfall in the vain hope that

Suleiman Al-Jama's secret base was somewhere in the desert wastes beyond.

The truck was loaded with enough water and food to last the party three days. They had brought only one tent, but Alana felt comfortable enough with her companions that it wouldn't be a problem. They also carried a fifty-gallon drum of fuel strapped in the bed, with enough diesel to extend their range a further three hundred miles, depending on how much they used up running the drill.

No one was optimistic about their chances. The waterfall was simply too tall for a sailing ship to navigate. However, they were desperate. The Tripoli Accords were fast approaching. Alana was aware that the Secretary of State was flying in to Libya this very day for a brief round of preliminary talks, so she felt the added pressure.

"Do you have to hit every pothole and rock?" Greg asked from the rear bench seat of the open-topped truck.

"As a matter of fact, I do," Mike deadpanned.

Greg shifted to the right so he was behind Alana. "Then hit them with the left-side tires, will ya?"

It was another sparkling-clear day, which meant the temperature hit one hundred and eight degrees when they stopped for lunch. Alana handed out chilled bottles of water from the cooler and gave each man a sandwich the camp staff had prepared. According to the odometer, they had come seventy miles, and if she remembered correctly the falls were a further thirty.

"What do you think about over there?" Mike asked with his mouth full of food. He used his sandwich like a pointer to indicate the far bank of the old river. Where usually they were hemmed in by steep cliffs, here, in a curve in the watercourse, erosion had carved into the bank so it was a ramp up to the desert floor.

"Looks to be a sixty percent grade, or steeper," Greg said.

"If we can find something on top to secure the winch, we should be able to pull ourselves up, no problem."

Alana nodded. "I like it."

As soon as they finished their meal, something the heat made unappealing to them all, Mike drove the truck to the base of the riverbank. Seen up close, the gradient appeared steeper than they had originally estimated, and the height a good thirty feet more. He forced the truck up the bank until the rear wheels lost traction and began to throw off plumes of dust. Alana and Greg leapt from the vehicle. She began to unspool the braided-steel cable from the winch mounted to the front bumper, while Greg Chaffee, the fittest of the bunch, threw himself into the task of climbing the slope. His boots kicked up small avalanches of loose dirt and pebbles with each step, and he was quickly forced to scramble up the hill using his hands and arms as well as his legs. He cursed when his big straw hat went flying away, rolling down the hill behind him. With no choice, he clipped the hook to the back of his belt and kept going, scraping his fingers raw on the rough stone.

It took Greg nearly ten minutes to reach the summit, and, when he did, the back of his shirt was soaked through with perspiration, and he could feel the bald spot on the crown of his head parboiling. He vanished from sight for a moment, dragging the wire behind him.

When he reemerged, he shouted down to the other two, "I looped the wire around an outcropping of rock. Give it a try, and pick up my hat on the way up."

The winch could be controlled from inside the truck's cab, so Alana fetched the hat before it blew away and hopped back into her seat. Mike jammed the transmission into first, fed the engine some gas, and engaged the winch's toggle. While not especially powerful, the winch's motor ran through enough gears to give it the torque it needed. The truck started a slow, stately ascent up the bank. Alana and Mike exchanged grins, while above them Greg gave a triumphant shout.

The flick of a shadow crossing her face drew Alana's attention. She glanced skyward, expecting to see a hawk or vulture.

A large twin-engine jet was passing overhead at less than a thousand feet. Incongruously, Alana could barely hear the roar of its exhaust. It was as if the engines were shut down and the jet was gliding. She knew of no landing fields in the area, at least on this side of the Libyan border, and guessed correctly that the plane was in trouble.

She noticed two details as the jet banked slightly away. One was a jagged hole near the tail that was stained with what she guessed was hydraulic fluid. The other thing she saw were words written along the aircraft's fuselage: UNITED STATES OF AMERICA.

Greg had stopped whooping. He placed his hand above his eyes, shading them from the sun, and he turned in place, tracking the path of the crippled government jet.

Alana gasped aloud when she realized what plane that was and who was on it.

Concentrating on getting the truck up the hill, Mike Duncan hadn't seen a thing, so when Alana sucked in a lungful of air he thought something was happening with the tow cable, and asked, "What is it?"

"Get to the top of the hill as fast as you can."

"I'm working on it. What's the rush?"

"The Secretary of State's plane is about to crash."

Of course, there was nothing Mike could do. They were at the mercy of the slowly turning winch.

Alana shouted up to Greg, "Can you see anything?"

"No," he replied over the rig's snarling engine. "The plane flew over some hills a couple miles from here. I don't see any smoke or anything. Maybe the pilot was able to set it down safely."

For eight agonizing minutes, the truck climbed up the hill like a fly crawling over a crust of bread. Greg kept reporting that he saw no smoke, which was a tremendous relief.

They finally emerged from the dry riverbed. Greg unsnapped the tow hook from the cable and unwound it from a sandstone projectile the size of a locomotive. The cable had cut deeply into the soft stone, and he had to brace his foot against the rock to pull it free.

"It could have come down in Libya," Mike muttered.

"What was that?" Alana asked.

"I said the plane could have come down across the border in Libya." He spoke loudly enough for Greg to hear as well.

Alana was the team leader but she looked to Chaffee for validation, her suspicions that he was from the CIA making him the expert in this type of situation.

"We could be the only people for fifty or more miles," Greg said. "If they managed to land, there could be injuries, and we have the only vehicle out here."

"Who do you really work for?" asked Alana.

"We're wasting time."

"Greg, this is important. If we have to cross into Libya, I need to know who you work for."

"I'm with the Agency, all right. The CIA. My job is to keep an eye on you three. Well, the two of you, since the good Dr. Bumford hasn't left camp since we arrived. You recognized the plane, didn't you?" Alana nodded. "So you know who's on board?"

"Yes."

"Are you willing to let her die out here because you're afraid we might run into a Libyan patrol? Hell, they invited her. They aren't going to do anything to us if we're trying to rescue her, for God's sake."

Alana looked over at Mike Duncan. The rangy oilman's face was a blank mask. They could be discussing the weather, for all the concern he showed. "What do you think?" she asked.

"I'm no hero, but I think we should probably check it out."

"Then let's go," Alana replied.

They started off across the open desert. It was like driving on the surface of the moon. There was no hint of human habitation, no inkling they were on the same planet even. From the river to the string of hills Greg mentioned was nothing but a boulder-strewn plain devoid of life. This deep in the desert, only a few insects and lizards could survive, and they had the good sense to remain in their burrows during the torturous afternoons.

As they drove, Greg tried unsuccessfully to reach his superiors on his satellite phone. His had a dedicated government communications system, the same one used by the military, so there was no reason he shouldn't get through but he couldn't. He replaced the chargeable battery with another he carried in a knapsack.

"This piece of junk," he spat. "Thirty-billion-a-year budget and they send me out with a five-year-old phone that doesn't work. I should have known. Listen, you guys, you ought to know that this wasn't really a priority mission. If we found Al-Jama's papers, great. But if not, the conference was going ahead anyway."

"But Christie Valero said—"

"Anything to get you to agree to come. Hey, Mike and I both know from playing the ponies that long shots sometimes pay, too, but this has been a farce since day one. For me, this mission is punishment for a screwup I made in Baghdad a few months ago. For you guys . . . I have no idea, but they sent me out here with crap equipment, so you figure it out."

After Greg's revealing outburst, the team drove on in silence, the mood in the truck somber. Alana was torn between thinking about what Greg had said and what they would find when they came across Secretary Katamora's plane. Both options were grim. She had never met Fiona Katamora, but she admired her tremendously. She was the kind of role model America needed. To think of her dead in a plane crash was just too horrible to contemplate.

But to consider Greg's words was painful, too, so she decided he was simply wrong. Who knew what baggage he carried that made him so jaded. Christie Valero and St. Julian Perlmutter had laid out a convincing case. Being able to undercut the justifications Islamic radicals used to validate their murderous actions would be perhaps the greatest stride yet in the war on terror. More than ever, she was certain that this mission, while admittedly a long shot, was critical to the upcoming peace talks, and she didn't care what Greg said about it.

Mike steered them into a canyon between the hills, shaded and much cooler than the open desert. It snaked through the low mountains for a half mile before they emerged on the other side. There still wasn't any evidence that the Secretary's plane had crashed, no column of black smoke rising up into the sky. Considering how low the plane had been flying, it had to be on the ground by now, so Alana let herself hope it had landed safely.

They continued on for another hour, knowing that they had passed the unmarked border at some point and were now in Libyan territory illegally. Her only solace was Greg's fluency in Arabic. If they ran into a patrol, it would be up to him to talk their way out of trouble.

The desert rose and fell in unending dunes of gravel and dirt that sent off shimmering curtains of heat. It made the distant horizon look fluid. The truck crested another anonymous hill, and Mike was about to take them down the far side when he braked suddenly. He rammed the gearbox into reverse and twisted in his seat to look behind them.

"What is it?" Alana cried as the vehicle plunged back down the hill they had climbed moments earlier.

Her answer came not from Mike but from Greg. "Patrol!"

Alana looked ahead as a military vehicle came over the hill, a soldier propped up in a hatch in the truck's roof. He was hanging on to a wicked-looking machine gun. With its tall suspension, balloon tires, and boxy cab, the truck looked perfectly suited for the desert.

"Forget it, Mike," Greg shouted over the keening engine. "Running from them is only going to make it worse."

Mike Duncan looked undecided for a moment, then nodded. He knew Chaffee was right. He eased off the gas and applied the brake. When the truck came to a stop, he killed the engine and left his hands on the wheel.

The Libyan patrol vehicle stopped twenty yards away, giving the roof gunner an optimal position to cover the trio. Back doors were thrown open and four soldiers dressed in desert fatigues rushed out, their AKs at the ready.

Alana had never been so frightened in her life. It was the suddenness of it all. One second they had been alone and the next they were looking down the barrel of a gun. Multiple guns, in fact.

The Libyan soldiers were shouting and gesturing with their weapons for them to get out of the truck. Greg Chaffee was trying to speak to them in Arabic, but his efforts had no effect. One soldier stepped back a pace and raked the ground with automatic fire, the bullets kicking up geysers of sand that blew away on the wind.

The sound was staggering, and Alana screamed.

Mike, Greg, and Alana threw their hands over their heads in the universal signal of surrender. A soldier grabbed Alana's wrist and yanked her from the open cab. Mike made a move to protest the rough treatment and had the butt of an AK slammed into his shoulder hard enough to numb his arm to the fingertips.

Alana sprawled in the dirt, her pride injured more than her body. Greg jumped from the rear seat, keeping his arms pointed skyward.

"Please," he said in Arabic, "we didn't know we had traveled into Libya."

"Tell them about the plane," Alana said, getting to her feet and dusting off her backside.

"Oh, right." Chaffee addressed the soldiers again. "We saw an aircraft that looked like it was about to crash. We were trying to see if it had."

Though none were wearing insignia on their uniforms, one of the soldiers was clearly their leader. He asked, "Where did you see this?"

Greg was relieved he had opened a dialogue. "We are part of an archaeological expedition working just across the border in Tunisia. The plane flew over where we were working at no more than a thousand feet—ah, three hundred meters."

"Did you see the plane crash?" the unshaved soldier asked.

"No. We didn't. We think it might have actually found someplace to land in the desert, because we haven't seen any smoke."

"That is good news for you," was his non sequitur reply.

"What's that supposed to mean?" Greg asked.

The Libyan ignored the question and stepped back to his patrol vehicle. He came back a moment later with something in his hands. None of the Americans could tell what he had until he handed them over to one of his men. Handcuffs.

"What are you doing?" Alana demanded in English when one of the soldiers grabbed her shoulders from behind. "We haven't done anything wrong."

When the warm steel snapped around her wrist, she turned and spat in the face of her captor. The man backhanded her hard enough to send her sprawling.

Mike pushed aside a soldier, getting ready to cuff him, and had taken two strides toward where Alana lay semiconscious, when the group's leader reacted to the aggressive move. He drew a pistol from a holster at his hip and calmly put a bullet between the oilman's eyes.

Mike Duncan's head snapped back, and his body toppled a couple of feet from Alana. Dazed by the blow, she could do nothing but stare at the obscene third eye in Mike's forehead. A trickle of dark fluid oozed from it.

She felt herself lifted to her feet but could do nothing to either resist or assist when she was manhandled into the back of the patrol truck. Greg Chaffee, too, seemed to be in shock as he was placed on a bench seat next to her. The interior was hot, hotter than even the open desert, and it was made worse when a soldier threw a dark cloth bag over her head.

The material absorbed Alana Shepard's tears as soon as they leaked from her eyes.

NINE

CORINTHIA BAB AFRICA HOTEL,
TRIPOLI, LIBYA

AMBASSADOR CHARLES MOON STOOD FROM BEHIND HIS DESK
as soon as his secretary opened his office door and stepped
aside. In a show of respect, Moon met his guest halfway across the
carpeted room.

"Minister Ghami, I appreciate you taking the time out of your
busy schedule to come see me in person." Moon's tone was grave.

"At a time like this, President Qaddafi wishes he could have
expressed our government's concern in person, but affairs of state
wait for no man. Please accept my humble presence as a sign that we
share your anxiety at this disastrous event." He held out his hand to
be shaken.

The U.S. Ambassador took his hand and motioned to the sofas
under the glass wall overlooking the sparkling waters of the Mediterranean. Near the horizon, a tanker was plowing westward. The
two men sat.

Where Moon was short in stature and wore his suit like a gun-
nysack, the Libyan Foreign Minister stood a solid six feet, with a
handsome face and perfectly coiffed hair. His suit had the distinctive
tailoring of Savile Row, and his shoes were shined to a mirror gloss.

His English was nearly flawless, with just a trace of an accent that added to his urbane sophistication. He crossed his legs, plucking at his suit pants so the fabric draped properly.

"My government wants to assure you that we have scrambled search-and-rescue teams to the area, as well as aircraft. We will not stop until we are certain what happened to Secretary Katamora's plane."

"We deeply appreciate that, Minister Ghami," Charles Moon replied formally. A career diplomat, Moon knew that the tone and timbre of their conversation was as important as the words. "Your government's response to this crisis is everything we could wish for. Your visit alone tells me how serious you feel toward what could turn out to be a terrible tragedy."

"I know the cooperative relationship between our two nations is in its infancy." Ghami made a sweeping gesture with his hand to encompass the room. "You don't even have a formal embassy building yet and must work out of a hotel suite, but I want this in no way to jeopardize what has been a successful rapport."

Moon nodded. "Since May of 2006, when we formalized relations once again, we have enjoyed nothing but support from your government, and at this time don't believe anything, ah, *deliberate* has occurred." He emphasized the word, and drove the point home further by adding, "Unless new information comes to light, we view this as a tragic accident."

It was Ghami's turn to nod. Message received. "A tragic accident indeed."

"Is there anything my government can do to help?" Moon asked, though he already knew the answer. "The aircraft carrier *Abraham Lincoln* is currently in Naples, Italy, and could aid in the search in a day or two."

"I would like nothing more than to take you up on your kind offer,

Ambassador. However, we believe that our own military and civilian search units are more than up for the task. I would hate to think of the diplomatic consequences if another aviation accident occurred. Further, the people of Libya have not forgotten the last time American warplanes were flying in our skies."

He was referring to the air strikes carried out by Air Force FB-111s and carrier aircraft on April 14, 1986, that leveled several military barracks and severely crippled Libya's air defense network. The strikes were in response to a spate of terrorist bombings in Europe that the U.S. had linked to a Libyan-backed group. Libya denied they had been involved, but history notes that there were no further such bombings until Al-Qaeda emerged a decade later.

Ghami gave a little smile. "Of course, we accept that you have most likely retasked some of your spy satellites to overfly our nation. If you happen to spot the plane, well, we would understand the source of that information should you choose to share it." Moon made to protest, but the Libyan cut him off with a gesture. "Please, Mr. Ambassador, you need not comment."

Moon smiled for the first time since the transponder on Fiona Katamora's plane went silent twelve hours earlier. "I was just going to say that we would doubtlessly share such information."

"There is one more thing we need to discuss," Ghami said. "At this time, and with your approval, I see no reason to cancel or even delay the upcoming peace conference."

"I spoke with the President this morning," Moon informed him, "and he expressed the same sentiment. If, God forbid, the worst has happened, it would do Secretary Katamora's memory a disservice by canceling what she believed was the greatest opportunity to achieve regional stability. She more than anyone, I believe, would want us to proceed."

"In the event that, well, as you say, the worst has occurred, do you know who would represent your government at the conference?"

"Frankly, no. The President refused to even speculate."

"I understand completely," Ghami said.

"He and Secretary Katamora were particularly close."

"I can well imagine. From what I've read and seen on the news, she was a remarkable woman. Forgive me, *is* a remarkable woman." Ghami stood, clearly irritated at his gaffe. "Mr. Ambassador, I won't take up any more of your day. I simply wanted to express our concern in person, and you have my word that as soon as I hear anything I will call you regardless of the time."

"I appreciate that."

"On a personal note, Charles"—Ghami used his Christian name deliberately—"if this is Allah's will, I certainly don't understand it."

Moon recognized that only the most heartfelt sentiment would cause Ghami to even suggest that he was questioning the will of his God. "Thank you."

The United States Ambassador led the Libyan Foreign Minister to the bank of elevators. Almost as an afterthought, Moon asked Ghami, "I wonder, if there is wreckage, how we should proceed."

"I don't understand."

"If the plane crashed, my government would most likely request that a team of American examiners inspect the remains in situ. People from the National Transportation Safety Board are experts at determining exactly what forces were in play to cause an airplane to crash."

"I see, yes." Ghami rubbed his jaw. "We have specialists who perform a similar function here. I can't see it as a problem. However, I'll need to consult with the President."

"Very well. Thank you."

A minute after Moon returned to his office, there was a knock on the door. "Come in."

"What do you think?" asked Jim Kublicki, the CIA station chief at the American Embassy. A former college football star, Kublicki had been with the agency for fifteen years. He was nearly as tall as the doorframe, which meant he would never be a covert operative because he stood out in any crowd, but he was a competent administrator, and the four agents assigned to the embassy liked and respected him.

"If they're involved in some way, Ali Ghami's out of the loop," Moon replied.

"From what I've heard, Ghami is Qaddafi's fair-haired boy. If they intentionally shot down that plane, he'd know."

"Then my gut tells me the Libyans didn't do anything and whatever has happened was an accident."

"We won't know for certain until they find the wreckage and get a team to examine it."

"Obviously."

"Did you ask him if we can bring over folks from the NTSB?"

"I did. Ghami agreed, but he wants to talk it over with Qaddafi. I think Ghami wasn't prepared for the question and wants a little time to figure out how to accept without admitting our people are better than his. They can't afford a diplomatic flap by refusing."

"If they do, that would surely tell us something," Kublicki said with a spook's inherent paranoia. "So, what's he like in person— Ghami, I mean?"

"I'd met him before, of course, but this time I got a better sense of the man behind the diplomatic niceties. He's charming and gracious, even in these circumstances. I could tell he was truly disturbed by what's happened. He's poured a lot of his own reputation into this conference, only to see it marred before it starts. He's really upset. It's hard to believe a regime like this could produce someone like that."

"Qaddafi saw the writing on the wall when we took down Saddam

Hussein. How long after we pulled him out of the spider hole did Libya agree to abandon its nuke program and disavow terrorism?"

"A matter of days, I believe."

"There you go. A leopard can change his spots once he sees the consequences of jerking around the good old U.S. of A."

The corners of Moon's mouth turned downward. He wasn't much for jingoism, and had been dead set against the Iraq invasion, though he acknowledged that without it the upcoming peace summit might never have been proposed. He shrugged. Who really knew? Events had unfolded the way they had and there was no use revisiting past actions. "Have you heard anything?" he asked Kublicki.

"NRO has shifted one of their spy birds from the Gulf to cover Libya's western desert. The imaging specialists have the first pictures now. If that plane's out there, they'll find it."

"We're talking thousands and thousands of square miles," Moon reminded. "And some of that is pretty mountainous."

Kublicki was undeterred. "Those satellites can read a license plate from a thousand miles up."

Moon was too upset about the situation to point out that being able to see details of a specific target had no relation to searching an area the size of New England. "Do you have anything else for me?"

Realizing he was being dismissed, Kublicki got to his feet. "No, sir. It's pretty much a wait-and-see kind of thing now."

"Okay, thanks. Could you ask my secretary to get me some aspirin?"

"Sure thing." The agent lumbered out of the office.

Charles Moon pressed his thumbs against his temples. Since hearing about the plane's disappearance, he had managed to keep his emotions in check, but exhaustion was cracking his professional façade. He knew without a doubt that if Fiona Katamora was dead, the Tripoli Accords didn't stand a chance in hell. He had lied to Ali

Ghami during their meeting. He and the President had discussed who would represent the United States. The President had told him that he would send the VP because an Undersecretary simply didn't carry enough clout. The problem was, the Vice President was a young, good-looking congressman who'd been put on the ticket to balance it out. He had no diplomatic experience and, everyone agreed, no brain either.

The VP had once met with Kurdish representatives at a White House function and wouldn't stop joking about bean curds. At a state dinner for the Chinese President, he'd held out his plate to the man and asked, "What do you call china in China?" Then there was the video clip, an Internet favorite for months, of him staring at an actress's cleavage and actually licking his lips.

Not one for praying, Charles Moon had the sudden urge to get on his knees and beg God for Fiona's life. And he wanted to pray for the untold hundreds and thousands who would keep dying in the seemingly unending cycle of violence if she was gone.

"Your aspirin, Mr. Ambassador," his secretary said.

He looked up at her. "Leave the bottle, Karen. I'm going to need it."

TEN

A S SOON AS THE POLISHED-BRASS ELEVATOR DOORS OPENED on the *Oregon*'s lowest deck, Juan Cabrillo felt the pulsing beat against his chest. It wasn't the ship's revolutionary engines producing the throbbing presence in the carpeted corridor but rather what had to be the most expensive stereo system afloat. To him, the music blaring from the only cabin in this section of the freighter sounded like a continuous explosion with a voice-over track that seemed to mimic a dozen cats fighting in a burlap bag. The wailing rose and fell in no relation to the beat, and every few seconds feedback from the musicians' amplifiers would shriek.

Mark Murphy's taste in music, if this could be called music, was the reason there were no other cabins in this part of the *Oregon*.

Cabrillo paused at the open door. Members of the Corporation had been given generous stipends to decorate their cabins any way they saw fit. His own was done in various types of exotic woods and resembled an English manor house more than a nautical suite. Franklin Lincoln, who had had nothing growing up on the streets of Detroit, and who had spent twenty years in the Navy sleeping wherever they told him to, furnished his cabin with a cot, a footlocker, and a pressed-metal wardrobe. The rest of his money went into a customized Harley. Max's cabin was a mishmash of unmatched furniture that looked like it had come from Goodwill.

And then there was Mark and his partner in crime, Eric Stone. Eric's room was a geek's fantasy, with every conceivable video-game console and controller. The walls were adorned with pinup girls and gaming posters. The floor was a static-dampening rubber that was crisscrossed with a couple thousand feet of cables. His bed was an unmade pile of sheets and blankets tucked into one corner.

Mark had gone for a minimalist vibe. The walls of his cabin were painted a matte gray, with a matching carpet. One wall was a video display system nearly eighteen feet across and composed of dozens of individual flat screens. There were two overstuffed leather chairs, a queen-sized bed, and a stark chest of drawers. The room's dominant feature was the speakers. The four of them stood seven feet tall and resembled Frank Gehry's Guggenheim Museum in Bilbao, Spain. Murph claimed that sharp angles in a speaker system affected the sound. Considering the garbage he listened to, Juan wasn't sure how his young weapons specialist could tell.

Murph and Stone were standing in front of the video display, looking at satellite imagery provided by Langston Overholt. With the *Oregon* driving hard for Libya, Cabrillo had finalized a contract with Lang to act as a covert search-and-rescue group and had gotten his people thinking about what they would find once they reached their destination. He had also asked for the raw satellite imagery that he was certain the National Reconnaissance Office had obtained within a few hours of Secretary Katamora's disappearance.

Mark and Eric had altered some basic pattern-recognition software to help them search the imagery for a downed aircraft. The NRO had a dedicated staff of dozens doing the same thing, with hardware and software more sophisticated than what was at his people's disposal, but Juan was confident they would find the downed 737 first.

Juan flipped the light switch to get their attention.

Murph pointed a remote at the stereo rack and muted the system.

"Thank you," Juan said. "Just so I don't buy the CD by mistake, who was that?"

"The Puking Muses," Mark replied as though Cabrillo should have known.

"Yeah, no way I'd make that mistake."

Mark was wearing ripped jeans, and a shirt that said PEDRO FOR PRESIDENT. His hair was a tangled dark mane, and to Juan's surprise he had shaved off the scraggly whiskers he called a beard. Eric was in his customary button-down shirt and chinos.

Cabrillo touched his chin and said, "About time you got rid of the dead bird on your face."

"This girl I'm chatting up on the net said I'd look better without it." Mark's cockiness had returned following the Chairman's rebuke over his mistake in Somalia. Sam Pryor, the wounded engineer, said he harbored no ill feelings but was going to make Murph his personal valet once he got out of Medical.

"Smart woman. Marry her. So what have you got so far? Wait. Before you answer, what is that?"

He pointed to the map on the screen where the Sahara desert met the Mediterranean, about fifty miles west of the recognizable urban sprawl of Tripoli and its suburbs. Where the coastline usually ran in a fairly even stroke, there was an area where the sea pushed inland in a perfectly shaped rectangle. It was obviously a man-made feature, and, from the scale on the monitors, enormous.

"A new kind of tidal power station," Eric said. "Just came online a month ago."

"I didn't think the Med has high enough tides," Juan mused.

"It doesn't, but this power station doesn't rely on the ebb and flow of the tides. The place they built the plant had been a narrow-mouthed bay that was much deeper than normal for the region. They built a seawall across its mouth and pumped it dry. They then expanded the dried-out bay so it was wider and deeper than it was originally. There is a series of sluice gates running along the seawall near its summit and sloping downward. During high tide, water pours through the gates, down pipes, and turns turbines to produce electricity."

"That doesn't make any sense. Eventually, the old bay will fill with water. I don't care how big they made it."

"You're forgetting the location." Eric had a little smirk on his face. When he'd first read about the project, he had intuitively grasped the facility's secret. When Juan stared back blankly, he added, "The desert."

The Chairman suddenly understood. "Evaporation. Brilliant."

"The reservoir had to be wide and broad but not necessarily deep. They calculated typical evaporation rates to get the right size for the amount of electricity they wanted to produce. By the time the sun goes down in the evening, the artificial lake is virtually empty. Then the tide rises, water pours in through the powerhouse, and the cycle is repeated."

"What about the . . ."

"Excess salt? It's trucked away at night, and sold to European municipalities as a deicing agent for roads. Completely renewable, clean energy, with the bonus of a few million dollars a year in road salt."

"There is a potential problem," Mark said, "Over time, the excess evaporation could change weather patterns downwind from the site."

"The report I read said it would be negligible," Eric said, defending the project from Mark's natural paranoia.

"That report was written by the Italian company that developed the plant in the first place. Of course, they're going to say it's negligible, but they don't really know."

"Not our problem," Cabrillo said before Mark could ramp up one of his conspiracy theories. "Finding the Secretary's plane is. What have you got so far?"

Murph chugged half a can of Red Bull before answering. "Okay, we've got a couple of scenarios. Number one is the plane exploded in midair, either the result of a catastrophic failure, like TWA 800 over Long Island south shore, or a missile strike, also like TWA 800, depending on who you believe. If that's the case, then we would have wreckage strewn over a hundred square miles when we factor in the plane's speed and altitude."

"It would be nearly impossible to spot any of it without knowing approximately where the event occurred," Eric said, wiping his glasses on the tail of his shirt.

"We know when their transponder and communications died," Mark pointed out. "A quick extrapolation of their course, speed, and estimated time of arrival at Tripoli International would have put the event just on Tunisia's side of the border with the wreckage landing on Libya's."

"Is that what you have there?" Juan asked, pointing to the desert imagery on the multipanel display.

Murph shook his shaggy head. "No, we already checked it out, and nada. We saw an abandoned truck and a lot of tire tracks left by what we assume are border patrols, but no plane."

"That's good news, then," Juan said. "Her aircraft didn't suffer a midair explosion."

"Good and bad," Eric replied. "Since we don't know the nature of the event, it becomes much more difficult to figure out. Did the oxygen system fail and kill the crew, so the plane just kept flying until it ran out of fuel? If that's the case, it could have struck five hundred miles or more to the east of Tripoli, possibly even in the Med. Or there could have been an engine failure. If that happened, the plane would have glided for miles before impact."

"But that wouldn't explain the radio silence," the Chairman pointed out. "The crew would have radioed an emergency."

"We know that," Mark said a little defensively. "Still, we have to investigate every possible theory to winnow—good word, eh?—to winnow down our target area. It's unlikely the radios would die the same moment as the engines, but stranger things have happened. Hey, that reminds me, have the feds talked to the ground people who serviced that plane last? You know, it could have been sabotaged."

"Lang said the FBI is conducting interviews as we speak."

"They should check out the flight crew, too. One of them could be Al-Qaeda or something."

"The crew's all Air Force personnel," Juan replied. "I doubt they are a security threat."

"The CIA said the same thing about Aldridge Ames, and I'm sure the FBI had vetted Robert Hanssen." Despite his genius intellect, or maybe because of it, Murph delighted in pointing out the mistakes of others. "There's no reason some Air Force guy couldn't be bought. He could have flown the plane to some remote Libyan base, where they're torturing the Secretary of State right at this moment." He looked to Eric, his eyes a little glassy with inspiration. "What do you bet they're waterboarding her? Good enough for the guys we have at Gitmo, right? Or they've attached electrodes to her—"

"Gentlemen, let's not get ahead of ourselves," Juan interrupted before they started coming up with more lurid torture techniques.

"Oh sure, sorry," Eric muttered, even though he had remained silent during Mark's excited outburst. "Um, well, if both engines failed, we factored speed, altitude, and estimated a fifteen-hundred-foot-per-minute descent rate. That gives us a target area of roughly eighty nautical miles."

"So that's what you have on the screen?" Cabrillo asked.

"Not exactly," Eric said.

Mark overrode his friend's next words, "Yes, we had to consider the engine failure–radio dying scenario, but we discounted it pretty quickly and came up with something better."

Juan was losing patience with his brain trust, but he kept it to himself. He knew Murph and Eric delighted at showing off their intellect, and he wouldn't rob them of their fun.

"So what's the answer?"

"The plane's tail came off."

"Or at least part of it," Eric amended.

"A structural failure in the tail could very likely damage the radio antennas, which would explain the blackout." Mark said. "It could also knock out the plane's transponder at the same time."

"Depending on the extent of the damage," Eric went on, "the aircraft could still fly for some distance. It would be highly unstable, and the pilot would have minimal control. He could only steer the plane by alternating thrust to each of its engines."

"The danger comes from the fact the 737 doesn't have fuel-dump capabilities. He would have had to fly in circles to burn off avgas or risk coming in too heavy." Juan made to ask a question, but Mark anticipated him. "They refueled in London when they stopped for a quick meeting with England's Foreign Secretary. By my calculations, they had enough to keep going for at least an hour after the plane went dark."

Cabrillo nodded. "Even throttled back, she could have cruised for a couple hundred miles."

"But they didn't," Eric said, "or they would have tried an emergency landing in Tripoli."

"Good point. So where the hell are they?"

"We combined two of our scenarios. Engine failure and the tail coming apart," Mark said proudly. "It's plausible. Highly unlikely, but it could happen. That narrowed our area to about a hundred square miles. We found one potential spot, but it turned out to be a vaguely airplane-shaped geologic formation." He pointed to the center screen. "And there, we found that."

Juan stepped forward. The screen showed a mountainous area, nearly inaccessible to anything other than a chopper or a serious four-wheel drive. Mark hit a button on the panel's control and the shot zoomed in. "There it is," the Chairman whispered.

Near the top of one of the mountains was the plane. Or what was left of it. The wreckage stretched for a half mile or more up the slope. He could see marks on the ground where it first impacted, rose up again, and then belly flopped, tearing itself apart as it decelerated. Fire had scorched the ground about halfway between the second impact and the main debris site. The fuselage, at least the two-thirds of it that had stayed together, was a charred tube surrounded by the shredded remains of the wings. One engine lay a hundred feet from the aircraft. Juan couldn't spot the second.

"Any signs there were survivors?" he asked, knowing the answer.

"Sorry, boss man," Eric said. "If there were, they haven't done anything to signal for help. Mr. Overholt said we should be getting another set of satellite images in about ten hours. We'll compare the two and see if anything at the site has changed. But look for yourself. It doesn't appear likely that anyone could have survived a crash like that, not with the fire and all."

"You're right. I know. I just don't like it. Fiona Katamora was one of the good ones. It's a damned shame for her to die like this. Especially on the eve of the Tripoli Accords." The certainty that she was dead was like a heavy stone in the pit of Cabrillo's stomach. "Listen, guys, good work finding the wreckage. Zap a quick note to my computer with the exact coordinates so I can pass them on. No sense wasting the government's imaging specialists' time searching if we've already found her. I'm sure Lang's going to want us to investigate the site before reporting it to the Libyans. By the way, where are they searching?"

"They're off by a few hundred miles," Mark said. "If you want my opinion, I think they're just going through the motions. They know we've got the satellites, so they're fumbling around until our government tells them where to look."

"Probably right," Juan agreed. "Anyway, we've got to be able to get up there and we can't use our chopper covertly, so map a route in for the Pig."

"Max doesn't like when you call it that," Eric reminded.

"He gave it the ridiculous name Powered Investigator Ground, so we'd call it the Pig. He just grumbles about the nickname because he likes to grumble." Juan tried to say this lightly, but his thoughts were on the victims of the plane crash.

If he closed his eyes, he could imagine the terror they must have all felt as the plane was about to barrel into the side of the mountain. He wondered what Fiona Katamora's last thoughts were.

An hour later, he was alone in his cabin, sitting with his feet propped up on his desk, a Cuban cigar between his index and middle fingers. He watched the smoke pool lazily along the coffered ceiling. Everything was set for their arrival in Tripoli the following night. He had gotten hold of a shadowy facilitator in Nicosia, Cyprus, who went by the name L'Enfant, the Baby, a man Juan had never met but who had contacts all over the Mediterranean. For a fee, the Baby had made all the customs arrangements for unloading the Pig. He had also gotten together the proper visas for the team Cabrillo would take with him into the mountains. Langston had been adamant that they verify that the Secretary of State was dead.

Juan didn't relish combing the wreckage, but he knew they had to be certain.

He again glanced at the hard copy of the satellite image sitting on his blotter. Something about the wreckage pattern bothered him, but he couldn't say what. He'd pulled up pictures of plane crashes from the Internet and saw no obvious discrepancies. Not that any two crashes were identical, but there was nothing glaringly out of place. Still, there was something.

With Cabrillo's fluency in Arabic, it was no surprise he had spent time in Libya during his years with the CIA. The two missions he'd been assigned hadn't been that dramatic. One had been helping a general and his family to defect. The other had been a secret meeting with a scientist who claimed he worked on Qaddafi's nuclear weapons program. It turned out the guy had virtually no useful information, so nothing came of it. Juan had liked the people he'd met and sensed that they weren't too keen on their government but were too frightened to do anything about it. Such was life in a police state.

He wondered if that had changed. Was Libya really opening up to the West or did they still see us as enemies? For all he knew, both factions coexisted within the halls of power. He made a decision anyway. He wasn't going to trust that what happened to Katamora's plane was an accident until he heard the flight voice recorder for himself. And he wasn't going to believe she was dead until he saw the DNA result from the samples Langston wanted them to gather.

He had been a success as a CIA agent because he had good instincts and knew to trust them. He'd done even better with the Corporation for the same reasons.

Something wasn't right, and he was determined to find out what.

ELEVEN

IT TURNED OUT THAT THE HARBOR PILOT ASSIGNED TO TAKE the *Oregon* into the Port of Tripoli was their contact. He was an affable man of medium height, with thick curly hair just beginning to gray. His eyebrows stretched across his forehead in an unbroken line, and one of his incisors was badly chipped. He worried at the tooth with his tongue whenever he wasn't talking, which led Juan to think it was a recent break. There was a little bruising at the corner of the man's mouth to bolster Cabrillo's assumption.

The man explained that he did what he did because he needed the extra money to take care of his extended family. His brother-in-law had recently lost his construction job in Dubai, so his family had moved into the man's house. His parents were both alive, blessings to Allah, but they ate him out of house and home. And he had two upcoming weddings to pay for. On top of that, he claimed he made regular contributions to an assortment of aunts, uncles, and cousins.

All this information had come in the time it took them to walk from the boarding ladder to Juan's topside cabin.

"You are indeed an honorable man, Mr. Assad," Juan said with a straight face. He didn't believe a word of it. He suspected that the proceeds from Assad's corruption went to maintaining a mistress, and either she or the wife had recently hit him hard enough to crack the tooth.

The pilot waved a dismissive hand, the cigarette clutched between his fingers moving like a meteorite in the dim cabin. The sun was well beyond the horizon, and the *Oregon* was far enough from the harbor that little light from the city filtered through the salt-rimed porthole. Juan had only turned on the anemic desk lamp. Although he had disguised himself a bit—a dark wig, glasses, and gauze in his cheeks to puff up his face—he didn't want Assad getting a good look at him, though he knew from experience that men like Assad didn't want to take a good look anyway.

"We do what we must to get by," Assad pontificated. He laid a well-used leather briefcase on Cabrillo's desk and popped the lid. "Our mutual friend in Cyprus said you wished to off-load a truck and needed visas and passport stamps for three men and a woman." He withdrew a handful of papers as well as a customs stamp. Juan knew the routine and gave him four passports. They had come from Kevin Nixon's Magic Shop and with the exception of the photographs bore no accurate information about the crew accompanying Cabrillo into the desert.

It took the harbor pilot a few minutes to record names, numbers, and other information before he stamped a fresh page in each of the passports and handed them back.

He then gave Juan some more papers. "Give these to the customs inspectors for your truck. And these"—he pulled out a pair of license plates and set them on the desk—"will make it much easier traveling in my country."

That saved Cabrillo the hassle of stealing a set from a vehicle in town. "Very thoughtful. Thank you."

The Libyan smiled. "All business is customer service, yes?"

"True enough," Juan agreed.

"How good are you at remembering numbers?"

"I beg your pardon?"

"Numbers. I want to give you a cell phone number, but I do not want you to write it down."

"Oh. Fine. Go ahead."

Assad rattled off a string of digits. "Give the person who answers a number where you can be reached, and I will call it within the hour." Assad chuckled. "Provided I am not with my wife, eh?"

Juan smiled dutifully at the joke. "I'm sure we won't need your services, but, again, thank you."

Assad's bonhomie suddenly faded and his eyes narrowed under his unibrow. "I don't see how three men and a woman in a truck can be any great danger to my country, but if I become suspicious about anything I hear in the news I will not hesitate to contact the authorities. I have ways that keep me out of it, understand?"

Juan wasn't angry at the warning. He'd been expecting it and had heard it from dozens of such men over the years. Some might actually have had the juice to back it up. Assad could be one of them. He had that look. And Juan knew that next on the agenda, if Assad held true to form, would be a little fishing expedition.

"The American government must be very upset about the death of their Secretary of State," Assad remarked.

How Juan loved a cliché. "I'm sure they are. But, as you saw from my passport, I am a Canadian citizen. I have no control over what happens with our neighbor to the south."

"Still, they must be anxious to locate the wreckage."

"I'm sure they are." Cabrillo was as stone-faced as a professional poker player.

"Where exactly are you from?" Assad asked suddenly.

"Saint John's."

"That is in Nova Scotia."

"Newfoundland."

"Ah, part of the Gaspe."

"It's an island."

Assad nodded. Test administered and passed. Perhaps the captain really was Canadian.

"Maybe your government is willing to help their southern friends in this matter," he probed.

Juan understood that Assad needed reassuring they were here about the plane crash and not something else. It was the only logical assumption Assad could make, given the timing of their arrival, and the Chairman saw no reason not to give the Libyan some peace of mind. "I am sure they would be more than willing to lend any assistance they could."

Assad's smile returned. "Foreign Minister Ghami was on television last night, calling for people with information about the crash to come forward immediately. It is in everyone's best interest the plane be found, yes?"

"I guess so," Juan replied. He was growing tired of Assad's questions. He opened a desk drawer. Assad leaned forward as Cabrillo pulled out a bulging envelope. "I think this takes care of our transaction."

He handed it across. Assad stuffed it into his briefcase without opening it. "Our mutual friend in Cyprus told me that you are an honorable man. I will take his word and not count the money."

It took all of Juan's self-control not to smirk. He knew full well that before Assad brought the *Oregon* into its berth, he would have counted the cash at least twice. "You said earlier that business is all about customer service. I will add, it's also about reputation."

"Too true." Both men got to their feet and shook hands. "Now, Captain, if you will kindly lead me to your bridge I will not delay you further."

"My pleasure."

*   *   *

CABRILLO HAD ALWAYS HELD the belief that organized crime had begun on the docks and quaysides of the ancient Phoenician seafarers when a couple of stevedores pilfered an amphora of wine. He imagined they had given a cup or two to the guards for looking the other way, and he also thought that someone saw them and extorted them to steal more. In that one simple act were the three things necessary for a crime racket—thieves, corrupt guards, and a boss demanding tribute. And the only thing that had changed in the thousands of years since was the scale of the theft. Ports were worlds unto themselves, and no matter how authoritarian the local rule they maintained levels of autonomy that only the corrupt could fully exploit.

He had seen it over and over in his years at sea, and had used the ingrained corruption of harbors as an entrée into the criminal underground in several cities during his tenure with the CIA. With so many goods entering and leaving, harbors were ripe for the picking. It was little wonder the Mafia was so heavily invested with the Teamsters Union back in its heyday.

Containerization of general cargo had temporarily quelled petty thievery because the goods were locked up in bonded boxes. But soon the bosses figured they might as well just steal entire containers.

Juan was standing on the wing bridge, overlooking the dock, with Max Hanley at his side. Fragrant smoke curled from Max's pipe and helped mask the smell of bunker fuel and rotting fish that permeated the port. Across from their berth, a mobile crane on crawler treads was swinging a container from a coastal freighter. There were no lights on the crane, and the overhead gantry lamps were shut off. The tractor trailer waiting to take the load didn't even have its headlights on. Only a single flashlight carried by a crewman standing near the container gave the scene any illumination. Mr. Assad had gone straight from the *Oregon* to oversee the unloading. Cabrillo could just make out his silhouette, standing with the ship's captain, on the dock. It was too dark to see the envelope exchange, but Eric had reported the act after watching with the *Oregon*'s low-light camera.

"Looks like *L'Enfant* knows his men," Max said. "Our Mr. Asssad is a busy boy."

"What was it Claude Rains said in *Casablanca*, 'I am only a poor corrupt official'?"

Cabrillo's walkie-talkie squawked. "Chairman, we have the hatch cover off. We're ready."

"Roger that, Eddie. Assad said we can use our own crane to unload the Pig, so get it fired up and ready."

"You got it."

Like the mysterious ship tied to the opposite dock, the *Oregon* was completely dark. On the other side of the harbor, tall cranes mounted on rails were off-loading a massive containership under the brutal glare of sodium-vapor lights. Beyond it stretched a field of stacked containers, and past that was a security fence and a series of warehouses and towering oil-storage tanks.

One of the *Oregon*'s only working deck cranes started swinging across the horizon, cable paying off the crane's drum as the crane's arm was positioned over the open hatch. The braided-steel cable vanished into the hold for five minutes before being drawn back up through the tackle. The boom took the weight easily.

Although he couldn't see details in the darkness, Juan recognized the shape of the Pig. The Powered Investigator Ground was Max's brainchild. From the outside, the Pig looked like a nondescript cargo truck emblazoned with the logo of a fictitious oil-exploration company, but under its rough exterior was a Mercedes Unimog chassis, the only unmodified part on the vehicle. Its turbodiesel engine had been bored, stroked, and tuned to produce nearly eight hundred horsepower, and, with a nitrous oxide boost, could push past a thousand. The heavily lugged, self-sealing tires were on an articulating suspension that could raise the vehicle up and give it almost two feet of ground clearance, six inches more than the Army's storied Humvee. The four-person cab squatting over the front tires was armored enough to take rifle fire at point-blank range. The boxy body was similarly protected.

When Eric and Mark first heard Max's plans for the Pig, they had called him Q, in honor of the armorer from the James Bond franchise. A .30 caliber machine gun was hidden beneath the front bumper. It was also fitted with guided rockets that launched from hidden racks that swung down from the truck's side, and a smoke generator could lay down a dense screen in its wake. From a seamless hatch on the roof, the Pig could fire mortar barrages, and could be mounted with another .30 cal or an automatic grenade launcher as well. The cargo area could be reconfigured to meet mission parameters—anything from a mobile surgical suite to a covert radar station to a troop carrier for ten fully kitted soldiers.

And yet, other than the larger than normal tires, not one aspect of the Pig gave away her true nature. She was the land-based version of the *Oregon* herself. If an inspector opened the rear doors, he would be confronted with the curved sides of six fifty-five-gallon drums stacked floor to ceiling. And if the inspector were really curious, the first row could be removed to reveal a second. The first ones were actually spare fuel tanks that gave the Pig an eight-hundred-mile range. The second row was a façade to shield the interior of the truck, so they played the odds that no one would ever ask to remove it.

"Well, Max old boy, I guess we get to see if this contraption of yours was worth the effort."

"Ye of little faith," Max replied dourly.

Cabrillo turned serious. "You're set on what to do?"

"As soon as you get clear of Tripoli, I'm leaving the harbor and steaming west. We'll take up a position in international waters due north of the crash site, with the chopper on ten-minute alert."

"I know you'll be at the helo's maximum range, but it's good to have a little insurance just in case. If things go as planned, you shadow us offshore when we make our escape into Tunisia."

"And if things don't go as planned?"

Juan gave him a look of mock horror. "When was the last time things didn't go as expected?"

"A couple days ago in Somalia, a few months ago in Greece, last year in the Congo, before that in—"

"Yeah, yeah yeah . . ."

A burst of static erupted from the speaker in the wheelhouse. Juan strode in, plucked the microphone off the wall, and said, "Cabrillo."

"Chairman, the Pig's on the dock and we're good to go. Latest intel puts the Libyan search-and-rescue a good three hundred miles from the crash site."

"Okay, Linda, thanks. I'll meet you at the gangway in five." He went back out onto the flying bridge.

Max tapped his pipe against the rail, unleashing a shower of sparks that tumbled down the side of the ship and winked out one by one. "See you in a couple of days."

"You got it." Rarely would they wish each other luck before a mission.

•   •   •

JUAN DROVE, WITH MARK MURPHY riding shotgun and Linda Ross and Franklin Lincoln occupying the rear bench seat. All four wore khaki jumpsuits, the ubiquitous uniform of oil workers all over North Africa and the Middle East. Linda had trimmed her hair and tucked it under a baseball cap. With her slender build, she could easily pass for a young man on his first overseas job.

It was still dark by the time the lights of Tripoli faded in the rearview mirror. Traffic on the coast road was nearly nonexistent, and after an hour they had yet to come upon any roadblocks. A police cruiser had slashed by, its dome lights flashing and its siren keening, but it passed the truck without incident and vanished into the distance.

Cabrillo was confident in their fake papers, but he preferred to remain anonymous as long as possible. He wasn't as worried about a legitimate stop by the authorities. What concerned him were corrupt cops setting up roadblocks to shake down motorists. He had cash on hand for such a situation; however, he knew things could spiral out of control quickly.

Mark had keyed in way points on the Pig's integrated navigation system to get them to the downed airliner, and it was just their luck that there was a roadblock less than a hundred feet from where they were supposed to leave the highway and begin their trek into the desert. Two police cars were parked so that they cut the two-lane road down to one. A cop wearing a reflective vest was leaning into a car headed in the opposite direction, his flashlight bathing the interior of the sedan. Juan could make out two more men in one of the cars. He suspected there was a fourth keeping himself out of view.

As he slowed, Juan asked, "Murph, can we pass through and turn farther down the road?"

The young weapons expert shook his head. "I mapped our route exactly from the satellite pictures. If we don't turn here, we come up against some pretty steep cliffs. You can't see it in the darkness, but there's a switchback trail just to our left that will get us to the top."

"So it's here or never, eh?"

"'Fraid so."

Cabrillo braked the big truck far enough from the makeshift roadblock so the car could pass him once the cops were satisfied. In a concealed pocket to the right of his seat he could feel the butt of his preferred handgun, the Fabrique Nationale (FN) Five-seveN. The military-grade SS190 rounds had unbelievable penetrating power, and, because of their small size, twenty could be loaded into a comfortable grip magazine. He left it for the moment.

At this distance, Juan could see it was a family in the car. The wife's head was covered in a scarf, so her face was a pale oval in the flashlight's glow. She held a baby over her shoulder and was bouncing it gently. He could hear its crying over the wind. A second child was standing in the backseat. Though he couldn't understand the words, he could hear the tension in the voices as the father argued with the cop.

"Is this stop legit or a case of *mordida*?" Linc asked, using the Spanish word for bite and the Mexican euphemism for bribery.

Juan was opening his mouth to reply when suddenly the cop pulled back from the open car window and yanked a pistol from his holster. The woman's startled scream echoed across the night, pitched even higher than the infant wailing in her lap. The husband in the driver's seat threw up his hands in supplication.

Car doors were flung open as the other two police officers jumped from their vehicles, both going for the automatics on their hips. One strode toward the passenger's side of the sedan while the other raced toward Cabrillo and his team, his pistol leveled at the cab.

Juan's wary apprehension turned into instant fury because he knew they were going to be too late.

Mark Murphy yanked open the glove compartment and a tray automatically slid out and opened to reveal a flat-panel display and a keyboard with a small joystick. As he fumbled to activate the forward-mounted machine gun, the cop who had been leaning into the car fired.

The hapless driver's head exploded in a red spray that coated the inside of the windshield with blood and gore. It obscured Cabrillo's view of the gunman firing twice more. The woman and her baby's cries were cut off mid-keen. A fourth shot, and Juan was certain the kid in the backseat was dead in what he now knew was a shakedown gone bad.

Instinct took over. Cabrillo jammed the transmission into gear and hit the pedal. Acceleration wasn't the Pig's strong suit, but it lurched from a standstill like a snarling animal. The cop running for them stopped and opened fire. His bullets gouged harmless craters into the safety glass or ricocheted off the truck's armored plate.

"Got it," Mark yelled.

Juan glanced over for a second. The video screen showed a camera mounted beneath the secreted machine gun that gave Mark an aiming reference. The gun had lowered itself so the barrel peeked from under the bumper.

"Do it!" Juan snapped.

Mark keyed the weapon, and a juddering vibration rattled the truck while a plume of fire erupted under the cab. Bullets tore into the road in a line aimed straight for the nearest gunman. The corrupt cop turned to run to his left but made his move too early. He gave Murph ample time to adjust his aim. The rounds took the cop in the calf, and then walked up his body, punching holes into him at a rate of four hundred rounds a minute. The kinetic force drove him to the asphalt and rolled him once so he lay faceup. His torso looked as if he'd been mauled by a lion.

The cop who had gunned down the family lunged for his car while the third retreated back to his. Mark lifted the trigger as soon as the first one was down and swiveled the barrel to take on the third killer. Rounds pummeled the car, blowing out its windshield and side windows and shredding the bodywork. Both tires deflated, and the vehicle settled closer to the road. The gunman found temporary cover behind the partially closed door but must have understood his position was untenable. He scrambled across the seat, threw open the far door, and fell to the ground on the opposite side of his cruiser. He hunkered behind the front tire and kept low as autofire raked the vehicle.

For the moment, he was neutralized, so Juan cranked the wheel over and steered for the other car. The triggerman was halfway into his seat when the Pig's powerful halogen lights swept across the car and then centered on him. He raised his pistol and fired as fast as the gun would allow. His rounds had no more effect than his partner's on the truck bearing down on him.

Cabrillo felt nothing but cold rage as he drove straight for the murderer.

"Brace yourselves," he said needlessly an instant before the Pig barreled into the cruiser.

There was a terrific crunch of metal as the door slammed into the gunman's body, cutting off one leg at the ankle, one arm at the wrist, and his head. The impact skidded the police cruiser until its tires hooked on the macadam and the car flipped on its roof.

"First car! First car!" Linda cried from the backseat.

Juan looked over to see the driver was reaching into the cruiser. No doubt going for his radio, he thought. He had no time to turn the ponderous truck to line up the .30 caliber, so he pulled the FN Five-seveN from its hiding place and tossed it back to Linda. She caught it one-handed while the other hand was cranking down her bulletproof window.

She thumbed off the safety and opened fire as soon as she had the room to stick the gun out the window. Linc reached over to keep cranking it down to give her a better field of fire.

Linda's angle was all wrong to hit the gunman, so as the window lowered she thrust her upper body out of the truck, bracing herself by gripping the big side mirror with her left hand. She then fired. She was cycling the trigger so fast the distinctive whip-crack of the Five-seveN sounded like a string of firecrackers.

Cabrillo was about to caution Linda that he suspected there was a fourth shooter manning the checkpoint when the crooked cop emerged from behind a dune near the shoulder of the road and opened up with a machine pistol. The weapon was woefully inaccurate at this range, and at five hundred rounds a minute it took only four seconds to unload its long magazine. Rounds whipped around the Pig, flying off when they struck the armor and starring the glass when they hit the windshield. One round flew through the open window over Linda's hunched backside and struck the doorframe an inch from Linc's head. The impact gouged a sliver of metal off the frame that sliced into the ex-SEAL's neck. Had the angle been just a few tenths of a degree different, the shrapnel would have sliced his jugular.

Pressing one hand to his bleeding neck, Linc had the wherewithal to grab Linda's ankles when Juan spun the wheel to put the armored side of the Pig between them and the shooter. He barely kept her from tumbling to the road.

"You're hit," she said when she saw the blood oozing through his fingers.

"I've cut myself worse shaving in the morning," Linc deadpanned. However, he didn't demur when Linda unclipped a first-aid kit stored under her side of the bench seat.

Cabrillo had spun the Pig in a tight turn to line up the underslung .30 caliber for another go. Linda's actions had bought them the few seconds they had needed. Her cover fire had pinned the gunman behind the cruiser once again, and only now was he reaching back in to work the radio.

Mark opened fire as soon as he had a shot. He wasn't aiming for the driver's compartment. The shooter was too well protected. Instead, Mark riddled the rear of the vehicle until gasoline gushed from the perforated tank. Because every seventh round was a magnesium-tipped tracer, it took only a second-long burst to ignite the growing lake. Flame blossomed from under the car in a concussive whoosh that was strong enough to lift the car's rear end off the asphalt. The Libyan started running for the desert but wasn't fast enough.

The mixture of fuel and air in the tank exploded spectacularly, flipping the car into the air, its undercarriage burning like a meteor as it cartwheeled. It crashed into the dirt a few feet from the fleeing gunman and kicked up a flaming spray of dust that engulfed the man. When it cleared, his clothes were burning, flaring like a torch. He dropped to the ground, trying to smother the flames, but he was soaked in gasoline and the fire refused to die.

Murph sent another burst from the machine gun into him. It was a mercy shot.

"Where's the last guy?" Juan shouted.

"I think he took off into the desert," Linc said. Linda had a gauze pad taped to his neck and was cleaning the blood from her hands.

Cabrillo cursed.

It was only a matter of time before another vehicle came along. But he had no choice. They couldn't afford to leave any witnesses behind. He heaved the wheel over and left the road.

The Pig's rugged suspension handled the soft sand with ease, and soon they were barreling along at forty miles per hour. The gunman's tracks were clearly visible in the beam of the halogen lamps, widely spaced divots that told him their guy was running with everything he had.

It took only another minute to spot the corrupt police officer sprinting like a startled hare. Even with the big truck bearing down on him, he made no effort to surrender. He just kept running. Juan brought the Pig up right on his heels so he would feel the engine heat burning into his back.

"What are we going to do with him?" Mark asked. There was genuine concern in his voice.

Juan didn't answer for a second. He'd seen and caused death in a hundred forms but hated killing in cold blood. He'd done it before, more times than he cared to think about, but he knew every time he did he lost a little more of his soul. He wished the Libyan would turn and fire at them, but Juan could see the man had abandoned his weapon back at the checkpoint. The smart thing would be to run him over and be done with it.

Cabrillo's ankle flexed to gun the engine and then relaxed again. There had to be another way. The gunman suddenly tried to dodge out of the way of the Pig. He lost his footing in the soft sand and went down. Juan slammed the brakes and turned the wheel sharply, skidding the truck in a desperate bid to avoid running the guy over. All four of them in the cab felt the impact.

Before the Pig had settled on its suspension, Juan had his door open and was jumping to the ground. He bent over the body. A quick glance told him everything he needed to know. He climbed back into the truck, his mouth a tight, fixed line.

Cabrillo focused his mind on the image of the man firing at the Pig, of Linda hanging out the window, of the flesh wound in Linc's neck, but nothing he knew would make him feel better about what had just happened. When they regained the road, he drove for the civilian vehicle. The one police cruiser was still burning.

Juan took back his pistol from Linda, rammed home a fresh magazine, and racked the slide. He jumped down from the cab, keeping the weapon pointed in a two-handed combat grip, swinging from one mangled police car to the next. He reached into the first one and yanked the radio microphone from its attachment point and tossed it into the desert, in case a Good Samaritan came along and wanted to call the authorities. The second would be a melted puddle of plastic, so he ignored it.

He approached the family sedan, taking a deep breath as he leaned in the window. The smell of blood was a coppery film that coated the back of his throat. The husband and wife, as well as their two children, were dead. The only solace he could find was the bullet wounds had been instantly fatal. That did nothing to lessen his anger at the senseless slaughter. He noticed a slim wallet sitting on the father's lap. Ignoring the blood splatter, he grabbed it. The driver's name was Abdul Mohammad. He had lived in Tripoli, and, according to his ID card, had been a high school teacher. Also in the wallet Juan found just a couple of dinar.

He didn't feel so bad about running down the fourth gunman.

The young family had died because they were too poor to pay a bribe.

TWELVE

S EVEN MONOTONOUS HOURS PASSED AS THE TEAM TRAVELED across the desert. Linc slept most of the time, his big body swaying to the rhythms of the Pig churning over the rough terrain. Linda had offered to drive for a while, but Cabrillo declined. He needed to keep focused and out of his head. Every time the image of the slaughtered family crept to the forefront of his mind, his knuckles would blanch as he gripped the steering wheel.

Mark and Eric Stone had done a fantastic job mapping their route through the mountains using the satellite photos, and the truck had delivered more than Max had promised. The engine barely strained going up the steepest inclines, and her brakes were more than ample to keep the Pig under control during the descents. Max Hanley had even rigged chains that could be lowered behind the rear tires like long mud flaps. The chains dragged across the ground and obliterated any sign of the vehicle's passage.

There was little fear they would be tracked from the checkpoint. However, there was a palpable sense of urgency. It wouldn't take the Libyan authorities long to figure out what had happened on the highway, and they would want to catch the people who killed the cops, corrupt or not.

Juan received regular updates from Max aboard the *Oregon*. The Navy was rotating a squadron of E-2C Hawkeyes thirty miles off the coast. The propeller-driven, early-warning aircraft were keeping an eye on Lybia's search-and-rescue efforts. These reports were shared with Cabrillo, so as the dawn flared and aircraft of the Libyan SAR teams once again took to the skies he knew if any were getting close to their location.

So far they had been in the clear. Once again the Libyans were concentrating their efforts more than a hundred miles from the crash site.

"GPS puts us two klicks from the wreckage," Mark said. "Stoney and I spotted a good place to hide the Pig near here."

Cabrillo looked around. They were in a shallow valley up in the mountains at an elevation of four thousand feet. Nothing grew on the bare, rocky slopes, and only sparse vegetation clung to the valley floor. This was a true wasteland.

"Turn left and go another five hundred yards," Murph ordered.

Juan followed his directions and they approached another rise in the elevation, but before they started climbing he spotted what his guys had seen on the satellite pictures. There was a narrow cleft in the rock, just wide enough and deep enough to hide the Pig from any observation except from directly overhead.

"Perfect," he muttered, and drove into the tight crevice. He killed the engine, noting they still had two-thirds of their fuel supply. The Pig got better cross-country mileage than Max had anticipated.

They sat for a moment, letting their hearing adjust to the lack of the growling diesel.

"Are we there yet?" Linc asked dreamily.

"Near enough, big man. Wakey, wakey."

Linc yawned, and stretched as much as he could. Linda reached behind them and toggled a hidden switch. The rear wall of the cab slid down to reveal the cargo hold. Because of the nature of this mission, they had brought a minimal amount of gear. Apart from a small arsenal of submachine guns and rocket-propelled grenade launchers, there were four knapsacks that had been prepacked with equipment aboard the *Oregon*. She reached in and started passing them back. As soon as she handed Cabrillo his, he jumped from the truck, knuckling kinks out of his spine.

Even in the sheltered fissure, the air was hot and dry and tasted of dust. He couldn't imagine how anyone could live out here, but he knew the Sahara had been inhabited for millennia. He considered it a testament to mankind's adaptability and ingenuity.

A moment later, the others joined him. Mark consulted the hand-held GPS device he carried and pointed north.

They had been mostly silent during the drive, and no one felt the need to talk now. Juan took point as they started climbing another nameless hill. A pair of wraparound sunglasses protected his eyes, but he could feel the heat rising on his neck. He plucked a handkerchief from his hip pocket and tied it loosely around his throat. It felt good to be walking after so many hours cooped up in the Pig.

Fifteen minutes later, they moved around a sharp rise in the topography and came across the first bit of wreckage. It was a mangled piece of aluminum the size of a trash-can lid—a section of a wing, perhaps. An aviation expert would have identified it as part of the hatch that covered the 737's front gear assembly.

Juan looked up the slope and saw it was littered with debris. In the distance, three-quarters of the way to the hill's summit, lay the largest section of the aircraft's fuselage. It looked to him like the aftermath of a tornado, where bits of some poor family's house lay scattered in no discernible order.

There was no denying the savagery of the impact. Apart from the fifty-foot length of charred fuselage, most of the chunks of metal and plastic were no bigger than the first they had come across. The ground has been torn up by the crash, leaving huge scars in the earth. The explosion of aviation kerosene had scorched most of the area as if a forest fire had passed by, only here there were no trees.

During their approach, the wind had been at their back, so they couldn't smell the stench of fuel. Now it lay heavy in the air, making breathing difficult. All four tied cloth around their noses and mouths in an effort to filter the worst of it.

They fanned out as they searched the scene. Mark was taking digital photographs of some of the larger pieces, focusing in on where the metal had torn. He took several of the sheared-off bolts that had once secured a row of seats to the cabin floor. He had already looked around in vain for the tail section, the part he and Eric Stone had suspected had come apart and caused the crash. If they were right, it would be miles from here.

"Chairman," Linda called. She was off to the left near the mangled remains of one of the plane's CFM International engines.

He was at her side in a moment. She pointed silently at the ground.

Juan looked closer. Half buried in the dirt was a severely burned human hand. It was little more than a twisted claw, but judging by the size it was male. Cabrillo snapped on a pair of latex gloves and bent over the severed member. From his knapsack, he took out a plastic tube. He popped open one end and extended a swab. He took a sample of blood from the ragged tear along the wrist and resealed the evidence-collection tube. He then slipped off the wedding band from the third finger and examined the inscription inside.

He handed it to Linda. She took it and read the inscription aloud. "FXM and JCF 5/15/88." She gave him a steady gaze. "Francis Xavier Maguire and Jennifer Catherine Foster. Married May fifteenth, 1988. I studied the crew and passenger manifest. He was on Katamora's Secret Service detail."

Any hope Juan had harbored that Secretary Katamora was still alive evaporated. It wasn't that he had seen anything suspicious in the satellite photographs. It was his own desire to see something that had tricked him into believing. As final confirmation, Linc approached, his expression dark.

"I found a partial identification tag on the port engine. The serial number checks out. This was their plane." He laid a meaty hand on Cabrillo's shoulder. "Sorry."

Juan felt as though he'd been kicked in the gut. He was well aware of the global implications of her death. He also knew that until a team of experts arrived they would never know the cause of the crash. The evidence was so badly damaged that he considered calling off their search. Their very presence here could contaminate the site for the group from the NTSB. But he had a contract to fulfill with Langston Overholt, and Cabrillo wasn't one to leave a job half finished no matter how futile.

"Okay," he finally said. "We'll keep getting samples. But be very careful."

He looked down at his feet. All of them wore shoes with no tread on the soles. They were leaving no footprints. He replaced the wedding band on the amputated hand and made sure it was in the exact position in which they'd found it.

Mark had already gone ahead to the large section of fuselage, so the three of them followed suit. The length of cabin ran from just aft of the cockpit and included half of the area where the wings attached to the aircraft. On the port side, where there would normally be a row of windows, the fuselage was torn open, so the aluminum bent inward like a long, obscene, lipless mouth. Severed wires and hydraulic lines dangled from the aircraft, and fluid had leaked from some of them to stain the rocky soil.

Beyond it, farther up the hill, was the shattered remains of the cockpit. The nose of the aircraft was punched in for a good eight feet, so the metal skin resembled the accordion joint of a tandem bus.

Juan climbed up into the fuselage. What once had been an opulent cabin befitting a cabinet secretary was now nothing but ruin. Puddles of melted plastic pooled all along the floor. Seats were identifiable only because of their metal frames.

He did a quick count and totaled up eleven corpses. Like the Secret Service agent's hand, they were burned beyond recognition. They were just genderless piles of charred flesh. No clothing remained, and because of the violence of the crash they lay scattered haphazardly. The stench of cooked meat and putrefaction was strong enough to overpower the smell of aviation fuel. The drone of flies rose and fell as they scattered and resettled when Juan moved from body to body.

The sudden jet of nausea-induced saliva forced him to swallow hard.

Mark Murphy was on his hands and knees peering under one of the burned-up club chairs with a miniature flashlight clamped between his teeth. Despite the grisly surroundings—or maybe because of them—he was humming to himself.

"Mr. Murphy," Juan said, "if you don't mind . . ."

The Chairman's voice startled Mark up from where he was working. He pulled the flashlight from his mouth. "This has got to be the best con job I have ever seen."

"Beg pardon?"

"The crash site is bogus, Juan. Someone's been here before us and tampered with the evidence."

"Are you sure? It looks about how I'd expect."

"Oh, the crash is legit all right. This is Fiona Katamora's plane, but someone has been fooling around with it."

Juan settled down on his haunches so he was eye level with Murphy. "Convince me."

Instead of addressing the Chairman, Mark called over to Linc. "You notice it yet?"

"What are you talking about?" Linc replied. "I notice a seriously messed-up airplane and some bodies that I'll be seeing in my nightmares for the rest of my life."

Mark said, "Take that rag off your face and sniff."

"No way, man."

"Do it."

"You are one squirrelly dude," Linc said, but lowered his bandanna and took a tentative breath. Detecting something, he breathed in deeper. A spark of recognition widened his eyes. "I'll be damned. You're right."

"What is it?" Juan asked.

"You wouldn't recognize it because I doubt very much you ever came across it during your CIA days, and neither would Linda because the Navy doesn't use it."

"Use what?"

"Jellied gasoline."

"Huh?"

"Like napalm," Linc said.

Mark nodded at the former SEAL. "Most likely, a good old-fashioned flamethrower. Here's the scenario as I see it. They somehow forced the plane to land somewhere inside Libyan territory and took the Secretary off. Then they flew it here and intentionally crashed it into this mountain, using either a retrofitted remote-controlled system or, more likely, a suicide pilot.

"When they came up here to make sure everything's okay and remove any trace of said pilot, they discovered the cabin hadn't burned as much as they'd like, so they squirted it with a flamethrower. If we hadn't come along the smell would have dissipated and would have been undetectable. The anomaly would only have shown up when the guys from the NTSB analyzed their samples under a gas chromatograph and discovered traces other than aviation fuel."

"You're both sure?" Juan asked, looking from one man to the other.

Linc nodded. "It's like the perfume of your first girlfriend."

"She must have been something," Linda quipped.

"Nah, it's one of those smells you never forget."

Juan felt like he was being given a second chance. His earlier pessimism sloughed off, and he felt a charge of energy surging through his body. And then he had another thought, and his mood soured. "Wait a second. What evidence do you have that the plane landed before the crash?"

"That should be in the landing gear. Follow me."

As a group, they climbed down out of the fuselage and clambered into the dim cargo area below the passenger cabin. It reeked of burned fuel, but they didn't have to contend with the smell of what a couple days in the desert did to the bodies. Mark went unerringly to an access panel set into the floor. He popped the toggles and heaved the hatch open on its long piano hinge. Below lay the large tires and truck of the 737's portside landing strut. Everything looked remarkably well, considering.

Murph jumped down into the well and played his flashlight beam on one of the tires. He crawled all the way around it, his eyes inches from the rubber.

"Nothing," he muttered, and hunkered even lower to check the other wheel.

He popped up a minute later, holding up a small piece of rock as if it were the Hope Diamond. "Here's your proof."

"A stone?" Linda queried.

"A piece of sandstone wedged into the tread. And there's sand on the bottom of the lower hatch." When he saw the look of confusion on the faces peering down at him, he added, "This plane supposedly took off from Andrews Air Force Base, flew to London, and then crashed, right? Where in the heck could it have picked up a lump of sandstone that looks exactly like every lump of rock for a thousand miles around us?"

"It landed in the desert," Juan said. "Murph, you did it. That *is* the proof."

Juan slipped the stone into his breast pocket. "In case the NTSB guys miss it, this needs to be analyzed to be certain, but I'd call it a smoking gun."

The sound came out of nowhere, and all four ducked instinctively as a large helicopter roared directly overhead. It was so low that its rotor wash kicked up a maelstrom of dust.

It had come in from the northeast, most likely a Libyan military base outside of Tripoli, and had to have flown nap-of-the-earth to avoid detection by the Navy's AWACS planes. That was why no one had called in a warning. As it began to slow into a landing hover, they could see it was a big Russian-built Mi-8 cargo chopper, capable of carrying nearly five tons. Its turbines changed pitch as it neared the top of the hill about five hundred yards from the truncated fuselage.

"You want further proof they know about this crash site?" Mark asked, and pointed at the khaki-painted helo. "That sucker knew right where he was headed."

"Come on." Juan started toward the rear of the cargo hold. "Let's find cover before the dust settles around their chopper."

They crawled through the fuselage and jumped to the ground on the far side. There was little natural cover near the remnants of the aircraft, so they ran down the slope until they came across a narrow dry wash that had served to drain rainwater off the mountain aeons ago. When everyone was settled, Juan buried them under a thin layer of sand and heaped as much onto himself as possible. Their view wasn't the best, but they were far enough away he doubted anyone from the chopper would wander by.

"What do you think's going on?" Mark asked in a whisper.

"I haven't the foggiest," Juan replied. "Linda? Linc?"

"No clue," Linc rumbled.

"Maybe someone realized their little stage setting isn't as good as they thought," Linda said, "and they've come back to tweak it."

Up at the summit, the turbines spooled into silence and the big rotor began to slow. In moments it was beating the air no harder than a ceiling fan. The large clamshell doors under the tail boom split open and men began to emerge. They wore matching desert-camouflage uniforms, and their heads were covered in red-and-white kaffiyehs, the wraparound scarves favored by Islamic militants throughout the Middle East.

"Regular army or guerillas?" Linc asked.

Juan watched for nearly a minute before answering. "Judging by how they're milling around, I'd say irregulars. Real soldiers would have been ordered into a parade formation by now. Just don't ask me what they're doing in a chopper with Libyan military markings."

To add more confusion to the situation, two men backed out of the helicopter, drawing on the reins of a camel. The dromedary fought them on shaky legs, growling at the men and spitting. Then it vomited onto one of its handlers, a copious display of what it thought of the flight. Laughter drifted down to the Corporation team.

"What the hell are they doing with that thing?" Mark asked. "It looks half dead."

Juan was no judge of camels, though he'd ridden them a few times, and while he preferred horses he hadn't found the experiences too bad. He did have to agree. Even at this distance, the animal didn't look healthy. Its coat was uneven and dull, and its hump was half of what it should be.

He had a suspicion about what was taking place but held his tongue and watched the events unfold.

After a few more minutes, the twenty or so men descended on the debris field. The two with the camel led it aimlessly over the area, tracking back and forth, laying fresh tracks over old so it would appear there had been more than one animal. It wasn't until Cabrillo realized that some of the men wore leather sandals that he was certain what was going on.

"Linda's right. They don't think the crash site will stand up under a thorough forensic review. They're contaminating it by pretending to be a group of nomads who wandered by."

They watched for nearly an hour as the men systematically trashed everything they could lay their hands on. They beat on the debris with sledgehammers, yanked out hundreds of yards of charred wiring, and moved chunks of the aircraft so nothing lay in proper relation to the rest. They got at the plane's big tires by prying open the landing gear doors and shot them flat with pistols. They also hauled parts of the plane up to the helicopter. When the helicopter was full, it flew off with a couple of the men and then returned twenty minutes later. Juan assumed they had dumped the detritus farther into the desert.

What had been a confusing jumble of aluminum, plastic, and

steel but would have been recognizable to crash experts was now completely ruined. They went so far as to dismember and then bury the bodies in several unmarked graves, and make a couple of cooking fires as though nomads had camped here for a few days. When they were finished with the camel, one of the men shot it between the eyes.

Finally, it looked as though they were about finished up. Several men scattered in different directions, presumably to find some privacy to relieve themselves before their return flight back to their base.

Juan turned to his team. "Here's what I want you to do. Get back to the Pig and make for the Tunisian border, but don't head for the coast right away. Wait for me to make contact through Max on the *Oregon*. Tell him what we've discovered and make sure he tracks me."

All Corporation operatives had tracking chips surgically implanted in their legs. The chip used the body's own energy as a power source, though it required an occasional transdermal recharge. Utilizing GPS technology, the chips could be localized to within a couple dozen yards.

"What are you doing?" Linda asked.

"I'm going with them."

"We don't even know who they are."

"Exactly why I'm going."

One of the masked men was coming to within a hundred yards of where they crouched. He was roughly the same height and build as Cabrillo, which had given him the idea. Juan's normally blond hair had been dyed dark, and he wore brown contacts. With his fluency in Arabic and the kaffiyeh covering his features, he might just pull off the switch.

He tossed the Pig's keys to Linc and had started to slide back from their concealed position when Linda grabbed his arm. "What do we do with the guy?"

"Leave him. I have a feeling the Libyan government is going to announce they've located the crash site within the next twenty-four hours. Pretty soon, this place will be crawling with people. Let him explain what the hell he's doing here."

With that, Cabrillo slipped away. Crawling on his elbows, he covered the distance to the unsuspecting man in under a minute. It helped that the distant helicopter's turbines were beginning to turn over with a whine keen enough to set his teeth on edge.

Screened from the others behind a hillock, Juan waited for the man to finish his business before rushing the last few yards. The man's back was turned, and just as he started to stand upright and reach to pull up his trousers Cabrillo struck him in the back of the head with a fist-sized stone. He'd recalled the Somali he'd struck in a similar fashion less than a week earlier and put enough behind the blow to collapse the Libyan in the dust.

Juan nodded to himself when he felt a pulse at the man's throat and started stripping off his clothes. Fortunately, the man was one of the few wearing boots. They would hide the shining titanium struts of his artificial leg. Removing the kaffiyeh revealed an average-looking guy in his late twenties or early thirties. There was nothing about his features to make Juan think he wasn't Libyan, though he couldn't be positive. There was no wallet in his uniform pockets or any other means of identification. The clothes didn't even have labels.

Cabrillo dragged the unconscious man farther from the crash site, and made certain his own satellite phone was secure behind his back. Without it, he never would have considered what he was doing. Then he waited, though not for long. Someone began shouting, bellowing over the roar of the chopper's engines.

"Mohammad! Mohammad! Come on!"

Now Juan knew the name of the man he was to impersonate. He tucked his scarf a little tighter around his face and emerged from behind the hill. The soldier they earlier identified as the leader of the twenty-man team stood fifty feet from the chopper. He waved Juan in. Cabrillo acknowledged him and started jogging.

"Another minute and we would have left you out here with the scorpions," Juan was told when they came abreast.

"Sorry, sir," Cabrillo said. "Something I ate earlier."

"Not to worry." The team leader slapped him on the shoulder, and together they climbed up into the chopper. Inside its rear cargo compartment, fold-down seats lined both walls. Juan slouched into one a little ways off from the others, making sure his pant cuff covered his metal ankle. He was pleased to note that not everyone had lowered their kaffiyehs, so he laid his head against the warm aluminum hull and closed his eyes.

He had no idea if he was in the middle of a regular Army platoon or surrounded by fanatical terrorists. In the end, if they discovered him, he decided it probably wouldn't matter. Dead was dead.

A moment later, they were airborne.

THIRTEEN

THE MUSIC CAME IN EVER-RISING WAVES AS IT NEARED ITS crescendo. The orchestra had never played better, never had more passion. The conductor's face glistened with sweat, and his baton whirled and flared. The audience beyond the bright spotlights was held rapt by the performance, knowing they were experiencing something magical. The rhythmic pounding from the percussion section sounded like an artillery barrage, but even that couldn't drown out the swelling notes from the violins and woodwinds.

Then came an off-key sound.

The musicians staggered in their play but somehow managed to find their place again.

The dull thud came again followed by a sharp click, and the music stopped entirely.

Fiona Katamora returned from the performance she had been playing in her head, her right hand poised with an imaginary bow, her left curled for her fingers to rest on the strings.

Practicing music in her mind had been the only way to keep herself sane since her capture.

Her cell was a featureless metal box with a single door and a chamber pot that was infrequently emptied. A low-wattage bulb protected by a wire cage gave the only illumination. They had taken her watch, so there was no way for her to know how long she'd been their prisoner. She guessed four days.

Moments before their aircraft made its emergency landing in the open desert, their pilot had come over the intercom to explain that they had spotted an old airfield. He managed to eke a few more miles out of their descent and set the aircraft down. The landing on the dirt strip was rough, but he had gotten them down in one piece. The cheer that went up when the wheels finally stopped rolling had been deafening. Everyone was up at once, hugging, laughing, and wiping at their joyous tears.

When the pilot and copilot stepped from the cockpit, their backs were slapped black-and-blue, and their hands shaken until they were probably ready to fall off. Frank Maguire had opened the main door, and a warm desert breeze had blown the stink of fear from the cabin.

And then his head had exploded, spraying blood and tissue onto the stewardess standing behind him.

A swarm of men emerged from along the length of the runway, where they had been hiding in foxholes covered with tarps and sand. They wore khaki uniforms, their heads swaddled in scarves. Several had ladders, and before anyone could think to reseal the cabin one of the ladders was set against the bottom sill. The pilot rushed to push it back, like a knight defending a castle wall. He was hit in the shoulder by the same sniper that killed Maguire. He went down clutching at the wound. An instant later, three men brandishing AK-47s had reached the cabin.

Fiona's assistant, Grace Walsh, screamed so shrilly that Fiona later recalled being annoyed with her at the same time she feared for her life.

It all happened so fast. They were herded back away from the open door to allow more men to enter the plane. The terrorists kept repeating in Arabic, "Down. Everybody get down."

Fiona somehow had managed to find her voice. "We will do whatever you say. There is no need for violence." And she had gotten down on her knees.

Seeing her take the lead, the crew and staff sank to the cabin floor.

One of the men yanked Fiona to her feet and pushed her toward the exit at the same time that another man was climbing the ladder. Unlike the others, he wore dark slacks and a white short-sleeved oxford shirt.

Fiona knew the moment she saw him she would never forget his face. It was angelic, with smooth coffee-colored skin and long curling lashes behind wire-framed glasses. He was no more than twenty years old, slender, and almost bookish. She had no idea how he related to the gun-wielding savages shouting at her people. Then she noted he had something in his hands. A set of Arab worry beads and a copy of the Koran.

He smiled shyly as he passed her and was led into the cockpit.

She looked back to see her people being handcuffed to their seats, understanding telescoping in on her so the horror hit like a physical blow.

"Please don't do this," she begged the man grasping her arm.

He shoved her even harder toward the ladder. Fiona went wild, clawing at his face with her fingernails and trying to ram her knee into his groin. She managed to rip off his kaffiyeh and saw he didn't have the classic Semitic features of a typical Libyan. She guessed he was Pakistani or Afghani. He balled up his fist and punched her hard enough that she momentarily lost consciousness. One second, she was scratching and kicking, and the next she was lying on the carpet, the left side of her face pulsing with pain. Men standing outside on the ladder started dragging her off the plane.

Fiona caught Grace's eye just before she was hauled away. She had somehow managed to stifle her tears. Grace, too, realized what was about to happen.

"God bless you," Grace mouthed.

"You, too," Fiona replied silently, and then she was outside, being manhandled down to the ground.

They took her about a hundred feet from the aircraft and forced her to her knees, her wrists cuffed behind her back. Through the small cockpit window she could see the young man fiddling with the controls. She also saw that there was a hole in the plane's tail section. It looked like a missile had struck the plane but hadn't exploded. Which, she assumed, was the point. They wanted her but wanted the world to think she was dead.

The last of the terrorists finished securing the people left aboard. The suicide pilot stepped from the cockpit and hugged the last gunman at the door's threshold. He paused there, waving to the others, who cheered him riotously. When the gunman was on the ground and the ladder hauled away, the pilot closed the hatch and retook his place in the cockpit.

Tears were running down Fiona's cheeks. She could see faces pressed to the aircraft's windows. Those were her people—men and women she had worked with for years. For them, she would show no weakness, and she willed herself to stop crying.

The working engine fired up, its howl building until it hurt her ears. There had been vehicles hidden along the dirt strip under camouflage tarps, one of which was a small utility tractor like those seen at airports the world over. It approached the big plane's front landing gear, and the driver attached a tow hook.

It took several minutes for him to position the plane at the foot of the compacted-earth airstrip. Another moment passed before the engine beat changed and the Boeing started accelerating down the runway.

Fiona prayed that the damage done by the missile strike was severe enough to prevent the aircraft from reaching its takeoff speed, but with so little fuel in the tanks and so few passengers on board she could see it gaining speed rapidly. It flashed by her, its exhaust like a reeking hot breath. The terrorists were firing their AKs into the air, cheering as the plane's nosewheel slowly lifted from the ground. It hung awkwardly for a long moment and then the tail struck the gravel strip, a result of the damage and the inexperience of the pilot.

The nose started to fall back to earth, and Fiona was sure her prayers had been answered. They were running out of graded runway. He wouldn't be able to take off.

And then the plane rose majestically into the air at a slight tilt. The cheering redoubled, and the amount of ammunition pumped into the sky was staggering.

Fiona bit her lip as the jetliner slowly gained altitude. She had no idea how far they were going to take it. For all she knew, they were headed for Tripoli, to crash it into the conference hall where the peace summit was to be staged. Yet none of the terrorists acted as though they were ready to leave. They all looked skyward as the aircraft shrank into the distance. She couldn't bear to watch but couldn't tear her eyes from it.

The plane started to wing over, its nose now pointed at a hill some distance away. The pilot made an effort to regain control, and for a moment the aircraft leveled. Then in one violent maneuver it flipped completely onto its back. It slammed into a hill with enough force to shake the ground. Chunks of it went spinning away. The wings separated from the fuselage before bursting into flame. One of the engines tore free of the conflagration and somersaulted up the hill, kicking up gouts of earth. Dust blown up by the impact obscured the scene for many moments before slowly dissipating. The wings burned on while the white tube of the fuselage rolled safely out of the fire's reach.

Fiona gasped while the men around her roared with approval.

Even from this distance, she knew no one had survived. Though they had been spared the horror of burning alive, no one could have lived through such a violent crash. Off to her side, just out of ear-shot, several of the terrorists began speaking in low, earnest tones. She could tell by their body language that they were disappointed that the plane hadn't burned more thoroughly, and were probably deciding how best to proceed.

Across the runway, a tarp was pulled off a large earthmoving machine. Its engine bellowed, and soon it began erasing the evidence of the landing by systematically tearing up the strip they had graded to lure Fiona's pilots into landing there. At the pace they were going, in just a few hours no trace of their presence would remain.

The meeting ended abruptly. The person Fiona assumed was the group's leader issued orders to the others. She missed most of it, but did hear, "Make sure to remove any trace that the plane was hit by a missile, and don't forget the handcuffs." He finally approached her where she knelt on the stony ground.

"Why have you done this?" she asked in Arabic.

He leaned in close. All she could see were his eyes, dark pools of insanity. "Because Allah willed it to happen." He called to one of his men. "Bring her. Suleiman Al-Jama will want to inspect his prize."

A hood was tossed over her head, and she was manhandled into the back of a truck. The next time she was allowed to see, she was here in this cell, covered in a kind of burqa she recognized as the Afghani *chadri*. Her entire body was covered except for her eyes, which were shielded by a fine mesh of lace.

The noise she had heard that ended the concert in her head was a key being rammed into the lock and the bolt thrown. The door squealed open. She had yet to see any of her captors' faces, other than the suicide pilot and the man she'd grappled with on the plane. The two men who filled the doorway were no different. They wore matching khaki uniforms without insignia and traditional headscarves.

One of them actually snarled when he saw she had managed to tear herself free of the burqa despite her cuffed hands. Averting his eyes so as not to look her in the face, he recovered it from where she'd been using it as a pillow and quickly draped it over her head and body.

"You will show respect," he said.

"I recognize your accent," Fiona replied. "You're from Cairo. The Imbaba slums, if I'm not mistaken."

He raised a hand to strike her but stopped himself. "Next time, my fist flies if you dare speak again."

The guards took her from her cell and led her outside the prison building. She was actually grateful for the lace mesh, which protected her eyes from the brutal glare of the sun pounding against the desert floor. She could tell by its angle that it was late morning, but the heat wasn't as bad as it should have been. They were higher in the mountains, she decided.

Keeping track of details like that and playing classical music in her head helped Fiona keep from dwelling on her predicament and the fate of her friends and staffers.

The terrorist camp looked like the hundreds she'd seen in surveillance pictures. There were a few wind-battered tents tucked up against a cliff that was pockmarked with countless caves. The largest, she knew, would be their last redoubt if the camp were ever attacked, and she had no doubt it was rigged with enough explosives to take down half the mountain.

A drill instructor was leading a batch of men through calisthenics on a parade ground. Judging by the crispness of their movements, they were nearing the end of their training cycle. A little ways off, in the lee of the mountain looming over the camp, another group was gathered to live fire AK-47s. The targets were too far away for Fiona to judge their accuracy, but with the amount of money funneled into terrorist groups such as Al-Jama's they could afford to waste rounds training even the worst recruit.

Beyond the shooting range she could see a half mile into a shallow valley, with an even larger massif of mountains on the far side. There was excavation work under way at the bottom of the valley, and a rail line. She could see several boxcars on a siding next to a row of dilapidated wooden buildings. On the far side of the structures hulked a monstrous diesel locomotive that dwarfed a smaller engine which was configured much like the truck used to bring her here. The burqa's mesh face screen made seeing details impossible.

Again, she had no intelligence on this place. A terrorist camp near a railhead had never been mentioned in any of the reports she read ad nauseam from the CIA, NSA, and FBI. This many years into the war on terror and they were still playing catch-up.

The guards led her into a cave a short way off from the main cavern. There were electric wires strung from the ceiling and bare lightbulbs every thirty or so feet. The air was noticeably colder and had that clammy feeling like an old basement in a long-disused building. They came to a wooden barrier built across the cave with an inset door. The guard who'd threatened to strike her knocked and waited until he was summoned.

He opened the door. They were at the very back of the cave. The room was ringed on three sides with rough stone. Thick Persian carpets were laid four or five deep on the floor, and a charcoal brazier smoldered in a corner, connected to the outside through a chimney tube that followed along next to the wires.

A man sat cross-legged in the middle of the room. He wore crisp white robes and a black-and-white kaffiyeh around his head. He was studying a book by the dim light—the Koran, she suspected. He didn't look up or acknowledge their presence.

If ever there was a posed scene, this was it, Fiona thought. Had this been her office, she would have been at her desk, bent over an important-looking document with a pen in hand. She'd kept people waiting for up to thirty seconds, but this man didn't look up for a full minute. His tactic of dominance was wasted on her.

"Do you know who I am?" he asked, closing the Koran with reverence.

"Ali Baba?" she said to goad him.

"Are you to be my Scheherazade?"

"Over my dead body."

"That isn't my particular predilection, but I'm sure it can be arranged."

Fiona had no desire to let him pretend to be anything other than the monster he was. "No one knows your real name, but you go by Suleiman Al-Jama. Your stated goals are the destruction of Israel and the United States and the formation of an Islamic State stretching from Afghanistan to Morocco, with you as . . . Sultan?"

"I'm not sure what title I'll take," Al-Jama said. "Sultan works, but it has decadent connotations, don't you think? Harems, palace intrigues, and all that."

He rose to his feet in a quick fluid motion and got tea from a brass urn placed near the brazier. His motions were graceful but predatory in their swiftness. He poured himself a glass but didn't offer any to Fiona.

Now that he was standing, she could see he was nearly six feet tall, with broad shoulders and, judging by the thickness of his bare wrists, strongly built. She couldn't see his features, and in the wavering light and through the burqa's lace she could discern little of his eyes, other than the impression that they were deep-set and dark.

"Your Jesus said, 'Blessed are the peacemakers.' Did you know he is a prophet in Islam? Not the last one, of course. That is Muhammad, peace be upon Him. But your 'Savior' is recognized as a great teacher."

"We both worship the God of Isaac and Abraham," Fiona said.

"But you do not believe in His final pronouncements to His last chosen Prophet, the holy words written through Muhammad and laid into the Koran."

"My faith begins and ends with a death and resurrection."

Al-Jama said nothing, but she could tell he had a stinging retort. He finally uttered, "Back to the quote. Do you think you are blessed?"

"If I can bring about the end of violence, I think the work itself is what is blessed, not those who participate."

He nodded. "Well said. But why? Why do you desire peace?"

"How can you ask that?" Despite her earlier reservations, she felt herself drawn into the conversation. She had expected a tirade on the evils of the West, not an intellectual Q-and-A session. It was obvious the self-styled Suleiman Al-Jama was well educated, so she was curious how he would justify his brand of mass murder. She'd listened to tapes of Bin Laden's ramblings, read transcripts of detainees at Guantánamo, and watched dozens of martyrdom videos. She wanted to know how he differed, although she already knew that the difference, if any, had no meaning at all.

Al-Jama said, "Peace equals stagnation, my esteemed Secretary. When man is at peace, his soul atrophies and his creative spirit is snuffed. It is only through conflict that we are truly the beings that Allah intended. War brings out bravery and sacrifice. What does peace bring us? Nothing."

"Peace brings us prosperity and happiness."

"Those are things of the flesh, not of the spirit. Your peace is about owning a better television set and fancier car."

"While your war brings suffering and despair," Fiona countered.

"Then you *do* understand. For these are things of the spirit, not the body. These are the things we are meant to feel. Not the comfort of a grand home but the experience of shared hardship. This is what brings us closer to Allah. Not your democracy, not your rock music, not your pornographic movies. They distract us from our true reason for existence. We serve no other purpose on earth than to subjugate ourselves to Allah's will."

"Who knows what His will is?" she asked. "Who decided you know His intentions more than anyone else? The Koran forbids suicide and yet you sent a young man to intentionally crash a planeload of people into a mountainside."

"He died a martyr."

"No," she said sharply. "You convinced some poor boy that he was dying a martyr and he would have his seventy-seven virgins in heaven, but don't tell me for one instant you believe it. You are nothing more than a cheap thug trying to wrest power from others and exploiting the blind faith of a few to obtain your goals."

Suleiman Al-Jama clapped his hands together and gave a delighted laugh. He switched to English. "Bravo, Secretary Katamora. Bravo."

Though he couldn't see it because of the burqa, a surprised look crossed Fiona's face. The sudden shift in language and the conversation's intensity momentarily confused her.

"You seem to recognize that this has always been about power on the world stage. Centuries ago, England gained it using her superior Navy. The United States has it now because of her wealth and nuclear arsenal. What do the nations of the Middle East have but the willingness of some of their citizens to blow themselves up? A crude weapon, yes. But let me ask how much your country has spent on Homeland Security since a handful of men with hardware-store knives took down two of your largest buildings? A hundred billion? Five hundred billion?"

The number was closer to a trillion, but Fiona said nothing. This wasn't going as she had expected at all. She had thought Al-Jama would spout a bunch of corrupted passages from the Koran to explain why he'd done what he had, not expose himself as a man bent on dominance.

"Before the attacks on the World Trade Center, one in five hundred thousand Muslims was willing to martyr himself. Since then, the number has doubled. That's ten thousand men and women ready to blow themselves up in the jihad against the West. Do you really think you can stop ten thousand attacks once they are unleashed? People like that boy who flew the plane and Bin Laden in his cave in Pakistan may believe in the cause of jihad, Madame Secretary, but they are mere pawns, tools to be exploited and discarded. We have a near-unlimited pool of willing martyrs now, and soon we will begin to use them in coordinated attacks that will see the world's boundaries redrawn in the way I have always envisioned."

He spoke not as a zealot but almost like a corporate president outlining growth projections for his company.

"You don't need to do this." Fiona found herself pleading.

"It's too late to stop." He pulled the kaffiyeh from down below his chin. Fiona had to will herself not to faint when she saw his face. "And your death will be the first strike."

FOURTEEN

No sooner had Linc gotten behind the wheel of the Pig and fired the engine than Mark Murphy opened the truck's voice-activated communications system.

"Call Max."

The ringing of a telephone sounded inside the off-road vehicle. The Pig was so well built, they could barely hear the engine as Linc guided the truck out of its hiding place and pointed its blunt snout toward the Tunisian border.

A voice no one recognized answered the call. "Max's Pizza. Is this for pickup or delivery?"

"Be something if they would deliver," Linc said. "I could go for a slice."

"Sorry. Wrong number." Mark cut the connection and tried again. "Call Max Hanley."

This time Max's voice muttered hello when the phone was answered.

"Max, it's Mark Murphy. I'm in the Pig with Linda and Linc."

"Glad you finally called," Max said. "The stuff's hit the fan since you went dark."

"I can imagine. Are you in the op center?"

"Yeah."

"Have someone pull up the screen for the bio tracking chips."

"Just a second." There was a moment's pause. While they waited, Mark used the Pig's computer to jack into the *Oregon*'s closed-circuit television system so the image of the futuristic control room popped up on his screen. Max was standing next to the communications station, watching over the duty officer's shoulder.

"That's interesting," Hanley muttered. "I have the three of you heading west at forty miles per hour, presumably in the Powered Investigator Ground, while the Chairman is going northeast at a hundred miles an hour. What happened, you guys get into an argument?"

"Funny. Make sure you stay on him. We're on our way to the Tunisian border. Juan's with the people we're certain brought down the Secretary's plane. We don't believe she's dead."

"Did you say the plane was brought down?"

"I did, and I don't think Fiona Katamora was on it when it crashed."

"How the hell did they pull that off? Tell me in a second. You'd better hightail it out of there. Twenty minutes ago, the Libyans announced that they've located the wreckage, and their government has given permission for a team from our NTSB to examine it. They had been prestaged in Cairo and will be in Tripoli by noon, but I'm sure the Libyans will be swarming that area sooner."

"They're not going to find anything," Mark told him. "A team of men came in on a chopper to demolish the site and ruin any chance of a reconstruction. They moved wreckage around, took some away, and smashed up just about everything they could lay their hands on. They even brought a lame camel to lay tracks all over the place."

"A lame camel?"

"To make it look like nomads had done the damage," Mark explained.

"Someone's thinking a couple of steps ahead," Max grunted.

"Is the NTSB coming to Libya general knowledge?" Linda asked.

"No. Langston told me it was cleared at the highest levels and kept under wraps."

"That means the tangos have a source in the government if they knew to come back and mess with the wreckage."

"Or they're government sponsored," Max countered. "Mark, you said you don't think Secretary Katamora was on the plane."

"There's pretty convincing evidence that the plane landed in the desert before the crash."

"You think they took her off?"

"Why else would they land it, take off again, and slam it into a mountaintop? They want the world to think she's dead."

"What do they gain by that?"

"Come on, Max," Linda said. "She's the damned Secretary of State. She's either an intelligence coup for these people or the best bargaining chip in history. Remember, she was the last President's National Security Advisor. If we think she's dead, we aren't going to be looking for her. They could extract information from now until doomsday and we'd never be the wiser."

There was a pause in the conversation as all of them digested the implications of Linda's theory. The terrorists getting their hands on Fiona Katamora was probably more damaging than if they had kidnapped the President. As a politician only in his first year of office, he was kept away from the operational minutia that went into fighting the war on terror. Because of the positions she'd held over the years, and the insatiable ability of her mind to absorb details, Fiona knew more about America's ongoing operations and the nation's plans for the future than the Chief Executive.

"We have to get her back," Max said.

There was no need to respond to such an obvious statement.

"Is there anything else going on that we need to be aware of?" Mark asked.

"Yeah. Langston forwarded information about a mission on behalf of the State Department being carried out in Tunisia very close to the Libyan border."

"State's running ops now?" Linc asked.

"It was cleared through Langley, and they sent a minder along with the team. It was given medium priority because there wasn't much of a chance for success."

"What are they doing in Tunisia?"

Max explained about the letter that first came to light through St. Julian Perlmutter and how it related to the historic pirate Suleiman Al-Jama during the Barbary Wars. He told them of the belief that the old corsair might have left writings in a hidden cave someplace along a dried-up river course that expounded on ways Islam and Christendom could coexist peacefully.

"Does sound like a long shot," Linda said when he finished. "Is this connected to the plane crash?"

"It's kind of coincidental that these two events happened around the same time and near the same place, but there's no hard evidence of a link. The Secretary wasn't even aware of the expedition. It was handled by an Undersecretary named Christie Valero. Apparently, she thought it was worth trying for. And for whatever it's worth, so do I. Pronouncements from influential clerics carry a tremendous amount of weight in the region. It was the Ayatollah Khomeini who declared that anyone who—"

"'—commits an act of suicide while engaged with the enemy shall be considered a martyr,'" Linda finished for him. "We know our history, Max. And I'm willing to bet you just learned that little factoid when you spoke with Overholt."

Hanley didn't deny it. "Anyway, three of the four people State sent to Tunisia are now considered missing. They had been given permission by the local government chaperone to stay away from the camp for seventy-two hours, but their truck's overdue."

"The supposition at Langley is that this is connected to Fiona's abduction, right?" Mark asked doubtfully.

"They're not supposing anything," Max replied with a tone that said he didn't give a whit for Mark's skepticism. "But Lang wants us to check it out anyway."

Linda said, "I don't think that's a good idea. We just saw Juan fly off with either a group of terrorists or members of Libya's Special Forces, but either way they're involved in the crash. We shouldn't be traipsing across the desert searching for lost archaeologists when he could need us at a moment's notice."

"Hold on a second," Murph interrupted, a hint of excitement in his voice. "Where's Stoney?"

"He's not on duty right now so he's probably in his cabin."

"Max, pipe this call down to him, and we'll be right back." Max made the switch. Eric Stone came up on a webcam a moment later, slurping from an energy drink. "Hey, how is it playing Lawrence of Arabia?" he said in greeting.

"Are you bogarting my Red Bull?" Murph accused.

Eric quickly pulled the can out of camera range. "Nope."

"Jerk. Listen, when we were checking the satellite pictures we spotted an abandoned truck out in the open desert not too far from our flight path estimates."

"I remember."

"Flash me a close-up and give me the GPS coordinates."

"Hold on." Eric glanced down from the webcam and started typing at his computer. Over his shoulder, an online gaming avatar that looked like a toad in medieval armor had been set by a macroprogram to grind out points by repeatedly arranging a basket of flowers.

"Looks like a real badass game you're playing, Eric," Linc remarked when he glanced over at the computer screen in front of Murph. "Let me guess, Sir Ribbet and the Bouquet of Death?"

Stone looked over his shoulder, saw that he could never explain what he was doing to a warrior like Linc, and killed that computer screen with a remote control. "Okay, I've e-mailed the GPS numbers and a zoom shot of the truck. I'm now looking at your tracking information. You're only about a hundred miles from it. Shouldn't take more than a couple of hours."

"As the crow flies, Stoney, not as the Pig crawls, but thanks. Would you also send that picture to the main screen in the op center and route this call back to Max?"

"On its way."

"Talk to you later."

"Is that their truck?" Mark asked Hanley as soon as he'd reestablished contact.

"Overholt said it had some kind of drill rig on the back, so I'd say it is. How did you know where to find a picture of it?"

"I'm a genius, Max," Murph replied without a trace of irony. "You know that."

"Okay, genius, you just bought yourself a detour. I want you guys to check out the truck, and then I need you to interview the fourth member of the search team, a Dr. Emile Bumford. He's still at the Roman archaeological site that the State Department team was using as cover. He's already spoken with the Undersecretary at State, who set this up. From what Lang told me Bumford's useless, but a face-to-face might get us something."

"What about the Chairman?" Linda persisted. "I feel like we're abandoning him."

"Sweetie," Max soothed, "this is Juan Cabrillo we're talking about. With his luck that chopper's headed to some five-star seaside resort, and ten minutes after they land he'll have a drink in one hand and a woman in the other."

•   •   •

IT TOOK THE BETTER part of eight hard hours to cross the desert to where Eric and Mark had spotted the abandoned drill truck on the satellite pictures. The landscape was a fractured plane of endless hillocks and riverbeds that rattled their organs until they felt their bodies were nothing more than liquid held in check by their skin.

Mark and Linda had switched places so she rode shotgun next to Linc. He drove in a loose-armed, relaxed pose, as if the rough terrain were no more bothersome than an occasional pothole on an interstate highway. As the sun hovered over the distant horizon, they were approaching the GPS coordinates Eric Stone had provided. The Pig was still performing as advertised, and their remaining fuel was just enough to get them across the border into Tunisia. There they would need to find diesel. Linc was hoping they could buy a supply at the archaeological site, but most likely it would need to be choppered in from the *Oregon*. He would have to call Max about making the arrangements so they could sling a bladder of diesel under the Corporation's new McDonnell Douglas MD-520N. With its hook-lifting capacity of a ton, George Adams, their pilot, could more than handle the fuel needed to fill the Pig's many tanks.

Something sticking up from the otherwise barren desert caught Linc's attention. It was less than a quarter mile off to their left. He wasn't sure what it was. From a distance and in the uncertain light, it appeared to be pulsating. He pointed it out to Linda and Mark. Neither knew what to make of it. They were a mile from the abandoned truck, but Linc felt it was worth a look, so he parked the Pig behind a low dune and killed the engine.

"Mark, grab me my REC7, will you?" Linc asked. Next to him, Linda drew a Glock 19, the compact version of the 17, one of the most popular combat pistols in the world.

Mark opened the door to the rear compartment and handed Linc his assault rifle. Not as proficient with small arms as he was with the *Oregon*'s state-of-the-art arsenal, Murph tucked an antique Model 1911 .45 caliber pistol into the small of his back when he unlimbered his lanky frame from the truck.

The three of them kept in a crouch and used natural cover to approach the unknown object thrust up from the ground. When they were fifty yards off, they heard an obscene crying sound, something that wasn't human but still reminded them all of an infant's scream.

"What the hell is that thing?" Mark asked with superstitious dread.

Linc was just ahead of the other two, his rifle tucked high against his shoulder, as he peered intently, trying to understand what he was seeing. The object looked like an inverted cross, but there were two dark shapes moving on either side of the cross, shuffling around in an ungainly motion.

Then one of the shapes spread a pair of wide black wings, and Linc knew immediately what he was seeing. A man had been crucified with his head pointed toward the ground, and a pair of bald-necked vultures was sitting on the crux of his underarms. The feathers around their heads were matted with gore, as they feasted upon the corpse. One had torn off a strip of flesh that now hung in its beak. It jerked its head back and forth to force the meat down its gullet.

Linc knew from an experience in central Africa when he was with the SEALs that no warning shot in the world would chase the repugnant birds from their favored carrion. He fired for effect, putting two rounds downrange, and the vultures were blown off their unholy perch. A couple of feathers drifted lazily on the slight breeze and settled a few feet away from their bodies.

"Oh, God . . . Oh, God . . . Oh, God," Mark Murphy kept repeating, but, to his credit, he stayed with Linc and Linda as they drew nearer.

The birds had inflicted unspeakable wounds to the body. They'd had days to tear and rip into the man's flesh, but there was enough recognizable to see he was Caucasian and he'd died from a single bullet to the head. Because of the blood that had soaked into the ground below the crucifix, it was impossible to tell if he'd been shot before or after he'd been strung up. Being only a mile from the drill truck, it wasn't a leap in logic to assume that this was what remained of one of the State Department people.

In Linc's mind he could concede that the terrorists might have felt that killing the man had been an operational necessity. But the desecration of his body in an intentional perversion of Christ's death had been done merely for the fun of it.

Without a word, Linc started back to the Pig to get a shovel.

The grisly task took twenty minutes in the soft soil, and when he was finished only a thin sheen of sweat greased his torso and shaved head. While he worked, Linda and Mark cast ahead for the truck only to discover it had been moved since the satellite flyby. They found clearly defined tire tracks leading off to the west. They also saw a second set of tracks from a vehicle lighter than the drill truck. Between the two sets of tracks was a single brass shell casing that still smelled of gunpowder, and a red-black stain in the earth that was being painstakingly cleared away one sand grain at a time by columns of ants.

When they told Linc what they'd seen, all agreed that the State Department team had inadvertently crossed the border into Libya, where they had been discovered by a patrol. For some reason, one of their party had been shot in the head and the others taken prisoner. The body had been driven a short distance and crucified.

"It's possible they saw Katamora's plane fly overhead," Mark suggested. "Realizing it was in trouble, they might have decided to investigate."

"And they just happened to run into a border patrol?" Linda's comment was more a dubious statement than a question.

"Not a border patrol," Linc countered, sensing where Linda was heading. "The terrorists sent out teams along the projected flight path to eliminate anyone who saw the plane."

"Judging from where the ambush took place, the State people were well south of their own base camp," Mark pointed out. "They were in the right place only it was the wrong time."

"What do you want us to do?" Linc asked Linda Ross.

As the Corporation's vice president of operations, she was the ranking member on the team. She considered calling Max and leaving the decision up to him, but Hanley hadn't seen the condition of the body, couldn't feel what she'd felt at that moment when she realized what it was. When it came to tactical matters, Linda rarely allowed her emotions to interfere with her decisions. No good commander does. However, this time, looking at her companions, she knew the right call was to go after the butchers who did this. With luck, they would take one alive. It was doubtful a foot soldier would know the overall plans these people had for the Secretary of State, but any intelligence was better than nothing.

"They've got a hell of a head start," she said, her jaw barely moving because of her anger.

"Don't matter to me," Linc said.

"If it makes it easier," Mark said, "there's a fifty-fifty chance the two other Americans were taken prisoner when the Libyans took their truck."

Linda hadn't thought of that, and it was the last piece of information to cement her decision. "Mount up."

Tracking the drill truck's tire tracks across the desert was as easy as following the dotted lines on a country road. The vehicle was heavy enough that the marks hadn't yet succumbed to the constant scouring of the wind. And when the sun sank over some distant mountains, Mark activated the Pig's FLIR system. Designed for attack helicopters, the Forward Looking Infrared system could detect ambient heat sources and would give them a warning many miles off if they approached the warm engine of the truck.

Linc strapped a pair of night vision goggles over his head. Using both passive and active near-infrared illuminators, he could drive comfortably in total darkness if necessary. However, the quarter moon rising behind them gave the third-generation system more than enough light.

No one spoke as they drove across the wasteland. There was no need. All three of them shared the same thoughts, the same concerns, and also the same desire to avenge the dead man. None of them cared about the bumps and ruts that the powerful truck bulled through. What the massive shock absorbers couldn't take, their bodies would.

"How far are we from the Tunisian border?" Linda asked after a couple of hours.

Mark checked their position on his computer. "About eight miles."

"Keep sharp. I doubt they'll cross it."

The ghostly shadows cast by the risen moon suddenly winked out as a curtain of clouds crossed in front of it. Linc's NVGs didn't have enough light to process, so he keyed the active illuminators, sending out wavelengths in the near-infrared spectrum that were undetectable to human vision but which showed clearly in his goggles.

They drove like that for another mile. Mark Murphy was well aware that the active signal from Linc's goggles could be seen by anyone else equipped with a night vision device, so he never took his eyes off the FLIR. So far, the desert ahead remained completely dark on the thermal scans.

And then a tiny blip showed itself. It was too small to be a man, he thought, and he dismissed it as some nocturnal animal when suddenly a burst of light exploded in the truck's cabin across nearly every wavelength.

The hot exhaust from an RPG showed like a streak of white lightning on Mark's screen while Linc's NVGs were nearly overwhelmed by the blast of the rocket motor. They had stumbled into a perfectly laid ambush, and had the man with the grenade launcher fired a moment sooner they would have been blown apart in the opening salvo.

FIFTEEN

THE PIG WAS AT THE CREST OF A HILL, SO THEY COMMANDED the high ground, but without cover it did them no good. Their forward momentum didn't give Linc enough time to jam the transmission into reverse, so he took the only option open to him. As the rocket came at them on its unguided, flat trajectory, the former SEAL mashed the accelerator and charged down the slope. He pressed a button on the dash to activate the hydraulic suspension, lowering the vehicle's center of gravity by pushing the wheels out well beyond the fenders.

Murph no longer had the ground clearance to engage the .30 caliber machine gun mounted under the front bumper, but Linc's move had given the truck enough stability to race across the face of the dune without tipping. Linc hit another switch to lower the curtain of chains behind the rear tires to cover their tracks. At the speeds he was hitting, the heavy lengths of chain hurled up a dense cloud of billowing dust, something their FLIR could see through but which the grenadier's NVGs could not.

The rocket-propelled grenade impacted the earth where the Pig had been seconds before, blasting a harmless fountain of dirt and debris into the air. Tracer fire began to knife out of the darkness, converging on the rampaging truck like fire hoses.

"Linda—" Linc started to say, but she cut him off.

"I'm on it."

She opened the door to the rear cargo area and launched herself through feetfirst. She went immediately for the switch that opened the top hatch, and the instant it was opened she pushed the secondary machine gun up and onto its roof mounts. The hatch covers gave her protection from the sides, so she aimed for the gunmen firing at them straight ahead. The .30 caliber roared in her hands, and spent brass arced away from the breach in a shimmering blur. She poured rounds into one particularly dense area of fire. In the darkness, she couldn't tell what was happening a hundred yards away, but the stream of tracers racing for the Pig withered away to nothing.

She swung the gun to counter Linc's erratic driving, ravaging another foxhole. There must have been a grenadier with the men firing assault rifles because the position was blown apart by an explosion that sent shattered bodies high into the sky.

Another RPG blasted out of the night, but the aim was so far off that Linc could afford to ignore it. He pointed the Pig at a long mound of sand that was giving several attackers perfect cover. He went up its face at an angle, and when he reached the top he threw the heavy truck into a four-wheel drift so that when they reached the bottom on the far side Linda had the entire row of gunmen in her sight's crosshairs. She walked her rounds up the defile, tearing apart the defensive positions in a fury of destruction.

"I've got a massive thermal image here," Mark said, staring at his computer.

"Range?"

"Five hundred yards. It's partially obscured by the topography, but there is something big out there, and it's getting hotter."

"Missiles," Linc ordered.

Even bouncing over the rough ground, Mark didn't miss a key-stroke as he worked his computer. Hydraulically operated pan-els opened along the Pig's sides just enough to reveal the blunt nose cones of four FGM-148 Javelin antitank missiles. Normally a shoulder-fired weapon, the Javelin carried a seventeen-pound war-head, and had proved capable of defeating any armored vehicle it had ever engaged.

The Javelin was an infrared-guided fire-and-forget weapon, so as soon as Mark locked his computer's targeting reticle on the unknown heat signature, the missile was ready.

"Fire in the hole," he shouted for Linda's benefit, and launched the rocket.

It came out of its tube in a gush of hot exhaust and streaked across the desert. Linc turned the wheel so Linda could engage another machine-gun nest that was peppering the Pig's flank with a steady barrage of fire. It seemed the only active enemy still willing to engage them.

The Javelin homed in on the heat source with single-minded determination, ignoring the battle raging around it and the futile attempts of a couple of men to shoot it down as it roared into a secret desert base. Fifty feet from its target, its seeker head suddenly lost the signal, though it picked up a cooler, and closer, contact. Still, it ignored the bait and maintained its original course.

What the missile didn't know was that a fuel truck had passed between it and its target, the cooler thermal image being its engine. The rocket slammed into the tank just behind the cab. The driver died in an instant as the fuel-air mixture detonated in a blossom-ing fireball that seemed to lick the heavens. A cluster of nearby tents was torn to shreds by the blast, their guy ropes turned to ribbons, and the poles reduced to split wood. Cargo netting strung up from date palms to hide the compound from satellite photography flared like tinder. Pieces of metal blown from the truck scythed down the ground crew that had been working at the base, but the shrapnel did nothing to the machine the crew had been servicing.

In the towering flames of the destroyed truck, Linc, Mark, and Linda saw two things at the same time. One was that the drill truck belonging to the State Department team had been blown onto its side by the explosion and its undercarriage was aflame. The second was what the perimeter guards had been protecting.

Nestled in a sandbag bunker was a Russian-built Mi-24 helicopter gunship, perhaps the most feared battlefield chopper in history. The heat from its twin Isotov turbines spooling up was what Mark had detected on the FLIR. The rotors were a blur as the pilot readied the flying tank killer for takeoff.

"Holy crap!" Murph cried. "If he gets that thing off the ground, we're toast."

Even as he said it, the chopper, code-named Hind, hauled itself into the sky. The pilot rotated the helo on its axis while still partially covered by the walls of sandbags. Mounted under the nose of the Hind was a four-barreled Gatling gun, and when it cleared the top of the walls it erupted.

Linda just managed to duck through her hatch when the desert around the Pig came alive with hundreds of .50 caliber rounds. Bullets pounded into the armored windshield with enough force to star the glass, and if the onslaught continued for even a few seconds more the glass would disintegrate.

Linc dropped a gear and hit the gas, throwing a rooster tail of sand in their wake. The ground just to the left of the Pig exploded as a fresh barrage chased after them. Then came the rockets, a half dozen of them, launched off pods slung under the Hind's stubby wings. It was like driving through a sandstorm. The unguided missiles tore into the hills all around them. Linc swerved as best he could, zigging and zagging between each impact, hoping to buy a few seconds more. One rocket hit the rear bumper, rocking the Pig on its suspension but doing little damage beyond mangling the hardened steel.

Linc looked over at Murph. "Ready?"

"Do it!"

Linc cranked the wheel and slammed the brakes with every ounce of his considerable strength. The Pig whipped around, sliding on the shifting sands, its wide stance keeping it from flipping. The instant the nose was pointed back toward the Hind, Mark unleashed a pair of Javelins, trusting their heat seekers to find the target because he couldn't take the time to aim properly.

The Hind's pilot lost his target in the swirling maelstrom of dust and held his fire for a moment so the wind would blow the dust away. It was from this impenetrable curtain that the two missiles emerged. The cryonic cooling system of one of them had failed to reach the proper temperature, so it couldn't acquire the target against the still-warm desert floor. It augered into the ground and exploded well shy of the chopper.

Pointed nose-on at the incoming rockets, the Hind posed a small thermal cross section because its hull shielded the exhaust from its turbines. The pilot knew this and did nothing, hoping that playing possum could cause the missile to fly past. But the Javelin locked on anyway. To its computer brain, the four glowing tubes hanging below the helicopter's chin were enticing enough to commit to attack.

The heat seeker sent minute corrections to the missile's fins, aiming it straight for the still-hot barrels of the Hind's Gatling gun. The pilot tried to pull up at the last second, so the Javelin missed the gun but impacted directly under the cockpit. The explosion tore the helicopter in half, its front section nearly disintegrating, while the hull and tail boom reared up from the force of the blast. Because the main rotor was still fully engaged, the chopper lost all stability and began to spin, smoke pouring from the blackened hole that had been the cockpit. When the chopper canted over almost ninety degrees, the blades lost lift, and the ten-ton Hind crashed to earth. Its aluminum rotors tore furrows into the ground until they blasted apart, sending shrapnel careening at near-supersonic speeds. So much grit was sucked into the Isotov turbines that they flared out and seized.

The chopper's self-sealing fuel tanks had done their job. There were no secondary explosions, and the flames around the engines' exhausts quickly starved for gas.

Mark blew out a long breath.

"Nice shooting, Tex," Linc drawled. He then called back to Linda, "You okay back there?"

"I know what James Bond's martini feels like."

"Sorry about that."

She poked her head back into the cabin. "You guys took down the Hind, so it was an observation, not a complaint. What is this place? Some sort of border station?"

"Probably," Linc replied.

"Take us over to the Hind, will you?" Mark asked. He was studying the downed chopper through the FLIR.

"That isn't such a good idea. We should clear out while the clearing's good."

"I don't think this is a border station," Murph said. "I need a closer look at the helo to be sure. Also, we have to do a sweep for any communications gear left intact. If there are survivors out here, the last thing we need is them calling in reinforcements."

Linc dropped the transmission into gear and drove the quarter mile to the wreckage. The Pig wasn't even stopped before Mark threw open his door. Like a primitive hunter approaching a dangerous prey that he wasn't sure was dead, Mark crept closer to the downed Hind. Linda was back up in the hatch, watching the smoldering ruins of the camp over her machine gun's iron sights.

"What are you looking for?" she asked without looking down from her perch.

"Not *for*," Mark corrected. "At."

"Okay, then, at."

"The air intakes aren't normal. They're oversized. Also, the stubs of the rotor blades."

"And?" Linc prompted from the Pig's cab.

Mark turned to look at him. "This chopper's modified for high-altitude operations. I bet if I checked the fuel lines for their turbines, they'll be larger than normal, too. And this"—he slapped a hard-point mount under the gunship's wing—"is the launch rail for an AA-7 Apex missile."

"So?"

"The Apex isn't part of the typical load-out for a Hind. These are ground-attack choppers. The Apex is designed for air-to-air combat, specifically for the MiG-23 Flogger."

"How can you be so sure?" Linda asked.

"Weapons design is what I did before coming to the Corporation. I lived and breathed this stuff," he replied. "You guys have put two and two together, right?"

"Air-to-air missile, high-altitude chopper"—Linc made a motion like he was balancing these two elements in his hands—"it isn't exactly a mystery worthy of Sherlock Holmes. They used this bird to shoot down the Secretary's plane."

Linda asked, "So is this place Libyan or some terrorist compound?"

"That's the million-dollar question," Mark replied, stepping back into the Pig. "Let's check it out and see if we can come up with an answer."

They drove into the confines of the desert base. The tents were little more than ash, and the fronds had burned off all the palm trees. Linc braked next to the body of one of the Hind's mechanics, placing the Pig between the corpse and the open desert. Mark jumped down and turned the body over. In the wavering light of the nearby fires, he could see a chunk of metal, probably from the tank of the fuel truck, was embedded in the man's chest. What Mark didn't find were rank insignia on the uniform or any kind of identification in the man's pockets, not even dog tags.

He checked several more corpses, never venturing far from the protection of the Pig. No one showed any rank or carried ID. He poked around the ruined tents, finding a satellite phone, which he pocketed, and a big radio transceiver, which had been destroyed by the blast, but nothing to indicate who these men were or whom they served.

"Well?" Linda asked when he clambered into the cab of the Pig and closed the door for the last time.

"This place is a complete cipher." He raked his hand though his stringy hair in a gesture of frustration. "We know the how of the crash, but we still don't know the who or the why."

"I'm not worried," Linc said as he started them away from the camp and toward the Tunisian border. "I bet the Chairman had those two questions pegged five minutes after landing in that other helo."

SIXTEEN

As SOON AS THE HELICOPTER'S CLAMSHELL DOORS OPENED and Juan's eyes adjusted to the bright light streaming in from outside, he knew he was into it. Deep.

Avoiding detection at a Libyan air base should have been relatively easy. There would be a thousand men stationed there, dozens of buildings to hide in, and the anonymity that came with the transient nature of military personnel who were shuffled from duty assignment to duty assignment.

But the Mi-8 hadn't landed at an Air Force facility. It had landed high in the mountains on a shielded plateau that still commanded views over several breathtaking valleys. Below the compacted-earth landing pad was a training camp. Exiting the rear of the helo with the others, he could see dozens of tents, a parade field, an obstacle course, and a shooting range.

Juan made sure not to jump to a conclusion. The fact that this appeared to be a terrorist camp didn't necessarily mean it wasn't government backed. He was still in Libya after all.

Off to one side of the compound was the mock-up of a three-story building constructed of metal scaffolding draped in burlap. The building it represented was large, like an office block, with a perimeter wall, a cantilevered porte cochere extending out over the circular drive, and a side wing that somehow made Juan think of a solarium, except the structure was too big for a private residence. The back of the building was an enclosed space, and while the men here hadn't landscaped it like the real place, they had erected burlap fences to represent hedges.

With the turbines winding down, Cabrillo heard generators chugging away below them and the cry of a muezzin calling the faithful to noontime prayers. Men were streaming across the camp, each carrying a prayer rug. They began assembling on the parade ground, orienting their mats to face east and the holy city of Mecca. He estimated there were at least two hundred men—a large number, to be sure, but not big enough for him to remain anonymous for long. Someone would eventually miss the real Mohammad, and a thorough search would be conducted.

As much as he needed to gather intelligence about this group, his only chance lay in ducking away early and hoping he could return for a nocturnal reconnaissance.

"Get moving," he was ordered from behind, and he shuffled off the chopper's rear ramp.

Off across the valley, Juan spied some sort of construction site or excavation. He tugged his headscarf tighter around his face and started for the footpath leading to the camp below. He stayed close to the man in front of him so no one could get a look at his eyes and made sure to walk in a slight stoop to hide the fact that he was taller than most of the others.

He didn't know if the men sent out to sabotage the downed airliner were stationed in the same barracks, but it stood to reason. He had watched them work, and while not as disciplined as professional soldiers they had a cohesiveness that came from working and training together in a tight group. Once they reached their billet, Juan knew his life would be measured in seconds.

The path wound along the edge of a steep ravine, its flank criss-crossed with countless intersecting gullies and wadis and covered with loose rock and sand. There was a shelf halfway down that sat atop a vertical cliff at least thirty feet high. Juan was judging the odds of his making it to the bottom alive as slim to nil when the team leader at the head of the little column turned around and started collecting their kaffiyehs.

The majority of the men knew this was coming and had already unwound their kaffiyehs from around their heads. Juan glanced down again at the camp to his left. No one had his head covered. It was a bonding tool, he knew. Only to outsiders would they be anonymous. Safe here at their camp and among their brothers, they showed themselves openly.

The odds no longer mattered.

He rammed the heels of his hands into the back of the man in front of him and snarled, "Watch yourself."

The man whirled, his eyes fierce. "What did you do that for?"

"You elbowed me in the stomach," Juan retorted. "I should kill you for the insult."

"What's going on back there?"

"This son of a pig pushed me," Juan shouted.

"Who is that?" the leader called. "Show yourself."

"Only when he apologizes."

"I will not. You hit me in the back first."

Juan swung at the Arab's face, a lazy roundhouse lacking a tenth of Juan's strength. The man saw it coming a mile away, ducked instinctively inside Juan's reach, and fired two quick punches into Juan's stomach. It was the excuse Juan needed. He yanked off the other man's headscarf, turning him so Juan's back was toward the rest of the men and no one could see his face.

"I don't know you!" Juan cried in mock surprise. "This man is an impostor, an infiltrator."

"Are you mad? I've been here for seven months."

"Liar," Cabrillo seethed.

The man went to push Juan. Rather than resist, Cabrillo grabbed his wrists and stepped back off the trail. His feet immediately began to slide. The gradient was gradual at first but quickly steepened. They started gaining speed, and when they reached a tipping point Juan fell backward, flipping the hapless terrorist over his head without relinquishing his grip, so the momentum tumbled him onto the man's chest like an acrobat. It was now the terrorist's body grinding against the sharp rocks, as they slid down the ravine with Juan lying on top.

They crashed into the first gully, and Cabrillo heard bones breaking against the hiss of gravel avalanching down the hill with them. The Libyan screamed in Juan's ear as their speed careened them into the gully. They went down like bobsledders, only the terrorist was the sled. All around them, more and more rocks were loosened by the pair's passage until, from above, the two must have been completely obscured by dust. Both of the man's legs were broken below the knee and flopped sickeningly, as he and Juan whooshed down the defile, swaying up and down the sides according to the vagaries of the terrain.

Cabrillo used his artificial leg as a sort of rudder to keep them in the center of the gully as best he could. Each time he extended the limb, it was like a sledgehammer blow against his stump, but without Juan bracing them they would have started to tumble uncontrollably.

More gravel and sand was building up around them, and then suddenly they were on top of the avalanche they had created. The friction of the terrorist's battered body scratching against the ground vanished without warning, and their speed seemed to double. Juan could no longer control their slide. When the gully began to twist to the left, the sheer volume of material rocketing down the hillside could no longer be contained and burst from its banks like a river in flood, bearing Juan and the Arab with it. They caught air as the ground dropped sharply away. When they came down, the terrorist was no longer screaming, and they had gained a few precious yards on the wall of gravel now in pursuit.

This new valley was wider and deeper than the first but twisted more often. Again, the avalanche caught up to them and again Juan rode the man as though he were straddling a tree trunk in a logging flume. Just ahead, he could see the debris cascading off the shelf he'd spotted from the top. He chanced a look up the slope. Behind the shifting thrust of gravel and sand, boulders tumbled in the avalanche, succumbing to the forces of gravity and the weight of dirt from above. It was like looking into the grinding mouth of an industrial wood chipper. The boulders banged and rattled against one another, pulverizing themselves as they fell.

He looked back downslope. The avalanche arced ten feet through space beyond the cliff before cascading to earth. Had it been water, Juan would have gone over the falls and had a good chance of swimming away at the bottom. But not here.

Cabrillo dug his prosthesis into the gravel, forcing it down into the avalanche until he felt solid ground beneath. Seconds before he and the Arab were carried over the precipice, he pushed off with everything he had, launching himself off the terrorist's corpse in an awkward lurch that carried him right to the edge of the avalanche.

He scrambled onto all fours and started clawing his way upward, fighting the remorseless downward plummet of the gravel under him. It was like crawling against a treadmill set on maximum. There was no way he could gain any ground. The avalanche was much too fast. He only hoped to buy himself a few precious seconds as he angled himself farther up the side of the gully, driving himself to get out of the landslide's grasp before it carried him over the cliff.

With ten feet to go, he was still mired in the fringes of avalanche. His bloodied fingers dug into it with machinelike tenacity, and his legs pistoned, kicking up dirt with each thrust. But it wasn't enough. He was too far from the slide's boundary to haul himself clear.

It wasn't in him to give up, and he made one last supreme effort. The cascade of loose debris claimed the shattered remains of his companion at the same instant his fingers felt solid ground. Cabrillo groped to find purchase, and his hands clasped something hard and round. With no choice, he grasped it in his left hand and swung to find purchase with his right.

He knew the first rule of rock climbing was never to trust vegetation. It could let go without a moment's notice. But with no other choice, he clung to the root of a gnarled tree left exposed to the sun.

Almost immediately, the root started to tear away from the earth as if he had yanked on the end of a rope that had been buried just beneath the surface. Though he had managed to drag all but his feet free of the landslide, he was relying entirely on the root, and the more its tangled subterranean connections snapped, the more he fell toward the edge of the cliff.

His legs went over the edge, and then his hips. He held on to the root with everything he had while less than a foot away a continuous torrent of sand and rock plummeted past his shoulder. His fall checked for an instant, he tried to pull himself upward, only to have more of the root break away. He slipped completely over the edge, dangling by his arms. Just before he went over, he saw that the wall of boulders and rocks was seconds away from cascading over the falls.

He forced himself to crab along the cliff face to his right, his head and shoulders pounded by the light rubble, lengthening the angle between himself and where the root was anchored on the side of the gulley. Then he raced back, running through the deluge seconds ahead of the boulders. He burst from the landslide, swinging like a pendulum. He reached out with his left hand and just managed to grasp a knuckle of rock in his fist.

His movements scraped the root against the razor-sharp edge of the cliff, like a length of string against a saw blade. Cabrillo had no time to gain a better purchase on the piece of sandstone in his hand when the root parted. His body crashed into the cliff. The tree root that had saved his life tumbled away, swallowed by the debris pouring down the mountainside.

Hanging by only one hand, he looked down in desperation. At first, the cliff appeared to be as smooth as a pane of glass and as perfectly vertical as the side of a skyscraper. But just a couple of inches below his feet was a shelf no wider than a paperback book.

The friable sandstone knuckle he was holding started to come apart in his grip.

Juan gathered a breath and let himself drop. There wasn't enough room to absorb the shock by bending his knees, and he could feel the void sucking at his heels. The satellite phone, which had stayed with him for his wild plummet, was dislodged by the impact, snaking down one pant leg and emerging from the cuff. There was nothing he could do when it clattered off the shelf and disappeared into the valley below.

He couldn't hear it land over the din of falling debris, but he knew it was a total loss. He clutched at the cliff face. The stone was warm on his cheek.

Next to him, curtains of dust rose from the rock and sand falling over the cliff, but already the landslide was slowing. With the steady wind swirling around the mountaintop, it wouldn't be long before the dust blew away, exposing Cabrillo to anyone observing from above. The vertical drop to the next part of the mountain slope was at least thirty feet, with an additional hundred of steep terrain to the valley floor.

He looked to his right. The avalanche was almost over. The largest of the boulders now littered the ground below while only a thin trickle of sand poured over the edge of the cliff.

The second rule of climbing was never descend a rock face unless you know the route.

Juan had no idea what lay below him, what handholds and toeholds he would find, but with twenty armed gunmen doubtless peering down the hill to see what had happened to their comrades the rules of safe climbing weren't particularly relevant.

He bent down as far as he dared and lowered a leg off the shelf, feeling with his toes for some kind of hold. He also locked the ankle joint of his artificial leg. His foot found a slight depression, barely big enough for all his toes, but it was enough to take his weight. He lowered himself farther still, so that his elbows rested on the narrow shelf. He switched feet in the little niche and again poked blindly for another irregularity in the rock. There was nothing to be felt. The stone was featureless.

A thick tangle of rope suddenly shot past his face, uncoiling as it fell. Looking up, he saw that the cliff hid him from the terrorists above. They weren't throwing him a lifeline, he realized, they were going to send someone down to check on survivors. It was just his good luck that they had chosen to send the climber exactly where he was clinging to the stone.

Juan quickly climbed back onto his shelf and carefully pulled off his boot. He yanked free some buttons of his uniform shirt and stuffed the boot against his chest. Then he wrapped the rope around the smooth molded foot of his prosthesis, looping it twice around, almost like the artificial limb was a pulley. He started to feel the rope dance and jerk in time with the movements of the man who had volunteered to check on his fallen teammates. Cabrillo grasped a handful of the line dangling over the void and stepped into empty space. With his back against the rock face, he slowly paid out rope through his hands. Because of the loops of rope around his foot and his locked ankle, he lowered himself down the cliff hand over hand, so smoothly that the guy above never felt him on the line.

It took less than a minute to reach the base of the cliff. If not for the artificial foot, a traditional descent would have alerted the terrorist of his presence or torn the flesh from his limb until all that remained was bone and gristle. He scrambled across the slope and hurled himself over a defile a moment before the climber reached the edge of the cliff and peered over.

His voice echoed across the valley. "I don't see anything but a pile of rocks. I think they're both dead."

Juan chanced looking up at him. The soldier—or terrorist, depending on what Cabrillo discovered about this place—regarded the pile of rubble for a moment longer, then started climbing back up the rope. Juan collapsed, allowing the first waves of pain to wash over him. Nothing felt broken, but he knew his body was a sea of black-and-blue. He allowed himself only a ten-minute rest—any longer and he would have stiffened to the point of immobility.

Juan considered it a sign of good fortune when he found his kaffiyeh half buried in a mound of sand. He slipped it over his head and unlocked his prosthetic ankle. His plan was to find a safe place to hole up for the day and then make his way up over the mountain on the other side of the construction site that he'd spotted in the next valley. Given its proximity to the terrorist training camp, he had to assume the two facilities were connected.

Once there, he would have to trust on luck again to find out what it was, and hope that Secretary Katamora was being held in one camp or the other.

Deep in the pit of his stomach, he knew no one was that lucky.

SEVENTEEN

L INDA ROSS AND FRANKLIN LINCOLN APPROACHED THE archaeological camp on foot an hour before dawn. Both were operating on too much adrenaline and too little sleep. Murph had taken the Pig off into the deep desert to rendezvous with George Adams, who was flying in the bladder of fuel they would need to complete their mission.

No one liked the idea of splitting up. Finding only the one body near the drill truck and no sign of the other two Americans at the helicopter service area meant they had been taken elsewhere. The guess was, wherever the Libyan cargo chopper had taken the Chairman. If that were the case, their interrogation would be swift, brutal, and more than likely successful. Even now, a team of terrorists could be headed toward the archaeological dig in the Mi-8 helicopter.

But time was ticking down. The summit was fast approaching, and, more important, the longer the Secretary was held, the more likely she would be tortured as well.

With the sun climbing the horizon, the camp began to stir. Linda and Linc noted the archaeologists were mostly grad students spending a summer doing fieldwork. There were a few older expedition members who they assumed were full professors and faculty advisers. The camp also supported a staff of roughly ten native Tunisians, one of whom was dressed in an ill-fitting suit and looked agitated and did very little, so they assumed he was the government minder.

They had to watch for nearly an hour before Dr. Emile Bumford emerged from his tent. For a man who had lost three-quarters of his team, the prissy doctor didn't appear overly upset. He yawned theatrically when he stepped into the sun, as if his sleep the night before had been untroubled. Wearing a ridiculous safari suit with a Panama hat, he ambled to the mess tent. Cooks worked over grills set behind the structure, and while the smell didn't carry to Linda or Linc both imagined the scent of eggs and country-fried potatoes. Their breakfast had been cold MREs. The meal went long; no doubt there had been a staff meeting after everyone ate. The students left the mess first, returning to their tents briefly to grab packs and hand tools and heading over a low rise to the Roman ruins. The teachers were a bit more leisurely, but they, too, vanished over the hill separating the camp from the archaeological site.

Bumford returned to his quarters after all the others had gone to work. He was inside for only a minute before settling himself on a chair under a sunshade just outside his tent's entrance. The book he cracked open was easily as thick as an encyclopedia volume. Linc wanted to sneak into the camp and grab Bumford now, but native workers were moving about, gathering laundry and tidying the students' tents.

"I took an archaeology class my junior year in college," Linda whispered. "We went on a dig for a long weekend. We never had servants like this."

"You didn't have the State Department paying extra to let some of their people tag along."

"Good point. So what do you make of Bumford?"

"If I were to guess, I'd say he's making a healthy per diem being out here and is in no hurry to find out what happened to Alana Shepard and the others."

"Nice," Linda said sarcastically.

The Tunisian representative approached Bumford about an hour after he'd settled into his chair. They spoke for only a moment. Bumford made elaborate gestures with his arms and ended the conversation with a nonchalant shrug.

Linc whispered in a thick, faintly Arabic accent, "'Professor Bumford, have you heard from your people?'" He then made his voice pinched and nasally. "'I have no idea what happened to them . . . Surely you have contacted your university and reported them missing . . . That isn't my responsibility. I am only here as a consultant . . . But aren't you concerned? They are several days overdue . . . Not my problem.' And local guy exits stage right."

Linc's pantomime and prediction was spot-on. Bumford didn't give the conversation a second's thought before returning to his book.

They waited twenty more minutes for the camp to quiet down. The native staff was nowhere to be seen, so Linc crept from his hiding place and threaded his way to the back of Bumford's tent. He slipped a knife from a deep pocket of his coveralls. It was an Emerson CQC-7A. The blade was so sharp that when he slit the nylon, it made no more sound than a knife cutting butter.

Stepping silently into the tent, he crossed over to the entrance. Bumford's back was toward him, less than a foot away, and the man had no idea anyone was looking over his shoulder. Linc glanced across to where Linda crouched behind barrels used to keep the camp's generator fueled. She held up a slim hand for Linc to wait while one of the cooks crossed the compound headed toward the pit latrine. As soon as he vanished, Linda clenched her fist.

Linc reached out and grabbed Bumford under his arms and heaved him into the tent in a fluid motion that sent the Ottoman specialist sprawling onto the dirt floor. Lincoln was on him like a dark wraith, one hand clamped over Bumford's mouth, the other poised with the knife so the portly professor could see it.

A moment later, Linda stepped into the tent through the hole Linc had cut. "Damn, you made that look easy. He must weigh two-fifty."

"Closer to two-seventy. That was my variation on the clean and jerk. I call it heave the jerk."

Linda hunkered low next to Bumford's head. The doctor's eyes were as big as saucers, and sweat beaded his domed forehead. "My colleague is going to remove his hand. You are not going to move or cry out. Understand?"

Bumford lay there like a gutted fish.

"Nod if you understand."

When he still didn't move, Linc prompted him by yanking his chin up and down. Bumford's eyelids fluttered as the first wave of terror ebbed, and he nodded vigorously.

When Linc pulled his hand away, Bumford whimpered, "Who are you?"

"Keep your voice down," Linda said. "We're here about Alana Shepard, Mike Duncan, and Greg Chaffee."

"Who are you?" Bumford repeated. "I don't recognize you. You aren't part of this group."

When Linda reached across him, Bumford seemed to try to burrow into the ground. She straightened his glasses on the bridge of his nose and curled one of the spectacles's arms around his ear where it had dislodged. "We're friends. We need to talk to you about the other members of your team."

"They aren't here."

"What is this guy, an idiot savant?" Linc asked.

"Professor Bumford," Linda opened again, as smoothly as she could, "we're here to ask you a few questions. We're part of an American search-and-rescue team."

"Like the military?"

"Strictly contract civilians, but people in Washington thought your mission important enough to hire us."

"It's a waste of time," Bumford said, regaining a little of his equilibrium, and his arrogance.

"Why do you say that?"

"You do know who I am, yes?"

Linda knew he was fishing for a little recognition to prime his ego. "You're Emile Bumford, one of the world's foremost experts on the Ottoman Empire."

"Then you must know I needn't explain my opinions. You may take them as fact. This expedition for the State Department is a complete waste of time."

"Then why in the hell did you come?" Linc asked.

Bumford didn't answer right away, and Linda saw the furtive look in his eye. "Don't lie," she cautioned.

With a sigh Bumford said, "I lost my tenure because of an affair with a student, and I'm now in the middle of a divorce. My soon-to-be-ex-wife's lawyer is treating my wallet like a piñata, and I didn't make that much teaching in the first place. Add that to the fact that I haven't published a book in ten years, and you figure it out."

"Money."

"The State Department is paying me five hundred dollars a day. I need it."

"That's why you're out here sitting on your butt even though the rest of your team is missing. You're just racking up your per diem." There was neither denial nor shame in Bumford's expression.

Linda wanted to slap his smug face but instead said as calmly as she could, "Well, it's time you start earning your money. Tell me exactly why you think this trip is a waste of time."

"Do you know the story of Suleiman Al-Jama we were told—about how he befriended an American sailor and had a change of heart concerning his jihad against the West?"

"We've heard it," Linda said.

"I don't believe it. Not for a second. I've studied everything Al-Jama ever wrote. It's almost as if I know the man. He wouldn't change. None of the Barbary corsairs would. They made too much money waging war against European shipping."

"I thought Al-Jama fought for ideological reasons, not monetary gain," Linc countered.

"Al-Jama was a man like any other. I'm certain he would've been tempted by the riches that raiding provided. He might have started off wanting to kill infidels for the sake of killing them, but in some of his later writings he talks about the 'rewards' he accumulated. His word, not mine."

"Reward doesn't necessarily mean treasure," Linda said, realizing that Bumford was interpreting Al-Jama through his own money-grubbing prism.

"Young lady, I was brought out here because I am the expert. If you don't care to listen to my explanations, please leave me be."

"I'm curious," Linc said. "Just how lucrative was piracy for the Barbary pirates?"

"What do you really know of them?"

"I know the Marines kicked some butt like the song says—'to the shores of Tripoli.'"

"That was actually five hundred mercenaries under the command of ex–American consul, William Eaton, and a handful of Marines who sacked the city of Dema, a backwater in the Bashaw of Tripoli's holdings. True, their action may have hastened a peace treaty, but it was far from a legendary battle worthy of a hymn."

Linc had some Marine Corps friends who would have killed the man for such a remark.

"Between the fifteenth and nineteenth centuries," Bumford continued, "the Barbary pirates had a stranglehold on the most lucrative sea routes in the world—the Mediterranean and the North Atlantic coast of Europe. During that time, those nations that wouldn't or couldn't pay the exorbitant tributes had their shipping fall prey to the pirates. Their cargos were stolen and their crews either ransomed or sold into slavery. Nations like England, France, and Spain paid the pirates millions in gold to protect maritime commerce. For a time, even the United States was paying them. And by some accounts, more than a tenth of the federal revenue went to various Barbary Coast rulers. The pirates also went on raiding parties to kidnap people from seaside villages as far north as Ireland. By some estimates, more than a million and a half Europeans were taken from their homes and sold into slavery. Can you imagine?"

"Yeah," Linc said with a trace of irony.

Bumford had warmed to his subject and chose to ignore the African-American's gibe. "We're talking about one of the preeminent naval powers of their time. And Suleiman Al-Jama was perhaps the most successful and by far the most ruthless pirate of them all. Though he had first studied to be an Imam, his family had a tradition of piracy that went back for generations. There are tales of his ancestors preying on ships returning from the Crusades. It was in Al-Jama's blood. I'm sorry, but from what I know of him, he would never renounce what he saw as a holy war against the Western powers any more than the modern terrorist of the same name would."

And Linda saw her mistake. His prism wasn't that of his own personal greed. He saw what they were trying to accomplish through the lens of the continuation of inevitable terrorism and the triumph of indefatigable Islamic dogma. She was speaking to a man defeated, a man who had never fired a shot in the war against extremists of a culture he professed to study but had never understood.

She went on anyway. "But this is when Thomas Jefferson decided the United States would no longer pay tribute. For the first time in their history, the pirates were facing a first-class navy that was willing to fight rather than hand over money. Surely Al-Jama must have understood their free rein was over. Jefferson's unilateral declaration of war against piracy was the beginning of the end for them. One nation had taken a stance against their form of savagery despite the rest of the world continuing to cower."

Even as she said it, the parallels to the present struggle against terrorism sent a chill down her spine. Europe had spent the latter part of the twentieth century living under the constant threat of terrorism. There'd been bombings in nightclubs, kidnappings, assassinations, and hijackings all across the continent, with very little response from the authorities.

The United States had taken a similar route following the first attack on the World Trade Center. The government had treated it as a criminal act rather than what it truly was: the opening salvo in a war. The perpetrators had been duly arrested and sent to prison, and the matter was largely forgotten until 9/11.

Rather than ignore the truth for a second time, the government had responded to the 2001 attack by taking the fight back to any and all who supported terrorism in its many forms. Like it had chosen two hundred years earlier, America had proclaimed to the world that it would rather fight than live in fear.

Bumford said, "Even if I grant the possibility that Al-Jama had a change of heart and found ways to reconcile the differences between Islam and Christianity, there is the practical matter of finding his ship, the *Saqr*. It is simply impossible that a vessel has remained hidden in the desert for two centuries. It would either have been destroyed by the elements or looted by nomads. Trust me, there is nothing left to find."

"For the sake of argument"—Linc cut in when he could tell Bumford's pessimism was about to make Linda snap—"if it somehow survived, would you have any clue where it might be?"

"From the letter I read back in Washington, I do believe it must be on the dry riverbed to the south of us, but Alana, Mike, and Greg have scoured it completely. They stopped only when they came to a waterfall that when the river was flowing would have been impassable. There is no Barbary pirate ship hidden out there."

"Was there any other clue in the letter? Something insignificant, even."

"Henry Lafayette said it was hidden in a large cavern that was accessible only through the use of, and I quote here, 'a clever device.' Please don't ask me what that means. Alana pestered me for weeks on end about it. The only other thing I have is a local legend that the ship is hidden beneath the black that burns."

"The what?" Linda asked.

"The black that burns. The tale comes from the journal of Al-Jama's second-in-command, Suleiman Karamanli. It survived because he happened to be the Bashaw of Tripoli's nephew, so it was housed with the Royal Archives. What it means, I'm afraid, is beyond me. I am sorry."

"So am I," Linda muttered.

If a trained archaeologist like Alana Shepard couldn't find Al-Jama's ship after spending weeks using sophisticated equipment, there was little hope she and Mark and Linc would discover it in the remaining days before the peace conference.

Linda glanced at her watch. They had an hour to hike back to where they were going to rendezvous with Mark and the Pig. After reporting that they'd struck out with Bumford, she was going to tell Max their best course of action now was to prestage the Pig to Juan's location in the hope that the Chairman had had better luck.

"Come on, Linc," she said. "Dr. Bumford, thank you for your time. And I don't think I need to remind you that we were never here."

"Yes, of course," the scholar said. "By the way, have you found any sign of the rest of my team?"

Linda bit back a barb about his concern for the others being an afterthought. "One of the men is dead. Either Greg Chaffee or Mike Duncan. Single gunshot to the head. The vultures didn't leave enough to make an ID. We don't know about the other two."

"Dear God. Is it safe for me to remain here? Maybe I should return to the States."

Linc grabbed her arm before she decked the Ottoman scholar. "Easy, girl. He ain't worth it. Let's go."

The two of them slipped out the back of the tent and made their way across the quiet camp. Neither noticed the small figure of a boy who'd listened to the conversation by crouching at the side of the tent. He waited until the pair disappeared over a sand embankment before scampering away to find the Tunisian representative. Twenty minutes later, the information was passed on to a contact in Tripoli for a healthy sum of money, and a further forty minutes after that the turbines of an Mi-8 helicopter at a remote mountaintop training camp began to shriek.

EIGHTEEN

W HEN AMBASSADOR MOON CAUGHT HIS FIRST GLIMPSE OF the debris field from the cabin of an executive helicopter, it took all his self-control not to throw up on the lap of his companion, Foreign Minister Ali Ghami. The devastation was nothing less than total. The remains of the State Department plane were strung out for almost a mile, and other than a fifty-foot section of the cabin and the engines there didn't appear to be any pieces larger than a suitcase.

"Allah, be merciful," Ghami said. It was his first time at the site as well.

Down on the ground, protected by a cordon of Libyan soldiers, men were examining the wreckage. This was the advance team from the NTSB as well as a couple of local aviation experts. They'd arrived only a short time before the American Ambassador, and their helicopter was parked a good mile from the wreckage.

"Mr. Minister," the pilot called over the intercom in the specially soundproofed cabin. "We will need to land near their chopper so our rotor wash doesn't disturb the site."

"That's fine," Ghami replied. "I think the walk and fresh air will do both the Ambassador and me some good."

"Understood, sir.

The Minister turned to Moon, resting a hand on the American's shoulder. "On behalf of my government, and myself, I am so sorry, Charles."

"Thank you, Ali. When you called with the news that the plane had been found, I held out hope." He gestured out the helo's Plexiglas window. "Now . . ." He let his voice trail off. There was nothing more to say.

The pilot settled the French-built EC155 executive chopper next to a utilitarian helicopter with military colors. Ghami's bodyguard, a tight-lipped, no-necked mountain of a man named Mansour, opened the helicopter's door while the blades still whirled overhead. Ignoring the blast of grit kicked up by the rotor wash, Ghami leapt down to the ground and paused while the more portly Moon followed.

They started walking toward the wreck. Moon was sweating after only a couple of paces, but neither the Libyan Minister nor his guard seemed affected by the heat and the blazing sun. The smell of charred plastic and aviation fuel carried over to them on the occasional slap of wind.

In Moon's estimation, approaching the debris on foot made it look worse than from the air. Everything was burned dark and warped by the fire that had consumed the plane. They paused at the cordon of soldiers and waited for the lead investigator from the NTSB. The investigator was moving slowly through the debris, snapping pictures with a digital camera, while a man with him was recording everything on a camcorder. When the investigator finally noted the dignitaries, he said a couple of words to his companion and trudged over. His face was long and gaunt, his mouth turned down at the corners.

"Ambassador Moon?" he called when he was within earshot.

"I'm Moon. This is Ali Ghami, Libya's Foreign Minister."

They shook hands. "I'm David Jewison."

Moon saw Ghami shift position ever so slightly at hearing the name.

"Can you, ah, tell us anything?" Moon invited.

Jewison glanced back over his shoulder and then returned his gaze to the Ambassador. "We weren't the first people to come here. That much is certain."

"What are you saying?" Ghami asked sharply.

Moon knew that Libya's handling of this crisis would have an impact on their relations with the United States and the Western powers far beyond the Tripoli Accords. Jewison's revelation doubtless put both Ghami and his government in a difficult position. If there was any evidence of tampering, then an accusation of a cover-up wouldn't be too far behind.

"From what we can tell, a group of nomads has been over the site. They left behind hundreds of footprints, as well as cooking fires, camp detritus consistent with their lifestyle, and the body of a camel that had been shot in the head. Our local guide said the camel appeared to be near the end of its life, judging by the wear on its teeth, and was probably put down because it no longer had value.

"Parts of the wreckage have been disturbed, some possibly removed. The passengers' remains have also been moved. I believe Muslim custom is to bury people within twenty-four hours of their deaths. My Libyan counterpart here says it's likely the nomads did just that. I have no reason to doubt his assessment, but we won't know for sure until we get some cadaver dogs up here."

"Do you have any preliminary ideas what happened to the plane?"

"From what we can tell—and this is very, very early—the aircraft lost part of its tail section sometime during the flight. We don't know why, because it has not been recovered here at the scene. We're sending out our chopper in a few minutes to visually search what we know to be the flight path. This damage could have caused a loss of hydraulic fluid as well as the failure of its rudder and elevators. Without the hydraulic system, the flaps, ailerons, slats, and spoilers on the main wings would have also failed. Had this been the case, the plane would have been difficult, if not impossible, to control."

Ghami asked, "Is there any indication why part of the tail was lost?"

"Nothing yet," Jewison replied. "We'll get an idea once we find it."

"And if you don't?" This was from Moon. The question wasn't a deliberate provocation, but he was curious about Ghami's reaction. Just because he personally liked the man didn't mean he had forgotten his role here.

"Barring some other evidence, it would officially be classified as reasons unknown."

Ghami looked to the Ambassador. "Charles, I promise you that it will be located and the reason for this tragedy explained."

"No offense, Minister," Jewison interrupted, "but that may not be a promise you can keep. I've been a crash investigator for eighteen years. I've seen everything there is to see, including an airliner that exploded in midair and was pulled out of the ocean off Long Island. That was a relatively straightforward investigation compared to this. We can't tell what damage was done by the crash and what was done by your people." Ghami made to protest, and Jewison staved him off with a gesture. "I mean the nomads. They're Libyan so they're your people, is all I mean."

"The nomads are citizens of no country but the desert."

"Either way, they messed with this scene so badly I don't know if even finding the tail will give us a definitive answer."

Ghami held the aviation expert's stare. "Ambassador Moon and other representatives of your government have explained to me that you are the best in the world at what you do, Mr. Jewison. I have their assurance and thus their confidence that you will find an answer. I am certain that you treat each and every airline disaster with your utmost efforts, but you must surely know the gravity of this situation and the importance of what you find."

Jewison looked from one man to the other. His expression was even more dour as he came to understand that politics was going to play as large a part in his search as forensic science.

"How long until the conference?" he asked.

"Forty-eight hours," Moon answered.

He shook his head with weary resignation. "*If* we can find the tail and *if* it hasn't been further damaged by nomads, I might have a preliminary report for you by then."

Ghami held out his hand, which Jewison took. "That's all any of us ask for."

• • •

THE *OREGON* HAD BEEN rigged for ultraquiet. There was little that could be done about the sound of waves lapping against the hull except to keep her bow into the wind. Other than that, nothing about the ship's position was left to chance. Max Hanley had surrounded the vessel at a distance of thirty miles with passive buoys that collected incoming radar energy and relayed that information via secure burst transmitters to the onboard computer. This gave them ample warning if another ship was in the area without the use of their own active radar suite. If a target appeared to be headed in their direction, the ship's dynamic positioning system would move the *Oregon* using power supplied by her massed banks of silver-zinc deep-cycle batteries, so she crept along with the barest whisper of water forced through her pump jets. With her hull and superstructure doped with radar-absorbent material, a passing ship would almost need to be in visual range to detect her.

A passive-sonar array dangled from the moon pool down at her keel. Capable of listening three hundred and sixty degrees, the acoustical microphones covered any threats lurking below the surface. Other sensors were vacuuming up electronic data and radio chatter from shipping, aircraft, and shore-based facilities along Libya's coast. This ability of drift and lift, or as Murph called it "lurk and work," was the exact type of mission Juan had designed the *Oregon* to perform. Her stealth capabilities allowed the crew to station the ship off a hostile coast for days—or weeks, if necessary—gathering intelligence on fleet movements, electronics signaling, or anything else her clients demanded.

They had lain off the coast of Cuba for twenty-eight days during the time that Fidel Castro's illness made it necessary for him to transfer power to his brother, Raul, listening in on everything taking place behind the closed doors of the communist dictator's private retreat. They had provided the American intelligence services unprecedented knowledge of the inner workings of the secretive regime and eliminated any uncertainty as to what was taking place.

Rigging the *Oregon* for ultraquiet also meant suspending all routine maintenance, which no one on the crew minded. However, the ship's fitness facility was closed to prevent weights from accidentally clanging together, and meals were reduced to prepackaged pouches boiled in a pot clamped to the stove in the galley. The culinary staff had outdone themselves in preparing the meals, but they remained a poor substitute for the gourmet dishes to which the men and women of the Corporation had grown accustomed. The normal silverware and fine china were replaced with paper plates and plastic knives and forks, and any television or radio had to be enjoyed with headphones.

Max Hanley was in his cabin working on a scratch-built model of a Swift boat, one of the fast riverine crafts he had commanded during Vietnam. Hanley wasn't a man who dwelled much on his past or gave in to the siren song of nostalgia. He stored the medals he'd won in a Los Angeles safe-deposit he hadn't visited in years and met up with former shipmates only at funerals. He was building the model simply because he could do it from memory and it kept his mind occupied with something other than his responsibilities.

Doc Huxley had suggested the hobby as a way of reducing stress and keeping his blood pressure in check. So far, he'd managed to stick to it longer than the yoga she'd prescribed before. He'd already built and presented a beautiful replica of the *Oregon* to Juan, which now sat under a plastic case in the executive conference room, and had plans for a Mississippi paddle wheeler when he was finished with the Swift boat.

The knock on his door was so soft that he knew it was Eric Stone taking the whole silent-rigging thing to the limit.

"Enter," Hanley called.

Eric stepped though the doorway, carrying a laptop computer and a large, flat portfolio. He looked like he hadn't slept in a week, which probably wasn't too far off the mark. Stone usually maintained a semblance of the military comportment drilled into him at Annapolis, but today his shirt was untucked, and his chinos were as wrinkled as a balled-up piece of aluminum foil.

While Max worried whenever they had people stuck out there in a hostile environment, Eric took it even further. Max had been Stoney's mentor when he'd first joined the Corporation, but since then he'd grown to idolize Juan Cabrillo, and Mark Murphy was like the brother he'd never had growing up. Fatigue lines etched his normally smooth face, and while he'd never had much of a beard it was obvious he hadn't shaved in a while.

"You have something?" Max asked without preamble.

He showed off the portfolio. "Detailed maps of Juan's location and a rundown of the place's history."

"I knew you could do it." Hanley cleared a wide space on his desk for Eric to lay out the map. He stood to give himself a better perspective. "Tell me what I'm looking at."

He could see a small training facility, built high in the mountains, roughly twenty miles from the coast. The camp was well hidden by the peaks, and, had it not been for its proximity to a large open pit of some kind, it would have been easy to overlook, even knowing its location because of Juan's implanted GPS transponder. There was a dark line snaking up from the shore to the pit that closely followed the contour of the land. Where the line met the coast were a couple of old buildings and a long jetty. There were other buildings along the rim of a valley where the earth had been excavated.

Eric pointed to the port area first. "This is what remains of a British-built coaling station dating back to the 1840s. It was updated with a bigger pier in 1914, possibly in anticipation of World War I. That pier was partially destroyed during Rommel's North Africa campaign, and the Germans rebuilt it to use as a staging area for their push toward Egypt. The dark line here is a railroad that linked the station to the coal mine here." His finger followed the railroad tracks to the buildings overlooking the open-pit mine. "There used to be a barge canal to transport the coal, but the aquifer dried up and the railroad was laid in."

"Looks to me like someone's reopening the place," Max remarked.

"Yes, sir. About five months ago. The rail line was refurbished to accommodate larger ore cars, with an eye toward extracting coal from the old mine."

"Did anyone ask if this makes sense in a country sitting on forty billion barrels of oil?"

"I did as soon as I figured out what this place was," Eric replied. "And, in a word, it doesn't. Especially in light of their government's attempts to go green with the tidal generating station farther down the coast."

"So what's going on here really?"

"The CIA thinks it's a cover for a new subterranean nuclear-research program."

"I thought Uncle Muammar gave up his nuke ambitions," Max remarked. "Besides, the CIA was probably convinced my mother-in-law was pursuing a nuclear program when she had a new root cellar dug."

Eric chuckled. "Foreign intelligence services dismiss the CIA estimate. They think this is a legit enterprise. Problem is, I can't dig up any corporate entities charged with working there. Which isn't all that surprising. The Libyans aren't known for their transparency. There was one article in a trade publication that said Libya is interested in pursuing coal gasification as an alternative to oil, and claims they have a system that will be cleaner than natural gas."

"You don't sound convinced," Max said.

"It took some digging, but I found records from ships that had once used the station back in the day. Building up a picture over time, it appears vessels that regularly refueled there showed a fifty percent increase in maintenance and a twenty percent reduction in efficiency."

As an engineer, Max immediately grasped the implications of Eric's findings. "The coal is filthy, isn't it?"

"An archived log from the captain of a coastal freighter called *Hydra* says he'd rather fill his bunkers with sawdust than use the coal from the station."

"There's no way any current gasification technology can make it clean. So what is this place, really?"

"The facility to the north of the mine was once used by the Libyan military as a training base."

"This whole thing is government sanctioned after all," Max said, jumping ahead.

"Not necessarily," Eric countered. "They stopped using it a couple of years ago."

"Back to square zero," Max said bitterly.

"'Fraid so. In the past two days, there have been suspicious military maneuvers in Syria, so our satellite coverage has gone east to keep an eye on them. This picture here is two months old, and is the most current I could find."

"What about getting some shots from a commercial satellite company?"

"Already tried and struck out. Even offering double their normal fees, we can't get new shots until a week from now."

"Too late for Juan or Fiona Katamora."

"Yup," Eric agreed.

"And you've tried everything to pierce the corporate veil of the company working on the rail line?"

"Do onions have layers? They're better shielded than anything I've ever seen before. I've hit dead end after dead end trying to trace ownership. But the thing I learned about companies working in Libya is, they are generally partnered with the government in a sort of quasi-nationalized arrangement."

"So we come full circle, and it's Libya's government behind all this?"

"You're familiar with Cosco, aren't you?"

"It's a Chinese shipping company."

"Which many suspect is actually owned by the People's Liberation Army. I'm wondering if we don't have something similar going on here."

"You're saying it's not Libya's central government that's involved but a segment of it?" Max asked, and Eric nodded. "The military?"

"Or the JSO, the Jamahiriya Security Organization, their principal spy agency. Ever since Qaddafi started playing nice, the JSO has been marginalized. This could be a play for them to regain some of their lost prestige."

"One hell of a gamble, since we know these people are somehow connected to the downing of Katamora's plane," Max said. Stone didn't argue, so Hanley went on. "What about terrorists paying this rogue faction to look the other way? That worked for Bin Laden in the Sudan, and then Afghanistan, until we toppled the Taliban."

"That was my next thought." Eric said. "We know Libya's sheltered terrorists in the past. The mine and railroad could be a terrorist front for a training camp, with an eye toward using the proceeds to fund their activities. Al-Qaeda had done that in Africa, trafficking conflict diamonds."

Max took a moment to light his pipe, using the familiar distraction to organize his thoughts. When it was drawing evenly and a wreath of smoke began to form a haze along the ceiling, he said, "We're spinning our wheels. There's no sense in you and me trying to guess who's doing what. Juan will probably have the answer. So as I see it, our priority is to get him out of there and find out what he's learned."

"Agreed."

"Any suggestions?" Hanley invited.

"Not at this time. We need to wait until he makes contact."

Max Hanley was known by the crew as a man who kept his own counsel, so Eric was surprised when he suddenly blurted in frustration, "I hate this."

"I know what you mean."

"Juan shouldn't have taken off like that."

"He saw it as a tactical necessity. How else would we know where they staged from?"

"There are better ways. We could have tracked the chopper on radar."

"We never saw them flying to the accident site," Eric replied. "How would we have tracked them out? They were flying nap-of-the-earth the whole way. Completely invisible to us from this distance. And before you say it, there wasn't time to get satellite coverage again. Juan made the only decision open to him."

Max raked his hand through his thinning ginger hair. "You're right. I know. I just don't like it. There are so many variables at play here that I don't know if we're coming or going. Is this state-sponsored terrorism, a rogue faction within Libya's government, or some garden-variety terrorist group, most likely Suleiman Al-Jama's outfit? We have no idea who we're up against or what they want. We don't know if Katamora's alive or dead. Basically, we don't know squat. Linc, Linda, and Mark discover a chopper that looks like it was armed to take the Secretary's plane down, but, again, we don't know who's behind it. Then we've got a group of missing archaeologists who may or may not be involved, and some other academic weenie who says they've all been navel-gazing so he can pay off an ex-wife. Did I miss any other pieces to this jigsaw puzzle? Oh yeah, the most important peace conference since Camp David is in a couple of days. And with Juan incommunicado, I don't know what piece fits where."

And there it was, Eric thought. The crux of Max's problem. Hanley wasn't a natural leader, not the way Cabrillo was. Give Max a technical challenge and he will work it until he has a solution, or present him with a plan and he will see it carried out to the letter.

But when it came to making the hard decisions, he agonized because it wasn't his forte. He wasn't a strategist or tactician, and he, more than anyone else, knew it.

"If it were up to me," Eric said diplomatically, "I would get Mark and the others to within striking distance of the mine–terrorist camp for when Juan calls."

"What about the archaeologists and the scrolls?"

"A distraction, for now. Our priorities are the Chairman and then Secretary Katamora."

Max's phone rang. He could tell from the display it was the communications duty officer. He hit the button to put the phone on speaker. "Hanley."

"Max, I just received a secure alert from Overholt."

"Now what?" he groused.

"A chopper fitting the description of the one Juan flew in earlier showed up at the Roman archaeology site across the border in Tunisia. Armed men kidnapped Professor Emile Bumford, the Tunisian government overseer, and one member of the camp staff, a local boy that may be related to him."

Max looked Eric in the eye, arching one of his bushy brows. "A distraction?" He then addressed the comm specialist. "Okay. Send an acknowledgment to Lang that we received his message." He snapped off the phone and leaned back into his padded chair. "Another damned piece that just won't fit."

Eric wisely didn't add that the piece might be part of an entirely different puzzle.

NINETEEN

HIS PRECIOUS FACE WAS A MIX OF DETERMINATION AND delight. His mouth was formed into a tiny O, and his eyes were open despite the chlorine sting. Beads of water clung to his impossibly long lashes like diamond chips. His body wriggled with the almost rhythm of his kicking legs, and the inflatable bands around his arms kept bumping into his chin with each awkward stroke.

Alana felt like her heart was going to explode, as she stood waist-deep in her condo's community pool, Josh striking out for her as she retreated a slow pace at a time. He knew the game, would complain bitterly if he tired out before reaching her, or beam with pride if he made it to the sanctuary of her waiting arms.

Her buttocks pressed against the pool's concrete side. Josh was a few feet away, his mouth now spreading into a triumphant grin. He knew he was going to make it. And then his water wings suddenly vanished, and his face fell into the water. Alana tried to push herself off the wall, but it was as though her skin and swimsuit were adhered to the concrete and tile.

Josh came up, sputtering. His eyes were wide with panic as the first choking cough shook his little body. Water and saliva bubbled from his lips. He managed to cry out "Mommy!" before his head slipped under the surface again.

Alana stretched her arms, feeling like they were pulling from their sockets, but she couldn't reach him. Couldn't move. There were people all around the pool area, lounging on chairs or sitting at the water's edge with their feet dangling in the cool water. She tried to call to them but no sound escaped her lips. They were oblivious to her plight.

Josh's thrashing became less frantic, his longish hair spreading around his head, swaying in the eddies like some sea creature. His hands were balled into little fists, as if trying to hang on, but there was nothing Alana could do. The pool's filtration system was pushing him farther from her. Her arms screamed with the strain of trying to reach him, and her head pounded with an unholy ache—the punishment for being a bad mother, she knew.

Her baby was dying.

She was dying.

And she would have accepted such a fate, but reality was much more cruel.

She came back from the nightmare.

The pain in her head was from being clubbed and momentarily stunned by one of the guards. Her arms ached because she was being dragged from the serving line, where moments earlier she had been slopping a thin gruel onto the tin plates of the other prisoners. Her backside felt numb because the ground was rough gravel and the man dragging her set a strong pace.

Another of the guards shouted at the man who had hit her. He stopped midstride and let her fall to the dirt. She paid no attention to the rapid-fire Arabic the two shot at each other. She simply lay still, hoping against hope that they would forget about her.

The image of her son drowning, something her imagination conjured up to add more pain to her already brutal existence, was like a dull ache in her chest. Josh was eleven now, not the five-year-old she had seen, and he was an excellent swimmer.

The shouting match between the two guards grew more heated until a third man entered the fray. She knew he was one of the senior people at the work camp, and a quiet word from him ended the discussion instantly. The man who had hit Alana toed her in the ribs to get her on her feet and motioned for her to retake her place at the trestle table that served as the prisoners' buffet. The servers were all women, while the people they fed were mostly men, men who were wasting away in the heat until their ragged clothes hung off their thin frames and their cheeks were shadowed hollows.

Alana had been here less than a week and already knew that most of these poor souls had been here for months. They looked no better than the prisoners liberated from Nazi concentration camps.

When she retook her place behind the table, the woman next to her muttered something in Arabic.

"I'm sorry, I don't understand."

The woman, who had once been heavyset, judging by the slabs of flesh that hung from her neck, pointed to Alana's eyes and then pointed down to the table. Don't look at the guards, she was trying to say. Or that was Alana's interpretation. Maybe, keep your eye on your work. Either way, when the next prisoner shuffled up to her, she lifted her gaze just enough to see the plate he held in one trembling hand.

After getting their food and a cup filled with water that was hot enough to scald the tongue, the prisoners ate on the ground. A few were lucky enough to be able to rest their backs against one of the old buildings. The buildings were all two and three stories high, with badly rusted iron roofs. Their sides were powdery clapboards that the sun and heat had curled and split. On the other side of the buildings were rail sidings holding a few railcars as well as two locomotives, one not much larger than a truck. Unlike the buildings and railcars, the locomotives were newer, though still coated in dust. A little farther down the main line, which vanished around a curve in the mountains a half mile away, was an enormous rusted-steel structure with old conveyor belts and metal chutes that sagged from neglect.

It hadn't taken her long to realize this was an old mine, and that the prisoners were working to reopen it. Gangs of the strongest detainees went off every morning to labor on the tracks to the north, while others toiled in the massive open pit at the bottom of the valley. There was little heavy equipment being used, only a crane mounted on a rail flatbed, to help lay track, and a couple of bulldozers. Everything else was done by hand under the watchful eye, and quick fists, of the guards.

A buzz of soft whispers suddenly swept through the prisoners while eating their meal, their eyes turned to the east, along the rim of the valley. A vehicle was approaching, coils of dust billowing from its tires as it negotiated the narrow trail.

The vehicle was identical to the one that had captured the two Americans, a desert-patrol truck with tall, knobby tires, and a machine gun mounted on its roof. As the truck drew closer, Alana could see a bundle of some kind roped to its hood. And closer still, she could tell it was the body of a man. His clothes were missing, and his once-dark skin was burned red and had begun to peel off in great sheets. She could tell an animal had gotten to the body, because there were bloody gouges all over his arms and chest. His face was a raw, pulpy mass.

The patrol had been sent out to track down an escaped prisoner.

The truck stopped just short of the trestle tables and the passenger's door flew open. The man who emerged spoke to the guard captain for a moment. He, in turn, made an announcement to the assembled prisoners. Alana didn't need to understand the language to know he was telling them that this is what happens to those who try to escape. He then drew a knife, cut the bindings holding the body to the truck, and strode away. The corpse hit the ground with a meaty sound, and the flies that were a constant swarm over the serving dishes suddenly found a more appetizing meal.

There wasn't enough food in Alana's stomach for her to throw up. Instead, she bent at the waist, braced her hands against her knees, and dry-heaved until her stomach was a knotted lump. When she straightened, a guard she didn't recognize eyed her with some interest.

A half hour later, the meal finished, Alana and the other women were cleaning the tin serving dishes, using fistfuls of sand to scour the metal. Not that the prisoners back laboring in the mine and along the railroad had left much behind on their plates. One of the principal means for the guards to maintain control was to keep all the captives on the verge of starvation.

She was kneeling on the ground, swirling sand inside a bowl, when a shadow loomed over her. She looked up. The other women working with her kept their attention on their work. Alana was suddenly yanked to her feet and turned around violently. It was the guard who had slapped her earlier. He was close enough that she could smell the tobacco on his breath and see that he wasn't much older than twenty, and that there was a lifelessness in his eyes. He didn't see her as another human being. There wasn't enough behind his gaze to make her think he saw her as an animate object at all.

The other guards meant to watch over the dozen women were purposefully looking away. An arrangement had been made, a deal struck. For however long he wished, Alana Shepard belonged to this man.

She tried to ram a knee into his groin but must have telegraphed her intentions because he turned aside adroitly and took the glancing blow to his thigh. The leering expression on his face didn't change, even when he slapped her on the same cheek that was already swollen and beginning to bruise.

Alana refused to cry out or collapse. She swayed on her feet until the stinging subsided and her head cleared. The guard spun her again, and with a bony hand clamped on her shoulder so that his fingers dug into her flesh he maneuvered her away from the others.

A hundred yards off was an old shed. Half the roof was missing, and the sides were bowed like the swayed back of an old horse. The door hung askew on a single rusted hinge. Just at the threshold, the guard shoved Alana hard enough to send her sprawling. She knew what was coming, had suffered the ordeal once before in college, and had vowed never to let it happen again. When she turned to face him from her supine position, her arm swept the floor to scoop up some pebbles and dirt.

He came forward in a rush and kicked her wrist. Her fingers opened reflexively and her arm went numb. Her meager weapon was scattered back to the ground. He said something in Arabic and chuckled to himself.

Alana opened her mouth to scream, and he was suddenly on her, one filthy hand clamped over her nose and mouth, the other she refused to think about. She tried to thrash under his weight, to bite his fingers, to block out the horror of what was about to happen, but he held her pressed to the earth. She couldn't breathe. His lunge had knocked the air from her lungs and his hand shut off her airways. Her head began to swim, and after just a few seconds of a defense she thought she would never give up her body betrayed her. Her motions became less frantic. Unconsciousness loomed like a black shadow.

Then came a loud crackle, like the staccato snap of a bunch of twigs, and she could turn away and draw breath. Above her, she saw the back of a man's hand and the back of her attacker's head. The guard was dragged off of her, and Alana could breathe more deeply, short, choppy gasps that nevertheless filled her lungs. The would-be rapist came to rest next to her, his face inches from hers. If it was possible, death brought a certain amount of life to his unblinking eyes.

Kneeling over her was the guard who had watched her dry-heave in the mess line. He had snapped the other man's neck with his bare hands.

He spoke in a soothing voice, and it took her a second to realize she recognized the words. He was speaking English. "You're okay now," he'd said. "His ardor has cooled. Permanently."

"Who? Who are you?" He'd pulled aside his kaffiyeh. He was older than all the other guards she had seen, his skin weathered by a lifetime of living outdoors. She noticed, too, that unlike any of the other people she'd seen recently, one of his eyes was brown and weepy while the other was a startling blue.

"My name is Juan Cabrillo, and if you want to live you and I have to get out of here right now."

"I don't understand."

Cabrillo got to his feet and extended a hand to Alana. "You don't need to. You just have to trust me."

●   ●   ●

AFTER A NIGHT OF moving by moonlight across the valley toward the construction site, gaining access to the facility had been simplicity itself. The guards had orders to keep people in. There was nothing about keeping men dressed like themselves out.

When Juan had been questioned about his presence, as he stood casually in line for breakfast with the other guards after sunrise prayer, he'd replied that he had been sent from the other camp as punishment for failing on the obstacle course. The young man who'd questioned him had judged the answer adequate and said nothing more.

Just like that, Cabrillo was part of the landscape—another Arab in desert fatigues, with half his face hidden by a checkered scarf. He had to be careful. During his tumble down the mountain, he had lost one of his brown contact lenses. The other he washed as best he could in his mouth, but it was ingrained with grit, and every time he blinked it felt like he was scratching his cornea with sandpaper. The eye streamed a constant flow of tears.

He spent the morning wandering the workings, staying close enough to other guards that he didn't attract anyone's attention. He quickly grasped that this was a forced-labor camp, and, judging by the prisoners' condition, it had either been here for a long time or they hadn't been in the best shape when they arrived. He believed more in the latter than the former, because it didn't look like a great amount of work had been accomplished.

And that was the point, he realized after a couple of hours. These people weren't meant to accomplish anything at all. The holes they had excavated at the bottom of the valley appeared random, with no oversight by a mining engineer. As best he could tell, reopening the facility was make-work, something to keep them tired and hungry and grateful for the meager meals they were given. But whoever sent them here didn't want them dead. At least not yet.

It made him think about Secretary Katamora and how she, too, currently existed in limbo. Neither dead nor alive, at least by any official designation.

By listening to the other guards, Juan built up a picture of the place, not what it was about—no one talked about that—but who staffed it. He heard Arabic in every accent imaginable, from the worst gutter talk of a Moroccan slum to the urbane polish of a university-educated Saudi. His belief that these were terrorists recruited from the far corners of the Middle East was confirmed by listening to the Babel of inflections and dialects.

At one point during the day, he'd gotten close enough to the command tent to hear who he believed to be the guard captain speaking into either a radio or, most likely, a satellite phone. Juan paused to tie his boot, watched by a guard stationed outside the tent's sealed flap, and was pretty sure he heard Suleiman Al-Jama's name. He knew better than to linger and moved away before the guard became suspicious.

It was during the noontime meal that he realized not all of the prisoners were Arabs. He spotted a fair-skinned man with thin blond hair among the detainees. The sun had burned him cruelly. And when one of the guards struck a serving woman, he saw that she, too, wasn't native to the region. She was petite, with closely cropped bangs peeking out from the headscarf she had been given, and her eyes were a brilliant green. She could have been Turkish, he guessed, but there was a girl-next-door, all-American wholesomeness to her that made him think otherwise.

He had kept an eye on her afterward and was in position when her attacker returned to avenge his humiliation at being dressed down by the guard captain in front of everyone.

Cabrillo was wearing what he dubbed his combat leg, a prosthetic crafted by Kevin Nixon in the Magic Shop with the help of the *Oregon*'s chief armorer. In its plastic-encased calf had been hidden a wire garrote, which he could have used but wanted to avoid the blood, as well as a compact Kel-Tec .380 pistol. The weapon didn't have a silencer, so it stayed in his pocket, and he'd resorted to snapping the man's neck.

•   •   •

"I GUESS I DON'T have a choice," Alana said as she took Juan's proffered hand.

The shed was far enough away from the rest of the compound

that none of the guards could see it directly. They knew what was supposed to be taking place within, so none made an effort to watch it overtly. Juan was able to lead Alana from the building to a low ridge beyond. Once over the ridge, they lay flat against the hot stone and waited, Cabrillo watching the camp for any sign they'd been seen.

Everything appeared to be normal.

After a few minutes, Juan judged it safe to move, and he and his new charge slid down the face of the ridge and started for the open desert, moving away from the distant terrorist training camp and deeper into the barren wastes.

He estimated they had at least an hour before anyone thought to look for the missing guard, and when they performed a head count of male prisoners capable of breaking another man's neck they would discover everyone accounted for. The confusion would add to the delay if they chose to send out patrols. However, once clear of the camp, he wasn't worried about pursuit. He'd seen the performance with the escapee during lunch and understood that the guards let the desert do the work for them and waited for the buzzards to lead them to their quarry.

Most likely, they would send out a patrol car in a day or two to search for circling vultures.

By then, he fully expected to be lounging in the copper tub in his cabin aboard the *Oregon*, with a drink in one hand and a Cuban cigar in the other. And because he'd lost his sat phone, there would be a blood-soaked bandage on his leg.

TWENTY

AN UNFAMILIAR ALARM WOKE DR. JULIA HUXLEY. HER cabin was located next to her office, with the door perpetually open. The alarm was coming from her computer, and when she glanced over she could see the screen coming to life, a milky glow that spilled across her tidy desk and glinted off the stainless steel arms of her rolling chair.

Julia threw aside her covers, her hands automatically bunching her hair into a ponytail and binding it with the elastic band sitting on her nightstand. In her one major, although secret, feminine conceit, she wore a hand-laced white satin nightgown that clung to her curves like a second skin. If she knew there would be a chance of a middle-of-the-night emergency, usually when the *Oregon* was gearing up for combat, she slept in an oversized T-shirt, but when things were quiet she had a whole closetful of clingy sleepwear. She'd nearly been found out a couple of times, but with a pair of clean scrubs folded at the foot of her bed she could change in seconds and no one was the wiser.

Julia padded in bare feet across her cabin and plopped herself in front of her computer. By the time she'd flicked on the articulated light clamped to her desk, she knew what the alarm was. One of the biometric tracking chips implanted in all shore operators' legs had failed. There were several tones the computer generated, depending on the nature of the failure. Most commonly, it was a dying electric charge, but what she heard sent a chill down her spine. The sharp electronic wail meant that either the chip in question had been removed or the owner was dead.

The story was writ across her computer screen.

Juan Cabrillo's tracking chip was no longer transmitting its location to the constellation of orbiting GPS satellites. She scrolled back to check his movements over the past several hours and saw he had left the general area of the terrorist camp and old mine, striking out to the south at a steady four miles per hour. He'd covered almost twenty-five miles. He had then stopped ten minutes earlier, and, without warning, the chip had ceased functioning.

She reached for the phone to call Max when the alarm stopped. The chip was transmitting once again. Julia typed in a command to run a system diagnostic, noting the Chairman hadn't moved. The tracking chips were still a new technology, and while they hadn't had too many problems, she understood they weren't infallible. According to the system, Cabrillo had either been dead for thirty-eight seconds or the chip had been pulled from his body and then returned to it, recontacting with pumping, oxygenated blood, completing the circuit it needed to transmit.

Just as suddenly as the alarm went silent, it started up again, keening for thirty or so seconds. And then it started dropping in and out, seemingly random.

Blip, beep beep. Blip, beep. Beep, blip, beep. Blip.
Blip, blip, beep. Blip, beep beep, blip.

Through the chaos of tones, she thought she recognized a pattern. Making sure her computer was recording the telemetry from Juan's chip, she opened an Internet connection and checked her hunch. It took her nearly a minute to decipher the first series of sounds even as more came in.

Wake . . . up . . .

Blip, blip, blip, blip. Blip, blip, beep. Beep, blip, blip, beep.

Hux . . .

Juan was interrupting the signal from the chip somehow and was sending a message in old-fashioned Morse code.

"You crafty SOB," Julia muttered in admiration.

And then the alarm shrieked a continuous cry that went on and on.

Julia knocked over a cup of pens reaching for the phone.

●   ●   ●

AFTER TREKKING THE FIRST four miles from the terrorist camp, Cabrillo had found a sheltered spot out of the sun's brutal gaze to hole up. He and his new charge, Alana Shepard, would need to wait until nightfall in order to tackle the open desert. He told her to sleep while he backtracked a mile to make sure their spoor had been obliterated by the wind. He knew Muslims didn't keep dogs, even for tracking purposes, so he felt confident that no one would be on their trail, at least for a while.

When they started out again shortly after sunset, he wanted to put much distance between themselves and the camp, sensing that once they stopped he wouldn't be able to walk much farther afterward. If he and Alana were still alone in the desert come dawn, the vultures would start circling. With food so scarce in the desert, the vultures would loiter for days waiting for their prey to die. It would be the same as raising a sign that said ESCAPEES HERE. If the terrorists sent out a patrol, especially the chopper, they would be spotted quickly.

One more thing he had to consider was Alana's endurance. She appeared in better condition than the other prisoners he had seen, but she still suffered from deprivation. He had swiped a couple of canteens during his earlier meanderings and allowed her to drink as much as she could, yet she remained sorely dehydrated. And there was nothing he could do for the rumbling in her belly that she felt compelled to keep apologizing for.

It was three in the morning when he could tell she was spent completely. She might make it another mile, but there was no real need. It was time now to rely on his people and not her stamina.

"So tell me more about the dig you were heading up," he invited to distract her, settling himself on the ground with his back against a rock. He had led her up a small outcrop of rock with a natural bowl at its summit that provided cover as well as a strong vantage point.

Because he had pushed the march so hard, they hadn't really spoken much beyond introductions.

"It's frustrating." She sipped from the canteen. Despite what must be a raging thirst, she had good survival instincts and drank sparingly. "The original source material strongly indicates the Suleiman Al-Jama's *Saqr* is still buried in a cave someplace, but I'll be darned if we could find any sign. For one thing, the geology is all wrong for caves or caverns."

"And for all you know, this guy Lafayette's bearings were off and you're searching the wrong riverbed," he said, finishing her thought. He rolled up his pant leg.

Alana stared at the molded titanium-and-plastic limb, saying nothing.

"Shaving cut," Juan said with a lopsided grin.

To her credit, she didn't miss a beat. "You should stick to depilatories. The third, and most likely, scenario is the Arab retainers Henry

Lafayette mentioned in his journal returned to the cave after Al-Jama's death, looted what they could, and destroyed the rest."

"That's actually the least likely of the three," Juan countered. From his combat leg, he pulled a throwing knife, basically a flat piece of surgical steel that had been balanced and honed to a razor's edge. He went on: "If they were that loyal to Al-Jama in life, the respect would have continued after death. A devout Muslim would no more desecrate a grave than he'd have ham for Easter dinner."

"But Muslims don't eat . . . Oh, I get it."

"If that one generation of servants kept quiet about the entombed ship, then I'm pretty sure it's still buried out there."

"Not where we've been looking." In the moonlight, her eyes dimmed. "Are we going to be able to rescue Greg Chaffee?"

He looked at her. "I'm not going to BS you. My team and I have another priority that trumps his rescue. I'm sorry. As soon as we're done, I will go back. That I can promise."

"You're searching for Fiona Katamora's plane, aren't you?" She took Juan's silence as confirmation. "We saw it going down. That's why Greg, Mike, and I crossed the border into Libya. We were look-ing for it, too."

"That explains why you were taken prisoner."

"A patrol found us. They . . . they killed Mike Duncan. Shot him dead for trying to come to my aid."

He could see tears glinting on her cheeks in the moonlight. Juan knew some women would want him to take them in his arms and comfort them, but there remained a defiant lift to Alana Shepard's chin. She didn't need his sympathy, only his help. His respect for her went up another notch.

"There's an important peace conference coming up," he said softly. "Her presence there would have pretty much guaranteed success."

"I know. It was the State Department that hired me to find Al-Jama's ship in the first place. They believed that some writing he left behind would help her during the meeting."

"So this isn't just about archaeology?" She shook her head. "Tell me everything from the beginning."

It took only a few minutes for her to lay out the story, from her summons to Christie Valero's office at the State Department to meeting with her and St. Julian Perlmutter to her capture by what she thought had been a routine border patrol.

"I know Perlmutter by reputation," Juan mentioned when she finished. "He's perhaps the best maritime researcher in the world, and if he's convinced the *Saqr*'s still buried in the desert that's good enough for me. I wonder why he didn't take this to NUMA. I thought he was some sort of consultant with them."

"I don't know. I'd never heard of him before. I did get the impression that because of the diplomatic angle he thought the State Department should handle it."

"Still, should have been NUMA," Juan said, thinking back to the professionalism he'd encountered with that Agency over the years. "I've been meaning to ask, do you have any idea who the other detainees were back at the labor camp?"

"No," Alana admitted. "Greg might have. He speaks Arabic. Other than mealtimes, I was kept away from the men, and none of the women I tried to speak with understood English or the little bit of Spanish I know."

"Another mystery for another time," he mused. "Now it's time to call in the cavalry."

Cabrillo unbuckled his belt and lowered his pants to expose his upper thighs. He had been such an enigma to Alana since first rescuing her that nothing he did surprised her. There was an inch-long red scar on the thickest point of his quadriceps.

Without so much as a calming breath, Juan sliced open the scar with the throwing knife. Dark blood welled from the open lips of the wound.

"What are you doing?" she asked, now suddenly alarmed.

"There's a tracking device in my leg," he replied. "I can use it to signal my people to come get us."

He plunged two fingers into the gash, fishing around, his mouth tight and set against the pain. A moment later, he withdrew the device, a black plastic object the size and shape of a cheap digital watch. He wiped its underside against his uniform shirt, waited silently for about thirty seconds to elapse, and then pressed it into the blood trickling out of his leg. He repeated what he'd just done, and then started moving quicker, dabbing and wiping so his hands were in constant motion.

"U . . . P . . . H . . . U . . . X," he said, transmitting each letter.

Like a desert djinn rising up from the ground, a spectral figure leapt over the rock parapet sheltering Juan and Alana. It crashed into Juan, the impact sending the slippery transmitter skittering off into the dark. Bony fingers clawed for his neck, the sharp nails digging into his flesh.

With an oozing wound in his leg and his pants pulled down to his knees, Cabrillo was at a complete disadvantage. The filthy creature made a guttural screech as it tried to ram its knees into Juan's chest while its feet raked across his legs like a cat trying to eviscerate its prey. Nails as tough as horn ripped out trenches of Juan's skin.

The Kel-Tec pistol was buried inside the pocket of his bunched-up pants, and the knife was out of reach. Juan reared his head back as far as he could and smashed it into his attacker's nose. He didn't have the leverage to break bone, so he had to find satisfaction in the spurts of blood that began to patter across his face and the howl of pain his blow elicited.

He twisted onto his stomach under the figure, gathered his legs under him, and thrust upward with everything he had. The creature was thrown from his back, sailing across the bowl and smashing into the far side. Cabrillo had already crouched and rolled to grab the knife, and he had it in his hand and cocked by the time the monstrosity crumpled into an untidy heap.

His knife arm came down, the blade glinting, and it would have flown true had two things not occurred to Cabrillo at the last instant. His attacker had been unbelievably light, and the man was dressed in the same rags he'd seen the prisoners wearing. It was too late to stop the throw, but he managed to angle it ever so slightly. The blade embedded itself into the sandstone an inch from the man's head.

Five seconds had passed since Juan was first attacked. In that time, Alana had managed to raise her hands to her mouth in alarm and nothing more.

Juan blew out a breath.

"Oh my God," Alana gasped. "Greg told me two prisoners escaped a couple of days ago. They only brought back one."

Juan considered the odds that they would come across the only other human within twenty miles and guessed they were actually pretty good. He had put the camp directly behind him as he and Alana had struck out, and they had followed the easiest terrain to gain distance. It had been the most logical choice, and the prisoner had done the exact same thing.

They had obviously moved faster than the man, and, considering his wasted condition, it was no surprise. The miracle was that he had made it this far at all. He must have been using the hillock as an observation post, spotted Alana and Juan walking toward him, and remained hidden until Cabrillo was at his most vulnerable.

Juan shuffled over to the prisoner and reached out a hand for Alana to pass him the canteen.

"Drink," Juan said in Arabic. "We're not going to hurt you."

Under the dirt and grime and weeks of matted beard, he saw the guy was about his own age, with a strong nose and broad forehead. His cheeks were hollow from hunger and dehydration, and his eyes had a dull sheen. But he had had the strength to hike this far and launch a pretty well thought out assault. Cabrillo was impressed.

"You've done well, my friend," he said. "Our rescue is close at hand."

"You are Saudi," the man rasped after drinking half the canteen. "I recognize your accent."

"No, I learned Arabic in Riyadh. I'm actually American."

"Praise be to Allah."

"And to His Prophet, Muhammad," Juan added.

"Peace be upon him. We are saved."

"We?"

TWENTY-ONE

JUAN NEVER TRANSMITTED AGAIN AFTER THE SALUTATION Julia had laboriously transcribed, so Max made the decision to have Linc, Linda, and Mark head to his final coordinates in the Pig.

It took the trio two hours of hard driving to reach the area.

Hanley was in the op center. The ship's computer was maintaining their position so there was no need for anyone other than a skeleton watch to be in the high-tech room, but a dozen men and women sat in the chairs or leaned against the walls. The only sounds were the rush of air through the vents and the occasional slurp of coffee. Eric Stone was at the helm, while next to him George Adams lolled in Mark Murphy's weapons station. With his matinee-idol looks and flight suit, the chopper pilot cut a dashing figure. He was one of the best poker players on the ship, after the Chairman himself, and his only tell was that he toyed with his drooping gunfighter mustache when he was really nervous. At the pace he was going on this night, he would have twisted the hair off his lip in another hour.

The main monitor over their heads showed a view of the predawn darkness outside the ship. There was the merest hint of color to the east. Not so much light but the absence of pitch-black. A smaller screen displayed the Pig's progress. The glowing dots representing the Pig and Juan's last position were millimeters apart.

When a phone rang, everyone startled. The tech sitting in Hali Kasim's communications center glanced at Max. Max nodded, and fitted a headset around his ears and adjusted the microphone.

"Hanley," he said, making sure to keep any concern out of his voice. He wouldn't give Juan the satisfaction of knowing how worried he'd been.

"Ah, Max. Langston Overholt."

Max grunted in irritation at the unexpected call. "You've caught us at a rather bad moment, Lang."

"Nothing serious, I hope."

"You know us. It's always serious. So are you at the tail end of a late night or just getting an early start?" It was midnight in Washington, D.C.

"To be honest, I don't even know anymore. It's all blended into one of the longest few days of my life."

"It's gotta be bad, then," Max said. "You were in the company during the Cuban Missile Crisis."

"Back then, I was still so wet behind the ears they wouldn't give me the code for the executive washroom."

Max Hanley and Langston Overholt had come from opposite poles of the American experience. Max was blue-collar all the way. His father had been a union machinist at a California aircraft plant, his mother a teacher. His commands during Vietnam had come through merit and ability. Overholt, on the other hand, had been born into a family from such old money they still considered the Astors nouveau riche. He was the result of twelve years of prep school, four years of Harvard, and three more of Harvard Law. Yet the two men had a strong respect for each other.

"Now I think one of the stalls is named after you," Max quipped.

"Enjoy your normal prostate while it lasts, my friend."

"So, what's up?"

"Libyans are reporting that a fighter jockey on a nighttime training exercise spotted something in the desert just inside their border with Tunisia. A patrol was sent out and discovered a secret base equipped with a Hind helicopter. The place had been hit hard. The gunship was destroyed, and there appeared to be no survivors."

"Yeah, I was meaning to tell you about that. Our people stumbled onto it. They took out the Hind and determined it had been modified to fire air-to-air missiles, specifically the"—he looked to Eric, who mouthed "Apex"—"Apex. It's Russkie-built."

"Damn it, Max, you should have told me about that when I told you Professor Bumford had been kidnapped."

"No offense, Lang, but you hired us to find the Secretary of State. I consider everything else to be collateral."

Max knew Overholt had to be calming himself, because he didn't say anything for almost thirty seconds. Max wasn't concerned. They hired the Corporation because they had no place else to turn. How missions were accomplished, the recent fiasco in Somalia notwithstanding, was up to his and Juan's discretion.

"You're right. Sorry. Sometimes I forget you guys get to operate with a level of autonomy I can only dream of."

"Don't worry about it. So what's this about the chopper?"

"The Libyans claim they found a computer buried under the command tent, or what was left of it."

Max opened his mouth to say that his people had gone over the site, but he knew their search was relatively cursory. Instead, he asked, "What was on the computer?"

"Links tying the chopper to Suleiman Al-Jama for one thing, and indications that they've opened a terrorist training camp right under the Libyans' noses using a dummy company purportedly opening up an old coal mine."

Max and Eric Stone shared a significant look. This was exactly as they had discussed the night before.

"How are we getting this information?" Hanley asked.

"Through a deliberate leak to the CIA station chief in Tripoli, a guy named Jim Kublicki. His contact is an opposite number in the JSO, the—"

"Jamahiriya Security Organization. We know who they are. How good is his source?"

"Given the level of cooperation we've gotten from the Libyans leading up to the summit and the help they provided trying to find Fiona Katamora's plane, I'd say pretty good."

"Or it could all be a trick. The damned Libyans could be into this up to their necks."

"Not according to the rest of my news."

"Max," the duty communications officer interrupted, "there's a call coming in from the Pig."

Max glanced at the overhead screen. The dot representing the Pig and the one for Cabrillo's last known location overlapped. "Wait one sec, Lang. Go ahead, patch through the new call. This is Hanley."

"Good morning, Max."

By the tone in Juan Cabrillo's voice, Hanley knew the Chairman was okay. "Hold the line, Juan." He flipped circuits back to Overholt. "Continue, Lang."

"What was that all about?"

"Nothing. Just Juan checking in. He can hold. What's the news that'll convince me this isn't the JSO or some other faction pulling a fast one?"

"Because the Libyans are going to hit the training camp in about two hours. Jim Kublicki is at one of their Air Force bases suiting up now to accompany them in a chopper for verification. If that's not enough, there's the possibility that Fiona Katamora is at the base as we speak. Also, the computer provided a clue to track down Al-Jama himself. The chopper and other equipment were funneled into the country with the help of a corrupt harbor pilot named Tariq Assad. They have a record that such a guy exists and has worked for the harbor authority for five years, but there's nothing in their system before then. No school records. No employment records. Nothing. They believe this Assad is actually a cover name for Al-Jama himself, and are already on their way to grab him."

The look Max and Eric exchanged this time was one of absolute horror.

Juan and the others were twenty-five miles from the terrorist training camp. They had more than enough time to find decent cover before the Libyan assault. The horror the two men shared stemmed from the fact that Eddie Seng and Hali Kasim had been shadowing Tariq Assad since the night the *Oregon* docked. With stakes as high as they were, Juan hadn't entirely trusted their Cypriot facilitator, *L'Enfant*, so he had ordered his best covert operative, Seng, and his only Arab, Kasim, to watch the man for any signs of treachery.

Other than the fact that Assad spent money like water on a string of mistresses all over Tripoli, they hadn't discovered anything suspicious. This was why the deadly shoot-out at the roadblock on the way out of the city that first night had been dismissed as a coincidence. Now Max realized Assad had set them up from the beginning.

Depending on how wide a net the JSO threw to capture him, Eddie and Hali were in real danger of being drawn into it.

Hanley finally found his voice. "Lang, what you've given me changes our tactical picture a hundred and eighty degrees. I need to coordinate with Juan or we're going to be in a world of hurt."

"Okay. Keep me pos—"

Max cut him off and switched phone lines. "Juan, you still there?"

"I don't know if I want to talk to you anymore," Cabrillo said, trying to sound sulky.

"We got trouble, my friend."

The gravity in Max's voice killed any of the playful relief Juan harbored from being rescued by Linc, Linda, and Mark. "What's happened?"

"The Libyans are two hours away from attacking the training camp where you just were. They think the Secretary might be there, so this is both a search-and-destroy mission and a rescue attempt. On top of that, they are going to arrest Tariq Assad because he's Suleiman Al-Jama."

"What about the mine?" Juan snapped.

"I'm not sure," Max admitted. "Why?"

Cabrillo didn't answer. Hanley could hear him breathing over the secure radio link. He understood the Chairman and knew he must be making a tough choice.

"Damn," Juan muttered, and then his voice firmed. "First thing is to get word to Eddie and Hali to watch themselves."

"Eric's on that now."

"There are more than two hundred tangos garrisoned at that training camp. If Fiona Katamora's there—which she may well be, for all I know—she is as good as dead. It'll take the Libyan strike force twenty or thirty minutes to secure the camp, plenty of time for someone to put a bullet in her head. We've got to even the odds."

"How?"

"I'm working on it. Where are you guys?"

"About eighty miles off the coast."

"And we've got two hours?"

"More or less."

"Okay, Max, I don't want to hear you grumble about your precious engines, but I need you on the coast as fast you can get here. Sound general quarters, and put Gomez Adams on fifteen-minute alert."

"Helm, give me emergency power," Max shouted. "All ahead flank. Get us to the coaling station dock. Don't worry, Juan. We'll get you out of there."

●　●　●

STRETCHED OUT on the back bench of the Pig, with Linc stitching up his leg under local anesthetic, Cabrillo looked across the front seat at the Libyan prisoner he and Alana had saved. Fodl was his name, and already the salt tablets and liter bottles of water he'd consumed had revived him tremendously.

"Yes, you will," Juan said to Fodl and Max. "All of us."

TWENTY-TWO

IN A COUNTRY THAT FOR ALL INTENTS AND PURPOSES WAS one hundred percent ethnically homogenous, Eddie Seng should have been at a disadvantage when the Chairman had given him and Hali Kasim the job of tailing their harbor pilot. He hadn't complained, though. Like Juan, he felt there was something suspicious about Assad, some quality that had made the hairs on the back of his neck stand erect.

Having a suspicion and proving it were two separate things, though, and there was no getting around the fact that every one of Eddie's relatives going back a couple hundred generations was Chinese and nearly all the people walking the streets of Tripoli were born in the Middle East.

But it wasn't quite all bad. There wasn't a city on the planet that didn't have an enclave of Chinese immigrants. And on that first night, while Hali trailed Tariq Assad, carrying a hand-lettered card proclaiming he was a mute to cover the fact that he spoke no Arabic, Eddie had gone off in search of Tripoli's Chinatown.

What he found came as a shock, though, upon reflection, it shouldn't have been. Buoyed by petrodollars, Libya, and especially

Tripoli, was undergoing a building boom, and a number of the projects were being erected by construction firms out of Hong Kong and Shanghai. Apart from the workers brought in, there was also a large support system of restaurants, bars, shops, and brothels, catering strictly to a Chinese clientele, that was nearly indistinguishable from Eddie's New York Chinatown home.

And, like New York, there were both legitimate and illegitimate layers of society. It had taken him only a few minutes of wandering to find gang symbols that he recognized spray-painted on a couple of the storefronts. And a few minutes more to see the symbol he wanted. It was small, just a few inches tall, and was sprayed in red paint on an otherwise plain gray metal door. The door was set in a heavy-duty structure of a warehouse, with a row of windows running only along the second floor.

Eddie knocked, using a code he knew from home. No one answered the door, so he knocked again, this time as a civilian would, a few hard raps with his knuckles. Judging by the dull echo he heard, he guessed the door was solid steel.

The door creaked open after a few seconds, and a boy of about ten poked his head around the jamb. There would be three or four armed men just out of sight. The boy didn't say a word.

Neither did Eddie.

He pulled out the tails of his shirt and turned, exposing his back up to the shoulder blades.

The boy gasped aloud, and suddenly Eddie felt other eyes on him. He slowly lowered his shirt again and faced the door. He took it as a good sign that the two gang members now studying him had their pistols lowered.

"Who are you?" one asked.

"A friend," Eddie replied.

"Who gave you the tattoo?" asked the second.

Eddie glanced at him with as much disdain as he dared. "No one gave it to me. I earned it."

On his back was inked an elaborate, though now-faded, tattoo of a dragon fighting a griffin. It was an old gang symbol of the Green Dragon Tong, from when they had battled a rival gang for control of the Shanghai docks back in the 1930s. Only senior members of the Tong or especially brave foot soldiers were allowed it on their skin, and, given the global reach of the Chinese underworld, Eddie had known it would gain him entrée here.

He just hoped they didn't test it because Kevin Nixon had applied the stencil only a few hours earlier from a catalog of gang and prison tattoos he kept aboard the *Oregon*.

"What are you doing here?" the first thug asked.

"There's a man who works at the harbor. He owes people I represent a great deal of money. I want to hire some of your guys to help me keep an eye on him until it's time to collect."

"You have money?"

Eddie didn't bother to answer. No one in their right mind would make such a request without being able to pay for it. "Four or five days. Eight or ten guys. Ten thousand dollars."

"Too tough to exchange. Make it euros. Ten thousand."

With the currency rates the way they were, that was almost fifty percent more. Eddie nodded.

And, just like that, he had enough men to keep Tariq Assad under twenty-four-hour watch, while he and Hali waited in a flea-bag hotel that the Tong controlled. The gang supplied updates on Assad's movements every six hours via disposable cell phones, so over the course of a few days they had a pretty good pattern of his movements.

Generally, Assad worked eight hours on the night shift at the dock, though he would usually take off for a couple if no ships were expected. On those nights, he went to an apartment not too far from the harbor where he kept a mistress. She wasn't the prettiest of the ones he frequented, but she was the most convenient.

After work he went home to be with his family, slept maybe six hours, and then went out to have coffee with coworkers before visiting other apartments dotted around Tripoli. Eddie asked his new employees to put together a list of the women's names, and when he asked Eric Stone to cross-reference them using the *Oregon*'s computer it came back that Assad was bedding the wives of midlevel government employees. Even the plain girl near the harbor was the sister of the deputy director of the Energy Ministry.

Given that Assad wasn't particularly attractive by anyone's standards, his conquests were all the more impressive.

Eddie and Hali both concluded that Assad was nothing more than a mildly corrupt harbor pilot with an overactive libido and one hell of a pickup line. That was until Max Hanley called with his bombshell announcement. Assad's ingratiation into the bedrooms of Libya's government took on a whole new and darker aspect.

•   •   •

JUAN LISTENED OVER THE phone as Eric Stone described the route the old rail spur took through the mountains toward the coast, twenty-odd miles away. The satellite pictures didn't give the gradient of the line, but Juan's tracking chip had put him at nearly a thousand feet above sea level when he'd gotten off the helicopter at the terrorists' training camp.

From the outline of a plan that was forming in his mind even as Eric spoke, Cabrillo decided it was going to be one hell of a wild ride.

Worse, though, the timing was going to be incredibly tight, and he could think of no excuse he could have Overholt pass on to the Libyans to delay their assault without tipping his hand.

Adding to his problems, he hadn't slept more than six hours out of the past forty-eight, and, judging by the appearance of his three shipmates, they weren't faring much better.

"What is it?" Linc asked, his surgical gloves covered with blood as he finished the last of the tight stitches. He had sewn the cut in Juan's leg by layering three rows of catgut, moving from the deepest part of the wound out to the skin, so there was no way it would reopen. With a local anesthetic keeping the pain to a dull ache, Juan felt confidence in his body's abilities.

"What?"

"You just chuckled," Linc replied, snapping off the gloves and stuffing them into a red biohazard-containment box.

"Did I? I was just thinking that we are so deep over our heads right now I don't know if what I have in mind is going to work."

"Not another of your infamous plan C's?" Linda groaned. She stood just outside of the Pig, looking over Linc's massive shoulder.

"That's why I laughed. Gallows humor. We're well past C and into D, E, or F."

There were two options facing Cabrillo but no real choices. He was about to put them all into a shooting gallery, with the Pig playing the role of sitting duck.

Linc duct-taped a gauze pad over Juan's wound, and said, "If Doc Huxley has a problem with my work, tell her to take it up with your HMO."

Juan struggled back into his pants. They were ripped in a dozen places, and so crusted with sand that they crackled when he drew them over his hips, but the Pig didn't carry any spare uniforms. He did a couple of deep knee bends when he leapt to the ground. The cut was tight, but both the stitches and the anesthesia held.

The sun had yet to show itself over the distant mountains, so the stars blazed cold and implacable overhead. Cabrillo studied them for a second, wondering—and not for the first time—if he would live to see them again.

"Mount up," he called. "The show's gonna be mostly over by the time the *Oregon* arrives, and we've got a lot of grim work ahead of us."

"Just curious, Juan," Linc said casually. "Who are these people we're going to rescue? Political prisoners, common criminals, what?"

"I think maybe they're the key to this whole thing."

Linc gave a little nod. "All right."

"If you ask me," Mark said and started to add, "I've got a bad feeling about—"

Cabrillo cut him off with a look.

Forty-eight minutes, by Juan's watch, ticked by before he judged they were ready. Barely. He had seen the quality of the guards looking after the prisoners and knew they weren't a serious threat in small numbers, but there were forty or so of them, and if his timing was off the two hundred more he hoped to lure from the training camp would reach the mine before everyone had made good their escape.

On their approach to the mine, they had left Linc to make his way to higher ground overlooking the stockyard behind the old administration buildings. With a Barrett .50 caliber sniper rifle, the ex-SEAL could have accurately hit targets from well over a mile away. His effective range with the smaller REC7 assault rifle was still an impressive seven hundred yards, and for what Juan had planned Linc would be taking significantly shorter shots than that. The Pig was just out of sight of the mining camp, atop the narrow trail where the day before the desert patrol had returned with the body of the escapee.

Dawn was a brushstroke in the distance, so darkness filled the hollows and gullies around them, and the air carried the chill of the distant sea.

Juan wished there was a way he could leave Alana and their new companion, Fodl, out of the fight, but he couldn't risk leaving them in the desert in case he and his team couldn't return. He had explained his plan to them, made sure they understood the dangers involved, and both were ready to do whatever he asked of them.

"Just so you fit in with all the other archaeologist-adventurers out there, I'll get you a fedora," he said, and smiled at Alana when she had told him she was game.

"And a whip?" she'd joked back.

"Kinky," he'd admonished with another grin.

"Comm check," Linc called over the tactical net.

"I've got you five by five, big man."

"I'm on top of the old ore-loading structure," the sniper reported. "The guards are starting to roust the prisoners for breakfast. It's now or never."

"Roger," Juan replied, and swallowed hard, his throat suddenly as dry as the desert sand. He looked across the driver's seat to Mark Murphy. The success or failure of Juan's plan hinged on Murph's virtuosity with the Pig's weapons systems. "Ready?"

Mark nodded.

"Tallyho!" Juan said.

Mark keyed up the Pig's roof-mounted mortars. They had already been sighted in with Linc's help, using a laser range finder. They fired simultaneously, and the weapon's autoloader had a second round dropped into each of the four tubes before the first rounds had traveled a hundred yards on their high, arcing parabolas.

The second fusillade launched with a comically hollow sound, and Mark shouted, "Go!"

Juan already had the Pig's engine revved, so that when he dropped it into gear, all four tires spun. They roared over a ridge, and the camp came into view. As he'd planned, no one had heard the mortars fire. Ragged prisoners were lining up for their pitifully small breakfast while guards casually harassed them. He saw one guard use a baton on a man, crashing it into the man's kidneys so hard his back bent like a bow at full stretch and he collapsed in the dust.

The mortar rounds hit the apex of their flight and started barreling earthward, each packed with a kilo of high explosives. Mark had spent part of the drive to the camp removing most of the shrapnel from each round to minimize the chance of hitting any of the detainees.

Linc laid the crosshairs of his REC7 on the guard who'd just clubbed the prisoner, let out half a breath, and squeezed the trigger. "We have pink mist," he reported when the guard's head exploded.

He took out another pair of guards before the first ripple of concern passed through the security contingent. The captain of the guards appeared from a tent. His chest was bare, and he wore his uniform pants bloused into his combat boots. Linc noted the radio antennae sticking up through a hole in the tent's roof and moved his aim onto another target.

Four mortar rounds struck the ground at precisely the same instant. The path leading down to the floor of the open-pit mine erupted in geysers of dirt and greasy fire. A moment later, more rounds hit even closer to the camp.

Both guards and prisoners alike pulled back, moving toward the large wooden buildings, while Linc continued to thin the ranks of terrorists, one shot—one kill—at a time. He made the ones carrying weapons his priority.

Cabrillo raced the Pig down on the camp like a rally driver dashing for the finish line. Next to him, Murph fought to keep the aiming reticle of the Pig's onboard missiles locked on one of the terrorists' trucks. He got tone and fired.

The rocket screamed off the rails, carving an erratic path through the air, and exploded against the truck's cab, snapping its chassis in half so it rose up like a ship that had been torpedoed.

The blast further corralled the frightened prisoners closer to the building, while the guards were rushing back to their tents where many had left their automatic weapons.

The Pig was a hundred yards from the camp when the freshly armed terrorists started running from the tents, brandishing their AKs and firing long strings of rounds in random directions. Up in the Pig's cupola, Linda watched them over the sights of her M60 machine gun. The weapon bucked in her arms, slamming into her shoulder like the business end of a jackhammer, but her aim never wavered.

The ground around the running gunmen came alive as rounds blew into their midst. Men fell, clutching at horrendous wounds, some struck by their own comrades who had whirled at this new threat and opened fire indiscriminately.

"He's had enough time," Juan yelled over the snarling engine. "Take out the command tent."

Cabrillo's plan had two goals. The first was to rescue as many of the prisoners as he could because he wasn't sure if the Libyan military would take the time to discern friend from foe. He wasn't even sure of their definition of those terms at this point. The second objective was to get as many terrorists as possible away from their training camp before the main attack. If Fiona Katamora was really there, then every gunman engaged at the mine was one less gunman trying to kill her before she was rescued.

This was why Linc had been told specifically to let the mine's garrison commander contact the training camp on the radio. They needed him to raise the alarm. But now that he had . . .

Mark put a missile through the command tent's front flap at just the right angle for it to hit the ground before it flew through the far side. The canvas rose up on a blossoming column of flame, and the piles of military gear stacked outside were blown flat by the concussion. The tent caught fire like flash paper and turned to ash that fell to the ground like dirty snow.

They were deep into the camp now. Above Juan and Murph, Linda continued to work the M60, taking out clusters of guards and using the tracer rounds to keep the prisoners moving toward the stockyard where the terrorists stored their railcars and train engines.

Cabrillo could tell that the guards' will had been broken by the sudden and furious assault. Many of them were running down into the mine or over the ridge and into the desert. Fifty or more prisoners were huddled against the side of the old mine office building. A gunman suddenly reared up from behind a bulldozer. He had a perfect bead on the defenseless men and women and an RPG-7 lifted to his shoulder.

Murph flipped the controls from missiles to gun, and the .30 cal under the Pig's snout chattered. The terrorist went down, but not before he fired his rocket-propelled grenade. The five-pound missile made it less than ten feet from the tube before it inexplicably exploded in midair.

"Damn, Linc," Juan said in awe, "was that you?"

"It's all a matter of knowing how to read them," Linc replied. He would later admit that he was shooting at the terrorist and the rocket flew into his bullet.

Juan whipped the Pig around the side of the building, braking hard so the big truck slid onto a set of tracks, its tail resting just a couple of feet from a boxcar with a handwheel on its roof for brakemen to mechanically slow the antique rolling stock. The track was a good foot narrower than the Pig's tires. Juan searched the dash for a second and found the control that could alter the vehicle's ground clearance by pulling in the wheels on articulated suspension joints.

He had to jockey the truck back and forth, as the wheels drew inward, until they were resting directly on the rails, and there was a full two feet of open space between the chassis and the crushed-rock ballast on the ground.

With another button, Juan deactivated the automatic tire-inflation system and then jumped from the cab. "Mark, Linda, get busy," he called over the tactical radio. "Linc, cover them. Fodl, with me."

He grabbed up a REC7 assault rifle, and had the FN Five-seveN pistol in his hand when he hit the ground. He fired at the left-side tires. The truck's weight made them go flat instantly, and, just like that, the steel rims were cradled around the rails, with the rubber acting as extra grip. He couldn't prevent a satisfied smile. Mating the Pig to the railroad tracks had been the cornerstone of his plan.

He ran for the corner of the building as his new Libyan friend clambered out of the Pig still wearing his prisoner's rags. Across the compound, he could see a few guards hunting for targets, but for the moment no one was paying the detainees any attention.

A couple of them who were pressed against the building looked at Juan fearfully when they saw his weapon. Then Fodl appeared at his side.

"Come with us," Fodl told them with an aura of command that didn't surprise the Chairman. "These people are here to help."

A few of the emaciated prisoners stared back at him uncertainly. "Go. That is an order."

Like a breached levee, the few heading toward the railcar that Linda held open turned into a flood. Cabrillo stood at the corner, sweeping the compound for any interested guards. If any looked their way, he put them down, while next to him Fodl waved in more of his people. A group of women appeared from under the overturned serving tables and raced for the building, only to have someone open fire at them from their flank. One of the women went down before Juan could counterfire, hammering home a steady burst into a pyramid of crates from where the shots had originated.

The other women helped the injured girl to her feet, supporting her under her arms and making her almost hopscotch to safety.

"Bless you," one of them said to Juan as they passed around the building and into protective cover.

Another prisoner paused at Juan's side. He gave the man a passing glance and then returned to scanning the compound. The prisoner touched Juan's sleeve, and he looked at him more carefully. He wasn't an Arab like all the others. His hair and face were pale, although his skin was burned raw by the sun.

"You Chaffee?" Juan asked.

"Yes. How did you know?"

"You've got Alana Shepard to thank for your rescue."

Chaffee sagged with relief. "Thank God. We were told last night she was shot for trying to escape."

"Are you in any condition to fight?"

The CIA agent tried to pull himself erect. "Give me a gun and watch me."

Juan pointed to where Mark Murphy was securing the old boxcar to the Pig's rear tow hooks. From this distance, the train car looked massive and the chain as thin as a silver necklace, but there was nothing he could do about it. "Report to that guy over there. He'll take care of you."

"Thank you."

Cabrillo looked at his watch. Eight minutes since the first shot fired. They had less than ten more before a horde of gunmen arrived from the training camp, and just an hour until the Libyan military arrived and opened fire on anything that moved.

Prisoners continued to stream toward the railcar, and no matter how Juan tried to urge them to hurry they just couldn't. They were so far gone from their ordeal that even the offer of freedom couldn't make their bodies move faster than a painful shuffle. He could almost hear his watch ticking.

Glancing over his shoulder, Juan watched them climb into the train, each one pausing when he or she was inside to help the next in line.

It wasn't his watch Juan thought he heard. It was the rhythmic *whomp-whomp-whomp* of an approaching helicopter. George Adams was still twenty minutes out. It had to be the terrorists' Mi-8.

It didn't matter that the train car was full anyway, and only one old woman was struggling to make it to the railhead from across the compound, while behind her tents and equipment burned, sending columns of smoke into the pinking sky.

Time had run out.

TWENTY-THREE

WHEN BULLETS PEPPERED THE GROUND IN THE OLD WOMAN'S wake, Cabrillo was slapping home a fresh magazine into the underside of his assault rifle. He hadn't expended the first, so there was no need to cock the weapon.

To Juan, at this moment, the more than one hundred people crowded into the boxcar didn't matter. Only the old woman.

It was perhaps a fault in his logic, a synapse that fired a little off. He made no distinction between the needs of the many versus the needs of the few. At that moment, her life meant as much to him as all the others.

He broke cover and fired from the hip, laying down a blistering barrage that silenced the terrorist's gun. The woman had frozen in place. *Deer caught in headlights*, flashed through Juan's mind.

He reached her in a dozen long strides, ducking as he approached so he could scoop her up over his left shoulder without pausing. She was a solid one hundred and eighty pounds, despite the starvation diet, and must have tipped the scales at two-fifty before her ordeal. Juan staggered under the weight, his wounded leg almost buckling. The woman gave a startled yelp but didn't struggle, as Cabrillo started back for the building, running awkwardly, half turning to watch their rear, his rifle held one-handed.

The woman suddenly screamed. Juan twisted back. A guard had appeared out of nowhere. He was armed only with a club, a suicide charge, but Cabrillo's rifle was still pointed in the wrong direction. As he spun, the old woman's feet missed the guard's head by inches, and when Juan came around to get his REC7 aimed the woman used his momentum to fire a solid punch to the guard's chin an instant before the club crashed down on her exposed neck.

The terrorist staggered back and was starting forward again when a round from Linc in the loading tower drilled him to the ground.

"Lady," Juan panted in Arabic, "you've got a right cross like Muhammad Ali."

"I always thought George Foreman had a better punch," she replied.

He almost dropped her when he started to laugh. He dumped her into the boxcar and nodded to Linda to slam the rolling door closed. "Murph, you set?" he called over the radio.

The sound of the approaching chopper grew by the second.

"I'm good to go."

"Linc, get ready. We're rolling in thirty seconds."

On his way to the passenger's seat, Mark Murphy flattened the Pig's right-side tires. It took him two shots each despite the point-blank range. Linda had already helped Fodl into the rear cargo compartment, and Greg Chaffee stood with his head and torso thrust out of the open top hatch.

Juan threw himself into the driver's seat. Ahead of them loomed a diesel-electric locomotive, a huge machine capable of hauling strings of ore cars up and down the mountain. He would have been concerned about it following them, but its engines were cold and would take at least a half hour to get running at temperature.

Max Hanley had designed the Pig with a twenty-four-gear transmission. Juan dropped it into low range and selected the lowest of the four reverse gears. Pressing his foot to the accelerator, he felt and heard the engine revs build while the twin turbos screamed. The railcar behind them weighed eighteen thousand pounds, according to the faded stencil on its side, and packed within was another five tons of humanity. From a dead stop, he had no idea if he could get such a load moving.

The truck shuddered as the deflated tires slipped against the slick steel rails.

Juan unclipped a safety device attached to the floor shifter and pushed down on a red knob. From the integrated NOS, nitrous oxide flowed into the engine's cylinders, breaking down in the extreme heat and releasing additional oxygen for combustion.

The Pig didn't have the torque, as Max had boasted, "to push the *Oregon* up Niagara Falls," but the two-hundred-horsepower boost provided by the nitrous oxide was the kick Juan needed to overcome the train's static inertia.

Starting out at barely a snail's pace, the Pig started pushing the laden railcar along the track, and each foot gained increased their speed fractionally. The digital speedometer on the dash ticked to one mile per hour, and had reached three when the train began to pass under the skeletal support frame of the old coal-loading station where Linc had made his sniper's nest.

When the Chairman had radioed they were ready to go, Linc had climbed down from the top of the rusted conveyor belt and stood poised over the open mouth of a coal chute straddling the tracks. The leading edge of the car rolled into view, and he dropped through space, landing and tumbling in one smooth motion. The coaling station had been designed for low-slung hopper cars, not the tall, boxy freight car, and as he pressed himself up to get to his feet he spotted the razor-sharp edge of another coal chute about to slice his head off.

He dropped flat, the chute passing an inch above his nose, and he remained perfectly still as they accelerated under a dozen more. Only when they had cleared the rusted bulk of the loading station did he dare draw a breath. "I'm aboard," he radioed.

"Good," Juan answered. "You've got more time behind the wheel of this thing. Get your butt down here and drive."

For the first mile out of the mine, the ground was dead level, and the Pig was accelerating smoothly, so Juan hit the cruise control and unlimbered himself from his seat. In the cargo bed, he stuffed extra magazines for his Barrett REC7 into his pant pocket. "How are you two holding up?" he asked Alana and Fodl without looking at them.

"You have given me hope for the first time in six months," the Libyan replied. "I have never felt better."

"Alana?" he asked, finally able to give her his attention. He'd strapped a double holster around his waist for a pair of FN Five-seveNs.

"I haven't done anything to deserve that fedora yet."

"You've done plenty."

"Ah, who's driving the train?" Linc asked as he lowered himself past Greg Chaffee and spotted Juan.

"First corner isn't for another half mile or more. We do this exactly like we talked about and we should make it. Oh, damn," Cabrillo said, suddenly remembering something. He ducked his head back into the Pig's cab. "Mark, the boxcar weighs nine tons. Throw in another five for the people. Math it."

"I need its dimensions."

"Guess."

Mark looked at him, incredulous. "Guess? Are you kidding?"

"Nope."

" 'Math it,' he says," Mark griped to Juan's departing form. " 'Guess.' Jeesh!"

Juan climbed out onto the Pig's roof. He estimated they were up to fifteen miles per hour and continuing to accelerate. So far, so good, he thought briefly before looking up and seeing no sign of the helicopter.

He stepped aft and was bracing himself to leap up onto the box-car's roof when Greg Chaffee opened up with the M60. Cabrillo turned to see a camouflaged truck careen toward the stockyard. It was the first of the terrorists from the training camp. There were a dozen holding on to the rails of the truck's open bed. Their gun barrels bristled.

The road they were on clung to the side of a hill running a little above and parallel to the rail line. Chaffee had been quick with the machine gun, firing at the truck's tires before the driver had regained full control of the vehicle. Rounds peppered the area near the front tire until it exploded, shedding rubber like a Catherine wheel throws sparks.

The truck swerved when the mangled rim gouged into the soft gravel shoulder. The men in back started to scream as the vehicle tipped further. Still moving dangerously fast, the truck flipped onto its side, skidding down the hill. Some of the terrorists were thrown clear, others clutched the supports to keep themselves inside when it rolled onto its roof. The cab plowed a furrow into the earth before it flipped again, barrel-rolling violently, sheet metal and men peeling away in a cloud of dust.

A second desert-patrol vehicle appeared before the first had settled back on its ruined undercarriage. The driver of this one caught a break. Greg Chaffee had blown through the last of the ammunition in the belt and stood impotently as Linda showed him how to swap it out. The truck dashed down the hill and braked for cover behind the hulking shadow of the locomotive. The men in the bed opened fire at extreme range, and a few lucky hits were close enough to make Linda and Chaffee duck.

Cabrillo had lost precious seconds watching the spectacle and roused himself with an angry shudder. The boxcar's roof was four feet above his head, and he needed a running start to launch himself so he hit the edge with his chest. Kicking at the smooth metal sides and straining with his arms, he hauled himself atop the car and looked forward. The first curve was a quarter mile away, and they had sped up to at least twenty miles an hour.

He knew from the map Eric had e-mailed from the *Oregon* that this was a long, sweeping corner taking the tracks around the very top of this mountain and that the grade started to fall away as soon as they entered it. Twenty miles an hour was okay going in, but if they continued to accelerate eventually they would lose control of the boxcar.

Juan moved all the way to the front of the car where a rusted, four-spoked metal wheel gave him control over the car's mechanical brakes. In the days before George Westinghouse invented his fail-safe pneumatic-braking system, teams of brakemen would ride atop trains and turn devices like this one to squeeze the pads against the wheels in an uncoordinated and often deadly ballet. Cabrillo prayed as he grasped the wheel that it wasn't frozen solid by rust, and that after the decades the car had been used on the line there were any brake pads remaining.

Prepared to heave with all his strength, he cursed when the wheel spun freely in his hands. It felt like it wasn't connected to anything, but then he heard the squeal of metal on metal as the old brakes clamped over the top of the car's wheels. They worked after all and had been recently greased. Grinning at his luck, he cranked the wheel another half turn, and his elation turned to dismay. The added pressure should have tightened the brake pads further and changed the pitch of the screech coming from the wheels. It didn't happen.

They had brakes, yes. But not much.

The Pig pushed the freight car into the turn, and Juan lost sight of the ore-loading superstructure as it vanished around the hilltop. To his right, he had a commanding view over another valley and, as if to remind him of their predicament, a string of ore cars that had left the tracks a hundred years before at its bottom, looking like discarded toys. If he had to guess, the steam engine that had gone over with them probably had five times the Pig's horsepower.

"Linc, you there?" he radioed.

"Yes."

"What's our speed?"

"Twenty-eight."

"Okay, don't let it go past thirty. We don't have much braking left on the boxcar."

"Is that bad?" Linda asked over the net.

"It ain't good."

There were ladder rungs welded to the front of the car, so Cabrillo climbed over and down. Next to him was the shaft that linked the wheel above to a worm gear that activated the brakes. Juan hooked his legs around the forward coupling and braced one hand on a stanchion so he could peer under the edge of the car. Creosote-blackened railroad ties zipped by inches from where he dangled. A stone was lodged between the turning rod and the worm gear. When he twisted the wheel, the stone had kicked the gear's teeth out of alignment so it turned without activating the brakes. Redoubling his grip, he stretched until his chest was under the car. Weeds growing in the old railbed whipped his cheek and face.

His fingers sank into the grease that coated the gear, but no matter how he tried he couldn't get a grip on the tightly wedged stone chip.

"Screw this," he muttered, and reached behind his back for one of his automatic pistols.

His body swayed as he drew it, and for a moment he was looking up the tracks. A metal jerry can had fallen from an earlier train or been left between the rails by one of the work crews. Juan was hurtling toward it at more than thirty miles per hour and didn't have the time or leverage to pull himself clear. Hanging practically upside down, he aimed at the can and opened fire as fast as the gun would cycle. The high-velocity bullets from the FN Five-seveN punched through the can's thin sides without moving it. He was ten feet from having his face smashed into the container when a round caught on one of its corner seams and sent the can skittering harmlessly away.

He twisted back and fired the last round at the worm gear. The rock popped free and fell away.

"Now, that's what I'm talking about," he crowed, high on accomplishment and adrenaline.

"Repeat that, Chairman," Linc asked.

"Nothing. I think I've fixed the brakes." He straightened himself up and reached for the ladder. "What's our speed?"

"Thirty-four. I'm using the Pig's brakes, so that carbon-fiber dust is blowing off the pads something fierce."

"No problem. This is why we started in reverse. Throw her into first gear and start slowing us using the engine. I'll get on the brake up here, and between the two we should be okay."

Juan reached the top of the boxcar. They had dropped a hundred feet or so from the mountain's summit as they curled around its flank. Above them, the hillside was sparse scrub. Then he saw that there was a road that ran parallel to and slightly higher than the railbed. He only noticed it because of the dun-colored truck that emerged from around a bend and started pacing the train as it glided down the tracks.

A man with his head wrapped in a ubiquitous kaffiyeh stood bracing himself in the back of the truck. Cabrillo had left his REC7 on the boxcar's roof when he'd crawled down to fix the brakes. He lunged up and over the front of the car at the same instant the fanatic leapt from the speeding truck.

His defiant scream was lost in the wind as he arced though the air. Juan's fingers had closed around the rifle's barrel when the man crashed onto the roof close enough to send the weapon skidding toward the side. Jacked up on even more adrenaline than Cabrillo, the man shouted a battle cry and kicked Juan full in the face.

Cabrillo's world went dark in an instant, and only started returning in painfully slow increments. When Juan was somewhat conscious of what was happening, the terrorist had pulled his AK-47 from around his back and was just lining up. Juan rolled over and scissor-kicked his legs, twisting on the hot steel roof enough to catch the man in the shin. The AK stitched four holes into the roof next to Juan's head, and inside the car someone screamed out in pain.

Goaded beyond fury, Cabrillo reached up and grasped the weapon by its forward grip. As he pulled down, the gunman reared back and actually helped pull the Chairman to his feet. Juan fired two punches into the gunman's face. The Arab was so intent on keeping his weapon that he didn't defend himself. Juan landed two more solid blows, and over the terrorist's shoulder saw two more men preparing to leap for the train.

He rammed his elbow into his opponent's stomach as he rolled into him, turning them both so that when he grabbed at the guy's right hand and forced his finger onto the trigger the AK's barrel was pointed back at the truck. The spray of tracers caught one of the men just as he gathered himself to jump. He fell out of the side of the truck and vanished under its rear wheels, his body making the vehicle bounce slightly on its suspension.

The second man flew like a bird and landed on the roof with the agility of a cat.

Cabrillo continued to spin the first terrorist, and when he let go the guy staggered back one pace, two, and then there was no more train roof. He went cartwheeling into space, his headscarf coming unwound and fluttering after him like a distracted butterfly.

Juan threw his empty pistol at his new opponent and charged him before the man could pull his assault rifle across his body on its canvas sling. Juan hit the guy low and reared up, lifting him nearly five feet into the air before letting go. The gunman crashed onto the roof, his breath exploding from his body in a rancid gush. If his back wasn't broken, he was still out for the duration.

Unless Linda or Linc had noticed the first guy go over the side of the boxcar, they weren't at the right angle to see what was happening behind them, and with Juan's radio dislodged from his ear he had no way of warning them. The Pig was giving its all to slow the train, but without the addition of the car's brakes they continued to accelerate. Juan guessed they were nearing forty-five miles an hour. The grade remained at a constant downward slope and the curve was still gentle, but if they got going much faster he feared that they wouldn't be able to slow when they hit the first sharp corner.

Three more terrorists jumped for the boxcar. Two landed on the roof. A third smashed into its side, his fingers clawing at the edge of the roof to keep himself from falling off.

One of the gunmen caromed into Juan when he landed, grabbed him tight, and slammed a hardened fist deep into the Chairman's kidney. Cabrillo's grunt at the staggering pain drove the man into a frenzy. He fired two more punches, grinding his knuckles into Cabrillo's flesh with each impact. Juan then felt his second FN

Five-seveN being pulled from its holster. He shifted violently just as the man fired at his spine. The bullet singed the cloth of Cabrillo's shirt and hit the second terrorist in the throat. Blood fountained from the wound in time to the man's wildly beating heart.

The sight of his comrade's life pumping from his body might have distracted the gunman, but it held no sway over Cabrillo. Juan yanked his pistol free from the man's slack grip, stepped back a pace, and put two through his heart.

Both bodies hit the roof at the same instant.

"Juan? Juan? Come in."

Cabrillo reset his earpiece and adjusted the mike so he could communicate. "Yeah."

"We need brakes," Linc was shouting. "Now."

Juan looked forward. They were coming out of the turn, and the tracks dipped for a hundred yards before another sharper bend to the right. He ran for the brake wheel and was nearly there when the terrorist who he thought had a broken back threw out an arm and tripped him. Cabrillo went sprawling and didn't have time to recover before the guy was on him, throwing punches with abandon. There was no power behind the shots, but all Juan could do was defend himself while the train hurtled for the corner.

He felt the sudden dip in the line and knew he had seconds. He tucked his legs to his chest, managing to plant his feet on the terrorist's chest, and in a judo move threw him over his head. The guy crashed down onto the roof on his back. Juan spun and, using his right hand to power his left elbow, drove it into the man's throat. The crushing of cartilage, sinew, and tissue was nauseating.

The instant Juan's fingers grasped the metal wheel, he started spinning it with everything he had. They were doing fifty on a corner meant to be taken at thirty. The brakes screamed and threw off showers of sparks as they entered the turn. Too late, Juan knew. Way too late.

The centrifugal force made the boxcar light on its outside wheels, and despite its massive weight they started losing contact with the rails. Juan cranked the brake wheel until it was locked tight. Behind him, the Pig's engine roared with the flood of nitrous oxide Linc had dumped into the cylinders, and rubber smeared off the deflated tires when they spun against the steel tracks. The freight car's outside wheels bumped and lifted, bumped and lifted, gaining centimeters with each judder. He wished there was some way he could communicate to the men and women inside the car. Their weight could make all the difference.

Inspiration born of desperation made Juan snatch up one of the terrorist's AK-47s and step to the outside edge of the car. The valley stretched below him seemingly forever. He aimed along the length of the train and loosened a full magazine. The bullets hit the steel flank at such an angle that they all ricocheted off into space, but the din inside was enough to frighten the prisoners over to the opposite side of the car above the bouncing wheels.

Their weight cemented the train back to the tracks.

The boxcar shot out of the turn and onto another gentle stretch of line. Juan shook his head to clear it and was about to sit down to give his body a rest when Mark's panicked voice exploded in his ears. "Take off the brake! Hurry!"

Cabrillo started turning the wheel to take pressure off the pads and chanced a look behind them. The road was no longer visible, the truck loaded with flying terrorists out of the picture at least for now, but farther up the line, barreling down the tracks, was another truck that had been modified to run on the rails. Unburdened by thirteen tons of train car and people, it came toward them at breakneck speed. Over its cab, Juan could see more men eager for the fight, and even at this distance he could tell they were armed with rocket-propelled grenades.

The Pig's windshield was so badly cracked, it wouldn't hold up to autofire, so he had no illusions what an RPG would do.

Linc had the transmission back in reverse, forgoing the low-range gears for the higher ones in hopes that the truck's power and the rolling stock's momentum would be enough to buy them some time. So long as they continued to sway through the gentle bends, the terrorists couldn't take a shot.

"When's our next tight turn?" Juan asked. He knew Mark had a scrolling map going on his laptop slaved to the Pig's GPS tracker.

"Two miles."

"Missiles?"

"Only one."

"Keep it. I've got an idea."

Juan raced aft, leaping from the train car onto the Pig's roof. Linda had replaced Greg Chaffee on the M60. Chaffee was sitting down in the cargo area with Alana and Fodl. He looked spent. "The instructors at the Farm would be proud, especially . . ." Juan mentioned the name of a legendary staffer at the CIA's training center, a name known only to those who'd gone through it.

Chaffee's eyes widened. "You're . . . ?"

"Retired."

Juan popped the hinge pins from one of the cabinets built into the inside wall of the Pig. The door was three feet square and weighed about sixty pounds. He passed it up through the hatch with Linda's help and then crawled onto the Pig's cab. His timing didn't necessarily have to be that good, but his luck had to hold. The train-truck was a quarter mile distant, gaining fast. Someone on it spotted Cabrillo out in the open and fired with his AK. Juan hauled up the metal door, using it like a screen, and bullets pinged off it like lead rain, their kinetic energy like sledgehammer blows.

The Pig went into another shallow curve, just enough for their pursuers to lose sight of them. Juan slid the sheet steel down along the retreating truck's nearly vertical windshield and let go.

The metal plate hit the outside track with a ringing crash and slid for several long seconds before its lip caught a tie and it spun to a stop. It came to rest across one of the rails.

Thirty seconds later, the truck showed itself from around the corner. It had to be doing sixty miles an hour. This time the Pig was too tempting a target for the men with the RPGs, and several made ready to let fly.

TWENTY-FOUR

T HE DRIVER OF THE HYBRID TRAIN-TRUCK HAD JUST SECONDS to react, and in saving his life he saved Cabrillo and the others. He spotted the piece of sheet steel sitting on the track and recognized immediately that hitting it would cause a derailment. Stomping the brakes, he yanked a lever on the floor next to his seat. Hydraulics raised the train wheels that sat just inside the truck's regular tires, and as the wheels tucked under the chassis the outside tires made contact with the railroad ties.

Between the brutal deceleration and the staccato impact of running over the raised ties, the gunmen leaning over the cab readying their RPGs had no chance to accurately fire. Rocket contrails arrowed away from the truck in every direction—skyward, where they corkscrewed like giant fireworks, or into the valley below, where they detonated harmlessly in the desert.

The truck bounced over the metal plate, and once they were clear the quick-thinking driver had to slow even further in order to mate the steel train wheels with the track once again.

Cabrillo's idea had gained them only a half mile or so, not the outcome he had hoped. The next tight corner was coming up, and he had to return to the brake wheel. He climbed over the back of the Pig, nearly gagging at the smell of burning rubber from the shredded tires. They were at forty miles an hour again, and the wind made leaping up to the boxcar a tricky maneuver. Below him, he could see the darkened ties blur by in the tight gap between the Pig and her ponderous charge.

The track rose slightly as they approached the turn, helping to slow the convoy, but it would quickly fall away again, and their speed was still too great to negotiate the bend. The uneven railbed had rattled the car so much that the bodies of the two terrorists had vanished over the side of the train. Only the corpse of the man whose throat Cabrillo had crushed lay where he'd left it.

The car crested the rise and, despite the Pig's awesome power, the train picked up more speed.

Juan stepped past the dead man's inert form and was reaching for the wheel when the terrorist lunged for him. Too late, Cabrillo remembered the man he had killed had been wearing a blue kaffiyeh, and this man's head was swathed in a red one. He remembered the three men leaping from the truck and how one hadn't seemed to make it. He had clambered aboard when Juan had been back in the Pig and had assumed the dead man's position.

Those thoughts flashed through his mind in less time than it takes to blink but time enough for his legs to be wrapped up and his body to be dragged down. He hit hard, unable to cushion the impact. It was when the terrorist pressed his weight against Juan's thighs that another realization hit him. His attacker was huge, easily outweighing him by fifty pounds.

Juan went for his remaining pistol. The fanatic saw him move and clamped a hand over Cabrillo's. Juan tore his hand free and tried to twist away. Ahead of the boxcar, the turn loomed closer and closer.

"If you don't let me go," he cried in desperation, "we both die."

"Then we both die," the man snarled, crashing an elbow into the back of Juan's leg. He seemed to have grasped the situation and was content to keep Cabrillo pinned on his stomach until the out-of-control train finished them both.

Juan torqued his body around so the tendons in his back screamed in protest, and he put everything he had into a punch that connected with his attacker's jaw at the point it attached to his skull. There was a sickening pop as his jaw dislocated, and for a fleeting moment Juan had the other guy dazed. Wriggling and kicking, Juan threw off the man's deadweight and landed another blow in the exact same spot. The Arab roared at the pain. Juan scrambled to his feet and grabbed the brake wheel, spinning it furiously.

He managed only a couple of revolutions before the guy had him in a choke hold. Juan bent his knees as soon as he felt the thick arm over his neck and then kicked upward, planting a foot on the wheel and kicking again. He went up and over the terrorist's back, breaking the grip and landing behind him. The giant towered a head taller than Cabrillo, so when the man turned Juan had to punch up to deliver a third blow to the jaw. This time, the bone snapped.

Blinded by pain, the man tried to get Cabrillo into a bear hug. Juan ducked below the outstretched arms, pounded the back of his fist into the man's groin, and went back to the wheel, knowing he had no time. He gained two more turns, forcing the overheated pads tighter against the wheels.

He sensed more than heard the next attack and had his pistol out before he turned. As his hand extended, his attacker clamped it under his arm, wrenching it up so that Juan was suddenly on his toes. The colossus brought an elbow down on Juan's shoulder, trying to break his collarbone. Juan shrugged before the blow hit and he took the impact on the socket joint rather than the vulnerable clavicle.

His attacker leered, knowing even the glancing blow was agonizing. Juan sagged in the man's grip, kicking up a leg and knee while fumbling behind his back. There were two straps that he used to keep his leg in place when he was going into combat, and his fingers deftly unhooked them. He pulled the prosthesis off his stump and swung it like a club. The steel toe of his boot glanced off the corner of the man's eye, tearing open enough skin to fill the socket with blood. The blow wasn't all that powerful, but coming from such an unexpected quarter it had the element of surprise.

Cabrillo's backhand follow-through hit him in the face again, loosening teeth, and also loosening his viselike grip on Juan's arm. When he tried to yank his arm free, his pistol was stripped from his fingers and clattered onto the roof, so he swung the leg again. The blow staggered his opponent, and Juan didn't waste a second. After so many years of having only one leg, his superior balance allowed him to hop after the man, swinging the artificial limb like a logger would an ax.

Left, right, left, right, reversing his grip with each blow. He bought himself just enough distance to release two safeties built into the leg and to press a trigger integrated into the ankle. There was a stubby .44 caliber single-shot pistol—little more than a barrel and firing pin—that fired through the prosthesis's heel. The Magic Shop's last refinement to Juan's combat leg had saved him on more than one occasion, and when it discharged he knew it had saved him again. The heavy bullet hit the terrorist's center mass and blew him over the side of the car as limp as a rag doll.

The train was just entering the turn by the time the Chairman applied the full brakes, and as before the timing had been cut so finely that the car's outside wheels started to skip off the rail. Someone inside the compartment must have understood the situation, because suddenly the wheels smacked down again and stayed there. They had used their mass as a counterweight to keep the rolling stock stable.

Cabrillo looked back to see the terrorists' train-truck crest the rise they had flashed over moments earlier. Smoke puffed from under the Pig's cab, and the sound of autofire reached the Chairman an instant later. Mark Murphy had locked the Pig's targeting computer on the rise and waited for their hunters to show themselves.

A stream of 7.62mm rounds raked the unarmored front of the pursuit vehicle. The windshield dissolved, flaying open the skin as shards were blown into the cab. The radiator was punctured a half dozen times. An eruption of steam from the grille enveloped the truck in a scalding cloud, and bullets found their way into the engine compartment. The vulnerable distributor was shredded, killing power to the engine, and one round severed the hydraulic line that kept the train wheels in the extended position.

The truck came down off its second set of wheels so hard and so fast that the driver couldn't react. The tires slammed into a railroad tie, lifting the rear of the vehicle high enough to throw two of the men in the cargo bed over the roof of the cab and onto the rail line. They vanished under the truck.

With its front suspension broken, the cab settled heavily into the ballast stones, and the oddball vehicle came to a complete stop in a haze of steam and dust.

Cabrillo whooped at the sight of their vanquished foe splayed across the tracks.

A deep blast echoed off the valley walls.

Air horn blaring, the diesel-electric locomotive that Juan was certain wouldn't be able to follow them came over the small rise like a rampaging monster. It towered fifteen feet above the railbed and tipped the scales at over a hundred tons. The smoke blowing from its exhaust was a greasy black, testimony to its poor maintenance, but the engine was more than up to the challenge of chasing down the fleeing prisoners.

A couple of the luckier men in the back of the train-truck leapt free before the locomotive smashed into the rear of the disabled vehicle. It came apart as if it had been packed with explosives. Sheet metal, engine parts, and the chassis burst from the collision, winging away as though they weighed nothing. The ruptured gas tank splashed flaming fuel into the mix so it looked like the train was charging through an inferno.

And then it was clear. The truck had been reduced to scrap metal and contemptuously shoved aside.

Juan spat a four-letter expletive, and started easing off the brake, deadly corner or no deadly corner.

From the side of the Pig, an arrow lanced out riding a fiery tail. Mark had fired their last missile in a snap shot. Juan held his breath as it ate the distance to the locomotive. The rocket connected an instant later. The resulting explosion was many times that of the impact with the truck. The engine was wreathed in fire, and the blast shook the very air. The locomotive looked like a meteor hurtling down the tracks, with flame and smoke boiling off its hide.

But for all its fury, the missile made no difference on the two-hundred-thousand-pound behemoth. It shook off the blast like a battle tank hit with a pellet gun and kept charging after the Pig.

Their little caravan was once again picking up speed, yet it was no match for the diesel-electric engine. It was bearing down on them at twice their velocity. For a fleeting second, Cabrillo considered jumping clear. But the idea was dismissed before it had fully formed. He would never abandon his shipmates to save his own skin.

The locomotive was fifty yards from the Pig, the flames all but blown out. There was a smoldering crater low on the engine cover and some blackened paint. Other than that, there was no visible evidence the four-pound shaped charge from their surface-to-surface missile had done anything at all.

However, what Juan couldn't see under the front of the locomotive, where the leading wheel truck was secured to the steel frame, was that the mounting pins had taken a direct hit from the jet of searing plasma produced by the warhead. The train hit one more jarring bump in the old rails and the pins failed entirely. The lead truck for the four front wheels derailed, the hardened wheels splintering the thick ties and peeling sections of track off their supports.

With its front end no longer held in by the rails, the locomotive broke free entirely, tipping in slow motion until it crashed onto its side. The added friction from plowing up ballast stones and yanking dozens of ties from the earth weren't enough to check its awesome momentum. Even in its death throes, it was going to collide with the Pig.

It was twenty feet from them, coming on as strong as ever. Linc had to have had his foot to the floor in a last-ditch effort to set them free. The Pig and boxcar continued to sweep through the turn, barely clinging to the tracks as they curved around the mountain.

Without the tracks to guide it, the locomotive kept going straight, driven by its massive weight and the speed it had built chasing its quarry. It passed no more than a yard in front of the Pig as it careened toward the edge of the steep valley. There were no guardrails, nothing to keep it on the man-made rail line. Its nose tore a wedge out of the ground when it reached the lip of the precipice and sent a shower of gravel pattering down the hillside, and then it barrel-rolled over.

Low down in the Pig's cab, Linc and Mark could no longer see it. But from his vantage high on the boxcar's roof, where he was already tightening the brakes again, Cabrillo watched the locomotive tumble down the hill, gaining speed with each revolution. Its huge belly tank split open, and fuel ignited off the hot manifolds. The resulting explosion and pall of dust obscured its final moments before it crashed into the rocky valley floor.

The freight car went around the last of the corner on its outside wheels only, at such an angle that Juan thought it would never recover. But somehow the plucky old antique finished the curve and flopped back onto the rails. Juan sagged against the brake wheel, catching his breath for a moment before strapping his artificial limb back on his stump.

He estimated there were only another ten or so miles to the coaling station and the dock where the *Oregon* would be waiting, and they were home free.

The only thing he didn't know, and couldn't understand, is what had happened to the Mi-8 helicopter that he was certain he'd heard before they'd escaped the mine depot. The tangos hadn't tried coming after them with it, which to Cabrillo made no sense. True, a cargo chopper wasn't the most stable platform to mount an assault, but considering the lengths the terrorists had gone to in order to stop them he would have thought they'd have launched the helo at them, too.

For the next five minutes, the train eased around several smooth turns, each so gentle that Juan barely had to work the brakes. He was just switching comm frequencies to patch through to Max aboard ship when they rounded another bend that had hidden his view of the tracks ahead.

His blood went cold.

The rail line left the relative safety of the mountain's flank and angled off over the valley across a bridge straight out of the Old West. It resembled a section of a wooden roller coaster and towered a hundred or more feet off the valley floor, an intricate lattice of timber beams bleached white by decades of sun and wind. And at its base, its rotors still turning at idle, sat the Mi-8.

Juan didn't need to see exactly what the men moving gingerly along the framework were doing to know they were planting explosives to blow the bridge to hell.

TWENTY-FIVE

W HEN THE PHONE WAS FINALLY ANSWERED, ABDULLAH, THE commander of the terror camp they irreverently referred to as East Gitmo, wasn't sure if he should be afraid or relieved.

"Go," a voice answered, a voice that in just one word conveyed a malevolence that was dredged up from a dank well which contained normal men's souls.

There was no need for Abdullah to identify himself. Only a handful of people had the number to this particular satellite phone. He hated to think the equipment was made by the cursed Israelis, but the phones were one hundred percent secure. "I need to speak with him."

"He is busy. Speak to me."

"This is urgent," Abdullah insisted but vowed he wouldn't press further if he was rebuffed. In the background, he could hear a ship's horn and the merry clanging of a buoy's bell. Other than those noises, his response was silence. He honored his promise to himself. "Very well. Tell the Imam that the prisoners are attempting to escape."

Abdullah didn't know the details himself, so he kept his briefing vague. "It appears they overpowered the guards and stole one of the

small trucks designed to ride on the old rail line as well as a boxcar."
Again, the man on the other end of the call said nothing. Abdullah plowed on. "Attempts to stop them at the mine failed, and a few
trainees from the camp haven't been able to stop them either. I dispatched some of our elite forces in the helicopter. They are going to
blow up the trestle bridge. That way, we are certain to get them all."

The terrorist commander swallowed audibly. "I, er, thought that
with the information we learned from the American archaeologist
our presence here is no longer necessary. We now know that our
belief that the original Suleiman Al-Jama's hidden base was in this
valley, to the south of the "black that burns," as the legend goes, is
wrong. Al-Jama and the *Saqr* based out of another old riverbed in
Tunisia. The men we sent there should have found it anytime now."

Again, all he could hear was the buoy clanging and an occasional
blast of an air horn.

"Where are you?" Abdullah asked impetuously.

"None of your concern. Continue."

"Well, since we no longer need the pretext of reopening the coal
mine, the burning black we mistook for the legendary sign, I figured blowing up the bridge was the best course of action. Two for
the price of one, as it were. We kill all of the escapees and begin to
dismantle our operation here."

"How many of our elite forces remain there?"

"About fifty," Abdullah answered at once.

"Do not risk those fighters on something as trivial as prisoners.
Send more of the less trained men, if you must. Tell them that to
martyr themselves on this mission will find them in Allah's special
graces in Paradise. The Imam so decrees."

Abdullah thought better of explaining that there wasn't time
to withdraw their crack troops from the bridge. Instead, he asked,
"What about the woman Secretary?"

"Helicopters should be arriving there in about thirty minutes. One of them has orders to take charge of her. Your primary concern is the prisoners' deaths and making certain that our forces in Tripoli are at full strength. There will be legitimate security personnel at the gathering who they will have to overcome to gain entrance to the main hall. Once inside, of course, the targeted government officials aren't armed. It will be a glorious bloodletting, and the end of this foolish bid for peace."

That was the longest Abdullah had ever heard the other man speak. He believed in their cause as much as any of them, as much as Imam Al-Jama himself. But even he had to admit there were levels of fanaticism on which he wouldn't dwell.

He'd often listen to the boys they had recruited chatting among themselves, youths from slum and privilege alike. They made almost a game of thinking up sadistic tortures for the enemies of Islam as a way to bolster one another's confidence. He'd done the same years earlier, during the Lebanese civil war, when he had come of age. But secretly each knew, though never admitted, that it was only a diversion, a way to boast of your dedication and hatred. In the end, most were too petrified to even hold a pistol properly, and suicide vests had to be made as idiotproof as possible.

But not so the man on the other end of the phone. Abdullah knew he reveled in slicing off Westerners' heads with a scimitar that reportedly dated back to the Crusades. He had roasted alive Russian soldiers in the desolate mountains of Chechnya and helped string up the mutilated bodies of American soldiers in Baghdad. He had recruited his own nephew, a teenager with the mind of a two-year-old who liked nothing more than to separate grains of sand into precise piles of one hundred, to walk into a Sunni laundromat in Basra carrying forty pounds of explosives and nails in order to flame sectarian violence. Fifty women and girls perished in the blast, and the reprisal and counterreprisals claimed hundreds more.

Abdullah would do his duty, as he saw it, for Allah. His contact within the Imam's inner circle, Al-Jama's personal bodyguard, killed and maimed because he enjoyed it. The open secret within Al-Jama's organization was that the man didn't even practice Islam. Though born a Muslim, he never prayed, never fasted during Ramadan, and ignored all the faith's dietary laws.

Why the Imam allowed such an abomination had been the subject of debate among senior commanders like Abdullah, until word of such discussions reached Al-Jama's ear. Two days later, the four who had questioned the Imam's choice of top lieutenant had their tongues cut out, their eyes plucked from their heads, their noses and fingertips removed, and their eardrums punctured.

The meaning had been clear. By talking about the man behind his back, they had shown they had no sense, so they would forevermore have no senses either.

"The Imam's will be done, peace be upon him," Abdullah said hastily when he realized he should have replied. The line was already dead.

*　*　*

"LINDA, GET YOUR BUTT up here with the M60," Juan shouted over the radio. "And as much ammo as you can carry. Mark, I need you to separate the Pig from the boxcar."

"What?" cried Murphy. "Why?"

"You can't go fast enough backward."

Linc came over the tactical net. "I thought our problem was slowing down this crazy caravan."

"Not anymore."

Seconds later, the .30 caliber machine gun from the Pig's roof cupola landed with a thud on the railcar's tarry roof. Cabrillo rushed back to give Linda a hand with the unwieldy weapon. Behind her Alana Shepard stood with an ammo belt slung around her neck like some deadly piece of jewelry. At her feet were two more boxes of rounds. She handed up the boxes, and he helped boost her up.

"Trying to earn that fedora, I see." Juan smiled.

Spying the bridge for the first time, Linda Ross understood why the Chairman needed the heavy firepower. As soon as she reached the front of the car, she extended the M60's stumpy bipod legs and was lying behind the weapon, ready for him to feed the first belt into the gun. With Alana pulling a second hundred-round belt from one of the boxes, Juan loaded the M60 and slammed the receiver closed. Linda racked back on the bolt and let fly.

The bridge was well beyond the weapon's effective range, but even random shots pattering against the wooden trestle would force the terrorists to find cover and hopefully buy them the time they needed.

Her whole body shook as if she were holding on to a live electric cable, and a tongue of flame jetted a foot from the muzzle. Watching the string of tracers arcing across the distance, she raised the barrel until the bead of phosphorus-tipped rounds found their mark. At this range, all Juan could see were small explosions of dust kicked off the blanched timbers when the rounds bored in. It took nearly a third of the first belt before the men working under the railbed realized what was happening. None had been hit, as far as they could tell, but soon they were all scrambling to hide themselves in the tangle of crossbeams.

Using controlled bursts to keep the barrel from overheating, Linda kept the men pinned, getting one lucky shot that yanked a terrorist off the delicate trestle. His body plummeted from the bridge, falling soundlessly and seemingly in slow motion, until he slammed into a beam and cartwheeled earthward. He hit the ground in a silent puff of dust that drifted lazily on the breeze.

Mark Murphy could hear the chattering .30 cal but had no idea what they were firing at. He had unhooked himself from his safety straps, climbed up and out of the Pig, and was now crouched over the rear bumper, trying not to notice the ties blurring under his feet.

He had woven a tow cable back and forth around the bumper and the railcar's coupling to keep them attached. Linc was accelerating slightly faster than the car was rolling down the tracks, so there was no tension on the line. Using a large pair of bolt cutters, he attacked the braided steel, snipping at it as fast as he could. If the car started pulling away from the Pig, the tension would snap the cable, and Mark's legs would most likely be taken off at the knees.

They started going through a curve. Murph noticed Linda's machine gun had gone silent and realized the hills were blocking her aim. The car also started picking up speed. The thin cable stretched taut, and braids began to part, curling off the line like silver smoke.

"Linc, goose it a little," Mark called, and Lincoln gave the Pig more gas.

As soon as the tension was off, Mark worked at it again, heaving on the big cutters with everything he had.

"When you're through the last cable," Juan shouted into the radio, "jump onto the coupling so we don't lose the time it'll take you to climb aboard the Pig."

Mark swallowed hard, not sure what he liked less—the prospect of clinging to the rusted coupling or the thought of what the Chairman knew about their situation to ask him to do it in the first place.

"You hear that, Linc," Cabrillo continued. "As soon as Mark's done, turn the Pig around and shove this boxcar with everything you've got. Hear me?"

"I'm through," Mark announced before the SEAL could respond.

In the Pig, Linc stood on the brakes, blowing off clouds of carbon dust from the nearly spent pads. He cranked the wheel as soon as he felt it safe enough. The tires hit the railroad ties with bone-jarring regularity, and the heavy truck grew light on one side. He rammed it into first before he'd come to a complete stop, kicking up twin sprays of ballast stones. The truck leapt after the runaway freight car, Linc aiming to put the wheels atop the rails once again. His vision blurred, and it felt like his molars were going to come loose from his jaw before he could center the Pig on the tracks.

Once the wheels were aligned, he chased down the car until the reinforced bumper kissed its coupling. He watched, amazed, as Mark Murphy planted one foot on the bumper and bent to strip off coils of towline from the Pig's forward winch and started to wrap it around the coupling to secure the two vehicles together. Linc had never doubted the kid's courage, but even he would have thought twice about the dangerous maneuver.

"Chairman," he called, "I'm around and pushing hard. Murph's tying us to the train car with the winch."

"Mark, have you run your calculations?" Cabrillo asked. He stood over the young weapons expert and watched him work.

Murph snapped the winch's hook around a couple of loops of cable and climbed up the Pig's windshield before turning to the Chairman and answering. "Yeah, just like you asked, I mathed it. The freight car's got enough buoyancy to hold us on the surface. The unknown is how fast water is going to fill it up."

"Max will just have to be quick with the *Oregon*'s derrick crane."

"Tell him he should switch from a lifting hook to the magnetic grapple."

Juan instantly saw the logic to Murph's suggestion. The big electromagnet wouldn't require crewmen to secure the crane to the
freight car.

Behind him, the train must have cleared another hill because
Linda opened up again with the M60. He caught whiffs of cordite
smoke in the air as the railcar continued to accelerate. He turned.
The bridge was still some distance away and looked as delicate as a
railroad hobbyist's model. Under the hail of tracers arcing in toward
the structure, the men setting the explosives hid behind the trestle
supports again. At the speed the Pig was pushing the old freight car,
they would be sweeping through another turn in seconds, and the
terrorists would be free to finish their work.

Cabrillo went ashen under his tan. He knew with certainty that
they weren't going to make it. The Pig snarled as it pushed the boxcar, but they were just too far away, and without a direct line of fire
to keep the sappers pinned they would be ready to blow the bridge at
about the same time the train hit the trestle.

He was just about to order Linc to stand on the brakes in the vain
hope that they could unload the passengers and make some sort of
stand when movement on the far side of the bridge caught his eye.
At first, he couldn't tell what he was seeing because the heavy timber
supports obscured his view.

And then without warning the Corporation's glossy black
McDonnell Douglas MD-520N helicopter roared over the bridge.
With its ducted exhaust eliminating the need for a rear rotor, and by
using every scrap of cover he could find, George "Gomez" Adams
had achieved complete surprise.

The sound of the rotors and Adams's rebel yell filled Cabrillo's
earpiece. The noise was quickly drowned out by the hammering of a
heavy machine gun. A figure silhouetted in the chopper's open rear
door had opened fire at near-point-blank range. The thick timber

supports had stood for more than a century, baking and curing in the relentless desert heat until they were as hard as iron. And yet chunks of wood exploded off the bridge under the relentless fire, leaving behind raw white wounds and a steady rain of dust and sand. Where the bullets met flesh, the damage was much, much worse.

"About time you showed up," Juan radioed.

"Sorry about the dramatic entrance," Gomez Adams replied. "Headwind the whole way here."

"Keep them pinned on the bridge until we cross, then fly cover for us until we hit the dock." Juan changed frequencies. "Max, you there?"

"Sure am," Max said breezily as if he didn't have a care in the world, which showed how worried he really was.

"What's your ETA?"

"We'll be alongside the dock about two minutes before you get here. Just so you know, it's a floating pier, and at the speed you're going to hit the rail bumpers at the end you're going to kill everyone in the boxcar."

"That's your idea of an FYI? You have a plan?"

"Of course. We've got it handled."

"All right," Juan said, trusting his second-in-command implicitly. With so much happening on and around the train, he would leave the details to Hanley.

They were barreling through the turn now. The engineers who'd built the line had carved a narrow shelf into the side of the hill, barely wide enough for the freight car. He imagined that when they normally took the big locomotive through the tight curve, they did so at a snail's pace. Living rock whizzed by the edge of the car with less than a hand span's clearance.

The tight tolerances saved their lives.

The train's outside wheels lifted off the track, and the top edge of the car slammed into the blasted-stone wall, gouging out a deep rent in the rock and showering Cabrillo with chips as sharp as glass shards. The impact forced the car's wheels back onto the rail, and for a moment they held before the incredible centrifugal forces acting on them lifted them up again. Again, the top edge of the car tore into the rock, but this time Juan turned so it was his back and not his exposed face blasted by debris.

"Chairman?" There was something in Franklin Lincoln's voice that Cabrillo had never heard. Fear.

"Don't you dare slow down now!" Juan said. Below him he could hear their passengers' screams of panic. As bad as it was riding on top of the car, he couldn't imagine what they were experiencing in the pitch-darkness inside.

Twice more, they hit the rock, before the turn started to lose its tight radius and the wheels stayed firmly planted on the hot iron rails. That was the last curve before they hit the bridge. Before them was a straight shot down a gentle defile, then across the trestle. A flash of light blazed off the binoculars of an observer in the valley below the bridge. Juan could almost sense the man's thoughts despite the distance. Seconds later, an order had to have been given, because the men rigging the bridge with explosives started swarming down the trestle, ignoring the blistering fire from Gomez Adams in the MD-540.

Cabrillo moved to the leading edge next to where Linda and Alana crouched behind the M60.

"I know I'm dating myself," Linda said, her face a little pale under its dusting of freckles, "but that's what I call an E-ticket ride. Makes the Matterhorn feel tame."

She no longer had an angle to fire at the men, but Adams was making their retreat hell.

"There's nothing more we can do," Juan shouted over the roar of wind filling his ears. They were pushing sixty miles per hour, and the rush of wind over the carriage threatened to blow them off if they rose above a crouch. "Let's get back to the Pig."

He hefted the big gun, with its necklace of shining brass shells dangling from the receiver, so Linda and Alana could crawl back to the rear of the car together. They lowered themselves down onto the Pig's cab and then vanished through the open hatch. Cabrillo paused for a moment, forcing his eyes to slits to look up the tracks. Adams ducked and weaved in the chopper, dancing away from enemy fire, while his door gunner—Cabrillo thought he recognized the beefy form of Jerry Pulaski—peppered the bridge supports whenever the helo was steady enough to shoot.

The tone of wheel against rail suddenly changed. They were on the first section of the bridge. A quick glance over the side of the car confirmed that the ground was beginning to recede from under them.

The explosion came farther along the bridge's length, on the valley floor near one of the trestle supports. Smoke and flame climbed the wooden members, mushrooming outward and upward like a deadly bloom. Cabrillo threw himself flat as the train barreled through the pulsing surge of fire and emerged on the other side with no more damage than some singed paint.

Behind them the blast had weakened the bridge's lattice framework, but Linda's and then Adams's sniping had prevented the terrorists from properly rigging the structure. The supports stood firm for a solid ten seconds after the train had rushed past, allowing them to get nearly to the end of the long span before the structure started to collapse. The great timbers fell in on themselves, the valley choking with dust thick enough to obscure the waiting Mi-8 helicopter and the tiny figures of running terrorists.

The bridge fell like dominoes, the steel rails sagging as though they had no more strength than piano wire. Linc had to have seen what was happening behind the Pig in the wing mirrors, because the engine beat changed when he flooded the cylinders with nitrous oxide.

Wood and iron tumbled in a rolling avalanche that chased after the fleeing boxcar. Cabrillo watched awestruck as the bridge vanished in their wake. He should have felt fear, but his fate wasn't in his hands, so he saw the spectacle with almost clinical detachment. And even as the Pig gained more speed, so, too, did the structure's incredible failure. A hundred feet behind their rear bumper, the rails quivered and then vanished into the boiling maelstrom of dust.

He didn't dare look ahead to see how much farther they had to travel. It was better, he thought fleetingly, not to know.

Just as the rails started to dip under them, the hollow sound of air rushing below the carriage changed once again and thick wooden ties appeared under the line. They had made it just as the last of the bridge crumpled into the valley, rending itself apart so that nothing showed above the billowing debris.

Cabrillo pumped his fist, shouting at the top of his lungs, and nearly lost his footing in his excitement. "That was a hell of a piece of driving," he called to Linc. "Is everyone okay?"

"We're all good," Lincoln replied.

There was something his voice, something Cabrillo didn't like. "What is it, big man?"

"I tore the guts out of the transmission the last time I hit the nitro. I'm looking down the tracks in the mirror and see we're laying one hell of an oil slick."

It was only after it was reported that Juan noticed he couldn't hear the motor's aggressive growl. Without gears, there was no reason to leave the engine running.

"Mark says the rest of the line is pretty gentle, but . . ." He let his voice trail off.

"And let me guess," Juan added, "our brakes are shot, too."

"I've got my foot pressed to the floorboards, for whatever good it'll do us."

Juan looked in the direction they were heading. The ocean was a slag-gray shimmer in the distance. The train tracks' terminus was hidden in a fold of land, though he estimated they had only a few more miles to go. He also agreed with Mark Murphy's assertion that the rest of the way was a gentle glide down to the sea. He could only hope that whatever reception Max had planned would work because when he clamped on the boxcar's brakes he could tell they, like the Pig's, were worn down to nothing.

"Max, do you read me?" he said into his mic.

"Loud and clear."

"Where are you?"

"We're in position and ready to pick you up."

"Any word on the choppers of the Libyan strike team?"

"No. I suspect they'll come in from the south, so we'll never see them. And more important, they'll never see us."

"As soon as you have us with the magnet, I want Eric to make best possible speed into international waters."

"Relax, Juan. Everything's ready. Doc Huxley and her people have set up the forward hold with cots, blankets, and plenty of IV drips. The cooking staff's been whipping up enough food to feed the people you've found, and I've got every weapons system on the ship locked and loaded in case someone wants to take them back."

"Okay. Okay, I get it. We'll be there in about three minutes."

The last section of the rail line came out of the mountains through a valley that ran right to the sea. The Corporation people, along with Alana, Greg Chaffee, and their new Libyan charge, Fodl, were strapped into the Pig, while the rest of the refugees in the boxcar had been given a shouted warning to brace themselves.

The old coaling station was a run-down ruin, little more than the metal framework of a couple of buildings with bits of wood still somehow clinging to their sides. The cranes that once filled freighters with coal were long gone, and the desert had hidden where the anthracite had once been mounded in the lee of a cliff.

The *Oregon* loomed over the newly installed floating dock. Her main cargo derrick was swung over into position, and the large electromagnet dangled less than twenty feet over the pier.

Juan's pride usually swelled a bit whenever he saw his creation, but this time his mind was on the speed the train was making as it raced for the station. He fought the urge to glance at the speedometer but guessed they were pushing seventy. He'd expected Max would have laid down some sort of barrier foam to slow the train, but he saw nothing on the tracks. Then he realized the dock was much lower in the water than he'd first thought. In fact, the far end of it was completely submerged.

He laughed aloud when the hurtling train left its old railbed and started along the pier. Max had holed the large interlocked plastic pods that made up the dock, most likely with the *Oregon*'s Gatling gun. The pier's own weight started it sinking, and as the boxcar pressed down the pier dipped deeper.

Two curling sheets of water peeled off the car's leading edge, and the ocean absorbed the train's momentum so smoothly that no one in the Pig felt their seat-belt tensioners react. Two-thirds the way down the pier, the Pig was down to twenty miles per hour, and the water was well above its lugged tires.

The boxcar was barely moving when it tipped off the edge of the pier, dragging the truck with it. The car bobbed in the water for only a few seconds before the magnet swooped over them, and when current was applied it stuck fast. Moments later, the old railcar, with the Pig dangling from its rear coupling, was pulled from the sea. Juan knew Max Hanley himself had to be at the controls because the operator had estimated the train's center of gravity perfectly.

With water pouring from the car, they were swung over the *Oregon*'s rail and set onto the deck. Juan threw open his door the instant the tires touched the deck plate. A crewman was standing by with an oxyacetylene cutting torch and was already slicing through the cables that bound the Pig to the boxcar. Juan rushed past him and nearly collided with Dr. Huxley in his haste to open the train's sliding door. With her were several teams of orderlies with gurneys at the ready.

"Looks like you don't think I've been earning my pay keeping your rogues patched up, eh?" she said. "You had to bring a train car full of patients for me."

Deep below his feet, Juan could feel the magnetohydrodynamics ramping up. "What else do you give a doctor as a gift after a little relaxing shore leave?"

Juan pulled back on the sliding door and a fresh cascade of water poured onto the deck. Then from the gloomy interior emerged the first skeletal prisoner, owl-eyed and soaking wet.

"You're safe now," Juan said in Arabic. "You are all safe. But you must hurry, understand?"

Fodl joined him and Dr. Huxley an instant later, and together they cajoled the shell-shocked men and women out of the car. There were a few injuries, sprains mostly, but a couple of broken limbs as well. And one man who'd caught a bullet in the wrist from one of the terrorists Cabrillo had fought on the car's roof. As was his custom, Juan would more regret hurting these people further than take satisfaction in saving their lives.

He spotted Mark Murphy. The lanky weapons expert had his

kit bag slung over one shoulder and a waterproof laptop case in his hand. He was heading for a hatchway that would lead him to his cabin. "Forget it, Mr. Murphy. As of this second, you and Mr. Stone are on a priority research job."

"Can't it wait until after I shower?"

"No. Now. I want to know everything there is to know about something called the Jewel of Jerusalem. Alana Shepard mentioned it may be buried with Suleiman Al-Jama but isn't really sure what it is."

"Sounds like a legend out of a trashy novel."

"It might just be. Find out. I want a report in an hour."

"Yes, boss," Mark said dejectedly, and shuffled away.

"Who are all these people?" Julia Huxley asked, passing a woman down to the waiting arms of an orderly.

"They were all in the upper levels of Libya's Foreign Ministry," Juan told her. "One of these poor souls should be the Minister himself."

"I don't understand. Why are they all prisoners?"

"Because unless I messed up my reasoning, the new Foreign Minister, the esteemed Ali Ghami, is Suleiman Al-Jama."

TWENTY-SIX

THE HELICOPTERS PAINTED WITH LIBYAN MILITARY COLORS swarmed out of the empty wastes of the southern desert like enraged wasps. Four of the five Russian-made choppers were done in mottled earth-toned camouflage, while the other wore the drab gray of the Libyan Navy.

In his fifteen years with the CIA, Jim Kublicki never thought he would be an observer on a Libyan helo assault of a terrorist base camp. Ambassador Moon had arranged his presence on the attack with Minister Ghami personally. On the surface, the new level of cooperation out of Tripoli was amazing, but both Moon and Kublicki harbored their doubts. The chief among them was the result of the eyes-only report that had been delivered from Langley. Kublicki had no idea how operatives had penetrated Libyan airspace during the height of the search for the Secretary of State's plane, but somehow they had. The evidence they found led to the only conclusion possible: Her plane had been forced down before the crash—presumably, to remove the Secretary herself. Then the Boeing was intentionally slammed into a mountaintop.

The report also documented how a team of men in a chopper had landed at the crash site and deliberately tampered with the scene.

The exact words from the document were "they tore through the wreckage like a twister through a trailer park."

The team from the National Transportation Safety Board had issued a secret and still-preliminary report backing up what Langley had said. Despite the best efforts of the terrorists, there were inconsistencies in the wreckage that could not be easily explained. When Moon had met with David Jewison of the NTSB and outlined the CIA report, he'd nodded, and said it was quite possible the plane had landed briefly before the crash.

When Kublicki had arrived at a remote air base outside of Tripoli where they were staging the assault, he'd met with the operation's leader, a Special Forces colonel named Hassad. He'd explained that the Libyan desert was dotted with hundreds of old training bases left over from the days when his government had allowed them sanctuary. In the few years since the government renounced terrorism, he and his men had destroyed most of the ones they knew of, but he admitted there were dozens more they did not.

Hassad sat in the right-hand seat next to their pilot, while Kublicki crammed his six-foot six-inch frame into a folding jump seat immediately behind the cockpit. There was only a handful of men in the rear section of the utility chopper. The bulk of the assault force was in the other helicopters.

The Libyan colonel clamped a hand over his helmet's boom mic and leaned back. He had to raise his voice over the whopping thrum of the rotor blades. "We're landing in about a minute."

Kublicki was a little taken aback. "What? I thought we were going in after the assault."

"I don't know about you, Mr. Kublicki, but I want a piece of these people for myself." Hassad shot him a wolfish grin.

"I'm with you there, Colonel, but the uniform you lent me didn't come with a weapon."

The Libyan officer unsnapped the pistol at his waist and handed it over butt first. "Just make sure that me giving you a sidearm doesn't make it into your report."

Kublicki smiled conspiratorially and popped the pistol's magazine to assure himself it was loaded. The narrow slit along the mag's length showed thirteen shiny brass cartridges. He rammed the clip home but wouldn't cock the pistol until they were on the ground.

From his low vantage strapped in behind the cockpit, Kublicki couldn't see through the windshield but knew they were about to land when his view of the sky was blocked by dust kicked up by the helicopter's powerful rotor wash. He hadn't been in a combat situation since the first Gulf War, but the combination of fear and exhilaration was a sensation he would never forget.

The craft settled on the ground, and Kublicki whipped off his safety belts. When he stood to peer over Hassad's shoulder, he saw the terrorist camp a good hundred yards away. Men in checkered kaffiyehs, brandishing AK-47s, were running toward them with abandon. He saw no sign of the soldiers from the other choppers in pursuit.

Fear began to wash away the exhilaration.

Hassad threw open his door and swung to the ground. He vanished from sight for a moment, and then the chopper's side door slammed back on its roller stop.

Kublicki blinked at the bright light flooding the hold.

The two men stared at each other for what to Kublicki felt like a long time but was only a few seconds. A current of understanding passed between them. The veteran CIA agent cocked the pistol and aimed it at the Libyan in one smooth motion. What had sounded like cries of fear from the gathering terrorists was actually exaltation, and it rose from a hundred throats.

Kublicki pulled the trigger four times before he realized the weapon hadn't fired. A gun barrel was jammed into his spine, and he sat frozen as Hassad reached across and yanked the pistol from his hand. "No firing pin." He repeated the phrase in Arabic, and the group of terrorists laughed in approval.

In the last seconds of life Jim Kublicki had remaining, he promised himself he wouldn't go down without a fight. Ignoring the assault rifle pressed to his back, he launched himself out of the chopper, his hands going for Hassad's throat. To his credit, he got within a few inches of his target before the gunman behind him opened fire. A one-second-long burst from the AK stitched his back from kidney to shoulder blade. The kinetic energy drove him to the ground at Hassan's feet. The Libyan stood over him in the stunned silence that followed the attack. Rather than salute a valiant foe who'd fallen into an impossible ambush, Hassad spat on the corpse, turned on his heal, and walked away.

He found the camp commander, Abdullah, outside his tent. The two men greeted each other warmly. Hassad cut through the polite period of small talk that was so much a part of Muslim life and struck to the heart of the matter.

"Tell me of the escapees."

The two men were of similar rank within Al-Jama's terror cell, but Hassan had the more forceful personality.

"We got them."

"All of them? Ah, yes, I heard you were going to blow up the bridge. It worked, eh?"

"No," Abdullah said. "They got past. But they were going so fast when they hit the end of the dock that they sailed off the end."

"Someone saw this happen?"

"No, but it was only fifteen or so minutes after they cleared the bridge that our chopper reached the old coaling station. There was no sign of the prisoners on the quay, so they didn't get off, and they spotted the boxcar about two hundred yards from shore. Only the roof was above water, and it sank completely as they watched."

"Excellent." Hassad clapped him on the shoulder. "The Imam, peace be upon him, won't be pleased he couldn't witness our former Foreign Minister's death, but he will be relieved the escape was foiled."

"There is one thing," Abdullah said. "The reports from my men aren't precise, but it appears the prisoners might have had help."

"Help?"

"A single truck, carrying several men and perhaps a woman, attacked the camp at the same time the prisoners were starting to make their break."

"Who were these people?"

"No idea."

"Their vehicle?"

"Presumably, it sank with the boxcar. Like I said, the eyewitness accounts come from some of our rawest recruits, and it's possible they mistook one of our own trucks for another in their enthusiasm."

Hassad chuckled humorlessly. "I'm sure some of these kids see Mossad agents behind every rock and hill."

"After tomorrow's attack, when we move from here to our new base in the Sudan, at least half of them are going to be left behind. Those who show promise will come with us. The rest aren't worth the effort."

"Recruiting numbers has never been our problem. Recruiting quality, well, that is something else. Speaking of . . ."

"Ah, yes."

Abdullah said a few words to a hovering aide. A moment later, the subaltern came back with another of their men. Gone were the dust-caked and tattered camouflage utilities and sweaty headscarf. The man wore a new black uniform, with the cuffs of his pants bloused into glossy boots. His hair was neatly barbered and his face was carefully shaved. The leatherwork of his pistol belt shone brightly from hours of careful cleaning, and the rank pips on his shoulders glinted like gold.

While the recruits trained with AK-47s that had knocked around the terrorist world since before many of the them had been born, the weapon this man carried at port arms was brand-new. There wasn't a scratch on the receiver or a nick in the polished wooden stock.

"Your credentials," Hassad barked.

The man shouldered his rifle smartly, and from a pocket on his upper arm produced a leather billfold. He snapped it open for inspection. Hassad looked at it carefully. The military identification had been made in the same office that produced the real ones by a sympathizer to the cause. Libya's military was riddled with them at every level, which was how they'd gotten the helicopters for today's operation and the Hind gunship they had used to disable Fiona Katamora's aircraft.

Opposite the ID was a pass authorizing the bearer to work the security detail for tomorrow's peace summit. It had been deemed too risky to try to get them from the issuing office, so these had been forged here at the camp. Hassad had friends in the Army who would be at the conference as part of the massive security force, and he'd studied their passes. What he saw before him was a flawless copy.

He handed back the papers, and asked, "What do you expect tomorrow?"

"To be martyred in the name of Islam and Suleiman Al-Jama."

"Do you believe you are worthy of such an honor?"

The answer was a moment in coming. "It is enough for me that the Imam believes I am worthy."

"Well said," Hassad remarked. "You and your compatriots are

going to strike a blow against the West that will take them years to recover from, if ever. Imam Al-Jama has decreed they will no longer be allowed to dictate to us how we should live our lives. The corruption they spread with their television and movies, their music, and their democracy, will no longer be allowed. Soon we will see the beginning of the end for them. They will finally understand their way of life is not for us, and that it is Islam that will take over the world. This is the honor of which Al-Jama believes you are worthy."

"I will not let him down," the terrorist said, his voice firm, his eyes steady.

"You are dismissed," Hassad said, and turned back to Abdullah. "Very well done, my old friend."

"The military training was relatively easy," the commander said. "Keeping them true to the cause without making them appear like wild-eyed fanatics was the difficult part."

Both men knew that countless suicide attacks had been thwarted because the perpetrators looked so nervous and out of place that even untrained civilians knew what was about to occur. And the fifty men they were sending to Tripoli today would be surrounded by legitimate security forces on full alert for the very type of attack they were attempting. They had culled through hundreds of recruits from training camps and madrasas all over the Middle East to find the right men.

Hassad glanced at his watch. "In eighteen hours, it will be over. The American Secretary of State will be dead, and the palace hall will be awash in blood. The tide of peace will once again be pushed back, and in its absence we will continue to spread our way of life."

"As the original Suleiman Al-Jama wrote, 'When in the struggle to keep our faith from corruption we find our will slacking, our resolve waning, our strength ebbing, we must, at that moment, make the supreme effort, and the supreme sacrifice if necessary, to show our enemies that we will never be defeated.'"

"I prefer another line, 'They who do not submit to Islam are an affront to Allah and worthy only of our bullets.'"

"Soon they shall have them."

"Now, why don't you introduce me to the American woman. I have a little time before she needs to board the frigate for her date with destiny, but I would like to gaze upon her."

TWENTY-SEVEN

C ABRILLO'S HOPE FOR A LONG BATH FOLLOWING HIS RETURN to the *Oregon* was not meant to be. He allowed himself a quick shower only after all the prisoners had been made as comfortable as possible in the hold. He had been introduced to Libya's ex–Foreign Minister by Fodl, who'd been his deputy. As it was nearing noon, Juan had shown him in which direction Mecca lay relative to the ship so they could all pray for the first time since their incarceration.

He was dressing when Max Hanley knocked on his cabin door and entered without waiting. In tow were Eric Stone and Mark Murphy, who still wore his filthy uniform.

On seeing Cabrillo, he said, "Man, that is totally not fair."

"Privilege of rank," Juan replied airily, and finished tying a pair of black combat boots. "What do you have for me?"

"They apparently bought the trick with the sinking railcar," Max said. "They sent out a chopper to investigate about fifteen minutes after you boarded. Mark's time estimation of it sinking was spot-on. They must have seen it seconds before it went under."

Eric cut in. "Then I swung the UAV back over the terrorist camp.

Because of the altitude I had to maintain so they wouldn't hear it, the camera's resolution wasn't the best, but we have a pretty good idea of what was happening."

"And?"

"You were right," Max replied. "The flight of Libyan military choppers landed with no opposition. It looks like there were only a few men aboard any of them."

"Sounds like transport back out to me," Juan guessed.

"That's our read, too," Eric replied. "They're going to be moving more men than they can carry in that old Mi-8 you flew on from the crash scene."

"What's the capacity of the choppers?"

"Fifty at least."

"Hell of an assault force."

Mark said, "The target has to be the peace conference."

Eric Stone shook his head. "Never happen. The security is impenetrable. There is no way a terrorist is going to get within a mile of a single dignitary."

"They would if the Libyan government's in on it," Max countered.

"That's the million-dollar question. If Minister Ghami is Suleiman Al-Jama, does Qaddafi know it?"

"How could he not? He appointed him."

"Okay, say he does, Max. That still doesn't mean he knows what Al-Jama is planning."

"What difference does it make?" Hanley asked.

"Maybe none, but it's something we need to know."

"And how do we find out?"

"I'll get to that in a minute. Mark, is there any chance we can take out those choppers?"

"We'd need to launch another UAV," Eric said before Mark could answer. "The first drone's out of fuel, and I had to ditch it. Though not before taking this."

He handed Juan a grainy still photograph from the drone's video camera. Details were murky to say the least, but it looked like two armed men escorting a third person toward one of the helicopters.

"Is that Secretary Katamora?"

"Possibly. Factoring the height of a typical Libyan male and comparing the middle figure to them, the height is right, and the build certainly fits. The person's head is covered so we can't see hair, which would have been a dead giveaway—hers flows to the middle of her back."

"Best guess?"

"It's her, and by the time we turn around she's going to be long gone."

Juan frowned. He'd made a conscious decision to save the Libyan prisoners rather than wait out the terrorists. The balance of one life versus one hundred tipped the same way no matter who sat on the scales. But being so close and not getting her irked. "Okay, what about taking out the other choppers?" he said to get the meeting back on course, his eyes lingering on the picture.

"We could laze them from the second UAV so I can guarantee a missile hit, but we have to consider collateral damage if Secretary Katamora's there."

"Options?"

"Nail the choppers in flight if they come out over the ocean. But, again, we risk her life if she's a hostage aboard one of them."

"They'll stick to the desert anyway," Eric said.

Max cleared his throat. "Listen, why not pass on what we know to Overholt and let him tell the other delegates about the possibility of a massive attack?"

"We'll tell Lang," Juan replied, "but I don't want that information disseminated."

"Why the hell not?"

"Two reasons. One, if they know the attack is coming, they will call off the conference, and the chance to get these people in a room talking peace again is zilch. The conference has to proceed. Second, we have nothing concrete linking Ghami to Al-Jama. This is our one and only chance to expose him and his entire operation."

"You're risking a lot of important lives."

"Mine, for one," Mark said.

"I admit it's the biggest toss of the dice we've ever attempted, but I know it's worth it. Overholt will agree. He understands that if we can nail Al-Jama on the eve of the peace conference, it will give it such a boost that the delegates are certain to hammer out a comprehensive and lasting treaty. In one blow, we take out the second-most-wanted terrorist on the planet and guarantee lasting peace."

"Boy, Juan. I'm not sure. The prize is awesome, yes. But the price, you know . . ."

"Trust me."

Still uncertain, but never one to doubt the Chairman, Max asked, "So how is this going to work?"

"In a minute." He turned his attention to Murph and Stoney. "What did you two come up with?"

"There's not a whole lot out there that doesn't fall into the realm of fantasy."

"Hold it," Max interrupted. "What did you have them research?"

"Alana said there might be something called the Jewel of Jerusalem stashed in the original Suleiman Al-Jama's tomb. She was told about it by St. Julian Purlmutter. Even he wasn't sure what it was. What did you guys find?"

"You haven't given us much time on this, so our report is sketchy at best. There are two schools of thought. Well, three, if you include the vast majority of scholars who think the whole thing is baloney. Anyway, one school says the jewel is a cabochon ruby about the size of a softball with some words carved into it. People believe it may be Sura 115 from the Koran, a final chapter to the Muslim holy book that appears nowhere else because Muhammad believed it so perfect and so special that it could only be written on a flawless jewel."

"Any idea what it says?" Juan asked.

"Depends on which side of the radical line you stand. The nut jobs think it says they should kill infidels all the livelong day. Moderates ascribe to the idea that it promotes peace between Islam and Christianity."

"So no one knows."

"Exactly," Mark said skeptically. "Take any object, give it the ability to bring special knowledge or power, and, voilà, you've got yourself a legend that'll last for generations. Kinda like the Ark of the Covenant. Total bunko, but people still look for it today."

"Skip the commentary and stick to the story."

"Okay. They say that Saladin first brought the jewel to Jerusalem following his siege of the city in 1187 and that the stone was kept in a cedar box in a cave beneath the Dome of the Rock. The legend says that any man who dared gaze upon the stone went blind or mad, or both. Convenient, eh?

"So the stone sits in its underground vault until the Sixth Crusade in 1228. During this one, Frederick II of the Holy Roman Empire made a treaty with the ruler of Egypt that turned over control of all Jerusalem to the Christians, except the Dome of the Rock and the nearby Al-Aqsa Mosque. It was during this period that German mercenaries working for the Knights Templar stormed the Dome and stole the jewel."

"Why would Christian knights want an Islamic relic?"

"Because they thought it was something else. Remember, I said there were two schools of thought. This is where their paths cross. You see, the Templars believed the Jewel of Jerusalem wasn't a ruby at all. They thought it was a pendant fashioned a thousand years earlier for a man named Didymus, or Judas Tau'ma."

"Never heard of him," Max grumbled.

Eric said, "You know him better as Doubting Thomas, one of Christ's twelve Apostles."

"And this pendant?" Juan prompted.

"As you know, in the Bible story Thomas didn't believe Christ's resurrection and demanded to touch the wound. The Bible doesn't say whether he did or didn't touch Him, but the Templars were convinced that he did. They believed the Jewel of Jerusalem was a crystal into which an alchemist called Jho'acabe had encapsulated the traces of blood left on Thomas's fingers. The crystal was then hung from a necklace that fell into Muslim control when Saladin took the city."

"If that were true wouldn't the Muslims have destroyed it?" Hanley asked.

"Actually, no," Eric replied. "By all accounts, Saladin treated the city's Christians and their churches respectfully. He might not have given back the pendant, but I doubt he would have intentionally destroyed it either."

"So now the jewel, either a ruby or a necklace, is in the hands of the Templars. How does it end up entombed with Suleiman Al-Jama?"

"Because the ship carrying them back to Malta—"

"—is attacked by Barbary pirates." Juan answered his own question.

"One of Al-Jama's ancestors, in fact," Eric said. "The cedar chest with the jewel inside gets passed from father to son until Al-Jama's death. Henry Lafayette left it in the tomb, and so it sits today."

"It's all crap," Mark spat. "Chairman, if you saw some of the websites where we found this stuff you'd know there's nothing to it. It's a myth like the Loch Ness Monster, or Bigfoot or the Lost Dutchman Mine."

"There was a kernel of truth behind the myth of Noah's Ark, if you recall from our little adventure a few months ago." The Chairman went quiet for a moment. "We know for a fact from Lafayette that in his later years Al-Jama saw there was hope of peace between Christians and Muslims. This has only recently come to light, right? It isn't something conspiracy buffs are privy to. Here's a little speculation. What if the first version of the story's right, about the jewel being an inscribed ruby, and Al-Jama read Muhammad's last words and that led to his change of heart. It does lend a little credence, yes?"

"Possibly. But come on. What are the chances it ends up in Al-Jama's possession?"

"Why not? He was a noted Imam from a family with a long history of piracy. Even if one of his ancestors wasn't part of the attack on the Templar ship, it's still possible the jewel was given to them as a tribute."

"Gentlemen, let's get back on course," Max suggested. "At this stage in the game, it doesn't really matter what the jewel is, or even where it is. Our focus should be on saving the Secretary and stopping Al-Jama's attack."

"Max, you said something about how the Libyans are claiming our old buddy at the harbor, Tariq Assad, is Al-Jama."

"Obviously, a smoke screen, if we're right."

"Has Eddie reported anything that makes you think Assad's involved with Al-Jama's faction?"

"No, but this morning they noted Assad's house and his office are surrounded by covert agents. The Libyans are making good on their promise to nab him."

"And when the dust settles, they'll have their scapegoat," Eric remarked. "They'll put on a quick show trial and execute him for the attack."

"The Libyans have to be targeting him for a reason. There must be something to this guy, right? Max, get on the horn and tell Eddie to pick up Assad. We need to question him."

Cabrillo studied Mark Murphy for a moment. Murph's jaw was blurred with stubble, and he slouched in his chair as if he were melted into it, but his eyes were still bright. In the past few months, after a lot of ribbing from the crew, he had embarked on the first exercise program of his life. He'd been through a lot in the past forty-eight hours, yet Juan suspected he was ready for more. "You up for another op?"

"I still want that shower first, but yeah."

"I want you and Eric over the border into Tunisia to find Al-Jama's tomb." Cabrillo didn't like losing his best helmsman at a time like this, but Murph and Stone worked together on such a deep, intuitive level that he felt it necessary to send both.

"Better take along a couple of gundogs," Max suggested. "Don't forget the tangos kidnapped the fourth member of Alana Shepard's team."

"Bumford," Mark said. "Emile Bumford. Linda and Linc say he's a tool."

"Just so you know what you're up against," Hanley continued, "the other archaeologists report that there were at least a dozen terrorists who snatched him."

"Gomez can chopper you over and be back in a couple of hours."

"We still have fuel left in the cache we set up in the desert when we first talked to Bumford."

"Good. I want you guys in the air in two hours. For now, all I want you to do is find the tomb. If they've beaten you there, stick close and watch. No matter what, don't engage them. Greg Chaffee's volunteered to fully debrief the prisoners, but from what I've been able to gather from them so far Al-Jama wants that tomb as badly as we do. His entire operation out in the desert was an attempt to find it. Be ready for anything."

"Ready is my middle name."

"Herbert's your middle name," Eric teased.

"It's better than Boniface."

Cabrillo's phone rang. It was the duty officer in the op center. "Chairman, I thought you'd want to know, radar picked up a low-flying aircraft parallel to the coast near the approximate position of the terrorist training camp."

"Could you track it?"

"Not really. It popped up only for a second and then vanished again. My guess is it's flying at wave-top height."

"Did you get its speed or bearing?"

"Nothing. Just the blip, and then it was gone."

"Okay. Thanks." He set the Bakelite handset back on its cradle. "Al-Jama's men are bugging out."

Max glanced at his watch. "Didn't take them long."

"I'd like to think our little fracas pushed their deadline," Juan said, "but I doubt that's the case." He went quiet for a moment. "What the hell were they doing near the coast?"

"Hmm?"

"The chopper. Why risk getting close to the coast where they could be spotted? Eric's right. They should stick to the empty desert.

Max, I want you to do a search on Libya's naval forces. I want to know where every ship capable of landing a helicopter is right now."

Hanley asked, "What about you?"

"I'm going to call Langston and convince him to stick to my script. Then I want Doc Huxley to look at where I gouged out my subdermal transmitter and give me another dose of local. I have a feeling I'm going to need it."

TWENTY-EIGHT

E DDIE SENG GENTLY CLOSED HIS CELL PHONE AND THOUGHT
he'd contained a sigh, but from across the sweltering hotel
room Hali Kasim asked, "What's up?"

Max had already briefed the pair about what had been happening, so the call had lasted for less than five seconds, but from the look
on Seng's face the news couldn't be good.

"The Chairman wants us to grab Tariq Assad."

"When? Tonight?"

"Now."

"Why?"

"Didn't ask."

Because the dingy room they rented from the Chinese gang lacked
air-conditioning or even running water, both men were stripped down
to their boxer shorts. Both their bodies ran with sweat, although Hali
seemed to be suffering the worst. His chest and upper shoulders were
a matted pelt of hair, a legacy of his Lebanese heritage.

Eddie had been leaning against one of the single bed's headboards
when his cell had chimed. He stood and started getting on his

clothes. He shook out the cockroaches before legging into his pants. A trickle of aromatic steam from the restaurant below the room rose from a seam in the old wooden floors.

"Are we really doing this?" Hali asked, a fresh wash of perspiration slicking his face.

"Juan says that Assad's the key, so, yeah, we're doing this."

"The key? Assad's the key? The guy's nothing more than a two-bit, two-timing corrupt official."

Seng looked across at the Corporation's communications specialist. "All the more reason to wonder why they've staked out his house, and his office at the dock. Max said yesterday that their government thinks he's tied in with Al-Jama's crew, even though that makes no sense. Assad's lifestyle is too conspicuous for him to be a terrorist. Real tangos don't carry on a half dozen romantic liaisons and draw potential police interest by taking bribes."

Hali thought for a moment. "Okay, I'll buy that. So if he's not with Al-Jama, why do the Libyans want him so badly?"

"For the same reason Juan does. He knows something about this whole mess, only no one knows what."

Kasim was on his feet, securing a compact Glock 19 to an ankle holster before slipping on his pants. "This is why I stay on the ship. There my job is easy. Radio call comes in, I answer it. Someone wants to talk to a guy on the other side of the world, I make it happen. Shore Operations need encrypted phones that look like cigarette packs, I can get 'em. Skulking around in broad daylight trying to abduct a man wanted by the Libyan secret police isn't exactly my cup of tea."

Putting on the accent of an elderly Chinese sage, Eddie said, "Broaden your appetites, grasshopper, and the world will feed your soul."

Seng was not noted for his sense of humor. It wasn't that he didn't enjoy a good joke but that he was rarely the source, so Hali's laugh was disproportionately loud and long. Telling it had been Eddie's way of reassuring Hali that he knew what he was doing.

"Don't worry. Our last report puts Assad at the house of girlfriend number three. The Libyan authorities are nowhere near there. By now, he has to know he's a wanted man, so anyone offering him a lifeline is going to seem like a godsend. We're just going to stroll up, explain to him he's out of options, and bring him back here. Piece of cake."

Assad's third mistress, the Rubenesque wife of a judge, lived with her husband in a neighborhood of four- and five-story buildings built of stone covered with stucco and dating back more than a hundred years. The windows and balconies were protected by wrought-iron grilles, and the flat roofs were seas of satellite dishes. The ground floors of most of the buildings were shops and boutiques that catered to the upscale residents.

The sidewalks were wide and generous, while the roads were narrow and twisting, a leftover from when the neighborhood was serviced by horses rather than cars. The meandering nature of the streets gave the neighborhood a feeling of exclusivity, a quiet little enclave in the otherwise bustling city.

The Chinese gang members they had hired to track Tariq Assad hid in plain sight with a broken-down delivery van. They were parked opposite the mistress's building, with the hood up and engine parts spread across a tarp on the nearby sidewalk. Men and women, some dressed in robes, others in Western fashion, moved around them without a glance.

Eddie found a spot for their rental car in front of a small grocery store down the street from the van. The smell of oranges from bins flanking the door filled the air.

He fumbled in the glove compartment while focusing on the

street, searching for anything out of the ordinary. Nothing seemed out of place, and his instincts, which had served him well over the years, told him the area was clear. The two old men playing backgammon at an outdoor café were what they appeared to be. The stock boy dusting a table in the front window of a furniture store kept his eyes on his job and not on passing traffic. No one was just sitting in his car as the afternoon sun beat down mercilessly. Other than the gang members, there were no vans for an observation team to use as a base.

At the end of the block was a large construction site with a crawler crane, hoisting material up the ten-story, steel-and-concrete framework of what would soon be luxury condominiums. Again, Eddie saw nothing suspicious about the parade of cement mixers and trucks moving through the gates.

"Ready?" he asked Hali.

Kasim blew out a breath so his cheeks puffed like a horn player's. "How do you and Juan and the others keep so calm?"

"Juan, for one, thinks out every possible scenario and makes sure he has a contingency plan for whatever crops up. Me? I don't think about it at all. I just clear my mind and react as needed. Don't worry, Hali. We'll be fine."

"Let's do this, then."

They opened their doors. Eddie adjusted his hat and dark glasses, the only form of disguise he was using to hide his Asian features. Both men wore baggy tan slacks and open-necked shirts, which was about as anonymous as one could get in many quarters of the Middle East.

As they strolled past the van, Eddie palmed a disposable cell phone off on one of the gang members. He whispered, "Push back your perimeter, and watch that red Fiat we drove here. Speed-dial one is my phone."

The Chinese youth gave no indication he heard anything other than the slam of the van's hood. Eddie and Hali walked on without breaking stride.

The front door to their target building wasn't locked, but there was a watchman in a dark uniform sitting on a sofa in the lobby, reading a newspaper. The pair had walked in as if one of them had just told a joke. Both were laughing, and they ignored the guard when he set aside his paper and asked something in Arabic that neither man understood.

Hali never saw the move. He didn't believe they were even close enough.

Eddie had lunged like a fencer, the fingers of his right hand held stiff and ridged. He connected with the hollow of the guard's throat just below the Adam's apple. He could have killed the man had he wanted, but the strike was measured. The Libyan started to gag, and Eddie threw another blow, the edge of his hand connecting on the side of the man's neck. The watchman's eyes rolled up until only the whites showed, and he crumpled back onto the couch.

Seng glanced out the glass door to see if anyone was paying attention, and then with Hali's help he dragged the unconscious watchman into a back room, where one wall was lined with mail cubbies.

"How long will he be out?"

"An hour or so." Eddie rifled the man's pocket, looking for ID. It said the guard's name was Ali. "Come on. Assad's on the fourth floor, front-side corner."

Both men drew their pistols as they climbed an interior stairwell. They weren't concerned about running into anyone. People who lived in buildings like this invariably used the elevator.

Eddie cautiously opened the door on the fourth-floor landing. The hallway beyond was carpeted and lit with wall sconces. The six apartment doors were solid, made of heavy carved wood—left over from a time of superior craftsmanship. He was relieved the doors didn't have peepholes.

He approached the door to the mistress's apartment and rapped respectfully. A moment later, he heard a muffled woman's voice. He assumed she was asking who it was, so he said, "Ali, *sayyidah*."

She spoke again, most likely asking what he wanted, so Eddie said the first thing that popped into his head, and prayed his pronunciation was close. *"Al-Zajal, sayyidah."* Federal Express, ma'am. He'd seen their distinctively colored trucks all over the city.

Eddie mouthed "Stay back" to Hali, while inside the apartment a chain rattled and a pair of locks disengaged. He slammed his shoulder into the door, meeting more resistance than he'd expected but managing to shove the woman aside. He dove low, and a bullet from a silenced pistol cut the air inches over his shoulder.

The woman screamed. Seng rolled once, coming to his knees behind a couch. "Tariq, don't shoot." He kept his voice as calm as the adrenaline dose would allow. "Please. We're here to help."

The woman's cry turned into slow blubbering, as a few seconds ticked away on the grandfather clock pressed up against one plaster wall.

"Who are you?" Tariq Assad asked.

"A couple of nights ago, you made arrangements for us to unload a large truck in the harbor."

"The Canadians?"

"Yes."

"Who was I contacted through?"

"L'Enfant."

"You may stand," Assad said.

Eddie got to his feet slowly, making certain Assad could see his finger was nowhere near his pistol's trigger. "We're here to help you get out."

Hali entered the room cautiously. Assad watched him for a moment, then turned his attention back to Eddie. Seng had removed his hat and glasses so the harbor pilot could see his features. "I recognize you from that night. You acted as helmsman. You know, since then I thought I was going insane. I've had the feeling of being watched, and everywhere I turn I see young Chinamen acting strangely. I guess you are the explanation."

"I hired some local boys to keep tabs on you," Eddie said, slipping his pistol into the waistband of his pants.

Assad crossed to the crying woman, helping her up onto her piano legs. She wiped at her nose with the back of her hand, smearing a wet trail through her fine mustache. Eddie guessed she tipped the scales above two hundred, and standing at a little over five feet she looked like a basketball in her burnt orange robe.

Tariq Assad was no Adonis, with his graying hair and single dense eyebrow, but he had a good personality and Eddie thought he could have done better than this rather bovine woman. If not love or lust, he guessed information. She was the wife of a judge, after all.

As the Libyan muttered reassurances into her cauliflower ear, Eddie surveyed the apartment. The judge's home was well furnished, with a new leather sofa and chairs and a marble-topped coffee table with a neatly arranged fan of glossy magazines. There was an impressive oriental rug on the hardwood floor, and shelves for matching leather-bound books. The walls were adorned with intricate needlework of geometric design framed under glass. Her handiwork, he assumed. A breeze worked the gauzy curtains near the balcony, and the apartment was high enough that the traffic below was a low-register thrum.

Assad patted his mistress on her ample rump to send her back to the bedroom.

"She's a good girl," he remarked before she was out of earshot.

"Not too bright, and a little rough on the eyes, yes, but a veritable tiger where it counts."

Eddie and Hali shuddered.

"May I get you gentlemen a drink?" Assad offered when the bedroom door closed. "The judge favors gin, but I brought Scotch whiskey. Oh, and I am sorry for firing at you. It was reflex. I thought it was him."

"I think you can drop the act, Mr. Assad."

No one spoke for a few seconds. Eddie could read Assad's face. He'd been out in the cold, in spy parlance, for a while, and was debating if the two strangers represented a way out.

His shoulders sagged slightly. "Okay. No more act." Though he still spoke English with an accent, it was subtly different. "I'm pretty screwed no matter what happens now, so it doesn't really matter anymore. Who are you people? I figured CIA, when I met with you on your ship."

"Near enough," Eddie replied. "That's Hali Kasim. My name's Eddie Seng."

"You're in Libya to find out what happened to your Secretary of State?"

"Yeah. But the mission's also morphed into a hunt for Suleiman Al-Jama."

"As I figured it would. His organization is like an octopus with its tentacles wrapped all through the Libyan government. They work in the shadows, infiltrating one high-ranking office after another."

"Who are you and what's your deal here?"

"My name's Lev Goldman."

Understanding hit Eddie like a punch to the gut. "My God, Mossad. We have information that says you've been here five years."

"No. My cover goes back that far. I arrived in Tripoli eighteen months ago. Tel Aviv suspected Al-Jama was going to take over a

North African country through slow subterfuge. They sent deep-cover agents into Morocco, Algeria, Tunisia, and here to keep an eye on the government. When it became clear that Libya was the target, the other agents were pulled and I remained."

"So these women?"

Goldman lowered his voice even further. "Lonely housewives of powerful men. Oldest trick in the book."

"And your work at the harbor?"

"Nothing goes in or out that I don't know about. Arms, supplies, everything Al-Jama's brought here. Including a modified Hind gunship they bought from the Pakistanis. It was used in the high mountains of Kashmir, and can reach elevations unheard of for a regular helicopter. I had no idea why they wanted it until Fiona Katamora's plane crashed."

"Members of our team took it out," Eddie told him. "They also rescued about a hundred people who used to work in Libya's Foreign Ministry."

"There were rumors of a purge when Ali Ghami was named Minister despite the press reports that everyone who left had retired or been transferred to other branches of the government. This is still a police state, so everyone knew not to question the official word."

"Listen, we can get into all of this later. We need to get you out of here. The secret police have staked out your home and office."

"Why do you think I was hiding here?"

"What's your exit strategy?"

"I have a couple, but I thought I'd have a little warning from some of my contacts. I'm flying by the seat of my pants now. I had planned to ambush the judge when he got home from work and steal his car. I have an electronic device that will broadcast my location to an Israeli satellite. My orders are to get out into the southern desert as far as I can and await extraction by an Army helicopter disguised as a relief agency helo doing charity work for Darfur refugees in Chad."

"We can get you out quicker and safer, but we have to leave now."

No sooner had Eddie spoken the words than his phone rang. He answered without speaking, listened for a few seconds, and cut the connection. "Too late. Our guys just reported a police van moving into the area. They also hear an approaching helicopter. They'll be establishing a wide perimeter before closing in."

"I have a secret exit from this building but it won't get us far enough away. I had it in case the judge ever came home early."

Eddie made a snap decision. "We're going to split up. Hali, stay with Lev. Get yourselves to an embassy, but not ours. Try Switzerland, or some other unallied country. You'll be safe there until this all blows over."

"What about you?"

"I'm the distraction. Lev, where's the master bathroom?"

"Through there." He pointed to the closed bedroom door.

All three men strode into the room. Lev and the judge's wife spoke for a few moments, he trying to reassure her, she accusing him of God knows what. Eddie ignored them and flipped on the bathroom light. He searched through several drawers until he found the items he wanted.

First, he moussed his hair to give it Goldman's curls and then sprinkled it with talcum powder so it matched his salt-and-pepper. He filled in the space between his eyebrows with a cosmetic pencil, and used a wad of toilet paper and the contents of a mascara bottle to give his face Goldman's heavy five o'clock shadow.

Goldman saw what Eddie was doing and had his harbor pilot shirt off and ready to swap. Eddie tossed Goldman his shirt and slipped on Goldman's.

The Israeli agent led them out of the bathroom and into the

woman's closet. He pushed aside a section of the hanging clothes, ignoring the increasing whine of her pleading questions. He moved a rather odorous shoe rack to reveal a piece of wood pressed up against the stucco wall. When he pulled it away, there was an open void about two feet across that ran the depth of the building. Opposite, they could see the backside of the laths for the next apartment. Budging plaster filled the gaps between the boards. Above, light filtered into the void from a pair of dusty skylights.

"This was left over from when the building was converted from offices," Lev explained. "I found it on the old blueprints. At the bottom, I cut another hole that leads to the garage."

"Okay, you two go down. Hali, get our car and pick up Lev in the garage. The cordon shouldn't be too tight yet, and with any luck the police will be focusing on me."

"If it is the police," Goldman said. "Remember, Al-Jama is running a shadow government inside Qaddafi's."

"Does it really matter?" Hali pointed out, thrusting a leg into the opening.

He braced a foot on each wall and slowly started making his way down. His motion kicked up a thick cloud of fine white dust, and his weight caused the old laths to bow. Chunks of plaster broke away and fell into the darkness below.

Goldman had to disentangle himself from his distraught mistress. Her eye makeup ran in dark smudges down her apple cheeks, and her heavy bosom heaved with each sob.

"Women," he remarked when he was finally free and crawling after Hali.

Eddie followed him, but rather than descend he moved laterally for a few feet, so any plaster he dislodged wouldn't hit the men below, and started climbing. It was only a single story, so it took just a few minutes before he was pressed up under one of the skylights. The heat in the shaft was stifling, a weight that pulled at him as surely as gravity.

He could hear the rotor beat of the police helicopter and judged he had a few more seconds. The glazing holding the panes of glass to the metal frame had dried rock hard and came away with just a little pressure.

A shadow passed over the skylight. The chopper.

Eddie swallowed hard and popped one of the large panes free. The sound of the helicopter doubled, and even though he was exposed to the noonday sun it felt like he was moving into air-conditioning.

He rolled onto the flat, tarry roof and got to his feet. The chopper was a couple blocks away, hovering a few hundred feet above the rooftops. Eddie had to wait almost a minute before he was spotted. The big machine twisted in the air and thundered toward him. Its side door was open, and a police sniper stood braced with a scoped rifle cradled against his shoulder.

Eddie ran for the wall separating this building from the next, his feet sinking slightly into the warm tar. The wall was built to chest height and topped with jagged bits of embedded glass to prevent people from doing what Seng was attempting. But unlike barbed wire, which never loses its keen edge, the glass had been scoured by wind for decades and was almost smooth. Pieces snapped flat when he vaulted over the wall. He landed on the other side.

This building's roof was virtually identical to the first, a wide area of a tar-gravel mix punctured by the elevator housing and dozens of satellite dishes and defunct antennae.

The chopper swooped low over the roof, and Eddie made certain the sniper saw his face and hoped it was a close enough match to Tariq Assad's. He got his answer a second later when a three-round burst from an automatic weapon pounded the roof at his feet.

Now that the police believed their suspect was on the roof, Hali and Goldman should be able to slip away undetected.

Eddie raced for the back of the building, cutting a serpentine path to throw off the sharpshooter, and almost threw himself from the edge before realizing that, unlike the mistress's apartment house, this one didn't have a proper fire escape. There was just a simple metal ladder bolted to the side of the structure, a death trap if he committed himself to it with the sniper hovering so close overhead.

He glanced back the way he came. He'd be running right for the circling chopper if he retreated, so instead he ran for the next building, vaulting the wall and opening a gash in his palm for the effort. Not all the glass had weathered the same.

More bullets pounded into the roof, kicking up hot clots of tar that burned against his cheek. He pulled his pistol and returned fire. The wide misses were still enough to force the pilot to retreat for a moment.

Sprinting flat out, he raced for the next building, throwing himself over the wall and almost dropping down. The next building was a story lower than the previous ones, and beyond that was the open expanse of the construction site. Dangling from his fingertips, he looked quickly to see if there was any evidence of a fire escape and saw none, not even a cable house for an elevator.

He made the decision to pull himself back over the wall and find some other route when the sniper zeroed in on his hands. Bullets tore into the brick and mortar, forcing Eddie to drop free. He rolled when he landed to absorb the impact, but surviving the ten-foot drop didn't mean he was any less trapped.

TWENTY-NINE

B Y THE TIME HALI KASIM REACHED THE BOTTOM OF THE air shaft, he was covered in dust, and his shoulders and knees ached mercilessly. He promised himself that when he returned to the *Oregon*, he'd spend more time in the ship's fitness center. He'd seen how effortlessly Eddie had climbed, and the former CIA agent was nearly a decade older.

The floor here was littered with fragments of plaster and dried layers of pigeon guano. Lev Goldman lowered himself the last few feet. Sweat had cut channels through the dirt caked on his face, and the dust coating his beard aged him twenty years.

"You okay?" Hali panted, resting his hands on his knees.

"Perhaps I should have thought up a better escape route," the Israeli admitted, fighting not to cough in the mote-filled air. "Come. This way."

He led Kasim toward the rear of the building and an area where the lath had been cut way low to the ground. Together they kicked at the two-foot-square spot. At first, the blows merely cracked the plaster. But then bits of it broke away. Goldman used his hands to tear out inch-thick chunks until the hole was big enough to crawl through.

They emerged into an underground garage. The lot was mostly vacant, with only a few cars, usually driven by the stay-at-home wives, sitting in their assigned spots. Had any of them been older models, Hali would have considered hot-wiring one of them, but they were all fairly new and would be equipped with alarms.

"Meet me at the exit and stay out of sight," he said. "Our car is right around the corner."

Hali dusted himself off as best he could as he jogged up the ramp and into the blazing sunshine. The street was a scene of pandemonium. The shots fired from the helicopter had forced everyone to find cover. Oranges from the grocer's littered the sidewalk where someone had run into the display. The chairs where the old men had played backgammon were overturned. Police vans were just now arriving.

It didn't take much acting for Hali to pretend to be just another frightened Libyan. He reached their rental car and opened the door. Sirens filled the air, drowning out even the heavy throb of the chopper's blades.

The Fiat's engine fired on the first try. Hali's hands were so slick that the wheel got away from him, and he clipped the rear bumper of the car parked in front of him, its alarm adding to the keening police sirens.

The first of the officers, outfitted in black tactical gear, began to emerge from a van. They would have the block surrounded in seconds. Yet none of them seemed interested in anything except the building's front door. Eddie's distraction was working. They thought they had their man cornered and ignored proper procedure.

Hali drove around the corner, slowed, but didn't stop for Lev Goldman, who threw himself into the passenger's seat, and eased into traffic on the next side street.

Every block they drove exponentially increased the area the police had to cover in order to find them. After eight stoplights, Goldman felt safe enough to pop his head up above the dashboard.

"Pull over into that gas station," he ordered.

"Can't you hold it?"

"Not for that. We need to switch seats. It is obvious you don't know the roads or how to drive like a local. No one here obeys the traffic rules."

Hali cranked the wheel into the gas station's lot and threw the car into park. Lev sat still for a moment, expecting Hali to jump out so he could slide over. Instead, he was forced out of the car, and Kasim took the passenger's seat.

He chuckled humorlessly when he engaged the transmission. "In a situation like that, Mossad training says driver should exit the vehicle."

Kasim looked at him skeptically. "Really? Doing it your way means there is no one at the wheel for several seconds longer. You should talk to your instructors."

"No matter." Lev grinned, this time with genuine amusement. "We made it."

He asked as they made random turns away from his mistress's neighborhood, "I am sorry, what is your name again?"

"Kasim. Hali Kasim."

"That is an Arab name. Where are you from?"

"Washington, D.C."

"No. I mean your family. Where were they from?"

They took what Hali assumed was a shortcut in an alley between two large, featureless buildings. "My grandfather emigrated from Lebanon when he was a boy."

"So are you Muslim or Christian?"

"What difference does that make?"

"If you are Christian, I wouldn't feel so bad about this."

The report was just a sharp spit in the confines of the Fiat's cramped interior. A fine mist of blood splattered the passenger's window when the bullet burst from Hali's rib cage. Goldman fired his silenced pistol again at the same instant the car hit a pothole. His aim was off, so the round missed entirely, blowing out the side window in a cascade of minuscule chips.

Hali had been so stunned in the first instant of the attack, he had done nothing to stop the second shot. His chest felt like a molten poker had been rammed through it from side to side, and he could feel hot wetness trickling past his belt line.

He grabbed for the gun as it recoiled up, forcing Goldman to let go of the wheel and throw an awkward body shot that still hit directly on the entrance wound. Hali screamed at the unimaginable agony of it, and he lost his grip on the handgun's warm barrel.

Rather than fight a battle he had no chance of winning, he used his elbow to push open the door release and let himself fall from the car. They were doing perhaps twenty-five miles per hour, and he landed right on his butt, so he didn't tumble but rather slid along the pavement, until skin smeared from his body.

The Fiat's brake lights lit up immediately, but by the time the car had come to a stop Hali had pulled his pistol from his ankle holster. He fired as soon as he saw Goldman's head emerge from the car. Hali missed, so he fired again, this time aiming through the car. Glass splintering sound like tiny bells. The pistol's recoil made him feel like he was being kicked, but he kept at it. Three more rounds hit the car, other rounds shot masonry off the building beyond. The man Hali thought was an Israeli agent decided killing him wasn't worth it.

"If you'd only gotten out at that gas station, I would have simply driven away," he said. The Fiat's door slammed, and the car sped off with a chirp of its tires.

Hali collapsed onto his back, his chest heaving as his blood pumped from both entrance and exit wounds. He yanked up his shirt to see the damage. There were tiny bubbles foaming from the right-side bullet hole. He didn't need Doc Huxley to tell him he had been shot in the lung, or that if he didn't get to a hospital soon he was a dead man.

The alley where he'd been both duped and dumped was long, and he couldn't see traffic crossing either entrance. This had been a perfect setup, he thought fleetingly, gritting his teeth against a fresh wave of pain when he levered himself to his feet. Whoever Goldman was, he had played them like a maestro.

Hali made it no more than a couple of paces before he collapsed against the building and dropped to the ground amid the broken bottles, thorny weeds, and trash.

His last thought before succumbing to oblivion was relief that Eddie would most likely make it out. Nothing could stop the wiry ex-agent.

●   ●   ●

EDDIE SENG COULD ONLY HOPE that Hali and Goldman were safe, because he was in serious trouble. The police helicopter roared into view overhead, and he put two bullets into its underside before it swept out of pistol range. The sniper wasn't so limited by his weapon and blazed away. Bullets pounded the wall behind Eddie, forcing him to run again. The marksman adjusted, leading Eddie ever so slightly, and put a round through the roof less than an inch from his right toe.

Eddie felt as exposed as an actor on an empty stage. Without any cover, it was only a matter of time before the bullets found their mark. Ahead of him, the roof ended in a low decorative cornice, and beyond was the skeletal framework of the new high-rise under construction. An Olympic long jumper would still miss the building by fifty feet from here. The boom of the crane that he and Hali had seen was closer, but there would be nothing to grab onto if he made it.

It was swinging across the sky and Eddie could see its cable reeling upward, but he had no idea what was being maneuvered to one of the building's upper floors.

At this point, it didn't matter.

Putting on a burst of speed, he raced for the horizon, running flat out without any deviation. The sniper high above zeroed in, laying down a rain of fire that chased Eddie's heels. Just before reaching the cornice, he saw down below that the crane was lifting a pallet of Sheetrock. He altered his speed slightly, put one foot on the cornice, and launched himself into space, leaping through a stinging cloud of exploding masonry.

He flew out and down, a forty-foot drop sucking at his body, his stomach lurching at the rapid earthward acceleration. The pallet of Sheetrock was twelve feet below him and rising when he leapt, so when he crashed into it the impact turned his ankle and he almost slid off the far side.

Before he could grab one of the cables, his weight unbalanced the load. It tipped, and he had to scramble on his bad leg. Sheets of gypsum board began to slide against one another as the angle increased. He lunged for the cable as the entire two tons slipped free. The sheets separated as they fell, spreading out as though a giant had tossed a deck of playing cards into the air.

Eddie's fingers clutched at the cable, his body jerking spasmodically because the cable was bouncing to adjust to losing the load. He managed to change his grip and loop a leg around the cable.

To his credit, the crane's operator was quick-thinking. He had been watching the lift from the cab, had seen the figure leap from the adjacent building, and understood why the heavy sheets had fallen. Rather than take the time to slowly lower the dangling figure to the ground, he locked the cable spool and continued to swing the boom toward the unfinished building.

The heavy hook at the end of the cable had enough weight to pendulum Eddie through the building's open side, and he let go, tumbling onto a concrete floor. The workers who'd seen his stunt were several floors above him. It would take them a few moments to come down the ladders leaning inside what would become a stairwell.

Favoring his sprained ankle, Eddie loped to the edge of the building, where a debris chute had been attached. He peered over the edge. The chute was a metal tube about twenty-four inches in diameter that ended just above a large green Dumpster sitting atop a flatbed truck. He stepped in, wedged his good foot against the wall, and braced his hands behind him. His descent was measured and controlled. His only real concern was that someone higher up might toss something in the Dumpster after him.

He landed lightly on chunks of concrete and rebar torn out from a cement pour gone wrong. Seconds later, he was over the side of the Dumpster and striding across the construction site. Everyone still assumed he was up on the third floor, so no one paid him the slightest attention. Most important, the hovering sniper was watching the building and not the lone figure crossing the construction yard.

Parked near a pump truck designed to force concrete up armored hoses to the upper stories was a cement mixer, its rear chute extended with cement flowing into the pump's hopper. Eddie leapt onto its front bumper, stepped onto its driver's-side fender, and grabbed the big wing-mirror support before the driver was aware of Eddie's presence. Eddie swung himself through the open window, caught the man on the jaw with his good foot, and dropped into the seat as the man collapsed sideways.

The whole truck vibrated with the power of the huge cement drum turning just behind the cab. Eddie kicked the unconscious man down into the passenger's footwell, yanked the gearshift into first, and started forward. He couldn't hear the shouts of the surprised workers, but he could see them running after the cement mixer in his wing mirrors.

He drove the truck across the site on the dedicated dirt road. In his wake, wet cement continued to fall from the chute like the mixer was some diarrheal mechanical monster. The chopper had to have alerted the ground forces that their man had leapt for the construction site, because a half dozen cops were rushing for the chain-link gate when Eddie smashed through, scattering men like bowling pins.

When he cranked the wheel over, the steel chute pivoted outward like a baseball bat at full swing, knocking over two more men and smashing out the windshield of a parked sedan. A police car charged after him, its siren wailing. When it pulled alongside, Eddie braked hard and turned the wheel. The cement mixer rode up onto the cruiser's hood. The massive weight of the truck and its load of concrete blew out the front tires and burst the radiator. The truck's rear wheels skidded into the patrol car so it blocked both the road's narrow lanes.

The move sent the chute flinging the other way and it tore through the glass of another car. It ricocheted back and forth like a metal tail, smashing into automobiles and keeping the pursuing police well back.

Eddie could see them pause to fire at the truck, but their shots were deflected by the enormous revolving drum, and he was increasing the range with every second. The problem wasn't them. It was the helicopter circling overhead. Eddie couldn't make his escape with them watching his every move and radioing his position

The street straightened and widened as he left the neighborhood. In the distance, approaching at nearly seventy miles per hour, were three more police cars, their lights winking rhythmically. Charging along with them was some sort of wheeled armored vehicle. Eddie assumed it would have a mounted heavy machine gun.

He pressed the accelerator to the floor, short shifting the transmission to build up his speed as quickly as possible. With a hundred feet separating him and the cruisers, Eddie slammed on the brakes and spun the wheel over hard. The front fender caught the rear corner of a big delivery truck, and it was enough to unbalance the cement mixer. It went up onto its outside wheels, even as it continued to careen sideways, and then it smashed over onto its side.

Eddie held on to the wheel to stop himself from tumbling onto the passenger's door, covering his face with his elbow to protect it from the flying glass of the shattered windshield. The truck's regular operator was sufficiently jammed into place that he was okay as glass rained down on him.

The collision with the ground was hard enough to snap the pins holding the cement drum in place and break the links of its chain drive. Momentum did the rest.

Eleven tons of steel and concrete began rolling down the street, wobbling slightly as the cement sloshed in the huge barrel. Two of the police cars had the good sense to peel out of the way and jump onto the curb, one smashing into a utility pole, the other coming to rest with its front end embedded in a wall. The armored car and the other cruiser were closer and didn't stand a chance. The barrel rolled up the armored car's front glacis and tore its small turret from its mount. The gunner would have been sliced in half had he not ducked at the last second.

The drum smashed back onto the road, cracking the asphalt before hitting the police cruiser in a glancing blow that was still enough to flatten it from the rear seat back. The barrel came to rest against the side of a building, with cement as stiff as toothpaste oozing from its open mouth.

Eddie grabbed a spare work shirt that had been hanging from a peg at the back of the cab and stepped through the shattered windshield. He was hidden from the view of the chopper by the truck, so he took a few seconds to wipe the cosmetics from his face and don the denim shirt. The pain radiating from his ankle was something he could contain and compartmentalize, so when he moved away from the truck he walked without a limp. He went no more than a few feet and stopped to stare with the people who'd poured out of shops and homes to see the accident. As simply as that, he was just another rubbernecker.

When the police arrived and began questioning witnesses, he was virtually ignored. They were looking for a Libyan, not an Asian man who spoke no Arabic. He slowly drifted away from the scene, and no one stopped him. Five minutes after calling their hired gang members, he was in the van headed away from the neighborhood entirely.

●　　●　　●

FIVE MILES AWAY IN the rented Fiat, Tariq Assad was on his cell phone.

"It's me. There was a raid today. The police almost got me. First, find out why I wasn't warned. This should have never happened. As it was, I had a little help in escaping from those people off that damned ship. I was pumping them for information when the police arrived."

He listened for a moment, and replied. "Watch your tone! You arranged the ambush on the coast road, and those were your hand-picked men. We've both seen a copy of the investigation report, thanks to our mole in the police. Rather than let vehicles pass unmolested, your supposedly well-trained men were shaking down motorists for bribe money. I don't know how these American mercenaries managed to kill them all, but they did. Then they proceeded to blow up our Hind, free most of our prisoners, and generally disrupt what had been a perfectly executed plan . . . What? Yes, I said free. Their cargo ship must have been berthed at the coaling station dock. Our men saw an empty train car sinking . . . How should I know? Maybe the vessel is faster than it looks or the men in the chopper were bigger fools than the ones you sent to stop their truck in the first place.

"I have to get out of the city now," he went on. "Actually, out of the country. I know a pilot who is sympathetic to our cause. I will ask him to fly me in his helicopter to where the men are searching for Suleiman Al-Jama's tomb, and I will take control personally. Despite the setbacks, it appears you have everything controlled from this end. Fiona Katamora should be in her execution chamber by now, and Colonel Hassad phoned to tell me our martyr force is en route.

"I won't speak to you again until it's over. So let me say that Allah's blessings be upon us all."

He killed the connection and tossed the encrypted phone on the seat next to him. He was a man who had always been able to keep a grip on his emotions. He wouldn't have lasted as long as he had if he couldn't. Today's close call enraged him. He hadn't been lying when he said they had spies and sympathizers in every level of the Libyan government. He'd had ample warning that the police were staking out his office and apartment, so he should have been told about the raid.

It seemed the supreme leader, Muammar Qaddafi, needed reminding that his autonomy remained limited.

THIRTY

OVING AS SLOWLY AS HE COULD, ERIC STONE REACHED under his chest and carefully turned the rock that had been digging into his ribs for the past fifteen minutes. He could feel the disapproval that he'd moved radiating off Franklin Lincoln, who was lying prone next to him. On his other side was Mark Murphy, and beside him was Linda Ross. Next to her was Alana Shepard.

Despite everything she'd been through and the dangers now presented by the terrorists, she had insisted on coming with them. Dr. Huxley had given her a brief medical exam and cleared her for the mission.

Because of her rank within the Corporation, Linda was in charge of the group, so it was her call. She'd figured Cabrillo would nix the idea, so she hadn't bothered asking when she'd agreed to let Alana come with them.

They were on a ridge overlooking the dry river valley where Alana and her team had spent so many weeks searching for Suleiman Al-Jama's lost tomb. Below them were a dozen terrorists from the training camp. They might have been proficient at killing and maiming, but they were useless when it came to archaeology. The squad leader had no idea what he was doing, so he had the men scrambling all over the wadi, moving random stones and climbing the steep banks looking for any clue as to the tomb's location. At their current pace, they'd reach the old waterfall Alana's team had found in four or five hours.

With them was Professor Emile Bumford. It was difficult to tell without binoculars, which they couldn't use for fear the sun would flash off the lens, but he didn't look the worse for wear. He was searching like the others, and while he moved slowly he wasn't limping or favoring any injury. There was no sign of the representative from the Tunisian Antiquities Ministry or his son. He'd been paid for betraying the Americans and was probably back in Tunis.

There was no sign of the old Mi-8 helicopter the terrorists were using as a base, so the team assumed it was farther down the river and would leapfrog the searchers when they reached a predetermined distance away.

Linc tapped Eric's leg, the signal for them to retreat off the ridge. He slithered back as carefully as he could, followed by Linda, Mark, and Alana. The former SEAL stayed in position for a couple more minutes, making certain no one below saw any movement.

He led them southward for twenty minutes before he judged it safe enough to talk, albeit in whispers.

"What do you think?" Mark asked.

"I guess we have to ask ourselves WWJD?"

Mark looked at him strangely. "What would Jesus do?"

"No. What would Juan do?"

"That's easy," Eric said. "Take out the bad guys, find the tomb, and somehow manage to bed a local Bedouin girl."

Alana had to cover her mouth to stifle a laugh.

"Seriously," Linc went on. "Now that we know where the bad guys are, we've only got a few hours before they reach the falls. Do you two geniuses have any idea how to find the tomb?"

"We need to see the falls to be sure, but, yeah, we've got some ideas."

This was the first Alana had heard of their plans, and she said, "Hold on a second. I've seen the old waterfall for myself. There's no way a sailing ship could have negotiated them. They're too steep. The top one is practically a vertical wall."

"You're not giving credit where it's due," Eric said mildly.

"Here's the plan." Linda made eye contact with each member of her team. "We're going to try to find the tomb. Linc, I want you to stay behind and keep an eye on these guys. Radio when you think there's an hour left before they reach the falls so we can bug out. Any questions?"

There were none.

Having already marched to the wadi from their chopper's distant landing zone, the two men and two women still made good time hiking the six miles to the first set of cataracts that blocked the unnamed river. They had stayed on top of the bluff overlooking the bed so when they reached the falls they had a bird's-eye view. Linda ordered Alana to stay with the men while she scouted the area. Mark and Eric took up a position overlooking the cliffs and scanned them methodically with binoculars.

It was only from above, a vantage Alana and her partners had never enjoyed, that the odd nature of the riverbed became apparent. Upstream from the first cataract, there was a natural bowl that spanned the full width of the river, a basin formed of living rock that had resisted the efforts of erosion for aeons. It was roughly a hundred feet long, and its upstream side was yet another cliff face, only this one was just four feet higher than its predecessor. A man-made wall constructed of dressed and mortared stone ran its length. Unlike the streambed, which had been scoured clean by the powerful currents that once washed between the banks, the basin floor was littered with water-rounded boulders.

Also from above, she could see the footings of another ancient wall that had long since vanished, stretching from the base of the first falls and extending another hundred or so feet downstream.

She borrowed a pair of binoculars from Eric when she first spied the boulders and spent several minutes observing them, as if she expected them to move. Nothing changed, and yet they were telling her a story about what was happening farther into the mountains.

"Those are basalt," she said, handing back the glasses. "Same with that wall."

"So?"

"It's the first indication of anything other than sandstone in this whole godforsaken country. It means there was volcanic activity someplace around here."

"And that means?" Mark prompted.

"The possibility of caves."

"Of that there is no doubt."

Her tone turned to disappointment. "But it doesn't make any difference. Al-Jama couldn't have gotten his ship above the falls. Period."

"You're looking at this place like a geologist, not an engineer." He turned his head to talk to Eric. "Where do you think?"

"They'd need them on both banks. The river's too wide for just one." He pointed to a flat ledge just above the riverbank. "There for our side, and that promontory twenty feet higher on the other side."

"Agreed."

"What are you talking about?" Alana asked. Her only experience with the Corporation was witnessing them as soldiers. She didn't know what to make of Eric Stone and Mark Murphy. To her they were techno-geeks, not mercenaries, and they seemed to speak in a private code only they understood.

"Derricks," they said simultaneously. Eric added, "We'll show you."

They made their way down to the ledge. It would have remained a few feet above the water level even at the height of the spring runoff. It was almost dead even with the first cliff spanning the river, and was large enough to accommodate a city bus. The two men scanned the ground intently. When something caught their eye, one would bend to brush at the dirt covering the sandstone.

"Got it," Mark cried softly. He was on his haunches, excavating sand from a perfectly round twelve-inch-wide hole that had been drilled into the rock. He didn't hit bottom even when lying on the ground and burying his arm to the shoulder.

"What is that?" Alana asked.

"This is where they stepped the mast for the derrick," Murph replied. "Most likely the dressed trunk of a tree. Attached to it would have been an angled boom that could reach halfway across the river. As you can see by the hole, the boom was massive and would have been capable of supporting several tons. There would have been another on the opposite bank."

"I don't get it. What are they for?"

"Using these they could lower stones into the river—"

"Not stones," Eric countered quickly. "We talked about this. They would have used woven baskets, or possibly bags made of sailcloth, that were filled with sand. This way they would eventually dissolve in the current and wash away."

"Fine," Mark said with a tinge of irritation. Alana might be a dozen years older, but she was attractive, and Murph's only real hope with women was showing off his intellect. "Large bags of sand were lowered onto the wall they'd constructed below the first fall to divide the river channel. That way they could dam up the downstream end on one side and not stop the river entirely. Their earthworks would never have withstood the full force of the current.

"With the *Saqr* tucked into what was essentially a shipping lock, they allowed a controlled amount of water into the chamber, building the walls higher as it filled until they could haul the boat forward into the second lock, the one nature had created and which most likely inspired old Suleiman's engineer in the first place."

"They would repeat the process again," Eric added, "and draw the *Saqr* onto the upper river."

"You guys figured this out without ever visiting this place?" There was respect in Alana's voice.

Mark opened his mouth to brag, but Eric beat him to the explanation, saying with his trademark earnestness, "A lock is the only thing that could possibly explain what Henry Lafayette had meant by 'clever device.' Knowing that, we studied satellite imagery to verify our hypothesis."

"I am impressed," Alana told them. "And a little mad at myself. I stared at this stupid pile of rocks for hours but never saw it."

Mark was about to use this as another opening to brag when Linda Ross approached so silently no one heard her until she was right behind them. "You boys need to be a little more aware of your surroundings. I wasn't even trying to be quiet. What have you found?"

"Just as we suspected," Mark said, giving Eric a look. "During a particularly dry spell, when the river stopped flowing entirely, Al-Jama's people converted the waterfall into a lock system so they could hide their ship where no one would ever think to look."

"So the cave is farther upstream?"

"Gotta be."

"Then let's start hiking," Linda said.

She radioed Linc to tell them what was happening and inform him they might lose radio contact because of the distance and topography. He must have been close enough to the terrorists not to risk replying. Her acknowledgment was two quick clicks in her earpiece.

They started southward, marching three-quarters of the way up the bank so as not to silhouette themselves against the distant horizon, as well as to shield themselves from the worst of the wind that had started to kick up. This region of the desert was enough to make anyone feel insignificant. The brassy sky towered over the party, and the relentless sun beat down on them as they trudged along. They each carried enough water for a day so that wasn't a concern, but three of the four were operating on minimal sleep and the effects of a punishing few days.

For the members of the Corporation, they pushed themselves because they saw it as their duty. For Alana, she marched with them because, if she didn't, she would never lose the image of Mike Duncan's lifeless eyes, as the petroleum geologist lay on the desert floor with blood leaking from the hole in his forehead. She was an archaeologist and mother, and her place was as far from here as possible, but she wouldn't be able to live with herself if she'd not come. The decision certainly wasn't rational. However, she'd never been more certain.

Her life was dictated by rules that the men who killed Mike and kidnapped her had broken, and, simply put, she wanted revenge.

Two miles above the falls, the riverbed changed dramatically. The sandstone banks gave way to a lighter gray rock that had been part of a saltwater reef millions of years ago but was now limestone.

"This has got to be it," Alana said when she recognized the geology. "Limestone is notorious for caves and caverns."

Mark tapped Eric on the arm and pointed to a spot across the dry wash. "What do you think?"

It was an area where a landslide had torn away some of the bank and dumped untold tons of rubble into the riverbed. The slide stretched for a hundred and fifty feet, and behind it the riverbank was significantly taller than anywhere else they had seen.

"Bingo," Stone said, and high-fived Murph. "The cave's riverine entrance was blasted and the cavern sealed. Behind that mess is Suleiman Al-Jama's corsair, the *Saqr*, his tomb, and just possibly the Jewel of Jerusalem."

The initial excitement of finding the tomb's location faded quickly.

Alana voiced the concern. "There's no way we can move that much debris without heavy construction equipment and several weeks' time."

"Don't you get us yet?" Mark asked her seriously.

"What do you mean?"

"Back door," Stone and Murphy said in perfect sync.

It took ten minutes to climb down to the riverbed and cross the river before they were standing atop the crushed section of bank. The backside of the hill facing the western desert was a folded warren of gullies and ravines that had been eroded when the Sahara had been a lush, subtropical jungle. They found the first cave entrance only moments after splitting up into pairs and starting their systematic search.

Eric pulled a small halogen flashlight from a pocket on his upper sleeve and stepped into the man-sized aperture. Ten feet in, the cave turned ninety degrees and petered out into a solid wall of rock.

Linda and Alana found a second cave that went a little deeper before it, too, came to an abrupt end. The third cave was smaller than the others, forcing Eric and Mark to crawl on their hands and knees. It ran deep into the hillside, twisting with the vagaries of the matrix stone. At times, they could stand and walk upright, and then the next moment they were forced to slither through the dust on their bellies. Stone used a piece of chalk to mark the walls when the cave began to branch off.

"What do you think?" Eric asked after they'd been underground for fifteen minutes. He was pointing to a carving on one wall. It was crude, done with a knifepoint or awl, and neither man could read it, but they recognized the looping Arabic script. "Al-Jama's version of 'Kilroy was here'?"

"This has got to be it," Murph replied. "We're going to need help exploring all these side tunnels." He tried radioing Linda but couldn't get reception this deep into the earth. "Rock, paper, scissors?"

The two men made their choices, paper-covered rock, so Mark turned himself around for the laborious climb back to the surface, his echoing grumbles diminishing as he retreated.

Eric Stone shut off his light to conserve batteries, but when the weight of darkness pressed in on him like a palpable sensation he quickly flicked it back on. He took a few calming breaths to steel himself, shut his eyes, and killed the light again.

It was a long thirty-minute wait until he heard the others crawling down the tunnel.

When Mark's light swept Eric's face, Murph chuckled. "Man, you are as white as a ghost."

"I've never been fond of tight spaces," Stone admitted. "It's okay with the lights on. Not so much in the dark."

Normally, Mark would have ribbed him more, but considering their situation all he said was, "Don't sweat it, dude."

Linda quickly drew up a plan of attack to survey the subterranean warren of interconnected tunnels and caves. Whenever they came to a fork, one team would check the left tunnel, the other would head right. They would meet back at the branch after ten minutes no matter what. Whichever option looked the most promising was the way they would all go.

Another hour passed as they laboriously checked each section. It was all the more difficult because of the weapons and extra ammunition the three Corporation people carried. Knees and palms were scraped raw from contact with the rough stone, and without proper equipment each one of them had struck his or her head at least once. Eric had a piece of gauze taped near his hairline where he'd gashed his skin. Blood had dried coppery brown in the furrows of his forehead.

The four of them were together walking down a long gallery with heaps of shattered stones on the floor when Eric happened to play his flashlight on the ceiling ten feet over their heads. At first he thought the hundreds of projections hanging down were stalactites formed from mineral-rich water seeping into the cavern, but then he saw one was wearing pants.

Horror crept up his spine. "Oh my God."

Alana looked up and gasped.

Hanging from the ceiling were dozens of pairs of mummified legs, some showing just the foot from the ankle down, others hanging from the upper thighs as if materializing from the living rock. One person was suspended on his side, half of the corpse contained within the matrix stone while the other half dangled grotesquely. The neck was bent at such an angle that the back of the skull was hidden, and the cadaverous face leered down at them through sightless eye sockets.

There were animal legs, too, long, awkward camel legs ending in big skeletal feet and horses' limbs with their distinctive fused hoofs. The dry air had retarded putrefaction, so skin hung from the bones as brittle as parchment and clothing remained intact.

Mark studied the uneven floor, stooped, and came back up holding a leather sandal that began to crumble almost immediately.

Linda asked, "What happened to them? How did they get fused in the rock?"

Over his initial shock, Eric studied the ceiling more carefully. Unlike the rest of the cave system, the ceiling here was black and glossy under a coat of dust.

"Everyone cover your ears," he said, and brought his assault rifle to his shoulder. The crack of the shot was especially brutal in the tight confines.

The bullet had knocked free a splinter of the ceiling. He retrieved it, looked at it for only a moment, and tossed it to Mark Murphy.

"Completely solidified," he commented. "When the cave below the pit collapsed it left them hanging."

"Of course," Alana said, examining the material.

"Little help for the nonscience types." Linda didn't bother looking at the rock sample. Her only exposure to geology was a "rocks for jocks" class back in college.

"Above us is the bottom of a tar pit," Eric answered, "like La Brea in L.A., only smaller and obviously dormant."

"It's actually asphaltic sand," Alana corrected.

"During the summer months, it warmed enough to get sticky and entrap the animals. My guess is, the people were thrown in as a form of execution. Then, at some point over the past two hundred years, the bottom of the pit collapsed—that's all this rubble on the floor— and exposed the victims at the very deepest part of the pit."

"There was something I was told by St. Julian Perlmutter a couple of days after our initial meeting," Alana said, suddenly remembering. "He'd come across one additional scrap of information. It comes from a local belief about Al-Jama's tomb. It is said he was buried beneath the 'black that burns.' That's why they had us digging in an abandoned coal mine. The terrorists thought the black was coal, but it was this."

Eric took the shard of hardened tar from her and held the flame of a disposable lighter to the thumb-sized lump. In seconds, it caught fire, and he dropped it to the ground. The four of them watched it burn silently.

Linda snuffed it out with her foot. "I would say we're getting close."

But another hour of exploration still hadn't revealed the hidden tomb.

Eric and Mark had separated from the women at yet another juncture. They approached the dead end of a particularly straight and easy section of tunnel deep under the river's original water level. Eric paused to take a sip from his canteen before they retreated to the rendezvous. The end of the tunnel sloped up in a perfectly flat ramp that met the ceiling. Something about it intrigued him, and he climbed up the incline until his face was inches from where it joined the roof.

Rather than solid rock, he saw a jagged line, a crack barely a millimeter wide, that ran the full width of the tunnel. He fumbled in his pocket for the disposable lighter, and called over his shoulder, "Kill your light."

"What? Why?"

"Just do it already."

He thumbed the lighter and held the flame close to the crack. There wasn't much of a flicker, but it was enough to convince him that there was an open space on the other side of the ramp and a slight breeze was getting through. He turned on his light again, examining every square inch of the incline. It was a neatly fitted piece of work. The cracks along the walls were almost invisible.

"This is man-made," he announced. "I think it's like a giant teeter-totter. Give me a hand."

They stood, stooped, as far up the ramp as they could go, with their backs braced against the ceiling.

"On three," Eric said. "One . . . two . . . three."

They pushed with everything they had. At first, nothing happened, and the sounds of their straining bodies filled the tunnel. Then, imperceptibly, the floor under them gave way slightly, pushed down by their combined strength. When they relaxed, it snapped back into position.

"Again. Harder."

Their second attempt pushed the big stone lever down about an inch, enough for Eric to see there was a large chamber beyond. He jammed the lighter into the crack just before they let go, but the weight of stone was too great and the plastic case was crushed.

"Good idea, though. I think the four of us should be able to do it. There's enough room to stand side by side."

They found Linda and Alana a few minutes later, sitting with their backs against a wall sharing a protein bar.

"Not to keep repeating myself," Linda said around a monstrous bite, "but we hit another dead end."

"Eric and I think we found something."

Moments later, Eric explained how the rock incline was a pivoting device, balanced in the middle, halfway up the ten-foot-high slope. The four got into position at the top of the ramp, standing side by side, their upper shoulders pressed to the ceiling.

"And go," Linda ordered.

Their combined strength made stone grate against stone, and the incline began to flatten out. What had been a tiny crack yawned into the entrance of another chamber, one they could see was partially lined with mud bricks. Harder they pushed, groaning at the effort. The lever dipped on its fulcrum, so the ramp became perfectly flat.

"You know once we're through, there's no going back," Linda grunted, fresh perspiration flushing her pixie face.

"I know," Mark replied. "Push."

The rock platform began to slope down into the bricked chamber beyond the tunnel, and they were able to shuffle back so they stood at its very lip, muscles quivering. They were only a couple feet above the sand-covered floor.

Linda judged they had enough clearance. "Ready? Go!"

The four leapt off the stone slab, tumbling into the dirt. Behind them the rock-slab lever crashed back to the ground with an echoing boom. There was a space under it like the nook beneath a flight of stairs. They could see the actual fulcrum was a thick length of log resting on notched-stone blocks. In the crease where the rock met the floor was another small wooden contraption whose purpose was unknown.

No sooner had the echoes died away than there came a new sound, a deep rumbling hiss from someplace above them. Eric flashed his light to the ceiling twenty feet over their heads just as sand began to pour out of dozens of manhole-sized openings.

"You've got to be kidding me," Mark said.

The wooden device was the trigger for a booby trap that activated when the pivot returned to its original position.

They cast their lights around the room. It was about ten feet square. Three of the walls were natural rock, part of the limestone cavern—one had the alcove for the lever device. The fourth wall was mud bricks laid with mortar between the joints. They ignored the rock and concentrated their attention on the brick. There were no holes or openings of any type, no handles or other kind of mechanism for getting out of the room.

In the five minutes they spent searching the wall, two feet of sand had built up on the floor in uneven piles that shifted and spread, with more dropping down from above. Linda pulled her knife from its sheath and pried at the mortar near one brick. It crumbled under the blade, and she was able to loosen the brick enough to work it out of the wall. Behind it was an identical layer. And, for all she knew, there were a half dozen more.

"We'll have to try to move the lever from underneath," Linda said. She accidentally backed into the stream of fine sand cascading from the ceiling and had to shake her head like a dog to dislodge the grit.

There were three holes directly in front of the alcove, and already it was half full of sand.

Eric countered, "With that much sand right in front we'll be buried before we can push it open."

"We're trapped," Alana said, panic making her voice crack. "What are we going to do?"

Stoney looked at Mark Murphy, and for the first time neither man had an answer.

THIRTY-ONE

T ARIQ ASSAD THANKED HIS PILOT FRIEND AND STEPPED from the helicopter. He closed the flimsy door, gave it a tap, and scurried from under the whirling blades. The small service chopper lifted off the desert floor in a dust storm of its own creation. Assad had to turn his back to it and keep his eyes tightly closed.

As soon as the helo had lifted clear, he strode toward the team commander. The seething anger he had felt in the wake of the police raid back in Tripoli had been replaced with unmitigated joy. He embraced the terrorist leader, kissing him on both cheeks effusively.

"Ali, this is going to be a great day." Assad grinned.

He'd radioed ahead that he was coming and saw with satisfaction that his orders had been carried out. The men were waiting at the rear cargo ramp of their Mi-8. When Assad waved, they gave him a rousing cheer. Their prisoner was bound to one of the bench seats, a rag tied over his mouth.

Ali noticed Assad's look. "When we do not gag him, he shrieks like a woman. If he wasn't such a supposed expert on Suleiman Al-Jama, blessings be upon him, I would put a bullet through that fat lout's head and be done with it."

"What a remarkable turn of events," Assad said, Emile Bumford's treatment all but forgotten. "A few hours ago, I was moments from being grabbed by the police, and now we will shortly discover the lost tomb."

"Tell me again how you found it," Ali invited. They strode to the waiting chopper, whose blades started to beat the super-heated air.

"Coming in on the helicopter, I had the pilot swing south when we crossed the border into Tunisia, and as we came down the old riverbed, flying just above it, I spotted an area where it appeared that a section of the bank had been blasted into the river. Had I known about the waterfall a little farther downstream, I wouldn't have paid it any attention, for surely a sailing ship couldn't have navigated it. But I didn't know, so I had the pilot set down so I could investigate."

"When was this?"

"Moments before I radioed you. What, a half hour ago? And when we landed, I saw evidence that people had been there recently. There were four distinct sets of shoe prints. Two are women, or maybe small men, but I think one might be the American archaeologist who worked with our guest there." He pointed across the cargo bay to Bumford.

The turbines' whine made it so Assad had to shout to be heard by the man sitting to his left. "The prints all disappeared into a cave located behind a hill along the river. They must all still be inside. We have them, Ali, the Americans who have disrupted our plans for the last time, and Suleiman's tomb."

* * *

JUAN ACCEPTED A CUP of coffee from Maurice, the *Oregon*'s chief steward.

"How are you feeling, Captain?" the dour Englishman asked.

"I think the expression is 'rode hard and put away wet,'" Juan said, taking a sip of the strong brew.

"An equine reference, I believe. Filthy creatures, only good for glue factories and betting at Ascot."

Cabrillo chuckled. "Dr. Huxley juiced my leg so it's feeling pretty good, and the handful of ibuprofen I scarfed down are kicking in. All in all, I'm not doing too badly."

The one secret about pain Juan had never shared with anyone other than Julia Huxley, as medical officer, was that he felt it constantly. Doctors call it phantom pain, but to him it was real enough. His missing leg, the one shot off by a Chinese gunboat all those years ago, ached every minute of every day. And on the good days it only ached. Sometimes he'd be hit with lances of agony that took all his self-control not to react to.

So when it came to dealing with the discomfort from where he'd cut out his tracking chip, it wasn't bravado that made him ignore it. It was practice.

Around them, the op center buzzed with activity. Max Hanley and a pair of technicians had an access panel removed under one of the consoles to replace a faulty computer monitor. The duty weapons officer was talking with teams working throughout the ship to make certain her suite of armaments was operating exactly to standards, while the helmsman maintained a steady course well beyond Libya's twelve-mile territorial limit.

The ship and crew were ready, only, for the time being, Cabrillo had nothing for them to do.

They still hadn't received an updated list of Libyan naval assets capable of landing a helicopter, and until they did there was nothing for *Oregon* to do but wait.

Juan hated to wait. Especially when he had people on the ground. His feelings toward them made it as though everything they went through exacted a physical price on him, too.

"Call coming through," the radio operator said over her shoulder.

Juan hit a switch on the arm of his chair, and from hidden speakers came the sound of heavy breathing, almost panting.

"You've picked a bad time for an obscene phone call," he said to the unknown person.

"Chairman, it's Linc," Franklin gasped. "We got trouble."

"What's happened?"

"You can forget your theories about Ali Ghami being Al-Jama." Lincoln continued to wheeze. It was obvious he was running. "Our old buddy Tariq Assad just showed up, and after a little Arab-style kissy face with the leader of the group searching for the tomb they beat it southward in that old Mi-8 of theirs. He's Al-Jama, Juan. I tried calling Linda but they're still underground. I'm now hightailing it after them, but I figure I got four or five miles to go."

"That confirms it." Agitated, Juan stood and began pacing the deck. "A couple hours ago, we got suspicious because Hali Kasim hadn't checked in, and his GPS chip hadn't moved in a while. I sent Eddie to find him. Hali'd been shot at such close range, there was GSR all over him. The last person with him was none other than Tariq Assad."

"Jesus, is Hali okay?"

"We don't know yet. Eddie said it was bad. All he could do was stabilize him and call for an ambulance. He stuck around long enough to follow it to a hospital, but he can't exactly barge in and start demanding answers."

A fax machine built into the communications center started whirring.

"For Assad to bug out like he did," Linc panted, "he must have seen something he liked in the same area as Linda and the others."

"I can get a backup team to you by chopper, but it's going to take a couple of hours," Juan offered lamely, for he knew it would be over long before then.

The communications officer handed him the fax. He glanced at it quickly. It was the report on Libya's Navy he'd been expecting for hours now.

"Nah. I'll be okay. I'm doing eight-minute miles so I'll have something in the tank when I get there. A dozen tangos in a cave when I have the element of surprise shouldn't be too difficult."

Juan was barely paying attention. He crossed to the navigation computer to punch in the GPS numbers and plot the vessels' coordinates and recent movements.

One leapt out at him immediately. His instincts screamed at him that they had found it. The ship would have been within helicopter range of the terrorist training camp, and, while all the others were converging on Tripoli for a military review as part of the peace conference, this particular vessel was loitering near the Tunisian border.

"Linc, call me back when you reach the cave. I've got to go."

"Roger that."

"Helm, plot me a course for that ship." He pointed at the blinking light on the overhead display. The edge in his voice caused those around him to stop their work and look. A wave of expectant energy swept the op center crew.

"Course laid in, Chairman."

"What's our ETA at best possible speed?"

"A little over three hours."

"Okay, hit it."

An alarm the crew was all too familiar with began to wail. When the ship was pushing near her maximum speed, the ride was usually rough, and every loose item from the saucers in the galley to the makeup pots in Kevin Nixon's Magic Shop had to be secured.

The acceleration was smooth as the *Oregon*'s revolutionary engines came online, the cryopumps whining a high-pitched tone that became inaudible to humans but would have sent a dog into paroxysms.

Juan returned to his central seat and called up the specifications for the Libyan vessel. She was a modified Russian frigate, purchased in 1999, weighing in at fourteen hundred tons. She was two-thirds the length of the *Oregon*—three hundred and thirteen feet—and the Corporation's ship outclassed the Libyan when it came to weapons systems. But the frigate *Khalij Surt* still packed a powerful punch, with four three-inch deck guns, multiple launchers for the SS-N-2c Styx ship-to-ship missiles, as well as an umbrella of Gecko rockets and rapid-fire 30mm cannons to ward off an air assault. The *Khalij Surt*, or *Gulf of Sidra*, could also fire torpedoes from deck launchers and lay mines from her stern.

Juan studied a picture of the vessel from *Jane's Defence Review*'s website. She was a lethal-looking craft, with a tall, flaring bow, and a radio mast festooned with antennae for her upgraded sensor systems behind her single funnel. The big cannons were paired in armored turrets fore and aft, and just behind the lead gun sat her antiship missile launchers.

Cabrillo had no doubt he could take her in an engagement. The *Oregon*'s ship-to-ship missiles had twice the range of the *Sidra*'s Styx system, but blowing the Libyan frigate out of the water with a missile shot from over the horizon wasn't the point.

He needed to board the *Sidra*, rescue Fiona Katamora if his hunch was right, and get her to safety.

"That her?" Max asked. He'd moved to Juan's side silently and was pointing at the computer monitor.

"Yup. What do you think?"

"Judging by the radar specs, they'll see a chopper coming fifty miles off. And it looks like she's loaded for bear, with triple-A and SAMs."

"Which means we're going to have to lay in alongside her and do this old-school."

"You mean go toe to toe with her, don't you?"

"We'll need a distraction to get in close, but, yeah, that's what I'm thinking."

Max was silent for a moment. Naval war-fighting doctrine had changed dramatically in the years since missiles had been perfected. No longer did heavily armored battleships pound at each other with their big guns, hoping for a hit. Sea battles now oftentimes were fought with the combatants hundreds of miles apart. The power of high-explosive-tipped missiles made thick plates of protective steel superfluous, so modern navies rarely bothered.

The *Oregon* had built-in protection, but not against the *Sidra*'s three-inch cannons, and certainly not if she managed to slam a couple of Styx missiles into *Oregon*'s side. Juan was proposing to get close enough to the Libyan frigate to send across a boarding party under the full onslaught of the *Sidra*'s guns and missiles.

"When was the last time two capital ships dueled it out like this?" Hanley finally asked.

"I'm thinking March ninth, 1862, at Hampton Roads, Virginia."

"The *Monitor* and the *Merrimack*?" Juan nodded. Max added, "They fought to a draw. We don't have that option. And you do realize that unless we sink her as soon as we have the Secretary, we're going to have just as tough a time getting clear again. We might get lucky sneaking up on their ship, but don't think the Libyans are gonna let us just sail away, you know?"

"Already thought about that."

"You have an idea?"

"No," Juan said airily. "But I *have* thought about it."

"And your distraction? Any ideas on that front?"

"Don't have the foggiest. But since we'll attack under the cover of darkness, we've got until dusk to come up with one. One thing, though . . ."

"Yeah?"

"A ship the size of the *Sidra* is going to take twenty minutes or more to sink, no matter how we do it. That's more than enough time to give the *Oregon* a missile enema."

Max put on a long-suffering expression. "Oh, you are just full of cheery news, aren't you?"

"I'll add insult to injury. Before we face the *Sidra*, we're loading our new Libyan friends into our lifeboats. I don't want them aboard when we go into battle. So if something goes wrong, we've got no way off the *Oregon*."

"Why did I ever take that first phone call from you all those years ago?" Max cried theatrically to the ceiling.

"Chairman," the comm officer said, "you have another call coming through."

"Linc?"

"No, sir. Langston Overholt."

"Thanks, Monica." Juan donned a headset and keyed his computer to accept the call. "Lang, it's Cabrillo."

"How are you feeling?"

"Good. Tired, but good."

"And your guests?"

"Grateful and ravenous. They've gone through half our stores in a single day."

"I'm calling for an update and to give you some news."

"Tariq Assad just showed up near where my people are looking for Suleiman's tomb."

"He's the official who Qaddafi's government said is Al-Jama?"

"And it would appear they were right, and we helped him escape and nearly lost a man doing so."

"Lost someone. Who?"

"Hali Kasim, my head communications officer, was shot in the chest. Eddie Seng got him to a hospital, but we have no idea yet on his condition."

"I'll get word to Ambassador Moon so he'll look into it."

"I'd appreciate that, thank you."

"Does this clear Minister Ghami from your list of suspects?"

"Not in the slightest. Terrorists might have taken down the Secretary's plane without government help, but there was a cover-up afterward. It could have easily been orchestrated from the top or manipulated from the shadows. If Al-Jama's people have infiltrated the Libyan government the way we suspect, then the tangos could have been tipped off early enough to put the cover-up in place."

"Or Ghami is high in Al-Jama's organization, and he ordered the destruction of the plane's wreckage as well as the convenient timing of its discovery."

"Exactly. And let's not forget that the person who Ghami replaced, plus most of his senior staff, were arrested and left to rot. That could have come from Ghami, or Qaddafi himself could have ordered a purge."

"What a mess." The CIA veteran sighed. "Despite our warnings, the Vice President is insisting on going to a scheduled reception tonight at Ghami's home for many of the conference's senior attendees."

"Bad idea," Juan snapped.

"I concur, but there isn't anything I can do about it. The Secret Service detail has been informed there may be an assault, but the VP is adamant he attend."

"The guy's a moron."

"I concur with that, too. However, it doesn't change the facts. On the plus side, Ghami's house is totally isolated, and the security personnel are the same people being used for the conference in Tripoli tomorrow morning. They've all been vetted. Even if Ghami is somehow connected to the terrorists, I think this dinner should be okay."

"Really? Why?"

"Would you stage a massive attack on your own home? Especially when you'll have the same people gathered together the next day with the world's press watching every move they make. You must remember the impact of Anwar Sadat's assassination being broadcast nearly live. If there's going to be an attack—"

"Not *if*, Lang," Juan said.

"*If* there's going to be an attack," Overholt persisted, "it'll be tomorrow, or sometime during the conference."

"I don't like this."

"Nobody does, but there isn't any other way. All of these leaders know they're putting their lives at risk by attending the conference, either there in Tripoli or back home when their own fundamentalists rouse themselves into a frenzy. In these troubled times, being the president of a Middle Eastern country is a dangerous occupation, especially for those willing to work on a peace deal. They all know it and are still willing to go ahead. That says something."

Overholt then changed tack as his way of saying that was the end of the discussion, and he asked, "How are you coming with finding Secretary Katamora?"

"I think we have a lead." Juan had already explained to Overholt about the radar blip they'd seen and his theory that she was being taken to a ship offshore. "She may be on a frigate called the *Gulf of Sidra*, or *Khalij Surt*, and we're on our way to her now."

"What are you planning to do?"

"Board her, rescue the Secretary, and put the *Sidra* on the bottom."

"Absolutely not!" Overholt roared. Juan winced. "You will not sink a naval vessel belonging to a sovereign nation. I can't even condone you boarding her."

"I'm not asking for permission, Lang," Juan retorted hotly.

"Juan, as God is my witness, if you sink that ship I will see to it that you are charged for piracy. I can authorize you to discover if she is aboard. After that, it falls on our diplomats, and possibly our military, to resolve the situation."

"Diplomats?" Juan scoffed. "These are terrorists. Murderers. You can't negotiate with them."

"Then our Navy will handle an assault, if it comes to that. Am I clear?"

"Might as well pack it in now, Lang, because if you follow that plan she's as good as dead."

"You don't think I know what's at stake?" Overholt shouted. "I know her life is probably forfeit, but I also have rules, and when *I* have them so do you. You were hired to find her, and if she's on the *Gulf of Sidra* you've done your job. Take your money and go."

"Damn it." Juan's anger spilled into his voice. He had no idea why the conversation had veered in this direction, but he wasn't going to take an insult. "This isn't about money, and you know it."

"Christ. I'm sorry," Lang replied contritely. "That was a low blow. It's just this whole situation."

"I understand. Marquis of Queensbury."

"What's that?"

"Just something Max said a while back. Don't worry. I won't destroy their ship, you have my promise. But if there's a chance I can get her back, I'm going for it. Okay?"

"All right. It's just that we can't handle another diplomatic incident with Libya right now. On the heels of the plane crash, they'll see the destruction of one of their frigates as retaliation no matter who was responsible, and they'll treat it as an act of war. You'll scuttle the conference before it even starts."

"We're on the same page, Lang. Relax, and I'll call you later." Juan killed the connection and turned to Max. "Good thing that wasn't a video call."

"Why's that?"

"He would have seen my fingers crossed."

THIRTY-TWO

WITH SO MUCH SAND POURING THROUGH THE CEILING, THE air in the subterranean chamber was becoming unbreathable, even though they had rags tied across their mouths. Their lights cast meager, murky beams through the choking pall. The glow was closer to burnt umber than the halogen's normal silver.

Doggedly, Linda, Alana, Eric, and Mark dug their way upward to stay atop the growing pile. The sand was coming so fast that even a few seconds' rest would see a limb buried. They moved on pure survival instinct, buying themselves a little more time before they were buried alive under the hissing onslaught. The mound was so deep now that they could no longer stand upright but had to stoop slightly against the ceiling.

Whoever had designed the trap those hundreds of years ago would find comfort in heaven or hell that it still worked after centuries.

The women were faring better than the men because their bodies were lighter and they helped Eric and Mark dig themselves free whenever they got into trouble.

Alana had just yanked Stoney's foot clear when a realization hit him. He shouted over to Murph, "Are you sure this room's below the old river level?"

"Pretty sure. Why?"

"We're idiots. One-point-six."

"One-point-six?"

"One-point-six," Eric confirmed. "And figure a fifty percent over-engineering factor."

"Of course. Why didn't I see that?"

"Do you mind explaining what's so important about one-point-six," Linda called over the sound of falling sand.

"Because this part of the tunnel is below the river, the trap was most likely designed to fill with water and drown its victims. Over the years, sand filled the reservoir."

"So?"

"Sand is one-point-six times heavier than water by volume."

Linda didn't see his point, and made an impatient gesture for him to continue.

"The brick wall was constructed to withstand the pressure of a certain amount of water. But now that this room is filling with sand, it's holding back one-point-six times more weight than its builders intended. Any good engineer will factor in an additional fifty percent safety margin to be certain. Even if they overbuilt the wall, the sand is still ten percent heavier than it can withstand. It's only a matter of time before it fails."

Skeptically, Linda looked from Eric to Mark. Both still struggled to stay ahead of the rising tide of sand, but the grim fatalism that had been etched on their faces moments before was gone. The two of them were certain they were getting out of the trap alive. That was good enough for her.

Moments later, the wall still hadn't collapsed, and the four were forced to their hands and knees. It was much more difficult to keep ahead of the sand in this position. Linda and Alana struggled right along with the men now. With their backs pressed to the ceiling, there was only twenty inches of space remaining before the chamber was completely full. Those last seconds would go fast.

Linda's brief elation that they were going to survive ebbed, though she would fight until the bitter end. Mark and Eric contorted themselves, digging frantically to keep above the rising tide of sand, but Alana Shepard had given up. They could hear her sobs over the cascade's din.

"Damn," was all Eric said. His cheek was mashed to the roof, and he had created a tiny air pocket around his mouth a moment before a wave of dirt buried his face.

Twenty feet below them, the multiple courses of brick at the wall's base bowed under the hundreds of tons of sand, the mortar cracked in places, and wispy trickles of grit dribbled through the crevasses.

All at once the entire ten-foot width of the wall gave way. The wall failed completely, collapsing and falling outward into another chamber beyond like a burst dam. A tidal wave of sand swept through the breach, pushing the wall's remnants like so much flotsam.

The four people who moments earlier were muttering their final prayers were borne along the tsunami and deposited unceremoniously in a tangle of limbs, the very sand that had been seconds from killing them cushioning their wild ride.

Mark was the first to recover, his booming whoop of joy bouncing from wall to wall in the large chamber. He reached across and held out a fist to Eric so they could tap knuckles. "Good call, my friend. Damned good call."

Eric was a little pale. "I wasn't so sure at the end."

"Never a doubt." Mark hoisted Stone to his feet, and they then helped Alana and Linda to theirs.

Alana threw her arms around Eric's neck and kissed him as if predicting the wall's collapse had made it happen. "Thank you," she breathed into his ear.

"You're welcome," he replied awkwardly.

It took a few minutes to find their weapons and clean the sand from the barrels and receivers. The assault rifles weren't designed to take this kind of punishment, so they had to be thorough.

They found themselves in another cave, still part of the same complex of limestone caverns riddling the hill above them. There was only one exit, a narrow cleft ten feet up the far wall and accessible by steps carved into the living rock.

"Now that we know this place is booby-trapped," Linda said at the base of the stairs, "I'm taking point. Eric, you're behind me, then Alana, then Mark. And from now on, we stick together, no exploring on your own. Everyone stay on your toes, and look for anything unusual—an odd rock, writing on the walls, anything."

They climbed into the tight cave. Headroom wasn't a problem, but the tunnel was so narrow it was difficult to walk without scraping their shoulders. The cave climbed steeply, and, with space so tight, their footing was uneven. A wrong step could twist an ankle. Linda was concentrating on her movements yet still aware of danger, and she spotted the trip wire well before she was going to trigger it.

It was a thin filament of copper that stretched across the tunnel at the level of her shins, with one end secured to the wall with an iron screw and the other vanishing up into the gloom ahead. She pointed it out to the others and cautiously stepped over it.

The sharply ascending tunnel ended another hundred feet from the trip wire in a small room with a low ceiling. They had to crawl under a wooden trestle built at the tunnel's exit. The wire wrapped around a metal lever built into a device that would fall back when it was tripped. This in turn would release a carved-stone ball sitting on the angled cradle. The ball was about three feet around and weighed in at half a ton. A direct hit, after rolling and bouncing down the shaft, would crush a man flat, while a glancing blow would surely break bone.

"We should trigger it," Mark said, mostly because the kid in him wanted to watch the stone hurtle down the tunnel.

"Leave it," Alana said. The archaeologist in her hated the idea of disturbing what was the find of her career.

"We'll compromise," Linda said. She plucked a stone from the ground and wedged it under the boulder. Even if someone hit the trip wire and the lever were released, the rock would prevent it from moving.

There were a few other man-made items in the room—a battered wooden chest missing its lid, an empty sword scabbard for one of the Barbary pirate's wicked scimitars made of beaten brass, a couple lengths of rope, and a half dozen thin metal shafts Mark identified as ramrods. They took the opportunity to change out their flashlight batteries, and started exploring further.

Three different tunnels branched off from what they called "the boulder room." They explored one tunnel without incident and were halfway down the second one when Linda placed a foot on a hidden trigger. There was just the tiniest give under her foot, but she knew they were in trouble.

Just under the surface of the sandy passage, a wooden board had been buried and cleverly concealed. Her weight rasped a piece of steel against flint under the plank to produce enough sparks to ignite a fuse. The cask of gunpowder was secreted farther in the hole, and contained enough explosive to kill all four of them.

Linda jumped back instantly and, in a tackle that would have done a pro football player proud, pushed her three companions back until the whole pile of them went down. But the blast never came. Instead, the powder ignited and burned unevenly, a flaring, sputtering cauldron of fire that filled the tunnel with noxious white smoke. In the two hundred years since the trap had been set, the powder's acidity had eaten through the wooden cask, so when it lit there was nothing to contain the fire and cause an explosive detonation.

"Everybody all right?" Linda asked when the last of the powder had burned itself out.

"I think so," Alana answered, stifling a cough.

"I feel like I just went three rounds with Eddie in his dojo," Eric replied, rubbing his ribs where Linda's shoulder had hit him. "I never knew someone so small could hit so hard."

"Amazing what a little adrenaline can do." She stood and brushed herself off. "The fact that this tunnel's booby-trapped tells me we're on the right path."

They kept going, and the tunnel started climbing. There was no way of knowing how deep they had gone or where they were in relation to the riverbank, but all of them felt they had to be getting close.

There was more evidence that people had spent a greater amount of time in this part of the cavern. There were marks in the sand coating the ground where men had walked, men who had constructed the elaborate traps they had already passed. Twice more, Linda stopped the party to check the ground, but they found no additional hidden bombs.

The tunnel turned sharply. Linda peered around the corner before committing herself and came up short. Around the bend stood an iron door embedded in the rock. The metal had a reddish hue, a tracery of rust having formed from exposure to damp air when the river still flowed. There was no lock or keyhole. The door was a featureless slab of metal, so they knew the hinges must be on the other side.

Linda dropped to one knee to dig through her pack.

Mark moved until he was directly in front of the door, spread his arms wide in a theatrical pose. "Open sesame," he intoned. The door didn't budge. He glanced over at Alana. "You know, I kind of thought that would work."

"This will." Linda straightened, holding a block of plastic explosives.

She used a piece of cardboard torn from a box in her first-aid kit to slip between the door and jamb to determine which side it hinged from and set her charges over the hinges. She selected a pair of two-minute timing pencils and rammed them home.

"Coming?" she called sweetly, and the four of them retreated fifty yards back down the tunnel. The distance muted the blast, but the pressure wave hit with enough force to ripple their clothes.

When they returned, the door had been blown from its hinges and tossed ten feet into the next section of the tunnel.

Unlike the claustrophobic nature of much of the cave, the chamber they found themselves standing in was vast. It was longer than the reach of their flashlights and equally broad. The ceiling lofted forty or more feet over their heads. Much of the cave was limestone like they'd been seeing since entering the earth, but the wall to their right was a vast mound of rubble, the debris blasted over the cave's entrance when Henry Lafayette started his long journey home.

On the left side of the cavern ran an elevated platform that looked like it had once served as Suleiman Al-Jama's pier. And tied to it, canted slightly because its keel rested on the ground and wasn't floating as it should, was the infamous pirate's ship, the *Saqr*.

Her mast had been lowered and her rigging stowed in order to enter the cave, but otherwise she looked fully capable of sailing once again. The dry air had perfectly preserved her wooden hull. She was facing away from them, so the mouths of her stern long guns looked like enormous black holes.

On closer inspection, as they peered down on her from the quay, they could see where she had sustained damage during her running battle with the American ketch *Siren*.

Chunks of her bulwarks had been blown apart by cannon shot, and there were a dozen places where fire had scorched the deck. One of her guns was missing, and, judging from the damage around its emplacement, it had exploded at some point during the battle and was lost over the side.

"This is absolutely amazing," Alana said breathlessly. "It's a piece of living history."

"I can almost hear the battle," Mark agreed.

There was so much more to explore, but for several minutes the four of them stared down on the corsair.

A flicker of movement to his right caught Eric's attention and broke him from his reverie. He cast the beam of his light back to the remnants of the mangled doorframe just as a figure slipped through. He was about to shout a challenge when an assault rifle opened up ten feet from the first man's position, its juddering flame winking in the darkness.

In the half second before he reacted, he saw several more gunmen in the uneven light. Bullets filled the air around them when more weapons opened up.

The four had no idea how Al-Jama's people had found them so quickly, but the fact was clear. They had arrived with almost three-to-one superiority, and more ammunition because they were prepared for a fight, and now they controlled the only way out of the cave.

THIRTY-THREE

JUAN TOOK A SECOND TO LOOK ACROSS THE SEA. IT WAS A view he would never tire of. To him, the ocean was mystery and majesty and the promise of what lay over the horizon. It could be the still, sultry waters of a tropical lagoon or the raging fury of an Asian cyclone tearing away the surface in sheets that stretched for miles. The sea was both siren and adversary, the duality making his love for it all the stronger.

When he'd conceived the Corporation, basing it aboard a ship had been the logical choice. It gave them mobility and anonymity. But he had been secretly pleased by the fact that they would need a vessel like the *Oregon* so he could indulge in moments like this.

There was a bare whisper of wind, and the waves were gently lapping against the hull as though the ship were a babe rocked in a cradle. This far from shore the air was fresh, tinged with a salt tang that reminded Juan of his childhood on the beaches of southern California.

"Captain, excuse me," a voice said. "I do not wish to disturb you, but I wanted to thank you again before we leave."

Juan turned. Standing before him in a suit provided by the Magic Shop was Libya's former Foreign Minister. He had his hand out.

Cabrillo shook it with genuine warmth. "Not necessary."

Juan wanted to make sure the escaped prisoners left the *Oregon* during daylight. He had full confidence in his ship and crew, but no captain ever likes to put people into lifeboats, and doing so at night only compounded the risks. He looked down from the bridge wing at the mass of humanity standing on the deck in the shadow of one of the boats.

They hadn't been able to provide everyone with new clothes, so many of them sported the rags they'd been wearing since their incarceration. At least they'd had the chance to eat and bathe. A few noted him looking down and waved. It quickly turned into a rousing cheer.

"They would all be dead without you," the Minister said.

Juan turned back to the diplomat. "Then their lives are thanks enough. We will be in contact with the crewmen I'm sending with you so you'll know exactly what's happening. And we should be able to pick you up at first light. If something goes wrong, my men will take you to Tunisia. From there, it'll be up to you where you go."

"I will return home," the Libyan said forcefully, "and somehow take back my job."

"How was it you were arrested? Was it Ghami who ordered it?"

"No. The Minister of Justice. A political rival of mine. One day I'm Foreign Minister, and the next I'm being shoved into a van and Ghami has my job."

"When was this?"

"February seventh."

"And what was Ghami before? He worked for your ministry, right?"

"That is something he wants people to believe. I don't know what he did before taking my office, but he didn't work in the Foreign Ministry. What I have been able to piece together is that he managed to get a meeting with President Qaddafi, which is difficult to say the least. The next day it was announced that I had been arrested and Ghami had been named my replacement."

"Could he have something on Qaddafi, some sort of leverage?"

"You cannot blackmail a man who is President for Life."

"Hold on one second." Juan stepped onto the bridge and keyed the wall-mounted microphone. The duty officer in the op center answered straightaway. "Do me a favor," Juan said. "Check international press reports of any crime involving Libyan nationals going back a month prior to February seventh of this year."

"What is it you suspect?" the diplomat asked when Juan stepped back outside.

"You don't give a job like yours to a complete unknown without a reason." Juan wanted to call Overholt and at the very least demand that the Vice President not attend this evening's dinner. "I still don't know if Ghami's tied to Suleiman Al-Jama, but I don't trust this guy one whit. He's put on a hell of a show in diplomatic circles, and orchestrating the summit is the achievement of a lifetime . . ." Juan's voice drifted off.

"What is it?"

"The timing and the fact you are who you are." His tone sharpened. "It isn't coincidence that you were in a terrorist camp run by Al-Jama. There is a link between him and Ghami. I'm certain of it."

"Captain, you must understand something about my country that I am not proud of. We have harbored many fighters so they may train on our soil, and allowing them use of our political prisoners is quite common."

"I thought your government had renounced terrorism."

"It has, but there are many who don't agree with that policy. Our own Justice Minister is one of them. I know for a fact that he has provided aid to Al-Jama in the past."

"So you're saying Ghami's legit?"

"As much as it pains me to say, it is possible. And I have more reason than you to think ill of him. The man took my job and even now lives in my house."

The intercom on the bridge squawked. Juan stepped through and punched the button. "Anything?"

"Nothing earth-shattering, if that's what you're looking for. A quick search shows a couple of Libyans arrested for smuggling heroin into Amsterdam, one killed in a traffic pileup that claimed four other people in Switzerland. A Libyan national living in Hungary was arrested for domestic abuse, and another for attempted murder stemming from a dispute with a shopkeeper just across the border in Tunisia."

"Okay. Thanks." Juan turned to the Minister. "Dead end."

"What were you thinking?"

"Truthfully, I don't know."

Below them the forty-seat lifeboat was lowered from its davits so the refugees could step through a gate built into the ship's rail. They would need to overload the boats to get all the people off the *Oregon*. The boats were fully enclosed and could weather a hurricane because of their self-righting hull design, so at worst the former prisoners would be cramped but not in any real danger.

Juan shook the diplomat's hand a second time. "Good luck."

Cabrillo watched until the last of the Libyans was safely aboard. He nodded to Greg Chaffee, who wasn't happy about being exiled with them. But, then again, Juan wasn't happy that Alana Shepard had snuck off with Linda and the others behind his back.

He waved to the general operations technician who would command the craft before the man ducked through the Plexiglas hatch and secured it behind him. The winches took up the strain and lowered the boat down the side of the *Oregon*'s hull. A moment later, the lines were disengaged from inside the boat and its motor fired. It started puttering away from the big freighter.

The second boat, lowered from the port side, met up with the first. The two would stay together throughout the night and hopefully would be back in their cradles in time for breakfast.

Juan took the secret elevator at the back of the pilothouse to the op center and settled into his seat. He still didn't have a plan for how they were going to make their final approach on the *Sidra* or how they were going to avoid sinking her after they had rescued the Secretary. One corner of the main view screen showed the radar plot. Because of the *Oregon*'s vastly superior sensor suite, the Libyans had no idea they were being watched as they cruised only about a mile off the coast, tracking eastward at a lazy eight knots. The only other ship on the plot was a supertanker heading on a parallel track, most likely making for the oil terminal at Az-Zāwiya.

He glanced at his watch. The diplomatic reception at Ali Ghami's house was scheduled to start in a little over an hour. The guests were probably already en route. Full darkness would follow two hours later. There was a quarter moon tonight that wouldn't rise until well after midnight, which severely tightened their window of opportunity.

To distract himself, and hopefully free his mind so inspiration would hit, Cabrillo checked the Internet for those police reports concerning Libyans. The car accident had been particularly brutal. Three of the victims were burned beyond recognition and had to be identified though dental records. The Libyan, a student, was IDed because he was driving a rental car.

He scanned a couple more reports, thinking about his conversation moments ago on deck. He called up a photograph of Libya's Justice Minister, and cringed. He was an ugly man, with a bulbous, misshapen nose, narrow eyes, and a skin condition of some sort that made his face appear pebbled.

On top of that, he'd been injured. Half his lower jaw was missing, and the grafts to cover the hole were taut, shiny cicatrices. The official bio said the wound came from the American bombing of Tripoli in 1986, but a little further digging in a CIA database Cabrillo still had access to told him that the Minister had been beaten to within an inch of his life by a cuckolded husband.

Cabrillo smirked. He compared this information to his impression of the ousted Foreign Minister. Now, that guy was a class act, he thought. He had lost his job, been imprisoned and forced to do hard labor, and yet wouldn't accuse Ghami of orchestrating the whole thing. He seemed more upset that Ghami was living in his house.

"Must be a hell of a place," Juan muttered to himself.

It took him a few minutes searching the Internet to find an article about Ghami's home that listed an address. He then found the GPS coordinates off a mapping site and keyed them into Google Earth. As the computer zoomed in on the precise location, pixels blurred for a moment. When they resolved, Cabrillo leapt from his chair so fast he startled the rest of the op center crew.

He mashed the intercom on his chair's arm. "Max, get up here now. We've got trouble."

Cabrillo looked again at the satellite image. The house sat alone in the desert, miles from any other building, and was ringed with a perimeter wall. The driveway ran up to the home before looping back on itself under a cantilevered porte cochere. There was a glass-enclosed solarium attached to one side, and the back lawns were a veritable maze of box hedges. On the roof was a satellite-uplink antenna.

He'd seen this exact layout for the first time as a mock-up less than forty-eight hours earlier.

He understood everything at that moment. The attack was planned for tonight. Al-Jama wanted to do it before the conference to show symbolically that peace never stood a chance. Knowing the terrorist mastermind's sense of the dramatic and penchant for beheadings, he was pretty sure what would start the attack. He envisioned Fiona Katamora's graceful neck bent and a man standing over her with a sword.

When he closed his eyes, the sword came down in a shining blur.

THIRTY-FOUR

T HE EXECUTIONER EXAMINED THE ROOM CRITICALLY. HE was alone for now, but there was plenty of space for witnesses, though they had been forced to use a lottery system to choose the lucky ones. The black backdrop, a piece of thick cloth hung from a pipe, was in place. The camera sat on its tripod and had already been tested. The uplink worked perfectly. There was thick plastic sheeting on the floor to make cleanup afterward a bit easier.

He recalled the first time he'd used a sword to decapitate a man. His victim's heart had been racing and his blood pressure dangerously high, so when the head came free it was like a fountain. So much blood erupted from the stump that they opted to abandon the safe house in Baghdad they had used rather than clean the mess.

Tonight would be his eleventh, and for him the most satisfying. He'd never killed a woman before—at least, not with a sword. Since taking up arms he'd killed dozens of women in bombings from Indonesia to Morocco. And in firefights with Americans in Afghanistan and Iraq, stray rounds had certainly hit others.

He gave them little thought. Al-Jama had issued orders and he had carried them out. There was no more weight on his conscience than had he been told to shake his victims' hands rather than blow them up.

Of course the irony, and open secret within the organization, was that he wasn't a practicing Muslim. He'd been born into the faith, but his parents hadn't been devout followers so he'd visited mosques only on holy days. He'd only come to Al-Jama after a hitch with the French Foreign Legion had given him a taste for combat that he had yet to slake. He fought and killed and maimed for himself, not for some insane religious conviction that slaughter was somehow Allah's will.

He didn't try to understand the motivations of those who fought with him so long as they followed orders. He did admit, however, that the fear of missing out on Paradise kept the fighters motivated to a degree only the best-trained armies could achieve. And the ability to talk people into blowing themselves up was a weapon unlike any other in the arsenals of the world. It went so against the West's precepts for the preservation of life that the effects rippled from the blast's epicenter to the very hearts of any who learned of it.

A subaltern knocked softly at the doorframe behind him. "Does everything meet your needs, Mansour?"

"Yes," he said absently. "This will be fine."

"When should we get the American whore?"

"Not until just before her execution. It's been my experience that they are most terrified in those first moments when they realize their death is upon them."

"As you wish. If you need anything further, I am just outside."

The executioner didn't bother to reply, and the man stepped out of view again.

He doubted there would be any pleas for mercy from the woman. He'd observed her only briefly but had a strong sense of her defi-

ance. He actually preferred it that way. The men loved the crying
and wailing, but he found it . . . bothersome. Yes, that was the word,
bothersome. Better to accept fate, he believed, than to demean yourself in worthless begging. He wondered if they actually believed carrying on would stop their execution. By the time they met him, their
death was an inevitability, and pleading was as useless as trying to
stave off an avalanche by raising your arms protectively.

No, the woman would not beg.

•   •   •

"WATCH THE RIGHT FLANK," Linda said, and fired a controlled
burst over the *Saqr*'s rail. "They're trying to get around us by crawling along the rubble wall."

The muzzle flash drew counterfire from four different points.

Eric had been ready for it, crouched twenty feet farther along the
deck. He raked the spot where one of the terrorists was hiding, but
in the cavern's absolute darkness he had no idea if he'd hit anything.

In the first furious seconds of the gunfight, both sides scrambled
to organize themselves after the surprise encounter. Linda quickly
ordered her people onto the *Saqr*, which offered the best cover on
short notice, while the terrorist leader shouted at his men to conserve
ammunition and prepare for an all-out assault.

They came swiftly, flicking their flashlights on and off like lightning bugs in order to see the terrain but not overly expose themselves.
The Corporation team concentrated their fire on the men with the
lights before realizing their mistake. The men carrying torches only
turned them on when they were behind cover. The beams were
meant for others scouting ahead.

"Come on, come on," Mark chided himself as he tore through his
pack, tossing aside gear with abandon. "I know it's in here."

Bullets stitched the side of the ship, several winging through a gunport and splintering wood inches from where he crouched.

Linda called to Eric. "On my mark. Go!"

They both popped up and let loose. In their scramble to find cover, a terrorist accidentally stepped into the beam of his partner's light. He was climbing the old riverbank to gain access to the pier. Had he reached it, he would have been able to hose the deck and end the battle single-handedly.

The beam barely caressed his leg, but it was enough. Linda adjusted her aim, approximated where his torso would be, and fired again. She was rewarded with a scream that echoed over the rattling assault rifles.

She and Eric both ducked down when rounds filled the air around them.

"This is crazy," Eric panted.

He couldn't see her saucy grin but heard it in her voice when she said, "I've never been in a firefight that wasn't."

Something heavy rattled against the *Saqr*'s stern.

"Down," Linda shouted.

An instant later, a grenade exploded. The shrapnel flew over the prone figures, tearing away more of the ship's woodwork.

Linda's ears rang, but she didn't let it distract her. The grenade was meant to keep them pinned for seconds only, and she was determined not to give them even that.

She peered over the rail. Lights flickered from one side of the cavern entrance to the other. Linda fought the raw fear running through her veins. It was really two against a dozen, since Alana didn't have a weapon, and Mark Murphy couldn't shoot to save his life.

She searched an ammo pouch hanging from her combat harness and pinched off a wad of plastique. By feel, she selected a sixty-second timing pencil, rammed it home, and tossed it over the side. She laid down another three-round burst and ducked back again.

"We've got to stop them flanking us," she called across to Eric. "I tossed some plastique. When it blows find some targets."

She took the opportunity to change out her magazine, uncertain how many rounds she'd fired. If they had time, she would have Alana consolidate the spare ammunition in fresh clips.

The blast came a moment later. The concussion was like a kick to the chest, and she'd been ready for it. The fireball crashed against the ceiling, bathing the cavern in demonic light.

Linda and Eric opened up. Terrorists who were caught in the open raced for cover, rounds screaming past them before the pair could zero in and put the men down.

Return fire came from eight different directions. Linda's chin was bloodied by a shard of wood torn from the rail, and as much as she didn't want to lose the last of the light she had to stay under cover from such a deadly barrage.

When it lessened, she fired blind at the riverbank below the quay in case anyone was tying to climb it again. Then, over the sharp stench of cordite, she smelled a familiar odor: wood smoke.

She looked aft just as the smoldering decking that had been hit by the grenade caught fire. The flame was low and smoky, but every second saw it grow. If it got out of control, they were as good as dead. The *Saqr* would become their funeral pyre.

"Mark, get that. We'll cover you."

Alana crawled from his side and approached Linda. "He's working on something. I've got it."

"Stay low," Linda cautioned, impressed with the archaeologist's courage.

The flames rose higher, first illuminating only the ship's stern. But, like a rising sun, the light's reach expanded rapidly. The terrorists used this to their advantage. They could see the vessel more clearly, and their accuracy improved.

Thirty feet from Linda, Alana slithered right to the edge of the burning section. She saw it wasn't the deck afire, but a bench for the helmsman. She swung onto her back, braced her feet under the burning seat, and heaved. Rather than fly over the side of the ship, the bench broke in two, showering her with embers.

Alana beat out the ashes where they seared her skin, ripped her T-shirt over her head, and with nothing to protect her skin but the thin cotton she worked on snuffing out the fire by hand. All the while, Linda and the gunmen traded shots over her head.

By the time Alana extinguished the last of the stubborn flames, her shirt had all but burned up, and most the skin on her palms was gone, leaving behind nothing but raw red meat that hurt like nothing she'd ever experienced in her life.

The pain was so intense, she couldn't crawl on her hands and knees, but rather had to slither like a snake to return to the others.

Linda shined a penlight on Alana's injuries and gasped.

"I'll be all right," Alana managed to say.

"Cover your ears," Mark Murphy whispered urgently.

He waited a beat, studying the array of winking flashlights over the touchhole of one of the *Saqr*'s great cannons. When he thought the time right, he slipped a timer pencil into the gun's touchhole, where it sank into the plastic explosives he'd rammed down the barrel. Between it and the muzzle was a cannonball made up of dozens of small metal spheres fused lightly together.

The timer went off, detonating the plastique, and the gun belched the grapeshot in a ten-foot tongue of flame. The ropes secured to the cannon to prevent the recoil from pushing it across the deck failed at full stretch, and the two tons of bronze rocketed through the opposite rail and plowed into the steep riverbank below the pier.

The impact of the grape was lost in the gun's mighty roar, but when Murphy looked out to where he'd aimed two of the three flashlights were no longer there.

It was as if the cannon's blast had signaled the end of round one and the beginning of the second. The gunmen opened up with renewed fury, rounds chewing at the *Saqr* as if to tear it apart piece by piece. The three Corporation operatives fired back, but the weight of the onslaught kept them pinned.

The cry of the terrorists' charge carried above the din. They were coming with everything they had.

Eric took a glancing bullet to the shoulder when he tried to shoot back and stem the tide. Unable to hold his rifle against the wound to aim, he flicked to full auto and raked the ground thirty feet from the *Saqr*'s side, creating a curtain of lead the terrorists couldn't penetrate.

When the rifle bolt snapped back on an empty magazine, Murphy took up the duty, blasting away in a desperate bid to break the charge. His gun, too, fell empty. Linda screamed like a Valkyrie as she hosed the dirt. It didn't matter if she hit anyone. The intention was just to keep the terrorists back long enough that their courage would fail and they'd retreat for cover.

Bullets whizzed all around her, but to her absolute relief she saw the muzzle flashes were coming from farther and farther away. The charge had broken. They had stopped them.

She slipped down below the bulwarks, her entire body vibrating as an aftereffect of her rifle's recoil, and she was covered in oily sweat. "You guys okay?" she called to her people as the gunmen's fire slowed.

"I took one to the shoulder," Eric reported from the darkness.

"I'm still pissed at myself for not grabbing the night vision goggles from Linc," Mark said bitterly. "We go spelunking, and I forget the most important piece of gear we would need."

"Alana?"

"I'm here," she called softly, her voice pinched with pain.

"Mark, give her something from your med kit." The sound of gunfire that had risen and fallen erratically over the past ten minutes dribbled away to silence.

Everyone's ears rang, but not badly enough to miss a man's voice calling out from the cavern entrance. "I will give you this one chance to give yourselves up."

"Holy crap," Eric exclaimed. "I know that voice."

"What? Who is it?"

"I listened in when he and the Chairman were talking aboard the *Oregon*. That's the harbor pilot, Hassad or Assad or something."

"That explains the ambush on the coast road," Murph surmised.

"Doesn't change anything for us, though." Linda thought for a moment, then shouted back, "I think General Austin McAuliffe said it best when he was asked to surrender during the Battle of the Bulge. In a word: nuts."

Murph grumbled sarcastically, "Oh, that'll go well for us."

Round three started in earnest.

THIRTY-FIVE

T HE FIRST PIECE OF GOOD NEWS CABRILLO HAD HEARD IN a while was that he was familiar with the supertanker slowly overtaking the Libyan frigate. She was the Petromax Oil ULCC *Aggie Johnston*, and several months earlier the *Oregon* had saved her from being hit by a couple of Iranian torpedoes by firing one of their own at the sub that had launched them.

They were close enough now that he had to assume all communications could be monitored by the *Gulf of Sidra*. To get around that, he found the ship's e-mail address on the Petromax website and sent its captain a note. It was far from convenient, and their exchanges went back and forth for nearly ten minutes before he could convince the captain that he was the commander of the freighter now shadowing them from a thousand yards away and not some lunatic kid e-mailing from his parents' basement in Anytown, USA.

As Juan waited for each reply, he lamented that Mark and Eric weren't aboard. Those two could have hacked the parent company's mainframe to issue the orders directly, and he wouldn't have to explain what he wanted from the floating behemoth and why.

A fresh e-mail appeared in his inbox.

Captain Cabrillo, It goes against my better instincts and my years of training, but I will agree to do what you've asked, provided we don't come within a half mile of that frigate and you provide the same sort of protection you did in the Straits of Hormuz if they fire on us.

As much as I want to do more, I must place the well-being of my ship and crew above my desire to help you unreservedly. I've spent the better part of my career operating out of Middle Eastern ports and hate what these terrorists have done to the region, but I can't allow anything to happen to my vessel. And as you can well imagine, if we were loaded with oil rather than running in ballast the answer would have been an unequivocal no.

All the best,

James McCullough.

PS: Give 'em one on the chin for me. Good hunting.

"Hot damn," Juan cried, "he'll do it."

Max Hanley was standing across the pilothouse chart table, the stem of his pipe clamped between his tobacco-stained teeth. "I wouldn't get that excited when you're contemplating playing chicken with a fully armed frigate."

"This will be perfect," Juan countered. "We'll be inside his defenses before they know what we're up to. We worked the vectors as we narrowed the gap and kept the tanker between us and the *Sidra* the whole time. As far as they know, there's only the one ship that's going to pass them. They have no idea we're here, and won't until the *Johnston* breaks off."

He typed a reply on a wireless-connected laptop as he spoke:

Captain McCullough, You are the key to saving the Secretary's life, and I can't thank you or your crew enough. I only wish that afterward you'd receive the accolades you so richly deserve, but this incident must remain secret. We will flash your bridge with our Aldis lamp when we want you to begin. That should be in about ten minutes.

Again, my sincerest thanks,

Juan Cabrillo.

Spread across the table was a detailed schematic of the Russian-built Koni-class frigate, showing all her interior passages. Also there were Mike Trono and Jerry Pulaski, who would be leading the assault teams. They were well-trained fire-eaters who'd seen more than their share of combat, but Juan wished Eddie Seng and Franklin Lincoln would be in on the attack with him. Behind Trono and Pulaski were the ten other men who would be boarding the Libyan ship.

Outside the starboard windows lurked the thousand-foot slab of steel that was the *Aggie Johnston*'s hull. With the *Oregon* ballasted down to lower her profile and the supertanker nearly empty, the *Johnston* seemed to loom over them even at this distance. The accommodation block at her stern was the size of an office building, and her squat funnel resembled an upended railroad tank car.

"Okay, back to this. Do we all agree the most likely place for the execution is the crew's mess?"

"It's the biggest open space on the ship," Mike Trono said. He was a slender man with fine brown hair who'd come to the Corporation after working as a pararescue jumper.

"Makes sense to me," Ski remarked. The big Pole was a former Marine who towered half a head over the others. Rather than wear combat clothing, the men had donned sailors' uniforms that Kevin Nixon's staff had modified to resemble the utilities worn by Libyan sailors. An instant of confusion on an opponent's part on seeing a familiar uniform but an unfamiliar face could mean the difference between life and death.

"Why a ship?" Mike asked suddenly.

"Sorry?"

"Why carry out the execution on a ship?"

"It'll be next to impossible to triangulate where the broadcast signal originates," Max replied. "And even if you can, the vessel's long gone by the time anyone comes out to investigate."

"We're going to enter the *Sidra* here," Juan said, pointing to an amidships hatch on the main deck. "We then move two doors down on the right to the first staircase. We take it down one flight, then it's left, right, left. The mess will be right in front of us."

"There's gonna be a lot of sailors in there to watch," Jerry predicted.

"I'd agree, normally," Juan said. "But as soon as we make our move, they'll go to general quarters. The hallways will be deserted, and anyone left in the mess is going to be a terrorist. The legitimate crew will be at their battle stations. We take out the tangos, grab Miss Katamora, and get off that tub before they know we were even there."

"There's still one problem with your plan," Max said, relighting his pipe. "You haven't explained our exit strategy. As soon as we pull away, *Sidra*'s going to nail us. I've been thinking about it, and I want to suggest that another team board her, carrying satchel charges. The *Oregon* can disable some of her armaments during the attack, and they can blow up what gets missed."

Hanley wasn't known for his tactical insights, so Juan was genuinely impressed. "Why, Max, what a well-reasoned and carefully considered plan."

"I thought so, too," he preened.

"Only thing is those men would get cut down long before they could approach the *Sidra*'s primary weapons systems." Juan pointed to the schematic again. "They've got emplacements for .30 caliber machine guns on all four corners of the superstructure. We can knock out the ones we can see, but the two on the far side are protected by the ship itself. Our boys would be cut to ribbons."

"Send Gomez up in the chopper and hit them with a missile," Hanley said, defensive that his plan was being questioned.

"SAM coverage is too tight. He'd never get close enough."

Max looked crestfallen, and his voice was a little sulky when he asked, "All right, smart guy, what's your idea?"

Juan peeled back the naval drawings. Beneath them was a chart of the Libyan coastline due south of their current position. Juan tapped his finger on a spot ten miles west of them. "This."

Max looked from Juan down to where he pointed and back up again. His smile was positively demonic. "Brilliant."

"Thought you'd like that. It's the reason we're delaying the attack for a few minutes. We need them close enough for this to work." Cabrillo added, "If there isn't anything else, we should all get into position."

"Let's do this," Mike Trono said.

The men descended the outside stairs to get to the main deck. Juan and Max lingered a moment.

"You still look a bit peevish," Cabrillo said to his best friend.

"You're going into the lion's den, Juan. This isn't like when we sneak into some warehouse in the middle of the night by knocking out a couple of rent-a-cops. There are some real bad apples on that ship, and I'm afraid as soon as they realize something's up they're going to kill her straightaway, and this'll all be for nothing."

A glib reply died on the Chairman's lips. He said somberly, "I know, but if we don't try they've already won. In a way, this war started in these waters two hundred years ago. We as a nation stood up back then for our core principles and said enough is enough.

Wouldn't it be something if we end it here, too, fighting for the very same things?"

"If nothing more, it would be rather poetic justice."

Juan slapped him on the back, grinning. "That's the spirit. Now, get down to the op center, and don't hurt my ship when I'm gone."

Max shook his head like an old bloodhound. "That's one promise you know I can't keep."

Once they gave Captain McCullough the signal, the massive tanker altered her course southward toward the Libyan frigate. It was done subtly and without warning, but inexorably the distance between the two vessels shrank. On her original course, the *Aggie Johnston* would have passed the *Sidra* with a five-mile separation, but as the trailing distance closed so, too, did the range. Staying tight to her flank, the *Oregon*, too, closed in on its prey.

The radios stayed quiet until the tanker was a mile astern and two miles north of the frigate. Juan had a portable handset as he waited in the shadow of the gunwales with his men. With the sun beginning to set behind them, the worst of the day's heat had abated, and yet the deck was still too hot to touch comfortably.

"Tanker approaching on my stern, this is the *Khalij Surt* of the Libyan Navy. You are straying too close for safe passage. Please alter your course and increase your separation before coming abeam."

"*Khalij Surt*, this is James McCullough of ULCC *Aggie Johnston*." McCullough had a smooth, cultured voice. Juan pictured him standing around six-two and, for some reason, bald as an egg. "We're experiencing a rogue ebb tide right now. I have the rudder over, and she's starting to respond. We will comply with your directive in time, I assure you."

"Very good," came the curt reply from the *Sidra*. "Please advise if you continue to have difficulties."

McCullough had stuck to Juan's script, and the first act of the play had gone perfectly. Of course, the tanker's captain would maintain his heading and, in the process, buy the *Oregon* more time.

Ten minutes went by, and the speeds of the ships relative to each other had narrowed the gap by another half mile. Juan thought the Libyans would have called much earlier. He considered it a good omen that there didn't seem to be any alarm.

"*Aggie Johnston, Aggie Johnston*, this is the *Khalij Surt*." The man's tone was still cool and professional. "Are you still experiencing difficulties?"

"A moment, please," McCullough radioed back as if pressed for time. When he didn't respond for two minutes, the Libyans repeated their request. This time, a bit more forcefully.

"Yes, sorry about that. The ebb intensified. We're coming out of it now."

"We did not experience this tidal action you seem to be facing."

"That's because our keel is forty feet down and stretches for three football fields."

Easy, Jimmy boy, Juan thought.

Juan and the captain had worked it out so the next call originated from McCullough. Two minutes after the last comment, he was on the horn again. "*Khalij Surt*, this is the *Aggie Johnston*. Please be advised our steering gear just failed. I have ordered an emergency stop, but at our current speed it will take us several miles. I calculate I will pass down your port beam with a half-mile clearance. May I suggest you alter your speed and heading."

Rather than slowing, the tanker began a steady acceleration, her single prop churning the water into a maelstrom at her fantail. This wasn't in the script, and Juan knew that McCullough was ignoring his own preset conditions in order to get the *Oregon* in as tight as he possibly could. Cabrillo vowed to find the man and buy him a drink when this was over.

The *Sidra* had begun to turn away and gain speed, but she was still going slow enough that her maneuvers were sluggish. The tanker dwarfed the warship as she started to cruise past, moving at eighteen knots only a third of a mile off the Libyans' rail.

Juan felt the *Oregon*'s deck shiver ever so slightly. Her big pumps were rapidly draining seawater from her saddle ballast tanks. They were going in.

In the op center, Max Hanley sat at the fore helm. Like Juan, he'd listened to the entire exchange, but unlike the Chairman he'd been able to at least watch some of the action. Next to him was the weapons tech. Every exterior door was folded back and every gun run out. The ship literally bristled.

He killed power to the pump jets, then reversed the flow.

Water exploded in a churning wave from the bow tubes, and the ship slowed so quickly her stern lifted slightly out of the water. As soon as she was clear of the *Aggie Johnston*, he cut reverse and applied forward pressure through the tubes. The cryopumps keeping the magnetohydrodynamics chilled to a hundred degrees below zero began to sing as the jets demanded more and more energy.

The *Oregon* accelerated like a racehorse, carving a graceful curve around the back of the tanker. In front of him was the low gray silhouette of the Libyan frigate.

He could imagine the consternation on the *Sidra*'s bridge when a ship twice its size suddenly appeared without warning from around the supertanker. After what had to have been a stunned thirty seconds, the airways came alive with expletives, demands, and threats.

Max nimbly tucked the *Oregon* between the two vessels even as McCullough turned sharply northward to gain sea room and safety.

"Identify yourself or we will open fire."

That was the second time Max had heard the challenge, and he doubted there would be a third. There was still a big enough gap for the *Sidra* to rake the *Oregon* with her three-inch cannons. He resisted the strong impulse to snatch up the handset and identify themselves as the USS *Siren*.

Watching on the monitor, he saw a cloud like a big cotton ball bloom in front of the *Sidra*'s forward gun. The shell shrieked by the bow and exploded in the sea fifty feet off her beam an instant before the concussion of the shot rumbled across the *Oregon*.

"Warning shot's free, my friend," Max said tightly. "Next one and the gloves come off."

The rear gun discharged this time, and an explosive shell slammed into the wing bridge, blowing it completely away.

Max could barely keep himself in his chair. "That's it. Fire at will."

The narrowing gulf between the two combatants came alive as the *Oregon*'s 30mm Gatling guns and bigger Bofors autocannon spewed out continuous streams of fire. The *Sidra*'s own antiaircraft guns added to the thunder of her main batteries, which were firing at a four-shot-a-minute clip.

The *Oregon* rang like a bell with each staggering impact. The rounds from the AAA penetrated her hull but were stopped by the next bulkhead. The deck guns' rounds burst through.

Already three cabins were in ruins, and slabs of marble had been ripped from the walls of the ballast tank that doubled as a swimming pool. Every impact saw more destruction. The boardroom where the senior staff met took a direct hit. The five-hundred-pound table was upended, and the leather chairs turned to kindling.

The automated fire-suppression system was battling a half dozen simultaneous blazes. Fire teams had been told to stay on the opposite side of the ship with the rest of the crew rather than risk themselves during the duel.

But the *Oregon* was giving as good as she got. All the *Sidra*'s bridge windows had been shot out, and enough tungsten rounds poured through the openings to mangle all the navigation and steering equipment. Rounds sparked off her armored hide. Her lifeboat shook like a rat in the jaws of a terrier when the Gatling hosed it. When it moved on, the craft was riddled with holes and hung drunkenly from one set of pulleys.

None of their smaller-caliber weapons could penetrate the armor protecting the turrets, so the weapons officer loosened the bow-mounted 120mm cannon. Because it used the same stability control system as an M1A2 main battle tank, this main gun had unbelievable accuracy. Its first round hit where the turret met the *Sidra*'s deck, and the entire mass jumped five feet into the air before smashing back again, greasy smoke billowing from the guns' barrels.

The two ships continued to pound on each other, each capable of absorbing tremendous punishment, as the gap grew narrower still. At point-blank range, there was no need to aim. Rounds impacted almost the instant they left the guns.

Nothing like this had been seen in the annals of naval warfare for a century, and despite the danger Max Hanley wouldn't have wanted to be anyplace else in the world.

Not so for the Chairman and the men on deck. They were hunkered behind a section of rail that had been triple reinforced, but when a 30mm autocannon raked the bulwark they all felt naked and exposed.

Juan couldn't imagine fighting this way as a normal course of events. Technology had sanitized warfare, made it cold and distant. The press of a button was all that was needed to vanquish your enemy. This was something else entirely. He could feel their hatred. It was as if each shot they took was an expression of personal loathing.

They wanted him dead. And not just dead but blown out of existence, as if he had never been born at all.

Another shell slammed into the armor plate, and for a moment it felt to Juan like his insides had liquefied. For a terrifying moment, he thought he had made a huge mistake.

Then he thought no, these people would not stop until someone stood up to them. If they wouldn't listen to reason, they would have to face the consequences of their own barbarity.

There came a brutal shudder. The *Oregon* was alongside the *Sidra*. Max had known to ballast their ship so the two railings were even. Juan snatched up his compact machine pistol and threw himself over the side.

The shimmering trail of an RPG launched from a concealed redoubt astern of the *Sidra*'s rear turret passed inches over his head and hit the armored plate just as the rest of his twelve-man team was following. The hit couldn't have been luckier or worse. Ten of the men were blown back by the blast, bloodied and suffering concussions, and two were tossed forward just as a wave separated the ships slightly. They plummeted down into the tight space and hit the water simultaneously.

Max had seen the disaster on the closed-circuit television system and immediately hauled the *Oregon* away from the *Sidra* so the hulls wouldn't slam together and smear the men into paste. He didn't know if they were alive or dead, but he ordered the rescue team standing by in the boat garage to immediately launch a Zodiac.

A tech moved a joystick to swivel the camera and scan the *Sidra*'s deck.

"There," Max shouted.

Cabrillo stood alone on the Libyan ship, his Heckler & Koch machine pistol smoking after taking out the gunman who was reloading his rocket launcher. It was almost as if he knew the camera was on him. He looked directly at it with the most savage expression Max had ever seen and then vanished alone through the frigate's hatchway.

THIRTY-SIX

Ambassador Charles Moon was failing one of his principal tasks for the evening. He'd been expressly directed by the President to make sure the VP didn't drink too much during the reception at Minister Ghami's home.

The VP had an alcoholic's lack of self-control but not the tolerance, and he'd downed four crystal flutes of champagne during the half hour they'd been here. It might have been understandable, had he known the house was the likely target of a terrorist attack, but the administration felt that the Vice President couldn't be trusted with that information if their plan was going to work.

Moon set his own untouched champagne on a marble-topped table to wipe his sweaty palms on the legs of his tuxedo. Next to him, Vice President Donner got to the punch line of an off-color joke. The group of ten guests who were within earshot waited a beat before giving him a smattering of polite laughter. His press secretary, who was filling the role as his date for the evening, pulled him slightly aside before he could launch into another.

Moon took the opportunity to look around the elegant reception hall. Minister Ghami's isolated home was stunning. Built of stone and stucco, it had the feel of a Moorish castle, massive and secure. The main entrance off the porte cochere opened all the way to the roof three stories up. Elegant wrought-iron balusters ringed the upper stories, and the staircase that spilled onto the ground floor was easily twenty feet wide. An orchestra was set up on the midpoint landing, where the steps divided left and right. They played classical music with an Arabic flair.

As impressive as the house was, it paled in comparison to the importance of the guests. Moon counted no fewer than ten heads of state among the elegantly dressed throng. In one corner, under a dramatically backlit potted palm, the Israeli Prime Minister was sharing some private words with Lebanon's President, and on the other side of the room Iraq's PM was conversing with Iran's Foreign Minister.

Moon expected these people to speak cordially at a reception such as this—these were politicians and diplomats, after all—but he had a feeling this went a little deeper. There was true optimism in the room that the Tripoli Accords would be a success.

Then the voice of gloom in his head overshadowed his brief moment of confidence. First, they needed to survive the night.

By far the biggest group of people stood around Ali Ghami as he held court near a bubbling mosaic-tiled fountain. The two men's eyes met for a moment. Ghami raised his glass slightly, a solemn gesture that told Moon he acknowledged the most important guest to him was the one who wasn't here.

Fiona Katamora was the topic of most conversations this night. Moon had been told that Qaddafi, wearing a civilian suit rather than a uniform, would make a speech about her loss.

Moon's bodyguard for the night, wearing a borrowed ill-fitting tux, tapped him on the arm and nodded in the direction of the open entrance to the adjoining living room. Tucked away unobtrusively near the ceiling was a video camera.

"I've counted five so far," the man said.

"For security?"

"Or posterity. You can best believe those are switched on right now and ready to record tonight's attack. I also noticed that the plasma television in the living room is a temporary setup. The wires are taped down to the floor rather than run under the Persian rug. This way, everyone here will be able to witness the beheading. It'll also bunch the crowd together nicely for the attack. I think this is going to be a two-way performance because I saw a small webcam sitting next to the TV."

"It's really going to happen, isn't it?"

"That's their plan, but don't worry. We know what we're doing."

"Have you been able to tell which are the legitimate security guards and which are the terrorists?" Moon asked.

"The tangos are still outside. The planners of this attack know they wouldn't be able to hold their cover for long if they were in here now." The bodyguard felt confident, but he carefully watched the few Libyan agents mingling with the guests.

Muammar Qaddafi climbed a couple steps to get above the crowd, a wireless microphone in his hand. The orchestra fell silent, and the men and women turned expectantly for his tribute to Fiona Katamora.

The Libyan leader was known to be almost as long-winded as Castro. After five rambling minutes, Moon tuned him out.

He'd wiped his hands twice during that brief period of time and knew that if he took off his jacket the stains under his arms would reach his belt line.

Amazingly, the guard at his side looked totally relaxed.

•   •   •

IN THE CAVERN'S DARKNESS, Eric changed out his ammo magazine by feel. Only two clips remained in the pouch strapped to his harness. His shoulder throbbed in time with his racing heart, and he hadn't had a chance to tend to it. Blood ran hot and sticky all the way to his fingertips.

Another grenade thrown blindly hit just below the *Saqr*'s gunwale and dropped to the dirt. The explosion was muffled by the hull, but it rocked the ship toward the pier, and they remained at a ten-degree list. This time, the desiccated wood caught fire immediately, and with the flames spreading outside the ship there was nothing they could do to stop it.

"As soon as it gets light enough, we're toast," Mark said grimly.

Already, Linda Ross could see his dim outline growing from the gloom. She knew he was right. The darkness had saved them until now, but when the fire reached a certain size and its light filled the cavern the advantage would shift to the terrorists. The question for her was whether they should wait it out and hope to somehow beat back the attack or retreat and find another way out of this trap.

She made her decision the moment she acknowledged her limited options. "Okay, we'll lay down a short burst of cover fire. Mark, Eric, take Alana, jump for the pier, and head away from the entrance. Try to find some defensible position. I'll give you a thirty-second head start. Hose 'em again, and I will be right behind you."

They quickly lined the *Saqr*'s rail. The fire burning aft of them wasn't yet big enough to illuminate the entire cave, but they could see ten or fifteen feet out. The body of a terrorist lay sprawled on the ground at the limit of their vision, a black stain pooled under his chest slowly soaking into the dirt.

"Fire," Linda ordered, and they loosened a blistering fusillade, raking the rubble that had been blasted to seal the cave from the river.

As soon as their guns emptied, Eric and Mark lifted Alana from the deck by her forearms. Linda was still shooting behind them, sniping into the darkness to keep the gunmen down. The three stepped up onto the *Saqr*'s rail and jumped the gap to the pier. Alana almost fell, and had Eric not grabbed her quickly she would have caught herself on her badly blistered hands.

Keeping as low as he could, Mark led them forward, his arms out in front of him. When he touched the cave's back wall, he turned right and groped his way along the uneven surface. Alana couldn't keep a hand on the rock, but behind her Eric laid one hand on her shoulder to keep her oriented.

They walked blindly for seventy-five feet, the staggering wall of sound from the renewed gun battle behind them never seeming to grow distant because of the confined acoustics.

Mark chanced flicking on his light. They were at the end of the pier. There was nautical gear piled just ahead of them, coils of rope mostly, but there was also some chain nestled in reed baskets as well as lengths of wood for spars. But what most caught his attention was the mouth of a side cave off the main cavern. A metal bar had been attached to the rock above it, and from it hung the tatters of what had once been a pair of tapestries that when closed would have afforded privacy inside.

"We might be okay," he said, and they all stepped into the new chamber.

Eric quickly drew the shades closed and changed out his magazine to stand guard while Mark played the flashlight around the room, keeping his fingers over the lens to defuse the harsh halogen light.

"This is incredible," Alana whispered reverently. For the moment, she forgot the pain radiating from her hands and the noise of the firefight raging outside.

The cave floor was covered with several layers of intricate oriental carpets to prevent cold from seeping through the rock. More tapestries covered much of the walls and gave the chamber the cheery feel of a tent. There were two rope beds on one side of the room, one of them neatly made, the other rumpled. Other furniture included several chests and a large writing table, complete with ink pots and feather quills, which had grown limp over the centuries and wilted over the sides of their solid gold stand. The desktop was inlaid with complex geometric patterns done in mother-of-pearl. Books were stacked on the floor around it and filled an adjacent set of shelves. An ornate Koran had the place of honor next to a tattered, dog-eared Bible.

There was an alcove next to the shelves. It was stacked floor to ceiling with chests. The lid for one of them was sprung, and when Mark shone the light in the crack the unmistakable flash of gold dazzled back at him.

He tried to see if there was an opening behind the chests, but with them so tightly packed it was impossible to tell without moving them. He shoved at the topmost trunk to dislodge it. The trunk wouldn't budge. If it was full of gold like the lower one, it would easily weigh a thousand pounds.

He gave the light to Alana, who tucked it under her arm because she couldn't trust her hands to hold it properly.

"There's no way out," Mark said, returning to Eric's side. Stoney had reloaded Murph's rifle and handed it across. "On the bright side, we're going to die rich. Must be a hundred million in gold shoved in a closet back there."

The firing outside remained relentless, although Linda had to be on the move because they couldn't hear her weapon over the sharp whip-cracks of the terrorists' AKs. The stern of the *Saqr* was a pyre now, with flames almost reaching the cave's ceiling and quickly filling the cave with smoke.

Eric kept whispering "Marco" into the gloom and was rewarded with a return call of "Polo."

Linda reached the entrance and ducked through long before the gunmen were aware she had moved. "Tell me the good news."

"We're rich," Mark offered. "But trapped."

●   ●   ●

THE TWO SHIPS WERE so close to each other that it was impossible to get off a shot, so they had fallen on a deadly stalemate, although the *Oregon* was using her superior size and power to start herding the Libyan frigate closer to shore. Whenever the hulls came together, the smaller naval vessel was forced to cut starboard to avoid being crushed under the freighter. Occasionally, a brave, or suicidal, terrorist would pop on deck and try to launch another RPG at the freighter, but the antiboarding .30 calibers were deployed and aimed before he could take an accurate shot. The two RPGs they managed to fire at the *Oregon* flew right over the ship, and the gunmen were cut down for their efforts.

The corridors inside the frigate were a scene of bedlam, with damage-control teams running in every direction. The air was smoky from a fire in the forward part of the ship, although the antiquated scrubbers were working to clear it. Alarms wailed, and men shouted orders over the strident cry.

It was all music to Fiona Katamora's ears, as she lay shackled to a bed frame in an officer's cabin. She had no idea what was happening around her other than that the men who'd kidnapped her were in trouble.

She knew she had been taken aboard a ship after the helicopter flight from the jihadists' training camp. She could tell from the salty air that wafted through the bag they had placed over her head and from the engine's thrum and the action of waves against the hull. She hadn't known which type of vessel until the cannons started firing.

It came as no surprise that Suleiman Al-Jama had been able to co-opt a Libyan warship. More likely, the entire crew were members of his organization.

Explosions wracked the frigate, and with each blast her sense of well-being grew. They would still kill her before it was over, she wasn't fooling herself about that, but the United States Navy would ensure they wouldn't have the chance to enjoy their victory.

A particularly loud explosion hit the ship, which seemed to stagger under the blow. When Fiona no longer heard the forward cannon firing, she knew the American warship had blown off one of the Libyan's main gun turrets.

The door to the cabin was hastily thrown open. Her jailors wore headscarves to mask their features and had AK-47s slung over their backs. Fiona's moment of well-being vanished as her cuffs were rearranged so her hands were bound behind her. Wordlessly, they yanked her from the room.

Uniformed sailors barely threw them a glance. They were too preoccupied with saving their ship to gloat over their prize. Fiona fell against a bulkhead when another fury of rounds slammed into the ship's side. The ferocity of the battle so distracted her for the walk down to another, larger room that she forgot to pray.

But when she saw the black cloth hanging across the back wall, the video camera, and the man holding a massive scimitar, the words fell from her lips. There were others in the room, terrorists, not Libyan sailors. One was standing behind the camera, another near him fiddled with the satellite-uplink controls. The rest of the masked men were here as witnesses. She recognized their khaki utilities from the desert base. The man with the sword wore all-black.

The alarm loudspeaker in the mess hall had been disabled, though it was still audible from other parts of the vessel.

"Far from saving you," the executioner said in Arabic, "that ship out there has pushed up our timeline by a few minutes." He stared hard at the Secretary, and she returned his defiance. "Are you ready to die?"

"For the sake of peace," Fiona replied, her voice as steady as she could keep it, "I was ready to die from the moment I understood the concept."

They secured her to a chair set before the drape. Plastic sheeting had been placed on the deck at her feet. A gag was tied across her mouth to deny her any parting words.

The executioner nodded to the cameraman and he began to film. The lens stayed focused on Fiona for a moment, to make sure the target audience knew exactly who was about to die. Then the swordsman stepped in front of her, holding the ornate scimitar so it was plainly visible.

"We, the servants of Suleiman Al-Jama, come before you today to rid the world of another infidel." He was reading from a typewritten script. "This is our answer to the Crusaders' efforts to thrust their decadence upon us. From this unholy woman has come the worst of their lies, and for that she must die."

Fiona willed herself to ignore the rant so in her head all she heard was "Our Father who art in heaven . . ."

• • •

SEEING HIS MEN HIT sent a lance of concern through Cabrillo's heart, but there was no chance to go back now. Rather than consider retreat, he went on single-handedly. None of the Libyan sailors paid him the slightest attention. With a handful of Al-Jama's terrorists using the ship as their base for Fiona Katamora's execution, an unfamiliar face in their midst wasn't cause for alarm. The few men moving around inside the ship were too focused on their jobs. When a fire-control team rushed toward him, Juan stopped running and flattened himself to a wall as any sailor would be trained to do.

"Come with us," the fire team leader shouted without breaking stride.

"Captain's orders," Juan replied over his shoulder, and raced away in the opposite direction.

He found the staircase and rushed down three at a time, bowling over a seaman clawing his way topside. On the next deck, he ran unerringly for the crew's mess. There were two armed guards posted outside the door. One was looking into the room, the other glanced at Cabrillo but dismissed him as part of the crew because of the uniform.

If Juan had needed confirmation he'd been right about a terrorist presence, it was these two, with their kaffiyehs and AKs.

Ten paces from them, Juan could hear a voice inside the mess saying ". . . killed our women and children in their homes, bombed our villages, and defied the very word of Allah."

It was enough for him. With a cold fury born of fighting for too long—for his entire life, it seemed—he whipped the compact machine pistol into view. The one terrorist's eyes widened, but that was the only reaction the Chairman allowed him. Cabrillo's weapon chattered in his hands, stitching both men across their torsos. One round blew off the top of a man's shoulder, the resulting blood splatter like obscene graffiti on the wall behind him.

Juan was moving so fast he had to push aside the collapsing bodies to get into the mess. Six armed men stood to his right beyond the sweep of a tripod-mounted camera. Two more were near the video equipment and another stood in front of it, a piece of paper in one hand, a curved sword in the other.

Fiona Katamora sat behind him, her mouth gagged but her eyes bright.

Cabrillo took in this tableau in the first half of a second and made his threat evaluation in the next. The executioner would need to move to make his killing stroke, and the men working the camera had left their weapons on the deck.

Juan skidded to his knees for a more stable firing position and then cut into the six terrorists. Two went down before they knew he was in the room. A third died as he tried to sweep his rifle into his hands. Because of the H&K's notorious barrel rise on full automatic, number five was a double-tap headshot that sent brain tissue spinning through the air.

Cabrillo had to release the trigger for an instant to adjust. Number six opened fire before he'd drawn a bead. Rounds pinked off the wall to Juan's right, chipping white paint off the metal and throwing ricochets in every direction.

The Chairman got his sight picture and let fly, drilling the gunman with a steady burst that threw him bodily into a bulkhead. He turned to the swordsman. The guy had the fastest reaction reflex Juan had ever seen. Four seconds had elapsed since he'd fired the first shots. Any normal human would have spent half that processing what his senses were telling him.

But not the swordsman.

He was moving the instant Juan's eyes had first swept past him. He drew back the sword, pirouetting in a graceful display, and had the blade arcing toward Fiona Katamora's exposed neck even before the sixth gunmen went down.

Hyped on adrenaline, Juan watched it happen like it was slow motion. He began swinging the H&K's stubby barrel, knowing it was too late. He fired anyway, and from across the room the videographer pulled a pistol from a holster Cabrillo hadn't seen.

A line of raging pain creased the side of Juan's head and his vision went black.

THIRTY-SEVEN

ALI GHAMI GLANCED AT HIS WATCH FOR ABOUT THE DOZENTH time since Qaddafi had started speaking. And he kept looking over at an assistant, who hovered near the front door, a radio bud in his ear. Every time he met the man's eyes, the aide would shake his head imperceptibly.

Charles Moon's bodyguard had pointed out the behavior to him, and as he studied the Libyan Minister more closely he saw other signs of his disquiet. Ghami was constantly shifting from foot to foot, or thrusting his hands into his jacket pocket only to remove them an instant later. Many guests were growing tired of the long speech, which was now closing in on a half hour, but Ghami seemed more agitated than bored.

He looked again at his aide. The suited man was turned slightly away, his hand to his ear to listen better over Qaddafi's droning voice. He turned back a moment later and nodded at Ghami, a smile of triumph spread across his face.

"Showtime," Moon's guard said nonchalantly.

Ghami climbed one of the steps to get the Libyan President's attention. When Qaddafi cut off his rambling praises of Fiona Ka-tamora, the Minister climbed higher and whispered into his ear.

Qaddafi visibly paled. "Ladies and gentlemen," he said, his voice, which had been so compassionate and clear moments earlier, quaver-ing. "I have just been given the worst news possible."

Moon translated for his companion's sake.

"It appears that the beloved American Secretary of State man-aged to survive the horrific airplane crash." This was met with a col-lective gasp, and conversations sprang up spontaneously all around the room. "Please, ladies and gentlemen, your attention, please. This is not what it seems. Following the crash, she was abducted by forces loyal to Suleiman Al-Jama. I have just been given word that they are about to carry out her execution. Minister Ghami also tells me they have a way of communicating with us in this house."

Qaddafi followed his Foreign Minister into the next room, and soon many of the more sangfroid of the guests were crammed into every corner. The guard had Moon hold back so they were still in the entry hall, peering over the shoulders of others. The televi-sion had been turned on, its pale glow making the people look like the blood had been drained from their bodies. Several women were crying.

An image suddenly sprang up on the monitor. Sitting in front of a black background was Secretary Katamora. Her hair was a tangled mess after her ordeal, and her wide dark eyes were red-rimmed. The gag tied across her mouth pulled her cheeks back in an ugly rictus, but still she looked beautiful.

The weeping intensified.

A man hiding his features with a checked kaffiyeh stepped into view. He carried a sword with a small nick in its blade. "We, the ser-vants of Suleiman Al-Jama, come before you tonight to rid the world of another infidel," he said. "This is our answer to the Crusaders' efforts to thrust their decadence upon us. From this unholy woman has come the worst of their lies, and for that she must die."

Moon's guard watched Ghami's reaction closely. Something about what was playing out on the television had him off-kilter.

Qaddafi picked up the small camera from the television stand and held it at arm's length. "My brother," he said. "My Muslim brother who basks in the light of Allah, peace be upon him. This is no longer the way. Peace is the natural order of the world. Bloodshed only begets bloodshed. Can you not see that taking her life will accomplish nothing? It will not end the suffering in the Muslim world. Only discourse can do that. Only when we sit facing our enemies and discussing what brought us to such a state can we ever hope to live in harmony.

"The Koran tells us there can be no harmony with the infidel."

"The Koran also tells us to love all life. Allah has given us this contradiction as a choice for each man to make. The time for choosing hatred is over. Our governments are meeting now so we make this same choice for all our people. I beg you to lay down your sword. Spare her life."

No one could see the swordsman's features because of the headscarf, but his body language was easy enough to read. His shoulders slumped, and he let the heavy scimitar fall from view.

Then, from the back of the reception hall, came the sound of running feet, dozens of them pounding across the marble floor.

The plan was falling apart.

Ali Ghami yanked the camera from Qaddafi's hand. "Mansour," he screamed at his bodyguard, "what are you doing? Our gunmen are here. Kill her! Do it now!"

Rather than take up his sword again to slice off her head, the figure on the television helped pull the gag from Secretary Katamora's mouth.

"Mansour," Ghami cried again. "No!"

Someone yanked the camera away from the Minister at the same time he felt the barrel of a pistol crammed into his spine. He looked over to see an Asian man, Charles Moon's bodyguard, standing behind him.

"Game's up, Suleiman," Eddie Seng said. "Take a look."

On the monitor, the man Ghami thought was his most trusted confidant pulled the kaffiyeh from around his head. "How'd it go?" Chairman Cabrillo asked, half his head swaddled in bandages.

"I think the term is red-handed."

The squad of President Qaddafi's personal bodyguards came to a halt in the entrance to report that they had overwhelmed the security personnel outside without needing to fire a shot.

Qaddafi, who'd been briefed on the operation by Charles Moon earlier in the afternoon, rounded on his Minister. "The charade is over. After receiving an anonymous tip this afternoon, members of the Swiss military raided the house where you've been holding my grandson after faking his death in an automobile accident. He is safe, so you can no longer sit like an asp at my breast threatening to strike if I don't allow you free rein.

"I truly did not know you were Al-Jama. I thought you black-mailed me to attain your current position for selfish gains of power. But now you have exposed yourself to the world. Your guilt is without question, and your execution will be swift. And I will work tirelessly to rid my government of anyone who even spoke of you highly."

Qaddafi spread his arms to encompass the important people in the room. "We stand united in rejecting your ways, and the failure of your plot to kill leaders from other Muslim nations will serve as notice to others who stand in the way of peace. Take this piece of garbage from my sight."

A burly Libyan soldier grabbed Ghami by the scruff of the neck and frog-marched him through the stunned crowd.

From the television came a woman's voice.

"Mr. President, I couldn't have said that better myself." Fiona Katamora was standing at Juan's side. "And I want to assure all the conference's attendees that I will be at the bargaining table tomorrow morning at nine o'clock sharp so together we can all usher in a new era."

• • •

THE BULLET THAT GRAZED the Chairman's head in the frigate's mess had knocked him out for only a second while the single round he'd managed to fire had done something far more remarkable. It had hit the sword as it swung, throwing off the executioner's aim. The blade had struck the metal back of the chair, knocking it sideways and tumbling Fiona to the deck.

Lying on the floor, Juan triggered off a pair of three-round bursts, killing the cameraman and his assistant. The swordsman had lost his weapon, and he backed away from Fiona, holding his hands over his head.

"Please," he begged. "I am unarmed."

"Uncuff her," Juan ordered. "And remove her gag."

Before he could comply, the man who'd been threatening her life moments ago wet himself.

"It's a little tougher facing armed men in combat than blowing up innocents, eh?" Juan mocked. When the gag came off, he asked the Secretary, "Are you okay?"

"Yes. I think so. Who are you?"

"Let's just say I'm the spirit of Lieutenant Henry Lafayette and leave it at that." Juan pulled the hand radio from his pant pocket. "Max, do you copy?"

"About damned time you called in," Max said so gruffly that Cabrillo knew he was beside himself with concern.

"I've got her and we're on our way out."

"Make it quick. The *Sidra*'s accelerating, and we've only got about two minutes for your extraction plan to work."

Fiona got to her feet, massaging her wrists where the cuffs had dug into her skin. She kept a wary distance from the swordsman but did the most astonishing thing Juan could imagine. She said, "I forgive you, and someday I pray you will come to see me not as your enemy but as your friend." She turned to Juan. "Do not kill this man."

Cabrillo was incredulous. "With all due respect, are you nuts?"

Without a backward glance, she strode from the room. Juan made to follow, turned back on the swordsman, and fired a single shot. He grabbed the script from the deck where it had fallen and noted the frequency the television camera was going to broadcast on, the final piece of his plan. When he caught up to her, he said, "I couldn't have him follow us, so I put one through his knee."

He took her hand, and together they raced for the main deck. The smoke, he noticed, was much thinner. A pair of sailors was on the top landing of the stairs. They didn't react until they recognized the Japanese-American Secretary of State. As if choreographed, they jumped at her simultaneously. Juan shot one as he flew, and the bullet's impact was enough to alter his trajectory. The second slammed into Juan's chest with enough force to blow the air from his lungs. Choking to refill them, Juan was defenseless for several moments, an opening the sailor took to throw a quick series of punches.

Fiona tried to wrestle him off her rescuer, and had she not been through the ordeal of the past few days she would have succeeded, but she was exhausted beyond her body's limit. The sailor shoved her aside contemptuously and threw a kick that caught Cabrillo on the chin.

From outside the confines of the ship came a roar that rattled the stairwell.

A missile had streaked off a hidden launch tube buried on the *Oregon*'s deck. It lifted into the growing darkness on a fiery column that seemed to split the sky. The explosive-tipped rocket began to topple almost immediately on its short projected flight.

The sound galvanized the Chairman, and he found a berserker's fury. The kick had rattled his brain, so he fought on instinct alone. He ducked as the next blow came at him and smashed his elbow down on the sailor's exposed shin with enough force to snap the bone.

The man screamed when he put weight on it and the shattered ends grated against one another. Juan gained his feet, rammed a knee into the sailor's groin, and pushed him down the rest of the steps. He grabbed Fiona's hand, and they rushed for the exit.

The hatch he had used to gain entry into the *Sidra*'s superstructure was closed, and when he opened it, expecting to see the *Oregon* hard against the frigate's side, he saw instead that his ship was a good thirty feet away. In her wake, the rocket's contrail hung in the air, a twisting snake that corkscrewed into the night.

From the far side of the frigate came an explosion much more powerful than anything felt since the battle had begun. The ship-to-shore rocket had impacted on the inside of the main sluice gates for the Zonzur Bay Tidal Power Station.

●   ●   ●

EIGHT ASSAULT RIFLES POURED their deadly fire into the mouth of the side cave. Stone chips and ricochets filled the air like a swarm of angry hornets. All four Americans were bleeding from multiple hits, though no one had as serious an injury as Eric Stone's shoulder.

There was so much coming in at them that there was no way they could return fire, so they hunkered near the entrance as the terrorists advanced behind a wall of lead.

One gunman suddenly burst into the cave, shouting wildly. He fired from the hip, raking the walls, tearing apart the bed, and blowing books off the shelves. Linda hit him with a three-round burst to the chest before he could aim at any of them, blowing his body back out into the main cavern.

It had been dumb luck that she had killed him before he got any of them, and she knew that wouldn't happen again. Next time, the entire team would rush them, and it would be over.

Linda checked her ammo. She had no spare magazines in her harness, and the clip jammed into her rifle's receiver was only half full. Eric was out of rounds and held his weapon like a club, ready to defend himself hand to hand. Mark Murphy couldn't have very many bullets left either, she knew.

A lifetime of defending her country had come down to this last stand in a dark cave far from home, fighting a bunch of fanatics who wanted nothing more than the right to keep on killing.

The firing outside the cave slackened slightly. They were preparing for the final push.

A grenade flew out of the smoke-filled passage and landed in the alcove loaded with chests. The wood absorbed half of the blast, belching splinters and glittering gold coins while the spray of shrapnel peppered the cave walls. Again, no one had been hit, but the concussion left them reeling. Bits of burning wood had landed on the beds and caught the linens on fire. In seconds, the air was choked with smoke.

Eric screamed something to Linda, but she couldn't hear him with her ringing ears. They would come now, she was certain. In the wake of the grenade's detonation, the terrorists had to know they had them. Filthy, aching, emotionally raw, she tightened her finger around the REC7's trigger.

But nothing happened for long seconds. Of the seven surviving terrorists, only one or two were firing into the cave now. They were waiting us out, Linda thought, knowing the smoke will force us to them, or hoping we die in the fire.

Lying prone to get out of the worst of it, Linda took tiny sips of the fouled air, but each breath seared her lungs. Assad's men were going to get their wish, she thought grimly. They couldn't stay here much longer. She looked over at Eric and Mark, her eyes questioning. They seemed to read her mind and both nodded their assent. Linda scrambled to her knees and launched herself onto her feet, her shipmates at her side.

"Let's go, Sundance," Mark shouted as they charged into the mouths of the waiting guns.

They sprinted past the burning drapery over the cave's entrance and made a good five feet and still hadn't drawn fire. Linda searched for a target in the wavering light of the ship burning in the distance but spotted no one standing to face them. There was a terrorist sprawled on the ground a few paces from her, a neatly drilled hole between his shoulder blades. Then she saw others they had somehow managed to hit. The cavern floor was littered with them. Her headlong rush slackened until she stood stock-still with a total of eight bodies at her feet.

She felt a superstitious tingle run the length of her spine.

One of the men moved weakly, clawing at the sand and gasping for air. Like the first, he'd been hit in the back. Mark kicked the AK out of the man's reach and rolled him over. Frothy blood from his ruptured lung bubbled from his lips. Linda had never seen Tariq Assad, so she didn't recognize his distinctive unibrow.

"How?" he gasped.

"Your guess is as good as ours, pal," Mark told him.

And then over the crackling of the burning *Saqr* and through the

428   C L I V E   C U S S L E R

ringing in their ears came a rich melodious baritone singing, "From the hall of Montezuma / To the shores of Tripoli, / We will fight our country's battles / In the air, on land and sea."

"Linc?" Linda cried.

"How you doing, sweet stuff?" He emerged from his cover position with his rifle cocked on his hip and a pair of night vision goggles pulled down around his neck. "Got here as fast as I could, but this bod wasn't made for running across the damned desert."

Linda threw her arms around the big man, sobbing into his chest, the depth of determination to face her enemies in a suicidal charge dissolving into profound relief at being alive. Mark and Eric pounded his back, laughing and choking on the smoke at the same time.

"Looks like you guys made a good show for yourselves." Which, from Linc, was his greatest sign of respect.

Alana staggered from the cave, her torso bare and once-white bra blackened with soot. She was holding a couple of books as gingerly as she could. Their pages smoldered. When one started burning, Mark took it from her, dropped it on the ground, and kicked sand over it to snuff the flames.

"I wanted to save more," she managed between coughs, "but the smoke. I couldn't. I did get this, though."

"What's that?" Linc asked.

Dangling from a crudely fashioned chain of silver was a small crystal nestled in a rudimentary setting. The piece of jewelry wasn't particularly attractive; in fact, it looked almost like a child's attempt at making a Mother's Day present out of pipe cleaners and paste. But there was something compelling about it beyond its obvious antiquity, an aura as if it were a presence there in the cave with them.

A bullet had shattered the stone, so it lay in its cradle in tiny shards no bigger than grains of sugar, and from it oozed a single claret drop.

"Holy God," Mark said, dropping to his knees to scoop up the soaked spot of sand. From a shirt pocket, he pulled out a power bar and ripped away its wrapping. He threw the food aside and carefully placed the tiny bit of mud on the paper and twisted it closed. There was a red streak on his palm that mingled with the blood from a deep cut he'd received at some point during the battle.

"When the covers burned away," Alana explained, "I realized there was a mummy on the bed, placed on his side facing Mecca as a good Muslim should. This was around his neck. Henry Lafayette must have placed Al-Jama like that when the old man died and left him with his greatest treasure. That is the Jewel of Jerusalem, isn't it? And that was His blood, preserved for two thousand years in a vacuum within that crystal."

"His blood?" Linc asked. "Who His?"

"Stuffed in that candy wrapper in Mark's hands may be the blood of Jesus Christ."

●   ●   ●

THE TIDAL STATION'S MASSIVE steel gate stretched for more than a hundred feet above the generating plant set in the desert depression. When the facility was operating at full capacity, the gate could be lowered more than thirty feet to allow water to flow into large-diameter pipes down into the long turbine room more than a hundred feet below sea level. With the sun setting rapidly to the west, the gate had been closed and the turbines idled so crews could remove excess salt left over by the sun's evaporation, the key to the zero-emissions facility.

The missile off the *Oregon* hit the exposed machinery that operated the gate dead center, blowing apart the hydraulic systems and smashing the gears that acted as a mechanical brake. Even the pressure of the ocean it was designed to withstand couldn't keep the heavy door pinned in place, and it started to lower on its own accord into a recess built into the artificial dike.

Water spilled over the top of the gate, first in thin erratic sheets tossed by waves lapping against the structure, and then in a solid curtain when it fell below the surface. With less surface exposed to the titanic forces holding back the Mediterranean, the gate accelerated downward. The curtain turned into a gush, and then into a torrent more powerful than the worst levee break on the Mississippi River. Millions of tons of seawater poured though the gap. The pipes to carry the water into the powerhouse were closed, saving the delicate turbines, so the deluge flowed wild and uncontained down the dike into the desert.

Even when the plant wasn't active, there was a two-mile exclusion zone around the facility for all shipping. It was a rule Max Hanley had gladly ignored. He'd been shepherding the *Gulf of Sidra* into the exact right position for when the missile hit. Up on the main view screen, he watched the ocean disappearing into the gap on the far side of the frigate, but, more important, he could feel the pull of the current in the way his beloved ship responded to his controls.

The *Sidra* had sheered away from the *Oregon* as soon as they were in the gravity-induced vortex, sucked toward the opening as surely as if she'd been aimed at it. Max goosed the directional thrusters and closed the gap, keeping one eye on the camera feed showing where Juan would appear.

"Come on, buddy. We don't have all day."

The Chairman suddenly burst through the frigate's hatchway, holding the hand of Secretary Katamora. Max steepened his angle and closed the gap, so the two ships brushed just enough to scrape a little paint off her hull. Juan was on the *Sidra*'s railing at that exact moment. He lifted Fiona off the deck and hurled her onto the *Oregon*, where she fell into the waiting arms of a still-woozy Mike Trono.

As soon as Juan's boots hit the deck, Max pulled the big freighter away from the stricken frigate and opened the throttles as far as they would go. The warship was also desperately trying to get clear of the maelstrom. Smoke belched from her stack and her props beat the water frantically, and yet she lost more ground with every passing moment.

The *Oregon*'s revolutionary engines gave her ten times the power, and once water was humming through the tubes her lateral motion checked and she started to pull away. Max even eased back on the controls a touch, never wanting to push his babies harder than he had to.

The *Sidra*'s hull slammed into the open sluice intake at a perfect broadside. Water continued to rush under her keel, but half the floodwaters were suddenly contained once again. Balanced precariously, with the sea pressing in on the hull so her steel moaned at the strain, the crew could do nothing as the ship that had foiled their perfect plan steamed serenely away.

On the *Oregon*'s deck, the Corporation operators who'd been blown back by the RPG clustered around the Chairman and his guest. So little time had elapsed since that fateful moment that medical staff hadn't even arrived, but it looked as if Doc Huxley and her team weren't going to be busy after all. The injuries appeared minor.

Juan stuck out a hand to formally introduce himself to Fiona. "I want to say it is an honor to meet you. My name's Cabrillo, Juan Cabrillo. Welcome aboard the *Oregon*."

She brushed aside his hands and hugged him tightly, repeating her thanks into his ear over and over again. The thing about adrenaline heightening one's senses was that it had that effect on *all* of them, so before Fiona realized how much Juan was enjoying the contact he gently untangled himself from her willowy arms.

"I know you're a woman of many accomplishments, but I wonder if acting is among them?"

She looked at him askance. "Acting? After what we just went through you're talking about acting. You call *me* nuts."

He slipped an arm around her waist to lead her into the ship's interior. "Don't worry, you get to play yourself, and we just practiced the scene I want to reproduce for Ali Ghami."

"You know?"

"I even know how he got leverage on Qaddafi. His grandson was in Switzerland on vacation when he was killed in a car crash. The crash was staged and the boy kidnapped. If Qaddafi ever wanted to see the kid alive again, he had to make Ghami Foreign Minister, not knowing that he had just made one of the worst terrorists in the world a senior government official and given him access to everything he needed to pull off his little caper."

"And you?" Fiona asked. "How do you fit in with all of this?"

He gave her a squeeze. "Just lucky, I guess."

THE SENIOR STAFF WAS ASSEMBLED ON THE AFT HELICOPTER pad when George Adams brought Hali Kasim back to the ship from a Tripoli hospital. Hux had a wheelchair standing by, and she turned away from the chopper as it flared in over the *Oregon*'s fantail.

The skids kissed dead center. Gomez killed the turbines. Everyone rushed forward under the spinning blades to pound on the rear door glass, laughing and aping for Hali as he sat strapped in, a johnny pulled loosely over his heavily bandaged chest. He'd undergone five hours of surgery to repair the damage Assad's bullet had done to his internal organs and endured a week of hospital food before his doctors would allow him to leave.

But he was the last of them home after what had been perhaps the toughest mission the Corporation had ever undertaken. At dawn, they had rendezvoused with their two wandering lifeboats full of ex-prisoners. The Foreign Minister already had his old job back and was at the conference. Adams had picked up Linda and the others from the desert cave not long afterward. When they had emerged from the cavern, they discovered Professor Emile Bumford bound and gagged at the entrance. The two gundogs who'd gone into the drink during the attack on the *Sidra* had been picked up, half-drowned, by the rescue Zodiac with nothing worse than flash burns on their hands and faces. Hux and her staff had patched them up, tended Alana's hands and Eric's shoulder, and removed what seemed like a pound of stone shrapnel from the group Mark dubbed the "Fantastic Four."

Alana had remained on the *Oregon* for just a night. She was anxious to return to Arizona and her son. Unfortunately, without any kind of provenance and with its crystal ruined, no one would risk their career by saying definitively if the necklace she'd found was indeed the fabled Jewel of Jerusalem. The real team of archaeologists who'd been excavating the Roman villa had been sent into the caverns after the pall of smoke had been extracted. The *Saqr* had been reduced to ashes, and only the gold remained in the side chamber. But it in itself was a numismatist's wildest dream come true. The gold was mostly in the form of coins from every nation of Europe and every corner of the old Ottoman Empire, stretching back hundreds of years. It was the accumulated hoard of generations of the Al-Jama family, and even the most conservative estimate put the coins' worth ten times higher than the value of the gold alone.

The delegates at the Tripoli Accords had already declared that the proceeds of the sale of so many perfectly preserved and diverse coins would help fund antipoverty programs across the Muslim world. And that was only the beginning of the sweeping reforms the leaders had on the table.

A half dozen helping hands eased Hali Kasim out of the chopper and into the waiting wheelchair.

"You don't look so bad to me," Max said, wiping at his eyes.

"I'm still on pain meds, so I don't feel so bad either," Hali replied with a grin.

"Welcome back." Juan shook his hand. "You sure took one for the team this time."

"I'll tell you, Chairman, I don't know what was worse: getting shot or getting so completely bamboozled. Mossad agent, my brown butt. I just hope he suffered in the end."

"Don't you worry about that," Linc said. "Lung shot's about the worst way to go."

The bright note about the archaeological finds from the tomb were the three books Alana had managed to save. One was Henry Lafayette's Bible, which he'd left with his mentor, and another was Suleiman Al-Jama's personal Koran. The third was a detailed treatise on ways the two great religions could and should coexist if all of the faithful were strong enough to live up to the moral standards set down in the sacred texts. The writing had already been authenticated, and while some of the diehards called it a forgery and a Western trick, others—many, many others—were heeding the Imam turned pirate turned peacenik's words.

No one kidded themselves, least of all Juan Cabrillo, that terrorism was about to end, but he was optimistic that it was on the wane. He'd have no problem with that, even if it meant that the *Oregon* would head for the breaker's yard and he would light out for a tropical retirement.

Everyone followed Hali as he was wheeled into the ship except for Max and Juan. They lingered over the fantail next to the Iranian flag their ship sported. Water churned in the big freighter's wake as she started to get under way again.

Max took out his pipe and jammed it between his teeth. The fantail was too windy and exposed to light it. "Couple pieces of good news for you. A team of NATO commandoes raided the new base Ghami's people were building in the Sudan. With their leader imprisoned, they put up only token resistance. Not so, however, the ones still in Libya. The last of them tried to storm the prison where he's being held."

"And . . ." Juan prompted.

"Shot dead, to a man. A single guard was killed by a suicide blast when he tried to take one of them prisoner. Oh, hey," Max exclaimed, suddenly remembering something, "I read your final report this morning about this whole fur ball. Question for you."

"Shoot."

"On the *Sidra*, when you went back after the Secretary told you not to shoot Ghami's bodyguard . . ."

"Mansour."

"Right, him. You wrote you kneecapped him. Is that true?"

"Absolutely," Juan said without taking his eyes off the horizon. "Marquis of Queensbury rules, remember? Those are the restrictions we've placed on ourselves. Come to think of it, actually, I could have been a little more detailed in the report. I didn't mention that Mansour was bent over one of his men trying to get his weapon in such a way that his head was on the other side of the knee I blew out. I don't believe the good Marquis ever said anything about bullets overpenetrating."

Max chuckled. "I think that's true. Say, what was it Hux told you just before Hali arrived?"

"I'm not sure if you want to know." There was an odd undercurrent in Juan's voice. "I'm still trying to get my mind around it."

"Go ahead, I can take it," Max said in a way to lighten the suddenly somber mood.

"She managed to analyze the fluid that leaked out of the jewel. It was pretty degraded, and there was only a minute amount, so she can't verify her findings. Her official report states 'inconclusive.'"

"But . . . ?"

"It was human blood."

"Could be anybody's. Al-Jama might've made that jewel himself and used his own."

"Carbon dating puts the sample between fifty B.C. and eighty A.D. The real kicker is, she only found female DNA."

"It's a woman's blood?"

"No, the chromosomes proved the blood came from a man, only he had one hundred percent mitochondrial DNA, even outside the mitochondria, and please don't ask me to explain. Hux tried and just gave me a headache. Bottom line is, the mitochondrial DNA is only passed on to us through our mothers."

Max felt a chill despite the balmy weather. "What does it mean?"

"It means that the mother of whoever that blood belonged to provided all his DNA. One hundred percent. The father made zero contribution. It was almost as if he didn't exist."

"What are you saying?"

"Her words were something like if she were to imagine the blood work of a person who was of virgin birth, what we found was it."

"Jesus."

Max said it as a blasphemous expression of awe, but Juan responded to his comment anyway. "Apparently."

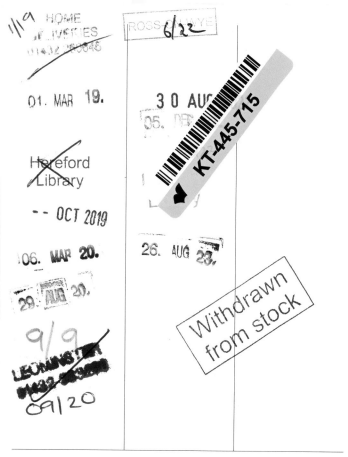

SPECIAL MESSAGE TO READERS

THE ULVERSCROFT FOUNDATION
(registered UK charity number 264873)

was established in 1972 to provide funds for research,
diagnosis and treatment of eye diseases.
Examples of major projects funded by
the Ulverscroft Foundation are:-

- The Children's Eye Unit at Moorfields Eye Hospital, London
- The Ulverscroft Children's Eye Unit at Great Ormond Street Hospital for Sick Children
- Funding research into eye diseases and treatment at the Department of Ophthalmology, University of Leicester
- The Ulverscroft Vision Research Group, Institute of Child Health
- Twin operating theatres at the Western Ophthalmic Hospital, London
- The Chair of Ophthalmology at the Royal Australian College of Ophthalmologists

You can help further the work of the Foundation
by making a donation or leaving a legacy.
Every contribution is gratefully received. If you
would like to help support the Foundation or
require further information, please contact:

THE ULVERSCROFT FOUNDATION
The Green, Bradgate Road, Anstey
Leicester LE7 7FU, England
Tel: (0116) 236 4325

website: www.foundation.ulverscroft.com

Jo Nesbø is one of the world's leading crime writers, which he claims only partly compensates for having a promising soccer career abruptly terminated when he tore ligaments in both knees at the age of eighteen. After he studied economics and financial analysis, he worked as a stockbroker by day and played with the band Di Derre ('Them There') at night. When commissioned by a publisher to write a memoir about life on the road with his band, he instead came up with the plot for his first Harry Hole crime novel, *The Bat*. His books are published in 50 languages and have sold over 40 million copies worldwide.

You can discover more about the author at www.jonesbo.co.uk

MACBETH

When a drug bust turns into a bloodbath in a
dark, rainy Scottish town, it's up to Inspector
Macbeth and his team to clean up the mess. He's
the best cop they've got, and he's rewarded for
his success. Power. Money. Respect. They're all
within reach. But he's also an ex-drug addict
with a troubled past — and a man like him won't
get to the top. Plagued by hallucinations and
paranoia, Macbeth starts to unravel. He's convinced he won't get what's rightfully his . . . unless
he kills for it — and then the ambitions of a
corrupt policeman are pitted against loyal colleagues, a drug-depraved underworld, and the
pull of childhood friendships.

Books by Jo Nesbø
Published by Ulverscroft:

THE LEOPARD
POLICE
THE SON
BLOOD ON SNOW
MIDNIGHT SUN

JO NESBØ

MACBETH

Translated from the Norwegian by Don Bartlett

HOGARTH
SHAKESPEARE

Complete and Unabridged

CHARNWOOD
Leicester

First published in Great Britain in 2018 by
Hogarth
An imprint of Vintage
London

First Charnwood Edition
published 2018
by arrangement with
Vintage
Penguin Random House
London

A catalogue record for this book is available
from the British Library.

ISBN 978–1–4448–3931–9

Published by
F. A. Thorpe (Publishing)
Anstey, Leicestershire

Set by Words & Graphics Ltd.
Anstey, Leicestershire
Printed and bound in Great Britain by
T. J. International Ltd., Padstow, Cornwall

This book is printed on acid-free paper

PART ONE

1

The shiny raindrop fell from the sky, through the darkness, towards the shivering lights of the port below. Cold gusting north-westerlies drove the raindrop over the dried-up riverbed that divided the town lengthwise and the disused railway line that divided it diagonally. The four quadrants of the town were numbered clockwise; beyond that they had no name. No name the inhabitants remembered anyway. And if you met those same inhabitants a long way from home and asked them where they came from they were likely to maintain they couldn't remember the name of the town either.

The raindrop went from shiny to grey as it penetrated the soot and poison that lay like a constant lid of mist over the town despite the fact that in recent years the factories had closed one after the other. Despite the fact that the unemployed could no longer afford to light their stoves. In spite of the capricious but stormy wind and the incessant rain that some claimed hadn't started to fall until the Second World War had been ended by two atom bombs a quarter of a century ago. In other words, around the time Kenneth was installed as police commissioner. From his office on the top floor of police HQ Chief Commissioner Kenneth had then misruled the town with an iron fist for twenty-five years, irrespective of who the mayor was and what he was or wasn't doing, or what the powers-that-be were saying or not saying over in Capitol, as the country's second-largest and once most important industrial centre sank into a quagmire of corruption, bankruptcies, crime and chaos. Six months ago Chief Commissioner Kenneth had fallen from a chair in his summer house. Three weeks later, he was dead. The funeral had been paid for by the town — a council decision made long ago that Kenneth himself had incidentally engineered. After a funeral worthy of a dictator the council and mayor had brought in Duncan, a broad-browed bishop's son and the head of Organised Crime in Capitol, as the new chief commissioner. And hope had been kindled amongst the city's inhabitants. It had been a surprising appointment because Duncan didn't come from the old school of politically pragmatic officers, but from the new generation of well educated police administrators who supported reforms, transparency, modernisation and the fight against corruption — which the majority of the town's elected get-rich-quick politicians did not.

And the inhabitants' hope that they now had an upright, honest and visionary chief commissioner who could drag the town up from the quagmire had been nourished by Duncan's replacement of the old guard at the top with his own hand-picked officers. Young, untarnished idealists who *really* wanted the town to become a better place to live.

The wind carried the raindrop over District 4 West and the town's highest point, the radio tower on top of the studio where the lone, morally indignant voice of Walt Kite expressed the hope, leaving no 'r' unrolled, that they finally had a saviour. While Kenneth had been alive Kite had been the sole person with the courage to openly criticise the chief commissioner and accuse him of some of the crimes he had committed. This evening Kite reported that the town council would do what it could to rescind the powers that Kenneth had forced through making the police commissioner the real authority in town. Paradoxically this would mean that his successor, Duncan the good democrat, would struggle to drive through the reforms he, rightly, wanted. Kite also added that in the imminent mayoral elections it was 'Tourtell, the sitting and therefore fattest mayor in the country, versus no one. Absolutely no one. For who can compete against the turtle, Tourtell, with his shell of folky joviality and unsullied morality, which all criticism bounces off?'

In District 4 East the raindrop passed over the Obelisk, a twenty-storey glass hotel and casino that stood up like an illuminated index finger from the brownish-black four-storey wretchedness that constituted the rest of the town. It was a contradiction to many that the less industry and more unemployment there was, the more popular it had become amongst the inhabitants to gamble away money they didn't have at the town's two casinos.

'The town that stopped giving and started taking,' Kite trilled over the radio waves. 'First of all we abandoned industry, then the railway so that no one could get away. Then we started selling drugs to our citizens, supplying them from where they used to buy train tickets, so that we could rob them at our convenience. I would never have believed I would say I missed the profit-sucking masters of industry, but at least they worked in respectable trades. Unlike the three other businesses where people can still get rich: casinos, drugs and politics.'

In District 3 the rain-laden wind swept across police HQ, Inverness Casino and streets where the rain had driven most people indoors, although some still hurried around searching or escaping. Across the central station, where trains no longer arrived and departed but which was populated by ghosts and itinerants. The ghosts of those — and their successors — who had once built this town with self-belief, a work ethic, God and their technology. The itinerants at the twenty-four hour dope market for brew; a ticket to heaven and certain hell. In District 2 the wind whistled in the chimneys of the town's two biggest, though recently closed, factories: Graven and Estex. They had both manufactured a metal alloy, but what it consisted of not even

5

those who had operated the furnaces could say for sure, only that the Koreans had started making the same alloy cheaper. Perhaps it was the town's climate that made the decay visible or perhaps it was imagination; perhaps it was just the certainty of bankruptcy and ruin that made the silent, dead factories stand there like what Kite called 'capitalism's plundered cathedrals in a town of drop-outs and disbelief'.

The rain drifted to the south-east, across streets of smashed street lamps where jackals on the lookout huddled against walls, sheltering from the sky's endless precipitation while their prey hurried towards light and greater safety. In a recent interview Kite had asked Chief Commissioner Duncan why the risk of being robbed was six times higher here than in Capitol, and Duncan had answered that he was glad to finally get an easy question: it was because the unemployment rate was six times higher and the number of drug users ten times greater.

At the docks stood graffiti-covered containers and run-down freighters with captains who had met the port's corrupt representatives in deserted spots and given them brown envelopes to ensure quicker entry permits and mooring slots, sums the shipping companies would log in their miscellaneous-expenses accounts swearing they would never undertake work that would lead them to this town again.

One of these ships was the MS *Leningrad*, a Soviet vessel losing so much rust from its hull in the rain it looked as if it was bleeding into the harbour.

The raindrop fell into a cone of light from a lamp on the roof of one two-storey timber building with a store-room, an office and a closed boxing club, continued down between the wall and a rusting hulk and landed on a bull's horn. It followed the horn down to the motorbike helmet it was joined to, ran off the helmet down the back of a leather jacket embroidered with

NORSE RIDERS in Gothic letters. And to the seat of a red Indian Chief motorbike and finally into the hub of its slowly revolving rear wheel where, as it was hurled out again, it ceased to be a drop and became part of the polluted water of the town, of everything.

Behind the red motorbike followed eleven others. They passed under one of the lamps on the wall of an unilluminated two-storey port building.

★   ★   ★

The light from the lamp fell through the window of a shipping office on the first floor, onto a hand resting on a poster: MS *GLAMIS* SEEKS GALLEY HAND. The fingers were long and slim like a concert pianist's and the nails well manicured. Even though the face was in shadow, preventing you from seeing the intense blue eyes, the resolute chin, the thin, miserly lips and nose shaped like an aggressive beak, the scar shone like a white shooting star, running diagonally from the jaw to the forehead.

'They're here,' Inspector Duff said, hoping his men in the Narcotics Unit couldn't hear the involuntary vibrato in his voice. He had assumed the Norse Riders would send three to four, maximum five, men to get the dope. But he counted twelve motorbikes in the procession slowly emerging from the darkness. The two at the back each had a pillion rider. Fourteen men to his nine. And there was every reason to believe the Norse Riders were armed. Heavily armed. Nevertheless, it wasn't the sight of superior numbers that had produced the tremor in his vocal cords. It was that Duff had achieved his dearest wish. It was that *he* was leading the convoy; finally *he* was within striking distance.

The man hadn't shown himself for months, but only one person owned that helmet and the red Indian Chief motorbike. Rumour had it the bike was one of fifty the New York Police Department had manufactured in total

7

secrecy in 1955. The steel of the curved scabbard attached to its side shone.

Sweno.

Some claimed he was dead, others that he had fled the country, that he had changed his identity, cut off his blond plaits and was sitting on a *terrazza* in Argentina enjoying his old age and pencil-thin cigarillos.

But here he was. The leader of the gang and the cop-killer who, along with his sergeant, had started up the Norse Riders some time after the Second World War. They had picked rootless young men, most of them from dilapidated factory-worker houses along the sewage-fouled river, and trained them, disciplined them, brainwashed them until they were an army of fearless soldiers Sweno could use for his own purposes. To gain control of the town, to monopolise the growing dope market. And for a while it had looked as if Sweno would succeed, certainly Kenneth and police HQ hadn't stopped him; rather the opposite, Sweno had bought in all the help he needed. It was the competition. Hecate's home-made dope, brew, was much better, cheaper and always readily available on the market. But if the anonymous tip-off Duff had received was right, this consignment was big enough to solve the Norse Riders' supply problems for some time. Duff had hoped, but not quite believed, what he read in the brief typewritten lines addressed to him was true. It was simply too much of a gift horse. The sort of gift that — if handled correctly — could send the head of the Narco Unit further up the ladder. Chief Commissioner Duncan still hadn't filled all the important positions at police HQ with his own people. There was, for example, the Gang Unit, where Kenneth's old rogue Inspector Cawdor had managed to hang on to his seat as they still had no concrete evidence of corruption, but that could only be a question of time. And Duff was one of Duncan's men. When there were signs that Duncan might be appointed

8

chief commissioner Duff had rung him in Capitol and clearly, if somewhat pompously, stated that if the council didn't make Duncan the new commissioner, and chose one of Kenneth's henchmen instead, Duff would resign. It was not beyond the bounds of possibility that Duncan had suspected a personal motive behind this unconditional declaration of loyalty, but so what? Duff had a genuine desire to support Duncan's plan for an honest police force that primarily served the people, he really did. But he also wanted an office at HQ as close to heaven as possible. Who wouldn't? And he wanted to cut off the head of the man out there.

Sweno.

He was the means *and* the end.

Duff looked at his watch. The time tallied with what was in the letter, to the minute. He rested the tips of his fingers on the inside of his wrist. To feel his pulse. He was no longer hoping, he was about to become a believer.

'Are there many of them, Duff?' a voice whispered.

'More than enough for great honour, Seyton. And one of them's so big, when he falls, it'll be heard all over the country.'

Duff cleaned the condensation off the window. Ten nervous, sweaty police officers in a small room. Men who didn't usually get this type of assignment. As head of the Narco Unit it was Duff alone who had taken the decision not to show the letter to other officers; he was using only men from his unit for this raid. The tradition of corruption and leaks was too long for him to risk it. At least that is what he would tell Duncan if asked. But there wouldn't be much cavilling. Not if they could seize the drugs and catch thirteen Norse Riders red-handed.

Thirteen, yes. Not fourteen. One of them would be left lying on the battlefield. If the chance came along.

Duff clenched his teeth.

'You said there'd only be four or five,' said Seyton, who had joined him at the window.

'Worried, Seyton?'

'No, but you should be, Duff. You've got nine men in this room and I'm the only one with experience of a stake-out.' He said this without raising his voice. He was a lean, sinewy, bald man. Duff wasn't sure how long he had been in the police, only that he had been in the force when Kenneth was chief commissioner. Duff had tried to get rid of Seyton. Not because he had anything concrete on him; there was just something about him, something Duff couldn't put his finger on, that made him feel a strong antipathy.

'Why didn't you bring in the SWAT team, Duff?'

'The fewer involved the better.'

'The fewer you have to share the honours with. Because unless I'm very much mistaken that's either the ghost of Sweno or the man himself.' Seyton nodded towards the Indian Chief motorbike, which had stopped by the gangway of *MS Leningrad*.

'Did you say Sweno?' said a nervous voice from the darkness behind them.

'Yes, and there's at least a dozen of them,' Seyton said loudly without taking his eyes off Duff. 'Minimum.'

'Oh shit,' mumbled a second voice.

'Shouldn't we ring Macbeth?' asked a third.

'Do you hear?' Seyton said. 'Even your own men want SWAT to take over.'

'Shut up!' Duff hissed. He turned and pointed a finger at the poster on the wall. 'It says here MS *Glamis* is sailing to Capitol on Friday at 0600 hours and is looking for galley staff. You said you wanted to take part in this assignment, but you hereby have my blessing to apply for employment there instead. The money and the food are supposed to be better. A show of hands?'

Duff peered into the darkness, at the faceless,

unmoving figures. Tried to interpret the silence. Already regretting that he had challenged them. What if some of them actually did put up their hands? Usually he avoided putting himself in situations where he was dependent on others, but now he needed every single one of the men in front of him. His wife said he preferred to operate solo because he didn't like people. There could have been something in that, but the truth was probably the reverse. People didn't like him. Not that everyone actively disliked him, although some did; there was something about his personality that put people off. He just didn't know what. He knew his appearance and confidence attracted a certain kind of woman, and he was polite, knowledgeable and more intelligent than most people he knew.

'No one? Really? Good, so let's do what we planned, but with a few minor adjustments. Seyton goes to the right with his three men when we come out and covers the rear half of them. I go to the left with my three men. While you, Sivart, sprint off to the left, out of the light, and run in an arc in the darkness until you're behind the Norse Riders. Position yourself on the gangway so that no one can escape into the boat. All understood?'

Seyton cleared his throat. 'Sivart's the youngest and — '

' — fastest,' Duff interrupted. 'I didn't ask for objections, I asked if my instructions were *understood*.' He scanned the blank faces in front of him. 'I'll take that as a yes.' He turned back to the window.

A short bow-legged man with a white captain's hat waddled down the gangway in the pouring rain. Stopped by the man on the red motorbike. The rider hadn't removed his helmet, he had just flipped up the visor, nor had he switched off his engine. He sat with his legs splayed obscenely astride the saddle and listened to the captain. From under the helmet

11

protruded two blond plaits, which hung down over the Norse Rider logo.

Duff took a deep breath. Checked his gun.

The worst was that Macbeth *had* rung. He had been given the same tip-off via an anonymous phone call and offered Duff the SWAT team. But Duff had turned down his offer, saying all they had to do was pick up a lorry, and had asked Macbeth to keep the tip-off quiet.

At a signal from the man in the Viking helmet one of the other bikers moved forward, and Duff saw the sergeant's stripes on the upper arm of his leather jacket when the rider opened a briefcase in front of the ship's captain. The captain nodded, raised his hand, and a second later iron screamed against iron, and light appeared in the crane swinging over its arm from the quayside.

'We're almost there,' Duff said. His voice was firmer now. 'We'll wait until the dope and the money have changed hands, then we'll go in.'

Silent nods in the semi-darkness. They had gone through the plans in painstaking detail, but they had imagined a maximum of five couriers. Could Sweno have been tipped off about a possible intervention by the police? Was that why they had turned up in such strength? No. If so, they would have called it all off.

'Can you smell it?' Seyton whispered beside him.

'Smell what?'

'Their fear.' Seyton had closed his eyes and his nostrils were quivering. Duff stared into the rainy night. Would he have accepted Macbeth's offer of the SWAT team now? Duff stroked his face with his long fingers, down the diagonal scar. There was nothing to think about now; he had to do this, he'd always had to do this. Sweno was here now, and Macbeth and SWAT were in their beds asleep.

★　★　★

Macbeth yawned as he lay on his back. He listened to the rain drumming down. Felt stiff and turned onto his side.

A white-haired man lifted up the tarpaulin and crept inside. Sat shivering and cursing in the darkness.

'Wet, Banquo?' Macbeth asked, placing the palms of his hands on the rough roofing felt beneath him.

'It's a bugger for a gout-ridden old man like me to have to live in this piss-hole of a town. I should grab my pension and move into the country. Get myself a little house in Fife or thereabouts, sit on a veranda where the sun shines, bees hum and birds sing.'

'Instead of being on a roof in a container port in the middle of the night? You've got to be joking?'

They chuckled.

Banquo switched on a penlight. 'This is what I wanted to show you.'

Macbeth held the light and shone it on the drawing Banquo passed him.

'There's your Gatling gun. Beautiful job, isn't she?'

'It's not the appearance that's the problem, Banquo.'

'Show it to Duncan then. Explain that SWAT needs it. Now.'

Macbeth sighed. 'He doesn't want it.'

'Tell him we'll lose as long as Hecate and the Norse Riders have heavier weaponry than us. Explain to him what a Gatling can do. Explain what *two* can do!'

'Duncan won't agree to any escalation of arms, Banquo. And I think he's right. Since he's been the commissioner there *have* been fewer shooting incidents.'

'This town is still being depopulated by crime.'

'It's a start. Duncan has a plan. And he wants to do what's right.'

'Yes, yes, I don't disagree. Duncan's a good man.' Banquo groaned. 'Naive though. And with this weapon we could clear up and — '

They were interrupted by a tap on the tarpaulin.

13

'They've started unloading, sir.' Slight lisp. It was SWAT's young new sharpshooter, Olafson. Along with the other equally young officer Angus, there were only four of them present, but Macbeth knew that all twenty-five SWAT officers would have said yes to sitting here and freezing with them without a moment's hesitation.

Macbeth switched off the light, handed it back to Banquo and slid the drawing inside his black SWAT leather jacket. Then he pulled away the tarpaulin and wriggled on his stomach to the edge of the roof.

Banquo crawled up beside him.

In front of them in the floodlights, over the deck of MS *Leningrad*, hovered a prehistoric-looking military-green lorry.

'A ZIS-5,' Banquo whispered.

'From the war?'

'Yep. The S stands for Stalin. What do you reckon?'

'I reckon the Norse Riders have more men than Duff counted on. Sweno's obviously worried.'

'Do you think he suspects the police have been tipped off?'

'He wouldn't have come if he did. He's afraid of Hecate. He knows Hecate has bigger ears and eyes than us.'

'So what do we do?'

'We wait and watch. Duff might be able to pull this off on his own. In which case, we don't go in.'

'Do you mean to say you've dragged these kids out here in the middle of the night to sit and *watch?*'

Macbeth chortled. 'It was voluntary, and I did say it might be boring.'

Banquo shook his head. 'You've got too much free time, Macbeth. You should get yourself a family.'

Macbeth raised his hands. His smile lit up the beard on his broad dark face. 'You and the boys are my family, Banquo. What else do I need?'

14

Olafson and Angus chuckled happily behind them.

'When's the boy going to grow up?' Banquo mumbled in desperation and wiped water off the sights of his Remington 700 rifle.

★   ★   ★

Bonus had the town at his feet. The glass pane in front of him went from floor to ceiling, and without the low cloud cover he would have had a view of absolutely the whole town. He held out his champagne glass, and one of the two young boys in riding jodhpurs and white gloves rushed over and recharged it. He should drink less, he knew that. The champagne was expensive, but it wasn't him paying. The doctor had said a man of his age should begin to think about his lifestyle. But it was so good. Yes, it was as simple as that. It was so good. Just like oysters and crawfish tails. The soft, deep chair. And the young boys. Not that he had access to them. On the other hand, he hadn't asked.

He had been picked up from reception at the Obelisk and taken to the penthouse suite on the top floor with a view of the harbour on one side and the central station, Workers' Square and Inverness Casino on the other. Bonus had been received by the great man with the soft cheeks, the friendly smile, the dark wavy hair and the cold eyes. The man who was called Hecate. Or the Invisible Hand. Invisible, as very few people had ever seen him. The Hand, as most people in the town over the last ten years had been affected in some way or other by his activities. That is, his product. A synthetic drug he manufactured himself called brew. Which, according to Bonus' rough estimate, had made Hecate one of the town's four richest men.

Hecate turned away from the telescope on the stand by the window. 'It's difficult to see clearly in this rain,' he said, pulling at the braces of his own jodhpurs, and took a pipe from the tweed jacket hanging over the back of the chair. If he'd known that they would turn out dressed as an English hunting party he would have chosen something other than a boring everyday suit, Bonus thought.

'But the crane's working, so that means they're unloading. Are they feeding you properly, Bonus?'

'Excellent food,' Bonus said, sipping his champagne. 'But I have to confess I'm a little unsure what it is we're celebrating. And why I'm entitled to be here.'

Hecate laughed and raised his walking stick, pointing to the window. 'We're celebrating the view, my dear flounder. As a seabed fish you've only seen the belly of the world.'

Bonus smiled. It would never have occurred to him to object to the way Hecate addressed him. The great man had too much power to do good things for him. And less good.

'The world is more beautiful from up here,' Hecate continued. 'Not more real but more beautiful. And then we're celebrating this, of course.' The stick pointed to the harbour.

'And this is?'

'The biggest single stash ever smuggled in, dear Bonus. Four and a half tons of pure amphetamine. Sweno has invested everything the club owns plus a little more. What you see below is a man who has put all his eggs in one basket.'

'Why would he do that?'

'Because he's desperate, of course. He can see that the Riders' mediocre Turkish product is outclassed by my brew. But with such a large quantity of quality speed from the Soviets, bulk discount and reduced transport costs will makes it competitive in price and quality per kilo.' Hecate rested the stick on the thick wall-to-wall carpet and caressed its gilt handle. 'Well calculated by Sweno, and if he succeeds it's enough to upset the balance of power in this town. So here's to our worthy competitor.'

He raised his glass, and Bonus obediently followed suit. But as Hecate was about to put it to his lips he studied the glass with a raised eyebrow, pointed to something and handed the glass back to one of the boys, who immediately cleaned it with his glove.

'Unfortunately for Sweno,' Hecate continued, 'it's difficult to obtain such a large order from a completely new source without someone in the same line of business catching wind of it. And unfortunately it seems this 'someone' may have passed on to the police an anonymous, though reliable, tip-off about where and when.'

'Such as you?'

Hecate smirked. Took the glass, turned his broad bottom towards Bonus and leaned down to the telescope. 'They're lowering the lorry now.'

Bonus got up and went over to the window. 'Tell me, why didn't you launch an attack on Sweno instead of watching from the sidelines? You would have got rid of your sole competitor and acquired four and a half tons of quality amphetamine at a stroke. And you could have sold it on the street for how many millions?'

Hecate sipped from his glass without raising his eye from the telescope. 'Krug,' he said. 'They say it's the best champagne. So it's the only one I drink. But who knows? If I'd been served something else I might have acquired a taste for it and switched brands.'

'You don't want the market to try anything else but your brew?'

'My religion is capitalism and the free market my creed. But it's everyone's right to follow their nature and fight for a monopoly and world domination. And society's duty to oppose us. We're just playing our roles, Bonus.'

'Amen to that.'

'Shh! Now they're handing over the money.' Hecate rubbed his hands. 'Showtime . . . '

★ ★ ★

Duff stood by the front door with his fingers around the handle listening to his breathing while trying to get eye contact with his men. They were standing in a line on the narrow staircase right behind him. Busy with their thoughts. Releasing the safety catch. A last word of advice to the man next to them. A last prayer.

'The suitcase has been handed over,' Seyton called down from the first floor.

'Now!' Duff shouted, wrenching open the door and hugging the wall.

The men pushed past him into the darkness. Duff followed. Felt the rain on his head. Saw figures moving. Saw a couple of motorbikes left unmanned. Raised the megaphone to his mouth.

'Police! Stay where you are with your hands in the air! I repeat, this is the police. Stay where — '

The first shot smashed the glass in the door behind him, the second caught the inside leg of his trousers. Then came a sound like when his kids made popcorn on a Saturday night. Automatic weapons. Fuck.

'Fire!' Duff screamed, throwing down the megaphone. He dived onto his stomach, tried to raise his gun in front of him and realised he had landed in a puddle.

'Don't,' whispered a voice beside him. Duff looked up. It was Seyton. He stood stationary with his rifle hanging down by his side. Was he sabotaging the action? Was he . . . ?

'They've got Sivart,' Seyton whispered.

Duff blinked filthy water from his eyes and kept looking, a Norse Rider in his sights. But the man was sitting calmly on his motorbike with his gun pointed at them, not shooting. What the hell was going on?

18

'Nobody move a fuckin' finger now and this'll be fine.'

The deep voice came from outside the circle of light and needed no megaphone. Duff saw first the abandoned Indian Chief. Then saw the two figures in the darkness merge into one. The horns sticking up from the helmet of the taller of the two. The figure he held in front of him was a head shorter. With every prospect of being another head shorter. The blade of the sabre glinted as Sweno held it to young Sivart's throat.

'What will happen now — ' Sweno's bass voice rumbled from out of the visor opening ' — is that we'll take our stuff with us and go. Nice and quietly. Two of my men will stay and make sure none of you does anything stupid. Like trying to come after us. Got that?'

Duff hunched up and was about to stand.

'If I were you I'd stay in the puddle, Duff,' Seyton whispered. 'You've screwed this up enough as it is.'

Duff took a deep breath. Let it out. Drew another. Shit, shit, shit.

★ ★ ★

'Well?' said Banquo, training the binoculars on the protagonists on the quayside.

'Looks like we'll have to activate the young ones after all,' Macbeth said. 'But not quite yet. We'll let Sweno and his men leave the scene first.'

'What? We're going to let them get away with the lorry and all the stash?'

'I didn't say that, dear Banquo. But if we start anything now we'll have a bloodbath down there. Angus?'

'Sir?' came the quick response from the lad with the deep blue eyes and the long blond hair unlikely to have been allowed by any other team leader but Macbeth. His emotions were written over all his open face. Angus

19

and Olafson had the training, now they just needed some more experience. Angus especially needed to toughen up. During his job interview Angus had explained that he had dropped out of training to become a priest when he saw there was no god; people could only save themselves and one another, so he wanted to become a policeman instead. That had been good enough for Macbeth; he liked the fearless attitude, the boy dealing with the consequences of his beliefs. But Angus also needed to learn how to master his feelings and realise that in SWAT they became practical men of action, the long, and rough, arm of the law. Others could take care of reflection.

'Go down the back, fetch the car and be ready by the door.'

'Right,' Angus said, got up and was gone.

'Olafson?'

'Yes?'

Macbeth glanced at him. The constant slack jaw, the lisping, the semi-closed eyes and his grades at police college meant that when Olafson had come to Macbeth, begging to be moved to SWAT, he had had his doubts. But the lad had *wanted* the move, and Macbeth decided to give him a chance, as he himself had been given a chance. Macbeth needed a sharpshooter, and even if Olafson was not spectacularly talented in theoretical subjects, he was a highly gifted marksman.

'At the last shooting test you beat the twenty-year-old record held by him over there.' Macbeth nodded to Banquo. 'Congratulations, that's a damn fine achievement. You know what it means right here and now?'

'Er . . . no, sir.'

'Good, because it means absolutely nothing. What you have to do here is watch and listen to Inspector Banquo and learn. You won't save the day today. That's for later. Understand?'

Olafson's slack jaw and lower lip were working but

were clearly unable to produce a sound, so he just nodded.

Macbeth laid a hand on the young man's shoulder. 'Bit nervous?'

'Bit, sir.'

'That's normal. Try to relax. And one more thing, Olafson.'

'Yes?'

'Don't mess up.'

★ ★ ★

'What's happening?' Bonus asked.

'I know what's going to happen,' Hecate said, straightening his back and swinging his telescope away from the quay. 'So I don't need this.' He sat down beside Bonus. Bonus had noticed that he often did that. Sat down beside you instead of opposite. As though he didn't like you looking straight at him.

'They've got Sweno and the amphetamine?'

'On the contrary. Sweno's seized one of Duff's men.'

'What? Aren't you worried?'

'I never bet on one horse, Bonus. And I'm more worried about the bigger picture. What do you think of Chief Commissioner Duncan?'

'His promise that you'll be arrested?'

'That doesn't concern me at all, but he's removed many of my former associates in the police and that's already created problems in the markets. Come on, you're a good judge of character. You've seen him, heard him. Is he as incorruptible as they say?'

Bonus shrugged. 'Everyone has a price.'

'You're right there, but the price is not always money. Not everyone is as simple as you.'

Bonus ignored the insult by not perceiving it as such. 'To know how Duncan can be bribed you have to know what he wants.'

'Duncan wants to serve the herd,' Hecate said. 'Earn the town's love. Have a statue erected he didn't order himself.'

'Tricky. It's easier to bribe greedy vermin like us than pillars of society like Duncan.'

'You're right as far as bribery is concerned,' Hecate said. 'And wrong with respect to pillars of society and vermin.'

'Oh?'

'The foundation of capitalism, dear Bonus. The individual's attempt to get rich enriches the herd. It's mechanics pure and simple and happens without us seeing or thinking about it. You and I are pillars of society, not deluded idealists like Duncan.'

'Do you think so?'

'The moral philosopher Adam Hand thought so.'

'Producing and selling drugs serves society?'

'Anyone who supplies a demand helps to build society. People like Duncan who want to regulate and limit are unnatural and in the long run harmful to us all. So how can Duncan, for the good of the town, be rendered harmless? What's his weakness? What can we use? Sex, dope, family secrets?'

'Thank you for your confidence, Hecate, but I really don't know.'

'That's a shame,' said Hecate, gently tapping his stick on the carpet as he observed one of the boys remove the wire from the cork of a new bottle of champagne. 'You see, I've begun to suspect Duncan has only one weak point.'

'And that is?'

'The length of his life.'

Bonus recoiled in his chair. 'I really hope you haven't invited me here to ask me to . . . '

'Not at all, my dear flounder. You'll be allowed to lie still in the mud.'

Bonus heaved a sigh of relief as he watched the boy

22

struggle with the cork.

'But,' Hecate said, 'you have the gifts of ruthlessness, disloyalty and influence that give you power over the people I need to have power over. I hope I can rely on you when help is needed. I hope you can be my invisible hand.'

There was a loud bang.

'There we are!' Bonus laughed, patting the boy on the back as he tried to get as much of the unrestrained champagne into the glasses.

★   ★   ★

Duff lay still on the tarmac. Beside him his men stood equally still watching the Norse Riders, less than ten metres away, preparing to leave. Sivart and Sweno stood in the darkness outside the cone of light, but Duff could see the young officer's body shaking and Sweno's sabre blade, which rested against Sivart's throat. Duff could see that the least pressure or movement would pierce the skin, the artery and drain the man's blood in seconds. And Duff could feel his own panic when he considered the consequences. Not only the consequences of having one of his men's blood on his hands and record, but the consequences of his privately orchestrated actions failing miserably just as the chief commissioner was about to appoint a head of Organised Crime. Sweno nodded to one of the Norse Riders, who dismounted from his motorbike, stood behind Sivart and pointed a gun at his head. Sweno pulled down his visor, stepped into the light, spoke to the man with the sergeant's stripes on his leather jacket, straddled his bike, saluted with two fingers to his helmet and rode off down the quayside. Duff had to control himself not to loose off a shot at him. The sergeant gave some orders and a second later the motorbikes growled off into the night. Only two unmanned motorbikes were left after

23

the others had followed Sweno and the sergeant.

Duff told himself not to give way to panic, told himself to think. Breathe, think. Four men in Norse Rider regalia were left on the quay. One stood behind Sivart in the shadows. One stood in the light keeping the police covered with an assault rifle, an AK-47. Two men, presumably the pillion riders, got into the lorry. Duff heard the continuous strained whine as the ignition key was turned and for a second he hoped that the old iron monster wouldn't start. Cursed as the first low growl rose to a loud rumbling rattle. The lorry moved off.

'We'll give them ten minutes,' shouted the man with the AK-47. 'Think of something pleasant in the meantime.'

Duff stared at the lorry's rear lights slowly fading into the darkness. Something pleasant? A mere four and a half tons of drugs heading away from him, along with what would have been the biggest mass arrest this side of the war. It didn't help that they *knew* Sweno and his people had been there right in front of them if they couldn't tell the judge and jury they had *seen* their faces and not just fourteen sodding helmets. Something *pleasant?* Duff closed his eyes.

Sweno.

He'd had him here in the palm of his hand. Shit, shit, shit!

Duff listened. Listened for something, *anything*. But all that could be heard was the meaningless whisper of the rain.

★   ★   ★

'Banquo's got the guy holding the lad in his sights,' Macbeth said. 'Have you got the other one, Olafson?'

'Yes, sir.'

'You have to shoot at the same time, OK. Fire on the

24

count of three. Banquo?'

'I need more light on the target. Or younger eyes. I might hit the boy as it is.'

'My target has lots of light,' Olafson whispered. 'We can swap.'

'If we miss and our lad is killed, we'd prefer it if it was Banquo who missed. Banquo, what's the maximum speed of a fully loaded Stalin lorry, do you reckon?'

'Hm. Sixty maybe.'

'Good, but time's getting short to achieve all our objectives. So we'd better do a bit of improvising.'

'Are you going to try your daggers?' Banquo asked Macbeth.

'From this distance? Thanks for your confidence. No, you'll soon see, old man. As in *see*.'

Banquo looked up from his binoculars and discovered that Macbeth had stood up and grabbed the pole on to which the light on the roof was bolted. The veins in Macbeth's powerful neck stood out and his teeth shone in either a grimace or a grin, Banquo couldn't decide which. The pole was screwed down to withstand the feisty north-westerlies that blew for eight of the year's twelve months, but Banquo had seen Macbeth lift cars out of snowdrifts before now.

'Three,' Macbeth groaned.

The first screws popped out of their sockets.

'Two.'

The pole came loose and with a jerk tore the cable away from the wall below.

'One.'

Macbeth pointed the light at the gangway.

'Now.'

It sounded like two whiplashes. Duff opened his eyes in time to see the man with the automatic weapon topple forward and hit the ground helmet first. Where Sivart stood there was now light, and Duff could see him clearly and also the man behind him. He was no longer holding a gun to Sivart's head but resting his chin on Sivart's shoulder. And in the light Duff also saw the hole in the visor. Then, like a jellyfish, he slid down Sivart's back to the ground.

Duff turned.

'Up here, Duff!'

He shaded his eyes. A peal of laughter rang out behind the dazzling light and the shadow of a gigantic man fell over the quay.

But the laughter was enough.

It was Macbeth. Of course it was Macbeth.

2

A seagull swept in over Fife through the silence and moonlight under a cloud-free night sky. Below, the river shone like silver. On the west of the river — like an immense fortress wall — a steep black mountain rose to the sky. Just short of the top a monastic order had once erected a large cross, but as it had been put up on the Fife side the silhouette appeared to be upside down to the residents of the town. From the side of the mountain — like a drawbridge over the fortress moat — jutted an impressive iron bridge. Three hundred and sixty metres long and ninety metres high at its tallest point. Kenneth Bridge, or the new bridge as most people called it. The old bridge was by comparison a modest but more aesthetically pleasing construction further down the river, and it meant a detour. In the middle of the new bridge towered an unlovely marble monument in the shape of a man, meant to represent former Chief Commissioner Kenneth, erected at his own orders. The statue stood inside the town boundary by a centimetre as no other county would give the rogue's posthumous reputation a centimetre of land for free. Even though the sculptor had complied with Kenneth's order to emphasise his visionary status by creating a characteristic horizon-searching pose, not even the most benevolent of artists could have refrained from drawing attention to the chief commissioner's unusually voluminous neck and chin area.

The seagull flapped its wings to gain height, hoping for better fishing on the coast across the mountain, even though that meant crossing the weather divide. From good to bad. For those wishing to travel the same way there was a two-kilometre-long narrow black hole from the new bridge through the mountain. A mountain and a partition many appeared to appreciate — neighbouring counties referred to the tunnel as a rectum with an anal orifice at each end. And indeed as the seagull passed over the mountain peak it was like flying from a world of quiet harmony into a freezing-cold filthy shower falling onto the foul-smelling town beneath. And as if to show its contempt the seagull shat, then continued to swerve between the gusts of wind.

The seagull shit hit the roof of a shelter, below which an emaciated trembling boy crept onto a bench. Although the sign beside the shelter indicated it was a bus stop the boy wasn't sure. So many bus routes had been stopped over the last couple of years. Because of the decreasing population, the mayor said, the fathead. But the boy had to get to the central station for brew; the speed he had bought from some bikers was just crap, icing sugar and potato flour rather than amphetamine.

The oily wet tarmac glinted beneath the few street lamps that still worked, and the rain lay in puddles on the potholed road leading out of town. It had been quiet, not a car to be seen, only rain. But now he heard a sound like a low gurgle.

He raised his head. Pulled on the string of his eyepatch, which had slipped over from his empty eye cavity and now covered the remaining eye. Perhaps he could hitch a lift to the centre?

But no, the sound came from the wrong direction.

He drew up his knees again.

The gurgle rose to a roar. He couldn't be bothered to move, besides he was already drenched, so he just covered his head with his arms. The lorry passed, sending a cascade of filthy water into the bus shelter.

He lay there thinking about life until he realised it was wiser not to.

The sound of another vehicle. This time?

He struggled upright and looked out. But no, it was coming from the town too. Also at great speed. He stared into the lights as they approached. And the thought came into his head: one step into the road and all his problems were solved.

The van passed him without going into any of the potholes. Black Ford Transit. Cops, three of them. Great. You don't want a lift with them.

$$\star \quad \star \quad \star$$

'There it is, ahead of us,' Banquo said. 'Step on it, Angus!'

'How do you know it's them?' Olafson asked, leaning forward between the front seats of the SWAT Transit.

'Diesel smoke,' Banquo said. 'My God, no wonder there's an oil crisis in Russia. Get right behind them so that they can see us in their rear-view mirror, Angus.'

Angus maintained his speed until they reached the black exhaust. Banquo rolled down his window and steadied his rifle on the wing mirror. Coughed. 'And now alongside, Angus!'

Angus pulled out and accelerated. The Transit drew alongside the snorting, groaning lorry.

A puff of smoke came from the lorry window. The mirror under Banquo's rifle barrel broke with a crack.

'Yes, they've seen us,' Banquo said. 'Get behind them again.'

The rain stopped suddenly and everything around them became even darker. They had driven into the tunnel. The tarmac and the hewn black walls seemed to swallow the lights of the headlamps; all they could see was the lorry's rear lights.

'What shall we do?' Angus asked. 'The bridge at the other end, and if they pass the middle . . . '

'I know,' Banquo said, lifting his rifle. The town stopped by the statue, their area of jurisdiction stopped, the chase stopped. In theory of course they could carry on, it had happened before: enthusiastic officers, rarely in the Narco Unit though, had arrested smugglers on the wrong side of the boundary. And every time they'd had a nice fat juicy case thrown out of court and had to face censure for gross misjudgement in the course of duty. Banquo's Remington 700 recoiled.

'Bull's eye,' he said.

The lorry began to swerve in the tunnel; bits of rubber flew off the rear wheel.

'Now you'll feel what a heavy steering wheel is *really* like,' Banquo said and took aim at the other rear tyre. 'Bit more distance, Angus, in case they go straight into the tunnel wall.'

'Banquo!' came a voice from the back seat.

'Olafson?' Banquo said, slowly pressing the trigger.

'Car coming.'

'Whoops.'

Banquo lifted his cheek off the rifle as Angus braked.

In front of them the ZIS-5 veered from side to side, alternately showing and cutting off the headlights of the oncoming car. Banquo heard the horn, the desperate hooting of a saloon car that saw a lorry bearing down on it and knew it was too late to do anything.

'Jesus . . . ' Olafson said in a lisped whisper.

The sound of the horn rose in volume and frequency.

Then a flash of light.

Banquo automatically glanced to the side.

Caught a glimpse of the back seat in the car, the cheek of a sleeping child, resting against the window.

Then it was gone, and the dying tone of the horn sounded like the disappointed groan of cheated spectators.

'Faster,' Banquo said. 'We'll be on the bridge in no time.'

Angus jammed his foot down, and they were back in the cloud of exhaust.

'Steady,' Banquo said while aiming. 'Steady . . . '

At that moment the tarpaulin on the back of the lorry was pulled aside, and the Transit's headlamps lit up a flatbed piled with plastic bags containing a white substance. The window at the back of the driver's cab had been smashed. And from the top of a gap between the kilo bags pointed a rifle.

'Angus . . . '

A brief explosion. Banquo caught sight of a muzzle flash, then the windscreen whitened and fell in on them.

'Angus!'

Angus had taken the point and swung the wheel sharply to the right. And then to the left. The tyres screamed and the bullets whined as the fire-spitting muzzle tried to track their manoeuvres.

'Jesus Christ!' Banquo shrieked and fired at the other tyre, but the bullet just drew sparks from the wing.

And suddenly the rain was back. They were on the bridge.

'Get him with the shotgun, Olafson,' Banquo yelled. 'Now!'

The rain pelted through the hole where the windscreen had been, and Banquo moved so that Olafson could lay the double-barrelled gun on the back of his seat. The barrel protruded above Banquo's shoulder, but disappeared again at the sound of a thud like a hammer on meat. Banquo turned to where Olafson sat slumped with his head tipped forward and a hole in his jacket at chest height. Grey upholstery filling fluffed up when the next bullet went right through Banquo's seat and into the seat beside Olafson. The guy on the lorry had got his eye in now. Banquo took the shotgun from Olafson's hands and in one swift movement swung it forward and fired. There was a white explosion on the back of the lorry. Banquo let go of the shotgun and raised his rifle. It was impossible for the guy on the lorry to see through the thick white

31

cloud of powder, but from the darkness rose the floodlit white marble statue of Kenneth, like an unwelcome apparition. Banquo aimed at the rear wheel and pulled the trigger. Bull's eye.

The lorry careered from side to side, one front wheel mounted the pavement, a rear wheel hit the kerb, and the side of the ZIS-5 struck the steel-reinforced fence. The scream of metal forced along metal drowned the vehicles' engines. But, incredibly, the driver in front managed to get the heavy lorry back on the road.

'Don't cross the bloody boundary, please!' Banquo yelled.

The last remnant of rubber had been stripped from the lorry's rear wheel rims and a fountain of sparks stood out against the night sky. The ZIS-5 went into a skid, the driver tried desperately to counter it, but this time he had no chance. The lorry veered across the road and skidded along the tarmac. It was practically at the boundary when the wheels gained purchase again and steered the lorry off the road. Twelve tons of Soviet military engineering hit Chief Commissioner Kenneth right under the belt, tore him off the plinth and dragged the statue plus ten metres or so of steel fencing along before tipping over the edge. Angus had managed to stop the Transit, and in the sudden silence Banquo observed Kenneth falling through the moonlight and slowly rotating around his own chin. Behind him came the ZIS-5, bonnet first, with a tail of white powder like some damned amphetamine comet.

'My God . . . ' the policeman whispered.

It felt like an eternity before everything hit the water and coloured it white for an instant, and the sound reached Banquo with a slight time delay.

Then the silence returned.

★   ★   ★

32

Sean stamped his feet on the ground outside the club house, staring out through the gate. Scratched the *NORSE RIDERS TILL I DIE* tattoo on his forehead. He hadn't been so nervous since he was in the hospital delivery room. Wasn't it just typical that he and Colin had drawn the short straw and had to stand guard on the night when excitement was at fever pitch? They hadn't been allowed to string along and collect the dope or go to the party either.

'Missus wants to call the kid after me,' said Sean, mostly to himself.

'Congrats,' said Colin in a monotone, pulling at his walrus moustache. The rain ran down his shiny pate.

'Ta,' said Sean. Actually he hadn't wanted either. A tattoo that would stamp him for life or a kid he knew would do the same. Freedom. That was the idea of a motorbike, wasn't it? But the club and then Betty had changed his notion of freedom. You can only truly be free when you belong, when you feel real solidarity.

'There they are,' Sean said. 'Looks like everything's gone well, eh?'

'Two guys missing,' Colin said, spitting out his cigarette and opening the high gate with barbed wire on top.

The first bike stopped by them. The bass rumbled from behind the horn helmet. 'We were ambushed by the cops, so the twins will come a bit later.'

'Right, boss,' Colin said.

The bikes roared through the gate one after the other. One of the guys gave a thumbs up. Good, the dope was safe, the club saved. Sean breathed out with relief. The bikes rolled across the yard past the shed-like single-storey timber house with the Norse Rider logo painted on the wall and disappeared into the big garage. The table was laid in the shed; Sweno had decided that the deal should be celebrated with a piss-up. And after a few minutes Sean heard the music turned up inside and the first shouts of celebration.

'We're rich.' Sean laughed. 'Do you know where they're taking the dope?'

Colin said nothing, just rolled his eyes.

He didn't know. Nobody did. Only Sweno. And those in the lorry, of course. It was best like that.

'Here come the twins,' Sean said, opening the gate again.

The motorbikes came slowly, almost hesitantly, up the hill towards them.

'Hi, João, what happ — ?' Sean began, but the bikes continued through the gate.

He watched them as they stopped in the middle of the yard as though considering leaving their bikes there. Then they nudged one another, nodded to the open garage door and drove in.

'Did you see João's visor?' Sean said. 'It had a hole in it.'

Colin sighed heavily.

'I'm not kidding!' Sean said. 'Right in the middle. I'll go and see what really happened down on the quay.'

'Hey, Sean . . . '

But Sean was off, ran across the yard and entered the garage. The twins had dismounted. Both stood with their backs to him, still wearing their helmets. One twin by the door leading straight from the garage into the club's function room held the door ajar, as though not wanting to show himself but seeing what the party was like first. João, Sean's best mate, stood by his bike. He had removed the magazine from his ugly-looking AK-47 and seemed to be counting how many bullets he had left. Sean patted him on the back. That must have been quite a shock because he spun round with a vengeance.

'What happened to your visor, João? Stone chip, was it?'

João didn't answer, just appeared to be busy inserting the magazine back into his AK-47. He was strangely clumsy. The other strange thing was that he seemed . . . taller. As though it wasn't João standing there, but . . .

'Fuck!' Sean shouted, took a step back and reached for his belt. He had realised what the hole in the visor was and that he wasn't going to see his best pal again. Sean pulled out his gun, released the safety catch and was about to point it at the man still struggling with the AK-47 when something struck him in the shoulder. He automatically swung the gun in the direction from which the blow had come. But there was no one there. Only the guy in the Norse Rider jacket standing over by the door. At that moment his hand seemed to wither and Sean dropped his gun to the floor.

'Not a peep,' a voice said behind him.

Sean turned again.

The AK was pointing at him, and in the reflection of the holed visor he saw a dagger sticking out of his shoulder.

★ ★ ★

Duff put the barrel of the AK to the tattoo on the guy's forehead. Looked into his gawping, ugly features. His finger squeezed the trigger, just a fraction . . . He heard the hiss of his own breathing inside the helmet and his heart pounding beneath the somewhat too tight leather jacket.

'Duff,' Macbeth said from the club-room doorway. 'Easy now.'

Duff squeezed the trigger a fraction more.

'Stop that,' Macbeth said. 'It's our turn to use a hostage.'

Duff let go of the trigger.

The man's face was as white as a sheet. From fear or loss of blood. Both probably. His voice shook. 'We don't save — '

35

Duff hit him across the tattoo with the gun barrel. Leaving a stripe that for a moment shone white like a copy of Duff's own trademark. Then it filled with blood.

'You shut up, son, and everything'll be fine,' said Macbeth, who had joined them. He grabbed the young man's long hair, pulled his head back and put the blade of his second dagger to his throat. Pushed him forward to the club-room door. 'Ready?'

'Remember Sweno's mine,' Duff said, making sure the curved magazine sat properly in the weapon, and strode after Macbeth and the Norse Rider.

Macbeth kicked open the door and went in with the hostage in front and Duff hard on his heels. Grinning and loud-mouthed, the Norse Riders were sitting at a long table in the large, open but already smoke-filled club-room. All of them with their backs to the wall facing the three doors that led from the room. Probably a club rule. Duff estimated there were twenty of them. The music was on loud. The Stones. 'Jumpin' Jack Flash'.

'Police!' Duff shouted. 'No one move or my colleague will cut the throat of this fine young man.'

Time seemed to come to an abrupt halt, and Duff saw the man at the end of the table raise his head as if in slow motion. A ruddy porcine face with visible nostrils and plaits so tight they pulled the eyes into two narrow hate-filled straight lines. From the corner of his mouth hung a long thin cigarillo. Sweno.

'We don't save hostages,' he said.

The young man lost consciousness and fell.

In the next two seconds everything in the room froze and all you could hear was the Rolling Stones.

Until Sweno took a drag of his cigarillo. 'Take them,' he said.

Duff registered at least three of the Norse Riders react at the same time and pulled the trigger of his AK-47. Held it there. Spraying chunks of lead with a diameter of 7.62 millimetres, which smashed bottles, raked the table, lashed the wall, carved flesh and stopped Mick Jagger between two *gasses*. Beside him Macbeth had reached for the two Glocks he had removed from the Norse Rider bodies on the quay. Along with their jackets, helmets and bikes. In Duff's hands, his gun felt warm and soft like a woman. Darkness fell gradually as lamps were shot to pieces. And when Duff finally let go of the trigger, dust and feathers hovered in the air, and one lamp swung to and fro from the ceiling sending shadows scurrying up the walls like fleeing ghosts.

3

'I looked around, and in the semi-darkness Norse Rider guys were strewn across the floor face down,' Macbeth said. 'Blood, broken glass and empty shell cases.'

'Jesus!' Angus shouted with a slur over the lively babble at the Bricklayers Arms, the SWAT's local behind the central station. The glazed blue eyes looked at Macbeth with what seemed to be adoration. 'You just swept them off the face of the earth! Holy Jesus! Cheers!'

'Now, now, careful with your language, you priest-in-waiting,' Macbeth said, but when many of the eighteen SWAT officers in attendance raised their beer mugs to him, he eventually smiled, shaking his head, and then raised his glass too. Took a long draught and looked at Olafson, who was holding a heavy Bricklayers Arms pint mug in his left hand.

'Does it hurt, Olafson?'

'It's all the better for knowing that one of them has a sore shoulder as well,' Olafson lisped and shyly straightened the sling when the others burst into loud laughter.

'The ones who actually got things rolling were Banquo and Olafson here,' Macbeth said. 'I was just holding the light like some bloody photographer's assistant for these two artists.'

'Keep going,' Angus said. 'You and Duff had all the Norse Riders on the floor. What happened then?' He flicked his blond hair behind his ears.

Macbeth gazed at the expectant faces around the table and exchanged glances with Banquo before continuing. 'Some of them screamed they were surrendering. The dust settled and the music system was shot to pieces, so it was finally quiet but still dark, and the situation was rather unclear. Duff and I started checking them out from our end of the room. There were no fatalities, but a number of them required medical attention, you might say. Duff shouted that he couldn't find Sweno.' Macbeth ran a finger through the condensation on the outside of his glass. 'I spotted a door behind the end of the table where Sweno had been sitting. At that moment we heard motorbikes starting up. So we left the others and charged out into the yard. And there we saw three motorbikes on their way out of the gate, one of them was red, Sweno's. And the guard, a bald guy with a moustache, jumped on his bike and followed. Duff was furious, wanted to give chase, but I said there were a few badly injured guys inside . . . '

'Did you think that would stop Duff?' a voice whispered. 'Bastards lying around bleeding when he could catch Sweno?'

Macbeth turned. The voice in question was sitting alone in the next booth, his face hidden in the shadow beneath the dart club's trophy cupboard.

'Did you think Duff would consider a few ordinary people's lives when a heroic exploit was within reach?' A beer mug was raised in the shadows. 'After all there are careers to consider.'

Macbeth's table had gone quiet.

Banquo coughed. 'To hell with careers. We in SWAT don't let defenceless people just die, Seyton. We don't know what you in Narco do.'

Seyton leaned forward and the light fell on his face. 'None of us in Narco quite know what we're doing either, that's the problem with a boss like Duff. But don't let me interrupt your story, Macbeth. Did you go back in and tend their wounds?'

'Sweno's a murderer who would kill again if he had the chance,' Macbeth said without letting go of Seyton's eyes. 'And Duff was worried they would escape across the bridge.'

'I was afraid they'd get across the bridge, as the lorry had tried to do,' Duff said. 'So we jumped back on our bikes. We rode them as hard as we could. Plus a bit more. One miscalculated bend on the wet tarmac . . . ' Duff pushed the golden half-eaten crème brûlée across Lyon's damask cloth, took the bottle of champagne from the cooler and refilled the other three's glasses. 'After the first hairpin bend at the bottom of the valley I saw the rear lights of four bikes and pressed on. In my mirror I saw Macbeth was still following.'

Duff cast a furtive glance at Chief Commissioner Duncan to see if his account was being well received. His gentle, friendly smile was hard to interpret. Duncan still hadn't directly commented on the night's stake-out, but wasn't the fact that he had come to this little celebration an acknowledgement in itself? Perhaps, but the chief commissioner's silence unsettled Duff. He felt more secure with the pale redhead leader of the Anti-Corruption Unit, Inspector Lennox, who with his customary enthusiasm leaned across the table swallowing every word. And the head of the Forensic Unit, Caithness, whose big green eyes told him she believed every scrap and crumb.

Duff put down the bottle. 'On the stretch leading to the tunnel we were side by side and the lights ahead were growing. As though they had slowed down. I could see the horns on Sweno's helmet. Then something unexpected happened.'

Duncan moved his champagne next to his red wine glass, which Duff didn't know whether to interpret as tension or just impatience. 'Two of the bikes turned off straight after the bus shelter, by the exit road to Forres, while the other two continued towards the tunnel. We were seconds away from the junction and I had to make a decision . . . '

Duff emphasised the word *decision*. Of course he could have said *make a choice*. But *choosing* was just something any idiot might be forced to do while *making a decision* is pro-active, it requires a mental process and character, it is taken by a leader. The kind of leader the chief commissioner needed when he appointed the head of the newly established Organised Crime Unit. The OCU was a grand merging of the Narco Unit and the Gang Unit, and a logical fusion as all the drug dealing in town was now split between Hecate and the Norse Riders, who had swallowed the other gangs. The question was who would lead the unit, Duff or Cawdor, the experienced leader of the Gang Unit, who had a suspiciously large fully paid-off house on the west side of town. The problem was that Cawdor had a supporting cast on the town council and among Kenneth's old conspirators at police HQ, and even though everyone knew Duncan was prepared to stick his neck out to get rid of the various Cawdors he also had to show some political nous so as not to lose control at HQ. What was clear was that one of Cawdor or Duff would emerge as the winner and the other would be left without a unit.

'I signalled to Macbeth that we should follow the Forres pair.'

'Really?' said Lennox. 'Then the other two would cross the county boundary.'

'Yes, and that was the dilemma. Sweno's a sly fox. Was he sending two men to Forres as decoys while he drove to the boundary as he's the only Norse Rider we've got anything on? Or was he counting on us thinking that was what he was thinking and he would therefore do the opposite?'

'Have we?' Lennox asked.

'Have we what?' Duff asked, trying to conceal his irritation at being interrupted.

'Got anything on Sweno? The Stoke Massacre is

time-barred, as far as I know.'

'The two post office robberies in District I five years ago,' Duff said impatiently. 'We've got Sweno's fingerprints and everything.'

'And the other Norse Riders?'

'Zilch. And we didn't get anything tonight either because they were all wearing helmets. Anyway, when we turned off for Forres we saw the helmet — '

'What's the Stoke Massacre?' Caithness asked.

Duff groaned.

'You probably weren't born then,' Duncan said in a friendly voice. 'It happened in Capitol straight after the war. Sweno's brother was about to be arrested for desertion and was stupid enough to draw a weapon. The two arresting policemen, who had both spent the war in the trenches, shot holes in him. Sweno avenged his brother several months later in Stoke. He went into the local police station and shot down four officers, among them one very pregnant woman. Sweno disappeared off our radar, and when he reappeared the case was time-barred. Please, Duff, continue.'

'Thank you. I thought they weren't aware we were so close on their tails that we could see Sweno's helmet when he turned off for Forres and the old bridge. We caught them up only a couple of kilometres or so later. That is, Macbeth fired two shots in the air when they were still a good way in front, and they stopped. So we stopped too. We had left the valley behind us, so it wasn't raining. Good visibility, moonlight, fifty to sixty metres between us. I had my AK-47 and ordered them to get off their bikes, walk five steps towards us and kneel down on the tarmac with their hands behind their heads. They did as we said, we got off our bikes and walked towards them.'

Duff closed his eyes.

He could see them now.

They were kneeling.

Duff's leather gear creaked as he walked towards them, and a drop of water hung in his peripheral vision from the edge of his open visor. Soon it would fall. Soon.

★   ★   ★

'There was probably a distance of ten to fifteen strides between us when Sweno pulled out a gun,' Macbeth said. 'Duff reacted at once. He fired. Hitting Sweno three times in the chest. He was dead before his helmet hit the ground. But in the meantime the second man had drawn his gun and aimed at Duff. Fortunately though he never managed to pull the trigger.'

'Holy shit!' Angus shouted. 'You shot him, did you?'

Macbeth leaned back. 'I got him with a dagger.'

Banquo studied his superior officer.

'Impressive,' whispered Seyton from the shadows. 'On the other hand, Duff reacted quicker than you when Sweno went for his gun? I'd have bet you'd be quicker, Macbeth.'

'But there you're wrong,' Macbeth said. *What was Seyton doing, what was he after?* 'Just like Duff,' Macbeth said, lifting his beer mug to his mouth.

★   ★   ★

'I made a mistake,' Duff said, signalling to the head waiter for another bottle of champagne. 'Not about shooting, of course. But choosing which bikes to follow.'

The head waiter came to the table and quietly informed them that unfortunately they would have to close, and it was illegal to sell alcohol after midnight. Unless the chief commissioner . . .

'Thank you, but no,' said Duncan, who was a master of the art of smiling roguishly while raising his eyebrows in reproof. 'We'll keep to the law.'

43

The waiter took his leave.

'Making the wrong choice can happen to the best of us,' Duncan said. 'When did you realise? When you removed his helmet?'

Duff shook his head. 'Immediately before, when I knelt down beside the body and happened to glance at his bike. It wasn't Sweno's bike, the sabre wasn't there. And the Riders don't swap bikes.'

'But they swap helmets?'

Duff shrugged. 'I should have known. After all, Macbeth and I had just employed the same trick ourselves. Sweno swapped his helmet, and they slowed down enough for us to see his helmet was on one of the Riders going to Forres. He himself went through the tunnel, over the bridge and escaped.'

'Smart thinking, no doubt about it,' Duncan said. 'Shame his people weren't as smart.'

'What do you mean?' Duff asked, looking down at the leather folder with the bill the waiter had placed before him.

'Why pull guns on the police when they know — as you yourself said — we have no evidence against anyone except Sweno? They could have just allowed themselves to be arrested and left the police station as free men a few hours later.'

Duff shrugged. 'Perhaps they didn't believe we were policemen. Perhaps they thought we were Hecate's men and we were going to kill them.'

'Or as the chief commissioner says,' Lennox said, 'they're stupid.'

Duncan scratched his chin. 'How many Norse Riders did we lock up?'

'Six,' Duff said. 'When we returned to the club house it was mainly the seriously injured who were still there.'

'I didn't think gangs like the Norse Riders left their injured for the enemy.'

'They knew they would get medical aid faster.

44

They're being treated now, but we're expecting to get more in custody tomorrow. And then they'll be questioned about Sweno. However much pain they're in. We'll find him, sir.'

'Fine. Four and a half tons of amphetamine. That's a lot,' said Duncan.

'It is indeed.' Duff smiled.

'So much that you almost have to ask yourself why you didn't inform me about the stake-out beforehand.'

'Time,' Duff replied quickly. He had weighed up the pros and cons of how to answer the inevitable question. 'There wasn't enough time between receiving the tip-off and going into action. As head of the unit I had to assess procedural regulations against the risk of not preventing four and a half tons of amphetamines from reaching the youths in this town.'

Duff met Duncan's eyes, which were contemplating him. The chief commissioner's index finger stroked the point of his chin to and fro. Then he moistened his lips.

'There's a lot of blood too. A lot of damage to the bridge. The fish in the river are probably already junkies. And Sweno's still on the loose.'

Duff cursed inwardly. The hypocritical, arrogant fool must be capable of seeing the bigger picture.

'But,' said the chief commissioner, 'six Norse Riders are in custody. And even if we do feel a little more invigorated than usual when eating fish over the next few weeks, better that than the dope ending up in our young people. Or — ' Duncan grabbed his champagne glass ' — in Seized Goods.'

Lennox and Caithness laughed. It was well known that the HQ warehouse was still unaccountably losing goods.

'So,' Duncan said, raising his glass, 'good police work, Duff.'

Duff blinked twice. His heart beat quickly and lightly. 'Thank you,' he said, draining his glass.

Duncan snatched the leather folder. 'This is on me.'

45

He took the bill, held it at arm's length and squinted. 'Although I can't see if I've been given the right bill.'

'Who has!' Lennox said with a stiff smile when no one laughed.

'Let me,' Caithness said, taking the bill and putting on her horn-rimmed granny glasses, which Duff knew she didn't need but wore because she thought they added a couple of years to her age and detracted from her appearance. Duncan had been brave to give Caithness the Forensic Unit. Not because anyone doubted her professional competence — she had been the best cadet at her police college and had also studied chemistry and physics — but she was younger than any of the other unit heads, single and simply too good-looking for suspicion of ulterior motives not to creep in. The candle flames made the water in her laughing eyes behind the glasses, the moisture of her full red lips and the wetness of her shining white teeth sparkle. Duff closed his eyes. The gleaming shine of the tarmac, the sound of tyres on the wet road. The spattering sound. The blood that had splashed to the floor when the man had pulled the dagger from his neck. It was a like a hand squeezing Duff's chest, and he opened his eyes with a gasp.

'Everything OK?' Lennox held a carafe of water over Duff's glass, and the dregs splashed in. 'Drink, Duff, so that you can dilute the champagne. You have to drive now.'

'No question of that,' Duncan said. 'I don't want my heroes arrested for drunk driving or killed on the road. My driver wouldn't object to a little detour.'

'Thank you,' Duff said. 'But Fife's — '

' — more or less on my way home,' Duncan said. 'And it's Mrs Duff and your two wonderful children who should thank me.'

'Excuse me,' Duff said, pushing his chair back and standing up.

'A stupendous police officer,' Lennox said as he watched Duff stagger towards the toilet door at the back of the room.

'Duff?' Duncan queried.

'Him too, but I was thinking about Macbeth. His results are impressive, his men love him, and even though he worked under Kenneth, we in the Anti-Corruption Unit know he's rock solid. It's a pity he doesn't have the formal qualifications necessary for a higher management post.'

'There's no requirement to have anything higher than police college. Look at Kenneth.'

'Yes, but Macbeth still isn't one of us.'

'Us?'

'Well,' Lennox lifted his champagne glass with a wry smile, 'you've chosen heads who — whether we like it or not — are seen as belonging to the elite. We all come from the western side of town or Capitol, have an education or a respectable family name. Macbeth is seen more as someone from the broader ranks of the populace, if you know what I mean.'

'I do. Listen, I'm a bit worried about Duff's unsteadiness on his feet. Could you . . . ?'

★ ★ ★

Fortunately the toilet was empty.

Duff did up his flies, stood by one of the sinks, turned on a tap and splashed water over his face. He heard the door go behind him.

'Duncan asked me to check how you were,' Lennox said.

'Mm. What do you think he thought?'

'Thought about what?'

Duff grabbed a paper and dried his face. 'About . . . how things went.'

'He probably thinks what we all think: you did a good job.'

Duff nodded.

Lennox chuckled. 'You really do want the Organised Crime job, don't you.'

Duff turned off the tap and soaped his hands while looking at the head of Anti-Corruption in the mirror.

'You mean I'm a climber?'

'Nothing wrong with climbing the ladder.' Lennox smirked. 'It's just amusing to see how you position yourself.'

'I'm qualified, Lennox. So isn't it simply my duty to this town and my and your children's future to do what I can for Organised Crime? Or should I leave the biggest unit to Cawdor? A person we both know must have both dirty and bloody hands to have survived under Kenneth for as long as he did.'

'Aha,' Lennox said. 'It's duty that drives you? Not personal ambition at all. Well, St Duff, let me hold the door open for you.' Lennox performed a deep bow. 'I presume you will refuse the salary increase and other concomitant privileges.'

'The salary, honour and fame are irrelevant to me,' Duff said. 'But society rewards those who contribute. Showing contempt for the salary would be like showing contempt for society.' He studied his face in the mirror. *How can you see when a person is lying?* Is it possible when the person in question has succeeded in convincing himself that what he says is the truth? How long would it take him to convince himself that it was the truth, the version he and Macbeth had arranged to give of how they had killed the two men on the road?

'Have you finished washing your hands now, Duff? I think Duncan wants to go home.'

★　★　★

48

The SWAT men took their leave of each other outside the Bricklayers Arms. 'Loyalty, fraternity,' Macbeth said in a loud voice.

The others answered him in slurred, to varying degrees, unison: 'Baptised in fire, united in blood.'

Then they walked away in every direction of the compass. Macbeth and Banquo to the west, past a street musician who was howling rather than singing 'Meet Me On The Corner' and through the deserted run-down concourses and corridors of the central station. A strangely warm wind picked up through the passages and swept litter between the once beautiful Doric pillars crumbling after years of pollution and lack of maintenance.

'Now,' Banquo said. 'Are you going to tell me what *really* happened?'

'You tell me about the lorry and Kenneth,' Macbeth said. 'Ninety-metre free fall!' His laughter resounded beneath the brick ceiling.

Banquo smiled. 'Come on, Macbeth. What happened out there on the country road?'

'Did they say anything about how long they would have to close the bridge for repairs?'

'You might be able to lie to them, but not to me.'

'We got them, Banquo. Do you need to know any more?'

'Do I?' Banquo waved away the stench from the stairs down to the toilets, where a woman of indeterminate age was standing bent over with her hair hanging down in front of her face as she clung to the handrail.

'No.'

'All right,' Banquo said.

Macbeth stopped and crouched down by a young boy sitting by the wall with a begging cup in front of him. The boy raised his head. He had a black patch over one eye and the other stared out from a doped-up state, a dream. Macbeth put a banknote in his cup and a hand

49

on his shoulder. 'How's it going?' he asked softly.

'Macbeth,' the boy said. 'As you can see.'

'You can do it,' Macbeth said. 'Always remember that. You can stop.'

The boy's voice slurred and slid from vowel to vowel. 'And how do you know that?'

'Believe me, it's been done before.' Macbeth stood up, and the boy called a tremulous 'God bless you, Macbeth' after them.

They went into the concourse in the eastern part of the station, where there was a conspicuous silence, like in a church. The druggies who weren't sitting, lying or standing by the walls or on the benches were staggering around in a land of slow dance, like astronauts in an alien atmosphere, a different gravitational field. Some stared suspiciously at the two police officers, but most just ignored them. As though they had X-ray eyes that had long-ago established that these two had nothing to sell. Most were so emaciated and ravaged it was hard to know exactly how long they had been alive. Or how long they had left.

'You're never tempted to start again?' Banquo asked.

'No.'

'Most ex-junkies dream of a last shot.'

'Not me. Let's get out of here.'

They walked to the steps in front of the west exit, stopped before they came to where the roof no longer sheltered them from the rain. Beside them, on black rails on a low plinth, stood what appeared in the darkness to be a prehistoric monster. Bertha, a hundred and ten years old, the first locomotive in the country, the very symbol of the optimism about the future that had once held sway. The broad, majestic, gently graded steps led down to the dark, deserted Workers' Square, where once there had been hustle and bustle, market stalls and travellers hurrying to and fro, but which was now ghostly, a square where the wind whistled and whined. At one end lights glittered in a venerable brick building which had at one time housed the offices of the National Railway Network but had fallen into disuse after the railway was abandoned, until it had been bought and renovated to become the most glamorous and elegant building the town had to offer: Inverness Casino. Banquo had been inside only once and immediately knew it was not his kind of place. Or, to be more precise, he wasn't their kind of customer. He was probably the Obelisk type, where customers were not so well dressed, the drinks were not so expensive and the prostitutes not so beautiful nor so discreet.

'Goodnight, Banquo.'

'Goodnight, Macbeth. Sleep well.'

Banquo saw a light shiver go through his friend's body, then Macbeth's white teeth shone in the darkness. 'Say hello to Fleance from me and tell him his father has done a great job tonight. What I wouldn't have given to see Kenneth in free fall from his own bridge . . .'

Banquo heard his friend's low chuckle as he disappeared into the darkness and rain on Workers' Square, but when his own laughter had faded too an unease spread through him. Macbeth wasn't only a friend and a colleague, he was like a son, a Moses in a basket whom Banquo loved almost as much as Fleance. So that was why Banquo waited until he saw Macbeth reappear on the other side of the square and walk into the light by the entrance to the casino, from which a tall woman with flowing flame-red hair in a long red dress emerged and hugged him, as though a phantom had warned her that her beloved was on his way.

Lady.

Perhaps she had caught wind of this evening's events. A woman like Lady wouldn't have got to where she was without informants who told her what she needed to know about everything that moved beneath the surface of this town.

They still had their arms around each other. She was a beautiful woman and might well have been even more beautiful once. No one seemed to know Lady's age, but it was definitely a good deal more than Macbeth's thirty-three years. But maybe it was true what they said: true love conquers all.

Or maybe not.

The older policeman turned and set off north.

★ ★ ★

In Fife the chief commissioner's chauffeur turned off onto the gravel lane as instructed. The gravel crunched under the car tyres.

'You can stop here. I'll walk the rest of the way,' Duff said.

The chauffeur braked. In the ensuing silence they could hear the grasshoppers and the sough of the deciduous trees.

'You don't want to wake them,' Duncan said, looking down the lane, where a small white farmhouse lay bathed in moonlight. 'And I agree. Let our dear ones sleep in ignorance and safe assurance. A lovely little place you've got here.'

'Thank you. And sorry about the detour.'

'We all have to take detours in life, Duff. The next time you get a tip-off, as with the Norse Riders, you make a detour towards me. OK?'

'OK.'

Duncan's index finger moved to and fro across his chin. 'Our aim is to make this town a better place for everyone, Duff. But that means all the positive powers have to work together and think of the community's best interests, not only their own.'

'Of course. And I'd just like to say I'm willing to do any job so long as it serves the force and the town, sir.'

Duncan smiled. 'In which case it's me who should

thank you, Duff. Ah, one last thing . . . '

'Yes?'

'You say fourteen Norse Riders including Sweno himself were more than you'd anticipated and it would have been more discreet of them to have just sent a couple of men to drive the lorry away?'

'Yes.'

'Has it struck you that Sweno might also have been tipped off? He might have suspected you'd be there. So your fear of a leak was perhaps not unfounded. Goodnight, Duff.'

'Goodnight.'

Duff walked down to his house breathing in the smell of the earth and grass where the dew had already fallen. He had considered this possibility and now Duncan had articulated it. A leak. An informant. And he, Duff, would find the leak. He would find him the very next day.

★ ★ ★

Macbeth lay on his side with his eyes closed. Behind him he heard her regular breathing and from down in the casino the bass line of the music, like muffled heartbeats. The Inverness stayed open all night, but it was now late even for crazed gamblers and thirsty drinkers. In the corridor overnight guests walked past and unlocked their rooms. Some alone, some with a spouse. Some with other company. This wasn't something Lady paid too much attention to as long as the women who frequented the casino complied with her unwritten rules of always being discreet, always well groomed, always sober, always infection-free and always, but always, attractive. Lady had once, not long after they had got together, asked why he didn't look at them. And laughed when he had answered it was because he only had eyes for her. It was only later she

53

understood he meant that quite literally. He didn't need to turn round to see her, her features were seared into his retinas; all he had to do — wherever he was — was close his eyes and she was there. There hadn't been anyone before Lady. Well, there had been women who made his pulse race and there were definitely women's hearts that had beaten faster because of him. But he had never been intimate with them. And of course there was one who had scarred his heart. When Lady had realised and had, laughing, asked him if she had been sent a genuine virgin, he told her his story. The story that hitherto only two people in the world had known. And then she had told him hers.

The suite's silk sheet felt heavy and expensive on his naked body. Like a fever, hot and cold at the same time. He could hear from her breathing that she was awake.

'What is it?' she whispered sleepily.

'Nothing,' he said. 'I just can't sleep.'

She snuggled up to him, and her hand stroked his chest and shoulders. Occasionally, like now, they breathed in rhythm. As though they were one and the same organism, like Siamese twins sharing lungs — that was exactly how it felt the time they had exchanged their stories, and he knew he was no longer alone.

Her hand slid down his upper arm, over the tattoos, down to his lower arm, where she caressed his scars. He had told her about them too. And about Lorreal. They quite simply kept no secrets from each other. They weren't secrets, but there were grim details he had begged her to spare him. She loved him, that was all that was important, that was all he *had* to know about her. He turned onto his back. Her hand stroked his stomach, stopped and waited. She was the queen. And her vassal obediently stood up under the silk material.

★ ★ ★

54

When Duff crept into bed beside his wife, listened to her regular breathing and felt the heat from her back, it was as though the memories of the night's events had already begun to recede. This place had that effect on him, it always had. They had met while he was a student. She came from an affluent family on the western side of town, and even though her parents had been initially sceptical, after a while they accepted the hard-working ambitious young man. And Duff came from a respectable family, in his father-in-law's opinion. The rest followed almost automatically. Marriage, children, a house in Fife, where the children could grow up without inhaling the town's toxic air, career, everyday grind. A lot of everyday grind with long days and promotion beckoning. And time flies by. That's the way it is. She was a good woman and wife, it wasn't that. Clever, caring and loyal. And what about him — wasn't he a good husband? Didn't he provide for them, save money for the children's education, build a cabin by the lake? Yes, neither she nor her father had much to complain about. He was the way he was, he couldn't help that. Anyway, there was a lot to say for having a home, having a family: it gave you peace. It had its own pace of life, its own agenda, and it didn't care much about what was on the outside. Not really. And he needed that perception of reality — or the lack of it — he *had* to have it. Now and then.

'You came home then — ' she mumbled.

'To you and the kids,' he said.

' — in the night,' she added.

He lay listening to the silence between them. Trying to decide whether it was good or bad. Then she laid a tender hand on his shoulder. Pressed her fingertips carefully against his tired muscles where he knew they would soothe.

Closed his eyes.

And he saw it again.

The raindrop hanging from the edge of his visor. The man kneeling in front of him. Not moving. The helmet with the horns. Duff wanted to say something to him, but he couldn't. Instead he lifted the gun to his shoulder. Couldn't the man at least move? The raindrop would soon fall.

'Duff,' Macbeth said behind him. 'Duff, don't . . . '

The drop fell.

Duff fired. Fired again. Fired again.

Three shots.

The man kneeling in front of him fell sideways.

The silence afterwards was deafening. He squatted down beside the dead man and removed his helmet. It was like having a bucket of ice-cold water thrown over him when he saw it wasn't Sweno. The young man's eyes were closed; he looked like he was sleeping peacefully where he lay.

Duff turned, glanced at Macbeth. Felt the tears filling his eyes, still unable to speak, just shook his head. Macbeth nodded in response and removed the other's helmet. Also a young man. Duff felt something pushing up into his throat and wrapped his hands around his face. Over his sobs he heard the man's pleas reverberate like gulls' cries across the uninhabited plains. 'No, don't! I haven't seen anything! I won't tell anyone! Please, no jury will believe me anyway. I under — '

The voice was cut off. Duff heard a body smack against the tarmac, a low gurgle, then everything went quiet.

He turned. Only now did he notice the other man was wearing white clothes. They were soaking up the blood running from the hole in his neck.

Macbeth stood behind the man, a dagger in his hand. His chest was heaving. 'Now,' he said gruffly. Cleared his throat. 'Now I've paid my debt to you, Duff.'

★   ★   ★

56

Duff pressed his fingertips against the place where he knew they didn't soothe. He held his other hand over the man's mouth to muffle his screams and forced him down onto the hospital bed. The man pulled desperately at the handcuffs shackling him to the bed head. From the daylight flooding in through the window Duff could clearly see the network of fine blood vessels around the big pupils, black with shock, in his wide-open eyes under the *NORSE RIDER TILL I DIE* tattoo on his forehead. Duff's forefinger and index finger went red where they pressed under the bandage into the shoulder wound, making squelching noises.

Any job, Duff thought, *as long as it serves the force and the town.*

And repeated the question: 'Who's your police informant?'

He took his hand away from the wound. The man stopped screaming. Duff took his hand off his mouth. The man didn't answer.

Duff ripped off the bandage and pressed all his fingers into the wound.

He knew he would get an answer, it was just a question of time. There is only so much a man can take before he gives in, before he breaks every tattooed oath and does everything — absolutely everything — he thought he would never do. For eternal loyalty is inhuman and betrayal is human.

4

It took twenty minutes.

Twenty minutes after Duff had walked into the hospital and poked his fingers into the shoulder wound of the man with the tattoo on his forehead, until he left, amazed, with enough information about whom, where and when for the relevant person to find it impossible to deny unless he was innocent. Amazed because — now things had got so bad that they had a mole in their midst — it was almost too good to be true.

It took thirty minutes.

Thirty minutes after Duff had got in his car, driven through the trickle of rain falling onto the town like an old man piddling, parked outside the main police station, received a gracious nod from the chief commissioner's anteroom lady to let him know he could pass, until he was sitting in front of Duncan and articulated the one word. Cawdor. And the chief commissioner leaned across his desk, asked Duff if he was sure, after all this was the head of the Gang Unit they were talking about — sat back, drew a hand over his face and for the first time Duff heard Duncan swear.

It took forty minutes.

Forty minutes from when Duncan had announced that Cawdor had a day off, lifted the phone and ordered Macbeth to arrest him, until eight SWAT men surrounded Cawdor's house, which lay on a big plot of land overlooking the sea so far to the west that refuse was still collected and the homeless removed, and Mayor Tourtell was his closest neighbour. The SWAT team parked some distance away and crept up to the house, two men from each direction.

Macbeth and Banquo sat on the pavement with their

backs against the high wall to the south of the house, beside the gates. Cawdor — like most of his neighbours — had cemented glass shards into the top of the wall, but SWAT had mats to overcome hindrances of that kind. The raid followed the usual procedure, the teams reporting via walkie-talkies when they were in their pre-arranged positions. Macbeth glanced across the street to where a boy of six or seven had been throwing a ball against a garage wall when they arrived. Now he stopped and stared at them with his mouth open. Macbeth put a finger to his lips, and the boy nodded back somnambulantly. The same expression as the white-clad young man kneeling on the tarmac the previous night, Macbeth reflected.

'Wake up.' It was Banquo whispering in his ear.

'What?'

'All the teams are in position.'

Macbeth breathed in and out a couple of times. Had to shut out other things from his mind now, had to get in the zone. He pressed the talk button: 'Fifty seconds to going in. North? Over.'

Angus's voice with that unctuous priest-like chanting tone: 'All OK. Can't see any movement inside. Over.'

'West? Over.'

'All OK.' That was the replacement's voice, Seyton. Monotone, calm. 'Hang on, the sitting-room curtain twitched. Over.'

'OK,' Macbeth said. He didn't even need to think; this was part of the what-if procedure they drilled day in, day out. 'We may have been seen, folks. Let's cut the countdown and go in. Three, two, one . . . go!'

And there it was, the zone. The zone was like a room where you closed the door behind you and nothing else but the mission, you and your men existed.

They got to their feet, and as Banquo threw the mat over the glass on the wall Macbeth noticed the boy with the ball wave slowly, robotically, with his free hand.

Within seconds they were over the wall and sprinting through the garden, and Macbeth had this feeling he could sense everything around him. He could hear a branch creak in the wind, could see a crow take off from the ridge of the neighbour's roof, could smell a rotting apple in the grass. They ran up the steps, and Banquo used the butt of his gun to smash the window beside the front door, slipped his hand through and unlocked the door from the inside. As they entered they heard glass breaking elsewhere in the house. Eight against one. When Macbeth asked Duncan if there was any reason to think Cawdor would put up resistance Duncan had answered that wasn't why he wanted a full-scale arrest.

'It's to send a signal, Macbeth. We don't treat our own more leniently. Quite the contrary. Smash glass, kick in doors, make a lot of noise and lead Cawdor out in handcuffs through the front entrance so that everyone can see and tell others.'

Macbeth went in first. Pressing an assault rifle to his shoulder as his gaze swept the hall. Stood with his back to the wall beside the sitting-room door. His eyes gradually adapted to the darkness after the sharp sunlight outside. All the curtains in the house appeared to be drawn. Banquo came up to his side and carried on into the sitting room.

As Macbeth pushed off from the wall to follow him, it happened.

The attacker came swiftly and silently from the darkness shrouding one of the two staircases, hit Macbeth in the chest and sent him flying backwards.

Macbeth felt hot air on his throat, but managed to get his gun barrel between him and the dog and knock its snout to the side so that the big teeth sank into his shoulder instead. He screamed with pain as an immense snarling head tore at skin and flesh. Macbeth tried to hit out, but his free hand was caught in his rifle strap. 'Banquo!' Cawdor wasn't supposed to have a dog. They always checked before operations of this kind. But this was definitely a dog, and it was strong. The dog shoved the gun barrel to the side. It was going for his throat. He would soon have his carotid artery severed.

'Banq — '

The dog went stiff. Macbeth turned his head and stared into dulled canine eyes. Then its body went limp and slumped on top of him. Macbeth pushed it off and looked up.

Seyton was standing over him holding out a hand.

'Thank you,' Macbeth said, getting to his feet without help. 'Where's Banquo?'

'He and Cawdor are inside,' Seyton answered, motioning towards the sitting room.

Macbeth went to the sitting-room door. They had opened the curtains, and in the bright light from behind he saw only Banquo's back as he stared up at the ceiling. Above him hovered an angel with a halo of sunshine and his head bowed as if in a plea for forgiveness.

★ ★ ★

It took an hour.

An hour from the moment Macbeth had said, 'Go!' until Duncan had gathered all the departmental and unit leaders together in the large conference room at HQ.

Duncan stood up on the podium and looked down at some papers; Duff knew he had written some words there the way he wanted them to be said but that he would ad-lib according to the moment and the situation. Not because the chief commissioner was a loose cannon, far from it. Duff knew he had the words under control, he was as much a man of heart as he was of mind, a man who spoke how he felt and vice versa. A man who understood himself and therefore others too,

61

Duff thought. A leader. Someone people would follow. Someone Duff wished he was, or could be.

'You all know what happened,' Duncan said in a low, solemn voice, yet it carried as though he had shouted. 'I just wanted to brief you fully before the press conference this afternoon. One of our most trusted officers, Inspector Cawdor, had a serious charge of corruption levelled against him. And at the present moment it appears this suspicion was justified. In the light of his close connection with the Norse Riders — against whom we launched a successful operation yesterday — there was clearly a risk that he, given the situation, might try to destroy evidence or flee. For that reason, at ten o'clock this morning I gave the order for SWAT to arrest Inspector Cawdor with immediate effect.'

Duff had hoped his name would be mentioned, but he was also aware that Duncan wouldn't divulge any details. For if there is one thing you learn in the police it is that rules are rules, even when unwritten. So he was surprised when Duncan looked up and said, 'Inspector Macbeth, would you be so kind as to come up here and briefly summarise the arrest?'

Duff turned and watched his colleague stride up between the lines of chairs to the podium. Obviously he had been caught by surprise as well. The chief commissioner didn't normally delegate in these contexts; he would usually say his piece, make it short and to the point and conclude the meeting so that everyone could get back to their job of making the town a better place to live.

Macbeth looked ill at ease. He was still wearing his black SWAT uniform, but the zip at the neck was undone far enough for them to see the bright white bandage on his right shoulder.

'Well,' he began.

Not exactly an elegant start, but then no one

expected the head of SWAT to be a wordsmith. Macbeth checked his watch as though he had an appointment. Everyone in the room knew why: it is the instinctive reaction of police officers who have been ordered to report back and feel unsure of themselves. They check their watches as though the obligatory time references for past events are written there or the watch face will jog their memory.

'At ten fifty-three,' Macbeth said and coughed twice, 'SWAT raided Inspector Cawdor's home. A terrace door was open, but there was no sign of a break-in or violence, or that anyone had been there before us. Apart from a dog. Nor any signs that anyone other than Cawdor himself had done it . . . ' Now Macbeth stopped looking at his watch and addressed the gathering. 'A chair was knocked over by the terrace door. I'm not going to anticipate the SOCOs' conclusions, but it looked as if Cawdor didn't just step off the chair when he hanged himself, he jumped, and when he swung back kicked the chair across the room. That tallies with the way the deceased's excrement was scattered across the floor. The body was cold. Suicide seems the obvious cause of death, and one of the guys asked if we could skip the procedures and cut the man down as Cawdor had been a police officer all his life. I said no . . . '

Duff noticed Macbeth's dramatic pause. As if to allow the audience to listen to his silence. It was a trick Duff might use himself, a method he had definitely seen Duncan use, but he hadn't imagined that the pragmatic Macbeth would have it in his repertoire. And perhaps he didn't, because he was studying his watch again.

'Ten fifty-nine.'

Macbeth looked up and pulled his sleeve over the watch in a gesture to suggest he had finished.

'So Cawdor's still hanging there. Not for any investigative purpose, but because he was a *corrupt* policeman.'

63

It was so quiet in the room that Duff could hear the rain lashing against the window high up the wall. Macbeth turned to Duncan and gave a cursory nod. Then he left the podium and went back to his seat.

Duncan waited until Macbeth had sat down before saying, 'Thank you, Macbeth. That won't form part of the press conference, but I think it's a suitable conclusion to this internal briefing. Remember that a condemnation of all that is weak and bad in us can also be seen as an optimistic tribute to all that is strong and good. So back to your good work, folks.'

★   ★   ★

The young nurse stood by the door and watched the patient take off his top. He had pulled his long black hair behind his head as the doctor unwound the blood stained bandage from his left shoulder. All she knew about the patient was that he was a police officer. And muscular.

'Oh my goodness,' the doctor said. 'We'll have to give you a few stitches. And you'll need a tetanus injection, we always do that with dog bites. But first a little anaesthetic. Maria, can you . . . ?

'No,' said the patient, staring stiffly at the wall.

'Sorry?'

'No anaesthetic.'

A silence ensued.

'No anaesthetic?'

'No anaesthetic.'

The doctor was about to say something about pain when she caught sight of the scars on his forearms. Old scars. But the type of scar she had seen all too often after she moved to this town.

'Right,' she said. 'No anaesthetic.'

★   ★   ★

Duff leaned back in his office chair and pressed the receiver to his ear.

'It's me, love. What are you all doing?'

'Emily's gone swimming with friends. Ewan has got toothache. I'll take him to the dentist.'

'OK. Love, I'm working late today.'

'Why's that?'

'I may have to stay over here.'

'Why's that?' she repeated. Her voice didn't reveal any annoyance or frustration. It just sounded as if this was information she would like, perhaps to explain his absence to the children. Not because she needed him. Not because . . .

'It'll soon be on the news,' he said. 'Cawdor has committed suicide.'

'Oh dear. Who's Cawdor?'

'Don't you know?'

'No.'

'The head of the Gang Unit. He was a strong candidate for the Organised Crime post.'

Silence.

She had never taken much interest in his work. Her world was Fife, the children and — at least when he was at home — her husband. Which was great for him. In the sense that he didn't have to involve them in the grimness of his work. On the other hand, her lack of interest in his ambition meant she didn't always show much understanding for what the job demanded of his time. For his sacrifice. For . . . what he needed, for goodness' sake.

'The head of Organised Crime, who will be number three in the chain of command at HQ, after Duncan and Deputy Commissioner Malcolm. So, yes, this is a big deal, and it means I have to be here. Probably for the next few days, too.'

'Just tell me you'll be here for the pre-birthday.'

The pre-birthday. Oh, hell! It was a tradition they

had, the day before the child's real birthday it was just the four of them, meat broth and Mum and Dad's presents. Had he really forgotten Ewan's birthday? Perhaps the date had slipped his mind with all the events of the last few days, but he had gone out to buy what Ewan said he wanted after Duff told him how the undercover officers worked in the Narco Unit — sometimes they donned a disguise so that they wouldn't be recognised. In the drawer in front of Duff there was a nicely wrapped gift box containing a false beard and glue, fake glasses and a green woolly hat, all adult sizes so that he could assure Ewan it was *exactly* what Daddy and the others in the Narco Unit wore.

A light flashed on his telephone. An internal call. He had an inkling who it might be.

'Just a mo, love.'

He pressed the button below the light. 'Yes?'

'Duff? Duncan here. It's about the press conference this afternoon.'

'Oh yes?'

'I'd like to show we haven't been rendered impotent by what's happened and we're thinking about the future, so I'm going to announce the name of the acting head of Organised Crime.'

'Organised Crime? Er . . . already?'

'I'd have done it at the end of the month anyway, but as the Gang Unit no longer has a leader it's expedient to appoint an acting head straight away. Can you come up to my office?'

'Of course.'

Duncan rang off. Duff sat staring at the extinguished light. It was unusual for the chief commissioner to ring personally; it was always his secretary or one of his assistants who called meetings. Acting head. Who would probably take over the post when the formalities — application phase, appointment board's deliberations and so on — were at an end. His gaze picked up another light. He had completely forgotten his wife was on hold.

'Love, something's happened. I've got to run.'

'Oh? Nothing awful, I hope.'

'No,' Duff laughed. 'Nothing awful. Not at all. I think you should switch on the radio news this afternoon and listen to what they say about the new appointment for Organised Crime.'

'Oh?'

'Kiss on the neck.' They hadn't used this term of endearment for years. Duff rang off and ran — he couldn't stop himself — out of his office and up the stairs to the top floor. Up, up, up, higher and higher.

The secretary told Duff to go straight in. 'They're waiting for you.' She smiled. Smiled? She never smiled.

Around the circular oak table in the chief commissioner's large, airy but soberly furnished office sat four people, not counting Duncan. Deputy Chief Commissioner Malcolm, prematurely grey and bespectacled. He had studied philosophy and economics at the university in Capitol, spoke accordingly and was seen by many as a strange bird in HQ. He was an old friend of Duncan's, who claimed he had brought him in because they needed his broad range of management skills. Others said it was because Duncan needed Malcolm's unqualified 'Yes' vote at management meetings. Beside Malcolm, Lennox leaned forward, as keen as ever, albino-pale. His section, the Anti-Corruption Unit, had been established during Duncan's reorganisation. There had been a brief discussion as to whether *anti* should be in the title, some arguing that they didn't say the Anti-Narcotics Unit or the Anti-Homicide Unit. Yet under Kenneth the Narcotics Unit had been known as the corruption unit in local parlance. On the other side of Duncan sat an assistant taking minutes of the meeting, and beside her, Inspector Caithness.

As Duncan didn't allow smoking in his office there

were no ashtrays on the table with cigarette ends to tell Duff roughly how long they had been sitting there, but he registered that some of the notepads on the table had coffee stains and some of the cups were nearly empty. And the open, gentle, almost relaxed atmosphere suggested they had reached a conclusion.

'Thank you for coming so quickly, Duff,' Duncan said, showing him to the last vacant chair with an open palm. 'Let me get straight to the point. We're pushing forward the merging of your Narcotics Unit with the Gang Unit to become the Organised Crime Unit. This is our first crisis since I took over the chair of — ' Duff looked in the direction Duncan was nodding, to the desk. The chief commissioner's chair was high-backed and large, but didn't exactly look comfortable. Bit too straight. No soft upholstery. It was a chair to Duff's taste ' — so I feel it's important we show some vim.'

'Sounds sensible,' Duff said. And regretted it at once. The remark made it seem as if he had been brought in to assess top management's reasoning. 'I mean, I'm sure you're right.'

There was a moment's silence around the table. Had he gone too far the other way, suggesting that he didn't have opinions of his own?

'We have to be absolutely one hundred per cent certain that the person is not corrupt,' Duncan said.

'Of course,' Duff said.

'Not only because we can't afford any similar scandals such as this one with Cawdor, but because we need someone who can help us to catch the really big fish. And I'm not talking Sweno but Hecate.'

Hecate. The silence in the room after articulating the name spoke volumes.

Duff straightened up in his chair. This was indeed a big mission. But it was clear this was what the job demanded: slaying the dragon. And it was magnificent. For it started here. Life as a different, better man.

'You led this successful attack on the Norse Riders,' Duncan said.

'I didn't do it on my own, sir,' Duff said. It paid dividends to show a bit of humility, and especially in situations where it wasn't required; it was precisely then you could afford to be humble.

'Indeed,' Duncan said. 'Macbeth helped you. Quite a lot, I understand. What's your general impression of him?'

'Impression, sir?'

'Yes, you were in the same year at police college. He's undoubtedly done a good job with SWAT, and everyone there is enthusiastic about his leadership qualities. But of course SWAT is a very specialised unit. You know him, and that's why we'd like to hear whether you believe Macbeth could be the man for the job.'

Duff had to swallow twice before he could get his vocal cords to produce a sound. 'If Macbeth could be the man to lead the Organised Crime Unit, you mean?'

'Yes.'

Duff needed a couple of seconds. He placed a hand over his mouth, lowered his eyebrows and forehead and hoped this made him look like a deep thinker — not a deeply disappointed man.

'Well, Duff?'

'It's one thing leading men in a raid on a house, shooting criminals and saving hostages,' Duff said. 'And Macbeth's good at that without any doubt. Leading an organised crime unit requires slightly different qualifications.'

'We agree,' Duncan said. 'It requires *slightly* different and not *completely* different qualifications. Leading is leading. What about the man's character? Is he trustworthy?'

Duff squeezed his top lip between thumb and first finger. Macbeth. Bloody Macbeth! What should he say? This promotion belonged to him, Duff, and not some

69

guy who could equally well have ended up as a juggler or knife thrower in a travelling circus! He focused his gaze on the painting on the wall behind the desk. Marching, loyalty, leadership and solidarity. He could see them in his mind's eye on the country road: Macbeth, himself, the two dead men. The rain washing the blood away.

'Yes,' Duff said. 'Macbeth is trustworthy. But above all he's a craftsman. That was perhaps clear from his performance on the podium today.'

'Agreed,' Duncan said. 'That was why I got him up there, to see how he would tackle it. Around the table we agreed unanimously that what he demonstrated today was an excellent example of a practitioner's respect for established reporting routines, but also a true leader's ability to enthuse and inspire. *Cawdor's still hanging there because he was a corrupt policeman.*'

Muted laughter around the table at Duncan's imitation of Macbeth's rough working-class dialect.

'If he really has these qualities,' Duff said, hearing an inner voice whispering that he shouldn't say this, 'you have to ask yourself why he hasn't got further since his police college years.'

'True enough,' Lennox said. 'But this is one of the strongest arguments in *favour* of Macbeth.' He laughed — an ill-timed, high-pitched trill. 'None of us sitting round this table had high posts under the last chief commissioner. Because we, like Macbeth, weren't in on the game, we refused to take bribes. I have sources who can say with *total* certainty that this stalled Macbeth's career.'

'Then you have answered the question already,' Duff said stiffly. 'And of course you've taken into consideration his relationship with the casino owner.'

Malcolm glanced at Duncan. Received a nod from him in return and spoke up. 'The Fraud Unit's now looking into businesses that were allowed to prosper

70

under the previous administration and, with respect to that, they've just carried out a thorough investigation of Inverness Casino. Their conclusion is unambiguous: the Inverness is run in exemplary fashion with regard to accounts, tax and employment conditions. Which is not a matter you can take for granted in gambling joints. At this moment they're taking a closer look at the Obelisk's — ' he smiled wryly ' — cards. And let me say quite openly that this is a different kettle of fish. To be continued, as they say. So, in other words, we have no objections to Lady and her establishment.'

'Macbeth's from the east end of town and an outsider,' Duncan said, 'while all of us around this table are considered to belong to an inner circle. We're known to have stood up to Kenneth, we represent a change of culture in the force, but we've also had private educations and come from privileged homes. I think it's a good signal to send. In the police, in *our* police force, everyone can get to the top, whatever background, whatever connections they have, as long as they work hard and are honest, with emphasis on the *honest*.'

'Good thinking, sir,' Lennox said.

'Fine.' Duncan brought his hands together. 'Duff, anything you'd like to add?'

Haven't you seen the scars on his arms?

'Duff?'

Haven't you seen the scars on his arms?

'Anything wrong, Duff?'

'No, sir. I have nothing to add. I'm sure Macbeth is a good choice.'

'Good. Then let me thank all of you for attending this meeting.'

★ ★ ★

Macbeth stared at the red traffic lights as the wipers went to and fro across the windscreen of Banquo's

71

Volvo PV544. The car was as small as Banquo, a good deal older than the others around them, but fully functional and reliable. There was something about the design of the car, especially the set-back bonnet and protruding lower front, that made it look a bit like a throwback to before the war. But internally and under the bonnet, according to its owner, it had everything a man could demand of a modern car. The wipers struggled to dispose of the rain, and the running water reminded Macbeth of melting glass. A boy in a wet coat ran across the road in front of them, and Macbeth saw the light for pedestrians had changed from a green man to red. A human body covered with blood from head to toe. Macbeth shuddered.

'What is it?' Banquo asked.

'I think I'm getting a temperature,' Macbeth said. 'I keep seeing things.'

'Visions and signs,' Banquo said. 'It's flu then. No wonder. Soaked all day yesterday and bitten by a dog today.'

'Talking about the dog, have we found out where it came from?'

'Only that it wasn't Cawdor's. It must have come in through the open veranda door. I was wondering how it died.'

'Didn't I tell you? Seyton killed it.'

'I know that, but I couldn't see any marks on it. Did he *strangle* it?'

'I don't know. Ask him.'

'I did, but he didn't give me a proper answer, just — '

'It's green, Dad.' The boy on the back seat leaned forward between the two men. Macbeth glanced at the lanky nineteen-year-old. Fleance had inherited more of his mother's modesty than his father's good-natured joviality.

'Who's driving, you or your dad, son?' Banquo said with a warm smile and accelerated. Macbeth looked at the people on the pavement, the housewives shopping, the unemployed men outside the bars. In the last ten years the town had become busier and busier in the mornings. It should have lent the town an atmosphere of hustle and bustle, but the opposite was true, the apathetic, resigned faces were more reminiscent of the living dead. He had searched for signs of change over recent months. To see whether Duncan's leadership had made any difference. The most glaring and brutal street crimes were perhaps rarer, probably because there were more patrols out. Or maybe they had simply shifted to the back streets, into the twilight areas.

'Afternoon lectures at police college,' Macbeth said. 'We didn't have them in my day.'

'It's not a lecture,' the boy said. 'Me and a couple of others have a colloquium.'

'A colloquium? What's that?'

'Fleance and some of the keener ones swot together before exams,' Banquo said. 'It's a good idea.'

'Dad says I have to study law. Police college isn't enough. What do you think, Uncle Mac?'

'I think you should listen to your dad.'

'But you didn't do law either,' the boy objected.

'And look where it got him.' Banquo laughed. 'Come on, Fleance. You have to aim higher than your wretched father and this slob.'

'You say I don't have leadership qualities,' Fleance said.

Macbeth arched an eyebrow and glanced at Banquo.

'Really? I thought it was a father's job to make his children believe they can do anything if they try hard enough?'

'It is,' Banquo said. 'And I didn't say he hasn't got leadership qualities, only skills. And that means he has to work on it. He's smart; he just has to learn to trust his own judgement, which means taking the initiative and not always following others.'

Macbeth turned to the back seat. 'You've got a hard nut of a father.'

Fleance shrugged. 'Some people always want to give orders and take charge while others aren't like that — is that so weird?'

'Not weird,' Banquo said. 'But if you want to get anywhere you have to try to change.'

'Have *you* changed?' asked Fleance with a touch of annoyance in his voice.

'No, I was like you,' Banquo said. 'Happy to let others take charge. But I wish I'd had someone to tell me my opinion was as good as anyone else's. And sometimes better. And if you've got better judgement you *should* lead, it's your damned duty to the community.'

'What do you think, Uncle? Can you just change and *become* a leader?'

'I don't know,' Macbeth said. 'I think some people are born leaders and become them as a matter of course. Like Chief Commissioner Duncan. People whose sense of conviction rubs off on you, who can make you die for something. While others I know have neither conviction nor leadership skills, they're just driven by the desire to climb and climb until they get the boss's chair. They might be intelligent, have charm and the gift of the gab, but they don't really understand people. Because they don't *see* them. Because they understand and see only one thing: themselves.'

'Are you talking about Duff?' Banquo smiled.

'Who's Duff?' Fleance pleaded.

'It doesn't matter,' Macbeth said.

'Yes, it does. Come on, Uncle. I'm here to learn, aren't I?'

Macbeth sighed. 'Duff and I were friends at an orphanage and at police college, and now he's head of the Narco Unit. Hopefully he'll learn the odd thing on the way and that will change him.'

'Not him.' Banquo laughed.

'The Narco Unit,' Fleance said. 'Is he the one with the diagonal scar across his mug?'

'Yes,' his father said.

'Where did he get it?'

'He was born with it,' Macbeth said. 'But here's the school. Be good.'

'Yeah, yeah, Uncle Mac.'

The 'Uncle' came from when Fleance was small; now he mostly used it ironically. But as Macbeth watched the boy sprinting through the rain to the gates of the police college it gave him a feeling of warmth anyway.

'He's a good lad,' he said.

'You should have children,' Banquo said, pulling away from the kerb. 'They're a gift for life.'

'I know, but it's a bit late for Lady now.'

'Then with someone younger. What about someone of your own age?'

Macbeth didn't answer, staring out the window rapt in thought. 'When I saw the red man at the lights I thought about death,' he said.

'You were thinking about Cawdor,' Banquo said. 'By the way, I spoke to Angus while he was staring at Cawdor dangling there.'

'Religious musings?'

'No. He just said he didn't understand rich, privileged people who took their own lives. Even if Cawdor had lost his job and maybe had to do a short stretch, he was still well set up for a long, carefree life. I had to explain to the boy that it's the fall that does it. And the disappointment when you see your future won't live up to your expectations. That's why it's important not to have such high expectations, to start slowly, not to have success too young. A planned rise, don't you think?'

'You're promising your son a better life than yours if he studies law.'

'It's different with sons. They're an extension of your life. It's their job to ensure a steady rise.'

'It wasn't Cawdor.'

'Eh?'

'It wasn't Cawdor I was thinking of.'

'Oh?'

'It was one of the young men on the country road. He was — ' Macbeth looked out of the window ' — red. Soaked in blood.'

'Don't think about it.'

'Cold blood.'

'Cold . . . what do you mean?'

Macbeth took a deep breath. 'The two men by Forres, they'd surrendered. But Duff shot the guy wearing Sweno's helmet anyway.'

Banquo shook his head. 'I knew it was something like that. And the other one?'

'He was a witness.' Macbeth grimaced. 'They'd run out of the party and he'd only been wearing a white shirt and white trousers. I took out my daggers. He started to plead; he knew what was coming.'

'I don't need to hear any more.'

'I stood behind him. But I couldn't do it. I stood there with a dagger in the air, paralysed. But then I saw Duff. He was sitting with his face in his hands sobbing like a child. Then I struck.'

A siren was heard in the distance. A fire engine. What the hell could be burning in this rain? Banquo thought.

'I don't know if it was because his clothes were drenched,' Macbeth said, 'but the blood covered *all* of him. All his shirt and trousers. And lying there on the tarmac with his arms down and slightly to the side, he reminded me of the traffic light. Stop now. Don't walk.'

They went on in silence, past the entrance to the garage under police HQ. Only unit leaders and higher-ranking officers had parking spots there. Banquo turned into the car park at the rear of the building. He stopped and switched off the engine. The rain beat down on the car roof.

'I understand,' Banquo said.

'What do you understand?'

'Duff knew that if you arrested Sweno, hauled him before a greedy judge in the country's most corrupt town, how long would he have got? Two years? Maximum three? Full acquittal? And I understand you.'

'Do you?'

'Yes. What would Duff have got if Sweno's lackey had taken the stand against him? Twenty years? Twenty-five? In the force we take care of our own. No one else does. And even more importantly, another police scandal would do so much harm just as we have a chief commissioner who's beginning to give the public back some faith in law and order. You have to see the bigger picture. And sometimes cruelty is on the side of the good, Macbeth.'

'Maybe.'

'Don't give it another thought, my friend.'

The water streaming down the windscreen had distorted the police headquarters building in front of them. They didn't move, as though what had been said had to be digested before they could get out.

'Duff should be grateful to you,' Banquo said. 'If you hadn't done that he would've had to do it himself, both of you knew that. But now you've both got something on each other. A balance of terror. That's what allows people to sleep at night.'

'Duff and I are not the US and the Soviet Union.'

'No? What are you actually? You were inseparable at police college, but now you barely talk. What happened?'

Macbeth shrugged. 'Nothing much. We were probably an odd couple anyway. He's a Duff. His family had property once, and that kind of thing lingers. Language, upper-class manners. At the orphanage it isolated and exposed him, then he seemed to gravitate towards me. We became a duo you didn't mess with, but at college you could see he was drawn to his own sort. He was released into the jungle like a tame lion. Duff studied at university, found himself an upper-class girl and got married. Children. We drifted apart.'

'Or did you just get sick of him behaving like the selfish, arrogant bastard he is?'

'People often get the wrong idea about Duff. At police college he and I swore we would get the big bad boys. Duff really *wants* to change this town, Banquo.'

'Was that why you saved his skin?'

'Duff's competent and hard-working. He has a good chance of getting Organised Crime, everyone knows that. So why should one mistake in the heat of battle stop the career of a man who can do something good for us all?'

'Because it's not like you to kill a defenceless man in that way.'

Macbeth shrugged. 'Maybe I've changed.'

'People don't change. But I see now you saw it simply as your soldier's duty. You, Duff and I are fighting on the same side in this war. You've cut short the lives of two Norse Riders so that they can't continue to cut short the lives of our children with their poison. But you don't perform your duty by choice. I know what it costs you when you start seeing your dead enemies in traffic lights. You're a better man than me, Macbeth.'

Macbeth smirked. 'You see more clearly than me in the mists of battle, old man, so it's some solace to me that I have your forgiveness.'

Banquo shook his head. 'I don't see better than anyone else. I'm just a chatterbox with doubt as my sole guide.'

'Doubt, yes. Does it eat you up sometimes?'

'No,' Banquo answered, staring through the windscreen. 'Not sometimes. All the time.'

* * *

Macbeth and Banquo walked from the car park up to the staff entrance at the rear of HQ, a two-hundred-year-old stone building in the centre of District 3 East. In its time the building had been a prison, and there was talk of executions and mumblings of torture. Many of those who worked late also claimed they felt an inexplicably cold draught running through the offices and heard distant screams. Banquo had said to Macbeth it was only the somewhat eccentric caretaker, who turned down the heating at five on the dot every day, and his screams when he saw someone leaving their desk without turning off the lamp.

Macbeth noticed two Asiatic-looking women shivering on the pavement among the unemployed men, looking around as if they were waiting for someone. The town's prostitutes used to gather in Thrift Street behind the National Railway Network offices until the council chased them out a few years ago, and now the market had split into two: those attractive enough to work the casinos, and those forced to endure the hard conditions of the streets, who felt safer wall to wall with the law. Moreover, when the police, after periodic pressure from politicians or the press, 'cleaned' the 'sex filth' off the streets with mass arrests, it was convenient for all sides if the clear-up was brief and quick. Soon everything would be back to normal, and you couldn't rule out the possibility that some of the girls' punters came from police HQ anyway. But Macbeth had politely declined the girls' offers for so long that they left him in peace. So when he saw the two women moving towards him and Banquo he assumed they were new to the area. And he would have remembered them. Even by the relatively low standard of these streets their appearance did not make a favourable impression. Now it was Macbeth's experience that it was difficult to put a precise age on

Asiatic women, but whatever theirs was, they must have been through hard times. It was in their eyes. They were the cold, inscrutable kind that don't let you see in, that only reflect their surroundings and themselves. They were stooped and dressed in cheap coats, but there was something else that caught his attention, something which didn't add up, the disfiguration of their faces. One opened her mouth and revealed a line of dirty, brown, neglected teeth.

'Sorry, ladies,' Macbeth said cheerfully before she managed to speak. 'We'd have liked to say yes, but I've got a frighteningly jealous wife and him there, he's got a terrible VD rash.'

Banquo mumbled something and shook his head.

'Macbeth,' said one of them in a staccato accent and squeaky doll-like voice at variance with her hard eyes.

'Banquo,' said the other woman — identical accent, identical voice.

Macbeth stopped. Both women had combed their long raven-black hair over their faces, probably to conceal them, but they couldn't hide the big un-Asiatic fiery-red noses hanging over their mouths like glass glowing beneath the glass-blower's pipe.

'You know our names,' he said. 'So how can we help you, ladies?'

They didn't answer. Just nodded towards a house on the other side of the street. And there, from the shadows of an archway, a third person stepped into the daylight. The contrast to the two others couldn't have been greater. This woman — if it was a woman — was as tall and broad-shouldered as a bouncer and dressed in a tight leopardskin-print outfit that emphasised her female curves the way a swindler emphasises the false benefits of his product. But Macbeth knew what she was selling, at least what she used to sell. And the false benefits. Everything about her was extreme: her height, width, bulging breasts, the claw-like red nails that bent around her strong fingers, the wide-open eyes, the theatrical make-up, boots up to her thighs with stiletto heels. To him the only shock was that she hadn't changed. All the years had passed without apparently leaving a mark on her.

She crossed the street in what seemed to be two gigantic steps.

'Gentlemen,' she said in a voice so deep Macbeth thought he could hear the glass panes behind him quiver.

'Strega,' Macbeth said. 'Long time, no see.'

'Likewise. You were a mere boy then.'

'So you remember me?'

'I remember all my clients, Inspector Macbeth.'

'And who are these two?'

'My sisters.' Strega smiled. 'We bring Hecate's congratulations.'

Macbeth saw Banquo automatically reach inside his jacket at the sound of Hecate's name, and he placed a guarded hand on his arm. 'What for?'

'Your appointment as head of Organised Crime,' Strega said. 'All hail Macbeth.'

'All hail Macbeth,' the sisters echoed.

'What are you talking about?' Macbeth said, scanning the unemployed men across the street. He had spotted a movement when Banquo went for his gun.

'One man's loss, another man's gain,' Strega said. 'Those are the laws of the jungle. More dead, more bread. And who will get the bread, I wonder, if Chief Commissioner Duncan dies?'

'Hey!' Banquo took a step towards her. 'If that's Hecate threatening us, then . . . '

Macbeth held him back. He had seen it now. Three of the men across the road had looked up, braced themselves. They were standing apart but among the others, and there was a similarity: they all wore grey lightweight coats. 'Just let her talk,' Macbeth whispered.

81

Strega smiled. 'There's no threat. Hecate won't do anything; he's just stating an interesting fact. He thinks you'll be the next chief commissioner.'

'Me?' Macbeth laughed. 'Duncan's deputy would take over of course, and his name's Malcolm. Be off with you.'

'Hecate's prophecies never err,' said the man-woman. 'And you know that.' She stood opposite Macbeth without moving, and Macbeth realised she was still taller than him.

'Well?' she said. 'Is your casino lady keeping you clean?'

Banquo saw Macbeth stiffen. And thought this Strega should be happy to be considered a woman. Macbeth snorted, looked as if he was going to say something but changed his mind. Shifted his weight from one foot to the other. Opened his mouth again. Nothing came out this time either. Then he turned and strode towards the entrance of police HQ.

The tall woman watched him. 'And as for you, Banquo, aren't you curious to know what's in store for you?'

'No,' he said and followed Macbeth.

'Or your son, Fleance?'

Banquo stopped in his tracks.

'A good, hard-working boy,' Strega said. 'And Hecate promises that if he and his father behave and follow the rules of the game, in the fullness of time he'll also become chief commissioner.'

Banquo turned to her.

'A planned rise,' she said. Gave a slight bow and smiled, turned and grabbed the other two under her arms. 'Come on, sisters.'

Banquo stared after this bizarre trio until they had rounded the corner of HQ. So out of place had they seemed that when they were gone he had to ask himself if they had really been there.

'Lots of fruitcakes on the streets nowadays,' Banquo said as he caught up with Macbeth in the foyer before the reception desk.

'Nowadays?' Macbeth said, pressing the lift button impatiently again. 'Fruitcakes have always prospered in this town. Did you notice the ladies had minders?'

'Hecate's invisible army?'

The lift doors glided open.

'Duff,' Macbeth said, stepping to the side. 'Now how . . . ?'

'Macbeth and Banquo,' said the blond man, striding past them towards the door to the street.

'Goodness me,' Banquo said. 'A stressed man.'

'That's what it's like when you've got the top job.' Macbeth smiled, walked in and pressed the button for the basement floor. The SWAT floor.

'Have you noticed how Duff's shoes always creak?'

'It's because he always buys shoes too big for him,' Macbeth said.

'Why?'

'No idea,' Macbeth replied and managed to stop the doors closing in front of the officer running over from reception.

'Just had a call from the chief commissioner's office,' he said, out of breath. 'Telling us to ask you to go up the minute you arrive.'

'Right,' Macbeth said and let go of the doors.

'Trouble?' Banquo asked after they had closed.

'Probably,' Macbeth said, pressing the button for the fourth floor. Feeling the stitches in his shoulder begin to itch.

5

Lady walked through the gaming room. The light from the immense chandeliers fell softly on the dark mahogany where they were playing blackjack and poker, on the green felt where the dice would dance later in the evening, on the spear-shaped gold spire that stood up like a minaret in the middle of the spinning roulette wheel. She'd had the chandeliers made as smaller copies of the four-and-a-half-ton chandelier in Dolmabahçe Palace in Istanbul, while the spire pointing from the middle of the ceiling down to the roulette table was a copy of the spire in the roulette wheel. The chandeliers were anchored with cords tied to the banisters of the mezzanine in such a way that they could be lowered every Monday and the glass cleaned. This was the kind of detail that passed straight over most customers' heads. Like the small, discreet lilies she'd had sewn into the thick, sound-muffling burgundy carpets she had bought in Italy for a tiny fortune. But they didn't go over *her* head, she saw the matching spires and only she knew what the lilies commemorated. That was enough. For this was hers.

The croupiers automatically stood up straight whenever she passed. They knew their jobs, they were efficient and careful, they treated the customers with courtesy but were firm, they had manicured hands, groomed hair and were immaculately dressed in Inverness Casino's elegant red and black croupier uniform, which was changed every year and tailor-made for every single member of staff. And, most important of all, they were honest. This wasn't something she assumed, it was something she *saw* and *heard. Saw* it in people's eyes, involuntary tics, muscular twitches or

84

theatrically relaxed states. *Heard* it in the tiny distinctions of quivering vocal cords. It was an innate sensitivity she had, inherited from her mother and grandmother. But while this sensitivity had led them as they aged into the dark shadows of insanity, Lady had used her skills to flush out dishonesty. Away from childhood's vale of woe, up to where she was today. The rounds of inspection had two functions. One was to keep her employees on their toes that little bit more so that every day, every night, they would show themselves to be at least one class higher than those at the Obelisk. The second was to uncover any dishonesty. Even though they had been honest and honourable yesterday, people were like wet clay: they were shaped by opportunity, motive and what you told them today, and they could blithely do what had been inconceivable the day before. Yes, that was the only thing that was fixed, the only thing you could count on: the heart was greedy. Lady knew that. She had that kind of heart herself. A heart she alternately cursed and counted herself lucky to have, which had brought her affluence but had also deprived her of everything. But it was the heart that beat in her chest. You can't change anything, you can't stop it, all you can do is follow it.

She nodded to the familiar faces gathered around the roulette table. Regular customers. They all had their reasons for coming here and playing. There were those who needed to switch off after a challenging working day and those who, after a boring working day, needed a challenge. And those who had neither work nor a challenge, but money. Those who had none of the above ended up at the Obelisk, where you were given a tasteless but free lunch if you gambled more than five hundred. You had idiots who thought they had a system which promised long-term gains, a breed that kept dying but curiously never died out. And then you had those who — and no casino-owner would admit this aloud — formed the bedrock of their business. Those who had to. Those who felt compelled to come here because they couldn't stop themselves risking everything, night after night, fascinated by the roulette ball whizzing around the shiny wheel like a little globe caught in the sun's gravitational field, the sun that gave them daily life but which in the end, with the inevitability of physics, would also burn them up. The addicted. Lady's bread and butter.

Talking about addiction. She looked at her watch. Nine. It was still a bit early in the evening, but she wished the tables were fuller. Reports from the Obelisk suggested they were continuing to take business away from her despite the heavy investment she had made in interior design, the kitchen and the upgrade of the hotel rooms. Some thought she was in the process of pricing herself out of the market and, because the three-year-old Obelisk was well established in people's minds as the more reasonable alternative, she could and should cut down on the standards and expenses. After all, she wouldn't lose her status as the town's exclusive option. But they didn't know Lady. They didn't know that for her it wasn't primarily about the bottom line but being the exclusive option. Not only more elegant than the Obelisk but better, whatever the comparison. Lady's Inverness Casino should be the place you wanted to be seen, the place you wanted to be associated with. And she, Lady, should be the person you wanted to be seen and associated with. The moneyed came here and the top politicians, actors and sports personalities from the celebrity firmament, writers, beauties, hipsters and intellectuals — everyone came to Lady's table, bowed respectfully, kissed her hand, met her discreet rejection of their equally discreet enquiry about gambling credit with a smile and gratefully accepted a Bloody Mary on the house. Profit or no profit, she hadn't come all this way to run a bloody bordello, as they were doing at the

Obelisk, so they could have the dregs, those she would rather not see beneath Inverness Casino's chandeliers. *Genuine* chandeliers. But of course the tide had turned. The creditors *had* started asking questions. And they hadn't liked her answer: what the Inverness needed was not cheaper drinks but more and bigger chandeliers.

Business wasn't on her mind now though. Addiction was. And the fact that Macbeth hadn't got here yet. He always said if he was going to be late. And what had happened during the Sweno raid had affected him. He didn't say so, but she could sense it. Sometimes he was strangely soft-hearted, it seemed to her — a man she had seen kill with her own eyes. She had seen the calculated determination before the killing, the cold efficiency during it and the remorseless smile afterwards.

But this had been different, she knew. The man had been defenceless. And even if on occasion she had problems understanding the code of honour men like Macbeth upheld, she knew this sort of issue could cause him to lose his bearings. She crossed the floor, caught the stares of two men at the bar. Both younger than her. But they didn't interest her. Although she had always done everything to feel desired she despised men who desired her. Apart from one man. It had surprised her at first that someone could fill her thoughts and heart so fully and completely. And often she had asked herself why she, who had never loved any man, loved this particular man. She had concluded it was because he loved that part of her which frightened other men. Her strength. Willpower. An intelligence that was superior to theirs and she couldn't be bothered to hide under a bushel. It took a man to love that in a woman. She stood by the large window facing Workers' Square, looked over towards Bertha, the black locomotive guarding the entrance to the disused station. To the swamp where, over the years, she had seen so many get stuck and sink. Could he — ?

'Darling.'

How many times had she heard this voice whisper this word in her ear? And yet every time was like the first. He lifted her long red hair to the side, and she felt currents run through her body as his lips touched her neck. It was unprofessional — she knew the two men at the bar were watching — but she let it go. He was here.

'Where've you been?'

'In my new office,' he said, wrapping an arm around her midriff.

'New office?' She caressed his forearm. Felt the scar tissue under her fingertips. He had told her the reason the scars were there was because he'd had to inject in the dark and couldn't see his veins, so he would feel his way to the wound from the previous injection and shoot up in the same spot. If you did that enough times, for several years, plus the unavoidable infection now and then, you ended up with forearms that looked like his, as though they had been dragged through barbed wire. But she couldn't feel any fresh wounds. It was some years ago now. So long that sometimes — in fits of childlike optimism — she considered him cured.

'I didn't think you called those coal bins in the cellar offices.'

'On the third floor,' Macbeth said.

Lady turned to him. 'What?'

His white teeth shone in his dark beard. 'You see before you the new head of Organised Crime in this town.'

'Is that true?'

'Yes.' He laughed. 'And now you look as shocked as I imagine I did in Duncan's office.'

'I'm not shocked, my love. I'm . . . I'm just happy. It's so deserved! Haven't I kept telling you? Haven't I said you're worth more than that office in the basement?'

'Yes, you have. Again and again, darling. But you

88

were the only one.' Macbeth leaned back and laughed again.

'And now we're going up, my love. Out of your cellar obscurity! I hope you demanded a good salary.'

'Salary? No, I forgot to ask. My sole demand was that I had Banquo as my deputy, and they both agreed. It's quite mad — '

'Mad? Not at all. It's a wise appointment.'

'Not the appointment. On the way to HQ we met three sisters sent by Hecate, who prophesied I would get the job.'

'Prophesied?'

'Yes!'

'They must have known.'

'No. When I got to Duncan's office he said the decision had been made just five minutes before.'

'Hm. Witchcraft, nothing less.'

'They were probably high on their own dope and talking nonsense. They said I'd be the chief commissioner, too. And do you know what? Duncan suggested we celebrate my appointment here, at the Inverness!'

'Hang on a moment. What did they say?'

'He wanted to celebrate it here. Wouldn't the chief commissioner choosing to organise a party in your casino be good for your reputation?'

'No, I mean the sisters. Did they say you'd be chief commissioner?'

'Yes, but forget it, darling. I suggested to Duncan that we make an evening of it, and he and all the people who live out of town can stay overnight in the hotel. You've got quite a lot of unoccupied rooms at the moment, so . . .'

'Of course we'll do that.' She stroked his cheek. 'I can hear you're happy, but you still look pale, my love.'

He shrugged. 'I don't know. I think I'm sickening for something. I see dead men in traffic lights.'

She put a hand under his arm. 'Come on. I've got what you need, my boy.'

He smiled. 'Yes, you do.'

They sailed through the casino. She knew it was her high heels that made her half a head taller than him. Knew her young figure, elegant evening gown and stately, lissom walk made the men at the bar still stare after her. Knew this was something they didn't have at the Obelisk.

★   ★   ★

Duff lay on the large double bed staring at the ceiling, at the crack in the paint he knew so well.

'Afterwards, as I was leaving the meeting, Duncan took me aside and asked if I was disappointed,' he explained. 'He said we both knew I'd have been the natural candidate for the post.'

The crack had offshoots spreading in an apparently random way, but when he scrunched up his eyes, thereby losing focus, the crack seemed to follow a pattern, form an image. He just couldn't work out what it was.

'And what did you answer?' came the voice over the running water in the bathroom. Even now, after having seen as much of each other as any two people can, she disliked him seeing her until she was ready. And that was fine by him.

'I answered that, yes, I was disappointed. When he said they wanted Macbeth *because* he didn't belong to the inner circle, my being one of those who had supported Duncan's project right from the start was used *against* me.'

'Well, that's true. What did — ?'

'Duncan said there was another reason, but he didn't want to mention it with the others present. The Sweno raid had only been partly successful as Sweno had got

90

away. And it turned out I had received the tip-off so early that there would have been enough time to inform him. I had almost undone a year's undercover work by what looked a lot like an ego trip. And Macbeth and SWAT had saved the whole operation. Therefore it would seem suspicious to choose me ahead of him. But at least he did give me a consolation prize.'

'He gave you the Homicide Unit, and that's not bad, is it?'

'It's smaller than Narco, but at least I escaped the humiliation of being a subordinate officer in Organised Crime.'

'Who persuaded Duncan anyway?'

'What do you mean?'

'Who argued Macbeth's case? Duncan's a listener; he likes consensus and goes for group decisions.'

'Believe me, my dearest, no one lobbies for Macbeth. I doubt he knows what the word means. All he wants in life is to catch baddies and make sure his casino queen is happy.'

'Speaking of which.' She posed by the bathroom door. The gauzy negligee revealed more than it hid of course. Duff liked a lot about this woman, some things he wasn't even able to articulate, but what he idolised was plain enough: her youth. The glow from the candles on the floor made the moisture in her eyes, on her red lips, on her shining teeth, sparkle. And yet tonight he needed something more. He wasn't in the mood. After what had happened he didn't feel like the buck he had been when he had started the day. But that could perhaps be changed.

'Take it off,' he said.

She laughed. 'I've just put it on.'

'It's an order. Stay where you are and take it off. Slowly.'

'Hm. Maybe. If I'm given a clearer order . . . '

'Caithness, you are hereby ordered by a superior

91

officer to turn your back, pull what you're wearing over your head, lean forward and take a good hold of the door frame.'

Duff heard her little girlie gasp of shock. Perhaps it was put on for his sake, perhaps not. It was fine by him. He was getting in the mood.

★   ★   ★

Hecate strode across the damp floor of the central station, between the peeling walls and mumbling drug addicts. He noticed the gaze of two guys stooped over a spoon and syringe they were obviously sharing. They didn't know him. No one knew him. Perhaps they were thinking the big man with the mustard-yellow cashmere coat, the carefully groomed, almost unnaturally black hair and the resplendent heavy Rolex looked like perfect prey which had just walked into the lion's den. Or they may have had suspicions; perhaps there was something about the self-assured, determined gait, something about the gold-capped walking stick, which made a rhythmic *tick-tock* in time with the stiletto heels of the tall broad-shouldered woman who walked two steps behind him. If she was a woman. There might also have been something about the three men, all wearing grey lightweight coats, who had entered the station immediately before him and taken up a position by the wall. Perhaps that was why they sensed that they were in his den. *He* was the lion.

Hecate stopped, and let Strega go first down the narrow stairs reeking of urine to the toilet. Saw the two druggies lower their heads and concentrate on the task in hand — heating and injecting. Addicts. For Hecate this was a statement of fact without contempt or irritation. After all, they were his bread and butter.

Strega opened the door at the bottom of the stairs, lifted a sleeping man to his feet, bared her teeth to show him her mood and a thumb to point him in the right direction. Hecate followed her in between the cubicles and the running sinks. The stench was so intense that Hecate could still get tears in his eyes. But it also had a function: it kept away curious eyes and made even the hardened addicts keep their visits as brief as possible. Strega and Hecate went into the furthest cubicle with the sign DO NOT USE on the door and a bowl filled to the brim with excrement. Furthermore, the neon tube in the ceiling above had been removed, so it was impossible to see or hit veins in there. Strega removed one of the tiles above the disconnected loo, turned a handle and pushed. The wall swung open, and they stepped inside.

'Close it quickly,' Hecate said and coughed. He looked around the room. It had been a railway storeroom, and the other door led to the tunnel for the southern lines. He had moved his production here two years after the train traffic had ceased. He'd had to chase out some tramps and junkies, and although no one ever came here and Chief Commissioner Kenneth had been their highest-ranking protector he had installed camouflaged CCTV in the tunnel and over the stairs down to the toilet. There were twelve people in total on the evening shift, all wearing masks and white coats. On this side of the glass partition dividing the room into two, brew was chopped up, weighed and packed into plastic bags by seven people. By the tunnel door sat two armed guards keeping an eye on the workers and the CCTV monitors. Inside the glass partition was what they called the inner sanctum or simply the kitchen. The tank was there, and only the sisters had access. The kitchen was hermetically sealed for many reasons. First, so that nothing outside could contaminate the processes inside and because some idiot might inadvertently flick a lighter or throw down a lit cigarette end, blowing them all to pieces. But mostly because everyone in the room would soon be hooked if they inhaled the molecules floating in the air on a daily basis.

Hecate had found the sisters in a Chinatown opium den in Bangkok, where the two had set up a home-made laboratory to make heroin from the opium in Chang Rai. He didn't know much about them, only that they had fled China with Chiang Kai-shek's people, the disease that had ravaged their faces had reportedly spread through the village they came from, and as long as he paid them punctually they would deliver whatever he asked. The ingredients were well known, the proportions the same, and others could follow the procedures through the glass window. Yet there was a mystery about the way they mixed and heated the ingredients. And Hecate saw no reason to deny the rumours that they used toads' glands, bumble bee wings, juice from rats' tails and even blew their noses into the tank. It created a sense of black magic, and if there was something that people would pay for in their all-too-real working lives, it was precisely that: black magic. And brew was going down a bomb. Hecate had never seen so many become so desperately addicted in such a short time. But it was equally obvious that the day the sisters produced a slightly less potent product he would have to get rid of them. That was how it was. Everything had its day, its cycle. Like the two decades under Kenneth. The good times. And now with Duncan, who if he was allowed to go his merry way would mean bad times for the magic industry. It is obvious that if the gods bring good and bad times, short human lives and death, you have to make sure you become a god yourself. It is easier than you might think. The obstacle to most people achieving god-like status is that they are afraid and superstitious, and in their anxiety-ridden submission they believe there is a morality, a set of heaven-sent rules that apply to all people. But these rules are made by precisely those that tell you they are gods, and in some strange way the rules serve these gods. Well, OK, not everyone can be a god, and every god needs followers, a client base. A market. A town. Many towns.

Hecate took up a position at the end of the room, placed both hands on the top of his stick and just stood there. This was his factory. Here he was the factory owner. In a growing industry. He would soon have to expand. If he didn't meet the demand others would, those were the simple rules of capitalism. He'd long had plans to take over one of the town's disused factories, set up some fictitious business as a cover while he concocted his brew in the back rooms. Guards, barbed-wire fences, his own lorries going in and out. He could increase production tenfold and export to the rest of the country. But it would be more visible and would require police protection. It would require a chief commissioner who was in his pocket. It would require a Kenneth. So what do you do if Kenneth is dead? You make a new one and clear a path for him.

He received stiff smiles and brief nods from his choppers and packers before they launched themselves at their tasks with renewed energy. They were frightened. That was the principal purpose of these inspections. Not to stop the cycle — it was inevitable — but to delay it. Everyone in this cellar room would at some point try to cheat him, take a few grams home and sell it themselves. They would be found out, and the sentence would be carried out speedily. By Strega. She seemed to enjoy her varied assignments. Like being a messenger together with the sisters.

'Well, Strega,' he said. 'Do you think the seed we sowed in Macbeth will grow?'

'Human ambition will always stretch towards the sun like a thistle and overshadow and kill everything around it.'

95

'Let's hope so.'

'They're thistles. They can't help themselves. They're evil and foolish. If people see the soothsayer's first prophecy fulfilled they'll believe the next one blindly. And now Macbeth has found out he's the new head of Organised Crime. The only question is whether Macbeth has enough of the thistle's ambition in him. And the necessary cruelty to go the whole way.'

'Macbeth doesn't,' Hecate said. 'But she does.'

'She?'

'Lady, his beloved dominatrix. I've never met her, yet I know her innermost secrets and understand her better than I understand you, Strega. All Lady needs is time to reach the inescapable conclusion. Believe me.'

'Which is?'

'That Duncan has to be got rid of.'

'And then?'

'Then,' Hecate said, tapping his stick on the ground, *tap-tap*. 'The good times will roll again.'

'Are you sure we can control Macbeth? Now he's clean he's probably . . . moralistic, isn't he?'

'My dear Strega, the only person more predictable than a junkie or a moralist is a love-smitten junkie and moralist.'

★   ★   ★

Banquo lay in the bedroom on the first floor listening to the rain, to the silence in the room, to the train that never came. The railway track ran past outside, and he visualised the wet, glistening gravel where some of the rails and the sleepers had been removed. Well, stolen. They had been happy here, he and Vera. They'd had good times. He had met Vera while she was working for the goldsmith Jacobs & Sons, where the finer folk went to buy wedding rings and gifts for each other. One evening the burglar alarm went off, and Banquo — who

96

was on patrol — arrived on the spot, sirens howling, within a minute. Inside, a terrified young woman was desperately shouting over the ear-piercing bell that she was only closing up, she was new and must have done something wrong when she was putting the alarm on. He had only caught the odd word here and there and had had all the more time to observe her. And when eventually she burst into tears he had put a gentle, consoling arm around her. She felt like a warm, tremulous, fledgling bird. During the next few weeks they went to the cinema, walked on the sunny side of the tunnel and he had kissed her at the gate. She came from a working-class family and lived at home. Right from a young girl she'd had to make a contribution and had worked at the Estex factory like her parents. Until she got a bad cough, unofficial advice from a doctor to work elsewhere and a job at Jacobs via recommendations.

'The pay's worse,' she said, 'but you live longer.'

'You still cough?'

'Only on rainy days.'

'We'd better make sure you get more sunshine. Another walk on Sunday?'

After six months Banquo went to the jeweller's shop and asked her if she had an engagement ring she could recommend. She looked so bewildered he had to laugh.

After getting married they moved into a poky two-bed flat, with neighbours beneath them on the ground floor. They had saved up for, bought and made love in the bed where he was lying now. Out of consideration for their neighbours, Vera — who was a passionate but shy woman — would wait for a train until she came. When a train thundered past, shaking the walls and ceiling lamps, she let herself go, screamed and dug her nails into his back. She did the same when she gave birth to Fleance in that very bed — waited until the train came and then screamed, dug her nails into his hand and squeezed out a son.

97

They bought the ground floor the following year to have more room. There were three of them and could soon be many more. But five years later there were only two of them: a boy and a man. It was her lungs. The doctors blamed the polluted air, all the toxins from the factories forced down by low-pressure weather systems hovering over the town like a lid. And with lungs that were already damaged . . . Banquo blamed himself. He hadn't been able to scrape enough money together to move the family to the other side of the tunnel, to Fife, to somewhere with a bit of sunshine and fresh air you could breathe.

Now they had too much room. He could hear the radio on downstairs and knew Fleance was doing his schoolwork. Fleance was conscientious, he wanted so much to do well. It was some consolation that those who found school easy and got off to a good start often lost their enthusiasm when life became tougher. And then students like Fleance, who was forced to employ strict working routines and knew that learning required effort, got their turn. Yes, it would all be fine. And, who knows, perhaps the boy would meet a girl and start a family. Here in this house, for example. Perhaps new and better times were coming. Perhaps they would be able to help Duncan even more, now that Macbeth was in charge of fighting organised crime in this town. The news had come as a huge surprise to Banquo and most at HQ. Down in the SWAT cellar Ricardo had put it bluntly: he couldn't imagine Macbeth and Banquo sitting behind their desks in suits and ties. Drawing diagrams and presenting budgets. Or making polite conversation at cocktail parties with chief commissioners, council members and other fine folk. But they would see. There wouldn't be any lack of will. And perhaps it was now the turn of people like Macbeth, who were used to having to put in a shift, to achieve their aims.

There was no one else at HQ apart from Duff who knew how addicted to speed Macbeth had been when he was a teenager, how crazy it had made him, how hopelessly lost he had been. Banquo had been on the beat, tramping round the rain-lashed streets, when he came across the boy curled up on a bench in a bus shelter, out of his head on dope. He woke him, wanting to move him on, but there was something about his pleading brown eyes. Something in his alert movements when he stood up, something about his fit, compact body that told Banquo he was going to waste. Something that might have been developing. Something that could still be saved. Banquo took the fifteen-year-old home that night, got him some dry clothes. Vera fed him and they put him to bed. The next day, a Sunday, Vera, Banquo and the boy drove through the tunnel, came out into sunshine on the other side and went for a long walk in the green hills. Macbeth talked with a stammer at first, then less so. He had grown up in an orphanage and dreamed about working in a circus. He showed them how he could juggle and then took five paces from a tall oak and threw Banquo's penknife into the tree, where it quivered. The boy found it more difficult to show them the scars on his forearm and talk about them. That didn't happen until later, when he knew Banquo and Vera were people he could trust. Even then he only said it had started after he fled the home, not how or what triggered it. After that there were more Sundays, more conversations and walks. But Banquo remembered the first especially well because Vera had whispered to him on the way home, 'Let's make a son like him.' And when, four years later, a proud Banquo had accompanied Macbeth to police college, Fleance had been three and Macbeth clean for just as long.

Banquo turned and looked at the photograph on the bedside table. It was of him and Fleance; they were standing under the dead apple tree in the garden. Fleance's first day at police college. He was wearing his uniform, it was early morning, the sun was out, and the shadow of the photographer fell across them.

He heard a chair scrape and Fleance stomping around. Angry, frustrated. It wasn't always easy to grasp everything straight off. It took time to acquire understanding. Like it took time and willpower to renounce drugs, the escape you had become so addicted to. Like it took time to change a town, to redress injustice, to purge the saboteurs, the corrupt politicians and the big-time criminals, to give the town's citizens air they could breathe.

It had all gone quiet downstairs. Fleance was back at his desk.

It was possible if you took one day at a time and did the work that was required. Then one day the trains might run again.

He listened. All he heard was silence. And rain. But if he closed his eyes, wasn't that Vera's breathing beside him in bed?

⋆ ⋆ ⋆

Caithness's panting slowly subsided.

'I have to call home,' Duff said, kissing her sweaty forehead and swinging his legs out of bed.

'Now?' she exclaimed. He could see from the way she bit her lower lip that it had come out more angrily than she had intended. Who said he didn't understand people?

'Ewan had toothache yesterday. I have to see how he is.'

She didn't answer. Duff walked naked through the flat. He usually did as it was an attic flat and no one could see in. Besides, being seen naked didn't bother him. He was proud of his body. Perhaps he was especially fond of his body because he had grown up feeling ashamed of the scar that divided his face. The flat was large, larger than you would have imagined a young woman working in the state sector would have. He had offered to help her with the rent as he spent so many nights there, but she said her father took care of that side of things.

Duff went into the study, closed the door after him and dialled the Fife number.

He listened to the rain drumming on the attic window right above his head. She answered after the third ring. Always after the third ring. Regardless of where she was in the house.

'It's me,' he said. 'How did it go with the dentist?'

'He's better now,' she said. 'I'm not sure if it was toothache.'

'Oh? What was it then?'

'There are other things that can hurt. He was crying, and when I asked him why, he wouldn't tell me and said the first thing that came into his head. He's in bed now.'

'Hm. I'll be home tomorrow and then I'll have a chat with him. What's the weather like?'

'Clear sky. Moonlight. Why?'

'We could go to the lake tomorrow, all of us. For a swim.'

'Where are you, Duff?'

He stiffened, there was something about her intonation. 'Where? At the Grand, of course.' And added in an exaggeratedly cheery voice, 'Beddy-byes for tired men, you know.'

'I rang the Grand earlier this evening. They said you hadn't booked in.'

He stood up straight with the phone in his hand.

'I rang you because Emily needed help with some maths. And, as you know, I'm not that good at putting two and two together. So where are you?'

'In my office,' Duff said, breathing through his

mouth. 'I'm sleeping on the sofa in the office. I'm up to my ears in work. I'm sorry I said I was at the Grand, but I thought you and the children didn't need to know how hard things were at the moment.'

'Hard?'

Duff gulped. 'All the work. And I still didn't get the Organised Crime post.' He curled his toes. He could hear how pathetic he sounded, as though he were asking her to let him off the hook out of sympathy.

'Well, you got the Homicide Unit anyway. And a new office, I hear.'

'What?'

'On the top floor. I can hear the rain drumming on a window. I'll ring off then.'

There was a click and she was gone.

Duff shivered. The room was chilly. He should have put on some clothes. Shouldn't have been so naked.

★　★　★

Lady listened to Macbeth's breathing and shivered.

It was as though a chill had passed through the room. A ghost. The ghost of a child. She had to get out of the darkness that weighed down on her, force her way out of the mental prison that had imposed itself on her mother and grandmother, up into the light. Fight for her liberation, sacrifice whatever had to be sacrificed to be the sun. To be a star. A shining mother who was consumed in the process and gave life to others. The centre of the universe as she burned up. Yes. Burned. As her breath and skin burned now, forcing the cold from the room. She ran a hand down her body, feeling her skin tingle. It was the same thought, the same decision as then. It had to be done, there was no way round it. The only way was onwards, straight on at whatever lay in their path, like a bullet from a gun.

She laid a hand on Macbeth's shoulder. He was

sleeping like a child. It would be the last time. She shook him.

He turned to her, mumbling, put out his hands. Always ready to serve. She held his hands firmly in hers.

'Darling,' she whispered, 'you have to kill him.'

He opened his eyes; they shone at her in the darkness. She let go of his hands.

Stroked his cheek. The same decision as then.

'You have to kill Duncan.'

6

Lady and Macbeth had first met one late summer's evening four years ago. It had been one of those rare days when the sun shone from a cloudless sky and Lady was sure she had heard a bird singing in the morning. But when the sun had set and the night shift came on an evil moon had risen above Inverness Casino. She had been standing outside the main entrance to the casino, in the moonlight, when he rolled up in a SWAT armoured vehicle.

'Lady?' he said, looking straight into her eyes. What did she see? Strength and determination? Maybe. Or perhaps it was because that was what she wanted to see at that moment.

She nodded. Thinking he seemed a little too young. Thinking the man behind him, an elderly man with white hair and calm eyes, looked more suited for the job.

'I'm Inspector Macbeth. Any changes in the situation, ma'am?'

She shook her head.

'OK, is there anywhere we can see them from?'

'The mezzanine.'

'Banquo, assemble the men and I'll recce.'

Before they went up the stairs to the mezzanine the young officer whispered that she should take off her high heels to make less noise. That meant she was no longer taller than him. On the mezzanine they first kept to the back, by the windows looking out over Workers' Square, so that they couldn't be seen from the gaming room below. Halfway along they moved towards the balustrade. They were partially hidden by the rope to the central chandelier and the genuine suit of

Maximilian armour from the sixteenth century which she had bought at an auction in Augsburg. The idea was that when gamblers saw it up there it would give them an unconscious sense of being either protected or watched. Their own conscience would determine which. Lady and the officer crouched and peered down into the room, where twenty minutes earlier customers and staff had fled in panic. Lady had been standing on the roof looking up at the full moon and instinctively felt the evil when she heard the crash and screams from down below. She went down, grabbed one of the fleeing waiters, who said that some guy had fired a gun into the chandelier and was holding Jack.

She had already calculated the cost of a new chandelier, but it was obvious that would be nothing compared to the cost of the gun — which was at present pointing at the head of Jack, her best croupier — being fired one more time. After all, part of what her casino offered was safe excitement and relaxation; for a while you didn't need to think about the crime in the streets outside. If the impression was created that Inverness Casino couldn't offer that, the gaming room would be as empty as it was now. The only two people left were sitting at the blackjack table below the mezzanine on the other side. Poor Jack was ramrod-stiff and as white as a sheet.

Right behind him, holding a gun, sat the customer.

'It would be hard to get a shot in from such a distance as long as he's hiding behind your croupier,' Macbeth whispered, taking out a little telescope from his black uniform. 'We have to get closer. Who is he and what does he want?'

'Ernest Collum. He says he'll kill my croupier unless he's given back everything he's lost at the casino.'

'And is that a lot?'

'More than we have in cash here. Collum's one of the addicts. An engineer and a number-crunching genius, so he knows the odds. They're the worst. I've told him we'll try and get the money, but the banks are closed, so it could take a while.'

'We don't have much time. I'm going in.'

'How do you know?'

Macbeth moved back from the balustrade and tucked the telescope inside his uniform. 'His pupils. He's high and he's going to shoot.' He pressed a button on his walkie-talkie. 'Code Four Six. Now. Take command, Banquo. Over.'

'Banquo in command. Over.'

'I'll go with you,' Lady said, following Macbeth.

'I don't think — '

'This is my the casino. My Jack.'

'Listen, ma'am — '

'Collum knows me, and women calm him down.'

'This is a police matter,' Macbeth said and ran down the stairs.

'I'm coming,' Lady said and ran after him.

Macbeth came to a halt and stood in front of her.

'Look at me,' he said.

'No, you look at me,' she said. 'Do I look as if I'm *not* going with you? He's expecting me to bring the money.'

He looked at her. He had a good look. Looked at her in a way other men had looked at her. But also in a way no men or women had looked at her. They looked at her with fear or admiration, respect or desire, hatred, love or subservience, measured her with their eyes, judged her, misjudged her. But this young man looked at her as though he had finally found something. Which he recognised. Which he had been looking for.

'Come on then,' he said. 'But keep your mouth shut, ma'am.'

The thick carpet muffled the sound of their feet as they entered the room.

The table where the two men were sitting was less well illuminated than usual because of the smashed chandelier. Jack's face, stiffened into a mask of transfixed shock, didn't change when he saw Lady and Macbeth coming towards him. Lady noticed the hammer of the gun rise.

'Who are you?' Collum's voice was thick.

'I'm Inspector Macbeth from SWAT,' said the policeman, pulling out a chair and taking a seat. Laying both palms on the table so that they were visible. 'My job is to negotiate with you.'

'There's nothing to negotiate, Inspector. I've been cheated by this bloody casino for years. It has ruined me. They fix the cards. *She* fixes the cards.'

'And you've arrived at that conclusion after taking brew?' Macbeth asked, tapping his fingers soundlessly on the felt. 'It distorts reality, you know.'

'The reality, Inspector, is that I have a gun and I see better than ever, and if you don't give me the money I'll first shoot Jack here, then you, as you'll try to draw a gun, and then Lady, so-called, who will at that point either try to flee or overpower me, but it will be too late for both. Then possibly myself, but we'll have to see whether I'm in a better mood after dispatching you three to hell and blowing this place sky-high.' He chuckled. 'I don't see any money, and these negotiations are thereby called off. So let's get started . . . '

The hammer rose higher. Lady automatically grimaced and waited for the bang.

'Double or quits,' Macbeth said.

'I beg your pardon?' Collum said. Immaculate pronunciation. Immaculate shave and immaculate dinner suit with a pressed white shirt. Lady guessed his underclothes were clean too. He had known this was unlikely to finish with him leaving the casino holding a suitcase full of money. He would be carried out as bankrupt as when he came in. But, well, immaculate.

'You and I play a round of blackjack. If you win, you get all the money you've lost here, times two. If I win, I

107

get your gun with all the bullets and you drop all your demands.'

Collum laughed. 'You're bluffing!'

'The suitcase with the money you asked for has arrived and is in the police vehicle outside. The owner has said she's willing to double up if we agree. Because we *know* there's been some jiggery-pokery with the cards, and fair's fair. What do you say, Ernest?'

Lady looked at Collum, at his left eye, which was all that was visible behind Jack's head. Ernest Collum was not a stupid man; quite the opposite. He didn't believe the story about the suitcase. And yet. Sometimes it seemed as if it was the most intelligent customers who refused to see the inevitability of chance. Given enough time everyone was doomed to lose against the casino.

'Why would you do this?' Collum said.

'Well?' Macbeth said.

Collum blinked twice. 'I'm the dealer and you're a player,' he said. 'She deals.'

Lady looked at Macbeth, who nodded. She took the pack, shuffled and laid two cards in front of Macbeth face up.

A six. And the king of hearts.

'Sweet sixteen.' Collum grinned.

Lady laid two cards in front of Collum, one face up. Ace of clubs.

'One more,' Macbeth said, stretching out a hand.

Lady gave him the top card from the pack. Macbeth held it to his chest, sneaked a look. Glanced up at Collum.

'Looks like you've bust, sweet sixteen,' Collum said. 'Let's see.'

'Oh, I'm pretty happy with my hand,' Macbeth said. Smiling at Collum. Then he threw the card to the right, where the table was in part-shadow. Collum automatically leaned across a fraction to see the card better.

The rest happened so fast Lady remembered it as a

flash. A flash of a hand in motion, a flash of steel that caught the light as it flew across the table, a flash of Collum's one eye staring at her, wide open in aggrieved protest, light glistening in a cascade of blood streaming out both sides of the blade that sliced his carotid artery. Then the sounds. The muffled sound of the gun hitting the thick, much-too-expensive carpet. The splash of blood landing on the table. Collum's deep gurgle as his left eye extinguished. Jack's one quavering sob.

And she remembered the cards. Not the ace, not the six. But the king of hearts. And, half in shadow, the queen of spades. Both sprayed with Ernest Collum's blood.

They came in wearing their black uniforms, quick, soundless, obeying his every sign. They didn't touch Collum; they led out a sobbing Jack. She pushed away an offer of help. Sat looking at the young head of SWAT, who leaned back in his chair looking content. Like someone thinking he had taken the last trick.

'Collum will take the last trick,' she said.

'What?'

'Unless we find it.'

'Find what?'

'Didn't you hear what he said? *After dispatching you three to hell and blowing this place sky-high.*'

He stared at her for a couple of seconds, first with surprise, then with something else. Acknowledgement. Respect. Then shouted, 'Ricardo! There's a bomb!'

Ricardo was a SWAT guy with calm self-assurance in his gaze, his movements and the softly spoken orders he gave. His skin was so black Lady thought she could see her reflection. It took Ricardo and his men four minutes to find what they were searching for, inside a locked toilet cubicle. A zebra-striped suitcase Collum had brought in after the doorman had checked the contents. Collum had explained it was four gold bars. He intended to use them as a stake at the exclusive poker table where, until the Gambling and Casino Committee had forbidden it, they had accepted cash, watches, wedding rings, mortgage deeds, car keys and anything else, provided that the players agreed. Behind the gold-painted iron bars engineer and numbers genius Collum had placed a home-made time bomb, which the SWAT bomb expert later praised for its craftsmanship. Exactly how many minutes were left on the timer Lady couldn't remember. But she remembered the cards.

The king of hearts and the queen of spades. That evening they met under an evil moon.

★   ★   ★

Lady invited him over for dinner at the casino the next evening. He accepted the invitation but refused the aperitif. No to wine, but yes to water. She had the table on the mezzanine laid with a view of Workers' Square, where the rain was trickling down and running quietly over the cobblestones from the railway station to the Inverness. The architects had built the station a few metres higher up because they thought the weight of all the marble and trains like Bertha would over time cause the floor to sink in the town's constantly waterlogged, marshy terrain.

They talked about this and that. Avoided anything too personal. Avoided what had happened the evening before. In short, they had a nice time. And he was — if not polite — so charming and witty. And unusually attractive in a grey a-little-too-tight suit that he said he had been given by his older colleague, Banquo. She listened to stories about the orphanage, a pal called Duff and a travelling circus which he had joined one summer as a boy. About the nervous lion-tamer who always had a cold, about the skinny sisters who were trapeze artists and only ate oblong food, about the magician who invited members of the audience into the ring and made their possessions — a wedding ring, a key or a watch — float in the air in front of their very eyes. And he listened with interest to Lady talking about the casino she had built from scratch. And finally, when she felt she had told him everything that could be told, she raised her glass of wine and asked, 'Why do you think he did it?'

Macbeth shrugged. 'Hecate's brew drives people crazy.'

'We ruined him, that's true, but there's no duplicity with the cards.'

'I didn't think there was.'

'But two years ago we had two croupiers who worked a number with players on the poker table and stole from others. I kicked them out of course, but I hear they've got together with some financiers and have applied to the council to have a new casino built.'

'The Obelisk? Yes, I've seen the drawings.'

'Perhaps you also know a couple of the players they worked with were politicians and Kenneth's men?'

'I've heard that, yes.'

'So the casino will be built. And I promise you people like Ernest Collum will have every reason to feel they're being cheated.'

'I'm afraid you're right.'

'This town needs new leaders. A new start.'

'Bertha,' Macbeth said, nodding towards the window facing the central station, where the old black locomotive stood glistening in the rain on the plinth by the main entrance, its wheels on eight metres of the original rails that ran to Capitol. 'Banquo says she needs to be started up again. We need to have a new, healthy activity. And there's good energy in this town too.'

'Let's hope so. But back to last night ... ' She twiddled her wine glass. Knew he was looking at her cleavage. She was used to men doing that and it didn't make her feel anything either way; she only knew that

111

her female attributes could be used now and then, sometimes should not be used, like any other business tool. But his eyes were different. *He* was different. He wasn't anyone she needed, merely a sweet policeman on a low rung of the ladder. So why was she spending time with him? Of course she could have shown him a sign of her appreciation other than her presence. She observed his hand as he took the glass of water. The thick veins on the suntanned hand. Obviously he made sure to get out of town when he could.

'What would you have done if Collum hadn't agreed to play blackjack?'

'I don't know,' he said, looking at her. Brown eyes. People in this town had blue eyes, but of course she had known men with brown eyes before. Not like these though. Not so . . . strong. And yet vulnerable. My God, was she falling for him? So late in life?

'You don't know?' she asked.

'You said he was an addict. I was counting on him not being able to resist the temptation to gamble one more time. With everything.'

'You've been to a lot of casinos, I can see.'

'No.' He laughed. A boy's laughter. 'I didn't even know whether my cards were any good.'

'Sixteen versus an ace? I would say they weren't. So how could you be so sure he would play? The story you told him wasn't exactly convincing.'

He shrugged. She looked into her glass of wine. And saw what she knew. He knew what addiction was.

'Did you at any point have any doubt you'd be able to stop him before he shot Jack?'

'Yes.'

'Yes?'

The young policeman sipped from his glass. He didn't seem to be relishing this topic of conversation. Should she let him off the hook? She leaned across the table. 'Tell me more, Macbeth.'

He put down his glass. 'For a man to lose consciousness before he has time to pull the trigger in such a situation, you have to either shoot him in the head or cut his carotid artery. As you saw, cutting his artery produced a brief but thick jet of blood, then the rest trickled out. Well, the oxygen the brain needed was in the first jet, so that meant he was unconscious before the blood even hit the table. There were two problems. Firstly, the ideal distance for throwing a knife is five paces. I was sitting much closer, but fortunately the daggers I use are balanced. That makes them harder to throw for someone without sufficient experience, but for an experienced thrower it's easier to adjust the rotation. The second problem was that Collum was sitting in such a way that I could only get at the artery on the left-hand side of his face. And I would have to throw with my right hand. I am, as you can see, left-handed. I was dependent on a bit of luck. And usually I'm not lucky. What was the card by the way?'

'Queen of spades. You lost.'

'See.'

'You're not lucky?'

'Definitely not at cards.'

'And?'

He considered. Then he shook his head. 'Nope. Not lucky in love either.'

They laughed. Toasted each other and laughed again. Listened to the falling rain. And she closed her eyes for a moment. She thought she had heard ice clinking in glasses at the bar. The click of the ball on wood spinning round the roulette wheel. Her own heartbeats.

★ ★ ★

'What?' He blinked in the dark bedroom.

She repeated the words: 'You have to kill Duncan.'

Lady heard the sound of her own words, felt them

grow in her mouth and drown her beating heart.

Macbeth sat up in bed, looking at her carefully. 'Are you awake or talking in your sleep, darling?'

'No. I'm here. And you know it has to be done.'

'You were having a bad dream. And now — '

'No! Think about it. It's logical. It's him or us.'

'Do you think he wishes us any harm? He's only just promoted me.'

'In name you may be the head of Organised Crime, but in practice you're at the mercy of his whims. If you want to close the Obelisk, if you want to chase the drug dealers out of the area around the Inverness and increase police presence on the streets so that people feel safe you have to be chief commissioner. And that's just the small things. Think of all the big things we could achieve with you in the top job, darling.'

Macbeth laughed. 'But Duncan wants to do big things.'

'I don't doubt that he honestly and genuinely wants to, but to achieve big things a chief commissioner must have broad support from the people. And for this town's inhabitants Duncan is just a snob who landed the top post, as Kenneth did too, as Tourtell did in the town hall. It isn't beautiful words that win over the populace, it's who you are. And you and I are part of them, Macbeth. We know what they know. We want what they want. Listen. *Of the people. For the people. With the people.* Do you understand? We are the only ones who can say that.'

'I understand, but . . . '

'But what?' She stroked his stomach. 'Don't you want to be in charge? Aren't you a man who wants to be at the top? Are you happy to lick the boots of others?'

'Of course not. But if we just wait we'll get there anyway. As head of Organised Crime I'm still number three.'

'But the chief commissioner's office is not for the

likes of you, my love! Think about it. You've been given this job so that it *looks* as if we're as good as them. They'll *never* give you the top job. Not willingly. We have to *take* it.'

He rolled over onto his other side, with his back to her. 'Let's forget this, darling. The way you've forgotten that Malcolm will be chief if anything happens to Duncan.'

She grabbed his shoulder, pulled him back over so that he lay facing her again.

'I haven't forgotten anything. I haven't forgotten that Hecate said you'll be the chief commissioner, and that means he has a plan. We take care of Duncan and he'll take care of Malcolm. And I haven't forgotten the evening you took care of Ernest Collum. Duncan is Collum, my sweet. He's holding a pistol to the head of our dream. And you have to find the courage you displayed that evening. You have to be the man you were that night, Macbeth. For me. For us.' She placed a hand on his cheek and softened her voice. 'Life doesn't give the likes of us that many opportunities, darling. We have to grasp the few that offer themselves.'

He lay there. Silent. She waited. Listened, but no words drowned out the beating of her heart now. He had ambition, dreams and the will, she knew that, they were what had raised him from the mess he had found himself in — they had turned a youth addicted to drugs into a police cadet and later the head of SWAT. That was the affinity they had: they had both made good, paid the price. Should he stop now, halfway there, before they could enjoy the rewards? Before they could enjoy the respect and admire the view? He was courageous and a ruthless man of action, but he had failings that could prove costly. A lack of evil. The evil that you needed, if only for one decisive second. The second when you have to cope with not having restrictive morality on your side, when you mustn't lose sight of the bigger picture, mustn't torment yourself by asking if you're doing the right thing in this, the smaller one. Macbeth loved what he called justice, and his loyalty to the rules of others was a weakness she could love him for. In times of peace. And despise him for now, when the bells of war were ringing. She ran her hand from his cheek to his neck, slowly over his chest and stomach. And back up. Listened. His breathing was regular, calm. He was asleep.

★ ★ ★

Macbeth breathed deeply, as though he were sleeping. She took away her hand. Moved to lie down along his back. She was breathing calmly too now. He tried to breathe in time with her. *Kill Duncan?* Impossible. Of course it was impossible.

So why couldn't he sleep? Why did her words persist, why did his thoughts whirl around in his head like bats?

Life doesn't give the likes of us that many opportunities, darling. We have to grasp the few that offer themselves. He thought of the opportunities life had given him. The one that night in the orphanage, which he hadn't grasped. And the one Banquo had given him, which he *had*. How the first one had almost killed him and the second had saved him. But isn't it that you don't take some opportunities that are offered because they will condemn you to unhappiness anyway, opportunities that will cause regret for the rest of your life whether you take them or not? Oh, the insidious dissatisfaction that will always poison the most perfect happiness. And yet. Had fate opened a door that would soon shut? Was his courage letting him down again, the way it had let him down that night in the orphanage? He visualised the man in the bed that time, asleep, unsuspecting. Defenceless. A man who stood between him and the freedom every human being deserved. Between him and the dignity every human being should crave. Between Macbeth and the power he would gain. And the respect. And the love.

Day had started to break when he woke Lady.

'If I did this . . . ' he said, 'I would be beholden to Hecate.'

She opened her eyes as though she had been awake the whole time. 'Why do you think like that, darling? Hecate has only prophesied that something will happen, so there is no debt to be paid.'

'So what has he to gain by my becoming chief commissioner?'

'You'd better ask him, but it's obvious — he must have heard that Duncan has sworn he won't rest until he has arrested Hecate. And he probably knows it's not inconceivable that you would prioritise action against the drugs gangs who use violence and shoot each other in the streets.'

'The Norse Riders, whose back has already been broken?'

'Or against establishments that cheat good people out of their savings.'

'The Obelisk?'

'For example.'

'Hm. You said something about the big things we could do. Were you thinking of something good for the town?'

'Of course. Remember the chief commissioner decides which politicians need to be investigated and which do not. And anyone who has any knowledge of the town council knows that everyone in a position of power during the last ten years has paid for services in ways that would not bear close scrutiny. And that they in turn have demanded payment. Under Kenneth they didn't need to bother to camouflage their corruption, the evidence was there for all to see. We know that, they know that, and it means we can control them as we wish, my love.'

She stroked his lips with her forefinger. She had told him the first night they spent together that she loved his lips. They were so soft and thin-skinned she could taste his blood with no more than a little nibble.

'Make them finally keep their promises to implement initiatives that would save this town,' he whispered.

'Exactly.'

'Get Bertha running again.'

'Yes.' She nibbled his lower lip, and he could feel the trembling, hers and his, their hearts racing.

He held her.

'I love you,' he whispered.

Macbeth and Lady. Lady and Macbeth. They were breathing in rhythm with each other now.

7

Lady looked at Macbeth. He was so handsome in a dinner jacket. She turned, checked that the waiter had put on white gloves as she had asked. And that the champagne flutes on the silver tray were the ones with the narrow bowls. She had, mostly for fun, put a small but elegant silver whisk on the tray, even though very few customers had seen one before and even fewer knew what it was for. Macbeth rocked back on his shoes as they sank into the deep carpet in the Inverness, and stared stiffly at the front door. He had seemed nervous all day. Only when they went through the practical details of the plan did he regain concentration and become the professional policeman of a rapid-response unit and forget the target had a name. Duncan.

The guards outside opened the door, and a gust of rain swept in.

The first guests. Lady switched on her happiest, most excited smile and placed her hand under Macbeth's arm. She felt him instinctively straighten up.

'Banquo, old friend!' she exclaimed. 'And you've brought Fleance. He's become such a good-looking young man — I'm jolly glad I don't have any daughters!' Hugs and clinking glasses. 'Lennox! You and I should have a little chat, but first some champagne. And there's Caithness! You look ravishing, my dear! Why can't I find dresses like that? Deputy Chief Commissioner Malcolm! But your title's simply too long. Is it all right if I just call you Chief? Don't tell anyone, but sometimes I tell Macbeth to call me Director General just to hear how it sounds.'

She had barely said a word to most of them before, yet she still managed to make them feel they had known

119

each other for years. Because she could see inside them, see how they wanted to be seen — it was the blessing of super-sensitivity among all its curses. It meant she could skip the preliminary skirmishes and get straight to the point. Perhaps it was her unpretentious manner that made them trust her. She broke the ice by telling them apparently intimate details of her life, which made them daring, and when they noticed their little secrets were rewarded with an 'Ah' and conspiratorial laughter, they ventured on to slightly bigger secrets. It was unlikely any other person in the town knew more about its inhabitants than this evening's hostess.

'Chief Commissioner Duncan!'

'Lady. Apologies for my late arrival.'

'Not at all. It is indeed your privilege. We don't want a chief commissioner who arrives first. I always ensure I arrive last, in case anyone should be in any doubt as to who is considered the queen.'

Duncan laughed quietly, and she laid a hand on his arm. 'You're laughing, so in my eyes the evening is already a success, but you should try our exquisite champagne, dear Chief Commissioner. I assume your bodyguards won't . . . '

'No, they'll probably be working all night.'

'All night?'

'When you publicly threaten Hecate you have to sleep with at least one eye open. I sleep with two pairs open.'

'Apropos sleeping. Your bodyguards have the adjacent room to your suite with an intervening door, as they requested. The keys are at reception. But I insist your guards at least taste my home-made lemonade, which I promise was not made using the town's drinking water.' She signalled to the waiter holding a tray bearing two glasses.

'We — ' one bodyguard said, clearing his throat.

'Refusals will be taken personally and as an insult,' Lady interrupted.

The bodyguards exchanged glances with Duncan, then they each took a glass, drained the contents and put it back on the tray.

'It's very magnanimous of you to host this party, ma'am,' Duncan said.

'It's the least I can do after you made my husband head of the Organised Crime Unit.'

'Husband? I didn't know you were married.'

She tilted her head. 'Are you a man to stand on formality, Chief Commissioner?'

'If by formality you mean rules, I probably am. It's in the nature of my work. As it is in yours, I assume.'

'A casino stands or falls on everyone knowing that the rules apply in all cases, no exceptions.'

'I have to confess I've never set foot in a casino before, ma'am. I know you have your hostess duties, but might I ask for a tiny guided tour when it suits you?'

'With pleasure.' Lady smiled and linked her arm with his. 'Come on.'

She led Duncan up the stairs to the mezzanine. If his eyes and secret thoughts were drawn to the high split in her dress as she strode ahead, he concealed them well. They stood at the balustrade. It was a quiet evening. Four customers at the roulette table; the blackjack tables were empty; four poker players at the table underneath them. The others at the party had gathered by the bar, which they had almost to themselves. Lady watched Macbeth nervously fidgeting with his glass of water as he stood with Malcolm and Lennox, trying to look as though he was listening.

'Twelve years ago this was a water-damaged vandalised ruin after the railway administration moved out. As you know we're the only county in the land to allow casinos.'

'Thanks to Chief Commissioner Kenneth.'

'Bless his blackened soul. Our roulette table was built according to the Monte Carlo principle. You can put your bets on identical slots on both sides of the wheel, which is made of mostly mahogany, a little rosewood and ivory.'

'It is, frankly, very impressive what you've created here, Lady.'

'Thank you, Chief Commissioner, but it has come at a cost.'

'I understand. Sometimes you wonder what drives us humans.'

'So tell me what drives you.'

'Me?' He deliberated for a second or two. 'The hope that this town may one day be a good place to live.'

'Behind that. Behind the fine principles we can so easily articulate. What are your selfish, emotional motives? What is your dark motive, the one that whispers to you at night and haunts you after all the celebratory speeches have been made?'

'That's a searching question, Lady.'

'It's the *only* question, my dear Chief Commissioner.'

'Maybe.' He rolled his shoulders inside his dinner jacket. 'And maybe I didn't need such a strong motivation. I was dealt good cards when I was born into a relatively affluent family where education, ambition and career were a matter of course. My father was unambiguous and plain-spoken about corruption in the public sector. That was probably why he didn't get very far. I think I just carried on where he left off and learned from the strategic mistakes he made. Politics is the art of the possible, and sometimes you have to use evil to fight evil. I do whatever I have to do. I'm not the saint the press likes to portray me as, ma'am.'

'Saints achieve little apart from being canonised. I'm more for your school of tactics, Chief Commissioner. That's always been my way.'

'I can understand that. And although I don't know any details of your life, I do know you've had a longer and steeper path to tread than me.'

Lady laughed. 'You'll find me in the faded files of your archives. I supported myself on the oldest profession in the world for a few years — that's not exactly a secret. But we all have a past and have — as you put it — done what we had to do. Does the Chief Commissioner gamble? If so, I'd like you to do so on the house tonight.'

'Thank you for your generosity, Lady, but it would break my rules to accept.'

'Even as a private individual?'

'When you become chief commissioner your private life ceases to exist. Besides, I don't gamble, ma'am. I prefer not to rely on the gods of fate but to merit any winnings I might make.'

'Nevertheless you got where you are — as you yourself said — because the gods of fate dealt you good cards at birth.'

He smiled. 'I said *prefer*. Life's a game where you either play with the cards you have or throw in your hand.'

'May I say something, Chief Commissioner? Why are you smiling?'

'At your question, ma'am. I think you'll ask anyway.'

'I just wanted to say that I think you, my dear Duncan, are a thoroughly decent person. You're a man with spine, and I respect who you are and what you stand for. Not least because you have dared to give an unknown quantity like Macbeth such a prominent position in your management team.'

'Thank you, ma'am. Macbeth has only himself to thank.'

'Does the appointment form part of your anti-corruption campaign?'

'Corruption is like a bedbug. Sometimes you have to demolish the whole house to get rid of the plague. And start building again with non-infected materials. Like Macbeth. He wasn't part of the establishment, so he isn't infected.'

'Like Cawdor.'

'Like Cawdor, ma'am.'

'I know what it costs to pare away the infected flesh. I had two disloyal servants in my employ.' She leaned over the balustrade and nodded towards the roulette table. 'I still cried when I sacked them. Being tempted by money and wealth is a very common human weakness. And I was too soft-hearted, so instead of crushing the bedbugs under my heel I let them go. And what was my thanks? They used *my* ideas, the expertise *I* had given them and probably money they had stolen from here to start a dubious establishment that is not only destroying the reputation of the industry but taking bread from the mouths of the people who created this market, from us. If you chase away bedbugs they come back. No, I'd have done the same as you, Chief Commissioner.'

'As me, ma'am?'

'With Cawdor.'

'I couldn't let him get away with working with Sweno.'

'I mean, you did the job properly. All you had on him was the testimony of a Norse Rider who even the most stupid judge and jury know would have been willing to tell the police whatever he needed to keep himself out of prison. Cawdor could have got away.'

'We had a bit more on him than that, ma'am.'

'But not enough for a watertight conviction. Cawdor the bedbug *could* have come back. And then the scandal would have dragged on interminably. A court case with one hell of a shit-storm that could easily have left stains here and there. Not exactly what the police need when they're trying to win back the town's trust. You have my full support, Chief Commissioner. You have to crush them. One turn of your heel and it's over.'

Duncan smiled. 'That's quite a detailed analysis, but I hope you're not suggesting I had anything to do with

Cawdor's premature demise, ma'am.'

'No, God forbid.' She placed a hand on the chief commissioner's arm. 'I'm only saying what Banquo usually says: there are several ways to skin a cat.'

'Such as?'

'Hm. Such as ringing a man and telling him that Judgement Day has come. The evidence is so overwhelming he'll have SWAT at his door in minutes; he'll be publicly humiliated, stripped of all his honours, his name will be dragged through the gutters to the stocks. He has only a few minutes.'

Duncan studied the poker table beneath. 'If I had some binoculars,' he said. 'I'd be able to see their cards.'

'You would.'

'Where did you get your binoculars, ma'am? A gift from birth?'

She laughed. 'No, I had to buy them. With experience. Dearly bought.'

'Of course I haven't said anything, but Cawdor served in the force for many years. Like most of us he was neither a-hundred-per-cent good nor a-hundred-per-cent bad. Perhaps he deserved, perhaps his family deserved, to have had a choice as to which way out he took.'

'You're a nobler person than me, Chief Commissioner. I'd have done the same, but exclusively for selfish reasons. *Santé.*'

They raised glasses and clinked.

'Talking about binoculars,' Lady said, nodding towards the others in the bar. 'I see Inspector Duff and young Caithness have their antennae tuned in.'

'Oh?' Duncan arched an eyebrow. 'They're standing at opposite ends of the bar, from what I can see.'

'Exactly. They're keeping the maximum distance between them. And still checking every fifteen seconds where the other is.'

'Not much escapes your eye, does it?'

'I saw something when I asked you what your dark, selfish motive was.'

Duncan laughed. 'Can you see in the dark too?'

'My sensitivity to the darkness is inherited, Chief Commissioner. I sleepwalk in the darkest night without hurting myself.'

'I suppose the motive for the best charitable work can be called selfish, but my simple view is that the end justifies the motive.'

'So you'd like a statue like the one Kenneth got? Or the love of the people, which he didn't get?'

Duncan held her gaze, checked the bodyguards behind them were still outside hearing range, then emptied his glass and coughed. 'For myself I wish to be at peace in my soul, ma'am. The satisfaction of having done my duty. Of having maintained and improved my forefathers' house, so to speak. I know it's perverse, so please don't tell anyone.'

Lady took a deep breath, pushed off from the balustrade and lit up in a big happy smile. 'But what is your hostess doing? Interrogating her guests when there's supposed to be a party! Shall we go and meet the others? And then I'll go down to the cellar and get a bottle that has been waiting for an occasion just like this.'

★　★　★

After enduring Malcolm's lengthy analysis of the loopholes in the new tax law Duff made an excuse and went to sit at the bar to reward himself with a whisky.

'Well?' said a voice behind him. 'How was your day off with the family?'

'Fine, thanks,' he said without turning. Pointed to a bottle for the waiter and showed with two fingers that he wanted a double.

'And tonight?' Caithness asked. 'You still want to stay over at . . . the hotel?'

126

The code word for her bed. But he could hear the question was not only about tonight but the nights to come. She wanted him to repeat the old refrain: the assurance that he wanted her, he *didn't* want to return to his family in Fife. But this all took time, there were many aspects to consider. It was incomprehensible to him that Caithness didn't know him any better, that she doubted this could be what he really wanted. Perhaps that was why he answered with a certain defiance that he had been offered a bed at the casino.

'And do you want that? To stay here?'

Duff sighed. What did women want? Were they all going to tie him up, tether him to the bed head and feed him in the kitchen so that they could milk his wallet and testicles to overwhelm him with more offspring and a guilty conscience?

'No,' he said, looking at Macbeth. Considering he was the focus of the party, he seemed strangely burdened and ill at ease. Had the responsibility and gravity of his new post already intimidated the happy, carefree boy in him? Well, now it was too late, both for Macbeth and for himself. 'If you go first I'll wait a suitable length of time and follow you.'

He noticed her hesitate behind him. He met her eyes in the mirror behind the shelves of bottles. Saw she was about to touch him. Sent her an admonitory glance. She desisted. And left. *Jesus.*

Duff knocked back his drink. Got up to go over to Macbeth, who was leaning on the end of the bar. Time to congratulate him properly. But right at that moment Duncan came between them; people flocked around him, and Macbeth was lost in the melee. And when Duff saw him again, Macbeth was on his way out, rushing after Lady's skirt tails, which he saw leaving the room.

★ ★ ★

Macbeth caught Lady up as she was unlocking the wine cellar.

'I can't do it,' he said.

'What?'

'I can't kill my own chief commissioner.'

She looked at him.

She grabbed the lapels of his jacket, pulled him inside and closed the door. 'Don't fail me now, Macbeth. Duncan and his guards are set up in their rooms. Everything's ready. You've got the master key, haven't you?'

Macbeth took the key from his pocket and held it up for her. 'Take it. I can't do this.'

'Can't or won't?'

'Both. I *won't* do it to because I *can't* find the will for such villainy. It's wrong. Duncan's a good chief commissioner, and I can't do anything better than him. So what's the point, apart from feeding my ambition?'

'*Our* ambition! Because after hunger, cold, fear and lust there is nothing more than ambition, Macbeth. Because honour is the key to respect. And that is the master key. Use it!' She was still holding his lapels, and her mouth was so close to his he could taste the fury in her breath.

'Darling — ' he began.

'No! If you think Duncan is such an honourable man listen to how he killed Cawdor to spare himself the embarrassing revelations that might have leaked out if Cawdor had lived.'

'That's not true!'

'Ask him yourself.'

'You're only saying that to . . . to . . . '

'To steel your will,' she said. She let go and instead pressed her palms against the lapels as if to feel his heartbeat. 'Just think that you're going to kill a murderer, the way you killed the Norse Rider, then it'll be easy.'

'I don't *want* it to be easy.'

'If it's your morals that are getting the better of you, then just remember you're bound by the promise you made me last night, Macbeth. Or are you telling me that what I saw and interpreted as courage when you killed Ernest Collum was just a young man's recklessness because it wasn't your life at stake but my croupier's? While now, when you have to risk something yourself, you flee like a cowardly hyena.'

Her words were unreasonable but still hit home. 'You know that's not how it is,' he said in desperation.

'So how *can't* you keep the promise you made to me, Macbeth?'

He gulped. Searched feverishly for words. 'I . . . Can you say you keep *all* your promises?'

'Me? *Me?*' She emitted a piercing laugh of astonishment. 'To keep a promise to myself I wrenched my suckling child from my breast and smashed its head against a wall. So how could I break a promise to you, my only beloved?'

Macbeth stood looking at her. He was inhaling her breath now, her poisonous breath. He felt it weakening him second by second. 'But you don't realise, do you, that if this fails Duncan will cut your head off too?'

'It won't fail. Listen. I'm going to give Duncan a glass of this burgundy, and I'll insist that his bodyguards at least *taste* it. They won't notice anything, but they might become a little muddled later in the evening. And sleep like logs when they go to bed . . . '

'Yes, but — '

'Shh! You'll be using your daggers so there's no chance of them waking. Afterwards smear the blood on the blades all over the guards and leave the daggers in their beds. And later when you wake them — '

'I remember our plan. But it has weaknesses, and — '

'It's *your* plan, my love.' She grasped his chin with one hand and bit the lobe of his ear hard. 'And it's perfect. Everyone will realise the guards have been bought by Hecate; they were just too drunk to hide the traces of their crime.'

Macbeth closed his eyes. 'You can only give birth to boys, can't you?'

Lady gave a low chuckle. Kissed him on the neck.

Macbeth held her shoulders and pushed her away. 'You'll be the death of me, Lady, do you know that?'

She smiled. 'And you know everywhere you go, I go.'

8

The dinner was held in the casino restaurant. Duff was placed next to the hostess, who had Duncan on her other side. Macbeth sat opposite them with Caithness as his neighbour. Duff noticed that neither Caithness nor Macbeth spoke or ate much, but the atmosphere was still good and the table so wide it was hard to have a conversation across it. Lady chatted and seemed to be enjoying herself with Duncan, while Duff listened to Malcolm and concentrated on not yawning.

'Caithness looks beautiful tonight, doesn't she?'

Duff turned. It was Lady. She smiled at him, her large blue eyes innocent beneath fiery red hair.

'Yes, nearly as beautiful as you, ma'am,' Duff said but could hear his words lacked the spark that could have brought them to life.

'She's not only beautiful,' Lady said. 'I suppose, as a woman in the police, she must have sacrificed a lot to get where she is. Having a family, for example. I can see she's sacrificed having a family. Can't you too, Duff?'

Grey eyes. They were grey, not blue.

'All women who want to get on have to sacrifice something, I suppose,' Duff said, lifting his wine glass and discovering it was empty again. 'Family isn't the be-all and end-all for everyone. Don't you agree, ma'am?'

Lady shrugged. 'We humans are practical. If decisions we made once can't be changed, we do our best to defend them so that our errors won't haunt and torment us too much. I think that's the recipe for a happy life.'

'So you're afraid you'd be haunted if you saw your decisions in a true light?'

'If a woman is to get what she wants, she has to think

and act like a man and not consider the family. Her own or others'.'

Duff recoiled. He tried to catch her eye, but she had leaned forward to fill the glasses of the guests around her. And the next moment Duncan tapped his glass, stood up and coughed.

Duff watched Macbeth during the inspired thank-you speech, which paid homage not only to the hostess's dinner and the host's promotion but to the mission they had all signed up to: to make the town a place where it was possible to live. And he rounded off by saying that after a long week they deserved the rest the merciful Lord had granted them and they would be wise to use it because there was a good chance the chief commissioner wasn't going to be such a merciful god in the weeks to come.

He wished them a good night, stifled a yawn and proposed a toast to their hosts. During the ensuing applause Duff glanced across at Macbeth, wondering if he would return the toast — after all Duncan was the chief commissioner. But Macbeth just sat there, pale-faced and as stiff as a board, apparently caught off guard by the new situation, his new status and the new demands that he would have to face.

Duff pulled out Lady's chair for her. 'Thank you for everything this evening, ma'am.'

'Likewise, Duff. Have you got the key for your room?'

'Mm, I'll be staying . . . elsewhere.'

'Back home in Fife?'

'No, with a cousin. But I'll be here early tomorrow morning to pick up Duncan. We live in Fife, not far apart.'

'Oh, what time?'

'At seven. Duncan and I both have children and . . . Well, it's the weekend. All go, you know how it is.'

'Actually I don't,' Lady said with a smile. 'Sleep well and my regards to your cousin, Duff.'

One by one the guests left the bar and the gaming tables and went to their rooms or homes. Macbeth stood in reception shaking hands and mumbling hollow goodbyes, but at least there he didn't have to make conversation with the stragglers in the bar.

'You really don't look well,' Banquo said with a slight slur. He had just come out of the toilet and placed a heavy paw on Macbeth's shoulder. 'Get to bed now, so you don't infect other folk.'

'Thanks, Banquo. But Lady's still in the bar entertaining.'

'It's almost an hour now since the chief went to bed, so you're allowed to go too. I'll just drink up in the bar, then Fleance and I will go too. And I don't want to see you standing here like a doorman. OK?'

'OK. Goodnight, Banquo.'

Macbeth watched his friend walk somewhat unsteadily back to the bar. Looked at his watch. Seven minutes to midnight. It would happen in seven minutes. He waited for three. Then he straightened up, looked through the double doors to the bar, where Lady was standing and listening to Malcolm and Lennox. At that moment, as though she had felt his presence, she turned and their eyes met. She gave an imperceptible nod and he nodded back. Then she laughed at something Malcolm said, countering with something that made both of the men laugh. She was good.

Macbeth went up the stairs, let himself into his and Lady's suite. Put his ear to the door of the bodyguards' room. The snoring from inside was even, safe. Almost artless. He sat on the bed. Ran his hand over the smooth bedcover. The silk whispered beneath his rough fingertips. Yes, she was good. Better than he would ever be. And perhaps they could pull this off — perhaps the two of them, Macbeth and Lady, could make a difference, shape the town in their image, carry on what Duncan had started and take it further than he would ever have managed. They had the will, they had the strength and they could win people over. Of the people. For the people. With the people.

His fingers stroked the two daggers he had laid out on the bed. But for the fact that power corrupts and poisons, they wouldn't have needed to do this. If Duncan's heart had been pure and idealistic they could have discussed it, and Duncan would have seen that Macbeth was the best man to realise his dream of leading the town out of the darkness. For whatever dreams Duncan had, the common people of the town wouldn't follow an upper-class stranger from Capitol, would they? No, they needed one of their own. Duncan could have been the navigator, but Macbeth would have to be the captain — as long as he could get the crew to obey, to guide the boat to where they both wanted, into a safe harbour. But even if he accepted that a transfer of power was in the best interests of the town, Duncan would never surrender his post to Macbeth. Duncan, for all his virtue, was no better than any other person in power: he put his personal ambitions above everything else. See how he killed those who could damage his reputation or threaten his authority. Cawdor's body had still been warm when they got there.

Wasn't that so? Yes, it was. It was, it was.

Twelve o'clock.

Macbeth closed his eyes. He had to get into the zone. He counted down from ten. Opened his eyes. Swore, closed them again and counted down from ten again. Looked at his watch. Grabbed the daggers, stuffed them in the especially made shoulder holster with sheaths for two knives, one on each side. Then he went into the corridor. Passed the bodyguards' door and stopped outside Duncan's. Listened. Nothing. He drew a deep breath. Evaluations of a variety of scenarios had been done beforehand; the only thing left was the act itself. He inserted the master key into the lock, saw his reflection in the shiny door knob of polished brass, then gripped it and turned. Observed what he could in the corridor light, then he was inside and had closed the door behind him.

He held his breath in the darkness and listened to Duncan's breathing.

Calm, even.

Like Lorreal's. The director of the orphanage.

No, don't let that thought out now.

Duncan's breathing told him he was in bed and asleep. Macbeth went to the bathroom door, switched on the light inside and left the door slightly ajar. Enough light for what he was going to do.

What he was going to do.

He stood beside the bed and looked down at the unsuspecting sleeping man. Then he straightened up. What an irony. He raised a dagger. Killing a defenceless man — could anything be easier? The decision had been taken, now all he had to do was carry it out. And hadn't he already killed his first defenceless victim on the road to Forres, wasn't his virginity already gone, hadn't he paid his debt to Duff there and then, paid him back in the same currency Duff had run it up: cold blood. Seen Lorreal's hot blood streaming onto the white sheet, the blood that had looked black in the darkness. So what was stopping him now? How was this conspiracy different from when he and Duff had changed the crime scene so that all the evidence found in Forres would tally with the story they agreed they would tell? And the story at the orphanage they agreed they would tell. *And sometimes cruelty is on the side of the good, Macbeth.* He looked up from the blade glinting in the light from the bathroom.

He lowered the dagger.

He didn't have it in him.

But he had to do it. He *had* to. He had to have it in him. But what could he do if he wasn't up to it even in the zone?

He had to become the other Macbeth, the one he had buried so deep, the crazy flesh-eating corpse he had sworn he would never be again.

★   ★   ★

Banquo stared at the big, lifeless locomotive as he unbuttoned his flies. He swayed in the wind. He was a bit drunk, he knew that.

'Come on, Dad,' came Fleance's voice from behind him.

'What's the time, son?'

'I don't know, but the moon's up.'

'Then it's past twelve. There's a storm forecast tonight.' The gun holster hanging between the first and second loops on his belt was in his way. He unhooked it and passed it to Fleance.

His son took it with a resigned groan. 'Dad, this is a public place. You can't — '

'It's a public urinal, that's what it is,' Banquo slurred and at that moment registered a black-clad figure coming round the steam engine. 'Give me the gun, Fleance!'

The light fell on the man's face.

'Oh, it's just you.'

'Ah, it's you, is it?' Macbeth said. 'I was out for some air.'

'And I just had to air the old fella,' Banquo slurred. 'No, I *wasn't* about to piss on Bertha. After all, that would be — now they've closed St Joseph's Church — desecrating the last holy thing in this town.'

'Yes, maybe.'

'Is there anything up?' Banquo said, trying to relax. He always found it difficult to get going with strangers

136

nearby, but Macbeth and his son?

'No,' Macbeth said in a strangely neutral tone.

'I dreamed about the three sisters last night,' Banquo said. 'We haven't talked about it, but they got their prophecies spot on, didn't they. Or what do you reckon?'

'Oh, I'd forgotten them. Lets's talk about it another time.'

'Whenever,' Banquo said, sensing the flow coming.

'Well,' Macbeth said. 'Actually I was going to ask you — now you're my deputy in Organised Crime — but suppose something like that did happen, just as the sisters said it would?'

'Yes?' Banquo groaned. He had lost patience, started forcing it, and with that the flow stopped.

'I'd appreciate it if you joined me then too.'

'Become your deputy CC? Ha ha, yes, pull the other one.' Banquo suddenly realised that Macbeth wasn't joking. 'Of course, my boy, of course. You know I'm always willing to follow anyone who'll fight the good fight.'

They looked at each other. And then, as if a magic wand had been waved, it came. Banquo looked down, and there was a majestic golden jet splashing intrepidly over the locomotive's large rear wheel and running down onto the rail beneath.

'Goodnight, Banquo. Goodnight, Fleance.'

'Goodnight, Macbeth,' answered father and son in unison.

'Was Uncle Mac drunk?' Fleance asked when Macbeth had gone.

'Drunk? You know he doesn't drink.'

'Yes, I know, but he was so strange.'

'Strange?' Banquo grinned grimly as he watched the continuous stream with satisfaction. 'Believe me, that boy isn't *strange* when he gets high.'

'What is he then?'

'He goes crazy.'

The jet was suddenly swept to the side by a strong gust of wind.

'The storm,' Banquo said, buttoning up.

★   ★   ★

Macbeth went for a walk around the central station. When he came back Banquo and Fleance had gone, and he went into the large waiting room.

He scanned the room and instantly sorted the individuals there into the four relevant categories: those who sold, those who used, those who did both and those who needed somewhere to sleep, shelter from the rain and would soon be joining one of the first three. That was the path he himself had followed. From orphanage escapee receiving food and drink from officers of the Salvation Army to user who financed dope and food by selling.

Macbeth went over to an older, plump man in a wheelchair.

'A quarter of brew,' he said, and just the sound of the words made something that had been hibernating in his body wake up.

The man in the wheelchair looked up. 'Macbeth,' he said, spitting the name out in a shower of saliva. 'I remember you and you remember me. You're a policeman, and I don't sell dope, OK? So get the hell away from me.'

Macbeth walked on to the next dealer, a man in a checked shirt who was so hyped up he couldn't stand still.

'Do you think I'm an idiot?' he shouted. 'I am by the way. Otherwise I wouldn't be here, would I. But selling to a cop and ending up in clink for twenty-four hours when you know you can't go four hours without a fix?' He leaned back, and his laughter echoed beneath the ceiling. Macbeth went further in, along the corridor to the departures hall, and heard the dealer's cry resound behind him: 'Undercover cop coming, folks!'

'Hi, Macbeth,' came a thin, weak voice.

Macbeth turned. It was the young boy with the eyepatch. Macbeth went over to him and crouched down by the wall. The black patch had ridden up, allowing Macbeth to see inside the cavity's mysterious darkness.

'I need a quarter of brew,' Macbeth said. 'Can you help me?'

'No,' said the boy. 'I can't help anyone. Can you help me?'

Macbeth recognised something in his expression. It was like looking into a mirror. What the hell was he actually doing? He had, with the help of good people, managed to get away, and now he was back to this? To perform an act of villainy even the most desperate drug addict would shy away from? He could still refuse. He could take this boy with him to the Inverness. Give him food, a shower and a bed. Tonight could be very different from the way he had planned it, there was still that possibility. The possibility of saving himself. The boy. Duncan. Lady.

'Come on. Let's — ' Macbeth started.

'Macbeth.' The voice coming from behind him rumbled like thunder through the corridor. 'Your prayers have been heard. I have what you need.'

Macbeth turned. Lifted his eyes higher. And higher. 'How did you know I was here, Strega?'

'We have our eyes and ears everywhere. Here you are, a present from Hecate.'

Macbeth gazed down at the little bag that had dropped into his hand. 'I want to pay. How much?'

'Pay for a present? I think Hecate would take that as an insult. Have a good night.' Strega turned and left.

'Then I won't take it,' Macbeth called out and threw

the bag after her, but she had already been swallowed up the darkness.

'If you don't . . . ' said the one-eyed reedy voice. 'Is it OK if I . . . ?'

'Stay where you are,' Macbeth snarled without moving.

'What do you want to do?' the boy asked.

'Want?' Macbeth echoed. 'It's never what you *want* to do, but what you have to do.'

He walked towards the bag and picked it up. Walked back. Passing the boy's outstretched hand.

'Hey, aren't you going . . . ?'

'Go to hell,' Macbeth growled. 'I'll see you there.'

★ ★ ★

Macbeth went down the stairs to the stinking toilet, chased out a woman sitting on the floor, tore open the bag, sprinkled the powder onto the sink below the mirrors, crushed the lumps with the blunt side of a dagger and used the blade to chop it up into finer particles. Then he rolled up a banknote and sniffed the yellowy-white powder first up one nostril, then the other. It took the chemicals a surprisingly short time to pass through the mucous membranes into his blood. And his last thought before the dope-infected blood entered his brain was that it was like renewing an acquaintance with a lover. A much too beautiful, much too dangerous lover who hadn't aged a day in all these years.

★ ★ ★

'What did I tell you?' Hecate banged his stick on the floor by the CCTV monitors.

'You said there was nothing more predictable than a love-smitten junkie and moralist.'

'Thank you, Strega.'

140

* * *

Macbeth stopped at the top of the steps in front of the central station. Workers' Square swayed like a sea ahead of him; the breakers crashed beneath the cobblestones, sounding like the chattering of teeth as they rose and fell. And down below the Inverness there was a paddle steamer filled with the noise of music and laughter, and the light made it sparkle in the water running from its slowly rotating, roaring wheel.

Then he set off. Through the black night, back to the Inverness. He seemed to be gliding through the air, his feet off the ground. He floated through the door and into the reception area. The receptionist looked at him and gave him a friendly nod. Macbeth turned to the gaming room and saw that Lady, Malcolm and Duff were still talking in the bar. Then he went up the stairs as though he were flying, along the corridor until he stopped outside Duncan's door.

Macbeth inserted the master key in the lock, turned the knob and went in.

He was back. Nothing had changed. The bathroom door was still ajar, and the light inside was on. He walked over to the bed. Looked down at the sleeping police officer, put his left hand inside his jacket and found the handle of the dagger.

He raised his hand. It was so much easier now. Aimed for the heart. The way he had aimed at the heart carved into the oak tree. And the knife bored a hole between the names there. Meredith and Macbeth.

'Sleep no more! Macbeth is murdering sleep.'

Macbeth stiffened. Was it the chief commissioner, the dope or he himself who had spoken?

He looked down at Duncan's face. No, the eyes were still closed and his breathing calm and even. But as he watched, Duncan's eyes opened. Looked at him quietly. 'Macbeth?' The chief commissioner's eyes went to the dagger.

'I thought I heard s-s-sounds coming from here,' Macbeth said. 'I'll check.'

'My bodyguards . . . '

'I h-h-heard them snoring.'

Duncan listened for a few moments. Then he yawned. 'Good. Let them sleep. I'm safe here, I know. Thanks, Macbeth.'

'Not at all, sir.'

Macbeth walked towards the door. He wasn't floating any longer. A sense of relief, *happiness* even, spread through his body. He was saved. The chief commissioner had liberated him. Lady could do and say what she liked, but this stopped here. Five paces. He grabbed the door knob with his free hand.

Then a movement in the reflection on the polished brass.

As if in a fairground mirror and in the light from the bathroom door he saw — like in some absurd, distorted film — the chief commissioner pull something from under his pillow and point it at his back. A gun. Five paces. Throwing distance. Macbeth reacted instinctively. Whirled round. He was off balance, and the dagger left his hand while he was still moving.

9

Of course it had been Duff who had approached the two girls and asked to join them at their table. Macbeth went to the bar and bought them all beers, came back and heard Duff sounding off about Macbeth and him being the best two cadets in the final year at police college. Their future prospects looked more than rosy, and the girls should make a move if they knew what was good for them, he said. The two girls laughed, and the eyes of the girl called Meredith glinted, but she looked down when Macbeth tried to hold her gaze. When the bar closed, Macbeth accompanied Meredith to the gate and was rewarded with a friendly handshake and a telephone number. While, next morning, Duff went into great detail about how he had serviced the friend, Rita, in a narrow bed at the nurses' hall of residence, Macbeth rang Meredith the same evening and in a trembling voice invited her out for dinner.

He had ordered a table at Lyon's and knew it was a mistake the moment he saw the head waiter's knowing gaze. The elegant suit Duff had lent him was much too big, so he'd had to go for Banquo's, which was two sizes too small and twenty years out of date. Fortunately Meredith's dress, beauty and calm polite nature compensated. The only part of the French menu he understood was the prices. But Meredith explained and said that was how the French were: they refused to accept that they spoke a language that was no longer international, and they were so bad at English they couldn't bear the double ignominy of appearing idiots in their rivals' tongue.

'Arrogance and insecurity often go together,' she said.

143

'I'm insecure,' Macbeth said.

'I was thinking of your friend Duff,' she said. 'Why are you so insecure?'

Macbeth told her about his background. The orphanage. Banquo and Vera. Police college. She was so easy to talk to he was almost tempted to tell her everything, for one crazy moment even about Lorreal. But of course he didn't. Meredith said she had grown up in the western part of town, with parents who made sure their children lacked for nothing but who also made demands on them and were ambitious on their behalf, especially for her brothers.

'Protected, privileged and boring,' she said. 'Do you know I've never been to District 2 East.' She laughed when Macbeth refused to accept that could be true. 'Yes, it is! I never have!'

So after dinner he took her down to the riverbed. Walking along the potholed road alongside the run-down houses as far as Penny Bridge. And when he said goodnight outside the gate she leaned forward and kissed him on the cheek.

When he returned to his room Duff was still up. 'Spill the beans,' he ordered. 'Slowly and in detail.'

Two days later. Cinema. *Lord of the Flies*. They walked home under the same umbrella, Meredith's hand under his arm. 'How can children be so cruel and bloodthirsty?' she said.

'Why should children be any less cruel than adults?'

'They're born innocent!'

'Innocent and without any sense of morality. Isn't peaceful passivity just something that adults force children to learn so that we recognise our place in society and let them do what they like with us?'

They kissed at the gate. And on Sunday he took her for a walk in the woods on the other side of the tunnel. He had packed a picnic basket.

'You can cook!' she exclaimed excitedly.

'Banquo and Vera taught me. We used to come to this very spot.'

Then they kissed, she panted and he put his hand up her cotton dress.

'Wait . . . ' she said.

And he waited. Instead he carved a heart in the big oak and used the point of his knife to write their names. Meredith and Macbeth.

'She's ready to be plucked,' Duff told Macbeth when he came home and told him the details. 'I'm going to Rita's on Wednesday. Invite her here.'

Macbeth had opened a bottle of wine and lit candles when Meredith rang at the door. He was prepared. But not for what happened — for her loosening his belt as soon as they were inside the door and stuffing her hand down his trousers.

'D-d-don't,' he said.

She looked at him in surprise.

'S-s-stop.'

'Why are you stammering?'

'I d-d-don't want you to.'

She withdrew her hand, her cheeks burning with shame.

Afterwards they drank a glass of red wine in silence.

'I have to get up early tomorrow,' she said. 'Exams soon and . . . '

'Of course.'

Three weeks passed. Macbeth tried ringing several times, but the few times he got an answer Rita said that Meredith wasn't at home.

'You and Meredith are no longer dating, I take it,' Duff said.

'No.'

'Rita and I aren't either. Do you mind if I meet Meredith?'

'You'd better ask her.'

'I have.'

Macbeth gulped. It was as if he had a claw around his heart. 'Oh yes? And what did she say?'

'She said yes.'

'Did she? And when are you . . . ?'

'Yesterday. Just for a bite to eat, but . . . it was nice.'

The day after, Macbeth woke up and was sick. And it was only later he realised what this sickness was and that there was no remedy for a broken heart. You had to suffer your way through it and he did. Suffered in silence without mentioning her name to anyone but an old oak tree on the healthy side of the tunnel. And after a while the symptoms passed. Almost completely. And he discovered that it wasn't true what people said, that we can only fall in love once. But unlike Meredith, Lady was the sickness and remedy in one. Thirst and water. Desire and satisfaction. And now her voice reached him from across the sea, from across the night.

'Darling . . . '

Macbeth drifted through water and air, light and darkness.

'Wake up!'

'He opened his eyes. He was lying in bed. It had to be night still, for the room was dark. But there was a grainy element, a kind of imperceptible greyness that presaged dawn.

'At last!' she hissed in his ear. 'Where have you been?'

'Been?' Macbeth said, trying to hold on to a scrap of the dream. 'Haven't I been here?'

'Your body has, yes, but I've been trying to wake you for hours. It's as if you've been unconscious. What have you done?'

Macbeth was still holding on to the dream, but suddenly he didn't know whether it was a good dream or a nightmare. Duncan . . . He let go, and images whirled in the darkness.

'Your pupils,' she said, holding his face between her hands. 'You've taken dope, that's why.'

146

He squirmed away, from her, from the light. 'I needed it.'

'But you've done it?

'It?'

She shook him hard. 'Macbeth, darling, answer me! Have you done the deed you promised you would?'

'Yes!' He groaned and ran a hand across his face. 'No, I don't know.'

'You don't know?'

'I can see him in front of me with a dagger in him, but I don't know if it really happened or I just dreamed it.'

'There's a clean dagger here on the bedside table. You were supposed to have put both daggers in with the bodyguards after killing Duncan, one with each of them.'

'Yes, yes, I remember.'

'Is the other dagger with them? Pull yourself together!'

'Sleep no more. Macbeth is murdering sleep.'

'What?'

'He said that. Or I dreamed it.'

'We'd better go in and check.'

Macbeth closed his eyes, reached out for the dream — perhaps it could tell him. Rather that than go back in. But the dream had already slipped through his fingers. When he reopened his eyes Lady was standing with an ear to the wall.

'They're still snoring. Come on.' She grabbed the dagger from the bedside table.

Macbeth breathed in deeply. The day and its revealing light would soon be here. He swung his legs out of bed and discovered he was still fully dressed.

They went into the corridor. Not a sound to be heard. Those who stayed at the Inverness didn't usually get up early.

Lady unlocked the guards' room, and she and

Macbeth went in. Each was lying asleep in an armchair. But there were no daggers anywhere, and there was no blood smeared over their suits and shirts, as per their plan.

'I only dreamed it,' Macbeth whispered. 'Come on, let's drop this.'

'No!' Lady snarled and strode off to the door connecting to Duncan's room. Shifted the dagger to her right hand. Then, without any sign of hesitation, she tore open the door and went in.

Macbeth waited and listened.

Nothing.

He walked over to the door opening.

Grey light seeped in through the window.

She was standing on the opposite side of the bed with the dagger raised by her mouth. Squeezing the handle with both hands, her eyes wide with horror.

Duncan was in the bed. His eyes were open and seemed to be staring at something by the other door. Everything was sprayed with blood. The duvet, the gun lying on the duvet, the hand on the gun. And the handle of the dagger sticking out of Duncan's neck like a hook.

'Oh darling,' Lady whispered. 'My man, my hero, my saviour, Macbeth.'

Macbeth opened his mouth to say something, but at that moment the total Sunday silence was broken by a barely audible but continuous ringing sound from below.

Lady looked at her watch. 'That's Duff. He's early! Darling, go downstairs and keep him busy while I sort this out.'

'You've got three minutes,' Macbeth said. 'Don't touch the blood. It's semi-coagulated and will leave prints. OK?'

She angled back her head and smiled at him. 'Hi,' she said. 'There you are.'

And he knew what she meant. At last he was there. The zone.

Standing in front of the door to the Inverness, Duff shivered and longed to be back in Caithness's warm bed. He was about to press the bell a second time when the door opened.

'Sir, the entrance to the casino is down there.'

'No, I'm here to collect Chief Commissioner Duncan.'

'Oh, right. Come in. I'll ring and say you're here. Inspector Duff, isn't it?'

Duff nodded. They had really first-class staff at the Inverness. He sank down into one of the deep armchairs.

'No answer, sir,' said the receptionist. 'Neither there nor in his bodyguards' room.'

Duff looked at his watch. 'What's the chief commissioner's room number?'

'Two thirteen, sir.'

'Would you mind if I went up to wake him?'

'Not at all.'

Duff was on his way up the stairs when a familiar figure came bounding down towards him.

'Morning, Duff,' Macbeth called cheerily. 'Jack, could you go to the kitchen and get us both a cup of strong coffee.'

The receptionist went off.

'Thanks, Macbeth, but I've been told to collect Duncan.'

'Is it that urgent? And aren't you a bit early?'

'We've arranged a time to be home, and I remembered that Kenneth Bridge was still out of action, so we'll have to take the detour over the old bridge.'

'Relax.' Macbeth laughed, grabbing Duff under the arm. 'She won't be setting a stopwatch, will she? And you look exhausted, so if you're driving you'll need some strong coffee. Come on, let's sit down.'

Duff hesitated. 'Thanks, my friend, but that'll have to wait.'

'A cup of coffee and she won't notice the smell of whisky quite as easily.'

'I'm considering becoming a teetotaller like you.'

'Are you?'

'Booze leads to three things: a colourful nose, sleep and pissing. In Duncan's case, obviously sleep. I'll go up and — '

Macbeth held on to his arm. 'And booze is lust's dupe, I've heard. Increases your lust but reduces performance. How was your night? Tell me. Slowly and in detail.'

Duff arched an eyebrow. Slowly and in detail. Was he using the interrogation term from their police college days as a jokey parody or did he know something? No, Macbeth didn't talk in riddles. He didn't have the patience or the ability. 'There's not much to tell. I stayed with a cousin.'

'Eh? You never told me you had any family. I thought your grandfather was the last relation you had. Look, here's the coffee. Just put it on the table, Jack. And try ringing Duncan again.'

Reassured that the receptionist was on the case, Duff went down the steps and greedily reached for the coffee. But stayed standing.

'The family, yes,' Macbeth said. 'It's a source of a constant guilty conscience, isn't it?'

'Yes, maybe,' said Duff, who had burned his tongue with his first sip and was now blowing on the coffee.

'How are they? Are they enjoying Fife?'

'Everyone enjoys Fife.'

'Duncan still isn't answering his phone, sir.'

'Thanks, Jack. Keep trying. Lots of people will have heavy heads this morning.'

Duff put down his cup. 'Macbeth, I think I'll wake

him first and drink coffee afterwards, so we can get going.'

'I'll go up with you. He's next to us,' Macbeth said, taking a sip of his coffee. He spilled it on his hand and jacket sleeve. 'Whoops. Have you got a paper towel, Jack?'

'I'll just — '

'Hang about, Duff. That's it, yes. Thanks, Jack. Come on, let's go.'

They walked up the stairs.

'Have you hurt yourself?' Duff asked.

'No. Why?'

'I've never seen you climb stairs so slowly.'

'I might have pulled a muscle during the Norse Rider chase.'

'Hm.'

'Otherwise. Sleep well?'

'No,' Duff said. 'It was a terrible night. Thunder, lightning and rain.'

'Yes, it was a bad night.'

'So you didn't sleep either?'

'Well, I did — '

Duff turned and looked at him.

' — after the worst of the storm had died down,' Macbeth finished. 'Here we are.'

Duff knocked. Waited and knocked again. Grabbed the door knob. The door was locked. And he had a sense, a sense something was not as it should be.

'Is there a master key?'

'I'll go and ask Jack,' Macbeth said.

'Jack!' Duff shouted. And then again, from the bottom of his lungs: 'Jack!'

After a few seconds the receptionist's head appeared over the edge of the stairs. 'Yes, sir?'

'Have you got a master key?'

'Yes, sir.'

'Come here and open the door at once.'

The receptionist ran up to them, taking short steps,

rummaged in his jacket pocket and pulled out a key, put it in the lock and twisted.

Duff opened the door.

They stood staring. The first person to speak was the receptionist.

'Holy shit.'

★   ★   ★

Macbeth examined the scene, conscious of the door threshold pressing against the sole of his foot, and heard Duff smash the glass of the fire alarm, which immediately began to howl. The dagger had been removed from the right-hand side of Duncan's neck and Lady had added a stab on the left. The gun on the duvet had also been removed. Otherwise everything appeared to be how it had been.

'Jack!' Duff called over the howl. 'Get everyone out of their rooms and assemble them in reception now. Not a word about what you've seen, all right?'

'All r-right, sir.'

Doors down the corridor opened. Out of the closest came Lady, barefoot and in her dressing gown.

'What's up, darling? Is there a fire?'

She was good. They were back following the plan, he was still in the zone, and Macbeth felt at this second, at this moment, with everything apparently in chaos, that everything was actually on track. Right now he and the woman he loved were unbeatable, right now they were in total control — of the town, fate, the orbit of the stars. And he felt it now, it was like a high, as strong as anything Hecate could offer.

'Where on earth are his bodyguards?' Duff shouted, furious.

They hadn't imagined it would be Duff in the role of witness to what was about to happen, but one of the more perplexed and frightened overnight guests they had placed in neighbouring rooms, such as Malcolm. But now Duff was here he was impossible to ignore.

'In here, darling,' Macbeth said. 'You too, Duff.'

He pushed them into Duncan's room and closed the door. Took his service pistol from the holster on his trouser belt. 'Listen carefully now. The door was locked and there was no sign of a break-in. The only person who has a master key to this room is Jack . . . '

'And me,' said Lady. 'I think so anyway . . . '

'Apart from that, there's only one possibility.' Macbeth pointed to the door to the adjacent room.

'His own bodyguards?' Lady said in horror and put a hand to her mouth.

Macbeth cocked his gun. 'I'm going in to check.'

'I'll go with you,' Duff said.

'No, you won't,' Macbeth said. 'This is my business, not yours.'

'And I choose to ma — '

'You'll choose to do what I tell you, Inspector Duff.'

Macbeth initially saw surprise in Duff's face. Afterwards it slowly sank in: the head of Organised Crime outranked the head of Homicide.

'Take care of Lady, will you, Duff?'

Without waiting for an answer Macbeth opened the door to the guards' room, stepped inside and closed the door behind him. The bodyguards were still in their chairs. One of them grunted; perhaps the fire alarm was penetrating the heavy veil of drugs.

Macbeth struck him with the back of his hand.

One eye half-opened, its gaze floated around the room and landed on Macbeth. It remained there before gradually taking in his body.

★ ★ ★

Andrianov registered that his black suit jacket and white shirt were covered with blood, then he felt that

153

something was missing. The weight of his gun in its holster. He put a hand inside his jacket and down into the holster, where his fingers found instead of his service pistol cold sharp steel and something sticky . . . The bodyguard removed his hand and looked at it. Blood? Was he still dreaming? He groaned, a section of his brain received what it interpreted as signals of danger, and he desperately tried to collect himself, automatically looked around, and there, on the floor beside his chair he saw his gun. And his colleague's gun, beside the chair where he lay, apparently asleep.

'What . . . ' Andrianov mumbled, looking into the muzzle of the gun held by the man in front of him.

'Police!' the man shouted. It was Macbeth. The new head of . . . of . . . 'Hold the guns where I can see them or I'll shoot.'

Andrianov blinked in his confusion. Why did it feel as if he was lying in a bog? What had he taken?

'Don't point that gun at me!' Macbeth shouted. 'Don't . . . '

Something told Andrianov that he shouldn't reach for the gun on the floor. The man in front of him wouldn't shoot him if he sat still. But it didn't help. Perhaps all the hours, days, years as a bodyguard had created an instinct, a reaction which was no longer steered by will, *to protect without a thought for your own life*. Or perhaps that was just how he was and why he had applied to work in this branch of service.

Andrianov reached out for the gun, and his life and reasoning were interrupted by a bullet that bored through his forehead, brain and the back of the chair and didn't stop until it met the wall with the golden-thread wallpaper that Lady had bought for a minor fortune in Paris. The explosion sent a convulsion through his colleague's body, but he never managed to regain consciousness before he too got a bullet through the forehead.

Duff made for the door as the first shot went off.

But Lady held him back. 'He said you — '

A second shot rang out, and Duff freed himself from her grasp. Ripped open the door and charged in. And stood in the middle of the floor looking around. Two men, each in a chair with a third eye in his forehead.

'Norse Riders,' Macbeth said, putting the smoking gun back in its holster. 'Sweno's behind this.'

There was shouting and banging on the corridor door.

'Let them in,' Macbeth said.

Duff did as he was told.

'What's going on?' Malcolm gasped, out of breath. 'Heavens above, are they . . . ? Who . . . ?'

'Me,' said Macbeth.

'They pulled their guns,' Duff said.

Malcolm's eyes jumped in bewilderment from Duff back to Macbeth. 'On you? Why?'

'Because I was going to arrest them,' Macbeth said.

'What for?' Lennox asked.

'Murder.'

'Sir,' Duff said, looking at Malcolm, 'I'm afraid we have bad news.'

He could see Malcolm's eyes narrowing behind the square glasses as he leaned forward like a boxer bracing himself for the punch he wouldn't see yet sensed was on its way. Everyone turned to the figure that had appeared in the doorway to the next room.

'Chief Commissioner Duncan is dead,' Lady said. 'Stabbed with a knife while he was sleeping.'

The last sentence made Duff automatically turn towards Macbeth. Not because it said anything he didn't already know, but because it was an echo of the same sentence uttered early one morning in an

155

orphanage so many years ago.

Their eyes met for a brief instant before both of them looked away.

PART TWO

10

The morning Chief Commissioner Duncan was found dead in bed at Inverness Casino was the second time in its history that Lady had immediately ordered the building to be cleared of customers and a CLOSED sign to be hung up outside.

Caithness arrived with everyone she could muster from Forensics and they closed the whole of the first floor.

The other officers who had stayed the night gathered around the roulette table in the empty gaming room.

Duff looked at Deputy Chief Commissioner Malcolm sitting at the end of the makeshift conference table. He had taken off his glasses, perhaps to clean them, at least that was what he was doing as he stared fixedly at the green felt, as though answers to all the questions lay there. Malcolm was the highest-ranking officer present, and Duff had occasionally wondered whether the reason he walked with such a stoop was that Malcolm, a bureaucrat surrounded by people with practical police experience, felt he was on such thin ice that he automatically leaned forward to catch any advice, any whispered hints. And perhaps Malcolm's wan complexion was not down to the previous night's drinking but the fact that he had suddenly become acting chief commissioner.

Malcolm breathed on his glasses and kept cleaning them. He didn't look up. As though he didn't dare meet the gazes directed at him, colleagues waiting for him to speak.

Duff was perhaps too harsh. Everyone knew that in chiselling out Duncan's programme Malcolm had been both the chisel and the hammer. But could he lead them? The others had years of experience leading their respective units, while Malcolm had spent days running two stooped paces behind Duncan like a kind of overpaid assistant.

'Gentlemen,' Malcolm said, staring at the green felt. 'A great man has left us. And at this juncture that's all I intend to say about Duncan.' He put on his glasses, raised his head and studied those around the table. 'As chief commissioner he would not have allowed us to sink into sentimentality and despair at such a pass, he would have demanded that we did what we're employed to do: find the guilty party, or parties, and put them under lock and key. Tears and commemorative words will have to come afterwards. At this meeting let's plan and coordinate what to do first. The next meeting will be at HQ at six this evening. I suggest the first thing you do after this meeting is to ring your wives and so on — '

Malcolm's gaze landed on Duff, but Duff couldn't work out if there was any intentional subtext.

' — and say you're unlikely to be home for a while.' He paused for a moment. 'Because first of all you're going to arrest the person who took Chief Commissioner Duncan from us.' Long pause. 'Duff, you've got the Homicide Unit. I want an interim report for the meeting in an hour, including whatever Caithness and her team have or haven't found at the crime scene.'

'Right.'

'Lennox, I want a full background check on the bodyguards and details of their movements before the murder. Where they were, who they spoke to, what they bought, any changes in their bank accounts, some tough questioning of family and friends. Requisition any resources you need.'

'Thank you, sir.'

'Macbeth, you've already contributed a lot to this case, but I need more. See if Organised Crime can link this with the big players, those who would profit most from getting rid of Duncan.'

'Isn't it pretty obvious?' Macbeth said. 'We've dumped Sweno's dope in the river, killed two and arrested half the Norse Riders. This is Sweno's revenge, and — '

'It's not obvious,' Malcolm said.

The others stared at the deputy chief commissioner in surprise.

'Sweno has everything to gain by Duncan continuing his project.' Malcolm tapped on some gambling chips that had been left on the cloth after the hasty evacuation. 'What was Duncan's first promise to this town? He was going to arrest Hecate. And now, with the Norse Riders down for the count, Duncan would have focused all the police resources on precisely that. And if Duncan had succeeded what would he have done?'

'He would have cleaned up the market for Sweno so that he could make a comeback,' Lennox said.

'Quite honestly,' Macbeth said, 'do you really think a vindictive Sweno would think that rationally?' Malcolm raised an eyebrow a fraction. 'A man from the working classes, with no education or any other help, who has run one of the most profitable businesses in this town for more than thirty years. Could he be financially rational? Is he capable of putting aside a thirst for revenge when he can see what's good for business?'

'OK,' Duff said. 'Hecate's the one with the most to gain from Duncan's removal, so you assume he's behind this.' He was looking at Malcolm.

'I'm not assuming anything, but Duncan's extreme prioritisation of the hunt for Hecate has been, as we know, much debated, and from Hecate's point of view anyone who succeeds Duncan would be preferable.'

'Especially if his successor were someone Hecate had tabs on,' Duff said. Realising at once what he had insinuated, he closed his eyes. 'Sorry. I didn't mean to . . . '

161

'That's fine,' Malcolm said. 'We can speak and think freely here, and what you said follows from my reasoning. Hecate might think he would have an easier time than under Duncan. So let's show him how wrong he is.' Malcolm pushed all the chips onto black. 'So our provisional hypothesis is Hecate, but let's hope we know more by six o'clock. To work.'

★　★　★

Banquo could feel sleep letting go. Felt the dream letting go. Felt Vera letting go. He blinked. Was it the church bells that had woken him? No. There was someone in the room. A person sitting by the window and looking down at the framed photograph, who, without looking up, asked, 'Hangover?'

'Macbeth? How . . . ?'

'Fleance let me in. He's taken over my room, I see. Even the winkle-pickers you bought me.'

'What's the time?'

'And there was me thinking pointed shoes were way out of fashion.'

'That was why you left them here. But Fleance will wear anything if he knows it was once yours.'

'Books and school stuff everywhere. He's hard-working, he's got the right attitude to get to the top.'

'Yes, he's getting there.'

'But, as we know, that's not always enough to get to the top. You're one of many, so it's a question of opportunity. Having the skill and the courage to strike when the opportunity presents itself. Do you remember who took this picture?'

Macbeth held it up. Fleance and Banquo under the dead apple tree. The shadow of the photographer falling across them.

'You did. What do you want?' Banquo rubbed his face. Macbeth was right: he did have a hangover.

'Duncan's dead.'

Banquo's hands dropped to the duvet. 'What was that you said?'

'His bodyguards stabbed him in the neck while he was asleep at the Inverness last night.'

Banquo felt nausea on the march and had to breathe in several times to stop himself throwing up.

'This is the opportunity,' Macbeth said. 'That is, it's a parting of the ways. From here one way goes to hell and the other to heaven. I'm here to ask which you'll choose.'

'What do you mean?'

'I want to know if you'll follow me.'

'I've already answered that. And the answer's yes.'

Macbeth turned to him. Smiled. 'And you can say that without asking whether it'll lead to heaven or hell?' His face was pale, his pupils abnormally small. Had to be the sharp morning light because if Banquo hadn't known Macbeth better he would have said he was back on dope. But the moment he was about to push that thought away the certainty broke over him like a sudden freezing-cold deluge.

'Was it you?' Banquo said. 'Was it you who killed him?'

Macbeth tilted his head and studied Banquo. Studied him the way you study a parachute before you jump, a woman before you try to kiss her for the first time.

'Yes,' he said. 'I killed Duncan.'

Banquo had difficulty breathing. Squeezed his eyes shut. Hoping that Macbeth, that *this* would be gone when he opened them again. 'And what now?'

'Now I have to kill Malcolm,' he heard Macbeth say. 'That is, *you* have to kill Malcolm.'

Banquo opened his eyes.

'For me,' Macbeth said. 'And for my crown prince, Fleance.'

11

Banquo sat in the frugal light of the cellar listening to Fleance stamping to and fro upstairs. The boy wanted to go out. Meet friends. Maybe a girl. It would be good for him.

Banquo let the chain slide through his fingers.

He had said yes to Macbeth. Why? Why had he crossed this boundary so easily? Was it because of Macbeth's promise that he was of the people, with the people and for the people, in a way that an upper-class man like Malcolm could never be? No. It was because you simply couldn't say no when it was about a son. And even less when it was about two.

Macbeth had described it as following fate's call, clearing a path to the chief commissioner's office. He hadn't said anything about Lady being the brains behind it. He hadn't needed to. Macbeth preferred simple plans. Plans that didn't require too much thinking in critical situations. Banquo closed his eyes. Tried to imagine it. Macbeth taking over as chief commissioner and running the town with absolute power, the way Kenneth had done but with the honest aim of making the town a better place for all its inhabitants. If you want to make all the drastic changes that are needed, the slowness of democracy and the free rein it gives simple-mindedness are no good. A strong, just hand. And so, by the time Macbeth is too old, he will let Fleance take over at the helm. By then Banquo will have died of old age, happy. Perhaps that was why he couldn't imagine it.

Banquo heard the front door slam.

But it's obvious, even if visions of this nature take time to become completely clear.

He put on his gloves.

★　★　★

It was half past five and the rain was hammering down on the cobblestones and on the windscreen of Malcolm's Chevelle 454 SS as he wound his way through the streets. He was aware it was stupid to buy a petrol guzzler in the middle of an oil crisis, and even if he had bought it second-hand for what he considered a reasonable price, he had fallen short in the responsibility argument. First of all, with his ecology-conscious daughter, then with Duncan, who had underscored the significance of leaders showing moderation. In the end Malcolm had said what he felt: he had loved these American exaggerations of cars ever since he was a boy, and Duncan had said that at least it showed economists were humans too.

He had quickly popped home to have a shower and change his clothes, which fortunately didn't take long because it was a Sunday and there was very little traffic. A large press gathering awaited him at the entrance to HQ, probably hoping for a comment or a better picture than they would get at the press conference at half past seven. The mayor, Tourtell, had already been on TV to make a statement. 'Incomprehensible', 'tragedy', 'our thoughts go out to the family' and 'the town must stand united against this evil' was what he had said, only accompanied by a great many more words. Malcolm's, by contrast, minimal comment had been to ask the press for their understanding; his focus was now on the investigation, and he referred them to the press conference.

Malcolm drove down the ramp to the basement garage, nodded to the guard, who opened the barrier, and swung in. The distance from your parking slot to the lift was in direct proportion to your place in the hierarchy. And when Malcolm backed into his slot it struck him that, from a formal point of view, he *could*

165

have actually parked in the one that was closest.

He was about to take out the ignition key when the door on the passenger side opened and someone slipped into the back, sliding over behind the driver's seat. And for the first time since Duncan's murder Malcolm confronted the thought. With the chief commissioner's job came not only a parking slot closer to the lift but also a death threat, whenever, wherever; security was a privilege accorded to those who parked further away.

'Start up the car,' the person in the back seat said.

Malcolm looked in the rear-view mirror. The person had moved so quickly and so soundlessly that he could only conclude SWAT training was effective. 'Anything wrong, Banquo?'

'Yes, sir. We've uncovered plans for an attack on your life.'

'Inside police HQ?'

'Yes. Drive slowly, please. We have to get away. We don't know who is involved in the force yet, but we think they're the same people who killed Duncan.'

Malcolm knew he should be frightened. And he *was*. But not as frightened as he could have been. Often it was trivial situations — like standing on a ladder or being surrounded by angry wasps — that could trigger pathetic panic-like reactions. But now, just like this morning, it was as though the situation didn't permit that type of fear; on the contrary it sharpened your ability to think fast and rationally, strengthened your resolve and, paradoxically, calmed him down.

'If that's the case, how do I know you're not one of them, Banquo?'

'If I'd wanted to kill you, you would already be dead, sir.'

Malcolm nodded. Something about Banquo's tone told him that the physically smaller and much older man would probably have been able to do so with his bare hands if he so wished.

'So where are we going?'

'To the container harbour, sir.'

'Why not home to — '

'You don't want your family caught up in this mess, sir. I'll explain when we're there. Drive. I'll slump down in the seat. Best no one sees me and realises you've been informed.'

Malcolm drove out, received a nod from the guard, the barrier was lifted and he was back out in the rain.

'I have a meeting in — '

'That'll be taken care of.'

'And the press conference?'

'That too. What you should think about now is you. And your daughter.'

'Julia?' Malcolm could feel it now. The panic.

'She'll be taken care of, sir. Just drive now. We'll soon be there.'

'What are we going to do?'

'Whatever has to be done.'

Five minutes later they drove through the gates of the container harbour, which in recent years had been left open as all attempts to keep the homeless and thieves out had achieved had been smashed fences and locks. It was Sunday and the quay was deserted.

'Park behind the shed there,' Banquo said.

Malcolm did as instructed, parking beside a Volvo saloon.

'Sign this,' Banquo said, holding a sheet of paper and a pen between the front seats.

'What is it?' Malcolm said.

'A few lines written on your typewriter,' Banquo said. 'Read it aloud.'

'*The Norse Riders threatened they would kill my daughter — *' Malcolm stopped.

'Carry on,' Banquo said.

Malcolm cleared his throat. ' *— Julia, if I didn't help them to kill the chief commissioner,*' he read. '*But now they have a hold on me and they've told me to perform* other services for them, too. I know that for as long as I'm alive the threat to my daughter will always be there. That is why — and because of the shame I feel for what I've done — I've decided to drown myself.'

'That is in fact true,' Banquo said. 'Only the signature on that letter can save your daughter.'

Malcolm turned to Banquo on the back seat. Stared into the muzzle of the gun he was holding in his gloved hand.

'There isn't any attempt on my life. You lied.'

'Yes and no,' Banquo said.

'You tricked me into coming here so that you could kill me and dump me in this canal.'

'You'll drown yourself, as it says in the letter.'

'Why should I?'

'Because the alternative is that I shoot you in the head now, drive to your house and then the suicide letter looks like this.' Banquo passed him another sheet of paper. 'Just the ending has been changed.'

'For as long as my daughter and I are alive, the threat will always be there. That's why I've chosen to take our lives and spare her the shame of what I've done and a life of endless fear.' Malcolm blinked. He understood the words, they made sense, yet still he had to reread the letter.

'Sign now, Malcolm.' Banquo's voice sounded almost comforting.

Malcolm closed his eyes. It was so quiet in the car that he could hear the creak of the trigger springs in Banquo's gun. Then he opened his eyes, grabbed the pen and signed his name on the first letter. Metal rattled on the back seat. 'Here,' said Banquo. 'Put them around your waist under your coat.'

Malcolm appraised the tyre chains Banquo held out. A weight.

He took them and wrapped them around his waist while his brain tried to find a way out.

'Let me see,' Banquo said, tightening the chains. Then he threaded through a padlock and clicked it shut. Placed the signed letter on the passenger seat and on top a key Malcolm assumed was for the padlock.

'Come on.' They got out into the rain. With his gun Banquo prodded Malcolm along the edge of the quay following a narrow canal that cut in from the main docks. Containers stood like walls on both sides of the canal. Even if people were out walking on the quay they wouldn't see Malcolm and Banquo where they were.

'Stop,' Banquo said.

Malcolm stared across the black sea, which lay flat, beaten down and tamed by the lashing rain. Lowered his gaze and looked down into the oil-covered greenish-black water, then turned his back to the sea and fixed his eyes on Banquo.

Banquo raised his gun. 'Jump, sir.'

'You don't look like someone intending to kill, Banquo.'

'With all due respect, sir, I don't think you know what such people look like.'

'True enough. But I'm a fairly good judge of character.'

'Have been up to now.'

Malcolm stretched his arms out to the side. 'Push me then.'

Banquo moistened his lips. Changed his grip on the gun.

'Well, Banquo? Show me the killer in you.'

'You're cool for a suit, sir.'

Malcolm lowered his arms. 'That's because I know something about loss, Banquo. Just like you. I've learned that we can afford to lose most things. But then there are some we cannot, that will stop us existing even more than if we lose our own lives. I know that you lost your wife to the illness which this town has given to its inhabitants.'

'Oh yes? How do you know that?'

'Because Duncan told me. And he did so because I lost my first wife to the same illness. And we talked about how we could help to create a town where this wouldn't happen, where even the town's most powerful industrial magnates would face trial for breaking the law, where a murder is a murder, whether it's with a weapon or by gassing the town's inhabitants until their eyes go yellow and they smell like a corpse.'

'So you've already lost the unloseable.'

'No. You can lose your wife and your life still has meaning. Because you have a child. A daughter. A son. It's our children who are unloseable, Banquo. If I save Julia by dying now, that's the way it has to be, it's worth it. And there will be others after me and Duncan. You might not believe me, but this world is full of people who want what is good, Banquo.'

'And who decides what is good? You and the other big bosses?'

'Ask your heart, Banquo. Your brain will deceive you. Ask your heart.'

Malcolm saw Banquo shift his weight from one foot to the other. Malcolm's mouth and throat were dry, he was already hoarse. 'You can hang as many chains on us as you like, Banquo, it won't make any difference because we'll float to the surface. What is good rises. I swear I'm going to float to the surface somewhere and reveal your misdeeds.'

'They aren't mine, Malcolm.'

'Hecate. Yours. You're in the same boat. And we both know which river that boat will cross and where you'll soon end up.'

Banquo nodded slowly. 'Hecate,' he said. 'Exactly.'

'What?'

Banquo seemed to be staring at a point on Malcolm's forehead. 'You're right, sir. I work for Hecate.' Malcolm tried to decipher Banquo's faint smile. Water was running down his face as though he were crying, Malcolm thought. Was he hesitating? Malcolm knew he would have to continue talking, to make Banquo talk, because every word, every second prolonged his life. Increased the fading tiny chance that Banquo might change his mind or someone might appear.

'Why drowning, Banquo?'

'Eh?'

'Shooting me in the car and making it look like suicide would be easier.'

Banquo shrugged. 'There are many ways to skin a cat. The crime scene is underwater. No traces if they suspect murder. And drowning is nicer. Like going to sleep.'

'What makes you think that?'

'I know. I almost drowned twice in my youth.'

The barrel of Banquo's gun had sunk a fraction. Malcolm estimated the distance between them.

Malcolm swallowed. 'Why did you almost drown, Banquo?'

'Because I grew up on the east side of town and never learned to swim. Isn't it funny that here in a town on the edge of the sea there are people who die if they fall in? So I tried to teach my boy to swim. The odd thing is he didn't learn either. Perhaps because it was a non-swimmer trying to teach him. If we sink, they sink, that's how our fates are passed on. But people like you can swim, Malcolm.'

'Hence the chains, I assume.'

'Yes.' The gun barrel was raised again. The hesitation was gone and the determination back in Banquo's eyes. Malcolm took a deep breath. The chance had been there and now it wasn't.

'Good people or not,' Banquo said, 'you have the buoyancy we lack. And I have to be sure you will stay under the water. And never rise to the surface again. If you don't I won't have done my job. Do you understand?'

'Understand?'

'Give me your police badge.'

Malcolm took the brass badge from his jacket pocket and gave it to Banquo, who immediately threw it. It flew over the edge of the quay, hit the water and sank. 'It's brass. It's shiny but will sink right to the bottom. That's gravity, sir, it drags everything with it into the mud. You have to disappear, Malcolm. Disappear for ever.'

★   ★   ★

In the meeting room Macbeth looked at his watch. Twenty-nine minutes past six. The door opened again, and a person Macbeth recognised as Lennox's assistant stuck her head in, said it still wasn't possible to get in contact with Malcolm; all they knew was he arrived at HQ, turned round in the garage and left, and no one, not even his daughter Julia, knew where he was.

'Thanks, Priscilla,' Lennox said and turned to the others. 'Then I think we should start this meeting by — '

Macbeth knew this was the moment. The moment Lady had spoken about, the moment of the leadership void, when everyone would unconsciously regard the person who took the initiative as the new leader. For that reason his interruption came over loud and clear.

'Excuse me, Lennox.' Macbeth turned to the door. 'Priscilla, could you organise a search for Malcolm and his car? For the time being, radio only patrol cars. And phrase it as low key as possible. HQ wishes to contact him ASAP. That kind of thing, thank you.' He turned to the others. 'Sorry to requisition your assistant, Lennox, but I think most of us here share my unease. OK, let's start the meeting. Anyone object if I chair it until Malcolm arrives?'

He scanned the table. Caithness. Lennox. Duff. Saw how they had to think before they concluded what

Lennox said stiffly after a clearing of the throat: 'You're the next in command, Macbeth. Away you go.'

'Thank you, Lennox. Would you mind, by the way, closing the window behind you? Let's start with the bodyguards. Has Anti-Corruption got anything there?'

'Not yet,' Lennox said, trying to close the latches. 'There's nothing to suggest irregularities or anything one might deem suspicious. In fact, the lack of irregularities is the only suspicious thing.'

'Nothing suspicious, new connections, no sudden purchasing of luxury goods or bank account movements?'

Lennox shook his head. 'They seem as clean as shining armour.'

'My guess is they *were* clean,' Duff said. 'But even the cleanest knights can be poisoned and corrupted if you can find the chink in their armour. And Hecate found that gap.'

'Then we can, too,' Macbeth said. 'Keep searching, Lennox.'

'I will.' His tone suggested a space for *sir* at the end. It wasn't spoken, but everyone had heard it.

'You mentioned you spoke to the undercover guys in your old section, Duff?'

'They say the murder came as a shock to everyone working on the street. No one knew anything. But everyone takes it as a foregone conclusion that Hecate's behind it. A young guy down at the central station mentioned something about a police officer asking for dope — I don't know if it was one of our undercover drugs men, but it definitely wasn't either of the bodyguards. We'll continue to look for clues that could lead us to where Hecate is. But it's — as we know — at least as hard as finding Sweno.'

'Thanks, Duff. Crime scene investigation, Caithness?'

'Predicted finds,' she said, looking at the notes in front of her. 'We've identified various fingerprints in the deceased's room and they match those of the three maids, the bodyguards and those who were in the room — Lady, Macbeth and Duff. As well as a set of prints we couldn't identify for a while, but now we have a match with the prints of the previous occupants of the room. So when I say predicted finds that's not exactly true; usually hotel rooms are full of unidentified fingerprints.'

'The owner of the Inverness takes cleaning very seriously,' Macbeth said drily.

'Pathology confirms that the direct cause of death was two stab wounds. The wounds match the daggers that were found. And although the daggers were cleaned on the sheet and the bodyguards' own clothing there was still more than enough blood on the blades and handles to establish it came from the deceased.'

'Can we say Duncan?' Macbeth asked. 'Instead of deceased.'

'As you wish. One dagger is bloodier than the other as it was the one that cut the dece — erm Duncan's carotid artery, hence the splash of blood over the duvet, as you can see on this photograph.' Caithness pushed a black-and-white photo into the middle of the table, which the others dutifully examined. 'Full autopsy report will be ready tomorrow morning. We can say more then.'

'More about what?' Duff asked. 'What he had for dinner? As we all know, we had the same. Or what illnesses he had that he *didn't* die of? If we're going to keep up the pace it's essential now that we focus on information that's important.'

'An autopsy,' Caithness said, and Macbeth noticed the quiver in her voice, 'can confirm or deny the assumed sequence of events. And I'd assume that was pretty important.'

'It is, Caithness,' Macbeth said. 'Anything else?'

She showed some more photos, talked about other

medical and technical evidence, but none of it pointed in a direction that was different from the general consensus around the table: that the two bodyguards had killed Duncan. There was also agreement that the guards didn't seem to have a motive, therefore other forces must have been behind the murder, but the consequent discussion about whether anyone else apart from Hecate could have been responsible was brief and unproductive.

Macbeth suggested postponing the press conference until ten o'clock pending the location and briefing of Malcolm. Lennox pointed out that nine was a better time for the press as they had early deadlines on a Sunday.

'Thank you, Lennox,' Macbeth said. 'But our agenda is what counts and not sales figures early tomorrow.'

'I think that's stupid,' Lennox said. 'We're the new management team, and it's unwise to make ourselves unpopular with the press at the very first opportunity.'

'Your view has been noted,' Macbeth said. 'Unless Malcolm appears and says anything to the contrary, we meet here at nine and go through what has to be said at the press conference.'

'And who will give the press conference?' Duff asked.

Before Macbeth had the chance to answer, the door opened. It was Priscilla, Lennox's assistant.

'Sorry to interrupt,' she said. 'A patrol car has reported that Malcolm's car is parked at the container harbour. It's empty and there's no sign of Malcolm.'

Macbeth felt the silence in the room. Savoured the knowledge that they didn't share. And the control it gave him.

'Where in the container harbour?' Macbeth asked.

'On the quay by one of the canals.'

Macbeth nodded slowly. 'Send divers.'

'Divers?' Lennox said. 'Isn't that a bit premature?'

'I think Macbeth's right,' Priscilla interrupted, and the others turned to her in astonishment. She gulped. 'They found a letter on the car seat.'

12

The press conference started at ten precisely. When Macbeth entered Scone Hall and walked to the podium, flashes fired off from all angles and cast grotesque fleeting shadows of him on the wall behind. He placed his papers on the lectern in front of him, looked down at them for a few seconds, then coughed and scanned the full rows of seats. He had never enjoyed speaking in front of audiences. Once, long ago, the very thought of it had been worse than the most hazardous mission. But it had got better. And now, this evening, he felt happy. He would enjoy it. Because he was in control and knew something they didn't. And because he had just inhaled a line of brew. That was all he needed.

'Good evening, I'm Inspector Macbeth, head of the Organised Crime Unit. As you know, Chief Commissioner Duncan was found murdered at Inverness Casino this morning at 6.42. Immediately afterwards the two provisional suspects in the case, Duncan's bodyguards Police Officer Andrianov and Police Officer Hennessy, were shot and killed by the police in the adjacent room when they resisted arrest. An hour ago you were given a detailed account of the course of events, our current findings and assumptions about the case, so this can be dealt with quickly. But I would like to add a couple of things of a more technical nature.'

Macbeth held his breath and one journalist was unable to restrain himself:

'What do you know about Malcolm?' the question resounded.

'Is he dead?' another journalist lobbed in.

Macbeth looked down at his notes. Put them to the side.

'If these questions mean the press considers we've covered our responsibility to report on the murder of Chief Commissioner Duncan, we can now talk about the disappearance of the deputy chief commissioner.'

'No, but first things first,' shouted one of the older journalists. 'We have deadlines looming.'

'OK,' Macbeth said. 'Deputy Chief Commissioner Malcolm didn't show up — as you appear to know — at our meeting in police HQ at six. On a day when the chief commissioner has been found dead that is of course disturbing. So we instigated a search, and Malcolm's car was located this afternoon in the container harbour. Subsequently the area was searched, also by divers. And they found — '

'The body?'

' — this.' Macbeth held up a round piece of metal that glinted in the glare of the TV lamps. 'This is Malcolm's police badge, and was found on the seabed by the quay.'

'Do you think someone has killed him?'

'Possibly,' Macbeth said, without batting an eyelid, in the deafening silence that followed. 'If by *someone* we include Malcolm himself.' He ran his eye over the audience and continued: 'A letter was found on the front seat of his car.'

Macbeth addressed the letter. Cleared his throat.

'*The Norse Riders threatened they would kill my daughter, Julia, if I didn't help them to kill the chief commissioner. But now they have a hold on me and they've told me to perform other services for them, too. I know that for as long as I'm alive the threat to my daughter will always be there. That is why — and because of the shame I feel for what I've done — I've decided to drown myself.* It is signed by the deputy chief commissioner.'

Macbeth looked up at the assembled journalists. 'The first question we — and I presume you, too — are asking is of course whether the letter is genuine. Our Forensics Unit has confirmed that the letter was written on Malcolm's typewriter at HQ. The paper bears Malcolm's fingerprints and the signature is Malcolm's.'

It was as though the room needed a few seconds to digest the information. Then came shrill voices.

'Do you know if there's anything else to confirm Malcolm was behind Duncan's murder?'

'How could Malcolm have helped the Norse Riders to murder Duncan?'

'What's the connection between Malcolm and the bodyguards?'

'Do you think there are any other police officers involved?'

Macbeth held up his palms. 'I won't answer any questions about Duncan's murder now, as it is all speculation. Only questions about Malcolm's disappearance. One at a time, please.'

Silence. Then the only female journalist in the room said, 'Are we to understand that you've found Malcolm's police badge, but *not* Malcolm?'

'We have a muddy seabed to contend with, and the water in our harbour is not the cleanest. A light brass badge doesn't necessarily sink into the mud the way a body does, and brass reflects light. It will take the divers time to find Malcolm.'

Macbeth watched the journalists as they threw themselves over their pads and made notes.

'Isn't the most obvious reason for that the current carrying away the body?' said a voice with rolled 'r's.

'Yes,' Macbeth replied, and he spotted the face behind the voice. One of the few who wasn't taking notes. Walt Kite. He didn't need to; the radio station microphone was placed in front of Macbeth.

'If Malcolm killed Duncan and regretted it, why — '

'Stop.' Macbeth raised a palm. 'As I said, I won't answer any questions about Duncan's murder until we know more. And now please understand that we have to return to work. The number one priority for us is to investigate this case as quickly and efficiently as we can with the resources at our disposal. We also have to appoint a chief commissioner as soon as possible so that we have continuity in the rest of the work the police are doing for this town.'

'Is it correct that you're the acting chief at this moment, Macbeth?'

'In formal terms, yes.'

'And in practice?'

'In practice . . . ' Macbeth paused. Looked down quickly at his sheet. Moistened his lips. 'We're a group of experienced unit heads who have already taken the helm, and I'm not afraid to say we are in control. Nor, however, am I afraid to say that filling Duncan's shoes will take some doing. Duncan was a visionary man, a hero who died in the fight against the powers of evil, who think today they have won a victory.' He gripped the lectern and leaned forward. 'But all they have achieved is to make us even more determined that this lost battle will be the start of progress towards the final victory for the power of good. For justice. For security. And through that for rebuilding, re-establishing and regaining prosperity. But we can't do that alone; to do that we need your trust and the town's trust. If we have that we will continue the work that Chief Commissioner Duncan started. And I would — ' he stopped to raise his hand as if swearing an oath ' — like to guarantee personally that we will not stop until we have achieved the goals that Duncan set for this town and all — *all* — its inhabitants.'

Macbeth let go of the lectern and straightened up. Looked at the faces, which blurred into a sea of eyes and open mouths before him. No, he wasn't afraid. He saw the effect and was still savouring the sound of his own words. Lady's words. He had leaned forward exactly when he was supposed to. She had instructed him in front of a mirror and explained how aggressive body language gave the impression of spontaneous passion and hunger for a fight, and that body language was more important than the words he used because it bypasses the brain and speaks directly to the heart.

'The next press conference is tomorrow morning at eleven here in Scone Hall. Thank you.'

Macbeth collected his papers, and there was a groan of disappointment before a hail of protests and questions. Macbeth peered across the room. He wanted to stay there a couple more seconds. He managed — with some difficulty — to stop the incipient smile at the last moment.

He looks like the bloody captain of a boat, thought Duff, sitting in the front row. A captain fearlessly looking across the stormy sea. Someone has taught him that. It's not the Macbeth I know. Knew.

Macbeth nodded briefly, marched across the podium and disappeared through the door held open by Priscilla.

'Well, what do you reckon, Lennox?' Duff asked while the journalists were still shouting for an encore behind them.

'I'm moved,' said the redhead inspector. 'And inspired.'

'Exactly. That was more like an election speech than a press conference.'

'You can interpret it like that or you can interpret it as a clever and responsible tactical move.'

'Responsible?' Duff snorted.

'A town, a country, rests on notions. Notions that banknotes can be exchanged for gold, notions that our leaders think about you and me and not their own good, that crimes will be punished. If we didn't believe in those notions civilised society would disintegrate in a frighteningly short time. And in a situation where anarchy is knocking on the door Macbeth has just reassured us that the town's public institutions are fully intact. It was a speech worthy of a statesman.'

'Or stateswoman.'

'You think those were Lady's words, not Macbeth's?'

'Women understand hearts and how to speak to them. Because the heart is the woman in us. Even if the brain is bigger, talks more and believes that the husband rules the house, it's the heart that silently makes the decisions. The speech touched your heart and the brain gladly follows. Believe me, Macbeth doesn't have it in him; the speech is her work.'

'So what? We all need a better half. As long as the result is what we want it doesn't matter if the devil himself is behind it. You're not jealous of Macbeth, are you, Duff?'

'Jealous?' Duff snorted. 'Why would I be? He looks and speaks like a real leader, and if he acts like one as well, it's obviously best for all of us that he leads and no one else.'

Chairs scraped back behind them. Macbeth hadn't returned and their deadline was approaching.

★　★　★

It was an hour to midnight. The wind had dropped, but litter and wreckage from last night's storm were still being blown through the streets. The damp north-westerly was compressed and accelerated through the corridors of the station concourse, past a bundle lying beside the wall and — a few metres further down — a man with a scarf wrapped over his nose and mouth.

Strega went over to him.

'Afraid you'll be recognised, Macbeth?'

'Shh, don't say my name. I gave a speech this evening and I'm afraid I lost my anonymity.'

'I saw the evening news, yes. You looked good up

there. I believed almost everything you said. But then a handsome face has always had that effect on me.'

'How come you appear as soon as I show up here, Strega?'

She smiled. 'Brew?'

'Have you got anything else? Speed? Cocaine? I'm seeing things and get such terrible dreams from brew.'

'It was the storm, not brew, that gave you such bad dreams, Macbeth. I don't touch the stuff, yet I dreamed that all the dogs went mad from the thunder. I saw them going for each other with foam coming from their jaws. And while they were still alive they were eating each other. I was covered in sweat and relieved when I woke up.'

Macbeth pointed at the bundle further up the corridor. 'There you have your dream.'

'What is it?'

'It's the corpse of a half-eaten dog, can't you see?'

'I think you're seeing things again. Here.' She put a little bag in his hand. 'Brew. Don't go crazy now, Macbeth. Remember the path is simple, it runs straight ahead.'

★　★　★

As Macbeth passed Bertha and hurried down across the deserted Workers' Square where it sloped down towards Inverness Casino's illuminated facade he saw a figure standing in the darkness and rain. And on getting closer he saw to his surprise that it was Banquo.

'What are you doing here?' Macbeth said.

'Waiting for you,' Banquo said.

'Midway between Bertha and the Inverness, where neither can give you shelter?'

'I couldn't make up my mind,' Banquo said.

'Which way to go?'

'What to do with Malcolm.'

182

'You didn't put the chains around him, is that it?'

'What?'

'The divers haven't found the body yet. Without some weight the current will have taken him.'

'It's not that.'

'No? Let's go to the Inverness then instead of standing here and getting cold and wet.'

'For me it's too late. I'm chilled to the very bottom of my heart. I was waiting for you here because there are journalists outside the casino. They're waiting for you, the new chief commissioner.'

'Then we'd better do this quickly. What happened?'

'I skinned the cat in a different way. You have nothing to fear. Malcolm's gone for ever and will never come back. And even if he did he has no idea you've played a part in this. He thinks Hecate's behind everything.'

'What are you talking about? Is Malcolm *alive*?'

Banquo shivered. 'Malcolm thinks I'm in Hecate's pocket and it was me who influenced Duncan's bodyguards. I know this wasn't what we agreed. But I solved our problem and I saved the life of a good man.'

'Where's Malcolm now?'

'Gone.'

'Where?' Macbeth said and saw from Banquo's face that he had raised his voice.

'I drove him to the airport and put him on a plane to Capitol. From there he'll go abroad. He knows that if he tries to contact anyone or gives the smallest sign of being alive, his daughter Julia will be liquidated at once. Malcolm is a father, Macbeth. And I know what that means. He will never risk his daughter's life, *never*. He'd rather let a town go to the dogs. Believe me, even in the draughtiest attic a flea-bitten Malcolm will wake up every morning hungry, cold and lonely and thank his maker that his daughter can live another day.'

Macbeth raised his hand and then saw something in Banquo's eyes he had only ever seen once before. Not in all the operations they had carried out together against desperadoes or lunatics who had taken children as hostages. Not the times Banquo had faced an adversary who was bigger, stronger and he knew would — and did — give him a beating. Macbeth had only seen this expression on Banquo's face once, and it was the time he came home after visiting Vera in hospital and the doctor had told him the result of the latest tests. Fear. Sheer, unadulterated fear. And for that reason Macbeth suspected it wasn't for himself that Banquo was afraid.

'Thank you,' Macbeth said. He laid his hand heavily on Banquo's shoulder. 'Thank you, my dear friend, for being kind where I was not. I thought one man was a small sacrifice for such an immense objective as ours. But you're right: a town can't be saved from going to the dogs by letting good men die without need. This one could be spared and so he should be spared. And perhaps you've saved us both from ending up in hell for such a gross act of cruelty.'

'I'm so glad you see it that way,' Banquo exclaimed, and Macbeth could feel the trembling muscles in Banquo's shoulder relax under his hand.

'Get off home and sleep now, Banquo. And say hello to Fleance from me.'

'I will. Goodnight.'

Macbeth crossed the square, pensive. Sometimes good men did die for no need, he thought. And sometimes there was a need. He entered the light from the Inverness, ignored the journalists' barked questions about Malcolm, about Duncan's bodyguards, about whether it really was he who had shot them both.

Inside, Lady received him.

'They broadcast the whole of the press conference live on TV, and you were fantastic,' she said and hugged him. He wouldn't let her go again. He held her until he could feel heat returning to his body. Felt the wonderful electric currents down his back as her lips touched his ear and she whispered, 'Chief Commissioner.'

Home. With her. The two of them. This, this was all he wanted. But to have this you had to merit it. That is how it is in this world. And, he thought, also in the next.

★   ★   ★

'Are you home?'

Duff turned in the doorway to the children's room, to the surprised voice behind him. Meredith had put on a dressing gown and stood with her arms crossed, shivering.

'Just popped by,' he whispered. 'I didn't want to wake you. Doesn't Ewan want to sleep in his own room?' He nodded towards his son, who lay curled up in the bed beside his big sister.

Meredith sighed. 'He's started going to Emily when he can't sleep. I thought you would be staying in town while you're working on these dreadful things?'

'Yes. Yes, but I had to escape for a while. Get some clean clothes. See if you all still existed. I thought I'd sleep a couple of hours in the guest room and then be on my way.'

'All right, I'll make up the bed. Have you eaten?'

'I'm not hungry. I'll have a sandwich when I wake up.'

'I can make you some breakfast. I can't sleep anyway.'

'You go and sleep, Meredith. I'll be up for a bit, then I'll make up the bed.'

'As you like.' She stood there with her arms crossed looking at him, but in the darkness he couldn't see her eyes. She turned and went.

13

'But I want to know *why*,' Duff said, placing his elbows on the table and his chin in his hands. 'Why didn't Andrianov and Hennessy run off? Why would two treacherous bodyguards first kill their boss and then lie down for a sleep in the adjacent room, covered in blood and evidence from here to hell? Come on, you're detectives, you must have some bloody *suggestions* at least!'

He looked around. Several of the Homicide Unit's twelve detectives sat in the room in front of him, but the only one who opened his mouth did so to yawn. It was Monday morning — perhaps that was why they were so uncommunicative, looked so ill-at-ease and switched off? No, these faces would look just as tired tomorrow unless someone got a grip on things. There was a reason the Homicide Unit had been without a formal leader for the two months that had passed since Duncan had given the previous head an ultimatum: resign or an internal enquiry will be set up to investigate suspected corruption. There were no qualified applicants. Under Kenneth, the Homicide Unit had had the lowest clear-up rate in the country, and corruption was not the only reason. While the Homicide Unit in Capitol got the best in the field, the Homicide Unit at police HQ had only the dregs: the apathetic and the dysfunctional.

'This has to be turned round,' Duncan had said. 'The success or failure of the Homicide Unit determines to a large extent people's confidence in the police. That's why I'm putting one of our finest officers on the case. You, Duff.'

Duncan had known how to serve up bad news to his staff in an inspiring way. Duff groaned. He had a pile of reports beside him worth less than the paper they were written on — meaninglessly detailed interviews with guests at Inverness Casino all telling the same story: they hadn't seen or heard anything apart from the hellish weather. Duff knew the silence around the table might be because they were simply afraid of his fury, but he didn't give a damn. This wasn't a popularity contest, and if they had to be frightened into doing something, fine by him.

'So we think the guilty bodyguards just slept the sleep of the innocent, do we? As it had been a long day at work. Which of you idiots votes for that?'

No reaction.

'And who *doesn't* believe that?'

'Not of the innocent,' said Caithness, who had just breezed in through the door. 'Of the medicated. Apologies for my late arrival, but I had to pick up this.' She waved something horribly resembling a report. Which it was, Duff established as it landed in front of the pile on the table with a thud. More precisely, a forensic report. 'Blood samples taken from Andrianov and Hennessy show they had enough benzodiazepines in their bodies to sleep for twelve hours.' Caithness sat down on one of the unoccupied chairs.

'Bodyguards who take sleeping tablets?' Duff said in disbelief.

'They calm you down,' said one guy rocking on a chair at the back of the room. 'If you're going to assassinate your boss, you're probably a bit shaky. Lots of bank robbers take benzos.'

'And that's why they fuck it up,' said a detective with nervous twitches around his nose wearing a shoulder holster over a white polo neck.

Laughter. Short-lived.

'What do you reckon, Caithness?' Duff said.

She shrugged. 'Detection is not my field of expertise, but to me it seems pretty obvious that they needed to take something to calm their nerves, but they don't know a lot about drugs, so they messed up the dosage.

187

During the murder the drugs worked as intended. Their reflexes were still fast, but the nervousness was gone, and the clean cuts show a steady hand. But after the murder, when the chemical really kicked in, they lost control of the situation. They wandered around getting blood all over themselves and in the end both simply fell asleep in chairs.'

'Typical,' said the polo neck. 'Once we nabbed two doped-up bank robbers who had fallen asleep in their getaway car at the lights. I'm not kidding. Criminals are so bloody stupid you can — '

'Thank you,' Duff interrupted. 'How do you know their reflexes were still fast?'

Caithness shrugged. 'Whoever made the first stab managed to remove their hand from the knife before the blood spurted out. Our blood-spatter analyst says the blood on the handle is from the spurt. It didn't run, drip or get smeared on.'

'In which case I agree with all your other conclusions,' Duff said. 'Who disagrees?'

No reaction.

'Anyone agree?'

Mute nods.

'Good, let's say that answers that then. Now let's go to the other loose thread. Malcolm's suicide.' Duff stood up. 'His letter says that the Norse Riders threatened to kill his daughter if he didn't help them kill Duncan. My question is: instead of doing as Sweno and the Norse Riders want and taking his own life, why not go to Duncan and have his daughter moved to a safe house? Threats aren't exactly something new for the police. What do you think?'

The others looked at the floor, each other and out of the window.

'No opinions? Really? A whole Homicide Unit of detectives and no — '

'Malcolm knows Sweno has contacts in the police,'

said the chair rocker. 'He knows Sweno would have found his daughter anyway.'

'Good, we're up and running,' Duff said, bent over and pacing to and fro in front of them. 'Let's assume Malcolm thinks his daughter can be saved by doing as Sweno says. Or by dying so that Sweno no longer has any reason to kill his daughter. OK?' He saw that none of those present had a clue where he was going.

'So if Malcolm — as the letter suggests — cannot live if either he loses his daughter or he becomes an accessory to Duncan's murder, why didn't he commit suicide *before* Duncan was murdered and save them both?'

The faces gaped at him.

'If I might . . . ' Caithness began.

'Please, Inspector.'

'Your question might be logical, but the human psyche doesn't work like that.'

'Doesn't it?' Duff replied. 'I think it does. There's something about Malcolm's apparent suicide that doesn't tally. Our brains will always — with great accuracy and based on available information — weigh up the pros and cons and then make an irrefutably logical decision.'

'If the logic's irrefutable, why, despite having no new information, do we sometimes feel remorse?'

'Remorse?'

'Remorse, Inspector Duff.' Caithness looked him straight in the eye. 'It's a feeling in people with human qualities that tells us we wish something that we've done, undone. We can't exclude the possibility that Malcolm was like that.'

Duff shook his head. 'Remorse is a sign of illness. Einstein said proof of insanity is when someone goes through the same thought process again hoping to get a different answer.'

'Then Einstein's contention can be refuted if, over time, we draw different conclusions. Not because the information has changed in any way, but because people can do that.'

'People don't change!'

Duff noticed that the officers in the room had woken up and were following attentively now. They perhaps suspected that this exchange with Caithness was no longer only about Malcolm's death.

'Perhaps Malcolm changed,' Caithness said. 'Perhaps Duncan's death changed him. That can't be ruled out.'

'Nor can we rule out the possibility that he left a suicide letter, threw his police badge in the sea and did a runner,' Duff said. 'As regards human qualities and all that.'

The door opened. It was an officer from the Narcotics Unit. 'Phone call for you, Inspector Duff. He says it's about Malcolm and it's urgent. And he *only* wants to speak to you.'

★ ★ ★

Lady stood in the middle of the bedroom looking at the man sleeping in her bed. In *their* bed. It was gone nine o'clock, she'd had her breakfast a long time ago, but there was still no life in the body under the silk sheets.

She sat down on the side of the bed, stroked his cheek, tugged at his thick black curls and shook him. A narrow strip of white appeared under his eyelids.

'Chief Commissioner! Wake up! The town's on fire!'

She laughed as Macbeth groaned and rolled onto his side, his back to her. 'What's the time?'

'Late.'

'I dreamed it was Sunday.'

'You dreamed a lot, I think.'

'Yes, that bloody . . . '

'What?'

'Nothing. I heard storm bells. But then I realised they were church bells. Summoning churchgoers to confession and a christening.'

'I told you not to say that word.'

'Christening?'

'Macbeth!'

'Sorry.'

'The press conference is in less than two hours. And they'll be wondering what's happened to their chief commissioner.'

He swung his legs out of bed. Lady stopped him, held his face between her hands and inspected him carefully. The pupils were small. Again.

She pulled a stray hair from his eyebrow.

'Also we've got a dinner this evening,' she said, searching for more. 'You haven't forgotten, have you?'

'Is it really right to have it so close after Duncan's passing-away?'

'It's a dinner to cultivate connections, not a banquet. And we still have to eat, darling.'

'Who's coming?'

'Everyone I've asked. The mayor. Some of your colleagues.' She found a grey hair, but it slipped between her long red nails. 'We're going to discuss how to enforce the regulations for the casinos. It's in today's leader column that the Obelisk is apparently running a prostitution racket under cover of the casino and that therefore it should be closed.'

'It doesn't help that your editor chum writes what you want him to if no one reads his newspapers.'

'No. But now I've got a chief commissioner as my husband.'

'Ow!'

'You should get a few more grey hairs. They look good on bosses. I'll talk to my hairdresser today. Perhaps he can discreetly dye your temples.'

'My temples aren't visible.'

'Exactly. That's why we'll get your hair cut — so they are.'

'Never!'

'Mayor Tourtell might think his town should have a chief commissioner who looks like a grown man, not a boy.'

'Oh? Are you worried?'

Lady shrugged. 'Normally the mayor wouldn't interfere with the police hierarchy, but he's the one who appoints the new chief commissioner. We just have to be sure he doesn't get any funny ideas.'

'And how can we do that?'

'Well, we might have to ensure we have some hold over Tourtell in the unlikely event that he cuts up rough. But don't you worry about that, darling.'

'All right. Apropos cutting up rough . . .'

She stopped searching for unruly hairs. She recognised the tone. 'Is there something you haven't told me, dearest?'

'Banquo . . .'

'What about him?'

'I've begun to wonder whether I can trust him. Whether he hasn't made some cunning plan for himself and Fleance.' He took a deep breath, and she knew he was about to tell her something important. 'Banquo didn't kill Malcolm yesterday, he sent him off to Capitol. He made some excuse about this not being a life we risked anything by sparing.'

She knew he was waiting for her reaction. When none was forthcoming he remarked she didn't seem so dumbfounded.

She smiled.

'This is not the time to be dumbfounded. What do you think he's planning?'

'He claims he's frightened Malcolm into silence, but I'm guessing the two of them have concocted something that will give Banquo a better and surer pay-off than he's getting with me.'

'Darling, surely you don't think that nice old Banquo has any ambition to become chief commissioner?'

'No, no, Banquo has always been someone who wants to be led, not to lead. This is about his son, Fleance. I'm only fifteen years older than Fleance, and by the time I retire Fleance will be old and grey himself. So it's better for him to be the crown prince to an older man like Malcolm.'

'You're just tired, my love. Banquo's much too loyal to want to do anything like that. You said yourself he would burn in hell for you.'

'Yes, he has been loyal. And so have I to him.' Macbeth got up and stood in front of the big gold-framed mirror on the wall. 'But if you take a closer look, hasn't this mutual loyalty been more advantageous for Banquo? Hasn't he been the hyena who follows the lion's footprints and eats prey he hasn't killed himself? I made him second-in-command in SWAT and my deputy in Organised Crime. I would say he's been well paid for the small services he's performed for me.'

'All the more reason why you can count on his loyalty, darling.'

'Yes, that's what I thought too. But now I see . . . ' Macbeth frowned and went closer to the mirror. Placed a hand on its surface to check if there was something there. 'He loved me like a father loves a son, but that love turned to hatred when he drank the poison of envy. I passed him on the way up, and instead of him being my boss I became his. And as well as obeying my orders he has had to tolerate the unspoken contempt of his own blood, Fleance, who has seen his father bow his head to the cuckoo in the nest, Macbeth. Have you ever looked into a dog's faithful brown eyes as it looks up at you, wagging its tail and hoping for food? It sits there, still, waiting, because that's what it's been trained to do. And you smile at it, pat its head, and you can't see the hatred behind the obedience. You can't see that if it got the opportunity, if it saw its chance to escape punishment, it would attack you, it would tear at your throat; your death would be its breath of freedom and it would leave you half-eaten in some filthy corridor.'

'Darling, what *is* the matter with you?'

'That's what I dreamed.'

'You're paranoid. Banquo really is your friend! If he was planning to betray you he could have just gone to Malcolm and told him about your schemes.'

'No, he knows he'll be stronger if he plays his ace at the end. First kill me, a dangerous murderer, and then bring back Malcolm as chief commissioner. What a heroic deed! How can you reward a man like that and his family?'

'Do you really believe this?'

'No,' said Macbeth. He was standing close to the mirror now, his nose touching the glass, which had misted up. 'I don't believe it, I *know* it. I can *see*. I can see the two of them. Banquo and Fleance. I have to forestall them, but how?' Suddenly he turned to her. 'How? You, my only one, you have to help me. You have to help *us*.'

Lady crossed her arms. However warped Macbeth's reasoning sounded, there was some sense in it. He *might* be right. And if he wasn't, Banquo was still a fellow conspirator and a potential witness and blabber. The fewer there were of them, the better. And what real *use* did they have for Banquo and Fleance? None. She sighed. As Jack would say, *If you've got less than twelve in blackjack you ask for another card. Because you can't lose.*

'Invite them here one evening,' she said. 'Then we know where they are.'

'And we do it here?'

'No, no, there have been enough murders at the Inverness; one more would cast suspicion on us and also frighten away the clientele. We'll do it on the road.'

Macbeth nodded. 'I'll ask Banquo and Fleance to come by car. I'll tell them we've promised someone a lift home with them. I know exactly the route he'll take, so if I tell them to be punctual we'll know to the minute where on the route they'll be. Do you know what, woman of my dreams?'

Yes, she thought, as he embraced her, but let him say it anyway.

'I love you above everything on this earth and in the sky above.'

★   ★   ★

Duff found the young boy sitting on a bollard at the edge of the quay. There was a break in the rain, and more light than usual penetrated the layer of white cloud above them. But out in the river new troops of bluish-grey clouds stood lined up ready to ride in on the north-westerly wind against them — all you could rely on in this town.

'I'm Duff. Are you the person who rang about Malcolm?'

'Cool scar,' the boy said, straightening his eyepatch. 'They said you weren't the head of Narco any more?'

'You said it was urgent.'

'It's always urgent, Mr Narco Boss.'

'Suits me fine. Spit it out.'

'*Fork* it out, I think we say.'

'Oh, so that's why it's urgent. When do you have to have your next shot?'

'A couple of hours ago. And as this is important enough for the boss himself to show up, I think we'll say you pay for not only the next one, but the next ten.'

'Or I wait half an hour and you'll happily spit it out for half the price. Another half an hour and it'll cost half again . . .'

'I cannot deny this, Mr Narco Boss, but the question is: which of us is in a greater hurry? I read about Malcolm in the papers this morning and recognised him in the photo. Drowned, kind of. Deputy chief commissioner and shit. Heavy stuff.'

'Come on, lad, and I'll pay you what it's worth.'

The one-eyed boy chuckled. 'Sorry, Mr Narco Boss, but I've stopped trusting the fuzz. Here's your first bite. I wake up after nodding off, sitting between the lines of containers you can see over there, where you can shoot up and have a trip without being robbed, know what I mean? No one sees me, but I can see him, Malcolm, on the other side of the canal. Well, Narco Boss? First shot's for free, the next one will cost you big time. Heard that one before?' The boy laughed.

'Not sure I'm hooked there,' Duff said. 'We know Malcolm was here, we found his car.'

'But you didn't know he wasn't alone here. Or who was here with him.'

From bitter experience Duff knew a junkie told more lies than the truth, especially if that way they could finance their next shot. But, as a rule, a junkie preferred easier and quicker ways of tricking you than ringing HQ and insisting on talking to one of the unit heads, then waiting an hour in the rain, and all of that without a guaranteed payment.

'And you know that, do you?' Duff asked. 'Who this person is?'

'I've seen him before, yes.'

Duff took out his wallet. Produced a wad, counted, passed the banknotes to the boy.

'I was thinking of calling Macbeth himself,' the boy said as he recounted. 'But then I realised he would probably refuse to believe me when I told him who it was.'

'Personal?'

'That Malcolm was talking to Macbeth's sidekick,' the boy said. 'Old guy, white hair.'

Duff gasped involuntarily. 'Banquo?'

'I dunno what his name is, but I've seen him with

Macbeth at the station.'

'And what were Banquo and Malcolm talking about?'

'They were too far away for me to hear.'

'What erm . . . did it seem as if they were talking about? Were they laughing? Or were there loud, angry voices?'

'Impossible to say. The rain was hammering down on the containers and mostly they had their backs to me. They might have been arguing. The old boy was waving his shooter for a while. But then things quietened down, they got into a Volvo and drove off. The old boy was driving.'

Duff scratched his head. Banquo and Malcolm in cahoots?

'This is too much,' the boy said, holding up a note.

Duff looked down at him. A junkie giving him change? He took the note. 'You didn't tell me this just for the money for another shot, did you?'

'Eh?'

'You said you'd read the papers and knew this was heavy stuff. And it is. So heavy that if you'd rung a journalist with this story you'd have got ten times more than from a policeman. So either it's Hecate who sent you to spread false info or you've got another agenda.'

'Go to hell, Mr Narco Boss.'

Duff grabbed the junkie's collar and pulled him off the bollard. The boy weighed almost nothing.

'Listen to me,' Duff said, trying to avoid inhaling the boy's stinking breath. 'I can put you behind bars, and let's see then what you think when you hit cold turkey and you know you've got two days in the wilderness in front of you. Or you tell me now why you came to me. You've got five seconds. Four . . . '

The boy glared back at Duff.

'Three . . . '

'You piece of cop shit, you're fuckin' . . . '

'Two . . . '

'My eye.'

'One . . . '

'My eye, I said!'

'What about it?'

'I only wanted to help you catch the man that took my eye.'

'Who was it?'

The boy snorted. 'The same guy that's busting your arse. Don't you know who's behind all this shit? There's only one person in this town who can kill a chief commissioner and get away with it, and that's the Invisible Hand.'

Hecate?

14

Macbeth drove along the dirty road between the old factories. The cloud hung so low and Monday-grey over the chimneys that it was difficult to see which were smoking, but some of the gates had CLOSED signs or chains secured across them like ironic bow ties.

The press conference had passed painlessly. Painlessly because he had been too high to feel anything. He had concentrated on sitting back in a relaxed manner with his arms crossed and leaving the questions to Lennox and Caithness. Apart from those directed at him personally, which he had answered with, 'We cannot comment on that at the present time,' delivered with an expression that said they had much too much information and were in full control. Calm and assured. That was the impression he hoped he had given. An acting chief commissioner who did not allow himself to be affected by the hysteria around him, who answered journalists' shrill questions — 'Doesn't the public have the right to know?' — with a somewhat resigned, tolerant smile.

Although then Kite, the reporter with the rolled 'r's, had said in his radio programme right after the press conference that the acting chief commissioner had yawned a lot, seemed uninvolved and looked at his watch a lot. But to hell with Kite. In the Patrols Section they definitely thought the new chief commissioner was involved enough as he had personally dropped in and redirected the patrols from District 2 West to District 1 East. He explained it was time the neighbourhoods of normal people were also patrolled. It was an important signal to send: the police didn't prioritise districts with money and influence. And if Kite had been annoyed,

Banquo had at least been happy to receive a dinner invitation with instructions to bring along Fleance.

'Good for the lad to get used to mixing with the big boys,' Macbeth had said. 'And then I think you should decide what you'd like to do. Take over SWAT, Organised Crime or become the deputy chief commissioner.'

'Me?'

'Don't get stressed now, Banquo. Just give it some thought, OK?'

And Banquo had chortled and shaken his head. Gentle, as always. As though he didn't have an evil thought in his mind. Or at least he didn't have a conscience about having one. Well, tonight the traitor would meet his maker and destroyer.

No one was on the gate of the Norse Riders' club house. They probably didn't have anyone left to stand guard.

Macbeth got out of his car and went into the club-room. Stopped in the doorway and looked around. It felt like a strangely long time ago since he had stood there beside Duff and scanned the same room. Now the long table had gone, and at the bar stood three men with low-slung paunches in the club's leather jackets and two women with high-slung breasts. One was holding a baby, who was wriggling around under a muscular maternal arm tattooed with the name SEAN.

'Colin, isn't that the . . . ?' she whispered.

'Yes,' said the completely bald man with the walrus moustache in a low voice. 'That's the one who got Sean.'

Macbeth remembered the name from the report. It was strange how he kept forgetting the names of people he met, but never those that appeared in reports. Sean. He was the one who had been on guard at the gate, the one Macbeth had knifed in the shoulder and whom they had used as a hostage, one of those who was still in custody.

The man glared at the police officer in slack-jawed

200

fury. Macbeth took a deep breath. It was so quiet he could hear the floorboards creak under his heels as he walked over to the bar. He addressed the leather jacket behind the counter and caught himself thinking as he opened his mouth that he shouldn't have sniffed that last line before leaving HQ. Brew had a tendency to make him cocky. And his concern was confirmed by what came out: 'Hello, not many people here, where is everybody? Oh, yes, that's right. In the slammer. Or the morgue. A Glendoran, please.'

Macbeth saw the barman's eyes flit across, knew an attack was imminent from his left and he still had oceans of time. Macbeth had always had good reflexes, but with brew he was like a fly — he could yawn, scratch his back and study his watch with its incredibly slow second hand while a fist was on its way. But then, as Colin with the walrus moustache thought he was about to connect, Macbeth swayed back, and the fist that was heading for his newly trimmed temple met air. Macbeth lifted and swung his elbow to the side, barely felt the impact, only heard a groan, the crunch of cartilage, staggering footsteps and bar stools toppling over.

'On the rocks,' Macbeth said.

Then he turned to the man beside him, in time to see he had clenched his right hand and drawn his shoulder back to deliver a punch. As it arrived, Macbeth lifted his hand and met Colin's halfway. But instead of the expected crunch of bone on bone, there came the smooth sound of steel in flesh followed by a dull thud when Colin's knuckles hit the hilt. Then his long drawn-out scream when he saw the dagger running up through his clenched hand into his forearm. Macbeth pulled out the dagger with a jerk.

' . . . and some soda.'

The man with the walrus moustache fell to his knees.

'What the hell is going on?' said a voice.

This came from the door to the garage. The man had a big beard and a leather jacket with three chevrons on each shoulder. Plus a sawn-off shotgun in his hands.

'I'm ordering,' Macbeth said, turning to the barman, who still hadn't moved.

'Ordering what?' said the man, coming closer.

'Whisky. Among other things.'

'And what else?'

'You're the sergeant. You run the shop when Sweno's not here, don't you? By the way, where's he hiding this time?'

'Say what you came to say and get outta here, cop scum.'

'I won't hear a bad word about the place, but the service could be friendlier and quicker. What about you and me doing this in peace and quiet, in a back room, Sarge?'

The man looked at Macbeth for some moments. Then he lowered the gun barrel. 'There's not much more damage you can do here anyway.'

'I know. And Sweno's going to like my commission, I can guarantee you that.'

The sergeant's little office — for that's what it was — had posters of motorbikes on the walls and a very small selection of engine parts on the shelves. With a desk, telephone and in and out trays. And a chair for visitors.

'Don't make yourself too comfortable, cop.'

'My order is for a hit job.'

If the sergeant was shocked he didn't show it. 'Wrong address. We don't do that stuff for cops any more.'

'So the rumour's true? You used to do hit jobs for Kenneth's men?'

'If there was nothing else . . . '

'Only this time it isn't a competitor you would have to dispatch into the beyond,' Macbeth said, leaning forward in his chair. 'It's two cops. And the payment is your Norse Riders being set free immediately afterwards and all charges dropped.'

The sergeant raised an eyebrow. 'And how would you do that?'

'Procedural error. Spoiled evidence. This shit happens all the time. And if the chief commissioner says we haven't got a case, we haven't got a case.'

The sergeant crossed his arms. 'Carry on.'

'The person who has to be dispatched is the guy who ensured the dope you were going to live off ended up in the river. Inspector Banquo.' Macbeth watched the sergeant nod slowly. 'The other is a cop sprog who will be in the same car.'

'And why are they to be expedited?'

'Is that important?'

'Usually I wouldn't ask, but this is police officers we're talking about, and that means there's going to be loads of trouble.'

'Not with these ones. We know Inspector Banquo is working with Hecate, we just can't prove it, so we have to get rid of him another way. This is the best option from our point of view.'

The sergeant nodded again. Macbeth had counted on him understanding this logic.

'How do we know you'll keep your part of a potential deal?'

'Well,' Macbeth said, squinting at the calendar girl above the sergeant's head. 'We have five witnesses in the bar who can vouch for Acting Chief Commissioner Macbeth being here in person and giving you a commission. You don't think I'd want to give you any reason to make that public, do you?'

The sergeant leaned back in his chair so far it touched the wall, studying Macbeth while making growling noises and pulling at his beard. 'And when and where would this job potentially take place?'

'Tonight. You know Gallows Hill in District 2 West?'

'That's where they hanged my great-great-grandfather.'

'On the main road above the lanes where the West Enders go shopping there's a big junction.'

'I know the one you mean.'

'They'll be in a black Volvo at the lights some time between half past six and ten to seven. Probably at exactly a quarter to. He's a punctual man.'

'Hm. There are always a lot of patrol cars there.'

Macbeth smiled. 'Not tonight there won't be.'

'Oh, really? I'll think about it and give you an answer at four.'

Macbeth laughed. '*Sweno* will think about it, you mean. Great. Pick up a pen, and I'll give you my phone number and the registration number of the Volvo. And one more thing.'

'Uhuh?'

'I want their heads.'

'Whose?'

'The two cops. I want their heads. Delivered to the door.'

The sergeant stared at Macbeth as if he considered him insane.

'The customer requires a receipt,' Macbeth said. 'Last time I ordered a hit job I didn't ask for a receipt and that was an error. I didn't get what I ordered.'

★　★　★

Late in the afternoon Duff made a decision.

His thoughts had been churning for hours in a brain where the traffic felt as slow-moving as that on the road in front of him and the way ahead as full of choices. They still hadn't replaced the railings on Kenneth Bridge, so the traffic eastbound was being redirected to the old bridge and the queue backed up to District 2, where Duff's car moved forward at a snail's pace from junction to junction, which all threw up the question:

left, right, straight ahead, what's the fastest?

Duff's own particular junction was this.

Should he go to Macbeth and the others with what he had found out on the quayside? Should he keep it to himself? But suppose the one-eyed boy wasn't telling the truth or Banquo was able to deny the accusations? What would the consequences be for Duff if in this chaotic situation he made false accusations against Banquo, who, with Macbeth, had suddenly become a powerful figure?

Duff could of course simply present the information the way he had been given it and let Lennox and Macbeth evaluate it themselves, but then he would lose the chance to register a badly needed personal triumph by single-handedly arresting and unmasking Banquo.

On the other hand, he couldn't afford another blunder after his raid on the container harbour. It had cost him the Organised Crime appointment; another blunder could easily cost him his job.

Another junction: Organised Crime would be up for grabs again if Macbeth became chief commissioner, and if Duff seized the opportunity now, dared and won, the unit could be his.

He had weighed up asking Caithness for her opinion, but then the cat would be out of the bag, he couldn't play innocent and would be forced to do *something*. Take a risk.

The way he had chosen in the end was one where he didn't risk much, but where he would still get the credit if it all went as he hoped.

Duff turned off the little railway bridge and into the yard in front of the modest brick building on the other side. It had taken him more than three quarters of an hour to cover the short distance from HQ to Banquo's address.

'Duff,' said Banquo, who opened the door seconds after Duff had rung the bell. 'What gives?'

'A party by the looks of it,' Duff said.

'Yes, and that's why I can't decide whether to take this or not.' Banquo held up the holster with his service gun.

'Leave it behind. It'll only make a bulge in your suit. But that tie knot is no good.'

'Isn't it?' Banquo said, pressing his chin down against his white shirt collar in a futile attempt to see the knot. 'It's been good enough for fifty years, ever since I was confirmed.'

'That's a poor man's knot, Banquo. Come on, let me show you . . . '

Banquo warded off Duff's helping hand by covering the knot. 'I *am* a poor man, Duff. And I assume you came here to get help, not offer it.'

'That's true enough, Banquo. Can I come in?'

'I'd have liked to offer you help and coffee, but I'm afraid we're on our way out.' Banquo put his gun holster on the hat shelf behind him and called up the stairs: 'Fleance!'

'Coming!' was the response.

'We can go outside in the meantime,' Banquo said, buttoning up his coat.

They stood on the covered white steps. Rain gurgled cheerily down from the gutters while Banquo offered Duff a cigarette and lit his own when the inspector declined.

'I was back in the container harbour today,' Duff said. 'I met a boy, one of our young drug addicts, who wanted to talk to me. He's got only one eye. He told me how he lost the other one.'

'Mmhm.'

'He'd been driven crazy with his craving for dope but was broke. Down at central station he met an old man and begged him for some money. The old man had a walking stick with a gold tip.'

'Hecate?'

'The old man stopped, took out a bag which he dangled in front of the boy and said it was top-quality brew straight from the pot. The boy could have it if he would do two things for him. The first was to answer the question: which sense would you be most afraid to lose? When the boy replied it would be his eyesight, the old man said he wanted one of his eyes.'

'That *was* Hecate.'

'When the boy asked the old man why he wanted his eye, Hecate answered that he had everything, so all that was left for him was what was most valuable to the buyer, not to himself. And after all it was only half his eyesight, well, not even that. And think how much more valuable his second eye would be afterwards. Indeed loss and gain would almost be equal.'

'I don't understand that.'

'Maybe not, but that's the way some people are. They desire power itself more than what it can give them. They'd rather own a worthless tree than the edible fruit that grows on it. Just so that they can point to it and say, 'That's mine.' And then cut it down.'

Banquo blew out a cloud of smoke. 'What did the boy decide to do?'

'He was helped by a man-woman, who was with the old man, to take out the eye. And when he got his shot afterwards all the pain he had ever known was gone — it smoothed all the scars, removed all the bad memories. The boy said it was so wonderful that even today he can't say he has any regrets. He's still chasing after it, the perfect shot.'

'And what was he after today when you met him?'

'The same. Plus the person who had taken his eye just because he could.'

'He'll have to take his place in the queue of Hecate-chasers.'

'He was thinking instead that he would help us catch Hecate.'

'And how would a poor brew slave do that?'

'Malcolm's so-called suicide letter tries to finger the Norse Riders. But the boy thinks Hecate's behind everything. Both the letter and the murder of Duncan. And Hecate's in league with Malcolm. And perhaps others in the force.'

'A popular theory nowadays.' Banquo flicked the ash off the cigarette and looked at his watch. 'Was he paid for that?'

'No,' Duff said. 'He wasn't paid for anything until he told me he'd seen Malcolm down on the quay before he went missing. And he'd been with you.'

The cigarette on its way to Banquo's mouth stopped. He laughed. 'Me? I don't believe it.'

'He described you and your car.'

'Neither I nor my car was there. And I find it difficult to believe you could have paid public money for such a claim. So which of you is bluffing? This junkie then or you now?'

A gust of cold wind blew, and Duff shivered. 'The boy says he saw Malcolm and an older man he'd seen with Macbeth. A Volvo saloon. And a gun. Wouldn't you have paid for that information, Banquo?'

'Only if I was desperate.' Banquo stubbed his cigarette out on the iron railing which flanked the steps. 'And not even then if it concerned a police colleague.'

'Because you always rate loyalty very high, don't you?'

'A police force cannot function without the loyalty of individuals. It's a prerequisite.'

'So how far does your loyalty to the force stretch?'

'I'm a simple man, Duff, and I don't understand what you mean.'

'If you mean what you say about loyalty then you have to give us Malcolm. For the sake of the force.'

Duff pointed out into the grey soup of rain and mist in front of them. 'For this town's sake. Where is

Duncan's murderer hiding in Capitol?'

Banquo blew the ash from the cigarette end and put it in his coat pocket. 'I know nothing about Malcolm. Fleance! Sorry, Inspector, but we're going out to dinner.'

Duff ran after Banquo, who had walked down the three steps into the rain. 'Speak to me, Banquo! I can see you're weighed down by guilt and a bad conscience. You're not an evil, cunning person. You've just been led into temptation by someone higher in rank than you by trusting their judgement. And so you've been betrayed. He *has* to be arrested, Banquo!'

'Fleance!' Banquo screamed in the direction of the house as he unlocked the car in the yard.

'Do you want us to continue in this downward spiral into chaos and anarchy, Banquo? Our forefathers built railways and schools. We build brothels and casinos.'

Banquo got into the car and hooted the horn twice. The house door opened, and a suited Fleance emerged onto the steps struggling to open an umbrella.

Banquo cracked open the window, presumably because the car was misting up inside, and Duff put his hands on the window and tried to press it down further while talking through the narrow opening. 'Listen, Banquo. If you do this, if you confess, there's not a lot I can do for you, you know that. But I promise you no one will be allowed to hurt Fleance. His prospects won't be those of a traitor's son but those of the son of a man who sacrificed himself for the town. You have my word.'

'Hi. Inspector Duff, isn't it?'

Duff straightened up. 'Hi, Fleance. That's right. Have a nice dinner.'

'Thanks.'

Duff waited until Fleance had got into the passenger's seat and Banquo had started the engine. Then he set off for his car.

'Duff!'

He turned.

Banquo had opened his door. 'It's not as you think,' he shouted.

'Isn't it?'

'No. Meet me by Bertha at midnight.'

Duff nodded.

The Volvo was put into gear, and father and son went through the gate into the mist.

15

Lady went up the last metal rungs of the ladder to the door leading to the flat roof of Inverness Casino. She opened it and stared into the darkness. All that could be heard was the mumbled whisper of the rain. It seemed that everything and everyone had secrets. She was about to turn and go back in when a crackle of lightning lit up the roof, and she saw him. He was standing by the edge of the roof and looking down into Thrift Street, at the back of the casino. Before she had persuaded the town council to clean it up, the prostitutes had stood there in the barely lit street and not only offered themselves but often performed their services right there, in the archways, in cars, on cars or up against walls. When the National Railway Network had been here it was said that the boss had had all the windows facing Thrift Street bricked up so that his subordinates could concentrate on work and not the filth outside.

She opened her umbrella and went over to Macbeth.

'Out here getting wet, darling? I've been looking for you. The guests for dinner will be here soon.' She looked down the smooth black windowless walls like a fortress that led down to Thrift Street. She knew every yard of the street. And that was reason enough to keep the windows bricked up.

'What can you see down there?'

'An abyss,' he said. 'Fear.'

'My dearest, don't be so gloomy.'

'No?'

'What would the point of all our victories be if they didn't bring a smile to our lips?'

'We've won only a couple of battles. The war has barely begun. And already I'm being consumed by this

211

fear. God knows where it comes from. Give me an armed biker gang coming towards me rather than this serpent we've slashed at but haven't killed.'

'Stop it, my love. No one can catch us now.'

'Duncan. I can see him down there. And I envy him. He's dead — I've granted him peace — while all he gives me is anxiety and these nightmares.'

'It's brew, right? It's brew that gives you nightmares.'

'Darling . . .'

'Do you remember what you said about Collum? You said brew drove people crazy. You have to stop taking it or you'll lose everything we've won! Do you hear me? Not another grain of brew!'

'But the nightmares aren't a product of my imagination. The sergeant called me. The deal is done. Or have you forgotten the grave deed we have planned for this evening? Have you repressed the thought that my only father and best friend are going to be slaughtered?'

'I don't know what you're talking about and nor do you. When what's done is done, there'll be nothing to brood over. And brew won't give you consolation or courage. Now your soul will receive its reward. So no more brew! Put a tie on now, my love. And a smile.' She took his hand. 'Come on, let's charm them to pieces.'

★　★　★

Caithness sat in an armchair with a glass of red wine in her hand listening to the rain on the attic window and Kite on the radio. He was talking about the problem of an acting chief commissioner in practice having more power than a democratically elected mayor, all because of Kenneth's tampering with the town's laws and statutes. She liked the way he rolled his 'r's and his calm voice. Liked the way he wasn't afraid to shine with his knowledge and intelligence. But most of all she liked the

212

way he was always *against* something. Against Kenneth, against Tourtell, yes, even against Duncan, who himself had been against so much. It had to be a lonely furrow. And who would want to be lonely if they had a choice?

She had occasionally wondered whether to send an anonymous letter to his radio station, saying how reassuring it was that there were still principled people like him, someone who took on the job of a lone, fearless watchdog. Speaking of which. Wasn't that the second time she had heard that sound from the front door? She turned down the radio. Listened. There it was again. She crept over to the door and put her ear against it. A familiar creaking sound. She opened the door.

'Duff. What are you doing?'

'I . . . erm . . . am standing here. And thinking.' He had his hands stuck deep down in his coat pockets and was rocking on his much-too-large shoes with the creaking soles.

'Why didn't you ring the bell?'

'I have,' Duff said. 'I . . . The bell obviously doesn't work.'

She opened the door wide, but he still seemed to be caught in two minds.

'Why so glum, Duff?'

'Am I glum?'

'Sorry, I know there's not much to be cheery about right now, but are you coming or going?'

His eyes flitted around. 'Can I stay until midnight?'

'Of course, but come in, will you? I'm cold.'

★　★　★

The sergeant rested his hands on the handlebars of his Honda CB450 'Black Bomber'. It was less than five years since he had bought it, and on good days he could squeeze a ton out of it. Nevertheless it felt a bit old now that the Honda CB750 superbike was on the market.

He looked at his watch. Sixteen minutes to seven. The rush hour had subsided now, and darkness had fallen early. Waiting beside the road, he could see every single car that came towards the Gallows Hill junction. Sweno had sent them reinforcements from the club down south: three members, cousins they called them, had jumped on their bikes and arrived in town in less than three hours. They were sitting on their bikes, ready, by the pumps at the petrol station on the road along which the car was supposed to be coming. Appraising the models and number plates. Down the road, on the other side of the junction, he could see Colin standing on climbing irons up one of the posts by the junction box. The only entertainment they'd had so far was when they had done a trial run, and Colin had stuck a screwdriver in and turned. Brakes squealed on the road when the lights, without any warning, had changed from green to red. And seconds later, when they had changed back to green, engine revs had risen hesitantly and carefully, and cars crept across the junction while the sergeant flashed his headlights to signal to Colin that things were working as they should.

The sergeant looked at his watch again. A quarter to seven.

Sweno had needed a little time to make the decision, but the sergeant had the feeling that was more for reasons of caution than doubt. And that was confirmed when the three cousins from the south had drawn up in front of the club gate, a Harley Davidson chopper with high handlebars, a Harley FL 1200 Electra Glide and a Russian Ural with a sidecar and mounted machine gun. The guy on the Electra Glide had a sword with him, not curved like Sweno's sabre, but it would do the job.

Fourteen minutes to seven.

★   ★   ★

'Fleance . . . '

Something in his father's voice made Fleance glance across. His father was always calm, but when something was wrong he had this voice that was even calmer. Like the time Fleance was seven and his father came home from the hospital after visiting Mum and said his name in that same eerily calm way.

'Change of plans for this evening.' His father shifted lane, tucked in behind a Ford Galaxy. 'And the next few days.'

'Really?'

'You're going to Capitol. Tonight.'

'Capitol?'

'Something's happened. You'll have lots of questions, my lad, but you won't get any answers just yet. Drop me off at the Inverness, then you drive on at once. Pop home, take only what you need with you and go to Capitol. Drive steadily, not too fast, and you'll get there late tomorrow. Got that?'

'Yes, but what — '

'No questions. You should stay there a few days, maybe weeks. As you know, your mother inherited a little flat. Take the notepad from the glove compartment.'

'The one-room flat she called the rat hole?'

'Yes. No wonder we never managed to sell it. Fortunately, I have to say now. The address is 66 Tannery Street, District 6. Right next to the Dolphin Nightclub. Second floor on the right. You're safe there. Have you written that down?'

'Yes.' Fleance tore out the page and put the notepad back in the glove compartment. 'But I'll need a key, won't I? I mean, who'll let me in if it's empty?'

'It's not empty.'

'Tenants?'

'Not exactly; I've let poor old cousin Alfie stay there. He's so old and deaf he might not open up when you ring the bell, so you'll have to improvise.'

'Dad?'

'Yes?'

'Has this got anything to do with what Duff was after? He seemed very . . . intense.'

'Yes, but no more questions, Fleance. You'll just have to stay there, study some school books you take with you, get bored, but no phone calls, no letters, don't say a peep to anyone about where you are. Just do as I say, and I'll send for you when it's safe to return.'

'Are *you* safe then?'

'You heard what I said.'

Fleance nodded.

They drove in silence, the worn rubbers of the windscreen wipers squeaking and sounding as if they wanted to tell them something.

'Yes,' Banquo said, 'I'm safe. But take no notice of the news from now on, probably just lies. There's someone else staying there as well at the moment. I think he's got a mattress on the floor, so you take the sofa. If the rats haven't eaten it.'

'Funny guy. Do you promise me you're safe?'

'Don't you worry . . . '

'The lights are red!'

Banquo jumped on the brakes and almost ended up on the rear bumper of the Galaxy, which obviously hadn't seen the lights change either.

'Here,' Banquo said, passing his son a thick worn wallet. 'Take the money, then you've got enough to make ends meet for a while.'

Fleance took out the notes

'Bloody long time on red . . . ' he heard his father mutter.

Fleance glanced in the side mirror. There was already a long queue behind them. On the outside of the queue a line of motorbikes was coming towards them.

'Strange,' his father said. Again his much-too-calm

216

voice. 'Looks like the road ahead is on red too. And has been for a while.'

'Dad, there are some motorbikes coming.'

Fleance saw his father glance in the rear-view mirror for a second. Then he put his foot down on the accelerator, wrenched the steering wheel to the right and let go of the clutch. The old car spun on the wet, oily tarmac, but squeezed out to the right of the queue. The hubcaps hit the high kerb, and both cars screamed as if hurt when the Volvo scraped alongside the Galaxy and knocked off its side mirror as they passed.

A huge roar came from the street ahead. The lights had changed to green.

'Dad! Stop!'

But his father didn't stop; on the contrary, he slammed his foot down. They raced into the junction on a collision course with a lorry from the left and a bus from the right. And heard two horns blaring, one from either side, roaring a jarring chord as they emerged from between them. Fleance stared in the mirror as they shot down from Gallows Hill towards the centre, and the painful music sank in pitch behind them. He saw the traffic lights had changed back to green and the motorbikes were already across the junction.

★   ★   ★

Macbeth stood with both feet firmly planted on the solid tiles at the entrance to Inverness Casino yet still felt he was at sea. In front of him an overweight man in a black suit struggled to get out of the rear seat of a limousine. The Inverness's red-clad doorman held the car door open and an umbrella in his hand as he hesitated between offering to pull him up or letting him retain his dignity. After the man had finally managed to complete the job without help but with some panting, Lady rushed forward.

217

'Our very own . . . my very own mayor!' She laughed and embraced him. Which was no mean feat, Macbeth thought, hearing himself let slip a silly snigger as he watched Lady's slender hands grasp Tourtell's well padded turtle shell.

'You become more handsome and more virile every time we meet,' she twittered.

'And you, Lady, more beautiful and more mendacious. Macbeth . . . '

Macbeth shook hands, fascinated by how the flesh on the mayor's hand oozed away from under his thumb.

'And who's this young man?' Lady asked.

A brown-eyed, smooth-skinned boy with girlish good looks, so young he must have been in his teens, scurried around the limousine from the rear door on the opposite side. He smiled tentatively at Tourtell as if for help.

'This, Lady, is my son,' Tourtell said.

'Silly billy, you don't have any children,' Lady said, smacking the mayor on the lapel of his jacket.

'My *extra-marital* son,' Tourtell amended, stroking the base of the boy's spine and winking at Macbeth with a chuckle. 'I've only just found out about him, you know. You can see the likeness though, can't you, Lady?'

'You are and always will be a sly fox, dear Tourtell. Shall we give him a name?'

'What about Kasi Tourtell Junior?' said the mayor, stroking his Salvador Dalí moustache and emitting a booming laugh when Lady rolled her eyes.

'Get yourselves some refreshment in the warm,' Lady said.

The two of them went through the door as she came to stand next to Macbeth.

'How dare he, the perverted pig,' Macbeth said. 'I thought Tourtell was one of the respectable guys.'

'He's one of the respected guys, and that's all that counts, dear. Power gives you the freedom to do what you want without people losing their respect for you. At least now you're smiling.'

'Am I?'

'Like an unhinged clown.' Lady was already beaming at the taxi drawing up to the entrance. 'Don't overdo the grin, darling. This is Janovic, a property investor from Capitol.'

'Another scavenger buying up our factory sites for a song?'

'He looks at the casinos. Be nice and say hello, and at some point let drop a comment assuring him that street crime is already on its way down.'

★　★　★

Fleance screamed instinctively and ducked when the rear window exploded.

'How many?' his father asked calmly and swerved hard to the right, down a cobbled side street. Fleance turned. The roar of the bikes behind them rose in volume like an enraged dragon.

'Five or six,' Fleance shouted. 'Give me your gun!'

'It wanted to stay at home tonight,' Banquo said. 'Hold tight.' He twisted the steering wheel; the wheels hit the kerb, and the Volvo jumped and cut the corner in front of a posh clothes shop as they turned left down an even narrower street. Fleance understood the strategy: in these one-way alleys at least the bikers couldn't come alongside and finish them off. But they were getting unremittingly close. Another bang behind them. Fleance hadn't as yet learned to differentiate between all types of firearm, which he knew his father could, but even he knew that was a shotgun. Which after all was better than —

A hail of bullets hammered against the car body.

— an automatic weapon.

His father executed another sudden turn with

authority, as though he knew where he was going. They were well into the shopping area now, but the shops were closed and the streets almost deserted in the rain. Did his father know a way out of this labyrinth? In response Banquo suddenly steered the car to the right, past a sign bearing bad news.

'Dad, this is a cul-de-sac!'

Banquo didn't react.

'Dad!'

Still no reaction, only his eyes staring ahead in deep concentration, his hands clutching the wheel. Fleance only discovered now that blood was running down his father's face and inside the neck of his shirt, where its white collar, like blotting paper, had assumed a pink colour from the welling blood. And there was something missing from where the blood was seeping out of his father's head. Fleance shifted his gaze to the steering wheel. That was why he wasn't answering. His ear. It lay stuck to the dashboard, a small, pale scrap of skin, shreds of flesh and blood.

Fleance raised his eyes to the windscreen. And there he saw, quite literally, the end. The blind alley culminated in a solid-looking timber house. The ground floor was a large partially illuminated shop window. It was approaching fast, and they showed no signs of stopping.

'Belt on, Fleance.'

'Dad!'

'Now.'

Fleance grabbed his seat belt, pulled it across his chest and just managed to buckle it before the front wheels hit the kerb and they reared up. The bonnet hit the shop window in the middle, and Fleance had the feeling it had opened and they were flying through a curtain of white glass into whatever was inside. Then, as he looked around in amazement, knowing something was dislocated, there was a break in the course of events and he knew he must have passed out. There was an infernal ringing in his ears. His father lay motionless with his head on the wheel.

'Dad!'

Fleance shook him.

'Dad!'

No reaction. The windscreen was gone, and something on the bonnet was shining. Fleance had to blink before he realised it was what it looked like. Rings. Necklaces. Bracelets. And in front of him on the wall was written in gold letters: JACOBS & SONS. JEWELLERS. They had driven into a bloody jewellery shop. And the ringing he could hear wasn't coming from his head, it was the burglar alarm. Now it dawned on him. The burglar alarm. All the town's banks, the casinos and larger jewellery shops were connected to the central switchboard at police HQ. Who immediately contacted patrol cars in the district. Dad had known where he was going after all.

Fleance tried to undo his seat belt, but couldn't. He yanked and tugged, but the buckle refused to move.

★ ★ ★

The sergeant sat on his bike, counted the seconds and looked at the car protruding from the shop in front of them. The alarm drowned most sounds, but he could see from the smoke coming out of the exhaust pipe that the engine was running.

'Whad are we waidin' for, eh?' asked the guy on the Electra Glide. There was something irritating about the way he spoke. 'Led's go ged 'em.'

'We'll wait a while longer,' the sergeant said and counted. 'Twenty-one, twenty-two.'

'How long, eh?'

'Until we know the guy who ordered this job has kept his promise,' said the sergeant. Twenty-five, twenty-six.

221

'Doh. I wanna finish this head-choppin' stuff and leave this shide down.'

'Wait.' The sergeant quietly observed him. The guy looked like a grown man. Two grown men. The guy was as broad as a barn door and had muscles everywhere, even in his face. Yet he wore a brace on his teeth, like a boy. The sergeant had seen it before, in prison, where the inmates who pumped iron and took anabolic steroids grew such powerful jawbones that their teeth curled. Twenty-nine, thirty. Thirty seconds and no sirens. 'Away you go,' the sergeant said.

'Thanks.' The barn door pulled a long-barrelled Colt from his waistband and the sword from its sheath, dismounted his bike and set off towards the car. He nonchalantly ran the sword blade along the wall and over the post of the NO PARKING sign. The sergeant studied the back of his leather jacket. A pirate flag with the skull over a swastika. No style. He sighed. 'Cover him with the shotgun, Colin.'

Colin smoothed his walrus moustache with a bandaged hand, then broke open a short-barrelled shotgun and inserted two shells.

The sergeant saw a couple of faces appear in windows across the road, but still heard no sirens, only the monotonous, unceasing burglar alarm as the guy entered the shop and approached the car. He put the sword under his arm, pulled open the passenger door with his free hand and pointed the revolver at the person sitting there. The sergeant automatically clenched his teeth as he waited for the bang.

⋆ ⋆ ⋆

Fleance tore at the belt, but the infuriating buckle was stuck. He tried to wriggle out. Fleance raised his knees to his chin, swung himself round in the seat and placed his feet against the passenger door to push himself over

222

towards his father and the driver's seat. At that moment he caught sight of the man stepping into the shop with a sword and a revolver in his hands. It was too late to get away now, and Fleance didn't even have time to think how frightened he was.

The passenger door was wrenched open. Fleance saw the gleam of a dental brace and a revolver being raised and realised the man was out of reach for the kick he had planned. So instead he reached out with one foot for the opened door in sheer desperation. A normal shoe wouldn't have fitted behind the internal door handle, but the long thin toe of Macbeth's old winkle-pickers slipped in easily. He glimpsed the blackness of eternity in the revolver muzzle, then pulled the door to as hard as he could. There was a smack as the door hit the man's wrist and jammed it in the opening. And a muffled thud as the revolver hit the floor.

Fleance heard swearing, slammed the door shut with one hand while searching for the revolver with the other.

The door was torn open again, and there stood the dental-brace man with a sword raised over his head. Fleance patted the floor everywhere — under the seat — where the hell had the gun gone? Dental Brace then obviously realised that the door opening was too narrow for him to swing the sword and he would have to stab with it. He brought his elbow back, aimed the point at Fleance and leaped at him. Fleance lashed out and met him halfway with two outstretched legs, which sent the guy staggering backwards through the room to finally topple back and smash a glass counter in his fall.

★ ★ ★

'Colin,' sighed the sergeant. 'Please go in and bring this vaudeville to an end.'

'Right, boss.' Before dismounting Colin checked he would still be able to pull the trigger with the hand Macbeth had impaled with a dagger.

* * *

Fleance had given up his struggle, realising that he was trapped, he wouldn't be able to free himself from the seat belt before it was too late. So he lay sideways on the seat, watched the guy with the sword stand up from behind the smashed counter, fragments of glass falling from his broad shoulders. He was more careful this time. Took up a position beyond Fleance's reach. Checked he had a good grip on the sword. Fleance knew he was aiming for where he could do most instant damage and remain out of Fleance's reach. His groin.

'Bloody shide down,' the man snarled, spat on the sword, brought back his arm, took the necessary step closer and bared a row of clenched teeth. The soft, warm shop lighting made his brace sparkle, which for one instant looked like it belonged to the shop's inventory. Fleance raised the gun and fired. Glimpsed a surprised expression and a small black hole in the middle of the brace before the man fell.

* * *

The pianoforte's soft, discreet tones tickled Macbeth's ears.

'Dear guests, acquaintances, colleagues and friends of the casino,' he said, looking at the faces surrounding him, 'even if not everyone has arrived yet, I'd like on behalf of the woman you all know and fear — ' muted polite laughter and nods to a laughing Lady ' — to wish you a warm welcome and propose a toast before we take our seats at the table.'

Colin stopped when he saw his cousin from the south fall to the floor. The noise of the shot had drowned the alarm, and he saw a hand holding a revolver sticking out of the car-door opening. He reacted quickly. Fired one barrel. Saw the shell hit, saw the light-coloured inside of the door turn red, the window in the door explode and the revolver fall to the shop floor.

Colin walked quickly towards the motionless car. Adrenaline had made his senses so receptive that he took everything in. The faint vibration of the exhaust pipe, the absence of any heads in the smashed rear window and a sound he just recognised through the drone of the alarm. The belching sound of revving. *Shit!*

Colin ran the last steps to the door opening. On the passenger seat sat a suit-clad boy in a strangely distorted position. With his seat belt on, a blood-covered hand and his left foot stretched over to where the driver lay lifeless slumped over the wheel. Colin raised the shotgun as the engine raced, caught traction and the car rushed backwards. The open door hit Colin in the chest, but he managed to stick out his left hand and cling to the top of the door. They raced out of the shop, but Colin didn't let go. He still had the shotgun in his aching right hand, but to get a shot into the car he would have to move it to under his left arm . . .

★ ★ ★

Fleance had managed to get his foot over to the pedals, push his father's foot away and press the clutch so that he could move the gear lever out of neutral and into reverse. Then he gradually raised his heel off the clutch while pressing the accelerator with the tip of his shoe. The open passenger door had hit some guy who was still hanging on, but now they were out of the shop, on their way back. Fleance couldn't see a damn thing, but he gave it full throttle and hoped they wouldn't crash into anything.

The guy on the door was struggling to do something, and in a flash he saw what. The muzzle of a shotgun was protruding from under his arm. The next moment it went off.

Fleance blinked.

The guy with the gun was gone. Also the passenger door. He looked over the dashboard and saw the door and the guy wrapped around the post of the NO PARKING sign.

And he saw a side street.

He stamped on the brake and pressed the clutch before the engine died. Checked his mirror. Saw four men dismounting from their motorbikes and coming towards him. Their bikes were parked side by side barricading the narrow street; the Volvo wouldn't be able to reverse over them. Fleance grabbed the gear lever, noticed now that his hand was bleeding, tried to find first gear but couldn't, probably because from the position he was in he couldn't press the clutch right down. *Fuck, fuck, fuck.* The engine coughed and spluttered, about to breathe its last. He saw in his mirror they had drawn guns. No, machine guns. This was it. This was where it ended. And a strange thought struck him. How bitter it was that he wouldn't be taking his final exam in law now that he had finally cracked the code and understood the thinking: the difference between wrong and illegal, moral and regulation. Between power and crime.

He felt a warm hand on his, on top of the gear stick.

'Who's driving, son? You or your dad?'

Banquo's eyes were a little dimmed, but he sat upright in the seat with both hands on the wheel. And the next second the engine's old voice rose to a hoarse roar, and they skidded away on the cobblestones as the machine guns popped and crackled behind them as if it were Chinese New Year.

★   ★   ★

Macbeth looked at Lady. She sat two seats away from him enthusiastically making conversation with her dinner partner, Jano-something-or-other. The property shark from Capitol. She had placed her hand on his arm. Last year one of the town's powerful factory owners had sat in the shark's chair and captured her attention. But this year the factory was closed and its owner was not invited.

'You and I should have a chat,' Tourtell said.

'Yes,' Macbeth said, turning to the mayor, who was pushing a heavily laden fork of veal into his open jaws. 'What about?'

'What about? About the town, of course.'

Macbeth watched with fascination as the mayor's many chins expanded and compressed as he chewed, like an accordion of flesh.

'About what's best for the town,' Tourtell said with a smile. As though that was a joke. Macbeth knew he should concentrate on the conversation, but he couldn't keep his thoughts together, hold them here, down on the earth. Now for example he was wondering whether the calf's mother was still alive. And if so, if she could sense that now, right now, her child was being eaten.

'There's this radio reporter,' Macbeth said. 'Kite. He spreads malicious gossip and obviously has an unfortunate agenda. How do you neutralise a person like that?'

'Reporters,' Tourtell said, rolling his eyes. 'Now look, that's difficult. They answer only to their editors. And even if the editors in turn answer to owners who want to earn money, reporters are solemnly convinced that they're serving a higher purpose. Very difficult. You're not eating, Macbeth. Worried?'

'Me? Not at all.'

'Really? With one chief commissioner dead, another missing and all the responsibility on your shoulders? If you aren't worried, *I'd* be worried, Macbeth!'

'I didn't mean it like that.' Macbeth looked for help from Lady, who was sitting on the mayor's other side, but she was now engaged in conversation with a woman who was the town council's financial adviser or something.

'Excuse me,' Macbeth said and stood up. Got a quizzical, slightly concerned look from Lady and strode quickly into reception.

'Give me the phone, Jack.'

The receptionist passed him the phone, and Macbeth dialled the number of the HQ switchboard. It answered on the fifth ring. Was that a long or a short time to wait for an answer from the police? He didn't know, he had never considered it before. But now he would have to. Think about that sort of thing. As well. 'Put me through to Patrols.'

'OK.'

He could hear he had been put through, and the phone at the other end began to ring. Macbeth looked at his watch. They were taking their time.

'I never see you in the gaming room, Jack.'

'I don't work as a croupier any more, sir. Not after . . . well, that night, you know.'

'I see. It takes a while to get over.'

Jack shrugged. 'It's not just that. In fact, I think being a receptionist suits me better than being a croupier. So it's no tragedy.'

'But don't you earn a good deal more as a croupier?'

'If you're a fish out of water, it doesn't matter how much you earn. The fish can't breathe and dies beside a fat bagful of money. That's a tragedy, sir.'

Macbeth was about to answer when a voice

announced that he had got through to Patrols.

'Macbeth here. I was wondering if you'd had any reports about a shooting in Gallows Hill during the last hour.'

'No. Should we have done?'

'We have a customer here who said he'd just driven by and heard a loud bang. Must have been a puncture.'

'Must have been.'

'So there's nothing in District 2 West?'

'Only a break-in at a jeweller's, sir. The closest patrol car was some distance away, but we're heading there now.'

'I see. Well, have a good evening.'

'You, too, Inspector.'

Macbeth rang off. Stared down at the carpet, at the strange needlework, the flowery shapes. He had never thought about them, but now it was as if they were trying to tell him something.

'Sir?'

Macbeth looked up. Jack had a worried expression on his face.

'Sir, you've got a nosebleed.'

Macbeth put a hand to his top lip, realised the receptionist was right and hurried to the toilet.

★ ★ ★

Banquo accelerated down the main road. The wind howled outside the doorless passenger side. They passed the Obelisk. It wouldn't be long before they were at the central station now.

'Can you see them?'

Fleance said something.

'Louder!'

'No.'

Banquo couldn't hear in the ear on Fleance's side, either because the auditory canal was blocked with blood or because the bullet had taken his hearing as well. However it wasn't that shot which bothered him. He looked at the petrol gauge — the indicator had dropped remarkably in the four or five minutes since they had left the shopping area. The machine guns might have *sounded* harmless, but they had holed the petrol tank. But it wasn't those shots that bothered him either; they had enough petrol to get to the Inverness and safety.

'Who are they, Dad? Why are they after us?'

There, in front of them, was the central station.

'I don't know, Fleance.' Banquo concentrated on the road. And breathing. He had to breathe, get air into his lungs. Carry on. Carry on until Fleance was safe. That, and nothing else, was what mattered. Not the road that had begun to blur in front of him, not the shot that had hit him.

'Someone must have known we would come that way, Dad. The traffic lights, that wasn't normal. They knew exactly when we would pass Gallows Hill.'

Banquo had worked that one out. But it meant nothing now. What did mean something was that they had passed the central station and that the lights of the Inverness lay before them. Park in front of the entrance, get Fleance inside.

'I can see them now, Dad. They're at least two hundred metres behind us.'

More than enough if they didn't get held up. He should have had the blue light and the siren in the car. Banquo stared at the Inverness. Light. He could drive across Workers' Square at a pinch. The sirens. Something stuck in his throat. Stuck in his mind.

'Did you hear any sirens, Fleance?'

'Eh?'

'Sirens. Patrol cars. Did you hear them at the jeweller's?'

'No.'

'Absolutely sure? There are always loads of patrol cars in District 2 West.'

'Absolutely sure.'

Banquo felt the pain and darkness come. 'No,' he whispered. 'No, Macbeth, my boy . . . ' He held the wheel and turned left.

'Dad! This isn't the way to the Inverness.'

Banquo pressed the horn, pulled the Volvo out from behind the car in front and accelerated. He could feel the paralysing pain from his back spreading to his chest. Soon he wouldn't be able to keep his right hand on the wheel. The bullet probably hadn't made a big hole in the seat, but it had hit it. And that was the shot that worried him.

In front of them there was nothing. Only the container harbour, the sea and darkness.

But there was one last possibility.

★   ★   ★

Macbeth studied himself in the mirror above the sink. The bleeding had stopped, but he knew what it meant. That his mucous membranes couldn't take any more brew, and he should give it up for a while. It was different when he was young: then his body could take any amount of punishment. But if he continued now his nose would ache and bleed and his brain would spin until his head unscrewed itself from his neck. What he needed was a break. So why, thinking this, did he roll up a banknote and place it at the right-hand end of the line of powder on the sink? Because this was the exception. This was the critical point when he needed it. The point when he had to tackle the fat perverted mayor on the one side and the Norse Rider brigand who it seemed hadn't managed to keep to their agreement on the other. And Lady on the third. No, she wasn't a problem, she was the alpha and the omega, his birth, life and death. His reason for *being*. But just as their love could give him a tremulous joy, he could also feel the pain when he thought of what might be taken from him — her power now consisted in *not* loving him as much as loving him. He inhaled, sucked the brew up into his brain, hard, until it hit the inside of his scalp, or so it felt. Again looked at himself in the mirror. His face contorted and changed. He had white hair. A woman's red lips. A scar grew across his face. New chins extended under his chin. Tears filled his eyes and ran down his cheeks. He had to stop now. He had seen people who had sniffed so much they had ended up with prosthetic noses. Had to stop while there was still time, while there was something to save. He had to switch to a syringe.

★   ★   ★

The sergeant saw the rear lights of the Volvo gradually coming nearer. He opened the throttle knowing the others would find it difficult to keep up now even though his engine was only 450 cc. On wet oily tarmac experience and sensitivity were more important for road-holding than engine size. It was therefore with some surprise that he saw a bike approaching fast in his mirror. And with disbelief he recognised it. And the rider's helmet. The red Indian Chief passed so close to the sergeant that the point of a horn almost brushed against him. His headlight was reflected in the sabre when the bike overtook him. Where had he come from? How did he know? How did he always know when they needed him? The sergeant slowed down. Let Sweno ride at the front and lead them.

★   ★   ★

Banquo drove the same way they had when they were following the Russian lorry, overtaking dangerously a couple of times and temporarily increasing their

232

distance from the motorbikes. They would soon catch up again, but perhaps there was still time. There was a barrier in front of the tunnel and a sign to say the bridge was closed due to repairs. Splinters flew as the front of the Volvo smashed into the barrier and its headlights bored into the tunnel's darkness. He drove with one hand on the wheel; the other lay in his lap like a corpse. They could already see the exit when they heard the angry yapping of the motorbike engines entering the tunnel behind them.

Banquo braked approaching the sharp bend onto the bridge and then speeded up again.

And soon they were out on it, to a sudden silence beneath a clear sky and in the moonlight, which made the river glitter like copper below, far beneath them. All that could be heard was the Volvo's engine working as hard as it could. And then the whine of rubber on tarmac as Banquo braked suddenly in the middle of the bridge where the statue of Kenneth had once been and turned onto the shoulder where the breeze flapped the Highway Agency's red cordon tape, marking the spot the ZIS-5 had plunged down with the railing. Surprised, Fleance turned to his father, who had put the car into neutral. Banquo leaned over his son with a pocket knife in his hand and cut his seat belt.

'What . . . ?'

'We've got a leak, son. Soon we won't have any petrol, so listen to me. I've never been much of a preacher, you know that, but I want to say this to you . . . ' Banquo leaned against the door on his side, lifted his knees and swung round in his seat as Fleance had done.

'You can be whatever you want, Fleance. So don't be what I was. Don't be a lackey for lackeys.'

'Dad . . . '

'And land on your feet.'

He placed the soles of his shoes against his son's hip and shoulder, saw Fleance try to grab on to something, then shoved him with all his might. The son screamed in protest, in fear as he had done when he was born, but then he was out, the last umbilical cord severed, alone in the big wide world, in free fall towards his fate.

Banquo groaned with pain as he swung himself back, put the car in gear and accelerated towards his own fate.

When he ran out of petrol three kilometres after leaving the bridge they had almost caught him up. The car rolled the last metres, and Banquo could feel he was sleepy and laid his head back. A chill had spread down his whole back and into his stomach and was moving towards his heart. He thought about Vera. And when it finally rained on this side of the tunnel, it rained lead. Lead that pierced the car, seats and Banquo's body. He stared out of the side window, up the mountainside. There, almost at the top, he could see what looked like from the town side a tribute to evil. But here it was a Christian cross that shone in the light of the moon. It was so close. It showed the way. The gate was open.

'A planned rise,' Banquo mumbled. A plann — '

16

Duff listened to Caithness's breathing as it slowly quietened. Then he freed himself from her embrace and turned to the bedside table.

'Well, Cinders?' she whispered. 'Is it almost midnight?'

'We've got plenty of time, but I can't arrive late.'

'You've been looking at the clock every half an hour ever since you got here. Anyone would think you were dying to leave.'

He turned to her again. Put his hand behind her neck. 'That's not why, my beautiful woman, it's just that I lose all concept of time when I'm here with you.' He kissed her lightly on the lips.

She chuckled. 'You can sweet-talk, you can, Romeo. But I've been thinking.'

'Sounds scary.'

'Stop it. I've been thinking I love you. And — '

'Scary.'

'Stop it, I said. And I don't just want you here and now. I don't want you always disappearing like a half-dreamed dream.'

'I don't want to either, my love, but — '

'No more buts, Duff. You always say you'll tell her about us, but then there's the constant but, which means you have to postpone doing it, which you say is out of consideration for her, for the children, for — '

'But there are considerations, Caithness. You have to understand that. I've got a family and with it come — '

' — *Responsibilities I can't run away from*,' she mimicked. 'What about some consideration for me? You never seem to have any problem running away from me.'

'You know very well it's not like that. But you're young, you've got alternatives.'

'Alternatives? What do you mean? I love *you*!'

'I only mean that Meredith and the children are vulnerable right now. If we wait until the children are a year older, it'll be easier, then I can — '

'No!' Caithness smacked her hand down on the duvet. 'I want you to tell her now, Duff. And do you know what? That's the first time you've mentioned her by name.'

'Caithness . . . '

'Meredith. It's a nice name. I've envied her that name for a long time.'

'Why such a hurry all of a sudden?'

'I've realised something over the last few days. To get what you want you can't wait for someone to give it to you. You have to be tough, possibly inconsiderate, but a clean cut is best. Believe me, it isn't easy for me to ask you to do this, to sacrifice your family — it affects innocent people, and that's not in my nature.'

'No, Caithness, it's not in your nature, so where have you got this from, this idea of a clean cut?'

'Duff.' She sat up, cross-legged, in the middle of the bed. 'Do you love me?'

'Yes! Jesus, yes.'

'So will you do it? Will you do this for me?'

'Listen to me, Caithness — '

'I like Meredith better.'

'Darling. I love you more than anything else. I would give my life for you. My very own life, yes, without hesitation. But others' lives?' Duff shook his head. Inhaled to speak but let his breath back out. A clean cut. Did it have to be now? The idea of it surprised him. Had he unwittingly been on his way there all the time? On his way from Caithness, on his way home to Fife? He took another deep breath.

'My mother — whom I never knew — sacrificed her

236

life for me. Sacrificed hers so that I could live. So even if it's in my nature — as it was in my mother's nature — to sacrifice a life for love, love for a child is the greatest love. Just the *thought* of having to sacrifice anything smaller for my children — taking their family away from them for my selfish love for another woman — is like spitting on my mother's memory.'

Caithness put her hand to her mouth and an involuntary sob escaped her as her eyes filled with tears. Then she stood up and left the bedroom.

Duff closed his eyes. Banged his head on the pillow behind him. Then he followed her. He found her in the sitting room, where she was standing by one of the attic windows and staring out. Naked and shimmeringly white in the neon light from outside, which made the trails of raindrops on the window look like tears running down her cheeks.

He stood behind her and put an arm around her naked body. Whispered into her hair. 'If you want me to go now, I will.'

'I'm not crying because I can't have all of you, Duff. I'm crying because of my own hard heart. While you, you're a man with a real heart, darling. A man a child can trust. I can't stop loving you. Forgive me. And if I can't have everything, give me what you can of your pure heart.'

Duff didn't answer, just held her. Kissed her neck and held her. Her hips began to move. He thought of the time. Of Banquo. Their meeting by the locomotive. But it was still a long time to midnight.

★ ★ ★

'Inverness Casino, Jack speaking.'

'Good evening, Jack. I'd like to talk to Macbeth.'

'He's at a dinner. Can I give him a — '

'Get him, Jack. Come on.'

237

Pause.

The sergeant looked at the motorbikes gathered around the telephone box. Their shapes were distorted by the thick snakes of water coiling down the outside of the glass, but still the sight was the most beautiful he knew — engines on two wheels. And the brothers who rode them.

'I can ask, sir. Who can I say is calling?'

'Just say this is the call he was expecting.'

'I see, sir.'

The sergeant waited. Shifting his weight from one foot to the other. Switching the blood-stained parcel from one arm to the other.

'Macbeth.'

'Good evening. I'm just calling to say the fish has been caught and gutted, but the fry swam away.'

'Where?'

'Now the chances of a single fry surviving are a thousand to one against, and I think in this case we can be satisfied that it's dead and lying at the bottom of the sea.'

'Right. So?'

'The fish head's on its way. And I'd say you've won my respect, Macbeth. There are few who have the palate or stomach for this kind of delicacy.'

★ ★ ★

Macbeth put down the phone and held on to the counter as he breathed quickly in and out.

'Are you sure you're well this evening, sir?'

'Yes, thank you, Jack. Just a bit giddy.'

Macbeth repressed his thoughts and images one by one. Then he adjusted his jacket and tie and went back to the dining room.

The guests at the long table were talking and toasting, but there wasn't a great atmosphere. Now

238

perhaps these people didn't celebrate as loudly and passionately as they did in SWAT, but he wondered whether the shadow of Duncan's death didn't lie more heavily over the casino than Lady would have admitted. The mayor had seen Macbeth and waved him over. He saw that someone was sitting on his chair and assumed it was Tourtell's companion. But when Macbeth saw that he was wrong he came to a sudden halt. It felt as if his heart had stopped beating.

Banquo.

He was sitting there. Now.

'What is it, my love?' It was Lady. She had turned and was looking at him in surprise. 'Sit down.'

'My place is taken,' he said.

Tourtell also turned. 'Come on, Macbeth. Sit down.'

'Where?'

'On your chair,' Lady said. 'What's the matter?'

Macbeth screamed as Banquo turned his head like an owl. Above his white collar ran a long, continuous wound that seemed to run completely around his neck. Blood ran from the wound, like from the rim of a full glass of wine someone was continuing to fill.

'Who . . . who did this to you?' Macbeth groaned and placed both hands around Banquo's neck. Squeezed to stop the blood, but it was thin and trickled between his fingers like diluted wine.

'What are you doing, my love?' Lady laughed in a strained voice.

Banquo's mouth opened. 'It . . . was . . . you . . . my son.' The words were delivered in a monotone, his face expressionless like a ventriloquist's doll.

'No!'

'I . . . saw . . . you . . . master . . . I . . . am . . . waiting . . . for . . . you . . . master.'

'Be quiet!' Macbeth squeezed harder.

'You . . . are . . . strangling . . . me . . . Murderer-beth.'

Macbeth, terrified, let go. He felt someone pull hard at his arm.

'Come on.' It was Lady. He was about to tear his arm away when she hissed into his ear, 'Now! While you're still chief commissioner.'

She put her hand under his arm, as though she was following him, and like this they sailed out of the dining hall as if blown by the expressions of their guests.

'What's the matter?' she hissed when she had locked them in their suite.

'Didn't you see him? Banquo! He was sitting in my chair.'

'My God, you're high. You're seeing things! Do you want the mayor to think he's got a lunatic as his chief commissioner?'

'*His?*'

'Where's your wretched brew? Where?' She thrust her hand into his trouser pocket. 'This is going out now!'

Macbeth grabbed her wrist. '*His* chief commissioner?'

'Tourtell's going to appoint you, Macbeth. I put you two together because I thought at least you wouldn't destroy the impression that you were the right man for the job. Ow, let go!'

'Let Mayor Tourtell do what he likes. I've got enough on him to lock him up tomorrow. And if I don't, I can get it. I'm the chief commissioner, woman! Don't you understand what that means? I'm in command of six thousand people, two thousand of them armed. An army, darling!'

Macbeth saw her eyes were softening.

'All right, yes,' she whispered. 'Now you're talking sense again, love.'

He was still gripping her fine, slender wrist, but her hand had started moving in his pocket.

'Now I can feel you again,' she said.

'Come on, let's — '

'No, not now,' she interrupted and pulled her hand

away. 'We've got guests. But I have something else for you. A present to celebrate your appointment.'

'Oh?'

'Look in the bedside-table drawer.'

Macbeth took out a case. Inside it was a bright, shiny dagger. He lifted it to the light. 'Silver?'

'I was going to give it to you after the dinner, but I think you need it now. Silver, as is well known, is the only material that can kill ghosts.'

'Thank you, my sweet.'

'It's a pleasure. So tell me Banquo is dead.'

'Banquo's dead. He's dead.'

'Yes, and we'll mourn later. Now let's join the others. You tell them it was an inside joke between us. Come on.'

★ ★ ★

It was ten minutes past eleven.

Caithness was still in bed, while Duff had got dressed and was standing by the kitchen worktop. He had made a cup of tea and found a lemon in the fridge, but the only clean knife was more suited to stabbing than slicing a lemon. He stuck the point in the peel and a fine spray came out. So late at night it would normally take half the usual time to get to the central station, find a parking spot and get to Bertha. He had no intention of being late. Banquo didn't seem as if he needed an excuse *not* to tell him what he knew. On the other hand, Duff had seen Banquo wanted to talk. Wanted to unburden himself of . . . of what? The guilt? Or just what he knew? Banquo was no bellwether, he was a sheep, no more than a link. And soon Duff hoped he would know who the others were. And armed with that he would . . . The silence was broken by the telephone on the wall beside the cork board.

'Phone!' he shouted.

241

'Heard it. I'll take it here,' Caithness answered from the bedroom. She had a phone in every room, one of the things that could make him feel old when he was with her. They were perhaps a little old-fashioned, Meredith and him, but they thought that one phone per household was enough — it didn't hurt to have to run. He found a cloth and wiped his hand. Listened for her voice to determine what kind of conversation it was, who was ringing so late at night. Meredith? The thought came to him, and he rejected it at once. The second thought lingered for longer. A lover. Another lover, younger. No, an admirer, a potential lover. Someone standing in the wings, ready to step in if Duff hadn't given her the answer she wanted this evening. Yes, that was the reason for the sudden hurry. And Duff hadn't complied with her demands, while his ultimatum had been turned round to become her own. And she had chosen him. The moment he articulated the thought he half-wished it was an admirer. How strange are we humans?

'Could you repeat that?' he heard Caithness say from the bedroom. Her professional voice. Only more excited than usual. 'I'm on my way. Call the others.'

Definitely work. SOCO work.

He heard her rummaging around in her room. He hoped the job wasn't in Fife and she would suggest he drove her. His hand was sweaty. He licked it while looking down at the lemon. The juice had got into one of the cuts he had received when he fell on the tarmac at the quay. He was still for a second. Then he pulled the knife out and stabbed the lemon again. Hard and fast this time. Let go of the knife quickly and pulled his hand away, but it stung again. It was impossible. Impossible to stab and remove your hand before the spray.

Caithness rushed into the kitchen with a black doctor's bag in her hand.

'What is it?' Duff asked when he saw her expression.

'It was HQ. Macbeth's deputy from SWAT . . . '

'Banquo?' Duff felt his throat constrict.

'Yes,' she said, pulling open a drawer. 'He's been found on Kenneth Bridge.'

'Found? Do you mean . . . ?'

'Yes,' she said, rummaging angrily in the drawer.

'How?' The questions that accumulated were too numerous, and Duff helplessly grabbed his forehead.

'I don't know yet, but the police at the scene say his car's riddled with bullets. And his head's been removed.'

'Removed? As in . . . cut off?'

'We'll soon see,' she said, taking a pair of latex gloves from the drawer and putting them in the bag. 'Can you drive me?'

'Caithness, I've got this meeting, so . . . '

'You didn't say where, but if it's a long detour . . . '

He looked at the knife again.

'I'll go with you,' he said. 'Of course I will. I'm head of the Homicide Unit, and this case is top priority.'

Then he turned and threw the knife hard at the cork board. It spun one and a half times on its axis before hitting the board handle first and falling to the kitchen floor with a clatter.

'What are you trying to do?' she asked.

Duff stared at the knife. 'Something you need a lot of practice at before you succeed. Come on.'

17

'So, Seyton,' Macbeth said, 'what can I do for you?'

The rays of sunshine had found a break in the clouds and were now angled through the grimy windows of the chief commissioner's office and fell on his desk, on his photo of Lady, on the calendar showing it was a Tuesday, on the drawing of the Gatling gun and, sitting in front of Macbeth's desk, the polished, shiny pate of the lean, sinewy officer.

'You need a bodyguard,' Seyton said.

'Do I? And what kind of bodyguard do I need?'

'One who can fight evil with evil. Duncan had two, and after this business with Banquo, God bless his soul, there's every reason to assume they're after you as well, Chief Commissioner.'

'Who are *they?*'

Seyton looked at Macbeth with puzzlement in his eyes before answering. 'The Norse Riders. My understanding is that they're behind this execution.'

Macbeth nodded. 'Witnesses in District 2 say they saw bikers, some of them wearing Norse Rider jackets, shooting at a Volvo outside a jewellery shop the car had driven into. We presume it was Banquo's car.'

'If Malcolm was involved, the threat to the chief commissioner may come from inside the force. I don't trust all our so-called leaders. In my opinion, Duff is someone who lacks spine and morality. Of the threats outside the force there's obviously Hecate.'

'Hecate's a businessman. Being suspected of murder is rarely good for business. Sweno, on the other hand, has a motive which trumps business sense.'

'Revenge.'

'Good old-fashioned revenge, yes. Some of our

economists seem to undervalue the human tendency to follow our basest instincts instead of the bank book. When the black widow's lover is lying on her back, sated and exhausted by love-making, he *knows* he'll soon be eaten. Yet he would never be able to make any other choice. And there you have Sweno.'

'So you're less afraid of Hecate?'

'I've told you today that resources should be distributed more sensibly, the witch-hunt aimed at Hecate has to be scaled down so that we can sort out other more pressing problems for the town.'

'Such as?'

'Such as honest, hard-working people being openly cheated and robbed of their savings by one of our more dubious casinos. But back to the point. Former chief commissioners have had bad experiences with body-guards, but I haven't forgotten how effective and brave you were when I was attacked by that dog at Cawdor's. So let me sleep on this, Seyton. Actually, I'd been thinking of giving you a different post, one which is not so different from the one you were requesting, actually.'

'Oh?'

'Now I'm chief commissioner and Banquo's gone, SWAT doesn't have a head. You, Seyton, are the oldest officer with the most experience.'

'Thank you, Chief Commissioner. That is really an unexpected honour and statement of trust. The problem is that I don't know if I'm worthy of the trust. I'm not a politician, nor a leader of men.'

'No, I know the type. You're a watchdog who needs a master and a mistress, Seyton. But SWAT is a kind of watchdog. You'd be surprised at the detail of the instructions you get. I barely needed to think about how to apprehend the bad guys. And given the murders over the last two days it's clear that the threat to someone sitting in my chair is such that SWAT will have to be used to actively protect the head of police HQ.'

'Are you saying that SWAT will become the chief commissioner's personal bodyguard?'

'I can't imagine that an arrangement of that kind would meet any resistance that can't be quelled. In which case, we would be killing two birds with one stone. Your wishes and mine would be met. What do you say, Seyton?'

The sun was going down, and perhaps it was the sudden darkness falling in the room that made Seyton lower his voice so it sounded like a conspiratorial whisper: 'As long as my orders come directly and in detail from you personally, Chief Commissioner.'

Macbeth studied the man in front of him. *God bless his soul*, Seyton had said about Banquo. Macbeth wondered what kind of blessing it had been.

'My orders, loyal Seyton, will be unambiguous. As far as quelling protests is concerned, I've just ordered two of these Gatling guns.' He passed Seyton the drawing. 'Express delivery. Bit more expensive, but we'll get them in two days. What do you think?'

Seyton ran his eye over the drawing, nodding slowly. 'Tasty,' he said. 'Beautiful in fact.'

★   ★   ★

Duff yawned as he drove from a clear sky to dark clouds.

Ewan had woken him when he jumped up into the guest bed, with his sister hard on his heels.

'Daddy, you're home!'

They'd had breakfast in the kitchen with the morning sun low over the lake. Meredith had told the children to stop fighting to sit on Daddy's lap and eat; they had to go to school. She hadn't managed to put on the strict voice Duff knew she wanted to, and he had seen the smile in her eyes.

Now he passed the crime scene, where the

246

bullet-riddled car had been towed away and the blood on the tarmac had been cleaned up. Caithness and her people had worked efficiently and found what evidence there was. And there hadn't been much for him to do apart from state the obvious: that Banquo had been shot and beheaded. There was no trace of Fleance, but Duff had noticed that the seat belt on the passenger seat had been cut. That could mean anything at all; for the time being all they could do was put out a general missing-person alert for Banquo's young son. It was a deserted stretch of road, as the bridge was closed, and it was unlikely there had been any witnesses in the vicinity, so after an hour Duff had decided that since he was halfway home he may as well sleep in Fife.

Where he had lain awake thinking to the accompaniment of the grasshoppers' song outside. He had known. Known but hadn't understood. It wasn't that he had suddenly seen the bigger picture; it wasn't that all the interlocking pieces had suddenly fitted into the jigsaw puzzle. It had been one simple detail. The knife in Caithness's kitchen. But while he had been brooding the other pieces had emerged and slowly fitted in. Then he had fallen asleep and woken to the children's ambush at dawn.

Duff drove over the old bridge. It was narrow and modest in comparison with Kenneth Bridge, but solidly built, and many thought it would stand for longer.

The problem was: who should he talk to?

It had to be someone who not only had enough power, influence and dynamism, but also someone he could trust, who *wasn't* involved.

He drove down to the garage under HQ as the break in the clouds closed and the sun's short visit was over.

Lennox looked up from his typewriter as Duff came in. 'Lunch soon, and you're yawning as if you've just got up.'

'For the last time, is that thing genuine?' Duff asked,

nodding at the tarnished stick with a lump of rusty metal on the end that Lennox used as a paperweight. Duff slumped down in a chair beside the door.

'And for the last time — ' Lennox sighed ' — I inherited it from my grandfather, who had it thrown at his head in the Somme trenches. Fortunately, as you can see, the German forgot to pull the detonator pin. His soldier pals laughed a lot at that story.'

'Are you saying they laughed a lot in the Somme?'

'According to my grandfather the worse it got, the more they laughed. He called it the laughter of war.'

'I still think you're lying, Lennox. You're not the type to have a live grenade on your desk.'

Lennox smiled as he went on typing. 'Grandad kept it in his house all his life. He said it reminded him of the important things — the transience of life, the role of chance, his own mortality and others' incompetence.'

Duff motioned to the typewriter. 'Haven't you got a secretary to take care of that?'

'I've started writing my own letters and leaving the building to post them myself. Yesterday I was told by the Public Prosecutor's Office that one of my letters appeared to have been opened and resealed before they received it.'

'I'm not shocked. Thanks for receiving me at such short notice.'

'*Receiving* me? That sounds very formal. You didn't say what this was about on the phone.'

'No. As I said, I'm not shocked that someone opens letters.'

'The switchboard. Do you think — '

'I don't think anything, Lennox. I agree with you that there's no point taking risks with the situation as it is now.'

Lennox nodded slowly and tilted his head. 'And yet, good Duff, that's precisely why you've come here?'

'Maybe. I have some evidence concerning who killed Duncan.'

Lennox's chair creaked as he straightened his back. He pushed himself away from the typewriter and rested his elbows on the desk. 'Close the door.'

Duff stretched out his arm and closed it.

'What kind of evidence? Tangible?'

'Funny you should use that word . . . ' Duff took the letter opener from Lennox's desk and weighed it in his hand. 'As you know, at both crime scenes, Duncan's and the bodyguards', everything was apparently kosher.'

'The word *apparently* is used when something seems fine on the surface but isn't.'

'Exactly.' Inspector Duff placed the knife across his forefinger so that it balanced and formed a cross with his finger. 'If you stabbed a man in the neck with a dagger to kill him, wouldn't you hold on to the dagger in case you missed the carotid artery and had to stab again?'

'I suppose so,' Lennox said, staring at the letter opener.

'And if you hit the artery straight away, as we know one dagger did, enormous quantities of blood would shoot out in a couple of brief spurts, the victim's blood pressure would fall, the heart would stop beating, and the rest would just trickle out.'

'I follow. I think.'

'Yet the handle of the dagger we found on Hennessy was completely covered in blood; his prints were in the blood, and the inside of his hand was also covered with Duncan's blood.' Duff pointed to the handle of the letter opener. 'That means the murderer wasn't holding the handle when the blood spurted from Duncan's neck, but grabbed the handle afterwards. Or that someone pressed his hand around the handle later. Because someone — someone else — *threw* the dagger at Duncan's neck.'

'I see,' Lennox said, scratching his head. 'But throw or stab, what's the difference? The result's the same.'

Duff passed Lennox the letter opener. 'Try and throw this knife so that it sticks in the noticeboard over there.'

'I . . .'

'Come on.'

Lennox stood up. The distance to the board was probably two metres.

'You have to throw it hard,' Duff said. 'It requires strength to pierce a man's neck.'

Lennox threw. The knife hit the board and bounced off onto the floor with a clatter.

'Try ten times,' Duff said, picking up the knife and letting it balance on his finger. 'I bet you a bottle of good whisky you can't get the point to stick in.'

'You don't have much confidence in my ability or my luck?'

'If I'd given you a knife that wasn't balanced, with either a heavy handle or a heavy blade, I'd have made the odds better. But just like the dagger in Duncan's neck this is a balanced knife. You have to be an expert to throw one. And no one I've spoken to in this building has ever seen or heard anything to suggest Duncan's bodyguards were knife-throwers. To tell the truth, only one person I know was. Someone who actually almost ended up in a circus doing just that. And who was at Inverness Casino that evening.'

'Who's that?'

'The man you gave Organised Crime. Macbeth.'

Lennox stood stock still gaping at a point on Duff's forehead. 'Are you telling me . . . ?'

'Yes, I am. Chief Commissioner Duncan was killed by Macbeth. And the murder of those innocent body-guards was cold-blooded murder carried out by the same man.'

'God have mercy on us,' Lennox said, sitting down with a bump. 'Have you spoken to Forensics and Caithness about this?'

Duff shook his head. 'They noticed there was blood

on the handle, but they think that was down to quick reflexes when the dagger was let go, not that the dagger was thrown. Reasonable enough theory. After all, it's very rare for anyone to have that skill. And it's only Macbeth's closest colleagues who know he's one of them.'

'Good. We mustn't mention this to anyone. *No one.*' Lennox clenched his hands and chewed his knuckles. 'Are you aware of the situation this puts me in, Duff?'

'Yes. Now you know what I know, that can't be changed, and now your head's on the block with mine. I apologise for not giving you a choice, but what else could I do? Our moment of truth has come, Lennox.'

'Indeed. If what you say is correct and Macbeth is the monster you believe, a wounding shot is not enough — that would make him doubly dangerous. He must be felled with a single, decisive shot.'

'Yes, but how?'

'With cunning and caution, Duff. I'll have to give this some thought, and I'm no genius, so it will take time. Let's meet again. Not here where the walls have ears.'

'At six,' Duff said, getting up. 'The central station. By Bertha.'

'The old train? Why there?'

'That's where I was going to meet Banquo. He was going to tell me all I've worked out anyway.'

'So that's a suitable meeting place. See you.'

★   ★   ★

Macbeth stared at the telephone on his desk.

He had just put down the receiver after talking to Sweno.

His nerves were jerking and twitching under his skin. He needed *something*. Not *something*, he knew what. He snatched the big hat Lady had bought him. Priscilla smiled as Macbeth strode towards the anteroom. 'How

251

long will the chief commissioner be out?'

She had, at Macbeth's behest, been moved up from Lennox's office, the whole process taking less than two hours. He had wanted to give Duncan's old assistant the heave-ho, but instead had moved her down a floor after the head of admin explained to him that in the public sector not even a chief commissioner could dismiss employees at the drop of a hat.

'An hour,' Macbeth said. 'Or two.'

'I'll say two to callers then,' she said.

'You do that, Priscilla.'

He walked into the lift and pressed G for the ground floor. *To callers.* Not *if anyone calls.* Because people did call, non-bloody-stop. Unit heads, judges, council representatives. He didn't have the slightest clue what half of them did, apart from pester him with questions he couldn't fathom, and that meant a queue of callers. Journalists. Duncan's death, Malcolm's disappearance. And now another policeman, plus his son. Was everything spinning out of control? they asked. Could the chief commissioner assure them that . . . ? *No comment. May I refer you to the next press conference, which* . . .

And then there was Sweno.

The lift doors opened; two uniformed policemen on their way in stopped and backed out again. It was a rule Kenneth had introduced, and Duncan had abolished, that the chief commissioner should have the lift to himself. But before Macbeth could say they were welcome the lift doors had closed again and he continued down on his own.

On the pavement outside headquarters he bumped into a man in a grey coat reading a newspaper who mumbled, 'Sorry, Macbeth.' Not so strange because when Macbeth looked up he saw his own face on the front page. THIRD OFFICER TAKES THE HELM. Not a bad headline. Might have been Lady's suggestion. The editor was putty in her hands.

Macbeth pulled the big hat down over his face and walked with long strides. Now, in the middle of the day, the streets were so chock-a-block with traffic it was faster to walk than drive to the central station. And besides it was just as well no one saw the chief commissioner's limousine there.

God knows what Sweno had said to Priscilla to be put through. At any rate he hadn't said his name when Macbeth had him on the line, he hadn't needed to. If you heard his voice once you didn't forget it. The bass made the plastic in the receiver quiver. He said that Macbeth's promise had been the *immediate* release of the Norse Riders, and twelve hours had already passed. Macbeth had answered that it wasn't that simple: papers had to be signed by judges and lawyers as a prosecution had already been raised. But Sweno could safely prepare a welcome speech for the homecoming party in two days.

'That's two days too many,' Sweno had said. 'And the two last days you will ever get from me. The day after tomorrow, at eleven o'clock on the dot, one of our members will ring the home of one of the town's judges, I won't say which, and confess his involvement in Banquo's murder and how we knew exactly where Banquo and Fleance would be.'

'One of your kamikaze pilots?'

'In addition, we have seven witnesses that saw you come to our club house.'

'Relax and think about your speech, Sweno. We'll drop your boys outside the club gate tomorrow afternoon at half past three.'

And with that Macbeth rang off.

At the foot of the steps to the central station Macbeth scoured the area. Saw another grey coat, but not the same one. The hat hid his face, and he was after all only one of many smartly dressed men who ran up these steps every day to buy whatever they needed to function as surprisingly well as they did.

He stood where he had last stood, in the corridor, by the stairs down to the toilet. The young boy was nowhere to be seen. Macbeth hopped from foot to foot impatiently. It was many hours since he had felt the need, but it was only now, as he was about to satisfy his need, that it was really bad.

She appeared after what felt like an hour, but his watch told him only ten minutes had passed. She had a white stick in her hand, whatever that was supposed to mean.

'I need two bags,' he said.

'You need to meet someone,' Strega said. 'Put these in your ears and wear these.' She held out a pair of earplugs and some glasses that looked like a cross between swimming and welding goggles, the type he had seen blind people wear.

'Why should I?'

'Because if you don't you won't get any brew.'

He hesitated. No, he didn't hesitate, he just took his time. He would have walked on his hands if that was what they demanded. The goggles were painted, so he could see nothing at all. Strega held him and whirled him round several times, evidently so that he would lose his sense of direction. Then she handed him the white stick and led him off. Ten minutes later he knew they had walked in the rain, people and traffic had been around them, the ear-plugs didn't shut out all sound. Strega had helped him up onto a cement edge a metre and a half high and from there they had walked on gravel or sand. Then up onto another cement edge and inside somewhere, he guessed — at least it was warmer and the air was drier. And he had been sat down on a chair where someone took out the earplugs and told him to keep the goggles on.

He heard someone approaching, and a *tap-tap* sound

stopped right in front of him.

'I regret to have to bring you here in this way.' The voice was unusually gentle and soft and sounded as if it belonged to an elderly man. 'But I thought — all things taken into account — it was best to meet face to face. That is, you can't see mine of course, but if I were you, Macbeth, I would be glad of that.'

'I understand. It means you intend to let me leave alive.'

'You're not smart, but you're more smart than stupid, Macbeth. That was why we chose you.'

'Why am I here?'

'Because we're concerned. We knew of course of your affection for stimulants before we chose you, but we weren't aware that it would take over so completely and so quickly. In short, we have to find out if you're trustworthy or we will have to swap you.'

'Swap me for what?'

'Do you imagine you're unique? I hope the chief commissioner title hasn't gone to your head and that you realise it's only a front. Without me you're nothing. Duncan thought he could manage without me, indeed, that he could fight me. Do you believe that too, Macbeth?'

Macbeth gritted his teeth and swallowed his anger. He only wanted the bags and to get away. He took a deep breath. 'As far as I can see, we have a form of collaboration we both profit from, Hecate. You may have triggered events that led to me becoming chief commissioner, and I will get rid of Sweno and ensure that the police don't bother you and your monopoly too much.'

'Hm. So you have no moral scruples?'

'Of course I do, but I'm a pragmatist. In any town of this size there will be a market for dream sellers like you. If it isn't you or Sweno, it'll be someone else. Our cooperation will at least keep other and perhaps worse drug dealers away. I accept you as the means to the end of building a good future for this town.'

The old man chuckled. 'Sounds like words taken straight from Lady's mouth. Light and sweet to the taste but insubstantial. I'm at a crossroads here, Macbeth. And to decide my way I will have to make an assessment of your suitability. I see the newspapers are using metaphors about the third officer taking over the helm from the captain. Well, your ship is in a hurricane right now. Duncan, Banquo and a police cadet have been executed. Cawdor, Malcolm and two bodyguards are dead and assumed corrupt. Your ship is already a physical and moral wreck, Macbeth, so if I'm going to help you I have to know specifically how you're going to steer it into calmer waters.'

'The guilty parties will of course be apprehended and punished.'

'I'm glad to hear that. And who are the guilty parties?'

'That's obvious. The Norse Riders. They forced Malcolm and his guards to cooperate.'

'Good. In which case we shall be acquitted, you and I. But what if Sweno can prove his innocence with respect to Duncan's murder?'

'I have a feeling he won't be able to.'

'Hm. I hope you've got the energy to follow up what you've said, Macbeth.'

'I have, Hecate. And I hope I can demand the same of you.'

'What do you mean? I've carved out a path for you as chief commissioner, isn't that enough?'

'Not if I'm not protected. What I can see now is that everyone's out to get me: judges, journalists, criminals and probably colleagues too. With guns or words as weapons. The phone never stops. And look. I can be kidnapped or abducted like a blind man in the middle of the day.'

'Haven't you got SWAT to keep an eye on you?'

'Who knows if I can rely on everyone there. I need more protection.'

'I understand. And here's my answer. You already have my protection. You've already had it for some time. You just haven't seen it.'

'Where is it?'

'Don't even think about it. You should know Hecate protects his investments. The person I am, what I stand for, is the guarantee that no one, absolutely no one in this town, can hurt you as long as you're mine, Macbeth.'

'No one?'

'I promise you, the person isn't born that can harm a hair on your beautiful head. And old Bertha will roll again before anyone can push you out of office. Isn't that good enough for you, Macbeth?'

'Yes, I'm happy with both of those promises.'

'Good. Because there's one last thing I have to say. And that is, watch out for Inspector Duff.'

'Oh?'

'He knows it was you who killed Duncan.'

Macbeth knew he should feel alarm. Fear. Panic. But all he had space for was the familiar, hated craving.

'Fortunately for you there is at the moment only one man who knows what Duff knows.'

'Who's that?' Macbeth asked.

'The same man who launched and supported your candidature for head of Organised Crime, at my instruction. So discreetly that Duncan thought afterwards it had been his idea.'

'And who was that?'

'See for yourself.'

A chair leg scraped as Macbeth was turned round. Then his goggles were removed. Macbeth's first thought was that he was looking into a soundproofed interview room. It had the same one-way window that meant the interrogee neither saw nor heard those outside. The difference was that this resembled a large laboratory with glass flasks, tubes and pipes leading to an enormous tank. The tank made an almost comical contrast with all the modern equipment and reminded Macbeth of cartoons showing cannibals boiling people alive. On the wall behind the tank hung a sign with the words NO SMOKING. In front of the tank in the harshly illuminated room, close to the glass, sat a pale red-haired man upright in a recliner. One shirtsleeve was rolled up, his face turned to the ceiling, his mouth half-open, his eyes half-shut. He sat so close to them that Macbeth could see the blue half-irises under the man's eyelids trembling. He recognised one of the Chinese sisters, who was holding a syringe with the needle sticking into Inspector Lennox's forearm.

The gentle voice behind Macbeth said, 'Lennox sowed the idea in Duncan's mind, the idea that he should appoint someone who didn't belong to the elite, but a man people in the town felt was one of them.'

'Lennox told Duncan he should appoint me head of Organised Crime?'

'Of course Lennox said the opposite. Duncan couldn't take you because you had no formal qualifications and were too popular. That's how you manipulate stubborn old mules with big egos.'

'You said *jump* and Lennox jumped?'

'And Lennox didn't say *jump* and Duncan jumped.' There came a gurgle of laughter from behind Macbeth, as though someone were pouring whisky. 'The labyrinths of the human mind, Macbeth. Broad avenues, above all, easy to navigate. Lennox has been mine for more than ten years. A loyal toiler, Inspector Lennox.'

Macbeth tried to see the reflection of the man behind him, but he saw only Strega, as though Hecate himself could not be reflected. But he was standing there because Macbeth heard his voice by his ear:

'But when I say *jump*, it means jump.'

'Oh?'

'Kill Duff.'

Macbeth swallowed. 'Duff's my friend. But you probably knew that.'

'Banquo was a father to you, but that didn't stop you. Killing Duff is a necessity, Macbeth. Besides I have a better friend for you. Her name is power.'

'I don't need any new friends.'

'Yes, you do. Brew makes you unstable and quirky. You've had hallucinations, haven't you?'

'Maybe. Maybe this is a hallucination. What's power?'

'A new yet ancient product. Brew is a poor man's power. Power is seven times stronger and half as damaging. It sharpens and strengthens your mind. And that's what these times demand.'

'I prefer brew.'

'What you prefer, Macbeth, is to continue as chief commissioner.'

'And this new drug, will it make me dependent?'

'I told you it was ancient. And power will replace everything you're already dependent on. So what do you think? Duff versus power?'

Macbeth saw Lennox's head tip forward. He heard Strega whisper something behind him. The sister laid Lennox back on the recliner and went to the tank.

'Give it to me.'

'Sorry?'

Macbeth cleared his throat: 'Give it to me, I said.'

'Give him the bags,' Hecate said.

Macbeth heard the *tap-tap* fade as his goggles were put back on and the world around him disappeared.

18

'She's beautiful, isn't she?' Lennox said, stroking the curves.

'No,' Duff said. 'Bertha is many things, but she isn't beautiful.'

Lennox laughed and looked down at his hand, which was now covered with soot. 'Everyone says Bertha, but her full name is Bertha Birnam. Named after a black-haired construction site cook, she was the only employee with them throughout the years it took to build the line from here to Capitol.'

'How do you know that?'

'Because my grandfather worked on the line. From here to Capitol.'

'So your grandfather swung a sledgehammer and dragged sleepers?'

'No, of course not, he helped to *finance* the railway.'

'That sounds more likely.' Duff looked across at Inverness Casino's welcoming lights in the afternoon darkness.

'Yep, we Lennoxes are really bankers. In fact, I'm a kind of black sheep. What about your origins, Duff?'

'The usual.'

'Police.'

'As far as the eye can see.'

'I know lots of Duffs in town, but none of them is in the police.'

'I took the name from my maternal grandfather when I moved here.'

'And he's . . . '

'Dead. Orphanage after that. Then police college.'

'If you're not from here why didn't you go to the police college in Capitol? It's better, and so are the weather and air.'

'The big fish are here. The Norse Riders, Hecate . . . '

'I see. You really wanted Organised Crime, didn't you?'

'Yes, I probably did.'

'Well, it's still free. And when we've arrested Macbeth as Duncan's murderer, you'll just have to point to which unit you want. We'll be hailed as the saviours of the town, Duff.'

'Will we? Do you really think they care?' Duff nodded to the square, where people were scurrying to get out of sight as fast as possible, into the shadows to find shelter.

'I know what you mean, but it's a mistake to underrate the general public in this town.'

'There are two ways to tackle a problem, Lennox. By solving it or ignoring it. Kenneth taught this town to do the latter. Apathy towards corruption and shoving responsibility for the community onto others. Watching them escape, like cockroaches when the light comes on.'

'A contemptible town with contemptible inhabitants, and yet you're willing to risk everything?'

Lennox watched Duff shaking his head.

'My God, Lennox, what makes you think this is for the *town*? The town. It's just a way of speaking they use when they want to be elected to the town hall or become the chief commissioner. Tell me what you've turned up since we last met.'

'OK. I've spoken to a judge in Capitol — '

'We shouldn't talk to *anyone*!'

'Take it easy now, Duff. I didn't say what or who it was about, only that it concerned corruption at a high level. The point is that this judge is reliable. He lives elsewhere, so he's out of Macbeth, Sweno or Hecate's control. As a judge in a federal court of law he can hook up with the federal police, so we can leapfrog HQ and prosecute in Capitol, where Macbeth can't pull any strings. The judge is coming here in three days and he's agreed to meet us in total secrecy.'

'What's his name?'

'Jones.'

Lennox saw Duff staring at him.

'Lars Jones,' Lennox said. 'Anything wrong?'

'You've got pupils like a junkie.'

Lennox moistened his tongue and laughed. 'That's how it is when you're born half-albino. Eyes sensitive to light. That's one reason my family prefers indoor jobs.'

Duff shivered in his coat. Looked over at Inverness Casino again. 'So, three days. What shall we do in the meantime?'

Lennox shrugged. 'Keep our heads down. Don't rock the boat. And . . . I can't think of a third way to say that.'

'I'm already dreading my next meeting with Macbeth.'

'Why's that?'

'I'm no actor.'

'You've never fooled anyone?'

'Yes, but people always see through me.'

Lennox glanced at Duff. 'Oh? At home?'

Duff shrugged. 'Even my lad, who'll be nine in a couple of days, knows when his dad's telling fibs. And Macbeth knows me better than anyone.'

'Strange,' Lennox said, 'that two people who are so different have been such close friends.'

'We'll have to talk later,' Duff said, looking to the west. 'If I set off now I'll be in Fife by sunset.'

Lennox stood looking in the same direction as Duff. And thought it was good that nature had arranged things in such a way that rain showers always hid the view from those who were behind so that you could always be optimistic about a quick improvement in the weather.

★ ★ ★

'I have a feeling we're over the worst,' Macbeth said, stretching for the lighter on the bedside table and lighting his cigarette. 'Everything will get better now, my sweet. We're back where we should be. This town is ours.'

Lady rested a hand on her chest, felt her still-racing heart under the silk sheet. And talked between breaths: 'If your newly acquired enthusiasm is an indicator of your strength, darling — '

'Mm?'

' — then we're unbeatable. Are you aware how much they love you out there? People in the casino talk about you, say you're the town's saviour. And do you read the papers? Today *The Times* suggested in its leader that you should stand in the mayoral elections.'

'Was that your friend, the editor?' Macbeth grinned. 'Because you asked him?'

'No, no. The leader wasn't about you. It was a comment piece on Tourtell not having a real rival and being re-elected despite being unpopular.'

'You don't become popular by being Kenneth's lackey.'

'So your name was mentioned as someone who theoretically could challenge Tourtell. What do you say to that?'

'To standing as mayor? Me?' Macbeth laughed and scratched his forearm. 'Thank you, but no thank you. I've got a big enough office and now we have more than enough power to do what we want.' His nail rasped over the little hole in his skin. Power. He had injected himself with a syringe, and the sales pitch hadn't exaggerated.

'You're right, darling,' she said. 'But muse on it a little anyway. When the idea matures it will perhaps feel different — who knows? By the way, Jack received a parcel for you this morning. A biker brought it. Heavy and very well packed.'

Macbeth waited for the feeling of ice in his veins, but

it didn't come. Must have been the effect of the new dope. 'Where did you put it?'

'On the hat shelf in your wardrobe,' she said, pointing.

'Thank you.'

He slowly smoked his cigarette listening to her fall asleep beside him. Stared at the solid brown oak door of the wardrobe. Then he laid his head on the pillow and blew rings up into the beams of moonlight from the window, saw them twist and wreathe like an Arab belly dancer. He wasn't afraid. He had SWAT protecting him, he had Hecate protecting him, the gods of destiny were smiling on him. He lifted his head and stared at the wardrobe again. Not a sound came from it. The ghosts had made themselves scarce. And it was perfectly still outside, no drumming on the window. For sunshine did follow the rain. Love did purge you of the blood of battle. Forgiveness did come after sin.

19

'Good morning, everyone,' Macbeth said, meeting the eyes of everyone around the table. 'Except that it isn't a good morning, but the second one Banquo has been dead and the thirty-sixth hour his murderer has been wandering around free and unpunished. Let's start with a minute's silence for Banquo.'

Duff closed his eyes.

It was unusual to see Macbeth enter a room with such a serious expression; he used to greet every day and every person with a smile, come rain or come shine, whether he knew them or not. Like the first time they met at the orphanage. He must have looked at Duff, at his clothes and hair, how different the two of them were, but he had smiled as if they shared something that went deeper than such external matters, something that bound them together, that made them secret brothers. Perhaps he made everyone feel like that with this unconditional, white smile. It had conveyed a naive belief that the people around him wished one another the best and made Duff feel like a cold cynic even then. And what wouldn't Duff have given for a smile that could rub off on those around him.

'Duff?' Someone had whispered his name. He turned and looked into Caithness's clear green eyes. She nodded to the end of the meeting table, where Macbeth was looking at him.

'I asked if we could have an update on where we are in the investigation, Duff.'

Duff sat up on his chair, coughed, blushed and knew it. Then he began. He talked about the witnesses who had seen members of the Norse Riders and — judging by the logos on their leather jackets — another bikers' club shoot at the Volvo outside the jewellers' shop, Jacobs & Sons. About the jacket and Fleance's wallet, which were found by the bank below Kenneth Bridge, but no body as yet. Caithness had given a comprehensive account of the forensic evidence, which only confirmed what they already knew — that Sweno's gang had murdered Banquo and possibly Fleance.

'There's some evidence to suggest Sweno was personally present at the execution,' Duff said. 'The end of a cigarillo on the tarmac beside the car.'

'Lots of people smoke cigarillos, Lennox remarked.

'Not Davidoff Long Panatellas,' Duff answered.

'You *know* what Sweno smokes?' Lennox said with an arched eyebrow.

Duff didn't respond.

'We cannot allow this,' Macbeth said. 'The town cannot allow us to allow it. Killing a police officer is an attack on the town itself. For the heads of units sitting in this room to have the town's confidence tomorrow, something has to happen today. For that reason we cannot afford to hesitate, we have to strike with all the strength we have, even at the risk of losing police lives. This is a war and so we have to use the rhetoric of war. And, as you know, it doesn't consist of words but bullets. Accordingly I have appointed a new head of SWAT and given them extended powers regarding the use of weapons and also in their instructions for fighting organised crime.'

'Excuse me,' Lennox said. 'And what are the instructions?'

'You'll see soon. They're being worked on as we speak.'

'And who's writing them?' Caithness asked.

'Police Officer Seyton,' Macbeth said, 'SWAT's new head.'

'He's writing his own instructions?' Caithness asked. 'Without us — '

'It's time to act,' Macbeth interrupted. 'Not to polish formulations of instructions. You'll soon see the result, and I'm sure you'll be as happy as me. And the rest of the town.'

'But — '

'Naturally, you'll be able to comment on the instructions when they're available. This meeting is terminated. Let's get down to work, folks!' And there it was. The smile. 'Duff, can I have a few words with you?'

Chairs scraped back tentatively.

'You can go too, Priscilla,' Macbeth said. 'And please close the door after you. Thank you.'

The room emptied. Duff braced himself.

'Come here. Sit closer,' Macbeth said.

Duff stood up and moved to the chair beside him. Tried to be relaxed, breathed calmly and avoided involuntarily tensing his face muscles. Conscious that he was sitting within spitting distance of the man who killed Duncan.

'I've been thinking of asking you about something,' Macbeth said. 'And I want you to be absolutely honest.'

Duff could feel his throat constrict and his heart race.

'I wanted to offer someone else the post of head of Organised Crime. I know your first reaction is disappointment — '

Duff nodded, his mouth was so dry he wasn't sure his voice would obey.

' — but only because I want you to be my deputy. How do you feel about that?'

Duff cleared his throat. 'Thank you,' he said hoarsely.

'Aren't you well, Duff?' Macbeth wore an expression of concern and placed a hand on Duff's shoulder. 'Or just a wee bit disappointed? I know how much you wanted Organised Crime, and I can understand you'd prefer an operational post to helping an awkward bugger like me find his words and feet.' He smiled the white smile as Duff did his best to answer.

'You're my friend, Duff, and I want you close by. How does that proverb go?'

Duff coughed. 'Which proverb?'

'Proverbs are your domain, Duff, but never mind. If you insist on Organised Crime I'll give it some thought. I haven't said anything to Lennox yet. You look really dreadful. Shall I get you a glass of water?'

'No, thanks, I'm fine. I'm just a bit exhausted. I barely slept before the raid and I haven't had a wink of sleep since Duncan's murder.'

'Only a *bit* exhausted?'

Duff pondered. Shook his head. 'No, I'd actually been wondering whether I could have the next two days off. I know we're in the middle of an investigation, but Caithness can . . . '

'Of course, of course, Duff. No point riding a horse to death just because the rider's in a hurry. Go back home to Fife. Say hello to Meredith from me and tell her you have to stay in bed for two days at least. And those are, believe it or not, the chief commissioner's orders.'

'Thank you.'

'I warn you I'll come and check you're resting in Fife.'

'Fine.'

'And then you come back with an answer regarding the deputy position in three days.'

'Deal.'

Duff went straight to a toilet and threw up in the bowl.

His shirt was drenched with sweat and it was only an hour later, as he was finally driving over the old bridge, that his pulse dropped back to normal.

★ ★ ★

Lady walked through the restaurant and gaming room. She counted nine customers. Tried to tell herself that straight after lunch was the quietest time. She went to see Jack in reception.

'Any new clients today?'

'Not yet, ma'am.'

'Not yet? Will there be any later today?'

He smiled apologetically. 'Not that I know of.'

'Did you pop into the Obelisk, as I asked?'

'Of course, ma'am.'

'And there it was . . . ?'

'Quiet, I would say.'

'You're lying, Jack.'

'Yes, ma'am.'

Lady had to laugh. 'Jack, you're always a comfort to me. Is it the murders here, do you think?'

'Maybe. But someone also rang asking specifically for the room Duncan died in. At a pinch, the bodyguards' room.'

'People are sick in the head. And talking about sick, I'd like you to do a bit of probing around this boy Tourtell had with him. Find out how old he is.'

'So you think . . . ?'

'Let's hope for the boy's sake he's over sixteen. And for ours he's under.'

'Any special reason for this information, ma'am?'

'Storing up ammo just in case, Jack. The mayor appoints the chief commissioner, and even if the mayor usually follows the pecking order, in a case like this we can never be too sure, can we?'

'That's all?'

'Well, we'd like to see Tourtell put more pressure on the Gambling and the Casino Board to scrutinise the Obelisk's business practices, of course. I've been patient and tried the kind approach, but if it doesn't produce any results soon, we'll have to take more drastic action.'

'I'll see what I can find out.'

'Jack?'

'Yes, ma'am?'

'Have I been sleepwalking recently?'

'Not on my shifts, ma'am.'

'Are you lying again?'

'You might have popped down to reception last night, but I wasn't sure whether you were asleep or not.'

She laughed. 'Jack, Jack, if only everyone was as good as you. I had a suspicion. The key was in the lock on the outside of the door when I woke up.'

'Anything in particular on your mind? You only sleepwalk when something's bothering you.'

'Is there anything else but bother?' Lady sighed.

'And dreams? Do you have the same dream again and again?'

'I've told you, Jack. It isn't a dream, it's a memory.'

'Sorry, but you can't *know* that, ma'am. You can't know it happened exactly like that if you see it every night. Then the dream becomes a memory. For all you know, the child died a natural death.'

'The eternal comforter. But I don't need comfort. I don't need to forget. Quite the opposite, I need to *remember*. Remember what I've given up to be where I am, to put a price on my childless life every single morning when I wake up between silk sheets beside a man I've chosen to spend the night with, and can go downstairs to my place, to a life I've created for myself. Where I'm respected for what I am, Jack.'

'None of us is respected for what we are, ma'am. We're respected for what we can do. Especially if there's something we can do *to* the person we want respect from — '

'You're too clever to be a receptionist, Jack.'

' — and unfortunately that's why a receptionist's wisdom doesn't gain much respect. He's a harmless observer, a eunuch and occasionally a comfort to those who are respected.'

'I'm glad you never had children, Jack. You're the only person I can talk to about neglecting your own baby without it arousing the shocked revulsion it would from parents. You're a clever, tolerant man who prefers understanding to condemnation.'

'What is there to condemn? A young girl growing up in impoverished circumstances, who's raped when she's thirteen, becomes pregnant and — abandoned and without a roof over her head — gives birth to a child she cannot keep alive?'

'What if I didn't try hard enough?'

'What if you had died in the process, you mean? You were thirteen. Not an adult, but with a sharp mind. Should your future be sacrificed for a newborn baby, a seed which still isn't aware it's alive, which still doesn't feel longing, guilt, shame, true love, indeed is not really human, just a millstone around the neck of a young girl whom life has punished enough as it is? That this thirteen-year-old was unable to keep both of you alive, but survived herself, has to be called good luck within the bad luck. Because look what she achieved afterwards. She set up a little brothel. Set up a bigger, more luxurious one, which catered to the needs of everyone from the police commissioner to the town's most important politicians. Sold it and established the town's best the casino. And now — hey presto — she's the queen of the town.'

Lady shook her head. 'That's taking it too far, Jack. Embellishing my motives and granting me an amnesty for my misdeeds. What is a casino, what are the dreams of idiots against a real child's life? If I'd demanded less of my life I might have been able to save hers.'

'Did you demand so much in reality?'

'I demanded acceptance from others. No, more — respect. Yes, and love. Those are gifts that are not granted to everyone, but I demanded to be one of the few. And the price is having to lose my child again and again, night after night.'

Jack nodded. 'And if you could choose again, ma'am?'

271

Lady looked at him. 'Perhaps we're all, good or bad, only slaves of our desires, Jack. Do you believe that?'

'I don't know, ma'am, but with respect to slaves of desires I'll check out this boy of Tourtell's tomorrow.'

★   ★   ★

Macbeth exited the lift in the basement and stood for a couple of seconds inhaling the smell of leather, gun oil and male sweat. Looked at SWAT's motto under a fire-breathing red dragon: LOYALTY, FRATERNITY, BAPTISED IN FIRE, UNITED IN BLOOD. My God, it felt like a minor eternity since then.

He walked through the door to the SWAT common room.

'Olafson! Angus! Hey, what is this? Sit down, don't jump up like a couple of recruits. Where's Seyton?'

'In there,' Angus said in his unctuous priest-like tone. 'Sad to hear about Banquo. The lads are collecting money for a wreath, but you probably aren't — '

'One of the boys any more? Of course I am.' Macbeth pulled out his wallet. 'Thought you were on sick leave, Olafson. Where's the sling?'

'Slung it.' Olafson's lisp made him sound Spanish. 'The doctor thought I'd destroyed all the tendons in my shoulder and would never be able to shoot again. But then Seyton looked at it and suddenly it was fine again.'

'There you go. Don't trust doctors.' Macbeth passed Olafson a wad of notes.

'That's too much, sir.'

'Take it.'

'It's enough for a coffin.'

'Take it!'

Macbeth went into his old office. Which wasn't actually an office but a workshop with gun parts and ammunition on shelves and benches, where the type-writer had been moved unused to a chair.

'Well?' Macbeth said.

'The boys are briefed,' Seyton said, sitting with a thick instruction manual in front of him. 'And ready.'

'And our two Gatling girls?' Macbeth nodded to the manual.

'The machine guns are coming at about eight, early tomorrow morning. You spoke to the harbour master, I take it, so that the boat could jump the queue?'

'We couldn't have the girls coming late to the party. And there'll be a little job for you lads later tomorrow.'

'Fine. Where?'

'In Fife.'

20

Thursday morning. Fife was bathed in sunshine.

Duff was swimming.

Full, muscular breaststroke, ploughing a path through the cold heavy water.

He had long preferred the saltwater of the river, it felt lighter to swim in. Which actually was strange because he had learned that saltwater gave you more buoyancy, which had to mean it had greater density, which in turn had to mean it was heavier than freshwater. Nevertheless, until recently he had preferred the river, which as well as being freezing cold was so polluted that he felt dirty every time he emerged from it. But now he was clean. He had got up early, done his exercises on the cold wooden floor beside the guest bed, made breakfast for the family, sung a little birthday song for Ewan, driven the children to school and afterwards walked with Meredith the half a mile or so down to the lake. She had talked about how many apples there were on the trees this autumn, their daughter getting her first love letter — though Meredith was privately very disappointed it was from a boy who was three years younger than her — and Emily wanting a guitar for her twelfth birthday. Ewan had been in a fight in the school playground and had brought home a note for his parents. He had agreed with Mum that he would have to tell Dad himself, but it could wait until after his birthday party today — there would be plenty of time then. Duff asked if postponing the evil moment wouldn't mean Ewan would be dreading it for an unnecessarily long time.

'I don't know what he does most.' Meredith smiled. 'Look forward to something or dread it. The boy he had a fight with yesterday is in the class above him, and Ewan said the boy kicked little Peter first.'

'Who?'

'Ewan's best friend.'

'Oh, him,' Duff lied.

'Ewan said he was sorry but he had to defend his pal; Dad would have done the same. So he's keen to hear what you have to say.'

'I'll have to be balanced then. Condemn his behaviour but praise his courage. Say something about taking the initiative to make up instead of waging war. Reconciliation, right?'

'I'd appreciate that.'

And as he and Meredith glided out through the water Duff decided there and then that he would never swim anywhere except in their little lake in Fife.

'Here it is,' Meredith panted behind him.

Duff turned onto his back so that he could watch her while he floated, moving his hands and kicking his feet. His body was pale with a greenish tint under the water whereas hers, even in this light, was golden brown. He spent too much time in town; he had to get more sun.

She swam past him and crawled ashore onto a large water-smoothed rock.

Not any rock. Their rock. The rock where their daughter was conceived one summer's day eleven years ago. They had come to Fife to escape the town and had found this lake almost by chance. They had stopped because they saw an abandoned little farm Meredith thought looked so sweet. And from there they saw the water glitter, walked for ten to fifteen minutes and found the lake. Although the only other creatures by the lake were a couple of cows, they had swum to this hidden rock across the water where it was unlikely anyone would see them. A month later Meredith had told him she was pregnant, and in total euphoria they went back, bought the house midway between the lake

275

and the main road and after their second child, Ewan, was born, the plot by the lake where the cabin now stood.

Duff clambered up next to her on the rock. From where they sat they could see over to the red cabin.

He lay on his back on the sun-warmed rock. Closed his eyes and felt waves of pleasure run through his body. Sometimes it was worth getting cold to enjoy warming up afterwards, he thought.

'Are you home again now, Duff?'

When you lose something and find it again, the pleasure is greater than before you lost it.

'Yes,' he said.

Her shadow fell over him.

And when they kissed he wondered why he now — and not before — thought a woman's lips wetted by freshwater tasted better than wetted by saltwater, but concluded that it must be the body at some point telling you that freshwater can be drunk but not saltwater.

Afterwards when they lay entwined and sweaty from the sun and making love, he said he had to go to town.

'Right. It's broth at the usual time.'

'I'll be back in good time before. I just have to pick up Ewan's present. It's in the desk drawer in my office.'

'He wanted the undercover cop outfit, didn't he?'

'Yes, and there's one other thing I have to sort out ASAP.'

She stroked a finger down his forehead and nose. 'Something come up?'

'Yes and no. I should have sorted it out ages ago.'

'In which case — ' her finger, which knew him so well, caressed his lips ' — you do whatever you think you have to do. I'll wait for you here.'

Duff sat up on his elbows and looked down at her. 'Meredith.'

'Yes?'

'I love you.'

276

'I know, Duff. You just forgot for a while.'

Duff smiled. Kissed her freshwater lips again and stood up. Went to dive in, then stopped. 'Meredith?'

'Yes?'

'Did Ewan say who won the fight?'

★ ★ ★

'Did the chief commissioner say why they have to be driven to their club house?' the driver asked.

The prison warder looked down at the bunch of keys to find the right one for the next cell. 'Not enough evidence to keep them in custody.'

'Not enough evidence? Bloody hell, the whole town *knows* it was the Norse Riders who picked up the dope at the harbour. And they *know* it was the Norse Riders who killed that policeman and his son. But I didn't ask why they were being set free — I'm used to that malarkey — I was wondering why we don't just let them go. When I drive prisoners it's usually from one prison to another, not as a bloody taxi service so they don't have to walk home.'

'Don't ask me,' the warder said, unlocking the cell. 'Hey, Sean! Off your bed and home to your missus and daughter!'

'All hail Macbeth!' came a cry from inside the cell.

The warder shook his head and turned to the driver. 'You'd better bring the bus to the exit and we'll assemble there. We'll send two armed officers with you.'

'Why? Aren't these boys free?'

'The chief commissioner wants to be sure they're delivered where they're going with no trouble.'

'Can I put leg shackles on them too?'

'Not according to the book, but do as you like. Hey! Do up your shoes. We haven't got all day.'

'Do you mean it? Are the good times back, like under Kenneth?'

'Heh, heh. It's a bit early to say, but Macbeth's shaping up well, they say.'

'His problem is the unsolved police murders. If you don't fix things smartish you're soon out on your arse.'

'Maybe. Kite said on the radio today that Macbeth's a catastrophe.' He repeated 'catastrophe' exaggerating the rolled 'r', and the driver laughed. And gave a shudder when he saw the tattoo on the forehead of the prisoner who came out.

'Livestock transport,' he mumbled as the warder pushed the prisoner in the direction they were going.

★　★　★

Duff popped into his office, stuffed the parcel for Ewan in his jacket and hurried out. At Forensics on the second floor he was told that Caithness was in the darkroom in the garage. He took the lift down and let himself in. At some point when Caithness was sharing a flat with a girlfriend Duff had persuaded the caretaker that as head of Narco it would be useful if he had a key to the garage where Forensics had a firing range for ballistic analysis, a chemistry room, a darkroom to develop crime scene photographs, plus an open area inside the garage door facing the street where they could keep larger objects, such as cars, that had to be examined for evidence. After work hardly anyone did overtime in the cold damp basement; they went up to the offices on the second floor. For a year Duff and Caithness had had a regular rendezvous after work in the basement, as well as their weekly lunchtime meeting in Room 323 under the name of Mittbaum at the Grand Hotel. After Caithness had acquired her attic flat, strangely enough, Duff had missed these rushed trysts.

And opening the door and feeling the raw air hit him, he thought they must have been very much in love. In

278

the middle of the garage stood Banquo's bullet-ridden Volvo. It was covered with a tarpaulin, presumably because the door on the passenger side had been torn off and they wanted to protect possible evidence in the car from the rats that roamed the basement at night. Duff stopped outside the darkroom and took a deep breath. The decision was made. Now it was just the deed that needed doing. The deed. He pressed down the door handle and went into the darkness. Closed the door after him. Stood inhaling the ammonia smell from the fixer liquid, waiting for his pupils to expand.

'Duff?' he heard from the darkness. The same friendly, slightly tentative voice that had woken him in the meeting room yesterday morning. The same friendly, slightly tentative voice that had woken him on so many mornings in her attic flat. The friendly, tentative voice he wouldn't hear any more, not in the same way, not there.

'Caithness, we can't — '

'Roy,' she said, 'can you leave us alone for a while?'

Duff's eyes got used to the darkness in time for him to see the forensic photographer leave.

'Have you seen these?' asked Caithness, pointing a red light at the three recent dripping exposures hanging on a line.

One showed Banquo's car. The second, Banquo's headless body on the tarmac outside the car. The third was a close-up of the skin of Banquo's neck where it had been severed. She pointed to the last one. 'We think it was cut by a large blade, like the sabre you said Sweno has.'

'I see,' Duff said, staring at the picture.

'We found traces of other blood on the spine. Isn't that interesting?'

'What do you mean?'

'Sweno, or whoever it is, clearly hasn't been very particular about washing his sabre, so as the sabre cut through the spine here — ' she pointed ' — it scraped old dried blood off the blade. If we can determine which blood group it is, it might help us in other murder cases.'

Duff's stomach was on the point of turning, and he clutched the bench.

'Still feeling ill?' Caithness asked.

Duff took some deep breaths. 'Yes. No. I just had to get away. We have to talk.'

'What about?' He could hear in her voice she already knew. She had probably already known when he burst in; talking about the photos had been a kind of panic reaction.

'About meeting,' he said. 'It won't work any longer.'

He tried to see her face, but it was too dark.

'Is that all we've done?' she said. Her voice was tearful. 'Meet?'

'No,' he said. 'No, you're right of course — it was more than meeting. And all the more reason for it to stop.'

'You want to stop, dump me, here, at work?'

'Caithness — '

Her bitter laugh interrupted him. 'Well, that's very fitting. A relationship that has taken place in a dark room is concluded in a darkroom.'

'I'm sorry. It's out of consideration for — '

'You. You, Duff. Not the children, not the family, but you. You're the most selfish person I've ever met, so don't try to tell me it's out of consideration for anyone else but you.'

'As you like. It's out of consideration for me.'

'And out of *which* consideration are you dumping me, Duff? Is there an even younger, even more naive girl out there, who you know won't nag you to commit, to sacrifice something? Not *yet* anyway.'

'Does it help if I say I'm only thinking about the personal, selfish well-being I hope to feel when I imagine I'm doing the right thing for those I have obligations towards? If I'm breaking up with you because I'm scared stiff not to be included among the saved souls on the Day of Judgement?'

'Do you think you will be?'

'No. But the decision has been taken, Caithness, so just tell me how you want me to pull the tooth, slowly or all in one go?'

'Why should the torment stop now? Come to my flat at four.'

'What's the point?'

'To hear me cry, curse and beg. I can't do that here.'

'I've promised to eat with the family at five.'

'If you don't come, first of all I'll throw all your possessions out on the street, then I'll ring and tell your wife about your escapades — '

'She knows already, Caithness.'

' — and your parents-in-law. Tell them how you deceived their daughter and grandchildren.'

Duff gulped. 'Caithness — '

'Four o'clock. If you're nice and listen you'll get to your bloody meal.'

'OK, OK, I'll come. But don't think this will change anything.'

The crime photographer was leaning against the garage door and smoking when Duff came out.

'Nasty?' he asked.

'Sorry?'

'Cutting off his head like that.'

'Murder's always nasty,' Duff said, making for the exit.

★　★　★

Lady was in the bedroom, standing in front of the door to Macbeth's wardrobe. Listening to the sound of wet rats scurrying across the wooden floor. She told herself

281

the sounds were only in her imagination; the floor was thickly carpeted. Sounds in her imagination. Soon it would be voices. The voices her mother had talked about that wouldn't leave her in peace, the same voices her mother's mother had heard — their forefathers speaking, commanding them to sleepwalk at night, to hurtle towards death. She had been so afraid when she saw Macbeth hallucinating at the table during the dinner. Had she infected her only true love with this illness?

The scurrying rat feet had been in her imagination a long time now and they didn't want to disappear.

All she could do was scurry herself. Away from the sounds, away from her imagination.

She opened the wardrobe door.

Pulled out the drawer under the shelf. There was a little bag of powder inside. Macbeth's escape. Did it work? Would she escape if she went to the same place he went? She didn't think so. She closed the drawer again.

Looked up at the hat shelf. At the parcel Jack had been given. It was wrapped in paper, tied with twine and with transparent plastic on top. It was only a parcel. And yet it was as though it was staring down at her.

She opened the drawer again and took out the bag. Sprinkled a tiny bit of powder on the table in front of the mirror, rolled up a banknote and — unsure of how you actually did it — put one end in one nostril and held the other above the powder and breathed in, half with her nose, half with her mouth. As that didn't work, and after a couple more attempts, she arranged the powder in a line, inserted the note in her nostril and inhaled hard while running the note along the line, vacuuming it up. She sat for a while studying herself in the mirror. The sound of scurrying rats disappeared. Then she went to the bed and lay down.

★ ★ ★

'Here they come!' the sarge shouted. He stood in the Norse Riders gateway watching the yellow prison bus come up the road. It was half past three, bang on time. He glanced over at those who had gathered outside the club house in the drizzle. Everyone in the club was duty-bound to welcome back the injured they'd had to leave to the police that night. The women had also turned up — the girls who had a boyfriend among the released prisoners and those who did the rounds. The sergeant smiled at the laughing baby in Betty's arms; Betty was looking for her Sean. Even their cousins from the south had decided to join them again for this party, which already promised to be legendary. Sweno had given orders that there should be enough booze and dope to entertain the average village because they were celebrating more than just the release of their comrades. The Norse Riders had avenged the losses they had suffered with the dispatching of Banquo and — even more importantly — gained a new and gold-plated alliance. As Sweno had said, by making a personal appearance at the club house and ordering a hit job, Macbeth had sold his soul to the devil, and there was no right of cancellation on that. Now he was in their pocket just as much as they were in his.

The sarge went into the street and signalled to the bus to pull up outside the gate. No one except one-hundred-per-cent-ID'd members were allowed inside, that was the new club rule.

And then they trooped off the bus as the stereo in the club house was turned up. 'Let's Spend the Night Together'. Some walked and some danced to the gate, where they were received with clapping and raised fists by comrades and hugs and wet kisses by the women.

'This is fun,' shouted the sergeant, 'but the booze is inside.'

Calls and laughter. They moved inside. But the sarge stood at the doorway, scanning their surroundings one more time. The bus on its way down the road again. Chang, who had been joined by two men, guarding the gate. The empty factory buildings around, which they had checked to make sure no one was watching the club. The sky to the west, where it actually seemed that a little blue was on the way. Now perhaps he could relax a little. Perhaps Sweno was right: perhaps better times really were coming their way.

The sergeant went in, refused spirits and put a mug of beer to his mouth. Party or not, these were critical times. He looked around. Sean and Betty were smooching in the corner with the baby squeezed between them, and the sarge thought it would be a bizarre way to end a young life. But there were plenty of things a lot bloody worse than being suffocated by undiluted love.

'Norse Riders!' he shouted. The music was turned down, and conversations died away.

'This is a day of happiness. And a day of sadness. We haven't forgotten the fallen. But there's a time to cry and a time to laugh, and today we're partying. Cheers!'

Cheering and raised glasses. The sergeant took a huge swig and wiped the foam from his beard.

'And this is a new start,' he continued.

'To the speech?' shouted Sean, and everyone laughed.

'We lost a few men; they lost a few men,' the sergeant said. 'The drugs from Russia are water under the bridge.' No laughter. 'But as a man whose name you all know said to me today, 'With this head-case as the chief commissioner better times are coming our way.''

More cheering. The sarge felt as if he could talk for quite some time yet, say a few things about the club, about comradeship and sacrifice. But he had taken up enough time and space. No one but the sergeant knew that Sweno was waiting in the wings somewhere right now. It was time for the evening's grand entrance.

'And with these words,' he said, 'let me pass you over — '

In the dramatic pause that followed he heard something. The deep growl of a lorry with a powerful engine and in too low a gear. Well, there were lots of poor drivers out there.

' — to — '

He heard a roar. And knew the gate had flown off its hinges. And that the evening's grand entrance had a rival.

★ ★ ★

Duff stood outside the grey five-storey block of flats. He looked at his watch. Five minutes to four. He could still make it to the birthday party by quite a margin. He rang the bell.

'Come up,' said Caithness's voice from the intercom.

After their conversation in the darkroom he had gone to the Bricklayers Arms, sat in one of the booths and had a beer. He could of course have spent the time working in his office, but Macbeth's orders had been to stay at home in Fife. And then he had another. Giving himself time to think.

Now he walked up the stairs, not with the plodding, heavy steps of someone going to the scaffold, but with the quick, light steps of someone wanting to get a scene over with and survive. And who had another life he wanted to get back to.

The flat door was open.

'Come in,' he heard Caithness shout from somewhere. He gave a sigh of relief when he saw she had collected all his possessions on the table in the hall. A toilet bag. A shaver. A couple of shirts and underwear. The tennis racket she had bought him as they both played, though it had never been used. A necklace and pearl earrings. Duff's fingers caressed the jewellery he had bought her. It had been worn often.

'In here,' she shouted. From the bedroom.

The stereo was on. Elvis. 'Love Me Tender'.

Duff walked towards the open bedroom door, hesitating, not so light-footed now. He could smell her perfume from where he was.

'Duff,' she said with a sniffle when he appeared in the doorway. 'I'm giving you back what you gave me, but I expect a farewell present.'

She lay on the bed in a black corset and nylons. Also bought by him. At the bed head there was a champagne cooler containing an open bottle, which she was obviously well into. He absorbed the sight of her. She was the most beautiful, most gorgeous woman he had ever been with. Every single time he saw her he was struck by her beauty, as though it were the first time. And he could feel every caress they had exchanged, every wild ride they'd had. And now he was renouncing this. Now and for ever.

'Caithness,' Duff said, feeling his throat thicken. 'My dear, dear, beautiful Caithness.'

'Come here.'

'I can't . . . '

'Of course you can. You've been able to for so long, so many times, this is just the last. You owe me that.'

'You won't enjoy it. Neither of us will.'

'I don't want to enjoy it, Duff. I want closure. I want *you* to crawl, for once. I want you to swallow your virtue and do as *I* want. And now this is what I want. Just this. And afterwards you can go to hell and home to the meal with the wife you no longer love. Come on now. I can see from here you're ready for — '

'No, Caithness. I can't. You said you'd be satisfied with what you could have of my heart. But I can't just give you a bit of that, Caithness. Then I would be cheating twice, both you and the mother of my children. And what you said about me not loving her any more isn't true.' He inhaled. 'Because I'd forgotten. But then I remembered. That I love her and I always have. And

286

I've been unfaithful to you with my own wife.'

He saw the words hit home. Saw the thin, false veneer of seduction melt into deep shock. Then tears sprang from her eyes, and she curled up, pulled up the sheet and covered herself.

'Goodbye, Caithness. Hate me as I should be hated. I'm leaving now.'

At the front door Duff took the clothes and toiletries under his arm. The racket could stay. You don't play tennis on a smallholding. He stood looking at the earrings and necklace. Heard Caithness's pained sobs from the bedroom. It was expensive jewellery — it had cost him more than strictly speaking he could afford — but now, in his hand, it had no value. There was no one he could give it to anyway, except a pawnbroker. But could he bear the thought of this jewellery being worn by a stranger?

He hesitated. Looked at his watch. Then he put down the other things, took the jewellery and went back to the bedroom.

She stopped crying when she saw him. Her face was wet with tears, black with make-up. Her body shook with a last sob. One stocking had slipped down, also a shoulder strap.

'Duff . . . ' she whispered.

'Caithness,' he said with a gulp. Sugar in his stomach, blood rushing in his head. The jewellery fell on the floor.

★   ★   ★

The sergeant grabbed the rifle from behind the bar and ran to the window; the rest of the club members were already on their way to the arms cupboard. Outside there was a lorry standing side on to the club house. The engine was running and the club gate was still hanging off its front bumper. As was Chang. The sergeant put the rifle to his shoulder as the tarpaulin over the back of the lorry dropped. And there were SWAT in their ugly black uniforms, their guns raised. But there was something even uglier on board, something which made the blood in the sergeant's veins turn to ice. Three monsters. Two of them made of steel and on stands, with ammunition feeds, rotating barrels and cooling chambers. The third stood between them, a bald, lean, sinewy man the sergeant had never seen before but knew he had always known, had always been close to. And now this man raised his hand and shouted, 'Loyalty, fraternity!'

The others responded: 'Baptised in fire, united in blood!'

Then a single command: 'Fire.' Of course. Fire.

The sergeant got him in his sights and pulled the trigger. One shot. The last.

★　★　★

The raindrop fell from the sky, through the mist, towards the filthy port below. Heading for an attic window beneath which a couple were making love. The man was silent as his hips went up and down, slowly but with force. The woman beneath him clawed the sheet as, sobbing and impatient, she received him. The gramophone record had stopped playing its sweet melody some time ago, and the stylus kept bumping monotonously, like the man, against the record label with the command *Love Me Tender*. But the lovers didn't appear to notice, didn't appear to notice anything apart from the repetitive motion they were caught up in, didn't even notice each other as they banged away, banging out demons, banging out reality, the world around them, this town, this day, for these few minutes, this brief hour. But the raindrop never reached the window pane above them. A cold gust from the north-west drew the drop east of the river that split the town lengthways and south of the disused railway line dividing the town diagonally. It fell on the factory district, past Estex's extinguished chimneys and further east towards the fenced-in low timber building between the closed factories. There the drop ended its passage through the air and hit the shiny skull of a lean man, ran down his forehead, stopped for an instant in his short eyelashes, then fell like a tear down one cheek that had never known real tears.

★ ★ ★

Seyton didn't notice he had been hit. Not by a random raindrop, nor by the sergeant's bullet. He stood there, legs planted wide, his hand raised, feeling only the vibrations through the lorry as the Gatling guns opened up, feeling them spread from the soles of his shoes up to his hips, feeling the sound pound evenly on his eardrums, a sound that rose from a chattering mumble to a roar and then to a concerted howl as the barrels spat out bullets faster and faster. And as time passed, as the club house in front of them was shot to pieces, he felt the heat from the two machines. Two machines from hell with one function, to swallow the metal they were fed and spit it out again like bulimic robots, but faster than anything else in the world. So far the machine-gunners hadn't seen much damage, but gradually it became apparent as windows and doors fell off and parts of the walls simply dissolved. A woman appeared on the floor inside the door. Sections of her head were missing, while her body was shaking as if from electric shocks. Seyton sensed he had an erection. Must be the vibrations of the lorry.

One machine gun stopped firing.

Seyton turned to the gunner.

'Anything wrong, Angus?'

'The job's done now,' Angus shouted back, pulling his blond fringe to the side.

'No one stops until I say so.'

'But — '

'Is that understood?' Seyton yelled.

Angus swallowed. 'For Banquo?'

'That's what I said! For Banquo! Now!'

Angus's machine gun opened up again. But Seyton could see that Angus was right. The job was done. There wasn't a square decimetre in front of them that wasn't perforated. There was nothing that wasn't destroyed. Nothing that wasn't dead.

He still waited. Closed his eyes and just listened. But it was time to let the girls have a rest.

'Stop!' he shouted.

The machine guns fell silent.

A cloud of dust rose from the obliterated club house. Seyton closed his eyes again and breathed in the air. A cloud of souls.

'What's up?' lisped Olafson from the end of the lorry.

'We're saving ammo,' Seyton said. 'We've got a job this afternoon.'

'You're bleeding, sir! Your arm.'

Seyton looked down at his jacket, which was stuck to his elbow where blood was pouring from a hole. He placed a hand on the wound. 'It'll be all right,' he said. 'Handguns at the ready, everyone. We'll go in and do a body count. If you find Sweno, tell me.'

'And if we find any survivors?' Angus asked.

Someone laughed.

Seyton wiped a raindrop from his cheek. 'I repeat. Macbeth's order was that none of Banquo's murderers should survive. Is that a good enough answer for you, Angus?'

21

Meredith was hanging sheets on the line over the veranda by the front door. She loved this house, the rural, unpretentious, traditional, sober but practical essence of it. When people heard that she and Duff lived on a farm in Fife they automatically assumed it was a luxurious estate and probably thought she was being coy when she described how simply they lived. What would a woman with her surname be doing on a disused smallholding, they must have thought.

She had washed all the bedlinen in the house so that Duff wouldn't think she had only done the sheets of the marital bed. Where they would sleep tonight. Forget the bad stuff, repress what had been. Reawaken what they'd had. It had been dormant, that was all. She felt her stomach grow warm at the thought. The intimacy they had shared on the rock this morning had been so wonderful. As wonderful as in the first years. No, more wonderful. She hummed a tune she had heard on the radio — she didn't know what it was — hung up the last sheet and ran her hand over the wet cotton, inhaled the fragrant perfume. The wind blew the sheet high in the air, and the sunshine swept over her face and dress. Warm, pleasant, bright. This is how life should be. Making love, working, living. This was what she had been brought up to do, this was still her credo.

She heard a seagull scream and shaded her eyes. What was it doing here, so far from the sea?

'Mum!'

She had hung the washing over several lines, so she had to move between them, skip her way to the front door.

'Yes, Ewan?'

Her son was sitting on a bench, his chin propped on one hand, looking into the distance. Squinting into the low afternoon sun. 'Won't Dad be here soon?'

'Yes, he will. How's the soup doing, Emily?'

'It was ready aeons ago,' the daughter said, dutifully stirring the big pot.

Broth. Simple, nutritious peasant food.

Ewan stuck out his lower lip. 'He said he'd be here *before* the meal.'

'You hang him up by his toes for breaking his promise,' Meredith said, stroking his fringe.

'Should people be hung for lying?'

'Without exception.' Meredith looked at her watch. There might be hold-ups in the rush-hour traffic, now that only the old bridge was open.

'Who by?' the boy asked.

'What do you mean who by?'

'Who should hang people who lie?' Ewan's eyes had a faraway look, as though he were talking to himself.

'The honest joes of course.'

Ewan turned to his mother. 'Then liars are stupid because there are lots more of them than there are honest joes. They could beat the joes and hang them instead.'

'Listen!' Emily said.

Meredith pricked up her ears. And now she could hear it too. The distant rumble of an engine getting closer.

The boy jumped down from the bench. 'Here he comes! Emily, let's hide and give him a fright.'

'Yes!'

The children disappeared into the bedroom while Meredith went to the window. Tried to shade her eyes from the sun. She felt an unease she couldn't explain. Perhaps she was afraid the Duff who came home wouldn't be the same one who had left that morning.

Duff put his car in neutral and let it roll the last part of the gravel track to the house. The gravel murmured and fretted like subterranean trolls beneath the wheels. He had driven like a man possessed from Caithness, had broken a principle he had always adhered to, never to misuse the blue light he kept in the glove compartment. With the light on the roof he had managed to jump the queue on the road to the old bridge, but once there the carriageway was so narrow that even with the light he'd had to grit his teeth as they moved forward at a snail's pace. He braked hard and the subterranean voices died. Switched off the engine and got out. The sun was shining on the white sheets on the veranda welcoming him home with a wave. She had done the washing. All the bedlinen so that he wouldn't think she had only done the sheets on the marital bed. And even though he was sated with love-making, the notion warmed his heart. Because he had left Caithness. And Caithness had left him. She had stood in the door, wiping a last tear, given him a last goodbye kiss and said that now the door was closed to him. She could do this now that she had made up her mind. One day maybe someone else would come through the door he was leaving. And he replied that he hoped so, and the 'someone else' would be a very lucky man. On the street he had leaped in the air with relief, happiness and freedom regained. Yes, imagine that — free. To be with his wife and children! life is strange. And wonderful.

He walked towards the veranda. 'Ewan! Emily!' Usually when he came home they ran out to meet him. But sometimes they also hid to launch a surprise attack on him.

He dodged between the lines of sheets.

'Ewan! Emily!'

He stopped. He was hidden between the sheets,

which cast long shadows that moved across the veranda floor. He inhaled the soap's perfume and the freshwater in which they had been washed. There was another smell too. He smiled. Broth. His smile became even broader as he remembered the good-natured discussion they'd had when Ewan insisted on having the beard glued on *before* he ate his soup. It was perfectly still. The ambush could come at any second.

There were tiny dots of sunshine in the shadows the sheets cast.

He stood staring at them.

Then down at himself. At his sweater and trousers covered with tiny dots of sunshine. He felt his heart skip a beat. Ran a finger over a sheet. It found a hole at once. And another. He stopped breathing.

Pulled the sheet at the back to the side.

The kitchen window was gone. The wall was holed so badly it looked more like a hole than a wall. He looked in through where the window had been. The pot on the hotplate looked like a sieve. The stove and the floor around were covered with a steaming yellowish-green broth.

He wanted to go inside. He *had* to go inside. But he couldn't; it was as if his feet were frozen to the veranda floor and his willpower was deactivated.

But there's no one in the kitchen, he told himself. Empty. Perhaps the rest of the house was empty too. Destroyed but empty. Perhaps they had escaped to the cabin. Perhaps. Perhaps he hadn't lost everything.

He forced himself to pass through the opening where the door had been. He went into the children's rooms. First Emily's, then Ewan's. Checked the cupboards raked with machine gun fire and under the beds. No one. Nor in the guest room. He went towards the last room, his and Meredith's bedroom, with the broad soft double bed where on Sunday mornings they made room for all four of them, lay on their sides, tickled bare toes to the children's loud shrieks, gently scratched each other's backs, talked about all sorts of weird and wonderful things and fought to decide who should get up first.

The bedroom door hadn't been shot away, but the gaps between the bullet holes were the same as elsewhere in the house. Duff took a deep breath.

Perhaps not all was lost yet.

He gripped the handle. Opened the door.

Of course he knew he had been lying to himself. He had become good at it: the more he had practised self-deception the easier it had been to see what he wanted to see. But in the last few days the scales had fallen from his eyes and now he was there and couldn't not see what lay before his eyes. The feathers from the mattress were everywhere, as though snow had been falling. Perhaps that was why everything seemed so peaceful. Meredith looked as if she had tried to keep Ewan and Emily warm as they sat on the floor in the far corner with her arms around them. Red feathers were stuck to the walls around them.

Duff's breathing came in gasps. And then came a sob. One single, bitter, raging sob.

Everything was lost.

Absolutely everything was lost.

22

Duff remained standing in the doorway. Saw the blanket on the bed. He knew it wouldn't help if he waded into the feathers; all he would do was contaminate the crime scene and potentially destroy the evidence. But he had to cover them up. Cover them up for a last time, they couldn't stay like that. He stepped inside, then stopped.

He had heard a sound. A shout.

He backed out and strode into the sitting room, over to the smashed window facing south-east, towards the lake. There was the cry again. So far away he couldn't see who was shouting, but sound carried well out there in the afternoon. The voice sounded angry. It had repeated the same word, but Duff couldn't make out what it was. He pulled out the remains of a chest drawer, took out the binoculars kept there, focused on the cabin. One lens of the binoculars was pierced, but the other was good enough for him to see a fair-haired man hurrying towards the house on the narrow road. Behind him, in front of the cabin, stood a lorry, on the back of which was a man whose face he recognised. Seyton. He was standing between what looked like two enormous meat-mincers on stands. Duff remembered Macbeth's words. *Stay in bed for two days at least . . . an order.* Macbeth had known. Known that Duff was about to reveal that he had killed Duncan. *Lennox.* Lennox, the traitor. There was no judge from Capitol coming to town tomorrow.

Duff saw Seyton's mouth moving before the sound reached him. The same furious word: 'Angus!'

Duff moved back from the window so that the glass

in the binoculars wouldn't reflect the sun and give him away. He had to escape.

★   ★   ★

As darkness fell over the town, news of the massacre at the Norse Riders' club house was already spreading. And at nine o'clock most of the town's journalists, TV and radio crews were gathered in Scone Hall. Macbeth stood in the wings listening to Lennox welcome them to the press conference.

'We would ask you not to use flash until the chief commissioner has finished, and please ask questions by raising a hand and speaking. And now here is this proud town's chief commissioner, Macbeth.'

This introduction — and possibly the rumours of the victory over the Norse Riders in the battle at the club house — were cause enough for a couple of the less experienced journalists to clap when Macbeth appeared on the podium, but the thin applause died under the eloquent gazes of the more seasoned members of the audience.

Macbeth walked up to the lectern. No, he *took the lectern by force*, that was how it felt. It was strange that this — speaking to an audience — was what he had feared most; now he didn't just like it, he longed for it, he *needed* it. He coughed, looked down at his papers. Then he started.

'Today the police carried out two armed operations against those behind the recent murders of our officers, among them Chief Commissioner Duncan. I'm pleased to say that the first operation, given the circumstances, was one-hundred-per-cent successful. The criminal gang known as the Norse Riders has ceased to exist.' A single hurrah from the audience broke the silence. 'This was a planned action based on new information that emerged after the release of some Norse Rider members. The circumstances were that the Norse Riders fired shots at SWAT, and we had no choice but to hit back hard.'

A shout from the back of the hall: 'Is Sweno among the dead?'

'Yes,' said Macbeth. 'He is indeed one of the bodies that cannot be identified because of the comprehensive nature of his injuries, but I think you all recognise this . . . ' Macbeth held up a shiny sabre. More hurrahs, and now some of the more experienced journalists joined in the spontaneous applause. 'And with it an era is over. Fortunately.'

'There are rumours that women and children are among the dead.'

'Yes and no,' Macbeth said. 'Adult women who had chosen to associate with the club, yes. Many of them have what we might call a sullied record and none of them did anything to stop the Norse Riders firing at us. As for children, that's just nonsense. There were no innocent victims here.'

'You mentioned a second operation. What was that?'

'It took place out of town, in Fife, straight after the first, in a relatively deserted area, so you may not have heard about it, but this was an attempt to arrest someone we now know had been working with the Norse Riders for some time. It is of course regrettable that such an officer could be found within our ranks, but it also proves that Chief Commissioner Duncan was not infallible when he handed the Narcotics Unit and later the Homicide Unit to this man, Inspector Duff. And we're not infallible either. We considered his family and assumed he would do the same and give himself up. So when we arrived, Police Officer Seyton, the head of SWAT, went towards the house and asked Duff to come out alone and give himself up. Duff responded by shooting at Seyton.'

He nodded towards Seyton, who was standing under

298

the light by the door at the front of the hall so that everyone could see him with his arm in a sling.

'Luck would have it that the shot wasn't fatal. Police Officer Seyton soon received medical attention and there's every chance that he'll escape permanent injury. However, despite the seriousness of his injury, Police Officer Seyton led the attack. Unfortunately, Duff, in his desperation and cowardice, chose to use his family as a shield, with the tragic result that they paid with their lives, while Duff managed to escape from the back of the house and make a getaway in his car. He's a wanted man, and we have commenced a search. I promise to you here and now that we *will* find and punish Duff. Incidentally, let me use this opportunity to announce that we'll soon be able to address Police Officer Seyton as Inspector Seyton.'

More joined in the applause this time. Once it had died down there was a cough, and a voice with rolled 'r's said, 'This is all very well, Macbeth, but where is the evidence — ' the questioner pronounced '*evidence*' slowly with ultra-clear diction as though it were a difficult foreign word ' — against the people you have mown down?'

'As far as the Norse Riders are concerned, we have witnesses who saw them shooting at Banquo's car, and we have fingerprints on and inside the car, also blood on Banquo's seat identical to the types of some of those found dead in the club house this evening. Forensics can also confirm that fingerprints found on the inside of the windscreen, on the driver's side, match those of — ' Macbeth paused ' — Inspector Duff.'

A ripple went through the hall.

'At this juncture I'd like to praise the SOC officers. Duff went to the crime scene just after the murder. This was odd as no one at Homicide had been able to get hold of Duff to inform him of the murder. Obviously he turned up with the intention of erasing his fingerprints

299

and other clues he must have known he'd left behind. But the Forensics Unit didn't let anyone, no one at all, go near the body and contaminate the evidence. Personally, I can add that my suspicion that Duff was working with the Norse Riders grew during the raid on the container harbour. Both the Narcotics Unit and we at SWAT had received such a clear tip-off that Duff couldn't have ignored it without arousing suspicion that he was protecting them. Duff cleverly set up a raid that was doomed to fail, with inexperienced officers from his own unit in insufficient numbers, without seeking the assistance of SWAT, which is the normal procedure in such cases. Luckily the raid came to our attention, so SWAT reacted independently, and I think I can say without blowing our own trumpet that this was the start of the Norse Riders' and Duffs downfall. The Norse Riders and Inspector Duff dug their own graves when they avenged the loss of the drugs consignment and five of their members by killing first Duncan and then Banquo and his son. And this is, incidentally, the last time I will mention Duff by rank, which in our police force is considered an honour regardless of whether it is the highest or the lowest.' Macbeth noticed to his dismay that the slightly tremulous indignation in his voice was genuine, completely genuine.

'Do you really mean to say, Macbeth — '

'Hand up before you . . . ' Lennox started to say, but Macbeth raised his palms and nodded for Kite to continue. He was ready to take on this insubordinate querulous bastard now.

'Do you really mean to say, Macbeth, that you, the police, cannot be criticised for *anything* during these operations? In the course of one afternoon you killed seven people you'd released from prison an hour earlier, nine other gang members, most of whom had no record, plus six women who, as far as we know, had nothing to do with any crimes committed by the Norse

Riders. Then you tell us there's also a family in Fife who are by definition innocent victims. And you consider that you didn't make a single error?'

Macbeth observed Kite. The radio reporter had dark hair surrounding a bald head and a moustache that formed a sad mouth around his own. Always bad news. Macbeth wondered what fate awaited such a man. He shuffled his papers. Found the page he had drafted and to which Lady, later Lennox, had added detail. Breathed in. Knew he was in perfect equilibrium. Knew his medication was perfect. Knew he had received the perfect serve.

'He's right,' Macbeth said, looking across the assembled journalists. 'We've made mistakes.' Waited, waited until it was even quieter than quiet, until the silence was unbearable, you couldn't breathe, until the silence demanded *sound*. He looked down at his speech. He had to bring it alive, make it seem as if he wasn't just quoting the text he had in front of him.

'In a democracy,' he began, 'there are rules which determine when suspects must be released from custody. We obeyed them.' He nodded as an amen to his declaration. 'In a democracy there are rules which state that the police can and must arrest suspects when there is *new* evidence in a case. We obeyed them.' More nodding. 'In a democracy there are rules which set out how the police should react if suspects resist arrest and, as in this case, shoot at the police. And we obeyed them.' He could of course have continued like this, but three instances of 'We obeyed them' were enough. He raised a forefinger. 'And that's all we've done. Some have already called what we did heroic. Some have already called it the most effective and eagerly awaited police operation in the history of this town's suffering. And some have called it a turning point in the fight against crime on our streets.' He saw how his nodding had rubbed off on the listeners, he even heard a couple of mumbled yeses. 'But the way I see it as chief commissioner is that we were only doing the job we'd been given. Nothing more than you can ask of us as police officers.'

In the empty gallery he saw Lennox standing ready by the projector while following the speech in his copy of the manuscript.

'But I have to admit it makes me feel good this evening,' Macbeth said, 'to be able to say *police officers* and do so with pride. And now, goodness me, folks, let's put the formalities to one side for a moment. The fact is we had a big clean-up today. We paid Sweno and his murderers back in their own coin. We showed them what they can expect if they take our best men from us . . . '

The light shone brighter around him, and he knew the slide of Duncan had come up on the screen behind him; soon it would shift to Banquo and Fleance in uniform under the apple tree in the garden behind their house.

'But, yes, we made errors. We made an error by not starting this clean-up *before*! Before it was too late for Chief Commissioner Duncan. Before it was too late for Inspector Banquo, who served this town all his life. And his son, Police Cadet Fleance, who was looking forward to doing the same.' Macbeth had to take deep breaths to control the tremor in his voice. 'But this afternoon we showed that this is a new day. A new day when criminals are no longer in charge. A new day when the citizens of this town have stood up and said no. No, we won't allow this. And now this is the evening of the first of these new days. And in the days to come we will continue to clean up the streets of this town because this big clean-up isn't over.'

When Macbeth had finished and said, 'Thank you,' he stayed on his feet. Stood there in the storm of applause that broke out as chairs scraped and people rose and the ovation continued with undiminished vigour. And he could feel his eyes going misty at the cynical journalists' genuine response to his falsehoods. And when Kite also stood up and clapped, albeit in a rather more sedate tempo, he wondered if that was because the guy knew what was good for him. Because he saw that Macbeth had won their love now. Won power. And he could see and hear that the new chief commissioner was a man who was unafraid to use it.

★ ★ ★

Macbeth strode down the corridor behind Scone Hall.

Power. He could feel it in his veins; the harmony was still there. Not as perfect as a while ago — the unease and restlessness were already on the verge of returning — but he had more than enough medicine for the moment. And he would just enjoy tonight. Enjoy the food and drink, enjoy Lady, enjoy the view of the town, enjoy everything that was his.

'Good speech, sir,' Seyton said, who seemed to have no problem keeping up with Macbeth's pace.

Lennox ran up alongside him.

'Fantastic, Macbeth!' he exclaimed, out of breath. 'There are some journalists here from Capitol to see you. They'd like to interview you and — '

'Thank you but no,' Macbeth said without slowing down. 'No victory interviews, no laurels until we've achieved our goal. Any news of Duff?'

'His car's been found in the town, parked beside the Obelisk. The roads out of town, the airport, passenger boats — everything has been under surveillance since half an hour after we saw him driving towards the town from Fife, so we know he's still here somewhere. We've checked Banquo's house, his parents-in-law, and he's not there. But in this weather a man *has* to have a roof over his head at night, so we'll go through every hotel, every boarding house, pub and brothel with a toothcomb. Everyone, absolutely everyone is chasing Duff tonight.'

'Chasing's good, catching's better.'

'Oh, we'll catch him. It's just a question of time.'

'Good. Could you leave us alone for a minute?'

'OK.' Lennox stopped and was soon far behind them.

'Something bothering you, Seyton? The wound?'

'No, sir.' Seyton took his arm out of the sling.

'No? The sergeant shot you in the arm, didn't he?'

'I have unusually good healing tissue,' Seyton said. 'It's in the family.'

'Indeed?'

'Good healing tissue?'

'Family. There's something else eating you then?'

'Two things.'

'Out with it.'

'The baby we found and removed from the club house after the shooting.'

'Yes?'

'I don't really know what to do with it. I've got it locked in my office.'

'I'll take care of it,' Macbeth said. 'And the other thing?'

'Angus, sir.'

'What about him?'

'He didn't obey orders in Fife. He refused to fire and in the end left before the op was finished. He called it slaughter. He hadn't joined SWAT to take part in *this kind of thing*. I think there's a risk he might blab. We have to do something.'

They stopped in front of the lift.

Macbeth rubbed his chin. 'So you think Angus has lost the belief? If so, it won't be the first time. Has he told you he studied theology?'

'No, but I can smell it. And he walks about with this bloody ugly cross around his neck.'

'You're in charge of SWAT now, Seyton. What do you think should be done?'

'We have to get rid of him, boss.'

'Death?'

'You said yourself we're at war, sir. In war traitors and cowards are punished with death. We'll do what we did with Duff: we'll leak that he's corrupt and make it look like he resisted arrest.'

'Let me chew on it. Right now we're in the spotlight and we need to show loyalty and unity. Cawdor, Malcolm, Duff and now Angus. It's too many. The town likes dead criminals better than duplicitous policemen. Where is he?'

'He's sitting alone moping in the basement. He won't talk to anyone.'

'OK. Let me have a chat with him before we make a move.'

★ ★ ★

Macbeth found Angus in the SWAT common room. He was sitting with his head in his hands and barely reacted when Macbeth put a large shoebox before him on the table and sat down in the chair directly opposite.

'I heard what happened. How are you?'

No answer.

'You're a principled lad, Angus. That's part of what I like about you. Principles are important to you, aren't they?'

Angus raised his head and looked at Macbeth with bloodshot eyes.

'I can see them burning in your eyes right now,' Macbeth said. 'Righteous indignation, it warms your heart, doesn't it? Makes you feel like the person you want to be. But when the brotherhood demands a real sacrifice it's sometimes exactly that that we want, Angus. Your principles. For you to renounce the cosy warmth of a good conscience, for you to be wakened by the same nightmares as us, for you to give up what is most valuable to you, the way your former god demanded that Abraham give up his son.'

Angus cleared his throat, but his voice was still hoarse. 'I can give. But for what?'

'For the long-term goal. For the community's good. For the town, Angus.'

Angus snorted. 'Can you explain to me how killing innocent people is for the community's good?'

'Twenty-five years ago an American president dropped the atom bomb on two Japanese towns populated by children, civilians and innocents. It stopped a war. That's the kind of paradox God torments us with.'

'That's easy to say. You weren't there.'

'I know what it costs, Angus. Recently I cut the throat of an innocent person for the good of the community. I don't sleep well at night. The doubt, the shame, the sense of guilt, they're part of the price we have to pay if we really want to do something good and not just bathe in the cosy, safe warmth of self-righteousness.'

'God doesn't exist and I'm no president.'

'That's correct,' Macbeth said, taking the lid off the shoebox. 'But as I'm both in this building I'll give you a chance to make up for the mistake you made in Fife.'

Angus peeped into the box. And recoiled in his chair in shock.

'Take this and burn it in the furnace at Estex tonight.'

Angus swallowed, as pale as death. 'That's the b-b-baby from the club house . . . '

'Front-line soldiers, like you and me, know that innocent lives have to be lost in war, but they don't know that at home — the people we fight for. That's why we keep such things hidden from them, so they don't get hysterical. Do you get hysterical, Angus?'

'I-I . . . '

'Listen. I'm showing my confidence in you by giving you this assignment. You can go to Estex or you can use this to report your brothers here in SWAT. I'm giving you the choice. Because I need to know that I can trust you.'

Angus shook his head, a sob escaped him. 'You need to make me an *accessory* to know you can trust me!'

Macbeth shook his head. 'You're already an accessory. I only need to know that you're strong enough to take and carry the guilt without those at home finding out the price we pay to defend them. Only then will I know if you're a real man, Angus.'

'You make it sound as if we, and not the child, are the victims. I can't do it! I'd rather be shot.'

Macbeth looked at Angus. He didn't feel any anger. Perhaps because he liked Angus. Perhaps because he knew Angus couldn't hurt them. But mostly because he was sorry for him. Macbeth put the lid back on the shoebox and stood up.

'Wait,' Angus said. 'H-how are you going to punish me?'

'Oh, you'll punish yourself,' Macbeth said. 'Read what it says on our flag. It's not the child's screaming you'll hear when you wake up sweaty after a nightmare, but the words: *Loyalty, fraternity, baptised in fire, united in blood.*'

He took the shoebox and left.

★　★　★

There was still more than an hour to midnight when Macbeth let himself into the suite.

Lady was standing by the window with her back to him. The room was sparsely illuminated by a single wax candle, and she was dressed in a nightdress. He put the shoebox on the table under the mirror, went over to her and kissed her neck.

'The electricity went when I arrived,' he said. 'Jack's checking the fuse box. Hope none of the customers are using the opportunity to make off with the kitty.'

'The electricity has gone in over half the town,' she said, leaning back and resting her head on his shoulder. 'I can see from here. What have you got in the shoebox?'

'What do you normally have in a shoebox?'

'You're carrying it as if it were a bomb.'

At that moment a huge streak of lightning flashed like a white luminous vein across the sky, and they caught a glimpse of the town. Then it was dark again and thunder rolled in.

'Isn't it beautiful?' he said, inhaling the scent of her hair.

'I don't know what it is, you know.'

'I meant the town. And it will be more beautiful. When Duff's no longer in it.'

'It will still have a mayor who makes it ugly. Won't you tell me what's in the box?' Her voice was thick, as though she had just woken up.

'Just something I have to burn. I'll ask Jack to take it up to the furnaces at Estex tomorrow.'

'I want to be burned too, darling.'

Macbeth stiffened. What had she said? Was she sleepwalking? But sleepwalkers couldn't hold conversations, could they?

'So you haven't found Duff yet?' she said.

'Not yet, but we're looking everywhere.'

'Poor man. Losing his children and now he's all alone.'

'Someone's helping him. Otherwise we'd have found him. I don't trust Lennox.'

'Because you know he serves Hecate and brew?'

'Because Lennox is basically weak. He might be getting soft and conspiratorial, the way Banquo became. Perhaps he's hiding Duff. I should arrest him. Seyton tells me that under Kenneth they used to give arrestees an electric shock in the groin if they didn't talk. And another one to *stop* them talking.'

'No.'

'No?'

'No. Arresting one of your own unit commanders would look bad now. For the time being the general impression is that you've nabbed two rotten apples in Duff and Malcolm. Three would make it look like a purge. Purges raise questions not only about the unpurged but also the leader, and we don't want to give Tourtell any reason to hesitate in appointing you. And as for electric shocks, right now there's no electricity in this part of town.'

'So what do I do?'

'You wake the electrician and ask him to fix it.'

'You're difficult this evening, my love. This evening you should be uniting with me, acclaiming me as a hero.'

'And you me as a heroine, Macbeth. Have you checked out Caithness?'

'Caithness? What makes you think she's involved?'

'During the dinner that night Duff said he was staying with a cousin.'

'Yes, he mentioned that.'

'And you weren't surprised that an orphanage boy had an uncle in town?'

'Not all uncles can take on . . . ' Macbeth frowned as he stood behind her. 'You mean Duff and Caithness . . . ?'

'Dear Macbeth, my hero, you are and will always be a simple man without a woman's eye for how two secretly enamoured people look at each other.'

Macbeth blinked into the darkness. Then he put his arms around her, closed his eyes and pulled her to him. How would he have survived without her? 'Only when we two stand in front of the mirror,' he whispered in her ear. 'Thank you, darling. Go to bed now and I'll tell

Lennox to go to Caithness's at once.'

'It's back,' she said.

'What is?'

'The electricity. Look. Our town is lit up again.'

Macbeth opened his eyes and looked at her illuminated face. Looked down at both of their bodies. They glowed red from the neon Bacardi lights on the building across Thrift Street.

★ ★ ★

'Lennox?' Caithness was already so frozen that her teeth were chattering as she stood with her arms crossed in the doorway to her flat. 'Police Officer Seyton?'

'*Inspector* Seyton,' the lean policeman said, pushed her aside and went in.

'What's this about?' she asked.

'I'm sorry, Caithness,' Lennox said. 'Orders. Is Duff here?'

'Duff? Why on earth would he be here?'

'And why on earth would you say yes?' Seyton said, directing the four machine-gun-toting men in SWAT uniforms to the four rooms in the flat. 'If he's here it's because you're hiding him. You know very well he's a wanted man.'

'Feel free,' she said.

'Thank you so much for your permission,' Seyton said acidly. Studying her in a way that made her wish she had more on than her thin nightdress. Then he smiled. Caithness shuddered. His mouth arced up behind his slightly slanting eyes, making him look like a snake.

'Are you trying to hold us up?' he said.

'Hold you up?' she said, hoping he didn't notice the fear in her voice.

'Sir?' It was one of the men. 'There's a door to a fire escape here.'

'Oh, is there?' Seyton intoned without taking his eyes

310

off Caithness. 'Interesting. So when we rang your doorbell down on the street you let the cat out through the flap, did you?'

'Not at all,' she said.

'You are of course familiar with the penalty for lying to the police — in addition to that for hiding a criminal?'

'I am *not* lying, Police Officer Seyton.'

'*Inspec* — ' He paused, regained his smile. 'This is SWAT you're dealing with, Miss Caithness. We know our job. Such as examining the drawings of buildings before we enter.' He lifted his walkie-talkie to his mouth. 'Alpha to Charlie. Any sign of Duff by the fire escape door? Over.'

The brief sibilance when he pressed the button of the walkie-talkie made her think of waves lapping on a beach somewhere far far away.

'Not yet, Alpha,' came the answer. 'Conditions for a controlled arrest are good here, so can we confirm that the object should be shot on sight? Over.'

Caithness saw Seyton's eyes harden and heard his voice sharpen. 'Duff's dangerous. The order comes straight from the chief commissioner and must be followed to the letter.'

'Roger. Over and out.'

The four men came back into the sitting room. 'He's not here, sir.'

'Nothing?'

'I found this lying on the bedroom floor by the door to the fire escape.' One of them held up a tennis racket and jewellery.

Seyton took the racket and leaned over the hand holding the jewellery. To Caithness it looked as if he was sniffing them. Then he turned back to her holding the handle of the racket in an obscene way.

'Big racket for a little hand like yours, Miss Caithness. And do you make a habit of throwing your earrings on the floor?'

Caithness straightened. Breathed in. 'I think it's a common habit, Police Officer. Casting pearls before swine. But in time one learns, hopefully. If you've finished looking and the cat on the stairs has been executed, I'd like to go back to sleep. Goodnight, gentlemen.'

She saw Seyton's eyes go black and his mouth open, but he held his tongue when Lennox placed a hand on his shoulder.

'We apologise for the disturbance, Caithness. But as a colleague you will understand that absolutely no stone must be left unturned in this case.'

Lennox and the rest headed towards the front door, but Seyton stood his ground. 'Even if we don't always like the filth we find under them,' he said. 'So he didn't buy you a wedding ring then, I suppose?'

'What do you want, Seyton?'

His repulsive smile returned. 'Yes, what do we want?' Then he turned and left.

She closed the door behind him. Pressed her back against it. Where was Duff? Where was he last night? And what did she wish for him? The hell he had to be in or the redemption he didn't deserve?

★   ★   ★

Lennox stared through the rain pouring down the windscreen. The refracted light made the red traffic lights blur and distort. God, how he longed to get these hours, this shift, this night over and done with. God, how he longed to relax in his sitting room, pour himself a glass of whisky and inject some brew. He wasn't addicted. Not to the extent that it was a problem anyway. He was a user, not a misuser; *he* was in control, not the dope. One of the lucky few who could take drugs and still function in a demanding job as well as be a father and a husband. Yes, dope did actually help him to function. Without the breaks at work he wasn't sure he would have managed. Balancing everything, watching his step. Making compromises where he had to, eating shit with a smile, not rocking the boat, understanding who was in charge, bending with the wind. But one day it would probably be his turn to take charge. And if it wasn't, other things were more important. His family — that was who he was working for. So that he and Sheila could have a spacious house in a safe neighbourhood in the west of town, send their three lovely kids to a good school with healthy values, take a well-deserved Mediterranean holiday once a year, cover the health insurance, dentist and all that kind of thing. God, how he loved his family. Sometimes he would put down the newspaper and just look at them sitting in the lounge, all of them busy, and then he would think, *This is a gift I never thought I would have the good fortune to receive.* The love of others. He, the one they called Albert Albino, was beaten up in every school break until he got a doctor's note saying he couldn't tolerate daylight and had to stay in the classroom alone during breaks. White, small and delicate he may have been, but he had a big mouth on him. That was how he had got Sheila — he talked loudly and volubly for both of them. And even more when he had tried cocaine for the first time. It was coke that had made him a better version of himself, energetic, dogged and unafraid. At least for a while. Later it had become a necessity so that he wouldn't become a bad version of himself. Then he had changed drug in the hope that there was another way other than the dead-end street that cocaine was. Maximum one shot a day. No more. Some needed five. The dysfunctional. He was a long way from that. His father was wrong, he did have a spine. He had control.

'Everything under control?'

Lennox started. 'Eh?'

313

'Your list,' Seyton said from the back seat. 'What's left?'

Lennox yawned. 'HQ. That's the last stop.'

'Police HQ's massive.'

'Yes, but according to the caretaker Duff has only three keys. One for Narco and one for Homicide.'

'And the third?'

'The Forensics garage. But I hardly think he'd want to catch pneumonia in the cellar if he can hide under a table in a warm dry office.'

The police radio crackled, and a nasal voice informed them that all the rooms at the Obelisk, including the penthouse suite, had been searched without success.

The caretaker stood waiting for them with a big bunch of keys outside the staff entrance to HQ. It took Lennox, Seyton and eight officers less than twenty minutes to search the Narco rooms. Less to trawl through Homicide. And they had even checked behind the ceiling boards and the pipes in the ventilation system.

'That's that then.' Lennox yawned. 'That's it, folks. Grab a few hours' sleep. We'll continue tomorrow.'

'The garage,' Seyton said.

'As I said — '

'The garage.'

Lennox shrugged. 'You're right. Won't take long. Lads, you go home, and Seyton, Olafson and I will check the garage.'

The three of them took the lift down to the basement floor with the caretaker, who let them in and switched on the lights.

In the silence as the electricity worked to get the phosphates in the neon tubes to fluoresce Lennox heard something.

'Did you hear that?' he whispered.

'No,' the caretaker said. 'But it'll be rats if it's anything.'

Lennox had his doubts. It hadn't been a rattling or a

314

scurrying, it had been a creak. As if from shoes.

'A plague,' the caretaker sighed. 'Can't get rid of 'em, not down here.'

The large cellar room was empty apart from a trolley carrying various tools and Banquo's Volvo covered with a tarpaulin by the garage door. Ranged along the wall there were five closed doors.

'If you want to get rid of rats,' Seyton said, releasing the safety catch on his machine gun, 'just contact me. Olafson, let's start from the left.'

Lennox watched as the bald man moved quickly and nimbly across the room with Olafson hard on his heels. They took the doors one by one as if in a precisely choreographed and practised dance. Seyton opened, Olafson went in with his gun to his shoulder, sank to his knees while Seyton followed and passed him. Lennox counted the minutes. It was getting late for his shot, he could feel. There, the final room at last. Seyton pressed the handle.

'Locked!' he shouted.

'Oh yes, the darkroom is always locked,' the caretaker said. 'Photos are considered evidence. Duff hasn't got a key for this room. At least, he didn't get it from me.'

'Let's go then,' Lennox said.

Seyton and Olafson came towards them with the short barrels of their machine guns lowered as the caretaker held the door open.

At last.

Seyton held out his hand. 'The key.'

'What?'

'To the darkroom.'

The caretaker hesitated, glanced at Lennox, who sighed and nodded. The caretaker removed a key from his bunch and gave it to Seyton.

'What's he doing?' asked the caretaker as they watched Seyton and Olafson walk past the Volvo to the darkroom door.

'His job,' growled Lennox.

'I mean with his nose. Looks like he's sniffing, like an animal.'

Lennox nodded. Thinking he wasn't alone in noticing that Seyton could assume the shape of a . . . he didn't know what. Something that wasn't human anyway.

★ ★ ★

Seyton could smell him now. That smell. The same as the one in the house in Fife and Caithness's flat. Either he was here or he had been here recently. Seyton unlocked the door and opened it. Olafson went in and sank to his knees. When the caretaker turned on the switch at the front door all the lights in the garage and the side rooms had come on as well, but in here it was still dark. Of course. A darkroom.

Seyton went in. The stench of chemicals drowned the smell of the prey, of Duff. He found the light switch on the inside of the door, twisted it on, but still no light came. Maybe the fuse had gone during the power cut. Or someone had removed the bulb. Seyton switched on his torch. The wall above the table was covered with big photos hanging from a line. Seyton shone his torch across them. They showed a dagger with a blood-stained blade and handle. Duff had been here. Seyton was absolutely sure.

'Hey! What's going on?' It was Lennox. The little albino wimp wanted to go home. He was sweating and yawning. The bloody old woman.

'Coming,' Seyton shouted, switching off the torch. 'Come on, Olafson.'

Seyton let Olafson pass. Shut the door hard after him and stood inside the door. Listened in the darkness. Until Duff thought the coast was clear and relaxed. Seyton lifted his gun to the photos. Pressed the trigger. The weapon shook in his hands, the sound reverberated against his eardrums. He drew a cross with the burst. Then he switched on his torch again, walked over to the perforated photos and pulled them aside.

Stared at the bullet holes in the wall behind.

No Duff.

The explosions were still ringing in his ears. He noted that one of the holes was extra-deep — must have been two bullets hitting the same spot. Chance.

Of course.

Seyton marched out towards the others.

'What was that?' Lennox asked.

'I didn't like the photos,' Seyton said. 'There's one place we've forgotten.'

'Yes,' Lennox groaned. 'Our beds.'

'Duff thinks like they did during the bomb attacks in the war. He hides in a bomb crater because he believes two bombs can't hit exactly the same place.'

'What the hell . . . ?'

'He's back in his house in Fife. Come on!'

★ ★ ★

The rat darted out of its hiding place after the light in the garage had gone off, it had heard the door slam and the steps fade away. It padded over the damp brick floor to the car in the middle. There was blood on the driver's seat, which attracted it. Sweet, nutritious and days old. It just had to get through the tarpaulin spread over the car. The rat had almost got through before when it was disturbed. But now it gnawed through the last part and was inside. It ran across the floor on the passenger side, past the gear stick and down onto the rubber mat on the driver's side. Over a pair of leather shoes. Recoiled when one leather shoe creaked and rose. It reared up onto its legs and hissed. The lovely bloodstained driver's seat was occupied.

★ ★ ★

Duff heard the rustle of the fleeing rat. Then he loosened his tensed grip on the wheel. He could feel his heart wasn't pounding any more, only beating. It had been hammering so hard while Seyton and his men were in the garage he was sure they must have heard. He looked at his watch. Still five hours to daybreak. He tried to shift position, but his trousers were stuck to the blood on the seat. Banquo's blood. It glued him to this place. But he had to get away. Move on.

But where? And how?

When he fled his idea had been that it would be easier to drive to town and disappear in the crowds there than escape along a country road. He had abandoned his car in a street not far from the Obelisk and gone into the casino, which was the only place besides the Inverness he knew stayed open all night. He couldn't rent a room of course; overnight accommodation would be the first place Macbeth would check. But he could sit among the great swathe of one-armed bandits, as lonely and undisturbed as the person on the nearest machine, feeding it with coins and slowly allowing himself to be robbed. And he had done that while thinking — *trying to think* — about how he could escape and staring at the images of the odds spinning round in the three small windows. A heart. A dagger. A crown. After a few hours he went to the bar for a beer to see if that could brighten his mood and saw on the muted TV above the barman the press conference at police HQ, and suddenly a familiar face appeared on the screen, with a white scar running diagonally across it like a traffic sign. A close-up of himself, with the word WANTED written over it. Duff made for the exit with his collar turned up and head bent. And the cold night air cleared his brain enough for him to remember their old love nest, the garage, which was his best overnight option.

318

But soon Friday would dawn, a working day, and he would have to get out before the staff arrived, and outside the news-stands would be adorned with his face.

Duff put his hand into his jacket pocket. Felt the glossy paper under his fingers. Pulled out the package. Couldn't stop himself, imagined Ewan's face when he saw that he had been given what he asked for. Duff heard his own wild sobbing. Stop! He mustn't! He had promised himself he wouldn't think about them now. Grieving was a privilege he could grant himself later if he survived. He switched on the Volvo's inside light, dried his tears, removed the wrapping paper, took out the false beard, opened the glue tube and squeezed out the shiny glue, which he spread over his chin, around his lips and inside the beard. Used the rear-view mirror to stick it on. Pulled the tight woollen hat over his forehead so that the upper part of his scar was hidden. Then he put on the glasses. The comically wide frames covered the scar on his cheek above the beard. In the mirror he saw he had glue on his cheek. Searched in vain through his pockets for something to wipe it off with, opened the glove compartment, found a notebook, took it out and was about to tear off the top page. Stopped. In the light he saw depressions in the paper. Someone had recently written in the notebook. So what? He tore off the sheet, wiped the glue from his cheek. Scrunched up the paper and put it in his jacket pocket. Put the notebook back in the glove compartment.

So.

Leaned back in the seat. Closed his eyes.

Five hours. Why had he put on the beard so early? It already itched. He started thinking again. Fought to keep his mind off Fife. He had to find himself a place to hide in town. All the roads out would be closed. Besides he didn't have any bolt-holes outside town or in Fife, no

319

hostels or hotels that wouldn't be warned, no one out of town who would hide a wanted cop-killer. And then it struck him. He didn't know anyone who would help him. Not here, not anywhere. He was the type of person people got on with; they didn't necessarily actively dislike him. They just didn't like him. And why would they? What had he ever done to help them that hadn't also helped himself? He had alliances, not friends. And now, when Duff really needed help, a friend, a shoulder to cry on, Duff was a man with no creditworthiness, a lost cause. He examined his pathetic, stiff, hirsute reflection. The fox. The hunters were closing in on him, Macbeth's new chief hound, Seyton, already barking at his heels. He had to get away. But where, where could the fox find a foxhole?

Five hours to daybreak. To Friday. To Ewan's birth . . .

No! Don't cry! Survive! A dead man can't avenge anything.

He had to stay awake until it became light, then find himself somewhere else. One of the disused factories perhaps. No, he had already rejected that idea. Macbeth knew as well as he did where he would try to hide. Shit! Now he was going round in circles, crossing his own tracks, the way people did when they got lost.

He was so tired, but he had to stay awake until it was light. Ewan had never turned ten. Shit! He tried to find something to distract himself. He read all the gauges in front of him. Took the crumpled sheet from his jacket pocket, uncrumpled it and smoothed the page. Tried to read. Rummaged through the glove compartment until he found a pencil. Held it sideways over the paper and shaded over the depressions. What had been writen on the paper, on the sheet above, which had been taken, shone white against black: *Dolphin. 66 Tannery St, District 6. Alfie. Safe haven.*

An address. There was a Tannery Street in town, but

no District 6. And there was only one other town that was divided into districts. Capitol. When could this note have been written? He had no idea how long it took for an impression made by a pencil to disappear. And what did it mean by *Safe haven?*

Duff switched off the light and closed his eyes. A little nap maybe?

Capitol. Friday. He had seen this combination somewhere quite recently.

Duff was slipping into a dream with associations to the two words when he woke with a start.

He switched the light back on.

23

'Meredith and I are getting married,' Duff said. A sun seemed to be shining out of his eyes.

'Really? That was . . . erm quick.'

'Yes! Will you be my best man, Macbeth?'

'Me?'

'Of course. Who else?'

'Erm. When . . . ?'

'Sixth of July. At Meredith's parents' summer place. Everything's sorted. Invitations were sent out today.'

'It's kind of you to ask, Duff. I'll give it some thought.'

'Thought?'

'I've . . . planned a longish trip in July. July's difficult for me, Duff.'

'Trip? You didn't say anything about this to me.'

'No, I might not have done.'

'But then we haven't spoken for a while. Where have you been? Meredith was asking after you.'

'Was she? Oh, here and there. Been a bit busy.'

'And where will this trip take you?'

'To Capitol.'

'Capitol?'

'Yes, I've . . . erm never been there. Time to see our capital, isn't it? It's supposed to be so much nicer than here.'

'Listen to me now, my dear Macbeth. I'll pay for a return air ticket from Capitol. Can't have my best pal not being there when I get married. It'll be the party of the year! Imagine all Meredith's single girlfriends . . . '

'And from Capitol I'm going abroad. It's a long trip, Duff. I'll probably be away all July.'

'But . . . Has this got anything to do with the little

flirtation you and Meredith had once?'

'So if we don't see each other for a bit, all the best with the wedding and . . . well, everything.'

'Macbeth!'

'Thanks, Duff, but I won't forget I owe you dragon blood. Say hello to Meredith and thank her for the little flirtation.'

'Macbeth, sir!'

Macbeth opened his eyes. He was lying in bed. A dream. Nevertheless. Were those the words they had used then? *Dragon blood*. Lorreal. Had he really said that?

'Macbeth!?'

The voice came from the other side of the bedroom door and now it was accompanied by frenetic banging. He looked at the clock on the bedside table. Three o'clock in the morning.

'Sir, it's Jack!'

Macbeth turned the other way. He was alone. Lady wasn't there.

'Sir, you have to — '

Macbeth tore open the door. 'What's up, Jack?'

'She's sleepwalking.'

'So? Aren't you keeping an eye on her?'

'It's different this time, sir. She . . . You've got to come.'

Macbeth yawned, switched on the light, donned a dressing gown and was about to leave the room when his gaze fell on the table under the mirror. The shoebox was gone.

'Quick. Show me the way, Jack.'

They found her on the roof. Jack paused on the threshold of the open metal door. It had stopped raining, and all that could be heard was the wind and the regular rumble of the traffic that never slept. She was standing right on the edge, in the light of the Bacardi sign, with her back to them. A gust of wind caught her thin nightdress.

'Lady!' Macbeth said and was about to rush over to her, but Jack held him back. 'The psychiatrist said she mustn't be woken up when she's sleepwalking, sir.'

'But she could fall over the edge!'

'She often comes up here and stands just there,' Jack said. 'She can see even if she's asleep. The psychiatrist says sleepwalkers rarely come to harm, but if you wake them they can become disorientated and hurt themselves.'

'Why has no one told me she comes up here? I've been given the impression she basically strolls up and down the corridor.'

'She told me in no uncertain terms that I was not to say what she does in her sleep, sir.'

'And what does she do?'

'Sometimes she strolls up and down the corridor as you say. Otherwise she goes into the washroom and uses the strong soap there. Scrubs her hands, occasionally until her skin goes red. Then she comes up on the roof.'

Macbeth looked at her. His beloved Lady. So exposed and vulnerable out in the wind-blown night. So alone in the darkness of her mind, the darkness she had told him about but where she couldn't take him. There was nothing he could do. Just wait and hope she would choose to come back in from the night. So near and so out of reach.

'What makes you think she might take her life tonight?'

Jack glanced at Macbeth in surprise. 'I don't think she will, sir.'

'So what was it then, Jack?'

'What was what, sir?'

'What made you so worried that you called me?'

At that moment the moonlight broke through a gap in the cloud. And as if at an agreed signal Lady turned and walked towards them.

'That, sir.'

'God help us,' Macbeth whispered and hurriedly took a step back.

She was holding a bundle in her arms. She had pulled her nightdress to expose one breast, which she held to the open end of the bundle. Macbeth saw the back of a baby's head. He counted four black holes in it.

★ ★ ★

'Is she asleep?' Macbeth asked.

'I think so,' Jack whispered.

They had followed her closely off the roof, down the stairs and into the suite. Now they were standing by her bed, where she lay with the blanket pulled up over her and the child.

'Shall we take it off her?'

'Let her keep it,' Macbeth said. 'What harm can it do? But I want you to sit here and watch over her tonight. I have an important radio interview early tomorrow morning and have to sleep, so just give me a key for another room.'

'Of course,' Jack said. 'I'll ring for someone to take over at reception.'

While Jack was away Macbeth stroked the baby's cheek. Cold, stiff, a destroyed baby. What Lady and he had been. But they had managed to repair themselves. No. Lady had managed to repair herself. Macbeth had had help. From Banquo. And before that, at the orphanage, from Duff. Had Duff not killed Lorreal, Macbeth would probably have committed suicide sooner or later. Even when he escaped from the home he still had four black holes in his heart. Four holes that had to be filled with something. Brew was the quickest and easiest available sealant. But at least he kept himself alive. Thanks to Duff, the bastard.

And then there was Lady of course. Who had shown

him that hearts can be sealed with love, and pain can be eased with love-making. He stroked her cheek. Warm. Soft.

Were there ways back or had they forgotten to plan for a possible retreat? Had they planned only for victories? Yes, and they'd had victories. But what if the victory leaves a bitter taste, what if it comes at too great a cost and you would prefer a cheap defeat? What do you do then? Do you abdicate, renounce the royal trappings, ask humbly for forgiveness and return to your daily chores? When you step off the edge of the roof, and the cobbles of the red-light district rush towards you, do you ask gravity if you can retrace your ill-considered step? No. You take what's coming. Make the best of it. Make sure you land on your feet and perhaps break a leg or two. But you survive. And you become a better person who has learned to tread more carefully the next time.

Jack came in. 'I've found someone for reception,' he said and handed Macbeth a key.

Macbeth looked at it. 'Duncan's room?'

Jack put a hand to his mouth in horror. 'I thought it was the best room, but you might prefer . . . '

'That's fine, Jack. I'm close by in case there is anything. Besides I don't believe in ghosts. And as everyone knows I have nothing to fear from Duncan's ghost.'

'No, nothing.'

'Indeed, nothing at all. Goodnight.'

★   ★   ★

They came as soon as he closed his eyes.

Duncan and Malcolm. They were lying under the duvet either side of him.

'There isn't room for us all,' Macbeth screamed and kicked them out onto the floor, where they hissed until rat tails rustled alongside the wall and they were gone.

But then the door opened, and in crept Banquo, Fleance and Duff, each with a dagger in hand, poised ready to strike.

'What do you want?'

'Justice and our sleep back.'

'Ha, ha, ha!' Macbeth laughed, writhing in his bed. 'The person who can hurt me hasn't been born! Only Bertha can unseat me as chief commissioner! I am immortal! Macbeth is immortal! Out, you dead mortals!'

24

Fred Ziegler yawned.

'Fred, you need a cup of coffee.' The captain of MS *Glamis* chuckled. 'We can't have a harbour pilot falling asleep in this weather. Tell me, are you always tired?'

'Busy days, not enough sleep,' Fred said. He could hardly tell the captain the reason he was always yawning was that he was frightened. Fred had seen the same symptom in his dog, but fortunately yawning was usually regarded as indicating that you were totally at ease. Bored. Or, indeed, you hadn't slept enough. The captain pressed the intercom, and his order for coffee went down the cable to the galley, deck after deck after deck. MS *Glamis* was a big ship. A tall ship. And that was what bothered Fred Ziegler.

He stifled another yawn and stared across the river. He knew every reef, every shallow and every tiny paragraph in the port authority rulebook about sailing into and out of the harbour — where the current flowed strong, where the waves broke, where you could lie in shelter and where every bollard on the quay was. That didn't bother him. The river was grey; he could guide ships in and out blindfolded, and often had, or as good as. The weather didn't bother him either. A near gale was blowing, and the glass in front of them was already white with spray and salt. But he had guided bigger and smaller ships in hurricanes and worse without needing a beacon, a spar buoy or a lookout. The trip in the little pilot boat that would take him ashore didn't trouble him, even though it was as seaworthy as a cow — a fresh breeze and it took in water, the hint of a gale and it could turn round if the coxswain didn't hit the waves right.

Fred Ziegler yawned because he dreaded the ship lowering the red and white flag that showed they had a pilot on board. Or to be more precise, having to leave the ship. Going down the rope ladder.

For twelve years he had worked as a pilot and still he hadn't got used to going up and down the side of a ship. It didn't bother him that he might end up in the drink, although he knew he ought to have been afraid because he couldn't swim.

No, what bothered him was the height.

The paralysing fear when he would have to step out backwards from the ship's side. Even in this weather the ship was so big that climbing down the ladder on the leeward side wasn't difficult from a purely technical point of view. However, seeing or just knowing that there was fifteen metres of thin air between him and the abyss bothered him. It had always been like this and always would be. Every bloody working day was bound up with this minor hell: it was the first thing on his mind when he woke up in the morning and the last before he went to sleep. But what the heck, there was nothing unusual about it — all around him he saw people who lived their whole lives doing jobs or in positions they weren't cut out for.

'You must have come out of the harbour so many times now that you could ask the coastguard just to let you go,' Fred said.

'Let me go?' the captain said. 'I wouldn't have your company then, Fred. What is it? Don't you like me?'

I don't like your ship, Fred thought. I'm a small man who doesn't like big ships.

'By the way, you're going to see less of me in the future,' the captain said.

'Oh?'

'Not enough cargo. Last year we lost Graven when they went bankrupt and then Estex closed down. What we have on board now is the last remaining stock.'

Fred had noticed by the way the ship lay in the water there was less cargo than usual.

'Shame,' Fred said.

'No, makes no odds,' the captain said gloomily. 'Knowing this toxic stuff we've been transporting for all these years is paid for with our fellow citizens' lives . . . Believe me, I haven't always slept well and I've sometimes wondered what it must have been like being the captain of a slave ship. You have to be creative to find good enough excuses for yourself. Perhaps we know the difference between right and wrong even without using this wonderful big brain of ours. But with it we can assemble some really sophisticated arguments which, individually, sound good and, as a whole, can lead us to exactly where we want to go, regardless of how steeped in insanity this all is. No, Fred, I don't want to ask the coastguards for permission to navigate these contaminated waters without a pilot. On Wednesday we were queueing up to come in when a message came from the harbour master himself saying that we had top priority. Free of charge.'

'That must have been a nice surprise.'

'Yes. Then I took a closer look at the bill of lading. Turned out we'd been transporting two Gatling guns. This is beginning to resemble how it was under Kenneth. Hey, careful! Are you trying to scald our pilot, son?'

The man in the chequered galley outfit had lost his balance as the ship pitched into a wave and had spilled coffee on the pilot's black uniform. The guy mumbled an apology into his beard, put down the cups and hurried out.

'Sorry, Fred. Even here, where half the town is unemployed, it's hard to find crew with sea legs. This bloke came to us this morning claiming he'd worked in a galley before but had lost his papers.'

Fred slurped from the cup. 'He's not been on board a

330

boat before and he can't make coffee either.'

'Oh well,' the captain sighed. 'We'll manage as we're only going to Capitol. That's the Isle of Hanstholm behind us and now we're over the worst. I'll call up your boat and tell them to throw out the ladder.'

'OK,' Fred said, swallowing. 'Then we're over the worst.'

★ ★ ★

Macbeth was sitting on a chair in the corridor wringing his hands and staring at the door to the suite. 'What's he actually doing in there?'

'I don't know much about psychiatry,' Jack said. 'Shall I get some more coffee, sir?'

'No, stay where you are. But he's good, you say?'

'Yes, Dr Alsaker's supposed to be the best in town.'

'That's good, Jack. That's good. Terrible, terrible.' Macbeth leaned forward on the chair and hid his face in his hands. There was still an hour to go to the radio interview. He had woken before dawn to screams from Lady's room. And when he dashed in she had been standing beside the bed pointing at the dead baby.

'Look!' she shrieked. 'Look what I've done!'

'But it wasn't you, my love.' He tried to hold her, but she tore herself away and fell to her knees sobbing.

'Don't call me *my love*! I can't be loved, a child killer *shouldn't* be loved!' Then she turned to Macbeth and looked at him through those crazed black eyes of hers. 'Not even a child killer should love a child killer. Get out!'

'Come and lie down with me, darling.'

'Get out of my bedroom! And don't *touch* the child!'

'This is insanity. It's going to be burned today.'

'Touch the child and I'll kill you, Macbeth, I swear I will.' She took the body in her arms and rocked it.

He swallowed. He needed his morning shot. 'I'll take

331

some clothes and leave you in peace,' he said, going to the wardrobe. Pulled out a drawer. Stared.

'Sorry,' she said. 'You'll have to go and get some more. We need it, both of us.'

He left and instead of going for some more power he had got Jack to call for psychiatric assistance.

Now Macbeth looked at his watch again. How long could it take to fix the little short circuit she'd obviously had?

In response the door opened and Macbeth jumped up from his chair. A little man with a wispy grey beard and eyelids that appeared to be one size too large came out.

'Well?' Macbeth asked. 'Doctor . . . er . . . '

'Dr Alsaker,' Jack said.

'I've given her something to calm her down,' the psychiatrist said.

'What's wrong with her?'

'Hard to say.'

'Hard? You're supposed to be the best.'

'That's nice to hear, but not even the very best know all the labyrinths of the mind, Mr Macbeth.'

'You *have* to cure her.'

'As I said, with the little we really know about the human mind that's a lot to ask . . . '

'I'm not *asking*, Doctor. I'm giving you an ultimatum.'

'An ultimatum, Mr Macbeth?'

'If you don't make her normal again, I'll have to arrest you as a charlatan.'

Alsaker looked at him from under his oversized eyelids. 'I can see that you have slept badly and you're beside yourself with worry, Chief Commissioner. I recommend you take a day off work. Now as for your wife — '

'You're mistaken,' Macbeth said, taking a dagger from his shoulder holster. 'And the punishment for not doing your job is draconian during the present state of emergency.'

'Sir . . . ' Jack started to say.

'Surgery,' Macbeth said. 'That's what's needed, that's what a real doctor does: he cuts away what is pernicious. He excludes any thought of the patient's pain because that only makes him vacillate. You remove and destroy the offending item, a tumour or a rotting foot, to save the whole. It's not that the tumour or the foot are evil in themselves, they simply have to be sacrificed. Isn't that so, Doctor?'

The psychiatrist tilted his head. 'Are you sure it's your wife who needs to be examined and not yourself, Mr Macbeth?'

'You have your ultimatum.'

'And I'm leaving now. So you'd better stab me in the back with that thing if you need to.'

Macbeth watched Alsaker turn his back and set off towards the stairs. He stared at the dagger in his hand. What on earth was he doing?

'Alsaker!' Macbeth ran after the psychiatrist. Caught up with him and knelt down before him. 'Please, you *have* to, you have to help her. She's all I have. I must have her back. *You* must get her back. I'll pay whatever it costs.'

Alsaker held his beard between his thumb and forefinger. 'Is it brew?' he asked.

'Power,' Macbeth said.

'Naturally.'

'You know it?'

'Under a variety of sobriquets, but the chemicals are the same. People think it's an anti-depressant because it acts as an upper the first few times until the episodes become psychotic.'

'Yes, yes, that's what she takes.'

'I asked what *you* take, Mr Macbeth. And now I can see. How long have you been taking power?'

'I . . .'

'Not long evidently. The first thing to go is your teeth. Then your mind. And it's not easy to escape from the prison of psychosis. Do you know what they call you when you're completely hooked on power? A POW.'

'Now listen here — '

'A prisoner of war. Neat, isn't it?'

'I'm not your patient now, Alsaker. I beg you not to leave until you've done all you can.'

'I promise to return, but I have other patients to attend to now.'

'Jack,' Macbeth said without moving or taking his eyes off the psychiatrist.

'Yes, sir.'

'Show him.'

'But . . .'

'He's bound by the Hippocratic oath.'

Jack unwound the cloth from the bundle and held it out for the doctor. He took a step back covering his nose and mouth with his hand.

'She thinks it's hers,' Macbeth said. 'If not for my sake and hers, then for the town's, Doctor.'

★   ★   ★

Macbeth felt a strange pressure in his ears as the door closed behind him. Finally, he thought, I'm in the nuthouse. The walls of the little square room, where three people sat observing him, were padded, although there was a window.

'Don't be afraid,' said the man at the table in front of him. 'I'm just going to ask a few questions. It'll all be over soon.'

'It's not the questions I'm frightened of,' Macbeth said, sitting down, 'it's the answers.'

The man smiled, the music from the speaker above the window died, and he put a finger to his mouth as a red light on the wall came on.

'This is *Rolling News* with Walt Kite,' the man trilled, turning to the mike in front of him. 'We have a visit from the town's new favourite, Chief Commissioner Macbeth, who after wiping out one of the town's most notorious drugs gangs, the Norse Riders, is now tirelessly chasing their corrupt collaborators inside the police's own ranks. He has won the hearts of the people and lifted their hopes with inspiring speeches in which he says we're entering new times. Chief Commissioner Macbeth, isn't this just rhetoric?'

Macbeth cleared his throat. He was up for this. He was a new man. Once again he was perfectly medicated. 'I'm a simple man and I don't know much about rhetoric, Walt. I've only said what was on my mind. And that is that if this town has the will it has the muscle power to raise itself. But neither the chief commissioner nor politicians can lift a town; its citizens have to do that themselves.'

'But they can be inspired and led?'

'Naturally.'

'You're already being touted as mayor material. Is this something that might tempt you, Chief Commissioner Macbeth?'

'I'm a police officer and I wish only to serve the town in the job I have been appointed to.'

'As a humble servant of the people, in other words. Your predecessor, Duncan, also saw himself as a servant of the people, though he wasn't so humble. He promised to catch the town's most powerful criminal, Hecate, also known as the Invisible Hand, within a year. Now, you've dealt with the Norse Riders. What deadline have you set yourself for Hecate?'

'First, let me say there is a reason for the name the Invisible Hand. We know very little about Hecate, only that he's *probably* behind the manufacturing of the drug called brew. But given its widespread production and distribution it's equally probable that we're talking about a network or a shared supply chain.'

'Do I hear you saying you're not going to prioritise the arrest of Hecate as highly as Duncan did?'

'What you hear is a chief commissioner refusing to use all his resources on arrests that might make headlines, bring honour to the police and lead to clinking champagne glasses in the town hall, but in reality do little for people's everyday lives. If we arrest a man by the name of Hecate others will take over his market unless we tackle the town's real problem.'

'Which is?'

'Jobs, Walt. Giving people work. That's the best and the cheapest initiative against crime. We can fill our prisons, but as long as we have people walking the streets without food . . . '

'Now you really sound as if you're considering standing for election.'

'I don't care what it sounds like. I only want this town back on an even keel.'

'And how will you do that?'

'We can do that by ensuring this becomes a town where we take account of both investors and workers. Investors mustn't get away with not paying taxes into the common pot or bribing their way to privileges. But the town can give them the sure knowledge that rules are being followed. And workers should know that their workplace isn't poisoning them. Our recently deceased hero Banquo lost his wife Vera several years ago. She had breathed in poisonous fumes at the factory where she worked for many years. Vera was a lovely hard-working wife and mother. I knew her personally and loved her. As chief commissioner I *promise* the town that none of its future workplaces will take the lives of any more Veras. There are other ways of finding employment for people. *Better* ways. Which will give them a *better* life.'

Macbeth could see from Walt Kite's grin that he was impressed. Macbeth was impressed himself. He had never been so clear-thinking. It had to be the new powder, delivering the words, so concise and logical, from the brain to the tongue.

'Your popularity has grown quickly — exponentially — Chief Commissioner. Is that why you dare to make statements that, if I were Mayor Tourtell, I would regard as a challenge? Formally speaking, he is your boss and has to endorse your appointment to the post of chief commissioner. Otherwise you don't have a job.'

'I have more bosses than the mayor, Walt, among them my own conscience and the citizens of this town. And for me my conscience and this town are above a comfy chair in the chief commissioner's office.'

'In four months there are elections for a new mayor, and the closing date for nominations is in three weeks.'

'If you say so, Walt.'

Walt Kite laughed and raised an arm above his head. 'And with that we say thank you to Chief Commissioner Macbeth. I'm not so sure he's telling us the truth when he says he knows *nothing* about rhetoric. And now here's Miles Davis . . . ' He dropped his arm and pointed to the window. The red light went out, and the sound of a soft, dry trumpet filled the speakers.

'Thank you.' Kite smiled. '*No one will take the lives of any more Veras?* You are aware that you could be elected as mayor on that sound bite alone, aren't you?'

'Thanks for the interview,' Macbeth said without moving.

Kite glanced at him questioningly.

'Did I hear you aright?' Macbeth said slowly in a low voice. 'Did you accuse me of lying at the end there?'

Kite blinked, taken aback. 'Lying?'

'*I'm not so sure he's telling us the truth when he . . .* '

'Oh, but that — ' the reporter's Adam's apple jumped ' — was just a joke of course, a . . . erm, way of speaking, a . . . '

'I was just teasing.' Macbeth smiled and got up. 'See you.'

As Macbeth left the radio building in the rain he felt that Walt Kite wouldn't be a problem any more. And as he sat in the back of the limousine he felt that the Obelisk, Duff and Lady's illness weren't going to be problems any more either. Because he was thinking more clearly than ever.

'Drive a bit more slowly,' he said.

He wanted to enjoy the trip through the town. *His* town.

True enough, it wasn't his yet, but it soon would be. Because he was invincible. And perfectly medicated.

While they were waiting at some red lights his gaze fell on a man waiting by the crossing, although the pedestrian light was green. His upper body and face were hidden by a large black umbrella, so all Macbeth could see was his light-coloured coat, brown shoes and the big black dog he was holding on a lead. And a thought struck Macbeth. Did the dog wonder why he was owned, why he was on a lead? He gets a little food, his allotted portion, just enough for him to prefer security to insecurity, to be kept in check. That is all that stops the dog from trotting over to the owner while he is asleep, tearing out his throat and taking over the house. For that is all he has to do. Once you realise how to open the pantry door it is actually the natural response.

PART THREE

25

'Our finest-quality wool,' the assistant said, respectfully stroking the material of the black suit on the clothes hanger.

Outside the windows of the outfitters it was drizzling and on the river the waves had started to settle after the gales of the previous days.

'What do you think, Bonus?' Hecate said. 'Would it fit Macbeth?'

'I thought you were going for a dinner jacket, not a dark suit.'

'You never wear, as of course you know, a dinner jacket in church, and Macbeth has many funerals to attend this week.'

'So no dinner jacket today?' the assistant asked.

'We need both, Al.'

'I'd just like to point out that if this is for the gala banquet, full evening dress is de rigueur, sir.'

'Thank you, Al, but this isn't the royal palace, just the local town hall. What do you say, Bonus, aren't tails a bit — ' Hecate clicked his tongue ' — pretentious?'

'Agreed,' Bonus said. 'It's when the new rich dress themselves in old-money attire that they really look like clowns.'

'Good, a dark suit and a dinner jacket. Will you send a tailor to Inverness Casino, Al? And put everything on my account.'

'It will be done, sir.'

'And then we need a dinner jacket for this gentleman.'

'For me?' Bonus said in astonishment. 'But I've already got a wond — '

'Thank you. I've seen it and, believe me, you need a new one.'

'Do I?'

'Your position requires an impeccable appearance, Bonus, and you're working for me, what's more.'

Bonus didn't answer.

'Will you run and get me some more dinner jackets, Al?'

'Right away,' said the assistant, and dutifully ran a few bow-legged steps to the stairs down to the shop.

'I know what you're thinking,' Hecate said. 'And I admit that dressing you up is a way of displaying my power, the way kings dress up their soldiers and servants. But what can I say? I like it.'

Bonus had never been one-hundred-per-cent sure if the abnormally white, even teeth in the old man's smile were his own. If they were dentures, they were quite eccentric because they came equipped with three big gold crowns.

'Speaking of displayed power,' Hecate said, 'that attractive young boy who was at the dinner at the Inverness, is his name Kasi?'

'Yes.'

'How old is he?'

'Fifteen and a half,' Bonus said.

'Hm. That's young.'

'Age is — '

'I have no moral scruples, but neither do I have your taste for young boys, Bonus. I'm just pointing out that that's *illegally* young. And that it could potentially cause great harm. But I see this makes you uncomfortable, so let's change the topic of conversation. Lady is sick, I understand?'

'That's what the psychiatrist says. Serious psychosis. It can take time. He's afraid she might be suicidal.'

'Don't doctors take an oath?'

'Dr Alsaker may also soon be in need of a new dinner jacket.'

Hecate laughed. 'Just send me the bill. Can he cure her?'

'Not without hospitalisation,' he says. 'But we don't want that, do we?'

'Let's wait and see. I believe it's well known that Lady is one of the chief commissioner's most important advisers, and during these critical days there would be unfortunate consequences if it became public knowledge that she'd gone mad.'

'So psychosis is . . . ?'

'Yes?'

Bonus swallowed. 'Nothing.' What was it about Hecate that always made him feel like a dithering teenager? It was more than the display of real power; there was something else, something that terrified Bonus but he couldn't quite put his finger on. It wasn't what he could see in Hecate's eyes, it was more what he *couldn't* see. It was the blood-curdling certainty of a nothingness. Wasteland and numbingly cold nights.

'Anyway,' Hecate said, 'what I wanted to discuss was Macbeth. I'm concerned about him. He's changed.'

'Really?'

'I fear he's hooked. Not so strange, maybe, after all it is the world's most addictive dope.'

'Power?'

'Yes, but not the type that comes in powder form. Real power. I didn't think that he would be hooked quite so quickly. He's already managed to divest himself of any emotions that tie him to morality and humanity; now power is his new and only lover. You heard the radio interview the other day. The brat wants to be mayor.'

'But in practice the chief commissioner has more power.'

'As chief commissioner he will of course make sure that real power is returned to the town hall before he occupies the mayoral office. Truly, Macbeth is dreaming of taking over this town. He thinks he is invincible now. And that he can challenge me too.'

343

Bonus looked at Hecate in surprise. He had folded his hands over the golden top of his stick and was studying his reflection.

'Yes, Bonus, it should be the other way round: it should be you telling me that Macbeth is after me. That's what I pay you for. And now your little flounder brain is wondering how I can know this. Well, just ask me.'

'I . . . er . . . How do you know?'

'Because he said so on the radio programme you also listened to.'

'I thought he said the opposite, that pursuing Hecate *wouldn't* have the same priority as under Duncan.'

'And when did you last hear anyone with political ambitions say on radio what they *weren't* going to do for the electorate? He could have said he was going to arrest Hecate *and* create jobs. Sober politicians always promise everything under the sun. But what he said wasn't meant for voters, it was meant for me, Bonus. He didn't need to, yet he committed himself publicly and pandered to me. And when people pander you have to watch out.'

'You think he wants to gain your confidence — ' Bonus looked at Hecate to see if he was on the right track ' — because he hopes that way you will let him in close and he can then dispose of you?'

Hecate pulled a black hair from a wart on his cheek and studied it. 'I could crush Macbeth under my heel this minute. But I've invested a lot in getting him where he is now, and if there's one thing I hate it's a bad investment, Bonus. Therefore I want you to keep your eyes and ears open to find out what he's planning.' Hecate threw up his arms. 'Ah! Look, here's Al with more jackets. Let's find one to fit your long tentacle arms.'

Bonus gulped. 'What if I don't find out anything?'

'Then I have no more use for you, dear Bonus.'

It was said in such a casual way and made even more innocuous with a little smile. Bonus's eyes searched behind the smile. But he found nothing there except night and chill.

★ ★ ★

'Look at the watch,' Dr Alsaker ordered and let his pocket watch swing in front of the patient's face. 'You're relaxing, your arms and legs are feeling heavy, you're tired and you're falling asleep. And you won't wake until I say *chestnut*.'

She was easy to hypnotise. So easy that Alsaker had to check a couple of times that she wasn't pretending. Whenever he came to the Inverness he was followed up to the suite by the receptionist, Jack. There she sat ready in her dressing gown — she refused to wear anything else. Her hands were red from compulsive daily scrubbing, and even if she insisted she wasn't taking anything, he could see from her pupils that she was under the influence of some drug or other. It was one of several disadvantages of being refused permission to admit her to a psychiatric ward, where he could have kept an eye on her medication, sleep and meals and observed her behaviour.

'Let's begin where we left off last time,' Alsaker said, looking at his notes. Not that he needed them to remember; the details were of such a brutal nature they had seared themselves into his memory. He needed his notes to *believe* what she had actually told him. The first lines were not unusual; on the contrary they were a common refrain in many similar cases. 'Unemployed, alcoholic father and depressive and violent mother. You grew up by the river in what you call a hovel or a rats' nest. Literally. You told me your first memories were watching rats swimming towards your house when the sun set, and you remember thinking it was the rats'

345

house. You slept in their bed, you had eaten their food, when they came up into your bed you understood why they bit you.'

Her voice was soft and low. 'They just wanted what was theirs.'

'And your father said the same when he got into your bed.'

'He just wanted what was his.'

Alsaker skimmed his notes. It wasn't the first abuse case he had treated, but this one had some details that were particularly disturbing.

'You became pregnant when you were thirteen and gave birth to a child. Your mother called you a whore. She said you should chuck the misbegotten child into the river, but you refused.'

'I just wanted to have what was mine.'

'So you and the child were thrown out of the house, and you spent the next night with the first man you met.'

'He said he'd kill the baby if it didn't stop screaming, so I took it into the bed. But then he said it ruined his concentration because it was *watching*.'

'And while he was sleeping you stole money from his pockets and food from the kitchen.'

'I just took what was mine.'

'And what is yours?'

'What everyone else has.'

'What happened then?'

'The river ran dry.'

'Come on, Lady. What happened then?'

'More factories were built. More workers came to town. I earned a bit more money. Mum came to see me and told me Dad was dead. His lungs. It had been a painful death. I told her I'd have liked to have been there to see his pain.'

'Don't skirt around it, Lady. Get to the *point*. What happened to the baby?'

'Have you seen how babies' faces change, almost from one day to the next. Well, suddenly, one day it had his face.'

'Your father's.'

'Yes.'

'And what did you do then?'

'I gave it extra milk so that it was smiling blissfully at me when it fell asleep. Then I smashed its head against the wall. A head smashes easily, you know? How fragile a human life is.'

Alsaker swallowed and cleared his throat. 'Did you do it because the child's face was like your father's?'

'No. But it finally made it possible.'

'Does that mean you'd been thinking about it for a while?'

'Yes, of course.'

'Can you tell me why you say *of course?*'

She was silent for a moment. Alsaker saw her pupils twitch, and this reminded him of something. Frogspawn. A tadpole trying to break free from a sticky egg.

'If you want to achieve your aims you have to be able to renounce what you love. If the person you climb with to reach the peak weakens, you have to either encourage him or cut the rope.'

'Why?'

'Why? If he falls he'll drag both of you down. If you want to survive, your hand has to do what your heart refuses to do.'

'Kill the person you love?'

'The way Abraham sacrificed his son. Let the blood flow. Amen.'

Alsaker shivered and took notes. 'What is there at the peak that you want?'

'The peak is the top. Then you're up. Higher than everything and everyone.'

'Do you *have* to go there?'

'No. You can crawl around in the lowlands. On the

rubbish heap. In the muddy riverbed. But once you've started climbing there's no way back. It's the peak or the abyss.'

Alsaker put down his pen. 'And for this peak you're willing to sacrifice everything — also what you love? Is survival above love?'

'Naturally. But recently I've seen that we can live without love. So all this survival will be the death of me, Doctor.'

Her eyes had a sudden clarity which for an instant made Alsaker think she wasn't psychotic after all. But it may have been just the hypnosis or a temporary awakening. Alsaker had seen this many times before. How a patient in deep psychosis or depression can apparently perk up, like a drowning person coming to the surface with an effort of will, giving both relatives and an inexperienced psychiatrist hope. They can stay afloat for several days, only to use this last effort of will to do what they had been threatening or just sink back into the darkness whence they came. But no, it must have been the hypnosis because now the frogspawn membrane was over her eyes again.

★ ★ ★

'It says in the paper here that after the radio interview people are waiting for you to announce you're standing in the mayoral election,' Seyton said. He had spread the newspaper over a coffee table and was dropping his fingernail clippings onto it.

'Let them write,' Macbeth said, looking at his watch. 'Tourtell should have been here ten minutes ago.'

'But will you, sir?' There was a loud, clear snip as the long, pointed nail on his forefinger was cut.

Macbeth shrugged. 'You have to ponder something like that. Who knows? When the idea matures it might feel different.'

The door creaked. In the narrow opening Priscilla's sweet over-made-up face appeared. 'He's here, sir.'

'Good. Let him in.' Macbeth stood up. 'And get us some coffee.'

Priscilla smiled, and her eyes disappeared into her chubby cheeks, then she disappeared too.

'Shall I go?' Seyton asked, making a move to rise from the sofa.

'You stay,' Macbeth said.

Seyton resumed his nail-cutting.

'But stand up.'

Seyton rose to his feet.

The door opened wide. 'Macbeth, my friend!' roared Tourtell, and for a moment Macbeth wondered whether the doorway would be wide enough. Or his ribs strong enough, when the mayor slapped his chunky hand against his back.

'You've really got things buzzing here, Macbeth.'

'Thank you. Please, take a seat.'

Tourtell nodded briefly to Seyton and sat down. 'Thank you. And thank you, Chief Commissioner, for receiving me at such short notice.'

'You're my employer, so it's me who should feel honoured that you've made the time. And, importantly, that you've come here instead of the other way round.'

'Oh, that. I don't like to give people the feeling they've been summoned.'

'Does that mean I've been summoned?' Macbeth asked.

The mayor laughed. 'Not at all, Macbeth. I only wanted to see how things were going. Whether you were finding your feet. I mean it is a bit of a transition. And with all that's happened in the last few days . . . ' Tourtell rolled his eyes. 'That could have been a mess.'

'Do you mean it has? Been a mess?'

'No, no, no. Not at all. I think you've tackled everything beyond all expectation. After all, you're new to this game.'

'New to the game.'

'Yes. Things move fast. You have to react on the hoof. Comment. And then you can say things you don't even think.'

Priscilla came in, put a tray on the table, poured coffee, curtseyed awkwardly and left.

Macbeth sipped his coffee. 'Hm. Is that a reference to the radio interview?'

Tourtell reached for the bowl of sugar lumps, took three and put one in his mouth. 'Some of what you said could be interpreted as criticism of the town council and me. And that's fine — we appreciate a chief commissioner who calls a spade a spade — no one wears a muzzle here. The question is of course whether the criticism came across as a bit harsher than it was meant. Or what?'

Macbeth placed his forefinger under his chin and stared into the air pensively. 'I didn't consider it overly harsh.'

'There you go. That's exactly what I thought. You didn't mean to be harsh! You and I, we want the same things, Macbeth. What's best for the town. To get the wheels moving, to bring down unemployment. A lower jobless rate we know from experience will bring down crime and hit the drugs trade, which in turn reduces property crime. Soon prisoner numbers are drastically down, and everyone asks themselves how Chief Commissioner Macbeth has achieved what none of his predecessors managed. As you know, a mayor can only serve two terms of office. So after I've been elected, hopefully, and then finished my second term, it's a new man's turn. And then perhaps the town will feel this is the kind of man they need, someone who has produced results as a chief commissioner.'

'More coffee?' Macbeth poured the brown liquid into Tourtell's already full cup until it ran over into the saucer. 'Do you know what my friend Banquo used to say? Kiss the girl while she's in love.'

'Which means?' Tourtell said, staring at the saucer.

'Feelings change. The town loves me now. And four years is a long time.'

'Maybe. But you have to choose your battles, Macbeth. And your decision now is whether to challenge the incumbent mayor — which historically seldom leads to success — or wait for four years and be supported in the election by the departing mayor — which historically very *often* leads to success.'

'That kind of promise is easily made and more easily broken.'

Tourtell shook his head. 'I've based my long political career on strategic alliances and cooperation, Macbeth. Kenneth made sure that the chief commissioner's office had such extensive powers that I as mayor was — and am — completely dependent on the chief commissioner's goodwill. Believe me, I *know* a broken promise would cost me dear. You're an intelligent man and you learn quickly, Macbeth, but you lack experience in the complicated tactical game called politics. Instant popularity and a couple of juicy sound bites on radio aren't enough. My support isn't enough either, but it's more than you can hope to achieve on your own.'

'You wouldn't have come here to persuade me not to throw my hat in the ring for the upcoming elections if you didn't see me as a serious challenger.'

'You might think so,' Tourtell said, 'because you still don't have enough experience of politics to see the bigger picture. And the bigger picture is that when I continue as mayor and you as chief commissioner over the next four years, then the town will have a problem if its two most powerful men have had an agonising electoral struggle which makes it difficult for them to work together. And it would also make it impossible for me to support your candidature later. I'm sure you understand.'

I'm sure you understand. Ever so slightly condescending. Macbeth opened his mouth to object, but the thought that was supposed to form the words didn't come.

'Let me make a suggestion,' Tourtell said. 'Don't stand for election, and you won't have to wait four years for my support.'

'Oh?'

'Yes. The day you arrest Hecate — which will be an immense victory for us both — I'll go public and say I hope you'll be my successor at the elections in four years. What do you say to that, Macbeth?'

'I think I said on the radio that Hecate isn't our top priority.'

'I heard you. And I interpreted that as you saying you didn't want the pressure that Duncan put on himself and the police by making such optimistic and all-too-specific promises. Now, the day you arrest him will simply be a bonus. That's what you've planned, isn't it?'

'Of course,' Macbeth said. 'Hecate's a difficult man to arrest, but if the opportunity should offer itself — '

'My experience, I'm afraid to say, is that opportunities don't offer themselves,' Tourtell said. 'They have to be created and then grasped. So what's your plan for arresting Hecate?'

Macbeth coughed, played with his coffee cup. Tried to collect his thoughts. He had noticed he could suddenly have difficulty doing this, as though it were too much: there were too many balls to keep in the air at once, and when one ball fell, they all fell, and he had to start anew. Was he taking too much power? Or too little? Macbeth's eyes sought Seyton's, who had sat down at the coffee table, but there was no help to be found there. Of course not. Only she could help him. Lady. He would have to give up the drugs, talk to her. Only she could blow away the fog, clarify his thinking.

'I want to lure him into a trap,' Macbeth said.

'What kind of trap?'

'We haven't got the details worked out yet.'

'We're talking about the town's number-one enemy, so I would appreciate it if you keep me informed,' Tourtell said and stood up. 'Perhaps you could give me the plan in broad outline at Duncan's funeral tomorrow? Along with your decision regarding the election.'

Macbeth took Tourtell's outstretched hand without getting up. Tourtell nodded to the wall behind him. 'I've always liked that painting, Macbeth. I'll find my own way out.'

Macbeth watched him. Tourtell seemed to have grown every time he saw him. He hadn't touched the coffee. Macbeth swivelled on his chair to face the picture. It was big and showed a man and a woman, both dressed as workers, walking hand in hand. Behind them came a procession of children and behind that the sun was high in the sky. The bigger picture. He guessed Duncan had hung it; Kenneth had probably had a portrait of himself. Macbeth angled his head to one side but still couldn't work out what it meant.

'Tell me, Seyton. What do *you* think?'

'What I think? To hell with Tourtell. You're more popular than he is.'

Macbeth nodded. Seyton was like him, not a man with an eye for the bigger picture. Only she had that.

* * *

Lady had locked herself in her room.

'I need to talk to you,' Macbeth said.

No answer.

'Darling!'

'It's the child,' Jack said.

Macbeth turned to him.

353

'I took it from her. It was beginning to smell, and I didn't know what else to do. But she thinks you ordered me to take it.'

'Good. Well done, Jack. It's just that I needed her advice on a case and . . . Well . . . '

'She can hardly give you the advice you need in the state she's in right now, sir. May I ask — no. Sorry, I was forgetting myself. You aren't Lady, sir.'

'Did you think I was Lady?'

'No, I just . . . Lady usually airs her thoughts with me and I help in any way I can. Not that I have much to offer, but sometimes hearing yourself say something to someone can clear your mind.'

'Hm. Make us both a cup of coffee, Jack.'

'At once, sir.'

Macbeth went to the mezzanine. Looked down into the gaming room. It was a quiet evening. He saw none of the usual faces. Where were they?

'At the Obelisk,' Jack said, passing Macbeth a cup of steaming coffee.

'What?'

'Our regulars. They're at the Obelisk. That was what you were wondering, wasn't it?'

'Maybe.'

'I was in the Obelisk yesterday and I counted five of them. And spoke to two of them. Turns out I'm not the only one spying. The Obelisk's got its people here too. And they've seen who our regular customers are and have offered them better deals.'

'Better deals?'

'Credit.'

'That's illegal.'

'Unofficially, of course. It won't appear in any of the Obelisk's ledgers and if they're confronted they'll swear blind they don't give credit.'

'Then we'd better offer the same.'

'I think the problem runs deeper than that, sir. Can

you see how few there are in the bar downstairs? In the Obelisk there are queues. Beer and cocktails cost thirty-per-cent less, and that not only increases the number of customers and the turnover in the bar, it makes people less guarded in the gaming rooms.'

'Lady thinks we appeal to a different, more quality-conscious clientele.'

'The people who go to casinos in this town can be divided broadly into three groups, sir. You have the out-and-out gamblers who don't care about the quality of the carpets or expensive cognac; they want an efficient croupier, a poker table with visiting country cousins they can fleece and — if it's possible — credit. The Obelisk has this group. And then you have the country folk I mentioned, who usually come here because we have the reputation of being the *real* casino. But now they've discovered they prefer the simple more fun-filled sinful atmosphere at the Obelisk. These are people who tend to go to bingo rather than the opera.'

'And we're the opera?'

'They want cheap beer, cheap women. What's the point of an outing into town otherwise?'

'And the last group?'

Jack pointed down to the room. 'West Enders. The ones who don't want to mingle with the dregs. Our last loyal customers. So far. The Obelisk plans to open a new gaming room next year with a dress code, higher minimum stakes and more expensive brands of cognac in the bar.'

'Hm. And what do you suggest we do?'

'Me?' Jack laughed. 'I'm just a receptionist, sir.'

'And a croupier.' Macbeth looked down at the blackjack table where he, Lady and Jack had first met. 'Let me ask you for some advice, Jack.'

'A croupier just watches people placing bets, sir. They never give advice.'

'Fine, you'll have to listen then. Tourtell came to tell

355

me he didn't want me to stand as mayor.'

'Had you planned to do that, sir?'

'I don't know. I've probably half-thought about doing it and half-rejected it and then half-thought about it again. Especially after Tourtell so patronisingly explained to me what politics was *really* about. What do you think?'

'Oh, I'm sure you'd be a brilliant mayor, sir. Think of all the things you and Lady could do for the town!'

Macbeth studied Jack's beaming face — the undisguised happiness, the naive optimism. Like a reflection of the person he had once been. And a strange thought struck him: he wished he were Jack, the receptionist.

'But I have a lot to lose as well,' Macbeth said. 'If I don't stand now Tourtell will support me next time. And Tourtell's right about the sitting mayor invariably being elected.'

'Hm,' Jack said, scratching his head. 'Unless there's a scandal just before the elections, that is. A scandal so damaging that the town can't possibly let Tourtell continue.'

'For example?'

'Lady asked me to check out the young boy Tourtell brought to the dinner. My sources tell me Tourtell's wife has moved to their summer cottage in Fife, while the boy has moved in. And he's underage, sexually. What we need is concrete evidence of indecent behaviour. From employees in the mayor's residence, for instance.'

'But, Jack, this is fantastic!' Excitement at the thought of skewering Tourtell warmed Macbeth's cheeks. 'We gather the evidence, and I get Kite to set up a live election debate, and then I can throw this unseemly relationship straight in Tourtell's face. He won't be prepared for that. How about that?'

'Maybe.'

'Maybe? What do you mean?'

'I was just thinking, sir, that you yourself moved into

356

the house of a childless man when you were fifteen. The mayor would be able to come back with that.'

Macbeth felt the blood rising in his face again. 'What? Banquo and I . . . ?'

'Tourtell won't hesitate if you throw the first stone, sir. All's fair in love and war. At the same time it would be unfortunate if it looked as if you'd used your position to spy on Tourtell's private life.'

'Hm, you're right. So how would you do it?'

'Let me mull it over.' Jack took a sip of coffee. And another. Then he put his cup down on the table. 'The information about the boy must be leaked via roundabout means. But if you're standing against Tourtell you'll still be suspected of being the source. So the leak should happen before you announce your candidature. In fact, to be sure you avoid suspicion you should perhaps announce you're *not* standing, at least not for four years. You've got a job to do as chief commissioner first. Then, when the scandal disqualifies Tourtell, you'll say rather reluctantly that as the town needs a leader at short notice you'll put yourself at its disposal. You'll refuse to comment on the Tourtell scandal when journalists ask, showing that you're above that kind of behaviour, and only focus on how to get the town . . . er . . . You used such a good expression on the radio, sir, what was it again?'

'Back on an even keel,' Macbeth said. 'Now I understand why Lady uses you as an adviser, Jack.'

'Thank you, sir, but don't exaggerate my significance.'

'I'm not, but you have an unusually lucid eye for these matters.'

'It may be easier to be a croupier and observer than a participant, with all the risk and strong emotions involved, sir.'

'And I think you're one hell of a croupier, Jack.'

'And as a croupier I'd advise you to study your cards

357

even more carefully to see if they can be employed better than this.'

'Oh?'

'Tourtell promised you his support at the next election if you didn't stand now, but that won't be worth much if he's outed as a paedophile, will it?'

Macbeth stroked his beard. 'True enough.'

'So you should ask for something else now. Tell Tourtell you're not even sure you'll stand at the next election. And that you'd rather have something specific he can give you now.'

'For example?'

'What would you like, sir?'

'What would I . . . ?' Macbeth saw Jack motion towards the gaming room. 'Erm, more customers?'

'Yes. The Obelisk's clientele. But as chief commissioner you don't have the authority to close the Obelisk even if you had proof of illegal credit being given.'

'Don't I?'

'As a croupier I happen to know that the police can charge individuals, but it's only the Gambling and Casino Board that can close a whole casino, sir. And they're subject to the jurisdiction of . . . '

'The town hall. Tourtell.'

Macbeth could see it clearly now. He didn't need power; he should flush what he had down the toilet. A bell rang somewhere.

'Sounds like we've got customers, sir.' Jack got up.

Macbeth grabbed his arm. 'Just wait till Lady hears what we've cooked up. I'm sure it'll make her feel better in a flash. How can we thank you, Jack?'

'No need, sir.' Jack smiled wryly. 'It's enough that you saved my life.'

26

Duff swallowed his vomit. It was his fourth day on board, but there was no sign of improvement yet. One thing was the sea, quite another the stale smell in the galley. Inside, behind the swing door, it was a mixture of rancid fat and sour milk; on the other side, in the mess where the men sat eating, it was sweat and tobacco. The steward had left breakfast to Duff, saying he ought to be able to manage that on his own. Put out bread and assorted meats and cheese, boil eggs and make coffee, even a seasick first-timer could cope with that.

Duff had been woken at six, and the first thing he did was to throw up in the bucket beside his bed. He still hadn't had two nights in the same cabin as lack of berths meant he had had to borrow the beds of those who were on duty. Luckily he had only had lower bunks, so he didn't have to actually sleep with the bucket. He had just got his sweater over his head when the next wave of nausea came. On his way down to the galley he'd had pit stops to vomit in the toilet beside the first mate's cabin and in the sink before the last steep staircase.

Breakfast had been served, and those of the crew who were on duty had finished, it seemed. Time to clear away before they started making lunch.

Duff inhaled three stomachfuls of dubious air, got up and went out into the mess.

Four people were sitting at the nearest table. The speaker was a loud, slightly overweight engineer with hairy forearms, an Esso T-shirt stained with oil and sweat rings under his arms and a striped Hull City Tigers cap on his head. When he spoke he sniffed before and afterwards, like a form of inverted commas. What came between them was always denigration of those lower on the ladder. 'Hey, Sparks,' the engineer shouted to be sure everyone realised he was referring to the young boy with glasses at the end of the table, 'hadn't you better ask the new galley boy if he can heat you up some fish pie so you can stuff your dick in and enjoy the closest you'll ever get to cunt.' He sniffed before starting to laugh. This raised no more than short-lived, forced laughter from the others. The young radio-telegrapher smiled fleetingly and ducked his head even lower into his plate. The engineer, whom Duff had heard the others call Hutch, sniffed. 'But judging by today's breakfast I doubt you know how to heat up a fish pie, do you, lad?' Another sniff.

Duff kept his head down, like the telegrapher. That was all he had to do until they reached the docks in Capitol. Keep a low profile, mouth shut, mask on.

'Tell me, galley boy! Do you call this scrambled egg?'

'Anything wrong?' Duff said.

'Wrong?' The engineer rolled his eyes and turned to the others. 'The greenhorn asks me if something's wrong. Only that this scrambled egg looks and tastes like vomit. *Your* vomit. From your green, seasick gills.'

Duff looked at the engineer. The guy was grinning, and there was an evil glint in his shiny eyes. Duff had seen it before. Lorreal, the director of the orphanage.

'I'm sorry the scrambled egg didn't live up to your expectations,' Duff said.

'*Didn't live up to your expectations,*' the engineer mimicked, and sniffed. 'Think you're at some posh fuckin' restaurant, do you? At sea we want food, not muck. What do you reckon, guys?'

The men around him chuckled their agreement, but Duff saw two of them keep their heads down in embarrassment. Presumably they played along so as not to become targets.

'The steward's on duty at lunch,' Duff said, putting

360

plates of food and milk cartons on a tray. 'Let's hope it's better then.'

'What isn't any better,' the engineer said 'is the way you look. Have you got lice? Is that why you wear that hat? And what about those cunt pubes that pass for a beard? What happened, galley boy? Get your mother's cunt where others got a face?'

The engineer looked around expectantly, but this time all the others were studying the floor.

'I've got a suggestion,' Duff said. Knowing he shouldn't speak. Knowing he had promised himself he wouldn't. 'Sparks can stuff his wanger under your arm. That way he can feel what a cunt's like and you finally get some dick.'

The table went so quiet all that could be heard was the noise of Duff putting the plates of cheese, sausage and cucumber onto the tray. No sniff this time.

'Let me repeat the bit that might interest you most,' Duff said, putting down the tray. 'You finally get some dick.' He stressed the consonants so that no one would be in any doubt as to what he had said. Then Duff turned to the table. The engineer had risen to his feet and was coming towards him.

'Take off your glasses,' he said.

'Can't see fuck all without them,' Duff said. 'See a fuckwit with them.'

The engineer wound back his arm, announcing where the blow would come from, and swung. Duff retreated a step, swayed and, when the engineer's oil-black fist had passed, took two steps forward, grabbed the engineer, who was now off balance, by his other hand, forced it back against his wrist, grabbed the engineer's elbow and let his momentum take him forward while Duff slipped behind. The engineer screamed, automatically bending forward to relieve the painful pressure on his wrist as Duff steered him into a wall head first. Duff pulled the engineer back. Rammed him forward again. Against the bulkhead. Duff pushed the helpless engineer's arm higher, knowing that soon something would have to give, something would break. The engineer's scream rose to a whine, and his fingers lunged desperately at Duff's hat. Duff rammed his head against the wall for the third time. Was steadying himself for a fourth when he heard a voice.

'That's enough, Johnson!'

It took Duff a second to remember that was the name he had given when he signed on. And to realise the voice was the captain's. Duff looked up. The captain was standing right in front of them. Duff let go of the engineer, who fell to his knees with a sob.

'What's going on here?'

Duff noticed only now that he was panting. The provocation. The anger. 'Nothing, Captain.'

'I know the difference between nothing and something, Johnson. So what is this? Hutchinson?'

Duff wasn't sure, but it sounded like the man on his knees was crying.

Duff cleared his throat. 'A friendly bet, Captain. I wanted to show that the Fife grip is more effective than a Hull haymaker. I might have got carried away.' He patted the engineer's shaking back. 'Sorry, pal, but we agree that Fife beat Hull on this occasion, don't we?'

The engineer nodded, still sobbing.

The captain took off his hat and studied Duff. 'The Fife grip, you say?'

'Yes,' Duff answered.

'Hutchinson, you're needed in the engine room. You others have got jobs to do, haven't you?'

The mess cleared quickly.

'Pour me a cup of coffee and sit down,' the captain said.

Duff did as he said.

The captain raised his cup to his mouth a couple of times. Looked down at the black liquid and mumbled something. Just as Duff was beginning to wonder whether the captain had forgotten he was there, he raised his head.

'Generally I don't consider it worth the effort to delve into individuals' backgrounds, Johnson. Most of the crew are simple, with limited intellects; they have pasts best left unprobed and futures that won't be on board MS *Glamis*. As they won't be under my command or be my problem for long, I know it's not worth getting too involved. All that concerns me is how they function as a group, as my crew.'

The captain took another sip and grimaced. Duff had no idea if this was due to the coffee, pain or the conversation.

'You seem like a man with education and ambition, Johnson, but I won't ask how you ended up here. I doubt I would hear the truth anyway. But my guess is you're someone who knows how groups function. You know that there'll always be a pecking order, and everyone will have their role in that order, their place. The captain at the top, the rookie at the bottom. As long as everyone accepts their own and others' positions in the order we have a working crew. Exactly as I want it. At the moment, however, we have some confusion at the lower end of the pecking order on MS *Glamis*. We have three potential chickens at the bottom. Sparks because he's the youngest. You because it's your first time. And Hutchinson because he's the most stupid and very difficult to like.'

Another sip.

'Sparks will survive this trip as the bottom chicken. He's young, intelligent enough and he'll learn. And you, Johnson, have moved up the order, I've just seen, after what you did to Hutchinson. For all I know, it was a situation you initiated to achieve just this. But if I know Hutch, he started it. Like the stupid idiot he is, he set himself up for another fall. And that's why he's looking

363

for someone to be under him. It'll probably be some poor soul who signs on in Capitol, where we're going to need a couple of new men as people sign off all the time. Do you understand?'

Duff shrugged.

'And this is my problem, Johnson. Hutch is going to keep trying, but he is the permanent bottom chicken. And I would prefer another bottom chicken, one who would quietly accept his fate. But as Hutch is an ill-natured troublemaker who considers he's been given enough beatings in life and now it's someone else's turn, he's going to continue to create a bad atmosphere on board. He's not a bad engineer, but he makes my crew work worse than it would be without him.'

A loud slurp.

'So why don't I get rid of him, you say. And you say that because you're not a seaman and know nothing about Seafarers' Union employment contracts, which mean I'm stuck with Hutch until I can get something on him that would give me a so-called objective reason to offload him. Physically attacking a colleague would be one such objective reason . . . '

Duff nodded.

'So? All I need from you is a yes and a signature for the Seafarers' Union. I can get the rest from the witnesses.'

'We were only playing, Captain. It won't happen again.'

'No, it won't.' The captain scratched his chin. 'As I said, I don't make a habit of delving into my crew's backgrounds unnecessarily. But I have to say I've only seen the grip you had on Hutch used twice before: by the military police and the port police. The common denominator is police. So now I'd like to hear the truth.'

'The truth?'

'Yes. Did he attack you?'

Duff eyed the captain. He presumed he had known

364

from the start his real name wasn't Cliff Johnson and that the galley boy hadn't worked in any restaurant. All he was asking for was a yes and a false signature. If and when there was ever any discussion of the real identity of this Johnson he would be over the hills and far away.

'I see. Here's the truth,' Duff said, watching the captain lean across the table. 'We were only playing, Captain.'

The captain leaned back. Put the coffee cup to his mouth. His gaze above the cup was firmly fixed on Duff. Not on Duff's eyes but higher, on his forehead. The captain's Adam's apple went up and down as he swallowed. Then he brought the empty cup hard down on the table.

'Johnson.'

'Yes, Captain?'

'I like you.'

'Captain?'

'I have no reason to believe you like Hutch any more than the rest of us. But you're no snitch. That's bad news for me as a captain, but it shows integrity. And I respect that, so I won't mention this matter again. You're seasick and you're lying, but I could use more people like you in my crew. Thanks for the coffee.'

The captain got up and left.

Duff remained seated for a couple of seconds. Then he took the empty cup to the galley and put it in the sink. Closed his eyes, placed his hands on the cold shiny metal and swallowed his nausea. What was he doing? Why hadn't he told him the truth, that Hutch was a bully?

He opened his eyes. Saw his reflection in the saucepan hanging from the shelf in front of him. His heart skipped a beat. His hat had ridden up to his hairline without him noticing. Hutchinson must have clipped it when he swung. The scar shone against his skin like a thick white vapour trail after a plane in the sky. The scar. That was what the captain had been staring at before he put down his cup.

Duff closed his eyes, told himself to relax and think through the whole business.

Their departure had been so early the newspapers wouldn't have been out on the streets the day they left, so the captain couldn't have seen any WANTED pictures of him. Unless he had seen Duff's face on the TV broadcast of the press conference the evening before. But had there been any sign of shock in the captain's eyes when he saw the scar — if he had seen it? No. Because the captain was a good actor and didn't want to show that he had recognised him until they set upon him later? As there was little he could do about that, he decided the captain hadn't realised, but what about the others? No, he had been standing with his back to them until the captain had ordered them out. Apart from Hutchinson, lying in front of him. If he had seen the scar he didn't strike Duff as the type to scour the news.

Duff opened his eyes again.

In two days, on Wednesday, they would dock.

Forty-eight hours. Stay low for two days. He must be able to do that.

★ ★ ★

The organ music started, and standing between the rows of benches in the cathedral he could feel the hairs rise all over his body. It wasn't because of the music, nor the priest's or the mayor's eulogies, nor Duncan's coffin being borne down the aisle by six men, nor was it the fact that he hadn't taken any power. It was because of the dreadful new uniform he was wearing. Whenever he moved, the coarse wool rubbed against his skin and gave him the shivers. His old one had been cheaper material and was more worn-in and comfortable. He could of course have chosen the new black suit

366

delivered to police HQ, which could only have come from Hecate. The quality of the wool cloth was much better, but strangely enough it itched even more than the uniform. Besides, it would have been a breach of tradition to turn up to a police funeral in anything but a uniform.

The coffin passed Macbeth's row. Duncan's wife and two sons followed it with lowered heads, but when one son happened to look up and met his eyes, Macbeth automatically looked down.

Then they all filed out into the aisle and joined the cortège. Macbeth positioned himself in such a way that he was walking beside Tourtell.

'Fine speech,' Macbeth said.

'Thank you. I'm really sorry the town hall didn't agree to the town paying for the funeral. With closed factories and falling tax revenues, I'm afraid such demonstrations of honour are way down the list. Still pretty uncivilised, if you ask me.'

'The town hall has my sympathy.'

'I don't believe Duncan's family feel the same way. His wife rang me and said we should have driven his coffin through the streets and given people the opportunity to show how much they cared. They wanted what Duncan wanted.'

'Do you think people would have done that?'

Tourtell shrugged. 'I honestly don't know, Macbeth. My experience is that people in this town don't care about so-called reforms unless they see them putting food on the table or providing enough for an extra beer. I thought change was beginning to take place in the town, but if so the murder of Duncan would have made people seething mad. Instead it seems as if people have accepted that in this town good always loses. The only person who's opened his mouth is Kite. Are you going to Banquo and his son's funeral tomorrow?'

'Of course. Down in the Workers' Church. Banquo

wasn't particularly religious, but his wife, Vera, is buried there.'

'But Duff's wife and children are going to be buried in the cathedral, I've been informed.'

'Yes. I won't be there personally.'

'Personally?'

'We're going to have officers posted here in case Duff decides to pitch up.'

'Oh yes. You should accompany your children to their graves. Especially if you know you're partly responsible.'

'Yes, it's funny how guilt marks you for life, while honour and glory come out in the wash the same night.'

'Now, for a second there, Macbeth, you sounded like a man who knows a bit about guilt.'

'So let me confess right here and now that I've killed my nearest and dearest, Tourtell.'

The mayor stopped for a moment and looked at Macbeth. 'What was that you said?'

'My mother. She died in childbirth. Let's keep walking.'

'And your father?'

'He ran away to sea when he heard Mum was pregnant and was never seen again. I grew up in an orphanage. Duff and I. We shared a room. But you've probably never seen a room in an orphanage, have you, Tourtell?'

'Oh, I have opened an orphanage or two.'

They had come out onto the cathedral steps, where the wet north-westerly gale met them. On the gravel path Macbeth saw the coffin teeter dangerously.

'Well, well,' Tourtell said. 'The sea is also a way to escape.'

'Are you criticising my father, Tourtell?'

'Neither of us knew him. I'm just saying the sea is full of them — men who don't accept the responsibilities nature has placed on them.'

'So men like you and me should take even more

responsibility, Tourtell.'

'Exactly. So what have you decided?'

Macbeth cleared his throat. 'I can see that for the good of the town it's best the chief commissioner continues to be chief commissioner and carries on his good, close cooperation with the mayor.'

'Wise words, Macbeth.'

'So long as this cooperation functions of course.'

'And you're referring to?'

'The rumours that the Obelisk is running a prostitution racket under the auspices of the casino and giving credit illegally to some gamblers.'

'The former is an old accusation, the latter new. But, as you know, it's difficult to get to the bottom of such rumours, so they tend to stay that way and don't go anywhere.'

'I have a specific suspicions relating to at least two gamblers, and with effective interviewing methods and the promise of an amnesty I'm sure I can establish whether the Obelisk has offered them credit or not. Thereafter the Gambling and Casino Board will presumably have to close the place while the extent of the irregularities is examined more closely.'

The mayor pulled at the lowest of his chins. 'You mean close down the Obelisk in return for not standing?'

'I mean only that the town's political and administrative leaders have to be consistent in their enforcement of laws and regulations. If they don't want to be suspected of being bought and paid for by those who evade them.'

The mayor clicked his tongue. Like a child with an olive, Macbeth thought. The kind of food that takes you years to like. 'We're not talking about a series of possible irregularities,' Tourtell said as if to himself. 'And, as I said, it's difficult to get to the bottom of such rumours. It can take time.'

'A long time,' Macbeth said.

'I'll prepare the board by saying there's some information on its way which may necessitate closing the casino down. Where's Lady, by the way? I would imagine, as she and Duncan . . . '

'She doesn't feel well, I'm afraid. Temporary.'

'I see. Say hello and wish her well. We'd better go down and offer our condolences to the family.'

'You go first. I'll follow.'

Macbeth watched Tourtell waddle down the stairs and grasp Mrs Duncan's hand in both of his, watched his lips move as he inclined his head in the deepest sympathy. He really did look like a turtle. But there was something Tourtell had said. The sea was full of them. Men who had run off.

'Everything OK, sir?' It was Seyton. He had been waiting outside. He couldn't stand churches, he said, and that was fine; those who had it in for the chief commissioner would hardly be inside.

'We checked all the passenger boats leaving town,' Macbeth said, 'but did anyone think of checking the other ships?'

'For stowaways, you mean?'

'Yes. Or simply people who'd got a job on board.'

'Nope.'

'Send a precise description of Duff to all the boats which have left since yesterday. Now.'

'Right, sir.' Seyton took the steps in two strides and disappeared around the corner.

Meredith. Meredith had ceased to exist. But the scar on his heart was still there. And yet Macbeth wasn't going to the funeral. Because it was a long time since she had ceased to exist, so long that he had forgotten who she was. So long that he had forgotten who he himself had been then.

He shifted his weight, felt the material against the inside of his thigh, smelled wet wool. And shivered.

27

Duff stood in the galley looking at the men in the mess. They had eaten lunch and now they were rolling cigarettes and talking in low voices, laughing, lighting their cigarettes, drinking their coffee. Only one man sat on his own. Hutchinson. A big skin-coloured plaster on his forehead told those who hadn't been present about the beating he had been given. Hutchinson tried to look as though he were thinking about something that required concentration as he puffed on his roll-up, but his acting ability wasn't good enough for him to look anything but lost.

'We'll be docking tomorrow,' the steward said, who himself had lit a cigarette and was leaning against the cooker. 'You've learned fast. Fancy some more peggy?'

'Sorry?'

'Are you staying on for the next trip?'

'No,' Duff said. 'But thank you for asking.'

The steward shrugged. Duff watched someone who was late for lunch balance his soup dish and make for Hutchinson's table, look up, see who was sitting there and instead squeeze onto a full table. And Duff saw that Hutchinson had registered this and was now concentrating on his fag even harder while blinking furiously.

'Any of that cheesecake left from yesterday?'

Duff turned. It was the first engineer; he was standing in the doorway with a hopeful expression on his face.

'Sorry,' the steward said. 'All gone.'

'Hang about,' Duff said. 'I think I wrapped up a small slice.' He went into the freezer room, found a plate wrapped in foil and came back. Passed it to the first engineer. 'It's a bit cold.'

'That's OK,' said the first engineer, licking his lips. 'I like it cold.'

'One thing . . . '

'Yes?'

'Hutchinson . . . '

'Hutch?'

'Yes. He looks a bit . . . erm downcast. I was wondering about something the captain said to me. He said he was a good engineer. Is that right?'

The first engineer rocked his head from side to side looking at Duff a little uncertainly. 'He's good enough.'

'Perhaps it'd be a good idea to tell him.'

'Tell him what?'

'He's good enough.'

'Why?'

'I think he needs to hear it.'

'I don't know about that. If you build people up they just want more money and longer breaks.'

'When you were a young engineer did you have a first engineer who gave you the feeling you were doing a good job?'

'Yes, but I was.'

'Try and remember how good you *really* were then.'

The first engineer stood with his mouth ajar.

At that moment the boat rolled. Screams came from the mess, and there was a loud bang behind Duff.

'Fuckin' Ada!' the steward shouted, and when Duff turned he saw the big soup tureen had fallen on the floor. Duff stared at the thick, green, pea soup oozing out. Without warning his stomach lurched, he felt the nausea in his throat and just managed to grab the doorframe as it spurted from his mouth.

'Well, rookie,' said the first engineer, 'any other good advice?' He turned and left.

'Bloody hell, Johnson. Haven't you finished with all that?' the steward groaned, handing Duff a kitchen roll.

'What happened?' Duff asked, wiping his mouth.

'Hit a swell,' the steward said. 'It happens.'

'Have a breather. I'll clean up here.'

When Duff had finished scrubbing the floor, he went into the mess to collect the dirty crockery. Only three guys were sitting at one table, plus Hutch, who hadn't stirred from his place.

Duff listened to their chit-chat as he piled dishes and glasses on a tray.

'That breaker must have come from an earthquake or a landslide or something,' one of them said.

'Perhaps it was a nuclear test,' suggested one of the others. 'The Soviets are supposed to have some shit going on in the Barents Sea and shock waves apparently go all the way round the world.'

'Any messages about that, Sparks?'

'No.' Sparks laughed. 'The only excitement is a search for a guy with a white scar right across his face.'

Duff stiffened. Kept piling dishes as he listened.

'Yeah, it's gonna be good to get ashore tomorrow.'

'Is it hell. Missus says she's pregnant again.'

'Don't look at me.'

Good-natured laughter around the table.

Duff turned with the tray in his hands. Hutchinson had lifted his head and suddenly sat bolt upright. The few times they had met after their skirmish Hutchinson had looked down and avoided Duff's face, but now he was staring at Duff with wide-open eyes. Like a vulture that has unexpectedly and happily spotted a helpless, injured animal.

Duff shoved open the door to the galley with his foot and heard it clatter behind him. Put the tray down on the worktop. Damn, damn, damn! Not now, not with less than twenty-hours to land.

★   ★   ★

373

'Not too fast here,' Caithness said, looking through the windscreen.

The taxi driver took his foot off the accelerator, and they drove slowly past the Obelisk, where people were streaming into the street from the main entrance. Two police cars were parked on the pavement. The blue lights rotated idly.

'What's going on?' Lennox said and thrust his blue face between the two front seats. He was — like Caithness — still wearing his uniform, as the taxi had collected them from outside the church straight after Duncan's funeral. 'Has the fire alarm gone off?'

'The Gambling and Casino Board closed the place today,' Caithness said. 'Suspicion of breaching the Casino Act.'

They saw one of the policemen leading out an angrily gesticulating man in a light suit and flowery shirt with impressive sideburns. It looked as if the man was trying to explain something to the policeman, who was obviously turning a deaf ear.

'Sad,' the driver said.

'What's sad?' Lennox asked. 'Law enforcement?'

'Sometimes. At the Obelisk you could at least have a beer and a game of cards without dressing up and coming home ruined. By the way, do you know that the factory you want to go to is closed?'

'Yes,' Caithness answered. Thinking that was all she knew about it. Police Officer Angus had rung that morning and implored her to bring Inspector Lennox from the Anti-Corruption Unit with her to Estex. They would find out the rest when they got there. It was about corruption at the highest level and for the moment they mustn't mention their meeting to anyone. When she said she didn't know any Police Officer Angus, he had explained to her that he was the guy in SWAT with the long hair who she smiled at and said hello to in the lift. She remembered him. He was cute.

Looked more like an affable, unworldly hippie than a SWAT man.

They glided through the streets. She saw the unemployed men leaning against the walls sheltering from the rain, fags in mouths, wet coats, hungry, weary eyes. Hyenas. Not because they were born like that; it was the town. Duncan had said if carrion was all there was on the menu, you ate carrion, whoever you thought you were. And irrespective of what they did at police HQ the best way to reduce crime was to get the town's citizens back to work.

'Are you opening Estex again?' the driver asked, squinting at Caithness.

'What makes you think that?'

'I think Macbeth is smarter than Duncan, the blockhead.'

'Oh?'

'Closing a great factory just because it's leaking some gunge? Christ, everyone who worked there smokes. They'll die anyway. That was five thousand jobs. Five thousand jobs this town needed! Only some upper-class twit from Capitol could be so snobbish. Macbeth, on the other hand, is one of us — he understands and he does something. Let Macbeth take charge for a bit and maybe people will be able to afford a taxi again in this town.'

'Talking of Macbeth,' Caithness said, turning to the back seat. 'He's cancelled the morning meeting two days in a row and he looked very pale in church. Is he ill?'

'Not him,' Lennox said, 'but Lady. He's barely been at HQ.'

'Of course it's good of him to look after her, but he's the chief commissioner and we have a town in our charge.'

'Good job he has us there.' Lennox smiled.

The taxi stopped in front of the gate, from which

hung a chain with a padlock. The CLOSED sign had fallen onto the potholed tarmac. Caithness got out, stood by the driver's open window and scanned the abandoned industrial wasteland while waiting for her change. No telephone boxes, and the telephones at Estex had probably been cut off.

'How will we get hold of a taxi when we want to go back?' she asked.

'I'll park here and wait,' the driver said. 'There's no work in town anyway.'

Inside the factory gate was a rusty fork-lift truck and a tower of rotting wooden pallets. The pedestrian entrance beside the big retractable door was open.

Caithness and Lennox stepped into the factory building. It was cold outside, even colder under the high vaulted roof. The furnaces stood like gigantic pews inside the rectangular hall as far as the eye could see.

'Hello?' Caithness called, and the echo sent shivers down her spine.

'Here!' came the answer from up on the wall where the foreman's office and surveillance platform were located. Like a watchtower in a prison, Caithness thought. Or a pulpit.

The young man standing up there pointed to a steel staircase.

Caithness and Lennox went up the steps.

'Police Officer Angus,' he said shaking hands with them. His open face displayed his nervousness, but also determination.

They followed him into the foreman's office, which smelled of a marinade of dried sweat and tobacco. The large windows facing the factory floor had a strange yellow frosted glaze which looked as if it had been burned into the glass. On the tables there were open files that had clearly been taken from the shelves along the walls. The young man was unshaven and wearing tight faded jeans and a green military jacket.

'Thank you for coming at such short notice,' Angus said, indicating the peeling wooden chairs.

'I don't want to pressurise you, but I hope this is important,' Lennox said, taking a seat. 'I had to leave an important meeting.'

'As you haven't got much time, indeed as none of us has got much time, I'll get straight to the point.'

'Thank you.'

Angus crossed his arms. His jaws were working, and his eyes roamed, but there was a determination about him — he was like a man who *knows* he is right.

'Twice I've been a believer,' Angus said, swallowing, and Caithness knew he was memorising something he had written and rehearsed for the occasion. 'And twice I've lost that belief. The first was in God. The second in Macbeth. Macbeth is no saviour, he's a corrupt murderer. I wanted to say that first so that you know why I'm doing this. This is to rid the town of Macbeth.'

In the ensuing silence they could hear the deep sighs as drops of water hit the floor of the factory. Angus breathed in.

'We were — '

'Stop!' Caithness said. 'Thank you for your honesty, Angus, but before you say any more, Inspector Lennox and I have to decide whether we want to hear.'

'Let Angus finish,' Lennox said. 'Then we can discuss it later without anyone else present.'

'Wait,' Caithness said. 'There's no way back if we receive information which — '

'We were sent to the club house to kill everyone,' Angus said.

'I don't want to hear this,' Caithness said and stood up.

'No one was going to be arrested,' Angus said in a louder voice. 'We started shooting at the Norse Riders, and they managed to fire off one — ' he held up a forefinger which trembled as much as his voice ' — one single bloody shot in self-defence! Unlike at — '

Caithness stamped on the floor to drown out Angus's voice, opened the door, was about to step outside and leave when she heard his name and froze.

' — Duff's place in Fife. Not a single shot was fired there. Because he wasn't at home. When we entered the house after we'd shot it to pieces we found a girl and a boy and their mother — ' Angus's voice failed him.

Caithness turned to him. The young man leaned against the table and squeezed his eyes shut, ' — who had tried to cover them with her own body in the bedroom.'

'Oh, no, no, no,' Caithness heard herself whisper.

'Macbeth gave the order,' Angus said, 'and Seyton ensured it was carried out to the letter by SWAT, including — ' he coughed ' — me.'

'Why on earth would Macbeth give orders for these . . . liquidations?' Lennox asked with disbelief in his voice. 'He could have just arrested them, both Duff and the Norse Riders?'

'Maybe not,' Angus said. 'Maybe they had something on Macbeth, something that made him need to silence them.'

'Such as what?'

'Haven't you asked yourselves why the Norse Riders took their revenge on Banquo? Why not kill the person who gave the orders, Macbeth himself?'

'Simple,' Lennox snorted. 'Macbeth is better protected. Have you any proof at all?'

'These eyes,' Angus said, pointing.

'They're yours, and the same applies to your accusations. Give me one reason why we should believe you.'

'There's one reason,' Caithness said, walking slowly back to her chair. 'It's easy enough to get Angus's accusations confirmed or denied by the other SWAT officers, and if they're false, he'll lose his job, find himself on a charge and, to put it mildly, his future prospects will be poor. And he knows that.'

Angus laughed.

Caithness raised an eyebrow. 'Excuse me, did I say something stupid?'

'It's SWAT,' Lennox said. 'Loyalty, brotherhood, baptised in fire, united in blood.'

'Sorry?'

'You'll never get anyone in SWAT to say a word that will harm Macbeth,' Angus said. 'Or Seyton. Or any of the brothers.'

Caithness dropped her hands to her sides. 'So you come to us with these claims of executions even though you know there's no way to prove them?'

'Macbeth asked me to burn the body of a baby killed in the club house massacre,' Angus said. He fidgeted with his necklace. 'Here, in one of the furnaces.'

Caithness shuddered. And regretted staying. Why hadn't she turned on her heel? Why wasn't she already sitting in the taxi leaving this behind her?

'I said no,' Angus continued. 'But that means some-one else has done it. Perhaps he did it himself. I've looked through the furnaces and one of them has been used recently. I thought that if you got your Forensics people to examine the furnace you might find clues. Fingerprints, remains of bones, what do I know? And if you did, the Anti-Corruption Unit could take the case further.'

Lennox and Caithness exchanged glances.

'The police can't investigate their own chief commissioner,' Lennox said. 'Didn't you know?'

Angus frowned. 'But . . . the Anti-Corruption Unit, isn't it . . . ?'

'No, we can't do internal enquiries,' Lennox said. 'If you want to go after the chief commissioner you'll have to present your case to the town council and Tourtell.'

Angus shook his head desperately. 'No, no, no, they're bought and paid for, the whole bunch of them! We have to do this off our own bat. We have to bring Macbeth down from the inside.'

Caithness didn't answer. Confirming only that Angus was right. No one on the town council, Tourtell included, would dare to come out into the open against Macbeth. Kenneth had made sure that the chief commissioner had the legal authority to stamp down hard on that kind of political rebellion.

Lennox looked at his watch. 'I have a meeting in twenty minutes. I recommend you drop the matter until you've got something concrete, Angus. Then you can take your chances with the town council, can't you.'

Angus blinked in disbelief. 'My chances?' he said in a thick voice. He turned to Caithness. Despair, supplication, fear and hope flitted across his face like a narrative. And instantly she realised that Angus hadn't only asked her to come along because he needed Forensics to examine the furnaces. Angus needed a witness, a third person to ensure that Lennox couldn't pretend he hadn't received the information and, regardless of the outcome, then make his life uncomfortable. Angus had chosen Caithness simply because she had smiled at him in the lift. Because she looked like someone he could trust.

'Inspector Caithness?' he begged in a low voice.

She took a deep breath. 'Lennox is right, Angus. You're asking us to attack a bear and all we have is a cardboard sword.'

Angus's eyes were watery. 'You're frightened,' he stuttered. 'You believe me. Otherwise you wouldn't still be here. But you're frightened. You're frightened *because* you believe me. Because I've shown you what Macbeth is capable of.'

'Let's agree that this meeting never took place,' Lennox said, making for the door. Caithness was about to follow when Angus grabbed her arm.

'A baby,' he whispered, close to tears. 'It was in a shoebox.'

380

'It was an innocent victim in the fight against a crime syndicate,' she said. 'It happens. Macbeth wanting to hide it from the press to avoid a police scandal doesn't make him a murderer.'

Caithness saw Angus let go of her arm as if he had burned himself. He took a step back and stared at her. Caithness turned and left.

On the steel staircase to the factory floor the chill hit her warm cheeks.

As she made for the exit she stopped by one of the furnaces. There were stripes and marks made of grey dust.

Lennox stood in the factory doorway waving to the taxi to drive through the gate so that they wouldn't have to walk through the driving rain. 'What do you think Angus is after?' he asked.

'After?' Caithness turned and looked up at the foreman's shed-like office.

'He must know he's too young for a management post,' Lennox said. 'Hey! Over here! Is it about honour and fame?'

'Perhaps it's what he said. Someone has to stop Macbeth.'

'Duty calls?' Lennox chuckled, and Caithness heard the crunch of tyres on gravel. 'Everyone wants something, Caithness. Are you coming?'

'Yes.' Caithness could just make out the shape of Angus behind the window — he hadn't moved since they left him. He was just standing there. Waiting for something, it seemed.

How long would it be before Lennox informed Macbeth about this attempted mutiny?

What was she going to do with what Angus had told them?

She put her hand to her cheek. She knew why it was warm. She was blushing. Blushing with shame.

Lennox took the short cut through the station concourse. He liked short cuts. Always had. He had bought sweets to make friends, lied about diving off the crane on the harbour quay and about paying for a hand job from the girl working at the Indigo kiosk. He had worn higher platform shoes than anyone else, cheated in exams and still had to blag up his grade when the results came out. His father used to say — generally at family gatherings and without any attempt to conceal who he was referring to — that only a man with no spine would take short cuts. When his father had given a smallish gift to the town's private university, thereby saving himself and Lennox the disgrace of his son studying in the public sector, Lennox had also forged his degree certificate. Not to show potential employers but his father, who had asked to see it. Of course this was a fiasco because Lennox didn't have the spine to resist his father's suspicious looks and questions, and his father told him he didn't know how a mollusc like Lennox could stand up straight; he didn't have a single bone in his body!

Fair enough, but he definitely had enough spine to ignore the drug dealers who came up to him mumbling their offers. They recognised a user when they saw one. However, this wasn't how he got his brew; he had it sent in anonymous brown envelopes. Or when he occasionally asked for special treatment, they blindfolded him and led him — like a prisoner of war to a firing squad — to the secret kitchen, where he got his shot straight from the pot.

He passed Bertha Birnam, where Duff had fallen for his bluff about the judge from Capitol. But Hecate hadn't said anything about Macbeth killing Duff's wife and children. Lennox stepped up his tempo across Workers' Square, as though he had to hurry before something happened. Something inside him.

'Macbeth's busy,' said the little receptionist at Inverness Casino.

'Say it's Inspector Lennox. It's important and will only take a minute.'

'I'll ring up, sir.'

While Lennox waited he looked around. He couldn't put his finger on what, but there was something missing. Some final touch. Perhaps it was only the atmosphere that had changed; perhaps it was that some less well-dressed guys were laughing too loudly as they walked into the gaming room. This type of customer was new.

Macbeth came down the stairs.

'Hello, Lennox.'

'Hello, Chief Commissioner. The casino's busy today.'

'Daytime gamblers straight from the Obelisk. The Gambling and Casino Board closed down their place a few hours ago. I haven't got much time. Shall we sit here?'

'Thank you, sir. I just wanted to inform you about a meeting that took place today.'

Macbeth yawned. 'Oh yes?'

Lennox breathed in. Hesitated. Because there were millions of ways to start. Thousands of ways to formulate the same message. Hundreds of first words. And yet only two options.

Macbeth frowned.

'Sir,' the receptionist said. 'Message from the blackjack table. They're asking if we can provide them with another croupier. There's a queue.'

'I'm coming, Jack. Sorry about the interruption, Lennox. Lady usually deals with this. Well?'

'Yes. The meeting . . . ' Lennox thought about his family. Their house. The garden. The safe neighbour-hood, where the kids hadn't got involved in any nastiness. The university they would go to. The pay cheque that made all this possible. Plus the cash on the side that had now become a necessity to make ends meet. This wasn't for him; it was for the family, the family, the family. *His* family, not a house in Fife, not . . .

'Yes?'

The front door went.

'Sir!'

They turned. It was Seyton. He was out of breath. 'We've got him, boss.'

'We've found . . . ?'

'Duff. And you were right. He's on board a boat that sailed from here. The MS *Glamis*.'

'Fantastic!' Macbeth turned to Lennox. 'This will have to wait, Inspector. I'll have to be off now.'

Lennox remained seated as the other two went through the door.

'A busy man,' the receptionist smiled. 'A coffee, sir?'

'No, thanks,' Lennox said, staring ahead. Darkness had already started to fall, but there were still several hours before his next shot. An eternity. 'I think I'll take you up on that coffee. Yes, please.' An eternity for a man with no spine.

28

'Where are you going?' whispered Meredith.

'I don't know,' Duff said, trying to stroke her cheek, but he couldn't reach. 'I've got an address, but I don't know whose it is.'

'So why are you going there?'

'It was written down just before Banquo and Fleance died. It says *Safe haven*, and if they were on the run it might be safe for me too. I don't know. It's all I have, love.'

'In that case . . . '

'Where are you?'

'Here.'

'Where's *here?* And what are you doing?'

Meredith smiled. 'We're waiting for you. It's still the birthday.'

'Did it hurt?'

'A bit. It was soon over.'

Duff felt his throat thicken. 'Ewan and Emily, were they frightened?'

'Shh, darling, we're not talking about that now . . . '

'But — '

She laid a hand over his mouth. 'Shh, they're asleep. You mustn't wake them.'

Her hand. He couldn't breathe. He tried to move it, but she was too strong. Duff opened his eyes.

In the darkness above him he saw a figure, and the figure was pressing a hand against his mouth. Duff tried to scream and grab the hairy wrist, but the other person was too strong. Duff knew who it was when he heard the sniff. It was Hutchinson. Who leaned over him and whispered in his ear.

'Not a sound, Johnson. Or to be more accurate, Duff.'

His cover was blown. Was there a price on his head, dead or alive?

Hutchinson's moment for revenge had come. Knife? Bradawl? Hammer?

'Listen to me, Johnson. If we wake the guy in the bunk above, you're done for. OK?'

Why had the engineer woken him? Why hadn't he killed him?

'The police will be waiting for you when we dock in Capitol.' He removed his hand from Duff's mouth. 'Now you know and we're quits.'

The cabin was lit up for a moment as the door opened. Then it closed, and he was gone.

Duff blinked in the darkness, thinking for a moment that Hutchinson had also been part of his dream. Someone coughed in the bunk above. Duff didn't know who it was. The steward had explained the lack of bunks was because they had transported 'some very important boxes of ammo' on the last trip. They'd had to remove some bunks and use two of the cabins as the regulations only allowed them to store a certain quantity of explosives in one place on a boat. Only crew with stripes on their uniform had cabins of their own. Duff swung his legs onto the floor and hurried into the corridor. Saw the back of a dirty Esso T-shirt on its way down the ladder to the engine room.

'Wait!'

Hutchinson turned.

Duff trotted up to him.

The engineer's eyes were shiny now too. But the evil glint was gone.

'What are you talking about?' Duff said. 'Police? Quits?'

Hutchinson crossed his arms. Sniffed. 'I went in to see Sparks to . . . ' another sniff ' . . . to apologise. The captain was talking on the radio. They had their backs to me and didn't hear me.'

Duff felt his heart stop and crossed his arms. 'Carry on.'

'The captain said he had a Johnson who matched the description. You had a scar on your face and had signed up on the relevant date. The voice on the radio said the captain shouldn't do anything, as Duff was dangerous and the police would be ready when we came ashore. The captain answered he was glad to hear that after seeing you in action in the mess.' Hutchinson ran two fingers across his forehead.

'Why are you tipping me off?'

The engineer shrugged. 'The captain told me to apologise to Sparks. He said the only reason I still had a job was that you'd refused to squeal on me. And I'd like to keep this job . . . '

'And you will?'

The engineer sniffed. 'Probably. It's the only thing I'm any good at, according to the first engineer.'

'Oh? Did he say that?'

Hutchinson grinned. 'He came over to me this evening and said I shouldn't go getting any airs. I was a pimple on the arse of this boat, but I was a good engineer. Then he walked off. Pretty weird fellas on this boat, eh?' He laughed. Almost looked happy. 'I'd better go where I'm needed.'

'Wait,' Duff said. 'What good is it if you tell a doomed man he has a noose around his neck? I can't escape until we've docked.'

'That's not my problem, Johnson. We're quits.'

'Are we? This boat transported the machine guns that killed my wife and children, Hutchinson. No, it's not your problem, and it wasn't my problem when the captain asked me to give him a reason to fire you.'

Sniff. 'Jump in the sea then and swim away. It's not far. ETA in nine hours, Johnson.' Sniff.

Duff stood watching the engineer disappear into the belly of the ship.

Then he went to a porthole and looked at the sea. Day was dawning. Eight hours until they were in harbour. The waves were high. How long would he survive in such weather, in such cold water? Twenty minutes? Thirty? And when they were approaching land the captain was sure to have someone keeping an eye on him. Duff leaned his brow against the glass.

There was no way out.

He went back into the cabin. Looked at his watch. A quarter to five. There were still fifteen minutes until he had to turn out, as they said. He lay on his bunk and closed his eyes. He could see Meredith: she was waving from the rock, across the water. Waving to him to join her.

'We're waiting for you.'

★   ★   ★

As if in a dream, Macbeth thought. Or like swimming in a grotto under the water. That must be roughly what it was like sleep-walking. He held the torch in one hand and Lady with the other. Shone the light across the roulette table and the empty chairs. Shadows moved like ghosts across the walls. The false crystal above them gleamed.

'Why's no one here?' Lady asked.

'Everyone's gone home,' Macbeth said, shining the torch on a half-full glass of whisky on a poker table, and instinctively his mind went to dope. The absence of it had begun to make itself felt, but he was holding firm. He was strong, stronger than ever. 'It's just you and me, my love.'

'But we never close, do we?' She let go of his hand. 'Have you closed the Inverness down? And you've changed everything. I don't recognise anything! What's that?'

They had come into another room, where the cone of

388

light caught a line of one-armed bandits. There they were, standing in a row down the room. Like an army of small, sleeping robots, Macbeth thought. Mechanical boxes that would never wake again.

'Look, children's coffins,' Lady said. 'And so many, so many . . . ' Her voice faded, and soundless sobbing took over.

Macbeth drew her close, away from the machines. 'We're not in the Inverness, darling, this is the Obelisk. I wanted to show you what I've done for you. Look, it's closed. They've even cut off the electricity. Look, this is our victory. This is the foe's handsome battlefield, darling.'

'It's ugly, it's hideous! And it stinks. Can you smell it? It stinks of bodies. The stench is coming from the wardrobe!'

'Darling, darling, it's from the kitchen. The police threw everyone out at one so that no one could spoil the evidence. Look, there are still steaks on plates.'

Macbeth shone the torch over the tables: white cloths, burned-down candles and half-eaten meals. He stiffened when the light was reflected in two luminous yellow eyes staring at them. Lady screamed. He reached inside his jacket, but only glimpsed a lean, sinewy body before it was gone in the darkness. And discovered that he was holding a silver dagger in his hand.

'Relax, darling,' he said. 'It was only a dog. It must have smelled the food and got in somehow. There, there, it's gone now.'

'I want to go! Get me out! I want to go away!'

'OK, we've seen enough. We'll go back to the Inverness now.'

'Away, I said!'

'What do you mean? Away where?'

'Away!'

'But . . . ' He didn't complete the sentence, only the thought. They had nowhere else to go. They never had, but it hadn't struck him until now. Everyone else had a family, a childhood home, relatives, a summer cottage, friends. They only had each other and the Inverness. But it had never occurred to him that this wouldn't be enough. Not until now, after they had challenged the world and he was about to lose her. She had to come back; she had to wake up; he had to get her out of this dark place where she was trapped — that was why he had brought her here. But even their triumph was unable to jolt her back to reality. And he needed her now, needed her clear brain, her firm hand, not this woman crying silent tears who had no sense of what was happening around her.

'We've found Duff,' he said leading her quickly through the darkness towards the exit. 'Seyton's flown to Capitol, and at two MS *Glamis* will be docking.' There was light outside, but at the Obelisk all the windows had blinds, it was eternal night and party time. Gambling tables he didn't remember from when they had passed through before appeared suddenly in the torchlight and blocked their way. The sound of their footsteps was muffled by the carpet and he thought he heard the snarling and snapping of dogs' jaws behind them. *Shit! Where is it?* Where was the exit?

★　★　★

Lennox stood in the green grass. He had parked his car up on the main road and put on his sunglasses.

This was one of the reasons he would never settle in Fife. The light was too bright. He could already feel the sun burning his pale pink skin, as though he were going to be set alight like some damn vampire.

But he wasn't a vampire, was he. Some things you didn't see until you got close. Like the white farmhouse in front of him. It wasn't until you got close that you saw the whiteness was peppered with small black holes.

29

'Welcome aboard,' said the captain of MS *Glamis* as the pilot entered the bridge. 'I'd like us to be on time today. We've got someone waiting for us.'

'No problem,' the pilot said, shook the captain's hand and took up a position beside him. 'If the engines are working.'

'Why wouldn't they be?'

'One of your engineers asked to go back on my boat. He had to get hold of a part the first engineer wants.'

'Oh?' the captain said. 'I hadn't been told that.'

'Probably a minor detail.'

'Who was the engineer?'

'Hutch-something-or-other. There they are.' The pilot pointed to the boat rapidly moving away from them.

The captain took his binoculars. On the aft deck he saw a striped cap over the back of an Esso T-shirt.

'Anything wrong?' the pilot asked.

'No one leaves the ship without my permission,' the captain said. 'At least not today.' He pressed the intercom button for the galley. 'Steward!'

'Captain,' came the response from the other end.

'Send Johnson up with two cups of coffee.'

'I'm coming, Captain.'

'Johnson, I said.'

'He's got stomach cramps, Captain, so I let him rest until we dock.'

'Check he's in his cabin.'

'Righty-ho.'

The captain took his finger off the button.

'Three degrees port,' the pilot said.

'Aye aye,' said the first mate.

Inspector Seyton had said the safest option was for

391

the captain and the telegrapher to remain the only ones in the know so that Duff didn't realise his cover had been blown. Seyton and two of his best men would be ready on the quay when they docked, board the boat and overpower Duff. And Seyton had stressed that when it happened he wanted the crew well clear so that no one would be hurt if shots were fired. Although to the captain it sounded like *when* shots were fired.

'Captain!' It was the steward. 'Johnson's sleeping like a baby in his bunk. Shall I wake — '

'No! let him sleep. Is he alone in his cabin?'

'Yes, Captain.'

'Good, good.' The captain looked at his watch. In an hour everything would be over and he could go home to his wife. Soon have a couple of days off. Just that summons to the shipping line tomorrow concerning the insurance company report about a suspiciously high number of cases of the same type of illness in the crew who had worked in the hold over the last ten years. Something to do with blood.

'Course is fine,' the pilot said.

'Let's hope so,' the captain mumbled. 'Let's hope so.'

★ ★ ★

Ten minutes past one. Ten minutes ago a large elk head had come out of an elk clock and mooed. Angus looked around. He regretted the choice of place. Even if it was only unemployed layabouts and drunks at the Bricklayers Arms during the day now, it was the SWAT local, and if someone from police HQ saw him and the reporter talking it would soon get to Macbeth's ears. On the other hand, it was less suspicious than sitting in some bar hidden in the back streets.

But Angus didn't like it. Didn't like the elk. Didn't like it that the journalist still hadn't arrived. Angus would have gone long ago if this hadn't been his last chance.

'Sorry for being late.'

The rolled 'r's. Angus looked up. It was only the voice that reassured him the man standing there in yellow oilskins was Walter Kite. Angus had read that this radio reporter consistently said no to TV and being pictured in newspapers and celeb magazines, as he considered a person's appearance a distraction from the story. The word was everything.

'Rain and traffic,' Walt Kite said, undoing his jacket. Water ran from his thin hair.

'It's always rain and traffic,' Angus said.

'That's the excuse we use anyway,' the radio reporter said and sat down opposite him in the booth. 'The truth is the chain came off my bike.'

'I thought Walter Kite didn't lie,' Angus said.

'Kite, the radio reporter, never lies,' Kite said with a wry smile. 'Walter, the private person, is a long way behind.'

'Are you alone?'

'Always. Tell me what you didn't say on the phone.'

Angus drew a deep breath and began to speak. He experienced nothing of the nerves he had felt when he had presented his information to Lennox and Caithness. Perhaps because the die was already cast; there was no way back. He used more or less the same words he had at Estex the day before, but also told Kite about the meeting with Lennox and Caithness. He gave Kite everything. The names. The details about the club house and Fife. The order to burn the baby's body. While they were speaking Kite took a serviette from the box on the table and tried to wipe the black oil off his hands.

'Why me?' Kite asked, taking a second serviette.

'Because you're considered to be a brave reporter with integrity,' Angus said.

'Nice to hear people think so,' Kite said, studying Angus. 'Your language is more elevated than other young police officers'.'

'I studied theology.'

'So that explains both the language and why you want to expose yourself to this. You believe in salvation for good deeds.'

'You're mistaken, Mr Kite. I don't believe in either salvation or divinity.'

'Have you spoken to any other journalists — ' he smirked ' — with or without integrity?'

Angus shook his head.

'Good. Because if I work on this case I need total exclusivity. So not a word to other journalists, not to anyone. Are we in agreement?'

Angus nodded.

'Where can I get hold of you, Angus?'

'My phone number — '

'No phones. Address.'

Angus wrote it down on Kite's oil-stained serviette. 'What happens now?'

Kite heaved a sigh. Like a man who knew there was an immense amount of work in front of him.

'I have to check a few things first. This is a big case. I wouldn't like to be caught presenting false information or be suspected of being part of someone's agenda.'

'My only agenda is that the truth should come out and that Macbeth is stopped.'

Angus knew he had raised his voice when Kite looked around the sparse clientele to make sure no one had heard. 'If it's true, you're lying when you say you don't believe in divinity.'

'God doesn't exist.'

'I'm thinking about divinity in *humans*, Angus.'

'You mean the humanity in humans, Kite. Wanting goodness is as human as sinning.'

Kite nodded slowly. 'You're the theologian. Although

I have to confess I believe you, I'll have to check out the story — and you as a person. I think that's what's called — ' he got to his feet and buttoned up his oilskin jacket ' — integrity.'

'When do you think this can appear in print?' Angus breathed in and then let it out again. 'I don't trust Lennox. He'll go to Macbeth.'

'I'll prioritise the story,' Kite said. 'It should be mainly finished in two days.' He took out his wallet.

'Thank you. I'll pay for my own coffee.'

'Right.' Kite put his wallet back in his jacket. 'You're a rare bird in this town, you know.'

'Definitely in danger of extinction.' Angus smiled weakly.

He watched the reporter until he was out of the door. Looked around the pub. No one conspicuous. Everyone seemed occupied with their own business. Two days. He had to try and stay alive for two days.

★   ★   ★

Seyton didn't like Capitol. Didn't like the broad avenues, the magnificent old parliamentary buildings and all the other shit — the green parks, the libraries and the opera house, the street artists, the tiny Gothic churches and the ridiculously extravagant cathedral, the smiling people in the pavement restaurants and the expensive national theatre with its pompous plays, incomprehensible dialogue and megalomaniac kings who die in the last act.

That was why he preferred to stand like this, with his back to the town and his eyes across the sea.

They were inside the harbour office and could see MS *Glamis* now.

'Sure you don't want any help?' asked the policeman with the CAPITOL POLICE patch on his uniform. There had been a discussion about jurisdiction before they

395

arrived, but Capitol's chief commissioner had been cooperative, partly, he had said, because they felt the murder
of a policeman in another town affected them, partly
because you can make exceptions on board vessels.

'Thank you again, but I'm very sure,' Seyton said.

'Fine, but when he's been arrested and brought
ashore, we take over.'

'Absolutely. As long as you keep an eye on the
gangway and the ship.'

'He won't get away, Inspector.' The Capitol policeman pointed to the plain-clothes policemen in two rowing
boats fifty metres from the quay. The officers were
pretending to fish, but were ready to catch Duff if he
jumped overboard.

Seyton nodded. It wasn't so long since he had been
standing waiting in another harbour office. That time it
had been Duff who had refused help, the stupid idiot.
But the roles were changed now. And he would make
sure Duff knew. He would make him *feel* it. For some
endlessly long seconds. The Capitol Police knew nothing of Macbeth's orders of course: Duff was not to be
brought but carried ashore. In a body bag.

The *Glamis* reversed, and the sea was whipped white
below the surface, then the white water rose and
bubbled like champagne. Seyton loaded his MP-5.
'Olafson. Ricardo. Ready?'

The two SWAT men nodded. They had drawings of
the boat showing the cabin where Duff was.

Hawsers were thrown from the *Glamis* onto the quay,
one from the bow and one from the stern, coiled around
bollards and tightened. The side of the boat pushed
gently against screaming tyres. A gangway was lowered.

'Now,' Seyton said.

They ran out across the quay and up the gangway.
The crew stared at them open-mouthed; the captain
had obviously managed to keep the secret. They rushed
down an iron ladder past what was labelled the first

mate's cabin. Further down. And further down. Stopped outside the door of cabin 12.

Seyton listened but heard only his own breathing and the rumble of the engines. Ricardo had taken up a position further down the corridor where he could keep an eye on the nearby doors, in case Duff was in a different cabin, heard them and tried to make a getaway.

Seyton switched on his torch and nodded to Olafson. Then he went in. The torch was redundant; there was enough light inside. Duff was lying on the lower bunk, turned to the wall with a blanket over him. He was wearing the green hat the captain said 'Johnson' never took off and always kept pulled down to his big glasses. Apart from once when it had ridden up and the captain had seen the scar. Seyton took out the gun that would be placed in Duff's hand and fired two shots into the wall behind them. The explosions temporarily deprived him of hearing, and for a couple of seconds all Seyton heard was a high-pitched squeak. Duff had gone rigid in his bunk. Seyton put his mouth to Duff's ear.

'They screamed,' he said. 'They screamed, and it was wonderful to hear. You can scream a little too, Duff. Because I've decided to shoot you in the stomach first. For old acquaintance's sake, you arrogant prick.'

A strong smell rose from Duff. Seyton breathed it in. But it wasn't the delicious scent of fear. It was . . . sweat. Stale, old masculine sweat. Older than the few days that Duff had been missing.

The man in the bunk turned his face to him.

It wasn't Duff's face.

'Eh?' said the man, and the blanket fell off revealing a naked chest and a hairy forearm.

Seyton put the barrel of his machine gun to the man's forehead. 'Police. What are you doing here and where's Duff?'

The man sniffed. 'I'm *sleeping*, as you can see. And I have no idea who Duff is.'

'Johnson,' Seyton said, pressing the muzzle into the man's brow so hard his head fell back onto the pillow.

Another sniff. 'The galley boy? Have you checked the galley? Or the other cabins? We just take any bunk that's free on this trip. What's Johnson done, eh? Something serious by the look of it. If you're gonna make a dent in my head you'd better shoot, arsehole.'

Seyton pulled his gun away.

'Olafson, take Ricardo and search the boat.' Seyton studied the bloated face in front of him. Smelled him. Was the man really so unafraid or was it the composite stench of other body functions that drowned the smell of fear?

Olafson was still standing behind him.

'Search the boat!' Seyton yelled. And heard Olafson and Ricardo's boots pounding down the corridor and the sound of cabin doors being pulled open.

Seyton stretched. 'What's your name and why are you wearing Johnson's hat?'

'Hutchinson. And you can have the hat. You look like you need something to wank in.'

Seyton hit out. The gun opened the skin on the man's cheek and blood leaked out. But the guy didn't turn a hair even though his eyes filled with tears.

'Answer me,' Seyton hissed.

'I woke up cold and was going to put on my T-shirt. I left it on the chest over there. Both my T-shirt and cap were gone; instead there was this hat. It was cold, so I took it, OK?' Hutchinson's voice shook, but the hatred shone through the tears. Fear and hatred, hatred and fear, it was always the same, Seyton thought, wiping the blood off the muzzle of his MP-5.

Angry voices came from the corridor. Seyton already knew. They would search the whole boat, every nook and cranny, in vain. Duff had already gone.

30

Duff hurried down broad avenues past magnificent old buildings, through parks, passing street musicians and portrait painters. A smiling couple at a pavement restaurant pointed him in the right direction when he showed them the address on the slip of paper. Stared at his beard, which had started to come unstuck on one side. Duff, trying not to run, passed Capitol Cathedral.

Hutchinson had turned round.

Turned round as he was on his way down the ladder. Came back up. Had listened to Duff's story. And even when Duff told him details he himself would not have believed if someone else had told him, Hutchinson had kept nodding as if in recognition. As though nothing was alien to him with regard to what humans were capable of doing to one another. And when Duff had finished, the engineer presented an escape plan. Without any hesitation, so simple and obvious Duff assumed the engineer must have hatched it for himself at some point. Duff would put on Hutchinson's clothes and stand by the railing ready.

'Just make sure you have your back to the bridge so the captain can't see your face and thinks it's me. The boatman will leave the ladder to you if you're standing ready. Throw it out early, climb down and stand at the bottom when the pilot's boat comes alongside. Tell him you need to be ashore before the *Glamis* docks because you have to pick up a spare part at the shipping office which we need for the winch that tightens the hawsers on the quay.'

'Why?'

'Eh?'

'Why are you doing this for me?'

Hutchinson shrugged his shoulders. 'I was on the detail to load up the ammo boxes. There was a skinny, bald police bloke with his arms crossed who looked as if he wanted to spit on us as we loaded them onto his truck.'

Duff waited. For the rest of his explanation.

'People do things for each other,' Hutchinson said and sniffed. 'It seems.' Sniff. 'And if I've understood you right, you're alone against — ' he pointed to the decks above them ' — them. And I know a bit about how that feels.'

Alone. Them.

'Thank you.'

'No worries, Johnson.' The engineer shook Duff's hand. Briefly, almost shyly. And then he ran his hand over the plaster on his forehead. 'Next time I'll be ready, and it'll be your turn for a beating.'

'Of course.'

Duff was east of the centre now.

'Sorry. District 6?'

'Over there.'

He passed a kiosk with a news-stand. The houses were becoming smaller, the streets narrower.

'Tannery Street?'

'Down to the lights and the second or third left.'

A police siren rose and sank. They had a different sound here in the capital, not so harsh or sharp. And a different tune. Not as gloomy, not so piercingly disharmonious.

'Dolphin?'

'The nightclub? Isn't it closed? Anyway, do you see that café there? Right next to it.' But the eyes lingered too long on the scar, trying to remember something.

'Thank you.'

'Not at all.'

Number 66 Tannery Street.

Duff studied the names next to the bells by the

rotting big wooden door. None of them meant a thing to him. He pulled at the door. Open. Or to be more precise, a smashed lock. It was dark inside. He stood still until his pupils began to widen. A staircase. Wet newspaper, smell of urine. Sound of tuberculous coughing from behind a door. A sound like a hard wet slap. Duff set off up the stairs. There were two front doors on every floor, as well as a low door on every landing. He rang one of the doorbells. From inside came the angry barking of a dog and shuffling steps. A small, almost comical, wrinkled lady opened the door. No safety chain.

'Yes, love?'

'Hello, I'm Inspector Johnson.'

She eyed him sceptically. Duff assumed she could smell Hutchinson from the Esso T-shirt. The scent appeared to have quietened the little fluffball of a dog anyway.

'I'm looking for — ' Yes, what was he looking for?' — someone a friend of mine, Banquo, gave me an address for.'

'Sorry, young man. I don't know any Banquo.'

'Alfie?'

'Oh, Alfie. He lives on the second floor, right-hand side. Excuse me, but you . . . erm . . . you're losing your beard.'

'Thank you.'

Duff tore off the beard and glasses as he went up to the second floor. The door to the right had no name on it, just a bell with a button hanging from a spiral metal spring.

Duff knocked. Waited. Knocked again, harder. Another wet slap from the ground floor. He pulled at the door. Locked. Should he wait and see if anyone came? It was a better alternative than showing his face on the street.

Low cough. The sound came from behind the low

401

door on the landing. Duff walked down the five steps and turned the door knob. It moved a little, as though someone was holding on to it on the inside. He knocked.

No answer.

'Hello? Hello, is anyone there?'

He held his breath and put his ear to the door. He heard something which sounded like the rustle of paper. Someone was hiding in there.

Duff went down the stairs with loud, heavy footsteps, took off his shoes on the floor below and tiptoed back.

He grabbed the door knob and gave it a sharp pull. Heard something go flying as the door swung open. A piece of string.

He stared at himself.

The picture wasn't particularly big and positioned to the right at the bottom of the page underneath the headline.

The newspaper was lowered, and Duff stared into the face of an old man with a long, unkempt beard. He was sitting leaning forward with his trousers around his ankles.

A splash box. Duff had seen them before, in the old workers' blocks of flats along the river. He assumed they got their name from the sound made when shit from the upper floors hit the container on the ground floor. Like a wet slap.

'Sorry,' Duff said. 'Are you Alfie?'

The man didn't answer, just stared at Duff. Then he slowly turned the page of the newspaper, looked at the photo and back up at Duff. Moistened his lips. 'Louder,' he said, pointing to his ear with one hand.

Duff raised his voice. 'Are you Alfie?'

'Louder.'

'Alfie!'

'Shh. Yes, he's Alfie.'

Perhaps it was because of the shouting that Duff

didn't hear someone come. He just felt a hard object being pressed against the back of his head, and there was something vaguely familiar about the voice that whispered in his ear: 'And yes, this is a gun, Inspector. So don't move; just tell me how you found us and who sent you.'

Duff made to turn, but a hand pushed his face forward again, to face Alfie, who clearly regarded the situation as resolved and had resumed his reading.

'I don't know who you are,' Duff said. 'I found the impression of an address on a notepad in Banquo's car. And no one sent me. I'm alone.'

'Why have you come here?'

'Because Macbeth's trying to kill me. I'm fairly sure he had Banquo and Fleance killed. So if Banquo had an address he thought was a safe haven, it might be good for me too.'

A pause. For thought, it seemed.

'Come with me.'

Duff was turned, but in such a way that the person with the gun was still behind him. Then he was prodded up the stairs to the door where he had rung the bell. It was now open, and he was pushed into a big room that smelled stale even though the windows were wide open. The room contained a large table with three chairs, a kitchen counter with a sink, a fridge, a narrow bed, a sofa and a mattress on the floor. And one other person. He was sitting on a chair with his forearms and hands on the table and staring straight at Duff. The glasses were the same, also the long legs protruding from under the table. But there was something different about him. Perhaps it was the beard. Or his face had become thinner.

'Malcolm,' Duff said. 'You're alive.'

'Duff. Sit down.'

Duff sat down on the chair opposite the deputy chief commissioner. Malcolm took off his glasses. Cleaned them. 'So you thought I drowned myself after I took Duncan's life, did you?'

'At first I thought so. Until I realised that Macbeth was behind Duncan's murder. Then I also realised that he had probably drowned you to clear his path to the chief commissioner's office. And that the suicide letter was a forgery.'

'Macbeth threatened to kill my daughter if I didn't sign it. What do you want, Duff?'

'He says — ' the voice behind Duff started.

'I heard you,' Malcolm interrupted. 'And I see that the newspapers are making out that Macbeth is after you, Duff. But of course you could be working with him, and the scribblings are a plant so you can infiltrate us.'

'Killing my family was a cover operation?'

'I read about that too, but I don't trust anything any longer, Duff. If Macbeth and the police really were so keen to catch you they would already have done so.'

'I was lucky.'

'And then you came here.' Malcolm drummed his fingers on the table. 'Why?'

'Safe haven.'

'Safe?' Malcolm shook his head. 'You're a police officer, Duff, and you know that if you can find us that easily then so can Macbeth. A moderately intelligent wanted person sits tight. He doesn't visit other people also on the wanted list. So give me a better answer. Why here?'

'What do you think?'

'Let me hear you say it. The gun's pointing at where you have, or don't have, a bleeding heart.'

Duff gulped. Why had he come here? It had been a lot to hope for. But it had also been the only hope he had. The odds had been poor, but the calculation simple. Duff took a deep breath.

'Banquo was supposed to meet me to tell me

something the night he died. And he was the last person to see you the day you disappeared. I thought there was a chance I might find you here. And we could help each other. I have proof Macbeth killed Duncan. Macbeth knows and that's why he's trying to kill me.'

Malcolm arched an eyebrow. 'And how can we help each other? You don't imagine the police here in Capitol can help us, do you?'

Duff shook his head. 'They've been instructed to arrest us and send us back to Macbeth at once. But we can bring Macbeth down together.'

'To avenge your family.'

'Yes, that was my first thought.'

'But?'

'There's something bigger than revenge.'

'The chief commissioner's job?'

'No.'

'What then?'

Duff nodded towards the open window. 'Capitol is an elegant town, isn't she? It's difficult not to like her. To fall in love with her even — such a smiling blonde beauty with sunshine in her eyes. But you and I can never love her, can we? For we've given our hearts to the foul, rotten city up on the west coast. I've disowned her, thought she didn't mean anything to me. Me and my career were more important than the town that has done nothing but darkened our moods, corrupted our hearts and shortened our lives. Absurd, wasted love, I thought. But that's how it is. Too late we realise who we really love.'

'And you're willing to sacrifice yourself for a town like that?'

'It's easy.' Duff smiled. 'I've lost everything. There's not much left to sacrifice other than my life. What about you, Malcolm?'

'I have my daughter to lose.'

'And you can only save her if we bring Macbeth

down. Listen. You're the man who can carry on Duncan's work. And that's why I'm here to follow you, if you're willing to take over as chief commissioner and rule justly.'

Malcolm eyed him cautiously. 'Me?'

'Yes.'

Malcolm laughed. 'Thank you for the moral support, Duff, but let me make a few things clear first.'

'Yes?'

'The first is I've never liked you.'

'Understandable,' Duff said. 'I've never paid a thought to anyone else but myself. I'm not saying I'm a changed man, but what has happened has definitely given me new insights. I'm still not a clever man, but perhaps a little less stupid than I was.'

'Possibly, although you may only be saying what you want me to hear. But what I don't want to hear is any conversion nonsense. You might be slightly changed, but the world is the same.'

'What do you mean?'

'I'm pleased you regard me as relatively decent. But if I'm going to have you as part of my team I have to know your angel wings don't prevent you from keeping your feet on the ground. Surely you don't think you can get to me without turning a blind eye to some things? Accepting some . . . established practices for who gets away with something and who doesn't, and who gets the brown envelopes. If you take everything from a badly paid policeman overnight how are you going to get his loyalty? And isn't it better to win a few small battles now and then rather than to insist on always losing the big ones?'

Duff looked at the man with the beard as if to make sure this really was Malcolm. 'You mean, don't go after Hecate but his small competitors?'

'I mean, be realistic, my dear Duff. No one gains anything with a chief commissioner who doesn't know how things work in this world. We have to make a better and cleaner town than those who came before us, Duff, but for this job we damn well have to be paid.'

'Take payment, you mean?'

'We can't win against Hecate, Duff. Not yet. In the meantime we can let him pay some of our wages so that we're equipped to fight all the other crime in the town. God knows there's enough of it.'

At first Duff felt a weariness. And a strange relief. The fight was over; he could give in, could rest now. With Meredith. He shook his head. 'I can't accept that. You aren't the person I'd hoped you were, Malcolm, so that's my last hope gone.'

'Do you think there are better men? Are *you* a better man?'

'Not me, but I've met men in the belly of a boat who are better than you or me, Malcolm. So now I'm going to leave. You'd better make up your mind whether you're going to let me go or shoot me.'

'I can't let you go now as you know where I am. Unless you swear not to reveal my whereabouts.'

'A promise between traitors wouldn't be worth much, Malcolm. I still won't swear though. Please shoot me in the head — I have a family waiting for me.'

Duff got up, but Malcolm did too, put both hands on his shoulders and forced him back down onto the chair.

'You've asked me quite a few questions, Duff. And in an interview the questions are often truer and more revealing than the answers. I've been lying to you, and your questions were the right ones. But I wasn't sure if your righteous indignation was genuine until now, when you were willing to take a bullet for a clean police force and town.'

Duff blinked. His body was so heavy all of a sudden, he was close to fainting.

'There are three men in this room,' Malcolm said. 'Three men willing to sacrifice everything to carry on what Duncan stood for.' He put on the glasses he had been cleaning. 'Three men who may not be better than any others — perhaps we've already lost so much that it doesn't cost us much to sacrifice the rest. But this is the seed and the logic of the revolution, so let's not get carried away by our own moral excellence. Let's just say we have the will to do the right thing irrespective of whether the fuel powering our will is a sense of justice — ' he shrugged ' — a family man's lust for revenge, a traitor's shame, the moral exaltation of a privileged person or a God-fearing horror of burning in hell. For this *is* the right path and what we need now is the will. There are no simple paths to justice and purity, only the difficult one.'

'Three men,' Duff said.

'You, me and . . . ?'

'And Fleance,' Duff said. 'How did you manage it, lad?'

'My father kicked me out of the car and off the bridge,' the voice said behind him. 'He taught me how to do what he never succeeded in teaching Macbeth. How to swim.'

Duff looked at Malcolm, who sighed then smiled. And to his surprise Duff felt himself smiling too. And felt something surge up his throat. A sob. But he realised it was laughter, not tears, only when he saw Malcolm also burst into laughter and then Fleance. The laughter of war.

'Wozzup?'

They turned to see old Alfie standing in the doorway with a bewildered expression on his face and the newspaper in his hand, and they laughed even louder.

31

Lennox was standing by the window staring out. Weighing the grenade in his hand. Angus, Angus. He still hadn't told anyone about the meeting at Estex. Why, he didn't know. He only knew he hadn't done a thing all day. Or yesterday. Or the day before. Whenever he tried to read a report he lost concentration. It was as though the letters moved and made new words. *Reforming* became *informing* and *portrayal* became *betrayal*. Whenever he lifted the phone to make a call the receiver weighed a ton and he had to cradle it again. He had tried to read the newspaper and found out that old Zimmerman was standing for mayor. Zimmerman was neither controversial nor charismatic; he was respected for his competence, as far as that went, but he was not a serious challenger to Tourtell. Lennox had also started reading an article about the increase in drug trafficking, which according to the UN had turned it into the biggest industry after arms dealing, before realising he was only looking at sentences, not reading them.

Eight days had gone by since Duff had evaded capture in Capitol. When Lennox and Seyton had stood before him in the chief commissioner's office Macbeth had been so furious that he was literally foaming at the mouth. White bubbles of saliva gathered at the corners of his mouth as he ranted on about what an idiot he had been made to look in the capital. And if Lennox and Seyton had done their jobs and caught Duff while he was still in town then this would never have happened. And yet Lennox felt this paradoxical relief that Duff was still alive and free.

There wasn't much light left outside, but his eyes

smarted. Perhaps he needed an extra shot today. Just to get through this one day; tomorrow everything would be better.

'Is that really a hand grenade or is it supposed to be an ashtray?'

Lennox turned to the voice at the door.

Macbeth was in an odd pose, leaning forward with his arms down by his sides as though he were standing in a strong wind. His head was bowed, his pupils at the top of his eyes as he stared at Lennox.

'It was thrown at my grandfather in the First World War.'

'Lies.' Macbeth grinned, coming in and closing the door behind him. 'That's a German Model 24 *Stielhandgranate*, stick grenade. It's an ashtray.'

'I don't think my grandfather — '

Macbeth took the grenade out of Lennox's hand, grasped the cord at the end of the handle and began to pull.

'Don't!'

Macbeth raised an eyebrow and eyed the frightened head of the Anti-Corruption Unit, who continued: 'It will d-detonate — '

' — your grandfather's story?' Macbeth put the cord back into the handle and placed the grenade on the table. 'We can't have that, can we. So what were you thinking about, Inspector?'

'Corruption,' Lennox said, putting the grenade in a drawer. 'And anti-corruption.'

Macbeth pulled the visitor's chair forward. 'What is corruption actually, Lennox? Is a solemnly committed revolutionary paid to infiltrate our state machinery corrupt? Is an obedient but passive servant who does nothing but receive his regular and somewhat unreasonably high salary in a system he knows is based on corruption corrupt?'

'There are many grey areas, Chief Commissioner. As

a rule you know yourself if you're corrupt or not.'

'You mean it's a matter of feelings?' Macbeth sat down, and Lennox followed suit so as not to tower over him.

'So if you don't *feel* corrupt because the family you're providing for is dependent on your income, you're not corrupt? If the motive is good — for the family or town's benefit — we can just paraphrase the word *corruption* — say, well, *pragmatic politics*, for instance.'

'I think it's the other way round,' Lennox said. 'I think when you know greed and nothing else is at the root, then you resort to paraphrases for yourself. While the morally justified crime requires no paraphrase. We can live with it going by its right name. Corruption, robbery, murder.'

'So this is what you do? Spend your time in here thinking,' Macbeth said, holding his chin in his fingertips. 'Wondering whether you're corrupt or not.'

'Me?' Lennox chuckled. 'I'm talking about the people we investigate of course.'

'And yet we always talk about ourselves. And I'd still maintain that desperate situations make people call their own corruption by another name. And the payment you receive to take advantage of your position is not money but charity. Life. Your family's life, for instance. Do you understand?'

'I don't know . . . ' Lennox said.

'Let me give you an example,' Macbeth said. 'A radio reporter who is known for his integrity is contacted by a young police officer who thinks he has a story to tell that could bring down a chief commissioner. What this perfidious officer, let's call him Angus, doesn't know is that this radio reporter has a certain . . . relationship with the chief commissioner. The reporter, with good reason, fears for his family if he doesn't do as this chief commissioner wishes. So the reporter informs said chief commissioner about the officer's seditious plans. The reporter promises to get back to the young officer, and the chief commissioner tells the reporter to meet the officer where no one can see or hear them. Where the boss or his people can . . . well, you know.'

Lennox didn't answer. He wiped his hands on his trousers.

'So the boss is safe. But he wonders, naturally enough, who the corrupt person is here: the young officer, the radio reporter or . . . or who, Lennox?'

Lennox cleared his throat, hesitated. 'The chief commissioner?'

'No, no, no.' Macbeth shook his head. 'The third person. The one who should have informed the chief commissioner right from the start. The third person who knew about Angus's plans, who isn't part of them yet still is, indirectly, for as long as he fails to go to his boss and fails to save him. Which he hasn't done yet. Because he has to think. And think. And while he's thinking, he's becoming corrupt himself, or isn't he?'

Lennox tried to meet Macbeth's eyes. But it was like staring at the sun.

'The meeting at Estex, Lennox. I don't know when you were considering telling me about it.'

Lennox couldn't stop blinking. 'I . . . I've been thinking.'

'Yes, it's difficult to stop. Thoughts just come, don't they? And no matter how free we think our will is, it's governed by thoughts, bidden or unbidden. Tell me who came to you, Lennox.'

'This person — '

'Say the name.'

'He's — '

'Say the name!'

Lennox took a deep breath. 'Police Officer Angus.'

'Carry on.'

'You know Angus. Young. Impulsive. And with all that's happened recently anyone can react a little irrationally. I thought that before I came to you with these serious accusations I'd try to talk some common sense into him. Let him cool down a bit.'

'And in the meantime keep me in ignorance? Because you assumed that your judgement of the situation was better than mine? That I wouldn't let Angus, whom I employed in SWAT, have another chance? That I would have his overheated, though otherwise innocent, head chopped off straight away?'

'I . . . ' Lennox searched for words to complete his sentence.

'But you're wrong, Lennox. I always give my subordinates two chances. And that rule applies to both you and Angus.'

'I'm pleased to hear that.'

'I believe in magnanimity. So I would have forgotten the whole business if Angus had shown signs of regret and refused to meet the reporter when he rang to set up a second meeting. I wouldn't have given it another thought. Life would have gone on. Unfortunately Angus didn't do that. He accepted. And I don't have a third cheek.'

Macbeth got up and walked to the window.

'Which brings me to *your* second chance, Lennox. My reporter has been informed that you and Seyton are going to this meeting. It'll take place at the Estex factory this evening, where Angus believes there will also be a photographer to take pictures of a furnace where he believes a child's body has been burned. And there you will personally punish the traitor.'

'Punish?'

'I'll leave you to mete out the punishment at your own discretion. My only demand is that death should be the outcome.' Macbeth turned to Lennox, who was breathing through his mouth.

'And afterwards Seyton will help you dispose of the body.'

'But — '

'Third chances probably exist. In heaven. How's your family by the way?'

Lennox opened his mouth, and a sound emerged.

'Good,' Macbeth said. 'Seyton will pick you up at six. Depending on the punishment you choose it should all be over within an hour and a half, so I suggest you ring your charming wife to say you'll be a little late for tea. I've been told her shopping indicates she's giving you black pudding.'

Macbeth closed the door quietly behind him as he left.

Lennox put his head in his hands. A mollusc. A creature without a bone in his body.

A fix. He had to have a shot.

⋆ ⋆ ⋆

Macbeth crashed his heels down on the floor as he strode along the corridor. Trying to drown the voice shouting he had to have power. Or brew. Or anything. He had managed to stay clean for more than a week now. It would get worse before it got better, but it *would* get better. He had done it before and would do it again. There was just the awful sweat — it stank, stank of displeasure, fear and pain. But it would pass. Everything would pass. *Had* to pass. He walked into the anteroom to his office.

'Chief Commissioner — '

'No messages, no phone calls, Priscilla.'

'But — '

'Not now. Later.'

'You've got a visitor.'

Macbeth pulled up sharp. 'You let someone in — ' he pointed to the office door ' — there?'

'She insisted.'

Macbeth looked at Priscilla's desperate expression.

'It's your wife.'

'What?' came his astonished response. He did up the lowest button on his uniform and went into his office.

She was standing behind his desk examining the painting on the wall. 'Darling! You really have to do something about the art in here.'

Macbeth stared at Lady in disbelief. She was wearing a plain, elegant outfit under a fur coat; she had obviously come straight from the hairdresser's and looked relaxed and energetic. He approached her with caution. 'How . . . are you, darling?'

'Excellent,' she said. 'I can see this picture is propaganda, but what's it trying to say actually?'

Macbeth couldn't take his eyes off her. Where was the crazy woman he had seen yesterday? Gone.

'My love?'

Macbeth gazed at the painting. Saw the workers' coarse features. 'It was put there by someone else. I'll get it changed. I'm so glad you feel better. Have you . . . taken your medicine?'

She shook her head. 'No medicine. I've stopped my medicine. All of it.'

'Because there's none left?'

She smiled fleetingly. 'I saw the drawer was empty. You've stopped too.' She sat in his chair. 'This is a bit . . . cramped, isn't it?'

'Maybe.' Macbeth sat down on one of the visitor's chairs. Perhaps her madness had just been a labyrinth and she had found her way out.

'Glad you agree. I had a chat with Jack this morning. About the plan you made regarding the mayoral elections.'

'Yes. Well, what do you think?'

She pouted and waggled her head. 'You've done the best you can do, but you've forgotten one thing.'

'What's that?'

'Your thinking is that we should leak information about Tourtell's relationship with this boy just before

415

the elections. And then you, the Sweno-killer, will quickly fill the vacuum before people go to the ballot box.'

'Yes?' said Macbeth, full of enthusiasm.

'The problem is that the vacuum was filled when Zimmerman announced that he was standing.'

'That bore? No one cares about him.'

'Zimmerman doesn't have great appeal, it's true, but people know him and know what they can expect. So they feel safe with him. And it's important for people to feel safe in these dramatic times. That's why Tourtell will be re-elected.'

'Do you really think Zimmerman could beat me?'

'Yes,' Lady said. 'Unless you're officially supported by a Tourtell who has not been damaged by scandal and you've also dealt with Hecate. Get those two things organised and you're unbeatable.'

Macbeth felt a wearied relief. She was out of the labyrinth. She was here, back with him.

'Fine, but how?'

'By giving Tourtell an ultimatum. He can either voluntarily withdraw, giving advancing age and poor health as reasons, and lend you his unreserved, official support. Or we can force him to withdraw by threatening to unmask him as the perverted pig he is, after which he'll be arrested and thrown into jail, where he knows what happens to pederasts. Shouldn't be the most difficult decision to make.'

'Hm.' Macbeth scratched his beard. 'We'll have made an enemy.'

'Tourtell? On the contrary. He understands power struggles and will be grateful we gave him a merciful alternative.'

'Let me think about it.'

'No need, darling. There's nothing to consider. Then there's the puppeteer, Hecate. It's time he was got rid of.'

'I'm not so sure that's wise, darling. Remember he's our guarantor and will support us if we come up against opponents.'

'Hecate still hasn't demanded his pound of flesh for making you chief commissioner,' Lady said. 'But soon the day of reckoning will come. And then you'll do this.' She raised an elbow as though it were attached to a string. 'And this.' A foot shot out. 'Do you want to be Hecate's puppet, my love? Curtailing the campaign against him won't be enough; he'll want more and more, and in the end everything — that's what people such as him are like. So the question is whether you want to let Hecate control the town through you? Or — ' she placed her elbows on the desk ' — do you want to be the puppeteer yourself? Be the hero who caught Hecate and became mayor?'

Macbeth fixed her with his eyes. Then he nodded slowly.

'I'll invite Tourtell to a private game of blackjack,' Lady said, getting up. 'And you send a message to Hecate telling him you wish to meet him face to face.'

'And why do you think he'll say yes?'

'Because you'll hand him a suitcase full of gold as thanks for him getting us the chief commissioner's job.'

'And he'll swallow the bait, do you think?'

'Some people are blinded by power, others by money. Hecate belongs to the latter group. You'll get the details later.'

Macbeth accompanied her to the door. 'Darling,' he said, laying a hand on her back, stroking the thick fur, 'it's good to have you back.'

'Likewise,' she said, letting him kiss her on the cheek. 'Be strong. Let's make each other strong.'

He watched her as she sailed through the anteroom, wondering if he would ever fully understand who she was. Or if he wanted to. Wasn't it that which made her so irresistible to him?

Lennox and Seyton had parked in the road on the opposite side from Estex. It was so dark that Lennox couldn't see the drizzle; he only heard it as a whisper on the car roof and windscreen.

'There's the reporter,' Seyton said.

The light from a bike wobbled across the road. Turned in through the gate and was gone.

'Let's give him two minutes,' Seyton said, checking his machine gun.

Lennox yawned. Luckily he had managed to get a shot.

'Now,' Seyton said.

They stepped out, ran through the darkness, through the gate and into the factory building.

Voices were coming from the foreman's office high up on the wall.

Seyton sniffed the air. Then he motioned towards the steel staircase.

They tiptoed up, and Lennox felt a wonderful absence of thought and the steel of the railing which was so cold it burned the palms of his hands. They stood just outside the door. The high gave him that sense of sitting in a warm safe room and watching himself. The buzz of voices inside reminded him of his parents in the sitting room when he was small and had gone to bed.

'When will it appear in print?' Angus was speaking.

The answer came with drawled arrogance and long rolled 'r's: 'Disregarding the fact that on radio we don't refer to *print*, I hope — '

When Seyton opened the door it was as if someone had pressed the stop button on a cassette player. Walt Kite's eyes behind his glasses were large. With fear. Excitement. Relief? Not surprise anyway. Lennox and Seyton had been punctual.

'Good evening,' Lennox said, feeling a warm smile spread across his face.

Angus stood up and knocked his chair over as he reached for something inside his jacket. But froze when he caught sight of Seyton's machine gun.

In the silence that followed Kite buttoned up his yellow oilskin jacket. It was like being in a gentlemen's toilet: no looks were exchanged, no words were said; he just left them quickly with his head lowered. He had done his bit. Left the others with the stench.

'What are you waiting for, Lennox?' Angus asked.

Lennox became aware of his outstretched arm and the gun on the end of it. 'For the reporter to be so far away he won't hear the shot,' he said.

Angus's Adam's apple went up and down. 'So you're going to shoot me?'

'Unless you have another suggestion. I've been given a free hand as to how this should happen.'

'OK.'

'OK as in *I understand* or as in *Yes, I want to be shot?*'

'As in — '

Lennox fired. In the enclosed space he felt the physical pressure of the explosion on his eardrums. He opened his eyes again. But Angus was still standing in front of him, open-mouthed now. There was a hole in the file on the shelf behind him.

'Sorry,' Lennox said, walking two steps closer. 'I thought a sudden shot to the head would be the most humane solution here. But heads are very small. Stand still, please . . . ' An involuntary giggle escaped his lips.

'Inspector Lennox, without — '

The second shot hit the target. And the third.

'Without wishing to criticise,' Seyton said, looking down at the dead body, 'it would have been more practical if you'd ordered him down to the furnaces and done it there. Now we'll have to carry him.'

419

Lennox didn't answer. He was studying the growing pool of blood seeping out of the young man's body towards him. There was something strangely beautiful about the shapes and colours, the sparkling red, the way it extended in all directions, like red balloons. They carried Angus down to the factory floor and then picked up the empty shell casings, washed the floor and dug the first bullet out of the wall. Downstairs they removed his watch, a chain with a gold cross and manoeuvred the body into a furnace, closed it and fired it up. Waited. Lennox stared at the gutter that went from the bottom of the furnace to a tub on the floor. A low hissing sound came from the furnace.

'What happens to . . . ?'

'It evaporates,' Seyton said. 'Everything evaporates or turns to ash when the temperature's more than two thousand degrees. Except metal, which just melts.'

Lennox nodded. He couldn't take his eyes off the gutter. A grey trembling drop appeared with a membrane over it, like a coating.

'Lead,' Seyton said. 'Melts at three hundred and fifty.'

They waited. The hissing inside had stopped.

Then a golden drop came.

'We've topped a thousand now,' Seyton said.

'What . . . what's that?'

'Gold.'

'But we removed — '

'Teeth. Let's wait until it's over sixteen hundred, in case there's any steel in the body. After that all we have to do is hoover up the ash. Hey, are you OK?'

Lennox nodded. 'Bit dizzy. I've never . . . erm . . . shot anyone before. You have, so I'm sure you remember what it felt like the first time.'

'Yes,' Seyton said quietly.

Lennox was going to ask what it had felt like, but the glint in Seyton's eyes made him change his mind.

32

Macbeth stood on the roof of Inverness Casino looking to the east through a pair of binoculars. It wasn't easy to distinguish in the darkness, but wasn't that smoke coming from the top of the brick chimney at Estex? If so, the matter had been dealt with. And they would have two more men in their spider's web, two men with blood on their hands. Kite and Lennox. Kite could be useful to have around in the mayoral elections. If there were any other candidates standing. And Lennox would soon need someone else to get him dope. Before much longer Hecate would be no more than a saga as well.

Macbeth had waited by the stairs to the toilet in the central station for fifteen minutes before Strega turned up. At first he had rejected the bags of power and said he only wanted to pass on a message to Hecate. He wanted to meet him as soon as possible, inform him about his future plans and also give him a present as a token of Macbeth and Lady's gratitude for what Hecate had done for them. A present he was sure that Hecate — if the rumours about him liking gold were true — would appreciate.

Strega had said he would hear from her. Perhaps.

Yes, there was smoke coming from the chimney.

'Darling, Tourtell's here.'

Macbeth turned. Lady was standing in the doorway. She had put on her red dress.

'I'm coming. You look pretty, did I say?'

'You did. And that's all you'll say for a while, my love. Let me do the talking so we follow the plan.'

Macbeth laughed. Yes, she was back all right.

The gaming room and the restaurant were so full of customers that they literally had to force their way through to the gaming table they'd had set up in the separate small room at the end of the restaurant where Tourtell was waiting.

'Alone this evening?' Macbeth said, pressing the mayor's hand.

'Young ones have to study for exams.' Tourtell smiled. 'I saw there was a queue outside.'

'Since six o'clock,' Lady said, sitting down beside him. 'We're so full I had to persuade Jack here to be our croupier.'

'Which tells me there ought to be room for two casinos in this town,' Tourtell said, fidgeting with his black bow tie. 'You know how unhappy voters get when they aren't allowed to go out and waste their money.'

'Agreed,' Lady said, beckoning a waiter. 'Has the mayor had a lucky evening, Jack?'

'Bit early to say,' Jack said, smiling from where he stood in his red croupier's jacket. 'Another card, Mr Mayor?'

Tourtell looked at the two cards he had been given. 'Nothing ventured, nothing gained. Isn't that right, Lady?'

'You are so right. And that's why I've decided to tell you about a consortium which is keen to invest its capital by not only taking over the Obelisk but also renovating and reopening it as the most attractive casino in the country. It is of course a financial risk given that the Obelisk's reputation is being dragged through the mud right now, but we're willing to put our faith in a new owner and a new profile changing that.'

'We, Lady?'

'I'm in the consortium, yes. Together with Janovic, a property investor from Capitol. It's important, as you said, for the town to have the Obelisk up and running again. Just think of all the taxable income it will bring in from the neighbouring counties. And when we open the newly renovated, spectacular Obelisk in a few months' time it will be a tourist attraction. People will travel from Capitol to gamble in our town, Tourtell.'

Tourtell looked at the card Jack had given him and sighed. 'Doesn't look like this is going to be my night.'

'It still could be,' Lady said. 'The shares in the consortium haven't all been taken up, and we've considered you as a potential investor. You also need something to fall back on after your mayoralty is over.'

'Investor?' He laughed. 'As mayor I'm afraid I don't have the legal ability or the money to buy shares in companies, so the undoubted share-fest will have to take place without me.'

'Shares can be paid for in a variety of ways,' Lady said. 'For example, with services rendered.'

'What are you suggesting, my beautiful duchess?'

'That you publicly support Macbeth's candidature for mayor.'

Tourtell looked at his cards again. 'I've already promised I would and I'm famous for keeping my promises.'

'We mean in *this* election.'

Tourtell glanced up from his cards, at Macbeth. 'This election?'

Lady placed a hand on the mayor's arm and leaned against him. 'Yes, because you won't be standing.'

He blinked twice. 'I won't be?'

'It's true you intimated you would, but then you changed your mind.'

'And why was that?'

'Your health isn't the best, and the job of mayor requires an energetic man. A man of the future. And as soon as you're not the mayor you'll be free to join a consortium which in practice will have a monopoly over the casinos in this town and, unlike the cards you have in your hand, will make you a very rich man.'

'But I don't want to — '

'You recommend the voters elect Macbeth as your

successor because he's a man *of* the people, who works *for* the people and leads *with* the people. And because he, in his role as chief commissioner, has brought down both Sweno and Hecate and shown that he gets things *done.*'

'Hecate?'

'Macbeth and I are anticipating events here a little, but Hecate's a dead man. We're going to propose a meeting with Hecate, which he won't leave alive. This is a promise, and I'm famous for keeping promises too, my dear Mr Mayor.'

'And if I don't go along with this — ' he spat the words out like a rotten grape ' — *share deal?*'

'That would be a shame.'

Tourtell pushed his chair back, took one of his chins between his forefinger and middle finger. 'What else have you got, woman?'

'Sure we shouldn't stop there?' Lady asked.

Jack coughed, tapped his forefinger on the pack. 'Enough cards, Mr Mayor?'

'No!' Tourtell snarled without taking his eyes off Lady.

'As you wish,' she sighed. 'You'll be arrested and accused of unseemly behaviour with an underage boy.' She nodded to the card Jack had placed in front of him. 'See, you went too far. Bust.'

Tourtell stared at her with his heavy cod-eyes. His protruding wet lip twitched. 'You won't get me,' he hissed. 'Do you hear me? You won't get me!'

'If we can get Hecate, we can certainly get you.'

Tourtell stood up. Looked down at them. His chins, his scarlet face, indeed his whole body was shaking with fury. Then he spun on his heel and marched out, the inside thighs of his trousers rubbing against each other.

'What do you think?' Macbeth said after he had gone.

'Oh, he'll do what we want,' Lady said. 'Tourtell's no young fool. He just needs a bit of time to work out the odds before he makes his play.'

Caithness dreamed about Angus. He had rung her, but she didn't dare lift the receiver because she knew someone had been tampering with her phone and it would explode. She woke up and turned to the alarm clock on the bedside table beside the ringing telephone. It was past midnight. It had to be a murder. She hoped it was a murder, an everyday murder and not . . . She lifted the receiver.

'Hello?' She heard the click which had been there ever since the meeting at Estex.

'Sorry for ringing so late.' It was an unfamiliar, young man's voice. 'I just wanted to confirm that you're coming to 323 at the usual time tomorrow, Friday?'

'I'm doing what?'

'Sorry, perhaps I have the wrong number. Is that Mrs Mittbaum?'

Caithness sat up in bed, wide awake. She moistened her lips. Imagined the reels of the tape recorder in a room somewhere, perhaps the Surveillance Unit on the first floor of HQ.

'I'm not her,' she said. 'But I wouldn't worry. People with German surnames are generally punctual.'

'My apologies. Goodnight.'

'Goodnight.'

Caithness lay in bed, her heart pounding.

323. The room in the Grand Hotel where she and Duff used to have their lunchtime trysts, booked in the name of Mittbaum.

33

Hecate swung the telescope on its stand. The morning light leaked between the clouds and descended like pillars into the town. 'So Macbeth said he was planning to kill me during the meeting?'

'Yes,' Bonus said.

Hecate looked through the telescope. 'Look at that. Already a queue outside the Inverness.'

Bonus looked around. 'Are the waiters here today?'

'The boys, you mean? I book them only when I need them, same as with this penthouse suite. Owning things is tying yourself to them. And people, Bonus. But when you notice your car is so full of junk that it's slowing you down, you get rid of the junk, not the car. That's what Macbeth hasn't realised. That I'm the car, not the junk. Did you ring Macbeth, Strega?'

The tall man-woman, who had just entered the room, stepped out of the shadows.

'Yes.'

'And what did you arrange?'

'He'll come here alone tomorrow at six to meet you.'

'Thank you.'

She merged back into the shadows.

'I wonder how he dares,' Bonus said.

'Dares?' Hecate said. 'He can't stop himself. Macbeth has become like a moth drawn helplessly to the light, to power.'

'And like a moth he'll burn.'

'Maybe. What Macbeth has most to fear is — like the moth — himself.'

★ ★ ★

426

Caithness looked at her watch. Twelves minutes to twelve. Then she directed her gaze at the hotel door in front of her. She would never forget the brass numbers, however long she lived and however many men she met, loved and shared days and nights with.

323.

She could still turn back. But she had come here. Why? Because she thought she would meet Duff again and something had changed? The only thing that had changed was that now she knew she would be able to manage perfectly well without him. Or was it because she suspected that behind the door there could be another chance, a chance to do the right thing? Which she had failed to do when she walked away from Angus at Estex. She had got hold of his private phone number but there had been no answer.

She raised her hand.

The door would explode if she knocked.

She knocked.

Waited. Was about to knock again when the door opened. A young man stood there.

'Who are you?' she asked.

'Fleance, son of Banquo.' The voice was the same as on the phone. He stepped aside. 'Please come in, Mrs Mittbaum.'

The hotel room was as before.

Malcolm was as before.

But not Duff. He had aged. Not only in the months and years since she had last seen him sitting on the plush-covered hotel bed waiting for her like now, but in the days that had passed since he had left her flat for the last time.

'You came,' Duff said.

She nodded.

Malcolm coughed and cleaned his glasses. 'You don't seem particularly surprised to see us here, Caithness.'

'I'm most surprised that *I'm* here,' she said. 'What's going on?'

'What are you hoping is going on, Caithness?'

'I'm hoping we're going to remove Macbeth.'

★ ★ ★

Seyton pushed down the lever on the iron door and opened it. Macbeth stepped inside and twisted the switch. The neon tubes blinked twice before casting a cold blue light on the shelves of ammunition boxes and various weapons. On the floor in the square room were a safe and two half-dismantled Gatling guns. Macbeth went over to the safe, twirled the dial and opened it. Pulled out a zebra-striped suitcase. 'The ammo room was the only place with thick enough walls where we dared to keep it,' he said. 'And even then, in a safe.'

'So it's a bomb?'

'Yep,' said Macbeth, who had crouched down and opened the suitcase. 'Disguised as a case of gold.' He lifted out the bars covering the bottom. 'The bars are actually iron with a gold coating, but the bomb in the space beneath — ' he opened the lid to the false bottom ' — is genuine enough.'

'Look at that,' Seyton said with a low whistle. 'Your classic IED time bomb.'

'Ingenious, eh? The gold means no one will be suspicious about the weight. This was designed to blow up the Inverness.'

'Aha, it's that case. And why wasn't the bomb destroyed?'

'My idea,' Macbeth said, studying the clockwork machinery. 'It's a fantastically intricate piece of work and we had it fully disarmed. I thought we at SWAT might find a use for it one day. And now we have . . . '
He touched a matchstick-size metal pin. 'You just have to pull this, and the clock counts down. It looks easy,

but it took us almost forty minutes to defuse it, and there are only twenty-five minutes and fifty-five seconds left on the clock, so if I pull this out there's no way back.'

'Your discussions with Hecate will have to be quick then.'

'Oh, it won't be a long meeting. I'll say that the gold is proof of my gratitude for what he's already done and there'll be more if he helps me to be elected as mayor.'

'Will he, do you think?'

'I don't know, and he'll be dead ten minutes later anyway. The point is that he mustn't suspect anything, and he knows that in this town you don't get anything for nothing. I'll ask him to think about it, look at my watch, say I have a meeting with a management group — which is true — and go.'

'Sorry . . . ' They turned to the door. It was Ricardo. 'Telephone.'

'Tell them I'll ring back,' Seyton said.

'Not for you, for the chief commissioner.'

Macbeth heard the almost imperceptible coldness in the voice. He had felt it when he came to SWAT before. How the men had dutifully mumbled a greeting but had looked away seemingly busy with other things.

'For me?'

'Your receptionist has put it through. She says it's the mayor.'

'Show me the way.'

He followed the SWAT veteran. Something about Ricardo's narrow, aristocratic face, the shiny blackness of his skin and the suppleness of his majestic gait had always made Macbeth think the officer must be descended from a lion-hunting tribe. What was it called again? A loyal man of honour. Macbeth knew Ricardo would be willing to follow his brothers to the death if necessary. A man worth his weight in gold. Genuine gold.

'Anything wrong, Ricardo?'

'Sir?'

'You seem quiet today. Anything I should know?'

'We're a bit worried about Angus, that's all.'

'I heard he'd been off colour. This job isn't for everyone.'

'My worry is he hasn't appeared for work, and no one knows where he is.'

'He'll turn up soon enough. He probably needed some time out for a think. But, yes, I can see you're concerned he might have done something drastic.'

'Something drastic has happened to . . . ' Ricardo stopped by the open office door. Inside a telephone receiver lay on a desk. 'I don't think Angus has done anything.'

Macbeth stopped and looked at him. 'So what do you think?'

Their eyes met. And Macbeth saw nothing of the admiration and happiness directed at him that he was used to from his men in SWAT. Ricardo lowered his eyes. 'I don't know, sir.'

Macbeth closed the office door behind him and took the phone.

'Yes, Tourtell?'

'I lied about being the mayor so I'd be put through. The way you lied. You promised me no one would die.'

Macbeth thought it was strange how fear trumped arrogance. There wasn't a trace left of the latter in Walt Kite's voice.

'You must have misunderstood,' Macbeth said. 'I meant no one *in your family* would die.'

'You — '

'And they won't. If you continue to do as I say. I'm busy, so if there was nothing else, Kite.'

All he heard at the other end was an electric crackle.

'Good job we cleared that up,' Macbeth said and rang off. Looked at the photograph pinned to the wall above the desk. Showing the whole of the SWAT gang at the Bricklayers Arms. The broad smiles and the raised beer mugs testifying to the celebration of another successful mission. There was Banquo. Ricardo. Angus and the others. And Macbeth himself. So young. Such a stupid smile. So ignorant. So blissfully powerless.

★　★　★

'So that's the plan,' Malcolm said. 'And apart from you, we three are the only ones who know about it. What do you say, Caithness? Are you with us?'

They sat close to one another in the cramped hotel room, and Caithness looked from one face to the next. 'And if I say the plan's crazy and I won't have anything to do with it, will you let me stroll away, so that I can blab to Macbeth?'

'Yes,' Malcolm said.

'Isn't that naive?'

'Well. If you were thinking of running to Macbeth I assume you would have first told us it was a brilliant plan and that you were in. And *then* you would have blabbed. We know asking you is a calculated risk. But we refuse to believe there aren't good people out there, people who care, who put the town before their own good.'

'And you think I'm one of them?'

'Duff thinks you're one of them,' Malcolm said. 'He puts it stronger than that in fact: he says he *knows* you are. He says you're better than him.'

Caithness looked at Duff.

'It's a brilliant idea and I'm in,' she said.

Malcolm and Fleance laughed, and yes, even in Duff's sad, lifeless eyes she saw a brief glimpse of laughter.

34

At five minutes to six Macbeth entered the reception area at the Obelisk hotel. The spacious lobby was empty apart from a doorman, a couple of bellboys and three receptionists in black suits talking in low voices, like undertakers.

Macbeth headed straight for the lift, which was open, went in and pressed the button for the nineteenth floor. Clenched his teeth and blew out to equalise the pressure. The fastest lift in the country — they had even advertised it, probably to appeal to the country cousins. The handle of the suitcase felt slippery against his hand. Why had Collum, the unlucky gambler, chosen zebra stripes to disguise a bomb?

The lift door slid open and he walked out. He knew from drawings of the building that the stairs to the penthouse suite were to the left. He trotted up the fifteen steps and along a short corridor to the only door on the floor. Raised his hand to knock. But stopped and studied his hand. Did he detect a tremble, the tremble veterans said they got after around seven years at SWAT? The seven-year tremble. He couldn't see one. They said it was worse if there *wasn't* one, then it was definitely time to get out.

Macbeth knocked.

Heard footsteps.

His own breathing.

He didn't have any weapons on him. He would be searched, and there was no reason to make anyone jumpy, after all this was supposed to resemble a business meeting. Repeated to himself that he was only going to say he was standing for mayor and hand over the suitcase as thanks for services rendered and future favours. That explanation should be plausible.

'Mr Macbeth, sir?' It was a young boy. He was wearing jodhpurs and white gloves.

'Yes?'

The boy stepped to the side. 'Please come in.'

The penthouse suite had views in all directions. It had stopped raining, and in the west, behind the Inverness, the thin cloud cover was coloured orange by the afternoon sun. Macbeth's eyes roamed further, over the harbour in the south and the factory towers to the east.

'Mr Hand said he would be a little delayed, but not by much,' the boy said. 'I'll bring you some champagne.'

The door closed gently and Macbeth was alone. He sat down in one of the leather chairs by the round Plexiglass table. 'Mr Hand. Right.'

Macbeth looked at his watch. It was precisely three minutes and thirty-five seconds since he had been sitting with Seyton in the SWAT car and had pulled out the pin to activate the countdown. Twenty-two minutes and twenty seconds to detonation.

He got up, went over to the big brown fridge standing by one wall and opened it. Empty. Same with the wardrobe. He peered into the bedroom. Untouched. No one lived here. He went back to the leather chair and sat down.

Twenty minutes and six seconds.

He tried not to think, but thoughts came anyway.

They said that time ran out.

That darkness thickened.

That death drew closer.

Macbeth breathed deeply and calmly. And what if death came now? It would of course be a meaningless end, but isn't that the case with all ends? We're interrupted in mid-sentence in the narrative about ourselves, and the end hangs in the air, with no meaning, no conclusion, no unravelling final act. A short echo of the last, semi-articulated word and you're forgotten. Forgotten, forgotten, not even the biggest statue can change that. The person you were, the person you *really* were, disappears faster than concentric rings in water. And what was the point of this short, interrupted guest appearance? Of playing along as best you can, seizing the pleasures and happiness life has to offer while it lasts? Or leaving a mark, changing the direction of things, making the world a slightly better place before you yourself have to leave it? Or perhaps the point is to reproduce, to put more suitable small creatures on the earth in the hope that humans will at some point become the demi-gods they imagine they are? Or is there simply no meaning? Perhaps we're just detached sentences in an eternal chaotic babble in which everyone talks and no one listens, and our worst premonition finally turns out to be correct: you are alone. All alone.

Seventeen minutes.

Alone. Then Banquo had come along and taken him to his heart, made him part of his family. And now he had got rid of him. Got rid of everyone. And was alone again. Him and Lady. But what did he want with all this? *Did* he want it? Or did he want to give it to someone? Was it for her, for Lady?

Fourteen minutes.

And did he really think it would last? Wasn't it all as fragile as Lady's mind, wasn't it doomed to crash to the ground, this empire they were building, wasn't it just a question of time? Perhaps, but what else do we have but time, a little time, the frustratingly temporary nature of impermanence?

Eleven minutes.

Where was Hecate? It was already too late to take the suitcase to the harbour and heave it into the sea. The alternative was to dump it under a manhole cover in the street, but it was bright daylight, and the chances of

Macbeth being recognised were high after the recent news programmes and press exposure.

Seven minutes.

Macbeth made up his mind. If Hecate wasn't here in two minutes he would go. Leave the suitcase. Hope Hecate arrived before the bomb went off.

Five minutes. Four minutes.

Macbeth got up and went to the door. Listened.

Nothing.

Time to withdraw.

He gripped the door handle. Pulled. Pulled harder. Locked. He was locked in.

⋆　⋆　⋆

'Do you mean you were cheated, sir?' Lady was standing by the roulette table. She had been called because a customer was beginning to cause trouble. The man wasn't completely sober, nor was he drunk though. Creased tweed jacket. She didn't have to guess even: ex-Obelisk customer from bumpkin land.

'Of course I was,' the man said as Lady surveyed the room. It was just as full this evening. She would have to take on more staff, they needed at least two more in the bar. 'The ball lands on fourteen three times in a row. What are the chances of that, eh?'

'Exactly the same as they are for three, twenty-four and then sixteen,' Lady said. 'One in fifty thousand. Exactly the same as for any combination of numbers.'

'But — '

'Sir.' Lady smiled, lightly touching his arm. 'Has anyone ever told you that during a bombing raid you should hide in a bomb crater because lightning never strikes twice in the same place? That was when you were cheated. But now you're in Inverness Casino, sir.' She passed him a ticket. 'Have a drink at the bar at my expense. Please consider the logic of what I've just said

435

and we can talk afterwards, OK?'

The man leaned back and scrutinised her. Took the ticket and was gone.

'Lady.'

She turned. Above her towered a tall broad-shouldered woman. Or man.

'Mr Hand would like to speak to you.' The man-woman nodded towards an elderly man standing a few metres away. He wore a white suit, had dyed dark hair and was leaning on a gilded walking stick while examining the chandelier above him with interest.

'If this could wait for a couple of minutes . . . ' Lady smiled.

'He also has a nickname. Starting with H.'

Lady stopped.

'He prefers Hand.' The man-woman smiled.

Lady walked over to the old man.

'Baccarat crystal or Bohemian?' he asked without taking his eyes off the chandelier.

'Bohemian,' she said. 'It is, as you can see, a slightly smaller copy of the chandelier in Dolmabahçe Palace in Istanbul.'

'Unfortunately I've never been there, ma'am, but I was once in a chapel in a small place in Czechoslovakia. After the Black Death they had so many skeletons lying around there wasn't enough room for them. So they employed this one-eyed monk to tidy up and stack the remains. But instead of doing that he used them to decorate the chapel. They have an attractive chandelier there made out of skulls and human bones. Some might think that shows little respect to the dead; I would maintain the opposite.' The old man shifted his gaze from the chandelier to her. 'What greater gift can mankind receive than the touch of immortality inherent in retaining a function even after death, ma'am? Like becoming a coral reef. A chandelier. Or a symbol and guiding star, a chief commissioner who dies so prematurely that people still have this notion of a good person, a selfless leader, so bless-edly prematurely that there was never time to unmask him as another megalomaniacal corrupt king. I'm of the opinion that we need such deaths, ma'am. I hope the one-eyed monk received the gratitude he deserved.'

Lady swallowed. Usually she could see something in a person's eyes which she could interpret, understand and then use. But behind this man's eyes she saw nothing — it was like looking into the eyes of a blind man. 'How may I be of assistance, Mr Hand?'

'As you know, I should be at a meeting with your husband. He's sitting in a hotel suite waiting to kill me.'

Lady felt her windpipe contract and knew that if she spoke now her voice would be high and squeaky. So she refrained.

'But as I can't see that I'd be serving any good purpose dead, I thought instead I'd talk sense with the sensible one of you two.'

Lady looked at him. He nodded and smiled a sad, gentle smile, like a wise grandfather. Like someone who understood her and told her that excuses were unnecessary and pointless anyway.

'I see,' Lady said with a hefty cough. 'I think I need a drink. What can I offer you?'

'Well, if your bartender knows how to make a dirty martini . . . ?'

'Come with me.'

They went to the bar, where people were queueing. Lady ploughed her way to behind the bar counter, grabbed two martini glasses, poured from the gin bottle and then the Martini bottle, mixed the cocktails on the worktop beneath the counter. Less than a minute later she was back and handing the old man his glass. 'I hope it's dirty enough.'

He tasted. 'Definitely. But unless I'm mistaken it has an extra ingredient.'

'Two. It's my own recipe. This way?'

'And what are the ingredients?'

'That's a business secret of course, but let me put it this way: I think drinks should have a local touch.' Lady led the old man and the tall man-woman into the empty room behind the restaurant.

'Naturally, a man in my position has some sympathy with you wanting to protect your business secrets,' Hecate said, waiting for the man-woman to pull out a chair for him. 'So please excuse me if I've revealed your intentions to take over my town. I respect ambition, but I have other plans.'

Lady sipped her martini. 'Are you going to kill my husband?'

Hecate didn't answer.

She repeated the question.

★　★　★

Macbeth stared at the door and felt his mouth go dry. Locked in. He imagined he could *hear* the bomb ticking behind him now. There was no other way out — exits were one of the things he always checked when he examined drawings of buildings. Outside the windows the smooth wall dropped twenty floors to the tarmac.

Locked in. Trapped. Hecate's trap. His own trap.

He breathed through his mouth and tried to shut out the mounting panic.

His eyes swept the room. There was nowhere to hide, the bomb was too powerful. His eyes fell on the door again. On the thumb turn lock under the handle.

The thumb turn. He let his breath out in a long, relieved hiss. Shit, what was wrong with him? He laughed. A hotel door is *supposed* to lock when it closes. He lived in a hotel himself, for Christ's sake. All you had to do was turn the lock to open the door.

He reached out a hand. Hesitated. Why was something telling him it couldn't be so easy? That it never was, that where he was it would be impossible to get out, and that he was doomed to blow himself sky-high?

He could feel his fingers slippery with sweat as they closed round the lock. Turned.

The lock turned.

He pressed the handle.

Pushed open the door.

Went out. Rushed down the stairs and along the corridor, cursing quietly.

Stood in front of the lift and pressed the button.

Saw on the wall display it was on its way up from the ground floor.

Looked at his watch. Two minutes and forty seconds.

The lift was approaching. Could he hear something? A clinking, voices? Were there people in the lift? What if Hecate was there? There was no time to go back to the suite and talk now.

Macbeth ran. According to the drawings the fire escape was round the corner to the left.

It was.

He pushed open the door as he heard a *pling* signalling that the lift had arrived. Held his breath and the door as he waited.

Voices. High-pitched, boys' voices.

'I don't quite understand what — '

'Mr Hand isn't coming. We've just been told to delay the man in there for half an hour. Hope he likes champagne.'

The sound of trolley wheels.

Macbeth closed the door behind him and ran down the stairs.

On every floor there was a number.

He stopped at seventeen.

★ ★ ★

Lady nodded. Breathed. 'But you're going to kill him another day?'

'That depends. Did you put apple juice in?'

'No. Depends on what?'

'If this is just temporary confusion. You both seem to have stopped using my products, and that's perhaps best for all parties.'

'You won't kill him because you need him as chief commissioner. And now you've exposed Macbeth's plans once, you reckon he's learned his lesson. A dog isn't trained until it's been disobedient and has received its punishment.'

The old man turned to the man-woman. 'Do you now see what I mean when I say she's the smart one of the two?'

'So what do you want from me, Mr Hand?'

'Ginger? No, the recipe's a secret you said, so your answer won't be reliable. I just wanted to make you aware of the choice you have. Obey and I'll protect Macbeth against anything that can harm him. He'll be your Tithonos. Disobey and I'll kill both of you the way you do with dogs which turn out to be untrainable. Look around, Lady. Look at all you stand to lose. You have everything you've ever dreamed of. So you don't have to dream any more. As for recipes, if your dreams are too big they're a recipe for disaster.' The old man knocked back the rest of the drink and put the glass on the table. 'Pepper. That's one of the two ingredients.'

'Blood,' Lady said.

'Really?' He laid his hands on the walking stick and levered himself into a standing position. 'Human blood?'

Lady shrugged. 'Is that so important? You believe it is, and you seemed to like the recipe.'

The old man laughed. 'You and I could be very good friends if circumstances were different, Lady.'

'In another life,' she said.

'In another life, my little Lily.' He banged his stick twice on the floor. 'Stay where you are. We'll find our way out.'

Lady retained her smile until he was out of sight. Then she gasped for breath, felt the room whirling, had to hold on to the chair arm. *Lily.* He knew. How *could* he know?

★   ★   ★

Seventeenth floor.

Macbeth looked at his watch. One minute left. So why had he stopped? They must be carrying the trolley up the steps. They would be there when the bomb went off. So what? They were Hecate's boys. They had to be part of the whole set-up, so what was the problem? No one in this town was innocent. So why had this *something* come into his mind right now? Was it something from a speech? Written by Lady, given by him? Or was it from even longer ago, an oath they had sworn when they graduated from police college? Or before that too, something Banquo had said to him? Something, there was something, but he couldn't remember what. Just that . . .

Shit, shit, shit!
Fifty seconds.
Macbeth ran.
Up the stairs.

35

'Come with me!' Macbeth screamed.

The two young boys stared at the man who had suddenly appeared in the doorway to the penthouse suite. One of them was holding a bottle of champagne and had started loosening the wire from the cork.

'Now!' Macbeth shouted.

'Sir, we — '

'You've got thirty seconds if you don't want to die!'

'Calm down, sir.'

Macbeth grabbed the champagne cooler and hurled it at the window. The ice cubes bounced and ricocheted with a crackle across the parquet floor. He lowered his voice in the following silence: 'A bomb will go off inside here in twenty-five seconds.'

Then he turned and set off at a run. Down the stairs. With the clatter of footsteps in his ears. Sprinted past the lift. Held the door to the stairs open for the two boys.

'Run! Run!'

Closed the door behind them and charged after them.

Fifteen seconds. Macbeth had no idea how big the blast would be, but if the bomb had been made to destroy a building as solid as the Inverness they would need to get as far away as possible. Sixteenth floor. He noticed a headache coming on as though he could already feel the pressure of the explosion on his eardrums, eyeballs, inside his mouth. Fourteenth. He checked his watch. It was fifteen seconds over.

Eleventh floor. Still nothing. The countdown mechanism might not have been quite accurate or a deliberate delay had been built in. The two boys in front of him began to slow down. Macbeth yelled and they speeded up again.

On the eighth floor they burst through the fire escape door into a corridor, but Macbeth continued downwards, using the main stairs. The lift was a death trap. When he reached the ground floor the bomb was almost three minutes overdue.

He walked into reception. The same members of staff were there, hovering over the counter as though nothing had happened, unaware of him. He went out into the rain. Looked up. Stood like that until his neck hurt. Then he started across the deserted square towards Seyton and the waiting car. What the hell had happened? Or rather, what hadn't happened? Had the bomb got damp in the police HQ basement? Had someone managed to stop the countdown after he left the penthouse suite? Or had it detonated, but with much less power than SWAT's bomb expert had given him to believe? And what now? He pulled up. What if Hecate or his people went to the suite and discovered he had left a bomb there? He had to go back and fetch the suitcase.

Macbeth turned. Took two paces. Saw his shadow outlined on the cobbles and heard a dull boom like thunder. For a moment he thought it was hail. White granules hit him on the face and hands, pitter-pattered on the cobbles around him and danced on the parked cars. A shower head smacked to the ground a few metres from him. He glanced upwards, then was sent flying as he heard something crash beside him. Macbeth raised his arms to protect himself, but the man who had tackled him had already got up, brushed down his grey coat and run off. Macbeth saw a smashed brown fridge where he had been standing a second ago.

He rested his head on the cool cobbles.

Flames rose from the top of the Obelisk, and black smoke billowed into the sky. Something bounced over the cobbles towards him and came to rest beside his head. He picked it up. It was still wrapped in its wire cage.

443

* ⋆ ⋆

'What the hell happened?' Seyton said as Macbeth got in the car.

'Tourtell,' Macbeth said. 'He warned Hecate. Drive.'

'Tourtell?' Seyton said, pulling away from the pavement as the wipers swept small fragments of white glass from the windscreen.

'Tourtell's the only person who knew about our plan, and he must have informed Hecate hoping that he would kill me instead.'

'And Hecate didn't try to kill you?'

'No. Quite the contrary. He saved me.'

'How come?'

'He needs his puppets.'

'What?'

'Nothing, Seyton. Drive to the Inverness.'

Macbeth scanned the pavement, scanned the people gawping up. He searched for grey coats. How many were there? Did they all wear grey coats or only some of them? Were they always there? He closed his eyes. Immortal. As immortal as a wooden puppet. The pressure inside his head rose. And a strange thought whirled past. Hecate's promise to make him invulnerable was not a blessing but a curse. He could feel the wire on his skin as he rolled the cork from the champagne bottle between his fingers and heard the first police siren.

Seyton had stopped in front of the Inverness and Macbeth was about to get out of the car when he heard Tourtell's voice.

'Turn up the radio,' Macbeth said and got back in.

' . . . and to counter the rumours and out of respect for you, my dear fellow citizens, and your right to know about your elected representatives, I have today decided to tell you that fifteen years ago I had a brief extramarital affair which led to the birth of a son. In agreement with the relevant parties — that is, my son's mother and my wife — it was decided to keep this out of the public eye. I've always stayed in close contact with my son and his mother and maintained them using my own means. Not going public at that time was a judgement, taking several parties into consideration. The town was not one of them as at that juncture I wasn't in office and didn't need to answer to anyone except those closest to me and to myself. Now, however, things are different, and now is the right time to disclose this information. My son's mother is seriously ill, and with her consent two months ago he came to live with me. Since then I have taken Kasi with me to public events, where I have introduced him as my son, but paradoxically it seems my honesty has led to other rumours. The truth, as we know, is the last thing to be believed. I am not proud of being unfaithful fifteen years ago, but beyond having sought the forgiveness of those closest to me, there's little I can do about it. Just as little as I can do about people judging my abilities as a leader on the basis of my private life. All I can do is ask you for your trust as indeed I trust you now by making public details which are extremely painful and precious to me. I may not have always acted in ways that make me feel proud; however, I am proud of my fifteen-year-old son, Kasi. Last night I had a long talk with him, and he told me to do what I'm doing now. To tell the whole of this town that I'm his father.' Tourtell took a deep breath before concluding with a clear vibrato in his voice, 'And that he's my son.' He coughed. 'And to win the coming mayoral election.'

Pause. A woman's voice, also clearly moved.

'That was an announcement from Mayor Tourtell. Now back to the news. There has been a major explosion in District 4, to be precise at the top of the

Obelisk Casino. No one has been reported dead or injured, but — '

Macbeth switched off the radio.

'Damn,' he said. Then he burst into laughter.

36

Lady lay back against the pillows and stretched a foot out from under her dressing gown. Towards Macbeth, who was sitting on a low stool by the end of the bed. She had hung up two red dresses. He stroked her slim ankle and her smooth shaved leg.

'So Hecate knew about our plans,' he said. 'Did he say who had told him?'

'No,' Lady said. 'But he said you would be my Tithonos if we behaved.'

'Who's Tithonos?'

'A handsome Greek who was granted eternal life. But he also said that if we don't obey he'll kill us like dogs that don't respond to training.'

'Hm. It could only have been Tourtell who told him.'

'That's the third time you've said that, darling.'

'And not only did the slippery bugger blab. The boy really is his son. The question is now whether people in this town want a lecher as their mayor.'

'One single affair fifteen years ago?' Lady said. 'Which Tourtell admitted at the time, begged forgiveness for and has since paid for by looking after mother and son? And now when she's ill St Tourtell takes his son in? People will love him for it, darling. He's made a mistake most people will understand and shown shame and kindness afterwards. Tourtell has become of the people. This announcement is a stroke of genius. They're going to turn out in full force to vote for him.'

'Tourtell's going to stand and win. So what can we do?'

'Yes, what can we do? Well, first things first. Which dress, Jack?'

'The Spanish one,' Jack said, taking a cup of tea from

the tray and placing it on Lady's bedside table.

'Thank you. What about Tourtell and Hecate, Jack? Shall we do something or is it too risky?'

'I'm no strategist, ma'am. But I've read that when you have enemies on two fronts there are two classic strategies. One is to negotiate an armistice with one enemy, then concentrate your forces to knock out the other and attack without warning. The second is to set the two enemies against each other, wait until they are both weakened and then strike.'

He gave a cup of coffee to Macbeth.

'Remind me to promote you,' Macbeth said.

'Oh, he's already been promoted,' Lady said. 'We're fully booked for the next two weeks, so Jack now has an assistant. An assistant who'll address him as sir.'

Jack laughed. 'This wasn't my idea.'

'It's mine,' Lady said. 'And it's not an idea. It's only sensible to have rules for forms of address. It reminds everyone about the hierarchy so that misunderstandings can be avoided. If a mayor declares a state of emergency, it's important for example to know who runs the town. And who does?'

Jack shook his head.

'The chief commissioner,' Macbeth said, sipping his coffee. 'Until the chief commissioner suspends the state of emergency.'

'Really?' Jack said. 'And what if the mayor dies? Does the chief commissioner take over then too?'

'Yes,' Macbeth said. 'Until a new mayor is elected.'

'These are rules Kenneth introduced right after the war,' Lady said. 'At that time they placed a lot of emphasis on dynamic, assertive leadership in crises.'

'Sounds sensible,' Jack said.

'The great thing about a state of emergency is that the chief commissioner runs absolutely everything. He can suspend the justice system, censor the press, defer elections indefinitely; he is in brief . . . '

'A dictator.'

'Exactly, Jack.' Lady stirred her tea. 'Unfortunately, Tourtell will hardly agree to declare a state of emergency, so we'll have to make do with the next best option.'

'Which is?'

'Tourtell dying, of course.' Lady sipped her tea.

'Dying? As in . . . ?'

'An assassination,' Macbeth said, squeezing her calf muscle gently. 'That's what you mean, isn't it, my love?'

She nodded. 'The chief commissioner announces that he's taking over the running of the town while the assassination is investigated. Could there be political motives behind it? Hecate? Did it have anything to do with Tourtell's infidelity? The investigation drags on of course.'

'I can only rule temporarily,' Macbeth said, 'until a new mayor is elected.'

'But, darling, look, there's blood on the streets. Police officers murdered and politicians assassinated. The chief commissioner, who now functions as mayor, would probably decide to declare a state of emergency. And postpone the election indefinitely until things have calmed down. And it's the chief commissioner who determines when things have calmed down.'

Macbeth felt the same childish pleasure as when he and Duff had been kings of the castle in the school playground at the orphanage, and even the tough older kids had to accept it. 'In practice we'd have limitless power for as long as we wanted. And you're sure Capitol can't intercede?'

'Darling, I've had a long and interesting conversation with one of our Supreme Court judges today. Capitol has few or no sanctions, provided that the measures Kenneth introduced don't conflict with federal laws.'

'I see.' Macbeth rubbed his chin. 'Interesting indeed. So all that's needed is for Tourtell to die or declare a state of emergency himself.'

Jack coughed. 'Anything else, ma'am?'

'No, thanks, Jack.' Lady cheerfully waved him away.

Macbeth heard the hollow bass from the ground floor as Jack opened the door to the corridor and the wailing siren of an ambulance that followed after he closed it.

'Tourtell's making plans to stop us,' Lady said. 'The assassination will have to be soon.'

'What about Hecate? If this snake is Tourtell and Hecate, then Tourtell is the tail and Hecate the head. And cutting off the tail only makes it more dangerous. We have to tackle the head first!'

'No.'

'No? He says he'll kill us if we don't obey. Do you want to be his trained dog?'

'Sit still and listen to me now, darling. You heard Jack. Arrange an armistice with one party and attack the other. This is not the moment to challenge Hecate. What's more, I'm not sure that Hecate and Tourtell actually work together. If so, Hecate would have said we should stay away from Tourtell and the mayoral office. But he hasn't, not even after the speculation that you would stand. As long as Hecate thinks we've been taught a lesson and we're now his obedient dogs he'll only applaud us — and indirectly himself — taking political control of the town. Do you understand? We take care of one enemy now and get what we want. Then we decide what we have to do about Hecate afterwards.'

Macbeth ran his hand up her leg, past her knee. She fell quiet, closed her eyes, and he listened to her breathing. The breathing that with non-verbal commands determined what his hand should and shouldn't do.

★ ★ ★

450

Through the afternoon and night the rain continued to wash the town that was never clean. Hammered down on the roof of the Grand Hotel, where Fleance, Duff, Malcolm and Caithness had agreed they would stay until it was over. It was two o'clock in the morning when Caithness was woken by knocking on the door to her room. At once she knew who it was.

It wasn't the number of knocks, the interval between them or the force of them. It was the style. He knocked with a flat hand. And she knew the hand, every crease and cranny of it.

She opened the door a fraction.

Rain dripped from Duff's clothes and hair, his teeth were chattering and his face was so pale the scar was barely visible. 'Sorry, but I need a really hot shower.'

'Haven't you . . . ?'

'Fleance and I share a room with bunk beds and a sink.'

She opened the door a bit more, and he slipped in.

'Where have you been?' she asked.

'To the cemetery,' he said from inside the bathroom.

'In the middle of the night?'

'Not so many people out and about.' She heard the water being switched on. She stood close to the bathroom door. 'Duff?'

'Yes.'

'I just wanted to say I'm sorry.'

'What?' he shouted.

She cleared her throat and raised her voice. 'About your family.'

She listened to the beating of the water, which muffled her words, and stared into the steam that hid him from her.

When Duff came out again in the dressing gown that hung in the bathroom and with his wet clothes over one arm Caithness was dressed and lying on the broad bed. He pulled a soggy packet of cigarettes from the pocket

451

of his wet trousers. She nodded, and he lay beside her. Caithness rested her head on his arm and looked up at the domed yellow glass ceiling light. The bowl was dotted with dead insects.

'That's what happens when you get too close to the light,' he said. So he still had the ability to guess what she was thinking.

'Icarus,' she said.

'Macbeth,' he said and lit a cigarette.

'I didn't know you'd started smoking again,' she said.

'Well, it's a little strange. I've actually never liked this shit.' He grimaced and blew a big fat smoke ring up at the ceiling.

She sniggered. 'So why did you start?'

'Have I never told you?'

'There's a lot you've never told me.'

He coughed and passed her the cigarette. 'Because I wanted to be like Macbeth.'

'I'd have thought he wanted to be like you.'

'He looked so damned good. And was so . . . free. In harmony with himself and happy, so happy in his own skin. I never was.'

'But you had intellect.' She inhaled and passed the cigarette back. 'And the ability to persuade people you were right.'

'People don't like to realise they're wrong. And I didn't have the ability to persuade them to like me. He did.'

'Cheap charm, Duff. Look who he is now. He duped everyone.'

'No.' Duff shook his head. 'No, Macbeth didn't dupe anyone. He was straight-talking and upfront. No saint, but no ulterior motives — what you saw was what you got. Perhaps he didn't impress everyone with his wit or originality when he spoke, but you trusted every word. And rightly so.'

'Trust? He's an unfeeling murderer, Duff.'

'You're wrong. Macbeth is full of feelings. That's why he can't hurt a fly. Or to be accurate, especially not a fly. An aggressive wasp, yes, but a defenceless fly? Never, regardless of how annoying it is.'

'How can you defend him, Duff? You who have lost — '

'I'm not defending him. Of course he's a murderer. All I'm saying is he can't kill anyone who can't defend himself. It's happened only once. And he did it to save me.'

'Oh yes?' she said. 'Are you going to tell me about it?'

He sucked hard on the cigarette. 'It was when he killed the Norse Rider on the country road out by Forres. A young guy who'd just seen me kill his comrade, who I'd mistaken for Sweno.'

'So they didn't pull guns on you?'

Duff shook his head.

'But then Macbeth's no better than you,' Caithness said.

'Yes, he was. I killed for my own sake. He did it for someone else.'

'Because that's what we do in the police. We take care of each other.'

'No, because he thought he owed it to me.'

Caithness sat up on her elbows. 'Owed it to you?'

Duff held his cigarette up to the ceiling, pinched one eye shut and aimed above the glow with the other. 'When Grandad died and I ended up in the orphanage, I was almost too old — I was fourteen. Macbeth and I were the same age, but he'd been there since he was five. Macbeth and I shared a room and became friends straight away. In those days Macbeth stammered. And especially when Saturday night approached, which was when he disappeared from the room in the middle of the night and returned an hour later. He would never tell me where he'd been; it was only when I jokingly threatened to report him to the home's feared director,

Lorreal, that he said he doubted that would do much good.' Duff pulled hard on the cigarette. 'Because that was where he'd been.'

'You mean . . . the director —— '

' —— had been abusing Macbeth for as long as he could remember. I couldn't believe my ears. Lorreal had done things to him . . . you can't imagine anyone would do to another person or find any enjoyment in. The one time Macbeth had stood up against him Lorreal had half-killed him and kept him locked up for two weeks in the so-called correction room in the cellar, a genuine cell. I was so furious I cried. Because I knew every word was true. Macbeth never lies. So I said we had to kill Lorreal. I would help him. And Macbeth agreed.'

'You planned to *kill* him?'

'No,' Duff said, passing her the cigarette. 'We didn't plan so much. We just killed him.'

'You . . . '

'We went to his room one Thursday. Checked at the door that Lorreal was snoring. Went in. Macbeth knew the room inside out. I kept watch inside the door while Macbeth went to the bed and raised a knife. But time passed, and when my eyes had got used to the darkness I saw he was standing there as rigid as a pillar of salt. Then he crumpled and came over to me, whispering that he c-c-couldn't do it. So I took the knife, went over to Lorreal and thrust it hard into his snoring mouth. Lorreal twitched one more time, then he stopped snoring. There wasn't much blood. We left straight after.'

'My God.' Caithness was curled up in the fetal position. 'What happened afterwards?'

'Not much. There were two hundred young suspects to choose from. No one noticed that Macbeth was stammering more than before. And when he did a runner a couple of weeks later, no one connected that with the murder. Kids ran away all the time.'

'And then you and Macbeth met up again?'

'I saw him a couple of times down by the central station. I wanted to talk to him, but he legged it. You know, like a bankruptee from a creditor. Then we met several years later at police college. By then he was clean and had completely stopped stammering — he was a very different boy. The boy *I* wanted to be.'

'Because he was a clean-living kind-hearted man without a murder on his conscience like you?'

'Macbeth has never seen being able to murder in cold blood as a virtue but a weakness. In all his time at SWAT he killed only if he, or any of his men, was attacked.'

'And all these murders?'

'He ordered others to carry them out for him.'

'Killing women and children. I think he's become a different man from the one you knew, Duff.'

'People don't change.'

'*You've* changed.'

'Have I really?'

'If not, you wouldn't be here. Fighting this fight. Spoken as you have about Macbeth. You're a total egoist. Ready to ride roughshod over everything and everyone who's in your way. Your colleagues, your family. Me.'

'I can only remember really wanting to change once, and that was when I wanted to be like Macbeth. And when I realised that was impossible I had to become something better. Someone who could take what he wanted, even if it had less value for me than for who it belonged to, the way Hecate took that boy's eye. Do you know when I fell in love with Meredith?'

Caithness shook her head.

'When all four of us were sitting there — Macbeth, me, Meredith and her girlfriend — and I saw the way Macbeth was looking at Meredith.'

'Tell me this isn't true, Duff.'

'I regret to say it is.'

'You're a petty man, Duff.'

'That's what I'm trying to tell you. So when you say I'm fighting this fight for others, I don't know if it's true or I only want to take something away from Macbeth that I know he wants.'

'But he doesn't want it, Duff. The town, power, wealth — he couldn't care less about them. He wants only her love.'

'Lady.'

'Everything's about Lady. Haven't you realised?'

Duff blew a deformed smoke ring up to the ceiling. 'Macbeth's driven by love while I'm driven by envy and hatred. Where he has shown mercy, I've killed. And tomorrow I'm going to kill the person who was once my best friend — ambush him — and mercy and love will have lost again.'

'That's just cynicism and your self-loathing talking, Duff.'

'Hm.' He stubbed out the cigarette in the ashtray on the bedside table. 'You forgot self-pity.'

'Yes, I did. And self-pity.'

'I've been an arrogant egoist all my life. I can't understand how you could have loved me.'

'Some women have a weakness for men they think can save them, others for men they think they can save.'

'Amen,' Duff said, getting up. 'You women don't understand that we men don't change. Not when we discover love, not when we realise we're going to die. Never.'

'Some use false arrogance to cover up their lack of confidence, but your arrogance is genuine, Duff. It's down to total confidence.'

Duff smiled and pulled on his wet trousers. 'Try to sleep now. We have to have our wits about us tomorrow.'

After he had left, Caithness got up, pulled the curtain to one side and looked down at the street. The swish of tyres through pools of water. Faded adverts for Joey's Hamburger Bar, Peking Dry-Cleaners and the Tandrella Bingo Hall. A cigarette glowing for a second in an alleyway.

In a few hours day would break.

She wouldn't be able to go back to sleep now.

37

Saturday arrived with more rain. The front pages of both the town's newspapers carried Tourtell's announcement and the explosion on top of the Obelisk. *The Times* commented in its leader that Macbeth's radio interview had to be understood as him not categorically rejecting standing for mayor. And said Tourtell wasn't available for comment as he was at his son's mother's bedside in St Jordi's Hospital. Late that morning the rain cleared.

'You're home early,' Sheila said, wiping her hands on her apron in the hall and looking at her husband with a little concern.

'I couldn't find anything to do. I think I was the only person at work,' Lennox said, putting his bag by the chest of drawers, taking a clothes hanger from the wardrobe and hanging up his coat. Two years had passed since the town council had adopted the five-day week for the public sector, but at police HQ it was an unspoken rule that if you wanted to get on you had to show your face on Saturdays as well.

Lennox kissed his wife lightly on the cheek, noticed a new, unfamiliar perfume and a hitherto un-thought notion fluttered through his brain: what if he had caught her in bed with another man? He rejected this at once. First because she wasn't the type. Second because she wasn't attractive enough — after all there was a reason why she had ended up with a diminutive albino. The third and strongest reason for rejecting the notion was, however, simple: it was too hard to bear.

'Is there anything wrong?' she asked and followed him into the sitting room.

'Not at all,' he said. 'I'm just tired. Where are the kids?'

'In the garden,' she said. 'Finally some decent weather.'

He stood by the big window. Watching his children as they romped around screaming and laughing and playing a game the point of which he couldn't work out. Escaping, it seemed. Good skill to learn. He looked up at the sky. Decent? A little break before the piss came hammering down again. He slumped into an armchair. How long could he carry on like this?

'Lunch won't be ready for an hour,' she said.

'That's fine, love.' He looked at her. He genuinely liked her, but had he ever been in love with her? He couldn't remember and perhaps it wasn't that important. She hadn't said a word one way or the other, but he was fairly sure she hadn't been in love with him either. Generally Sheila didn't say much. Perhaps that was why she had given in to his persuasion and in the end said yes to being his girlfriend and eventually his wife. She had found someone who could talk for them both.

'Sure there's nothing wrong?'

'Absolutely sure, sweetheart. That smells good. What is it?'

'Erm, cod,' she said, her frown framing a question.

He was going to explain that he meant her perfume, not the lunch she had barely started, but she went to the kitchen and he swung his chair round to face the garden. His elder daughter saw him, beamed and shouted something to the other two. He waved to them. How could two such unattractive people have such beautiful children? And that was when the notion struck him again: *If they really were his.*

Infidelity and treachery.

Now his son was calling to him — what, he couldn't hear — but when he saw he had caught his father's attention he did a cartwheel on the grass. Lennox applauded with his hands raised high in the air, and now all three of them were doing cartwheels. Impress their daddy, impress the daddy they still admired, the daddy they thought was worth emulating. Shouting, laughter and frolics. Lennox thought of the silence out in Fife, the sunshine, the curtains fluttering in a window that had been shot to pieces, the gentle breeze whistling a barely audible doleful note through one of the holes in the wall. All the unbearable thoughts. There were so many ways to lose those you loved. What if one day they found out, realised, what kind of person their husband or father really was? Would the wind sing the same lament then?

He closed his eyes. Bit of a rest. Bit of decent weather.

He sensed someone was there, standing over him and breathing on him. He opened his eyes. It was Sheila.

'Didn't you hear me shouting?' she said.

'What?'

'There's a phone call for you. Some Inspector Seyton.'

Lennox went into the hall, picked up the receiver from the table. 'Hello?'

'Home early, Lennox? I'll need some help this evening.'

'I'm not well. You'd better try someone else.'

'The chief commissioner said to take you.'

Lennox swallowed. His mouth tasted of lead. 'Take me where?'

'To a hospital. Be ready in an hour. I'll pick you up.' There was a click. Lennox had rung off. Lead.

'What is it?' Sheila called from the kitchen.

A pale metal shaped by its environment, which poisons and kills, a heavy but unresisting material that melts at three hundred and fifty degrees.

'Nothing, sweetheart. Nothing.'

★ ★ ★

460

Macbeth woke from a dream about death. There was a knock at the door. Something about the knocking told him it had been going on for a long time.

'Sir!' It was Jack's voice.

'Yes,' Macbeth grunted, looking around. The room was flooded with daylight. What was the time? He had been dreaming. Dreaming he had been standing over the bed with a dagger in his hand. But whenever he blinked the face on the pillow changed.

'It's Inspector Caithness on the phone, sir. She says it's urgent.'

'Put her through,' Macbeth said, rolling over towards the bedside table. 'Caithness?'

'Sorry to ring you on a Saturday, but we've found a body. I'm afraid we'll have to ask you to help.' She sounded out of breath.

'Why's that?'

'Because we think it could be Fleance, Banquo's son. The body is in a bad way, and as he has no close relatives in town it seems you're the best person to identify him.'

'Oh,' Macbeth said, feeling his throat tighten.

'Sorry?'

'Yes, I suppose I am,' Macbeth said and pulled the duvet tighter around him. 'When a body's been in seawater for so long . . . '

'That's the point.'

'What's the point?'

'We didn't find the body in the sea but in an alleyway between 14th and 15th Streets.'

'What?'

'That's why we want to be absolutely sure it's Fleance before we go any further.'

'14th and 15th, you say?'

'Go to 14th and Doheney. I'll wait for you outside Joey's Hamburger Bar.'

'OK, Caithness. I'll be there in twenty minutes.'

'Thank you, sir.'

Macbeth rang off. Lilies. The flowers in the carpet were lilies. Lily. That was the name of Lady's child. Why hadn't he made the connection before? Dead. Because he hadn't seen, tasted, eaten and slept so much death before. He closed his eyes. Recalled the changing faces from the dream. Orphanage Director Lorreal's unknowing face as he snored with his mouth open became Chief Commissioner Duncan's, eyes that opened and stared at him, knowing. Then Banquo's stiff, brutal glare. No bodies, only the head on the pillow. Then the nameless young Norse Rider's panic-stricken expression as he knelt on the tarmac staring at his already dead comrade and Macbeth coming towards him. He looked at the ceiling. And remembered all the times he had woken from a nightmare and breathed a sigh of relief. Relieved to find in reality he wasn't drowning in quicksand or being eaten by dogs. But sometimes he *thought* he had woken from a nightmare but was still dreaming, still drowning, and he had to break through several layers before he reached consciousness. He shut his eyes tight. Opened them again. Then he got up.

★ ★ ★

The buxom black woman in reception at St Jordi's Hospital looked up from the ID card Lennox showed her.

'We've been told that no one has access . . . ' She checked the card again. 'Inspector.'

'Police matter,' he said. 'Top priority. The mayor has to be informed at once.'

'If you leave a message I can — '

'Confidential matter, urgent.'

She sighed.

'Room 204, first floor.'

Mayor Tourtell and the young boy sat side by side on

wooden chairs next to one of the beds in the large ward. The older man held the boy around the shoulder and they both looked up as Lennox stood behind them and coughed. In the bed lay a wan, thin-haired, middle-aged woman, and Lennox saw at once the likeness with the boy. 'Good evening, sir. You won't remember me, but we met at the dinner at Inverness Casino.'

'Inspector Lennox, isn't it? Anti-Corruption Unit.'

'Impressive. I apologise for bursting in like this.'

'How can I help, Lennox?'

'We've had a credible tip-off of an imminent assassination attempt against you.'

The boy gave a start, but Tourtell didn't bat an eyelid. 'More details, Inspector.'

'We don't have any more for the present, but we're taking it seriously and I'm to escort you from here to a safer place.'

Tourtell raised an eyebrow. 'And what could be safer than a hospital?'

'The newspapers say you're here, Mr Mayor. Anyone has access here. Let me accompany you to your car and follow you until you're safe within your own four walls. Then I hope we'll have time to delve deeper. So if you wouldn't mind coming with me . . . '

'Right now? As you see — '

'I can see and I apologise, but it's your duty and mine to protect the person of the mayor.'

'Stand by the door and keep watch, Lennox, so — '

'These aren't my orders, sir.'

'They are now, Lennox.'

'Go.' The whispered, barely audible word came from the woman in the bed. 'Go, and take Kasi with you.'

Tourtell laid a hand on hers. 'But Edith, you — '

'I'm tired, my dear. I want to be alone now. Kasi's safer with you. Listen to the man.'

'Are you — '

'Yes, I'm sure.'

The woman closed her eyes. Tourtell patted her hand and turned to Lennox. 'OK, let's go.'

They left the room. The boy a few steps in front of them.

'Does he know?' Lennox asked.

'That she's dying? Yes.'

'And how's he taking it?'

'Some days are harder than others. He's known for a while.' They went down the stairs towards the kiosk and the exit. 'But he says it's fine. It's fine as long as he has one of us. I'm just going to get some cigarettes. Will you wait for me?'

★ ★ ★

'There she is,' Macbeth said, pointing.

Jack pulled in to the kerb opposite the Grand Hotel, between a dry-cleaner's and a hamburger bar. They both got out, and Macbeth ran his eye up and down the empty street.

'Thanks for coming so quickly,' Caithness said.

'No problem,' Macbeth said. She smelled of strong perfume. He couldn't remember having noticed that before.

'Show me,' Macbeth said.

Macbeth and Jack followed her down the street. Saturday evening was just warming up. Under a flashing neon sign that read NUDE WOMEN a suited doorman gave Caithness the once-over, then threw his cigarette end to the tarmac and ground it in with his heel.

'I thought you would bring Seyton with you,' Caithness said.

'He had to go to St Jordi's this evening. Is it here?'

Caithness had stopped by the entrance to a narrow alley cordoned off with orange Homicide Unit tape. Macbeth peered down. It was so narrow that the dustbins outside the back doors on both sides were close. And it was too dark to see anything at all.

'I was here first. The rest of the SOC team is coming later. That's the way it is at the weekend. They're scattered to the four winds.' Caithness pushed up the tape and Macbeth ducked underneath. 'If you could go in and have a look at the body alone, sir. I've covered it with a sheet, but please don't touch anything else. We want as few prints as possible in there. Your driver can wait here while I go back to Joey's and meet the pathologist. He's supposed to be just around the corner.'

Macbeth looked at her. He saw nothing in her face. Yet. She had thought Seyton would be coming. Strong perfume. Which camouflaged any other smell she might be secreting.

'OK,' he said and set off down the alley.

He hadn't walked more than ten metres before all the sounds from the main street disappeared and all that could be heard was the whirr of fans, coughing from an open window and the drone of a radio: Todd Rundgren, 'Hello, It's Me'. He sneaked between the dustbins, creeping forward without quite knowing why. Habit, he supposed.

The body lay in the middle of the alley, half inside the cone of light from a wall lamp. He could make out 15th Street at the other end, but it was too far away for him to see if the alley was taped off there as well.

A pair of feet stuck out from under the white sheet. He immediately recognised the winkle-pickers.

He went over to the sheet. Took a deep breath. The air contained the sweet smell of dry-cleaning chemicals coming from a noisy extractor fan above the door right behind him. He grasped the sheet in the middle and pulled it away.

'Hi, Macbeth.'

Macbeth stared into the muzzle of the shotgun raised towards him by the man lying on his back in the

465

darkness. The scar shone on his face. Macbeth released the air from his lungs.

'Hi, Duff.'

★　★　★

Duff studied Macbeth's hands as he spoke. 'Macbeth, you are hereby arrested. If you move a finger I'll shoot you now. Your choice.'

Macbeth looked towards 15th Street. 'I'm the chief commissioner in this town, Duff. You can't arrest me.'

'There are other authorities.'

'The mayor?' Macbeth laughed. 'I don't think you can rely on him living that long.'

'I'm not talking about anyone in this town.' Duff got to his feet without the shotgun veering a centimetre from Macbeth.

'You've been arrested for involvement in the murders committed in Fife, and you will be transported there to stand trial. We've spoken with them. You will be charged with the murder of Banquo, which took place in Fife. Hold your hands above your head and face the wall.'

Macbeth did as instructed. 'You've got nothing on me and you know it.'

'With Inspector Caithness's statement about what Angus told her, we have enough to keep you in custody in Fife for a week. And a week without you at the helm will give us enough time to indict you here too. For the murder of Duncan. We have forensic evidence.' Duff took out his handcuffs. 'Turn round, put your hands behind — You know the drill.'

'Are you really not going to shoot me, Duff? Come on, you're a man who lives for revenge.'

Duff waited until Macbeth had turned his back and linked his hands behind his head, then approached.

'I know it affected you finding out the man you killed wasn't Sweno, Duff. But now you're sure you have the right man in front of you, aren't you going to avenge Meredith and the children? Or did your mother mean more to you than them?'

'Stand still and shut your mouth.'

'I've kept my mouth shut for years, Duff. I know the female officer Sweno killed in Stoke was your mother. What year was the business in Stoke? You can't have been very old.'

'I was young.' Duff closed the handcuffs around Macbeth's wrists.

'And why did you take your maternal grandfather's surname of instead of your parents' name?'

Duff turned Macbeth so that they stood face to face.

'You don't need to answer,' Macbeth said. 'You did it so that no one in the police or the Norse Riders could link your name to the Stoke massacre. No one would know that you didn't become an officer to serve the town and all that shit we swear to. It was all about catching Sweno, about you getting your revenge. Hatred drove you, Duff. At the orphanage when you killed Lorreal, it was easy, wasn't it? You saw Sweno in front of you. Lorreal was another man who had destroyed a childhood.'

'Maybe.' Duff was so close he could see his reflection in Macbeth's brown eyes.

'So what's happened, Duff? Why don't you want to kill now? I'm the man who took your family, and now this is your chance.'

'You'll have to take responsibility for what you've done.'

'And what have I done?'

Duff cast a quick glance in the direction of 15th Street, where the car with Malcolm and Fleance was waiting. Caithness was on her way there. 'You've killed innocent people.'

'It's our damned *duty* to kill innocent people, Duff. As long as it serves a greater purpose we have to

467

overcome our sentimental, compliant natures. The man whose throat I cut out on the country road, that wasn't for you, it wasn't repayment for you killing Lorreal for me. I made myself a murderer so that no one would drag the police force through the mud. It was for the town, against anarchy.'

'Come on. Let's go.'

Duff grabbed Macbeth's arm, but Macbeth twisted away. 'Has your lust for power become greater than your lust for revenge, Duff? Do you think you're going to get Organised Crime by arresting the chief commissioner himself?'

Duff pressed the muzzle of the shotgun under Macbeth's chin. 'I could of course tell them you resisted arrest.'

'Difficult decision?' Macbeth whispered.

'No,' Duff said, lowering the gun. 'This town doesn't need more bodies.'

'So you didn't love them, eh? Meredith, the children? Oh no, I forgot, you can't love — '

Duff hit out. The shotgun barrel struck Macbeth in the mouth. 'Remember I've never had your problem about killing a defenceless man face to face, Macbeth.'

Macbeth laughed and spat blood. What must have been a tooth bounced into the darkness. 'Then prove it. Shoot the only friend you've ever had. Come on. Do it for Meredith!'

'Don't even say her name.'

'Meredith! Meredith!'

Duff heard the blood throbbing in his ears, felt his heart pounding, heavy and painful. He mustn't — Macbeth's forehead hit Duff's nose with a crunch. But they were standing too close for Macbeth to have the momentum and power to knock him down. Duff stepped back two paces and raised the shotgun to his shoulder.

At that moment the door behind Macbeth flew open.

A silhouette in the doorway. The arm of a grey coat shot out, grabbed the handcuffs behind Macbeth's back and pulled. The force was so great that Macbeth's feet left the ground as he disappeared through the door into the darkness behind.

Duff fired.

The explosion met his eardrums and quivered between the walls of the alley.

Half-deafened, Duff stepped over the threshold into the darkness.

Something whirled in the air which he breathed in and spat out. People seemed to be lined up in front of him. The smell of perchlorethylene was overwhelming. His free hand found a light switch on the wall by the door. The people lined up were stands holding jackets and coats, each under a plastic cover with a note stating a name and date. In front of him a hole had been blasted in a plastic cover and a brown fur coat, and Duff realised he had been spitting out animal hair. He stood listening but heard only the drone of the green Garrett dry-cleaning machine by the wall. Then a ringing, like a bell above a shop door. He threw himself against the wall of clothes, ploughed past stand after stand through a door to the rear of a counter where a Chinese couple stared at him, scared out of their wits. He ran past them and onto the street. Looked up and down. The Saturday evening rush had started. A man bumped into him and for a moment Duff lost his balance. He cursed as the man apologised and continued down the pavement.

He heard laughter behind him. Turned and saw a guy in rags, filthy, a few stumps of teeth in an open mouth.

'You been robbed, mister?'

'Yes,' Duff said, lowering the shotgun. 'I have been robbed.'

38

Lennox stood outside the hospital entrance with Kasi. Glanced towards the kiosk where Tourtell was queueing to buy cigarettes, then focused on the car park. A light came on inside Tourtell's limousine. The distance was probably a hundred metres. Around the same distance as up to the roof of the multi-storey car park to the left. Lennox shivered. Clear weather often came with a rare north-easterly wind, but also the cold. And if it blew a bit more now the sky would be free of clouds. In moonlight Olafson could probably have shot Tourtell from anywhere, but in the darkness the plan was that it would happen in the car park, under one of the lights.

He checked his watch again. The cold was eating into his body, and he coughed. His lungs. He couldn't stand the sun and he couldn't stand the cold. What did God actually mean by sending someone like him to earth, a lonely suffering heart without armour, a mollusc without a shell?

'Thanks for helping us.'

'Sorry?' Lennox turned to the boy.

'Thank you for saving my father.'

Lennox stared at him. Kasi was wearing the same kind of denim jacket as his own son wore. And Lennox couldn't prevent the next thought coming. Here was a boy, not much older than his own, about to lose his mother. And his father. *He says it's fine as long as he has one of us.*

'Let's go, shall we?' Tourtell said as he came out puffing a cigarette he had just bought.

'Yes,' Lennox said. They crossed the road and went into the car park. Lennox moved to the left of Tourtell. Kasi was a few steps in front of them. All Lennox had to do was to stop as they went through the light under the first lamp so that he was out of the line of fire, and then the rest was up to Olafson.

Lennox felt a strange numbness in his tongue, fingers and toes.

★ ★ ★

'They're coming,' Seyton said, lowering the binoculars.

'I can see them,' Olafson lisped. He stood with one knee on the concrete of the car-park roof. One eye was shut, the other wide open behind the telescopic sights of the rifle resting on the parapet in front of them. Seyton scanned the roof behind them to make sure they were still alone. Their car was the only one up there. People didn't seem to visit the sick on a Saturday evening. He could hear the music from the streets below them and smell the perfume and testosterone from right up there.

Down in the car park the boy was walking in front of Tourtell and Lennox and out of the line of fire. Good. He could hear Olafson take a deep breath. The two men walked into the light under a lamp.

Seyton felt his heart give a leap of joy.

Now.

But there was no shot.

The two men walked out of the circle of light and became vague outlines in the darkness again.

'What happened?' Seyton asked.

'Lennox was in the line of fire,' Olafson said.

'I suppose he'll get out of the way when they pass under the next light.'

Seyton raised his binoculars again.

★ ★ ★

'Any idea who could be after me, Lennox?'

'Yes,' Lennox said. There were two lamps left before

471

they reached the limousine.

'Really?' Tourtell said in surprise and slowed down. Lennox made sure to do the same.

'Don't look up at the multi-storey behind me, Tourtell, but on the roof there's an expert marksman and right now we're in his sights. To be more precise, *I* am. So walk at the exact same speed as me. If not, you'll be shot in the head.'

He could see from Tourtell's look that the mayor believed him. 'The boy . . .'

'He's not in any danger. Keep walking. Don't let on.'

Lennox saw Tourtell open his mouth as though it were the only way his big body could get enough oxygen as his heart rate increased. Then the mayor nodded and walked faster, taking short steps.

'What's your role in this, Lennox?'

'The rogue,' Lennox said, and saw the driver, who must have been keeping his eye on them, get out of the car to open the rear door. 'Is it bulletproof?'

'I'm the mayor, not the president. Why are you doing this if you're the rogue?'

'Because someone has to save this town from Macbeth. I can't, so you'll have to, Tourtell.'

★ ★ ★

'What the fuck's Lennox up to?' Seyton said, snatching the binoculars from his eyes to check that what he had seen through them tallied with the reality down in the car park. 'Is he *intentionally* standing in front of Tourtell?'

'Don't know, boss, but this is becoming critical. They'll soon be by the car.'

'Your bullets, would they go through Lennox?'

'Boss?'

'Will they go through Lennox and kill Tourtell?'

'I use FMJ bullets, boss.'

'Yes or no?'

'Yes!'

'Then shoot the traitor.'

'But — '

'Shh,' Seyton whispered.

'What?' Sweat had broken out on the young officer's brow.

'Don't talk and don't think, Olafson. What you just heard was an order.'

★ ★ ★

The driver had walked around the car and smiled as he opened the rear door. A smile which disappeared when he saw Tourtell's expression. The boy walked to the rear door on the left-hand side.

'Get in and duck,' Lennox hissed. 'Driver, get out of here. Now!'

'Sir, what — '

'Do as he says,' Tourtell said. 'It — '

Lennox felt the shot to his back before he heard the *thwack*. His legs withered beneath him, he collapsed and automatically put his arms around Tourtell, who was dragged down as he fell.

Lennox registered the tarmac coming up to meet them. He didn't feel it as it hit them, but he smelled it all: dust, petrol, rubber, urine. He couldn't move and couldn't produce a sound, but he could hear. Hear the panting of Tourtell from underneath him on the tarmac. The driver's shocked 'Sir, sir?'

And Tourtell's 'Run, Kasi, run!'

They had almost made it. One more metre and they would have been covered by the car. Lennox tried to say something, the name of an animal, but still nothing came from his mouth. He tried in vain to move his hand. He was dead. Soon he would be floating up and looking down on his own body. One metre. He registered the sound of running feet quickly distancing themselves and the driver bending over them and trying to drag him off Tourtell. 'I'll get you in the car, sir!' Another *thwack* and Lennox was blinded by something wet in his eyes. He blinked, so at least his eyelids could move. The driver lay beside them staring vacantly into the air. His forehead was gone.

'Turtle,' Lennox whispered.

'What?' Tourtell gasped from underneath him.

'Crawl. I'm your shell.'

★ ★ ★

'That's got the driver,' Olafson said, pushing another cartridge into the chamber.

'Hurry. Tourtell's crawling behind the car,' Seyton said. 'And the boy's run off.'

Olafson loaded. He rested the butt against his shoulder and shut one eye.

'I've got the boy in my sights.'

'I don't give a fuck about the boy!' Seyton snarled. 'Shoot Tourtell!'

Seyton watched Olafson's rifle barrel swing back and forth, saw him blink a bead of sweat from his eyelashes.

'I can't see him, boss.'

'Too late!' Seyton slapped his hand against the parapet. 'They're behind the car. We'll have to go down and finish the job.'

★ ★ ★

Lennox heard Tourtell groan as he extricated himself. Lennox rolled onto the wet tarmac. He was lying on his stomach, helpless, his legs sticking out past the rear of the car. Until Tourtell grabbed his arms and pulled him to safety.

Rubber screamed on tarmac. A car was heading for them. Lennox looked under the car, but all he saw was the body of the driver on the other side. Tourtell had sat down with his back to the side of the car. Lennox tried to open his mouth to tell Tourtell to get in the car and escape, to save himself, but it was no use. It was the same old story, as though his whole life could be summed up in one sentence: he was unable to do what his brain and heart wanted.

A car stopped and doors opened.

Footsteps on the tarmac.

Lennox tried to move his head but couldn't. From the corner of his eye he saw the barrel of a gun parallel with a pair of trouser legs.

They were goners. In some strange way it felt like a relief.

The trouser legs came a step closer. A hand gripped his neck. He was going to be killed silently, strangulation. Lennox held his gaze on the shoes. They went out of fashion a while ago. Winkle-pickers.

'This one's dead,' said a familiar voice from the other side of the car.

'Tourtell's unhurt,' said the man holding him in a stranglehold. 'Lennox isn't moving, but he's got a pulse. Where did they shoot from?'

'The top of the multi-storey,' Tourtell sobbed. 'Lennox saved my life.'

Saved?

'Get over to this side, Malcolm!'

The hand removed itself, and a face came into Lennox's field of vision.

Duff stared him in the eye.

'Is he conscious?' asked a woman behind him. Caithness.

'Paralysed or in shock,' Duff said. 'His eyes are moving, but he can't move or talk. We need to get him into the hospital.'

'Car,' a voice said. A young boy. 'Coming out of the multi-storey car park.'

'Looks like a SWAT car,' Duff said, getting up and putting the shotgun to his shoulder.

There was silence for a couple of seconds. The sound of the car engine faded away.

'Let them go,' Malcolm said.

'Kasi.' Tourtell's voice.

'What?'

'You've got to find Kasi.'

★　★　★

Kasi ran. His heart was beating in his throat and his feet pummelling the wet tarmac, faster and faster. Until they were running as fast as the song that used to play in his head when he was afraid. 'Help'. He had been getting in the car when he heard the thud and saw the shot hit the pale-faced policeman in the back. He had fallen over Dad and Dad had told him to run.

He automatically took the road down towards the area where he had grown up, by the river. There was a burned-out house where they used to play, the rat house they called it.

The burned-out house was white with patches of soot around the door and windows, like a decrepit over-made-up whore. Down by the river the small houses lay huddled together as if searching for shelter with each other. Apart from one, which was on its own, as though the others were shunning it. It was timber-framed and painted blue; and around it the grass had grown high. Kasi ran up the steps into the door-less hall to what once had been a kitchen but now was an empty, urine-stinking shell with names and dirty words scribbled on the walls. He continued up the narrow stairs to the bedrooms. A mouldy mattress lay on the floor of one. He'd had his first kiss on it among empty spirit bottles and the stiff carcasses of river rats scattered around the floor. One afternoon when he was ten or eleven he and two friends had sat on it and tasted their first cigarette — in between coughing fits — in the sunset, and watched rats come towards the house, padding across the cracked and litter-strewn mud of the dry riverbed. Perhaps they came here to die.

Should he go back? No, Dad had said he should get away. And the other man, Lennox, was from the police, and there must be more of them there if they knew of plans to assassinate the mayor.

He would hide until it was all over, then go home.

Kasi opened the big wardrobe in the corner. It was empty, stripped of everything. He huddled inside and closed the door. Leaned his head back against the wood. Softly hummed the song in his mind. 'Help!' Thought of the film where the Beatles were running around helter-skelter and having fun in comic fast-forward motion, a world where nothing really horrible happened. And no one could find him here. Not unless they knew where he was. And anyway, he wasn't the mayor, only a boy who hadn't done anything bad in his life apart from smoke a few cigarettes on the quiet, share half a bottle of diluted whisky and kiss a couple of girls who had boyfriends.

His heart gradually slowed.

He listened. Nothing. But he would have to wait some time. He had got his breath back, enough to inhale through his nose now. He didn't know how many years it was since clothes had hung here, but he could still smell them. The smell, the ghosts of lives unknown. God knows where they were now. Mum said it had been an unhappy house, with alcohol, beatings and much worse. He should thank his lucky stars he had a father who loved him and had never laid a hand on him. And Kasi *had* thanked his lucky stars. No one had known his father was the mayor, and he didn't tell anyone either, neither those who called him a brat, nor the other brats who never saw their fathers or even knew who they

477

were. He felt sorry for them. He had told his father that one day he would help them. Them and all the others in difficulty after Estex closed. And Dad had patted him on the head and laughed, as other fathers would have done. He had listened attentively and said that if Kasi really wanted to do something, when the time came he would help him. He had promised. And who knows, one day Kasi might become mayor, greater wonders had come to pass, Dad had said and called him Tourtell Junior.

'Help!'

But the world wasn't like that. The world hadn't been made for good deeds and funny pop singers in films. You couldn't help anyone. Not your father, not your mother, not other children. Only yourself.

★ ★ ★

Olafson braked as the bus in front of them stopped. Young people, mostly women, streamed onto the pavement. Looking their best. Saturday night. That was what he would have done tonight: had a beer and danced with a girl. Drunk and danced away the sight of the driver. Beside him Seyton stretched out a hand and turned off the radio and Lindisfarne's 'Meet Me on the Corner'.

'Where the hell did they come from? Duff. Malcolm. Caithness. And the young guy I could have sworn was Banquo's son.'

'Back to HQ?' Olafson asked. It still wasn't too late for a decent Saturday night.

'Not yet,' Seyton said. 'We've got to catch the boy.'

'Tourtell's son?'

'I don't want to go back to Macbeth empty-handed, and the boy can be used. Turn left here. Drive even more slowly.'

Olafson swung the car down the narrow street and

glanced at Seyton, who had opened the window and was inhaling the air, his nostrils opening and closing. Olafson was about to ask if Seyton could sniff out where the boy had run to, but refrained. If this man could heal a shoulder by touching it he was probably capable of smelling his way to where someone had gone. Was he afraid of his new commander? Maybe. He had definitely asked himself whether he preferred his predecessor. But he hadn't known it could come to this. All he knew was that the surgeon at the hospital had pointed to an X-ray of his shoulder and explained that the bullet had destroyed the joint; he was an invalid and would have to get used to never working as a marksman for SWAT again. In a few moments the surgeon had deprived Olafson of all he had ever dreamed about doing. Then it had been easy to agree when Seyton said he could fix it if Olafson agreed to a deal. He hadn't even meant it because who could fix something like that in a day? And what did he have to lose? He had already sworn allegiance to the brotherhood that was SWAT, so what Seyton wanted from him was in many ways something he already had.

No, there was no point having regrets now. And just look what had happened to his best pal, Angus. He had betrayed SWAT, the idiot. Betrayed the most precious thing they had, all they had. *Baptised in fire and united in blood* wasn't an empty phrase, it was how they had to be, there were no alternatives. He wanted this. To know there was some meaning in what he did, that he meant something to people. To his comrades. Even when he couldn't see any meaning in what they did. That was a job for other people. Not for Angus, the bloody fool. He must have lost the plot. Angus had tried to persuade him to join him, but he had told him to go to hell, he didn't want anything to do with someone who betrayed SWAT. And Angus had stared at him and asked him how his shoulder had healed so quickly — a gunshot wound like that didn't heal in a couple of days. But Olafson hadn't answered. He just showed him the door.

The street ended. They had reached the riverbed.

'We're getting warmer,' Seyton said. 'Come on.'

They got out and walked by the hovels between the road and the riverbed. Passing house after house as Seyton sniffed the air. At a red building he stopped.

'Here?' Olafson asked.

Seyton sniffed in the direction of the house. Then he said aloud, 'Whore!' And walked on. They passed a burned-out house, a garage with a wrought-iron gate and came to a blue timber house with a cat on the steps. Seyton stopped again.

'Here,' he said.

'Here?'

★　★　★

Kasi looked at his watch. He had been given it by his father and the hands shimmered green in the darkness, the way he imagined wolves' eyes did in the night, from the light of a fire. More than twenty minutes had passed. He was fairly sure no one had followed him when he ran from the car park; he had looked back several times and hadn't seen anyone. The coast ought to be clear now. He knew the area like the back of his hand, that was why he had run straight here. He could go down to Penny Bridge and take the 22 bus from there, go west. Back home. Dad would be there. He *had* to be there. Kasi stiffened. Had he heard something? The staircase creaking? That was the only wood that had survived the fire, he didn't know why, just that it creaked when the wind blew or there was a change in the weather. Or if someone came. He held his breath. Listened. No. Probably the weather changing.

Kasi counted slowly to sixty.

Then he pushed the door open with his foot.

Stared.

'You're frightened,' said the man standing outside and looking at him. 'Smart thinking, hiding in a wardrobe. It keeps in the smell. Almost.' He stretched his arms out to the side with his palms up. Inhaled. 'But the air here is wonderful and full of your fear, boy.'

Kasi blinked. The man was lean, and his eyes were like the hands on Kasi's watch. Wolf eyes. And he had to be old. Not that he looked that old, but Kasi just knew that this man was very, very old.

'Hel — ' Kasi started to shout, before the man's hand shot out and grabbed him by the throat. Kasi couldn't breathe, and now he knew why he had come here. He was like the river rats. He had come here to die.

39

Duff looked at his watch, yawned and slumped even deeper in the chair. His long legs stretched almost across the hospital corridor, to Caithness and Fleance. Duff's eyes met Caithness's.

'You were right,' she said.

'We were both right,' he said.

It was less than an hour since he had jumped into the car in 15th Street, cursing, and said Macbeth had got away. And that something was afoot. Macbeth had said the mayor wouldn't live that long.

'An assassination,' Malcolm had said. 'A takeover. He's gone completely insane.'

'What?'

'The Kenneth Laws. If the mayor dies or declares a state of emergency, the chief commissioner takes over until further notice and in principle has unlimited power. Tourtell has to be warned.'

'St Jordi's,' Caithness had said. 'Seyton's there.'

'Drive,' Duff had shouted, and Fleance stamped on the accelerator.

It had taken them less than twenty minutes, and they heard the first shot from the car park when they stopped in front of the hospital's main entrance and were on their way up the steps.

Duff closed his eyes. He hadn't slept, and this should have been over now. Macbeth should have been behind lock and key in Fife.

'Here they are,' Caithness said.

Duff opened his eyes again. Tourtell and Malcolm were walking down the corridor towards them.

'The doctor says Lennox will live,' Malcolm said and sat down. 'He's fully conscious and can talk and move his hands. But he's paralysed from the middle of the back down, and it'll probably be permanent. The bullet hit his spine.'

'It was *stopped* by his spine,' Tourtell said. 'Otherwise it would have gone through him and hit me.'

'His family are in the waiting room,' Malcolm said. 'They've been in to see him, and the doctor said that's enough for today. He's had morphine and needs to rest.'

'Heard anything from Kasi?' Caithness asked.

'He hasn't come home yet,' Tourtell said. 'But he knows his way around. He may have gone to friends or hidden somewhere. I'm not worried.'

'You're not?'

Tourtell pulled a grimace. 'Not yet.'

'So what do we do now?' Duff asked.

'We wait a few minutes until the family has gone,' Malcolm said. 'Tourtell persuaded the doctor to give us two minutes with Lennox. We need a confession as soon as possible from Lennox so that we can get Capitol to issue a federal arrest warrant for Macbeth.'

'Aren't our witness statements good enough?' Duff asked.

Malcolm shook his head. 'None of us has received death threats directly from Macbeth or personally heard him give an order to murder.'

'What about blackmail?' Caithness asked. 'Tourtell, you just said that when you were playing blackjack in the private room at the Inverness Macbeth and Lady tried to force you to withdraw from the elections, dangling the bait of shares in the Obelisk and threatening to go public with a story of indecent behaviour with an underage boy.'

'In my line of work we call that kind of blackmail politics,' Tourtell said. 'Hardly punishable.'

'So Macbeth's right?' Duff said. 'We've got nothing on him.'

'We hope Lennox has something,' Malcolm said.

'Who should talk to him?'

'Me,' Duff said.

Malcolm regarded him pensively. 'Fine, but it's just a question of time before someone here recognises you or me, and raises the alarm.'

'I know how Lennox looks when he lies,' Duff said. 'And he knows I know.'

'But can you persuade him to reveal his cooperation and thus . . . ?'

'Yes,' Duff said.

'Don't persuade him the way you did the Norse Rider patient, Duff.'

'That was a different person who did that, sir. I'm not him any more.'

'Aren't you?'

'No, sir.'

Malcolm held Duff's gaze for a few seconds. 'Good. Tourtell, could you please take Duff?'

'Out of curiosity,' Duff said when he and Tourtell had got some way down the corridor, 'when Macbeth gave you his ultimatum why didn't you tell him Kasi was your son?'

Tourtell shrugged. 'Why tell the person pointing a gun at you it isn't loaded? They'll only start looking around for another weapon.'

The doctor was waiting for them outside a closed door. He opened it.

'Just him,' Tourtell said, pointing to Duff.

Duff stepped inside.

Lennox was as white as the sheets he was lying between. Tubes and wires led from his body to drip bags on a stand and machines emitting beeps. He looked like a surprised child, staring up at Duff with wide-open eyes and mouth. Duff took his hat and glasses off.

Lennox blinked.

'We need you to go public and say Macbeth is behind this,' Duff said. 'Are you willing to do that?'

484

Thin, shiny saliva ran from one corner of Lennox's mouth.

'Listen, Lennox. I've got two minutes, and — '

'Macbeth's behind this,' Lennox said. His voice was hoarse, husky, as though he had aged twenty years. But his eyes cleared. 'He ordered Seyton, Olafson and me to execute Tourtell. Because he wanted to take over the reins of the town. And because he thinks Tourtell is Hecate's informant. But he isn't.'

'So who is the informant?'

'I'll tell you if you do me a favour.'

Duff breathed hard through his nose. Concentrated on controlling his speech. 'You mean I might have to owe you a favour?'

Lennox closed his eyes again. Duff saw a tear forced out. Pain from his wound, Duff assumed.

'No,' Lennox whispered in a fading voice.

Duff leaned forward. There was a nauseous, sweet smell coming from Lennox's mouth, like the acetone breath of a diabetic, as he whispered, '*I'm* Hecate's informant.'

'You?' Duff tried to digest the information, tried to make it fit.

'Yes. How do you think Hecate slipped through our fingers all these years, how he was always a step ahead?'

'You're a spy for both — '

' — Hecate and Macbeth. Without Macbeth knowing. But that's how I know Tourtell's not in Hecate's pocket. Or Macbeth's. But it wasn't me who warned Hecate, so there must be another informant as well. Someone close to Macbeth.'

'Seyton?'

'Maybe. Or perhaps not a man.'

'A woman? Why do you think that?'

'I don't know. Something invisible, something that's just *there*.'

Duff nodded slowly. Raised his eyes and looked into

the darkness outside the window.

'How does it feel?'

'How does what feel?'

'To say it out loud finally. That you're a traitor. Is it a relief or does it weigh more heavily on you when the words make you realise it's true, the damage is your fault?'

'Why do you want to know?'

'Because I was wondering about it myself,' Duff said. The sky outside was dark, covered, giving no answer or sign. 'How it would feel to tell my family everything.'

'But you didn't,' Lennox said. 'We don't. Because we'd rather destroy ourselves than see the pain in their faces. But you didn't have the chance to choose.'

'Yes, I did. I chose. Every day. To be unfaithful.'

'Will you help me, Duff?'

Duff was torn out of his thoughts. Blinked. He needed to sleep soon. 'Help?'

'A favour. The pillow. Put it over my face and hold it there. It'll look as if I died of my wounds. And will you tell my children that their father, murderer and traitor that he was, repented?'

'I . . .'

'You're the only person I know who might understand me, Duff. That you can love someone so much and still betray them. And when it's too late, it's too late. All you can do is . . . what is right, but it's too late.'

'Like saving the life of the mayor.'

'But that isn't enough, is it, Duff?' Lennox's dry laughter turned into a bout of coughing. 'A last desperate act which, seen from the outside, is a sacrifice, but which deep down you hope will be rewarded with the forgiveness of your sins and the opening of heaven's gates. But that's too much, Duff. You don't think you can ever make amends for everything, do you.'

'No,' Duff said. 'No, I can't make amends. But I can start by forgiving you.'

'No!' Lennox said.

'Yes.'

'No, you can't! Don't do that, don't . . . ' His voice crumbled away. Duff looked at him. Small shiny tears rolled down his white cheeks.

Duff took a deep breath. 'I'll consider not forgiving you on one condition, Lennox.'

Lennox nodded.

'That you agree to give a radio interview this evening in which you tell everything and clear Malcolm.'

Lennox raised a hand with difficulty and wiped his cheeks. Then he placed his tear-wet hand round Duff's wrist. 'Ring Priscilla and ask her to come here.'

Duff nodded, got up and freed his wrist. Looked down at Lennox for a last time. Wondering if he saw a man who had changed or was just taking the easiest way out.

'Well?' Tourtell said, getting up from a chair against the corridor wall when Duff came out.

'He's confirmed that Macbeth was trying to kill you and he'll do the interview,' Duff said. 'But Hecate has an informant, an infiltrator close to Macbeth. It could be anyone at police HQ . . . '

'Anyway,' Tourtell boomed as they hurried down the corridor, 'with Lennox's statement Macbeth's finished! I'll ring Capitol and have a federal arrest warrant issued.'

A nurse came towards them. 'Mr Mayor, sir?'

'Yes?'

'We've had a call from Agnes, your maid. She says Kasi still hasn't come home.'

'Thank you,' Tourtell said. They continued walking. 'You'll see, he's gone to some friends and is waiting until the coast is clear.'

'Probably,' Duff said. 'Your maid . . . '

'Yes?'

'I've never had servants, but I assume that after a while they become part of the furniture. You speak freely and don't think they'll repeat stuff that shouldn't go beyond your four walls, isn't that right?'

'Agnes? Yes. Yes, at least when I was sure I could trust her. But that took time.'

'And yet you can never know for sure what another person thinks and feels, can you?'

'Hm. You're wondering if Macbeth has a personal secretary at HQ who might . . .'

'Priscilla?' Duff said. 'Well, as you said, it takes time to trust someone.'

'And?'

'You said you played blackjack in a private room as Macbeth and Lady made plans to kill Hecate. But doesn't it need a fourth person?'

'Sorry?'

'Blackjack. Don't you need a croupier?'

★ ★ ★

'Jack?'

'Yes, Lady?' Jack took his hand away. It had been casually placed on Billy's arched back as the two of them stood over the guestbook and Jack had explained how new customers should be entered.

'I have to talk to you about something, Jack. Let's go upstairs.'

'Of course. Will you hold the fort, Billy?'

'I'll do my best, Mr Bonus.'

Jack smiled and knew he held the newly employed boy's eyes a moment too long. Then he dashed up the stairs after Lady.

'What do you think of the new boy?' she asked after he had caught her up.

'Bit early to say, ma'am. A little young and

488

inexperienced, but he doesn't seem impossible.'

'Good. We need two waiters for the restaurant. The two who came today were utterly hopeless. How are young people going to survive in this world if they can't take things seriously and *learn* something? Do they think everything's going to be served to them on a silver platter?'

'True,' Jack said and went into the suite, Lady holding the door open for him. Turning, he saw she had closed the door and collapsed in tears on a chair.

'Lady, what's the matter?'

'Lily,' she sobbed. 'Lily. He said her name.'

'Lily? As in the flower, ma'am?'

Lady hid her face in her hands, and sobs racked her body.

Jack was at a loss to know what to do. He went towards her but then stopped. 'Would you like . . . to talk about it?'

'No!' she exclaimed. Took a tremulous breath. 'No, I don't want to talk about it. Dr Alsaker wanted to talk about it. He's crazy, did you know that? He told me himself. But that doesn't make him a bad psychiatrist, he says, more the opposite. I don't need words, Jack, I've heard them all. My own and those of others, and they don't soothe any more. I need medicine.' She sniffed and wiped under her eyes carefully with the back of her hand. 'Quite simply, medicine. Without it I can't be the person I have to be.'

'And who's that?'

'Lady, Jack.' She looked at the mascara smeared on her hand. 'The woman who lives and lets die. But Macbeth has stopped using medicine and so there's nothing here. Imagine. He's stronger than me. You wouldn't have guessed that, would you? So you'll have to go and buy some for me, Jack.'

'Lady . . . '

'Otherwise everything will collapse here. I hear a

child crying all the time, Jack. I go into the gaming room and smile and talk.' Tears started rolling again. 'Talk loudly and laugh to drown out the sound of the crying child, but now I can't do it any longer. He knew the name of my child. He said my final words to her.'

'What do you mean?'

'Hecate. He knew. The words I said before I smashed the head with the questioning blue eyes. *In another life, my little Lily.* I've never told that to a living soul. Never! At least not in a conscious state. But perhaps when I've been dreaming. Perhaps when I've been sleepwa — ' She stopped. Frowned as if she had realised something.

'Hypnosis,' Jack said. 'You said it during the hypnosis. Hecate knows it from Dr Alsaker.'

'Hypnosis?' She nodded slowly. 'Do you think so? Do you think Alsaker betrayed me? And was paid for it, you mean?'

'People are greedy, that's their nature, ma'am. Without greed man wouldn't have won the fight on earth. Just look what you've created, ma'am.'

'You mean it's down to *greed?*'

'Not for money, ma'am. I think different people are greedy for different things. Power, sex, admiration, food, love, knowledge, fear . . . '

'What are you greedy for, Jack?'

'Me?' He shrugged. 'I like happy, satisfied customers. Yes, I'm greedy for the happiness of others. Such as your own, ma'am. When you're happy, I'm happy.'

She fixed him with her gaze. Then she got up, went over to the mirror and grabbed the hairbrush lying on the table beneath. 'Jack . . . '

He didn't like the sound of her voice but met her eyes in the mirror. 'Yes, ma'am.'

'You ought to know something about loneliness.'

'You know I do, ma'am.'

She started to brush her long flame-red hair, which men had been attracted by or had taken as a warning,

490

according to circumstances. 'But do you know what is lonelier than never having anyone? It is believing you had someone, but then it turns out that the person you thought was your closest friend never was.' The brush got stuck, but she forced it through the thick unruly hair. 'That you've been deceived the whole time. Can you imagine how lonely that is, Jack?'

'No, I can't, ma'am.'

Jack looked at her. He didn't know what to do or say.

'Be happy you haven't been deceived, Jack.' She put down the brush and passed him some notes. 'You're like a suckerfish: you're too small to be deceived, you can only deceive. The shark lets you hang on because you clean off other, worse, parasites. In return, it takes you across the oceans of the world. And that's how you travel, to the mutual benefit of both, and the relationship is so intimate and close that it can be confused with friendship. Until a bigger, healthier shark swims by. Go on, Jack. Go and buy me some brew.'

'Are you sure, ma'am?'

'Say you want something that works. Something strong. That can take you up high and far away. So high that you would crush your skull if you fell. For who wants to live in a cold, friendless world like this one?'

'I'll do my best, ma'am.'

He closed the door behind him without a sound.

'Oh, I'm sure you know where to find it, Jack Bonus,' she whispered to the reflection in the mirror. 'Say hello to Hecate, by the way.' A tear ran down her cheek, in the salty trail of the previous one. 'My good, dear Jack. My poor little Jack.'

★ ★ ★

'Mr Lennox?'

Lennox opened his eyes. Looked at his watch. An hour and a half to midnight. His eyelids went again. He

491

had begged for more morphine. All he wanted was sleep, even the tormented sleep of the guilty.

'Mr Lennox.'

He opened his eyes again. The first thing he saw was a hand holding a microphone. Behind it he glimpsed something yellow. Slowly it came into focus. A man in a yellow oilskin jacket sitting on a chair beside a hospital bed.

'You?' he whispered. 'Of all the reporters in this world they sent you?'

Walt Kite straightened his glasses. 'Tourtell, Malcolm and the others know that I . . . that I . . . '

'That you're in Macbeth's pocket?' Lennox lifted his head from the pillow. They were alone in the room. He squirmed to reach the alarm button by the bed head, but the radio reporter placed his hand over it.

'No need,' Kite said calmly.

Lennox tried to pull Kite's hand away from the alarm, but he didn't have the strength.

'So that you can feed me to Macbeth?' Lennox snorted. 'The way you fed Angus to us?'

'I was in the same predicament as you, Lennox. I had no choice. He threatened my family.'

Lennox gave up and slumped back. 'And what do you want now? Have you got a knife with you? Poison?'

'Yes. This.' Kite waved the microphone.

'Are you going to kill me with *that*?'

'Not you, but Macbeth.'

'Oh?'

Walt Kite put down the microphone, unbuttoned his jacket and wiped the fug from his glasses.

'When Tourtell rang I knew they had enough to get him. Tourtell persuaded the doctor to give me five minutes, so we have to hurry. Give me the story, and I'll go straight to the radio station and broadcast it, raw and unedited.'

'In the middle of the night?'

'I can do it before midnight. And it's enough for some people to hear it. Hear that it's irrefutably your voice. Listen, I'm breaking all the principles of good journalism — the right to respond, the duty to check statements — to save — '

'Your own skin,' Lennox said. 'To swap sides again. To be sure you're on the winning team.'

He saw Kite open his mouth and close it again. Swallow. And blink behind his still fugged-up glasses.

'Admit it, Kite. It's fine. You're not alone. We're not heroes. We're completely normal people who perhaps dream about being heroes, but confronted with the choice between life and the principles we sound off about, we're pretty normal.'

Kite flashed a brief smile. 'You're right. I've been an arrogant, big-mouthed, cowardly moralist.'

Lennox drew breath, no longer sure whether it was him or the morphine talking. 'But if you had the chance do you think you could do things any differently?'

'What do you mean?'

'Could you be a different person? Could you make yourself sacrifice something for a higher entity than your own esteem?'

'Such as what?'

'Such as doing something which is really heroic because it will reduce the respected journalist Kite's reputation to rubble?'

★ ★ ★

Macbeth closed his eyes. He hoped that when he opened them again he would wake up from the bad dream and the much-too-long night. All while the voice coming from the radio on the shelf behind his desk droned away. Every rolled 'r' sounded like a machine-gun volley.

'So, Inspector Lennox, to sum up. You maintain that

Chief Commissioner Macbeth is behind the murders of Chief Commissioner Duncan and Inspector Banquo, the massacre at the Norse Riders' club house, the murder of Inspector Duff's family, plus the execution of Police Officer Angus carried out at Macbeth's orders by you and Inspector Seyton. And that earlier this afternoon Chief Commissioner Macbeth with the head of SWAT, Inspector Seyton, and Police Officer Olafson were behind the failed attempt on Mayor Tourtell's life.'

'That is correct.'

'With that we say thank you to Inspector Lennox, who was speaking from his bed in St Jordi's Hospital. This recording has been made with witnesses present so that it can be used in a court of law, even if Lennox is also murdered. And so, dear listeners, finally I will add that I, Walt Kite, was an accessory to the murder of Police Officer Angus in that I placed the integrity you have honoured me with at the disposal of the chief commissioner and murderer, Macbeth. In the law court where I will be judged and in the conversations I will be having with my nearest and dearest, one mitigating circumstance might be that I and my family were threatened. However, professionally, this will not count. I have shown that I can be threatened, used and manipulated to lie to you. I have let myself down and I have let you down, and that means this is the last time you will hear from me, Walt Kite, radio reporter. I will miss you more than you will miss me. Show that you are better citizens than me. Take to the streets and depose Macbeth. Goodnight and God bless our town.'

The signature tune.

Macbeth opened his eyes. But he was still in his office, Seyton was still on the sofa, Olafson still on the chair and the radio was on.

Macbeth got up and turned it off.

'Well?' said Seyton.

'Shh,' Macbeth said.

'What?'

'Shut up for a second!' He held the bridge of his nose between his thumb and first finger. He was tired, so tired it was difficult to think as clearly as he needed to. Because he did need to. The next decisions he made were going to be momentous, the next few hours would decide the struggle for the town.

'My name,' Olafson said.

'What?'

'They said my name on the radio.' He smiled sheepishly. 'I don't think anyone in my family has ever had their name mentioned on the radio.'

Macbeth listened to the silence. The traffic, where was the regular booming drone of the traffic? It was as though the town was holding its breath. He got up. 'Come on.'

They took the lift down to the basement.

Passed the SWAT flag with the red dragon.

Seyton unlocked the ammo room and switched on the light.

The boy was sitting between the machine-gun stands, gagged and tied to the safe. The brown irises of his eyes were just a thin ring around the pupils, which were large and black with fear.

'We're taking him to the Inverness,' Macbeth said.

'The Inverness?'

'We're not safe here any longer, none of us. But from the Inverness we can bring Tourtell to his knees.'

'Who's we?'

'The last of the faithful. Those who will be rewarded when the victory is won.'

'You, me and Olafson? Are we going to bring the town to its knees?'

'Trust me.' Macbeth stroked Kasi's head as if he were a loyal dog. 'Hecate needs us and is protecting us.'

'Against the whole of the town?' Olafson said.

'Hecate's helpers constitute an army, Olafson.

They're as invisible as he is, but they're there — they've already saved me twice. And we have the Gatling sisters and the Kenneth Laws on our side. When Tourtell gives in and declares a state of emergency the town is mine. Well? Loyalty, fraternity?'

Olafson closed his eyes. 'Baptised in fire,' he whispered. The 's' lisped around the concrete walls.

Seyton scowled at them. But then, slowly, a smile spread across his narrow lips. 'United in blood.'

40

Duff was sitting on the sofa in Tourtell's living room. The four of them looked nervously at the mayor as he stood with the telephone to his ear. It was two minutes to midnight. Pressure had built up and up and thunder had started to rumble. The town would soon be punished for the hot day. The mayor alternated between 'Yes' and 'No' on the phone. Then he cradled the receiver. Smacked his lips as though what he had heard had to be chewed and swallowed.

'Well?' said Malcolm impatiently.

'Good and bad news. The good news is that Supreme Court Judge Archibald says that, based on what we have, he's fairly sure they should be able to issue a federal warrant for Macbeth's arrest, and that accordingly they can send federal police here.'

'And the bad news?' Malcolm asked.

'It's a politically delicate matter and will take time,' Tourtell said. 'No one wants to arrest a chief commissioner if it turns out the case won't hold water. In concrete terms all we have is a radio interview with Lennox, who himself has confessed to being an accessory to murder. Archibald says quite a bit more persuasion is needed for him to succeed, but the best-case scenario is that they'll get a ruling tomorrow afternoon.'

'But it'll be decided then,' Caithness said. 'So we just have to hold out tonight and a few hours tomorrow.'

'Looks like it,' Malcolm said. 'Shame the circumstances don't allow for a celebration.'

'On the contrary,' Tourtell said, turning to the maid, who had just come into the room. 'During the war, the more the victories cost us, the harder we celebrated. Champagne, Agnes!'

'Yes, sir, but there's someone on the other line.'

Tourtell brightened up. 'Kasi?'

'I'm afraid it's Mr Macbeth.'

They looked at each other.

'Put the call through here,' Tourtell said.

* * *

Macbeth leaned back in the chair with the phone to his ear. Staring up at the ceiling, at the inverted gold spire on the chandelier hanging over him and the empty gaming room. He was alone. He could hear Seyton and Olafson still in the process of assembling the Gatlings on the mezzanine, but he was alone just the same. Lady wasn't here. They had got to work as soon as they arrived back from HQ. It had taken them half an hour to get all the gamblers and diners out. They had tried to do it in a relaxed way. But games had to be finished, chips had to be cashed and some customers insisted on drinking up even though they weren't asked to pay. The last customers had protested that it was a Saturday night and literally had to be pushed out. Lady would of course have managed it in a more elegant way. But Jack, whom Macbeth had sent up to the suite to get her, had returned unaccompanied. That was fine, she needed her sleep, and this was going to be a long fight. They had removed the bars from the windows and sited the machine guns at each end of the mezzanine.

'Tourtell here.' The voice struggled to sound neutral.

'Good evening, Mayor. All well?'

'I'm alive.'

'Good, good. I'm glad we saved you from the assassination attempt. I suspect Hecate was behind it. Sorry your driver had to pay for it with his life. And that Lennox has lost his senses from the injury he brought on himself.'

Tourtell gave a dry laugh. 'You're finished, Macbeth. Do you realise?'

'These are indeed wild times, don't you think, Tourtell? Explosions on rooftops, shooting in the streets, assassination attempts on the chief commissioner and mayor. I rang because I think you should declare a state of emergency at once.'

'That won't happen, Macbeth. What will happen is that a federal arrest warrant is being issued in your name.'

'You've called in the cavalry from Capitol? I thought you would. But the warrant won't be issued before I have control of this town, and then it's too late. I will have immunity. Chief Commissioner Kenneth had more foresight than many give him credit for.'

'You're going to rule the town like the dictators before you?'

'In this storm it's probably best to have a stronger hand on the till than yours, Tourtell.'

'You're mad, Macbeth. Why on earth would I declare a state of emergency and hand power to you?'

'Because I have your illegitimate son and will cut his head off if you don't do what I say.'

Macbeth heard a sharp intake of breath.

'So don't go to sleep, Tourtell. I'll give you a few hours to write and sign the declaration of a state of emergency. And it will come into effect before the sun rises tomorrow. If I haven't heard it broadcast on radio before the first ray of sun hits my eyes, Kasi will die.'

Pause. Macbeth had a feeling Tourtell wasn't alone. According to Seyton, Duff, Malcolm and Caithness were three of the four who had prevented them from completing the job at St Jordi's Hospital.

'And how do you think you will get away with killing my son, Macbeth?'

The tone was tough but couldn't quite conceal his helplessness. And Macbeth noticed he hadn't been prepared for such utter despair. But he shook it off. The mayor's shaking voice confirmed what he had hoped for: Tourtell was willing to do anything at all for the boy.

'Immunity. State of emergency. That'll do the trick, Mayor.'

'I don't mean escaping a court of law. I was thinking of your conscience. You've become a monster, Macbeth.'

'We never become what we aren't already, Tourtell. You too, you'll always be willing to sell your favours and soul to the highest bidder.'

'Can't you hear the thunder outside your house, Macbeth? How can you, in this situation, in this town, still believe there will be sunshine at daybreak?'

'Because I've given orders that there will be. But if you're not a believer, let the sunrise times in this year's almanac be your guide. Until then . . . '

Macbeth rang off. Light played on the crystal above him. Which had to mean it was moving. Perhaps it was rising heat, perhaps it was the strange tremors in the ground or perhaps it was the light outside changing. But there was of course a fourth possibility. That it was he himself who was moving. Who saw things from a different angle. He took the silver dagger from inside his jacket. It was perhaps not the most effective weapon against tanks and thick skin, but Lady was right: silver worked against ghosts. He hadn't seen Banquo, Meredith, Duncan or the young Norse Rider on his knees for a couple of days. He held the dagger up to the light.

'Jack!'

No answer. Louder: 'Jack!'

Still no answer.

'Jack! Jack!' He yelled in such a wild, uncontrolled way that he imagined he could feel the inside of his throat tearing.

A door opened at the end of the room. 'You called,

sir?' Jack's voice echoed.

'Still no sign of life from Lady?'

'No, sir. Perhaps you should wake her?'

Macbeth ran a finger across the tip of the dagger. How long had he been clean now? And how much had he longed for sleep, the deep, dark, dreamless kind? He could go up there, lie down beside her and say that now we're going, you and I, we're going to a place where this, the Inverness and the town, doesn't exist, where nothing else but you and I exist. She wanted to, wanted to as much as he did. They had lost their way, but there had to be a way back, back to where they had come from. Yes, of course there was; he just couldn't see it right now. He had to talk to her, get her to show him where it was, as she always did. So what was stopping him? What strange premonition was stopping him from going up there, holding him back, making him prefer to sit in this cold empty room rather than lie in the warm arms of his beloved?

He turned and looked at the boy. Seyton had chained Tourtell's son to the shiny pole in the middle of the room, with a leg manacle around the boy's long, slim neck. Like a dog. And like a dog he lay motionless on the floor looking at Macbeth with his imploring brown eyes. The way they had stared unflinchingly at him ever since they arrived.

Macbeth stirred from the chair with an exclamation of annoyance.

'Let's go and see her then,' he said.

His own and Jack's soundless footsteps on the thick carpets gave Macbeth the sense they were floating like ghosts up the stairs and along the corridor. It took Macbeth ages to find the right key on Jack's ring. He examined every single one of them as though they held a code, the answer to a question he didn't yet know.

Then he opened the door and went in. The lamp in the room was switched off, but moonlight shone through gaps in the curtains. He stood listening. The thunder had stopped. It was so still, as though everything was holding its breath.

Her skin was so pale, so bloodless. Her hair spread across the pillow like a red fan and her eyelids seemed to be transparent.

He went over to her and placed his hand on her brow. There was still some warmth in her. Next to her, on the quilt, lay a piece of paper. He picked it up. She had written only a few lines.

Tomorrow, tomorrow and tomorrow. The days crawl in the mud, and in the end all they have accomplished is to kill the sun again and bring all men closer to death.

Macbeth turned to Jack, who had remained in the doorway.

'She's gone.'

'Wh . . . what, sir?'

Macbeth pulled a chair to the bed and sat down. Not to be close to her; she wasn't there any more. He just wanted to sit.

He heard Jack's cry of shock behind him and knew he had seen it, the syringe still hanging from her forearm.

'Is she . . . ?'

'Yes, she's d-d-dead.'

'How long . . . ?'

'A l-l-long time.'

'But I was talking to — '

'She started d-d-dying the night she found the baby in the shoebox, Jack. She simulated life for a while, but it was only the convulsions of death. She saw her child, saw that she would have to travel into death to see her again. That was when we lost Lady, when she fell for that consoling notion that we meet our loved ones on the other side.'

Jack took a step closer. 'But you don't believe it?'

'Not when the sun is shining from a clear sky. But we live in a town without sun, where we take all the consolation we can get. So, by and large, I believe.'

Macbeth examined himself, amazed that he felt neither sorrow nor despair. Perhaps because he had long known that this is how it would end. He had known it and closed his eyes. And all he felt was emptiness. He was sitting in a waiting room in the middle of the night, he was the only passenger, and his train had been announced but it hadn't arrived. Announced but it hadn't arrived. And what does the passenger do then? He waits. He doesn't go anywhere, he reconciles himself to what is happening and waits for what is to come.

Macbeth picked up the piece of paper again.

The days crawl in the mud, and in the end all they have accomplished is to kill the sun again and bring all men closer to death.

41

The lift took Duff, Malcolm and the caretaker down to the basement at police HQ.

'I know it's a weekend, but are you sure there isn't anyone else here?' Duff said to the caretaker, whom Malcolm had spoken to at length on the phone from Tourtell's house.

'On the contrary,' the caretaker answered. 'They're waiting for you.'

Duff was unable to react before the lift arrived and the doors opened in front of him. Three people were there, all armed and dressed in the black SWAT uniform. Duff held his breath.

'Thank you,' Malcolm said. 'For coming at such short notice.'

'For the town,' said one of them.

'For Angus,' said the second.

'For the chief commissioner,' said the third, an erect, dark-skinned man. 'In our book his name is now Malcolm.'

'Thank you, Ricardo,' Malcolm said, exiting the lift.

The stiff-backed officer led the way. 'Have you spoken to anyone else, sir?'

'I've been on the phone all evening. It shouldn't be easy to persuade people to risk their lives and jobs to fight against a conspiracy they only have my word for. Especially when I add that we cannot expect any immediate help from Capitol. However, I have around thirty officers from the police, ten to fifteen from Civil Defence and maybe ten from the Fire Service.'

'The case may not sound very convincing, but *you* are, Malcolm.'

'Thank you, Ricardo, but I think Macbeth's actions speak for themselves.'

'I wasn't thinking about your words, sir. Your courage speaks louder.'

'I had everything taken from me and didn't have much to lose, Ricardo. Nevertheless I had to come back and fetch my daughter, who has been taken to safety now. It's you who show courage. You're not controlled by a father's heart, you're acting freely, governed by your own sense of justice. Which proves that in this town there are people who want what is good.'

They passed the dragon flag.

'And where's the mayor?' Ricardo asked.

'He's got other things on his mind at the moment.'

Ricardo stopped in front of a massive iron door, like the entrance to an air-raid shelter. It was open. 'Here.'

The shelves inside were laden with iron boxes and firearms. In the middle of the floor there was a safe. Malcolm took one of the machine guns from a shelf.

'Someone's taken the Gatling guns and their ammo,' Ricardo said. 'So this is all we have. Plus an armoured car. I can have it brought down to the central station straight away. There aren't enough guns for everyone, but the firemen don't have any weapon training anyway. My men and I can strike tonight, though.'

'We'd far prefer Macbeth to surrender voluntarily,' Malcolm said. 'The numbers tell us he probably has two men with him: Seyton and Olafson. When he sees how many we've mobilised outside I hope he will release Kasi and capitulate.'

'Negotiations.' Ricardo nodded. 'Modern tactics in hostage situations.'

'Precisely.'

'Modern and useless, as far as Macbeth is concerned. I've had him as a boss, sir. He has the two best marksmen in the country and two Gatling guns on his side. While we have very little time.'

'What can you do against two Gatling guns?' Malcolm asked, taking down a bazooka.

Duff stiffened. He had seen what was behind the bazooka.

'It's not very accurate over a long distance,' Ricardo said. 'But I'd be happy to draw up a plan of how we can take the Inverness if Macbeth won't surrender.'

'Good,' Malcolm said, looking at what Duff had found. 'Jesus, where's that from?'

'The ruins after the raid on the Norse Riders,' Ricardo said. 'It's a weapon, even if it's only a sabre.'

'It's not just any sabre,' Duff said, gripping the handle tightly. He swung it and felt the weight of the steel. 'It's Sweno's sabre.'

'You're not thinking of taking it, are you? It can't do any harm.'

'Wrong.' Duff ran his forefinger over the blade. 'It can slice open women's stomachs and children's faces.'

Malcolm turned to Ricardo. 'Can you have the weapons transported to the central station an hour before sunrise?'

'Consider it done.'

'Thank you. Let's see if the rest of us can catch a couple of hours' shut-eye?'

★ ★ ★

'Sir?'

Macbeth lifted his head from Lady's cold chest and looked up. It was Jack. He had returned and was standing in the doorway.

'There's someone down in reception who'd like to talk to you.'

'Have you let s-s-someone in?'

'He's alone and he kept knocking. I had to let him in. And now he doesn't want to go away.'

'Who is it?'

'A young man by the name of Sivart.'

'Sivart?'

'He says you saved his life down by the quay during the raid on the Norse Riders.'

'Oh, the hostage. Wh-wh-what does he want?'

'To volunteer. He says he's been contacted by Malcolm, and Malcolm is getting people together to launch an attack on the Inverness.'

'Then,' Macbeth said, resting his head back on Lady's chest and closing his eyes, 't-t-tell him to go.'

'He won't, sir.'

Macbeth sighed heavily, got to his feet and held out a hand. 'Lend me the gun I gave you, Jack.'

They went down to reception, where the young man was nervously waiting. From the stairs Macbeth pointed the gun at him. 'Out!'

'Chief Commissioner . . . ' the man stammered.

'Out! You've been sent by Malcolm to kill me. Now out!'

'No, no, I . . . '

'Now! I'll count to three! One . . . '

The man stumbled backwards, grabbed the door handle, but it was locked.

'Two!'

Jack rushed forward with the key and helped the man to open the door.

'Three!'

The door slammed behind the man and they heard running footsteps fade in the distance.

'Do you really think he — '

'No,' Macbeth said, handing back the gun to Jack. 'But a young man like him here would have just got in the way.'

'There aren't many of you, and he's the same age as Olafson, sir.'

'Have you done what I asked you to do, Jack?'

'I'm still doing it, sir.'

'Tell me when you've finished. I'm in the gaming room.'

Macbeth opened the double doors to the casino. The night grew old and grey behind the tall windows to the east.

42

The sun was hidden behind the mountain, but it had sent a red harbinger of its arrival. Inspector Lennox thought he had never seen a finer daybreak in the town. Or perhaps he had, but had never noticed it. Or perhaps it was the morphine more than the sun that coloured everything. The streets were adorned with smashed beer bottles, stinking piles of spew and cigarette ends after a lively Saturday night, but no one was about, only a little man in a black maritime uniform and white hat, who hurried past them. Everyone else, as the town's fate was decided, lay at home in bed with the blankets pulled over their heads. And despite this he had never seen his town looking more beautiful.

Lennox gazed down at the tartan blanket Priscilla had spread over his knees. They were approaching the modest eastern entrance to the central station. He noticed the wheelchair was moving more slowly. She was hesitant; he guessed she had hardly ever been to the station before.

'There's nothing to be afraid of, Priscilla. They only want to sell dope. Or buy it.' He saw from her shadow as they passed under a street light that she had straightened up. Their speed increased.

As arranged, she had picked him up while it was still dark outside, before the corridors were full of nurses and doctors who would have stopped them. And she had brought various things from the office which he had requested. He didn't even need to persuade her or explain anything to her; she had immediately done what he had said, even if officially he was no longer her boss.

'That's fine,' she had said. 'You'll always be my boss.

509

And Macbeth won't continue as chief commissioner, will he?'

'Why not?'

'He's off his trolley, isn't he.'

They passed cigarette-smoking pushers and junkies dozing on blankets who woke up and automatically reached out a begging hand.

But Priscilla didn't stop until they were in front of the stairs by the toilets.

It was here they used to collect him. All he had to do was stand there and they came. Lennox had never worked out where they took him because they not only put goggles on him but also gave him earplugs so that he couldn't speculate from the background noises.

It was a part of the agreement. When he needed a real trip, one that couldn't happen at home or at the office in the evening without the risk of being caught, they took him into the kitchen, the place where they made brew. And there he was given the purest drug that could be produced, injected by specialists. He was placed in a reclining chair, a bit like they did in the old days in opium dens, and after sleeping off his high in safe surroundings he could go into town and move around for a while like a new and better man.

In a way which he would never be able to do again.

He had felt how helpless he was when Priscilla freed him from all the wires and tubes and manoeuvred him across into the wheelchair. How useless he had become. How little he could be expected to do.

'Go,' he said now.

'What? Are we going?'

'You are.'

'And just leave you here, you mean?'

'It'll be fine. I'll ring you. Go now.'

She didn't move.

'It's an order, Priscilla — ' he smiled ' — from the man who will always be your boss.'

She sighed. Gently placed a hand on his shoulder. Then she left.

Less than ten minutes passed before Strega was standing in front of him with her arms crossed. 'Wow!' was all she said.

'I know,' Lennox said. 'It's an ungodly hour.'

She laughed briefly. 'You're in good humour despite the wheelchair. What can I do for you?'

'Something to stop the pain and an hour in the recliner.'

She passed him the earplugs and the goggles.

'My legs are not what they were, so you might have to help me get there.'

'A feather like you?' she said.

'I need the wheelchair with me.'

'We'll have to skip the car trip today.'

She pushed him. The pains had come and gone all morning, but when she lifted him out of the wheelchair a few minutes later and lowered him onto what felt like crushed stone it hurt so much he cried. He felt Strega's muscular arms around him, the almost overwhelming scent of her. After she managed to get him back in the wheelchair she began to push it. Every metre the wheelchair hit something in the gravel. A sleeper. There was a smell of tar and burned metal. He was being pushed along a railway track.

Fancy not realising. The other times they had ridden in a car, not a long way, but clearly in a circle, back to their starting point at the central station. He had known before that they were under cover as he hadn't felt the rain, but not that the brewing took place in one of the disused tunnels right under their noses! He groaned with impotence as Strega lifted him and laid him cheek down on something cold and damp. Concrete. Then she put him back in the wheelchair. Pushed it. The air was getting warmer, drier. They were approaching the kitchen now, the easily recognisable smells activating something in his brain which made his heart beat faster and gave him a foretaste of the trip. Someone removed the goggles and earplugs and he caught the tail end of Strega's sentence.

' . . . wash the trail of blood after him.'

'All right,' said one of the sisters stirring the tank.

Strega was about to lift him into the reclining chair, but Lennox waved her away and rolled up his left shirtsleeve. Brew straight from the pot. It didn't get any better than that. A junkie's heaven. This was where he wanted to go. Or not. He would see. Or not.

'Isn't that Inspector Lennox from the Anti-Corruption Unit?' Jack said. He was standing by the one-way glass looking in at the kitchen and the man in the wheelchair.

'Yes,' Hecate said. He was wearing a white linen suit and hat. 'It's not enough to have eyes and ears in the Inverness.'

'Did you hear that Lennox has accused Macbeth of murder? Doesn't he know Macbeth is your instrument?'

'No one's allowed to know more than they have to, not even you, Bonus. But back to the matters in hand. Lady has taken her own life, but Macbeth seems paralysed rather than upset, would you say?'

'That's my interpretation.'

'Hm. And if Tourtell declares a state of emergency, do you think Macbeth in his present state of mind will manage to take power, to do what has to be done to establish himself as the town's leader?'

'I don't know. He seems . . . not to care. As though nothing is very important any more. Either that or he believes himself to be invulnerable. You will save him whatever happens.'

'Hm.' Hecate tapped his stick on the floor twice. 'Without Lady the value of Macbeth as chief commissioner has sunk.'

'He'll still obey.'

'He might succeed in taking power now, but without her he won't be able to keep it. She was the one who understood the game, could see the wood for the trees, knew what manoeuvres were required. Macbeth can throw daggers, but someone has to tell him why and at whom.'

'I could become his new adviser,' Jack said. 'I'm winning his confidence.'

Hecate laughed. 'I can't quite make up my mind whether you're a mud-eating flounder or actually a sly predatory fish, Bonus.'

'I am a fish though, I gather.'

'Even if you could bolster his impaired ability to rule, I doubt you could do much about his will. He lacks Lady's lust for power. He seems to desire things you and I have not been dependent on, dear Bonus.'

'Brew?'

'Lady. Women. Friends maybe. You know, this love between humans. And now that Lady's dead he's no longer driven by the desire to satisfy her hunger for power.'

'Lady also needed love,' Jack said quietly.

'The desire to be loved and the ability to love, which give humans such strength, are also their Achilles heel. Give them the prospect of love and they move mountains; take it from them and a puff of wind will blow them over.'

'Maybe, maybe.'

'If the wind blows Macbeth over, what do you think about him there as chief commissioner?' Hecate nodded towards the glass. One of the sisters was drying Lennox's left arm with an alcohol swab and searching for a vein while holding a syringe ready.

'Lennox?' Jack said. 'Are you serious?'

Hecate smacked his lips. 'He's the man who brought Macbeth down. The hero who sacrificed his mobility to save the town's mayor. And no one knows that Lennox works for me.'

'But Malcolm's back. And everyone knows Lennox runs Macbeth's errands.'

'Lennox followed orders like a loyal policeman should. And Malcolms and Duffs can disappear again. Roosevelt won a world war from a wheelchair. Yes, I could get Lennox into the chief commissioner's office. What do you reckon?'

Jack looked at Lennox. Without answering.

Hecate laughed and laid a big soft hand on Jack's narrow shoulder. 'I know what you're thinking, flounder. What about you? Who will employ you if Macbeth has gone? So let's hope Macbeth rides the storm, eh? Come on, let me show you out.'

Jack cast a final glance at Lennox, then he turned and walked back with Hecate to the toilet door and the station.

★　★　★

'Wait,' Lennox said as the sister placed the needle against his skin. He put his free right hand into the big side pocket of the wheelchair. Pulled the cord from the end of the handle.

'Now,' he said.

She pushed the needle in and pressed the plunger as he took his hand from the pocket, swung his arm low alongside the chair and let go. What Priscilla had brought from the office rumbled along the concrete floor and disappeared under the table bearing the flasks, tubes and pipes beside the tank.

'Hey, what was that?' Strega asked.

'According to my grandfather, it was a grenade he had thrown at his head,' Lennox said, feeling the high, which would never be like the first time but still made him shiver with pleasure. Which was, after all these years of searching, still the closest he had come to the meaning of life. Unless it was this. The full stop.

'It might be a Model 24 *Stielhandgranate*. Or an ashtr — '

That was as far as he got.

★   ★   ★

Jack was halfway up the stairs when the explosion sent him flying. He picked himself up and turned back to the toilet. The door had been blown off and smoke was drifting out. He waited. When there were no more explosions he walked slowly down the stairs and into the toilet. The cubicle and door to the kitchen had gone. There was a fierce fire inside, and in the light of the flames he could see everything had been destroyed. The kitchen and those inside didn't exist any more. And five seconds earlier he had been —

'Bonus . . . '

The voice came from directly in front of him. And there, from under the steel door on the floor, it crawled out. A smashed cockroach in a white linen suit. The soft face was covered with shit and his eyes were black with shock.

'Help me . . . '

Bonus grabbed hold of the old man's hands and pulled him across the floor to the toilet door. There he turned Hecate onto his back. He was a wreck. His stomach was slashed open and blood was pouring out. The immortal Hecate. The Invisible Hand, he couldn't have many minutes or seconds left to live. All the blood . . . Jack turned away.

'Hurry, Jack. Find something you can — '

'I have to get a doctor,' Jack said.

'No! Find something to close the wound with before I run out of blood.'

'You need medical help. I'll hurry.'

'Don't leave me, Jack! Don't . . . ' The body in front of Jack arced and let out a howl.

515

'What?'

'Stomach acid! Something's leaking. Christ, I'm burning up. Help, Jack! Hel — ' The shout morphed into another hoarse howl. Jack watched him, unable to move. He did look like a cockroach lying on its back, its arms and legs thrashing helplessly.

'I'll be back soon,' Jack said.

'No, no!' Hecate screamed and made a grab for his legs.

But Jack stepped away, turned and left.

At the top of the stairs he stopped, looked left, west towards the Inverness. Towards Macbeth. Towards St Jordi's. There was a phone box in the waiting area that way. He turned to the east. To the mountain. To the other side. To new waters. Dangerous, open waters. But these were decisions a man — and a suckerfish — had to make sometimes to survive.

Jack breathed in. Not because he was hesitant, but because he needed air.

Then he headed east.

★ ★ ★

The crystal murmured and sang above Macbeth's head. He looked up. The chandelier swung back and forth, tugging at the ropes from which it hung.

'What was that?' yelled Seyton from the mezzanine, from the Gatling gun in the south-eastern corner of the Inverness.

'The end of the world,' Macbeth said. And added, in a low voice and to himself, 'I hope.'

'It came from the station,' Olafson shouted from the machine gun in the south-west corner. 'Was that an explosion?'

'Yessir!' Seyton sang. 'They're bringing up the artillery.'

'Are they?' Olafson said, shocked.

Seyton's laughter echoed between the walls. When they had discussed how the Inverness should be defended it had been easy to conclude that any attack would have to come from Workers' Square, as the bricked-up, windowless side facing Thrift Street was nothing less than a fortress wall.

'I can smell your fear from over here, Olafson. Can you smell it down there, boss?'

Macbeth yawned. 'I can barely remember the smell of fear, Seyton.' He rubbed his face hard. He had dropped off and dreamed he was lying on the bed next to Lady when the door to the suite slid silently open. The figure in the doorway was wearing a cloak, with a hat pulled so low that it was only when the figure stepped in and the light fell on him that he could see it was Banquo. One eye was gone and white; worms were wriggling out of his cheek and forehead. Macbeth had reached inside his jacket, drawn a dagger from his double shoulder holster and thrown. It bored into Banquo's brow with a soft thud as if the bone behind had already been eaten up. But it didn't stop the ghost advancing towards the bed. Macbeth screamed and shook Lady.

'She's dead,' the ghost said. 'And you have to throw a silver dagger, not steel.' It wasn't Banquo's voice. It was . . .

Banquo's head toppled from under the hat, fell on the floor and rolled under the bed, and from the hat Seyton's face laughed at him.

'What do you want?' Macbeth whispered.

'What you want, sir. To give you both a child. Look, she's waiting for me.'

'You're crazy.'

'Trust me. I don't want much in return.'

'She's dead. Go away.'

'We're all dead. Do it now, sow your seeds. If you don't I'll sow mine.'

'Get away!'

'Move over, Macbeth. I'll take her like Duff took Meredi — '

The second dagger hit Seyton in his open mouth. He clenched his teeth, grasped the handle, broke it off and passed it back to Macbeth. Showed him his bloody, sliced tongue and laughed.

★   ★   ★

'Anything on the radio?'

Macbeth gave a start. It was Seyton, shouting.

'Nothing,' Macbeth said, rubbing his face hard and turning up the volume on the radio. 'Still twenty minutes to sun-up.' He looked at the white line of finely chopped powder on the mirror he had placed on the felt in front of him. Saw his face reflected. The line of power ran like a scar across the shiny surface.

'And then will we really kill the boy?' Olafson shouted.

'Yes, Olafson!' Seyton shouted back. 'We're men, not cissies!'

'But . . . what then? We'll have nothing to negotiate with.'

'Does that sound familiar, Olafson?' More laughter from the south-east.

'We have nothing to fear,' Macbeth said.

'What's that, sir?'

'No man born can harm me. Hecate promised me I'll be chief commissioner until Bertha comes to get me. You can say a lot about Hecate, but he keeps his word. Relax. Tourtell will give in.' Macbeth looked at Kasi, who sat quietly with his back to the pole, staring into the distance. 'What can you see, Seyton?'

'People have gathered up by Bertha. They look like police officers and civilians. A few automatic weapons, some rifles and handguns. Shouldn't be much of a problem if they attack with those.'

'Can you see any grey coats?'

'Grey coats? No.'

'And your sector, Olafson?'

'None here either, sir.'

But Macbeth knew that they were there. Watching over him.

'Have you heard of Tithonos, Seyton?'

'Nope. Who's he?'

'A Greek. Lady told me about him. I looked him up. Eos was this goddess of the dawn and she stole a young lover, a pretty ordinary guy called Tithonos. Made sure the boss himself, Zeus, gave the guy eternal life, like her. The guy didn't ask for it, he just had it forced on him. But the goddess had forgotten to ask for eternal youth for the guy. Do you understand?'

'Maybe, but I don't understand where you're going with this, sir.'

'Everything disappears, everyone else dies, but there's Tithonos rotting away in his old age and loneliness. He hasn't been given anything, the opposite in fact — he's in prison, his eternal life is a bloody curse.'

Macbeth got up so quickly he felt giddy. This was just gloom and a hangover from the dope talking. He had a town lying at his feet, and soon it would be irrevocably his, only his, and he could have his every slightest wish fulfilled. Then all he would need to think about were desires and pleasures. Desires and pleasures.

★　★　★

Duff ran a finger over the crack in the base in front of Bertha's nose. Heard Malcolm's voice: 'Sorry, let me through!'

He looked up and saw Malcolm forcing his way through the crowd up to the top of the steps.

'Did you hear that too?' he asked, out of breath.

'Yes,' Caithness said. 'I thought the roof was going to

come down. Felt like an underground test explosion.'

'Or an earthquake,' Duff said, pointing to the crack.

'Looks like a bigger turnout than I'd planned,' Malcolm said, scanning the people who had gathered at the foot of the steps behind the barricade of police cars and a big red fire engine. 'Are all these people firemen and police officers?'

'No,' said a man coming up the steps. Malcolm examined his black uniform.

'Naval captain?'

'Pilot,' said the little man. 'Fred Ziegler.'

'What's a pilot doing here?'

'I heard Kite on the radio last night, rang around and heard rumours about what was going to happen here. Tell me what I can do.'

'Have you got a weapon?'

'No.'

'Can you shoot?'

'I was in the marines for ten years.'

'Good. Go to the man in the police uniform down there and he'll give you a rifle.'

'Thank you.' The pilot put three fingers to his white cap and left.

'What does Tourtell say?' Duff asked.

'Capitol has been informed about the hostage,' Malcolm said. 'But they can't help us until an arrest warrant has been issued this afternoon.'

'Jesus, there are people's lives at risk here.'

'One life. That doesn't qualify for federal intervention unless our chief commissioner requests it.'

'Bloody politics! And where's Tourtell now?' Duff stared to the east. At the edge of the mountain the pale blue sky was getting redder and redder.

'He went to the radio studio,' Caithness said.

'He's going to declare a state of emergency,' Malcolm said. 'We have to attack Macbeth now while we can still act under the mayor's orders. As soon as a state of emergency's declared we'll be lawless revolutionaries and none of these people will be with us.' He nodded towards the crowd.

'Macbeth has barricaded himself in,' Caithness said. 'People's lives will be lost.'

'Yes.' Malcolm put the megaphone to his mouth. 'My good men and women! Take up your positions!'

The crowd ran to the barricade at the foot of the steps. Rested their weapons on car roofs, took cover behind the SWAT armoured car and the fire engine and aimed at the Inverness.

Malcolm pointed the megaphone in the same direction. 'Macbeth! This is Deputy Chief Commissioner Malcolm speaking. You know, and we know, you're in a hopeless situation. All you can achieve is to defer the inevitable. So release the hostage and give yourself up. I'll give you one, I repeat, one minute.'

★ ★ ★

'What did he say?' Seyton shouted.

'He's giving me a minute,' Macbeth said. 'Can you see him?'

'Yes, he's standing at the top of the steps.'

'Olafson, take your rifle and shut Malcolm up.'

'Do you mean — '

'Yes, I mean exactly that.'

'All hail Macbeth!' Seyton laughed.

'Listen,' Macbeth said.

★ ★ ★

Duff alternated between looking at the mountain, his watch and the men around him. His elbows and shoulders twitched with nerves. They were shifting position because of his knees and calves, which had started to shake. Apart from the six SWAT volunteers

521

and some of the other policemen, the crowd was made up of people with ordinary jobs in accounting offices and fire stations, who had never fired a shot in anger. Or been shot at. And yet they had come here. They were willing, despite their inadequacy, to sacrifice everything. He counted down the final three seconds.

Nothing happened.

Duff exchanged glances with Malcolm and shrugged. Malcolm sighed and lifted the megaphone to his mouth.

Duff hardly heard the bang.

Malcolm staggered back, and the megaphone fell to the ground with a clang.

Duff and Fleance reacted at once, throwing themselves over Malcolm and covering him as he fell to the ground. Duff felt for blood and a pulse.

'I'm fine,' Malcolm groaned. 'I'm fine. Up you get. He hit the megaphone. That was all.'

★ ★ ★

'When you said shut him up, I thought you meant permanently,' Seyton shouted. 'Now they'll think we're weak, sir.'

'Wrong,' Macbeth said. 'Now they know we mean business, but we're sane. If we'd killed Malcolm we'd have given them an excuse to attack us with the fury of righteousness. Now they'll still hesitate.'

'I think they're going to attack anyway,' Olafson said. 'Look, there's our armoured car. It's coming towards us.'

'Well, that's different. A chief commissioner is allowed to defend himself. Seyton?'

'Yes?'

'Let the Gatling girls speak.'

★ ★ ★

Duff peeped from behind Bertha and followed the lumpen armoured car — known as a *Sonderwagen* — as it made its way across the square towards the Inverness. Thick, heavy diesel smoke drifted up from the vehicle's exhaust. German engineering, steel plates and bullet-proof glass. Ricardo's plan followed usual tactics. The six SWAT volunteers would drive up to the entrance in the *Sonderwagen*, dismount to fire tear-gas canisters through the windows, then break down the doors and storm the building wearing gas masks. The critical point was when they emerged from the armoured car to fire the tear gas. This would take only seconds, but in those seconds they needed covering fire from the others.

Malcolm's walkie-talkie crackled, and they heard Ricardo's voice.

'Covering fire in three . . . two . . . one . . . '

'Fire!' Malcolm roared.

It sounded like a drum roll as the weapons fired from the barricade. From an all-too-small drum, Duff thought. And the sound was drowned by a rising howl from the other side.

'Holy Jesus,' Caithness whispered.

At first it resembled a shower of rain whipping up dust from the cobbles in front of the *Sonderwagen*. Then with a cackle it hit the vehicle's grille, its armour, the windscreen and the roof. The vehicle seemed to sag at the knees and sink.

'The tyres,' Fleance said.

The vehicle kept moving, but more slowly, as though it were driving into a hurricane.

'It's fine. It's an armoured car,' Malcolm said.

The vehicle advanced more and more slowly. And stopped. The side mirrors and bumper fell off.

'It *was* an armoured car,' Duff said.

'Ricardo?' Malcolm called on the walkie-talkie. 'Ricardo? Withdraw!'

No answer.

Now the vehicle seemed to be dancing.

Then the barrage stopped. Silence fell over the square, broken only by a seagull's lament as it flew over. Smoke, like red vapour, rose from the armoured car.

'Ricardo! Come in, Ricardo!'

Still no answer. Duff stared at the vehicle, at the wreck. There were no signs of life. And now he knew how it had been. That afternoon in Fife.

'Ricardo!'

'They're dead,' Duff said. 'They're all dead.'

Malcolm sent him a sidelong glance.

Duff ran a hand over his face. 'What's the next move?'

'I don't know, Duff. That was the move.'

'The fire engine,' Fleance said.

The others looked at the young man.

He shrank beneath their collective gaze and for a moment seemed to stagger under the weight of it. But he straightened up and said with a slight quiver of his vocal cords, 'We have to use the fire engine.'

'It's no good,' Malcolm objected.

'No, but if we drive it round to the back, to Thrift Street.' Fleance paused to swallow before continuing. 'You saw they hit the armoured car with both machine guns, and that must mean they're not covering their rear.'

'Because they know we can't get in there,' Duff said. 'There are no doors and no windows, there's only brick, which you'd need a pneumatic drill or heavy artillery to go through.'

'Not through,' Fleance said. His voice was firmer now.

'Round?' Duff queried.

Fleance pointed a finger to the sky.

'Of course!' Caithness said. 'The fire engine.'

'Spit it out. What's so obvious?' growled Malcolm, snatching a glance at the mountain.

'The ladder,' Duff said. 'The roof.'

★ ★ ★

'They're moving the fire engine,' Seyton shouted.

'Why?' Macbeth yawned. The boy was sitting on the floor with his legs crossed and eyes closed. Calm and silent, he seemed to have reconciled himself to his fate and was just waiting for the end. Like Macbeth.

'I don't know.'

'What about you, Olafson?'

'I don't know, sir.'

'All right,' Macbeth shouted. He had taken out the silver dagger and whittled a match to a point. He poked it between his front teeth. Left the dagger on the felt. Picked up two chips and began to flip them between the fingers of each hand. He had learned how to do this at the circus. It was an exercise to balance the difference between the motor functions of his left and right hands. He sucked the matchstick, flipped the chips and examined what he was feeling. Nothing. He tried to work out what he was thinking. He wasn't thinking about Banquo and he wasn't thinking about Lady. He was just thinking that he didn't feel anything. And he thought one more thing: *Why? Why . . . ?*

He thought about that for a while . . .

Then he closed his eyes and began to count down from ten.

★ ★ ★

'This is not like a ladder against a house. It's going to sway more the higher we go,' said the man in the harbour pilot's uniform to Fleance and the two other volunteers. 'But make only one movement at a time, one hand, then one foot. Nothing to be afraid of.'

The pilot yawned loudly and smiled quickly before grasping the ladder and starting to climb.

Fleance watched the little man, wishing he was

equally unafraid. Thrift Street was empty apart from the fire engine with its fifteen-metre ladder pointing up the windowless wall.

Fleance followed the pilot, and strangely enough the fear diminished with every step. The worst was over, after all. He had spoken. And they had listened. Nodded and said they understood. Then they had got into the fire engine and driven east from the station in a great arc through the Sunday-still streets, arriving at the rear of the Inverness unseen.

Fleance looked up and saw the harbour pilot signalling from the roof that the way was clear.

They had gone through the drawings of the Inverness so thoroughly last night that Fleance knew exactly where everything was. The flat roof led to a door, and inside it there was a narrow ladder down to a boiler room with a door leading to the top corridor in the hotel. There they would split up, two men would take the northern staircase, two the southern. Both led down to the mezzanine. In a few minutes they would start shooting from the station and keep the machine-gunners' attention focused on Workers' Square, drowning out any sounds made by Fleance and the three others, who would sneak up from behind and eliminate the machine-gunners. The three volunteers had synchronised their watches with Fleance's without a word of protest that they were being led by a police cadet. The cadet seemed to know the odd thing about such actions. What was it his dad had said? *And if you've got better judgement you should lead, it's your damned duty to the community.*

Fleance heard them open fire from the station.

'Follow me.'

They approached the roof door, pulled. Locked. As expected. He nodded to one of the policemen, a guy from the Traffic Unit, who rammed a crowbar into the crack between the door and its frame and pushed hard.

The lock broke at the first attempt.

It was dark inside, but Fleance felt the heat coming from the boiler room beneath. The other policeman, a white-haired guy from the Fraud Unit, wanted to go first, but Fleance held him back. 'Follow me,' he whispered and stepped in over the high metal threshold. In vain he tried to distinguish shapes in the darkness and had to lower his machine gun as he groped for the railing of the ladder. The metal ladder sang as he took his first tentative step and then found the next rung. He froze, dazzled by a light. A torch had been switched on below him and shone at his face.

'Bang,' said a voice from behind the torch. 'You're dead.'

Fleance knew he was standing in the line of fire of the three behind him. And he knew he wouldn't have time to fire his machine gun. Because he knew whose the voice was.

'How did you know . . . ?'

'I wondered to myself, *Why oh why would you move a fire engine when there's no fire alarm to be heard?*' The voice in the darkness became a low chuckle. 'Still wearing my shoes, I see.' Uncle Mac sounded drunk. 'Listen, Fleance, you can save lives today. Your own and those of the other three mutineers with you. Back out now and get behind the barricade. You'll have a better chance of getting me from there.'

Fleance ran his tongue around his mouth searching for moisture. 'You killed Dad.'

'Maybe,' the voice slurred. 'Or perhaps it was the circumstances. Or perhaps it was Banquo's ambitions for his family. But probably — ' in the pause came the sound of a deep sigh ' — it was me. Go now, Fleance.'

Fluttering through Fleance's brain were all those pretend-fights he'd had with Uncle Mac at home on the sitting-room floor, when he had let Fleance get the upper hand, only to whisk him round at the last minute and pin him flat on the floor. This wasn't due to his uncle's strength, but his speed and precision. But how drunk was Uncle Mac now? And how much better coordinated was Fleance? Perhaps he had a chance after all? If he was quick, perhaps he could get a shot in. Save Kasi. Save the town. Avenge —

'Don't do it, Fleance.'

But it was too late. Fleance had already grabbed his machine gun, and the sound of a brief volley hammered against the eardrums of all five men in the cramped boiler room.

'Agh!' Fleance yelled.

Then he fell from the ladder.

He didn't feel himself hit the floor, felt nothing until he opened his eyes again. And then he saw nothing, although there was a hand against his cheek and a voice close to his ear.

'I told you not to.'

'Wh . . . where are they?'

'They left as instructed. Sleep now, Fleance.'

'But . . . ' He knew he had been shot. A leak. He coughed, and his mouth filled.

'Sleep. Say hello to your dad when you arrive and tell him I'm right behind you.'

Fleance opened his mouth, but all that came out was blood. He felt Macbeth's fingers on his eyelids, gentle, careful. Closing them. Fleance sucked in air as if for a dive. As he had done when he fell from the bridge into the river, into the black water, to his grave.

★　★　★

'No,' Duff said when he saw the fire engine driving towards them. 'No!'

He and Malcolm ran to meet the vehicle, and when it stopped they tore open the doors on each side. The driver, two police officers and the harbour pilot tumbled out.

'Macbeth was waiting for us,' groaned the pilot, still breathless. 'He shot Fleance.'

'No, no, no!' Duff leaned back and squeezed his eyes shut.

Someone laid a hand on his neck. A familiar hand. Caithness's.

Two men in black SWAT uniforms ran over and halted in front of Malcolm. 'Hansen and Edmunton, sir. We heard about this and came as soon as we could. And there are more coming.'

'Thank you, guys, but we're finished.' Malcolm pointed. They couldn't see the sun yet, but the silhouette of the upside-down cross at the top of the mountain had already caught its first rays. 'Now it's up to Tourtell.'

'Let's exchange hostages,' Duff said. 'Let Macbeth have who he wants, Malcolm. Us two. In exchange for Kasi.'

'Don't you think I've considered that?' Malcolm said. 'Macbeth will never exchange a mayor's son for small change like you and me. If Tourtell declares a state of emergency Kasi will be spared. You and I will be executed whatever. And who will lead the fight against Macbeth then?'

'Caithness,' Duff said, 'and all those people in this town you say you have such belief in. Are you afraid or . . . ?'

'Malcolm's right,' Caithness said. 'You're worth more to this town alive.'

'Damn!' Duff tore himself away and went towards the fire engine.

'Where are you going?' Caithness shouted.

'The plinth.'

'What?'

'We have to smash the plinth. Hey, Chief!'

The man who had driven the fire engine stood up. 'Erm, I'm not — '

'Have you got any fire axes or sledgehammers in the vehicle?'

'Of course.'

'Look!' Seyton shouted. 'The sun's shining on the top of the Obelisk. The boy has to die!'

'We all have to die,' Macbeth said softly and put one chip under the heart symbol on the red part of the felt, the other on black. Leaned to the left and took the ball from the roulette wheel.

'What actually happened up on the roof?' Seyton shouted.

'Banquo's boy,' Macbeth shouted back and spun the wheel. Hard. 'I took care of it.'

'Is he dead?'

'I took care of it, I said.' The roulette wheel spun in front of Macbeth, the individual numbers blurring as they formed a clear, unbroken circle. Unclear and yet clear. He had counted down to the zone and he was still there. The wheel whirled. This time it would never stop, this time he would never leave the zone — he had closed the door behind him and locked it. The wheel. Round and round towards an unknown fate, yet so familiar. The casino always wins in the end. 'What's that banging out there, Seyton?'

'Why don't you come up for a look yourself, sir?'

'I prefer roulette. Well?'

'They've started banging away at Bertha, the poor thing. And now the sun's out, sir. I can see it. Nice and big. The time's up. Shall we — '

'Are they smashing up Bertha?'

'The base she's standing on, anyway. Keep an eye on the square and shoot at everything approaching, Olafson.'

'Right!'

Macbeth heard the pad of feet on the stairs and looked up. The reddish tint to Seyton's face was more noticeable than usual, as though he was sunburned. He walked past the roulette table and over to the pole, where Kasi was sitting hunched with his head lowered and his hair hanging in front of his face.

'Who said you could leave your post?' Macbeth said.

'Won't take long,' Seyton said, pulling a black revolver from his belt. Put it to Kasi's head.

'Stop!' Macbeth said.

'We said to the second, sir. We can't — '

'Stop, I said!' Macbeth turned up the volume of the radio behind him.

' . . . Mayor Tourtell speaking to you. Last night I was given an ultimatum by Chief Commissioner Macbeth, who has recently been responsible for a number of murders, including that of Chief Commissioner Duncan. Last night he kidnapped my son, Kasi, after a failed attempt to kill me. The ultimatum is that unless I declare a state of emergency, thereby giving Macbeth unlimited power and preventing federal intervention, my son will be killed when the sun rises above our town. But *we* don't want, *I* don't want, *you* don't want, *Kasi* doesn't want, *this town* doesn't want another despot in power. For this, good men have sacrificed their lives over the last few days. And their sons. Sacrificed their sons the way we in this and other towns did during world wars when our democracy was threatened. And now the sun is rising and Macbeth is sitting by his radio waiting for me to confirm that this day and this town are his. Here's my message to you, Macbeth. Take him. Kasi is yours. I'm sacrificing him as I know and hope he would have sacrificed me or the son he will never have. And if you can hear me, Kasi, goodbye, apple of my eye.' Tourtell's voice thickened. 'You are loved not only by me but by a whole town, and we'll burn candles at your grave for as long as democracy exists.' He coughed. 'Thank you, Kasi. Thank you, citizens of this town. And now the day is ours.'

After a short silence there was a crackly recording of a man's sonorous voice singing 'A Mighty Fortress Is Our God'.

Macbeth switched off the radio.

531

Seyton laughed and applied pressure to the trigger. The hammer rose. 'Surprised, Kasi? A whore's son isn't worth much to a whoremonger, you know. But if you surrender your soul to me now I promise you a painless shot in the head instead of the stomach. Plus revenge over the whoremonger and his gang. What do you say, boy?'

'No.'

'No?' Seyton fixed his disbelieving eyes on the source of the answer.

'No,' Macbeth repeated. 'He mustn't be killed. Put down your revolver, Seyton.'

'And let them out there get what they want?'

'You heard me. We don't shoot defenceless children.'

'Defenceless?' Seyton snarled. 'What about us? Aren't we defenceless? Are we going to let Duff and Malcolm piss all over us again, as they always have? Are you planning to abandon your cause now that — '

'Your revolver's pointing at me, Seyton.'

'Perhaps it is. Because I'm not going to let you stop the kingdom that is coming, Macbeth. You're not the only one with a calling. I'm going — '

'I know what you're going to do, and if you don't put that revolver away, you're a dead man. A dead something anyway.'

Seyton laughed. 'There are things you don't know about me, Macbeth. Such as you can't kill me.'

Macbeth looked into the muzzle of the revolver. 'Do it then, Seyton. Because only you can send me to her. You're not born of woman, you were made. Made of bad dreams, evil and whatever it is that wants to break and destroy.'

Seyton shook his head and pointed the revolver at Kasi's head without taking his eyes off Macbeth. At that moment the first ray of sun penetrated the large windows on the mezzanine. Macbeth saw Seyton raise a hand to shade his eyes as the ray hit his face.

Macbeth threw at the sunshine on the tree trunk out there on the other side, at the heart carved into the wood. Knowing it would hit, for lines, veins from his fingertips, went to that heart.

There was a thud. Seyton wobbled and looked down at the handle of the dagger protruding from his chest. Then dropped the revolver and grabbed the dagger as he sank to his knees. Raised his eyes and looked at Macbeth with a fogged gaze.

'Silver,' Macbeth said, poking the matchstick between his front teeth again. 'It's said to work.'

Seyton fell forward and lay with his head by the boy's naked feet.

Macbeth placed the white ivory ball on the wooden frame around the rotating roulette wheel and sent it hard in the opposite direction.

★ ★ ★

'Keep going!' Duff shouted to the men beating away with sledgehammers and fire axes at the front of the plinth, where they had already dislodged big lumps of concrete.

And then the plinth cracked, and the locomotive's plough-shaped cow catcher dropped with an almighty bang. Duff almost fell forward in the driver's cab, but grabbed a lever and managed to hold on tight. The locomotive's nose, in front of him, was pointing downwards, but it didn't move.

'Come on!'

Still nothing.

'Come on then, you old woman!'

And Duff felt something through his feet. It had moved. Hadn't it? Or . . . He heard a sound like a low lament. Yes, it *had* moved, for the first time in eighty years Bertha Birnam had moved, and now the wailing of its movable metal parts rose, rose in a crescendo to a scream of protest. Years of rust and the laws of friction and inertia tried to hold on, but gravity was invincible.

'Keep clear!' Duff shrieked, tightening the strap of his machine gun and holding the butt of the reserve weapon he had tucked inside his belt.

The steam engine's wheels turned, wrenched out of their torpor, rolled slowly down the eight-metre length of rail and tipped off the plinth. The front wheels hit the top of the steps and the flagstones broke with a deafening crunch. For a moment it seemed the train would stop there, but then Duff heard the next step crack. And the next. And he knew that nothing could now stop this slowly accelerating massive force.

Duff stared fixedly ahead, but from the corner of his eye he registered that someone had jumped onto the train and was standing beside him.

'Single to the Inverness, please.' It was Caithness.

★ ★ ★

'Sir!' It was Olafson.

'Yes?' Macbeth's gaze followed the ivory's rumbling revolutions.

'I think it . . . it's . . . coming.'

'What's coming?'

'The . . . train.'

Macbeth raised his head. 'The train?'

'Bertha! She's coming . . . here! It's — '

The rest was drowned. Macbeth got up. From where he was standing in the gaming room he couldn't see up to the station building, only the sloping square outside the tall window. But he could hear. It sounded like something was being crunched to pieces by a bellowing monster. And it was coming closer.

And then, crossing the square in front of the Inverness, it came into his field of vision.

He gulped.

Bertha was coming.

'Fire!'

★   ★   ★

Deputy Chief Commissioner Malcolm stared in disbelief. Because he knew that whatever happened now he was never going to see the like of this again in his lifetime. A steam engine eating stone and making its own track across Workers' Square. A form of transport their forefathers had built with iron, too heavy and solid to be held back, with ball bearings that didn't rust or dry out after a mere eighty years of neglect, a locomotive against which a hail of bullets from a Gatling gun produced sparks but was repelled like water as it held its course straight towards Inverness Casino.

'That is one solid building,' someone said next to him.

Malcolm shook his head. 'It's just a gambling den,' he said.

★   ★   ★

'Hold on tight!' Duff yelled.

Caithness had sat down on the iron floor with her back to the side of the cab to avoid ricochets from the bullets screaming over their heads. She shouted something, her facial muscles tensed and her eyes closed.

'What?' yelled Duff.

'I love — '

Then they hit the Inverness.

Macbeth enjoyed the sight of Bertha filling the window before she smashed through. He had a feeling the whole building — the floor he was sitting on, the air in the room — everything was pushed back as the train broke through the wall into the room. The noise lay like

535

a coating on his eardrums. The funnel on the steam engine cut through the eastern part of the mezzanine and its cow catcher dug into the floor. The Inverness had braked her, but Bertha was still eating her way forward, metre by metre. She stopped half a metre in front of him, with the funnel against the railing of the west mezzanine and the cow catcher touching the roulette table. For a moment there was total silence. Then came a rattle of crystal. And Macbeth knew what that was. Bertha had sliced the ropes holding the chandelier above him. He made no attempt to move, he didn't even look up. All he noticed before everything went black was that he was covered in Bohemian glass.

Duff climbed up onto the train with the machine gun in his hands. The low rays of sun shone through the dust filling the air.

'The Gatling gun in the south-east corner is unmanned!' Caithness shouted behind him. 'What about — '

'Unmanned on the south-west too,' Duff said. 'Seyton's lying by the roulette table with a dagger in him. Looks pretty dead.'

'Kasi's here. Looks like he's unharmed.'

Duff scanned what once had been a gaming room. Coughed because of the dust. Listened. Apart from the frenetic rolling of a roulette ball in the wheel, there was silence. Sunday morning. In a few hours the church bells would peal. He clambered down. Stepped over Seyton's body to the chandelier. Used the sabre to sweep away the bits of glass from Macbeth's face.

Macbeth's eyes were wide open with surprise, like a child's. The point of the chandelier's gilt spire had disappeared into his right shoulder. Not much blood ran from the wound, which contracted rhythmically as if sucking from the light fitting.

'Good morning, Duff.'

'Good morning, Macbeth.'

'Heh heh. Do you remember we used to say that

every morning when we got up in the orphanage, Duff?
You were in the top bunk.'

'Where are the others? Where's Olafson?'

'Clever lad, that Olafson. He knows when the time's right to scarper. Like you.'

'Your SWAT men don't scarper,' Duff said.

Macbeth sighed. 'No, you're right. Would you believe me if I said he's behind you and will kill you in . . . erm, two seconds?'

Duff eyed Macbeth for a moment. Then he whirled round. Up where the mezzanine was cut in two, he saw two figures against the morning sun shining in through the hole in the east wall. One was a medieval suit of armour. The second, Olafson, kneeling with his rifle resting on the balustrade. Fifteen metres. Olafson could hit a penny from there.

A shot rang out.

Duff knew he was dead.

So why was he still standing?

The echo of the shot resounded through the room.

Macbeth saw Olafson fall against the suit of armour, which toppled back, fell through the gap in the mezzanine and clattered to the gaming-room floor. On the mezzanine Olafson lay with his face pressed to the railing. His cheek was pushed over one eye, the other was closed, as though he had fallen asleep over his Remington 700 rifle.

'Fleance!' Caithness shouted.

Duff turned to the northern end of the mezzanine.

And there, up where the stairs came down from the upper floors, stood Fleance. His shirt was drenched with blood, he was swaying and clinging to a still-smoking gun.

'Caithness, get Kasi and Fleance out,' Duff said. 'Now.'

Duff slumped into the chair beside the roulette table. The ball in the wheel was slowing; the sound had changed.

'What happens now?' Macbeth groaned.

'We wait here until the others come. They'll patch you up at the hospital. Custody. Federal case. They'll be talking about you for years, Macbeth.'

'Still think you've got the top bunk, do you, Duff?'

Crystal rattled. Duff looked up. Macbeth had raised his left hand.

'You know I have the speed of a fly. Before you've let go of that sabre and reached for your gun you'll have a dagger in your chest. You know that, don't you?'

'Possibly,' Duff said. Instead of feeling fear he felt just an immense weariness creeping over him. 'And you'll still lose, as always.'

Macbeth laughed. 'And why's that?'

'It's just one of those self-fulfilling things. You've always known, all your life, you're doomed to lose in the end. That certainty is and always has been you, Macbeth.'

'Oh yes? Haven't you heard? No man born of woman can kill me. That's Hecate's promise, and he's shown several times that he keeps his promises. So do you know what? I can just get up from here and go.' He tried to lever himself up into a sitting position, but the weight of the chandelier pressed down on him.

'Hecate forgot to take me into account when he made you that promise,' Duff said, keeping an eye on Macbeth's left hand. 'I can kill you, so just lie still.'

'Are you hard of hearing, Duff? I said — '

'But I wasn't born of woman,' Duff wheezed.

'You weren't?'

'No. I was cut out of my mother, not born.' Duff leaned forward and ran his forefinger down the scar over his face.

Macbeth was blinking with his child-eyes. 'You . . . you weren't born when Sweno killed her?'

'She was pregnant with me. I was told she was trying to stop the bleeding at the house of an officer when

538

Sweno swung this — ' Duff raised the sabre ' — and cut open her stomach.'

'And your face.'

Duff nodded slowly. 'You won't get away from me, Macbeth. You've lost.'

'Loss after loss. We start off having everything and then we lose everything. I thought it was the only thing that was certain, the amnesty of death. But not even that is guaranteed. Only you can give me death and send me to where I can be reunited with my beloved, Duff. Be my saviour.'

'No. You're under arrest and will rot alone in a prison.'

Macbeth chuckled. 'I can't, and you can't stop yourself. You couldn't stop yourself trying to kill me in the alley and you can't now. We are as we are, Duff. Free will is an illusion. So do what you have to do. Do what you *are*. Or shall I help you and say their names? Meredith, Emily and — '

'Ewan,' Duff said. 'You're the one who can't change from the person you've always wanted to be, Macbeth. That's how I knew there was still hope for Kasi even though the sun had risen over the mountain. You've never been able to kill a defenceless man. And even if you're remembered as more brutal than Sweno, more corrupt than Kenneth, it is your good qualities that have brought you down, your lack of brutality.'

'I was always the reverse of you, Duff. And hence your mirror image. So kill me now.'

'Why the hurry? The place awaiting the likes of you is hell.'

'So let me go.'

'If you ask for your sins to be forgiven, maybe you'll escape.'

'I've sold that chance, Duff. And happily, because I'm looking forward to meeting my beloved again, even if it's to burn together for all eternity.'

'Well, you'll get a fair trial and your sentence will be neither too severe nor too mild. It will be the first proof that this town can be civilised. It can become whole again.'

'You fatuous idiot!' Macbeth screamed. 'You're fooling yourself. You believe you're thinking the thoughts you *want* to think, you believe you're the person you *want* to be, but your brain's desperately searching right now for a pretext to kill me as I lie here defenceless, and that's precisely why something in you resists. But your hatred is like that train: it can't be stopped once it has got going.'

'You're mistaken, Macbeth. We *can* change.'

'Oh yes? Then taste this dagger, free man.' Macbeth's hand reached inside his jacket.

Duff reacted instinctively, folded both hands round the handle of the sabre and thrust.

He was surprised by how easily the blade sliced through Macbeth's chest. And when it met the floor beneath, he felt a tremble spread from Macbeth's body to the sabre and himself. A long sigh issued from Macbeth's lips, and a fine spray of pink blood came from his mouth and settled on Duff's hands like warm rain. He looked down into Macbeth's eyes, not knowing what he was after, only that he didn't find it. All he saw was a light extinguishing as the pupils grew and slowly ousted the irises.

Duff let go of the sabre and stepped back two paces.

Stood there in silence.

Sunday morning.

Heard voices approaching from Workers' Square.

He didn't want to. But he knew he would have to. So he did. Pulled Macbeth's jacket open.

Macbeth's left hand lay flat on his chest. There was nothing there, no shoulder holster, no dagger, only a white shirt gradually turning red.

A pecking sound. Duff turned. It came from the

roulette table. He got to his feet. On the felt a chip lay on red, under the heart, another on black. But the sound came from the wheel, which was still spinning but more and more slowly. The white ball danced between the numbers. Then it came to rest, finally trapped.

In the one green slot, which means the house takes all.

None of the players wins.

43

Church bells pealed in the distance. The one-eyed boy stood in the waiting room at the central station looking out into the daylight. It was a strange sight. From the waiting room Bertha had always blocked the view of the Inverness, but now the old steam engine skewered the facade of the casino. Even in the sharp sunlight he could see the rotating blue lights of the police cars and the flashes of the press photographers. People had flocked to Workers' Square, and occasionally there was a glimpse of light behind the windows in the Inverness too. That would be the SOC team taking pictures of the dead.

★　★　★

The boy turned and went down the corridor. As he approached the stairs down to the toilet he heard something. A low continuous howl, as if from a dog. He had heard it before, a penniless junkie who hadn't had his fix. He peered over the railing and saw pale clothes shining in the fetid darkness below. He was about to go on when he heard a cry, like a scream: 'Wait! Don't go! I've got money!'

'Sorry, Grandad. I haven't got any dope and you haven't got any money. Have a not very nice day.'

'But I've got your eye!' The boy stopped in his tracks. Went back to the railing. Stared down. That voice. Could it really be . . . ? He went over to the stairs, looked around. There was no one else there. Then he descended into the cold damp darkness. The stench got worse with every step.

The man was lying across the threshold of the men's

542

toilet. Wearing what had perhaps once been a white linen suit. Now it was the ragged remains soaked in blood. Just like the man himself. Ragged, blood-soaked remains. A triangular shard of glass protruded from his forehead under a dark fringe. And there was the stick with the gilt handle. *It damn well was him!* The man he had been searching for all these years. Hecate. The boy's eye gradually got used to the darkness and he saw the gaping wound, a tear across stomach and chest. It was pumping out blood, but not so much, as though he was running dry. Between each new surge of blood he could see the slimy pale-pink intestines inside.

'Bring my suffering to an end,' the old man rasped. 'Then take the money I have in my inside pocket.'

The boy eyed the man. The man from all his dreams, his fantasies. Tears of pain ran down the old man's soft cheeks. If the boy wanted, he could take out the short flick knife that he used to chop powder, the one with the narrow blade that had once removed an eye. He could stick it into the old man. It would be poetic justice.

'Has your stomach sprung a leak?' the boy asked, reaching inside the man's jacket. 'Is there acid in the wound?' He examined the contents of the wallet.

'Hurry!' the old man sobbed.

'Macbeth's dead,' the boy said, quickly counting the notes. 'Do you think that makes the world a better place?'

'What?'

'Do you think Macbeth's successors will be any better, fairer or more compassionate? Is there any reason to think they will be?'

'Shut up, boy, and get it over with. Use the stick if you want.'

'If death is what's most precious for you, Hecate, I won't take death from you as you took my eye. Do you know why?'

The old man frowned, stared, and the boy saw signs of recognition in his tear-filled eyes.

'Because I think we have the ability to change and become better people,' the boy said, putting the wallet in his ragged trousers. 'That's why I think Macbeth's successors will be a little better. Small, small steps, but a little better. A little more humane. Isn't it strange, by the way, that we use the word *humane*, human really, to describe what is good and compassionate?' The boy pulled his knife, and the blade sprang out. 'Bearing in mind all we've done to one another all the way through history, I mean?'

'Here,' groaned the old man, pointing to his throat. 'Quickly.'

'Do you remember that I had to cut out my eye myself?'

'What?'

The boy pressed the handle of the knife into the man's hand. 'Do it yourself.'

'But you said . . . more humane . . . I can't do it . . . please!'

'Small steps, small steps,' the boy said, getting up and patting his pocket. 'We're getting better, but we won't be saints overnight, you know.'

The howls followed the boy through the station, all the way until he emerged into the radiant sunshine.

44

The shiny raindrop fell from the sky, through the darkness, towards the shivering lights of the port below. North-westerly gusts of wind drove the raindrop east of the slow-flowing river that divided the town in two and south of the busy train line that split the town diagonally. The wind carried the raindrop over District 4 to the Obelisk and a new building, the Spring, two hotels where business people from Capitol stayed. Occasionally a yokel wandered into the Obelisk and asked whether this hadn't been a casino before. Most had forgotten, but they all remembered the other casino, the one that had been in the railway building which now housed the recently opened town library. The raindrop drifted over police HQ, where lights burned in Chief Commissioner Malcolm's office as he held a management meeting about restructuring. At first there had been some frustration among staff that Mayor Tourtell and the town council were demanding downsizing — a consequence of the statistics showing a strong fall in crime rates. Was this how you rewarded the police for doing such a good job over the last three years? But they realised that Malcolm was right: the job of the police was, as far as possible, to make themselves redundant. Of course this predominantly affected the Narcotics Unit and those departments that had an indirect link to the collapse of the drugs trade, such as the Homicide Unit. Staff numbers remained the same at Anti-Corruption, while the new Financial Crime Unit was the only one allowed to employ more staff. This was because of increased financial activity as a consequence of the town attracting more business and a recognition that white-collar criminals had had it too easy, contributing to a feeling that the police first and foremost served the rich. Duff had defended the size of the Organised Crime Unit by saying that he needed resources to prevent crime and that if professional criminals were to gain a foothold in the town again, this would be far more expensive to clear up. But he understood that he, like everyone else, had to accept cuts. The head of the Homicide Unit, Caithness — who had argued convincingly that with present officer numbers they could finally offer citizens a satisfactory level of efficiency in murder investigations — had even been forced to resign. So Duff was happy it was finally the weekend, and he and Caithness had planned a picnic in Fife. He was both looking forward to it and dreading it. The house had been demolished and he had let the plot grow wild. But the cabin was still there. He wanted them to lie there in the boiling sun and smell the fragrance of the tar in the planks. And listen to see if the echo of Emily and Ewan's laughter and joyous shouts still hung there. And then he wanted to swim alone out to the smooth rock. They say there are no roads back to the places — and the person — you were. He just had to find out if this was true. Not to forget. But so that he could finally look ahead.

The raindrop continued eastwards, over the expensive shopping streets in District 2 West before descending towards a forest-clad hillside next to the ring road, which glittered like a gold necklace around the town's neck this evening. There, at the top of Gallows Hill, the raindrop fell between the trees until with a splash it hit a large green oak leaf. Ran to the tip of the leaf, hung, collecting gravity, ready to fall the last few metres onto two men standing in the darkness under the tree.

'It's changed,' a deep voice said.

'You've been gone a long time, sir,' a higher-pitched one answered.

'Gone. Exactly. That's what I thought I was. And you haven't told me how you found me, Mr Bonus.'

'Oh, I keep my eyes and ears open. I listen and look, that's kind of my talent. The only one, I'm afraid.'

'I don't know if I believe you entirely there. Listen — I'll make no bones about it — I don't like you, Mr Bonus. You remind me a bit too much of those creatures you find in the water that attach themselves to bigger animals and suck.'

'Suckerfish, sir?'

'I was thinking of leeches. Horrible little things. Though harmless enough. So if you think you can help me to get my town back you can suck a bit by all means. Just watch it though. If you suck too hard I'll cut you off. Now tell me.'

'There are no competitors in the market. Many of the junkies moved to Capitol when the dope dried up here. The town council and the chief commissioner have finally begun to lower their guard. Downsizing. The timing's perfect. The potential for new, young customers is unlimited, and I've also found the sister who survived when Hecate's drug factory exploded. And she still has the recipe. Customers won't have alternatives to what we can offer them, sir.'

'And why do you need me?'

'I don't have the capital, the dynamism or your leadership qualities, sir. But I have . . . '

'Eyes and ears. And a suckermouth.' The old man threw down a half-smoked Davidoff Long Panatella as the raindrop on the branch above him lengthened. 'I'll think about it. Not because of what you've said, Mr Bonus. All towns are potentially good markets if you've got a good product.'

'I see. So why here?'

'Because this town took my brother from me, my club house — everything. So I owe it something.'

The raindrop let go. Landed on an animal's horn. Ran down it to the shiny surface of a biker's helmet. 'I owe it hell on earth.'

HOGARTH
SHAKESPEARE

'He was not of an age, but for all time' Ben Jonson

For more than four hundred years, Shakespeare's works have been performed, read, and loved throughout the world. They have been reinterpreted for each new generation, whether as teen films, musicals, science-fiction flicks, Japanese warrior tales, or literary transformations.

The Hogarth Press was founded by Virginia and Leonard Woolf in 1917 with a mission to publish the best new writing of the age. In 2012 Hogarth was launched in London and New York to continue the tradition. The Hogarth Shakespeare project sees Shakespeare's works retold by acclaimed and bestselling novelists of today.

Margaret Atwood, *The Tempest*
Tracy Chevalier, *Othello*
Gillian Flynn, *Hamlet*
Howard Jacobson, *The Merchant of Venice*
Jo Nesbo, *Macbeth*
Edward St Aubyn, *King Lear*
Anne Tyler, *The Taming of the Shrew*
Jeanette Winterson, *The Winter's Tale*

We do hope that you have enjoyed reading
this large print book.

Did you know that all of our titles
are available for purchase?

We publish a wide range of high quality
large print books including:
Romances, Mysteries, Classics
General Fiction
Non Fiction and Westerns

Special interest titles available in
large print are:
The Little Oxford Dictionary
Music Book
Song Book
Hymn Book
Service Book

Also available from us courtesy of
Oxford University Press:
Young Readers' Dictionary
(large print edition)
Young Readers' Thesaurus
(large print edition)

For further information or a free
brochure, please contact us at:
Ulverscroft Large Print Books Ltd.,
The Green, Bradgate Road, Anstey,
Leicester, LE7 7FU, England.
Tel: (00 44) 0116 236 4325
Fax: (00 44) 0116 234 0205

MIDNIGHT SUN

Jo Nesbø

Jon is on the run. He has betrayed Oslo's biggest crime lord, the Fisherman. Fleeing to an isolated corner of Norway, to a mountain town so far north that the summer sun never sets, Jon hopes to find sanctuary among a local religious sect. Hiding out in a shepherd's cabin in the wilderness, all that stands between him and his fate are Lea, a bereaved mother, and her young son, Knut. But while Lea provides a rifle, and Knut brings essential supplies, the midnight sun is slowly driving Jon to insanity. And then he discovers that the Fisherman's men are getting closer . . .